Grace Livingston Hill,
Collection novels

In this book:
The Enchanted Barn
The Girl from Montana
A Voice in the Wilderness
Exit Betty
Cloudy Jewel
The Mystery of Mary
Marcia Schuyler

Grace Livingston Hill (1865 — 1947) was an early 20th-century novelist and wrote both under her real name and the pseudonym Marcia Macdonald. She wrote over 100 novels and numerous short stories. Her characters were most often young female Christian women or those who become so within the confines of the story. Hill's messages are quite simplistic in nature: good versus evil. As Hill believed the Bible was very clear about what was good and evil in life, she reflected that cut-and-dried design in her own works. She wrote about a variety of different subjects, almost always with a romance worked into the message and often essential to the return to grace on the part of one or several characters.

In this book:

The Enchanted Barn

CHAPTER I

Shirley Hollister pushed back the hair from her hot forehead, pressed her hands wearily over tired eyes, then dropped her fingers again to the typewriter keys, and flew on with the letter she was writing.

There was no one else in the inner office where she sat. Mr. Barnard, the senior member of the firm, whose stenographer she was, had stepped into the outer office for a moment with a telegram which he had just received. His absence gave Shirley a moment's respite from that feeling that she must keep strained up to meet his gaze and not let trouble show in her eyes, though a great lump was choking in her throat and the tears stung her hot eyelids and insisted on blurring her vision now and then. But it was only for an instant that she gave way. Her fingers flew on with their work, for this was an important letter, and Mr. Barnard wanted it to go in the next mail.

As she wrote, a vision of her mother's white face appeared to her between the lines, the mother weak and white, with tears on her cheeks and that despairing look in her eyes. Mother hadn't been able to get up for a week. It seemed as if the cares of life were getting almost too much for her, and the warm spring days made the little brick house in the narrow street a stifling place to stay. There was only one small window in mother's room, opening against a brick wall, for they had had to rent the front room with its two windows.

But, poor as it was, the little brick house had been home; and now they were not to have that long. Notice had been served that they must vacate in four weeks; for the house, in fact, the whole row of houses in which it was situated, had been sold, and was to be pulled down to make way for a big apartment-house that was to be put up.

Where they were going and what they were going to do now was the great problem that throbbed on Shirley's weary brain night and day, that kept her from sleeping and eating, that choked in her throat when she tried to speak to Mr. Barnard, that stared from her feverish eyes as she looked at the sunshine on the street or tried to work in the busy monotony of the office.

They had been in the little house nearly a year, ever since the father died. It had taken all they could scrape together to pay the funeral expenses, and now with her salary, and the roomer's rent, and what George got as cash-boy in a department store they were just barely able to get along. There was not a cent over for sickness or trouble, and nothing to move with, even if they had anywhere to move, or any time to hunt for a place. Shirley knew from her experience in hunting for the present house that it was going to be next to impossible for them to find any habitable place for as little rent as they were now paying, and how *could* they pay more? She was only a beginner, and her salary was small. There were three others in the family, not yet wage-earners. The problem was tremendous. Could it be that Carol, only fourteen years old, must stop school and go to work somewhere to earn a pittance also? Carol was slender and pale, and needed fresh air and nourishing food. Carol was too young to bear burdens yet; besides, who would be housekeeper and take care of mother if Carol had to go to work? It was different with George; he was a boy, strong and sturdy; he had his school in the department store, and was getting on well with his studies. George would be all right. He belonged to a baseball team, too, and got plenty of chances for exercise; but Carol was frail, there was no denying it. Harley was a boisterous nine-year-old, always on the street these days when he wasn't in school; and who could blame him? For the narrow, dark brick house was no place for a lively boy. But the burden and anxiety for him were heavy on his sister's heart, who had taken over bodily all the worries of her mother. Then there was the baby Doris, with her big, pathetic eyes, and her round cheeks and loving ways. Doris, too, had to be shut in the dark little house with the summer heat coming on, and no one with time enough or strength enough to take her to the Park. Doris was only four. Oh, it was terrible, *terrible*! and Shirley could do nothing but sit there, and click those keys, and earn her poor little inadequate salary! Some day, of course, she would get more—but some day might be too late!

She shuddered as the terrible thought flashed through her mind, then went on with her work again. She must shake off this state of mind and give attention to her duty, or she would lose even this opportunity to help her dear ones.

The door of the outer office opened, and Mr. Barnard entered.

"Miss Hollister," he said hurriedly, "if you have those letters ready, I will sign them at once. We have just had word that Mr. Baker of the firm died last night in Chicago, and I must go on at once. The office will be closed for the rest of the day. You can let those other matters that I spoke of go until to-morrow, and you may have the day off. I shall not be at the office at the usual hour to-morrow morning, but you can come in and look after the mail. I will leave further directions with Mr. Clegg. You can mail these letters as you go down."

Ten minutes later Shirley stood on the street below in the warm spring sunshine, and gazed about her half dazed. It seemed a travesty on her poor little life just now to have a holiday and no way to make it count for the dear ones at home. How should she use it, anyway? Should she go home and help Carol? Or should she go out and see whether she could find a house somewhere that they could possibly afford to move to? That, of course, was the sensible thing to do; yet she had no idea where to go. But they did not expect her home at this time of day.

3

Perhaps it was as well that she should use this time and find out something without worrying her mother. At least, she would have time to think undisturbed.

She grasped her little package of lunch that she had brought from home with her and looked about her helplessly. In her little thin purse was the dime she always carried with her to pay her car-fare in case something happened that she had to ride either way—though she seldom rode, even in a storm. But her mother insisted on the dime. She said it was not safe to go without any money at all. This dime was her capital wherewith to hunt a house. Perhaps the day had been given her by a kind heavenly Father to go on her search. She would try to use it to the best of her ability. She lifted her bewildered heart in a feeble petition for light and help in her difficult problem, and then she went and stood on the corner of the street where many trolley-cars were passing and repassing. Which one should she take, and where should she go? The ten cents must cover all her riding, and she must save half of it for her return.

She studied the names on the cars. "Glenside Road" one read. What had she heard about that? Ah! that it was the longest ride one could take for five cents within the limits of the city's roads! Her heart leaped up at the word. It sounded restful anyway, and would give her time to think. It wasn't likely, if it went near any glens, that there would be any houses within her means on its way; but possibly it passed some as it went through the city, and she could take notice of the streets and numbers and get out on her return trip to investigate if there proved to be anything promising; or, if it were too far away from home for her to walk back from it, she could come another time in the evening with George, some night when he did not have school. Anyhow, the ride would rest her and give her a chance to think what she ought to do, and one car was as good as another for that. Her resolve was taken, and she stepped out and signalled it.

There were not many people in the car. It was not an hour when people rode out to the suburbs. Two workmen with rolls of wall-paper slung in burlap bags, a woman and a little girl, that was all.

Shirley settled back in her seat, and leaned her head against the window-sash wearily. She felt so tired, body and soul, that she would have been glad to sleep and forget for a little while, only that there was need for her to be up and doing. Her room had been oppressively warm the night before; and Doris, who slept with her, had rolled from one side of the bed to the other, making sleep well-nigh impossible for the elder sister. She felt bruised and bleeding in her very soul, and longed for rest.

The car was passing through the thickest of the city's business thoroughfare, and the noise and confusion whirled about her ears like some fiendish monotonous music that set the time for the mad dance of the world. One danced to it whether one would or not, and danced on to one's death.

Around the city hall the car passed, and on up Market Street. They passed a great fruit-store, and the waft of air that entered the open windows came laden with the scent of over-ripe bananas, late oranges and lemons; a moment later with sickening fumes it blended into a deadly smell of gas from a yawning hole in the pavement, and mingled with the sweat of the swarthy foreigners grouped about it, picks in hand. It seemed as though all the smells in creation were met and congregated in that street within four or five blocks; and one by one they tortured her, leather and paint and metal and soap, rank cheese in a fellow traveller's market-basket, thick stifling smoke from a street engine that was champing up the gravel they fed it to make a new patch of paving, the stench from the cattle-sheds as they passed the railroad and stock-yards, the dank odor of the river as they crossed the bridge, and then an oilcloth-factory just beyond! The faint sweet breath of early daffodils and violets from an occasional street vendor stood no chance at all with these, and all the air seemed sickening and dreadful to the girl as she rested wearily against the window with closed eyes, and tried to think.

They slipped at last into the subway with a whir and a swish, where the cool, clean smell of the cement seemed gradually to rise and drown the memory of the upper world, and came refreshingly in at the windows. Shirley had a passing thought, wondering whether it would be like that in the grave, all restful and sweet and quiet and clean, with the noisy, heartless world roaring overhead. Then they came up suddenly out of the subway, with a kind of triumphant leap and shout of brakes and wheels, into the light and sunshine above, and a new world. For here were broad streets, clean pavements, ample houses, well-trimmed lawns, quiet people walking in comfort, bits of flower-boxes on the window-sills filled with pansies and hyacinths; and the air was sweet and clean. The difference made Shirley sit up and look about her, and the contrast reminded her of the heaven that would be beyond the grave. It was just because she was so tired and disheartened that her thoughts took this solemn form.

But now her heart sank again, for she was in the world of plenty far beyond her means, and there was no place for such as she. Not in either direction could she see any little side streets with tiny houses that would rent for fifteen dollars a month. There were such in the city, she knew; but they were scarce, and were gobbled up as soon as vacant.

But here all was spaciousness, and even the side streets had three stories and smug porches with tidy rockers and bay windows.

She looked at the great plate-glass windows with their cobwebby lace draperies, and thought what it would be if she were able to take her mother and the children to such a home as one of those. Why, if she could afford that,

George could go to college, and Doris wear a little velvet coat with rose-buds in her bonnet, like the child on the sidewalk with her nurse and her doll-carriage.

But a thing like that could never come to her. There were no rich old uncles to leave them a fortune; she was not bright and gifted to invent some wonderful toy or write a book or paint a picture that would bring the fortune; and no one would ever come her way with a fortune to marry her. Those things happened only in story-books, and she was not a story-book girl; she was just a practical, every-day, hard-working girl with a fairly good complexion, good blue eyes and a firm chin. She could work hard and was willing; but she could not bear anxiety. It was eating into her soul, and she could feel a kind of mental paralysis stealing over her from it, benumbing her faculties hour by hour.

The car glided on, and the houses grew less stately and farther apart. They were not so pretentious now, but they were still substantial and comfortable, with more ground and an air of having been there always, with no room for newcomers. Now and then would come a nucleus of shops and an old tavern with a group of new groceries and crying competition of green stamps and blue stamps and yellow stamps posted alluringly in their windows. Here busy, hurried people would swarm, and children ran and shouted; but every house they passed seemed full to overflowing, and there was nowhere any place that seemed to say, "Here you may come and find room!"

And now the car left the paved and built-up streets, and wandered out between the open fields, where trees arched lavishly overhead, and little new green things lifted up unfrightened heads, and dared to grow in the sunshine. A new smell, the smell of rich earth and young green growing things, of skunk-cabbage in bloom in the swamps, of budding willows and sassafras, roused her senses; the hum of a bee on its way to find the first honey-drops came to her ears. Sweet, droning, restful, with the call of a wild bird in the distance, and all the air balmy with the joy of spring. Ah! This was a new world! This indeed was heaven! What a contrast to the office, and the little narrow stifling brick house where mother lay, and Doris cut strings of paper dolls from an old newspaper and sighed to go out in the Park! What a contrast! Truly, this was heaven! If she could but stay, and all the dear ones come!

She had spent summers in the country, of course; and she knew and loved nature, but it had been five years since she had been free to get outside the city limits for more than a day, and then not far. It seemed to her now that she had never sensed the beauty of the country as to-day; perhaps because she had never needed it as now.

The road went on smoothly straight ahead, with now a rounding curve, and then another long stretch of perfect road. Men were ploughing in the fields on one side, and on the other lay the emerald velvet of a field of spring wheat. More people had got into the car as it left the city. Plain, substantial men, nice, pleasant women; but Shirley did not notice them; she was watching the changing landscape and thinking her dismal, pitiful thoughts. Thinking, too, that she had spent her money—or would have when she returned, with nothing to show for it, and her conscience condemned her.

They were coming now to a wide, old-fashioned barn of stone, with ample grassy stone-coped entrance rising like a stately carpeted stairway from the barn-yard. It was resting on the top of a green knoll, and a great elm-tree arched over it protectingly. A tiny stream purled below at one side, and the ground sloped gradually off at the other. Shirley was not noticing the place much except as it was a part of the landscape until she heard the conductor talking to the man across the aisle about it.

"Good barn!" he was saying reflectively. "Pity to have it standing idle so long; but they'll never rent it without a house, and they won't build. It belongs to the old man's estate, and can't be divided until the youngest boy's of age, four 'r five years yet. The house burned down two years ago. Some tramps set it afire. No, nobody was living in it at the time. The last renter didn't make the farm pay,—too fur from the railroad, I guess,—and there ain't anybody near enough round to use the barn since Halyer built his new barn," and he indicated a great red structure down the road on the other side. "Halyer useta use this,—rented it fer less'n nothing, but he got too lazy to come this fur, and so he sold off half his farm fer a dairy and built that there barn. So now I s'pose that barn'll stand idle and run to waste till that kid comes of age and there's a boom up this way and it's sold. Pity about it, though; it's a good barn. Wisht I had it up to my place; I could fill it."

"Make a good location for a house," said the other man, looking intently at the big stone pile. "Been a fine barn in its time. Old man must uv had a pile of chink when he built it. Who'd ya say owned it?"

"Graham, Walter Graham, big firm down near the city hall—guess you know 'em. Got all kinds of money. This ain't one, two, three with the other places they own. Got a regular palace out Arden way fer summer and a town house in the swellest neighborhood, and own land all over. Old man inherited it from his father and three uncles. They don't even scarcely know they got this barn, I reckon. It ain't very stylish out this way just yet."

"Be a big boom here some day; nice location," said the passenger.

"Not yetta while," said the conductor sagely; "railroad station's too far. Wait till they get a station out Allister Avenue; then you can talk. Till then it'll stay as it is, I reckon. There's a spring down behind the barn, the best water in the county. I useta get a drink every day when the switch was up here. I missed it a lot when they moved the switch to the top of the hill. Water's cold as ice and clear as crystal—can't be beat this side the soda-fountain. I sometimes stop the car on a hot summer day now, and run and get a drink—it's great."

The men talked on, but Shirley heard no more. Her eyes were intent on the barn as they passed it—the great, beautiful, wide, comfortable-looking barn. What a wonderful house it would make! She almost longed to be a cow to enter this peaceful shelter and feel at home for a little while.

The car went on, and left the big barn in the distance; but Shirley kept thinking, going over almost unconsciously all the men had said about it. Walter Graham! Where had she seen that name? Oh, of course in the Ward Trust Building, the whole fourth floor. Leather goods of some sort, perhaps, she couldn't just remember; yet she was sure of the name.

The man had said the barn rented for almost nothing. What could that mean translated in terms of dollars? Would the fifteen dollars a month that they were now paying for the little brick house cover it? But there would be the car-fare for herself and George. Walking that distance twice a day, or even once, would be impossible. Ten cents a day, sixty cents a week—twice sixty cents! If they lived out of the city, they couldn't afford to pay but twelve dollars a month. They never would rent that barn for that, of course, it was so big and grand-looking; and yet—it was a *barn*! What did barns rent for, anyway?

And, if it could be had, could they live in a barn? What were barns like, anyway, inside? Did they have floors, or only stalls and mud? There had been but two tiny windows visible in the front; how did they get light inside? But then it couldn't be much darker than the brick house, no matter what it was. Perhaps there was a skylight, and hay, pleasant hay, to lie down on and rest. Anyhow, if they could only manage to get out there for the summer somehow, they could bear some discomforts just to sit under that great tree and look up at the sky. To think of Doris playing under that tree! And mother sitting under it sewing! Mother could get well out there in that fresh air, and Doris would get rosy cheeks again. There would not likely be a school about for Carol; but that would not hurt her for the summer, anyway, and maybe by fall they could find a little house. Perhaps she would get a raise in the fall. If they could only get somewhere to go now!

But yet—a barn! Live in a barn! What would mother say? Would she feel that it was a disgrace? Would she call it one of Shirley's wild schemes? Well, but what were they going to do? They must live *somewhere*, unless they were destined to die homeless.

The car droned on through the open country coming now and then to settlements of prosperous houses, some of them small; but no empty ones seemed to beckon her. Indeed, they looked too high-priced to make her even look twice at them; besides, her heart was left behind with that barn, that great, beautiful barn with the tinkling brook beside it, and the arching tree and gentle green slope.

At last the car stopped in a commonplace little town in front of a red brick church, and everybody got up and went out. The conductor disappeared, too, and the motorman leaned back on his brake and looked at her significantly.

"End of the line, lady," he said with a grin, as if she were dreaming and had not taken notice of her surroundings.

"Oh," said Shirley, rousing up, and looking bewilderedly about her. "Well, you go back, don't you?"

"Yes. Go back in fifteen minutes," said the motorman indulgently. There was something appealing in the sadness of this girl's eyes that made him think of his little girl at home.

"Do you go back just the same way?" she asked with sudden alarm. She did want to see that barn again, and to get its exact location so that she could come back to it some day if possible.

"Yes, we go back just the same way," nodded the motorman.

Shirley sat back in her seat again contented, and resumed her thoughts. The motorman took up his dinner-pail, sat down on a high stool with his back to her, and began to eat. It was a good time now for her to eat her little lunch, but she was not hungry. However, she would be if she did not eat it, of course; and there would be no other time when people would not be around. She put her hand in her shabby coat-pocket for her handkerchief, and her fingers came into contact with something small and hard and round. For a moment she thought it was a button that had been off her cuff for several days, But no, she remembered sewing that on that very morning. Then she drew the little object out, and behold it was a five-cent piece! Yes, of course, she remembered now. It was the nickel she put in her pocket last night when she went for the extra loaf of bread and found the store closed. She had made johnny-cake instead, and supper had been late; but the nickel had stayed in her coat-pocket forgotten. And now suddenly a big temptation descended upon her, to spend that nickel in car-fare, riding to the barn and getting out for another closer look at it, and then taking the next car on into the city. Was it wild and foolish, was it not perhaps actually wrong, to spend that nickel that way when they needed so much at home, and had so little? A crazy idea,—for how could a barn ever be their shelter?

She thought so hard about it that she forgot to eat her lunch until the motorman slammed the cover down on his tin pail and put the high stool away. The conductor, too, was coming out of a tiny frame house, wiping his mouth with the back of his hand and calling to his wife, who stood in the doorway and told him about an errand she wanted him to do for her in the city.

Shirley's cheeks grew red with excitement, for the nickel was burning in her hand, and she knew in her heart that she was going to spend it getting off that car near that barn. She would eat her lunch under the tree by the brook! How exciting that would be! At least it would be something to tell the children about at night! Or no! they would think her crazy and selfish, perhaps, to waste a whole day and fifteen cents on herself. Still, it was not on herself; it was really for them. If they could only see that beautiful spot!

When she handed her nickel to the conductor, she felt almost guilty, and it seemed as if he could see her intention in her eyes; but she told herself that she was not sure she was going to get off at all. She could decide as she came near the place. She would have to get off either before she got there or after she had passed and walk back. The conductor would think it strange if a young girl got off the car in the country in front of an empty barn. How would she manage it? There had been houses on the way, not far from the barn. What was the name the conductor had mentioned of the man who had built another barn? She might get off at his house, but still—stay— what was that avenue where they had said the railroad would come some day with a station? They had called it out as they stopped to let off the woman and the little girl. Allister Avenue! That was it. She would ask the conductor to let her off at Allister Avenue.

She watched the way intently; and, as they neared the place where Allister Avenue ought to be, her heart pounded so that she felt quite conscious, as if she were going to steal a barn and carry it home in her coat-pocket.

She managed to signal the car to stop quite quietly, however, and stepped down to the pavement as if it were her regular stopping-place. She was aware of the curious gaze of both motorman and conductor, but she held her head up, and walked a few steps up Allister Avenue until the car had whirred on out of sight. Then she turned anxiously, looking down the road, and there to her joy saw the stone gable of the great barn high on its knoll in the distance.

CHAPTER II

Shirley walked down the dusty road by the side of the car-track, elation and excitement in her breast. What an adventure! To be walking alone in this strange, beautiful spring country, and nobody to interfere! It was her Father's beautiful out-of-doors, and she had paid her extra nickel to have a right to it for a little while. Perhaps her mother would have been worried at her being alone in the country, but Shirley had no fears. Young people seldom have fears. She walked down the road with a free step and a bright light in her eyes. She had to see that barn somehow; she *just had to*!

She was almost breathless when she reached the bottom of the hill at last, and stood in front of the great barn. The up car passed her just as she got there, and the people looked out at her apathetically as they would at any country girl. She stood still a minute, and watched the car up the hill and out of sight, then picked her way across the track, and entered the field where the fence was broken down, walking up the long grassy slope to the front of the barn and standing still at the top in front of the big double doors, so grim and forbidding.

The barn was bigger than it looked in the distance. She fell very small; yet her soul rejoiced in its bigness. Oh, to have plenty of room for once!

She put her nose close to the big doors, and tried to find a crack to look through; but the doors were tight and fitted well. There was no use trying to see in from there. She turned and ran down the long grassy slope, trying to pretend it was a palatial stairway, then around the side to the back of the barn, and there at last she found a door part way ajar, opening into what must have been the cow-stables, and she slipped joyously in. Some good angel must have been protecting her in her ignorance and innocence, for that dark basement of the barn would have been an excellent hiding-place for a whole regiment of tramps; but she trod safely on her way, and found nothing but a field-mouse to dispute her entrance; and it scurried hastily under the foundation, and disappeared.

The cow-stables evidently had not been occupied for a number of years, for the place was clean and littered with dry straw, as if it had fallen and sifted from the floor above. The stalls were all empty now, and old farm implements, several ploughs, and a rickety wagon occupied the dusty, cobwebby spaces beyond the stalls. There were several openings, rude doorways and crude windows; and the place was not unpleasant, for the back of it opened directly upon a sloping hill which dropped away to the running brook below, and a little stone spring-house, its mossy roof half hidden by a tangle of willows. Shirley stood in a doorway and gazed with delight, then turned back to her investigation. This lower place would not do for human habitation, of course; it was too low and damp, and the floor was only mud. She must penetrate if possible to the floor above.

Presently she found a rough ladder, cleats nailed to uprights against the wall; and up this she crept cautiously to the opening above, and presently emerged into the wide floor of the real barn.

There were several small windows, left open, and the sweet spring air swept gently in; and there were little patches of pale sunshine in the misty recesses of the great dim room. Gentle motes floated in the sharp lances of sunshine that stole through the cracks; another ladder rose in the midst of the great floor to the loft above; and festoons of ancient hay and cobwebs hung dustily down from the opening above. After Shirley had skipped about the big floor and investigated every corner of it, imagining how grand it would be to set the table in one end of the room and put mother's bed behind a screen in the other end, with the old piano somewhere in the centre and the big parlor chair, mended, near by, the old couch covered with a portière standing on the other side, she turned her attention to the loft, and, gathering courage, climbed up there.

There were two great openings that let in the light; but they seemed like tiny mouse-holes in the great place, and the hay lay sweet and dim, thinly scattered over the whole big floor. In one corner there was quite a luxurious lot of it, and Shirley cast herself down upon it for a blessed minute, and looked up to the dark rafters, lit with beams of sunlight creeping through fantastic cracks here and there, and wondered how the boys would enjoy sleeping up here, though there was plenty of room down-stairs for a dozen sleeping-rooms for the matter of that.

Foolish, of course, and utterly impossible, as all daydreams always had been; but somehow it seemed so real and beautiful that she could scarcely bring herself to abandon it. Nevertheless, her investigation had made her hungry, and she decided at last to go down and eat her lunch under the big tree out in the sunshine; for it was dark and stuffy inside, although one could realize how beautiful it would be with those two great doors flung wide, and light and air let in.

The day was perfect, and Shirley found a beautiful place to sit, high and sheltered, where she would not be noticed when the trolley-cars sped by; and, as she ate her sandwiches, she let her imagination build a beautiful piazza where the grassy rise came up to the front of the barn, and saw in thought her mother sitting with the children at the door. How grand it would be to live in a home like this, even if it were a barn! If they could just get out here for the summer, it would do wonders for them all, and put new heart into her mother for the hard work of the winter. Perhaps by fall mother would be well enough to keep boarders as she longed to do, and so help out with the finances more.

Well, of course, this was just one of her wild schemes, and she must not think any more about it, much less even speak of it at home, for they would never get done laughing and teasing her for it.

She finished the last crumb of the piece of one-egg cake that Carol had made the day before for her lunch, and ran down to the spring to see whether she could get a drink, for she was very thirsty.

There proved to be an old tin can on the stones in the spring-house, doubtless used by the last tramp or conductor who came that way; but Shirley scrubbed it carefully in the sand, drank a delicious draught, and washed her hands and face in the clear cold water. Then she went back to the barn again, for a new thought had entered her mind. Supposing it were possible to rent that place for the summer at any reasonable price, how could they cook and how keep warm? Of course there were such things as candles and oil-lamps for lighting, but cooking! Would they have to build a fire out-of-doors and play at camping? Or would they have to resort to oil-stoves? Oil-stoves with their sticky, oily outsides, and their mysterious moods of smoke and sulkiness, out of which only an expert could coax them!

But, though she stood on all sides of that barn, and gazed up at the roof, and though she searched each floor diligently, she could find no sign of a chimney anywhere. Her former acquaintance with barns had not put her into a position to judge whether this was a customary lack of barns or not. There were two wooden, chimney-like structures decorating the roof, but it was all too evident that they were solely for purposes of ornament. Her heart sank. What a grand fireplace there might have been right in the middle of the great wall opposite the door! Could anything be more ideal? She could fancy mother sitting in front of it, with Harley and Doris on the floor playing with a kitten. But there was no fireplace. She wondered vaguely whether a stovepipe could be put out of the window, and so make possible a fire in a small cook-stove. She was sure she had seen stovepipes coming out of all sorts of odd places in the cities. But would the owners allow it? And would any fire at all perhaps make it dangerous and affect the fire-insurance? Oh, there were so many things to think about, and it was all so impossible, of course.

She turned with heavy heart, and let herself down the ladder. It was time she went home, for the afternoon was well on its way. She could hear the whir of the trolley-car going up. She must be out and down the road a little way to get the next one that passed it at the switch when it came back.

So with a wistful glance about the big dusty floor she turned away, and went down to the ground floor and out into the afternoon sunshine.

Just as she crossed the knoll and was stepping over the broken fence, she saw a clump of clover, and among the tiny stems one bearing four leaves. She was not superstitious, nor did the clover mean any special omen to her; but she stooped, smiling, and plucked it, tucking it into the button-hole of her coat, and hurried down the road; for she could already hear the returning trolley-car, and she wished to be a little farther from the barn before it overtook her. Somehow she shrank from having people in the car know where she had been, for it seemed like exposing her audacious wish to the world.

Seated in the car, she turned her eyes back to the last glimpse of the stone gables and the sweeping branches of the budding tree as the car sped down the hill and curved away behind another slope.

After all, it was but half-past four when the car reached the city hall. Its route lay on half a mile nearer to the little brick house, and she could stay in it, and have a shorter walk if she chose. It was not in the least likely anybody would be in any office at this hour of the day, anyway; that is, anybody with authority; but somehow

8

Shirley had to signal that car and get out, long walk or not. A strong desire seized her to put her fate to the test, and either crush out this dream of hers forever, or find out at once whether it had a foundation to live.

She walked straight to the Ward Trust Building and searched the bulletin-board in the hallway carefully. Yes, there it was, "Graham-Walter—Fourth floor front."

With rapidly beating heart she entered the elevator and tried to steady her voice as she said, "Fourth"; but it shook in spite of her. What was she doing? How dared she? What should she say when they asked her what she wanted?

But Shirley's firm little lips were set, and her head had that tilt that her mother knew meant business. She had gone so far she would see the matter to the finish, even if it was ridiculous. For now that she was actually on the elevator and almost to the fourth floor it seemed the most extraordinary thing in the world for a girl to enter a great business office and demand that its head should stoop to rent her an old barn out in the country for the infinitesimal sum she could offer. He would perhaps think her crazy, and have her put out.

But she got out of the elevator calmly, and walked down the hall to where a ground-glass door proclaimed in gold letters the name she was hunting. Timidly she turned the knob, and entered a large room, spacious and high ceiled, with Turkish rugs on the inlaid floor, leather chairs, and mahogany desks.

There was no one in the office but a small office-boy, who lolled idly on one elbow on the table, reading the funny page of the afternoon paper. She paused, half frightened, and looked about her appealingly; and now she began to be afraid she was too late. It had taken longer than she had thought it would to get here. It was almost a quarter to five by the big clock on the wall. No head of a business firm was likely to stay in his office so late in the day as that, she knew. Yet she could hear the steady click of typewriter keys in an inner office; he might have remained to dictate a letter.

The office-boy looked up insolently.

"Is Mr. Graham in?" asked Shirley.

"Which Mr. Graham?"

"Why," hesitating and catching the name on the door, "Mr. Walter Graham."

"No, he isn't here. Never here after four o'clock." The boy dropped on his elbow again, and resumed his reading.

"Oh!" said Shirley, dismayed now, in spite of her fright, as she saw all hope fading from her. "Well, is there another—I mean is the other—Mr. Graham in?"

Someone stirred in the inner office, and came across to the door, looking out, someone with an overcoat and hat on. He looked at the girl, and then spoke sharply to the boy, who stood up straight as if he had been shot.

"Edward! See what the lady wants."

"Yes, sir!" said Edward with sudden respect.

Shirley caught her breath, and plunged in.

"I would like to see *some* Mr. Graham if possible for just a moment." There was something self-possessed and businesslike in her voice now that commanded the boy's attention. Her brief business training was upon her.

The figure from the inner room emerged, and took off his hat. He was a young man and strikingly handsome, with heavy dark hair that waved over his forehead and fine, strong features. His eyes were both keen and kind. There was something luminous in them that made Shirley think of Doris's eyes when she asked a question. Doris had wonderfully wise eyes.

"I am Mr. *Sidney* Graham," said the young man, advancing. "What can I do for you?"

"Oh, I wanted to ask you about a barn," began Shirley eagerly, then stopped abashed. How could she ask this immaculate son of luxury if he would rent a young girl his barn to live in during the summer? She could feel the color mounting in her cheeks, and would have turned and fled gladly if a way had been open. She was aware not only of the kind eyes of the man upon her, but also of the gaping boy taking it all in, and her tongue was suddenly tied. She could say no more.

But the young man saw how it was, and he bowed as gracefully as if asking about barns was a common habit of young women coming into his office.

"Oh, certainly," he said; "won't you just step in here a moment and sit down? We can talk better. Edward, you may go. I shall not need you any longer this evening."

"But I am detaining you; you were just going out!" cried Shirley in a panic. "I will go away now and come again—perhaps." She would do anything to get away without telling her preposterous errand.

"Not at all!" said young Mr. Graham. "I am in no hurry whatever. Just step this way, and sit down." His tone was kindness itself. Somehow Shirley had to follow him. Her face was crimson now, and she felt ready to cry. What a fool she had been to get herself into a predicament like this! What would her mother say to her? How could she tell this strange young man what she had come for? But he was seated and looking at her with his nice eyes, taking in all the little pitiful attempts at neatness and style and beauty in her shabby little toilet. She was awfully conscious of a loose fluff of gold-glinted hair that had come down over one hot cheek and ear. How dishevelled she must look, and how dusty after climbing over that dirty barn! And then she plunged into her subject.

9

CHAPTER III

"I'm sure I don't know what you will think of my asking," said Shirley excitedly, "but I want very much to know whether there is any possibility that you would rent a beautiful big stone barn you own out on the old Glenside Road, near Allister Avenue. You do own it, don't you? I was told you did, or at least that Mr. Walter Graham did. They said it belonged to 'the estate.'"

"Well, now you've got one on me," said the young man with a most engaging smile. "I'm sure I don't know whether I own it or not. I'm sorry. But if it belongs to grandfather's estate,—his name was Walter, too, you know.—why, I suppose I do own part of it. I'm sorry father isn't here. He of course knows all about it—or the attorney—of course he would know. But I think he has left the office. However, that doesn't matter. What was it you wanted? To rent it, you say?"

"Yes," said Shirley, feeling very small and very much an impostor; "that is, if I could afford it. I suppose perhaps it will be way ahead of my means, but I thought it wouldn't do any harm to ask." Her shy eyes were almost filled with tears, and the young man was deeply distressed.

"Not at all, not at all," he hastened to say. "I'm just stupid that I don't know about it. Where did you say it was? Out on the Glenside Road? A barn? Come to think of it, I remember one of my uncles lived out that way once, and I know there is a lot of land somewhere out there belonging to the estate. You say there is a barn on it?"

"Yes, a beautiful barn," said Shirley anxiously, her eyes dreamy and her cheeks like two glowing roses. "It is stone, and has a wide grassy road like a great staircase leading up to it, and a tall tree over it. There is a brook just below,—it is high up from the road on a little grassy hill."

"Oh, yes, yes," he said, nodding eagerly, "I see! It almost seems as if I remember. And you wanted to rent it for the summer, you say? You are—ah—in the agricultural business, I suppose?" He looked at her respectfully. He knew the new woman, and honored her. He did not seem at all startled that she wanted to rent a barn for the summer.

But Shirley did not in the least understand. She looked at him bewildered a moment.

"Oh, no! I am only a stenographer myself—but my mother—that is——" she paused in confusion.

"Oh, I see, your mother is the farmer, I suppose. Your home is near by—near to the barn you want to rent?"

Then she understood.

"No, oh, no!" she said desperately. "We don't want to use the barn for a barn at all. I want to use it for a house!"

It was out at last, the horrible truth; and she sat trembling to see his look of amazement.

"Use it for a house!" he exclaimed. "Why, how could you? To live in, do you mean? or just to take a tent and camp out there for a few days?"

"To *live in*," said Shirley doggedly, lifting her eyes in one swift defiant look and then dropping them to her shabby gloves and thin pocketbook, empty now even of the last precious nickel. If he said anything more, she was sure she should cry. If he patronized her the least little bit, or grew haughty, now that he saw how low she was reduced, she would turn and fly from the office and never look him in the face.

But he did neither. Instead, he just talked in a natural tone, as if it were the most common thing in the world for a girl to want to live in a barn, and nothing to be surprised over in the least.

"Oh, I see," he said pleasantly. "Well, now, that might be arranged, you know. Of course I don't know much about things, but I could find out. You see, I don't suppose we often have calls to rent the property that way——"

"No, of course not," said Shirley, gathering up her scattered confidence. "I know it's queer for me to ask, but we have to move—they are going to build an apartment-house where we are renting now, and mother is sick. I should like to get her out into the country, our house is so little and dark; and I thought, if she could be all summer where she could see the sky and hear the birds, she might get well. I want to get my little sisters and brothers out of the city, too. But we couldn't likely pay enough rent. I suppose it was silly of me to ask."

"Not at all!" said the young man courteously, as though she had been a queen whom he delighted to honor. "I don't see why we shouldn't be able to get together on some kind of a proposition—that is, unless father has other plans that I don't know about. A barn ought not to be worth such a big price. How much would you feel like paying?"

He was studying the girl before him with interested eyes; noting the well-set head on the pretty shoulders, even in spite of the ill-fitting shabby blue coat; the delicate features; the glint of gold in the soft brown hair; the tilt of the firm little chin, and the wistfulness in the big blue eyes. This was a new kind of girl, and he was disposed to give her what she wanted if he could. And he *could*. He knew well that anything he willed mightily would not be denied him.

The frightened color came into the delicate cheeks again, and the blue eyes fluttered down ashamedly.

"We are only paying fifteen a month now," she said; "and I couldn't pay any more, for we haven't got it. I couldn't pay *as much*, for it would cost sixty cents a week apiece for George and me to come in to our work from there. I couldn't pay more than twelve! and I know that's ridiculous for such a great big, beautiful place, but—I *had* to ask."

She lifted her eyes swiftly in apology, and dropped them again; the young man felt a glow of sympathy for her, and a deep desire to help her have her wish.

"Why, certainly," he said heartily. "Of course you did. And it's not ridiculous at all for you to make a business proposition of any kind. You say what you can do, and we accept it or not as we like. That's our lookout. Now of course I can't answer about this until I've consulted father; and, not knowing the place well, I haven't the least idea what it's worth; it may not be worth even twelve dollars." (He made a mental reservation that it *should* not be if he could help it.) "Suppose I consult with father and let you know. Could I write or phone you, or will you be around this way any time to-morrow?"

Shirley's breath was fairly gone with the realization that he was actually considering her proposition in earnest. He had not laughed at her for wanting to live in a barn, and he had not turned down the price she offered as impossible! He was looking at her in a kindly way as if he liked her for being frank.

"Why, yes," she said, looking up shyly, "I can come in to-morrow at my noon hour—if that would not be too soon. I always have a little time to myself then, and it isn't far from the office."

"That will be perfectly all right for me," smiled young Graham. "I shall be here till half-past one, and you can ask the boy to show you to my office. I will consult with father the first thing in the morning and be ready to give you an answer. But I am wondering if you have seen this barn, I suppose you have, or you would not want to rent it; but I should suppose a barn would be an awfully unpleasant place to live, kind of almost impossible. Are you sure you realize what the proposition would be?"

"Yes, I think so," said Shirley, looking troubled and earnest. "It is a beautiful big place, and the outlook is wonderful. I was there to-day, and found a door open at the back, and went in to look around. The up-stairs middle floor is so big we could make several rooms out of it with screens and curtains. It would be lovely. We could live in picnic style. Yes, I'm sure mother would like it. I haven't told her about it yet, because if I couldn't afford it I didn't want to disappoint her; so I thought I would wait till I found out; but I'm just about certain she would be delighted. And anyhow we've *got* to go *somewhere*."

"I see," said this courteous young man, trying not to show his amazement and delight in the girl who so coolly discussed living in a barn with curtains and screens for partitions. He thought of his own luxurious home and his comfortable life, where every need had been supplied even before he realized it, and, wondering again, was refreshed in soul by this glimpse into the brave heart of the girl.

"Then I will expect you," he said pleasantly, and, opening the door, escorted her to the elevator, touching his hat to her as he left her.

Shirley would not have been a normal girl if she had not felt the least flutter in her heart at the attention he showed her and the pleasant tones of his voice. It was for all the world as if she had been a lady dressed in broadcloth and fur. She looked down at her shabby little serge suit—that had done duty all winter with an old gray sweater under it—half in shame and half in pride in the man who had not let it hinder him from giving her honor. He was a *man*. He must be. She had bared her poverty-stricken life to his gaze, and he had not taken advantage of it. He had averted his eyes, and acted as if it were just like other lives and others' necessities; and he had made her feel that she was just as good as any one with whom he had to deal.

Well, it was probably only a manner, a kind of refined, courteous habit he had; but it was lovely, and she was going to enjoy the bit of it that had fallen at her feet.

On the whole, Shirley walked the ten blocks to her narrow little home feeling that she had had a good day. She was weary, but it was a healthy weariness. The problem which had been pressing on her brain for days, and nights too, did not seem so impossible now, and hope was in her heart that somehow she would find a way out. It had been good to get away from the office and the busy monotony and go out into the wide, open out-of-doors. It was good also to meet a real nobleman, even if it were only in passing, and on business.

She decided not to tell her mother and the children of her outing yet, not until she was sure there were to be results. Besides, it might only worry her mother the more and give her a sleepless night if she let out the secret about the barn.

One more little touch of pleasantness there came to make this day stand out from others as beautiful. It was when she turned into Chapel Street, and was swinging along rapidly in order to get home at her usual time and not alarm her mother, that a car rolled quickly past to the middle of the block, and stopped just under a street-light. In a moment more a lady came out of the door of a house, entered the car, and was driven away. As she closed the car-door, Shirley fancied she saw something drop from the lady's hand. When Shirley reached the place she found it was two great, luscious pink rosebuds that must have slipped from the lady's corsage and fallen on the pavement. Shirley picked them up almost reverently, inhaling their exotic breath, and taking in their delicate curves and texture. Then she looked after the limousine. It was three blocks away and just turning into another street. It would be impossible for her to overtake it, and there was little likelihood of the lady's returning for two roses. Probably she would never miss them. Shirley turned toward the house, thinking she ought to take them in, but discovered that it bore the name of a fashionable modiste, who would, of course, not have any right to the roses, and Shirley's conscience decided they were meant by Providence for her. So, happily, she hurried on to the little brick house, bearing the wonderful flowers to her mother.

She hurried so fast that she reached home ten minutes earlier than usual, and they all gathered around her eagerly as if it were some great event, the mother calling half fearfully from her bedroom up-stairs to know whether anything had happened. She was always expecting some new calamity like sickness, or the loss of their positions by one or the other of her children.

"Nothing at all the matter, mother dear!" called Shirley happily as she hung up her coat and hat, and hugged Doris. "I got off earlier than usual because Mr. Barnard had to go away. Just see what a beautiful thing I have brought you—found it on the street, dropped by a beautiful lady. You needn't be afraid of them, for she and her limousine looked perfectly hygienic; and it wasn't stealing, because I couldn't possibly have caught her. Aren't they lovely?"

By this time she was up in her mother's room, with Doris and Carol following close behind exclaiming in delight over the roses.

She kissed her mother, and put the flowers into a glass beside the bed.

"You're looking better to-night, I believe, dear," said the mother. "I've been worried about you all day. You were so white and tired this morning."

"Oh, I'm feeling fine, mother dear!" said Shirley gayly, "and I'm going down to make your toast and poach you an egg while Carol finishes getting supper. George will be here in ten minutes now, and Harley ought to be in any minute. He always comes when he gets hungry. My! I'm hungry myself! Let's hurry, Carol. Doris, darling, you fix mother's little table all ready for her tray. Put on the white cloth, take away the books, set the glass with the roses in the middle very carefully. You won't spill it, will you, darling?"

Doris, all smiles at the responsibility accorded her, promised: "No, I yun't spill it I'll move it tarefully."

There was something in Shirley's buoyant air that night that lifted them all above the cares that had oppressed them for weeks, and gave them new hope. She flew around, getting the supper things together, making her mother's tray pretty, and taking little extra pains for each one as she had not felt able to do before. Carol caught the contagion, and mashed the potatoes more carefully, so that there wasn't a single lump in them.

"Goodness! But it's been hot in this kitchen all day, Shirley," said Carol. "I had the back door open, but it just seemed stifling. I got the ironing all done except a table-cloth, and I guess I can finish that this evening. I haven't got much studying to do for to-morrow. Nellie Waite stopped, and left me my books. I don't believe I'll have to stay at home another day this week. Mother says she can get along. I can leave her lunch all ready, and Doris can manage."

Shirley's conscience gave a sudden twinge. Here had she been sitting under a lovely tree by a brook, eating her lunch, and dreaming foolish day-dreams about living in a barn, while Carol stayed at home from school and toiled in the kitchen! Perhaps she ought to have come home and sent Carol back to school. And yet perhaps that nice young Mr. Graham would be able to do something; she would not condemn herself until the morrow, anyway. She had tried to do her best. She had not gone off there selfishly just to have a good time by herself when her dear ones were suffering. It had been for their sake.

Then George came in whistling, and Harley banged in gayly a minute later, calling to know whether supper was ready.

"'Cause I gotta date with the fellas this evening, and I gotta beat it," he declared impatiently.

The shadow of anxiety passed over Shirley's face again at that, but she quieted her heart once more with her hopes for to-morrow. If her plan succeeded, Harley would be away from "the fellas," and wouldn't have so many questionable "dates" to worry them all.

George was in a hurry, too.

"Gee, Shirley, I gotta be at the store all evening," he said, bolting his food hurriedly. "I wouldn't 'a' come home, only I knew you'd worry, and mother gets so upset. Gee, Shirley, what we gonta do about a house? It's getting almost time to move. I went to all those places you suggested at noon to-day, but there wasn't a vacant spot anywhere. There's some rooms on Louden Street, but there's all sorts in the house. Mother wouldn't like it. It's dirty besides. I suppose if we look long enough we could find rooms; but we'd have to get along with only two or three, for they come awful high. We'd have to have three anyway, you girls and mother in one, us boys in the other, and one for parlor and kitchen together. Gee! Wouldn't that be fierce? I oughtta get a better job. We can't live that way."

"Don't worry, George; I think we'll find something better," said Shirley with a hopeful ring in her voice. "I've been thinking out a plan. I haven't got it all just arranged in my mind yet, but I'll tell you about it pretty soon. You don't have school to-morrow night, do you? No, I thought not. Well, maybe we can talk it over then. You and I will have to go out together and look up a place perhaps," and she smiled an encouraging smile, and sent him off to his school happily.

She extracted a promise from Harley that he would be in by nine o'clock, discovered that he was only going to a "movie" show around the corner with one of the fellows who was going to "stand treat" on account of a wonderful ball game they had won, found out where his lessons were for the morrow, promised to help him when he returned, and sent him away with a feeling of comfort and responsibility to return early. She washed the dishes and ironed the table-cloth so Carol could go to her lessons. Then she went up and put Doris to bed with a story about a little bird that built a nest in a tall, beautiful tree that grew beside the place where the little girl lived; a little bird that drank from a little running brook, and took a bath on its pebbly shore, and ate the crumbs and berries the little girl gave it, and sat all day on five little blue eggs.

Harley came in at five minutes after nine, and did his lessons with her help. George came home just as they finished. He was whistling, though he looked tired. He said "the prof." had been "the limit" all the evening. Shirley fixed her mother comfortably for the night, and went at last to her own bed, more tired than she had been for weeks, and yet more happy. For through it all she had been sustained by a hope; inspired by a cultured, pleasant voice, and eyes that wanted to help, and seemed to understand.

As she closed her eyes to sleep, somehow that pleasant voice and those kind eyes mingled with her dreams, and seemed to promise relief from her great anxieties.

It was with a feeling of excitement and anticipation that she dressed the next morning and hurried away. Something was coming, she felt sure, some help for their trying situation. She had felt it when she knelt for her usual prayer that morning, and it throbbed in her excited heart as she hurried through the streets to the office. It almost frightened her to feel so sure, for she knew how terrible would be the disappointment if she got her hopes too high.

There was plenty to be done at the office, a great many letters to answer, and a telegram with directions from Mr. Barnard. But she worked with more ease than for some time, and was done by half-past eleven. When she took the letters out to Mr. Clegg to be signed, he told her that she would not be needed the rest of the day, and might go at once if she chose.

She ate her bit of lunch hurriedly, and made herself as fresh and tidy as was possible in the office. Then she took her way to the fourth floor of the Ward Trust Building. With throbbing heart and glowing cheeks she entered the office of Walter Graham, and asked for Mr. Sidney Graham.

The office-boy had evidently received instructions, for he bowed most respectfully this time, and led her at once to the inner office.

CHAPTER IV

The afternoon before, when Mr. Sidney Graham had returned to his office from seeing Shirley to the elevator, he stood several minutes looking thoughtfully at the chair where she had sat, while he carefully drew on his gloves.

There had been something interesting and appealing in the spirited face of the girl, with her delicate features and wistful eyes. He could not seem to get away from it. It had left an impression of character and a struggle with forces of which in his sheltered life he had had only a vague conception. It had left him with the feeling that she was stronger in some ways than himself, and he did not exactly like the sensation of it. He had always aimed to be a strong character himself; and for a young man who had inherited two hundred and fifty thousand dollars on coming of age, and double that amount two years later, with the prospect of another goodly sum when his paternal grandfather's estate was divided, he had done very well indeed. He had stuck to business ever since leaving college, where he had been by no means a nonentity either in studies or in athletics; and he had not been spoiled by the adulation that a young man of his good looks and wealth and position always receives in society. He had taken society as a sort of duty, but had never given it an undue proportion of his time and thoughts. Notably he was a young man of fine balance and strong self-control, not given to impulsive or erratic likes and dislikes; and he could not understand why a shabby little person with a lock of gold over one crimson cheek, and tired, discouraged lights in her had made so strong an impression upon him.

It had been his intention just before Shirley's arrival to leave the office at once and perhaps drop in on Miss Harriet Hale. If the hour seemed propitious, he would take her for a spin in his new racing-car that even now waited in the street below; but somehow suddenly his plan did not attract him deeply. He felt the need of being by himself. After a turn or two up and down his luxurious office he took the elevator down to the street floor, dismissed his chauffeur, and whirled off in his car, taking the opposite direction from that which would have taken him to the Hale residence. Harriet Hale was a very pretty girl with a brilliant mind and a royal fortune. She could entertain him and stimulate him tremendously, and sometimes he almost thought the attraction was strong enough to last him through life; but Harriet Hale would not be able to appreciate his present mood nor explain to him why the presence in his office for fifteen minutes of a nervy little stenographer who was willing to live in a barn should have made him so vaguely dissatisfied with himself. If he were to try to tell her about it, he felt sure he would meet with laughing taunts and brilliant sarcasm. She would never understand.

He took little notice of where he was going, threading his way skilfully through the congested portion of the city and out into the comparatively empty highways, until at last he found himself in the suburbs. The name of the street as he slowed up at a grade crossing gave him an idea. Why shouldn't he take a run out and hunt up that barn for himself? What had she said about it, where it was? He consulted the memorandum he had written down for his father's edification. "Glenside Road, near Allister Avenue." He further searched his memory. "Big stone barn, wide approach like a grand staircase, tall tree overhanging, brook." This surely ought to be enough to help him identify it. There surely were not a flock of stone barns in that neighborhood that would answer that description.

He turned into Glenside Road with satisfaction, and set a sharp watch for the names of the cross-avenues with a view to finding Allister Avenue, and once he stopped and asked a man in an empty milk-wagon whether he knew where Allister Avenue was, and was informed that it was "on a piece, about five miles."

There was something interesting in hunting up his own strange barn, and he began to look about him and try to see things with the eyes of the girl who had just called upon him.

Most of the fields were green with spring, and there was an air of things doing over them, as if growing were a business that one could watch, like house-cleaning and paper-hanging and painting. Graham had never noticed before that the great bare spring out-of-doors seemed to have a character all its own, and actually to have an attraction. A little later when the trees were out, and all the orchards in bloom, and the wild flowers blowing in the breeze, he could rave over spring; but he had never seen the charm of its beginnings before. He wondered curiously over the fact of his keen appreciation now.

The sky was all opalescent with lovely pastel colors along the horizon, and a few tall, lank trees had put on a soft gauze of green over their foreheads like frizzes, discernible only to a close observer. The air was getting chilly with approaching night, and the bees were no longer proclaiming with their hum the way to the skunk-cabbages; but a delicate perfume was in the air, and though perhaps Graham had never even heard of skunk-cabbages, he drew in long breaths of sweetness, and let out his car over the smooth road with a keen delight.

Behind a copse of fine old willows, age-tall and hoary with weather, their extremities just hinting of green, as they stood knee-deep in the brook on its way to a larger stream, he first caught sight of the old barn.

He knew it at once by something indefinable. Its substantial stone spaciousness, its mossy roof, its arching tree, and the brook that backed away from the wading willows, up the hillside, under the rail fence, and ran around its side, all were unmistakable. He could see it just as the girl had seen it, and something in him responded to her longing to live there and make it into a home. Perhaps he was a dreamer, even as she, although he passed in the world of business for a practical young man. But anyhow he slowed his car down and looked at the place intently as he passed by. He was convinced that this was the place. He did not need to go on and find Allister Avenue— though he did, and then turned back again, stopping by the roadside. He got out of the car, looking all the time at the barn and seeing it in the light of the girl's eyes. As he walked up the grassy slope to the front doors, he had some conception of what it must be to live so that this would seem grand as a home. And he showed he was not spoiled by his life in the lap of luxury, for he was able to get a glimpse of the grandeur of the spot and the dignity of the building with its long simple lines and rough old stones.

The sun was just going down as he stood there looking up. It touched the stones, and turned them into jewelled settings, glorifying the old structure into a palace. The evening was sweet with the voices of birds not far away. One above the rest, clear and occasional, high in the elm-tree over the barn, a wood-thrush spilling its silver notes down to the brook that echoed them back in a lilt. The young man took off his hat and stood in the evening air, listening and looking. He could see the poetry of it, and somehow he could see the girl's face as if she stood there beside him, her wonderful eyes lighted as they had been when she told him how beautiful it was there. She was right. It was beautiful, and it was a lovely soul that could see it and feel what a home this would make in spite of the ignominy of its being nothing but a barn. Some dim memory, some faint remembrance, of a stable long ago, and the glory of it, hovered on the horizon of his mind; but his education had not been along religious lines, and he did not put the thing into a definite thought. It was just a kind of sensing of a great fact of the universe which he perhaps might have understood in a former existence.

Then he turned to the building itself. He was practical, after all, even if he was a dreamer. He tried the big padlock. How did they get into this thing? How had the girl got in? Should he be obliged to break into his own barn?

He walked down the slope, around to the back, and found the entrance close to the ladder; but the place was quite dark within the great stone walls, and he peered into the gloomy basement with disgust at the dirt and murk. Only here and there, where a crack looked toward the setting sun, a bright needle of light sent a shaft through to let one see the inky shadows. He was half turning back, but reflected that the girl had said she went up a ladder to the middle floor. If she had gone, surely he could. Again that sense that she was stronger than he rebuked him. He got out his pocket flashlight and stepped within the gloom determinedly. Holding the flash-light above his head, he surveyed his property disapprovingly; then with the light in his hand he climbed in a gingerly way up the dusty rounds to the middle floor.

As he stood alone in the dusky shadows of the big barn, with the blackness of the hay-loft overhead, the darkness pierced only by the keen blade of the flash-light and a few feebler darts from the sinking sun, the poetry suddenly left the old barn, and a shudder ran through him. To think of trying to live here! How horrible!

Yet still that same feeling that the girl had more nerve than he had forced him to walk the length and breadth of the floor, peering carefully into the dark corners and acquainting himself fully with the bare, big place; and also to climb part way up the ladder to the loft and send his flash-light searching through its dusty hay-strewn recesses.

With a feeling utterly at variance with the place he turned away in disgust, and made his way down the ladders again, out into the sunset.

In that short time the evening had arrived. The sky had flung out banners and pennants, pencilled by a fringe of fine saplings like slender brown threads against the sky. The earth was sinking into dusk, and off by the brook the frogs were tinkling like tiny answering silver rattles. The smell of earth and growing stole upon his senses, and even as he gazed about him a single star burned into being in the clear ether above him. The birds were still now, and the frogs with the brook for accompaniment held the stage. Once more the charm of the place stole over him; and he stood with hat removed, and wondered no longer that the girl was willing to live here. A conviction grew within him that somehow he must make it possible for her to do so, that things would not be right and as they ought to be unless he did. In fact, he had a curiosity to have her do it and see whether it could be done.

He went slowly down to his car at last with lingering backward looks. The beauty of the situation was undoubted, and called for admiration. It was too bad that only a barn should occupy it. He would like to see a fine house reared upon it. But somehow in his heart he was glad that it was not a fine house standing there against the evening sky, and that it was possible for him to let the girl try her experiment of living there. Was it possible? Could there be any mistake? Could it be that he had not found the right barn, after all? He must make sure, of course.

But still he turned his car toward home, feeling reasonably sure that he had found the right spot; and, as he drove swiftly back along the way, he was thinking, and all his thoughts were woven with the softness of the spring evening and permeated with its sounds. He seemed to be in touch with nature as he had never been before.

At dinner that night he asked his father:

"Did Grandfather Graham ever live out on the old Glenside Road, father?"

A pleasant twinkle came in the elder Graham's eyes.

"Sure!" he said. "Lived there myself when I was five years old, before the old man got to speculating and made his pile, and we got too grand to stay in a farmhouse. I can remember rolling down a hill under a great big tree, and your Uncle Billy pushing me into the brook that ran at the foot. We boys used to wade in that brook, and build dams, and catch little minnows, and sail boats. It was great sport. I used to go back holidays now and then after I got old enough to go away to school. We were living in town then, but I used to like to go out and stay at the farmhouse. It was rented to a queer old dick; but his wife was a good sort, and made the bulliest apple turnovers for us boys—and doughnuts! The old farmhouse burned down a year or so ago. But the barn is still standing. I can remember how proud your grandfather was of that barn. It was finer than any barn around, and bigger. We boys used to go up in the loft, and tumble in the hay; and once when I was a little kid I got lost in the hay, and Billy had to dig me out. I can remember how scared I was when I thought I might have to stay there forever, and have nothing to eat."

"Say, father," said the son, leaning forward eagerly, "I've a notion I'd like to have that old place in my share. Do you think it could be arranged? The boys won't care, I'm sure; they're always more for the town than the country."

"Why, yes, I guess that could be fixed up. You just see Mr. Dalrymple about it. He'll fix it up. Billy's boy got that place up river, you know. Just see the lawyer, and he'll fix it up. No reason in the world why you shouldn't have the old place if you care for it. Not much in it for money, though, I guess. They tell me property's way down out that direction now."

The talk passed to other matters, and Sidney Graham said nothing about his caller of the afternoon, nor of the trip he had taken out to see the old barn. Instead, he took his father's advice, and saw the family lawyer, Mr. Dalrymple, the first thing in the morning.

It was all arranged in a few minutes. Mr. Dalrymple called up the other heirs and the children's guardian. An office-boy hurried out with some papers, and came back with the signatures of heirs and guardians, who happened all to be within reach; and presently the control of the old farm was formally put into the hands of Mr. Sidney Graham, he having signed certain papers agreeing to take this as such and such portion of his right in the whole estate.

It had been a simple matter; and yet, when at about half-past eleven o'clock Mr. Dalrymple's stenographer laid a folded paper quietly on Sidney Graham's desk and silently left the room, he reached out and touched it with more satisfaction than he had felt in any acquisition in a long time, not excepting his last racing-car. It was not the value the paper represented, however, that pleased him, but the fact that he would now be able to do as he pleased

15

concerning the prospective tenant for the place, and follow out a curious and interesting experiment. He wanted to study this girl and see whether she really had the nerve to go and live in a barn—a girl with a face like that to live in a barn! He wanted to see what manner of girl she was, and to have the right to watch her for a little space.

It is true that the morning light might present her in a very different aspect from that in which she had appeared the evening before, and he mentally reserved the right to turn her down completely if she showed the least sign of not being all that he had thought her. At the same time, he intended to be entirely sure. He would not turn her away without a thorough investigation.

Graham had been greatly interested in the study of social science when in college, and human nature interested him at all times. He could not but admit to himself that this girl had taken a most unusual hold upon his thoughts.

CHAPTER V

As the morning passed on and it drew near to the noon hour Sidney Graham found himself almost excited over the prospect of the girl's coming. Such foolish fancies as a fear lest she might have given up the idea and would not come at all presented themselves to his distraught brain, which refused to go on its well-ordered way, but kept reverting to the expected caller and what he should say to her. When at last she was announced, he drew back his chair from the desk, and prepared to meet her with a strange tremor in his whole bearing. It annoyed him, and brought almost a frown of sternness to his fine features. It seemed not quite in keeping with his dignity as junior member of his father's firm that he should be so childish over a simple matter like this, and he began to doubt whether, after all, he might not be doing a most unwise and irregular thing in having anything at all to do with this girl's preposterous proposition. Then Shirley entered the office, looked eagerly into his eyes; and he straight-way forgot all his reasoning. He met her with a smile that seemed to reassure her, for she drew in her breath half relieved, and smiled shyly back.

She was wearing a little old crêpe de chine waist that she had dyed a real apple-blossom pink in the wash-bowl with a bit of pink crepe-paper and a kettle of boiling water. The collar showed neatly over the shabby dark-blue coat, and seemed to reflect apple-blossom tints in her pale cheeks. There was something sky-like in the tint of her eyes that gave the young man a sense of spring fitness as he looked at her contentedly. He was conscious of gladness that she looked as good to him in the broad day as in the dusk of evening. There was still that spirited lift of her chin, that firm set of the sweet lips, that gave a conviction of strength and nerve. He reflected that he had seldom seen it in the girls of his acquaintance. Was it possible that poverty and privation and big responsibility made it, or was it just innate?

"You—you have found out?" she asked breathlessly as she sat down on the edge of the chair, her whole body tense with eagerness.

"Sure! It's all right," he said smilingly. "You can rent it if you wish."

"And the price?" It was evident the strain was intense.

"Why, the price will be all right, I'm sure. It really isn't worth what you mentioned at all. It's only a barn, you know. We couldn't think of taking more than ten dollars a month, if we took that. I must look it over again; but it won't be more than ten dollars, and it may be less."

Young Graham wore his most businesslike tone to say this, and his eyes were on the paper-knife wherewith he was mutilating his nice clean blotter pad on the desk.

"Oh!" breathed Shirley, the color almost leaving her face entirely with the relief of his words. "Oh, *really*?"

"And you haven't lost your nerve about living away out there in the country in a great empty barn?" he asked quickly to cover her embarrassment—and his own, too, perhaps.

"Oh, no!" said Shirley with a smile that showed a dimple in one cheek, and the star sparks in her eyes. "Oh, no! It is a lovely barn, and it won't be empty when we all get into it."

"Are there many of you?" he asked interestedly. Already the conversation was taking on a slightly personal tinge, but neither of them was at all aware of it.

"Two brothers and two sisters and mother," said the girl shyly. She was so full of delight over finding that she could rent the barn that she hardly knew what she was answering. She was unconscious of the fact that she had in a way taken this strange young man into her confidence by her shy, sweet tone and manner.

"Your mother approves of your plan?" he asked. "She doesn't object to the country?"

"Oh, I haven't told her yet," said Shirley. "I don't know that I shall; for she has been quite sick, and she trusts me entirely. She loves the country, and it will be wonderful to her to get out there. She might not like the idea of a barn beforehand; but she has never seen the barn, you know, and, besides, it won't look like a barn inside when I get it fixed up. I must talk it over with George and Carol, but I don't think I shall tell her at all till we take her out there and surprise her. I'll tell her I've found a place that I think she will like, and ask her if I may keep it a surprise. She'll be willing, and she'll be pleased, I know!" Her eyes were smiling happily, dreamily; the dreamer was uppermost in her face now, and made it lovely; then a sudden cloud came, and the strong look returned, with courage to meet a storm.

"But, anyhow," she finished after a pause, "we *have* to go there for the summer, for we've nowhere else to go that we can afford; and *anywhere* out of the city will be good, even if mother doesn't just choose it. I think perhaps it will be easier for her if she doesn't know about it until she's there. It won't seem so much like not going to live in a house."

"I see," said the young man interestedly. "I shouldn't wonder if you are right. And anyhow I think we can manage between us to make it pretty habitable for her." He was speaking eagerly and forgetting that he had no right, but a flush came into the sensitive girl's cheek.

"Oh, I wouldn't want to make you trouble," she said. "You have been very kind already, and you have made the rent so reasonable! I'm afraid it isn't right and fair; it is such a *lovely* barn!"

"Perfectly fair," said Graham glibly. "It will do the barn good to be lived in and taken care of again."

If he had been called upon to tell just what good it would do the barn to be lived in, he might have floundered out of the situation, perhaps; but he took care not to make that necessary. He went on talking.

"I will see that everything is in good order, the doors made all right, and the windows—I—that is, if I remember rightly there were a few little things needed doing to that barn that ought to be attended to before you go in. How soon did you want to take possession? I'll try to have it all ready for you."

"Oh, why, that is very kind," said Shirley. "I don't think it needs anything; that is, I didn't notice anything, but perhaps you know best. Why, we have to leave our house the last of this month. Do you suppose we could have the rent begin a few days before that, so we could get things moved gradually? I haven't much time, only at night, you know."

"We'll date the lease the first of next month," said the young man quickly; "and then you can put your things in any time you like from now on. I'll see that the locks are made safe, and there ought to be a partition put in—just a simple partition, you know—at one end of the up-stairs room, where you could lock up things. Then you could take them up there when you like. I'll attend to that partition at once. The barn needs it. This is as good a time as any to put it in. You wouldn't object to a partition? That wouldn't upset any of your plans?"

He spoke as if it would be a great detriment to the barn not to have a partition, but of course he wouldn't insist if she disliked it.

"Oh, why, no, of course not," said Shirley, bewildered. "It would be lovely. Mother could use that for her room, but I wouldn't want you to do anything on our account that you do not have to do anyway."

"Oh, no, certainly not, but it might as well be done now as any time, and you get the benefit of it, you know. I shouldn't want to rent the place without putting it in good order, and a partition is always needed in a barn, you know, if it's to be a really good barn."

It was well that no wise ones were listening to that conversation; else they might have laughed aloud at this point and betrayed the young man's strategy, but Shirley was all untutored in farm lore, and knew less about barns and their needs than she did of Sanskrit; so the remark passed without exciting her suspicion.

"Oh, it's going to be lovely!" said Shirley suddenly, like an eager child, "and I can't thank you enough for being so kind about it."

"Not at all," said the young man gracefully. "And now you will want to go out and look around again to make your plans. Were you planning to go soon? I should like to have you look the place over again and see if there is anything else that should be done."

"Oh, why," said Shirley, "I don't think there could be anything else; only I'd like to have a key to that big front door, for we couldn't carry things up the ladder very well. I was thinking I'd go out this afternoon, perhaps, if I could get George a leave of absence for a little while. There's been a death in our firm, and the office is working only half-time to-day, and I'm off again. I thought I'd like to have George see it if possible; he's very wise in his judgments, and mother trusts him a lot next to me; but I don't know whether they'll let him off on such short notice."

"Where does he work?"

"Farwell and Story's department store. They are pretty particular, but George is allowed a day off every three months if he takes it out of his vacation; so I thought I'd try."

"Here, let me fix that. Harry Farwell's a friend of mine." He caught up the telephone.

"Oh, you are very kind!" murmured Shirley, quite overcome at the blessings that were falling at her feet.

Graham already had the number, and was calling for Mr. Farwell, Junior.

"That you, Hal? Oh, good morning! Have a good time last night? Sorry I couldn't have been there, but I had three other engagements and couldn't get around. Say, I want to ask a favor of you. You have a boy there in the store I want to borrow for the afternoon if you don't mind. His name is George Hollister. Could you look him up and send him over to my office pretty soon? It will be a personal favor to me if you will let him off and not dock his pay. Thank you! I was sure you would. Return the favor sometime myself if opportunity comes my way. Yes, I'll hold the phone till you hunt him up. Thank you."

Graham looked up from the phone into the astonished grateful girl's eyes, and caught her look of deep admiration, which quite confused Shirley for a moment, and put her in a terrible way trying to thank him again.

"Oh, that's all right. Farwell and I went to prep school together. It's nothing for him to arrange matters. He says it will be all right. Now, what are your plans? I wonder if I can help in any way. How were you planning to go out?"

"Oh, by the trolley, of course," said Shirley. How strange it must be to have other ways of travelling at one's command!

"I did think," she added, half thinking aloud, "that perhaps I would stop at the schoolhouse and get my sister. I don't know but it would be better to get her judgment about things. She is rather a wise little girl."

She looked up suddenly, and seeing the young man's eyes upon her, grew ashamed that she had brought her private affairs to his notice; yet it had seemed necessary to say something to fill in this embarrassing pause. But Sidney Graham did not let her continue to be embarrassed. He entered into her plans just as if they concerned himself also.

"Why, I think that would be a very good plan," he said. "It will be a great deal better to have a real family council before you decide about moving. Now I've thought of something. Why couldn't you all go out in the car with me and my kid sister? I've been promising to take her a spin in the country, and my chauffeur is to drive her down this afternoon for me. It's almost time for her to be here now. Your brother will be here by the time she comes. Why couldn't we just go around by the schoolhouse and pick up your sister, and all go out together? I want to go out myself, you know, and look things over, and it seems to me that would save time all around. Then, if there should be anything you want done, you know——"

"Oh, there is nothing I want done," gasped Shirley. "You have been most kind. I couldn't think of asking for anything at the price we shall be paying. And we mustn't impose upon you. We can go out in the trolley perfectly well, and not trouble you."

"Indeed, it is no trouble whatever when I am going anyway." Then to the telephone: "Hello! He's coming, you say? He's on his way? Good. Thank you very much, Harry. Good-by!"

"That's all right!" he said, turning to her, smiling. "Your brother is on his way, and now excuse me just a moment while I phone to my sister."

Shirley sat with glowing cheeks and apprehensive mind while the young man called up a girl whom he addressed as "Kid" and told her to hurry the car right down, that he wanted to start very soon, and to bring some extra wraps along for some friends he was going to take with him.

He left Shirley no opportunity to express her overwhelming thanks, but gave her some magazines, and hurried from the room to attend to some matters of business before he left.

CHAPTER VI

Shirley sat with shining eyes and glowing cheeks, turning over the leaves of the magazines with trembling fingers, but unable to read anything, for the joy of what was before her. A real automobile ride! The first she had ever had! And it was to include George and Carol! How wonderful! And how kind in him, how thoughtful, to take his own sister, and hers, and so make the trip perfectly conventional and proper! What a nice face he had! What fine eyes! He didn't seem in the least like the young society man she knew he must be from the frequent mention she had noticed of his name in the papers. He was a real gentleman, a real nobleman! There were such. It was nice to know of them now and then, even though they did move in a different orbit from the one where she had been set. It gave her a happier feeling about the universe just to have seen how nice a man could be to a poor little nobody when he didn't have to. For of course it couldn't be anything to him to rent that barn—at ten dollars a month! That was ridiculous! Could it be that he was thinking her an object of charity? That he felt sorry for her and made the price merely nominal? She couldn't have that. It wasn't right nor honest, and—it wasn't respectable! That was the way unprincipled men did when they wanted to humor foolish little dolls of girls. Could it be that he thought of her in any such way?

Her cheeks flamed hotly and her eyes flashed. She sat up very straight indeed, and began to tremble. How was it she had not thought of such a thing before? Her mother had warned her to be careful about having anything to do with strange men, except in the most distant business way; and here had she been telling him frankly all the private affairs of the family and letting him make plans for her. How had it happened? What must he think of her? This came of trying to keep a secret from mother. She might have known it was wrong, and yet the case was so desperate and mother so likely to worry about any new and unconventional suggestion. It had seemed right. But of course it wasn't right for her to fall in that way and allow him to take them all in his car. She must put a stop to it somehow. She must go in the trolley if she went at all. She wasn't sure but she had better call the whole thing off and tell him they couldn't live in a barn, that she had changed her mind. It would be so dreadful if he had taken her for one of those girls who wanted to attract the attention of a young man!

In the midst of her perturbed thoughts the door opened and Sidney Graham walked in again. His fine, clean-cut face and clear eyes instantly dispelled her fears again. His bearing was dignified and respectful, and there was something in the very tone of his voice as he spoke to her that restored her confidence in him and in his impression of her. Her half-formed intention of rising and declining to take the ride with him fled, and she sat quietly looking at the pictures in the magazine with unseeing eyes.

"I hope you will find something to interest you for a few minutes," young Graham said pleasantly. "It won't be long, but there are one or two matters I promised father I would attend to before I left this afternoon. There is an article in that other magazine under your hand there about beautifying country homes, bungalows, and the like. It may give you some ideas about the old barn. I shouldn't wonder if a few flowers and vines might do a whole lot."

He found the place in the magazine, and left her again; and strangely enough she became absorbed in the article because her imagination immediately set to work thinking how glorious it would be to have a few flowers growing where Doris could go out and water them and pick them. She grew so interested in the remarks about what flowers would grow best in the open and which were easiest to care for that she got out her little pencil and notebook that were in her coat-pocket, and began to copy some of the lists. Then suddenly the door opened again, and Graham returned with George.

The boy stopped short on the threshold, startled, a white wave of apprehension passing over his face. He did not speak. The boy-habit of silence and self-control in a crisis was upon him. He looked with apprehension from one to the other.

Shirley jumped to her feet.

"Oh, George, I'm so glad you could come! This is Mr. Graham. He has been kind enough to offer to take us in his car to see a place we can rent for the summer, and it was through his suggestion that Mr. Farwell let you off for the afternoon."

There was a sudden relaxing of the tenseness in the young face and a sigh of relief in the tone as the boy answered:

"Aw, gee! That's great! Thanks awfully for the holiday. They don't come my way often. It'll be great to have a ride in a car, too. Some lark, eh, Shirley?"

The boy warmed to the subject with the friendly grasp the young man gave him, and Shirley could see her brother had made a good impression; for young Graham was smiling appreciatively, showing all his even white teeth just as if he enjoyed the boy's offhand way of talking.

"I'm going to leave you here for ten minutes more until I talk with a man out here in the office. Then we will go," said young Graham, and hurried away again.

"Gee, Shirley!" said the boy, flinging himself down luxuriously in a big leather chair. "Gee! You certainly did give me some start! I thought mother was worse, or you'd got arrested, or lost your job, or something, finding you here in a strange office. Some class to this, isn't there? Look at the thickness of that rug!" and he kicked the thick Turkish carpet happily. "Say, he must have some coin! Who is the guy, anyway? How'd ya get onto the tip? You don't think he's handing out Vanderbilt residences at fifteen a month, do you?"

"Listen, George. I must talk fast because he may come back any minute. Yesterday I got a half-holiday, and instead of going home I thought I'd go out and hunt a house. I took the Glenside trolley; and, when we got out past the city, I heard two men talking about a place we were passing. It was a great big, beautiful stone barn. They told who owned it, and said a lot about its having such a splendid spring of water beside it. It was a beautiful place, George; and I couldn't help thinking what a thing it would be for mother to be out in the country this summer, and what a wonderful house that would make——"

"We couldn't live in a barn, Shirl!" said the boy, aghast.

"Wait, George. Listen. Just you don't say that till you see it. It's the biggest barn you ever saw, and I guess it hasn't been used for a barn in a long time. I got out of the trolley on the way back, and went in. It is just enormous, and we could screen off rooms and live like princes. It has a great big front door, and we could have a hammock under the tree; and there's a brook to fish in, and a big third story with hay in it. I guess it's what they call in books a hay-loft. It's great."

"Gee!" was all the electrified George could utter. "Oh, gee!"

"It is on a little hill with the loveliest tree in front of it, and right on the trolley line. We'd have to start a little earlier in the morning; but I wouldn't mind, would you?"

"Naw!" said George, "but could we walk that far?"

"No, we'd have to ride, but the rent is so much lower it would pay our carfare."

"Gee!" said George again, "isn't that great? And is this the guy that owns it?"

"Yes, or at least he and his father do. He's been very kind. He's taking all this trouble to take us out in his car to-day to make sure if there is anything that needs to be done for our comfort there. He certainly is an unusual man for a landlord."

"He sure is, Shirley. I guess mebbe he has a case on you the way he looks at you."

"George!" said Shirley severely, the red staining her cheeks and her eyes flashing angrily. "George! That was a *dreadful* thing for you to say. If you ever even think a thing like that again, I won't have anything to do with him or the place. We'll just stay in the city all summer. I suppose perhaps that would be better, anyway."

Shirley got up and began to button her coat haughtily, as if she were going out that minute.

"Aw, gee, Shirley! I was just kidding. Can't you take a joke? This thing must be getting on your nerves. I never saw you so touchy."

"It certainly is getting on my nerves to have you say a thing like that, George."

Shirley's tone was still severe.

"Aw, cut the grouch, Shirley. I tell you I was just kidding. 'Course he's a good guy. He probably thinks you're cross-eyed, knock-kneed——"

"George!" Shirley started for the door; but the irrepressible George saw it was time to stop, and he put out an arm with muscles that were iron-like from many wrestlings and ball-games with his fellow laborers at the store.

"Now, Shirley, cut the comedy. That guy'll be coming back next, and you don't want to have him ask what's the matter, do you? He certainly is some fine guy. I wouldn't like to embarrass him, would you? He's a peach of a looker. Say, Shirley, what do you figure mother's going to say about this?"

Shirley turned, half mollified.

"That's just what I want to ask you, George. I don't want to tell mother until it's all fixed up and we can show if to her. You know it will sound a great deal worse to talk about living in a barn than it will to go in and see it all fixed up with rugs and curtains and screens and the piano and a couch, and the supper-table set, and the sun setting outside the open door, and a bird singing in the tree."

"Gee! Shirley, wouldn't that be some class? Say, Shirley, don't let's tell her! Let's just make her say she'll trust the moving to us to surprise her. Can't you kid her along and make her willing for that?"

"Why, that was what I was thinking. If you think there's no danger she will be disappointed and sorry, and think we ought to have done something else."

"What else could we do? Say, Shirley, it would be great to sleep in the hay-loft!"

"We could just tell her we were coming out in the country for the summer to camp in a nice place where it was safe and comfortable, and then we would have plenty of time to look around for the right kind of a house for next winter."

"That's the dope, Shirley! You give her that. She'll fall for that, sure thing. She'll like the country. At least, if it's like what you say it is."

"Well, you wait till you see it."

"Have you told Carol?" asked George, suddenly sobering. Carol was his twin sister, inseparable chum, and companion when he was at home.

"No," said Shirley, "I haven't had a chance; but Mr. Graham suggested we drive around by the school and get her. Then she can see how she likes it, too; and, if Carol thinks so, we'll get mother not to ask any questions, but just trust to us."

"Gee! That guy's great. He's got a head on him. Some lark, what?"

"Yes, he's been very kind," said Shirley. "At first I told him I couldn't let him take so much trouble for us, but he said he was going to take his sister out for a ride——"

"A girl! Aw, gee! I'm going to beat it!" George stopped in his eager walk back and forth across the office, and seized his old faded cap.

"George, stop! You mustn't be impolite. Besides, I think she's only a very little girl, probably like Doris. He called her his 'kid sister.'"

"H'm! You can't tell. I ain't going to run any risks. I better beat it."

But George's further intentions were suddenly brought to a finish by the entrance of Mr. Sidney Graham.

"Well, Miss Hollister," he said with a smile, "we are ready at last. I'm sorry to have kept you waiting so long; but there was something wrong with one of my tires, and the chauffeur had to run around to the garage. Come on, George," he said to the boy, who hung shyly behind now, wary of any lurking female who might be haunting the path. "Guess you'll have to sit in the front seat with me, and help me drive. The chauffeur has to go back and drive for mother. She has to go to some tea or other."

George suddenly forgot the possible girl, and followed his new hero to the elevator with a swelling soul. What would the other fellows at the store think of him? A whole half-holiday, an automobile-ride, and a chance to sit in the front and learn to drive! But all he said was:

"Aw, gee! Yes, sure thing!"

20

The strange girl suddenly loomed on his consciousness again as they emerged from the elevator and came out on the street. She was sitting in the great back seat alone, arrayed in a big blue velvet coat the color of her eyes, and George felt at once all hands and feet. She was a slender wisp of a thing about Carol's age, with a lily complexion and a wealth of gold hair caught in a blue veil. She smiled very prettily when her brother introduced her as "Elizabeth." There was nothing snobbish or disagreeable about her, but that blue velvet coat suddenly made George conscious of his own common attire, and gave Shirley a pang of dismay at her own little shabby suit.

However, Sidney Graham soon covered all differences in the attire of his guests by insisting that they should don the two long blanket coats that he handed them; and somehow when George was seated in the big leather front seat, with that great handsome coat around his shoulders, he did not much mind the blue velvet girl behind him, and mentally resolved to earn enough to get Carol a coat like it some day; only Carol's should be pink or red to go with her black eyes and pink cheeks.

After all, it was Shirley, not George, who felt embarrassment over the strange girl and wished she had not come. She was vexed with herself for it, too. It was foolish to let a child no older than Carol fluster her so, but the thought of a long ride alone on that back seat with the dainty young girl actually frightened her.

But Elizabeth was not frightened. She had been brought up in the society atmosphere, and was at home with people always, everywhere. She tucked the robes about her guest, helped Shirley button the big, soft dark-blue coat about her, remarking that it got awfully chilly when they were going; and somehow before Shirley had been able to think of a single word to say in response the conversation seemed to be moving along easily without her aid.

"Sid says we're going to pick up your sister from her school. I'm so glad! How old is she? About my age? Won't that be delightful? I'm rather lonesome this spring because all my friends are in school. I've been away at boarding-school, and got the measles. Wasn't that too silly for a great big girl like me? And the doctor said I couldn't study any more this spring on account of my eyes. It's terribly lonesome. I've been home six weeks now, and I don't know what to do with myself. What's your sister's name? Carol? Carol Hollister? That's a pretty name! Is she the only sister you have? A baby sister? How sweet! What's her name? Oh, I think Doris is the cutest name ever. Doris Hollister. Why don't we go and get Doris? Wouldn't she like to ride, too? Oh, it's too bad your mother is ill; but of course she wouldn't want to stay all alone in the house without some of her family."

Elizabeth was tactful. She knew at a glance that trained nurses and servants could not be plentiful in a family where the young people wore such plain, old-style garments. She gave no hint of such a thought, however.

"That's your brother," she went on, nodding toward George. "I've got another brother, but he's seventeen and away at college, so I don't see much of him. Sid's very good to me when he has time, and often he takes me to ride. We're awfully jolly chums, Sid and I. Is this the school where your sister goes? She's in high school, then. The third year? My! She must be bright. I've only finished my second. Does she know she's going with us? What fun to be called out of school by a surprise! Oh, I just know I'm going to like her."

Shirley sat dumb with amazement, and listened to the eager gush of the lively girl, wondered what shy Carol would say, trying to rouse herself to answer the young questioner in the same spirit in which she asked questions.

George came out with Carol in a very short time, Carol struggling into her coat and trying to straighten her hat, while George mumbled in her ear as he helped her clumsily:

"Some baby doll out there! Kid, you better preen your feathers. She's been gassing with Shirley to beat the band I couldn't hear all they said, but she asked a lot about you. You should worry! Hold up your head, and don't flicker an eyelash. You're as good as she is any day, if you don't look all dolled up like a new saloon. But she's some looker! Pretty as a red wagon! Her brother's a peach of a fellow. He's going to let me run the car when we get out of the city limit; and say! Shirley says for me to tell you we're going out to look at a barn where we're going to move this summer, and you're not to say a word about it's being a barn. See? Get onto that sky-blue-pink satin scarf she's got around her head? Ain't she some chicken, though?"

"Hush, George! She'll hear you!" murmured Carol in dismay. "What do you mean about a barn? How could we live in a barn?"

"You just shut up and saw wood, kid, and you'll see. Shirley thinks she's got onto something pretty good."

Then Carol was introduced to the beautiful blue-velvet girl and sat down beside her, wrapped in a soft furry cloak of garnet, to be whirled away into a fairy-land of wonder.

CHAPTER VII

Carol and Elizabeth got on very well together. Shirley was amazed to see the ease with which her sister entered into this new relation, unawed by the garments of her hostess. Carol had more of the modern young America in her than Shirley, perhaps, whose early life had been more conventionally guarded. Carol was democratic, and, strange to say, felt slightly superior to Elizabeth on account of going to a public school. The high-school girls were in the habit of referring to a neighboring boarding-school as "Dummy's Retreat"; and therefore Carol was not at all awed by the other girl, who declared in a friendly manner that she had always been crazy to go to the public school, and asked rapid intelligent questions about the doings there. Before they were out of the city limits the two girls were talking a steady stream, and one could see from their eyes that they liked each other. Shirley, relieved, settled back on the comfortable cushions, and let herself rest and relax. She tried to think how it would feel to own a car like this and be able to ride around when she wanted to.

On the front seat George and Graham were already excellent friends, and George was gaining valuable information about running a car, which he had ample opportunity to put into practice as soon as they got outside the crowded thoroughfares.

They were perhaps half-way to the old barn and running smoothly on an open road, with no one in sight a long way ahead, when Graham turned back to Shirley, leaving George to run the car for a moment himself. The boy's heart swelled with gratitude and utmost devotion to be thus trusted. Of course there wasn't anything to do but keep things just as he had been told, but this man realized that he would do it and not perform any crazy, daring action to show off. George set himself to be worthy of this trust. To be sure, young Graham had a watchful eye upon things, and was taking no chances; but he let the boy feel free, and did not make him aware of his espionage, which is a course of action that will win any boy to give the best that is in him to any responsibility, if he has any best at all.

It was not the kind of conversation that one would expect between landlord and tenant that the young girl and the man carried on in these brief sentences now and then. He called her attention to the soft green tint that was spreading over the tree-tops more distinctly than the day before; to the lazy little clouds floating over the blue; to the tinting of the fields, now taking on every hour new colors; to the perfume in the air. So with pleasantness of passage they arrived at last at the old barn.

Like a pack of eager children they tumbled out of the car and hurried up to the barn, all talking at once, forgetting all difference in station. They were just young and out on a picnic.

Graham had brought a key for the big padlock; and clumsily the man and the boy, unused to such manoeuvres, unlocked and shoved back the two great doors.

"These doors are too heavy. They should have ball bearings," remarked young Graham. "I'll attend to that at once. They should be made to move with a light touch. I declare it doesn't pay to let property lie idle without a tenant, there are so many little things that get neglected."

He walked around with a wise air as if he had been an active landowner for years, though indeed he was looking at everything with strange, ignorant eyes. His standard was a home where every detail was perfect, and where necessities came and vanished with the need. This was his first view into the possibilities of "being up against it," as he phrased it in his mind.

Elizabeth in her blue velvet cloak and blue cloudy veil stood like a sweet fairy in the wide doorway, and looked around with delight.

"Oh Sid, wouldn't this be just a dandy place for a party?" she exclaimed eagerly. "You could put the orchestra over in that corner behind a screen of palms, and decorate with gray Florida moss and asparagus vine with daffodils wired on in showers from the beams, and palms all around the walls, and colored electrics hidden everywhere. You could run a wire in from the street, couldn't you? the way they did at Uncle Andy's, and serve the supper out on the lawn with little individual rustic tables. Brower has them, and brings them out with rustic chairs to match. You could have the tree wired, too, and have colored electrics all over the place. Oh! wouldn't it be just heavenly? Say, Sid, Carol says they are coming out here to live, maybe; why couldn't we give them a party like that for a house-warming?"

Sidney Graham looked at his eager, impractical young sister and then at the faces of the three Hollisters, and tried not to laugh as the tremendous contrast of circumstances was presented to him. But his rare tact served him in good stead.

"Why, Elizabeth, that would doubtless be very delightful; but Miss Hollister tells me her mother has been quite ill, and I'm sure, while that might be the happiest thing imaginable for you young folks, it would be rather trying on an invalid. I guess you'll have to have your parties somewhere else for the present."

"Oh!" said Elizabeth with quick recollection, "of course! They told me about their mother. How thoughtless of me! But it would be lovely, wouldn't it, Miss Hollister? Can't you see it?"

She turned in wistful appeal to Shirley, and that young woman, being a dreamer herself, at once responded with a radiant smile:

"Indeed I can, and it would be lovely indeed, but I've been thinking what a lovely home it could be made, too."

"Yes?" said Elizabeth questioningly, and looking around with a dubious frown. "It would need a lot of changing, I should think. You would want hardwood floors, and lots of rugs, and some partitions and windows——"

"Oh, no," said Shirley, laughing. "We're not hardwood people, dear; we're just plain hard-working people; and all we need is a quiet, sweet place to rest in. It's going to be just heavenly here, with that tree outside to shade the doorway, and all this wide space to walk around in. We live in a little narrow city house now, and never have any place to get out except the street. We'll have the birds and the brook for orchestra, and we won't need palms, because the trees and vines will soon be in leaf and make a lovely screen for our orchestra. I imagine at night the stars will have almost as many colors as electrics."

Elizabeth looked at her with puzzled eyes, but half convinced.

"Well, yes, perhaps they would," she said, and smiled. "I've never thought of them that way, but it sounds very pretty, quite like some of Browning's poetry that I don't understand, or was it Mrs. Browning? I can't quite remember."

Sidney Graham, investigating the loft above them, stood a moment watching the tableau and listening to the conversation, though they could not see him; and he thought within himself that it might not be a bad thing for his little sister, with her boarding-school rearing, to get near to these true-hearted young working people, who yet were dreamers and poets, and get her standards somewhat modified by theirs. He was especially delighted with the gentle, womanly way in which Shirley answered the girl now when she thought herself alone with her.

George and Carol had grasped hold of hands and run wildly down the slope to the brook after a most casual glance at the interior of the barn. Elizabeth now turned her dainty high-heeled boots in the brook's direction, and Shirley was left alone to walk the length and breadth of her new abode and make some real plans.

The young man in the dim loft above watched her for a moment as she stood looking from one wall to the other, measuring distances with her eye, walking quickly over to the window and rubbing a clear space on the dusty pane with her handkerchief that she might look out. She was a goodly sight, and he could not help comparing her with the girls he knew, though their garments would have far outshone hers. Still, even in the shabby dark-blue serge suit she seemed lovely.

The young people returned as precipitately as they had gone, and both Carol and George of their own accord joined Shirley in a brief council of war. Graham thoughtfully called his sister away, ostensibly to watch a squirrel high in the big tree, but really to admonish her about making no further propositions like that for the party, as the young people to whom he had introduced her were not well off, and had no money or time for elaborate entertainments.

"But they're lovely, Sid, aren't they? Don't you like them just awfully? I know you do, or you wouldn't have taken the trouble to bring them out here in the car with us. Say, you'll bring me to see them often after they come here to live, won't you?"

"Perhaps," said her brother smilingly. "But hadn't you better wait until they ask you?"

"Oh, they'll ask me," said Elizabeth with a charming smile and a confident little toss of her head. "I'll make them ask me."

"Be careful, kid," he said, still smiling. "Remember, they won't have much money to offer you entertainment with, and probably their things are very plain and simple. You may embarrass them if you invite yourself out."

Elizabeth raised her azure eyes to her brother's face thoughtfully for a moment, then smiled back confidently once more.

"Don't you worry, Sid, dear; there's more than one way. I won't hurt their feelings, but they're going to ask me, and they're going to want me, and I'm going to come. Yes, and you're going to bring me!"

She turned with a laughing pirouette, and danced down the length of the barn to Carol, catching her hand and whirling her after her in a regular childish frolic.

"Well, do you think we ought to take it? Do you think I dare give my final word without consulting mother?" Shirley asked her brother when they were thus left alone for a minute.

"Sure thing! No mistake! It's simply *great*. You couldn't get a place like this if you went the length and breadth of the city and had a whole lot more money than you have to spend."

"But remember it's a barn!" said Shirley impressively. "Mother may mind that very much."

"Not when she sees it," said Carol, whirling back to the consultation. "She'll think it's the sensiblest thing we ever did. She isn't foolish like that. We'll tell her we've found a place to camp with a shanty attached, and she can't be disappointed. I think it'll be great. Just think how Doris can run in the grass!"

"Yes," put in George. "I was telling Carol down by the spring—before that *girl* came and stopped us—I think we might have some chickens and raise eggs. Harley could do that, and Carol and I could raise flowers, and I could take 'em to town in the morning. I could work evenings."

Shirley smiled. She almost felt like shouting that they agreed with her. The place seemed so beautiful, so almost heavenly to her when she thought of the close, dark quarters at home and the summer with its heat coming on.

"We couldn't keep a lodger, and we'd have that much less," said Shirley thoughtfully.

"But we wouldn't have their laundry nor their room-work to do," said Carol, "and I could have that much more time for the garden and chickens."

"You mustn't count on being able to make much that way," said Shirley gravely. "You know nothing about gardening, and would probably make a lot of mistakes at first, anyway."

"I can make fudge and sandwiches, and take them to school to sell," declared Carol stoutly; "and I'll find out how to raise flowers and parsley and little things people have to have. Besides, there's watercress down by that brook, and people like that. We could sell that."

"Well, we'll see," said Shirley thoughtfully, "but you mustn't get up too many ideas yet. If we can only get moved and mother is satisfied, I guess we can get along. The rent is only ten dollars."

"Good *night*! That's cheap enough!" said George, and drew a long whistle. Then, seeing Elizabeth approaching, he put on an indifferent air, and sauntered to the dusty window at the other end of the barn.

Sidney Graham appeared now, and took Shirley over to the east end to ask her just where she thought would be a good place to put the partition, and did she think it would be a good thing to have another one at the other end just like it? And so they stood and planned, quite as if Shirley were ordering a ten-thousand-dollar alteration put into her ten-dollar barn. Then suddenly the girl remembered her fears; and, looking straight up into the interested face of the young man, she asked earnestly:

"You are sure you were going to put in these partitions? You are not making any change on my account? Because I couldn't think of allowing you to go to any trouble or expense, you know."

Her straightforward look embarrassed him.

"Why, I——" he said, growing a little flushed. "Why, you see I hadn't been out to look things over before. I didn't realize how much better it would be to have those in, you know. But now I intend to do it right away. Father put the whole thing in my hands to do as I pleased. In fact, the place is mine now, and I want to put it in good shape to rent. So don't worry yourself in the least. Things won't go to wrack and ruin so quickly, you know, if there is someone on the place."

He finished his sentence briskly. It seemed quite plausible even to himself now, and he searched about for a change of topic.

"You think you can get on here with the rough floor? You might put padding or something under your carpets, you know, but it will take pretty large carpets——" He looked at her dubiously. To his conventional mind every step of the way was blocked by some impassable barrier. He did not honestly see how she was going to do the thing at all.

"Oh, we don't need carpets!" laughed Shirley gayly. "We'll spread down a rug in front of mother's bed, and another one by the piano, and the rest will be just perfectly all right. We're not expecting to give receptions here, you know," she added mischievously. "We're only campers, and very grateful campers at that, too, to find a nice, clean, empty floor where we can live. The only thing that is troubling me is the cooking. I've been wondering if it will affect the insurance if we use an oil-stove to cook with, or would you rather we got a wood-stove and put the pipe out of one of the windows? I've seen people do that sometimes. Of course we could cook outdoors on a camp-fire if it was necessary, but it might be a little inconvenient rainy days."

Graham gasped at the coolness with which this slip of a girl discoursed about hardships as if they were necessities to be accepted pleasantly and without a murmur. She actually would not be daunted at the idea of cooking her meals on a fire out-of-doors! Cooking indeed! That was of course a question that people had to consider. It had never been a question that crossed his mind before. People cooked—how did they cook? By electricity, gas, coal and wood fires, of course. He had never considered it a matter to be called in any way serious. But now he perceived that it was one of the first main things to be looked out for in a home. He looked down at the waiting girl with a curious mixture of wonder, admiration, and dismay in his face.

"Why, of course you will need a fire and a kitchen," he said as if those things usually grew in houses without any help and it hadn't occurred to him before that they were not indigenous to barns. "Well, now, I hadn't thought of that. There isn't any chimney here, is there? H'm! There ought to be a chimney in every barn. It would be better for the—ah—for the hay, I should think; keep it dry, you know, and all that sort of thing. And then I should think it might be better for the animals. I must look into that matter."

"No, Mr. Graham," said Shirley decidedly. "There is no necessity for a chimney. We can perfectly well have the pipe go through a piece of tin set in the back window if you won't object, and we can use the little oil-stove when it's very hot if that doesn't affect the insurance. We have a gas stove, of course, that we could bring; but there isn't any gas in a barn."

Graham looked around blankly at the cobwebby walls as if expecting gas-jets to break forth simultaneously with his wish.

"No, I suppose not," he said, "although I should think there ought to be. In a *barn*, you know. But I'm sure there will be no objection whatever to your using any kind of a stove that will work here. This is a stone barn, you know, and I'm sure it won't affect the insurance. I'll find out and let you know."

Shirley felt a trifle uneasy yet about those partitions and the low price of the rent, but somehow the young man had managed to impress her with the fact that he was under no unpleasant delusions concerning herself and that he had the utmost respect for her. He stood looking down earnestly at her for a moment without saying a word, and then he began hesitatingly.

"I wish you'd let me tell you," he said frankly, "how awfully brave you are about all this, planning to come out here in this lonely place, and not being afraid of hard work, and rough floors, and a barn, and even a fire out-of-doors."

Shirley's laugh rang out, and her eyes sparkled.

"Why, it's the nicest thing that's happened to me in ages," she said joyously. "I can't hardly believe it's true that we can come here, that we can really *afford* to come to a great, heavenly country place like this. I suppose of course there'll be hard things. There always are, and some of them have been just about unbearable, but even the hard things can be made fun if you try. This is going to be grand!" and she looked around triumphantly on the dusty rafters and rough stone walls with a little air of possession.

"You are rather"—he paused—"unusual!" he finished thoughtfully as they walked toward the doorway and stood looking off at the distance.

But now Shirley had almost forgotten him in the excitement of the view.

"Just think of waking up to that every morning," she declared with a sweep of her little blue-clad arm toward the view in the distance. "Those purply hills, the fringe of brown and green against the horizon, that white spire nestling among those evergreens! Is that a church? Is it near enough for us to go to? Mother wouldn't want us to be too far from church."

"We'll go home that way and discover," said Graham decidedly. "You'll want to get acquainted with your new neighborhood. You'll need to know how near there is a store, and where your neighbors live. We'll reconnoitre a little. Are you ready to go?"

"Oh, yes. I'm afraid we have kept you too long already, and we must get home about the time Carol usually comes from school, or mother will be terribly worried. Carol is never later than half-past four."

"We've plenty of time," said the driver of the car, looking at his watch and smiling assurance. "Call the children, and we'll take a little turn around the neighborhood before we go back."

And so the little eager company were reluctantly persuaded to climb into the car again and start on their way.

CHAPTER VIII

The car leaped forward up the smooth white road, and the great barn as they looked back to it seemed to smile pleasantly to them in farewell. Shirley looked back, and tried to think how it would seem to come home every night and see Doris standing at the top of the grassy incline waiting to welcome her; tried to fancy her mother in a hammock under the big tree a little later when it grew warm and summery, and the boys working in their garden. It seemed too heavenly to be true.

The car swept around the corner of Allister Avenue, and curved down between tall trees. The white spire in the distance drew nearer now, and the purplish hills were off at one side. The way was fresh with smells of spring, and everywhere were sweet scents and droning bees and croaking frogs. The spirit of the day seemed to enter into the young people and make them glad. Somehow all at once they seemed to have known one another a long time, and to be intimately acquainted with one another's tastes and ecstasies. They exclaimed together over the distant view of the misty city with the river winding on its far way, and shouted simultaneously over a frightened rabbit that scurried across the road and hid in the brushwood; and then the car wound round a curve and the little white church swept into view below them.

> "The little white church in the valley
> Is bright with the blossoms of May,
> And true is the heart of your lover
> Who waits for your coming to-day!"

chanted forth George in a favorite selection of the department-store victrola, and all the rest looked interested. It was a pretty church, and nestled under the hills as if it were part of the landscape, making a home-centre for the town.

"We can go to church and Sunday-school there," said Shirley eagerly. "How nice! That will please mother!"

Elizabeth looked at her curiously, and then speculatively toward the church.

"It looks awfully small and cheap," said Elizabeth.

"All the more chance for us to help!" said Shirley. "It will be good for us."

"What could you do to help a church?" asked the wondering Elizabeth. "Give money to paint it? The paint is all scaling off."

"We couldn't give much money," said Carol, "because we haven't got it. But there's lots of things to do in a church besides giving. You teach in Sunday-school, and you wait on table at suppers when they have Ladies' Aid."

"Maybe they'll ask you to play the organ, Shirley," suggested George.

"Oh George!" reproved Shirley. "They'll have plenty that can play better than I can. Remember I haven't had time to practise for ages."

"She's a crackerjack at the piano!" confided George to Graham in a low growl. "She hasn't had a lesson since father died, but before that she used to be at it all the time. She c'n sing too. You oughtta hear her."

"I'm sure I should like to," assented Graham heartily. "I wonder if you will help me get her to sing sometime if I come out to call after you are settled."

"Sure!" said George heartily, "but she mebbe won't do it. She's awful nutty about singing sometimes. She's not stuck on herself nor nothing."

But the little white church was left far behind, and the city swept on apace. They were nearing home now, and Graham insisted on knowing where they lived, that he might put them down at their door. Shirley would have pleaded an errand and had them set down in the business part of the town; but George airily gave the street and number, and Shirley could not prevail upon Graham to stop at his office and let them go their way.

And so the last few minutes of the drive were silent for Shirley, and her cheeks grew rosy with humiliation over the dark little narrow street where they would presently arrive. Perhaps when he saw it this cultured young man would think they were too poor and common to be good tenants even for a barn. But, when they stopped before the little two-story brick house, you would not have known from the expression on the young man's face as he glanced at the number but that the house was a marble front on the most exclusive avenue in the city. He handed down Shirley with all the grace that he would have used to wait upon a millionaire's daughter, and she liked the way he helped out Carol and spoke to George as if he were an old chum.

"I want you to come and see me next Saturday," called Elizabeth to Carol as the car glided away from the curb; "and I'm coming out to help you get settled, remember!"

The brother and two sisters stood in front of their little old dark house, and watched the elegant car glide away. They were filled with wonder at themselves that they had been all the afternoon a part of that elegant outfit. Was it a dream? They rubbed their eyes as the car disappeared around the corner, and turned to look up at the familiar windows and make sure where they were. Then they stood a moment to decide how they should explain to the waiting mother why they happened to be home so early.

It was finally decided that George should go to hunt up a drayman and find out what he would charge to move their things to the country, and Shirley should go to a neighbor's to inquire about a stove she heard they wanted to sell. Then Carol could go in alone, and there would be nothing to explain. There was no telling when either George or Shirley would have a holiday again, and it was as well to get these things arranged as soon as possible.

Meantime Elizabeth Graham was eagerly interviewing her brother, having taken the vacant front seat for the purpose.

"Sid, where did you find those perfectly dear people? I think they are just great! And are they really going to live in that barn? Won't that be dandy? I wish mother'd let me go out and spend a month with them. I mean to ask her. That Carol is the nicest girl ever. She's just a dear!"

"Now, look here, kid," said Graham, facing about to his sister. "I want you to understand a thing or two. I took you on this expedition because I thought I could trust you. See?"

Elizabeth nodded.

"Well, I don't want a lot of talk at home about this. Do you understand? I want you to wait a bit and go slow. If things seem to be all right a little later on, you can ask Carol to come and see you, perhaps; but you'll have to look out. She hasn't fine clothes to go visiting in, I imagine, and they're pretty proud. I guess they've lost their money. Their father died a couple of years ago, and they've been up against it. They do seem like awfully nice people, I'll admit; and, if it's all right later on, you can get to be friends, but you'll have to go slow. Mother wouldn't understand it, and she mustn't be annoyed, you know. I'll take you out to see them sometime when they get settled if it seems all right, but meantime can you keep your tongue still?"

Elizabeth's face fell, but she gave her word immediately. She and her brother were chums; it was easy to see that.

"But can't I have her out for a week-end, Sid? Can't I tell mother anything about her? I could lend her some dresses, you know."

"You go slow, kid, and leave the matter to me. I'll tell mother about them pretty soon when I've had a chance to see a little more of them and am sure mother wouldn't mind. Meantime, don't you fret. I'll take you out when I go on business, and you shall see her pretty soon again."

Elizabeth had to be content with that. She perceived that for some reason her brother did not care to have the matter talked over in the family. She knew they would all guy him about his interest in a girl who wanted to rent his barn, and she felt herself that Shirley was too fine to be talked about in that way. The family wouldn't understand unless they saw her.

"I know what you mean, Sid," she said after a thoughtful pause. "You want the folks to see them before they judge what they are, don't you?"

"That's just exactly the point," said Sidney with a gleam of satisfaction in his eyes. "That's just what makes you such a good pal, kid. You always understand."

The smile dawned again in Elizabeth's eyes, and she patted her brother's sleeve.

"Good old Sid!" she murmured tenderly. "You're all right. And I just know you're going to take me out to that barn soon. Aren't you going to fix it up for them a little? They can't live there that way. It would be a dandy place to live if the windows were bigger and there were doors like a house, and a piazza, and some fireplaces. A great big stone fireplace in the middle there opposite that door! Wouldn't that be sweet? And they'll have to have electric lights and some bathrooms, of course."

Her brother tipped back his head, and laughed.

"I'm afraid you wouldn't make much of a hand to live in a barn, kid," he said. "You're too much of an aristocrat. How much do you want for your money? My dear, they don't expect tiled bathrooms, and electric lights, and inlaid floors when they rent a barn for the summer."

"But aren't you going to do anything, Sid?"

"Well, I can't do much, for Miss Hollister would suspect right away. She's very businesslike, and she has suspicions already because I said I was going to put in partitions. She isn't an object of charity, you know. I imagine they are all pretty proud."

Elizabeth sat thoughtful and still. It was the first time in her life she had contemplated what it would be to be very poor.

Her brother watched her with interest. He had a feeling that it was going to be very good for Elizabeth to know these Hollisters.

Suddenly he brought the car to a stop before the office of a big lumber-yard they were passing.

"I'm going in here, kid, for just a minute, to see if I can get a man to put in those partitions."

Elizabeth sat meditatively studying the office window through whose large dusty panes could be seen tall strips of moulding, unpainted window-frames, and a fluted column or two, evidently ready to fill an order. The sign over the door set forth that window-sashes, doors, and blinds were to be had. Suddenly Elizabeth sat up straight and read the sign again, strained her eyes to see through the window, and then opened the car door and sprang out. In a moment more she stood beside her brother, pointing mutely to a large window-frame that stood against the wall.

"What is it, kid?" he asked kindly.

"Sid, why can't you put on great big windows like that? They would never notice the windows, you know. It would be so nice to have plenty of light and air."

"That's so," he murmured. "I might change the windows some without its being noticed."

Then to the man at the desk:

"What's the price of that window? Got any more?"

"Yes," said the man, looking up interested; "got half a dozen, made especially for a party, and then he wasn't pleased. Claimed he ordered sash-winders 'stead of casement. If you can use these six, we'll make you a special price."

"Oh, take them, Sid! They're perfectly lovely," said Elizabeth eagerly. "They're casement windows with diamond panes. They'll just be so quaint and artistic in that stone!"

"Well, I don't know how they'll fit," said the young man doubtfully. "I don't want to make it seem as if I was trying to put on too much style."

"No, Sid, it won't seem that way, really. I tell you they'll never notice the windows are bigger, and casement windows aren't like a regular house, you know. See, they'll open wide like doors. I think it would be just grand!"

"All right, kid, we'll see! We'll take the man out with us; and, if he says it can be done, I'll take them."

Elizabeth was overjoyed.

"That's just what it needed!" she declared. "They couldn't live in the dark on rainy days. You must put two in the front on each side the door, and one on each end. The back windows will do well enough."

"Well, come on, kid. Mr. Jones is going out with me at once. Do you want to go with us, or shall I call a taxi and send you home?" asked her brother.

"I'm going with you, of course," said Elizabeth eagerly, hurrying out to the car as if she thought the thing would be done all wrong without her.

So Elizabeth sat in the back seat alone, while her brother and the contractor discoursed on the price of lumber and the relative values of wood and stone for building-purposes, and the big car went back over the way it had been before that afternoon.

They stopped on the way out, and picked up one of Mr. Jones's carpenters who was just leaving a job with his kit of tools, and who climbed stolidly into the back seat, and sat as far away from the little blue-velvet miss as possible, all the while taking furtive notes to tell his own little girl about her when he went home.

Elizabeth climbed out, and went about the barn with them, listening to all they had to say.

The two men took out pencils and foot rules, and went around measuring and figuring. Elizabeth watched them with bright, attentive eyes, putting a whispered suggestion now and then to her brother.

"They can't go up and down a ladder all the time," she whispered. "There ought to be some rough stairs with a railing, at least as good as our back stairs at home."

"How about it?" said Graham aloud to the contractor. "Can you put in some steps, just rough ones, to the left? I'm going to have a party out here camping for a while this summer, and I want it to be safe. Need a railing, you know, so nobody will get a fall."

The man measured the space up with his eye.

"Just want plain steps framed up with a hand-rail?" he said, squinting up again. "Guess we better start 'em up this way to the back wall and then turn back from a landing. That'll suit the overhead space best. Just pine, you want 'em, I s'pose?"

Elizabeth stood like a big blue bird alighted on the door-sill, watching and listening. She was a regular woman, and saw big possibilities in the building. She would have enjoyed ordering parquetry flooring and carved newel-posts and making a regular palace.

The sun was setting behind the purply hill and sending a glint from the weather-vane on the little white church spire when they started back to the city. Elizabeth looked wistfully toward it, and wondered about the rapt expression on Shirley's face when she spoke of "working" in the church. How could one get any pleasure out of that? She meant to find out. At present her life was rather monotonous, and she longed to have some new interests.

That night after she had gone to her luxurious little couch she lay in her downy nest, and tried to think how it would be to live in that big barn and go to sleep up in the loft, lying on that hay. Then suddenly the mystery of life was upon her with its big problems. Why, for instance, was she born into the Graham family with money and culture and all the good times, and that sweet, bright Carol-girl born into the Hollister family where they had a hard time to live at all?

CHAPTER IX

Quite early the next morning Sidney Graham was in his office at the telephone. He conferred with the carpenter, agreeing to meet him out at the barn and make final arrangements about the windows in a very short time. Then he called up the trolley company and the electric company, and made arrangements with them to have a wire run from the road to his barn, with a very satisfactory agreement whereby he could pay them a certain sum for the use of as much light as he needed. This done, he called up an electrician, and arranged that he should send some men out that morning to wire the barn.

He hurried through his morning mail, giving his stenographer a free hand with answering some of the letters, and then speeded out to Glenside.

Three men were already there, two of them stone-masons, working away under the direction of the contractor. They had already begun working at the massive stone around the windows, striking musical blows from a light scaffolding that made the old barn look as if it had suddenly waked up and gone to house-cleaning. Sidney Graham surveyed it with satisfaction as he stopped his car by the roadside and got out. He did delight to have things done on time. He decided that if this contractor did well on the job he would see that he got bigger things to do. He liked it that his work had been begun at once.

The next car brought a quartette of carpenters, and before young Graham went back to the city a motor-truck had arrived loaded with lumber and window-frames. It was all very fascinating to him, this new toy barn that had suddenly come into his possession, and he could hardly tear himself away from it and go back to business. One would not have supposed, perhaps, that it was so very necessary for him to do so, either, seeing that he was already so well off that he really could have gotten along quite comfortably the rest of his life without any more money; but he was a conscientious young man, who believed that no living being had a right to exist in idleness, and who had gone into business from a desire to do his best and keep up the honorable name of his father's firm. So after he had given careful directions for the electric men when they should come he rushed back to his office once more.

The next two days were filled with delightful novelties. He spent much time flying from office to barn and back to the office again, and before evening of the second day he had decided that a telephone in the barn was an absolute necessity, at least while the work was going on. So he called up the telephone company, and arranged that connection should be put in at once. That evening he wrote a short note to Miss Shirley Hollister, telling her that the partitions were under way and would soon be completed, and that in a few days he would send her the key so that she might begin to transport her belongings to the new home.

The next morning, when Graham went out to the stone barn, he found that the front windows were in, and gave a very inviting appearance to the edifice, both outside and in. As Elizabeth had surmised, the big latticed windows opening inwards like casement doors seemed quite in keeping with the rough stone structure. Graham began to wonder why all barns did not affect this style of window, they were so entirely attractive. He was thoroughly convinced that the new tenants would not be likely to remember or notice the difference in the windows; he was sure he shouldn't have unless his attention had been called to them in some way. Of course the sills and sashes were rather new-looking, but he gave orders that they should at once be painted an unobtrusive dark green which would well accord with the mossy roof, and he trusted his particular young tenant would not think that he had done anything pointed in changing the windows. If she did, he would have to think up some excuse.

But, as he stood at the top of the grassy slope and looked about, he noticed the great pile of stones under each window, from the masonry that had been torn away to make room for the larger sashes, and an idea came to him.

"Mr. Jones!" he called to the contractor, who had just come over on the car to see how the work was progressing. "Wouldn't there be stones enough all together from all the windows to build some kind of a rude chimney and fireplace?" he asked.

Mr. Jones thought there would. There were stones enough down in the meadow to piece out with in case they needed more, anyway. Where would Mr. Graham want the fireplace? Directly opposite the front doors? He had thought of suggesting that himself, but didn't know as Mr. Graham wanted to go to any more expense.

"By all means make that fireplace!" said the young owner delightedly. "This is going to be a jolly place when it gets done, isn't it? I declare I don't know but I'd like to come out here and live."

"It would make a fine old house, sir," said the contractor respectfully, looking up almost reverently at the barn. "I'd like to see it with verandys, and more winders, and a few such. You don't see many of these here old stone buildings around now. They knew how to build 'em substantial in those old times, so they did."

"H'm! Yes. It would make a fine site for a house, wouldn't it?" said the young man, looking about thoughtfully. "Well, now, we'll have to think about that sometime, perhaps. However, I think it looks very nice for the present"; and he walked about, looking at the improvements with great satisfaction.

At each end of the barn a good room, long and narrow, had been partitioned off, each of which by use of a curtain would make two very large rooms, and yet the main section of the floor looked as large as ever. A simple stairway of plain boards had been constructed a little to one side of the middle toward the back, going up to the loft, which had been made safe for the children by a plain rude railing consisting of a few uprights with strips across. The darkening slats at the small windows in the loft had been torn away and shutters substituted that would open wide and let in air and light. Rough spots in the floor had been mended, and around the great place both up-stairs and down, and even down in the basement underneath, electric wires ran with simple lights and switches conveniently arranged, so that if it became desirable the whole place could be made a blaze of light. The young man did not like to think of this family of unprotected women and children coming out into the country without all the arrangements possible to make them feel safe. For this reason also he had established the telephone. He had talked it over with the agent, paying a certain sum for its installation, and had a telephone put in that they could pay for whenever they desired to use it. This would make the young householder feel more comfortable about leaving her mother out in the country all day, and also prevent her pride from being hurt. The telephone was there. She need not use it unless necessity arose. He felt he could explain that to her. If she didn't like it, of course she could have it taken away.

There were a lot more things he would like to do to make the place more habitable, but he did not dare. Sometimes even now his conscience troubled him. What did he know about these people, anyway? and what kind of a flighty youth was he becoming that he let a strange girl's appealing face drive him to such lengths as he was going now? Telephone, and electric lights, and stairs, and a fireplace in a barn! It was all perfectly preposterous; and, if his family should hear of it, he would never hear the last of it; that he was certain.

At such times he would hunt up his young sister and carry her off for a long drive in the car, always ending up at Glenside Road, where she exclaimed and praised to his heart's satisfaction, and gave anew her word not to tell anybody a thing about it until he was ready.

Indeed, Elizabeth was wild with delight. She wanted to hunt up some of her mother's old Turkish rugs that were put away in dark closets, to decorate the walls with pictures and bric-à-brac from her own room, and to smother the place in flowering shrubs for the arrival of the tenants; but her brother firmly forbade anything more being done. He waited with fear and trembling for the time when the clear-eyed young tenant should look upon the changes he had already made; for something told him she would not stand charity, and there was a point beyond which he must not go if he wished ever to see her again.

At last one morning he ventured to call her up on the telephone at her office.

"My sister and I were thinking of going out to see how things are progressing at the Glenside place," he said after he had explained who he was. "I was wondering if you would care to come along and look things over. What time do you get through at your office this afternoon?"

"That is very kind of you, Mr. Graham," said Shirley, "but I'm afraid that won't be possible. I'm not usually done until half-past five. I might get through by five, but not much sooner, and that would be too late for you."

"Not at all, Miss Hollister. That would be a very agreeable time. I have matters that will keep me here quite late to-night, and that will be just right for me. Shall I call for you, then, at five? Or is that too soon?"

"Oh, no, I can be ready by then, I'm sure," said Shirley with suppressed excitement. "You are very kind——"

"Not at all. It will be a pleasure," came the answer. "Then I will call at your office at five," and the receiver clicked at the other end, leaving Shirley in a whirl of doubt and joy.

How perfectly delightful! And yet ought she to go? Would mother think it was all right? His little sister was going, but was it quite right for her to accept this much attention even in a business way? It wasn't at all customary or necessary, and both he and she knew it. He was just doing it to be nice.

And then there was mother. She must send a message somehow, or mother would be frightened when she did not come home at her usual time.

She finally succeeded in getting Carol at her school, and told her to tell mother she was kept late and might not be home till after seven. Then she flew at her work to get it out of the way before five o'clock.

But, when she came down at the appointed time, she found Carol sitting excitedly in the back seat with Elizabeth, fairly bursting with the double pleasure of the ride and of surprising her sister.

"They came to the school for me, and took me home; and I explained to mother that I was going with you to look at a place we were going to move to. I put on the potatoes, and put the meat in the oven, and mother is going to tell George just what to do to finish supper when he gets home," she exclaimed eagerly. "And, oh, isn't it lovely?"

"Indeed it is lovely," said Shirley, her face flushing with pleasure and her eyes speaking gratitude to the young man in the front seat who was opening the door for her to step in beside him.

That was a wonderful ride.

The spring had made tremendous advances in her work during the ten days since they went that way before. The flush of green that the willows had worn had become a soft, bright feather of foliage, and the maples had sent out crimson tassels to offset them. Down in the meadows and along the roadside the grass was thick and green, and the bare brown fields had disappeared. Little brooks sang tinklingly as they glided under bridges, and the birds darted here and there in busy, noisy pairs. Frail wavering blossoms starred the swampy places, and the air was sweet with scents of living things.

But, when they came in sight of the barn, Elizabeth and her brother grew silent from sheer desire to talk and not act as if there was anything different about it. Now that they had actually brought Shirley here, the new windows seemed fairly to flaunt themselves in their shining mossy paint and their vast extent of diamond panes, so that the two conspirators were deeply embarrassed, and dared not face what they had done.

It was Carol who broke the silence that had come upon them all.

"Oh! Oh! Oh!" she shouted. "Shirley, just look! New, great big windows! Isn't that great? Now you needn't worry whether it will be dark for mother days when she can't go out! Isn't that the best ever?"

But Shirley looked, and her cheeks grew pink as her eyes grew starry. She opened her lips to speak, and then closed them again, for the words would not come, and the tears came instead; but she drove them back, and then managed to say:

"Oh, Mr. Graham! Oh, you have gone to so much trouble!"

"No, no trouble at all," said he almost crossly; for he had wanted her not to notice those windows, at least not yet.

"You see it was this way. The windows were some that were left over from another order, and I got a chance to get them at a bargain. I thought they might as well be put in now as any time and you get the benefit of them. The barn really needed more light. It was a very dark barn indeed. Hadn't you noticed it? I can't see how my grandfather thought it would do to have so little light and air. But you know in the old times they didn't use to have such advanced ideas about ventilation and germs and things——" He felt he was getting on rather famously until he looked down at the clear eyes of the girl, and knew she was seeing right straight through all his talk. However, she hadn't the face to tell him so; and so he boldly held on his way, making up fine stories about things that barns needed until he all but believed them himself; and, when he got through, he needed only to finish with "And, if it isn't so, it ought to be" to have a regular Water-Baby argument out of it. He managed to talk on in this vein until he could stop the car and help Shirley out, and together they all went up the now velvety green of the incline to the big door.

"It is beautiful! beautiful!" murmured Shirley in a daze of delight. She could not yet make it seem real that she was to come to this charmed spot to live in a few days.

Graham unlocked the big doors, and sent them rolling back with a touch, showing what ball bearings and careful workmanship can do. The group stepped inside, and stood to look again.

The setting sun was casting a red glow through the diamond panes and over the wide floor. The new partitions, guiltless of paint, for Graham had not dared to go further, were mellowed into ruby hangings. The stone fireplace rose at the opposite side of the room, and the new staircase was just at the side, all in the ruddy evening glow that carried rich dusky shadows into the corners, and hung a curtain of vagueness over blemishes.

Then all suddenly, before they had had time to take in the changes, more than the fact of the partitions which they expected, Graham stepped to the side of the door, and touched a button, and behold a myriad of lights burst forth about the place, making it bright like noontime.

"Oh! Oh! Oh!" breathed Carol in awe and wonder, and "Oh!" again, as if there were nothing else to say. But Shirley only looked and caught her breath. It seemed a palace too fine for their poor little means, and a sudden fear gripped hold upon her.

"Oh Mr. Graham! You have done too much!" she choked. "You shouldn't have done it! We can never afford to pay for all this!"

"Not at all!" said young Graham quickly. "This isn't anything. The electric people gave permission for this, and I thought it would be safer than lamps and candles, you know. It cost scarcely anything for the wiring. I had our regular man do it that attends to the wiring and lights at the office. It was a mere trifle, and will make things a lot more convenient for you. You see it's nothing to the company. They just gave permission for a wire to be run from the pole there. Of course they might not do it for every one, but I've some pretty good friends in the company; so it's all right."

"But the fireplace!" said Shirley, going over to look at it. "It's beautiful! It's like what you see in magazine pictures of beautiful houses."

"Why, it was just the stones that were left from cutting the windows larger. I thought they might as well be utilized, you know. It wasn't much more work to pile them up that way while the men were here than if we had had them carted away."

Here Carol interrupted.

"Shirley! There's a telephone! A real telephone!"

Shirley's accusing eyes were upon her landlord.

"It was put in for our convenience while the workmen were here," he explained defensively. "It is a pay phone, you see, and is no expense except when in use. It can be taken out if you do not care to have it, of course; but it occurred to me since it was here your mother might feel more comfortable out here all day if she could call you when she needed to."

Shirley's face was a picture of varying emotions as she listened, but relief and gratitude conquered as she turned to him.

"I believe you have thought of everything," she said at last. "I have worried about that all this week. I have wondered if mother would be afraid out in the country with only the children, and the neighbors not quite near enough to call; but this solves the difficulty. You are sure it hasn't cost you a lot to have this put in?"

"Why, don't you know the telephone company is glad to have their phones wherever they can get them?" he evaded. "Now, don't worry about anything more. You'll find hardships enough living in a barn without fretting about the few conveniences we have been able to manage."

"But this is real luxury!" she said, sitting down on the steps and looking up where the lights blazed from the loft. "You have put lights up there, too, and a railing. I was so afraid Doris would fall down some time!"

"I'm glad to find you are human, after all, and have a few fears!" declared the owner, laughing. "I had begun to think you were Spartan through and through and weren't afraid of anything. Yes, I had the men put what lumber they had left into that railing. I thought it wasn't safe to have it all open like that, and I didn't want you to sue me for life or limb, you know. There's one thing I haven't managed yet, and that is piping water up from the spring. I haven't been able to get hold of the right man so far; but he's coming out to-morrow, and I hope it can be done. There is a spring on the hill back of us, and I believe it is high enough, to get the water to this floor. If it is it will make your work much easier and be only the matter of a few rods of pipe."

"Oh, but, indeed, you mustn't do anything more!" pleaded Shirley. "I shall feel so ashamed paying such a little rent."

"But, my dear young lady," said Graham in his most dignified business manner, "you don't at all realize how much lower rents are in the country, isolated like this, than they are in the city; and you haven't as yet realized what a lot of inconveniences you have to put up with. When you go back to the city in the winter, you will be glad to get away from here."

"Never!" said Shirley fervently, and shuddered. "Oh, never! You don't know how dreadful it seems that we shall have to go back. But of course I suppose we shall. One couldn't live in a barn in the winter, even though it is a palace for the summer"; and she looked about wistfully. Then, her eyes lighting up, she said in a low tone, for the young man's benefit alone:

"I think God must have made you do all this for us!" She turned and walked swiftly over to one of the new casement windows, looking out at the red glow that the sun in sinking had left in the sky; and there against the fringes of the willows and maples shone out the bright weather-vane on the spire of the little white church in the valley.

"I think God must have sent you to teach me and my little sister a few things," said a low voice just behind Shirley as she struggled with tired, happy tears that would blur her eyes. But, when she turned to smile at the owner of the voice, he was walking over by the door and talking to Carol. They tumbled joyously into the car very soon, and sped on their way to the city again.

That night the Hollister children told their mother they had found a place in which to live.

CHAPTER X

The crisis was precipitated by Shirley's finding her mother crying when she came up softly to see her.

"Now, little mother, *dear*! What can be the matter?" she cried aghast, sitting down on the bed and drawing her mother's head into her lap.

But it was some time before Mrs. Hollister could recover her calmness, and Shirley began to be frightened. At last, when she had kissed and petted her, she called down to the others to come up-stairs quickly.

They came with all haste, George and Harley with dish-towels over their shoulders, Carol with her arithmetic and pencil, little Doris trudging up breathless, one step at a time, and all crying excitedly, "What's the matter?"

"Why, here's our blessed little mother lying here all by herself, crying because she doesn't know where in the world we can find a house!" cried Shirley; "and I think it's time we told our beautiful secret, don't you?"

"Yes," chorused the children, although Harley and Doris had no idea until then that there was any beautiful secret. Beautiful secrets hadn't been coming their way.

"Well, I think we better tell it," said Shirley, looking at George and Carol questioningly. "Don't you? We don't want mother worrying." So they all clustered around her on the bed and the floor, and sat expectantly while Shirley told.

"You see, mother, it's this way. We've been looking around a good deal lately, George and I, and we haven't found a thing in the city that would do; so one day I took a trolley ride out of the city, and I've found something I think will do nicely for the summer, anyway, and that will give us time to look around and decide. Mother dear, would you mind camping so very much if we made you a nice, comfortable place?"

"Camping!" said Mrs. Hollister in dismay. "Dear child! In a tent?"

"No, mother, not in a tent. There's a—a—sort of a house—that is, there's a building, where we could sleep, and put our furniture, and all; but there's a lovely out-of-doors. Wouldn't you like that, for Doris and you?"

"Oh, yes," sighed the poor woman; "I'd like it; but, child, you haven't an idea what you are talking about. Any place in the country costs terribly, even a shanty——"

"That's it, mother, call it a shanty!" put in Carol. "Mother, would you object to living in a shanty all summer if it was good and clean, and you had plenty of out-of-doors around it?"

"No, of course not, Carol, if it was perfectly respectable. I shouldn't want to take my children among a lot of low-down people——"

"Of course not, mother!" put in Shirley. "And there's nothing of that sort. It's all perfectly respectable, and the few neighbors are nice, respectable people. Now, mother, if you're willing to trust us, we'd like it if you'll just let us leave it at that and not tell you anything more about it till we take you there. George and Carol and I have all seen the place, and we think it will be just the thing. There's plenty of room, and sky, and a big tree, and birds; and it only costs ten dollars a month. Now, mother, will you trust us for the rest and not ask any questions?"

The mother looked in bewilderment from one to another, and, seeing their eager faces, she broke into a weary smile.

"Well, I suppose I'll have to," she said with a sigh of doubt; "but I can't understand how any place you could get would be only that price, and I'm afraid you haven't thought of a lot of things."

"Yes, mother, we've thought of everything—and then some," said Shirley, stooping down to kiss the thin cheek; "but we are sure you are going to like this when you see it. It isn't a palace, of course. You don't expect plate-glass windows, you know."

"Well, hardly," said Mrs. Hollister dryly, struggling with herself to be cheerful. She could see that her children were making a brave effort to make a jolly occasion out of their necessity, and she was never one to hang back; so, as she could do nothing else, she assented.

"You are sure," she began, looking at Shirley with troubled eyes. "There are so many things to think of, and you are so young."

"Trust me, mudder dearie," said Shirley joyously, remembering the fireplace and the electric lights. "It really isn't so bad; and there's a beautiful hill for Doris to run down, and a place to hang a hammock for you right under a big tree where a bird has built its nest."

"Oh-h!" echoed the wondering Doris. "And could I see de birdie?"

"Yes, darling, you can watch him every day, and see him fly through the blue sky."

"It's all right, mother," said George in a businesslike tone. "You'll think it's great after you get used to it. Carol and I are crazy over it."

"But will it be where you can get to your work, both of you? I shouldn't like you to take long, lonely walks, you know," said the troubled mother.

"Right on the trolley line, mother dear; and the difference in rent will more than pay our fare."

"Besides, I'm thinking of buying a bicycle from one of the fellows. He says he'll sell it for five dollars, and I can pay fifty cents a month. Then I could go in on my bike in good weather, and save that much." This from George.

"Oh, gee!" said Harley breathlessly. "Then I could ride it sometimes, too."

"Sure!" said George generously.

"Now," said Shirley with her commanding manner that the children called "brigadier-general," "now, mother dear, you're going to put all your worries out of your head right this minute, and go to sleep. Your business is to get strong enough to be moved out there. When you get there, you'll get well so quick you won't know yourself; but you've got to rest from now on every minute, or you won't be able to go when the time comes; and then what will happen? Will you promise?"

Amid the laughing and pleading of her children the mother promised, half smilingly, half tearfully, and succumbed to being prepared for the night. Then they all tiptoed away to the dining-room for a council of war.

It was still two weeks before they had to vacate the little brick house, plenty of time to get comfortably settled before they took their mother out there.

It was decided that George and Shirley should go out the next evening directly from their work, not waiting to return for supper, but eating a lunch down-town. Now that the place was lighted and they had been told to use the light as freely as they chose, with no charge, the question of getting settled was no longer a problem. They could do it evenings after their work was over. The first thing would be to clean house, and for that they needed a lot of things, pails, pans, brooms, mops and the like. It would be good to take a load of things out the next day if possible.

So George went out to interview the man with the moving-wagon, while Shirley and Carol made out a list of things that ought to go in that first load. George came back with the report that the man could come at half past four in the afternoon; and, if they could have the things that were to go all ready, he would have his son help to load them, and they could get out to Glenside by six o'clock or seven at the latest. Harley might go along if he liked, and help to unload at the other end.

Harley was greatly excited both at the responsibility placed upon him and at the prospect of seeing the new home. It almost made up for the thought of leaving "the fellows" and going to live in a strange place.

The young people were late getting to bed that night, for they had to get things together so that Carol would not have her hands too full the next day when she got home from school. Then they had to hunt up soap, scrubbing-pails, rags, brushes and brooms; and, when they went to bed at last, they were much too excited to sleep.

Of course there were many hindrances to their plans, and a lot of delay waiting for the cartman, who did not always keep his word; but the days passed, and every one saw some little progress toward making a home out of the big barn. Shirley would not let them stay later in the evenings than ten o'clock, for they must be ready to go to work the next morning; so of course the work of cleaning the barn progressed but slowly. After the first night they got a neighbor to sit with their mother and Doris, letting Carol and Harley come out on the car to help; and so with four willing workers the barn gradually took on a nice smell of soap and water.

The old furniture arrived little by little, and was put in place eagerly, until by the end of the first week the big middle room and the dining-room and kitchen began really to look like living.

It was Saturday evening of that first week, and Shirley was sitting on the old couch at the side of the fireplace, resting, watching George, who was reeling out a stormy version of chopsticks on the piano, and looking about on her growing home hopefully. Suddenly there came a gentle tapping at the big barn door, and George as the man of the house went to the door with his gruffest air on, but melted at once when he saw the landlord and his sister standing out in front in the moonlight.

"Are you ready for callers?" asked Graham, taking off his hat in greeting. "Elizabeth and I took a spin out this way, and we sighted the light, and thought we'd stop and see if we could help any. My, how homelike you've made it look! Say, this is great!"

Sidney Graham stood in the centre of the big room, looking about him with pleasure.

The young people had put things in apple-pie order as far as they had gone. A fire was laid in the big stone fireplace, all ready for touching off, and gave a homelike, cleared-up look to the whole place as if it were getting ready for some event. On each side of the chimney stood a simple set of bookshelves filled with well-worn volumes that had a look of being beloved and in daily intimate association with the family. On the top of the shelves Carol had placed some bits of bric-à-brac, and in the centre of each a tall vase. Beside them were a few photographs in simple frames, a strong-faced man with eyes that reminded one of Shirley and a brow like George's; a delicate-featured, refined woman with sweet, sensitive mouth and eyes like Carol's; a lovely little child with a cloud of fair curls.

The old couch was at one side of the fireplace, at a convenient angle to watch the firelight, and yet not hiding the bookshelves. On the other side, with its back toward the first landing of the rude staircase, stood an old upright piano with a pile of shabby music on the top and a book of songs open on the rack. On the floor in the space between was spread a worn and faded ingrain rug, its original colors and pattern long since blended into neutral grays and browns, which strangely harmonized with the rustic surroundings. A few comfortable but shabby chairs were scattered about in a homelike way, and a few pictures in plain frames were hung on the clean new partitions. Under one stood a small oak desk and a few writing-materials. A little further on a plain library table held a few magazines and papers and a cherished book or two. There had been no attempt to cover the wide bare floor spaces, save by a small dingy rug or two or a strip of carpet carefully brushed and flung here and there in front of a chair. There was no pretension and therefore no incongruity. The only luxurious thing in the place was the bright electric light, and yet it all looked pleasant and inviting.

"Say, now, this is great!" reiterated the young owner of the place, sinking into the nearest chair and looking about him with admiration. "Who would ever have imagined you could make a barn look like this? Why, you're a genius, Miss Hollister. You're a real artist."

Shirley in an old gingham dress, with her sleeves rolled high and her hair fluffing wilfully in disorder about her hot cheeks, stood before him in dismay. She had been working hard, and was all too conscious of the brief time before they must be done; and to have company just now—and such company—put her to confusion; but the honest admiration in the young man's voice did much to restore her equilibrium. She began to pull down her sleeves and sit down to receive her callers properly; but he at once insisted that she should not delay on his account, and, seeing her shyness, immediately plunged into some questions about the water-pipes, which brought about a more businesslike footing and relieved her embarrassment. He was soon on his way to the partitioned corner which was to be the kitchen, telling Shirley how it was going to be no trouble to run a pipe from the spring and have a faucet put in, and that it should be done on the morrow. Then he called to Elizabeth.

"Kid, what did you do with those eats you brought along? I think it would be a good time to hand them out. I'm hungry. Suppose you take George out to the car to help you bring them in, and let's have a picnic!"

Then, turning to Shirley, he explained:

"Elizabeth and I are great ones to have something along to eat. It makes one hungry to ride, you know."

The children needed no second word, but all hurried out to the car, and came back with a great bag of most delicious oranges and several boxes of fancy cakes and crackers; and they all sat down to enjoy them, laughing and chattering, not at all like landlord and tenants.

"Now what's to do next?" demanded the landlord as soon as the repast was finished. "I'm going to help. We're not here to hinder, and we must make up for the time we have stopped you. What were you and George doing, Miss Carol, when we arrived?"

"Unpacking dishes," giggled Carol, looking askance at the frowning Shirley, who was shaking her head at Carol behind Graham's back. Shirley had no mind to have the elegant landlord see the dismal state of the Hollister crockery. But the young man was not to be so easily put off, and to Carol's secret delight insisted upon helping despite Shirley's most earnest protests that it was not necessary to do anything more that evening. He and Elizabeth repaired to the dining-room end of the barn, and helped unpack dishes, pans, kettles, knives, and forks, and arrange them on the shelves that George had improvised out of a large old bookcase that used to be his father's. After all, there was something in good breeding, thought Shirley, for from the way in which Mr. Graham handled the old cracked dishes, and set them up so nicely, you never would have known but they were Haviland china. He never seemed to see them at all when they were cracked. One might have thought he had been a member of the family for years, he made things seem so nice and comfortable and sociable.

Merrily they worked, and accomplished wonders that night, for Shirley let them stay until nearly eleven o'clock "just for once"; and then they all piled into the car, Shirley and Carol and Elizabeth in the back seat, George and the happy Harley with Graham in the front. If there had been seven more of them, they would have all happily squeezed in. The young Hollisters were having the time of their lives, and as for the Grahams it wasn't quite certain but that they were also. Certainly society had never seen on Sidney Graham's face that happy, enthusiastic look of intense satisfaction that the moon looked down upon that night. And, after all, they got home almost as soon as if they had gone on the ten-o'clock trolley.

After that on one pretext or another those Grahams were always dropping in on the Hollisters at their work and managing to "help," and presently even Shirley ceased to be annoyed or to apologize.

The east end of the barn had been selected for bedrooms. A pair of cretonne curtains was stretched across the long, narrow room from wall to partition, leaving the front room for their mother's bed and Doris's crib, and the back room for Shirley and Carol. The boys had taken possession of the loft with many shouts and elaborate preparations, and had spread out their treasures with deep delight, knowing that at last there was room enough for their proper display and they need feel no fear that they would be thrown out because their place was wanted for something more necessary. Little by little the Hollisters were getting settled. It was not so hard, after all, because there was that glorious big "attic" in which to put away things that were not needed below, and there was the whole basement for tubs and things, and a lovely faucet down there, too, so that a lot of work could be done below the living-floor. It seemed just ideal to the girls, who had been for several years accustomed to the cramped quarters of a tiny city house.

At last even the beds were made up, and everything had been moved but the bed and a few necessities in their mother's room, which were to come the next day while they were moving their mother.

That moving of mother had been a great problem to Shirley until Graham anticipated her necessity, and said in a matter-of-fact way that he hoped Mrs. Hollister would let him take her to her new home in his car. Then Shirley's eyes filled with tears of gratitude. She knew her mother was not yet able to travel comfortably in a trolley-car, and the price of a taxicab was more than she felt they ought to afford; yet in her secret heart she had been intending to get one; but now there would be no necessity.

Shirley's words of gratitude were few and simple, but there was something in her eyes as she lifted them to Graham's face that made a glow in his heart and fully repaid him for his trouble.

The last thing they did when they left the barn that night before they were coming to stay was to set the table, and it really looked very cozy and inviting with a white cloth on it and the dishes set out to look their best. Shirley looked back at it with a sweeping glance that took in the great, comfortable living-room, the open door into the dining-room on one hand and the vista of a white bed on the other side through the bedroom door. She smiled happily, and then switched off the electric light, and stepped out into the sweet spring night. Graham, who had stood watching her as one might watch the opening of some strange, unknown flower, closed and locked the door behind them, and followed her down the grassy slope to the car.

"Do you know," he said earnestly, "it's been a great thing to me to watch you make a real home out of this bare barn? It's wonderful! It's like a miracle. I wouldn't have believed it could be done. And you have done it so wonderfully! I can just see what kind of a delightful home it is going to be."

There was something in his tone that made Shirley forget he was rich and a stranger and her landlord. She lifted her face to the stars, and spoke her thoughts.

"You can't possibly know how much like heaven it is going to be to us after coming from that other awful little house," she said; "and you are the one who has made it possible. If it hadn't been for you I know I never could have done it."

"Oh, nonsense, Miss Hollister! You mustn't think of it, I haven't done anything at all, just the simplest things that were absolutely necessary."

"Oh, I understand," said Shirley; "and I can't ever repay you, but I think God will. That is the kind of thing the kingdom of heaven is made of."

"Oh, really, now," said Graham, deeply embarrassed; he was not much accustomed to being connected with the kingdom of heaven in any way. "Oh, really, you—you over-estimate it. And as for pay, I don't ask any better than the fun my sister and I have had helping you get settled. It has been a great play for us. We never really moved, you see. We've always gone off and had some one do it for us. I've learned a lot since I've known you."

That night as she prepared to lie down on the mattress and blanket that had been left behind for herself and Carol to camp out on, Shirley remembered her first worries about Mr. Graham, and wondered whether it could be possible that he thought she had been forward in any way, and what her mother would think when she heard the whole story of the new landlord; for up to this time the secret had been beautifully kept from mother, all the children joining to clap their hands over wayward mouths that started to utter tell-tale sentences, and the mystery grew, and became almost like Christmas-time for little Doris and her mother. It must, however, be stated that Mrs. Hollister, that last night, as she lay wakeful on her bed in the little bare room in the tiny house, had many misgivings, and wondered whether perchance she would not be sighing to be back even here twenty-four hours later. She was holding her peace wonderfully, because there really was nothing she could do about it even if she was going out of the frying-pan into the fire; but the tumult and worry in her heart had been by no means bliss. So the midnight drew on, and the weary family slept for the last night in the cramped old house where they had lived since trouble and poverty had come upon them.

CHAPTER XI

Shirley was awake early that morning, almost too excited to sleep but fitfully even through the night. Now that the thing was done and they were actually moved into a barn she began to have all sorts of fears and compunctions concerning it. She seemed to see her delicate mother shrink as from a blow when she first learned that they had come to this. Try as she would to bring back all the sensible philosophy that had caused her to enter into this affair in the first place, she simply could not feel anything but trouble. She longed to rush into her mother's room, tell her all about it, and get the dreaded episode over. But anyhow it was inevitable now. They were moved. They had barely enough money to pay the cartage and get things started before next pay-day. There was nothing for it but to take her mother there, even if she did shrink from the idea.

Of course mother always had been sensible, and all that; but somehow the burden of the great responsibility of decision rested so heavily upon her young shoulders that morning that it seemed as if she could not longer bear the strain.

They still had a good fire in the kitchen range, and Shirley hastened to the kitchen, prepared a delicate piece of toast, a poached egg, a cup of tea, and took it to her mother's room, tiptoeing lightly lest she still slept.

But the mother was awake and glad to see her. She had been awake since the first streak of dawn had crept into the little back window. She had the look of one who was girded for the worst. But, when she saw her daughter's face, the mother in her triumphed over the woman.

"What's the trouble, little girl? Has something happened?"

The tenderness in her voice was the last straw that broke Shirley's self-control. The tears suddenly sprang into her eyes, and her lip trembled.

"Oh mother!" she wailed, setting the tray down quickly on a box and fumbling for her handkerchief. "I'm so worried! I'm so afraid you won't like what we've done, and then what shall we do?"

"I *shall* like it!" said the mother with instant determination. "Don't for a minute think of anything else. Having done something irrevocably, never look back and think you might have done something better. You did the best you could, or you thought you did, anyway; and there didn't seem to be anything else at the time. So now just consider it was the very best thing in the world, and don't go to fretting about it. There'll be *something* nice about it, I'm sure, and goodness knows we've had enough unpleasant things here; so we needn't expect beds of roses. We are just going to *make* it nice, little girl. Remember that! We are going to like it. There's a tree there, you say; so, when we find things we don't like, we'll just go out and look up at our tree, and say, 'We've got *you*, anyway, and *we're glad of it!*'"

"You blessed little mother!" laughed Shirley, wiping her tears away. "I just believe you will like it, maybe, after all, though I've had a lot of compunctions all night. I wondered if maybe I oughtn't to have told you all about it; only I knew you couldn't really judge at all until you had seen it yourself, and we wanted to surprise you."

"Well, I'm determined to be surprised," said the brave little woman; "so don't you worry. We're going to have a grand good time to-day. Now run along. It's almost time for your car, and you haven't had any breakfast yet."

Shirley kissed her mother, and went smiling down to eat her breakfast and hurry away to the office.

There was a big rush of work at the office, or Shirley would have asked for a half-holiday; but she did not dare endanger her position by making a request at so busy a season. She was glad that the next day was Sunday and they would have a whole day to themselves in the new home before she would have to hurry away to the office again. It would serve to make it seem less lonely for her mother, having them all home that first day. She meant to work fast to-day and get all the letters written before five if possible. Then she would have time to get home a few minutes before Graham arrived with his car, and see that her mother was all comfortably ready. It was a good deal to put upon Carol to look after everything. It wasn't as if they had neighbors to help out a little, for they were the very last tenants in the doomed block to leave. All the others had gone two or three weeks before.

Thinking over again all the many details for the day, Shirley walked down to the office through the sunshine. It was growing warm weather, and her coat felt oppressive already. She was so thankful that mother would not have to sleep in those breathless rooms after the heat began. The doctor had said that her mother needed rest and air and plenty of sunshine more than anything else. She would at least have those at the barn, and what did other things matter, after all? Mother was game. Mother wouldn't let herself feel badly over such a silly thing. They certainly were going to be more comfortable than they had been for several years. Think of that wonderful electric light. And clear cold water from the spring! Oh, it was great! And a little thrill of ecstasy passed over her, the first she had let herself feel since she had taken the great responsibility of transplanting her family to a barn.

After all, the day passed very quickly; and, when at half-past four the telephone-bell rang and Graham's voice announced that he would be down at the street door waiting for her in half an hour, that she needn't hurry, he would wait till she was ready, her heart gave a little jump of joy. It was as if school was out and she was going on a real picnic like other girls. How nice of him! How perfectly lovely of him! And yet there hadn't been anything but the nicest friendliness in his voice, such as any kindly disposed landlord might use if he chose, nothing that she need feel uncomfortable about. At least, there was the relief that after to-night mother would know all about it; and, if she didn't approve, Shirley could decline any further kindness, of course. And now she was just going to take mother's advice and forget everything but the pleasant part.

At home Carol and Harley bustled about in the empty house like two excited bumble-bees, washing up the few dishes, putting in an open box everything that had been left out for their last night's sleeping, getting lunch, and making mother take a nap. Doris, vibrating between her mother's room and down-stairs, kept singing over to herself: "We goin' to tuntry! We goin' to tuntry! See birdies an' twees and walk on gween gwass!"

After lunch was over and the dishes were put carefully into the big box between comfortables and blankets Carol helped her mother to dress, and then made her lie down and take a good long nap, with Doris asleep by her side. After that Carol and Harley tiptoed down to the bare kitchen, and sat on a box side by side to converse.

"Gee! Ain't you tired, Carol?" said the boy, pushing his hair back from his hot face. "Gee! Don't it seem funny we aren't coming back here any more? It kind of gets my goat I sha'n't see the fellows so often, but it'll be great to ask 'em to see us sometimes. Say, do you suppose we really can keep chickens?"

"Sure!" said Carol convincingly. "I asked Mr. Graham if we might,—George said we ought to, he was such a good scout you'd want to be sure he'd like it, and he said, 'Sure, it would be great.' He'd like to come out and see them sometimes. He said he used to keep chickens himself when he was a kid, and he shouldn't wonder if they had a few too many at their place they could spare to start with. He told me he'd look it up and see soon's we got settled."

"Gee! He's a peach, isn't he? Say, has he got a case on Shirl?"

"I don't know," said the girl thoughtfully; "maybe he has, but he doesn't know it yet, I guess. But anyhow you must promise me you will never breathe such a word. Why, Shirley would just bust right up if you did. I said a little something to her like that once; it wasn't much, only just that he was awfully nice and I guessed he liked her by the way he looked at her, and she just fairly froze. You know the way her eyes get when she is sore at us? And she said I must never, *never* even *think* anything like that, or she would give the place right up, and get a few rooms down on South Street, and stay in the city all summer! She said Mr. Graham was a gentleman, and she was only a working girl, and it would be a disgrace for her to accept any favors from him except what she could pay for, and an insult for him to offer them, because she was only a working girl and he was a gentleman, you know."

"H'm!" growled Harley. "I guess our sister's as good as he is any day."

"Of course!" snapped Carol; "but then he might not think so."

"Well, if he don't, he can go to thunder!" bristled Harley wrathfully. "I'm not going to have him looking down on Shirley. She's as good as his baby-doll sister with her pink cheeks, and her little white hands, and her high heels and airs, any day! She's a nut, she is."

"Harley! You stop!" declared Carol, getting wrathful. "Elizabeth's a dear, and you're not going to talk about her that way. Just because she is pretty and doesn't have to work."

"Well, you said her brother looked down on our sister," declared Harley.

"I did not! I only said he *might*! I only meant that was the way *some* gentlemen would. I only said people kind of expect gentlemen to do that."

"Not if they're real gentlemen, they won't. And anyhow *he* won't. If I find him looking down on my sister Shirley, I'll punch his face for him. Yes, I will! I'm not afraid. George and I could beat the stuffing out of him, and we will if he does any looking-down stunts, and don't you forget it!"

"Well, I'm sure he doesn't," said Carol pacifically, trying to put a soothing sound into her voice as wise elder sisters learn to do. "You see if he did look down on her, Shirley would know it; right away she'd know it. Nobody would have to tell *her*! She'd see it in his voice and smile and everything. And, if he had, she wouldn't have gone out there to live in the place he owns, you know. So I guess you can trust Shirley. *I* think he's been just dandy, fixing up that fireplace and stairs and lights and water and everything."

"Well, mebbe!" said Harley grudgingly. "Say, this is slow. I'm going out to meet the fellows when they come from school, and see what the score of the game is. Gee! I wish I could play to-day!"

"You'll be sure to come back in time?" asked Carol anxiously.

"Sure! You don't suppose I'd miss going out in that car, do you?" said the brother contemptuously. "Not on your tintype!"

"Well, maybe there won't be room for you. Maybe Elizabeth'll come along, and you'll have to go in the trolley with George."

"No chance!" declared the boy. "Mr. Graham said I should ride with him in the front seat, and he looks like a man that kept his word."

"You see! *You* know he's a gentleman!" triumphed Carol. "Well, I think you'd better stay here with me. You'll forget and be late, and make a mess waiting for you."

"No, I won't!" said the restless boy. "I can't be bothered sticking round this dump all afternoon"; and Harley seized his cap, and disappeared with a whoop around the corner. After he was gone Carol found she was tired out herself, and, curling up on a mattress that was lying ready for the cartman, was soon asleep. It was so that Harley found her when he hurried back an hour later, a trifle anxious, it must be confessed, lest he had stayed too long. He stirred up the small household noisily, and in no time had Carol in a panic brewing the cup of tea that was to give her mother strength to take the journey, dressing Doris, smoothing her own hair, putting the last things into bags and baskets and boxes, and directing the cartman, who arrived half an hour sooner than he promised. Carol was quite a little woman, going from one thing to another and taking the place of everybody.

Meantime Elizabeth Graham and her brother had been spending the afternoon in business of their own. It was Elizabeth who had suggested it, and her brother saw no reason why she should not carry out her plan and why he should not help her.

She came down in the car after lunch, the chauffeur driving her, a great basket of cut and potted flowers from the home conservatory in the tonneau beside her, carefully wrapped in wax-paper. She stopped at the office for her brother, and together they went about to several shops giving orders and making purchases. When they had finished they drove out to Glenside to unpack their bundles and baskets. Graham left Elizabeth with the old servant to help her, and drove rapidly back to his office, where he telephoned to Shirley.

Certainly Elizabeth had never had such fun in her life. She scarcely knew which delightful thing to do first, and she had only about two hours to complete her arrangements before the family would arrive.

She decided to decorate first, and the great hamper of flowers was forthwith brought into the barn, and the chauffeur set to work twining ropes and sprays of smilax and asparagus fern over doorways and pictures, and training it like a vine about the stone chimney. Then came the flowers. Pots of tall starry lilies, great, heavy-headed, exquisite-breathed roses, pink, white, yellow, and crimson; daffodils and sweet peas, with quantities of sweet violets in the bottom of the basket. Elizabeth with deft fingers selected the flowers skilfully, putting pots of lilies on the window-sills, massing a quantity of pink roses in a dull gray jar she found among the kitchen things, that looked to the initiated amazingly as though it might once have been part of a water-filter, but it suited the pink roses wonderfully. The tall vases on the bookcases each Bide of the fireplace held daffodils. Sweet peas were glowing in small vases and glasses and bowls, and violets in saucers filled the air with fragrance. White and yellow roses were on the dining-table, and three exquisite tall crimson rosebuds glowed in a slender glass vase Elizabeth had brought with her. This she placed in Mrs. Hollister's room on the little stand that she judged would be placed beside the bed when the bed arrived. The flowers certainly did give an atmosphere to the place in more senses than one; and the girl was delighted, and fluttered from one spot to another, changing the position of a vase or bowl, and then standing off to get the effect.

"Now bring me the big bundle, Jenkins, please," she said at length when she was satisfied with the effect. "Oh, and the little long box. Be careful. It is broken at one end, and the screws may fall out."

Jenkins was soon back with the things.

"Now, you get the rods put up at the windows, Jenkins, while I get out the curtains," and she untied the big bundle with eager fingers.

Jenkins was adaptable, and the rods were simple affairs. He was soon at work, and Elizabeth ran the rods into the curtains.

They were not elegant curtains. Graham had insisted that she should get nothing elaborate, nothing that would be out of keeping with the simplicity. They were soft and straight and creamy, with a frost-like pattern rambling over them in threads of the same, illuminated here and there with a single rose and a leaf in color. There was something cheerful and spring-like to them, and yet they looked exceedingly plain and suitable, no ruffles or trimming of any kind, just hems. To Elizabeth's mind they had been very cheap. Shirley would have exclaimed over their beauty wistfully and turned from them with a gasp when she heard their price. They were one of those quiet fitting things that cost without flaunting it. They transformed the room into a dream.

"Oh, isn't it *beautiful*!" exclaimed Elizabeth, standing back to look as the first curtain went up.

"Yes, Miss, it's very stunning, Miss," said the man, working away with good will in his face.

When the curtains were all up, Elizabeth pinned one of her cards to the curtain nearest the front door, inscribed, "With love from Elizabeth."

Then in a panic she looked at her watch.

"Oh Jenkins! It's almost six o'clock," she cried in dismay. "They might get here by half-past, perhaps. We must hurry! Bring the other things in quick now, please."

So Jenkins brought them in, bundles and bags and boxes, an ice-cream freezer, and last of all the cooking-outfit belonging to their touring-car.

"Now you get the hot things ready, Jenkins, while I fix the table," directed the girl.

Jenkins, well trained in such things, went to work, opening cans and starting his chafing-dish fire. Elizabeth with eager fingers opened her parcels.

A great platter of delicious triangular chicken sandwiches, a dish of fruit and nut salad surrounded by crisp lettuce leaves, a plate of delicate rolls, cream puffs, chocolate éclairs, macaroons, a cocoanut pie, things she liked herself; and then because she knew no feast without them there were olives, salted almonds, and bonbons as a matter of course.

Delicious odors from the kitchen end of the room began to fill the air. Jenkins was heating a pail of rich soup—chicken with rice and gumbo—from one of the best caterers in the city. He was making rich cocoa to be eaten with whipped cream that Elizabeth was pouring into a glass pitcher; the pitcher came from the ten-cent store if she had only known it. Jenkins was cooking canned peas and heating lovely little brown potato croquettes. The ice-cream freezer was out in full sight, where they could never miss it. Everything was ready now.

"Jenkins, you better light up that queer stove of theirs now if you're sure you know how,—she said it was just like a lamp the way it worked,—and put those things in the oven to keep warm. Then we'll pack up our things, and hide them out in the grass where they can't see, and get them in the car when they get out. Hurry, for they'll be here very soon now, I think."

Elizabeth stuck a card in the middle of the rose-bowl that said in pretty letters, "Welcome Home," stood back a minute to see how everything looked, and then fluttered to the door to watch for the car.

CHAPTER XII

When Shirley came down to the street at five o'clock. Graham was waiting for her as he promised, and swung the car door open for her with as much eagerness as if he were taking the girl of his choice on a picnic instead of just doing a poor little stenographer a kindness.

"I telephoned to the store and sent a message to George. We're going to pick him up on our way," he said as the car wended its way skilfully through the traffic.

She was sitting beside him, and he looked down at her as if they were partners in a pleasant scheme. A strange sense of companionship with him thrilled through her, and was properly rebuked and fled at once, without really rippling the surface of her joy much. She had determined to have the pleasure out of this one evening ride at least, and would not let her thoughts play truant to suggest what wider, sweeter realms might be for other girls. She was having this good time. It was for her and no one else, and she would just enjoy it as much as she could, and keep it the sweet, sane, innocent pleasure that it really was. If she was not a fool, everything would be all right.

George was waiting in a quiver of pride and eagerness for them as they swept up to the employees' entrance, and a line of admiring fellow-laborers stood gaping on the sidewalk to watch his departure.

"Oh, gee! Isn't this great?" shouted George, climbing into the back seat hilariously. "Got a whole omnibus of a car this time, haven't you?"

"Yes, I thought we'd have plenty of room for your mother, so she could lie down if she liked."

"That was very kind of you," murmured Shirley. "You think of everything, don't you? I'm sure I don't see how we ever could have managed without your help. I should have been frightened a dozen times and been ready to give up."

"Not you!" said Graham fervently. "You're the kind that never gives up. You've taught me several valuable lessons."

As they turned the corner into the old street where the little brick house stood, Shirley suddenly began to have a vivid realization that she had told her mother nothing whatever about Mr. Graham. What would she think, and how could she explain his presence? She had expected to get there before Graham arrived and have time enough to make her mother understand, but now she began to realize that her real reason for leaving the matter yet unexplained was that she did not know just what to say without telling the whole story from beginning to end.

"I'll hurry in and see if mother is all ready," she said, as the car stopped in front of the house, and the children rushed out eagerly, Doris just behind the others, to see the "booful tar."

"Mother," said Shirley, slipping softly into the house and going over to the bed where she lay with hat and coat on, fully ready. "Mother, I sha'n't have time to explain all about it, but it's all right; so don't think anything. Mr. Graham, the man who owns the place where we are going, has been kind enough to offer to take you in his car. He thinks it will be easier for you than the trolley, and he is out at the door now waiting. It's perfectly all right. He has been very kind about it——"

"Oh daughter, I couldn't think of troubling any one like that!" said the mother, shrinking from the thought of a stranger; but, looking up, she saw him standing, hat in hand, just in the doorway. The children had led him to the door when he offered to help their mother out to the car.

"Mother, this is Mr. Graham," said Shirley.

Mrs. Hollister, a little pink spot on each cheek, tried to rise, but the young man came forward instantly and stooped over her.

"Don't try to get up, Mrs. Hollister. Your daughter tells me you haven't been walking about for several weeks. You must reserve all your strength for the journey. Just trust me. I'm perfectly strong, and I can lift you and put you into the car almost without your knowing it. I often carry my own mother up-stairs just for fun, and she's quite a lot larger and heavier than you. Just let me put my hand under your back so, and now this hand here. Now if you'll put your arms around my neck—yes, that way—no, don't be a bit afraid. I'm perfectly strong, and I won't drop you."

Little Mrs. Hollister cast a frightened look at her daughter and another at the fine, strong face bent above her, felt herself lifted like thistle-down before she had had time to protest, and found herself obediently putting her weak arms around his neck and resting her frightened head against a strong shoulder. A second more, and she was lying on the soft cushions of the car, and the young man was piling pillows about her and tucking her up with soft, furry robes.

"Are you perfectly comfortable?" he asked anxiously. "I didn't strain your back or tire you, did I?"

"Oh, no, indeed!" said the bewildered woman. "You are very kind, and I hardly knew what you were doing till I was here. I never dreamed of anything like this. Shirley didn't tell me about it."

"No," said the young man, smiling, "she said she wanted to surprise you; and I believe she thought you might worry a little if you heard the details of the journey. Now, kitten, are you ready to get in?" He turned a smiling face to Doris, who stood solemnly waiting her turn, with an expression of one who at last sees the gates of the kingdom of heaven opening before her happy eyes.

"Soor!" said Doris in a tone as like Harley's as possible. She lifted one little shabby shoe, and tried to reach the step, but failed, and then surrendered her trusting hands to the young man; and he lifted her in beside her mother.

"Sit there, kitten, till your sister comes out," he said, looking at her flower face admiringly.

Doris giggled.

"I ain't a kitty," she declared; "I'se a 'ittle gurrul!"

"Well, little girl, do you like to go riding?"

"Soor! I do 'ike to go widin'!" said Doris. "Oh! There goes muvver's bed!" as the drayman came out carrying the headboard.

Shirley meanwhile was working rapidly, putting the last things from her mother's bed into the box, tossing things into the empty clothes-basket that had been left for this purpose, and directing the man who was taking down the bed and carrying out the boxes and baskets. At last all the things were out of the house, and she was free to go. She turned for one swift moment, and caught a sob in her throat. There had not been time for it before. It had come when she saw the young man stoop and lift her mother so tenderly and bear her out to the car.

But the children were calling her loudly to come. She gave one happy dab at her eyes with her handkerchief to make sure no tears had escaped, and went out of the little brick house forever.

A little middle seat had been turned down for Carol, and Doris was in her lap. Graham turned the other middle seat down for Shirley; the boys piled into the front seat with him; and they were off. Mrs. Hollister in her wonder over it all completely forgot to look back into what she had been wont to call in the stifling days of summer her "frying-pan," or to wonder whether she were about to jump into the fire. She just lay back on her soft cushions, softer than any she had ever rested upon before, and felt herself glide along away from the hated little dark house forever! It was a wonderful experience. It almost seemed as if a chariot of fire had swooped down and gathered all her little flock with her, and was carrying them to some kind of gracious heaven where comfort would be found at last. A bit of hope sprang up within her, utterly unpremeditated and unreasonable, and persisted so that she could not help feeling happy. As yet it had not come to her to wonder who this handsome young man was that presumed to lift her and carry her like a baby, and move her on beds of down to utterly unknown regions. She was too much taken up with the wonder of it all. If Doris hadn't been prattling, asking questions of her, and the light breeze hadn't flapped a lock of hair into her eyes and tickled her nose, she might have thought she was dreaming, so utterly unreal did it all seem to her.

And now they passed out from the narrow streets, through crowded thoroughfares for a brief space, then out beyond, and free, into the wider reaches. Fair houses and glimpsed of green were appearing. The car was gliding smoothly, for the sake of the invalid not going at high speed; and she could see on every side. The trees were in full leaf; the sky was large and blue; the air was filled with freshness. She drew a long breath; and closed her eyes to pray, "Oh, my Father!" and then opened them again to see whether it was all true. Shirley, sensitive for her to the slightest breath, turned and drew the robes closer about her mother, and asked whether she were perfectly warm and whether she wanted another pillow under her head.

Graham did not intrude himself upon the family behind him. He was absorbed in the two boys, who were entirely willing to be monopolized. He told them all about the car, and discoursed on the mysteries of the different makes with a freedom that gave George the impression that he was himself almost a man to be honored by such talk.

It was nearly seven o'clock when they reached Glenside and the big stone barn came in sight, for they had travelled slowly to make it easier for the invalid.

Elizabeth had sighted the car far down the road below the curve; and, switching on every electric light in the place, she fled down the ladder to the basement, dragging the willing Jenkins after her. Here they waited with bated breath until the family had gone inside, when they made their stealthy way out the east end, across the little brook under the fence, and down the road, to be picked up by the car according to previous arrangement.

As the car came in sight of the barn a deep silence suddenly fell upon the little company. Even Doris felt it, and ceased her prattle to look from one to another. "Whatzie mattah?" she asked Shirley shyly, putting out her hand to pat Shirley's face in a way she had when she was uneasy or troubled. "*Whatzie mattah, Surly?*"

But Shirley only squeezed her hand reassuringly, and smiled.

As they drew near, the young people noticed that the bars of the fence in front of the barn had been taken down and the ditch filled in smoothly. Then they saw that the car was turning in and going straight up the grassy incline to the door.

Mrs. Hollister, lying comfortably among her cushions, was looking at the evening sky, hearing a bird that reminded her of long ago, and scarcely noticed they had turned until the car stopped. Then in silent joy the children swarmed out of the car, and with one consent stood back and watched mother, as the strong young man came to the open door and gathered her in his arms once more.

"Now we're almost home, Mrs. Hollister," he said pleasantly. "Just put your arms around my neck once more, and we'll soon have you beside your own fire." He lifted her and bore her in to the wide couch before the crackling fire that Elizabeth had started just before she went to look out the door the last time.

Then into the blazing light of the transformed barn they all stepped, and every one stood back and stared, blinking. What was this? What wondrous perfume met their senses? What luxury! What flowers! What hangings!

They stood and stared, and could not understand; and between them they forgot to wonder what their mother was thinking, or to do a thing but stupidly stare and say, "Why!" and "Oh!" and "Ah!" half under their breath.

"Just phone me if you need anything, Miss Hollister, please. I shall be glad to serve you," said Graham, stepping quickly over to the door. "Mrs. Hollister, I hope you'll be none the worse for your ride"; and he slipped out the door, and was gone.

The sound of the car softly purring its way backward down the slope brought Shirley out of her daze; but, when she turned and understood that he was gone, the car was just backing into the road, turning with a quick whirl, and was away before she could make him hear.

"Oh! He is *gone*!" she cried out, turning in dismay to the children. "He is gone, and we never thanked him!"

George was out down the road like a shot; and the rest, forgetful for the moment of the invalid who had been the great anxiety all day, crowded at the door to watch him. They could hear the throbbing of the machine; they heard it stop down the road and start again almost immediately, growing fainter with every whir as it went farther from them. In a moment more George came running back.

"He's gone. He meant to, I guess, so we could have it all to ourselves right at first. Elizabeth and the man were down the road waiting for him. They've been dolling the place up to surprise us."

"Oh!" said Shirley, turning to look around, her cheeks growing rosy. "Oh! Isn't it beautiful?" Then, turning swiftly to the couch and kneeling, she said, "Oh *mother*!"

"What does it all mean, daughter?" asked the bewildered mother, looking about on the great room that seemed a palace to her sad eyes.

But they all began to clamor at once, and she could make nothing of it.

"Oh Shirley, look at the curtains! Aren't they perfectly dear?" cried Carol ecstatically.

"Perf'ly deah!" echoed Doris, dancing up and down gleefully.

"And here's a card, 'With love from Elizabeth'! Isn't it sweet of her? Isn't she a perfect *darling*?"

"Who is Elizabeth?" asked Mrs. Hollister, rising to her elbow and looking around.

"Gee! Look at the flowers!" broke in George. "It's like our store at Easter! I say! Those lilies are pretty keen, aren't they, Shirl?"

"Wait'll you see the dining-room!" called Harley, who was investigating with the help of his nose. "*Some*supper-table! Come on quick; I'm starved. Hello! Hustle here quick. Here's another sign-board!"

They followed to the dining-room. Harley, still following his nose, pursued his investigations to the kitchen, discovered the source of the savory odors that were pervading the place, and raised another cry so appreciative that the entire family, with the exception of the invalid, followed him and found the supper steaming hot and crying to be eaten.

After the excitement was somewhat quieted Shirley took command.

"Now, children, you're getting mother all excited, and this won't do. And, besides, we must eat this supper right away before it spoils. Quiet down, and bring the hot things to the table while I get mother's things off. Then we will tell her all about it. There's plenty of time, you know. We're going to stay right here all summer."

"Aw, gee! Can't we bring mother out to the table?" pleaded George. "Harley and I could lift that couch just as easy."

"Why, I don't know," said Shirley, hesitating. "You know she isn't strong, and she will worry about your lifting her."

"Oh Shirley, let her come," pleaded Carol. "We could all take hold and wheel the couch out here; you know the floor is real smooth since those new boards were put in, and there are good castors on the couch."

"Mother! Mother! You're coming out to supper!" they chorused, rushing back to the living-room; and before the invalid realized what was happening her couch was being wheeled carefully, gleefully into the brilliantly lighted dining-room, with Doris like a fairy sprite dancing attendance, and shouting joyously:

"Mudder's tumin' to suppy! Mudder's tumin' to suppy adin!"

The mother gazed in amazement at the royally spread table, so smothered in flowers that she failed to recognize the cracked old blue dishes.

"Children, I insist," she raised her voice above the happy din. "I insist on knowing immediately what all this means. Where are we, and what is this? A hotel? And who was the person who brought us here? I cannot eat anything nor stay here another minute until I know. People can't rent houses like this for ten dollars a month anywhere, and I didn't suppose we had come to charity, even if I am laid up for a few days."

Shirley could see the hurt in her mother's eyes and the quick alarm in her voice, and came around to her couch, smiling.

"Now, mother dear, we'll tell you the whole thing. It isn't a hotel we're in, and it isn't a house at all. It's only an old barn!"

"A barn!" Mrs. Hollister sat up on her couch alertly, and looked at the big bowl of roses in the middle of the table, at the soft, flowing curtains at the window and the great pot of Easter lilies on the little stand in front, and exclaimed, "Impossible!"

"But it is, really, mother, just a grand old stone barn! Look at the walls. See those two over there are just rough stones, and this one back of you is a partition made of common boards. That's only an old brown denim curtain over there to hide the kitchen, and we've got the old red chenille curtains up to partition off the bedrooms. The boys are going to sleep up in the hay-loft, and it's going to be just great!"

Mrs. Hollister looked wildly at the stone walls, back at the new partition, recognized one by one the ancient chairs, the old bookcase now converted into a china-closet, the brown denim curtain that had once been a cover for the dining-room floor in the little brick house. Now it was washed and mended, and was doing its faded part to look like a wall and fit into the scheme of things. She darted questioning glances at the wealth of flowers, and the abundantly set table, then settled back on her pillow but half satisfied.

"They don't have curtains in a barn!" she remarked dryly.

"Those are a present from Elizabeth, the little sister of the landlord. She was out here with him when he came to see about things, and she got acquainted with Carol. She has put up those curtains, and brought the flowers, and fixed the table, for a surprise. See, mother!" and Shirley brought the card on which Elizabeth had printed her crude welcome.

Mrs. Hollister took the card as if it were some sort of a life-preserver, and smiled with relief.

"But this is a great deal to do for strangers," she said tremblingly, and tears began to glitter in her eyes. "They must be wealthy people."

"Yes, mother, I think they are," said Shirley, "and they have been most kind."

"But, daughter, wealthy people do not usually take the trouble to do things like that for nothing. And ten dollars a month for a barn could be nothing to them."

"I know, mother, but he seems very well satisfied with the price," said Shirley with a troubled brow. "I——"

"Something's burning!" yelled Harley at the top of his lungs from the kitchen, and immediately they all rushed out to rescue the supper, which took that moment to assert itself.

"Now, mother," said Shirley, coming in with a big tureen of soup, "we've got to eat this supper or it will spoil. You're not to ask another question till we are through."

They all settled expectantly down at the table, Doris climbing joyously into her high chair, calling:

"Suppy! Suppy! Oh goody!"

Such a clatter and a clamor, such shoutings over the sandwiches and such jumpings up and down to carry something to mother! Such lingering over the delicious ice-cream and fresh strawberries that were found in the freezer! Think of it! Real strawberries for *them* that time of year!

Then, when they had eaten all they could, and began to realize that it was time to get mother to bed, they pushed the chairs back, and all fell to clearing off the table and putting things away. It was Carol who discovered the big roasted fowl and the bowl of salad set away in the tiny ice-box ready for to-morrow. How had Elizabeth, who never kept house in her life, known just what would be nice for a family were all tired out with moving, and needed to lie back and rest before starting on with living?

The dishes were almost washed when the cart arrived with the last load of things, and the drayman helped George to put up mother's bed.

They wheeled the couch into the living-room after the big doors were closed and safely fastened for the night. Before the glowing fire Shirley helped mother to undress, then rolled her couch into the bedroom and got her to bed.

"Do you mind very much that it is only a barn, mother dear?" questioned Shirley, bending anxiously over her mother after she was settled.

"I can't make it seem like a barn, dear; it seems a palace!" said the mother with a tremble in her voice. "I'm glad it's a barn, because we could never afford a house with space like this, and air!" She threw out her hands as if to express her delight in the wide rooms, and drew in a breath of the delicious country air, so different from air of the dusty little brick house in the city.

"Daughter!" she drew Shirley down where she could whisper to her. "You're sure he is not looking on us as objects of charity, and you're sure he understands that you are a self-respecting girl earning her honorable living and paying her way? You know this is a wicked, deceitful world we live in, and there are all sorts of people in it."

"Mother dear! I'm sure. Sure as anybody could be. He has been a perfect gentleman. You didn't think he looked like one of those—those people—that go around misunderstanding girls, did you mother?"

The mother remembered the gentle, manly way in which the young man had lifted her and carried her to and from the car, and her heart warmed to him. Yet her fears lingered as she watched her sweet-eyed girl.

"No-o-o," she answered slowly; "but then, you can't always judge. He certainly was a gentleman, and he was very nice-looking." Then she looked sharply at Shirley.

"You won't go to getting any notions in your head, dear child?" Her eyes were wistful and sad as she searched the sweet, weary face of the girl. "You know rich young men follow whims sometimes for a few days. They don't mean anything. I wouldn't want your heart broken. I wish he was an old man with white hair."

"Oh mother dear!" laughed Shirley with heart-free ring to her voice, "did you think you had a young fool for a daughter? He was only being nice because he is a perfect gentleman; but I know he is not in the same universe as I am, so far as anything more than pleasant kindliness is concerned. We shall probably never see him again now that we are settled. But don't you think I ought to go and telephone thanks to his little sister? They will be home by this time, and it seems as if we ought to make some acknowledgment of her great kindness."

"By all means, dear; but how can you? Is there a pay-station near here? I thought you said this was out in the country."

"Why, we have a telephone of our own, muddy dear! Just think of the luxury of it! Us with a telephone! Mr. Graham had it put into the barn when he was making some repairs, so he could communicate with his workmen; and he said if we would like it we might keep it. It is one of those 'pay-as-you-go' phones, with a place to drop nickels and dimes in; so we are perfectly independent. Mr. Graham thought it would be a comfort to you when George or I had to stay late in town."

"How thoughtful of him! He must be a *wonderful* rich man! By all means telephone at once, and tell the little girl to say to her brother from me that I shall esteem it a privilege to thank him personally for all that he has done for my children, sometime when he is out this way. Think. A real rose by my bed!" She reached out a frail hand, and touched the exquisite petals lovingly. "It is wonderful!"

So Shirley went into the living-room to telephone, while all the children stood about to watch and comment and tell her what to say. Doris sat on a little cushion at her feet in awe, and listened, asking Carol with large eyes: "Is Sirley tautin to Dod? Vy doesn't see sut her yeyes?" for Shirley's conversation over the telephone sounded to the little sister much like a prayer of thanksgiving; only she was not accustomed to hearing that joyous laughter in the voice when people prayed.

Then Doris was put to bed in her own little crib, and the light in mother's room was switched off amid Doris's flood of questions.

"Vat makes it light? Vy did it do avay? Will it tum adin?"

At last she was asleep, and the other children tiptoed excitedly about preparing for bed, going up and downstairs softly, whispering back and forth for this or that they could not find, till quiet settled down upon the tired, happy household, and the bullfrogs in the distant creek droned out the nightly chorus.

CHAPTER XIII

It was beautiful to wake the next morning with the birds singing a matin in the trees, and a wonderful Sabbath quiet over everything. Tired out as she was and worn with excitement and care, Shirley was the first to waken, and she lay there quiet beside Carol for a little while with her eyes closed, listening, and saying a prayer of thanksgiving for the peace of the place, and the wonder that it had come into her life. Then suddenly a strange luminousness about her simply forced her to open her eyes.

The eastern window was across the room from her bed, and the sky was rosy, with the dawn, and flooding the room. It was the first time in years she had watched the sun rise. She had almost forgotten, in the little dark city house, that there was a sun to rise and make things glorious. The sun had seemed an enemy to burn and wilt and stifle.

But now here was a friend, a radiant new friend, to be waited for and enjoyed, to give glory to all their lives. She raised herself on one elbow and watched until the red ball had risen and burst into the brightness of day. Then she lay down softly again and listened to the birds. They seemed to be mad with joy over the new day. Presently the chorus grew less and less. The birds had gone about their morning tasks, and only a single bright song now and then from some soloist in the big tree overhead marked the sweet-scented silence of the morning.

In the quiet Shirley lay and went over events since she had first seen this spot and taken the idea of living in the barn. Her heart gave thanks anew that her mother had not disliked it as she had feared. There was no sense that it was a stable, no odor of living creatures having occupied it before, only sweet dusty clover like a lingering of past things put away carefully. It was like a great camping expedition. And then all those flowers! The scent of the lilies was on the air. How lovely of the young girl out of her luxury to think to pass on some of the sweet things of life! And the gracious, chivalrous man, her brother! She must not let him think she would presume upon his kindness. She must not let even her thoughts cross the line and dwell on the ground of social equality. She knew where he belonged, and there he should stay for all her. She was heart-free and happy, and only too glad to have such a kind landlord.

She drifted off to sleep again, and it was late when she awoke the next time. A silvery bell from the little white church in the valley was ringing and echoing distantly. Sabbath, real Sabbath, seemed brooding happily in the very air. Shirley got up and dressed hastily. She felt as if she had already lost too much of this first wonderful day in the country.

A thrush was spilling his liquid notes in the tree overhead when she tiptoed softly into her mother's room. Doris opened her eyes and looked in wonder, then whispered softly:

"Vat is dat, Sirley? Vat *is* dat pitty sound?"

"A birdie in the tree, dearie!" whispered Shirley.

"A *weel budie*! I yantta see it! Take Doris up, Sirley!"

So Shirley lifted the little maiden, wrapped a shawl about her, and carried her softly to the window, where she looked up in wonder and joy.

The boys came tumbling down from their loft in a few minutes, and there was no more sleep to be had. Carol was up and out, and the voice of one or the other of them was continually raised in a shout of triumph over some new delight.

"I saw a fish in the brook!" shouted Harley under his mother's window. "It was only a little fellow, but maybe it'll grow bigger some day, and then we can fish!"

"You silly!" cried George. "It was a minnow. Minnows don't grow to be big. They're only good for bait!"

"Hush, George, there's a nest in the big tree. I've been watching and the mother bird is sitting on it. That was the father bird singing a while ago." This from Carol.

George, Harley, and Carol declared their intention of going to church. That had likely been the first bell that rang, their mother told them, and they would have plenty of time to get there if they hurried. It was only half-past nine. Country churches rang a bell then, and another at ten, and the final bell at half-past ten, probably. Possibly they had Sunday-school at ten. Anyhow, they could go and find out. It wouldn't matter if they were a little late the first time.

So they ate some breakfast in a hurry, took each a sandwich left from the night before, crossed the road, climbed the fence, and went joyously over the green fields to church, thinking how much nicer it was than walking down a brick-paved street, past the same old grimy houses to a dim, artificially lighted church.

Shirley took a survey of the larder, decided that roast chicken, potato croquettes, and peas would all warm up quickly, and, as there was plenty of ice cream left and some cakes, they would fare royally without any work; so she sat beside her mother and told the whole story of her ride, the finding of the barn, her visit to the Graham office, and all that transpired until the present time.

The mother listened, watching her child, but said no wore of her inner thoughts. If it occurred to her that her oldest daughter was fair to look upon, and that her winning ways, sweet, unspoiled face, and wistful eyes had somewhat to do with the price of their summer's abode, it would be no wonder. But she did not mean to trouble her child further. She would investigate for herself when opportunity offered. So she quieted all anxieties Shirley might have had about her sanction of their selection of a home, kissed Shirley, and told her she felt it in her bones she was going to get well right away.

And, indeed, there was much in the fact of the lifting of the burden of anxiety concerning where they should live that went to brighten the eyes of the invalid and strengthen her heart.

When the children came home from church Shirley was putting dinner on the table, and her mother was arrayed in a pretty kimono, a relic of their better days, and ready to be helped to the couch and wheeled out to the dining-room. It had been pleasant to see the children coming across the green meadow in the distance, and get things all ready for them when they rushed in hungry. Shirley was so happy she felt like crying.

After the dinner things were washed they shoved the couch into the living-room among the flowers, where George had built up a beautiful fire, for it was still chilly. The children gathered around their mother and talked, making plans for the summer, telling about the service they had attended, chattering like so many magpies. The mother lay and watched them and was content. Sometimes her eyes would search the dim, mellow rafters overhead, and glance along the stone walls, and she would say to herself: "This is a barn! I am living in a barn! My husband's children have come to this, that they have no place to live but a barn!" She was testing herself to see if the thought hurt her. But, looking on their happy faces, somehow she could not feel sad.

"Children," she said suddenly in one of the little lulls of conversation, "do you realize that Christ was born in a stable? It isn't so bad to live in a barn. We ought to be very thankful for this great splendid one!"

"Oh mother, dear! It is so beautiful of you to take it that way!" cried Shirley with tears in her eyes.

"Doris, you sing your little song about Jesus in the stable," said Carol. "I'll play it for you."

Doris, nothing loath, got a little stool, stood up beside her mother's couch, folded her small hands demurely, and began to sing without waiting for accompaniment:

"Away in a manger,
No trib for His head,
The litta Lord Jesus
Lay down His sveet head.
The tars in the haaven
Look down vhere 'e lay—
The litta Lord Jesus
As'eep in the hay.
"The catta are lowing,
The poor baby wates;
But the litta Lord Jesus
No cwyin' He mates.
I love Thee, Lord Jesus;
Look down fum the sky,
An' stay by my trib,
Watching my lul-la-by!"

Shirley kissed Doris, and then they began to sing other things, all standing around the piano. By and by that distant bell from the valley called again.

"There's a vesper service at five o'clock. Why don't you go, Shirley? You and George and Harley," said Carol.

"Me 'ant do too!" declared Doris earnestly, and it was finally decided that the walk would not be too long; so the boys, Shirley and the baby started off across the fields, while Carol stayed with her mother. And this time Mrs. Hollister heard all about Elizabeth and how she wanted Carol to come and see her sometime. Heard, too, about the proposed dance, and its quiet squelching by the brother. Heard, and looked thoughtful, and wondered more.

"Mother is afraid they are not quite our kind of people, dear!" she said gently. "You mustn't get your heart bound up in that girl. She may be very nice, but she's a society girl, and you are not, you know. It stands to reason she will have other interests pretty soon, and then you will be disappointed when she forgets all about you."

"She won't forget, mother, I know she won't!" declared Carol stoutly. "She's not that kind. She loves me; she told me so. She wanted to put one of her rings on my finger to 'bind our friendship,' only I wouldn't let her till I had asked you, because I didn't have any but grandmother's to give her, and I couldn't give her that."

"That was right, dear. You can't begin things like that. You would find a great many of them, and we haven't the money to keep up with a little girl who has been used to everything."

Carol's face went down. Tears began to come in her eyes.

"Can't we have even *friends*?" she said, turning her face away to hide the quiver in her lip, and the tears that were rolling down her cheeks.

"Yes, dear," said the mother sorrowfully, "but don't choose them from among another people. People who can't possibly have much in common with us. It is sure to hurt hard when there are differences in station like that."

"But I didn't choose them. They chose us!" declared Carol. "Elizabeth just went wild over us the first time she saw us, and her brother told Shirley he was glad, that it would do Elizabeth a lot of good to know us. He said, 'We've learned a lot of things from you already'; just like that, he said it! I was coming down the stairs behind them when they stood here talking one day, and I couldn't help hearing them."

"Yes?" said Mrs. Hollister thoughtfully. "Well, perhaps, but, dear, go slow and don't pin your heart to a friendship like that, for it will most likely be disappointing. Just be happy in what she has done for us already, and don't expect anything more. She may never come again. It may just have been a passing whim. And I don't want you to be always looking for her and always disappointed."

"I shall not be disappointed, mamma," said Carol decidedly. "You'll see!" and her face brightened.

Then as if to make good her words a big car came whirring up the road and stopped in front of the barn, and almost before she could get to the window to look out Carol heard Elizabeth's voice calling softly:

"Carol! Car-*roll*! Are you there?" and she flung the door open and rushed into her new friend's arms.

Graham came more slowly up the incline, smiling apologetically and hoping he didn't intrude, coming so soon.

Carol led them over to the invalid and introduced her friend, and the young man came after them.

"I'm afraid this is rather soon to obey your summons, Mrs. Hollister," he said engagingly, "but Elizabeth couldn't stand it without coming over to see if you really found the ice-cream freezer, so I thought we'd just drop in for a minute and see whether you were quite comfortable."

Somehow, suddenly, Mrs. Hollister's fears and conclusions concerning these two young people began to vanish, and in spite of her she felt just as Shirley had done, that they were genuine in their kindliness and friendship. Carol, watching her, was satisfied, and a glow of triumph shone in her eyes. Nevertheless, Mrs. Hollister gathered her caution about her as a garment, and in dignified and pleasant phrases thanked the two in such a way that they must see that neither she nor her children would ever presume upon what had been done for them, nor take it for more than a passing kindliness.

But to her surprise the young man did not seem to be more than half listening to her words. He seemed to be studying her face with deep intention that was almost embarrassing. The soft color stole into her thin cheeks, and she stopped speaking and looked at him in dismay.

"I beg your pardon," he said, seeing her bewilderment, "but you can't understand perhaps how interested I am in you. I am afraid I have been guilty of staring. You see it is simply amazing to me to find a woman of your refinement and evident culture and education who is content—I might even say joyful—to live in a *barn*! I don't know another woman who would be satisfied. And you seem to have brought up all your children with just such happy, adaptable natures, that it is a great puzzle to me. I—I—why, I feel sort of rebuked! I feel that you and your children are among the great of the earth. Don't thank Elizabeth and me for the little we have been able to do toward making this barn habitable. It was a sort of—I might say homage, due to you, that we were rendering. And now please don't think anything more about it. Let's just talk as if we were friends—that is, if you are willing to accept a couple of humble strangers among your list of friends."

"Why, surely, if you put it that way!" smiled the little woman. "Although I'm sure I don't know what else we could do but be glad and happy over it that we had a barn like this to come to under a sweet blue sky, with a bird and a tree thrown in, when we literally didn't know where we could afford to lay our heads. You know beggars shouldn't be choosers, but I'm sure one would choose a spacious place like this any day in preference to most of the ordinary city houses, with their tiny dark rooms, and small breathless windows."

"Even if 'twas called a barn?"

"Even if 'twas called a barn!" said the woman with a flitting dance in her eyes that reminded him of the girl Shirley.

"Well, I'm learning a lot, I tell you!" said the young man. "The more I see of you all, the more I learn. It's opened my eyes to a number of things in my life that I'm going to set right. By the way, is Miss Hollister here? I brought over a book I was telling her about the other day. I thought she might like to see it."

"She went over to the vesper service at the little church across the fields. They'll be coming home soon, I think. It must be nearly over."

He looked at his watch.

"Suppose I take the car and bring them back. You stay here, Elizabeth. I'll soon be back. I think I can catch them around by the road if I put on speed."

He was off, and the mother lay on the couch watching the two girls and wishing with all her heart that it were so that her children might have these two fine young people for friends. But of course such things could not very well be in this world of stern realities and multitudinous conventionalities. What, for instance, would be said in the social set to which the Grahams belonged if it were known that some of their intimate friends lived in a barn? No, such things did not happen even in books, and the mother lay still and sighed. She heard the chatter of the two girls.

"You're coming home with me to stay over Sunday pretty soon. Sidney said he would fix it all up with your mother pretty soon. We'll sleep together and have the grandest times. Mother likes me to have friends stay with me, but most of the girls I know are off at boarding-school now, and I'm dreadfully lonesome. We have tennis-courts and golf links and a bowling-alley. Do you play tennis? And we can go out in the car whenever we like. It's going to be grand. I'll show you my dog and my pony I used to ride. He's getting old now, and I'm too big for him, but I love him just the same. I have a saddle-horse, but I don't ride much. I'd rather go motoring with Sid——"

And so she rattled on, and the mother sighed for her little girl who was being tempted by a new and beautiful world, and had not the wherewithal to enter it, even if it were possible for her to do so.

Out in the sunset the car was speeding back again with the seats full, Doris chirping gleefully at the ride, for her fat legs had grown very weary with the long walk through the meadow and Shirley had been almost sorry she had taken her along.

The boys were shouting all sorts of questions about dogs and chickens and cars and a garden, and Graham was answering them all good-humoredly, now and then turning around to throw back a pleasant sentence and a smile at the quiet girl with the happy eyes sitting in the back seat with her arm around her little sister.

There was nothing notable about the ride to remember. It was just one of those beautiful bits of pleasantness that fit into the mosaic of any growing friendship, a bit of color without which the whole is not perfect. Shirley's part in it was small. She said little and sat listening happily to the boys' conversation with Graham. She had settled it with her heart that morning that she and the young man on that front seat had nothing in future to do with each other, but it was pleasant to see him sitting there talking with her brothers. There was no reason why she should not be glad for that, and glad he was not a snob. For every time she looked on his clean, frank face, and saw his nice gray eyes upon her, she was surer that he was not a snob.

The guests stayed a little while after they all got back, and accepted quite as a matter of course the dainty little lunch that Carol and Elizabeth, slipping away unobserved, prepared and brought in on trays,—some of the salad left from dinner, some round rolls that Shirley had brought out with her Saturday, cut in two and crisply toasted, cups of delicious cocoa, and little cakes. That was all, but it tasted fine, and the two self-invited guests enjoyed it hugely. Then they all ranged themselves around the piano and sang hymns, and it is safe to say that the guests at least had not spent as "Sabbathy" a Sabbath in all their lives. Elizabeth was quite astonished when she suggested that they sing a popular song to have Carol answer in a polite but gently reproving tone, "Oh, not to-day, you know."

"Why not? Doesn't your mother like it?" whispered Elizabeth.

"Why, we don't any of us usually sing things like that on Sunday, you know. It doesn't seem like Sunday. It doesn't seem quite respectful to God." Carol was terribly embarrassed and was struggling to make her idea plain.

"Oh!" Elizabeth said, and stood looking wistfully, wonderingly at her friend, and finally stole out a soft hand and slipped it into Carol's, pressing her fingers as if to make her know she understood. Then they lifted up their voices again over the same hymn-book:

"Thine earthly Sabbaths, Lord, we love,
But there's a nobler rest above;
To that our longing souls aspire
With cheerful hope and strong desire."

Graham looked about on the group as they sang, his own fine tenor joining in the words, his eyes lingering on the earnest face of his little sister as she stood arm in arm with the other girl, and was suddenly thrilled with the thought of what a Sabbath might be, kept in this way. It had never appealed to him quite like that before. Sabbath-keeping had seemed a dry, thankless task for a few fanatics; now a new possibility loomed vaguely in his mind. He could see that people like this could really make the Sabbath something to love, not just a day to loll through and pass the time away.

When they finally went away there was just a streak of dull red left in the western horizon where the day had disappeared, and all the air was seething with sweet night sounds and odors, the dampness of the swamps striking coolly in their faces as the car sped along.

"Sidney," said Elizabeth after a long time, "did you ever feel as if God were real?"

"Why, how do you mean, kid?" asked the brother, rather embarrassed. These subjects were not discussed at all in the Graham household.

"Did you ever feel as if there really was a God somewhere, like a person, that could see and hear you and know what you did and how you felt to Him? Because they do. Carol said they didn't sing 'Tipperary' on Sunday because it didn't seem quite respectful to God, and I could see she really meant it. It wasn't just because her mother said she had to or anything like that. She thought so herself."

"H'm!" said Graham thoughtfully. "Well, they're rather remarkable people, I think."

"Well, I think so too, and I think it's about time you fixed it up with mamma to let Carol come and visit me."

"I'm going to get mother to go out there and call this week if I can," said Graham after another longer pause, and then added: "I think she will go and I think she will like them. After that we'll see, kid. Don't you worry. They're nice, all right." He was thinking of the look on Shirley's face as she sat at the piano playing for them all to sing.

The first few days in the new home were filled with wonder and delight for them all. They just could not get used to having plenty of room indoors, with all outdoors for a playground. Doris's cheeks took on a lovely pink, and her eyes began to sparkle. She and Harley spent all day out-of-doors. They were making a garden. Not that they had any experience or any utensils. There was an old hoe and a broken spade down in the basement of the barn, and with these Harley managed to remove a few square feet of young turf, and mellow up an inch or two of soil depth. In this they planted violet roots and buttercups and daisies which they found in the meadows. Doris had a corner all her own, with neat rows of tiny stones from the brook laid in elaborate baby-patterns around the edge, and in this she stuck twigs and weeds of all descriptions, and was never daunted, only pained and surprised when they drooped and died in a day or two and had to be supplanted by others.

It had been decided that Harley was to stop school and stay at home with mother and Doris, which indeed he was quite willing to do under the glamour of the new life. The school itself never had much attraction for him, and "the fellows" were almost forgotten in searching for angleworms and building dams in the creek.

Carol went to high school every morning with Shirley and George on the trolley. There were only six more weeks till the term was over, and it was better for Carol to finish out her year and get her credits. Shirley thought they could afford the extra carfare for just that little while, and so all day long mother and Doris and Harley kept quiet home in the old barn, and the meadows rang with Doris's shouts and Harley's answers.

One day the doctor came out in his machine to see Mrs. Hollister as he had promised to do, and found her so much better that he told her she might get up and go around a little while every day if she was very careful not to get over-tired. He prophesied a speedy return to health if she kept on looking happy and breathing this good air. He praised the good sense that brought her out into the country to live, in preference to any little tucked-up house in town, and said if she could only get well enough to work outdoors in the ground and have a flower-bed it would be the making of her. Her eyes brightened at that, for she loved flowers, and in the days of her youth had been extremely successful at making things grow.

The doctor was deeply interest in the barn. He walked about with his hands in his pockets, looking the rooms over, as delighted as a child at seeing a new mechanical toy.

"Well, now this is great!" he said heartily. "This is simply great! I admire you people for having the nerve to go against conventionality and come out here. If I had a few more patients who could be persuaded to go out into the country and take some of the unused old barns and fix them up to live in, I'd have to change my occupation. It's a great idea, and I mean to recommend it to others if you don't mind. Only I doubt if I find two others who have the nerve to follow your example."

The invalid laughed.

"Why, doctor, I can't see the nerve. We really hadn't any choice. We couldn't find a decent place that we could afford, and this was big and healthful and cost less than the worst little tenement that would have done in town. Any one would be a fool not to have come here."

"Mrs. Hollister, do you know that most people would rather starve and swelter, yes—and *die* in a conventional house, than to do such an unheard-of thing as to live in a barn, no matter how delightful that barn might be? You are a great little woman, Mrs. Hollister, and you deserve to get well, and to see your children prosper. And they will. They have the right spirit."

After his visit Mrs. Hollister began to get up a little while every day, and her improvement in health was rapid. She even ventured out to see Doris's garden and watch the "budie" in his nest in the tree.

One day a drayman stopped at the place and left several great rolls of chicken-wire, and a couple of big crates. One crate was bigger than the other and contained half a dozen big yellow hens and a beautiful rooster. The small crate held two lovely white rabbits.

The children hovered joyfully over the crates.

"Mine wabbits!" declared Doris solemnly. "Nice Mistah Dwaham give Doris wabbits."

"Did Mr. Graham say he was going to send you some rabbits?" questioned her mother.

"'Es. He did say he was goin' to sen' me some wabbits. On 'e way fum chutch in big oughtymobeel. He did say he would give me wabbits. Oh, mine wabbits!" Doris was in ecstasy.

Mrs. Hollister looked at the big rolls of wire questioningly:

"George and I told him we wanted some chickens. I guess that's why he sent 'em," announced Harley excitedly.

"I hope you boys didn't hint. That's very bad manners. You know I can't have Mr. Graham giving you such expensive presents; it won't do, dear."

"No, mother, we didn't hint. George just asked him if he minded if we kept chickens here, and he said no, indeed, he'd like to go into the business himself. He said he used to have a lot of his own when he was a boy, and he guessed there was a lot of wire from the old chicken-run around at his place yet. If there was, there wasn't any reason why it shouldn't be in use, and he'd look it up. He said, if it was, he and we'd go into business. He'd furnish the tools and we could do the work, and maybe some day we could sell eggs and make it pay."

"That's very kind of him, I'm sure. But, Harley, that looks like new wire. It isn't the least bit rusted."

"It's galvanized, mother. Galvanized wire doesn't rust, don't you know that?" said Harley in a superior, man's voice.

Harley and Doris were wild over their pets, and could do nothing all that day but hover about them, and the minute George arrived the boys went out to see about putting up some of the wire and making a temporary abode for the creatures until they could get time to plan an elaborate chicken-run.

Before dark Graham arrived. He had brought a book on chicken-raising and had a good many suggestions to offer. With him in the front seat of the car rode a great golden-brown dog with a white-starred face, great affectionate eyes, and a plumy white tail. He bounded floppily out after Graham and came affably up to the door as if he understood everything; and at sight of him the children went wild.

"I brought this fellow along, thinking perhaps you'd like him to help look after things here. He's only a puppy, but he's a good breed, and I think you'll find him a splendid watch-dog. You don't need to keep him, of course, if you don't want him, Mrs. Hollister, but I thought out in the country this way it might be as well for you to have him on guard, at night especially. He'll be good company for the children. We've got so many of them that we want to give this one away."

And what was there to do but accept him with thanks, a dog like that begging for a home, and a home like that really needing a dog?

So the dog was promptly accepted as a member of the family, was named Star, and accepted the overtures of his devoted worshippers in many amiable waggings of tail and a wide puppy laugh on his face. He stayed behind most contentedly when Graham departed after a long conference with George and Harley over the "chicken" book, and a long discussion in the back yard as to the best place for the chicken-run. He seemed to know from the start that he had come to stay, that this was his "job" and he was on it for life.

It must be admitted that Mrs. Hollister went to sleep that night with more content, knowing that big, floppy, deep-voiced dog was lying across the door out in the living-room. The hillside had seemed a bit lonely at night, though she had never admitted it even to herself before, and she was glad the dog had come. That night in the little prayer that she said every night with all her children gathered about her couch in front of the fire, she added, "We thank Thee, oh, Lord, for sending us such good kind friends to make the world so much happier for us."

A few days later Mrs. Graham came to call.

Her son did not explain to her anything about the Hollisters, nor say a word about the place where they were living. He merely remarked casually: "Mother, there are some people I'd like you to call on if you don't mind. They live out Glenside way, and I'll take you any afternoon you have time."

"I really haven't much time now before we go to the shore, Sidney," she said. "Couldn't they wait till the fall when we return?"

"No, mother, I'd like you to call now. It needn't take you long, and I think you'll like them—her—Mrs. Hollister, I mean. Can't you go this afternoon? I'll call for you with the car anywhere you say, along about half-past four or five o'clock. It will be a pleasant little drive and rest you."

"Shall I have to be much dressed?" asked the mother thoughtfully, "because I shouldn't have time for an elaborate toilet. I have to go to Madame's for a fitting, meet with the Red Cross committee, drop in at the hospital for a few minutes, and see Mrs. Sheppard and Mrs. Follette about our Alumni Anniversary banquet."

"Just wear something simple, mother. They are not society people. It's you I want to show them, not your clothes."

"You ridiculous boy! You're as unsophisticated as your father. Well, I'll be ready at half-past four. You may call for me then at the Century Building."

Elizabeth had been loyal to her brother's commands and had said nothing about her new-found friend, awaiting his permission. Graham earnestly discussed the pros and cons of woman's suffrage with his mother during the drive out, so that she was utterly unprejudiced by any former ideas concerning the Hollisters, which was exactly what her son desired her to be. He knew that his mother was a woman of the world, and hedged about by conventions of all sorts, but he also knew her to be fair in her judgments when once she saw a thing right, and a keen reader of character. He wanted her to see the Hollisters without the least bit of a chance to judge them beforehand.

So when the car drew up in front of the old barn Mrs. Graham was quite unprepared to have her son get out and open the car door and say, "Mother, this is the place: may I help you out?" She had been talking earnestly, and had thought he was getting out to look after something wrong about the car. Now she looked up startled.

"Why, Sidney! Why, you must have made a mistake! This isn't a house; it is a barn!"

"This is the place, mother. Just come right up this way."

Mrs. Graham picked her way over the short green turf up to the door and stood astonished while her son knocked. What in the world did he mean? Was this one of his jokes? Had he brought her out to see a new riding-horse? That must be it, of course. He was always taking a fancy to a horse or a dog. She really hadn't the time to spare for nonsense this afternoon, but one must humor one's son once in a while. She stepped back absent-mindedly, her eyes resting on the soft greens and purples of the foliage across the meadows, her thoughts on the next paper she intended to write for the club. This incident would soon be over, and then she might pursue the even tenor of her busy way.

Then the door slid back and she became aware of something unusual in the tenseness of the moment. Looking up quickly she saw a beautiful girl of about Elizabeth's age, with a wealth of dark wavy hair, lovely dark eyes, and vivid coloring, and by her side one of the loveliest golden-haired, blue-eyed babies she had ever seen in her life. In the wonder of the moment she forgot that the outside of the building had been a barn, for the curtain had risen on a new setting, and here on the very threshold there opened before her amazed eyes a charming, homelike room.

At first she did not take in any of the details of furnishings. Everything was tastefully arranged, and the dull tones of wall and floor and ceiling in the late afternoon light mellowed the old furniture into its background so perfectly that the imperfections and make-shifts did not appear. It was just a place of comfort and beauty, even though the details might show shabby poverty.

But her son was speaking.

"Mother, this is Miss Carol Hollister, and this little girl is her sister Doris——"

Doris put out a fat hand and gravely laid it in the lady's kid glove, saying carefully, with shy lashes drooped sideways, and blue eyes furtively searching the stranger's face.

"How oo do?"

Then as if she had performed her duty, she turned on her smiles and dimples with a flash, and grasping Graham's hand said,

"Now, Mistah Dwa'm, oo tum out an' see my wabbits!"

It was evident to the mother that her son had been here before. She looked at him for an explanation, but he only said to Carol,

"Is your mother able to see callers for a few minutes?"

"Oh, yes," said Carol with a glad little ring in her voice. "Mother is up in a chair this afternoon. See! The doctor says she may get up now, she is so much better!" and she turned and flung out her arm toward the big easy chair where her mother sat.

Mrs. Hollister arose and came forward to meet them.

She was dressed in a plain little gown of cheap gray challis, much washed and mended, but looking somehow very nice; and Carol had just finished fastening one of Shirley's sheer white fluffy collars around her neck, with a bit of a pink ribbon looped in a pretty knot. Her hair was tastefully arranged, and she looked every inch a lady as she stood to receive her unexpected guests. Graham had never seen her in any but invalid's garb before, and he stood amazed for a moment at the likeness between her and Shirley. He introduced his mother with a few words, and then yielded to Doris's eager, pulling hand and went out to see the bunnies.

The situation was a trifle trying for both ladies, but to the woman of the world perhaps the more embarrassing. She hadn't a clew as to who this was she had been brought to see. She was entirely used to dominating any situation, but for a moment she was almost confused.

Mrs. Hollister, however, tactfully relieved the situation, with a gentle, "Won't you sit here by the fire? It is getting a little cool this evening, don't you think?" and put her at once at her ease. Only her family would have guessed from the soft pink spots in her cheeks that she was at all excited over her grand guest. She took the initiative at once, leading the talk into natural channels, about the spring and its wonderful unfolding in the country, exhibited a vase with jack-in-the-pulpits, and a glass bowl of hepaticas blushing blue and pink, told of the thrush that had built a nest in the elm over the door, and pointed out the view over the valley where the sinking sun was flashing crimson from the weather-vane on the little white spire of the church. She said how much they had enjoyed the sunsets since coming out here to live, taking it for granted that her visitor knew all about their circumstances, and making no apologies or comments; and the visitor, being what her son called "a good sport," showed no hint that she had never heard of the Hollisters before, but smiled and said the right thing at the right moment. And somehow, neither knew just how, they got to the subject of Browning and Ibsen, and from there to woman's suffrage, and when Graham returned with Carol and Harley, Doris chattering beside him and the dog bounding in ahead, they were deep in future politics. Graham sat and listened for a while, interested to note that the quiet little woman who had spent the last few years of her life working in a narrow dark city kitchen could talk as thoughtfully and sensibly as his cultured, versatile mother.

The next trolley brought Shirley and George, and again the mother was amazed to find how altogether free and easy seemed to be the relation between all these young people.

She gave a keen look at Shirley, and then another at her son, but saw nothing which gave her uneasiness. The girl was unconscious as a rose, and sweet and gracious to the stranger guests as if she had been in society all her life. She slipped away at once to remove her hat, and when she came back her hair was brushed, and she looked as fresh as a flower in her clean white ruffled blouse. The older woman could not take her eyes from her face. What a charming girl to be set among all this shabbiness! For by this time her discriminating eyes had discovered that everything—literally *every*thing was shabby. Who were these people, and how did they happen to get put here?

The baby was ravishingly beautiful, the girls were charming, and the boys looked like splendid, manly fellows. The mother was a product of culture and refinement. Not one word or action had shown that she knew her surroundings were shabby. She might have been mistress of a palace for aught she showed of consciousness of the pitiful poverty about her. It was as if she were just dropped down for the day in a stray barn and making a palace out of it while she stayed.

Unconsciously the woman of the world lingered longer than was her wont in making calls. She liked the atmosphere, and was strangely interested by them all.

"I wish you would come and see me," she said cordially as she rose at last to go, and she said it as if she meant it,—as if she lived right around the corner and not twenty-two miles away,—as if she really wanted her to come, and not as if this other woman lived in a barn at all.

"Good old sport!" commented her son in his heart as he listened. He had known she must see their worth, and yet he had been strangely afraid.

Mrs. Hollister received the invitation with a flush of pleasure.

"Thank you," she answered graciously, "I'm afraid not. I seldom go anywhere any more. But I've been very glad to have had this call from you. It will be a pleasure to think about. Come sometime again when you are out this way. Your son has been most kind. I cannot find words to express my thanks."

"Has he?" and his mother looked questioningly at her son. "Well, I'm very glad———"

"Yes, and Elizabeth! She is a dear sweet girl, and we all love her!"

Revelations!

"Oh, has Elizabeth been here too? Well, I'm glad. I hope she has not been a nuisance. She's such an impulsive, erratic child. Elizabeth is quite a problem just now. She's out of school on account of her eyes, and her girl friends, most of them, being away at school, she is perfectly forlorn. I am delighted to have her with your children. I am sure they are charming associates for her." And her eyes rested approvingly on the sparkling Carol in her simple school dress of brown linen with its white collar and cuffs. There was nothing countrified about Carol. She looked dainty in the commonest raiment, and she smiled radiantly at Elizabeth's mother and won her heart.

"Would you let Elizabeth stay overnight with us here sometime?" she asked shyly.

"Why, surely! I presume she would be delighted. She does about as she pleases these days. I really don't see very much of her, I'm so busy this time of year, just at the end of the season, you know, and lots of committee meetings and teas and things."

They stopped at the doorway to look up into the big tree, in response to the earnest solicitations of Doris, who pulled at the lady's gloved hand insistently, murmuring sweetly:

"Budie! Budie! See mine budie in the twee!"

The Hollisters stood grouped at the doorway when at last the visitors got into their car and went away. Mrs. Graham looked back at them wistfully.

"What a lovely group they make!" she murmured. "Now, Sidney, tell me at once who they are and why they live in a barn, and why you brought me out here. I know you had some special object. I knew the minute I saw that charming woman."

"Mother, you certainly are great! I thought you'd have the good sense to see what they are."

"Why, I haven't spent a more delightful hour in a long time than I spent talking with her. She has very original ideas, and she expresses herself well. As for the children, they are lovely. That oldest girl has a great deal of character in her face. But what are they doing in a barn, Sidney, and how did you come to know them?"

And so, as they speeded out the smooth turnpike to their lovely home Sidney Graham told his mother as much of the story of Shirley Hollister and the old barn as he thought she would care to know, and his mother sat thoughtfully watching his handsome, enthusiastic face while he talked, and wondering.

One comment she made as they swept up the beautiful drive to their luxurious country home:

"Sidney dear, they are delightful and all that, and I'm sure I'm glad to have that little girl come to see Elizabeth, but if I were you I wouldn't go out there too often when that handsome oldest girl is at home. She's not exactly in your set, you know, charming as she is, and you wouldn't want to give her any ideas. A gentleman looks out for things like that, you know."

"What has being in our set got to do with it, mother dear? Do you know any girl in our set that is better-looking or has nicer manners, or a finer appreciation of nature and books? You ought to hear her talk!"

"Yes, but, Sidney, that isn't everything! She isn't exactly———"

"Mother, were you and father, when you used to have good times together? Now, mother, you know you are just talking twaddle when you let that idea about 'our set' rule your mind. Be a good sport, mother dear, and look the facts in the face. That girl is as good as any other girl I know, and you know it. She's better than most. Please admit the facts. Yet you never warned me to be careful about calling on any of the girls in our set. Do please be consistent. However, don't worry about me. I've no idea at present of paying any special attention to anybody," and he swung the car door and jumped down to help her out.

CHAPTER XV

A man arrived one morning with a horse and a plough and several other implements of farm life of which Harley didn't know the name, and announced that Mr. Graham had sent him to plough the garden. Would Mrs. Hollister please tell him where she wanted the ground broken, and how much? He volunteered the information that he was her next neighbor, and that if he was in her place he'd plough the south slope of the meadow, and if she wanted flower-beds a strip along the front near the road; the soil was best in those spots, and she wouldn't need so much fertilizer.

Mrs. Hollister asked him how much he would charge to do it, and he said a little job like that wasn't worth talking about; that he used to rent the barn himself, and he always did a little turn for Mr. Graham whenever he needed it. He did it for Mr. Graham, and it wouldn't cost her "nothin'."

Mrs. Hollister asked him how much he would charge to see where it would be best to have the ploughing done, and when she came in a few minutes later and dropped down on the couch to rest from her unusual fatigue a new thought was racing through her mind. They could have a garden, a real garden, with lettuce and green peas and lima beans and corn! She knew all about making them grow. She had been brought up in a little village home, where a garden was a part of every one's necessary equipment for living. She used to kelp her father every spring and all summer. Her own little patch always took the prize of the family. But for years she had been in the city without an inch of space. Now, however, the old fever of delight in gardening took possession of her. If she could get out and work in the ground, as the doctor had suggested, she would get well right away. And why, with Harley to help, and George and Carol to work a little every evening, couldn't they raise enough on all that ground to sell some? George could take things into town early in the morning, or they could find some private families who would buy all they had to sell. It was worth thinking about, anyway. She could raise flowers for sale, too. She had always been a success with flowers. She had always wanted a hothouse and a chance to experiment. She heard the children say there were some old window-sashes down under the barn. She would get George to bring them out, and see what she could do with a coldframe or two. Violets would grow under a coldframe, and a lot of other things. Oh, if they could only just live here always, and not have to go back to the city in the fall! But of course there was no way to heat the barn in winter, and that was out of the question. Nevertheless, the idea of making some money with growing things had seized hold of her mind and would not be entirely put by. She thought of it much, and talked of it now and then to Shirley and the other children.

Shirley brought home some packages of seeds she got at the ten-cent store, and there was great excitement planting them. Then Mr. Graham sent over a lot of seeds, of both vegetables and flowers, and some shrubs, cuttings and bulbs which he said were "left-overs" at their country house that he thought perhaps the children could use; and so before the Hollisters knew it they were possessed of a garden, which almost in a breath lifted up its green head and began to grow.

Life was very full for the Hollisters in those days, and those who went to the city for the day could hardly bear to tear themselves away from the many delights of the country. The puppy was getting bigger and wiser every day, tagging Doris and Harley wherever they went, or sitting adoringly at Mrs. Hollister's feet; always bounding out to meet the evening trolley on which George and Shirley came, and always attending them to the trolley in the morning.

Out behind the barn a tiny coop held a white hen and her seven little downy balls of chickens. Another hen was happily ensconced in a barrel of hay with ten big blue duck-eggs under her happy wings, and a little further down toward the creek a fine chicken-run ended in a trig little roosting-place for the poultry, which George had manufactured out of a packing-box and some boards. The feathered family had been increased by two white Leghorns and three bantams. George and Harley spent their evenings watching them and discussing the price of eggs and chickens per pound. They were all very happy.

Elizabeth came out to spend Sunday as she had promised. She got up early to see the sun rise and watch the birds. She helped get breakfast and wash the dishes. Then she went with the others across the fields to the little white church in the valley to Sunday-school and church. She was as hungry and eager as any of them when she came home, and joyfully helped to do the work, taking great pride in the potatoes she was allowed to warm up under careful tutelage. In the afternoon there was no more eager listener among them to the Bible story Shirley told to Doris and the book she read aloud to them all afterward; her voice was sweetest and clearest of them all in the hymns they sang together; and she was most eager to go with Shirley to the Christian Endeavor service.

"I shouldn't wonder if Sidney wishes he was here too," she remarked dreamily that evening, as she sat before the fire on a little cushion, her chin in her hands, her eyes on the fantastic shadows in the ashes.

She went to school with Carol the next morning, came home with her in the afternoon, and when her brother came for her in the evening she was most reluctant to go home to the big, lonely, elegant house again, and begged that Carol might soon come and see her.

Friday afternoon Elizabeth called up Mrs. Hollister.

"Please, Mrs. Hollister, let Carol come and stay with me till Monday. I'm so lonesome, and mamma says she will be so glad if you will let her come."

"Oh, my dear, that would be impossible. Carol isn't suitably dressed to make a visit, you know," answered the mother quickly, glad that she had so good an excuse for keeping her child from this venture into an alien world about which she had many grave doubts.

But the young voice at the other end of the telephone was insistent.

"Dear Mrs. Hollister, please! She doesn't need any other clothes. I've got lots of things that would fit her. She loaned me her gingham dress to make garden in, and why shouldn't I loan her a dress to wear on Sunday? I've got plenty of clean middy blouses and skirts and can fix her all out fresh for school, too, Monday morning, and if you'll just let her stay Sidney will take us both down to her school when he goes to the office. You've got all those children there at home, and I've only myself. Sidney doesn't count, you know, for he's grown up."

So, with a sigh, the mother gave her consent, and Carol found the Graham car waiting for her when she came out of school. Thus she started on her first venture into the world.

It was all like fairy-land that wonderful week-end to the little girl whose memories were full of burdens and sacrifices: the palatial home of many rooms and rich furnishings, the swarm of servants, the anticipation of every want, the wide, beautiful grounds with all that heart could wish in the way of beauty and amusement, the music-room with grand piano, harp, and violin lying mute most of the time, the great library with its walls lined with rare books, mostly unread. Everything there to satisfy any whim, reasonable or unreasonable, and nobody using any of it much.

"Not a room in the whole place as dear and cozy and homey as this!" sighed Carol happily, sinking into the old denim-covered couch before the fireplace in the barn-living-room that Monday night after she got home. "I declare, mother, I don't see how Elizabeth stands it. Her mother is nice, but she's hardly ever there, unless she has a swarm of people dinnering or teaing or lunching. She hardly ever has time to speak to Elizabeth, and Elizabeth doesn't seem to care much, either. She almost seems to think more of that old nurse Susan that took care of her when she was a baby than she does of her mother. I'm so glad I was sent to you instead of to her!" And Carol suddenly slipped across the room and buried her face in her mother's neck, hugging and kissing her, leaving a few bright tears on her mother's happy face.

It was a wonderful relief to Mrs. Hollister to find her child unspoiled by her first experience of the world and glad to get back to her home, after all the anxiety her mother heart had felt. Carol presently sat up and told them minutely all about her visit. The grand concert that Sidney had taken them to Friday evening in the Academy of Music, where a world-renowned pianist was the soloist with the great symphony orchestra; the tennis and riding Saturday morning; the luncheon at a neighboring estate, where there were three girls and a brother who were "snobs" and hadn't at all good manners; the party in the evening that lasted so late that they didn't get to bed till long after midnight; the beautiful room they slept in, with every imaginable article for the toilet done in sterling silver with monograms; the strange Sabbath, with no service in the morning because they woke up too late, and no suggestion of anything but a holiday,—except the vesper service in a cold, formal chapel that Carol had begged to go to; just a lot of worldly music and entertaining, with a multitude of visitors for the end of it. Carol told of the beautiful dresses that Elizabeth had loaned her, coral crêpe de chine accordion-plaited for the concert, white with an orange sash for the luncheon, pale yellow with a black velvet girdle for the party, a little blue silk affair and another lovely white organdie for Sunday, and all with their accompanying silk stockings and slippers and gloves, and necklaces and bands for her hair. It was most wonderful to her, and as they listened they marvelled that their Carol had come back to them so gladly, and rejoiced to see her nestling in her brown linen skirt and middy blouse close beside her mother's chair. She declared herself satisfied with her flight into the world. She might like to go again for a glimpse now and then, but she thought she would rather have Elizabeth out to Glenside. She hated to lose any of the time out here, it was so pretty. Besides, it was lonesome without them all.

About that time Shirley picked up the morning paper in her office one day to look up a matter for Mr. Barnard. Her eye happened to fall on the society column and catch the name of Sidney Graham. She glanced down the column. It was an account of a wedding in high circles in which Graham had taken the part of best man, with Miss Harriet Hale—in blue tulle and white orchids as maid of honor—for his partner down the aisle. She read the column hurriedly, hungrily, getting every detail, white spats, gardenia, and all, until in those few printed sentences a picture was printed indelibly upon her vision, of Graham walking down the lily-garlanded aisle with the maid in blue tulle and white orchids on his arm. To make it more vivid the lady's picture was in the paper along with Graham's, just under those of the bride and groom, and her face was both handsome and haughty. One could tell that by the tilt of chin, the short upper lip, the cynical curve of mouth and sweep of long eyelash, the extreme effect of her dress and the arrangement of her hair. Only a beauty could have stood that hair and not been positively ugly.

Shirley suddenly realized what she was doing and turned over the page of the paper with a jerk that tore the sheet from top to bottom, going on with her search for the real-estate column and the item she was after. All that morning her typewriter keys clicked with mad rapidity, yet her work was strangely correct and perfect. She was working under a tense strain.

By noon she had herself in hand, realized what she had been doing with her vagrant thoughts, and was able to laugh at Miss Harriet Hale—whoever or whatever she was. What mattered it, Miss Harriet Hale or somebody else? What was that to Shirley Hollister? Mr. Graham was her landlord and a kindly gentleman. He would probably continue to be that to her to the end of her tenancy, without regard to Miss Hale or any other intruding Miss, and what did anything else matter? She wanted nothing else of Mr. Graham but to be a kindly gentleman whenever it was her necessity to come in his way.

But although her philosophy was on hand and her pride was aroused, she realized just where her heart might have been tending if it had not been for this little jolt it got; and she resolved to keep out of the gentleman's way whenever it was possible, and also, as far as she was able, to think no more about him.

Keeping out of Sidney Graham's way was one thing, but making him keep out of her way was quite another matter, and Shirley realized it every time he came out to Glenside, which he did quite frequently. She could not say to him that she wished he would not come. She could not be rude to him when he came. There was no way of showing him pointedly that she was not thinking of him in any way but as her landlord, because he never showed in any way that he was expecting her to. He just happened in evening after evening, in his frank, jolly way, on one pretext or other, never staying very long, never showing her any more attention than he did her mother or Carol or the boys, not so much as he did to Doris. How was she to do anything but sit quietly and take the whole thing as a matter of course? It really was a matter to deal with in her own heart alone. And there the battle must be fought if ever battle there was to be. Meantime, she could not but own that this frank, smiling, merry young man did bring a lot of life and pleasure into their lives, dropping in that way, and why should she not enjoy it when it came, seeing it in no wise interfered with Miss Harriet Hale's rights and prerogatives? Nevertheless, Shirley withdrew more and more into quietness whenever he came, and often slipped into the kitchen on some household pretext, until one day he boldly came out into the kitchen after her with a book he wanted her to read, and was so frank and companionable that she led the way back to the living-room, and concluded it would be better in future to stay with the rest of the family.

Shirley had no intention whatever of letting her heart stray out after any impossible society man. She had her work in the world, and to it she meant to stick. If there were dreams she kept them well under lock and key, and only took them out now and then at night when she was very tired and discouraged and life looked hard and long and lonely on ahead. Shirley had no intention that Sidney Graham should ever have reason to think, when he married Miss Harriet Hale or some one equivalent to her, that any poor little stenographer living in a barn had at one time fancied him fond of her. No, indeed! Shirley tilted her firm little chin at the thought, and declined to ride with Graham and Elizabeth the next time they called at the office for her, on the plea that she had promised to go home in the trolley with one of the office girls. And yet the next time she saw him he was just as pleasant, and showed no sign that she had declined his invitation. In fact, the whole basis of their acquaintance was such that she felt free to go her own way and yet know he would be just as pleasant a friend whenever she needed one.

Matters stood in this way when Graham was suddenly obliged to go West on a trip for the office, to be gone three or four weeks. Mrs. Graham and Elizabeth went to the Adirondacks for a short trip, and the people at Glenside settled down to quiet country life, broken only by a few visits from their farm neighbors, and a call from the cheery, shabby pastor of the little white church in the valley.

CHAPTER XVI

Graham did not seem to forget his friends entirely while he was gone. The boys received a number of post-cards from time to time, and a lot of fine views of California, Yellowstone Park, the Grand Cañon, and other spots of interest. A wonderful picture-book came for Doris, with Chinese pictures, and rhymes printed on crêpe paper. The next morning a tiny sandalwood fan arrived for Carol with Graham's compliments, and a few days later a big box of oranges for Mrs. Hollister with no clew whatever as to their sender. Shirley began to wonder what her part would be and what she should do about it, and presently received—a letter! And then, after all, it was only a pleasant request that she would not pay the rent, about which she had always been so punctual, until his return, as no one else understood about his affairs. He added a few words about his pleasant trip and a wish that they were all prospering,—and that was all.

Shirley was disappointed, of course, and yet, if he had said more, or if he had ventured to send her even a mere trifle of a gift, it would have made her uncomfortable and set her questioning how she should treat him and it. It was the perfection of his behavior that he had not overstepped a single bound that the most particular might set for a landlord and his respected tenant. She drew a deep sigh and put the letter back into the envelope, and as she did so she spied a small card, smaller than the envelope, on which was an exquisite bit of scenery, a colored photograph, apparently, and underneath had been pencilled, "One of the many beautiful spots in California that I am sure you would appreciate."

Her heart gave an unforbidden leap, and was promptly taken to task for it. Yet when Shirley went back to her typewriter the bit of a picture was pinned to the wall back of her desk, and her eyes rested on it many times that day when she lifted them from her work. It is questionable whether Shirley remembered Miss Harriet Hale at all that day.

The garden was growing beautifully now. There would soon be lettuce and radishes ready to eat. George had secured a number of customers through people at the store, and was planning to take early trips to town, when his produce was ripe, to deliver it. They watched every night and looked again every morning for signs of the first pea blossoms, and the little green spires of onion tops, like sparse hairs, beginning to shoot up. Every day brought some new wonder. They almost forgot they had ever lived in the little old brick house, until George rode by there on his bicycle one noon and reported that it had been half pulled down, and you could now see the outline of where the stairs and closets had been, done in plaster, on the side of the next house. They were all very silent for a minute thinking after he told that, and Mrs. Hollister looked around the great airy place in which they were sitting, and then out the open door where the faint stain of sunset was still lingering against the horizon, and said:

"We ought all to be very thankful, children. George, get the Bible and read the thirty-fourth psalm." Wonderingly George obeyed, and they all sat listening as the words sank into their souls.

"Now," said the mother when the psalm was finished and those last words, "The Lord redeemeth the soul of his servants, and none of them that trust in him shall be desolate"; "now let us kneel down and thank Him."

And they all knelt while she prayed a few earnest, simple words of thanksgiving and commended them to God's keeping.

By this time Mrs. Hollister was so well that she went every day for a little while into the garden and worked, and was able to do a great deal in the house. The children were overjoyed, and lived in a continual trance of delight over the wild, free life they were living. Carol's school had closed and Carol was at home all day. This made one more to help in the garden. George was talking about building a little pigeon-house and raising squabs for sale. The man who did the ploughing had given him a couple to start with and told him there was money in squabs if one only went about it right. George and Harley pored over a book that told all about it, and talked much on the subject.

The weather was growing warm, and Shirley was wishing her vacation came in July or August instead of the first two weeks in September. Somehow she felt so used up these hot days, and the hours dragged by so slowly. At night the trolleys were crowded until they were half-way out to Glenside. She often had to stand, and her head ached a great deal. Yet she was very happy and thankful—only there was so much to be done in this world, and she seemed to have so little strength to do it all. The burden of next fall came occasionally to mar the beauty of the summer, and rested heavily upon her young shoulders. If only there wouldn't be any winter for just one year, and they could stay in the barn and get rested and get a little money ahead somehow for moving. It was going to be so hard to leave that wide, beautiful abiding-place, barn though it was.

One morning nearly four weeks after Graham left for California Shirley was called from her desk to the outer office to take some dictation for Mr. Clegg. While she was there two men entered the outer office and asked for Mr. Barnard. One of them was a short, thick-set man with a pretentious wide gray mustache parted in the middle and combed elaborately out on his cheeks. He had a red face, little cunning eyes, and a cruel set to his jaw, which somehow seemed ridiculously at variance with his loud, checked suit, sporty necktie of soft bright blue satin, set with a scarf-pin of two magnificent stones, a diamond and a sapphire, and with the three showy jewelled rings which he wore on his fat, pudgy hand. The other man was sly, quiet, gray, unobtrusive, obviously the henchman of the first.

Mr. Clegg told the men they might go into the inner office and wait for Mr. Barnard, who would probably be in shortly, and Shirley watched them as they passed out of her view, wondering idly why those exquisite stones had to be wasted in such an out-of-place spot as in that coarse-looking man's necktie, and if a man like that really cared for beautiful things, else why should he wear them? It was only a passing thought, and then she took up her pencil and took down the closing sentences of the letter Mr. Clegg was dictating. It was but a moment more and she was free to go back to her own little alcove just behind Mr. Barnard's office and connecting with it. There was an entrance to it from the tiny cloak-room, which she always used when Mr. Barnard had visitors in his office, and through this way she now went, having a strange repugnance toward being seen by the two men. She had an innate sense that the man with the gaudy garments would not be one who would treat a young girl in her position with any respect, and she did not care to come under his coarse gaze, so she slipped in quietly through the cloak-room, and passed like a shadow the open door into Mr. Barnard's office, where they sat with their backs toward her, having evidently just settled down and begun to talk. She could hear a low-breathed comment on the furnishings of the office as indicating a good bank-account of the owner, and a coarse jest about a photograph of Mr. Barnard's wife which stood on his desk. It made her wish that the door between the rooms was closed; yet she did not care to rise and close it lest she should call attention to herself, and of course it might be but a minute or two before Mr. Barnard returned. A pile of envelopes to be addressed lay on her desk, and this work she could do without any noise, so she slipped softly into her seat and began to work.

"Well, we got them Grahams good and fast now!" a coarse voice, that she knew for that of the man with the loud clothing, spoke. "The young feller bit all right! I thought he would. He's that kind." He stopped for a laugh of contempt, and Shirley's heart stood still with apprehension. What could it mean? Was it something about her Grahams? Some danger threatening them? Some game being played on them? He looked like the kind of man who lived on the blindnesses of others. What was it they called such? A parasite? Instinctively she was on the alert at once, and automatically she reached for the pad on which she took dictation and began to write down in shorthand what she had just heard. The voice in the other room went on and her fountain pen kept eager pace, her breath coming quick and short now, and her face white with excitement.

"He went out to see the place, you know, examine the mines and all that. Oh, he's awful cautious! Thought he took a government expert with him to test the ore. We fixed that up all right—had the very man on tap at the right minute, government papers all O.K.—you couldn't have told 'em from the real thing. It was Casey; you know him; he's a crackerjack on a job like that,—could fool the devil himself. Well, he swore it was the finest kind of ore and all that kind of dope, and led that Graham kid around as sweetly as a blue-eyed baby. We had a gang out there all bribed, you know, to swear to things, and took particular pains so Graham would go around and ask the right ones questions,—Casey tended to that,—and now he's come home with the biggest kind of a tale and ready to boost the thing to the skies. I've got his word for it, and his daddy is to sign the papers this morning. When he wakes up one of these fine days he'll find himself minus a hundred thousand or so, and nobody to blame for it, because how could anybody be expected to know that those are only pockets? He'll recommend it right and left too, and we'll clean out a lot of other fellers before we get done. Teddy, my boy, pat yourself on the back! We'll have a tidy little sum between us when we pull out of this deal, and take a foreign trip for our health till the fracas blows over. Now mind you, not a word of this to Barnard when he comes in. We're only going to pave the way this morning. The real tip comes from Graham himself. See?"

Shirley was faint and dizzy with excitement as she finished writing, and her brain was in a whirl. She felt as if she would scream in a minute if this strain kept up. The papers were to be signed that morning! Even now the deed might be done and it would be too late, perhaps, to stop it. And yet she must make no sign, must not have the men know that she was there and that they had been heard. She must sit here breathless until they were gone, so they would not know she had overheard them, or they might manage to prevent her getting word to Graham. How long would they stay? Would they talk on and reveal more? The other man had only grunted something unintelligible in reply, and then before more could be said an office boy opened the outer door and told them that Mr. Barnard had just phoned that he would not be back before two o'clock.

The men swore and went out grumbling. Suddenly Shirley knew her time had come to do something. Stepping quickly to the door she scanned the room carefully to make sure they were gone, then closing her own door she took up the telephone on her desk and called up the Graham number. She did not know just what she meant to say, nor what she would do if Sidney Graham were not in the office,—and it was hardly probable he would be there yet if he had only arrived home the day before. He would be likely to take a day off before getting back to work. Her throbbing heart beat out these questions to her brain while she waited for the number. Would she dare to ask for Mr. Walter Graham? And if she did, what would she say to him? How explain? He did not know her, and probably never heard of her. He might think her crazy. Then there was always the possibility that there was some mistake—and yet it seemed a coincidence that two men of the same name should both be going West at that time. It must be these Grahams that the plot was against. But how explain enough over the phone to do any good? Of course she must give them a copy of what she had taken down in shorthand, but first she must stop the signing of those papers, whatever they were, at all costs.

Then all at once, into the midst of her whirling confusion of thoughts, came a voice at the other end of the phone, "Hello!" and her frantic senses realized that it was a familiar one.

"Oh, is this,—this *is* Mr. Sidney Graham, isn't it? This is Shirley Hollister."

There was a catch in her voice that sounded almost like a sob as she drew in her breath with relief to know that he was there, and his answer came in swift alarm:

"Yes? Is there anything the matter, Miss Shirley? You are not ill, are you?"

There was a sharp note of anxiety in the young man's voice, and even in her excitement it made Shirley's heart leap to hear it.

"No, there is nothing the matter with me," she said, trying to steady her voice, "but something has happened that I think you ought to know at *once*. I don't know whether I ought to tell it over the phone. I'm not sure but I may be overheard."

"I will come to you immediately. Where can I find you?"

Her heart leaped again at his willingness to trust her and to obey her call.

"In Mr. Barnard's private office. If you ask for me they will let you come right in. There is one thing more. If there is anything important your father was to decide this morning, could you get him to wait till you return, or till you phone him?"

There was a second's hesitation, and the reply was politely puzzled but courteous:

"He is not in the office at present and will not be for an hour."

"Oh, I'm so glad! Then *please hurry*!"

"I will get there as soon as I can," and the phone clicked into place.

Shirley sat back in her chair and pressed her hands over her eyes to concentrate all her powers. Then she turned to her typewriter and began to copy off the shorthand, her fingers flying over the keys with more than their usual swiftness. As she wrote she prayed, prayed that nothing might have been signed, and that her warning might not come too late; prayed, too, that Mr. Barnard might not return until Mr. Graham had been and gone, and that Mr. Graham might not think her an utter fool in case this proved to have nothing whatever to do with his affairs.

CHAPTER XVII

When Graham entered the office Shirley came to meet him quietly, without a word of greeting other than to put her little cold hand into his that he held out to her. She began to speak in a low voice full of suppressed excitement. She had a vague fear lest the two men might be still lingering about the outer office, waiting for Mr. Barnard, and a momentary dread lest Mr. Barnard might enter the room at any minute. She must get the telling over before he came.

"Mr. Graham, two men were sitting in this room waiting for Mr. Barnard a few minutes ago, and I was in my little room just back there. I could not help hearing what they said, and when I caught the name of Graham in connection with what sounded like an evil plot I took down their words in shorthand. It may not have anything to do with your firm, but I thought I ought to let you know. I called you on the phone as soon as they left the office and would not hear me, and I have made this copy of their conversation. Read it quickly, please, because if it does have anything to do with you, you will want to phone your father at once, before those men can get there."

Her tone was very cool, and her hand was steady as she handed him the typewritten paper, but her heart was beating mildly, because there had been a look in his eyes as he greeted her that made her feel that he was glad to see her, and it touched an answering gladness in her heart and filled her both with delight and with apprehension. What a fool she was!

She turned sharply away and busied herself with arranging some papers on Mr. Barnard's desk while he read. She must still this excitement and get control of herself before he was through. She *must* be the cool, impersonal stenographer, and not let him suspect for a moment that she was so excited about seeing him again.

The young man stood still, reading rapidly, his face growing graver as he read. The girl snatched a furtive glance at him, and felt convinced that the matter was a serious one and had to do with him.

Suddenly he looked up.

"Do you know who those men were, Miss Shirley?" he asked, and she saw his eyes were full of anxiety.

"No," said Shirley. "But I saw them as they passed through the outer office, and stopped to speak to Mr. Clegg. I was taking dictation from Mr. Clegg at the time. I came back to my desk through the cloak-room, so they did not know I was within hearing."

"What kind of looking men were they? Do you remember?"

She described them.

Certainty grew in his face as she talked, and grave concern.

"May I use your phone a minute?" he asked after an instant's thought.

She led him to her own desk and handed him the receiver, then stepped back into the office and waited.

"Hello! Is that you, Edward?" she heard him say. "Has father come yet? Give me his phone, please. Hello, father; this is Sidney. Father, has Kremnitz come in yet? He has? You say he's waiting in the office to see you? Well, don't see him, father, till I get there. Something has turned up that I'm afraid is going to alter matters entirely. Yes, pretty serious, I'm afraid. Don't see him. Keep him waiting. I'll be there in five minutes, and come in from the back way directly to your office. Don't talk with him on any account till I can get there. Good-by."

He hung up the receiver and turned to Shirley.

"Miss Shirley, you were just in time to save us. I haven't time now to tell you how grateful I am for this. I must hurry right over. Do you suppose if we should need you it would be possible for you to come over and identify those men? Thank you. I'll speak to Mr. Clegg about it as I go out, and if we find it necessary we'll phone you. In case you have to come I'll have an office-boy in the hall to take your hat, and you can come right into the office as if you were one of our employees—just walk over to the bookcase as if you were looking for a book—any book.

Select one and look through it, meanwhile glancing around the room, and see if you find those men. Then walk through into my office. I'll be waiting there. Good-by, and thank you so much!"

He gave her hand one quick clasp and was gone, and Shirley found she was trembling from head to foot. She walked quickly into her own room and sat down, burying her face in her hands and trying to get control of herself, but the tears would come to her eyes in spite of all she could do. It was not the excitement of getting the men and stopping their evil plans before they could do any damage, although that had something to do with her nervous state, of course; and it was not just that she had been able to do a little thing in return for all he had done for her; nor even his gratitude; it was—she could not deny it to herself—it was a certain quality in his voice, a something in the look he gave her, that made her whole soul glow, and seemed to fill the hungry longing that had been in her heart.

It frightened her and made her ashamed, and as she sat with bowed head she prayed that she might be given strength to act like a sensible girl, and crush out such foolish thoughts before they dared lift their heads and be recognized even by her own heart. Then strengthened, she resolved to think no more about the matter, but just get her work done and be ready to enter into that other business if it became necessary. Mr. Barnard would be coming soon, and she must have his work finished. She had lost almost an hour by this matter.

She went at her typewriter pell-mell, and soon had Mr. Clegg's letters done. She was nearly through with the addressing that Mr. Barnard left for her to do when the telephone called her to Graham's office.

She slipped on her hat and hurried out.

"Will it be all right for me to take my noontime now, Mr. Clegg?" she said, stopping by his desk. "Mr. Graham said he spoke to you."

"Yes, he wants you to help him identify some one. That's all right. I'll explain to Mr. Barnard when he comes. There's nothing important you have to finish, is there? All done but those envelopes? Well, you needn't return until one o'clock, anyway. The envelopes can wait till the four-o'clock mail, and if Mr. Barnard needs anything in a hurry Miss Dwight can attend to it this time. Just take your time, Miss Hollister."

Shirley went out bewildered by the unusual generosity of Mr. Clegg, who was usually taciturn and abrupt. She realized, however, that his warmth must be due to Graham's visit, and not to any special desire to give her a holiday. She smiled to think what a difference wealth and position made in the eyes of the world.

The same office-boy she had met on her first visit to Graham's office was waiting most respectfully for her now in the hall when she got out of the elevator, and she gave him her hat and walked into the office according to programme, going straight to the big glass bookcase full of calf-bound volumes, and selecting one after running her finger over two rows of them. She was as cool as though her part had been rehearsed many times, although her heart was pounding most unmercifully, and it seemed as though the people in the next room must hear it. She stood and opened her book, casting a casual glance about the room.

There, sure enough, quite near to her, sat the two men, fairly bursting with impatience. The once immaculate hair of the loudly dressed one was rumpled as if he had run his fingers through it many times, and he played nervously with his heavy rings, and caressed half viciously his elaborate mustache, working his thick, sensuous lips impatiently all the while. Shirley took a good look at him, necktie, scarf-pin, and all; looked keenly into the face of the gray one also; then coolly closed the door of the bookcase and carried the book she had selected into Sidney Graham's office.

Graham was there, standing to receive her, and just back of him stood a kindly-faced elderly man with merry blue eyes, gray hair, and a stylishly cut beard. By their attitude and manner Shirley somehow sensed that they had both been watching her. Then Graham introduced her.

"This is my father, Miss Hollister."

The elder man took her hand and shook it heartily, speaking in a gruff, hearty way that won her from the first:

"I'm glad to know you, Miss Hollister. I certainly am! My son has been telling me what you've done for us, and I think you're a great little girl! That was bully work you did, and I appreciate it. I was watching you out there in the office. You were as cool as a cucumber. You ought to be a detective. You found your men all right, did you?"

"Yes, sir," said Shirley, much abashed, and feeling the return of that foolish trembling in her limbs. "Yes, they are both out there, and the short one with the rings and the blue necktie is the one that did the talking."

"Exactly what I thought," drawled the father, with a keen twinkle in his kindly eyes. "I couldn't somehow trust that chap from the start. That's why I sent my son out to investigate. Well, now, will you just step into my private office, Miss Hollister, and take your seat by the typewriter as if you were my stenographer? You'll find paper there in the drawer, and you can just be writing—write anything you choose, so it looks natural when the men come in. When we get to talking I'd like you to take down in shorthand all that is said by all of us. You're pretty good at that, I judge. Sid, will you phone for those officers now? I think it's about time for the curtain to rise." And he led the way into his own office.

Shirley sat down at the typewriter as she had been directed and began to write mechanically. Mr. Graham touched the bell on his desk, and told the office boy who answered to send in Mr. Kremnitz and his companion.

Shirley was so seated that she could get occasional glimpses of the men without being noticed, and she was especially interested in the twinkle that shone in the bright blue eyes of the elder Graham as he surveyed the men who thought he was their dupe. Her heart warmed to him. His kindly, merry face, his hearty, unconventional speech, all showed him to be a big, warm-hearted man without a bit of snobbishness about him.

The son came in, and talk began just as if the matter of the mine were going on. Mr. Kremnitz produced some papers which he evidently expected to be signed at once, and sat complacently answering questions; keen questions Shirley saw they were afterwards, and in the light of the revelation she had overheard in Mr. Barnard's office Kremnitz perjured himself hopelessly by his answers. Presently the office-boy announced the arrival of some one in the next room. Shirley had taken down minutely a great deal of valuable information which the Grahams had together drawn from their victim. She was surprised at the list of wealthy business men who were to have been involved in the scheme.

Then suddenly the quiet scene changed. The elder Graham gave a signal to his office-boy, which looked merely like waving him away, and the door was flung open, revealing four officers of the law, who stepped into the room without further word. Graham arose and faced his two startled callers, his hand firmly planted on the papers on his desk which he had been supposed to sign.

"Mr. Kremnitz," he said, and even in the midst of this serious business Shirley fancied there was a half-comic drawl to his words. He simply could not help letting his sense of humor come on top. "Mr. Kremnitz, it is not going to be possible for me to sign these papers this morning, as you expected. I do not feel satisfied that all things are as you have represented. In fact, I have the best evidence to the contrary. Officer, these are the gentlemen you have come to arrest," and he stepped back and waved his hand toward the two conspirators, who sat with startled eyes and blanched faces, appalled at the sudden developments where they had thought all was moving happily toward their desired end.

"Arrest! Who? On what charge?" flashed the little gaudy Kremnitz, angrily springing to his feet and making a dash toward the door, while his companion slid furtively toward the other end of the room, evidently hoping to gain young Graham's office before he was noticed. But two officers blocked their way and the handcuffs clanked in the hands of the other two policemen.

"Why, arrest *you*, my friend," said Graham senior, as if he rather enjoyed the little man's discomfiture. "And for trying to perpetrate the biggest swindle that has been attempted for ten years. I must say for you that you've worked hard, and done the trick rather neatly, but you made one unfortunate slip that saved all us poor rich men. It seems a pity that so much elaborate lying should have brought you two nothing but those bracelets you're wearing,—they don't seem to match well with your other jewels,—but that's the way things go in this world. Now, take them away, officer. I've no more time to waste on them this morning!" and he turned and walked over by Shirley's desk, while the curtain fell over the brief drama.

"Do you know how much money you've saved for us, little girl,—just plain *saved*? I'll tell you. A clean hundred thousand! That's what I was going to put into this affair! And as for other men, I expected to influence a lot of other men to put in a good deal also. Now, little girl, I don't know what you think about it, but I want to shake hands." He put out his hand and Shirley laid her own timid one in it, smiling and blushing rosily, and saying softly with what excited breath she had, "Oh, I'm so glad I got you in time!" Then she was aware that the man had gone on talking. "I don't know what you think about it," he repeated, "but I feel that you saved me a clean hundred thousand dollars, and I say that a good percentage of that belongs to you as a reward of your quickness and keenness."

But Shirley drew away her hand and stepped back, her face white, her head up, her chin tilted proudly, her eyes very dark with excitement and determination. She spoke clearly and earnestly.

"No, Mr. Graham, nothing whatever belongs to me. I don't want any reward. I couldn't think of taking it. It is utterly out of the question!"

"Well, well, well!" said the elder Graham, sitting down on the edge of his desk, watching her in undisguised admiration. "Now that's a new kind of girl that won't take what she's earned,—what rightly belongs to her."

"Mr. Graham, it was a very little thing I did,—anybody would have done it,—and it was just in the way of simple duty. Please don't say anything more about it. I am only too glad to have had opportunity to give a little help to people who have helped me so much. I feel that I am under deep obligation to your son for making it possible for us to live in the country, where my mother is getting well."

"Well, now I shall have to inquire into this business. I haven't heard anything about obligations, and for my part I feel a big one just now. Perhaps you think it was a very little thing you did, but suppose you *hadn't* done it. Suppose you'd been too busy, or it hadn't occurred to you to take down that conversation until it was too late; or suppose you hadn't had the brains to see what it would mean to us. Why, then it would have become a very big thing indeed, and we should have been willing, if we had known, to pay a mighty big sum to get that evidence. You see a hundred thousand dollars isn't exactly a very little thing when you're swindled out of it. It's the *swindling* that hurts more than the loss of the money. And you saved us from that. Now, young lady, I consider myself under obligation to you, and I intend to discharge it somehow. If I can't do it one way I shall another, but in the meantime I'm deeply grateful, and please accept our thanks. If you are willing to add one more to your kindness, I shall be glad if you will make a carbon copy of those shorthand notes you took. I may need them for evidence. And, by the way, you will probably be called upon to testify in court. I'm sorry. That may be unpleasant, but I guess it can't be helped, so you see before you get through you may not think you did so very small a thing after all. Sid, I think you better escort this young lady back to her office and explain to Barnard. He's probably been on the verge of being buncoed also. You said Kremnitz was waiting for him when the conversation took place? I guess you better go with Miss Hollister and clear the whole thing up. Say, child, have you had your lunch yet? No, of course not. Sidney, you take her to get some lunch before she goes back to the office. She's had an exciting morning. Now, good-by, little girl. I sha'n't forget what you've done for us, and I'm coming to see you pretty soon and get things squared up."

So that was how it came about that in spite of her protests Mr. Sidney Graham escorted Shirley Hollister into one of the most exclusive tea-rooms of the city, and seated her at a little round table set for two, while off at a short distance Miss Harriet Hale sat with her mother, eating her lunch and trying in vain to "place" the pretty girl she did not recognize.

It never occurred to her for a moment that Sidney Graham's companion might be a stenographer, for Shirley had a knack about her clothes that made her always seem well dressed. That hat she wore had seen service for three summers, and was now a wholly different shape and color from what it had been when it began life. A scrub in hot water had removed the dust of toil, some judiciously applied dye had settled the matter of color, and a trifling manipulation on her head while the hat was still wet had made the shape not only exceedingly stylish but becoming. The chic little rosette and strictly tailored band which were its sole trimming were made from a much-soiled waist-ribbon, washed and stretched around a bottle of hot water to dry it, and teased into the latest thing in rosettes by Shirley's witching fingers. The simple linen dress she wore fitted well and at a distance could not have been told from something better, and neither were gloves and shoes near enough to be inspected critically, so Miss Hale was puzzled, and jealously watched the pretty color come and go in Shirley's cheek, and the simple grace of her movements.

Fortunately, Shirley did not see Miss Hale, and would not have recognized her if she had from that one brief glimpse she had of her picture on the society page of the newspaper. So she ate her delectable lunch, ordered by Graham, in terms that she knew not, about dishes that she had never seen before. She ate and enjoyed herself so intensely that it seemed to her she would never be able to make the rest of her life measure up to the privileges of the hour.

For Shirley was a normal girl. She could not help being pleased to be doing just for once exactly as other more favored girls did constantly. To be lunching at Blanco's with one of the most-sought-after men in the upper set, to be treated like a queen, and to be talking beautiful things about travels and pictures and books, it was all too beautiful to be real. Shirley began to feel that if it didn't get over pretty soon and find her back in the office addressing the rest of those envelopes she would think she had died in the midst of a dream and gone to heaven.

There was something else too that brought an undertone of beauty, which she was not acknowledging even to her inmost self. That was the way Graham looked at her, as if she were some fine beautiful angel dropped down from above that he loved to look at; as if he really cared what she thought and did; as if there were somehow a soul-harmony between them that set them apart this day from others, and put them into tune with one another; as if he were glad, *glad* to see her once more after the absence! All through her being it thrilled like a song that brings tears to the throat and gladness to the eyes, and makes one feel strong and pure. That was how it seemed when she thought about it afterward. At the time she was just living it in wonder and thanksgiving.

At another time her sordid worldliness and pride might have risen and swelled with haughtiness of spirit over the number of people who eyed her enviously as they went out together; over the many bows and salutations her escort received from people of evident consequence, for she had the normal human pride somewhere in her nature as we all have. But just then her heart was too humble with a new, strange happiness to feel it or take it in, and she walked with unconscious grace beside him, feeling only the joy of being there.

Later, in the quiet of her chamber, her mother's warning came to her, and her cheeks burned with shame in the dark that her heart had dared make so much of a common little luncheon, just a mere courtesy after she had been able to do a favor. Yet through it all Shirley knew there was something fine and true there that belonged just to her, and presently she would rise above everything and grasp it and keep it hers forever.

She felt the distinction of her escort anew when she entered Barnard and Clegg's in his company, and saw Mr. Clegg spring to open the door and to set a chair for his young guest, saw even Mr. Barnard rise and greet him with almost reverence. And this honor she knew was being paid to money, the great demagogue. It was not the man that she admired to whom they were paying deference, it was to his money! She smiled to herself. It was the *man* she admired, not his money.

All that afternoon she worked with flying fingers, turning off the work at marvellous speed, amused when she heard the new note of respect in Mr. Barnard's voice as he gave her a direction. Mr. Barnard had been greatly impressed with the story Graham had told him, and was also deeply grateful on his own account that Shirley had acted as she had, for he had been on the verge of investing a large trust fund that was in his keeping in the new mining operation, and it would have meant absolute failure for him.

When Shirley left the office that night she was almost too tired to see which trolley was coming, but some one touched her on the arm, and there was Sidney Graham waiting for her beside his car,—a little two-passenger affair that she had never seen before and that went like the wind. They took a road they had not travelled together before, and Shirley got in joyously, her heart all in a tumult of doubts and joys and questions.

CHAPTER XVIII

What that ride was to Shirley she hardly dared let herself think afterwards. Sitting cozily beside Graham in the little racing car, gliding through the better part of town where all the tall, imposing houses slept with drawn blinds, and dust-covered shutters proclaimed that their owners were far away from heat and toil. Out through wide roads and green-hedged lanes, where stately mansions set in flowers and mimic landscapes loomed far back from road in dignified seclusion. Passing now and then a car of people who recognized Graham and bowed in the same deferential way as they had done in the tea-room. And all the time his eyes were upon her, admiring, delighting; and his care about her, solicitous for her comfort.

Once he halted the car and pointed off against the sunset, where wide gables and battlemented towers stood gray amidst a setting of green shrubbery and trees, and velvety lawns reached far, to high, trim hedges arched in places for an entrance to the beautiful estate.

"That is my home over there," he said, and watched her widening eyes. "I wish I had time to take you over to-night, but I know you are tired and ought to get home and rest. Another time we'll go around that way." And her heart leaped up as the car went forward again. There was to be another time, then! Ah! But she must not allow it. Her heart was far too foolish already. Yet she would enjoy this ride, now she was started.

They talked about the sunset and a poem he had lately read. He told her bits about his journey, referring to his experience at the mines, touching on some amusing incidents, sketching some of the queer characters he had met. Once he asked her quite abruptly if she thought her mother would be disturbed if he had a cement floor put in the basement of the barn some time soon. He wanted to have it done before cold weather set in, and it would dry better now in the hot days. Of course, if it would be in the least disturbing to any of them it could wait, but he wanted to store a few things there that were being taken out of the office buildings, and he thought they would keep drier if there was a cement floor. When she said it would not disturb any one in the least, would on the contrary be quite interesting for the children to watch, she was sure, he went easily back to California scenery and never referred to it again.

All through the ride, which was across a country she had never seen before, and ended at Glenside approaching from a new direction, there was a subtle something between them, a sympathy and quick understanding as if they were comrades, almost partners in a lot of common interests. Shirley chided herself for it every time she looked up and caught his glance, and felt the thrill of pleasure in this close companionship. Of course it was wholly in her own imagination, and due entirely to the nervous strain through which she had passed that day, she told herself. Of course, he had nothing in his mind but the most ordinary kindly desire to give her a good time out of gratitude for what she had done for him. But nevertheless it was sweet, and Shirley was loath to surrender the joy of it while it lasted, dream though it might be.

It lasted all the way, even up to the very stop in front of the barn when he took her hand to help her out, and his fingers lingered on hers with just an instant's pressure, sending a thrill to her heart again, and almost bringing tears to her eyes. Foolishness! She was overwrought. It was a shame that human beings were so made that they had to become weak like that in a time of pleasant rejoicing.

The family came forth noisily to meet them, rejoicing openly at Graham's return, George and Harley vying with each other to shout the news about the garden and the chickens and the dove-cote; Carol demanding to know where was Elizabeth; and Doris earnestly looking in his face and repeating:

"Ickle budie fy away, Mistah Gwaham. All gone! All ickle budies fy away!"

Even Mrs. Hollister came smiling to the door to meet him, and the young man had a warm word of hearty greeting and a hand-shake for each one. It was as if he had just got home to a place where he loved to be, and he could not show his joy enough. Shirley stood back for the moment watching him, admiring the way his hair waved away from his temples, thinking how handsome he looked when he smiled, wondering that he could so easily fit himself into this group, which must in the nature of things be utterly different from his native element, rejoicing over the deference he paid to her plain, quiet mother, thrilling over the kiss he gave her sweet little sister.

Then Mrs. Hollister did something perfectly unexpected and dreadful—she invited him to stay to dinner! Shirley stood back and gasped. Of course he would decline, but think of the temerity of inviting the wealthy and cultured Mr. Graham to take dinner in his own barn!

Oh! But he wasn't going to decline at all. He was accepting as if it were a great pleasure Mrs. Hollister was conferring upon him. *Sure*, he would stay! He had been wishing all the way out they would ask him. He had wondered whether he dared invite himself.

Shirley with her cheeks very red hurried in to see that the table-cloth was put on straight, and look after one or two little things; but behold, he followed her out, and, gently insisting and assisting, literally compelled her to come and lie down on the couch while he told the family what she had been through that day. Shirley was so happy she almost cried right there before them all. It was so wonderful to have some one take care of her that way. Of course it was only gratitude—but she had been taking care of other people so long that it completely broke her down to have some one take care of her.

The dinner went much more easily than she had supposed it could with those cracked plates, and the forks from which the silver was all worn off. Doris insisted that the guest sit next to her and butter her bread for her, and she occasionally caressed his coat-sleeve with a sticky little hand, but he didn't seem to mind it in the least, and smiled down on her in quite a brotherly way, arranging her bib when it got tangled in her curls, and seeing that she had plenty of jelly on her bread.

It was a beautiful dinner. Mother Hollister had known what she was about when she selected that particular night to invite unexpected company. There was stewed chicken on little round biscuits, with plenty of gravy and currant jelly, mashed potatoes, green peas, little new beets, and the most delicious custard pie for dessert, all rich, velvety yellow with a golden-brown top. The guest ate as if he enjoyed it, and asked for a second piece of pie, just as if he were one of them. It was unbelievable!

He helped clear off the table too, and insisted on Carol's giving him a wiping-towel to help with the dishes. It was just like a dream.

The young man tore himself reluctantly away about nine o'clock and went home, but before he left he took Shirley's hand and looked into her eyes with another of those deep understanding glances, and Shirley watched him whirling away in the moonlight, and wondered if there ever would be another day as beautiful and exciting and wonderful as this had been, and whether she could come down to sensible, every-day living again by morning.

Then there was the story of the day to tell all over again after he was gone, and put in the little family touches that had been left out when the guest was there, and there was: "Oh, did you notice how admiring he looked when he told mother Shirley had a remarkably keen mind?" and "He said his father thought Shirley was the most unspoiled-looking girl he had ever seen!" and a lot of other things that Shirley hadn't heard before.

Shirley told her mother what the senior Mr. Graham had said about giving her a reward, and her mother agreed that she had done just right in declining anything for so simple a service, but she looked after Shirley with a sigh as she went to put Doris to bed, and wondered if for this service the poor child was to get a broken heart. It could hardly be possible that a girl could be given much attention such as Shirley had received that day, from as attractive a young man as Graham, without feeling it keenly not to have it continue. And of *course* it was out of the question that it should continue. Mrs. Hollister decided that she had done wrong to invite the young man to stay to supper, and resolved never to offend in that way again. It was a wrong to Shirley to put him on so intimate a footing in the household, and it could not but bring her sadness. He was a most unusual young man to have even wanted to stay, but one must not take that for more than a passing whim, and Shirley must be protected at all hazards.

"Now," said the elder Graham the next morning, when the business of the day was well under way and he had time to send for his son to come into his office, "now, I want you to tell me all about that little girl, and what you think we ought to give her. What did she mean by 'obligations' yesterday? Have you been doing anything for her, son? I meant to ask you last night, but you came home so late I couldn't sit up."

And then Sidney Graham told his father the whole story. It was different from telling his mother. He knew no barn would have the power to prejudice his father.

"And you say that girl lives in the old barn!" exclaimed the father when the story was finished. "Why, the nervy little kid! And she looks as if she came out of a bandbox! Well, she's a bully little girl and no mistake! Well, now, son, what can we do for her? We ought to do something pretty nice. You see it wasn't just the money we might have lost. That would have been a mere trifle beside getting all those other folks balled up in the mess. Why, I'd have given every cent I own before I'd have had Fuller and Browning and Barnard and Wilts get entangled. I tell you, son, it was a great escape!"

"Yes, father, and it was a great lesson for me. I'll never be buncoed as easily again. But about Miss Hollister, I don't know what to say. She's very proud and sensitive. I had an awful time doing the little things I just had to do to that barn without her suspecting I was doing it especially for her. Father, you ought to go out there and meet the family; then you'd understand. They're not ordinary people. Their father was a college professor and wrote things. They're cultured people."

"Well, I want to meet them. Why don't we go out there and call to-day? I think they must be worth knowing."

So late that afternoon the father and son rode out to Glenside, and when Shirley and George reached home they found the car standing in front of their place, and the Grahams comfortably seated in the great open doorway, enjoying the late afternoon breeze, and seemingly perfectly at home in their own barn.

"I'm not going to swarm here every day, Miss Shirley," said the son, rising and coming out to meet her. "You see father hadn't heard about the transformation of the old barn, and the minute I told him about it he had to come right out and see it."

"Yes," said the father, smiling contentedly, "I had to come and see what you'd done out here. I've played in the hay up in that loft many a day in my time, and I love the old barn. It's great to see it all fixed up so cozy. But we're going home now and let you have your dinner. We just waited to say 'Howdy' to you before we left."

They stayed a few minutes longer, however, and the senior Graham talked with Shirley while he held Doris on his knee and stroked her silky hair, and she nestled in his arms quite content.

Then, although young Graham was quite loath to leave so soon, they went, for he could not in conscience, expect an invitation to dinner two days in succession.

They rode away into the sunset, going across country to their home without going back to town, and Doris, as she stood with the others watching them away, murmured softly:

"Nice favver-man! Nice Gwaham favver man!"

The "nice-Graham-father-man" was at that moment remarking to his son in very decided tones, as he turned to get a last glimpse of the old barn:

"That old barn door ought to come down right away, Sid, and a nice big old-fashioned door with glass around the sides made to fill the space. That door is an eyesore on the place, and they need a piazza. People like those can't live with a great door like that to open and shut every day."

"Yes, father, I've thought of that, but I don't just know how to manage it. You see they're not objects of charity. I've been thinking about some way to fix up a heating arrangement without hurting their feelings, so they could stay there all winter. I know they hate to go back to the city, and they're only paying ten dollars a month. It's all they can afford. What could they get in the city for that?"

"Great Scott! A girl like that living in a house she could get for ten dollars, when some of these feather-brained baby-dolls we know can't get on with less than three or four houses that cost from fifty to a hundred thousand dollars apiece! Say, son, that's a peach of a girl, do you know it? A peach of a girl! I've been talking with her, and she has a very superior mind."

"I know she has, father," answered the son humbly.

"I say, Sid, why don't you marry her? That would solve the whole problem. Then you could fix up the old barn into a regular house for her folks."

"Well, father, that's just what I've made up my mind to do—if she'll have me," said the son with a gleam of triumph in his eyes.

"Bully for you, Sid! Bully for you!" and the father gave his son's broad shoulder a resounding slap. "Why, Sid, I didn't think you had that much sense. Your mother gave me to understand that you were philandering around with that dolly-faced Harriet Hale, and I couldn't see what you saw in her. But if you mean it, son, I'm with you every time. That girl's a peach, and you couldn't get a finer if you searched the world over."

"Yes, I'm afraid mother's got her heart set on Harriet Hale," said the son dubiously, "but I can't see it that way."

"H'm! Your mother likes show," sighed the father comically, "but she's got a good heart, and she'll bowl over all right and make the best of it. You know neither your mother nor I were such high and mighties when we were young, and *we* married for *love*. But now, if you really mean business, I don't see why we can't do something right away. When does that girl have her vacation? Of course she gets one sometime. Why couldn't your mother just invite the whole family to occupy the shore cottage for a little while,—get up some excuse or other,—ask 'em to take care of it? You know it's lying idle all this summer, and two servants down there growing fat with nothing to do. We might ship Elizabeth down there and let 'em be company for her. They seem like a fine set of children. It would do Elizabeth good to know them."

"Oh, she's crazy about them. She's been out a number of times with me, and don't you remember she had Carol out to stay with her?"

"Was that the black-eyed, sensible girl? Well, I declare! I didn't recognize her. She was all dolled up out at our house. I suppose Elizabeth loaned 'em to her, eh? Well, I'm glad. She's got sense, too. That's the kind of people I like my children to know. Now if that vacation could only be arranged to come when your mother and I take that Western trip, why, it would be just the thing for Elizabeth, work right all around. Now, the thing for you to do is to find out about that vacation, and begin to work things. Then you could have everything all planned, and rush the work so it would be done by the time they came back."

So the two conspirators plotted, while all unconscious of their interest Shirley was trying to get herself in hand and not think how Graham's eyes had looked when he said good-night to her.

CHAPTER XIX

Since the pastor from the village had called upon them, the young people of the stone barn had been identified with the little white church in the valley. Shirley had taken a class of boys in the Sunday-school and was playing the organ, as George had once predicted. Carol was helping the primary teacher, George was assistant librarian and secretary, Harley was in Shirley's class, and Doris was one of the primaries.

Shirley had at once identified herself with the struggling little Christian Endeavor society and was putting new life into it, with her enthusiasm, her new ideas about getting hold of the young people of the community, and her wonderful knack of getting the silent ones to take part in the meetings. She had suggested new committees, had invited the music committee to meet her at her home some evening to plan out special music, and to coöperate with the social committee in planning for music at the socials. She always carried a few appropriate clippings or neatly written verses or other quotations to meeting to slip into the hands of some who had not prepared to speak, and she saw to it that her brothers and sisters were always ready to say something. Withal, she did her part so unobtrusively that none of the old members could think she was trying to usurp power or make herself prominent. She became a quiet power behind the powers, to whom the president and all the other officers came for advice, and who seemed always ready to help in any work, or to find a way out of any difficulty. Christian Endeavor in the little white church at once took great strides after the advent of the Hollisters, and even the idlers on the street corners were moved with curiosity to drop into the twilight service of the young people and see what went on, and why everybody seemed so interested. But the secret of it all, Shirley thought, was the little five-minute prayer service that the prayer-meeting committee held in the tiny primary room just before the regular meeting. Shirley as chairman of the prayer-meeting committee had started this little meeting, and she always came into the larger room with an exalted look upon her face and a feeling of strength in her heart from this brief speaking with her Master.

Shirley was somewhat aghast the next Sabbath to have Sidney Graham arrive and ask her to take a ride with him.

"Why, I was just going to church," she said, half hesitating, and then smiling bravely up at him; "besides, I have a Sunday-school class. I couldn't very well leave them, you know."

He looked at her for a moment thoughtfully, trying to bridge in his thoughts this difference between them. Then he said quite humbly,

"Will you take me with you?"

"To church?" she asked, and there was a glad ring in her voice. Would he really go to church with her?

"Yes, and to Sunday School if I may. I haven't been to Sunday School in years. I'd like to go if you'll only let me."

Her cheeks grew rosy. She had a quick mental picture of putting him in Deacon Pettigrew's Bible class.

"I'm afraid there isn't any class you would enjoy," she began with a troubled look. "It's only a little country church, you know. They don't have all the modern system, and very few teachers."

"I should enjoy going into your class very much if I might."

"Oh, mine are just boys, just little boys like Harley!" said Shirley, aghast.

"I've been a little boy once, you know I should enjoy it very much," said the applicant with satisfaction.

"Oh, but—I couldn't teach *you*!" There was dismay in her voice.

"Couldn't you, though? You've taught me more in the few months I've known you than I've learned in that many years from others. Try me. I'll be very good. I'll be a boy with the rest of them, and you can just forget I'm there and go ahead. I really am serious about it. I want to hear what you have to say to them."

"Oh, I couldn't teach with you there!" exclaimed Shirley, putting her hands on her hot cheeks and looking like a frightened little child. "Indeed I couldn't, really. I'm not much of a teacher. I'm only a beginner. I shouldn't know how to talk before any but children."

He watched her silently for a minute, his face grave with wistfulness.

"Why do you teach them?" he asked rather irrelevantly.

"Because—why, because I want to help them to live right lives; I want to teach them how to know God."

"Why?"

"So that they will be saved. Because it was Christ's command that His disciples should give the message. I am His disciple, so I have to tell the message."

"Was there any special stipulation as to whom that message should be given?" asked the young man thoughtfully. "Did He say you were just to give it to those boys?"

"Why, no; it was to be given to—all the world, every creature." Shirley spoke the words hesitatingly, a dimple beginning to show in her cheek as her eyelids drooped over her shy eyes.

"And don't I come in on that?" asked Graham, with a twinkle that reminded Shirley of his father.

Shirley had to laugh shamefacedly then.

"But I couldn't!" said Shirley. "I'd be so scared I couldn't think of a thing to say."

"You're not afraid of me, Miss Shirley? You wouldn't be scared if you thought I really needed to know the message, would you? Well, I really do, as much as any of those kids."

Shirley looked steadily into his earnest eyes and saw something there that steadied her nerve. The laughter died out of her own eyes, and a beautiful light of longing came into them.

"All right," she said, with a little lift of her chin as if girding up her strength to the task. "You may come, and I'll do the best I can, but I'm afraid it will be a poor best. I've only a little story to tell them this morning."

"Please give them just what you had intended. I want the real thing, just as a boy would get it from you. Will the rest of them come in the car with us?"

Shirley was very quiet during the ride to church. She let the rest do all the talking, and she sat looking off at the woods and praying for help, trying to calm the flutter of her frightened heart, trying to steady her nerves and brace herself to teach the lesson just as she had intended to teach it.

She watched him furtively during the opening exercises, the untrained singing, the monotonous prayer of an old farmer-elder, the dry platitudes of the illiterate superintendent; but he sat respectfully listening, taking it all for what it was worth, the best service these people knew how to render to their Maker.

Somehow her heart had gained the strength she needed from the prayers she breathed continually, and when the time for teaching the lesson arrived she came to her class with quietness.

There was a little awe upon the boys because of the stranger in their midst. They did not fling the hymn-books down with a noisy thud, nor send the lesson leaves flying like winged darts across the room quite so much as they were wont to do. They looked askance at Harley, who sat proudly by the visitor, supplying him with Bibles, hymn-books, lesson leaves, and finding the place for him officiously. But Graham sat among the boys without ostentation, and made as little of his own presence as possible. He smiled at them now and then, put a handful of silver into the collection envelope when they would have passed him by, and promised a ride to one fellow who ventured to ask him hoarsely if that was his car outside the church.

Shirley had made up her mind to forget as far as she could the presence of the visitor in the class, and to this end she fixed her eyes upon the worst little boy present, the boy who got up all the disturbances, and made all the noises, and was the most adorable, homely, sturdy young imp the Valley Church could produce. He sat straight across from her, while Graham was at the side, and she could see in Jack's eye that he meant mischief if he could overcome his awe of the stranger. So before Jack could possibly get started she began her story, and told it straight to Jack, never taking her eyes from his face from start to finish, and before she was half-way through she had her little audience enthralled. It was a story of the Bible told in modern setting, and told straight to the heart of a boy who was the counterpart in his own soul of the man whom Christ cured and forgave. What Graham was thinking or looking Shirley did not know. She had literally forgotten his existence after the first few minutes. She had seen the gleam of interest in the eyes of the boy Jack; she knew that her message was going home to a convicted young soul, and that he saw himself and his own childish sins in the sinful life of the hero of her tale. Her whole soul was bent on making him see the Saviour who could make that young life over. Not until the story was almost finished did any one of the listeners, unless perhaps Harley, who was used to such story-recitals, have a suspicion that the story was just a plain, ordinary chapter out of the Bible. Then suddenly one of the elder boys broke forth: "Aw! Gee! That's just the man in the Bible let down through the roof!" There was a slight stir in the class at the discovery as it dawned upon them that the teacher had "put one over on them" again, but the interest for the most part was sustained breathlessly until the superintendent's bell rang, and the heads drew together in an absorbed group around her for the last few sentences, spoken in a lower tone because the general hum of teaching in the room had ceased.

Graham's face was very grave and thoughtful as she finished and slipped away from them to take her place at the little organ. One could see that it was not in the teacher alone, but in her message as well, that he was interested. The boys all had that subdued, half-ashamed, half-defiant look that boys have when they have been caught looking serious. Each boy frowned and studied his toes, or hunted assiduously in his hymn-book to hide his confusion, and the class in various keys lifted up assertive young voices vigorously in the last hymn.

Graham sat beside Shirley in the little crowded church during the rather monotonous service. The regular pastor, who was a good, spiritual man if not a brilliant one, and gave his congregation solid, practical sermons, was on his vacation, and the pulpit was supplied by a young theologue who was so new to his work that his sermon was a rather involved effort. But so strong was the power of the Sunday-school lesson to which he had just listened that Graham felt as if he were sitting in some hallowed atmosphere. He did not see the red-faced, embarrassed young preacher, nor notice his struggles to bring forth his message bravely; he saw only the earnest-faced young teacher as she spoke the words of life to her boys; saw the young imp-faces of her boys softened and touched by the story she told; saw that she really believed and felt every word she spoke; and knew that there was something in it all that he wanted.

The seat was crowded and the day was warm, but the two who looked over the same hymn-book did not notice it. The soft air came in from the open window beside them, breathing sweet clover and wild honeysuckle, and the meadowlarks sang their songs, and made it seem just like a little bit of heaven.

Shirley's muslin frills trembled against Graham's hand as she reached to catch a fluttering leaf of the hymn-book that the wind had caught; once her hand brushed the coatsleeve beside her as they turned the page, and she felt the soft texture of the fine dark blue goods with a pleasant sense of the beautiful and fitting. It thrilled her to think he was standing thus beside her in her own little church, yielding himself to the same worship with her in the little common country congregation. It was wonderful, beautiful! And to have come to her! She glanced shyly up at him, so handsome, standing there singing, his hand almost touching hers holding the book. He felt her glance and answered it with a look and smile, their eyes holding each other for just the fraction of a second in which some inner thought was interchanged, some question asked and answered by the invisible flash of heart-beats, a mutual joining in the spiritual service, and then half-frightened Shirley dropped her eyes to the page and the soft roses stole into her cheeks again. She felt as if she had seen something in his eyes and acknowledged it in her own, as if she had inadvertently shown him her heart in that glance, and that heart of hers was leaping and bounding with an uncontrollable joy, while her conscience sought by every effort to get it in control. What nonsense, it said, what utter folly, to make so much of his coming to church with her once! To allow her soul to get into such a flutter over a man who had no more idea of noticing her or caring for her than he had for a bird on the tree.

And with all the tumult in her heart she did not even see the envious glances of the village maidens who stared and stared with all their might at the handsome man who came to church in an expensive car and brought the girl who lived in a barn! Shirley's social position went up several notches, and she never even knew it. In fact, she was becoming a great puzzle to the residents of Glenside.

It was good to know that for once the shabby collection-box of the little church was borne back to the altar laden with a goodly bill, put in with so little ostentation that one might have judged it but a penny, looking on, though even a penny would have made more noise in the unlined wooden box.

After the service was over Graham went out with the children, while Shirley lingered to play over an accompaniment for a girl who was going to sing at the vesper service that afternoon. He piled all the children in the back seat of the car, put the boy he had promised a ride in the seat beside him, took a spin around the streets, and was back in front of the church by the time Shirley came out. Then that foolish heart of hers had to leap again at the thought that he had saved the front seat for her. The boy descended as if he had been caught up into heaven for a brief space, and would never forget it the rest of his life.

There was that same steady look of trust and understanding in Graham's eyes whenever he looked at her on the way home, and once while the children were talking together in the back seat he leaned toward her and said in a low tone:

"I wonder if you will let me take you away for a little while this afternoon to a quiet place I know where there is a beautiful view, and let us sit and talk. There are some things I want to ask you, about what you said this morning. I was very much interested in it all, and I'm deeply grateful that you let me go. Now, will you go with me? I'll bring you back in time for the Christian Endeavor service, and you see in the meantime I'm inviting myself to dinner. Do you think your mother will object?"

What was there for Shirley to do but accept this alluring invitation? She did not believe in going off on pleasure excursions on the Sabbath, but this request that she ride to a quiet place out-of-doors for a religious talk could not offend her strongest sense of what was right on the Sabbath day. And surely, if the Lord had a message for her to bear, she must bear it to whomsoever He sent. This, then, was this man's interest in her, that she had been able to make him think of God. A glad elation filled her heart, something deep and true stirred within her and lifted her above the thought of self, like a blessing from on high. To be asked to bring light to a soul like this one, this was honor indeed. This was an answer to her prayer of the morning, that she might fulfil God's pleasure with the lesson of the day. The message then had reached his soul. It was enough. She would think no more of self.

Yet whenever she looked at him and met that smile again she was thrilled with joy in spite of herself. At least there was a friendliness here beyond the common acquaintance, a something that was true, deep, lasting, even though worlds should separate them in the future; a something built on a deep understanding, sympathy and common interests. Well, so be it. She would rejoice that it had been given her to know one man of the world in this beautiful way; and her foolish little human heart should understand what a high, true thing this was that must not be misunderstood.

So she reasoned with herself, and watched him during the dinner, among the children, out in the yard among the flowers and animals, everywhere, he seemed so fine and splendid, so far above all other men that she had ever met. And her mother, watching, trembled for her when she saw her happy face.

"Do you think you ought to go with him, daughter?" she asked with troubled eyes, when they were left alone for a moment after dinner. "You know it is the Sabbath, and you know his life is very different from ours."

"Mother, he wants to talk about the Sunday School lesson this morning," said Shirley shyly. "I guess he is troubled, perhaps, and wants me to help him. I guess he has never thought much about religious things."

"Well, daughter dear, be careful. Do all you can for him, of course, but remember, don't let your heart stray out of your keeping. He is very attractive, dear, and very unconventional for a wealthy man. I think he is true and wouldn't mean to trifle, but he wouldn't realize."

"I know; mother; don't you be afraid for me!" said Shirley with a lofty look, half of exultation, half of proud self-command.

He took her to a mossy place beside a little stream, where the light filtered down through the lacy leaves flecking the bank, and braided golden currents in the water; with green and purple hazy hills in the distance, and just enough seclusion for a talk without being too far away from the world.

"My little sister says that you people have a 'real' God," he said, when she was comfortably fixed with cushions from the car at her back against a tall tree-trunk. "She says you seem to realize His presence—I don't know just how to say it, but I'd like to know if this is so. I'd like to know what makes you different from other girls, and your home different from most of the homes I know. I'd like to know if I may have it too."

That was the beginning.

Shirley, shy as a bird at first, having never spoken on such subjects except to children, yet being well versed in the Scriptures, and feeling her faith with every atom of her being, drew out her little Bible that she had slipped into her pocket when they started, and plunged into the great subject.

Never had preacher more earnest listener, or more lovely temple in which to preach. And if sometimes the young man's thoughts for a few moments strayed from the subject to rest his eyes in tenderness upon the lovely face of the young teacher, and long to draw her into his arms and claim her for his own, he might well have been forgiven. For Shirley was very fair, with the light of other worlds in her face, her eyes all sparkling with her eagerness, her lips aglow with words that seemed to be given her for the occasion. She taught him simply, not trying to go into deep arguments, but urging the only way she knew, the way of taking Christ's promise on its face value, the way of being willing to do His will, trusting it to Him to reveal Himself, and the truth of the doctrine, and make the believer sure.

They talked until the sun sunk low, and the calling of the wood-birds warned them that the Endeavor hour was near. Before they left the place he asked her for the little Bible, and she laid it in his hand with joy that he wanted it, that she was chosen to give him a gift so precious.

"It is all marked up," she said apologetically. "I always mark the verses I love, or have had some special experience with."

"It will be that much more precious to me," he said gently, fingering the leaves reverently, and then he looked up and gave her one of those deep looks that seemed to say so much to her heart. And all at once she realized that she was on earth once more, and that his presence and his look were very precious to her. Her cheeks grew pink with the joy of it, and she looked down in confusion and could not answer, so she rose to her feet. But he, springing at once to help her up, kept her hand for just an instant with earnest pressure, and said in deeply moved tones:

"You don't know what you have done for me this afternoon, my—*friend*!" He waited with her hand in his an instant as if he were going to say more, but had decided it were better not. The silence was so compelling that she looked up into his eyes, meeting his smile, and that said so many things her heart went into a tumult again and could not quite come to itself all through the Christian Endeavor service.

On the way home from the church he talked a little about her vacation: when it came, how long it lasted, what she would do with it. Just as they reached home he said,

"I hope you will pray for me, *my friend*!"

There was something wonderful in the way he said that word "friend." It thrilled her through and through as she stood beside the road and watched him speed away into the evening.

"My friend! I hope you will pray for me, *my friend*!" It sang a glory-song down in her heart as she turned to go in with the vivid glory of the sunset on her face.

CHAPTER XX

The cement floor had been down a week and was as hard as a rock, when one day two or three wagon-loads of things arrived with a note from Graham to Mrs. Hollister to say that he would be glad if these might be stored in one corner of the basement floor, where they would be out of her way and not take up too much room.

Harley and George went down to look them over that evening.

"He said something about some things being taken from the office building," said Harley, kicking a pile of iron pipes with his toe.

"These don't look like any old things that have been used," said George thoughtfully. "They look perfectly new." Then he studied them a few minutes more from another angle, and shut his lips judiciously. He belonged to the boy species that has learned to "shut up and saw wood," whatever that expression may mean. If anything was to come out of that pile of iron in the future, he did not mean to break confidence with anybody's secrets. He walked away whistling and said nothing further about them.

The next day Mrs. Graham came down upon the Hollisters in her limousine, and an exquisite toilet of organdie and ribbons. She was attended by Elizabeth, wild with delight over getting home again. She begged Mrs. Hollister very charmingly and sincerely to take care of Elizabeth for three or four weeks, while she and her husband were away, and to take her entire family down to the shore and occupy their cottage, which had been closed all summer and needed opening and airing. She said that nothing would please Elizabeth so much as to have them all her guests during September. The maids were there, with nothing to do but look after them, and would just love to serve them; it really would be a great favor to her if she could know that Elizabeth was getting a little salt air under such favorable conditions. She was so genuine in her request and suggested so earnestly that Shirley and George needed the change during their vacation, and could just as well come down every night and go up every morning for a week or two more after the vacations were over, that Mrs. Hollister actually promised to consider it and talk it over with Shirley when she came home. Elizabeth and Carol nearly went into spasms of joy over the thought of all they could do down at the shore together.

When Shirley came home she found the whole family quite upset discussing the matter. Carol had brought out all the family wardrobe and was showing how she could wash this, and dye that, and turn this skirt upside down, and put a piece from the old waist in there to make the lower part flare; and Harley was telling how he could get the man next door to look after the hens and pigeons, and there was nothing needing much attention in the garden now, for the corn was about over except the last picking, which wasn't ripe yet.

Mrs. Hollister was saying that they ought really to stay at home and look up another place to live during the winter, and Carol was pleading that another place would be easier found when the weather was cooler anyway, and that Shirley was just awfully tired and needed a change.

Shirley's cheeks grew pink in spite of the headache which she had been fighting all day, when she heard of the invitation, and sat down to think it out. Was this, then, another of the kind schemes of her kind friend to make the way easier for her? What right had she to take all this? Why was he doing it? Why were the rest of the family? Did they really need some one to take care of Elizabeth? But of course it was a wonderful opportunity, and one that her mother at least should not let slip by. And Doris! Think of Doris playing in the sand at the seaside!

Supper was flung onto the table that night any way it happened, for they were all too excited to know what they were about. Carol got butter twice and forgot to cut the bread, and Harley poured milk into the already filled water-pitcher. They were even too excited to eat.

Graham arrived with Elizabeth early in the evening to add his pleading to his mother's, and before he left he had about succeeded in getting Mrs. Hollister's promise that she would go.

Shirley's vacation began the first of September, and George had asked for his at the same time so that they could enjoy it together. Each had two weeks. Graham said that the cost of going back and forth to the city for the two would be very little. By the next morning they had begun to say what they would take along, and to plan what they would do with the dog. It was very exciting. There was only a week to get ready, and Carol wanted to make bathing-suits for everybody.

Graham came again that night with more suggestions. There were plenty of bathing-suits down at the cottage, of all sizes and kinds. No need to make bathing-suits. The dog, of course, was to go along. He needed the change as much as anybody, and they needed him there. That breed of dog was a great swimmer. He would take care of the children when they went in bathing. How would Mrs. Hollister like to have one of the old Graham servants come over to sleep at the barn and look after things while they were gone? The man had really nothing to do at home while everybody was away, as the whole corps of servants would be there, and this one would enjoy coming out to the country. He had a brother living on a place about a mile away. As for the trip down there, Graham would love to take them all in the big touring-car with Elizabeth. He had been intending to take her down that way, and there was no reason in the world why they should not all go along. They would start Saturday afternoon as soon as Shirley and George were free, and be down before bedtime. It would be cool and delightful journeying at that hour, and a great deal pleasanter than the train.

So one by one the obstructions and hindrances were removed from their path, and it was decided that the Hollisters were to go to the seashore.

At last the day came.

Shirley and George went off in the morning shouting last directions about things. They were always having to go to their work whatever was happening. It was sometimes hard on them, particularly this day when everything was so delightfully exciting.

The old Graham servant arrived about three o'clock in the afternoon, and proved himself invaluable in doing the little last things without being told. Mrs. Hollister had her first gleam of an idea of what it must be to have plenty of perfectly trained servants about to anticipate one's needs. He entered the barn as if barns were his native heath, and moved about with the ease and unobtrusiveness that marks a perfect servant, but with none of the hauteur and disdain that many of those individuals entertain toward all whom they consider poor or beneath them in any way. He had a kindly face, and seemed to understand just exactly what was to be done. Things somehow moved more smoothly after he arrived.

At four o'clock came Graham with the car and a load of long linen dust-cloaks and veils. The Hollisters donned them and bestowed themselves where they were told. The servant stowed away the wraps and suitcases; Star mounted the seat beside Harley, and they were ready.

They turned to look back at the barn as the car started. The old servant was having a little trouble with the big door, trying to shut it. "That door is a nuisance," said Graham as they swept away from the curb. "It must be fixed. It is no fit door for a barn anyway." Then they curved up around Allister Avenue and left the barn far out of sight.

They were going across country to the Graham home to pick up Elizabeth. It was a wonderful experience for them, that beautiful ride in the late afternoon; and when they swept into the great gates, and up the broad drive to the Graham mansion, and stopped under the porte-cochère, Mrs. Hollister was quite overcome with the idea of being beholden to people who lived in such grandeur as this. To think she had actually invited their son to dine in a barn with her!

Elizabeth came rushing out eagerly, all ready to start, and climbed in beside Carol. Even George, who was usually silent when she was about, gave her a grin of welcome. The father and mother came out to say good-by, gave them good wishes, and declared they were perfectly happy to leave their daughter in such good hands. Then the car curved about the great house, among tennis courts, green-houses, garage, stable, and what not, and back to the pike again, leaping out upon the perfect road as if it were as excited as the children.

Two more stops to pick up George, who was getting off early, and Shirley, who was through at five o'clock, and then they threaded their way out of the city, across the ferry, through another city, and out into the open country, dotted all along the way with clean, pretty little towns.

They reached a lovely grove at sundown and stopped by the way to have supper. Graham got down and made George help him get out the big hamper.

There was a most delectable lunch; sandwiches of delicate and unknown condiments, salad as bewildering, soup that had been kept hot in a thermos bottle, served in tiny white cups, iced tea and ice-cream meringues from another thermos compartment, and plenty of delicious little cakes, olives, nuts, bonbons, and fruit. It seemed a wonderful supper to them all, eaten out there under the trees, with the birds beginning their vesper songs and the stars peeping out slyly. Then they packed up their dishes and hurried on their beautiful way, a silver thread of a moon coming out to make the scene more lovely.

Doris was almost asleep when at last they began to hear the booming of the sea and smell the salt breeze as it swept back inland; but she roused up and opened wide, mysterious eyes, peering into the new darkness, and murmuring softly: "I yant to see ze osun! I yant to see the gate bid watter!"

Stiff, bewildered, filled with ecstasy, they finally unloaded in front of a big white building that looked like a hotel. They tried to see into the deep, mysterious darkness across the road, where boomed a great voice that called them, and where dashing spray loomed high like a waving phantom hand to beckon them now and again, and far-moving lights told of ships and a world beyond the one they knew,—a wide, limitless thing like eternity, universe, chaos.

With half-reluctant feet they turned away from the mysterious unseen lure and let themselves be led across an unbelievably wide veranda into the bright light of a hall, where everything was clean and shining, and a great fireplace filled with friendly flames gave cheer and welcome. The children stood bewildered in the brightness while two strange serving-maids unfastened their wraps and dust-cloaks and helped them take off their hats. Then they all sat around the fire, for Graham had come in by this time, and the maids brought trays of some delicious drink with little cakes and crackers, and tinkling ice, and straws to drink with. Doris almost fell asleep again, and was carried up-stairs by Shirley and put to bed in a pretty white crib she was too sleepy to look at, while Carol, Elizabeth, George, and Harley went with Graham across the road to look at the black, yawning cavern they called ocean, and to have the shore light-houses pointed out to them and named one by one.

They were all asleep at last, a little before midnight, in spite of the excitement over the spacious rooms, and who should have which. Think of it! Thirty rooms in the house, and every one as pretty as every other one! What luxury! And nobody to occupy them but themselves! Carol could hardly get to sleep. She felt as if she had dropped into a novel and was living it.

When Graham came out of his room the next morning the salt breeze swept invitingly through the hall and showed him the big front door of the upper piazza open and some one standing in the sunlight, with light, glowing garments, gazing at the sea in rapt enjoyment. Coming out softly, he saw that it was Shirley dressed in white, with a ribbon of blue at her waist and a soft pink color in her cheeks, looking off to sea.

He stood for a moment to enjoy the picture, and said in his heart that sometime, if he got his wish, he would have her painted so by some great artist, with just that little simple white dress and blue ribbon, her round white arm lifted, her small hand shading her eyes, the sunlight burnishing her brown hair into gold. He could scarcely refrain from going to her and telling her how beautiful she was. But when he stepped quietly up beside her only his eyes spoke, and brought the color deeper into her cheeks; and so they stood for some minutes, looking together and drawing in the wonder of God's sea.

"This is the first time I've ever seen it, you know," spoke Shirley at last, "and I'm so glad it was on Sunday morning. It will always make the day seem more holy and the sea more wonderful to think about. I like best things to happen on Sunday, don't you, because that is the best day of all?"

Graham looked at the sparkling sea all azure and pearls, realized the Sabbath quiet, and marvelled at the beauty of the soul of the girl, even as her feeling about it all seemed to enter into and become a part of himself.

"Yes, I do," said he. "I never did before, but I do now,—and always shall," he added under his breath.

That was almost as wonderful a Sabbath as the one they had spent in the woods a couple of weeks before. They walked and talked by the sea, and they went to a little Episcopal chapel, where the windows stood open for the chanting of the waves and the salt of the breeze to come in freely, and then they went out and walked by the sea again. Wherever they went, whether resting in some of the many big rockers on the broad verandas or walking on the hard smooth sand, or sitting in some cozy nook by the waves, they felt the same deep sympathy, the same conviction that their thoughts were one, the same wonderful thrill of the day and each other's nearness.

Somehow in the new environment Shirley forgot for a little that this young man was not of her world, that he was probably going back soon to the city to enter into a whirl of the winter's season in society, that other girls would claim his smiles and attentions, and she would likely be forgotten. She lost the sense of it entirely and companioned with him as joyously as if there had never been anything to separate them. Her mother, looking on, sighed, feared, smiled, and sighed again.

They walked together in the sweet darkness beside the waves that evening, and he told her how when he was a little boy he wanted to climb up to the stars and find God, but later how he thought the stars and God were myths like Santa Claus, and that the stars were only electric lights put up by men and lighted from a great switch every night, and when they didn't shine somebody had forgotten to light them. He told her many things about himself that he had never told to any one before, and she opened her shy heart to him, too.

Then they planned what they would do next week when he came back. He told her he must go back to the city in the morning to see his father and mother off and attend to a few matters of business at the office. It might be two or three days before he could return, but after that he was coming down to take a little vacation himself if she didn't mind, and they would do a lot of delightful things together: row, fish, go crabbing, and he would teach her to swim and show her all the walks and favorite places where he used to go as a boy. Reluctantly they went in, his fingers lingering about hers for just a second at the door, vibrating those mysterious heart-strings of hers again, sweeping dearest music from them, and frightening her with joy that took her half the night to put down.

CHAPTER XXI

Sidney Graham went back to the city the next morning. They all stood out on the piazza to watch the big car glide away. Doris stood on the railing of the piazza with Shirley's arm securely about her and waved a little fat hand; then with a pucker of her lip she demanded:

"Fy does mine Mister Dwaham do way? I don't yant him to do way. I yant him to stay wif me aw-ways, don't oo, Sirley?"

Shirley with glowing cheeks turned from watching the retreating car and put her little sister down on the floor suddenly.

"Run get your hat, Doris, and we'll take a walk on the sand!" she said, smiling alluringly at the child, till the baby forgot her grievance and beamed out with answering smiles.

That was a wonderful day.

They all took a walk on the sand first, George pushing his mother in a big wheeled chair belonging to the cottage. Elizabeth was guide and pointed out all the beauties of the place, telling eager bits of reminiscence from her childhood memories to which even George listened attentively. From having been only tolerant of her George had now come to look upon Elizabeth as "a good scout."

When Mrs. Hollister grew tired they took her back to the cottage and established her in a big chair with a book. Then they all rushed off to the bath-houses and presently emerged in bathing-suits, Doris looking like a little sprite in her scarlet flannel scrap of a suit, her bright hair streaming, and her beautiful baby arms and legs flashing white like a cherub's in the sunlight.

They came back from their dip in the waves, hungry and eager, to the wonderful dinner that was served so exquisitely in the great cool dining-room, from the windows of which they could watch the lazy ships sailing in the offing.

Doris fell asleep over her dessert and was tumbled into the hammock to finish her nap. Carol and Elizabeth and the boys started off crabbing, and Shirley settled herself in another hammock with a pile of new magazines about her and prepared to enjoy a whole afternoon of laziness. It was so wonderful to lie still, at leisure and unhurried, with all those lovely magazines to read, and nothing to disturb her. She leaned her head back and closed her eyes for a minute just to listen to the sea, and realize how good it was to be here. Back in her mind there was a pleasant consciousness of the beautiful yesterday, and the beautiful to-morrows that might come when Sidney Graham returned, but she would not let her heart dwell upon them; that would be humoring herself too much, and perhaps give her a false idea of things. She simply would not let this wonderful holiday be spoiled by the thought that it would have to end some day and that she would be back at the old routine of care and worry once more.

She was roused from her reverie by the step of the postman bringing a single letter, for her!

It was addressed in an unknown hand and was in a fat long envelope. Wonderingly she opened it and found inside a bank book and blank check book with a little note on which was written:

Dear Little Girl:

This is just a trifle of that present we were talking about the other day that belongs to you. It isn't all by any means, but we'll see to the rest later. Spend this on chocolates or chewing-gum or frills or whatever you like and have a good time down at the shore. You're a bully little girl and deserve everything nice that's going. Don't be too serious, Miss Shirley. Play a little more.

Your   elderly   friend,
Walter K Graham.

In the bank book was an entry of five thousand dollars, on check account. Shirley held her breath and stared at the figures with wide eyes, then slipped away and locked herself in the big white room that was hers. Kneeling down by the bed she cried and prayed and smiled all in one, and thanked the Lord for making people so kind to her. After that she went to find her mother.

Mrs. Hollister was sitting on the wide upper piazza in a steamer chair looking off to sea and drawing in new life at every breath. Her book was open on her lap, but she had forgotten to read in the joy of all that was about her. To tell the truth she was wondering if the dear father who was gone from them knew of their happy estate, and thinking how glad he would be for them if he did.

She read the letter twice before she looked at the bank book with its astonishing figures, and heard again Shirley's tale of the happening in the office the morning of the arrest. Then she read the letter once more.

"I'm not just sure, daughter," she said at last with a smile, "what we ought to do about this. Are you?"

"No," said Shirley, smiling; "I suppose I'll give it back, but wasn't it wonderful of him to do it? Isn't it grand that there are such men in the world?"

"It certainly is, dear, and I'm glad my little girl was able to do something that was of assistance to him; and that she has won her way into his good graces so simply and sweetly. But I'm not so sure what you ought to do. Hadn't we better pray about it a bit before you decide? How soon ought you to write to him? It's too late to reach him before he leaves for California, isn't it?"

"Oh, yes, he's just about starting now," said the girl. "Don't you suppose he planned it so that I couldn't answer right away? I don't know his address. I can't do a thing till I find out where to write. I wouldn't like to send it to the office because they would probably think it was business and his secretary might open it."

"Of course. Then we'll just pray about it, shall we, dear? I'm not just sure in my mind whether it's a well-meant bit of charity that we ought to hand back with sincere thanks, or whether it's God's way of rewarding my little girl for her faithfulness and quickness of action. Our Father knows we have been—and still are—in a hard place. He knows that we have need of 'all these things' that money has to buy. You really did a good thing and saved Mr. Graham from great loss, you know, and perhaps he is the kind of man who would feel a great deal happier if he shared a little of it with you, was able to make some return for what you did for him. However, five thousand dollars is a great deal of money for a brief service. What do you think, dear?"

"I don't know, mother dear. I'm all muddled just as you say, but I guess it will come right if we pray about it. Anyhow, I'm going to be happy over his thinking of me, whether I keep it or not."

Shirley went thoughtfully back to her hammock and her magazines, a smile on her lips, a dream in her eyes. She found herself wondering whether Sidney Graham knew about this money and what he would wish her to do about it. Then suddenly she cast the whole question from her and plunged into her magazine, wondering why it was that almost any question that came into her mind promptly got around and entangled itself with Mr. Sidney Graham. What did he have to do with it, anyway?

The magazine story was very interesting and Shirley soon forgot everything else in the pleasure of surrendering herself to the printed page. An hour went by, another passed, and Shirley was still oblivious to all about her. Suddenly she became aware of a boy on a bicycle, riding almost up to the very steps, and whistling vigorously.

"Miss Shirley Hollister here?" he demanded as he alighted on one foot on the lower step, the other foot poised for flight as soon as his errand should have been performed.

"Why, yes," said Shirley, startled, struggling to her feet and letting a shower of magazines fall all about her.

"Long distance wants yer," he announced, looking her over apathetically. "Mr. Barnard, of Philadelphia, wants to talk to yer!" and with the final word chanted nasally he alighted upon his obedient steed and spun away down the walk again.

"But, wait! Where shall I go? Where is the telephone?"

"Pay station!" shouted the impervious child, turning his head over his shoulder, "Drug store! Two blocks from the post office!"

Without waiting to go upstairs Shirley, whose training had been to answer the telephone at once, caught up Elizabeth's parasol that lay on a settee by the door, rumpled her fingers through her hair by way of toilet and hurried down the steps in the direction the boy had disappeared, wondering what in the world Mr. Barnard could want of her? Was he going to call her back from her vacation? Was this perhaps the only day she would have, this and yesterday? There would always be yesterday! With a sigh she looked wistfully at the sea. If she had only known a summons was to come so soon she would not have wasted a second on magazines. She would have sat and gazed all the afternoon at the sea. If Mr. Barnard wanted her, of course she would have to go. Business was business and she couldn't afford to lose her job even with that fairy dream of five thousand to her credit in the bank. She knew, of course, she meant to give that back. It was hers for the day, but it could not become tangible. It was beautiful, but it was right that it must go back, and if her employer felt he must cut short her vacation why of course she must acquiesce and just be glad she had had this much. Perhaps it was just as well, anyway, for if Sidney Graham came down and spent a few days there was no knowing what foolish notions her heart would take, jumping and careening the way it had been doing lately when he just looked at her. Yes, she would go back if Mr. Barnard wanted her. It was the best thing she could do. Though perhaps he would only be calling her to ask where she had left something for which they were searching. That stupid Ashton girl who took her place might not have remembered all her directions.

Breathless, with possibilities crowding upon her mind, she hurried into the drug store and sought the telephone booth. It seemed ages before the connection was made and she heard Mr. Barnard's dry familiar tones over the phone:

"That you, Miss Hollister? This is Mr. Barnard. I'm sorry to disturb you right in the midst of your holiday, but a matter has come up that is rather serious and I'm wondering if you could help us out for a day or two. If you would we'd be glad to give you fifty dollars for the extra time, and let you extend your vacation to a month instead of two weeks. Do you think you could spare a day or two to help us right away?"

"Oh! Why, yes, of course!" faltered Shirley, her eyes dancing at the thought of the extra vacation and money.

"Thank you! I was sure you would," said Mr. Barnard, with relief in his voice. "You see we have got that Government contract. The news just came in the afternoon mail. It's rather particular business because it has to do with matters that the Government wishes to keep secret. I am to go down to-morrow morning to Washington to receive instructions, and I have permission to bring a trusted private secretary with me. Now you know, of course, that I couldn't take Miss Ashton. She wouldn't be able to do what I want done even if she were one I could trust not to say a word about the matter. I would take Jim Thorpe, but his father has just died and I can't very well ask him to leave. Neither can I delay longer than to-morrow. Now the question is, would you be willing to go to Washington in the morning? I have looked up the trains and I find you can leave the shore at 8.10 and meet me in Baltimore at ten o'clock. I will be waiting for you at the train gate, but in case we miss each other wait in the station, close to the telephone booths, till I find you. We will take the next train for Washington and be there a little before noon. If all goes well we ought to be through our business in plenty of time to make a four o'clock train home. Of course there may be delays, and it is quite possible you might have to remain in Washington over night, though I hardly think so. But in case you do I will see that you are safe and comfortable in a quiet hotel near the station where my wife's sister is staying this summer.

"Of course your expenses will all be paid. I will telegraph and have a mileage book put at your disposal that you can call for right there in your station in the morning. Are you willing to undertake this for us? I assure you we shall not forget the service."

When Shirley finally hung up the receiver and looked about the little country drug store in wonder at herself the very bottles on the shelves seemed to be whirling and dancing about before her eyes. What strange exciting things were happening to her all in such breathless haste! Only one day at the shore and a piece of another, and here she was with a trip to Washington on her hands! It certainly was bewildering to have things come in such rapid succession. She wished it had come at another time, and not just now when she had not yet got used to the great sea and the wonder of the beautiful place where they were staying. She did not want to be interrupted just yet. It would not be quite the same when she got back to it she was afraid. But of course she could not refuse. It never entered her head to refuse. She knew enough about the office to realize that Mr. Barnard must have her. Jimmie Thorpe would have been the one to go if he were available, because he was a man and had been with Barnard and Clegg for ten years and knew all their most confidential business, but of course Jimmie could not go with his father lying dead and his mother and invalid sister needing him; and there was no one else but herself.

She thought it all out on the way back to the cottage, with a little pang at the thought of losing the next day and of having perhaps to stay over in Washington a day and maybe miss the arrival of Sidney Graham, if he should come in a day or two, as he had promised. He might even come and go back again before she was able to return, and perhaps he would think her ungrateful to leave when he had been so kind to plan all this lovely vacation for her pleasure. Then she brought herself up smartly and told herself decidedly that it was nothing to him whether she was there or not, and it certainly had no right to be anything to her. It was a good thing she was going, and would probably be a good thing for all concerned if she stayed until he went back to the city again.

With this firm determination she hurried up to the veranda where her mother sat with Doris, and told her story.

Mrs. Hollister looked troubled.

"I'm sorry you gave him an answer, Shirley, without waiting to talk it over with me. I don't believe I like the idea of your going to a strange city, all alone that way. Of course Mr. Barnard will look after you in a way, but still he's a good deal of a stranger. I do wish he had let you alone for your vacation. It seems as if he might have found somebody else to go. I wish Mr. Graham was here. I shouldn't wonder if he would suggest some way out of it for you."

But Shirley stiffened into dignity at once.

"Really, mother dear, I'm sure I don't see what Mr. Graham would have to say about it if he were here. I shouldn't ask his advice. You see, mother, really, there isn't anybody else that could do this but Jimmie Thorpe, and he's out of the question. It would be unthinkable that I should refuse in this emergency. And you know Mr. Barnard has been very kind. Besides, think of the ducky vacation I'll have afterward, a whole month! And all that extra money! That shall go to the rent of a better house for winter! Think of it! Don't you worry, mother dear! There isn't a thing in the world could happen to me. I'll be the very most-discreetest person you ever heard of. I'll even glance shyly at the White House and Capitol! Come, let's go up and get dolled up for supper! Won't the children be surprised when they hear I'm really to go to Washington! I'm so excited I don't know what to do!"

Mrs. Hollister said no more, and entered pleasantly into the merry talk at the table, telling Shirley what she must be sure to see at the nation's capital. But the next morning just as Shirley was about to leave for the station, escorted by all the children, Mrs. Hollister came with a package of addressed postal cards which she had made George get for her the night before, and put them in Shirley's bag.

"Just drop us a line as you go along, dear," she said. "I'll feel happier about it to be hearing from you. Mail one whenever you have a chance."

Shirley laughed as she looked at the fat package.

"All those, mother dear? You must expect I am going to stay a month! You know I won't have much time for writing, and I fully expect to be back to-night or to-morrow at the latest."

"Well, that's all right," said her mother. "You can use them another time, then; but you can just put a line on one whenever it is convenient. I shall enjoy getting them even after you get back. You know this is your first journey out into the world alone."

Shirley stooped to kiss the little mother.

"All right, dear! I'll write you a serial story. Each one continued in our next. Good-by! Don't take too long a walk to-day. I want you rested to hear all I'll have to tell when I get back to-night!"

Shirley wrote the first postal card as soon as she was settled in the train, describing the other occupants of the car, and making a vivid picture of the landscape that was slipping by her windows. She wrote the second in the Baltimore station, after she had met Mr. Barnard, while he went to get seats in the parlor car, and she mailed them both at Baltimore.

The third was written as they neared Washington, with the dim vision of the great monument dawning on her wondering sight in the distance. Her last sentence gave her first impression of the nation's capital.

They had eaten lunch in the dining car, a wonderful experience to the girl, and she promised herself another postal devoted to that, but there was no time to write more after they reached Washington. She was put into a taxi and whirled away to an office where her work began. She caught glimpses of great buildings on the way, and gazed with awe at the dome of the Capitol building. Mr. Barnard was kind and pointed out this and that, but it was plain his mind was on the coming interview. When Shirley sat at last in a quiet corner of a big dark office, her pen poised, her note-book ready for work, and looked at the serious faces of the men in the room, she felt as if she had been rushed through a treasure vault of glorious jewels and thrust into the darkness of a tomb. But presently the talk about her interested her. Things were being said about the vital interests of the country, scraps of sentences that reminded her of the trend of talk in the daily papers, and the headings of front columns. She looked about her with interest and noted the familiarity with which these men quoted the words of those high up in authority in the government. With awe she began her work, taking down whatever Mr. Barnard dictated, her fingers flying over the tiny pages of the note-book, in small neat characters, keeping pace with the voices going on about her. The detail work she was setting down was not of especial interest to her, save that it was concerned with Government work, for its phraseology was familiar and a part of her daily routine office work at home; but she set every sense on the alert to get the tiniest detail and not to make the smallest mistake, understanding from the voices of the men about her that it was of vital interest to the country that this order should be filled quickly and accurately. As she capped her fountain pen, and slipped the rubber band on her note-book when it was over, she heard one of the men just behind her say in a low tone to Mr. Barnard:

"You're sure of your secretary of course? I just want to give you the tip that this thing is being very closely watched. We have reason to believe there's some spying planned. Keep your notes carefully and don't let too many in on this. We know pretty well what's going on, but it's not desirable just now to make any arrests until we can watch a little longer and round up the whole party. So keep your eyes peeled, and don't talk."

"Oh, certainly! I quite understand," said Mr. Barnard, "and I have a most discreet secretary," and he glanced with a significant smile toward Shirley as she rose.

"Of course!" said the other. "She looks it," and he bowed deferentially to Shirley as she passed.

She did not think of it at the time, but afterwards she recalled how in acknowledging his courtesy she had stepped back a little and almost stumbled over a page, a boy about George's age, who had been standing withdrawn into the shadow of the deep window. She remembered he had a keen intelligent look, and had apologized and vanished immediately. A moment later it seemed to be the same boy in blue clothes and gilt buttons who held the outer door open for them to pass out—or was this a taller one? She glanced again at his side face with a lingering thought of George as she paused to fasten her glove and slip her note-book into her hand-bag.

"I think I will put you into the taxi and let you go right back to the station while I attend to another errand over at the War Department. It won't take me long. We can easily catch that four-o'clock train back. I suppose you are anxious to get back to-night?"

"Oh, yes," said Shirley earnestly, "I must, if possible. Mother isn't well and she worries so easily."

"Well, I don't know why we can't. Then perhaps you can come up to town to-morrow and type those notes for us. By the way, I guess it would be better for me to take them and lock them in the safe to-night. No, don't stop to get them out now"—as Shirley began to unfasten her bag and get the note-book out—"We haven't much time if we want to catch that train. Just look after them carefully and I'll get them when we are on the train."

He helped her into the taxi, gave the order, "To the station," and touching his hat, went rapidly over to the War Department Building. No one saw a boy with a blue cap and brass buttons steal forth on a bicycle from the court just below the office, and circling about the asphalt uncertainly for a moment, shoot off across the park.

Shirley sat up very straight and kept her eyes about her. She was glad they were taking another way to the station so that she might see more. When she got there she would write another postal and perhaps it would go on the same train with her.

It was all too short, that ride up Pennsylvania Avenue and around by the Capitol. Shirley gathered up her bag and prepared to get out reluctantly. She wished she might have just one more hour to go about, but of course that would be impossible if she wished to reach home to-night.

But before the driver of the car could get down and open the door for her to get out a boy with a bicycle slid up to the curb and touching his gilt-buttoned cap respectfully said:

"Excuse me, Miss, but Mr. Barnard sent me after you. He says there's been some mistake and you'll have to come back and get it corrected."

"Oh!" said Shirley, too surprised to think for a minute. "Oh! Then please hurry, for Mr. Barnard wants to get back in time to get that four-o'clock train."

The driver frowned, but the boy stepped up and handed him something, saying:

"That's all right, Joe, he sent you this." The driver's face cleared and he started his machine again. The boy vanished into the throng. It was another of Shirley's after-memories that she had caught a glimpse of a scrap of paper along with the money the boy had handed the driver, and that he had stuffed it in his pocket after looking intently at it; but at the time she thought nothing of it. She was only glad that they were skimming along rapidly.

CHAPTER XXII

Shirley's sense of direction had always been keen. Even as a child she could tell her way home when others were lost. It was some minutes, however, before she suddenly became aware that the car was being driven in an entirely different direction from the place she had just left Mr. Barnard. For a moment she looked around puzzled, thinking the man was merely taking another way around, but a glance back where the white dome of the Capitol loomed, palace-like, above the city, made her sure that something was wrong. She looked at the buildings they were passing, at the names of the streets—F Street—they had not been on that before! These stores and tall buildings were all new to her eyes. Down there at the end of the vista was a great building all columns. Was that the Treasury and were they merely seeing it from another angle? It was all very confusing, but the time was short, why had the man not taken the shorter way?

She looked at her small wrist watch anxiously and watched eagerly for the end of the street. But before the great building was reached the car suddenly curved around a corner to the right,—one block,—a turn to the left,—another turn,—a confusion of new names and streets! New York Avenue! Connecticut Avenue! Thomas Circle! The names spun by so fast she could read but few of them, and those she saw she wanted to remember that she might weave them into her next postal. She opened her bag, fumbled for her little silver pencil in the pocket of her coat and scribbled down the names she could read as she passed, on the back of the bundle of postal cards, and without looking at her writing. She did not wish to miss a single sight. Here were rows of homes, pleasant and palatial, some of them even cozy. The broad avenues were enchanting, the park spaces, the lavish scattering of noble statues. Bah the time was hastening by and they were going farther and farther from the station and from the direction of the offices where she had been. She twisted her neck once more and the Capitol dome loomed soft and blended in the distance. A thought of alarm leaped into her mind. She leaned forward and spoke to the driver:

"You understood, didn't you, that I am to return to the office where you took me with the gentleman?"

The man nodded.

"All right, lady. Yes, lady!" And the car rushed on, leaping out upon the beautiful way and disclosing new beauties ahead. For a few minutes more Shirley was distracted from her anxiety in wondering whether the great buildings on her right belonged to any of the embassies or not. And then as the car swerved and plunged into another street and darted into a less thickly populated district, with trees and vacant lots almost like the country, alarm arose once more and she looked wildly back and tried to see the signs; but they were going faster still now upon a wide empty road past stretches of park, with winding drives and charming views, and a great stone bridge to the right, arching over a deep ravine below, a railroad crossing it. There were deer parks fenced with high wire, and filled with the pretty creatures. Everything went by so fast that Shirley hardly realized that something really must be wrong before she seemed to be in the midst of a strange world aloof.

"I am sure you have made a mistake!" The girl's clear voice cut through the driving wind as they rushed along. "I must go back right away to that office from which you brought me. I must go *at once* or I shall be too late for my train! The gentleman will be very angry!" She spoke in the tone that always brought instant obedience from the employees around the office building at home.

But the driver was stolid. He scarcely stirred in his seat to turn toward her. His thick voice was brought back to her on the breeze:

"No, lady, it's all right, lady! I had my orders, lady! You needn't to worry. I get you there plenty time."

A wild fear seized Shirley, and her heart lifted itself as was its habit, to God. "Oh, my Father! Take care of me! Help me! Show me what to do!" she cried.

Thoughts rushed through her brain as fast as the car rushed over the ground. What was she up against? Was this man crazy or bad? Was he perhaps trying to kidnap her? What for? She shuddered to look the thought in the face. Or was it the notes? She remembered the men in the office and what they had said about keeping still and "spying-enemies." But perhaps she was mistaken. Maybe this man was only stupid, and it would all come out right in a few minutes. But no, she must not wait for anything like that. She must take no chance. The notes were in her keeping. She must put them where they would be safe. No telling how soon she would be overpowered and searched if that was what they were after. She must hide them, and she must think of some way to send word to Mr. Barnard before it was toe late. No telling what moment they would turn from the main road and she be hidden far from human habitation. She must work fast. What could she do? Scream to the next passer-by? No, for the car was going too fast for that to do any good, and the houses up this way seemed all to be isolated, and few people about. There were houses on ahead beyond the park. She must have something ready to throw out when they came to them. "Oh God! Help me think what to do!" she prayed again, and then looking down at her bag she saw the postal cards. Just the thing! Quickly she scribbled, still holding her hand within the bag so that her movements were not noticeable:

"Help! Quick! Being carried off! Auto! Connecticut Ave.! Park. Deer. Stone bridge. Phone Mr. Clegg. Don't tell mother! Shirley."

She turned the card over, drew a line through her mother's name and wrote Carol's in its place. Stealthily she slipped the card up her sleeve, dropped her hand carelessly over the side of the car for a moment, let the card flutter from her fingers, and wrote another.

She had written three cards and dropped them in front of houses before it suddenly occurred to her that even if these cards should be picked up and mailed it would be sometime before they reached their destination and far too late for help to reach her in time. Her heart suddenly went down in a swooning sickness and her breath almost went from her. Her head was reeling, and all the time she was trying to tell herself that she was exaggerating this thing, that probably the man would slow up or something and it would all be explained. Yes, he was slowing up, but for what? It was in another lonely spot, and out from the bushes there appeared, as if by magic, another man, a queer-looking man with a heavy mustache that looked as if it didn't belong to him. He stood alertly waiting for the car and sprang into the front seat without waiting for it to stop, or even glancing back at her, and the car shot forward again with great leaps.

Shirley dropped out the two cards together that she had just written and leaned forward, touching the newcomer on the arm.

"Won't you please make this driver understand that he is taking me to the wrong place?" she said with a pleasant smile. "I must get back to an office two or three blocks away from the Treasury Building somewhere. I must turn back at once or I shall miss my appointment and be late for my train. It is quite important. Tell him, please, I will pay him well if he will get me back at once."

The stranger turned with an oily smile.

"That's all right, Miss. He isn't making any mistake. We're taking you right to Secretary Baker's country home. He sent for your man, Mr.—— What's his name? I forget. Barnard? Oh, yes. He sent for Mr. Barnard to come out there, sent his private car down for him; and Mr. Barnard, he left orders we should go after you and bring you along. It's something they want to change in those notes you was taking. There was a mistake, and the Secretary he wanted to look after the matter himself."

Shirley sat back with a sudden feeling of weakness and a fear she might faint, although she had never done such a thing in her life. She was not deceived for an instant now, although she saw at once that she must not let the man know it. The idea that Secretary Baker would pause in the midst of his multiplicity of duties to look into the details of a small article of manufacture was ridiculous! It was equally impossible that Mr. Barnard would have sent strangers after her and let her be carried off in this queer way. He had been most particular that she should be looked after carefully. She was horribly to blame that she had allowed herself to be carried back at all until Mr. Barnard himself appeared; and yet, was she? That surely had been the page from the office who came with the message? Well, never mind, she was in for it now, and she must do her best while there was any chance to do anything. She must drop all those postals somehow, and she must hide those notes somewhere, and perhaps write some others,—fake ones. What should she do first?

"Father, help me! Show me! Oh, don't let me lose the notes! Please take care of me!" Again and again her heart prayed as her hand worked stealthily in her bag, while she tried to put a pleasant smile upon her face and pretend she was still deceived, leaning forward and speaking to the strange man once more:

"Is Secretary Baker's home much farther from here?" she asked, feeling her lips draw stiffly in the frozen smile she forced. "Will it take long?"

"'Bout ten minutes!" the man answered graciously, with a peculiar look toward the driver. "Nice view 'round here!" he added affably with a leering look of admiration toward her.

Shirley's heart stood still with new fear, but she managed to make her white lips smile again and murmur, "Charming!"

Then she leaned back again and fussed around in her bag, ostentatiously bringing out a clean handkerchief, though she really had been detaching the pages which contained the notes from her loose-leaf note-book. There were not many of them, for she always wrote closely in small characters. But where should she hide them? Pull the lining away from the edge of her bag and slip them inside? No, for the bag would be the first place they would likely search, and she could not poke the lining back smoothly so it would not show. If she should try to drop the tiny pages down her neck inside her blouse, the men would very likely see her. Dared she try to slip the leaves down under the linen robe that lay over her lap and put them inside her shoe? She was wearing plain little black pumps, and the pages would easily go in the soles, three or four in each. Once in they would be well hidden, and they would not rattle and give notice of their presence; but oh, what a terrible risk if anything should happen to knock off her shoe, or if they should try to search her! Still she must take some risk and this was the safest risk at hand. She must try it and then write out some fake notes, giving false numbers and sizes, and other phraseology. Or stay! Wasn't there already something written in that book that would answer? Some specifications she had written down for the Tillman-Brooks Company. Yes, she was sure. It wasn't at all for the same articles, nor the same measurements, but only an expert would know that. She leaned down quite naturally to pick up her handkerchief and deftly managed to get five small leaves slipped into her right shoe. It occurred to her that she must keep her keepers deceived, so she asked once more in gracious tones:

"Would it trouble you any to mail a card for me as soon as possible after we arrive? I am afraid my mother will be worried about my delay and she isn't well. I suppose they have a post office out this way."

"Sure, Miss!" said the man again, with another leering smile that made her resolve to have no further conversation than was absolutely necessary. She took out her fountain pen and hurriedly wrote:

"Detained longer than I expected. May not get back to-night. S. H.," and handed the card to the man. He took it and turned it over, all too evidently reading it, and put it in his pocket. Shirley felt that she had made an impression of innocence by the move which so far was good. She put away her fountain pen deliberately, and managed in so doing to manipulate the rest of the leaves of notes into her left shoe. Somehow that gave her a little confidence and she sat back and began to wonder if there was anything more she could do. Those dropped postals were worse than useless, of course. Why had she not written an appeal to whoever picked them up? Suiting the action to the thought she wrote another postal card—her stock was getting low, there were but two more left.

"For Christ's sake send the police to help me! I am being carried off by two strange men! Shirley Hollister."

She marked out the address on the other side and wrote: "To whoever picks this up." She fluttered it to the breeze cautiously; but her heart sank as she realized how little likelihood there was of its being picked up for days perhaps. For who would stop in a car to notice a bit of paper on the road? And there seemed to be but few pedestrians. If she only had something larger, more attractive. She glanced at her belongings and suddenly remembered the book she had brought with her to read, one of the new novels from the cottage, a goodly sized volume in a bright red cover. The very thing!

With a cautious glance at her keepers she took up the book as if to read, and opening it at the flyleaf began to write surreptitiously much the same message that had been on her last postal, signing her name and home address and giving her employers' address. Her heart was beating wildly when she had finished. She was trying to think just how she should use this last bit of ammunition to the best advantage. Should she just drop it in the road quietly? If only there were some way to fasten the pages open so her message would be read! Her handkerchief! Of course! She folded it cornerwise and slipped it in across the pages so that the book would fall open at the fly leaf, knotting the ends on the back of the cover. Every moment had to be cautious, and she must remember to keep her attitude of reading with the printed pages covering the handkerchief. It seemed hours that it took her, her fingers trembled so. If it had not been for the rushing noise of wind and car she would not have dared so much undiscovered, but apparently her captors were satisfied that she still believed their story about going to Secretary Baker's country house, for they seemed mainly occupied in watching to see if they were pursued, casting anxious glances back now and then, but scarcely noticing her at all.

Shirley had noticed two or three times when a car had passed them that the men both leaned down to do something at their feet to the machinery of the car. Were they afraid of being recognized? Would this perhaps give her a chance to fling her book out where it would be seen by people in an oncoming car? Oh, if she but had the strength and skill to fling it *into* a car. But of course that was impossible without attracting the attention of the two men. Nevertheless, she must try what she could do.

She lifted her eyes to the road ahead and lo, a big car was bearing down upon them! She had almost despaired of meeting any more, for the road was growing more and more lonely and they must have come many miles. As soon as the two men in front of her sighted the car, they seemed to settle in their seats and draw their hats down a little farther over their eyes. The same trouble seemed to develop with the machinery at their feet that Shirley had noticed before, and they bobbed and ducked and seemed to be wholly engrossed with their own affairs.

Shirley's heart was beating so fast that it seemed as though it would suffocate her, and her hand seemed powerless as it lay innocently holding the closed book with the knotted handkerchief turned down out of sight; but she was girding herself, nerving herself for one great last effort, and praying to be guided.

The big car came on swiftly and was about to pass, when Shirley half rose and hurled her book straight at it and then sank back in her seat with a fearful terror upon her, closing her eyes for one brief second, not daring to watch the results of her act,—if there were to be any results.

The men in the front seat suddenly straightened up and looked around.

"What's the matter?" growled the man who had got in last in quite a different tone from any he had used before. "What you tryin' to put over on us?"

Shirley gasped and caught at her self-control.

"I've dropped my book," she stammered out wildly, "Could you stop long enough to pick it up? It was borrowed!" she ended sweetly as if by inspiration, and wondering at the steadiness of her tone when blood was pounding so in her throat and ears, and everything was black before her. Perhaps—oh, perhaps they would stop and she could cry out to the people for help.

The man rose up in his seat and looked back. Shirley cast one frightened glance back, too, and saw in that brief second that the other car had stopped and someone was standing up and looking back.

"Hell! No!" said her captor briefly, ducking down in his seat. "*Let her out!*" he howled to the driver, and the car broke into a galloping streak, the wheels hardly seeming to touch the ground, the tonneau bounding and swaying this way and that. Shirley had all she could do to keep in her seat. At one moment she thought how easy it would be to spring from the car and lie in a little still heap at the roadside. But there were the notes! She must not abandon her trust even for so fearful an escape from her captors. Suddenly, without warning, they turned a sharp curve and struck into a rough, almost unbroken road into the woods, and the thick growth seemed to close in behind them and shut them out from the world.

Shirley shut her eyes and prayed.

CHAPTER XXIII

The next trolley that passed the old barn after the Hollisters had left brought a maid servant and a man servant from the Graham place. The other old servant met them, and together the three went to work. They had brought with them a lot of large dust-covers and floor-spreads such as are used by housemaids in cleaning a room, and with these they now proceeded to cover all the large pieces of furniture in the place. In a very short space of time the rugs and bits of carpet were carefully rolled up, the furniture piled in small compass in the middle of the rooms, and everything enveloped in thick coverings. The curtains, bric-â-brac, and even the dishes were put away carefully, and the whole big, inviting home was suddenly denuded. The clothes from the calico-curtained clothes-presses were folded and laid in drawers, and everything made perfectly safe for a lot of workmen to come into the house. Even the hay-loft bedrooms shared in this process. Only a cot was left for the old servant and a few necessary things for him to use, and most of these he transported to the basement out of the way. When the work was done the man and maid took the trolley back home again and the other old man servant arranged to make his Sabbath as pleasant as possible in the company of his brother from the near-by farm.

Monday morning promptly at eight o'clock the trolley landed a bevy of workmen, carpenters, plasterers, plumbers, and furnace men, with a foreman who set them all at work as if it were a puzzle he had studied out and memorized the solution. In a short time the quiet spot was full of sound, the symphony of industry, the rhythm of toil. Some men were working away with the furnace that had been stored in the cellar; others were measuring, fitting, cutting holes for lead pipes; still others were sawing away at the roof, making great gashes in its mossy extent; and two men were busy taking down the old barn door. Out in front more men were building a vat for mortar, and opening bags of lime and sand that began to arrive. Three men with curious aprons made of ticking, filled with thin wire nails, were frantically putting laths on the uprights that the carpenters had already set up, and stabbing them with nails from a seemingly inexhaustible supply in their mouths. It was as if they had all engaged to build the tower of Babel in a day, and meant to win a prize at it. Such sounds! Such shoutings, such bangings, thumpings, and harsh, raucous noises! The bird in the tall tree looked and shivered, thankful that her brood were well away on their wings before all this cataclysm came to pass.

Presently arrived a load of sashes, doors, and wooden frames, and another load of lumber. Things can be done in a hurry if you have money and influence and the will to insist upon what you want. Before night there was a good start made toward big changes in the old barn.

Plumbers and gas-fitters and men who were putting in the hot-water heat chased one another around the place, each man seeking to get his pipes in place before the lathers got to that spot; and the contractor was everywhere, proving his right to be selected for this rush job. As soon as the lathers had finished with a room the plasterers took possession, and the old door was rapidly being replaced with a great glazed floor set in a frame of more sashes, so that the old darkness was gone entirely.

In the roof big dormer windows were taking the place of the two or three little eyebrow affairs that had given air to the hay heretofore, and the loft was fast becoming pleasanter than the floor below.

Outside laborers were busy building up a terrace, where a wide cement-floor piazza with stone foundations and low stone walls was to run across the entire front. Another chimney was rising from the region of the kitchen. A white enamel sink with a wide drain-shelf attached appeared next, with signs of a butler's pantry between kitchen and dining-room. A delightful set of china-closet doors with little diamond panes that matched the windows was put in one corner of the dining-room, and some bookcases with sliding doors began to develop along the walls of the living-room. Down in the basement a man was fitting stationary tubs for a laundry, and on both the first floor and the second bathrooms were being made. If the place hadn't been so big, the workmen would have got in one another's way. Closets big and little were being put in, and parts of a handsome staircase were lying about, until you wouldn't know the place at all. Every evening the old servant and the neighbor next door, who used to rent the old barn before he built his own new one, came together to look over what had been accomplished during the day, and to discourse upon this changing world and the wonders of it. The farmer, in fact, learned a great deal about modern improvements, and at once set about bringing some of them to bear upon his own modest farmhouse. He had money in the bank, and why shouldn't he "have things convenient for Sally"?

When Sidney Graham reached the city on Monday morning he scarcely took time to read his mail in the office and give the necessary attention to the day's work before he was up and off again, flying along the Glenside Road as fast as his car would carry him. His mind certainly was not on business that morning. He was as eager as a child to see how work at the old barn was progressing, and the workmen stood small chance of lying down on their job that week, for he meant to make every minute count, no matter how much it cost. He spent a large part of

Monday hovering about the old barn, gloating over each new sign of progress, using his imagination on more things than the barn. But when Tuesday arrived an accumulation of work at the office in connection with a large order that had just come in kept him close to his desk. He had hoped to get away in time to reach Glenside before the workmen left in the afternoon, but four o'clock arrived with still a great pile of letters for him to sign, before his work would be done for the day.

He had just signed his name for the forty-ninth time and laid his pen down with an impatient sigh of relief when the telephone on his desk rang. He hesitated. Should he answer it and be hindered again, or call his secretary and let her attend to it while he slipped away to his well-earned respite? A second insistent ring, however, brought him back to duty and he reached out and took up the receiver.

"Is this Mr. Sidney Graham? Long distance is calling!"

The young man frowned impatiently and wished he had sent for his secretary. It was probably another tiresome confab on that Chicago matter, and it really wasn't worth the trouble, anyway. Then a small scared voice at the other end of the wire spoke:

"Is that you, Mr. Graham? Well, this is Carol. Say, Mr. Graham, I'm afraid something awful has happened to Shirley! I don't know what to do, and I thought I'd better ask you." Her voice broke off in a gasp like a sob.

A cold chill struck at the young man's heart, and a vision of Shirley battling with the ocean waves was instantly conjured up.

"Shirley! Where is she? Tell me, quick!" he managed to say, though the words seemed to stick in his throat.

"She's down at Washington," answered Carol. "Mr. Barnard phoned her last night. There was something special nobody else could take notes about, because it was for a Government contract, and has to be secret. Mr. Barnard asked her to please go and she went this morning. Mother didn't like her to go, but she addressed a lot of postal cards for her to write back, and one came postmarked Baltimore in this afternoon's mail, saying she was having a nice time. But just now a call came for mother to go to the telephone. She was asleep and George was crabbing so I had to come. It was a strange man in Washington. He said he had just found three postal cards on the road addressed to mother, that all said 'Help! Quick! Two men were carrying off Shirley and please to phone to the police.' He took the postals to the police station, but he thought he ought to phone us. And oh, Mr. Graham, *what shall I do*? I can't tell mother. It will kill her, and how can we help Shirley?"

"Don't tell mother," said Graham quickly, trying to speak calmly out of his horror. "Be a brave girl, Carol. A great deal depends on you just now. Have you phoned Mr. Barnard? Oh, you say he's in Washington? He was to meet your sister in Baltimore? He *did* meet her you say? The postal card said she had met him? Well, the next thing is to phone Mr. Clegg and find out if he knows anything. I'll do that at once, and unless he has heard that she is all right I will start for Washington on the next train. Suppose you stay right where you are till half-past five. I may want to call you up again and need you in a hurry. Then you go back to the cottage as fast as you can and talk cheerfully. Say you went to take a walk. Isn't Elizabeth with you? Well, tell her to help keep your mother from suspecting anything. Above all things don't cry! It won't do any good and it may do lots of harm. Get George off by himself and tell him everything, and tell him I said he was to make some excuse to go down town after supper and stay at the telephone office till ten o'clock. I may want to call him up from Washington. Now be a brave little girl. I suspect your sister Shirley would tell you to pray. Good-by."

"I will!" gasped Carol. "Good-by!"

Graham pressed his foot on the bell under his desk and reached out to slam his desk drawers shut and put away his papers. His secretary appeared at the door.

"Get me Barnard and Clegg on the phone! Ask for Mr. Barnard or, if he isn't in, Mr. Clegg. Then go out to the other phone and call up the station. Find out what's the next express to Washington. Tell Bromwell to be ready to drive me to the station and bring my car back to the garage."

He was working rapidly as he talked; putting papers in the safe, jotting down a few notes for the next day's work, trying to think of everything at once. The secretary handed him the phone, quietly saying, "Mr. Clegg on the phone," and went out of the room.

Excited conference with Mr. Clegg brought out the fact that he was but just in receipt of a telegram from Police Headquarters in Washington saying that a book with Barnard and Clegg's address and an appeal from a young woman named Shirley Hollister who was apparently being kidnapped by two strange men in an auto, had been flung into a passing car and brought to them. They had sent forces in search of the girl at once and would do all in their power to find her. Meantime they would like any information that would be helpful in the search.

Mr. Clegg was much excited. He appeared to have lost his head. He seemed glad to have another cooler mind at work on the case. He spluttered a good deal about the importance of the case and the necessity for secrecy. He said he hoped it wouldn't get into the papers, and that it would be Barnard and Clegg's undoing if it did. He seemed more concerned about that and the notes that Shirley probably had, than about the girl's situation. When Graham brought him up rather sharply he admitted that there had been a message from Barnard that he would be detained over night probably, but he had attached no significance to that. He knew Barnard's usual hotel address in

Washington but hadn't thought to phone him about the telegram from police headquarters. Graham hung up at last in a panic of fury and dismay, ringing violently for his secretary again.

"The next train leaves at five o'clock," she said capably, as she entered. "Bromwell has gone after the car. I told him to buy you a mileage book and save your time at this end. You have forty minutes and he will be back in plenty of time."

"Good!" said Graham. "Now call up long distance and get me Police Headquarters in Washington. No! Use the phone in father's office please, I'll have to use this while you're getting them."

As soon as she had left the room he called up the shore again and was fortunate in getting Carol almost immediately, the poor child being close at hand all in a tremble, with Elizabeth in no less a state of nervousness, brave and white, waiting for orders.

"Can you give me an exact description of your sister's dress, and everything that she had with her when she started this morning?" asked Graham, prepared with pen and paper to write it down.

Carol summoned her wits and described Shirley's simple outfit exactly, even down to the little black pumps on her feet, and went mentally through the small hand-bag she had carried.

"Oh, yes!" she added, "and she had a book to read! One she found here in the cottage. It had a red cover and was called, "From the Car Behind.""

Graham wrote them all down carefully, asked a few more details of Shirley's plans, and bade Carol again to be brave and go home with a message to George to be at the phone from half-past eight to ten.

He was all ready to go to his train when the Washington call came in, and as he hurried to his father's office to answer it he found his heart crying out to an Unseen Power to help in this trying hour and protect the sweet girl in awful peril.

"Oh, God, I love her!" he found his heart saying over and over again, as if it had started out to be an individual by itself without his will or volition.

There was no comfort from Washington Police Headquarters. Nothing more had been discovered save another crumpled postal lying along the roadside. They received with alacrity, however, Mr. Barnard's Washington hotel address, and the description of the young woman and her belongings. When Graham had finished the hasty conversation he had to fly to make his train, and when at last he lay back in his seat in the parlor car and let the waves of his anxiety and trouble roll over him he was almost overwhelmed. He had led a comparatively tranquil life for a young man who had never tried to steer clear of trouble, and this was the first great calamity that had ever come his way. Calamity? No, he would not own yet that it was a calamity. He was hurrying to her! He would find her! He would not allow himself to think that anything had befallen her. But wherever she was, if she was still alive, no matter how great her peril, he was sure she was praying now, and he would pray too! Yes, pray as she had taught him. Oh, God! If he only knew how to pray better! What was it she had said so often? "Whatsoever ye ask in my name"—yes, that was it—"I will do it." What was that talismanic Name? Ah! Christ! "Oh, God, in the name of Christ—" But when he came to the thought of her she was too exquisite and dear to be put into words, so his petition went up in spirit form, unframed by words to weight it down, wafted up by the pain of a soul in torture.

At Baltimore it occurred to Graham to send a telegram to Barnard to meet him at the train, and when he got out at Union Station the first person he saw was Barnard, white and haggard, looking for him through the bars of the train gate. He grasped the young man's hand as if it were a last straw for a drowning man to cling to, and demanded in a shaking voice to know if he had heard anything from Miss Hollister.

One of the first questions that Graham asked was whether Barnard had been back to the office where Miss Hollister had taken the dictation, to report her disappearance.

"Well, no, I hadn't thought of that,'" said Barnard blankly. "What would they know about it? The fact is I was rather anxious to keep the facts from getting to them. You see they warned me that there were parties anxious to get hold of those specifications. It's Government work, you know."

"They should know at once," said Graham sternly. "They may have inside information which would give us a clew to follow. The secret service men are onto a lot of things that we common mortals don't suspect."

Mr. Barnard looked mortified and convinced.

"Well, what *have* you done so far? We would better understand each other thoroughly so as to save time and not go over old ground. You have been in communication with Police Headquarters, of course?" asked Graham.

"Why, no," said the older man apologetically. "You see, I got here just in time for the train, and failing to find the young lady in the station where we had agreed to meet, I took it for granted that she had used the extra time in driving about to see a few sights in the city, as I suggested, and had somehow failed to get back in time. I couldn't understand it because she had been quite anxious to get home to-night. I could have caught the train myself, but didn't exactly like to leave her alone in a strange city, though, of course, it's perfectly safe for a steady girl like that. Afterward it occurred to me that she might have gotten on the train and perhaps I should have done so too, but there was really very little time to decide, for the train pulled out two minutes after I reached the station. I waited about here for a time, and then went over to the Continental, where my sister is stopping, thinking I would ask her to stay in the station and watch for the young lady and I would go home; but I found my sister had run down to the shore for a few days; so I had something to eat and while I was in the dining-room your telegram came. I was hoping somehow you had seen Miss Hollister, or had word from her, and it was all right."

One could see the poor man had no conception of what was due to a lady in his care, and Graham looked at him for a moment with rage, wishing he could take him by the throat and shake some sense into him.

"Then you don't know that she's been kidnapped and the police are out on track for her?" said Graham dryly.

"No! You don't say!" exclaimed Barnard, turning white and showing he had some real feeling after all. "Kidnapped! Why—why—how *could* she? And she's got *those notes*! Why, Graham! You're fooling! Why, how came you to know?"

Graham told him tersely as he walked the man over to the telephone booths, and finished with:

"Now, you go in that booth and phone your Government man, and I'll call up police headquarters and see what's doing. We've got to work fast, for there's no telling what may have happened in the last three hours. It's up to us to find that girl before anything worse happens to her."

White and trembling Barnard tottered into the booth. When he came out again the sleuth-hounds of the Secret Service were on the trail of Shirley Hollister's captors.

CHAPTER XXIV

The car that was bearing Shirley Hollister through the lonely wooded road at a breathless speed suddenly came to a halt in the rear of an old house whose front faced on another road equally lonely. During the brief time that they had been in the woods, the sky seemed to have perceptibly darkened with the coming evening.

Shirley looked about her with increased fright. It was almost night and here was her prison, far from town or human dwelling place. Even the road was at some distance in front of the house, and there were more woods on either side.

"This here is Secretary Baker's summer home," announced the man who had done the talking, as he climbed out of the car and opened the door for her. "You can just step in the back door and go through to the parlor; the help's all out this afternoon. The Secretary'll be down presently. He always takes a nap afternoons about this time. I'll tell him you've come."

There seemed nothing to do but obey, and Shirley chose to let the farce continue. Surely the man must know she was not a fool, but it was better than open hostility. There was nothing to be gained by informing him that she knew he was guying her.

"Oh, Jesus Christ, I trust myself to you!" she breathed in her heart as she stepped across the leaf-strewn grass and looked about her, wondering whether she should ever walk the earth again after she had stepped into the dim tree-shrouded house. But why go in?

"I think I will remain out here," she said calmly, albeit her heart was pounding away like a trip-hammer. "Please tell Mr. Baker to come to me here. It is much pleasanter than in the house a day like this."

"Aw no! You won't neither! The Secretary don't receive in the open air even in summer," drawled the man, and she noticed that he and the driver straightened up and stepped closer to her, one on either side. She gave one wild glance toward the open space. There was simply no chance at all to run away even if she succeeded in eluding them at the start by a quick, unexpected dash. They were alert athletic men, and no telling how many more were hidden in the house.

"Oh, very well, of course, if it's a matter of etiquette!" said Shirley pleasantly, determined to keep up the farce as long as possible.

A cold, dark air met the girl as she stepped within the creaking door and looked about her. At her left was an old-fashioned kitchen, dusty and cobwebby. A long, narrow hall led to the front of the house and her guide pointed her toward a room on the right. There was something hollow and eerie in the sound of their footsteps on the old oaken floor. The room into which she was ushered was musty and dusty as the rest. The floor was covered with an ancient ingrain carpet. The table was covered with a magenta felt cover stamped with a vine of black leaves and riddled with moth holes. The walls were hung with old prints and steel engravings suspended by woollen cords and tassels. The furniture was dilapidated. Everything was covered with dust, but there were finger marks in the dust here and there that showed the place had been recently visited. Through an open doorway an old square piano was visible in what must be the parlor. The place seemed to Shirley fairly teeming with memories of some family now departed. She leaped to the quick conclusion that the house had been long deserted and had only recently been entered and used as a rendezvous for illegal conferences. It occurred to her that there might be an opportunity for her to hide her precious papers somewhere safely if it came to it that she must be searched. How about that piano? Could she slip some of them between the keys? But it was hardly likely that there would be opportunity for anything like that.

She felt strangely calm as she looked about upon her prison.

"H'm! He ain't come yet!" remarked her guide as he glanced into the front room. "Well, you can set down. He won't be long now. Joe, you jest look about a bit and see if you can find the Secretary, and tell him the young lady is here."

The man flung himself full length on the carpet-covered couch and looked at her with satisfaction.

"What train was that you said you must make? I'm afraid now you might be going to be just a trifle late if he don't get a hustle on, but you can't hurry a great man like that you know."

"Oh, it's no matter!" said Shirley coolly, looking around her with the utmost innocence. "What a quaint old house! Has it been in the family a long time?"

The man looked at her amusedly.

"You're a cute one!" he remarked affably. "I believe you're a pretty good sport! You know perfectly well you're in my power and can't do a turn to help yourself, yet you sail around here as calm as a queen! You're some looker, too! Blamed if I'm not enjoying myself. I wouldn't mind a kiss or two from those pretty lips——"

But Shirley had melted through the doorway into the other room and her voice floated back with charming indifference as if she had not heard, though she was ready to scream with loathing and fear of the man:

"Why, isn't this a delightful old piano? The keys are actually mother-of-pearl. Isn't it odd? Would Mr. Baker mind if I played on it?"

And before her astonished captor could get himself to the doorway she had sat down on the rickety old hair-cloth stool and swept the keys lightly. The old chords trembled and shivered as if awaking from a tomb, and uttered forth a quavering, sweet sound like ancient memories.

The man was too much astonished to stop her, amused too, perhaps, and interested. Her white fingers over the dusty pearls in the growing dusk had a strange charm for the hardened reprobate, like the wonder of a flower dropped into the foulness of a prison. Before he could recover, he was startled again by her voice soaring out in the empty echoing house:

> Rock of ages, cleft for me,
> Let me hide myself in Thee;
> Let the water and the blood
> From Thy riven side which flowed,
> Be of sin the double cure,
> Save me Lord and make me pure!

Perhaps those dim, gloomy walls had echoed before to the grand old tune, but never could it have been sung in dire strait, or with more earnest cry from a soul in distress. She had chosen the first words that seemed to fit the chords she had struck, but every syllable was a prayer to the God in whom she trusted. It may be the man felt the power of her appeal as he stood rooted in the doorway and listened while she sang through all the verses she could remember. But the last trembling note was broken harshly by Joe's voice at the kitchen door in sharp, rasping orders:

"Hist, there! Can that noise! Do you want to raise hell here? Wake up, Sam! Get onto your job. Hennie's comin'."

"That's all right, Joe! Dry up! This is good Sunday School dope! This won't rouse no suspicions. Go to the devil and mind your business! I know what I'm about!"

Shirley was almost ready to cry, but she drew a deep breath and started on another song:

> Jesus, Lover of my soul,
> Let me to Thy bosom fly,
> While the nearer waters roll,
> While the tempest still is high!
> Hide me, oh, my Saviour hide,
> Till the storm of life is past.

On through the time-worn words she sang, while the sin-hardened man stood silently and listened. His eyes had gradually lost their leer and grown soft and tender, as if some childhood memories of home and mother and a time when he was innocent and good were looking out his eyes, reminding him of what he once intended to be before he ate the apple of wisdom and became as the gods and devils. Shirley gradually became aware that she was holding her strange audience; and a power beyond herself steadied her voice, and kept her fingers from trembling on the old pearl keys, as she wandered on from song to song; perhaps happening on the very ones,—who knows?—that this man, standing in the dying twilight of the old gloomy house, had sung beside his mother's hearth or in church during his childhood? Certain it is that he stood there silent and listened for at least half an hour without an interruption, while the light in the big room grew dimmer and dimmer and all about the house seemed still as death in the intervals between her voice. She was just beginning:

> Abide with me,
> Fast falls the eventide,
> The darkness deepens,
> Lord, with me abide!

When the man put his hand in his pocket and brought out a candle. Scratching a match on his trousers, he lit the candle and set it carefully on the piano, where its light fell flickering, wavering over her worn young face; and who shall say that she was not a messenger from another world to this man who had long trodden the downward path?

They were interrupted, however, before this song was finished by a newcomer who entered like a shadow and stood at the end of the piano looking wonderingly from Shirley to the man, when she glanced up. She stopped, startled, for although he wore no brass buttons nor blue clothes she was quite sure those were the same gray eyes that had looked at her from the recess of the window in the Government office that afternoon, perhaps the same boy who had come after her car and sent her off on this long way into the wilderness.

The man Sam straightened up suddenly and looked about him half-ashamed with an apologetic grin:

"Oh, you've come, have you, Hennie? Well, you been a long time about it! But now I guess we'll get to work. Where's Joe? Out on the watch? All right then, Miss, if you've no objection, we'll just take a little vacation on the psalm singin' and turn our attention to worldly things. I calculate you're sharp enough to know what we brought you put here for? I acknowledge you can sing real well, and you sorta got my goat for a while there with all that mourning bench tra-la, for you certainly have got that holy dope down fine; but now the time's come for business, and you needn't to think that because I can enjoy a little sentiment now and then in a leisure moment that you can put anything over on me, for it can't be did! I mean business and I've got you in my power! We're ten miles from any settlement, and no neighbors anywhere's about. Everybody moved away. So it won't do any good to work any funny business on us. You can't get away. We're all armed, and no one knows where you are! If you behave yourself and do as you're told there won't be any trouble. We'll just transact our business and then we'll have a bit of supper, and mebbe a few more tunes—got any rag-time in your repitwar?—and then sometime after midnight, when the moon's good and dark, we'll get you back to civilization where you won't have no trouble in gettin' home. But if you act up and get funny, why you know what to expect. There was a young girl murdered once in this house and buried in the cellar and ever since folks say it's hanted and they won't come near it. That's the kind of a place we're in! So, now are you ready?"

Shirley sat cold and still. It seemed as if her life blood had suddenly congealed in her veins and for a second she felt as if her senses were going to desert her. Then the echo of her own song: "Hide me, oh, my Saviour hide!" seemed to cry out from her soul silently and she rallied once more and gained her self-control.

"Well, Miss," went on the man impressively, "I see you're ready for the question, and you've got your nerve with you, too, I'll hand you that! But I warn you it won't do no good! We brung you out here to get a hold of that note-book you wrote in this morning, and we're goin' to have it. We know that Mr. Barnard left it in your care. Hennie here heard him say for you to keep it. So it won't be of any use for you to lie about it."

"Of course!" said Shirley, standing up and reaching over for her hand-bag, which she had laid on the piano beside her while she played. "I understand perfectly. But I'd like to ask you a question, Mr.——?"

"Smith, or Jones, whichever you like to call it. Spit it out!"

"I suppose you are paid to bring me out here, Mr. Smith, and get my property away from me?" she said gravely.

"Well, yes, we don't calculate to do it just for sweet charity."

"And *I* am paid to look after my note-book, you see. It's a trust that has been given me! I just *have* to look after it. It's out of the question for me to desert it!" Shirley spoke coolly and held her little bag close in the firm grasp of her two hands. The man stared at her and laughed. The boy Hennie fairly gaped in his astonishment. "A girl with all that nerve!"

"Of course, I understand perfectly that you can murder me and bury me down in the cellar beside that other girl that was murdered, and perhaps no one will find it out for a while, and you can go on having a good time on the money you will get for it. But the day will come when you will have to answer for it! You know I didn't come here alone to-day——!"

Both men looked startled and glanced uneasily into the shadows, as if there might be someone lurking there.

"*God* came with me and *He* knows! He'll *make you remember* some day!"

The boy laughed out a nervous ha! ha! of relief, but the man seemed held, fascinated by her look and words. There was silence for a second while the girl held off the ruffian in the man by sheer force of her strong personality. Then the boy laughed again, with a sneer in the end of it, and the spell was broken. The leer came into the eyes of the man again. The sneer of the boy had brought him to himself,—to the self he had come to be.

"Nix on the sob-stuff, girlie!" he said gruffly. "It won't go down with me! We're here for business and we've been delayed too long already. Come now, will you hand out that note-book or will we have to search you?" He took one stride across to where she stood and wrenched the hand-bag from her grasp before she was aware of his intention. She had not meant to give it up without a struggle, much as she loathed the thought of one. She must make the matter last as long as possible, if perchance God was sending help to her, and must contest every inch of the way as far as lay in her power. Oh, had anyone picked up her cards? Had the book with its message reached any friendly eye?

Frail and white and stern she stood with folded arms while they turned out the contents of the little bag and scattered it over the piano, searching with clumsy fingers among her dainty things.

The note-book she had rolled within her handkerchiefs and made it hard to find. She feared lest her ruse would be discovered when they looked it over. The boy was the one who clutched for the little book, recognizing it as the one he had seen in the office that morning. The man hung over his shoulder and peered in the candlelight, watching the boy anxiously. It meant a good deal of money if they put this thing through.

"Here it is!" said the boy, fluttering through the leaves and carefully scrutinizing the short-hand characters. "Yes, that's the dope!"

He ran his eye down the pages, caught a word here and there, technicalities of manufacture, the very items, of course, that he wanted, if this had been the specifications for the Government order. Shirley remembered with relief that none of the details were identical, however, with the notes she carried in her shoes. The book-notes were in fact descriptive of an entirely different article from that demanded by the Government. The question was, would these people be wise enough to discover that fact before she was out of their power or not?

Furtively she studied the boy. There was something keen and cunning about his youthful face. He was thick-set, with blond hair and blue eyes. He might be of German origin, though there was not a sign of accent about his speech. He had the bull-dog chin, retreating forehead and eagle nose of the Kaiser in embryo. Shirley saw all this as she studied him furtively. That he was an expert in short-hand was proved by the ease with which he read some of her obscure sentences, translating rapidly here and there as he examined the book. Was he well enough informed about the Government contract to realize that these were not the notes she had taken in the office that morning? And should he fail to recognize it, was there perhaps some one higher in authority to whom they would be shown before she was released? She shivered and set her weary toes tight with determination over the little crinkling papers in her shoes. Somehow she would protect those notes from being taken, even if she had to swallow them. There surely would be a way to hide them if the need came.

Suddenly the tense strain under which she was holding herself was broken by the man. He looked up with a grin, rubbing his hands with evident self-gratulation and relief:

"That's all right, Girlie! That's the dope we want. Now we won't trouble you any longer. We'll have supper. Hennie, you go get some of that wood out in the shed and we'll have a fire on the hearth and make some coffee!"

But Shirley, standing white and tense in the dim shadow of the room, suddenly felt the place whirling about her, and the candle dancing afar off. Her knees gave way beneath her and she dropped back to the piano stool weakly, and covered her face with her hands, pressing hard on her eyeballs; trying to keep her senses and stop this black dizziness that threatened to submerge her consciousness. She must not faint—if this was fainting. She must keep her senses and guard her precious shoes. If one of those should fall off while she was unconscious all would be undone.

CHAPTER XXV

The man looked up from the paper he was twisting for a fire and saw Shirley's attitude of despair.

"Say, kid," he said, with a kind of gruff tenderness, "you don't need to take it that a-way. I know it's tough luck to lose out when you been so nervy and all, but you knew we had it over you from the start. You hadn't a show. And say! Girlie! I tell you what! I'll make Hennie sit down right now and copy 'em off for you, and you can put 'em in your book again when you get back and nobody be the wiser. We'll just take out the leaves. We gotta keep the original o' course, but that won't make any beans for you. It won't take you no time to write 'em over again if he gives you a copy."

Somehow it penetrated through Shirley's tired consciousness that the man was trying to be kind to her. He was pitying her and offering her a way out of her supposed dilemma, offering to assist her in some of his own kind of deception. The girl was touched even through all her other crowding emotions and weariness. She lifted up her head with a faint little smile.

"Thank you," she said, wearily, "but that wouldn't do me any good."

"Why not?" asked the man sharply. "Your boss would never know it got out through you."

"But *I* should know I had failed!" she said sadly. "If you had my notes I should know that I had failed in my trust."

"It wouldn't be your fault. You couldn't have helped it!"

"Oh, yes, I could, and I ought. I shouldn't have let the driver turn around. I should have got out of that car and waited at the station as Mr. Barnard told me to do till he came. I had been warned and I ought to have been on my guard. So you see it *was* my fault."

She drooped her head forward and rested her chin dejectedly on the palm of her hand, her elbow on her knee. The man stood looking at her for a second in half-indignant astonishment.

"By golly!" he said at last. "You certainly are some nut! Well, anyhow, buck up, and let's have some tea. Sorry I can't see my way clear to help you out any further, being as we're sort of partners in this job and you certainly have got some nerve for a girl, but you know how it is. I guess I can't do no more'n I said. I got my honor to think about, too. See? Hennie! Get a move on you. We ain't waitin' all night fer eats. Bring in them things from the cupboard and let's get to work."

Shirley declined to come to the table when at last the repast was ready. She said she was not hungry. In fact, the smell or the crackers and cheese and pickles and dried beef sickened her. She felt too hysterical to try to eat, and besides she had a lingering feeling that she must keep near that piano. If anything happened she had a vague idea that she might somehow hide the precious notes within the big old instrument.

The man frowned when she declined to come to supper, but a moment later stumbled awkwardly across the room with a slopping cup of coffee and set it down beside her.

"Buck up, girlie!" he growled. "Drink that and you'll feel better."

Shirley thanked him and tried to drink a few mouthfuls. Then the thought occurred to her that it might be drugged, and she swallowed no more. But she tried to look a bit brighter. If she must pass this strange evening in the company of these rough men, it would not help matters for her to give way to despair. So after toying with the teaspoon a moment, she put the cup down and began to play soft airs on the old piano again while the men ate and took a stealthy taste now and then from a black bottle. She watched them furtively as she played, marvelling at their softened expressions, remembering the old line:

"Music hath charms to soothe the savage breast," and wondering if perhaps there were not really something in it. If she had not been in such a terrifying situation she would really have enjoyed the character study that this view of those two faces afforded her, as she sat in the shadow playing softly while they ate with the flaring candle between them.

"I like music with my meals!" suddenly chanted out the boy in an interval. But the man growled in a low tone:

"Shut up! Ain't you got no manners?"

Shirley prolonged that meal as much as music could do it, for she had no relish for a more intimate tête-a-tête with either of her companions. When she saw them grow restless she began to sing again, light little airs this time with catchy words; or old tender melodies of home and mother and childhood. They were songs she had sung that last night in the dear old barn when Sidney Graham and Elizabeth were with them, and unconsciously her voice took on the wail of her heart for all that dear past so far away from her now.

Suddenly, as the last tender note of a song died away Joe stumbled breathlessly into the room. The boy Hennie slithered out of the room like a serpent at his first word.

"Beat it!" he cried in a hoarse whisper. "Get a move on! All hell's out after us! I bet they heard her singin'! Take her an' beat it! I'll douse the fire an' out the candle."

He seized a full bucket of water and dashed it over the dying fire. Shirley felt the other man grasp her arm in a fierce grip. Then Joe snuffed out the candle with his broad thumb and finger and all was pitch dark. She felt herself dragged across the floor regardless of furniture in the way, stumbling, choking with fear, her one thought that whatever happened she must not let her slippers get knocked off; holding her feet in a tense strain with every muscle extended to keep the shoes fastened on like a vise. She was haunted with a wild thought of how she might have slipped under the piano and eluded her captor if only the light had gone out one second sooner before he reached her side. But it was too late to think of that now, and she was being dragged along breathlessly, out the front door, perhaps, and down a walk; no, it was amongst trees, for she almost ran into one. The man swore at her, grasped her arm till he hurt her and she cried out.

"You shut up or I'll shoot you!" he said with an oath. He had lost all his suavity and there was desperation in his voice. He kept turning his head to look back and urging her on.

She tripped on a root and stumbled to her knees, bruising them painfully, but her only thought was one of joy that her shoes had not come off.

The man swore a fearful oath under his breath, then snatched her up and began to run with her in his arms. It was then she heard Graham's voice calling:

"Shirley! Where are you? I'm coming!"

She thought she was swooning or dreaming and that it was not really he, for how could he possibly be here? But she cried out with a voice as clear as a bell: "I'm here, Sidney, come quick!" In his efforts to hush her voice, the man stumbled and fell with her in his arms. There came other voices and forms through the night. She was gathered up in strong, kind arms and held. The last thought she had before she sank into unconsciousness was that God had not forgotten. He had been remembering all the time and sent His help before it was too late; just as she had known all along He must do, because He had promised to care for His own, and she was one of His little ones.

When she came to herself again she was lying in Sidney Graham's arms with her head against his shoulder feeling oh, so comfortable and tired. There were two automobiles with powerful headlights standing between the trees, and a lot of policemen in the shadowy background. Her captor stood sullen against a tree with his hands and feet shackled. Joe stood between two policemen with a rope bound about his body spirally, and the boy Hennie, also bound, beside his fallen bicycle, turned his ferret eyes from side to side as if he hoped even yet to escape. Two other men with hawk-like faces that she had not seen before were there also, manacled, and with eyes of smouldering fires. Climbing excitedly out of one of the big cars came Mr. Barnard, his usually immaculate pink face smutty and weary; his sparse white hair rumpled giddily, and a worried pucker on his kind, prim face.

"Oh, my dear Miss Hollister! How unfortunate!" he exclaimed. "I do hope you haven't suffered too much inconvenience!"

Shirley smiled up at him from her shoulder of refuge as from a dream. It was all so amusing and impossible after what she had been through. It couldn't be real.

"I assure you I am very much distressed on your account," went on Mr. Barnard, politely and hurriedly, "and I hate to mention it at such a time, but could you tell me whether the notes are safe? Did those horrid men get anything away from you?"

A sudden flicker of triumph passed over the faces of the fettered man and the boy, like a ripple over still water and died away into unintelligence.

But Shirley's voice rippled forth in a glad, clear laugh, as she answered joyously:

"Yes, Mr. Barnard, they got my note-book, but not the notes! They thought the Tilman-Brooks notes were what they were after, but the real notes are in my shoes. Won't you please get them out, for I'm afraid I can't hold them on any longer, my feet ache so!"

It is a pity that Shirley was not in a position to see the look of astonishment, followed by a twinkle of actual appreciation that came over the face of the shackled man beside the tree as he listened. One could almost fancy he was saying to himself: "The nervy little nut! She put one over on me after all!"

It was also a pity that Shirley could not have got the full view of the altogether precise and conventional Mr. Barnard kneeling before her on the ground, removing carefully, with deep embarrassment and concern, first one, then the other, of her little black pumps, extracting the precious notes, counting over the pages and putting them ecstatically into his pocket. No one of that group but Shirley could fully appreciate the ludicrous picture he made.

"You are entirely sure that no one but yourself has seen these notes?" he asked anxiously as if he hardly dared to believe the blessed truth.

"Entirely sure, Mr. Barnard!" said Shirley happily, "and now if you wouldn't mind putting on my shoes again I can relieve Mr. Graham of the necessity of carrying me any further."

"Oh, surely, surely!" said Mr. Barnard, quite fussed and getting down laboriously again, his white forelock all tossed, and his forehead perplexed over the unusual task. How did women get into such a little trinket of a shoe, anyway?

"I assure you, Miss Hollister, our firm appreciates what you have done! We shall not forget it. You will see, we shall not forget it!" he puffed as he rose with beads of perspiration on his brow. "You have done a great thing for Barnard and Clegg to-day!"

"She's done more than that!" said a burly policeman significantly glancing around the group of sullen prisoners, as Graham put her upon her feet beside him. "She's rounded up the whole gang for us, and that's more than anybody else has been able to do yet! She oughtta get a medal of some kind fer that!"

Then, with a dare-devil lift of his head and a gleam of something like fun in his sullen eyes, the manacled man by the tree spoke out, looking straight at Shirley, real admiration in his voice:

"I say, pard! I guess you're the winner! I'll hand you what's comin' to you if I do lose. You certainly had your nerve!"

Shirley looked at him with a kind of compassion in her eyes.

"I'm sorry you have to be—there," she finished. "You were—as fine as you could be to me under the circumstances, I suppose! I thank you for that."

The man met her gaze for an instant, a flippant reply upon his lips, but checked it and dropping his eyes, was silent. The whole little company under the trees were hushed into silence before the miracle of a girl's pure spirit, leaving its impress on a blackened soul.

Then, quietly, Graham led her away to his car with Barnard and the detectives following. The prisoners were loaded into the other cars, and hurried on the way to judgment.

CHAPTER XXVI

The ride back to the city was like a dream to Shirley afterward. To see the staid Mr. Barnard so excited, babbling away about her bravery and exulting like a child over the recovery of the precious notes, was wonder enough. But to feel the quiet protection and tender interest of Sidney Graham filled her with ecstasy. Of course it was only kindly interest and friendly anxiety, and by to-morrow she would have put it into order with all his other kindlinesses, but to-night, weary and excited as she was, with the sense of horror over her recent experience still upon her, it was sweet to feel his attention, and to let his voice thrill through her tired heart, without stopping to analyze it and be sure she was not too glad over it. What if he would be merely a friend to-morrow again! To-night he was her rescuer, and she would rest back upon that and be happy.

"I feel that I was much to blame for leaving you alone to go to the station with a bait like these notes in your possession," said Mr. Barnard humbly. "Though of course I did not dream that there was any such possibility as your being in danger."

"It is just as well not to run any risks in these days when the country is so unsettled," said the detective dryly.

"Especially where a lady is concerned!" remarked Graham significantly.

"I suppose I should have taken Miss Hollister with me and left her in the cab while I transacted my business at the War Department!" said Barnard with self-reproach in his tones.

"They would have only done the same thing in front of the War Department," said the detective convincingly. "They had it all planned to get those notes somehow. You only made it a trifle easier for them by letting the lady go alone. If they hadn't succeeded here, they would have followed you to your home and got into your office or your safe. They are determined, desperate men. We've been watching them for some time, letting them work till we could find out who was behind them. To-night we caught the whole bunch red-handed, thanks to the lady's cleverness. But you had better not risk her alone again when there's anything like this on hand. She might not come out so easy next time!"

Graham muttered a fervent applause in a low tone to this advice, tucking the lap robes closer about the girl. Barnard gave little shudders of apology as he humbly shouldered the blame:

"Oh, no, of course not! I certainly am so sorry!" But Shirley suddenly roused herself to explain:

"Indeed, you mustn't any of you blame Mr. Barnard. He did the perfectly right and natural thing. He always trusts me to look after my notes, even in the most important cases; and I heard the warning as much as he did. It was my business to be on the lookout! I'm old enough and have read enough in the papers about spies and ruffians. I ought to have known there was something wrong when that boy ordered me back and said Mr. Barnard had sent me word. I ought to have known Mr. Barnard would never do that. I did know just as soon as I stopped to think. The trouble was I was giving half my attention to looking at the strange sights out of the window and thinking what I would tell the folks at home about Washington, or I would not have got into such a position. I insist that you shall not blame yourself, Mr. Barnard. It is a secretary's business to be on her job and not be out having a good time when she is on a business trip. I hadn't got beyond the city limits before I knew exactly what I ought to have done. I should have asked that boy more questions, and I should have got right out of that car and told him to tell you I would wait in the station till you came for me. It troubled me from the start that you had sent for me that way. It wasn't like you."

Then they turned their questions upon her, and she had to tell the whole story of her capture, Graham and Barnard exclaiming indignantly as she went on, the detective sitting grim and serious, nodding his approval now and then. Graham's attitude toward her grew more tender and protective. Once or twice as she told of her situation in the old house, or spoke of how the man dragged her along in the dark, he set his teeth and drew his breath hard, saying in an undertone: "The villain!" And there was that in the way that he looked at her that made Shirley hasten through the story, because of the wild, joyous clamor of her heart.

As soon as the city limits were reached, Graham stopped the car to telephone. It was after eleven o'clock, and there was little chance that George would have stayed at the phone so long, but he would leave a message for the early morning at least. George, however, had stuck to his post.

"Sure! I'm here yet! What'd ya think? Couldn't sleep, could I, with *my sister* off alone with a fella somewhere *being kidnapped*? What'd ya say? Found her? She's all right? Oh, gee! That's good! I told Carol you would! I told her not to worry! What'd ya say? Oh, Shirley's going to talk? Oh, hello, Shirley! How's Washington? Some speed, eh? Say, when ya coming home? To-morrow? That's good. No, mother doesn't know a thing. She thinks I went to bed early 'cause I planned to go fishing at sunrise. She went to bed herself early. Say, Mister Graham's a prince, isn't he? Well, I guess I'll go to bed now. I might make the fishing in the morning yet, if I don't sleep too late. I sure am glad you're all right! Well, so long, Shirley!"

Shirley turned from the phone with tears in her eyes. It wasn't what George said that made her smile tenderly through them, but the gruff tenderness in his boy tones that touched her so. She hadn't realized before what she meant to him.

They drove straight to the station, got something to eat, and took the midnight train back to their home city. Graham had protested that Shirley should go to a hotel and get a good rest before attempting the journey, but she laughingly told him she could rest anywhere, and would sleep like a top in the train. When Graham found that it was possible to secure berths in the sleeper for them all, and that they would not have to get out until seven in the morning he withdrew his protests; and his further activities took the form of supplementing her supper with fruit and bonbons. His lingering hand-clasp as he bade her good-night told her how glad he was that she was safe; as if his eyes had not told her the same story every time there had been light enough for them to be seen!

Locked at last into her safe little stateroom, with a soft bed to lie on and no bothersome notes to be guarded, one would have thought she might have slept, but her brain kept time to the wheels, and her heart with her brain. She was going over and over the scenes of the eventful day, and living through each experience again, until she came to the moment when she looked up to find herself in Sidney Graham's arms, with her face against his shoulder. Her face glowed in the dark at the remembrance, and her heart thrilled wildly sweet with the memory of his look and tone, and all his carefulness for her. How wonderful that *he* should have come so many miles to find her! That he should have been the one to find her first, with all those other men on the hunt. He had forged ahead and picked her up before any of the others had reached her. He had not been afraid to rush up to an armed villain and snatch her from her perilous position! He was a man among men! Never mind if he wasn't her own personal property! Never mind if there were others in his own world who might claim him later, he was hers for to-night! She would never forget it!

She slept at last, profoundly, with a smile upon her lips No dream of villains nor wild automobile rides came to trouble her thoughts. And when she woke in the home station with familiar sounds outside, and realized that a new day was before her, her heart was flooded with a happiness that her common sense found it hard to justify. She tried to steady herself while she made her toilet, but the face that was reflected rosily from the mirror in her little dressing room would smile contagiously back at her.

"Well, then, have it your own way for just one more day!" she said aloud to her face in the glass. "But to-morrow you must get back to common sense again!" Then she turned, fresh as a rose, and went out to meet her fellow travellers.

She went to breakfast with Sidney Graham, a wonderful breakfast in a wonderful place with fountains and palms and quiet, perfect service. Mr. Barnard had excused himself and hurried away to his home, promising to meet Shirley at the office at half-past nine. And so these two sat at a little round table by themselves and had sweet converse over their coffee. Shirley utterly forgot for the time that she was only a poor little stenographer working for her bread and living in a barn. Sidney Graham's eyes were upon her, in deep and unveiled admiration, his spirit speaking to hers through the quiet little commonplaces to which he must confine himself in this public place. It was not till the meal was over and he was settling his bill that Shirley suddenly came to herself and the color flooded her sweet face. What was she better than any other poor fool of a girl who let a rich man amuse himself for a few hours in her company and then let him carry her heart away with him to toss with his collection? She drew her dignity about her and tried to be distant as they went out to the street, but he simply did not recognize it at all. He just kept his tender, deferential manner, and smiled down at her with that wonderful, exalted look that made her dignity seem cheap; so there was nothing to do but look up as a flower would to the sun and be true to the best that was in her heart.

She was surprised to find his own car at the door when they came out on the street. He must have phoned for it before they left the station. He was so kind and thoughtful. It was so wonderful to her to be cared for in this way. "Just as if I were a rich girl in his own social set," she thought to herself.

He gave his chauffeur the orders and sat beside her in the back seat, continuing his role of admirer and protector.

"It certainly is great to think you're here beside me," he said in a low tone as they threaded their way in and out of the crowded thoroughfare toward the office. "I didn't have a very pleasant afternoon and evening yesterday, I can tell you! I don't think we'll let you go off on any more such errands. You're too precious to risk in peril like that, you know!"

Shirley's cheeks were beautiful to behold as she tried to lift her eyes easily to his glance and take his words as if they had been a mere commonplace. But there was something deep down in the tone of his voice, and something intent and personal in his glance that made her drop her eyes swiftly and covered her with a sweet confusion.

They were at the office almost immediately and Graham was helping her out.

"Now, when will you be through here?" he asked, glancing at his watch. "What train were you planning to take down to the shore? I suppose you'll want to get back as soon as possible?"

"Yes," said Shirley, doubtfully, "I do. But I don't know whether I oughtn't to run out home first and get mother's big old shawl, and two or three other little things we ought to have brought along."

"No," said Graham, quickly, with a flash of anxiety in his face. "I wouldn't if I were you. They'll be anxious to see you, and if it's necessary you can run up again sometime. I think you'll find there are lots of shawls down at the cottage. I'm anxious to have you safely landed with your family once more. I promised Carol you'd be down the first train after you got your work done. How long is it going to take you to fix Mr. Barnard up so he can run things without you?"

"Oh, not more than two hours I should think, unless He wants something more than I know."

"Well, two hours. It is half-past nine now. We'll say two hours and a half. That ought to give you time. I think there's a train about then. I'll phone to the station and find out and let you know the exact time. The car will be here waiting for you."

"Oh, Mr. Graham, that's not a bit necessary! You have taken trouble enough for me already!" protested Shirley.

"No trouble at all!" declared Graham. "My chauffeur hasn't a thing to do but hang around with the car this morning and you might as well ride as walk. I'll phone you in plenty of time."

He lifted his hat and gave her a last look that kept the glow in her cheeks. She turned and went with swift steps in to her elevator.

Sidney Graham dropped his chauffeur at the station to enquire about trains and get tickets, with orders to report at his office within an hour, and himself took the wheel. Quickly working his way out of the city's traffic he put on all possible speed toward Glenside. He must get a glimpse of things and see that all was going well before he went to the office. What would Shirley have said if she had carried out her plan of coming out for her mother's shawl? He must put a stop to that at all costs. She simply must not see the old barn till the work was done, or the whole thing would be spoiled. Strange it had not occurred to him that she might want to come back after something! Well, he would just have to be on the continual lookout. For one thing he would stop at a store on the way back and purchase a couple of big steamer rugs and a long warm cloak. He could smuggle them into the cottage somehow and have the servants bring them out for common use as if they belonged to the house.

He was as eager as a child over every little thing that had been started during his absence, and walked about with the boss carpenter, settling two or three questions that had come up the day before. In ten minutes he was back in his car, whirling toward the city again, planning how he could best get those rugs and cloaks into the hands of the housekeeper at the shore without anybody suspecting that they were new. Then it occurred to him to take them down to Elizabeth and let her engineer the matter. There must be two cloaks, one for Shirley, for he wanted to take her out in the car sometimes and her little scrap of a coat was entirely too thin even for summer breezes at the shore.

Shirley met with a great ovation when she entered the office. It was evident that her fame had gone before her. Mr. Barnard was already there, smiling benevolently, and Mr. Clegg frowning approvingly over his spectacles at her, The other office clerks came to shake hands or called congratulations, till Shirley was quite overwhelmed at her reception. Clegg and Barnard both followed her into the inner office and continued to congratulate her on the bravery she had shown and to express their appreciation of her loyalty and courage in behalf of the firm. Mr. Barnard handed her a check for a hundred dollars as a slight token of their appreciation of her work, telling her that beginning with the first of the month her salary was to be raised.

When at last she sat down to her typewriter and began to click out the wonderful notes that had made so much trouble, and put them in shape for practical use, her head was in a whirl and her heart was beating with a childish ecstasy. She felt as if she were living a real fairy tale, and would not ever be able to get back to common every-day life again.

At half-past eleven Graham called her up to tell her there was a train a little after twelve if she could be ready, and the car would be waiting for her in fifteen minutes.

When she finally tore herself away from the smiles and effusive thanks of Barnard and Clegg and took the elevator down to the street she found Sidney Graham himself awaiting her eagerly. This was a delightful surprise, for he had not said anything about coming himself or mentioned when he would be coming back to the shore, so she had been feeling that It might be some time before she would see him again.

He had just slammed the door of the car and taken his seat beside her when a large gray limousine slowed down beside them and a radiant, well-groomed, much-tailored young woman leaned out of the car, smiling at Graham, and passing over Shirley with one of those unseeing stares wherewith some girls know so well how to erase other girls.

"Oh, Sidney! I'm so glad I met you!" she cried. "Mother has been phoning everywhere to find you. We are out at our country place for a couple of weeks, and she wants to ask you to come over this afternoon for a little tennis tournament we are having, with a dance on the lawn afterward."

"That's very kind of you, Harriet," said Graham pleasantly, "but I can't possibly be there. I have an engagement out of town for this afternoon and evening. Give my regards to your mother, please, and thank her for the invitation. I know you'll have a lovely time, you always do at your house."

"Oh, that's too bad, Sidney!" pouted the girl. "Why will you be so busy! and in the summer-time, too! You ought to take a vacation! Well, if you can't come to-night, you'll run down over the week-end, won't you? We are having the Foresters and the Harveys. You like them, and we simply can't do without you."

"Sorry," said Graham, smilingly, "but I've got all my week-ends filled up just now. Harriet, let me introduce you to Miss Hollister. Miss Hale, Miss Hollister!"

Then did Harriet Hale have to take over her unseeing stare and acknowledge the introduction; somewhat stiffly, it must be acknowledged, for Harriet Hale did not enjoy having her invitations declined, and she could not quite place this girl with the lovely face and the half-shabby garments, that yet had somehow an air of having been made by a French artist.

"I'm sorry, Harriet, but we'll have to hurry away. We're going to catch a train at twelve-fifteen. Hope you have a beautiful time this afternoon. Remember me to Tom Harvey and the Foresters. Sorry to disappoint you, Harriet, but you see I've got my time just full up at present. Hope to see you soon again."

They were off, Shirley with the impression of Harriet Hale's smile of vinegar and roses; the roses for Graham, the vinegar for her. Shirley's heart was beating wildly underneath her quiet demeanor. She had at last met the wonderful Harriet Hale, and Graham had not been ashamed to introduce her! There had been protection and enthronement in his tone as he spoke her name! It had not been possible for Miss Hale to patronize her after that. Shirley was still in a daze of happiness. She did not think ahead. She had all she could do to register new occurrences and emotions, and realize that her joy was not merely momentary. It had not occurred to her to wonder where Graham was going out of town. It was enough that he was here now.

When they reached the station Graham took two large packages out of the car, and gave some directions to the chauffeur.

"Sorry we couldn't have gone down in the car again," he said as they walked into the station, "but it needs some repairs and I don't want to take as long a run as that until it has been thoroughly overhauled."

Then he was going down too! He had declined Harriet Hale's invitation to go back to the cottage with her! Shirley's breath came in little happy gasps as she walked beside her companion down the platform to the train.

She found herself presently being seated in a big green velvet chair in the parlor car while the porter stowed away the two big packages in the rack overhead.

CHAPTER XXVII

There was only one other passenger in the car, an old man nodding behind a newspaper, with his chair facing in the other direction. Graham took a swift survey of him and turned happily back with a smile to Shirley:

"At last I have you to myself!" he said with a sigh of satisfaction that made Shirley's cheeks bloom out rosily again.

He whirled her chair and his quite away from the vision of the old man, so that they were at the nearest possible angle to each other, and facing the windows. Then he sat down and leaned toward her.

"Shirley," he said in a tone of proprietorship that was tender and beautiful, "I've waited just as long as I'm going to wait to tell you something. I know it's lunch time, and I'm going to take you into the dining-car pretty soon and get you some lunch, but I must have a little chance to talk with you first, please."

Shirley's eyes gave glad permission and he hurried on.

"Shirley, I love you. I guess you've been seeing that for some time. I knew I ought to hide it till you knew me better, but I simply couldn't do it. I never saw a girl like you, and I knew the minute I looked at you that you were of finer clay than other girls, anyway. I knew that if I couldn't win you and marry you I would never love anybody else. But yesterday when I heard you were in peril away off down in Washington and I away up here helpless to save you, and not even having the right to organize a search for you, I nearly went wild! All the way down on the train I kept shutting my eyes and trying to pray the way you told your Sunday School boys how to pray. But all I could get out was, 'Oh, God, I love her! Save her! I love her!' Shirley, I know I'm not one-half worthy enough for you, but I love you with all my heart and I want you for my wife. Will you marry me, Shirley?"

When she had recovered a little from her wonder and astonishment, and realized that he had asked her to marry him, and was waiting for his answer, she lifted her wondering eyes to his face, and tried to speak as her conscience and reason bade her.

"But I'm not like the other girls you know," she said bravely. Then he broke in upon her fervently.

"No, you're not like any other girl I know in the whole wide world. Thank God for that! You are one among a thousand! No, you're one among the whole earthful of women! You're the *only* one I could ever love!"

"But listen, please; you haven't thought. I'm not a society girl. I don't belong in your circle. I couldn't grace your position the way your wife ought to do. Remember, we're nobodies. We're poor! We live in a *barn*!"

"What do you suppose I care about that?" he answered eagerly. "You may live in a barn all your days if you like, and I'll love you just the same. I'll come and live in the barn with you if you want me to. My position! My circle! What's that? You'll grace my home and my life as no other girl could do. You heart of my heart! You strong, sweet spirit! The only question I'm going to ask of you is, Can you love me? If you can, I know I can make you happy, for I love you better than my life. Answer, please. Do you love me?"

She lifted her eyes, and their spirits broke through their glances. If the old man at the other end of the car was looking they did not know it.

They came back to the cottage at the shore with a manner so blissful and so unmistakable that even the children noticed. Elizabeth whispered to Carol at table: "My brother likes your sister a lot, doesn't he? I hope she likes him, too."

"I guess she does," responded Carol philosophically. "She oughtta. He's been awfully good to her, and to all of us."

"People don't like people just for that," said wise Elizabeth.

Harley, out on the veranda after dinner, drew near to Carol to confide.

"Say, kid, I guess he *has* got a case on her all right now. Gee! Wouldn't that be great? Think of all those cars!"

But Carol giggled.

"Good night! Harley! How could we ever have a wedding in a barn? And they're such particular people, too!"

"Aw, gee!" said Harley, disgusted. "You girls are always thinking of things like that! As if that mattered. You can get married in a chicken-run if you really have a case like that on each other! *You make me tired!*" and he stalked away in offended male dignity.

Meantime the unconscious subjects of this discussion had gone to Mrs. Hollister to confess, and the sea was forgotten by all three for that one evening at least, even though the moon was wide and bright and gave a golden pathway across the dark water. For a great burden had rolled from Mrs. Hollister's shoulders when she found her beloved eldest daughter was really loved by this young man, and he was not just amusing himself for a little while at her expense.

The days that followed were like one blissful fleeting dream to Shirley. She just could not get used to the fact that she was engaged to such a prince among men! It seemed as if she were dreaming, and that presently she would wake up and find herself in the office with a great pile of letters to write, and the perplexing problem before her of where they were going to live next winter. She had broached that subject once to Graham shyly, saying that she must begin to look around as soon as she got back to town, and he put her aside, asking her to leave that question till they all went back, as he had a plan he thought she might think well of, but he couldn't tell her about it just yet. He also began to urge her to write at once to Mr. Barnard and resign her position, but that she would not hear of.

"No," she said decidedly. "We couldn't live without my salary, and there are a lot of things to be thought out and planned before I can be married. Besides, we need to get to know each other and to grow into each other's lives a little bit. You haven't any idea even now how far I am from being fitted to be the wife of a man in your position. You may be sorry yet. If you are ever going to find it out, I want you to do it beforehand."

He looked adoringly into her eyes.

"I know perfectly now, dear heart!" he said, "and I'm not going to be satisfied to wait a long time for you to find out that you don't really care for me after all. If you've got to find that out, I believe I'd rather it would be after I have you close and fast and you'll *have* to like me anyway."

And then the wonder and thrill of it all would roll over her again and she would look into his eyes and be satisfied.

Still she continued quite decided that nothing could be done about prolonging her vacation, for she meant to go back to Barnard and Clegg's on the day set.

"You know I'm the man of the house," she said archly. "I can't quite see it at all myself—how I'm ever going to give up."

"But I thought I was going to be the man of the house," pleaded Sidney. "I'm sure I'm quite capable and eager to look out for the interests of my wife's family."

"But you see I'm not the kind of a girl that has been looking around for a man who will support my family."

"No, you surely are not!" said the young man, laughing. "If you had been, young lady, I expect you'd have been looking yet so far as I am concerned. It is because you are what you are that I love you. Now that's all right about being independent, but it's about time to fight this thing to a finish. I don't see why we all have to be made miserable just because there are a lot of unpleasant precedents and conventions and crochets in the world. Why may I not have the pleasure of helping to take care of your perfectly good family if I want to? It is one of the greatest pleasures to which I am looking forward, to try and make them just as happy as I can, so that you will be the happier. I've got plenty to do it with. God has been very good to me in that way, and why should you try to hinder me?"

And then the discussion would end in a bewildering look of worshipful admiration on Shirley's part and a joyous taking possession of her and carrying her off on some ride or walk or other on the part of Graham.

He did not care just now that she was slow to make plans. He was enjoying each day, each hour, to the full. He wanted to keep her from thinking about the future, and especially about the winter, till she got home, and so he humored her and led her to other topics.

One night, as they sat on the dark veranda alone, Graham said to George:

"If you were going to college, where would you want to prepare?"

He wondered what the boy would say, for the subject of college had never been mentioned with relation to George. He did not know whether the boy had ever thought of it. But the answer came promptly in a ringing voice:

"Central High! They've got the best football team in the city."

"Then you wouldn't want to go away to some preparatory school?"

"No, *sir*!" was the decided answer. "I believe in the public school every time! When I was a little kid I can remember my father taking me to walk and pointing out the Central High School, and telling me that some day I would go there to school. I used to always call that 'my school.' I used to think I'd get there yet, some day, but I guess that's out of the question."

"Well, George, if that's your choice you can get ready to enter as soon as you go back to the city."

"What?" George's feet came down from the veranda railing with a thud, and he sat upright in the darkness and stared wildly at his prospective brother-in-law. Then he slowly relaxed and his young face grew grim and stern.

"No chance!" he said laconically.

"Why not?"

"Because I've got my mother and the children to support. I can't waste time going to school. I've got to be a *man*."

Something sudden like a choke came in the young man's throat, and a great love for the brave boy who was so courageous in his self-denial.

"George, you're not a man yet, and you'll shoulder the burden twice as well when you're equipped with a college education. I mean you shall have it. Do you suppose I'm going to let my new brother slave away before his time? No, sir; you're going to get ready to make the best man that's in you. And as for your mother and the family, isn't she going to be my mother, and aren't they to be my family? We'll just shoulder the job together, George, till you're older—and then we'll see."

"But I couldn't take charity from anybody."

"Not even from a brother?"

"Not even from a brother."

"Well, suppose we put it in another way. Suppose you borrow the money from me to keep things going, and when you are ready to pay it back we'll talk about it then. Or, better still, suppose you agree to pass it on to some other brother when you are able."

They talked a long time in the dark, and Graham had quite a hard time breaking down the boy's reserve and independence, and getting a real brotherly confidence. But at last George yielded, saw the common sense and right of the thing, and laid an awkward hand in the man's, growling out:

"You're a pippin and no mistake, Mr. Graham. I can't ever thank you enough! I never thought anything like this would happen to me!"

"Don't try thanks, George. We're brothers now, you know. Just you do your best at school, and it's all I ask. Shirley and I are going to be wonderfully proud of you. But please don't call me Mr. Graham any more. Sid, or Sidney, or anything you like, but no more mistering."

He filing a brotherly arm across the boy's shoulders and together they went into the house.

Meantime the beautiful days went by in one long, golden dream of wonder. The children were having the time of their lives, and Elizabeth was never so happy. Shirley sat on the wide verandas and read the wealth of books and magazines which the house contained, or roamed the beach with the children and Star, or played in the waves with Doris, and wondered if it were really Shirley Hollister who was having all this good time.

CHAPTER XXVIII

The morning they all started back to the city was a memorable one. Graham had insisted that Shirley ask for a holiday until Tuesday morning so that she might go up with them in the car, and have the whole day to be at home and help her mother get settled. She had consented, and found to her surprise that Mr. Barnard was most kind about it. He had even added that he intended to raise her salary, and she might consider that hereafter she was to have ten dollars more per month for her services, which they valued very highly.

George had sent his resignation to the store and was not to go back at all. Graham had arranged that, for school began the day after his return and he would need to be free at once.

Elizabeth, to her great delight, was to go with the Hollisters and remain a few days until her parents returned. Mrs. Graham had written from the West making a proposition to Mrs. Hollister that Carol be allowed to go to school with Elizabeth the next winter, because Mrs. Graham felt it would be so good for Elizabeth to have a friend like that. Mrs. Hollister, however, answered that she felt it better for her little girl to remain with her mother a little longer; and that she did not feel it would be a good thing for her child, who would be likely to have a simple life before her with very few luxuries, to go to a fashionable finishing-school where the standards must all necessarily be so different from those of her own station in life, and, kind as the offer had been, she must decline it. She did not say that Carol had fairly bristled at the idea of leaving her beloved high school now when she was a senior and only one year before her graduation. That bit of horror and hysterics on Carol's part had been carefully suppressed within the four walls of her mother's room; but Elizabeth, deeply disappointed, had wept her heart out over the matter, and finally been comforted by the promise that Mrs. Hollister would write and ask Mrs. Graham to allow Elizabeth to go to school with Carol the coming winter. That proposition was now on its way West, together with an announcement of Sidney's engagement to Shirley. Sidney was confidently expecting congratulatory telegrams that morning when he reached the city. He had written his father in detail all about their plans for returning, and how the work at the old barn was progressing, and Mr. Graham, Senior, was too good a manager not to plan to greet the occasion properly. Therefore Graham stopped at his office for a few minutes before taking the family out to Glenside, and, sure enough, came down with his hands full of letters and telegrams, and one long white envelope which he put carefully in his breast pocket. They had a great time reading the telegrams and letters.

The way out to Glenside seemed very short now, watching as they did for each landmark. The children were as eager to get back as they had been to leave, and Star snuggled in between Harley's feet, held his head high, and smiled benevolently on everybody, as if he knew he was going home and was glad. They began to wonder about the chickens, and if the garden was all dried up, and whether the doves were all right. There was an undertone of sadness and suppressed excitement, for it was in the minds of all the Hollisters that the time in the old barn must of necessity be growing brief. The fall would soon be upon them, and a need for warmth. They must go hunting for a house at once. And yet they all wanted this one day of delight before they faced that question.

At last they reached the final curve and could see the tall old tree in the distance, and the clump of willows knee-deep in the brook. By common consent they all grew silent, watching for the first glimpse of the dear old barn.

Then they came around the curve, and there it was! But what was the matter?

Nobody spoke. It seemed as if they could not get their breath.

Shirley rubbed her eyes, and looked again. Mrs. Hollister gave a startled look from her daughter to Graham and back to the barn again. Elizabeth and Carol were utterly silent, grasping each other's hands in violent ecstasy. The boys murmured inarticulately, of which the only audible words were: "Good night! Some class!" Doris looked for a long second, puckered her lips as if she were going to cry, and inquired pitifully: "I yant my dear barn house home! I yant to doh home!" and Star uttered a sharp, bewildered bark and bounded from the car as if this were something he ought to attend to.

But before anybody could say anything more, Graham brought out the long white envelope and handed it to Shirley.

"Before you get out and go in I just want to say a word," he began. "Father and I both want Shirley to have the old barn for her very own, to do with as she pleases. This envelope contains the deed for the property made out in her name. We have tried to put it in thorough repair before handing it over to her, and if there is anything more she can think of that it needs we'll do that too. And now, welcome home to the old barn! Mother, may I help you out?"

"But there isn't any barn any more," burst forth the irrepressible Elizabeth. "The barn's gone! It's just a house!"

And, sure enough, there stood a stately stone mansion on a wide green terrace, where shrubs and small trees were grouped fittingly about, erasing all signs of the old pasture-land; and the old grassy incline to the door now rolled away in velvety lawn on either side of a smooth cement walk bordered with vivid scarlet geraniums. Trailing vines and autumn flowers were blossoming in jars on the wide stone railing. The old barn door had been replaced by glass which gave a glimpse of strange new rooms beyond, and the roof had broken forth in charming colonial dormer windows like a new French hat on a head that had worn the same old poke bonnet for years. No wonder Doris didn't recognize the dear old barn. It did seem as though a wizard had worked magic upon it. How was one to know that only a brief half-hour before the old gardener from the Graham estate set the last geranium in the row along the walk, and trailed the last vine over the stone wall; or that even now the corps of men who had been hastily laying and patting the turf in place over the terrace were in hiding down in the basement, with their wheelbarrows and picks and spades, having beat a hasty retreat at the sound of the car coming, and were only waiting till they could get away unobserved? For orders were orders, and the orders were that the work was to be *done* and every man out of sight by the time they arrived. A bonus to every man if the orders were obeyed. That is what money and influence can do in a month!

In due time they got themselves out of that car in a sort of bewildered daze and walked up the new cement path, feeling strangely like intruders as they met the bright stare of the geraniums.

They walked the length of the new piazza in delight. They exclaimed and started and smiled and almost wept in one another's arms. Graham stood and watched Shirley's happy face and was satisfied.

The first thing Doris did when she got inside the lovely glass door was to start to run for her own little willow chair and her own little old rag doll that had been left behind, and down she went on the slippery floor. And there, behold, the old barn floors too had disappeared under a coating of simple matched hardwood flooring, oiled and polished smoothly, and Doris was not expecting it.

She got up quickly, half ashamed, and looked around laughing.

"I vas skating!" she declared with a ringing laugh. "I skated yite down on mine nose."

Then she hurried more cautiously to the haven of her own chair, and with her old doll hugged to her breast she reiterated over and over as if to reassure herself: "Mine! Doris! Mine! Doris!"

Words would fail to describe all they said about the wonderful rooms, the walls all shining in a soft rough-finish plaster, tinted creamy on the upper half and gray below, and finished in dark chestnut trimmings; of the beautiful staircase and the wide bay window opening from the first landing like a little half-way room, with seats to rest upon. It was standing in this bay window that Graham first called Mrs. Hollister's attention to something strange and new outside behind the house. It was a long, low glass building with green things gleaming through its shining roof.

"There, mother," he said, coming up softly behind her. "There is your plaything. You said you had always wanted a hot-house, so we made you one. It is heated from a coil in the furnace, and you can try all the experiments with flowers you want to. We put in a few things to start with, and you can get more at your leisure."

Mrs. Hollister gave one look, and then turned and put her arms around the tall young man, reaching up on her tip-toes to do so, brought his handsome face down to hers, and kissed him.

"My dear son!" she said. That was all, but he knew that she had accepted him and given him a loving place with her own children in her heart.

There were shoutings and runnings up stairs and down by first one and then another. The bathrooms were discovered one by one, and then they had to all rush down into the basement by the new stairs to see the new laundry and the new furnace, and the entrance to the hot-house; and the hot-house itself, with its wealth of bloom transplanted from the Graham greenhouses.

They almost forgot the chickens and the doves, and the garden was a past Eden not to be remembered till long hours afterward.

The sunset was dying away in the sky, and the stars were large and few and piercing in the twilight night when Shirley and Sidney came walking up the terrace arm in arm, and found Doris sitting in the doorway cuddling her old rag doll and a new little gray kitten the farmer next door had brought her, and singing an evening song to herself.

Shirley and Sidney turned and looked off at the sky where a rosy stain was blending softly into the gray of evening.

"Do you remember the first night we stood here together?" Sidney said in a low tone, as he drew her fingers within his own. "I loved you then, Shirley, that first night——"

And then Doris's little shrill voice chimed above their murmurings:

"Oh, mine nice dear home! Mine kitty an' mine dolly! and mine piazza! and mine bafwoom wif a place to swim boats! an' mine fowers an' pitty house! No more barn! Barn *all dawn*! Never turn bat any moh! Oh, mine nice, pitty dear home!"

The Girl from Montana

CHAPTER I

THE GIRL, AND A GREAT PERIL

The late afternoon sun was streaming in across the cabin floor as the girl stole around the corner and looked cautiously in at the door.

There was a kind of tremulous courage in her face. She had a duty to perform, and she was resolved to do it without delay. She shaded her eyes with her hand from the glare of the sun, set a firm foot upon the threshold, and, with one wild glance around to see whether all was as she had left it, entered her home and stood for a moment shuddering in the middle of the floor.

A long procession of funerals seemed to come out of the past and meet her eye as she looked about upon the signs of the primitive, unhallowed one which had just gone out from there a little while before.

The girl closed her eyes, and pressed their hot, dry lids hard with her cold fingers; but the vision was clearer even than with her eyes open.

She could see the tiny baby sister lying there in the middle of the room, so little and white and pitiful; and her handsome, careless father sitting at the head of the rude home-made coffin, sober for the moment; and her tired, disheartened mother, faded before her time, dry-eyed and haggard, beside him. But that was long ago, almost at the beginning of things for the girl.

There had been other funerals, the little brother who had been drowned while playing in a forbidden stream, and the older brother who had gone off in search of gold or his own way, and had crawled back parched with fever to die in his mother's arms. But those, too, seemed long ago to the girl as she stood in the empty cabin and looked fearfully about her. They seemed almost blotted out by the last three that had crowded so close within the year. The father, who even at his worst had a kind word for her and her mother, had been brought home mortally hurt—an encounter with wild cattle, a fall from his horse in a treacherous place—and had never roused to consciousness again.

At all these funerals there had been a solemn service, conducted by a travelling preacher when one happened to be within reach, and, when there was none, by the trembling, determined, untaught lips of the white-faced mother. The mother had always insisted upon it, especially upon a prayer. It had seemed like a charm to help the departed one into some kind of a pitiful heaven.

And when, a few months after the father, the mother had drooped and grown whiter and whiter, till one day she clutched at her heart and lay down gasping, and said: "Good-by, Bess! Mother's good girl! Don't forget!" and was gone from her life of burden and disappointment forever, the girl had prepared the funeral with the assistance of the one brother left. The girl's voice had uttered the prayer, "Our Father," just as her mother had taught her, because there was no one else to do it; and she was afraid to send the wild young brother off after a preacher, lest he should not return in time.

It was six months now since the sad funeral train had wound its way among sage-brush and greasewood, and the body of the mother had been laid to rest beside her husband. For six months the girl had kept the cabin in order, and held as far as possible the wayward brother to his work and home. But within the last few weeks he had more and more left her alone, for a day, and sometimes more, and had come home in a sad condition and with bold, merry companions who made her life a constant terror. And now, but two short days ago, they had brought home his body lying across his own faithful horse, with two shots through his heart. It was a drunken quarrel, they told her; and all were sorry, but no one seemed responsible.

They had been kind in their rough way, those companions of her brother. They had stayed and done all that was necessary, had dug the grave, and stood about their comrade in good-natured grimness, marching in order about him to give the last look; but, when the sister tried to utter the prayer she knew her mother would have spoken, her throat refused to make a sound, and her tongue cleaved to the roof of her mouth. She had taken sudden refuge in the little shed that was her own room, and there had stayed till the rough companions had taken away the still form of the only one left in the family circle.

In silence the funeral train wound its way to the spot where the others were buried. They respected her tearless grief, these great, passionate, uncontrolled young men. They held in the rude jokes with which they would have taken the awesomeness from the occasion for themselves, and for the most part kept the way silently and gravely, now and then looking back with admiration to the slim girl with the stony face and unblinking eyes who followed them mechanically. They had felt that some one ought to do something; but no one knew exactly what, and so they walked silently.

Only one, the hardest and boldest, the ringleader of the company, ventured back to ask whether there was anything he could do for her, anything she would like to have done; but she answered him coldly with a "No!" that cut him to the quick. It had been a good deal for him to do, this touch of gentleness he had forced himself into. He turned from her with a wicked gleam of intent in his eyes, but she did not see it.

When the rude ceremony was over, the last clod was heaped upon the pitiful mound, and the relentless words, "dust to dust," had been murmured by one more daring than the rest, they turned and looked at the girl, who had all the time stood upon a mound of earth and watched them, as a statue of Misery might look down upon the world. They could not make her out, this silent, marble girl. They hoped now she would change. It was over. They felt an untold relief themselves from the fact that their reckless, gay comrade was no longer lying cold and still among them. They were done with him. They had paid their last tribute, and wished to forget. He must settle his own account with the hereafter now; they had enough in their own lives without the burden of his.

Then there had swept up into the girl's face one gleam of life that made her beautiful for the instant, and she had bowed to them with a slow, almost haughty, inclination of her head, and spread out her hands like one who would like to bless but dared not, and said clearly, "I thank you—all!" There had been just a slight hesitation before that last word "all," as if she were not quite sure, as her eyes rested upon the ringleader with doubt and dislike; then her lips had hardened as if justice must be done, and she had spoken it, "all!" and, turning, sped away to her cabin alone.

They were taken by surprise, those men who feared nothing in the wild and primitive West, and for a moment they watched her go in silence. Then the words that broke upon the air were not all pleasant to hear; and, if the girl could have known, she would have sped far faster, and her cheeks would have burned a brighter red than they did.

But one, the boldest, the ringleader, said nothing. His brows darkened, and the wicked gleam came and sat in his hard eyes with a green light. He drew a little apart from the rest, and walked on more rapidly. When he came to the place where they had left their horses, he took his and went on toward the cabin with a look that did not invite the others to follow. As their voices died away in the distance, and he drew nearer to the cabin, his eyes gleamed with cunning.

The girl in the cabin worked rapidly. One by one she took the boxes on which the rude coffin of her brother had rested, and threw them far out the back door. She straightened the furniture around fiercely, as if by erasing every sign she would force from memory the thought of the scenes that had just passed. She took her brother's coat that hung against the wall, and an old pipe from the mantle, and hid them in the room that was hers. Then she looked about for something else to be done.

A shadow darkened the sunny doorway. Looking up, she saw the man she believed to be her brother's murderer.

"I came back, Bess, to see if I could do anything for you."

The tone was kind; but the girl involuntarily put her hand to her throat, and caught her breath. She would like to speak out and tell him what she thought, but she dared not. She did not even dare let her thought appear in her eyes. The dull, statue-like look came over her face that she had worn at the grave. The man thought it was the stupefaction of grief.

"I told you I didn't want any help," she said, trying to speak in the same tone she had used when she thanked the men.

"Yes, but you're all alone," said the man insinuatingly; she felt a menace in the thought, "and I am sorry for you!"

He came nearer, but her face was cold. Instinctively she glanced to the cupboard door behind which lay her brother's belt with two pistols.

"You're very kind," she forced herself to say; "but I'd rather be alone now." It was hard to speak so when she would have liked to dash on him, and call down curses for the death of her brother; but she looked into his evil face, and a fear for herself worse than death stole into her heart.

He took encouragement from her gentle dignity. Where did she get that manner so imperial, she, born in a mountain cabin and bred on the wilds? How could she speak with an accent so different from those about her? The brother was not so, not so much so; the mother had been plain and quiet. He had not known her father, for he had lately come to this State in hiding from another. He wondered, with his wide knowledge of the world, over her wild, haughty beauty, and gloated over it. He liked to think just what worth was within his easy grasp. A prize for the taking, and here alone, unprotected.

"But it ain't good for you to be alone, you know, and I've come to protect you. Besides, you need cheering up, little girl." He came closer. "I love you, Bess, you know, and I'm going to take care of you now. You're all alone. Poor little girl."

He was so near that she almost felt his breath against her cheek. She faced him desperately, growing white to the lips. Was there nothing on earth or in heaven to save her? Mother! Father! Brother! All gone! Ah! Could she but have known that the quarrel which ended her wild young brother's life had been about her, perhaps pride in him would have salved her grief, and choked her horror.

While she watched the green lights play in the evil eyes above her, she gathered all the strength of her young life into one effort, and schooled herself to be calm. She controlled her involuntary shrinking from the man, only drew herself back gently, as a woman with wider experience and gentler breeding might have done.

"Remember," she said, "that my brother just lay there dead!" and she pointed to the empty centre of the room. The dramatic attitude was almost a condemnation to the guilty man before her. He drew back as if the sheriff had entered the room, and looked instinctively to where the coffin had been but a short time before, then laughed nervously and drew himself together.

The girl caught her breath, and took courage. She had held him for a minute; could she not hold him longer?

"Think!" said she. "He is but just buried. It is not right to talk of such things as love in this room where he has just gone out. You must leave me alone for a little while. I cannot talk and think now. We must respect the dead, you know." She looked appealingly at him, acting her part desperately, but well. It was as if she were trying to charm a lion or an insane man.

He stood admiring her. She argued well. He was half minded to humor her, for somehow when she spoke of the dead he could see the gleam in her brother's eyes just before he shot him. Then there was promise in this wooing. She was no girl to be lightly won, after all. She could hold her own, and perhaps she would be the better for having her way for a little. At any rate, there was more excitement in such game.

She saw that she was gaining, and her breath came freer.

"Go!" she said with a flickering smile. "Go! For—a little while," and then she tried to smile again.

He made a motion to take her in his arms and kiss her; but she drew back suddenly, and spread her hands before her, motioning him back.

"I tell you you must not now. Go! Go! or I will never speak to you again."

He looked into her eyes, and seemed to feel a power that he must obey. Half sullenly he drew back toward the door.

"But, Bess, this ain't the way to treat a fellow," he whined. "I came way back here to take care of you. I tell you I love you, and I'm going to have you. There ain't any other fellow going to run off with you—"

"Stop!" she cried tragically. "Don't you see you're not doing right? My brother is just dead. I must have some time to mourn. It is only decent." She was standing now with her back to the little cupboard behind whose door lay the two pistols. Her hand was behind her on the wooden latch.

"You don't respect my trouble!" she said, catching her breath, and putting her hand to her eyes. "I don't believe you care for me when you don't do what I say."

The man was held at bay. He was almost conquered by her sign of tears. It was a new phase of her to see her melt into weakness so. He was charmed.

"How long must I stay away?" he faltered.

She could scarcely speak, so desperate she felt. O if she dared but say, "Forever," and shout it at him! She was desperate enough to try her chances at shooting him if she but had the pistols, and was sure they were loaded—a desperate chance indeed against the best shot on the Pacific coast, and a desperado at that.

She pressed her hands to her throbbing temples, and tried to think. At last she faltered out,

"Three days!"

He swore beneath his breath, and his brows drew down in heavy frowns that were not good to see. She shuddered at what it would be to be in his power forever. How he would play with her and toss her aside! Or kill her, perhaps, when he was tired of her! Her life on the mountain had made her familiar with evil characters.

He came a step nearer, and she felt she was losing ground.

Straightening up, she said coolly:

"You must go away at once, and not think of coming back at least until to-morrow night. Go!" With wonderful control she smiled at him, one frantic, brilliant smile; and to her great wonder he drew back. At the door he paused, a softened look upon his face.

"Mayn't I kiss you before I go?"

She shuddered involuntarily, but put out her hands in protest again. "Not to-night!" She shook her head, and tried to smile.

He thought he understood her, but turned away half satisfied. Then she heard his step coming back to the door again, and she went to meet him. He must not come in. She had gained in sending him out, if she could but close the door fast. It was in the doorway that she faced him as he stood with one foot ready to enter again. The crafty look was out upon his face plainly now, and in the sunlight she could see it.

"You will be all alone to-night."

"I am not afraid," calmly. "And no one will trouble me. Don't you know what they say about the spirit of a man—" she stopped; she had almost said "a man who has been murdered"—"coming back to his home the first night after he is buried?" It was her last frantic effort.

The man before her trembled, and looked around nervously.

"You better come away to-night with me," he said, edging away from the door.

"See, the sun is going down! You must go now," she said imperiously; and reluctantly the man mounted his restless horse, and rode away down the mountain.

She watched him silhouetted against the blood-red globe of the sun as it sank lower and lower. She could see every outline of his slouch-hat and muscular shoulders as he turned now and then and saw her standing still alone at her cabin door. Why he was going he could not tell; but he went, and he frowned as he rode away, with the wicked gleam still in his eye; for he meant to return.

At last he disappeared; and the girl, turning, looked up, and there rode the white ghost of the moon overhead. She was alone.

CHAPTER II
THE FLIGHT

A great fear settled down upon the girl as she realized that she was alone and, for a few hours at least, free. It was a marvellous escape. Even now she could hear the echo of the man's last words, and see his hateful smile as he waved his good-by and promised to come back for her to-morrow.

She felt sure he would not wait until the night. It might be he would return even yet. She cast another reassuring look down the darkening road, and strained her ear; but she could no longer hear hoof-beats. Nevertheless, it behooved her to hasten. He had blanched at her suggestion of walking spirits; but, after all, his courage might arise. She shuddered to think of his returning later, in the night. She must fly somewhere at once.

Instantly her dormant senses seemed to be on the alert. Fully fledged plans flashed through her brain. She went into the cabin, and barred the door. She made every movement swiftly, as if she had not an instant to spare. Who could tell? He might return even before dark. He had been hard to baffle, and she did not feel at all secure. It was her one chance of safety to get away speedily, whither it mattered little, only so she was away and hidden.

Her first act inside the cottage was to get the belt from the cupboard and buckle it around her waist. She examined and loaded the pistols. Her throat seemed seized with sudden constriction when she discovered that the barrels had been empty and the weapons would have done her no good even if she could have reached them.

She put into her belt the sharp little knife her brother used to carry, and then began to gather together everything eatable that she could carry with her. There was not much that could be easily carried—some dried beef, a piece of cheese, some corn-meal, a piece of pork, a handful of cheap coffee-berries, and some pieces of hard corn bread. She hesitated over a pan half full of baked beans, and finally added them to the store. They were bulky, but she ought to take them if she could. There was nothing else in the house that seemed advisable to take in the way of eatables. Their stores had been running low, and the trouble of the last day or two had put housekeeping entirely out of her mind. She had not cared to eat, and now it occurred to her that food had not passed her lips that day. With strong self-control she forced herself to eat a few of the dry pieces of corn bread, and to drink some cold coffee that stood in the little coffee-pot. This she did while she worked, wasting not one minute.

There were some old flour-sacks in the house. She put the eatables into two of them, with the pan of beans on the top, adding a tin cup, and tied them securely together. Then she went into her little shed room, and put on the few extra garments in her wardrobe. They were not many, and that was the easiest way to carry them. Her mother's wedding-ring, sacredly kept in a box since the mother's death, she slipped upon her finger. It seemed the closing act of her life in the cabin, and she paused and bent her head as if to ask the mother's permission that she might wear the ring. It seemed a kind of protection to her in her lonely situation.

There were a few papers and an old letter or two yellow with years, which the mother had always guarded sacredly. One was the certificate of her mother's marriage. The girl did not know what the others were. She had never looked into them closely, but she knew that her mother had counted them precious. These she pinned into the bosom of her calico gown. Then she was ready.

She gave one swift glance of farewell about the cabin where she had spent nearly all of her life that she could remember, gathered up the two flour-sacks and an old coat of her father's that hung on the wall, remembering at the last minute to put into its pocket the few matches and the single candle left in the house, and went out from the cabin, closing the door behind her.

She paused, looking down the road, and listened again; but no sound came to her save a distant howl of a wolf. The moon rode high and clear by this time; and it seemed not so lonely here, with everything bathed in soft silver, as it had in the darkening cabin with its flickering candle.

The girl stole out from the cabin and stealthily across the patch of moonlight into the shadow of the shackly barn where stamped the poor, ill-fed, faithful horse that her brother had ridden to his death upon. All her movements were stealthy as a cat's.

She laid the old coat over the horse's back, swung her brother's saddle into place,—she had none of her own, and could ride his, or without any; it made no difference, for she was perfectly at home on horseback,—and strapped the girths with trembling fingers that were icy cold with excitement. Across the saddle-bows she hung the two flour-sacks containing her provisions. Then with added caution she tied some old burlap about each of the horse's feet. She must make no sound and leave no track as she stole forth into the great world.

The horse looked curiously down and whinnied at her, as she tied his feet up clumsily. He did not seem to like his new habiliments, but he suffered anything at her hand.

"Hush!" she murmured softly, laying her cold hands across his nostrils; and he put his muzzle into her palm, and seemed to understand.

She led him out into the clear moonlight then, and paused a second, looking once more down the road that led away in front of the cabin; but no one was coming yet, though her heart beat high as she listened, fancying every falling bough or rolling stone was a horse's hoof-beat.

There were three trails leading away from the cabin, for they could hardly be dignified by the name of road. One led down the mountain toward the west, and was the way they took to the nearest clearing five or six miles beyond and to the supply store some three miles further. One led off to the east, and was less travelled, being the way to the great world; and the third led down behind the cabin, and was desolate and barren under the moon. It led down, back, and away to desolation, where five graves lay stark and ugly at the end. It was the way they had taken that afternoon.

She paused just an instant as if hesitating which way to take. Not the way to the west—ah, any but that! To the east? Yes, surely, that must be the trail she would eventually strike; but she had a duty yet to perform. That prayer was as yet unsaid, and before she was free to seek safety—if safety there were for her in the wide world—she must take her way down the lonely path. She walked, leading the horse, which followed her with muffled tread and arched neck as if he felt he were doing homage to the dead. Slowly, silently, she moved along into the river of moonlight and dreariness; for the moonlight here seemed cold, like the graves it shone upon, and the girl, as she walked with bowed head, almost fancied she saw strange misty forms flit past her in the night.

As they came in sight of the graves, something dark and wild with plumy tail slunk away into the shadows, and seemed a part of the place. The girl stopped a moment to gain courage in full sight of the graves, and the horse snorted, and stopped too, with his ears a-quiver, and a half-fright in his eyes.

She patted his neck and soothed him incoherently, as she buried her face in his mane for a moment, and let the first tears that had dimmed her eyes since the blow had fallen come smarting their way out. Then, leaving the horse to stand curiously watching her, she went down and stood at the head of the new-heaped mound. She tried to kneel, but a shudder passed through her. It was as if she were descending into the place of the dead herself; so she stood up and raised her eyes to the wide white night and the moon riding so high and far away.

"Our Father," she said in a voice that sounded miles away to herself. Was there any Father, and could He hear her? And did He care? "Which art in heaven—" but heaven was so far away and looked so cruelly serene to her in her desolateness and danger! "hallowed be thy name. Thy kingdom come—" whatever that might mean. "Thy will be done in earth, as it is in heaven." It was a long prayer to pray, alone with the pale moon-rain and the graves, and a distant wolf, but it was her mother's wish. Her will being done here over the dead—was that anything like the will of the Father being done in heaven? Her untrained thoughts hovered on the verge of great questions, and then slipped back into her pathetic self and its fear, while her tongue hurried on through the words of the prayer.

Once the horse stirred and breathed a soft protest. He could not understand why they were stopping so long in this desolate place, for nothing apparently. He had looked and looked at the shapeless mound before which the girl was standing; but he saw no sign of his lost master, and his instincts warned him that there were wild animals about. Anyhow, this was no place for a horse and a maid to stop in the night.

A few loose stones rattled from the horse's motion. The girl started, and looked hastily about, listening for a possible pursuer; but everywhere in the white sea of moonlight there was empty, desolate space. On to the "Amen" she finished then, and with one last look at the lonely graves she turned to the horse. Now they might go, for the duty was done, and there was no time to be lost.

Somewhere over toward the east across that untravelled wilderness of white light was the trail that started to the great world from the little cabin she had left. She dared not go back to the cabin to take it, lest she find herself already followed. She did not know the way across this lonely plain, and neither did the horse. In fact, there was no way, for it was all one arid plain so situated that human traveller seldom came near it, so large and so barren that one might wander for hours and gain no goal, so dry that nothing would grow.

With another glance back on the way she had come, the girl mounted the horse and urged him down into the valley. He stepped cautiously into the sandy plain, as if he were going into a river and must try its depth. He did not like the going here, but he plodded on with his burdens. The girl was light; he did not mind her weight; but he felt this place uncanny, and now and then would start on a little spurt of haste, to get into a better way. He liked the high mountain trails, where he could step firmly and hear the twigs crackle under his feet, not this muffled, velvet way where one made so little progress and had to work so hard.

The girl's heart sank as they went on, for the sand seemed deep and drifted in places. She felt she was losing time. The way ahead looked endless, as if they were but treading sand behind them which only returned in front to

99

be trodden over again. It was to her like the valley of the dead, and she longed to get out of it. A great fear lest the moon should go down and leave her in this low valley alone in the dark took hold upon her. She felt she must get away, up higher. She turned the horse a little more to the right, and he paused, and seemed to survey the new direction and to like it. He stepped up more briskly, with a courage that could come only from an intelligent hope for better things. And at last they were rewarded by finding the sand shallower, and now and then a bit of rock cropping out for a firmer footing.

The young rider dismounted, and untied the burlap from the horse's feet. He seemed to understand, and to thank her as he nosed about her neck. He thought, perhaps, that their mission was over and they were going to strike out for home now.

The ground rose steadily before them now, and at times grew quite steep; but the horse was fresh as yet, and clambered upward with good heart; and the rider was used to rough places, and felt no discomfort from her position. The fear of being followed had succeeded to the fear of being lost, for the time being; and instead of straining her ears on the track behind she was straining her eyes to the wilderness before. The growth of sage-brush was dense now, and trees were ahead.

After that the way seemed steep, and the rider's heart stood still with fear lest she could never get up and over to the trail which she knew must be somewhere in that direction, though she had never been far out on its course herself. That it led straight east into all the great cities she never doubted, and she must find it before she was pursued. That man would be angry, *angry* if he came and found her gone! He was not beyond shooting her for giving him the slip in this way.

The more she thought over it, the more frightened she became, till every bit of rough way, and every barrier that kept her from going forward quickly, seemed terrible to her. A bob-cat shot across the way just ahead, and the green gleam of its eyes as it turned one swift glance at this strange intruder in its chosen haunts made her catch her breath and put her hand on the pistols.

They were climbing a long time—it seemed hours to the girl—when at last they came to a space where a better view of the land was possible. It was high, and sloped away on three sides. To her looking now in the clear night the outline of a mountain ahead of her became distinct, and the lay of the land was not what she had supposed. It brought her a furious sense of being lost. Over there ought to be the familiar way where the cabin stood, but there was no sign of anything she had ever seen before, though she searched eagerly for landmarks. The course she had chosen, and which had seemed the only one, would take her straight up, up over the mountain, a way well-nigh impossible, and terrible even if it were possible.

It was plain she must change her course, but which way should she go? She was completely turned around. After all, what mattered it? One way might be as good as another, so it led not home to the cabin which could never be home again. Why not give the horse his head, and let him pick out a safe path? Was there danger that he might carry her back to the cabin again, after all? Horses did that sometimes. But at least he could guide through this maze of perplexity till some surer place was reached. She gave him a sign, and he moved on, nimbly picking a way for his feet.

They entered a forest growth where weird branches let the pale moon through in splashes and patches, and grim moving figures seemed to chase them from every shadowy tree-trunk. It was a terrible experience to the girl. Sometimes she shut her eyes and held to the saddle, that she might not see and be filled with this frenzy of things, living or dead, following her. Sometimes a real black shadow crept across the path, and slipped into the engulfing darkness of the undergrowth to gleam with yellow-lighted eyes upon the intruders.

But the forest did not last forever, and the moon was not yet gone when they emerged presently upon the rough mountain-side. The girl studied the moon then, and saw by the way it was setting that after all they were going in the right general direction. That gave a little comfort until she made herself believe that in some way she might have made a mistake and gone the wrong way from the graves, and so be coming up to the cabin after all.

It was a terrible night. Every step of the way some new horror was presented to her imagination. Once she had to cross a wild little stream, rocky and uncertain in its bed, with slippery, precipitous banks; and twice in climbing a steep incline she came sharp upon sheer precipices down into a rocky gorge, where the moonlight seemed repelled by dark, bristling evergreen trees growing half-way up the sides. She could hear the rush and clamor of a tumbling mountain stream in the depths below. Once she fancied she heard a distant shot, and the horse pricked up his ears, and went forward excitedly.

But at last the dawn contended with the night, and in the east a faint pink flush crept up. Down in the valley a mist like a white feather rose gently into a white cloud, and obscured everything. She wished she might carry the wall of white with her to shield her. She had longed for the dawn; and now, as it came with sudden light and clear revealing of the things about her, it was almost worse than night, so dreadful were the dangers when clearly seen, so dangerous the chasms, so angry the mountain torrents.

With the dawn came the new terror of being followed. The man would have no fear to come to her in the morning, for murdered men were not supposed to haunt their homes after the sun was up, and murderers were always courageous in the day. He might the sooner come, and find her gone, and perhaps follow; for she felt that he was not one easily to give up an object he coveted, and she had seen in his evil face that which made her fear unspeakably.

As the day grew clearer, she began to study the surroundings. All seemed utter desolation. There was no sign that any one had ever passed that way before; and yet, just as she had thought that, the horse stopped and snorted, and there in the rocks before them lay a man's hat riddled with shot. Peering fearfully around, the girl saw a sight which made her turn icy cold and begin to tremble; for there, below them, as if he had fallen from his horse and rolled down the incline, lay a man on his face.

For the instant fear held her riveted, with the horse, one figure like a statue, girl and beast; the next, sudden panic took hold upon her. Whether the man were dead or not, she must make haste. It might be he would come to himself and pursue her, though there was that in the rigid attitude of the figure down below that made her sure he had been dead some time. But how had he died? Scarcely by his own hand. Who had killed him? Were there fiends lurking in the fastnesses of the mountain growth above her?

With guarded motion she urged her horse forward, and for miles beyond the horse scrambled breathlessly, the girl holding on with shut eyes, not daring to look ahead for fear of seeing more terrible sights, not daring to look behind for fear of—what she did not know.

At last the way sloped downward, and they reached more level ground, with wide stretches of open plain, dotted here and there with sage-brush and greasewood.

She had been hungry back there before she came upon the dead man; but now the hunger had gone from her, and in its place was only faintness. Still, she dared not stop long to eat. She must make as much time as possible here in this open space, and now she was where she could be seen more easily if any one were in pursuit.

But the horse had decided that it was time for breakfast. He had had one or two drinks of water on the mountain, but there had been no time for him to eat. He was decidedly hungry, and the plain offered nothing in the shape of breakfast. He halted, lingered, and came to a neighing stop, looking around at his mistress. She roused from her lethargy of trouble, and realized that his wants—if not her own—must be attended to.

She must sacrifice some of her own store of eatables, for by and by they would come to a good grazing-place perhaps, but now there was nothing.

The corn-meal seemed the best for the horse. She had more of it than of anything else. She poured a scanty portion out on a paper, and the beast smacked his lips appreciatively over it, carefully licking every grain from the paper, as the girl guarded it lest his breath should blow any away. He snuffed hungrily at the empty paper, and she gave him a little more meal, while she ate some of the cold beans, and scanned the horizon anxiously. There was nothing but sage-brush in sight ahead of her, and more hills farther on where dim outlines of trees could be seen. If she could but get up higher where she could see farther, and perhaps reach a bench where there would be grass and some shelter.

It was only a brief rest she allowed; and then, hastily packing up her stores, and retaining some dry corn bread and a few beans in her pocket, she mounted and rode on.

The morning grew hot, and the way was long. As the ground rose again, it was stony and overgrown with cactus. A great desolation took possession of the girl. She felt as if she were in an endless flight from an unseen pursuer, who would never give up until he had her.

It was high noon by the glaring sun when she suddenly saw another human being. At first she was not quite sure whether he were human. It was only a distant view of a moving speck; but it was coming toward her, though separated by a wide valley that had stretched already for miles. He was moving along against the sky-line on a high bench on one side of the valley, and she mounting as fast as her weary beast would go to the top of another, hoping to find a grassy stretch and a chance to rest.

But the sight of the moving speck startled her. She watched it breathlessly as they neared each other. Could it be a wild beast? No, it must be a horse and rider. A moment later there came a puff of smoke as from a rifle discharged, followed by the distant echo of the discharge. It was a man, and he was yet a great way off. Should she turn and flee before she was discovered? But where? Should she go back? No, a thousand times, no! Her enemy was there. This could not be the one from whom she fled. He was coming from the opposite direction, but he might be just as bad. Her experience taught her that men were to be shunned. Even fathers and brothers were terribly uncertain, sorrow-bringing creatures.

She could not go back to the place where the dead man lay. She must not go back. And forward she was taking the only course that seemed at all possible through the natural obstructions of the region. She shrank to her saddle, and urged the patient horse on. Perhaps she could reach the bench and get away out of sight before the newcomer saw her.

But the way was longer to the top, and steeper than it had seemed at first, and the horse was tired. Sometimes he stopped of his own accord, and snorted appealingly to her with his head turned inquiringly as if to know how long and how far this strange ride was to continue. Then the man in the distance seemed to ride faster. The valley between them was not so wide here. He was quite distinctly a man now, and his horse was going rapidly. Once it seemed as if he waved his arms; but she turned her head, and urged her horse with sudden fright. They were almost to the top now. She dismounted and clambered alongside of the animal up the steep incline, her breath coming in quick gasps, with the horse's breath hot upon her cheek as they climbed together.

At last! They were at the top! Ten feet more and they would be on a level, where they might disappear from view. She turned to look across the valley, and the man was directly opposite. He must have ridden hard to get there so soon. Oh, horror! He was waving his hands and calling. She could distinctly hear a cry! It chilled her senses, and brought a frantic, unreasoning fear. Somehow she felt he was connected with the one from whom she fled. Some emissary of his sent out to foil her in her attempt for safety, perhaps.

She clutched the bridle wildly, and urged the horse up with one last effort; and just as they reached high ground she heard the wild cry ring clear and distinct, "Hello! Hello!" and then something else. It sounded like "Help!" but she could not tell. Was he trying to deceive her? Pretending he would help her?

She flung herself into the saddle, giving the horse the signal to run; and, as the animal obeyed and broke into his prairie run, she cast one fearful glance behind her. The man was pursuing her at a gallop! He was crossing the valley. There was a stream to cross, but he would cross it. He had determination in every line of his flying figure. His voice was pursuing her, too. It seemed as if the sound reached out and clutched her heart, and tried to draw her back as she fled. And now her pursuers were three: her enemy, the dead man upon the mountain, and the voice.

CHAPTER III
THE PURSUIT

Straight across the prairie she galloped, not daring to stop for an instant, with the voice pursuing her. For hours it seemed to ring in her ears, and even after she was far beyond any possibility of hearing it she could not be sure but there was now and then a faint echo of it ringing yet, "Hello!"—ringing like some strange bird amid the silence of the world.

There were cattle and sheep grazing on the bench, and the horse would fain have stopped to dine with them; but the girl urged him on, seeming to make him understand the danger that might be pursuing them.

It was hours before she dared stop for the much-needed rest. Her brain had grown confused with the fright and weariness. She felt that she could not much longer stay in the saddle. She might fall asleep. The afternoon sun would soon be slipping down behind the mountains. When and where dared she rest? Not in the night, for that would be almost certain death, with wild beasts about.

A little group of greasewood offered a scanty shelter. As if the beast understood her thoughts he stopped with a neigh, and looked around at her. She scanned the surroundings. There were cattle all about. They had looked up curiously from their grazing as the horse flew by, but were now going quietly on about their business. They would serve as a screen if any should be still pursuing her. One horse among the other animals in a landscape would not be so noticeable as one alone against the sky. The greasewood was not far from sloping ground where she might easily flee for hiding if danger approached.

The horse had already begun to crop the tender grass at his feet as if his life depended upon a good meal. The girl took some more beans from the pack she carried, and mechanically ate them, though she felt no appetite, and her dry throat almost refused to swallow. She found her eyes shutting even against her will; and in desperation she folded the old coat into a pillow, and with the horse's bridle fastened in her belt she lay down.

The sun went away; the horse ate his supper; and the girl slept. By and by the horse drowsed off too, and the bleating sheep in the distance, the lowing of the cattle, the sound of night-birds, came now and again from the distance; but still the girl slept on. The moon rose full and round, shining with flickering light through the cottonwoods; and the girl stirred in a dream and thought some one was pursuing her, but slept on again. Then out through the night rang a vivid human voice, "Hello! Hello!" The horse roused from his sleep, and stamped his feet nervously, twitching at his bridle; but the relaxed hand that lay across the leather strap did not quicken, and the girl slept on. The horse listened, and thought he heard a sound good to his ear. He neighed, and neighed again; but the girl slept on.

The first ray of the rising sun at last shot through the gray of dawning, and touched the girl full in the face as it slid under the branches of her sheltering tree. The light brought her acutely to her senses. Before she opened her eyes she seemed to be keenly and painfully aware of much that had gone on during her sleep. With another flash her eyes flew open. Not because she willed it, but rather as if the springs that held the lids shut had unexpectedly been touched and they sprang back because they had to.

She shrank, as her eyes opened, from a new day, and the memory of the old one. Then before her she saw something which kept her motionless, and almost froze the blood in her veins. She could not stir nor breathe, and for a moment even thought was paralyzed. There before her but a few feet away stood a man! Beyond him, a few feet from her own horse, stood his horse. She could not see it without turning her head, and that she dared not do; but she knew it was there, felt it even before she noticed the double stamping and breathing of the animals. Her keen senses seemed to make the whole surrounding landscape visible to her without the moving of a muscle. She knew to a nicety exactly how her weapons lay, and what movement would bring her hand to the trigger of her pistol; yet she stirred not.

Gradually she grew calm enough to study the man before her. He stood almost with his back turned toward her, his face just half turned so that one cheek and a part of his brow were visible. He was broad-shouldered and well built. There was strength in every line of his body. She felt how powerless she would be in his grasp. Her only hope would be in taking him unaware. Yet she moved not one atom.

He wore a brown flannel shirt, open at the throat, brown leather belt and boots; in short, his whole costume was in harmonious shades of brown, and looked new as if it had been worn but a few days. His soft felt sombrero was rolled back from his face, and the young red sun tinged the short brown curls to a ruddy gold. He was looking toward the rising sun. The gleam of it shot across his brace of pistols in his belt, and flashed twin rays into her eyes. Then all at once the man turned and looked at her.

Instantly the girl sprang to her feet, her hands upon her pistol, her eyes meeting with calm, desperate defiance the blue ones that were turned to her. She was braced against a tree, and her senses were measuring the distance between her horse and herself, and deciding whether escape were possible.

"Good morning," said the man politely. "I hope I haven't disturbed your nap."

The girl eyed him solemnly, and said nothing. This was a new kind of man. He was not like the one from whom she had fled, nor like any she had ever seen; but he might be a great deal worse. She had heard that the world was full of wickedness.

"You see," went on the man with an apologetic smile, which lit up his eyes in a wonderfully winning way, "you led me such a desperate race nearly all day yesterday that I was obliged to keep you in sight when I finally caught you."

He looked for an answering smile, but there was none. Instead, the girl's dark eyes grew wide and purple with fear. He was the same one, then, that she had seen in the afternoon, the voice who had cried to her; and he had been pursuing her. He was an enemy, perhaps, sent by the man from whom she fled. She grasped her pistol with trembling fingers, and tried to think what to say or do.

The young man wondered at the formalities of the plains. Were all these Western maidens so reticent?

"Why did you follow me? Who did you think I was?" she asked breathlessly at last.

"Well, I thought you were a man," he said; "at least, you appeared to be a human being, and not a wild animal. I hadn't seen anything but wild animals for six hours, and very few of those; so I followed you."

The girl was silent. She was not reassured. It did not seem to her that her question was directly answered. The young man was playing with her.

"What right had you to follow me?" she demanded fiercely.

"Well, now that you put it in that light, I'm not sure that I had any right at all, unless it may be the claim that every human being has upon all creation."

His arms were folded now across his broad brown flannel chest, and the pistols gleamed in his belt below like fine ornaments. He wore a philosophical expression, and looked at his companion as if she were a new specimen of the human kind, and he was studying her variety, quite impersonally, it is true, but interestedly. There was something in his look that angered the girl.

"What do you want?" She had never heard of the divine claims of all the human family. Her one instinct at present was fear.

An expression that was almost bitter flitted over the young man's face, as of an unpleasant memory forgotten for the instant.

"It really wasn't of much consequence when you think of it," he said with a shrug of his fine shoulders. "I was merely lost, and was wanting to inquire where I was—and possibly the way to somewhere. But I don't know as 'twas worth the trouble."

The girl was puzzled. She had never seen a man like this before. He was not like her wild, reckless brother, nor any of his associates.

"This is Montana," she said, "or was, when I started," she added with sudden thought.

"Yes? Well, it was Montana when I started, too; but it's as likely to be the Desert of Sahara as anything else. I'm sure I've come far enough, and found it barren enough."

"I never heard of that place," said the girl seriously; "is it in Canada?"

"I believe not," said the man with sudden gravity; "at least, not that I know of. When I went to school, it was generally located somewhere in Africa."

"I never went to school," said the girl wistfully; "but—" with a sudden resolve—"I'll go now."

"Do!" said the man. "I'll go with you. Let's start at once; for, now that I think of it, I haven't had anything to eat for over a day, and there might be something in that line near a schoolhouse. Do you know the way?"

"No," said the girl, slowly studying him—she began to feel he was making fun of her; "but I can give you something to eat."

"Thank you!" said the man. "I assure you I shall appreciate anything from hardtack to bisque ice-cream."

"I haven't any of those," said the girl, "but there are plenty of beans left; and, if you will get some wood for a fire, I'll make some coffee."

"Agreed," said the man. "That sounds better than anything I've heard for forty-eight hours."

The girl watched him as he strode away to find wood, and frowned for an instant; but his face was perfectly sober, and she turned to the business of getting breakfast. For a little her fears were allayed. At least, he would do her no immediate harm. Of course she might fly from him now while his back was turned; but then of course he would pursue her again, and she had little chance of getting away. Besides, he was hungry. She could not leave him without something to eat.

"We can't make coffee without water," she said as he came back with a bundle of sticks.

He whistled.

"Could you inform me where to look for water?" he asked.

She looked into his face, and saw how worn and gray he was about his eyes; and a sudden compassion came upon her.

"You'd better eat something first," she said, "and then we'll go and hunt for water. There's sure to be some in the valley. We'll cook some meat."

She took the sticks from him, and made the fire in a businesslike way. He watched her, and wondered at her grace. Who was she, and how had she wandered out into this waste place? Her face was both beautiful and interesting. She would make a fine study if he were not so weary of all human nature, and especially woman. He sighed as he thought again of himself.

The girl caught the sound, and, turning with the quickness of a wild creature, caught the sadness in his face. It seemed to drive away much of her fear and resentment. A half-flicker of a smile came to her lips as their eyes met. It seemed to recognize a comradeship in sorrow. But her face hardened again almost at once into disapproval as he answered her look.

The man felt a passing disappointment. After a minute, during which the girl had dropped her eyes to her work again, he said: "Now, why did you look at me in that way? Ought I to be helping you in some way? I'm awkward, I know, but I can obey if you'll just tell me how."

The girl seemed puzzled; then she replied almost sullenly:

"There's nothing more to do. It's ready to eat."

She gave him a piece of the meat and the last of the corn bread in the tin cup, and placed the pan of beans beside him; but she did not attempt to eat anything herself.

He took a hungry bite or two, and looked furtively at her.

"I insist upon knowing why you looked—" he paused and eyed her—"why you look at me in that way. I'm not a wolf if I am hungry, and I'm not going to eat you up."

The look of displeasure deepened on the girl's brow. In spite of his hunger the man was compelled to watch her. She seemed to be looking at a flock of birds in the sky. Her hand rested lightly at her belt. The birds were coming towards them, flying almost over their heads.

Suddenly the girl's hand was raised with a quick motion, and something gleamed in the sun across his sight. There was a loud report, and one of the birds fell almost at his feet, dead. It was a sage-hen. Then the girl turned and walked towards him with as haughty a carriage as ever a society belle could boast.

"You were laughing at me," she said quietly.

It had all happened so suddenly that the man had not time to think. Several distinct sensations of surprise passed over his countenance. Then, as the meaning of the girl's act dawned upon him, and the full intention of her rebuke, the color mounted in his nice, tanned face. He set down the tin cup, and balanced the bit of corn bread on the rim, and arose.

"I beg your pardon," he said. "I never will do it again. I couldn't have shot that bird to save my life," and he touched it with the tip of his tan leather boot as if to make sure it was a real bird.

The girl was sitting on the ground, indifferently eating some of the cooked pork. She did not answer. Somehow the young man felt uncomfortable. He sat down, and took up his tin cup, and went at his breakfast again; but his appetite seemed in abeyance.

"I've been trying myself to learn to shoot during the last week," he began soberly. "I haven't been able yet to hit anything but the side of a barn. Say, I'm wondering, suppose I had tried to shoot at those birds just now and had missed, whether you wouldn't have laughed at me—quietly, all to yourself, you know. Are you quite sure?"

The girl looked up at him solemnly without saying a word for a full minute.

"Was what I said as bad as that?" she asked slowly.

"I'm afraid it was," he answered thoughtfully; "but I was a blamed idiot for laughing at you. A girl that shoots like that may locate the Desert of Sahara in Canada if she likes, and Canada ought to be proud of the honor."

She looked into his face for an instant, and noted his earnestness; and all at once she broke into a clear ripple of laughter. The young man was astonished anew that she had understood him enough to laugh. She must be unusually keen-witted, this lady of the desert.

"If 'twas as bad as that," she said in quite another tone, "you c'n laugh."

They looked at each other then in mutual understanding, and each fell to eating his portion in silence. Suddenly the man spoke.

"I am eating your food that you had prepared for your journey, and I have not even said, 'Thank you' yet, nor asked if you have enough to carry you to a place where there is more. Where are you going?"

The girl did not answer at once; but, when she did, she spoke thoughtfully, as if the words were a newly made vow from an impulse just received.

"I am going to school," she said in her slow way, "to learn to 'sight' the Desert of Sahara."

He looked at her, and his eyes gave her the homage he felt was her due; but he said nothing. Here evidently was an indomitable spirit, but how did she get out into the wilderness? Where did she come from, and why was she alone? He had heard of the freedom of Western women, but surely such girls as this did not frequent so vast a waste of uninhabited territory as his experience led him to believe this was. He sat studying her.

The brow was sweet and thoughtful, with a certain keen inquisitiveness about the eyes. The mouth was firm; yet there were gentle lines of grace about it. In spite of her coarse, dark calico garb, made in no particular fashion except with an eye to covering with the least possible fuss and trouble, she was graceful. Every movement was alert and clean-cut. When she turned to look full in his face, he decided that she had almost beautiful eyes.

She had arisen while he was watching her, and seemed to be looking off with sudden apprehension. He followed her gaze, and saw several dark figures moving against the sky.

"It's a herd of antelope," she said with relief; "but it's time we hit the trail." She turned, and put her things together with incredible swiftness, giving him very little opportunity to help, and mounted her pony without more words.

For an hour he followed her at high speed as she rode full tilt over rough and smooth, casting furtive, anxious glances behind her now and then, which only half included him. She seemed to know that he was there and was following; that was all.

The young man felt rather amused and flattered. He reflected that most women he knew would have ridden by his side, and tried to make him talk. But this girl of the wilderness rode straight ahead as if her life depended upon it. She seemed to have nothing to say to him, and to be anxious neither to impart her own history nor to know his.

Well, that suited his mood. He had come out into the wilderness to think and to forget. Here was ample opportunity. There had been a little too much of it yesterday, when he wandered from the rest of his party who had come out to hunt; and for a time he had felt that he would rather be back in his native city with a good breakfast and all his troubles than to be alone in the vast waste forever. But now there was human company, and a possibility of getting somewhere sometime. He was content.

The lithe, slender figure of the girl ahead seemed one with the horse it rode. He tried to think what this ride would be if another woman he knew were riding on that horse ahead, but there was very small satisfaction in that. In the first place, it was highly improbable, and the young man was of an intensely practical turn of mind. It was impossible to imagine the haughty beauty in a brown calico riding a high-spirited horse of the wilds. There was but one parallel. If she had been there, she would, in her present state of mind, likely be riding imperiously and indifferently ahead instead of by his side where he wanted her. Besides, he came out to the plains to forget her. Why think of her?

The sky was exceedingly bright and wide. Why had he never noticed this wideness in skies at home? There was another flock of birds. What if he should try to shoot one? Idle talk. He would probably hit anything but the birds. Why had that girl shot that bird, anyway? Was it entirely because she might need it for food? She had picked it up significantly with the other things, and fastened it to her saddle-bow without a word. He was too ignorant to know whether it was an edible bird or not, or she was merely carrying it to remind him of her skill.

And what sort of a girl was she? Perhaps she was escaping from justice. She ran from him yesterday, and apparently stopped only when utterly exhausted. She seemed startled and anxious when the antelopes came into sight. There was no knowing whether her company meant safety, after all. Yet his interest was so thoroughly aroused in her that he was willing to risk it.

Of course he might go more slowly and gradually, let her get ahead, and he slip out of sight. It was not likely he had wandered so many miles away from human habitation but that he would reach one sometime; and, now that he was re-enforced by food, perhaps it would be the part of wisdom to part with this strange maiden. As he thought, he unconsciously slackened his horse's pace. The girl was a rod or more ahead, and just vanishing behind a clump of sage-brush. She vanished, and he stopped for an instant, and looked about him on the desolation; and a great loneliness settled upon him like a frenzy. He was glad to see the girl riding back toward him with a smile of good fellowship on her face.

"What's the matter?" she called. "Come on! There's water in the valley."

The sound of water was good; and life seemed suddenly good for no reason whatever but that the morning was bright, and the sky was wide, and there was water in the valley. He rode forward, keeping close beside her now, and in a moment there gleamed below in the hot sunshine the shining of a sparkling stream.

"You seem to be running away from some one," he explained. "I thought you wanted to get rid of me, and I would give you a chance."

She looked at him surprised.

"I am running away," she said, "but not from you."

"From whom, then, may I ask? It might be convenient to know, if we are to travel in the same company."

She looked at him keenly.

"Who are you, and where do you belong?"

CHAPTER IV
THE TWO FUGITIVES

"I'm not anybody in particular," he answered, "and I'm not just sure where I belong. I live in Pennsylvania, but I didn't seem to belong there exactly, at least not just now, and so I came out here to see if I belonged anywhere else. I concluded yesterday that I didn't. At least, not until I came in sight of you. But I suspect I am running away myself. In fact, that is just what I am doing, running away from a woman!"

He looked at her with his honest hazel eyes, and she liked him. She felt he was telling her the truth, but it seemed to be a truth he was just finding out for himself as he talked.

"Why do you run away from a woman? How could a woman hurt you? Can she shoot?"

He flashed her a look of amusement and pain mingled.

"She uses other weapons," he said. "Her words are darts, and her looks are swords."

"What a queer woman! Does she ride well?"

"Yes, in an automobile!"

"What is that?" She asked the question shyly as if she feared he might laugh again; and he looked down, and perceived that he was talking far above her. In fact, he was talking to himself more than to the girl.

There was a bitter pleasure in speaking of his lost lady to this wild creature who almost seemed of another kind, more like an intelligent bird or flower.

"An automobile is a carriage that moves about without horses," he answered her gravely. "It moves by machinery."

"I should not like it," said the girl decidedly. "Horses are better than machines. I saw a machine once. It was to cut wheat. It made a noise, and did not go fast. It frightened me."

"But automobiles go very fast, faster than any horses And they do not all make a noise."

The girl looked around apprehensively.

"My horse can go very fast. You do not know how fast. If you see her coming, I will change horses with you. You must ride to the nearest bench and over, and then turn backward on your tracks. She will never find you that way. And I am not afraid of a woman."

The man broke into a hearty laugh, loud and long. He laughed until the tears rolled down his cheeks; and the girl, offended, rode haughtily beside him. Then all in a moment he grew quite grave.

"Excuse me," he said; "I am not laughing at you now, though it looks that way. I am laughing out of the bitterness of my soul at the picture you put before me. Although I am running away from her, the lady will not come out in her automobile to look for me. She does not want me!"

"She does not want you! And yet you ran away from her?"

"That's exactly it," he said. "You see, *I* wanted *her*!"

"Oh!" She gave a sharp, quick gasp of intelligence, and was silent. After a full minute she rode quite close to his horse, and laid her small brown hand on the animal's mane.

"I am sorry," she said simply.

"Thank you," he answered. "I'm sure I don't know why I told you. I never told any one before."

There was a long silence between them. The man seemed to have forgotten her as he rode with his eyes upon his horse's neck, and his thoughts apparently far away.

At last the girl said softly, as if she were rendering return for the confidence given her, "I ran away from a man."

The man lifted his eyes courteously, questioningly, and waited.

"He is big and dark and handsome. He shoots to kill. He killed my brother. I hate him. He wants me, and I ran away from him. But he is a coward. I frightened him away. He is afraid of dead men that he has killed."

The young man gave his attention now to the extraordinary story which the girl told as if it were a common occurrence.

"But where are your people, your family and friends? Why do they not send the man away?"

"They're all back there in the sand," she said with a sad little flicker of a smile and a gesture that told of tragedy. "I said the prayer over them. Mother always wanted it when we died. There wasn't anybody left but me. I said it, and then I came away. It was cold moonlight, and there were noises. The horse was afraid. But I said it. Do you suppose it will do any good?"

She fastened her eyes upon the young man with her last words as if demanding an answer. The color came up to his cheeks. He felt embarrassed at such a question before her trouble.

"Why, I should think it ought to," he stammered. "Of course it will," he added with more confident comfort.

"Did you ever say the prayer?"

"Why,—I—yes, I believe I have," he answered somewhat uncertainly.

"Did it do any good?" She hung upon his words.

"Why, I—believe—yes, I suppose it did. That is, praying is always a good thing. The fact is, it's a long time since I've tried it. But of course it's all right."

A curious topic for conversation between a young man and woman on a ride through the wilderness. The man had never thought about prayer for so many minutes consecutively in the whole of his life; at least, not since the days when his nurse tried to teach him "Now I lay me."

"Why don't you try it about the lady?" asked the girl suddenly.

"Well, the fact is, I never thought of it."

"Don't you believe it will do any good?"

"Well, I suppose it might."

"Then let's try it. Let's get off now, quick, and both say it. Maybe it will help us both. Do you know it all through? Can't you say it?" This last anxiously, as he hesitated and looked doubtful.

The color came into the man's face. Somehow this girl put him in a very bad light. He couldn't shoot; and, if he couldn't pray, what would she think of him?

"Why, I think I could manage to say it with help," he answered uneasily. "But what if that man should suddenly appear on the scene?"

"You don't think the prayer is any good, or you wouldn't say that." She said it sadly, hopelessly.

"O, why, certainly," he said, "only I thought there might be some better time to try it; but, if you say so, we'll stop right here." He sprang to the ground, and offered to assist her; but she was beside him before he could get around his horse's head.

Down she dropped, and clasped her hands as a little child might have done, and closed her eyes.

"Our Father," she repeated slowly, precisely, as if every word belonged to a charm and must be repeated just right or it would not work. The man's mumbling words halted after hers. He was reflecting upon the curious tableau they would make to the chance passer-by on the desert if there were any passers-by. It was strange, this aloneness. There was a wideness here that made praying seem more natural than it would have been at home in the open country.

The prayer, by reason of the unaccustomed lips, went slowly; but, when it was finished, the girl sprang to her saddle again with a businesslike expression.

"I feel better," she said with a winning smile. "Don't you? Don't you think He heard?"

"Who heard?"

"Why, 'our Father.'"

"O, certainly! That is, I've always been taught to suppose He did. I haven't much experimental knowledge in this line, but I dare say it'll do some good some where. Now do you suppose we could get some of that very sparkling water? I feel exceedingly thirsty."

They spurred their horses, and were soon beside the stream, refreshing themselves.

"Did you ride all night?" asked the girl.

"Pretty much," answered the man. "I stopped once to rest a few minutes; but a sound in the distance stirred me up again, and I was afraid to lose my chance of catching you, lest I should be hopelessly lost. You see, I went out with a party hunting, and I sulked behind. They went off up a steep climb, and I said I'd wander around below till they got back, or perhaps ride back to camp; but, when I tried to find the camp, it wasn't where I had left it."

"Well, you've got to lie down and sleep awhile," said the girl decidedly. "You can't keep going like that. It'll kill you. You lie down, and I'll watch, and get dinner. I'm going to cook that bird."

He demurred, but in the end she had her way; for he was exceedingly weary, and she saw it. So he let her spread the old coat down for him while he gathered some wood for a fire, and then he lay down and watched her simple preparations for the meal. Before he knew it he was asleep.

When he came to himself, there was a curious blending of dream and reality. He thought his lady was coming to him across the rough plains in an automobile, with gray wings like those of the bird the girl had shot, and his prayer as he knelt in the sand was drawing her, while overhead the air was full of a wild, sweet music from strange birds that mocked and called and trilled. But, when the automobile reached him and stopped, the lady withered into a little, old, dried-up creature of ashes; and the girl of the plains was sitting in her place radiant and beautiful.

He opened his eyes, and saw the rude little dinner set, and smelt the delicious odor of the roasted bird. The girl was standing on the other side of the fire, gravely whistling a most extraordinary song, like unto all the birds of the air at once.

She had made a little cake out of the corn-meal, and they feasted royally.

"I caught two fishes in the brook. We'll take them along for supper," she said as they packed the things again for starting. He tried to get her to take a rest also, and let him watch; but she insisted that they must go on, and promised to rest just before dark. "For we must travel hard at night, you know," she added fearfully.

He questioned her more about the man who might be pursuing, and came to understand her fears.

"The scoundrel!" he muttered, looking at the delicate features and clear, lovely profile of the girl. He felt a strong desire to throttle the evil man.

He asked a good many questions about her life, and was filled with wonder over the flower-like girl who seemed to have blossomed in the wilderness with no hand to cultivate her save a lazy, clever, drunken father, and a kind but ignorant mother. How could she have escaped being coarsened amid such surroundings. How was it, with such brothers as she had, that she had come forth as lovely and unhurt as she seemed? He somehow began to feel a great anxiety for her lonely future and a desire to put her in the way of protection. But at present they were still in the wilderness; and he began to be glad that he was here too, and might have the privilege of protecting her now, if there should be need.

As it grew toward evening, they came upon a little grassy spot in a coulee where the horses might rest and eat. Here they stopped, and the girl threw herself under a shelter of trees, with the old coat for a pillow, and rested, while the man paced up and down at a distance, gathering wood for a fire, and watching the horizon. As night came on, the city-bred man longed for shelter. He was by no means a coward where known quantities were concerned, but to face wild animals and drunken brigands in a strange, wild plain with no help near was anything but an enlivening prospect. He could not understand why they had not come upon some human habitation by this time. He had never realized how vast this country was before. When he came westward on the train he did not remember to have traversed such long stretches of country without a sign of civilization, though of course a train went so much faster than a horse that he had no adequate means of judging. Then, besides, they were on no trail now, and had probably gone in a most roundabout way to anywhere. In reality they had twice come within five miles of little homesteads, tucked away beside a stream in a fertile spot; but they had not known it. A mile further to the right at one spot would have put them on the trail and made their way easier and shorter, but that they could not know.

The girl did not rest long. She seemed to feel her pursuit more as the darkness crept on, and kept anxiously looking for the moon.

"We must go toward the moon," she said as she watched the bright spot coming in the east.

They ate their supper of fish and corn-bread with the appetite that grows on horseback, and by the time they had started on their way again the moon spread a path of silver before them, and they went forward feeling as if they had known each other a long time. For a while their fears and hopes were blended in one.

Meantime, as the sun sank and the moon rose, a traveller rode up the steep ascent to the little lonely cabin which the girl had left. He was handsome and dark and strong, with a scarlet kerchief knotted at his throat; and he rode slowly, cautiously, looking furtively about and ahead of him. He was doubly armed, and his pistols gleamed in the moonlight, while an ugly knife nestled keenly in a secret sheath.

He was wicked, for the look upon his face was not good to see; and he was a coward, for he started at the flutter of a night-bird hurrying late to its home in a rock by the wayside. The mist rising from the valley in wreaths of silver gauze startled him again as he rounded the trail to the cabin, and for an instant he stopped and drew his dagger, thinking the ghost he feared was walking thus early. A draught from the bottle he carried in his pocket steadied his nerves, and he went on, but stopped again in front of the cabin; for there stood another horse, and there in the doorway stood a figure in the darkness! His curses rang through the still air and smote the moonlight. His pistol flashed forth a volley of fire to second him.

In answer to his demand who was there came another torrent of profanity. It was one of his comrades of the day before. He explained that he and two others had come up to pay a visit to the pretty girl. They had had a wager as to who could win her, and they had come to try; but she was not here. The door was fastened. They had forced it. There was no sign of her about. The other two had gone down to the place where her brother was buried to see whether she was there. Women were known to be sentimental. She might be that kind. He had agreed to wait here, but he was getting uneasy. Perhaps, if the other two found her, they might not be fair.

The last comer with a mighty oath explained that the girl belonged to him, and that no one had a right to her. He demanded that the other come with him to the grave, and see what had become of the girl; and then they would all go and drink together—but the girl belonged to him.

They rode to the place of the graves, and met the two others returning; but there was no sign of the girl, and the three taunted the one, saying that the girl had given him the slip. Amid much argument as to whose she was and where she was, they rode on cursing through God's beauty. They passed the bottle continually, that their nerves might be the steadier; and, when they came to the deserted cabin once more, they paused and discussed what to do.

At last it was agreed that they should start on a quest after her, and with oaths, and coarse jests, and drinking, they started down the trail of which the girl had gone in search by her roundabout way.

CHAPTER V

A NIGHT RIDE

It was a wonderful night that the two spent wading the sea of moonlight together on the plain. The almost unearthly beauty of the scene grew upon them. They had none of the loneliness that had possessed each the night before, and might now discover all the wonders of the way.

Early in the way they came upon a prairie-dogs' village, and the man would have lingered watching with curiosity, had not the girl urged him on. It was the time of night when she had started to run away, and the same apprehension that filled her then came upon her with the evening. She longed to be out of the land which held the man she feared. She would rather bury herself in the earth and smother to death than be caught by him. But, as they rode on, she told her companion much of the habits of the curious little creatures they had seen; and then, as the night settled down upon them, she pointed out the dark, stealing creatures that slipped from their way now and then, or gleamed with a fearsome green eye from some temporary refuge.

At first the cold shivers kept running up and down the young man as he realized that here before him in the sage-brush was a real live animal about which he had read so much, and which he had come out bravely to hunt. He kept his hand upon his revolver, and was constantly on the alert, nervously looking behind lest a troop of coyotes or wolves should be quietly stealing upon him. But, as the girl talked fearlessly of them in much the same way as we talk of a neighbor's fierce dog, he grew gradually calmer, and was able to watch a dark, velvet-footed moving object ahead without starting.

By and by he pointed to the heavens, and talked of the stars. Did she know that constellation? No? Then he explained. Such and such stars were so many miles from the earth. He told their names, and a bit of mythology connected with the name, and then went on to speak of the moon, and the possibility of its once having been inhabited.

The girl listened amazed. She knew certain stars as landmarks, telling east from west and north from south; and she had often watched them one by one coming out, and counted them her friends; but that they were worlds, and that the inhabitants of this earth knew anything whatever about the heavenly bodies, she had never heard. Question after question she plied him with, some of them showing extraordinary intelligence and thought, and others showing deeper ignorance than a little child in our kindergartens would show.

He wondered more and more as their talk went on. He grew deeply interested in unfolding the wonders of the heavens to her; and, as he studied her pure profile in the moonlight with eager, searching, wistful gaze, her beauty impressed him more and more. In the East the man had a friend, an artist. He thought how wonderful a theme for a painting this scene would make. The girl in picturesque hat of soft felt, riding with careless ease and grace; horse, maiden, plain, bathed in a sea of silver.

More and more as she talked the man wondered how this girl reared in the wilds had acquired a speech so free from grammatical errors. She was apparently deeply ignorant, and yet with a very few exceptions she made no serious errors in English. How was it to be accounted for?

He began to ply her with questions about herself, but could not find that she had ever come into contact with people who were educated. She had not even lived in any of the miserable little towns that flourish in the wildest of the West, and not within several hundred miles of a city. Their nearest neighbors in one direction had been forty miles away, she said, and said it as if that were an everyday distance for a neighbor to live.

Mail? They had had a letter once that she could remember, when she was a little girl. It was just a few lines in pencil to say that her mother's father had died. He had been killed in an accident of some sort, working in the city where he lived. Her mother had kept the letter and cried over it till almost all the pencil marks were gone.

No, they had no mail on the mountain where their homestead was.

Yes, her father went there first because he thought he had discovered gold, but it turned out to be a mistake; so, as they had no other place to go to, and no money to go with, they had just stayed there; and her father and brothers had been cow-punchers, but she and her mother had scarcely ever gone away from home. There were the little children to care for; and, when they died, her mother did not care to go, and would not let her go far alone.

O, yes, she had ridden a great deal, sometimes with her brothers, but not often. They went with rough men, and her mother felt afraid to have her go. The men all drank. Her brothers drank. Her father drank too. She stated it as if it were a sad fact common to all mankind, and ended with the statement which was almost, not quite, a question, "I guess you drink too."

"Well," said the young man hesitatingly, "not that way. I take a glass of wine now and then in company, you know—"

"Yes, I know," sighed the girl. "Men are all alike. Mother used to say so. She said men were different from women. They had to drink. She said they all did it. Only she said her father never did; but he was very good, though he had to work hard."

"Indeed," said the young man, his color rising in the moonlight, "indeed, you make a mistake. I don't drink at all, not that way. I'm not like them. I—why, I only—well, the fact is, I don't care a red cent about the stuff anyway; and I don't want you to think I'm like them. If it will do you any good, I'll never touch it again, not a drop."

He said it earnestly. He was trying to vindicate himself. Just why he should care to do so he did not know, only that all at once it was very necessary that he should appear different in the eyes of this girl from, the other men she had known.

"Will you really?" she asked, turning to look in his face. "Will you promise that?"

"Why, certainly I will," he said, a trifle embarrassed that she had taken him at his word. "Of course I will. I tell you it's nothing to me. I only took a glass at the club occasionally when the other men were drinking, and sometimes when I went to banquets, class banquets, you know, and dinners—"

Now the girl had never heard of class banquets, but to take a glass occasionally when the other men were drinking was what her brothers did; and so she sighed, and said: "Yes, you may promise, but I know you won't keep it. Father promised too; but, when he got with the other men, it did no good. Men are all alike."

"But I'm not," he insisted stoutly. "I tell you I'm not. I don't drink, and I won't drink. I promise you solemnly here under God's sky that I'll never drink another drop of intoxicating liquor again if I know it as long as I live."

He put out his hand toward her, and she put her own into it with a quick grasp for just an instant.

"Then you're not like other men, after all," she said with a glad ring in her voice. "That must be why I wasn't so very much afraid of you when I woke up and found you standing there."

A distinct sense of pleasure came over him at her words. Why it should make him glad that she had not been afraid of him when she had first seen him in the wilderness he did not know. He forgot all about his own troubles. He forgot the lady in the automobile. Right then and there he dropped her out of his thoughts. He did not know it; but she was forgotten, and he did not think about her any more during that journey. Something had erased her. He had run away from her, and he had succeeded most effectually, more so than he knew.

There in the desert the man took his first temperance pledge, urged thereto by a girl who had never heard of a temperance pledge in her life, had never joined a woman's temperance society, and knew nothing about women's crusades. Her own heart had taught her out of a bitter experience just how to use her God-given influence.

They came to a long stretch of level ground then, smooth and hard; and the horses as with common consent set out to gallop shoulder to shoulder in a wild, exhilarating skim across the plain. Talking was impossible. The man reflected that he was making great strides in experience, first a prayer and then a pledge, all in the wilderness. If any one had told him he was going into the West for this, he would have laughed him to scorn.

Towards morning they rode more slowly. Their horses were growing jaded. They talked in lower tones as they looked toward the east. It was as if they feared they might waken some one too soon. There is something awesome about the dawning of a new day, and especially when one has been sailing a sea of silver all night. It is like coming back from an unreal world into a sad, real one. Each was almost sorry that the night was over. The new day might hold so much of hardship or relief, so much of trouble or surprise; and this night had been perfect, a jewel cut to set in memory with every facet flashing to the light. They did not like to get back to reality from the converse they had held together. It was an experience for each which would never be forgotten.

Once there came the distant sound of shots and shouts. The two shrank nearer each other, and the man laid his strong hand protectingly on the mane of the girl's horse; but he did not touch her hand. The lady of his thoughts had sometimes let him hold her jewelled hand, and smiled with drooping lashes when he fondled it; and, when she had tired of him, other admirers might claim the same privilege. But this woman of the wilderness—he would not even in his thoughts presume to touch her little brown, firm hand. Somehow she had commanded his honor and respect from the first minute, even before she shot the bird.

Once a bob-cat shot across their path but a few feet in front of them, and later a kit-fox ran growling up with ruffled fur; but the girl's quick shot soon put it to flight, and they passed on through the dawning morning of the first real Sabbath day the girl had ever known.

"It is Sunday morning at home," said the man gravely as he watched the sun lift its rosy head from the mist of mountain and valley outspread before them. "Do you have such an institution out here?"

The girl grew white about the lips. "Awful things happen on Sunday," she said with a shudder.

He felt a great pity rising in his heart for her, and strove to turn her thoughts in other directions. Evidently there was a recent sorrow connected with the Sabbath.

"You are tired," said he, "and the horses are tired. See! We ought to stop and rest. The daylight has come, and nothing can hurt us. Here is a good place, and sheltered. We can fasten the horses behind these bushes, and no one will guess we are here."

She assented, and they dismounted. The man cut an opening into a clump of thick growth with his knife, and there they fastened the weary horses, well hidden from sight if any one chanced that way. The girl lay down a few feet away in a spot almost entirely surrounded by sage-brush which had reached an unusual height and made a fine hiding-place. Just outside the entrance of this natural chamber the man lay down on a fragrant bed of sage-brush. He had gathered enough for the girl first, and spread out the old coat over it; and she had dropped asleep almost as soon as she lay down. But, although his own bed of sage-brush was tolerably comfortable, even to one accustomed all his life to the finest springs and hair mattress that money could buy, and although the girl had insisted that he must rest too, for he was weary and there was no need to watch, sleep would not come to his eyelids.

He lay there resting and thinking. How strange was the experience through which he was passing! Came ever a wealthy, college-bred, society man into the like before? What did it all mean? His being lost, his wandering for a day, the sight of this girl and his pursuit, the prayer under the open sky, and that night of splendor under the moonlight riding side by side. It was like some marvellous tale.

And this girl! Where was she going? What was to become of her? Out in the world where he came from, were they ever to reach it, she would be nothing. Her station in life was beneath his so far that the only recognition she could have would be one which would degrade her. This solitary journey they were taking, how the world would lift up its hands in horror at it! A girl without a chaperon! She was impossible! And yet it all seemed right and good, and the girl was evidently recognized by the angels; else how had she escaped from degradation thus far?

Ah! How did he know she had? But he smiled at that. No one could look into that pure, sweet face, and doubt that she was as good as she was beautiful. If it was not so, he hoped he would never find it out. She seemed to him a woman yet unspoiled, and he shrank from the thought of what the world might do for her—the world and its cultivation, which would not be for her, because she was friendless and without money or home. The world would have nothing but toil to give her, with a meagre living.

Where was she going, and what was she proposing to do? Must he not try to help her in some way? Did not the fact that she had saved his life demand so much from him? If he had not found her, he must surely have starved before he got out of this wild place. Even yet starvation was not an impossibility; for they had not reached any signs of habitation yet, and there was but one more portion of corn-meal and a little coffee left. They had but two matches now, and there had been no more flights of birds, nor brooks with fishes.

In fact, the man found a great deal to worry about as he lay there, too weary with the unaccustomed exercise and experiences to sleep.

He reflected that the girl had told him very little, after all, about her plans. He must ask her. He wished he knew more of her family. If he were only older and she younger, or if he had the right kind of a woman friend to whom he might take her, or send her! How horrible that that scoundrel was after her! Such men were not men, but beasts, and should be shot down.

Far off in the distance, it might have been in the air or in his imagination, there sometimes floated a sound as of faint voices or shouts; but they came and went, and he listened, and by and by heard no more. The horses breathed heavily behind their sage-brush stable, and the sun rose higher and hotter. At last sleep came, troubled, fitful, but sleep, oblivion. This time there was no lady in an automobile.

It was high noon when he awoke, for the sun had reached around the sage-brush, and was pouring full into his face. He was very uncomfortable, and moreover an uneasy sense of something wrong pervaded his mind. Had he or had he not, heard a strange, low, sibilant, writhing sound just as he came to consciousness? Why did he feel that something, some one, had passed him but a moment before?

He rubbed his eyes open, and fanned himself with his hat. There was not a sound to be heard save a distant hawk in the heavens, and the breathing of the horses. He stepped over, and made sure that they were all right, and then came back. Was the girl still sleeping? Should he call her? But what should he call her? She had no name to him as yet. He could not say, "My dear madam" in the wilderness, nor yet "mademoiselle."

Perhaps it was she who had passed him. Perhaps she was looking about for water, or for fire-wood. He cast his eyes about, but the thick growth of sage-brush everywhere prevented his seeing much. He stepped to the right and then to the left of the little enclosure where she had gone to sleep, but there was no sign of life.

At last the sense of uneasiness grew upon him until he spoke.

"Are you awake yet?" he ventured; but the words somehow stuck in his throat, and would not sound out clearly. He ventured the question again, but it seemed to go no further than the gray-green foliage in front of him. Did he catch an alert movement, the sound of attention, alarm? Had he perhaps frightened her?

His flesh grew creepy, and he was angry with himself that he stood here actually trembling and for no reason. He felt that there was danger in the air. What could it mean? He had never been a believer in premonitions or superstitions of any kind. But the thought came to him that perhaps that evil man had come softly while he slept, and had stolen the girl away. Then all at once a horror seized him, and he made up his mind to end this suspense and venture in to see whether she were safe.

CHAPTER VI

A CHRISTIAN ENDEAVOR MEETING IN THE WILDERNESS

He stepped boldly around the green barrier, and his first glance told him she was lying there still asleep; but the consciousness of another presence held him from going away. There, coiled on the ground with venomous fangs extended and eyes glittering like slimy jewels, was a rattlesnake, close beside her.

For a second he gazed with a kind of fascinated horror, and his brain refused to act. Then he knew he must do something, and at once. He had read of serpents and travellers' encounters with them, but no memory of what was to be done under such circumstances came. Shoot? He dared not. He would be more likely to kill the girl than the serpent, and in any event would precipitate the calamity. Neither was there any way to awaken the girl and drag her from peril, for the slightest movement upon her part would bring the poisoned fangs upon her.

He cast his eyes about for some weapon, but there was not a stick or a stone in sight. He was a good golf-player; if he had a loaded stick, he could easily take the serpent's head off, he thought; but there was no stick. There was only one hope, he felt, and that would be to attract the creature to himself; and he hardly dared move lest the fascinated gaze should close upon the victim as she lay there sweetly sleeping, unaware of her new peril.

Suddenly he knew what to do. Silently he stepped back out of sight, tore off his coat, and then cautiously approached the snake again, holding the coat up before him. There was an instant's pause when he calculated whether the coat could drop between the snake and the smooth brown arm in front before the terrible fangs would get there; and then the coat dropped, the man bravely holding one end of it as a wall between the serpent and the girl, crying to her in an agony of frenzy to awaken and run.

There was a terrible moment in which he realized that the girl was saved and he himself was in peril of death, while he held to the coat till the girl was on her feet in safety. Then he saw the writhing coil at his feet turn and fasten its eyes of fury upon him. He was conscious of being uncertain whether his fingers could let go the coat, and whether his trembling knees could carry him away before the serpent struck; then it was all over, and he and the girl were standing outside the sage-brush, with the sound of the pistol dying away among the echoes, and the fine ache of his arm where her fingers had grasped him to drag him from danger.

The serpent was dead. She had shot it. She took that as coolly as she had taken the bird in its flight. But she stood looking at him with great eyes of gratitude, and he looked at her amazed that they were both alive, and scarcely understanding all that had happened.

The girl broke the stillness.

"You are what they call a 'tenderfoot,'" she said significantly.

"Yes," he assented humbly, "I guess I am. I couldn't have shot it to save anybody's life."

"You are a tenderfoot, and you couldn't shoot," she continued eulogistically, as if it were necessary to have it all stated plainly, "but you—you are what my brother used to call 'a white man.' You couldn't shoot; but you could risk your life, and hold that coat, and look death in the face. *You* are no tenderfoot."

There was eloquence in her eyes, and in her voice there were tears. She turned away to hide if any were in her eyes. But the man put out his hand on her sure little brown one, and took it firmly in his own, looking down upon her with his own eyes filled with tears of which he was not ashamed.

"And what am I to say to you for saving my life?" he said.

"I? O, that was easy," said the girl, rousing to the commonplace. "I can always shoot. Only you were hard to drag away. You seemed to want to stay there and die with your coat."

"They laughed at me for wearing that coat when we started away. They said a hunter never bothered himself with extra clothing," he mused as they walked away from the terrible spot.

"Do you think it was the prayer?" asked the girl suddenly.

"It may be!" said the man with wondering accent.

Then quietly, thoughtfully, they mounted and rode onward.

Their way, due east, led them around the shoulder of a hill. It was tolerably smooth, but they were obliged to go single file, so there was very little talking done.

It was nearly the middle of the afternoon when all at once a sound reached them from below, a sound so new that it was startling. They stopped their horses, and looked at each other. It was the faint sound of singing wafted on the light breeze, singing that came in whiffs like a perfume, and then died out. Cautiously they guided their horses on around the hill, keeping close together now. It was plain they were approaching some human being or beings. No bird could sing like that. There were indistinct words to the music.

They rounded the hillside, and stopped again side by side. There below them lay the trail for which they had been searching, and just beneath them, nestled against the hill, was a little schoolhouse of logs, weather-boarded, its windows open; and behind it and around it were horses tied, some of them hitched to wagons, but most of them with saddles.

The singing was clear and distinct now. They could hear the words. "O, that will be glory for me, glory for me, glory for me—"

"What is it?" she whispered.

"Why, I suspect it is a Sunday school or something of the kind."

"O! A school! Could we go in?"

"If you like," said the man, enjoying her simplicity. "We can tie out horses here behind the building, and they can rest. There is fresh grass in this sheltered place; see?"

He led her down behind the schoolhouse to a spot where the horses could not be seen from the trail. The girl peered curiously around the corner into the window. There sat two young girls about her own age, and one of them smiled at her. It seemed an invitation. She smiled back, and went on to the doorway reassured. When she entered the room, she found them pointing to a seat near a window, behind a small desk.

There were desks all over the room at regular intervals, and a larger desk up in front. Almost all the people sat at desks.

There was a curious wooden box in front at one side of, the big desk, and a girl sat before it pushing down some black and white strips that looked like sticks, and making her feet go, and singing with all her might. The curious box made music, the same music the people were singing. Was it a piano? she wondered. She had heard of pianos. Her father used to talk about them. O, and what was that her mother used to want? A "cab'net-organ." Perhaps this was a cab'net-organ. At any rate, she was entranced with the music.

Up behind the man who sat at the big desk was a large board painted black with some white marks on it. The sunlight glinted across it, and she could not tell what they were; but, when she moved a little, she saw quite clearly it was a large cross with words underneath it—"He will hide me."

It was a strange place. The girl looked around shyly, and felt submerged in the volume of song that rolled around her, from voices untrained, perhaps, but hearts that knew whereof they sang. To her it was heavenly music, if she had the least conception of what such music was like. "Glory," "glory," "glory!" The words seemed to fit the day, and the sunshine, and the deliverance that had come to her so recently. She looked around for her companion and deliverer to enjoy it with him, but he had not come in yet.

The two girls were handing her a book now and pointing to the place. She could read. Her mother had taught her just a little before the other children were born, but not much in the way of literature had ever come in her way. She grasped the book eagerly, hungrily, and looked where the finger pointed. Yes, there were the words. "Glory for me!" "Glory for me!" Did that mean her? Was there glory for her anywhere in the world? She sighed with the joy of the possibility, as the "Glory Song" rolled along, led by the enthusiasm of one who had recently come from a big city where it had been sung in a great revival service. Some kind friend had given some copies of a leaflet containing it and a few other new songs to this little handful of Christians, and they were singing them as if they had been a thousand strong.

The singing ceased and the man at the big desk said, "Let us have the verses."

"'The eternal God is thy refuge, and underneath are the everlasting arms,'" said a careworn woman in the front seat.

"'He shall cover thee with his feathers, and under his wings shalt thou trust,'" said a young man next.

"'In the time of trouble he shall hide me in his pavilion; in the secret of his tabernacle shall he hide me,'" read the girl who had handed the book. The slip of paper she had written it on fluttered to the floor at the feet of the stranger, and the stranger stooped and picked it up, offering it back; but the other girl shook her head, and the stranger kept it, looking wonderingly at the words, trying to puzzle out a meaning.

There were other verses repeated, but just then a sound smote upon the girl's ear which deadened all others. In spite of herself she began to tremble. Even her lips seemed to her to move with the weakness of her fear. She looked up, and the man was just coming toward the door; but her eyes grew dizzy, and a faintness seemed to come over her.

Up the trail on horseback, with shouts and ribald songs, rode four rough men, too drunk to know where they were going. The little schoolhouse seemed to attract their attention as they passed, and just for deviltry they shouted out a volley of oaths and vile talk to the worshippers within. One in particular, the leader, looked straight into the face of the young man as he returned from fastening the horses and was about to enter the schoolhouse, and pretended to point his pistol at him, discharging it immediately into the air. This was the signal for some wild firing as the men rode on past the schoolhouse, leaving a train of curses behind them to haunt the air and struggle with the "Glory Song" in the memories of those who heard.

The girl looked out from her seat beside the window, and saw the evil face of the man from whom she had fled. She thought for a terrible minute, which seemed ages long to her, that she was cornered now. She began to look about on the people there helplessly, and wonder whether they would save her, would help her, in her time of need. Would they be able to fight and prevail against those four terrible men mad with liquor?

Suppose he said she was his—his wife, perhaps, or sister, who had run away. What could they do? Would they believe her? Would the man who had saved her life a few minutes ago believe her? Would anybody help her?

The party passed, and the man came in and sat down beside her quietly enough; but without a word or a look he knew at once who the man was he had just seen. His soul trembled for the girl, and his anger rose hot. He felt that a man like that ought to be wiped off the face of the earth in some way, or placed in solitary confinement the rest of his life.

He looked down at the girl, trembling, brave, white, beside him; and he felt like gathering her in his arms and hiding her himself, such a frail, brave, courageous little soul she seemed. But the calm nerve with which she had shot the serpent was gone now. He saw she was trembling and ready to cry. Then he smiled upon her, a smile the like of which he had never given to human being before; at least, not since he was a tiny baby and smiled confidingly into his mother's face. Something in that smile was like sunshine to a nervous chill.

The girl felt the comfort of it, though she still trembled. Down her eyes drooped to the paper in her shaking hands. Then gradually, letter by letter, word by word, the verse spoke to her. Not all the meaning she gathered, for "pavilion" and "tabernacle" were unknown words to her, but the hiding she could understand. She had been hidden in her time of trouble. Some one had done it. "He"—the word would fit the man by her side, for he had helped to hide her, and to save her more than once; but just now there came a dim perception that it was some other He, some One greater who had worked this miracle and saved her once more to go on perhaps to better things.

There were many things said in that meeting, good and wise and true. They might have been helpful to the girl if she had understood, but her thoughts had much to do. One grain of truth she had gathered for her future use. There was a "hiding" somewhere in this world, and she had had it in a time of trouble. One moment more out upon the open, and the terrible man might have seen her.

There came a time of prayer in which all heads were bowed, and a voice here and there murmured a few soft little words which she did not comprehend; but at the close they all joined in "the prayer"; and, when she heard the words, "Our Father," she closed her eyes, which had been curiously open and watching, and joined her voice softly with the rest. Somehow it seemed to connect her safety with "our Father," and she felt a stronger faith than ever in her prayer.

The young man listened intently to all he heard. There was something strangely impressive to him in this simple worship out in what to him was a vast wilderness. He felt more of the true spirit of worship than he had ever felt at home sitting in the handsomely upholstered pew beside his mother and sister while the choir-boys chanted the processional and the light filtered through costly windows of many colors over the large and cultivated congregation. There was something about the words of these people that went straight to the heart more than all the intonings of the cultured voices he had ever heard. Truly they meant what they said, and God had been a reality to them in many a time of trouble. That seemed to be the theme of the afternoon, the saving power of the eternal God, made perfect through the need and the trust of His people. He was reminded more than once of the incident of the morning and the miraculous saving of his own and his companion's life.

When the meeting was over, the people gathered in groups and talked with one another. The girl who had handed the book came over and spoke to the strangers, putting out her hand pleasantly. She was the missionary's daughter.

"What is this? School?" asked the stranger eagerly.

"Yes, this is the schoolhouse," said the missionary's daughter; "but this meeting is Christian Endeavor. Do you live near here? Can't you come every time?"

"No. I live a long way off," said the girl sadly. "That is, I did. I don't live anywhere now. I'm going away."

"I wish you lived here. Then you could come to our meeting. Did you have a Christian Endeavor where you lived?"

"No. I never saw one before. It's nice. I like it."

Another girl came up now, and put out her hand in greeting. "You must come again," she said politely.

"I don't know," said the visitor. "I sha'n't be coming back soon."

"Are you going far?"

"As far as I can. I'm going East."

"O," said the inquisitor; and then, seeing the missionary's daughter was talking to some one else, she whispered, nodding toward the man, "Is he your husband?"

The girl looked startled, while a slow color mounted into her cheeks.

"No," said she gravely, thoughtfully. "But—he saved my life a little while ago."

"Oh!" said the other, awestruck. "My! And ain't he handsome? How did he do it?"

But the girl could not talk about it. She shuddered.

"It was a dreadful snake," she said, "and I was—I didn't see it. It was awful! I can't tell you about it."

"My!" said the girl. "How terrible!"

The people were passing out now. The man was talking with the missionary, asking the road to somewhere. The girl suddenly realized that this hour of preciousness was over, and life was to be faced again. Those men, those terrible men! She had recognized the others as having been among her brother's funeral train. Where were they, and why had they gone that way? Were they on her track? Had they any clue to her whereabouts? Would they turn back pretty soon, and catch her when the people were gone home?

It appeared that the nearest town was Malta, sixteen miles away, down in the direction where the party of men had passed. There were only four houses near the schoolhouse, and they were scattered in different directions along the stream in the valley. The two stood still near the door after the congregation had scattered. The girl suddenly shivered. As she looked down the road, she seemed again to see the coarse face of the man she feared, and to hear his loud laughter and oaths. What if he should come back again? "I cannot go that way!" she said, pointing down the trail toward Malta. "I would rather die with wild beasts."

"No!" said the man with decision. "On no account can we go that way. Was that the man you ran away from?"

"Yes." She looked up at him, her eyes filled with wonder over the way in which he had coupled his lot with hers.

"Poor little girl!" he said with deep feeling. "You would be better off with the beasts. Come, let us hurry away from here!"

They turned sharply away from the trail, and followed down behind a family who were almost out of sight around the hill. There would be a chance of getting some provisions, the man thought. The girl thought of nothing except to get away. They rode hard, and soon came within hailing-distance of the people ahead of them, and asked a few questions.

No, there were no houses to the north until you were over the Canadian line, and the trail was hard to follow. Few people went that way. Most went down to Malta. Why didn't they go to Malta? There was a road there, and stores. It was by all means the best way. Yes, there was another house about twenty miles away on this trail. It was a large ranch, and was near to another town that had a railroad. The people seldom came this way, as there were other places more accessible to them. The trail was little used, and might be hard to find in some places; but, if they kept the Cottonwood Creek in sight, and followed on to the end of the valley, and then crossed the bench to the right, they would be in sight of it, and couldn't miss it. It was a good twenty miles beyond their house; but, if the travellers didn't miss the way, they might reach it before dark. Yes, the people could supply a few provisions at their house if the strangers didn't mind taking what was at hand.

The man in the wagon tried his best to find out where the two were going and what they were going for; but the man from the East baffled his curiosity in a most dexterous manner, so that, when the two rode away from the two-roomed log house where the kind-hearted people lived, they left no clue to their identity or mission beyond the fact that they were going quite a journey, and had got a little off their trail and run out of provisions.

They felt comparatively safe from pursuit for a few hours at least, for the men could scarcely return and trace them very soon. They had not stopped to eat anything; but all the milk they could drink had been given to them, and its refreshing strength was racing through their veins. They started upon their long ride with the pleasure of their companionship strong upon them.

"What was it all about?" asked the girl as they settled into a steady gait after a long gallop across a smooth level place.

He looked at her questioningly.

"The school. What did it mean? She said it was a Christian Endeavor. What is that?"

"Why, some sort of a religious meeting, or something of that kind, I suppose," he answered lamely. "Did you enjoy it?"

"Yes," she answered solemnly, "I liked it. I never went to such a thing before. The girl said they had one everywhere all over the world. What do you think she meant?"

"Why, I don't know, I'm sure, unless it's some kind of a society. But it looked to me like a prayer meeting. I've heard about prayer meetings, but I never went to one, though I never supposed they were so interesting. That was a remarkable story that old man told of how he was taken care of that night among the Indians. He evidently believes that prayer helps people."

"Don't you?" she asked quickly.

"O, certainly!" he said, "but there was something so genuine about the way the old man told it that it made you feel it in a new way."

"It is all new to me," said the girl. "But mother used to go to Sunday school and church and prayer meeting. She's often told me about it. She used to sing sometimes. One song was 'Rock of Ages.' Did you ever hear that?

of Ages,

ɔ hide ɾ

She said it slowly and in a singsong voice, as if she were measuring the words off to imaginary notes. "I thought about that the night I started. I wished I knew where that rock was. Is there a rock anywhere that they call the Rock of Ages?"

The young man was visibly embarrassed. He wanted to laugh, but he would not hurt her in that way again. He was not accustomed to talking religion; yet here by this strange girl's side it seemed perfectly natural that he, who knew so very little experimentally himself about it, should be trying to explain the Rock of Ages to a soul in need. All at once it flashed upon him that it was for just such souls in need as this one that the Rock of Ages came into the world.

"I've heard the song. Yes, I think they sing it in all churches. It's quite common. No, there isn't any place called Rock of Ages. It refers—that is, I believe—why, you see the thing is figurative—that is, a kind of picture of things. It refers to the Deity."

"O! Who is that?" asked the girt.

"Why—God." He tried to say it as if he had been telling her it was Mr. Smith or Mr. Jones, but somehow the sound of the word on his lips thus shocked him. He did not know how to go on. "It just means God will take care of people."

"O!" she said, and this time a light of understanding broke over her face. "But," she added, "I wish I knew what it meant, the meeting, and why they did it. There must be some reason. They wouldn't do it for nothing. And how do they know it's all so? Where did they find it out?"

The man felt he was beyond his depth; so he sought to change the subject. "I wish you would tell me about yourself," he said gently. "I should like to understand you better. We have travelled together for a good many hours now, and we ought to know more about each other."

"What do you want to know?" She asked it gravely. "There isn't much to tell but what I've told you. I've lived on a mountain all my life, and helped mother. The rest all died. The baby first, and my two brothers, and father, and mother, and then John. I said the prayer for John, and ran away."

"Yes, but I want to know about your life. You know I live in the East where everything is different. It's all new to me out here. I want to know, for instance, how you came to talk so well. You don't talk like a girl that never went to school. You speak as if you had read and studied. You make so few mistakes in your English. You speak quite correctly. That is not usual, I believe, when people have lived all their lives away from school, you know. You don't talk like the girls I have met since I came out here."

"Father always made me speak right. He kept at every one of us children when we said a word wrong, and made us say it over again. It made him angry to hear words said wrong. He made mother cry once when she said 'done' when she ought to have said 'did.' Father went to school once, but mother only went a little while. Father knew a great deal, and when he was sober he used to teach us things once in a while. He taught me to read. I can read anything I ever saw."

"Did you have many books and magazines?" he asked innocently.

"We had three books!" she answered proudly, as if that were a great many. "One was a grammar. Father bought it for mother before they were married, and she always kept it wrapped up in paper carefully. She used to get it out for me to read in sometimes; but she was very careful with it, and when she died I put it in her hands. I thought she would like to have it close to her, because it always seemed so much to her. You see father bought it. Then there was an almanac, and a book about stones and earth. A man who was hunting for gold left that. He stopped over night at our house, and asked for some, thing to eat. He hadn't any money to pay for it; so he left that book with us, and said when he found the gold he would come and buy it back again. But he never came back."

"Is that all that you have ever read?" he asked compassionately.

"O, no! We got papers sometimes. Father would come home with a whole paper wrapped around some bundle. Once there was a beautiful story about a girl; but the paper was torn in the middle, and I never knew how it came out."

There was great wistfulness in her voice. It seemed to be one of the regrets of her girlhood that she did not know how that other girl in the story fared. All at once she turned to him.

"Now tell me about your life," she said. "I'm sure you have a great deal to tell."

His face darkened in a way that made her sorry.

"O, well," said he as if it mattered very little about his life, "I had a nice home—have yet, for the matter of that. Father died when I was little, and mother let me do just about as I pleased. I went to school because the other fellows did, and because that was the thing to do. After I grew up I liked it. That is, I liked some studies; so I went to a university."

"What is that?"

"O, just a higher school where you learn grown-up things. Then I travelled. When I came home, I went into society a good deal. But"—and his face darkened again—"I got tired of it all, and thought I would come out here for a while and hunt, and I got lost, and I found you!" He smiled into her face. "Now you know the rest."

Something passed between them in that smile and glance, a flash of the recognition of souls, and a gladness in each other's company, that made the heart warm. They said no more for some time, but rode quietly side by side.

They had come to the end of the valley, and were crossing the bench. The distant ranch could quite distinctly be seen. The silver moon had come up, for they had not been hurrying, and a great beauty pervaded everything. They almost shrank from approaching the buildings and people. They had enjoyed the ride and the companionship. Every step brought them nearer to what they had known all the time was an indistinct future from which they had been joyously shut away for a little time till they might know each other.

CHAPTER VII
BAD NEWS

They found rest for the night at the ranch house. The place was wide and hospitable. The girl looked about her with wonder on the comfortable arrangements for work. If only her mother had had such a kitchen to work in, and such a pleasant, happy home, she might have been living yet. There was a pleasant-faced, sweet-voiced woman with gray hair whom the men called "mother." She gave the girl a kindly welcome, and made her sit down to a nice warm supper, and, when it was over, led her to a little room where her own bed was, and told her she might sleep with her. The girl lay down in a maze of wonder, but was too weary with the long ride to keep awake and think about it.

They slept, the two travellers, a sound and dreamless sleep, wherein seemed peace and moonlight, and a forgetting of sorrows.

Early the next morning the girl awoke. The woman by her side was already stirring. There was breakfast to get for the men. The woman asked her a few questions about her journey.

"He's your brother, ain't he, dearie?" asked the woman as she was about to leave the room.

"No," said the girl.

"O," said the woman, puzzled, "then you and he's goin' to be married in the town."

"O, no!" said the girl with scarlet cheeks, thinking of the lady in the automobile.

"Not goin' to be married, dearie? Now that's too bad. Ain't he any kind of relation to you? Not an uncle nor cousin nor nothin'?"

"No."

"Then how be's you travellin' lone with him? It don't seem just right. You's a sweet, good girl; an' he's a fine man. But harm's come to more'n one. Where'd you take up with each other? Be he a neighbor? He looks like a man from way off, not hereabouts. You sure he ain't deceivin' you, dearie?"

The girl flashed her eyes in answer.

"Yes, I'm sure. He's a good man. He prays to our Father. No, he's not a neighbor, nor an uncle, nor a cousin. He's just a man that got lost. We were both lost on the prairie in the night; and he's from the East, and got lost from his party of hunters. He had nothing to eat, but I had; so I gave him some. Then he saved my life when a snake almost stung me. He's been good to me."

The woman looked relieved.

"And where you goin', dearie, all 'lone? What your folks thinkin' 'bout to let you go 'lone this way?"

"They're dead," said the girl with great tears in her eyes.

"Dearie me! And you so young! Say, dearie, s'pose you stay here with me. I'm lonesome, an' there's no women near by here. You could help me and be comp'ny. The men would like to have a girl round. There's plenty likely men on this ranch could make a good home fer a girl sometime. Stay here with me, dearie."

Had this refuge been offered the girl during her first flight in the wilderness, with what joy and thankfulness she would have accepted! Now it suddenly seemed a great impossibility for her to stay. She must go on. She had a pleasant ride before her, and delightful companionship; and she was going to school. The world was wide, and she had entered it. She had no mind to pause thus on the threshold, and never see further than Montana. Moreover, the closing words of the woman did not please her.

"I cannot stay," she said decidedly. "I'm going to school. And I do not want a man. I have just run away from a man, a dreadful one. I am going to school in the East. I have some relations there, and perhaps I can find them."

"You don't say so!" said the woman, looking disappointed. She had taken a great fancy to the sweet young face. "Well, dearie, why not stay here a little while, and write to your folks, and then go on with some one who is going your way? I don't like to see you go off with that man. It ain't the proper thing. He knows it himself. I'm afraid he's deceivin' you. I can see by his clo'es he's one of the fine young fellows that does as they please. He won't think any good of you if you keep travellin' 'lone with him. It's all well 'nough when you get lost, an' he was nice to help you out and save you from snakes; but he knows he ain't no business travellin' 'lone with you, you pretty little creature!"

"You must not talk so!" said the girl, rising and flashing her eyes again. "He's a good man. He's what my brother called 'a white man all through.' Besides, he's got a lady, a beautiful lady, in the East. She rides in some kind of a grand carriage that goes of itself, and he thinks a great deal of her."

The woman looked as if she were but half convinced.

"It may seem all right to you, dearie," she said sadly; "but I'm old, and I've seen things happen. You'd find his fine lady wouldn't go jantin' round the world 'lone with him unless she's married. I've lived East, and I know; and what's more, he knows it too. He may mean all right, but you never can trust folks."

The woman went away to prepare breakfast then, and left the girl feeling as if the whole world was against her, trying to hold her. She was glad when the man suggested that they hurry their breakfast and get away as quickly as possible. She did not smile when the old woman came out to bid her good-by, and put a detaining hand on the horse's bridle, saying, "You better stay with me, after all, hadn't you, dearie?"

The man looked inquiringly at the two women, and saw like a flash the suspicion of the older woman, read the trust and haughty anger in the beautiful younger face, and then smiled down on the old woman whose kindly hospitality had saved them for a while from the terrors of the open night, and said:

"Don't you worry about her, auntie. I'm going to take good care of her, and perhaps she'll write you a letter some day, and tell you where she is and what she's doing."

Half reassured, the old woman gave him her name and address; and he wrote them down in a little red notebook.

When they were well started on their way, the man explained that he had hurried because from conversation with the men he had learned that this ranch where they had spent the night was on the direct trail from Malta to another small town. It might be that the pursuers would go further than Malta. Did she think they would go so far? They must have come almost a hundred miles already. Would they not be discouraged?

But the girl looked surprised. A hundred miles on horseback was not far. Her brother often used to ride a hundred miles just to see a fight or have a good time. She felt sure the men would not hesitate to follow a long distance if something else did not turn them aside.

The man's face looked sternly out from under his wide hat. He felt a great responsibility for the girl since he had seen the face of the man who was pursuing her.

Their horses were fresh, and the day was fine. They rode hard as long as the road was smooth, and did little talking. The girl was turning over in her mind the words the woman had spoken to her. But the thing that stuck there and troubled her was, "And he knows it is so."

Was she doing something for which this man by her side would not respect her? Was she overstepping some unwritten law of which she had never heard, and did he know it, and yet encourage her in it?

That she need fear him in the least she would not believe. Had she not watched the look of utmost respect on his face as he stood quietly waiting for her to awake the first morning they had met? Had he not had opportunity again and again to show her dishonor by word or look? Yet he had never been anything but gentle and courteous to her. She did not call things by these names, but she felt the gentleman in him.

Besides, there was the lady. He had told about her at the beginning. He evidently honored the lady. The woman had said that the lady would not ride with him alone. Was it true? Would he not like to have the lady ride alone with him when she was not his relative in any way? Then was there a difference between his thought of the lady and of herself? Of course, there was some; he loved the lady, but he should not think less honorably of her than of any lady in the land.

She sat straight and proudly in her man's saddle, and tried to make him feel that she was worthy of respect. She had tried to show him this when she had shot the bird. Now she recognized that there was a fine something, higher than shooting or prowess of any kind, which would command respect. It was something she felt belonged to her, yet she was not sure she commanded it. What did she lack, and how could she secure it?

He watched her quiet, thoughtful face, and the lady of his former troubled thoughts was as utterly forgotten by him as if she had never existed. He was unconsciously absorbed in the study of eye and lip and brow. His eyes were growing accustomed to the form and feature of this girl beside him, and he took pleasure in watching her.

They stopped for lunch in a coulee under a pretty cluster of cedar-trees a little back from the trail, where they might look over the way they had come and be warned against pursuers. About three o'clock they reached a town. Here the railroad came directly from Malta, but there was but one train a day each way.

The man went to the public stopping-place and asked for a room, and boldly demanded a private place for his "sister" to rest for a while. "She is my little sister," he told himself in excuse for the word. "She is my sister to care for. That is, if she were my sister, this is what I should want some good man to do for her."

He smiled as he went on his way after leaving the girl to rest. The thought of a sister pleased him. The old woman at the ranch had made him careful for the girl who was thus thrown in his company.

He rode down through the rough town to the railway station, but a short distance from the rude stopping-place; and there he made inquiries concerning roads, towns, etc., in the neighboring locality, and sent a telegram to the friends with whom he had been hunting when he got lost. He said he would be at the next town about twenty miles away. He knew that by this time they would be back home and anxious about him, if they were not already sending out searching parties for him. His message read:

"Hit the trail all right. Am taking a trip for my health. Send mail to me at ———"

Then after careful inquiry as to directions, and learning that there was more than one route to the town he had mentioned in his telegram, he went back to his companion. She was ready to go, for the presence of other people about her made her uneasy. She feared again there would be objection to their further progress together. Somehow the old woman's words had grown into a shadow which hovered over her. She mounted her horse gladly, and they went forward. He told her what he had just done, and how he expected to get his mail the next morning when they reached the next town. He explained that there was a ranch half-way there where they might stop all night.

She was troubled at the thought of another ranch. She knew there would be more questions, and perhaps other disagreeable words said; but she held her peace, listening to his plans. Her wonder was great over the telegram. She knew little or nothing about modern discoveries. It was a mystery to her how he could receive word by morning from a place that it had taken them nearly two days to leave behind, and how had he sent a message over a wire? Yes, she had heard of telegrams, but had never been quite sure they were true. When he saw that she was interested, he went on to tell her of other wonderful triumphs of science, the telephone, the electric light, gas, and the modern system of water-works. She listened as if it were all a fairy tale. Sometimes she looked at him, and wondered whether it could be true, or whether he were not making fun of her; but his earnest, honest eyes forbade doubt.

At the ranch they found two women, a mother and her daughter. The man asked frankly whether they could take care of this young friend of his overnight, saying that she was going on to the town in the morning, and was in his care for the journey. This seemed to relieve all suspicion. The two girls eyed each other, and then smiled.

"I'm Myrtle Baker," said the ranch-owner's daughter. "Come; I'll take you where you can wash your hands and face, and then we'll have some supper."

Myrtle Baker was a chatterer by nature. She talked incessantly; and, though she asked many questions, she did not wait for half of them to be answered. Besides, the traveller had grown wary. She did not intend to talk about the relationship between herself and her travelling companion. There was a charm in Myrtle's company which made the girl half regret leaving the next morning, as they did quite early, amid protests from Myrtle and her mother, who enjoyed a visitor in their isolated home.

But the ride that morning was constrained. Each felt in some subtle way that their pleasant companionship was coming to a crisis. Ahead in that town would be letters, communications from the outside world of friends, people who did not know or care what these two had been through together, and who would not hesitate to separate them with a firm hand. Neither put this thought into words, but it was there in their hearts, in the form of a vague fear. They talked very little, but each was feeling how pleasant the journey had been, and dreading what might be before.

They wanted to stay in this Utopia of the plains, forever journeying together, and never reaching any troublesome futures where were laws and opinions by which they must abide.

But the morning grew bright, and the road was not half long enough. Though at the last they walked their horses, they reached the town before the daily train had passed through. They went straight to the station, and found that the train was an hour late; but a telegram had arrived for the man. He took it nervously, his fingers trembling. He felt a premonition that it contained something unpleasant.

The girl sat on her horse by the platform, watching him through the open station door where he was standing as he tore open the envelope. She saw a deathly pallor overspread his face, and a look of anguish as if an arrow had pierced his heart. She felt as if the arrow had gone on into her own heart, and then she sat and waited. It seemed hours before he glanced up, with an old, weary look in his eyes. The message read:

"Your mother seriously ill. Wants you immediately. Will send your baggage on morning train. Have wired you are coming."

It was signed by his cousin with whom he had been taking his hunting-trip, and who was bound by business to go further West within a few days more.

The strong young man was almost bowed under this sudden stroke. His mother was very dear to him. He had left her well and happy. He must go to her at once, of course; but what should he do with the girl who had within the last two days taken so strong a hold upon his—he hesitated, and called it "protection." That word would do in the present emergency.

Then he looked, and saw her own face pale under the tan, and stepped out to the platform to tell her.

CHAPTER VIII
THE PARTING

She took the news like a Spartan. Her gentle pity was simply expressed, and then she held her peace. He must go. He must leave her. She knew that the train would carry him to his mother's bedside quicker than a horse could go. She felt by the look in his eyes and the set of his mouth that he had already decided that. Of course he must go. And the lady was there too! His mother and the lady! The lady would be sorry by this time, and would love him. Well, it was all right. He had been good to her. He had been a strong, bright angel God had sent to help her out of the wilderness; and now that she was safe the angel must return to his heaven. This was what she thought.

He had gone into the station to inquire about the train. It was an hour late. He had one short hour in which to do a great deal. He had very little money with him. Naturally men do not carry a fortune when they go out into the wilderness for a day's shooting. Fortunately he had his railroad return ticket to Philadelphia. That would carry him safely. But the girl. She of course had no money. And where was she going? He realized that he had failed to ask her many important questions. He hurried out, and explained to her.

"The train is an hour late. We must sell our horses, and try to get money enough to take us East. It is the only way. Where do you intend going?"

But the girl stiffened in her seat. She knew it was her opportunity to show that she was worthy of his honor and respect.

"I cannot go with you," she said very quietly.

"But you must," said he impatiently. "Don't you see there is no other way? I must take this train and get to my mother as soon as possible. She may not be living when I reach her if I don't." Something caught in his throat as he uttered the horrible thought that kept coming to his mind.

"I know," said the girl quietly. "You must go, but I must ride on."

"And why? I should like to know. Don't you see that I cannot leave you here alone? Those villains may be upon us at any minute. In fact, it is a good thing for us to board the train and get out of their miserable country as fast as steam can carry us. I am sorry you must part with your horse, for I know you are attached to it; but perhaps we can arrange to sell it to some one who will let us redeem it when we send the money out. You see I have not money enough with me to buy you a ticket. I couldn't get home myself if I hadn't my return ticket with me in my pocket. But surely the sale of both horses will bring enough to pay your way."

"You are very kind, but I must not go." The red lips were firm, and the girl was sitting very erect. She looked as she had done after she had shot the bird.

"But why?"

"I cannot travel alone with you. It is not your custom where you come from. The woman on the ranch told me. She said you knew girls did not do that, and that you did not respect me for going alone with you. She said it was not right, and that you knew it."

He looked at her impatient, angry, half ashamed that she should face him with these words.

"Nonsense!" said he. "This is a case of necessity. You are to be taken care of, and I am the one to do it."

"But it is not the custom among people where you live, is it?"

The clear eyes faced him down, and he had to admit that it was not.

"Then I can't go," she said decidedly.

"But you must. If you don't, I won't go."

"But you must," said the girl, "and I mustn't. If you talk that way, I'll run away from you. I've run away from one man, and I guess I can from another. Besides, you're forgetting the lady."

"What lady?"

"Your lady. The lady who rides in a carriage without horses."

"Hang the lady!" he said inelegantly. "Do you know that the train will be along here in less than an hour, and we have a great deal to do before we can get on board? There's no use stopping to talk about this matter. We haven't time. If you will just trust things to me, I'll attend to them all, and I'll answer your questions when we get safely on the train. Every instant is precious. Those men might come around that corner ever there any minute. That's all bosh about respect. I respect you more than any woman I ever met. And it's my business to take care of you."

"No, it's not your business," said the girl bravely, "and I can't let you. I'm nothing to you, you know."

"You're every—that is—why, you surely know you're a great deal to me. Why, you saved my life, you know!"

"Yes, and you saved mine. That was beautiful, but that's all."

"Isn't that enough? What are you made of, anyway, to sit there when there's so much to be done, and those villains on our track, and insist that you won't be saved?' Respect you! Why, a lion in the wilderness would have to respect you. You're made of iron and steel and precious stones. You've the courage of a—a—I was going to say a man but I mean an angel. You're pure as snow, and true as the heavenly blue, and firm as a rock; and, if I had never respected you before, I would have to now. I respect, I honor, I—I—I—pray for you!" he finished fiercely.

He turned his back to hide his emotion.

She lifted her eyes to his when he turned again, and her own were full of tears.

"Thank you!" She said it very simply. "That makes me—very—glad! But I cannot go with you."

"Do you mean that?" he asked her desperately.

"Yes," steadily.

"Then I shall have to stay too."

"But you can't! You must go to your mother. I won't be stayed with. And what would she think? Mothers are—everything!" she finished. "You must go quick and get ready. What can I do to help?"

He gave her a look which she remembered long years afterward. It seemed to burn and sear its way into her soul. How was it that a stranger had the power to scorch her with anguish this way? And she him?

He turned, still with that desperate, half-frantic look in his face, and accosted two men who stood at the other end of the platform. They were not in particular need of a horse at present; but they were always ready to look at a bargain, and they walked speculatively down the uneven boards of the platform with him to where his horse stood, and inspected it.

The girl watched the whole proceeding with eyes that saw not but into the future. She put in a word about the worth of the saddle once when she saw it was going lower than it should. Three other men gathered about before the bargain was concluded, and the horse and its equipments sold for about half its value.

That done, the man turned toward the girl and motioned to her to lead her horse away to a more quiet place, and set him down to plead steadily against her decision. But the talk and the horse-selling had taken more time than he realized. The girl was more decided than ever in her determination not to go with him. She spoke of the lady again. She spoke of his mother, and mothers in general, and finished by reminding him that God would take care of her, and of him, too.

Then they heard the whistle of the train, and saw it growing from a speck to a large black object across the plain. To the girl the sight of this strange machine, that seemed more like a creature rushing toward her to snatch all beauty and hope and safety from her, sent a thrill of horror. To the man it seemed like a dreaded fate that was tearing him asunder. He had barely time to divest himself of his powder-horn, and a few little things that might be helpful to the girl in her journey, before the train was halting at the station. Then he took from his pocket the money that had been paid him for his horse; and, selecting a five-dollar bill for himself, he wrapped the rest in an envelope bearing his own name and address. The envelope was one addressed by the lady at home. It had contained some gracefully worded refusal of a request. But he did not notice now what envelope he gave her.

"Take this," he said. "It will help a little. Yes, you must! I cannot leave you—I *will* not—unless you do," when he saw that she hesitated and looked doubtful. "I owe you all and more for saving my life. I can never repay you. Take it. You may return it sometime when you get plenty more of your own, if it hurts your pride to keep it. Take it, please. Yes, I have plenty for myself. You will need it, and you must stop at nice places overnight. You will be very careful, won't you? My name is on that envelope. You must write to me and let me know that you are safe."

"Some one is calling you, and that thing is beginning to move again," said the girl, an awesome wonder in her face. "You will be left behind! O, hurry! Quick! Your mother!"

He half turned toward the train, and then came back.

"You haven't told me your name!" he gasped. "Tell me quick!"

She caught her breath.

"Elizabeth!" she answered, and waved him from her.

The conductor of the train was shouting to him, and two men shoved him toward the platform. He swung himself aboard with the accustomed ease of a man who has travelled; but he stood on the platform, and shouted, "Where are you going?" as the train swung noisily off.

She did not hear him, but waved her hand, and gave him a bright smile that was brimming with unshed tears. It seemed like instant, daring suicide in him to stand on that swaying, clattering house as it moved off irresponsibly down the plane of vision. She watched him till he was out of sight, a mere speck on the horizon of the prairie; and then she turned her horse slowly into the road, and went her way into the world alone.

The man stood on the platform, and watched her as he whirled away—a little brown girl on a little brown horse, so stanch and firm and stubborn and good. Her eyes were dear, and her lips as she smiled; and her hand was beautiful as it waved him good-by. She was dear, dear, dear! Why had he not known it? Why had he left her? Yet how could he stay? His mother was dying perhaps. He must not fail her in what might be her last summons. Life and death were pulling at his heart, tearing him asunder.

The vision of the little brown girl and the little brown horse blurred and faded. He tried to look, but could not see. He brought his eyes to nearer vision to fix their focus for another look, and straight before him whirled a shackly old saloon, rough and tumble, its character apparent from the men who were grouped about its doorway and from the barrels and kegs in profusion outside. From the doorway issued four men, wiping their mouths and shouting hilariously. Four horses stood tied to a fence near by. They were so instantly passed, and so vaguely seen, that he could not be sure in the least, but those four men reminded him strongly of the four who had passed the schoolhouse on Sunday.

He shuddered, and looked back. The little brown horse and the little brown girl were one with the little brown station so far away, and presently the saloon and men were blotted out in one blur of green and brown and yellow.

He looked to the ground in his despair. He *must* go back. He could not leave her in such peril. She was his to care for by all the rights of manhood and womanhood. She had been put in his way. It was his duty.

But the ground whirled by under his madness, and showed him plainly that to jump off would be instant death. Then the thought of his mother came again, and the girl's words, "I am nothing to you, you know."

The train whirled its way between two mountains and the valley, and the green and brown and yellow blur were gone from sight. He felt as if he had just seen the coffin close over the girl's sweet face, and he had done it.

By and by he crawled into the car, pulled his slouch hat down over his eyes, and settled down in a seat; but all the time he was trying to see over again that old saloon and those four men, and to make out their passing identity. Sometimes the agony of thinking it all over, and trying to make out whether those men had been the pursuers, made him feel frantic; and it seemed as if he must pull the bell-cord, and make the train stop, and get off to walk back. Then the utter hopelessness of ever finding her would come over him, and he would settle back in his seat again and try to sleep. But the least drowsiness would bring a vision of the girl galloping alone over the prairie with the four men in full pursuit behind. "Elizabeth, Elizabeth, Elizabeth!" the car-wheels seemed to say.

Elizabeth—that was all he had of her. He did not know the rest of her name, nor where she was going. He did not even know where she had come from, just "Elizabeth" and "Montana." If anything happened lo her, he would never know. Oh! why had he left her? Why had he not *made* her go with him? In a case like that a man should assert his authority. But, then, it was true he had none, and she had said she would run away. She would have done it too. O, if it had been anything but sickness and possible death at the other end—and his mother, his own little mother! Nothing else would have kept him from staying to protect Elizabeth.

What a fool he had been! There were questions he might have asked, and plans they might have made, all those beautiful days and those moon-silvered nights. If any other man had done the same, he would have thought him lacking mentally. But here he had maundered on, and never found out the all-important things about her. Yet how did he know then how important they were to be? It had seemed as if they had all the world before them in the brilliant sunlight. How could he know that modern improvements were to seize him in the midst of a prairie waste, and whirl him off from her when he had just begun to know what she was, and to prize her company as a most precious gift dropped down from heaven at his feet?

By degrees he came out of his hysterical frenzy, and returned to a somewhat normal state of mind. He reasoned himself several times into the belief that those men were not in the least like the men he had seen Sunday. He knew that one could not recognize one's own brother at that distance and that rate of passing speed. He tried to think that Elizabeth would be cared for. She had come through many a danger, and was it likely that the God in whom she trusted, who had guarded her so many times in her great peril, would desert her now in her dire need? Would He not raise up help for her somewhere? Perhaps another man as good as he, and as trustworthy as he had tried to be, would find her and help her.

But that thought was not pleasant. He put it away impatiently. It cut him. Why had she talked so much about the lady? The lady! Ah! How was it the lady came no more into his thoughts? The memory of her haughty face no more quickened his heart-beats. Was he fickle that he could lose what he had supposed was a lifelong passion in a few days?

The darkness was creeping on. Where was Elizabeth? Had she found a refuge for the night? Or was she wandering on an unknown trail, hearing voices and oaths through the darkness, and seeing the gleaming of wild eyes low in the bushes ahead? How could he have left her? How could he? He must go back even yet. He must, he must, *he must*!

And so it went on through the long night.

The train stopped at several places to take on water; but there seemed to be no human habitation near, or else his eyes were dim with his trouble. Once, when they stopped longer than the other times, he got up and walked the length of the car and down the steps to the ground. He even stood there, and let the train start jerkily on till his car had passed him, and the steps were just sliding by, and tried to think whether he would not stay, and go back in some way to find her. Then the impossibility of the search, and of his getting back in time to do any good, helped him to spring on board just before it was too late. He walked back to his seat saying to himself, "Fool! Fool!"

It was not till morning that he remembered his baggage and went in search of it. There he found a letter from his cousin, with other letters and telegrams explaining the state of affairs at home. He came back to his seat laden with a large leather grip and a suitcase. He sat down to read his letters, and these took his mind away from his troubled thoughts for a little while. There was a letter from his mother, sweet, graceful, half wistfully offering her sympathy. He saw she guessed the reason why he had left her and gone to this far place. Dear little mother! What would she say if she knew his trouble now? And then would return his heart-frenzy over Elizabeth's peril. O to know that she was protected, hidden!

Fumbling in his pocket, he came upon a slip of paper, the slip the girl had given Elizabeth in the schoolhouse on Sunday afternoon. "For in the time of trouble he shall hide me in his pavilion; in the secret of his tabernacle shall he hide me."

Ah! God had hidden her then. Why not again? And what was that he had said to her himself, when searching for a word to cover his emotion? "I pray for you!" Why could he not pray? She had made him pray in the wilderness. Should he not pray for her who was in peril now? He leaned back in the hot, uncomfortable car-seat, pulling his hat down closer over his eyes, and prayed as he had never prayed before. "Our Father" he stumbled through as far as he could remember, and tried to think how her sweet voice had filled in the places where he had not known it the other time. Then, when he was done, he waited and prayed, "Our Father, care for Elizabeth," and added, "For Jesus' sake. Amen." Thereafter through the rest of his journey, and for days and weeks stretching ahead, he prayed that prayer, and sometimes found in it his only solace from the terrible fear that possessed him lest some harm had come to the girl, whom it seemed to him now he had deserted in cold blood.

CHAPTER IX
IN A TRAP

Elizabeth rode straight out to the east, crossing the town as rapidly as possible, going full gallop where the streets were empty. On the edge of the town she crossed another trail running back the way that they had come; but without swerving she turned out toward the world, and soon passed into a thick growth of trees, around a hill.

Not three minutes elapsed after she had passed the crossing of the trails before the four men rode across from the other direction, and, pausing, called to one another, looking this way and that:

"What d'ye think, Bill? Shall we risk the right hand 'r the left?"

"Take the left hand fer luck," answered Bill. "Let's go over to the ranch and ask. Ef she's been hereabouts, she's likely there. The old woman'll know. Come on, boys!"

And who shall say that the angel of the Lord did not stand within the crossing of the ways and turn aside the evil men?

Elizabeth did not stop her fierce ride until about noon. The frenzy of her fear of pursuit had come upon her with renewed force. Now that she was alone and desolate she dared not look behind her. She had been strong enough as she smiled her farewell; but, when the train had dwindled into a mere speck in the distance, her eyes were dropping tears thick and fast upon the horse's mane. So in the first heaviness of her loneliness she rode as if pursued by enemies close at hand.

But the horse must rest if she did not, for he was her only dependence now. So she sat her down in the shade of a tree, and tried to eat some dinner. The tears came again as she opened the pack which the man's strong hands had bound together for her. How little she had thought at breakfast-time that she would eat the next meal alone!

It was all well enough to tell him he must go, and say she was nothing to him; but it was different now to face the world without a single friend when one had learned to know how good a friend could be. Almost it would have been better if he had never found her, never saved her from the serpent, never ridden beside her and talked of wonderful new things to her; for now that he was gone the emptiness and loneliness were so much harder to bear; and now she was filled with a longing for things that could not be hers.

It was well he had gone so soon, well she had no longer to grow into the charm of his society; for he belonged to the lady, and was not hers. Thus she ate her dinner with the indifference of sorrow.

Then she took out the envelope, and counted over the money. Forty dollars he had given her. She knew he had kept but five for himself. How wonderful that he should have done all that for her! It seemed a very great wealth in her possession. Well, she would use it as sparingly as possible, and thus be able the sooner to return it all to him. Some she must use, she supposed, to buy food; but she would do with as little as she could. She might sometimes shoot a bird, or catch a fish; or there might be berries fit for food by the way. Nights she must stop by the way at a respectable house. That she had promised. He had told her of awful things that might happen to her if she lay down in the wilderness alone. Her lodging would sometimes cost her something. Yet often they would take her in for nothing. She would be careful of the money.

She studied the name on the envelope. George Trescott Benedict, 2—— Walnut Street, Philadelphia, Penn. The letters were large and angular, not easy to read; but she puzzled them out. It did not look like his writing. She had watched him as he wrote the old woman's address in his little red book. He wrote small, round letters, slanting backwards, plain as print, pleasant writing to read. Now the old woman's address would never be of any use, and her wish that Elizabeth should travel alone was fulfilled.

There was a faint perfume from the envelope like Weldwood flowers. She breathed it in, and wondered at it. Was it perfume from something he carried in his pocket, some flower his lady had once given him? But this was not a pleasant thought. She put the envelope into her bosom after studying it again carefully until she knew the words by heart.

Then she drew forth the papers of her mother's that she had brought from home, and for the first time read them over.

The first was the marriage certificate. That she had seen before, and had studied with awe; but the others had been kept in a box that was never opened by the children. The mother kept them sacredly, always with the certificate on the top.

The largest paper she could not understand. It was something about a mine. There were a great many "herebys" and "whereases" and "agreements" in it. She put it back into the wrapper as of little account, probably something belonging to her father, which her mother had treasured for old time's sake.

Then came a paper which related to the claim where their little log home had stood, and upon the extreme edge of which the graves were. That, too, she laid reverently within its wrapper.

Next came a bit of pasteboard whereon was inscribed, "Mrs. Merrill Wilton Bailey, Rittenhouse Square, Tuesdays." That she knew was her grandmother's name, though she had never seen the card before—her father's mother. She looked at the card in wonder. It was almost like a distant view of the lady in question. What kind of a place might Rittenhouse Square be, and where was it? There was no telling. It might be near that wonderful Desert of Sahara that the man had talked about. She laid it down with a sigh.

There was only one paper left, and that was a letter written in pale pencil lines. It said:

"*My dear Bessie:* Your pa died last week. He was killed falling from a scaffold. He was buried on Monday with five carriages and everything nice. We all got new black dresses, and have enough for a stone. If it don't cost too much, we'll have an angle on the top. I always thought an angle pointing to heaven was nice. We wish you was here. We miss you very much. I hope your husband is good to you. Why don't you write to us? You haven't wrote since your little girl was born. I s'pose you call her Bessie like you. If anything ever happens to you, you can send her to me. I'd kind of like her to fill your place. Your sister has got a baby girl too. She calls her Lizzie. We couldn't somehow have it natural to call her 'Lizabeth, and Nan wanted her called for me. I was always Lizzie, you know. Now you must write soon.

"Your   loving   mother,
ELIZABETH BRADY."

There was no date nor address to the letter, but an address had been pencilled on the outside in her mother's cramped school-girl hand. It was dim but still readable, "Mrs. Elizabeth Brady, 18—— Flora Street, Philadelphia."

Elizabeth studied the last word, then drew out the envelope again, and looked at that. Yes, the two names were the same. How wonderful! Perhaps she would sometime, sometime, see him again, though of course he belonged to the lady. But perhaps, if she went to school and learned very fast, she might sometime meet him at church—he went to church, she was sure—and then he might smile, and not be ashamed of his friend who had saved his life. Saved his life! Nonsense! She had not done much. He would not feel any such ridiculous indebtedness to her when he got back to home and friends and safety. He had saved her much more than she had saved him.

She put the papers all back in safety, and after having prepared her few belongings for taking up the journey, she knelt down. She would say the prayer before she went on. It might be that would keep the terrible pursuers away.

She said it once, and then with eyes still closed she waited a moment. Might she say it for him, who was gone away from her? Perhaps it would help him, and keep him from falling from that terrible machine he was riding on. Hitherto in her mind prayers had been only for the dead, but now they seemed also to belong to all who were in danger or trouble. She said the prayer over once more, slowly, then paused a moment, and added: "Our Father, hide him from trouble. Hide George Trescott Benedict. And hide me, please, too."

Then she mounted her horse, and went on her way.

It was a long and weary way. It reached over mountains and through valleys, across winding, turbulent streams and broad rivers that had few bridges. The rivers twice led her further south than she meant to go, in her ignorance. She had always felt that Philadelphia was straight ahead east, as straight as one could go to the heart of the sun.

Night after night she lay down in strange homes, some poorer and more forlorn than others; and day after day she took up her lonely travel again.

Gradually, as the days lengthened, and mountains piled themselves behind her, and rivers stretched like barriers between, she grew less and less to dread her pursuers, and more and more to look forward to the future. It seemed so long a way! Would it never end?

Once she asked a man whether he knew where Philadelphia was. She had been travelling then for weeks, and thought she must be almost there. But he said "Philadelphia? O, Philadelphia is in the East. That's a long way off. I saw a man once who came from there."

She set her firm little chin then, and travelled on. Her clothes were much worn, and her skin was brown as a berry. The horse plodded on with a dejected air. He would have liked to stop at a number of places they passed, and remain for life, what there was left of it; but he obediently walked on over any kind of an old road that came in his way, and solaced himself with whatever kind of a bite the roadside afforded. He was becoming a much-travelled horse. He knew a threshing-machine by sight now, and considered it no more than a prairie bob-cat.

At one stopping-place a good woman advised Elizabeth to rest on Sundays. She told her God didn't like people to do the same on His day as on other days, and it would bring her bad luck if she kept up her incessant riding. It was bad for the horse too. So, the night being Saturday, Elizabeth remained with the woman over the Sabbath, and heard read aloud the fourteenth chapter of John. It was a wonderful revelation to her. She did not altogether understand it. In fact, the Bible was an unknown book. She had never known that it was different from other books. She had heard it spoken of by her mother, but only as a book. She did not know it was a book of books.

She carried the beautiful thoughts with her on the way, and pondered them. She wished she might have the book. She remembered the name of it, Bible, the Book of God. Then God had written a book! Some day she would try to find it and read it.

"Let not your heart be troubled"; so much of the message drifted into her lonesome, ignorant soul, and settled down to stay. She said it over nights when she found a shelter in some unpleasant place or days when the road was rough or a storm came up and she was compelled to seek shelter by the roadside under a haystack or in a friendly but deserted shack. She thought of it the day there was no shelter and she was drenched to the skin. She wondered afterward when the sun came out and dried her nicely whether God had really been speaking the words to her troubled heart, "Let not your heart be troubled."

Every night and every morning she said "Our Father" twice, once for herself and once for the friend who had gone out into the world, it seemed about a hundred years ago.

But one day she came across a railroad track. It made her heart beat wildly. It seemed now that she must be almost there. Railroads were things belonging to the East and civilization. But the way was lonely still for days, and then she crossed more railroads, becoming more and more frequent, and came into the line of towns that stretched along beside the snake-like tracks.

She fell into the habit of staying overnight in a town, and then riding on to the next in the morning; but now her clothes were becoming so dirty and ragged that she felt ashamed to go to nice-looking places lest they should turn her out; so she sought shelter in barns and small, mean houses. But the people in these houses were distressingly dirty, and she found no place to wash.

She had lost track of the weeks or the months when she reached her first great city, the only one she had come near in her uncharted wanderings.

Into the outskirts of Chicago she rode undaunted, her head erect, with the carriage of a queen. She had passed Indians and cowboys in her journeying; why should she mind Chicago? Miles and miles of houses and people. There seemed to be no end to it. Nothing but houses everywhere and hurried-looking people, many of them working hard. Surely this must be Philadelphia.

A large, beautiful building attracted her attention. There were handsome grounds about it, and girls playing some game with a ball and curious webbed implements across a net of cords. Elizabeth drew her horse to the side of the road, and watched a few minutes. One girl was skilful, and hit the ball back every time. Elizabeth almost exclaimed out loud once when a particularly fine ball was played. She rode reluctantly on when the game was finished, and saw over the arched gateway the words, "Janeway School for Girls."

Ah! This was Philadelphia at last, and here was her school. She would go in at once before she went to her grandmother's. It might be better.

She dismounted, and tied the horse to an iron ring in a post by the sidewalk. Then she went slowly, shyly up the steps into the charmed circles of learning. She knew she was shabby, but her long journey would explain that. Would they be kind to her, and let her study?

She stood some time before the door, with a group of laughing girls not far away whispering about her. She smiled at them; but they did not return the salutation, and their actions made her more shy. At last she stepped into the open door, and a maid in cap and apron came forward. "You must not come in here, miss," she said imperiously. "This is a school."

"Yes," said Elizabeth gravely, smiling. "I want to see the teacher."

"She's busy. You can't see her," snapped the maid.

"Then I will wait till she is ready. I've come a great many miles, and I must see her."

The maid retreated at this, and an elegant woman in trailing black silk and gold-rimmed glasses approached threateningly. This was a new kind of beggar, of course, and must be dealt with at once.

"What do you want?" she asked frigidly.

"I've come to school," said Elizabeth confidingly. "I know I don't look very nice, but I've had to come all the way from Montana on horseback. If you could let me go where I can have some water and a thread and needle, I can make myself look better."

The woman eyed the girl incredulously.

"You have come to school!" she said; and her voice was large, and frightened Elizabeth. "You have come all the way from Montana! Impossible! You must be crazy."

"No, ma'am, I'm not crazy," said Elizabeth. "I just want to go to school."

The woman perceived that this might be an interesting case for benevolently inclined people. It was nothing but an annoyance to herself. "My dear girl,"—her tone was bland and disagreeable now,—"are you aware that it takes money to come to school?"

"Does it?" said Elizabeth. "No, I didn't know it, but I have some money. I could give you ten dollars right now; and, if that is not enough, I might work some way, and earn more."

The woman laughed disagreeably.

"It is impossible," she said. "The yearly tuition here is five hundred dollars. Besides, we do not take girls of your class. This is a finishing school for young ladies. You will have to inquire further," and the woman swept away to laugh with her colleagues over the queer character, the new kind of tramp, she had just been called to interview. The maid came pertly forward, and said that Elizabeth could not longer stand where she was.

Bewilderment and bitter disappointment in her face, Elizabeth went slowly down to her horse, the great tears welling up into her eyes. As she rode away, she kept turning back to the school grounds wistfully. She did not notice the passers-by, nor know that they were commenting upon her appearance. She made a striking picture in her rough garments, with her wealth of hair, her tanned skin, and tear-filled eyes. An artist noticed it, and watched her down the street, half thinking he would follow and secure her as a model for his next picture.

A woman, gaudily bedecked in soiled finery, her face giving evidence of the frequent use of rouge and powder, watched her, and followed, pondering. At last she called, "My dear, my dear, wait a minute." She had to speak several times before Elizabeth saw that she was talking to her. Then the horse was halted by the sidewalk.

"My dear," said the woman, "you look tired and disappointed. Don't you want to come home with me for a little while, and rest?"

"Thank you," said Elizabeth, "but I am afraid I must go on. I only stop on Sundays."

"But just come home with me for a little while," coaxed the wheedling tones. "You look so tired, and I've some girls of my own. I know you would enjoy resting and talking with them."

The kindness in her tones touched the weary girl. Her pride had been stung to the quick by the haughty woman in the school. This woman would soothe her with kindness.

"Do you live far from here?" asked Elizabeth.

"Only two or three blocks," said the woman. "You ride along by the sidewalk, and we can talk. Where are you going? You look as if you had come a long distance."

"Yes," said the girl wearily, "from Montana. I am going to school. Is this Philadelphia?"

"This is Chicago," said the woman. "There are finer schools here than in Philadelphia. If you like to come and stay at my house awhile, I will see about getting you into a school."

"Is it hard work to get people into schools?" asked the girl wonderingly. "I thought they would want people to teach."

"No, it's very hard," said the lying woman; "but I think I know a school where I can get you in. Where are your folks? Are they in Montana?"

"They are all dead," said Elizabeth, "and I have come away to school."

"Poor child!" said the woman glibly. "Come right home with me, and I'll take care of you. I know a nice way you can earn your living, and then you can study if you like. But you're quite big to go to school. It seems to me you could have a good time without that. You are a very pretty girl; do you know it? You only need pretty clothes to make you a beauty. If you come with me, I will let you earn some beautiful new clothes."

"You are very kind," said the girl gravely. "I do need new clothes; and, if I could earn them, that would be all the better." She did not quite like the woman; yet of course that was foolish.

After a few more turns they stopped in front of a tall brick building with a number of windows. It seemed to be a good deal like other buildings; in fact, as she looked up the street, Elizabeth thought there were miles of them just alike. She tied her horse in front of the door, and went in with the woman. The woman told her to sit down a minute until she called the lady of the house, who would tell her more about the school. There were a number of pretty girls in the room, and they made very free to speak to her. They twitted her about her clothes, and in a way reminded Elizabeth of the girls in the school she had just interviewed.

Suddenly she spoke up to the group. An idea had occurred to her. This was the school, and the woman had not liked to say so until she spoke to the teacher about her.

"Is this a school?" she asked shyly.

Her question was met with a shout of derisive laughter.

"School!" cried the boldest, prettiest one. "School for scandal! School for morals!"

There was one, a thin, pale girl with dark circles under her eyes, a sad droop to her mouth, and bright scarlet spots in her cheeks. She came over to Elizabeth, and whispered something to her. Elizabeth started forward, unspeakable horror in her face.

She fled to the door where she had come in, but found it fastened. Then she turned as if she had been brought to bay by a pack of lions.

CHAPTER X
PHILADELPHIA AT LAST

"Open this door!" she commanded. "Let me out of here at once."

The pale girl started to do so, but the pretty one held her back. "No, Nellie; Madam will be angry with us all if you open that door." Then she turned to Elizabeth, and said:

"Whoever enters that door never goes out again. You are nicely caught, my dear."

There was a sting of bitterness and self-pity in the taunt at the end of the words. Elizabeth felt it, as she seized her pistol from her belt, and pointed it at the astonished group. They were not accustomed to girls with pistols. "Open that door, or I will shoot you all!" she cried.

Then, as she heard some one descending the stairs, she rushed again into the room where she remembered the windows were open. They were guarded by wire screens; but she caught up a chair, and dashed it through one, plunging out into the street in spite of detaining hands that reached for her, hands much hindered by the gleam of the pistol and the fear that it might go off in their midst.

It took but an instant to wrench the bridle from its fastening and mount her horse; then she rode forward through the city at a pace that only millionaires and automobiles are allowed to take. She met and passed her first automobile without a quiver. Her eyes were dilated, her lips set; angry, frightened tears were streaming down her cheeks, and she urged her poor horse forward until a policeman here and there thought it his duty to make a feeble effort to detain her. But nothing impeded her way. She fled through a maze of wagons, carriages, automobiles, and trolley-cars, until she passed the whirl of the great city, and at last was free again and out in the open country.

She came toward evening to a little cottage on the edge of a pretty suburb. The cottage was covered with roses, and the front yard was full of great old-fashioned flowers. On the porch sat a plain little old lady in a rocking-chair, knitting. There was a little gate with a path leading up to the door, and at the side another open gate with a road leading around to the back of the cottage.

Elizabeth saw, and murmuring, "O 'our Father,' please hide me!" she dashed into the driveway, and tore up to the side of the piazza at a full gallop. She jumped from the horse; and, leaving him standing panting with his nose to the fence, and a tempting strip of clover in front of him where he could graze when he should get his breath, she ran up the steps, and flung herself in a miserable little heap at the feet of the astonished old lady.

"O, please, please, won't you let me stay here a few minutes, and tell me what to do? I am so tired, and I have had such a dreadful, awful time!"

"Why, dearie me!" said the old lady. "Of course I will. Poor child; sit right down in this rocking-chair, and have a good cry. I'll get you a glass of water and something to eat, and then you shall tell me all about it."

She brought the water, and a tray with nice broad slices of brown bread and butter, a generous piece of apple pie, some cheese, and a glass pitcher of creamy milk.

Elizabeth drank the water, but before she could eat she told the terrible tale of her last adventure. It seemed awful for her to believe, and she felt she must have help somewhere. She had heard there were bad people in the world. In fact, she had seen men who were bad, and once a woman had passed their ranch whose character was said to be questionable. She wore a hard face, and could drink and swear like the men. But that sin should be in this form, with pretty girls and pleasant, wheedling women for agents, she had never dreamed; and this in the great, civilized East! Almost better would it have been to remain in the desert alone, and risk the pursuit of that awful man, than to come all this way to find the world gone wrong.

The old lady was horrified, too. She had heard more than the girl of licensed evil; but she had read it in the paper as she had read about the evils of the slave-traffic in Africa, and it had never really seemed true to her. Now she lifted up her hands in horror, and looked at the beautiful girl before her with something akin to awe that she had been in one of those dens of iniquity and escaped. Over and over she made the girl tell what was said, and how it looked, and how she pointed her pistol, and how she got out; and then she exclaimed in wonder, and called her escape a miracle.

They were both weary from excitement when the tale was told. Elizabeth ate her lunch; then the old lady showed her where to put the horse, and made her go to bed. It was only a wee little room with a cot-bed white as snow where she put her; but the roses peeped in at the window, and the box covered with an old white curtain contained a large pitcher of fresh water and a bowl and soap and towels. The old lady brought her a clean white nightgown, coarse and mended in many places, but smelling of rose leaves; and in the morning she tapped at the door quite early before the girl was up, and came in with an armful of clothes.

"I had some boarders last summer," she explained, "and, when they went away, they left these things and said I might put them into the home-mission box. But I was sick when they sent it off this winter; and, if you ain't a home mission, then I never saw one. You put 'em on. I guess they'll fit. They may be a mite large, but she was about your size. I guess your clothes are about wore out; so you jest leave 'em here fer the next one, and use these. There's a couple of extra shirt-waists you can put in a bundle for a change. I guess folks won't dare fool with you if you have some clean, nice clothes on."

Elizabeth looked at her gratefully, and wrote her down in the list of saints with the woman who read the fourteenth chapter of John. The old lady had neglected to mention that from her own meagre wardrobe she had supplied some under-garments, which were not included in those the boarders had left.

Bathed and clothed in clean, sweet garments, with a white shirt-waist and a dark-blue serge skirt and coat, Elizabeth looked a different girl. She surveyed herself in the little glass over the box-washstand and wondered. All at once vanity was born within her, and an ambition to be always thus clothed, with a horrible remembrance of the woman of the day before, who had promised to show her how to earn some pretty clothes. It flashed across her mind that pretty clothes might be a snare. Perhaps they had been to those girls she had seen in that house.

With much good advice and kindly blessings from the old lady, Elizabeth fared forth upon her journey once more, sadly wise in the wisdom of the world, and less sweetly credulous than she had been, but better fitted to fight her way.

The story of her journey from Chicago to Philadelphia would fill a volume if it were written, but it might pall upon the reader from the very variety of its experiences. It was made slowly and painfully, with many haltings and much lessening of the scanty store of money that had seemed so much when she received it in the wilderness. The horse went lame, and had to be watched over and petted, and finally, by the advice of a kindly farmer, taken to a veterinary surgeon, who doctored him for a week before he finally said it was safe to let him hobble on again. After that the girl was more careful of the horse. If he should die, what would she do?

One dismal morning, late in November, Elizabeth, wearing the old overcoat to keep her from freezing, rode into Philadelphia.

Armed with instructions from the old lady in Chicago, she rode boldly up to a policeman, and showed him the address of the grandmother to whom she had decided to go first, her mother's mother. He sent her on in the right direction, and in due time with the help of other policemen she reached the right number on Flora Street.

It was a narrow street, banked on either side by small, narrow brick houses of the older type. Here and there gleamed out a scrap of a white marble door-step, but most of the houses were approached by steps of dull stone or of painted wood. There was a dejected and dreary air about the place. The street was swarming with children in various stages of the soiled condition.

Elizabeth timidly knocked at the door after being assured by the interested urchins who surrounded her that Mrs. Brady really lived there, and had not moved away or anything. It did not seem wonderful to the girl, who had lived her life thus far in a mountain shack, to find her grandmother still in the place from which she had written fifteen years before. She did not yet know what a floating population most cities contain.

Mrs. Brady was washing when the knock sounded through the house. She was a broad woman, with a face on which the cares and sorrows of the years had left a not too heavy impress. She still enjoyed life, oven though a good part of it was spent at the wash-tub, washing other people's fine clothes. She had some fine ones of her own up-stairs in her clothes-press; and, when she went out, it was in shiny satin, with a bonnet bobbing with jet and a red rose, though of late years, strictly speaking, the bonnet had become a hat again, and Mrs. Brady was in style with the other old ladies.

The perspiration was in little beads on her forehead and trickling down the creases in her well-cushioned neck toward her ample bosom. Her gray hair was neatly combed, and her calico wrapper was open at the throat even on this cold day. She wiped on her apron the soap-suds from her plump arms steaming pink from the hot suds, and went to the door.

She looked with disfavor upon the peculiar person on the door-step attired in a man's overcoat. She was prepared to refuse the demands of the Salvation Army for a nickel for Christmas dinners; or to silence the banana-man, or the fish-man, or the man with shoe-strings and pins and pencils for sale; or to send the photograph-agent on his way; yes, even the man who sold albums for post-cards. She had no time to bother with anybody this morning.

But the young person in the rusty overcoat, with the dark-blue serge Eton jacket under it, which might have come from Wanamaker's two years ago, who yet wore a leather belt with gleaming pistols under the Eton jacket, was a new species. Mrs. Brady was taken off her guard; else Elizabeth might have found entrance to her grandmother's home as difficult as she had found entrance to the finishing school of Madame Janeway.

"Are you Mrs. Brady?" asked the girl. She was searching the forbidding face before her for some sign of likeness to her mother, but found none. The cares of Elizabeth Brady's daughter had outweighed those of the mother, or else they sat upon a nature more sensitive.

"I am," said Mrs. Brady, imposingly.

"Grandmother, I am the baby you talked about in that letter," she announced, handing Mrs. Brady the letter she had written nearly eighteen years before.

The woman took the envelope gingerly in the wet thumb and finger that still grasped a bit of the gingham apron. She held it at arm's length, and squinted up her eyes, trying to read it without her glasses. It was some new kind of beggar, of course. She hated to touch these dirty envelopes, and this one looked old and worn. She stepped back to the parlor table where her glasses were lying, and, adjusting them, began to read the letter.

"For the land sakes! Where'd you find this?" she said, looking up suspiciously. "It's against the law to open letters that ain't your own. Didn't me daughter ever get it? I wrote it to her meself. How come you by it?"

"Mother read it to me long ago when I was little," answered the girl, the slow hope fading from her lips as she spoke. Was every one, was even her grandmother, going to be cold and harsh with her? "Our Father, hide me!" her heart murmured, because it had become a habit; and her listening thought caught the answer, "Let not your heart be troubled."

"Well, who are you?" said the uncordial grandmother, still puzzled. "You ain't Bessie, me Bessie. Fer one thing, you're 'bout as young as she was when she went off 'n' got married, against me 'dvice, to that drunken, lazy dude." Her brow was lowering, and she proceeded to finish her letter.

"I am Elizabeth," said the girl with a trembling voice, "the baby you talked about in that letter. But please don't call father that. He wasn't ever bad to us. He was always good to mother, even when he was drunk. If you talk like that about him, I shall have to go away."

"Fer the land sakes! You don't say," said Mrs. Brady, sitting down hard in astonishment on the biscuit upholstery of her best parlor chair. "Now you ain't Bessie's child! Well, I *am clear* beat. And growed up so big! You look strong, but you're kind of thin. What makes your skin so black? Your ma never was dark, ner your pa, neither."

"I've been riding a long way in the wind and sun and rain."

"Fer the land sakes!" as she looked through the window to the street. "Not on a horse?"

"Yes."

"H'm! What was your ma thinkin' about to let you do that?"

"My mother is dead. There was no one left to care what I did. I had to come. There were dreadful people out there, and I was afraid."

"Fer the land sakes!" That seemed the only remark that the capable Mrs. Brady could make. She looked at her new granddaughter in bewilderment, as if a strange sort of creature had suddenly laid claim to relationship.

"Well, I'm right glad to see you," she said stiffly, wiping her hand again on her apron and putting it out formally for a greeting.

Elizabeth accepted her reception gravely, and sat down. She sat down suddenly, as if her strength had given way and a great strain was at an end. As she sat down, she drooped her head back against the wall; and a gray look spread about her lips.

"You're tired," said the grandmother, energetically. "Come far this morning?"

"No," said Elizabeth, weakly, "not many miles; but I hadn't any more bread. I used it all up yesterday, and there wasn't much money left. I thought I could wait till I got here, but I guess I'm hungry."

"Fer the land sakes!" ejaculated Mrs. Brady as she hustled out to the kitchen, and clattered the frying-pan onto the stove, shoving the boiler hastily aside. She came in presently with a steaming cup of tea, and made the girl drink it hot and strong. Then she established her in the big rocking-chair in the kitchen with a plate of appetizing things to eat, and went on with her washing, punctuating every rub with a question.

Elizabeth felt better after her meal, and offered to help, but the grandmother would not hear to her lifting a finger.

"You must rest first," she said. "It beats me how you ever got here. I'd sooner crawl on me hands and knees than ride a great, scary horse."

Elizabeth sprang to her feet.

"The horse!" she said. "Poor fellow! He needs something to eat worse than I did. He hasn't had a bite of grass all this morning. There was nothing but hard roads and pavements. The grass is all brown, anyway, now. I found some cornstalks by the road, and once a man dropped a big bundle of hay out of his load. If it hadn't been for Robin, I'd never have got here; and here I've sat enjoying my breakfast, and Robin out there hungry!"

"Fer the land sakes!" said the grandmother, taking her arms out of the suds and looked troubled. "Poor fellow! What would he like? I haven't got any hay, but there's some mashed potatoes left, and what is there? Why, there's some excelsior the lamp-shade come packed in. You don't suppose he'd think it was hay, do you? No, I guess it wouldn't taste very good."

"Where can I put him, grandmother?"

"Fer the land sakes! I don't know," said the grandmother, looking around the room in alarm. "We haven't any place fer horses. Perhaps you might get him into the back yard fer a while till we think what to do. There's a stable, but they charge high to board horses. Lizzie knows one of the fellers that works there. Mebbe he'll tell us what to do. Anyway, you lead him round to the alleyway, and we'll see if we can't get him in the little ash-gate. You don't suppose he'd try to get in the house, do you? I shouldn't like him to come in the kitchen when I was getting supper."

"O no!" said Elizabeth. "He's very good. Where is the back yard?"

This arrangement was finally made, and the two women stood in the kitchen door, watching Robin drink a bucketful of water and eat heartily of the various viands that Mrs. Brady set forth for him, with the exception of the excelsior, which he snuffed at in disgust.

"Now, ain't he smart?" said Mrs. Brady, watching fearfully from the door-step, where she might retreat if the animal showed any tendency to step nearer to the kitchen. "But don't you think he's cold? Wouldn't he like a—a—shawl or something?"

The girl drew the old coat from her shoulders, and threw it over him, her grandmother watching her fearless handling of the horse with pride and awe.

"We're used to sharing this together," said the girl simply.

"Nan sews in an up-town dressmaker's place," explained Mrs. Brady by and by, when the wash was hung out in fearsome proximity to the weary horse's heels, and the two had returned to the warm kitchen to clean up and get supper. "Nan's your ma's sister, you know, older'n her by two year; and Lizzie, that's her girl, she's about 's old 's you. She's got a good place in the ten-cent store. Nan's husband died four years ago, and her and me've been livin' together ever since. It'll be nice fer you and Lizzie to be together. She'll make it lively fer you right away. Prob'ly she can get you a place at the same store. She'll be here at half past six to-night. This is her week to get out early."

The aunt came in first. She was a tall, thin woman with faded brown hair and a faint resemblance to Elizabeth's mother. Her shoulders stooped slightly, and her voice was nasal. Her mouth looked as if it was used to holding pins in one corner and gossiping out of the other. She was one of the kind who always get into a rocking-chair to sew if they can, and rock as they sew. Nevertheless, she was skilful in her way, and commanded good wages. She welcomed the new niece reluctantly, more excited over her remarkable appearance among her relatives after so long a silence than pleased, Elizabeth felt. But after she had satisfied her curiosity she was kind, beginning to talk about Lizzie, and mentally compared this thin, brown girl with rough hair and dowdy clothes to her own stylish daughter. Then Lizzie burst in. They could hear her calling to a young man who had walked home with her, even before she entered the house.

"It's just fierce out, ma!" she exclaimed. "Grandma, ain't supper ready yet? I never was so hungry in all my life. I could eat a house afire."

She stopped short at sight of Elizabeth. She had been chewing gum—Lizzie was always chewing gum—but her jaws ceased action in sheer astonishment.

"This is your cousin Bessie, come all the way from Montana on horseback, Lizzie. She's your aunt Bessie's child. Her folks is dead now, and she's come to live with us. You must see ef you can't get her a place in the ten-cent store 'long with you," said the grandmother.

Lizzie came airily forward, and grasped her cousin's hand in mid-air, giving it a lateral shake that bewildered Elizabeth.

"Pleased to meet you," she chattered glibly, and set her jaws to work again. One could not embarrass Lizzie long. But she kept her eyes on the stranger, and let them wander disapprovingly over her apparel in a pointed way as she took out the long hat-pins from the cumbersome hat she wore and adjusted her ponderous pompadour.

"Lizzie'll have to help fix you up," said the aunt noting Lizzie's glance. "You're all out of style. I suppose they get behind times out in Montana. Lizzie, can't you show her how to fix her hair pompadour?"

Lizzie brightened. If there was a prospect of changing things, she was not averse to a cousin of her own age; but she never could take such a dowdy-looking girl into society, not the society of the ten-cent store.

"O, cert!" answered Lizzie affably. "I'll fix you fine. Don't you worry. How'd you get so awful tanned? I s'pose riding. You look like you'd been to the seashore, and lay out on the beach in the sun. But 'tain't the right time o' year quite. It must be great to ride horseback!"

"I'll teach you how if you want to learn," said Elizabeth, endeavoring to show a return of the kindly offer.

"Me? What would I ride? Have to ride a counter, I guess. I guess you won't find much to ride here in the city, 'cept trolley-cars."

"Bessie's got a horse. He's out in the yard now," said the grandmother with pride.

"A horse! All your own? Gee whiz! Won't the girls stare when I tell them? Say, we can borrow a rig at the livery some night, and take a ride. Dan'll go with us, and get the rig for us. Won't that be great?"

Elizabeth smiled. She felt the glow of at last contributing something to the family pleasure. She did not wish her coming to be so entirely a wet blanket as it had seemed at first; for, to tell the truth, she had seen blank dismay on the face of each separate relative as her identity had been made known. Her heart was lonely, and she hungered for some one who "belonged" and loved her.

Supper was put on the table, and the two girls began to get a little acquainted, chattering over clothes and the arrangement of hair.

"Do you know whether there is anything in Philadelphia called 'Christian Endeavor'?" asked Elizabeth after the supper-table was cleared off.

"O, Chrishun'deavor! Yes, I used t' b'long," answered Lizzie. She had removed the gum from her mouth while she ate her supper, but now it was busy again between sentences. "Yes, we have one down to our church. It was real interesting, too; but I got mad at one of the members, and quit. She was a stuck-up old maid, anyway. She was always turning round and scowling at us girls if we just whispered the least little bit, or smiled; and one night she was leading the meeting, and Jim Forbes got in a corner behind a post, and made mouths at her behind his book. He looked awful funny. It was something fierce the way she always screwed her face up when she sang, and he looked just like her. We girls, Hetty and Em'line and I, got to laughing, and we just couldn't stop; and didn't that old thing stop the singing after one verse, and look right at us, and say she thought Christian Endeavor members should remember whose house they were in, and that the owner was there, and all that rot. I nearly died, I was so mad. Everybody looked around, and we girls choked, and got up and went out. I haven't been down since. The lookout committee came to see us 'bout it; but I said I wouldn't go back where I'd been insulted, and I've never been inside the doors since. But she's moved away now. I wouldn't mind going back if you want to go."

"Whose house did she mean it was? Was it her house?"

"O, no, it wasn't her house," laughed Lizzie. "It was the church. She meant it was God's house, I s'pose, but she needn't have been so pernickety. We weren't doing any harm."

"Does God have a house?"

"Why, yes; didn't you know that? Why, you talk like a heathen, Bessie. Didn't you have churches in Montana?"

"Yes, there was a church fifty miles away. I heard about it once, but I never saw it," answered Elizabeth. "But what did the woman mean? Who did she say was there? God? Was God in the church? Did you see Him, and know He was there when you laughed?"

"O, you silly!" giggled Lizzie. "Wouldn't the girls laugh at you, though, if they could hear you talk? Why, of course God was there. He's everywhere, you know," with superior knowledge; "but I didn't see Him. You can't see God."

"Why not?"

"Why, because you can't!" answered her cousin with final logic. "Say, haven't you got any other clothes with you at all? I'd take you down with me in the morning if you was fixed up."

CHAPTER XI

IN FLIGHT AGAIN

When Elizabeth lay down to rest that night, with Lizzie still chattering by her side, she found that there was one source of intense pleasure in anticipation, and that was the prospect of going to God's house to Christian Endeavor. Now perhaps she would be able to find out what it all had meant, and whether it were true that God took care of people and hid them in time of trouble. She felt almost certain in her own little experience that He had cared for her, and she wanted to be quite sure, so that she might grasp this precious truth to her heart and keep it forever. No one could be quite alone in the world if there was a God who cared and loved and hid.

The aunt and the grandmother were up betimes the next morning, looking over some meagre stores of old clothing, and there was found an old dress which it was thought could be furbished over for Elizabeth. They were hard-working people with little money to spare, and everything had to be utilized; but they made a great deal of appearance, and Lizzie was proud as a young peacock. She would not take Elizabeth to the store to face the head man without having her fixed up according to the most approved style.

So the aunt cut and fitted before she went off for the day, and Elizabeth was ordered to sew while she was gone. The grandmother presided at the rattling old sewing-machine, and in two or three days Elizabeth was pronounced to be fixed up enough to do for the present till she could earn some new clothes. With her fine hair snarled into a cushion and puffed out into an enormous pompadour that did not suit her face in the least, and with an old hat and jacket of Lizzie's which did not become her nor fit her exactly, she started out to make her way in the world as a saleswoman. Lizzie had already secured her a place if she suited.

The store was a maze of wonder to the girl from the mountains—so many bright, bewildering things, ribbons and tin pans, glassware and toys, cheap jewelry and candies. She looked about with the dazed eyes of a creature from another world.

But the manager looked upon her with eyes of favor. He saw that her eyes were bright and keen. He was used to judging faces. He saw that she was as yet unspoiled, with a face of refinement far beyond the general run of the girls who applied to him for positions. And he was not beyond a friendly flirtation with a pretty new girl himself; so she was engaged at once, and put on duty at the notion-counter.

The girls flocked around her during the intervals of custom. Lizzie had told of her cousin's long ride, embellished, wherever her knowledge failed, by her extremely wild notions of Western life. She had told how Elizabeth arrived wearing a belt with two pistols, and this gave Elizabeth standing at once among all the people in the store. A girl who could shoot, and who wore pistols in a belt like a real cowboy, had a social distinction all her own.

The novel-reading, theatre-going girls rallied around her to a girl; and the young men in the store were not far behind. Elizabeth was popular from the first. Moreover, as she settled down into the routine of life, and had three meals every day, her cheeks began to round out just a little; and it became apparent that she was unusually beautiful in spite of her dark skin, which whitened gradually under the electric light and high-pressure life of the store.

They went to Christian Endeavor, Elizabeth and her cousin; and Elizabeth felt as if heaven had suddenly dropped down about her. She lived from week to week for that Christian Endeavor.

The store, which had been a surprise and a novelty at first, began to be a trial to her. It wore upon her nerves. The air was bad, and the crowds were great. It was coming on toward Christmas time, and the store was crammed to bursting day after day and night after night, for they kept open evenings now until Christmas. Elizabeth longed for a breath from the mountains, and grew whiter and thinner. Sometimes she felt as if she must break away from it all, and take Robin, and ride into the wilderness again. If it were not for the Christian Endeavor, she would have done so, perhaps.

Robin, poor beast, was well housed and well fed; but he worked for his living as did his mistress. He was a grocer's delivery horse, worked from Monday morning early till Saturday night at ten o'clock, subject to curses and kicks from the grocery boy, expected to stand meekly at the curbstones, snuffing the dusty brick pavements while the boy delivered a box of goods, and while trolleys and beer-wagons and automobiles slammed and rumbled and tooted by him, and then to start on the double-quick to the next stopping-place.

He to be thus under the rod who had trod the plains with a free foot and snuffed the mountain air! It was a great come-down, and his life became a weariness to him. But he earned his mistress a dollar a week besides his board. There would have been some consolation in that to his faithful heart if he only could have known it. Albeit she would have gladly gone without the dollar if Robin could have been free and happy.

One day, one dreadful day, the manager of the ten-cent store came to Elizabeth with a look in his eyes that reminded her of the man in Montana from whom she had fled. He was smiling, and his words were unduly pleasant. He wanted her to go with him to the theatre that evening, and he complimented her on her appearance. He stated that he admired her exceedingly, and wanted to give her pleasure. But somehow Elizabeth had fallen into the habit ever since she left the prairies of comparing all men with George Trescott Benedict; and this man, although he dressed well, and was every bit as handsome, did not compare well. There was a sinister, selfish glitter in his eyes that made Elizabeth think of the serpent on the plain just before she shot it. Therefore Elizabeth declined the invitation.

It happened that there was a missionary meeting at the church that evening. All the Christian Endeavorers had been urged to attend. Elizabeth gave this as an excuse; but the manager quickly swept that away, saying she could go to church any night, but she could not go to this particular play with him always. The girl eyed him calmly with much the same attitude with which she might have pointed her pistol at his head, and said gravely,

"But I do not want to go with you."

After that the manager hated her. He always hated girls who resisted him. He hated her, and wanted to do her harm. But he fairly persecuted her to receive his attentions. He was a young fellow, extremely young to be occupying so responsible a position. He undoubtedly had business ability. He showed it in his management of

Elizabeth. The girl's life became a torment to her. In proportion as she appeared to be the manager's favorite the other girls became jealous of her. They taunted her with the manager's attentions on every possible occasion. When they found anything wrong, they charged it upon her; and so she was kept constantly going to the manager, which was perhaps just what he wanted.

She grew paler and paler, and more and more desperate. She had run away from one man; she had run away from a woman; but here was a man from whom she could not run away unless she gave up her position. If it had not been for her grandmother, she would have done so at once; but, if she gave up her position, she would be thrown upon her grandmother for support, and that must not be. She understood from the family talk that they were having just as much as they could do already to make both ends meet and keep the all-important god of Fashion satisfied. This god of Fashion had come to seem to Elizabeth an enemy of the living God. It seemed to occupy all people's thoughts, and everything else had to be sacrificed to meet its demands.

She had broached the subject of school one evening soon after she arrived, but was completely squelched by her aunt and cousin.

"You're too old!" sneered Lizzie. "School is for children."

"Lizzie went through grammar school, and we talked about high for her," said the grandmother proudly.

"But I just hated school," grinned Lizzie. "It ain't so nice as it's cracked up to be. Just sit and study all day long. Why, they were always keeping me after school for talking or laughing. I was glad enough when I got through. You may thank your stars you didn't have to go, Bess."

"People who have to earn their bread can't lie around and go to school," remarked Aunt Nan dryly, and Elizabeth said no more.

But later she heard of a night-school, and then she took up the subject once more. Lizzie scoffed at this. She said night-school was only for very poor people, and it was a sort of disgrace to go. But Elizabeth stuck to her point, until one day Lizzie came home with a tale about Temple College. She had heard it was very cheap. You could go for ten cents a night, or something like that. Things that were ten cents appealed to her. She was used to bargain-counters.

She heard it was quite respectable to go there, and they had classes in the evening. You could study gymnastics, and it would make you graceful. She wanted to be graceful. And she heard they had a course in millinery. If it was so, she believed she would go herself, and learn to make the new kind of bows they were having on hats this winter. She could not seem to get the right twist to the ribbon.

Elizabeth wanted to study geography. At least, that was the study Lizzie said would tell her where the Desert of Sahara was. She wanted to know things, all kinds of things; but Lizzie said such things were only for children, and she didn't believe they taught such baby studies in a college. But she would inquire. It was silly of Bessie to want to know, she thought, and she was half ashamed to ask. But she would find out.

It was about this time that Elizabeth's life at the store grew intolerable.

One morning—it was little more than a week before Christmas—Elizabeth had been sent to the cellar to get seven little red tin pails and shovels for a woman who wanted them for Christmas gifts for some Sunday-school class. She had just counted out the requisite number and turned to go up-stairs when she heard some one step near her, and, as she looked up in the dim light, there stood the manager.

"At last I've got you alone, Bessie, my dear!" He said it with suave triumph in his tones. He caught Elizabeth by the wrists, and before she could wrench herself away he had kissed her.

With a scream Elizabeth dropped the seven tin pails and the seven tin shovels, and with one mighty wrench took her hands from his grasp. Instinctively her hand went to her belt, where were now no pistols. If one had been there she certainly would have shot him in her horror and fury. But, as she had no other weapon, she seized a little shovel, and struck him in the face. Then with the frenzy of the desert back upon her she rushed up the stairs, out through the crowded store, and into the street, hatless and coatless in the cold December air. The passers-by made way for her, thinking she had been sent out on some hurried errand.

She had left her pocketbook, with its pitifully few nickels for car-fare and lunch, in the cloak-room with her coat and hat. But she did not stop to think of that. She was fleeing again, this time on foot, from a man. She half expected he might pursue her, and make her come back to the hated work in the stifling store with his wicked face moving everywhere above the crowds. But she turned not to look back. On over the slushy pavements, under the leaden sky, with a few busy flakes floating about her.

The day seemed pitiless as the world. Where could she go and what should she do? There seemed no refuge for her in the wide world. Instinctively she felt her grandmother would feel that a calamity had befallen them in losing the patronage of the manager of the ten-cent store. Perhaps Lizzie would get into trouble. What should she do?

She had reached the corner where she and Lizzie usually took the car for home. The car was coming now; but she had no hat nor coat, and no money to pay for a ride. She must walk. She paused not, but fled on in a steady run, for which her years on the mountain had given her breath. Three miles it was to Flora Street, and she scarcely slackened her pace after she had settled into that steady half-run, half-walk. Only at the corner of Flora Street she paused, and allowed herself to glance back once. No, the manager had not pursued her. She was safe. She might go in and tell her grandmother without fearing he would come behind her as soon as her back was turned.

CHAPTER XII

ELIZABETH'S DECLARATION OF INDEPENDENCE

Mrs. Brady was at the wash-tub again when her most uncommon and unexpected grandchild burst into the room.

She wiped her hands on her apron, and sat down with her usual exclamation, "Fer the land sakes! What's happened? Bessie, tell me quick. Is anything the matter with Lizzie? Where is she?"

But Elizabeth was on the floor at her feet in tears. She was shaking with sobs, and could scarcely manage to stammer out that Lizzie was all right. Mrs. Brady settled back with a relieved sigh. Lizzie was the first grandchild, and therefore the idol of her heart. If Lizzie was all right, she could afford to be patient and find out by degrees.

"It's that awful man, grandmother!" Elizabeth sobbed out.

"What man? That feller in Montana you run away from?" The grandmother sat up with snapping eyes. She was not afraid of a man, even if he did shoot people. She would call in the police and protect her own flesh and blood. Let him come. Mrs. Brady was ready for him.

"No, no, grandmother, the man—man—manager at the ten-cent store," sobbed the girl; "he kissed me! Oh!" and she shuddered as if the memory was the most terrible thing that ever came to her.

"Fer the land sakes! Is that all?" said the woman with much relief and a degree of satisfaction. "Why, that's nothing. You ought to be proud. Many a girl would go boasting round about that. What are you crying for? He didn't hurt you, did he? Why, Lizzie seems to think he's fine. I tell you Lizzie wouldn't cry if he was to kiss her, I'm sure. She'd just laugh, and ask him fer a holiday. Here, sit up, child, and wash your face, and go back to your work. You've evidently struck the manager on the right side, and you're bound to get a rise in your wages. Every girl he takes a notion to gets up and does well. Perhaps you'll get money enough to go to school. Goodness knows what you want to go for. I s'pose it's in the blood, though Bess used to say your pa wa'n't any great at study. But, if you've struck the manager the right way, no telling what he might do. He might even want to marry you."

"Grandmother!"

Mrs. Brady was favored with the flashing of the Bailey eyes. She viewed it in astonishment not unmixed with admiration.

"Well, you certainly have got spirit," she ejaculated. "I don't wonder he liked you. I didn't know you was so pretty, Bessie; you look like your mother when she was eighteen; you really do. I never saw the resemblance before. I believe you'll get on all right. Don't you be afraid. I wish you had your chance if you're so anxious to go to school. I shouldn't wonder ef you'd turn out to be something and marry rich. Well, I must be getting back to me tub. Land sakes, but you did give me a turn. I thought Lizzie had been run over. I couldn't think what else'd make you run off way here without your coat. Come, get up, child, and go back to your work. It's too bad you don't like to be kissed, but don't let that worry you. You'll have lots worse than that to come up against. When you've lived as long as I have and worked as hard, you'll be pleased to have some one admire you. You better wash your face, and eat a bite of lunch, and hustle back. You needn't be afraid. If he's fond of you, he won't bother about your running away a little. He'll excuse you ef 'tis busy times, and not dock your pay neither."

"Grandmother!" said Elizabeth. "Don't! I can never go back to that awful place and that man. I would rather go back to Montana. I would rather be dead."

"Hoity-toity!" said the easy-going grandmother, sitting down to her task, for she perceived some wholesome discipline was necessary. "You can't talk that way, Bess. You got to go to your work. We ain't got money to keep you in idleness, and land knows where you'd get another place as good's this one. Ef you stay home all day, you might make him awful mad; and then it would be no use goin' back, and you might lose Lizzie her place too."

But, though the grandmother talked and argued and soothed by turns, Elizabeth was firm. She would not go back. She would never go back. She would go to Montana if her grandmother said any more about it.

With a sigh at last Mrs. Brady gave up. She had given up once before nearly twenty years ago. Bessie, her oldest daughter, had a will like that, and tastes far above her station. Mrs. Brady wondered where she got them.

"You're fer all the world like yer ma," she said as she thumped the clothes in the wash-tub. "She was jest that way, when she would marry your pa. She could 'a' had Jim Stokes, the groceryman, or Lodge, the milkman, or her choice of three railroad men, all of 'em doing well, and ready to let her walk over 'em; but she would have your pa, the drunken, good-for-nothing, slippery dude. The only thing I'm surprised at was that he ever married her. I never expected it. I s'posed they'd run off, and he'd leave her when he got tired of her; but it seems he stuck to her. It's the only good thing he ever done, and I'm not sure but she'd 'a' been better off ef he hadn't 'a' done that."

"Grandmother!" Elizabeth's face blazed.

"Yes, *gran*'mother!" snapped Mrs. Brady. "It's all true, and you might's well face it. He met her in church. She used to go reg'lar. Some boys used to come and set in the back seat behind the girls, and then go home with them. They was all nice enough boys 'cept him. I never had a bit a use fer him. He belonged to the swells and the stuck-ups; and he knowed it, and presumed upon it. He jest thought he could wind Bessie round his finger, and he did. If he said, 'Go,' she went, no matter what I'd do. So, when his ma found it out, she was hoppin' mad. She jest came driving round here to me house, and presumed to talk to me. She said Bessie was a designing snip, and a bad girl, and a whole lot of things. Said she was leading her son astray, and would come to no good end, and a whole lot of stuff; and told me to look after her. It wasn't so. Bess got John Bailey to quit smoking fer a whole week at a time, and he said if she'd marry him he'd quit drinking too. His ma couldn't 'a' got him to promise that. She wouldn't even believe he got drunk. I told her a few things about her precious son, but she curled her fine, aristocratic lip up, and said, 'Gentlemen never get drunk.' Humph! Gentlemen! That's all she knowed about it. He got drunk all right, and stayed drunk, too. So after that, when I tried to keep Bess at home, she slipped away one night; said she was going to church; and she did too; went to the minister's study in a strange church, and got married, her and John; and then they up and off West. John, he'd sold his watch and his fine diamond stud his ma had give him; and he borrowed some money from some friends of his father's, and he off with three hundred dollars and Bess; and that's all I ever saw more of me Bessie."

The poor woman sat down in her chair, and wept into her apron regardless for once of the soap-suds that rolled down her red, wet arms.

"Is my grandmother living yet?" asked Elizabeth. She was sorry for this grandmother, but did not know what to say. She was afraid to comfort her lest she take it for yielding.

"Yes, they say she is," said Mrs. Brady, sitting up with a show of interest. She was always ready for a bit of gossip. "Her husband's dead, and her other son's dead, and she's all alone. She lives in a big house on Rittenhouse Square. If she was any 'count, she'd ought to provide fer you. I never thought about it. But I don't suppose it would be any use to try. You might ask her. Perhaps she'd help you go to school. You've got a claim on her. She ought to give you her son's share of his father's property, though I've heard she disowned him when he married our Bess. You might fix up in some of Lizzie's best things, and go up there and try. She might give you some money."

"I don't want her money," said Elizabeth stiffly. "I guess there's work somewhere in the world I can do without begging even of grandmothers. But I think I ought to go and see her. She might want to know about father."

Mrs. Brady looked at her granddaughter wonderingly. This was a view of things she had never taken.

"Well," said she resignedly, "go your own gait. I don't know where you'll come up at. All I say is, ef you're going through the world with such high and mighty fine notions, you'll have a hard time. You can't pick out roses and cream and a bed of down every day. You have to put up with life as you find it."

Elizabeth went to her room, the room she shared with Lizzie. She wanted to get away from her grandmother's disapproval. It lay on her heart like lead. Was there no refuge in the world? If grandmothers were not refuges, where should one flee? The old lady in Chicago had understood; why had not Grandmother Brady?

Then came the sweet old words, "Let not your heart be troubled." "In the time of trouble he shall hide me in his pavilion; in the secret of his tabernacle shall he hide me." She knelt down by the bed and said "Our Father." She was beginning to add some words of her own now. She had heard them pray so in Christian Endeavor in the sentence prayers. She wished she knew more about God, and His Book. She had had so little time to ask or think about it. Life seemed all one rush for clothes and position.

At supper-time Lizzie came home much excited. She had been in hot water all the afternoon. The girls had said at lunch-time that the manager was angry with Bessie, and had discharged her. She found her coat and hat, and had brought them home. The pocketbook was missing. There was only fifteen cents in it; but Lizzie was much disturbed, and so was the grandmother. They had a quiet consultation in the kitchen; and, when the aunt came, there was another whispered conversation among the three.

Elizabeth felt disapproval in the air. Aunt Nan came, and sat down beside her, and talked very coldly about expenses and being dependent upon one's relatives, and let her understand thoroughly that she could not sit around and do nothing; but Elizabeth answered by telling her how the manager had been treating her. The aunt then gave her a dose of worldly wisdom, which made the girl shrink into herself. It needed only Lizzie's loud-voiced exhortations to add to her misery and make her feel ready to do anything. Supper was a most unpleasant meal. At last the grandmother spoke up.

"Well, Bessie," she said firmly, "we've decided, all of us, that, if you are going to be stubborn about this, something will have to be done; and I think the best thing is for you to go to Mrs. Bailey and see what she'll do for you. It's her business, anyway."

Elizabeth's cheeks were very red. She said nothing. She let them go on with the arrangements. Lizzie went and got her best hat, and tried it on Elizabeth to see how she would look, and produced a silk waist from her store of garments, and a spring jacket. It wasn't very warm, it is true; but Lizzie explained that the occasion demanded strenuous measures, and the jacket was undoubtedly stylish, which was the main thing to be considered. One could afford to be cold if one was stylish.

Lizzie was up early the next morning. She had agreed to put Elizabeth in battle-array for her visit to Rittenhouse Square. Elizabeth submitted meekly to her borrowed adornings. Her hair was brushed over her face, and curled on a hot iron, and brushed backward in a perfect mat, and then puffed out in a bigger pompadour than usual. The silk waist was put on with Lizzie's best skirt, and she was adjured not to let that drag. Then the best hat with the cheap pink plumes was set atop the elaborate coiffure; the jacket was put on; and a pair of Lizzie's long silk gloves were struggled into. They were a trite large when on, but to the hands unaccustomed to gloves they were like being run into a mould.

Elizabeth stood it all until she was pronounced complete. Then she came and stood in front of the cheap little glass, and surveyed herself. There were blisters in the glass that twisted her head into a grotesque shape. The hairpins stuck into her head. Lizzie had tied a spotted veil tight over her nose and eyes. The collar of the silk waist was frayed, and cut her neck. The skirt-band was too tight, and the gloves were torture. Elizabeth turned slowly, and went down-stairs, past the admiring aunt and grandmother, who exclaimed at the girl's beauty, now that she was attired to their mind, and encouraged her by saying they were sure her grandmother would want to do something for so pretty a girl.

Lizzie called out to her not to worry, as she flew for her car. She said she had heard there was a variety show in town where they wanted a girl who could shoot. If she didn't succeed with her grandmother, they would try and get her in at the show. The girls at the store knew a man who had charge of it. They said he liked pretty girls, and they thought would be glad to get her. Indeed, Mary James had promised to speak to him last night, and would let her know to-day about it. It would likely be a job more suited to her cousin's liking.

Elizabeth shuddered. Another man! Would he be like all the rest?—all the rest save one!

She walked a few steps in the direction she had been told to go, and then turned resolutely around, and came back. The watching grandmother felt her heart sink. What was this headstrong girl going to do next? Rebel again?

"What's the matter, Bessie?" she asked, meeting her anxiously at the door. "It's bad luck to turn back when you've started."

"I can't go this way," said the girl excitedly. "It's all a cheat. I'm not like this. It isn't mine, and I'm not going in it. I must have my own clothes and be myself when I go to see her. If she doesn't like me and want me, then I can take Robin and go back." And like another David burdened with Saul's armor she came back to get her little sling and stones.

She tore off the veil, and the sticky gloves from her cold hands, and all the finery of silk waist and belt, and donned her old plain blue coat and skirt in which she had arrived in Philadelphia. They had been frugally brushed and sponged, and made neat for a working dress. Elizabeth felt that they belonged to her. Under the jacket, which fortunately was long enough to hide her waist, she buckled her belt with the two pistols. Then she took the battered old felt hat from the closet, and tried to fasten it on; but the pompadour interfered. Relentlessly she pulled down the work of art that Lizzie had created, and brushed and combed her long, thick hair into subjection again, and put it in its long braid down her back. Her grandmother should see her just as she was. She should know what kind of a girl belonged to her. Then, if she chose to be a real grandmother, well and good.

Mrs. Brady was much disturbed in mind when Elizabeth came down-stairs. She exclaimed in horror, and tried to force the girl to go back, telling her it was a shame and disgrace to go in such garments into the sacred precincts of Rittenhouse Square; but the girl was not to be turned back. She would not even wait till her aunt and Lizzie came home. She would go now, at once.

Mrs. Brady sat down in her rocking-chair in despair for full five minutes after she had watched the reprehensible girl go down the street. She had not been so completely beaten since the day when her own Bessie left the house and went away to a wild West to die in her own time and way. The grandmother shed a few tears. This girl was like her own Bessie, and she could not help loving her, though there was a streak of something else about her that made her seem above them all; and that was hard to bear. It must be the Bailey streak, of course. Mrs. Brady did not admire the Baileys, but she was obliged to reverence them.

If she had watched or followed Elizabeth, she would have been still more horrified. The girl went straight to the corner grocery, and demanded her own horse, handing back to the man the dollar he had paid her last Saturday night, and saying she had need of the horse at once. After some parley, in which she showed her ability to stand her own ground, the boy unhitched the horse from the wagon, and got her own old saddle for her from the stable. Then Elizabeth mounted her horse and rode away to Rittenhouse Square.

CHAPTER XIII
ANOTHER GRANDMOTHER

Elizabeth's idea in taking the horse along with her was to have all her armor on, as a warrior goes out to meet the foe. If this grandmother proved impossible, why, then so long as she had life and breath and a horse she could flee. The world was wide, and the West was still open to her. She could flee back to the wilderness that gave her breath.

The old horse stopped gravely and disappointedly before the tall, aristocratic house in Rittenhouse Square. He had hoped that city life was now to end, and that he and his dear mistress were to travel back to their beloved prairies. No amount of oats could ever make up to him for his freedom, and the quiet, and the hills. He had a feeling that he should like to go back home and die. He had seen enough of the world.

She fastened the halter to a ring in the sidewalk, which surprised him. The grocer's boy never fastened him. He looked up questioningly at the house, but saw no reason why his mistress should go in there. It was not familiar ground. Koffee and Sons never came up this way.

Elizabeth, as she crossed the sidewalk and mounted the steps before the formidable carved doors, felt that here was the last hope of finding an earthly habitation. If this failed her, then there was the desert, and starvation, and a long, long sleep. But while the echo of the cell still sounded through the high-ceiled hall there came to her the words: "Let not your heart be troubled.... In my Father's house are many mansions; if it were not so, I would have told you. I go to prepare a place for you.... I will come again and receive you." How sweet that was! Then, even if she died on the desert, there was a home prepared for her. So much she had learned in Christian Endeavor meeting.

The stately butler let her in. He eyed her questioningly at first, and said madam was not up yet; but Elizabeth told him she would wait.

"Is she sick?" asked Elizabeth with a strange constriction about her heart.

"O no, she is not up yet, miss," said the kind old butler; "she never gets up before this. You're from Mrs. Sands, I suppose." Poor soul, for once his butler eyes had been mistaken. He thought she was the little errand-girl from Madam Bailey's modiste.

"No, I'm just Elizabeth," said the girl, smiling. She felt that this man, whoever he was, was not against her. He was old, and he had a kind look.

He still thought she meant she was not the modiste, just her errand-girl. Her quaint dress and the long braid down her back made her look like a child.

"I'll tell her you've come. Be seated," said the butler, and gave her a chair in the dim hall just opposite the parlor door, where she had a glimpse of elegance such as she had never dreamed existed. She tried to think how it must be to live in such a room and walk on velvet. The carpet was deep and rich. She did not know it was a rug nor that it was woven in some poor peasant's home and then was brought here years afterward at a fabulous price. She only knew it was beautiful in its silvery sheen with gleaming colors through it like jewels in the dew.

On through another open doorway she caught a glimpse of a painting on the wall. It was a man as large as life, sitting in a chair; and the face and attitude were her father's—her father at his best. She was fairly startled. Who was it? Could it be her father? And how had they made this picture of him? He must be changed in those twenty years he had been gone from home.

Then the butler came back, and before he could speak she pointed toward the picture. "Who is it?" she asked.

"That, miss? That's Mr. John, Madam's husband that's dead a good many years now. But I remember him well."

"Could I look at it? He is so much like my father." She walked rapidly over the ancient rug, unheeding its beauties, while the wondering butler followed a trifle anxiously. This was unprecedented. Mrs. Sands's errand-girls usually knew their place.

"Madam said you was to come right up to her room," said the butler pointedly. But Elizabeth stood rooted to the ground, studying the picture. The butler had to repeat the message. She smiled and turned to follow him, and as she did so saw on a side wall the portraits of two boys.

"Who are they?" she pointed swiftly. They were much like her own two brothers.

"Them are Mr. John and Mr. James, Madam's two sons. They's both of them dead now," said the butler. "At least, Mr. James is, I'm sure. He died two years ago. But you better come right up. Madam will be wondering."

She followed the old man up the velvet-shod stairs that gave back no sound from footfall, and pondered as she went. Then that was her father, that boy with the beautiful face and the heavy wavy hair tossed back from his forehead, and the haughty, imperious, don't-care look. And here was where he had lived. Here amid all this luxury.

Like a flash came the quick contrast of the home in which he had died, and a great wave of reverence for her father rolled over her. From such a home and such surroundings it would not have been strange if he had grown weary of the rough life out West, and deserted his wife, who was beneath him in station. But he had not. He had stayed by her all the years. True, he had not been of much use to her, and much of the time had been but a burden and anxiety; but he had stayed and loved her—when he was sober. She forgave him his many trying ways, his faultfindings with her mother's many little blunders—no wonder, when he came from this place.

The butler tapped on a door at the head of the stairs, and a maid swung it open.

"Why, you're not the girl Mrs. Sands sent the other day," said a querulous voice from a mass of lace-ruffled pillows on the great bed.

"I am Elizabeth," said the girl, as if that were full explanation.

"Elizabeth? Elizabeth who? I don't see why she sent another girl. Are you sure you will understand the directions? They're very particular, for I want my frock ready for to-night without fail." The woman sat up, leaning on one elbow. Her lace nightgown and pale-blue silk dressing-sack fell away from a round white arm that did not look as if it belonged to a very old lady. Her gray hair was becomingly arranged, and she was extremely pretty, with small features. Elizabeth looked and marvelled. Like a flash came the vision of the other grandmother at the wash-tub. The contrast was startling.

"I am Elizabeth Bailey," said the girl quietly, as if she would break a piece of hard news gently. "My father was your son John."

"The idea!" said the new grandmother, and promptly fell back upon her pillows with her hand upon her heart. "John, John, my little John. No one has mentioned his name to me for years and years. He never writes to me." She put up a lace-trimmed handkerchief, and sobbed.

"Father died five years ago," said Elizabeth.

"You wicked girl!" said the maid. "Can't you see that Madam can't bear such talk? Go right out of the room!" The maid rushed up with smelling-salts and a glass of water, and Elizabeth in distress came and stood by the bed.

"I'm sorry I made you feel bad, grandmother," she said when she saw that the fragile, childish creature on the bed was recovering somewhat.

"What right have you to call me that? Grandmother, indeed! I'm not so old as that. Besides, how do I know you belong to me? If John is dead, your mother better look after you. I'm sure I'm not responsible for you. It's her business. She wheedled John away from his home, and carried him off to that awful West, and never let him write to me. She has done it all, and now she may bear the consequences. I suppose she has sent you here to beg, but she has made a mistake. I shall not have a thing to do with her of her children."

"Grandmother!" Elizabeth's eyes flashed as they had done to the other grandmother a few hours before. "You must not talk so. I won't hear it. I wouldn't let Grandmother Brady talk about my father, and you can't talk so about mother. She was my mother, and I loved her, and so did father love her; and she worked hard to keep him and take care of him when he drank years and years, and didn't have any money to help her. Mother was only eighteen when she married father, and you ought not to blame her. She didn't have a nice home like this. But she was good and dear, and now she is dead. Father and mother are both dead, and all the other children. A man killed my brother, and then as soon as he was buried he came and wanted me to go with him. He was an awful man, and I was afraid, and took my brother's horse and ran away. I rode all this long way because I was afraid of that man, and I wanted to get to some of my own folks, who would love me, and let me work for them, and let me go to school and learn something. But I wish now I had stayed out there and died. I could have lain down in the sage-brush, and a wild beast would have killed me perhaps, and that would be a great deal better than this; for Grandmother Brady does not understand, and you do not want me; but in my Father's house in heaven there are many mansions, and He went to prepare a place for me; so I guess I will go back to the desert, and perhaps He will send for me. Good-by, grandmother."

Then before the astonished woman in the bed could recover her senses from this remarkable speech Elizabeth turned and walked majestically from the room. She was slight and not very tall, but in the strength of her pride and purity she looked almost majestic to the awestruck maid and the bewildered woman.

Down the stairs walked the girl, feeling that all the wide world was against her. She would never again try to get a friend. She had not met a friend except in the desert. One man had been good to her, and she had let him go away; but he belonged to another woman, and she might not let him stay. There was just one thing to be thankful for. She had knowledge of her Father in heaven, and she knew what Christian Endeavor meant. She could take that with her out into the desert, and no one could take it from her. One wish she had, but maybe that was too much to hope for. If she could have had a Bible of her own! She had no money left. Nothing but her mother's wedding-ring, the papers, and the envelope that had contained the money the man had given her when he left. She could not part with them, unless perhaps some one would take the ring and keep it until she could buy it back. But she would wait and hope.

She walked by the old butler with her hand on her pistol. She did not intend to let any one detain her now. He bowed pleasantly, and opened the door for her, however; and she marched down the steps to her horse. But just as she was about to mount and ride away into the unknown where no grandmother, be she Brady or Bailey, would ever be able to search her out, no matter how hard she tried, the door suddenly opened again, and there was a great commotion. The maid and the old butler both flew out, and laid hands upon her. She dropped the bridle, and seized her pistol, covering them both with its black, forbidding nozzle.

They stopped, trembling, but the butler bravely stood his ground. He did not know why he was to detain this extraordinary young person, but he felt sure something wrong. Probably she was a thief, and had taken some of Madam's jewels. He could call the police. He opened his mouth to do so when the maid explained.

"Madam wants you to come back. She didn't understand. She wants to see you and ask about her son. You must come, or you will kill her. She has heart trouble, and you must not excite her."

Elizabeth put the pistol back into its holster and, picking up the bridle again, fastened it in the ring, saying simply, "I will come back."

"What do you want?" she asked abruptly when she returned to the bedroom.

"Don't you know that's a disrespectful way to speak?" asked the woman querulously. "What did you have to get into a temper for, and go off like that without telling me anything about my son? Sit down, and tell me all about it."

"I'm sorry, grandmother," said Elizabeth, sitting down. "I thought you didn't want me and I better go."

"Well, the next time wait until I send you. What kind of a thing have you got on, anyway? That's a queer sort of a hat for a girl to wear. Take it off. You look like a rough boy with that on. You make me think of John when he had been out disobeying me."

Elizabeth took off the offending headgear, and revealed her smoothly parted, thick brown hair in its long braid down her back.

"Why, you're rather a pretty girl if you were fixed up," said the old lady, sitting up with interest now. "I can't remember your mother, but I don't think she had fine features like that."

"They said I looked like father," said Elizabeth.

"Did they? Well, I believe it's true," with satisfaction. "I couldn't bear you if you looked like those lowdown —
—"

"Grandmother!" Elizabeth stood up, and flashed her Bailey eyes.

"You needn't 'grandmother' me all the time," said the lady petulantly. "But you look quite handsome when you say it. Take off that ill-fitting coat. It isn't thick enough for winter, anyway. What in the world have you got round your waist? A belt? Why, that's a man's belt! And what have you got in it? Pistols? Horrors! Marie, take them away quick! I shall faint! I never could bear to be in a room with one. My husband used to have one on his closet shelf, and I never went near it, and always locked the room when he was out. You must put them out in the hall. I cannot breathe where pistols are. Now sit down and tell me all about it, how old you are, and how you got here."

Elizabeth surrendered her pistols with hesitation. She felt that she must obey her grandmother, but was not altogether certain whether it was safe for her to be weaponless until she was sure this was friendly ground.

At the demand she began back as far as she could remember, and told the story of her life, pathetically, simply, without a single claim to pity, yet so earnestly and vividly that the grandmother, lying with her eyes closed, forgot herself completely, and let the tears trickle unbidden and unheeded down her well-preserved cheeks.

When Elizabeth came to the graves in the moonlight, she gasped, and sobbed: "O, Johnny, Johnny, my little Johnny! Why did you always be such a bad, bad boy?" and when the ride in the desert was described, and the man from whom she fled, the grandmother held her breath, and said, "O, how fearful!" Her interest in the girl was growing, and kept at white heat during the whole of the story.

There was one part of her experience, however, that Elizabeth passed over lightly, and that was the meeting with George Trescott Benedict. Instinctively she felt that this experience would not find a sympathetic listener. She passed it over by merely saying that she had met a kind gentleman from the East who was lost, and that they had ridden together for a few miles until they reached a town; and he had telegraphed to his friends, and gone on his way. She said nothing about the money he had lent to her, for she shrank from speaking about him more than was necessary. She felt that her grandmother might feel as the old woman of the ranch had felt about their travelling together. She left it to be inferred that she might have had a little money with her from home. At least, the older woman asked no questions about how she secured provisions for the way.

When Elizabeth came to her Chicago experience, her grandmother clasped her hands as if a serpent had been mentioned, and said: "How degrading! You certainly would have been justified in shooting the whole company. I wonder such places are allowed to exist!" But Marie sat with large eyes of wonder, and retailed the story over again in the kitchen afterwards for the benefit of the cook and the butler, so that Elizabeth became henceforth a heroine among them.

Elizabeth passed on to her Philadelphia experience, and found that here her grandmother was roused to blazing indignation, but the thing that roused her was the fact that a Bailey should serve behind a counter in a ten-cent

Store. She lifted her hands, and uttered a moan of real pain, and went on at such a rate that the smelling-salts had to be brought into requisition again.

When Elizabeth told of her encounter with the manager in the cellar, the grandmother said: "How disgusting! The impertinent creature! He ought to be sued. I will consult the lawyer about the matter. What did you say his name was? Marie, write that down. And so, dear, you did quite right to come to me. I've been looking at you while you talked, and I believe you'll be a pretty girl if you are fixed up. Marie, go to the telephone, and call up Blandeaux, and tell him to send up a hair-dresser at once. I want to see how Miss Elizabeth will look with her hair done low in one of those new coils. I believe it will be becoming. I should have tried it long ago myself; only it seems a trifle too youthful for hair that is beginning to turn gray."

Elizabeth watched her grandmother in wonder. Here truly was a new phase of woman. She did not care about great facts, but only about little things. Her life was made up of the great pursuit of fashion, just like Lizzie's. Were people in cities all alike? No, for he, the one man she had met in the wilderness, had not seemed to care. Maybe, though, when he got back to the city he did care. She sighed and turned toward the new grandmother.

"Now I have told you everything, grandmother. Shall I go away? I wanted to go to school; but I see that it costs a great deal of money, and I don't want to be a burden on any one. I came here, not to ask you to take me in, because I did not want to trouble you; but I thought before I went away I ought to see you once because—because you are my grandmother."

"I've never been a grandmother," said the little woman of the world reflectively, "but I don't know but it would be rather nice. I'd like to make you into a pretty girl, and take you out into society. That would be something new to live for. I'm not very pretty myself any more, but I can see that you will be. Do you wear blue or pink? I used to wear pink myself, but I believe you could wear either when you get your complexion in shape. You've tanned it horribly, but it may come out all right. I think you'll take. You say you want to go to school. Why, certainly, I suppose that will be necessary; living out in that barbarous, uncivilized region, of course you don't know much. You seem to speak correctly, but John always was particular about his speech. He had a tutor when he was little who tripped him up every mistake he made. That was the only thing that tutor was good for; he was a linguist. We found out afterwards he was terribly wild, and drank. He did John more harm than good, Marie, I shall want Elizabeth to have the rooms next mine. Ring for Martha to see that everything is in order. Elizabeth, did you ever have your hands manicured? You have a pretty-shaped hand. I'll have the woman attend to it when she comes to shampoo your hair and put it up. Did you bring any clothes along? Of course not. You couldn't on horseback. I suppose you had your trunk sent by express. No trunk? No express? No railroad? How barbarous! How John must have suffered, poor fellow! He, so used to every luxury! Well, I don't see that it was my fault. I gave him everything he wanted except his wife, and he took her without my leave. Poor fellow, poor fellow!"

Mrs. Bailey in due time sent Elizabeth off to the suite of rooms that she said were to be hers exclusively, and arose to bedeck herself for another day. Elizabeth was a new toy, and she anticipated playing with her. It put new zest into a life that had grown monotonous.

Elizabeth, meanwhile, was surveying her quarters, and wondering what Lizzie would think if she could see her. According to orders, the coachman had taken Robin to the stable, and he was already rolling in all the luxuries of a horse of the aristocracy, and congratulating himself on the good taste of his mistress to select such a stopping-place. For his part he was now satisfied not to move further. This was better than the wilderness any day. Oats like these, and hay such as this, were not to be found on the plains.

Toward evening the grave butler, with many a deprecatory glance at the neighborhood, arrived at the door of Mrs. Brady, and delivered himself of the following message to that astonished lady, backed by her daughter and her granddaughter, with their ears stretched to the utmost to hear every syllable:

"Mrs. Merrill Wilton Bailey sends word that her granddaughter, Miss Elizabeth, has reached her home safely, and will remain with her. Miss Elizabeth will come sometime to see Mrs. Brady, and thank her for her kindness during her stay with her."

The butler bowed, and turned away with relief. His dignity and social standing had not been so taxed by the family demands in years. He was glad he might shake off the dust of Flora Street forever. He felt for the coachman. He would probably have to drive the young lady down here sometime, according to that message.

Mrs. Brady, her daughter, and Lizzie stuck their heads out into the lamplighted street, and watched the dignified butler out of sight. Then they went in and sat down in three separate stages of relief and astonishment.

"Fer the land sakes!" ejaculated the grandmother. "Wall, now, if that don't beat all!" then after a minute: "The impertinent fellow! And the impidence of the woman! Thank me fer my kindness to me own grandchild! I'd thank her to mind her business, but then that's just like her."

"Her nest is certainly well feathered," said Aunt Nan enviously. "I only wish Lizzie had such a chance."

Said Lizzie: "It's awful queer, her looking like that, too, in that crazy rig! Well, I'm glad she's gone, fer she was so awful queer it was jest fierce. She talked religion a lot to the girls, and then they laughed at her behind her back; and they kep' a telling me I'd be a missionary 'fore long if she stayed with us. I went to Mr. Wray, the manager, and told him my cousin was awfully shy, and she sent word she wanted to be excused fer running away like that.

He kind of colored up, and said 'twas all right, and she might come back and have her old place if she wanted, and he'd say no more about it. I told him I'd tell her. But I guess her acting up won't do me a bit of harm. The girls say he'll make up to me now. Wish he would. I'd have a fine time. It's me turn to have me wages raised, anyway. He said if Bess and I would come to-morrow ready to stay in the evening, he'd take us to a show that beat everything he ever saw in Philadelphia. I mean to make him take me, anyway. I'm just glad she's out of the way. She wasn't like the rest of us."

Said Mrs. Brady: "It's the Bailey in her. But she said she'd come back and see me, didn't she?" and the grandmother in her meditated over that fact for several minutes.

CHAPTER XIV
IN A NEW WORLD

Meantime the panorama of Elizabeth's life passed on into more peaceful scenes. By means of the telephone and the maid a lot of new and beautiful garments were provided for her, which fitted perfectly, and which bewildered her not a little until they were explained by Marie. Elizabeth had her meals up-stairs until these things had arrived and she had put them on. The texture of the garments was fine and soft, and they were rich with embroidery and lace. The flannels were as soft as the down in a milkweed pod, and everything was of the best. Elizabeth found herself wishing she might share them with Lizzie,—Lizzie who adored rich and beautiful things, and who had shared her meagre outfit with her. She mentioned this wistfully to her grandmother, and in a fit of childish generosity that lady said: "Certainly, get her what you wish. I'll take you downtown some day, and you can pick out some nice things for them all. I hate to be under obligations."

A dozen ready-made dresses had been sent out before the first afternoon was over, and Elizabeth spent the rest of the day in trying on and walking back and forth in front of her grandmother. At last two or three were selected which it was thought would "do" until the dressmaker could be called in to help, and Elizabeth was clothed and allowed to come down into the life of the household.

It was not a large household. It consisted of the grandmother, her dog, and the servants. Elizabeth fitted into it better than she had feared. It seemed pleasanter to her than the house on Flora Street. There was more room, and more air, and more quiet. With her mountain breeding she could not get her breath in a crowd.

She was presently taken in a luxurious carriage, drawn by two beautiful horses, to a large department store, where she sat by the hour and watched her grandmother choose things for her. Another girl might have gone half wild over the delightful experience of being able to have anything in the shops. Not so Elizabeth. She watched it all apathetically, as if the goods displayed about had been the leaves upon the trees set forth for her admiration. She could wear but one dress at once, and one hat. Why were so many necessary? Her main hope lay in the words her grandmother had spoken about sending her to school.

The third day of her stay in Rittenhouse Square, Elizabeth had reminded her of it, and the grandmother had said half impatiently: "Yes, yes, child; you shall go of course to a finishing school. That will be necessary. But first I must get you fixed up. You have scarcely anything to put on." So Elizabeth subsided.

At last there dawned a beautiful Sabbath when, the wardrobe seemingly complete, Elizabeth was told to array herself for church, as they were going that morning. With great delight and thanksgiving she put on what she was told; and, when she looked into the great French plate mirror after Marie had put on the finishing touches, she was astonished at herself. It was all true, after all. She was a pretty girl.

She looked down at the beautiful gown of finest broadcloth, with the exquisite finish that only the best tailors can put on a garment, and wondered at herself. The very folds of dark-green cloth seemed to bring a grace into her movements. The green velvet hat with its long curling plumes of green and cream-color seemed to be resting lovingly above the beautiful hair that was arranged so naturally and becomingly.

Elizabeth wore her lovely ermine collar and muff without ever knowing they were costly. They all seemed so fitting and quiet and simple, so much less obtrusive than Lizzie's pink silk waist and cheap pink plumes. Elizabeth liked it, and walked to church beside her grandmother with a happy feeling in her heart.

The church was just across the Square. Its tall brown stone spire and arched doorways attracted Elizabeth when she first came to the place. Now she entered with a kind of delight.

It was the first time she had ever been to a Sabbath morning regular service in church. The Christian Endeavor had been as much as Lizzie had been able to stand. She said she had to work too hard during the week to waste so much time on Sunday in church. "The Sabbath was made for man" and "for rest," she had quoted glibly. For the first time in her life since she left Montana Elizabeth felt as if she had a real home and was like other people. She looked around shyly to see whether perchance her friend of the desert might be sitting near, but no familiar face met her gaze. Then she settled back, and gave herself up to delight in the service.

The organ was playing softly, low, tender music. She learned afterward that the music was Handel's "Largo." She did not know that the organ was one of the finest in the city, nor that the organist was one of the most skilful to be had; she knew only that the music seemed to take her soul and lift it up above the earth so that heaven was all around her, and the very clouds seemed singing to her. Then came the processional, with the wonderful voices of the choir-boys sounding far off, and then nearer. It would be impossible for any one who had been accustomed all his life to these things to know how it affected Elizabeth.

It seemed as though the Lord Himself was leading the girl in a very special way. At scarcely any other church in a fashionable quarter of the great city would Elizabeth have heard preaching so exactly suited to her needs. The minister was one of those rare men who lived with God, and talked with Him daily. He had one peculiarity which marked him from all other preachers, Elizabeth heard afterward. He would turn and talk with God in a gentle, sweet, conversational tone right in the midst of his sermon. It made the Lord seem very real and very near.

If he had not been the great and brilliant preacher of an old established church, and revered by all denominations as well as his own, the minister would have been called eccentric and have been asked to resign, because his religion was so very personal that it became embarrassing to some. However, his rare gifts, and his remarkable consecration and independence in doing what he thought right, had produced a most unusual church for a fashionable neighborhood.

Most of his church-members were in sympathy with him, and a wonderful work was going forward right in the heart of Sodom, unhampered by fashion or form or class distinctions. It is true there were some who, like Madam Bailey sat calmly in their seats, and let the minister attend to the preaching end of the service without ever bothering their thoughts as to what he was saying. It was all one to them whether he prayed three times or once, so the service got done at the usual hour. But the majority were being led to see that there is such a thing as a close and intimate walk with God upon this earth.

Into this church came Elizabeth, the sweet heathen, eager to learn all that could be learned about the things of the soul. She sat beside her grandmother, and drank in the sermon, and bowed her lovely, reverent head when she became aware that God was in the room and was being spoken to by His servant. After the last echo of the recessional had died away, and the bowed hush of the congregation had grown into a quiet, well-bred commotion of the putting on of wraps and the low Sabbath greetings, Elizabeth turned to her grandmother.

"Grandmother, may I please go and ask that man some questions? He said just what I have been longing and longing to know, and I must ask him more. Nobody else ever told me these things. Who is he? How does he know it is all true?"

The elder woman watched the eager, flushed face of the girl; and her heart throbbed with pride that this beautiful young thing belonged to her. She smiled indulgently.

"The rector, you mean? Why, I'll invite him to dinner if you wish to talk with him. It's perfectly proper that a young girl should understand about religion. It has a most refining influence, and the Doctor is a charming man. I'll invite his wife and daughter too. They move in the best circles, and I have been meaning to ask them for a long time. You might like to be confirmed. Some do. It's a very pretty service. I was confirmed myself when I was about your age. My mother thought it a good thing for a girl before she went into society. Now, just as you are a schoolgirl, is the proper time. I'll send for him this week. He'll be pleased to know you are interested in these things. He has some kind of a young people's club that meets on Sunday. 'Christian Something' he calls it; I don't know just what, but he talks a great deal about it, and wants every young person to join. You might pay the dues, whatever they are, anyway. I suppose it's for charity. It wouldn't be necessary for you to attend the meetings, but it would please the Doctor."

"Is it Christian Endeavor?" asked Elizabeth, with her eyes sparkling.

"Something like that, I believe. Good morning, Mrs. Schuyler. Lovely day, isn't it? for December. No, I haven't been very well. No, I haven't been out for several weeks. Charming service, wasn't it? The Doctor grows more and more brilliant, I think. Mrs. Schuyler, this is my granddaughter, Elizabeth. She has just come from the West to live with me and complete her education. I want her to know your daughter."

Elizabeth passed through the introduction as a necessary interruption to her train of thought. As soon as they were out upon the street again she began.

"Grandmother, was God in that church?"

"Dear me, child! What strange questions you do ask! Why, yes, I suppose He was, in a way. God is everywhere, they say. Elizabeth, you had better wait until you can talk these things over with a person whose business it is. I never understood much about such questions. You look very nice in that shade of green, and your hat is most becoming."

So was the question closed for the time, but not put out of the girl's thoughts.

The Christmas time had come and passed without much notice on the part of Elizabeth, to whom it was an unfamiliar festival. Mrs. Bailey had suggested that she select some gifts for her "relatives on her mother's side," as she always spoke of the Bradys; and Elizabeth had done so with alacrity, showing good sense and good taste in her choice of gifts, as well as deference to the wishes of the one to whom they were to be given. Lizzie, it is true, was a trifle disappointed that her present was not a gold watch or a diamond ring; but on the whole she was pleased.

A new world opened before the feet of Elizabeth. School was filled with wonder and delight. She absorbed knowledge like a sponge in the water, and rushed eagerly from one study to another, showing marvellous aptitude, and bringing to every task the enthusiasm of a pleasure-seeker.

Her growing intimacy with Jesus Christ through the influence of the pastor who knew Him so well caused her joy in life to blossom into loveliness.

The Bible she studied with the zest of a novel-reader, for it was a novel to her; and daily, as she took her rides in the park on Robin, now groomed into self-respecting sleekness, and wearing a saddle of the latest approved style, she marvelled over God's wonderful goodness to her, just a maid of the wilderness.

So passed three beautiful years in peace and quietness. Every month Elizabeth went to see her Grandmother Brady, and to take some charming little gifts; and every summer she and her Grandmother Bailey spent at some of the fashionable watering-places or in the Catskills, the girl always dressed in most exquisite taste, and as sweetly indifferent to her clothes as a bird of the air or a flower of the field.

The first pocket-money she had been given she saved up, and before long had enough to send the forty dollars to the address the man in the wilderness had given her. But with it she sent no word. It was like her to think she had no right.

She went out more and more with her grandmother among the fashionable old families in Philadelphia society, though as yet she was not supposed to be "out," being still in school; but in all her goings she neither saw nor heard of George Trescott Benedict.

Often she looked about upon the beautiful women that came to her grandmother's house, who smiled and talked to her, and wondered which of them might be the lady to whom his heart was bound. She fancied she must be most sweet and lovely in every way, else such as he could not care for her; so she would pick out this one and that one; and then, as some disagreeableness or glaring fault would appear, she would drop that one for another. There were only a few, after all, that she felt were good enough for the man who had become her ideal.

But sometimes in her dreams he would come and talk with her, and smile as he used to do when they rode together; and he would lay his hand on the mane of her horse—there were always the horses in her dreams. She liked to think of it when she rode in the park, and to think how pleasant it would be if he could be riding there beside her, and they might talk of a great many things that had happened since he left her alone. She felt she would like to tell him of how she had found a friend in Jesus Christ. He would be glad to know about it, she was sure. He seemed to be one who was interested in such things, not like other people who were all engaged in the world.

Sometimes she felt afraid something had happened to him. He might have been thrown from that terrible train and killed, perhaps; and no one know anything about it. But as her experience grew wider, and she travelled on the trains herself, of course this fear grew less. She came to understand that the world was wide, and many things might have taken him away from his home.

Perhaps the money she had sent reached him safely, but she had put in no address. It had not seemed right that she should. It would seem to draw his attention to her, and she felt "the lady" would not like that. Perhaps they were married by this time, and had gone far away to some charmed land to live. Perhaps—a great many things. Only this fact remained; he never came any more into the horizon of her life; and therefore she must try to forget him, and be glad that God had given her a friend in him for her time of need. Some day in the eternal home perhaps she would meet him and thank him for his kindness to her, and then they might tell each other all about the journey through the great wilderness of earth after they had parted. The links in Elizabeth's theology had been well supplied by this time, and her belief in the hereafter was strong and simple like a child's.

She had one great longing, however, that he, her friend, who had in a way been the first to help her toward higher things, and to save her from the wilderness, might know Jesus Christ as he had not known Him when they were together. And so in her daily prayer she often talked with her heavenly Father about him, until she came to have an abiding faith that some day, somehow, he would learn the truth about his Christ.

During the third season of Elizabeth's life in Philadelphia her grandmother decided that it was high time to bring out this bud of promise, who was by this time developing into a more beautiful girl than even her fondest hopes had pictured.

So Elizabeth "came out," and Grandmother Brady read her doings and sayings in the society columns with her morning coffee and an air of deep satisfaction. Aunt Nan listened with her nose in the air. She could never understand why Elizabeth should have privileges beyond her Lizzie. It was the Bailey in her, of course, and mother ought not to think well of it. But Grandmother Brady felt that, while Elizabeth's success was doubtless due in large part to the Bailey in her, still, she was a Brady, and the Brady had not hindered her. It was a step upward for the Bradys.

Lizzie listened, and with pride retailed at the ten-cent store the doings of "my cousin, Elizabeth Bailey," and the other girls listened with awe.

And so it came on to be the springtime of the third year that Elizabeth had spent in Philadelphia.

CHAPTER XV
AN EVENTFUL PICNIC

It was summer and it was June. There was to be a picnic, and Elizabeth was going.

Grandmother Brady had managed it. It seemed to her that, if Elizabeth could go, her cup of pride would be full to overflowing; so after much argument, pro and con, with her daughter and Lizzie, she set herself down to pen the invitation. Aunt Nan was decidedly against it. She did not wish to have Lizzie outshone. She had been working nights for two weeks on an elaborate organdie, with pink roses all over it, for Lizzie to wear. It had yards and yards of cheap lace and insertion, and a whole bolt of pink ribbons of various widths. The hat was a marvel of impossible roses, just calculated for the worst kind of a wreck if a thunder-shower should come up at a Sunday-school picnic. Lizzie's mother was even thinking of getting her a pink chiffon parasol to carry; but the family treasury was well-nigh depleted, and it was doubtful whether that would be possible. After all that, it did not seem pleasant to have Lizzie put in the shade by a fine-lady cousin in silks and jewels.

But Grandmother Brady had waited long for her triumph. She desired above all things to walk among her friends, and introduce her granddaughter, Elizabeth Bailey, and inadvertently remark: "You must have seen me granddaughter's name in the paper often, Mrs. Babcock. She was giving a party in Rittenhouse Square the other day."

Elizabeth would likely be married soon, and perhaps go off somewhere away from Philadelphia—New York or Europe, there was no telling what great fortune might come to her. Now the time was ripe for triumph if ever, and when things are ripe they must be picked. Mrs. Brady proceeded to pick.

She gathered together at great pains pen, paper, and ink. A pencil would be inadequate when the note was going to Rittenhouse Square. She sat down when Nan and Lizzie had left for their day's work, and constructed her sentences with great care.

"*Dear Bessie—*" Elizabeth had never asked her not to call her that, although she fairly detested the name. But still it had been her mother's name, and was likely dear to her grandmother. It seemed disloyalty to her mother to suggest that she be called "Elizabeth." So Grandmother Brady serenely continued to call her "Bessie" to the end of her days. Elizabeth decided that to care much about such little things, in a world where there were so many great things, would be as bad as to give one's mind entirely over to the pursuit of fashion.

The letter proceeded laboriously:

"Our Sunday school is going to have a picnic out to Willow Grove. It's on Tuesday. We're going in the trolley. I'd be pleased if you would go 'long with us. We will spend the day, and take our dinner and supper along, and wouldn't get home till late; so you could stay overnight here with us, and not go back home till after breakfast. You needn't bring no lunch; fer we've got a lot of things planned, and it ain't worth while. But if you wanted to bring some candy, you might. I ain't got time to make any, and what you buy at our grocery might not be fine enough fer you. I want you to go real bad. I've never took my two granddaughters off to anything yet, and your Grandmother Bailey has you to things all the time. I hope you can manage to come. I am going to pay all the expenses. Your old Christian Deaver you used to 'tend is going to be there; so you'll have a good time. Lizzie has a new pink organdie, with roses on her hat; and we're thinking of getting her a pink umbreller if it don't cost too much. The kind with chiffon flounces on it. You'll have a good time, fer there's lots of side-shows out to Willow Grove, and we're going to see everything there is to see. There's going to be some music too. A man with a name that sounds like swearing is going to make it. I don't remember it just now, but you can see it advertised round on the trolley-cars. He comes to Willow Grove every year. Now please let me hear if you will go at once, as I want to know how much cake to make.

"Your loving grandmother,
ELIZABETH BRADY."

Elizabeth laughed and cried over this note. It pleased her to have her grandmother show kindness to her. She felt that whatever she did for Grandmother Brady was in a sense showing her love to her own mother; so she brushed aside several engagements, much to the annoyance of her Grandmother Bailey, who could not understand why she wanted to go down to Flora Street for two days and a night just in the beginning of warm weather. True, there was not much going on just now between seasons, and Elizabeth could do as she pleased; but she might get a fever in such a crowded neighborhood. It wasn't in the least wise. However, if she must, she must. Grandmother

Bailey was on the whole lenient. Elizabeth was too much of a success, and too willing to please her in all things, for her to care to cross her wishes. So Elizabeth wrote on her fine note-paper bearing the Bailey crest in silver:

"Dear Grandmother: I shall be delighted to go to the picnic with you, and I'll bring a nice big box of candy, Huyler's best. I'm sure you'll think it's the best you ever tasted. Don't get Lizzie a parasol; I'm going to bring her one to surprise her. I'll be at the house by eight o'clock.

"Your loving granddaughter,
ELIZABETH."

Mrs. Brady read this note with satisfaction and handed it over to her daughter to read with a gleam of triumph in her eyes at the supper-table. She knew the gift of the pink parasol would go far toward reconciling Aunt Nan to the addition to their party. Elizabeth never did things by halves, and the parasol would be all that could possibly be desired without straining the family pocketbook any further.

So Elizabeth went to the picnic in a cool white dimity, plainly made, with tiny frills of itself, edged with narrow lace that did not shout to the unknowing multitude, "I am real!" but was content with being so; and with a white Panama hat adorned with only a white silken scarf, but whose texture was possible only at a fabulous price. The shape reminded Elizabeth of the old felt hat belonging to her brother, which she had worn on her long trip across the continent. She had put it on in the hat-store one day; and her grandmother, when she found how exquisite a piece of weaving the hat was, at once purchased it for her. It was stylish to wear those soft hats in all sorts of odd shapes. Madam Bailey thought it would be just the thing for the seashore.

Her hair was worn in a low coil in her neck, making the general appearance and contour of her head much as it had been three years before. She wore no jewelry, save the unobtrusive gold buckle at her belt and the plain gold hatpin which fastened her hat. There was nothing about her which marked her as one of the "four hundred." She did not even wear her gloves, but carried them in her hand, and threw them carelessly upon the table when she arrived in Flora Street. Long, soft white ones, they lay there in their costly elegance beside Lizzie's post-card album that the livery-stable man gave her on her birthday, all the long day while Elizabeth was at Willow Grove, and Lizzie sweltered around under her pink parasol in long white silk gloves.

Grandmother Brady surveyed Elizabeth with decided disapproval. It seemed too bad on this her day of triumph, and after she had given a hint, as it were, about Lizzie's fine clothes, that the girl should be so blind or stubborn or both as to come around in that plain rig. Just a common white dress, and an old hat that might have been worn about a livery-stable. It was mortifying in the extreme. She expected a light silk, and kid gloves, and a beflowered hat. Why, Lizzie looked a great deal finer. Did Mrs. Bailey rig her out this way for spite? she wondered.

But, as it was too late to send Elizabeth back for more fitting garments, the old lady resigned herself to her disappointment. The pink parasol was lovely, and Lizzie was wild over it. Even Aunt Nan seemed mollified. It gave her great satisfaction to look the two girls over. Her own outshone the one from Rittenhouse Square by many counts, so thought the mother; but all day long, as she walked behind them or viewed them from afar, she could not understand why it was that the people who passed them always looked twice at Elizabeth and only once at Lizzie. It seemed, after all, that clothes did not make the girl. It was disappointing.

The box of candy was all that could possibly be desired. It was ample for the needs of them all, including the two youths from the livery-stable who had attached themselves to their party from the early morning. In fact, it was two boxes, one of the most delectable chocolates of all imaginable kinds, and the other of mixed candies and candied fruit. Both boxes bore the magic name "Huyler's" on the covers. Lizzie had often passed Huyler's, taking her noon walk on Chestnut Street, and looked enviously at the girls who walked in and out with white square bundles tied with gold cord as if it were an everyday affair. And now she was actually eating all she pleased of those renowned candies. It was almost like belonging to the great élite.

It was a long day and a pleasant one even to Elizabeth. She had never been to Willow Grove before, and the strange blending of sweet nature and Vanity Fair charmed her. It was a rest after the winter's round of monotonous engagements. Even the loud-voiced awkward youths from the livery-stable did not annoy her extremely. She took them as a part of the whole, and did not pay much attention to them. They were rather shy of her, giving the most of their attention to Lizzie, much to the satisfaction of Aunt Nan.

They mounted the horses in the merry-go-rounds, and tried each one several times. Elizabeth wondered why anybody desired this sort of amusement, and after her first trip would have been glad to sit with her grandmother and watch the others, only that the old lady seemed so much to desire to have her get on with the rest. She would not do anything to spoil the pleasure of the others if she could help it; so she obediently seated herself in a great sea-shell drawn by a soiled plaster nymph, and whirled on till Lizzie declared it was time to go to something else.

They went into the Old Mill, and down into the Mimic Mine, and sailed through the painted Venice, eating candy and chewing gum and shouting. All but Elizabeth. Elizabeth would not chew gum nor talk loud. It was not her way. But she smiled serenely on the rest, and did not let it worry her that some one might recognize the popular Miss Bailey in so ill-bred a crowd. She knew that it was their way, and they could have no other. They were having a good time, and she was a part of it for to-day. They weighed one another on the scales with many jokes and much laughter, and went to see all the moving pictures in the place. They ate their lunch under the trees, and then at last the music began.

They seated themselves on the outskirts of the company, for Lizzie declared that was the only pleasant place to be. She did not want to go "way up front." She had a boy on either side of her, and she kept the seat shaking with laughter. Now and then a weary guard would look distressedly down the line, and motion for less noise; but they giggled on. Elizabeth was glad they were so far back that they might not annoy more people than was necessary.

But the music was good, and she watched the leader with great satisfaction. She noticed that there were many people given up to the pleasure of it. The melody went to her soul, and thrilled through it. She had not had much good music in her life. The last three years, of course, she had been occasionally to the Academy of Music; but, though her grandmother had a box there, she very seldom had time or cared to attend concerts. Sometimes, when Melba, or Caruso, or some world-renowned favorite was there, she would take Elizabeth for an hour, usually slipping out just after the favorite solo with noticeable loftiness, as if the orchestra were the common dust of the earth, and she only condescended to come for the soloist. So Elizabeth had scarcely known the delight of a whole concert of fine orchestral music.

She heard Lizzie talking.

"Yes, that's Walter Damrosch! Ain't that name fierce? Grandma thinks it's kind of wicked to pernounce it that way. They say he's fine, but I must say I liked the band they had last year better. It played a whole lot of lively things, and once they had a rattle-box and a squeaking thing that cried like a baby right out in the music, and everybody just roared laughing. I tell you that was great. I don't care much for this here kind of music myself. Do you?" And Jim and Joe both agreed that they didn't, either. Elizabeth smiled, and kept on enjoying it.

Peanuts were the order of the day, and their assertive crackle broke in upon the finest passages. Elizabeth wished her cousin would take a walk; and by and by she did, politely inviting Elizabeth to go along; but she declined, and they were left to sit through the remainder of the afternoon concert.

After supper they watched the lights come out, Elizabeth thinking about the description of the heavenly city as one after another the buildings blazed out against the darkening blue of the June night. The music was about to begin. Indeed, it could be heard already in the distance, and drew the girl irresistibly. For the first time that day she made a move, and the others followed, half wearied of their dissipations, and not knowing exactly what to do next.

They stood the first half of the concert very well, but at the intermission they wandered out to view the electric fountain with its many-colored fluctuations, and to take a row on the tiny sheet of water. Elizabeth remained sitting where she was, and watched the fountain. Even her grandmother and aunt grew restless, and wanted to walk again. They said they had had enough music, and did not want to hear any more. They could hear it well enough, anyway, from further off. They believed they would have some ice-cream. Didn't Elizabeth want some?

She smiled sweetly. Would grandmother mind if she sat right there and heard the second part of the concert? She loved music, and this was fine. She didn't feel like eating another thing to-night. So the two ladies, thinking the girl queer that she didn't want ice-cream, went off to enjoy theirs with a clear conscience; and Elizabeth drew a long breath, and sat back with her eyes closed, to test and breathe in the sweet sounds that were beginning to float out delicately as if to feel whether the atmosphere were right for what was to come after.

It was just at the close of this wonderful music, which the programme said was Mendelssohn's "Spring Song," when Elizabeth looked up to meet the eyes of some one who stood near in the aisle watching her, and there beside her stood the man of the wilderness!

He was looking at her face, drinking in the beauty of the profile and wondering whether he were right. Could it be that this was his little brown friend, the maid of the wilderness? This girl with the lovely, refined face, the intellectual brow, the dainty fineness of manner? She looked like some white angel dropped down into that motley company of Sunday-school picknickers and city pleasure-seekers. The noise and clatter of the place seemed far away from her. She was absorbed utterly in the sweet sounds.

When she looked up and saw him, the smile that flashed out upon her face was like the sunshine upon a day that has hitherto been still and almost sad. The eyes said, "You are come at last!" The curve of the lips said, "I am glad you are here!"

He went to her like one who had been hungry for the sight of her for a long time, and after he had grasped her hand they stood so for a moment while the hum and gentle clatter of talk that always starts between numbers seethed around them and hid the few words they spoke at first.

"O, I have so longed to know if you were safe!" said the man as soon as he could speak.

Then straightway the girl forgot all her three years of training, and her success as a débutante, and became the grave, shy thing she had been to him when he first saw her, looking up with awed delight into the face she had seen in her dreams for so long, and yet might not long for.

The orchestra began again, and they sat in silence listening. But yet their souls seemed to speak to each other through the medium of the music, as if the intervening years were being bridged and brought together in the space of those few waves of melody.

"I have found out," said Elizabeth, looking up shyly with a great light in her eyes. "I have found what it all means. Have you? O, I have wanted so much to know whether you had found out too!"

"Found out what?" he asked half sadly that he did not understand.

"Found out how God hides us. Found what a friend Jesus Christ can be."

"You are just the same," said the man with satisfaction in his eyes. "You have not been changed nor spoiled. They could not spoil you."

"Have you found out too?" she asked softly. She looked up into his eyes with wistful longing. She wanted this thing so very much. It had been in her prayers for so long.

He could not withdraw his own glance. He did not wish to. He longed to be able to answer what she wished.

"A little, perhaps," he said doubtfully. "Not so much as I would like to. Will you help me?"

"*He* will help you. You will find Him if you search for Him with all your heart," she said earnestly. "It says so in His book."

Then came more music, wistful, searching, tender. Did it speak of the things of heaven to other souls there than those two?

He stooped down, and said in a low tone that somehow seemed to blend with the music like the words that fitted it,

"I will try with all my heart if you will help me."

She smiled her answer, brimming back with deep delight.

Into the final lingering notes of an andante from one of Beethoven's sublime symphonies clashed the loud voice of Lizzie:

"O Bess! Bess! B-es-see! I say, Bessie! Ma says we'll have to go over by the cars now if we want to get a seat. The concert's most out, and there'll be a fierce rush. Come on! And grandma says, bring your friend along with you if you want." This last with a smirking recognition of the man, who had turned around wonderingly to see who was speaking.

With a quick, searching glance that took in bedraggled organdie, rose hat, and pink parasol, and set them aside for what they were worth, George Benedict observed and classified Lizzie.

"Will you excuse yourself, and let me take you home a little later?" he asked in a low tone. "The crowd will be very great, and I have my automobile here."

She looked at him gratefully, and assented. She had much to tell him. She leaned across the seats, and spoke in a clear tone to her cousin.

"I will come a little later," she said, smiling with her Rittenhouse Square look that always made Lizzie a little afraid of her. "Tell grandmother I have found an old friend I have not seen for a long time. I will be there almost as soon as you are."

They waited while Lizzie explained, and the grandmother and aunt nodded a reluctant assent. Aunt Nan frowned. Elizabeth might have brought her friend along, and introduced him to Lizzie. Did Elizabeth think Lizzie wasn't good enough to be introduced?

He wrapped her in a great soft rug that was in the automobile, and tucked her in beside him; and she felt as if the long, hard days that had passed since they had met were all forgotten and obliterated in this night of delight. Not all the attentions of all the fine men she had met in society had ever been like his, so gentle, so perfect. She had forgotten the lady as completely as if she had never heard of her. She wanted now to tell her friend about her heavenly Friend.

He let her talk, and watched her glowing, earnest face by the dim light of the sky; for the moon had come out to crown the night with beauty, and the unnatural brilliance of electric blaze, with all the glitter and noise of Willow Grove, died into the dim, sweet night as those two sped onward toward the city. The heart of the man kept singing, singing, singing: "I have found her at last! She is safe!"

"I have prayed for you always," he said in one of the pauses. It was just as they were coming into Flora Street. The urchins were all out on the sidewalk yet, for the night was hot; and they gathered about, and ran hooting after the car as it slowed up at the door. "I am sure He did hide you safely, and I shall thank Him for answering my prayer. And now I am coming to see you. May I come to-morrow?"

There was a great gladness in her eyes. "Yes," she said.

The Bradys had arrived from the corner trolley, and were hovering about the door self-assertively. It was most apparent to an onlooker that this was a good opportunity for an introduction, but the two young people were entirely oblivious. The man touched his hat gravely, a look of great admiration in his eyes, and said, "Good night" like a benediction. Then the girl turned and went into the plain little home and to her belligerent relatives with a light in her eyes and a joy in her steps that had not been there earlier in the day. The dreams that visited her hard pillow that night were heavenly and sweet.

"Now we're goin' to see ef the paper says anythin' about our Bessie," said Grandmother Brady the next morning, settling her spectacles over her nose comfortably and crossing one fat gingham knee over the other. "I always read the society notes, Bess."

Elizabeth smiled, and her grandmother read down, the column:

"Mr. George Trescott Benedict and his mother, Mrs. Vincent Benedict, have arrived home after an extended tower of Europe," read Mrs. Brady. "Mrs. Benedict is much improved in health. It is rumored they will spend the summer at their country seat on Wissahickon Heights."

"My!" interrupted Lizzie with her mouth full of fried potatoes. "That's that fellow that was engaged to that Miss What's-her-Name Loring. Don't you 'member? They had his picture in the papers, and her; and then all at once she threw him over for some dook or something, and this feller went off. I heard about it from Mame. Her sister works in a department-store, and she knows Miss Loring. She says she's an awfully handsome girl, and George Benedict was just gone on her. He had a fearful case. Mame says Miss Loring—what is her name?—O, Geraldine—Geraldine Loring bought some lace of her. She heard her say it was for the gown she was going to wear at the horse-show. They had her picture in the paper just after the horse-show, and it was all over lace, I saw it. It cost a whole lot. I forget how many dollars a yard. But there was something the matter with the dook. She didn't marry him, after all. In her picture she was driving four horses. Don't you remember it, grandma? She sat up tall and high on a seat, holding a whole lot of ribbons and whips and things. She has an elegant figger. I guess mebbe the dook wasn't rich enough. She hasn't been engaged to anybody else, and I shouldn't wonder now but she'd take George Benedict back. He was so awful stuck on her!"

Lizzie rattled on, and the grandmother read more society notes, but Elizabeth heard no more. Her hear had suddenly frozen, and dropped down like lead into her being. She felt as if she never would be able to raise it again. The lady! Surely she had forgotten the lady. But Geraldine Loring! Of all women! Could it be possible? Geraldine Loring was almost—well, fast, at least, as nearly so as one who was really of a fine old family, and still held her own in society, could be. She was beautiful as a picture; but her face, to Elizabeth's mind, was lacking in fine feeling and intellect. A great pity went out from her heart to the man whose fate was in that doll-girl's hands. True, she had heard that Miss Loring's family were unquestionable, and she knew her mother was a most charming woman. Perhaps she had misjudged her. She must have done so if he cared for her, for it could not be otherwise.

The joy had gone out of the morning when Elizabeth went home. She went up to her Grandmother Bailey at once, and after she had read her letters for her, and performed the little services that were her habit, she said:

"Grandmother, I'm expecting a man to call upon me to-day. I thought I had better tell you."

"A man!" said Madam Bailey, alarmed at once. She wanted to look over and portion out the right man when the time came. "What man?"

"Why, a man I met in Montana," said Elizabeth, wondering how much she ought to tell.

"A man you met in Montana! Horrors!" exclaimed the now thoroughly aroused grandmother. "Not that dreadful creature you ran away from?"

"O no!" said Elizabeth, smiling. "Not that man. A man who was very kind to me, and whom I like very much."

So much the worse. Immediate action was necessary.

"Well, Elizabeth," said Madam Bailey in her stiffest tones, "I really do not care to have any of your Montana friends visit you. You will have to excuse yourself. It will lead to embarrassing entanglements. You do not in the least realize your position in society. It is all well enough to please your relatives, although I think you often overdo that. You could just as well send them a present now and then, and please them more than to go yourself. But as for any outsiders, it is impossible. I draw the line there."

"But grandmother——"

"Don't interrupt me, Elizabeth; I have something more to say. I had word this morning from the steamship company. They can give us our staterooms on the Deutschland on Saturday, and I have decided to take them. I have telegraphed, and we shall leave here to-day for New York. I have one or two matters of business I wish to attend to in New York. We shall go to the Waldorf for a few days, and you will have more opportunity to see New York than you have had yet. It will not be too warm to enjoy going about a little, I fancy; and a number of our friends are going to be at the Waldorf, too. The Craigs sail on Saturday with us. You will have young company on the voyage."

Elizabeth's heart sank lower than she had known it could go, and she grew white to the lips. The observant grandmother decided that she had done well to be so prompt. The man from Montana was by no means to be admitted. She gave orders to that effect, unknown to Elizabeth.

The girl went slowly to her room. All at once it had dawned upon her that she had not given her address to the man the night before, nor told him by so much as a word what were her circumstances. An hour's meditation brought her to the unpleasant decision that perhaps even now in this hard spot God was only hiding her from worse trouble. Mr. George Benedict belonged to Geraldine Loring. He had declared as much when he was in Montana. It would not be well for her to renew the acquaintance. Her heart told her by its great ache that she would be crushed under a friendship that could not be lasting.

Very sadly she sat down to write a note.

"*My dear Friend*," she wrote on plain paper with no crest. It was like her to choose that. She would not flaunt her good fortune in his face. She was a plain Montana girl to him, and so she would remain.

"My grandmother has been very ill, and is obliged to go away for her health. Unexpectedly I find that we are to go to-day. I supposed it would not be for a week yet. I am so sorry not to see you again, but I send you a little book that has helped me to get acquainted with Jesus Christ. Perhaps it will help you too. It is called 'My Best Friend.' I shall not forget to pray always that you may find Him. He is so precious to me! I must thank you in words, though I never can say it as it should be said, for your very great kindness to me when I was in trouble. God sent you to me, I am sure. Always gratefully your friend,

"ELIZABETH."

That was all, no date, no address. He was not hers, and she would hang out no clues for him to find her, even if he wished. It was better so.

She sent the note and the little book to his address on Walnut Street; and then after writing a note to her Grandmother Brady, saying that she was going away for a long trip with Grandmother Bailey, she gave herself into the hands of the future like a submissive but weary child.

The noon train to New York carried in its drawing-room-car Madam Bailey, her granddaughter, her maid, and her dog, bound for Europe. The society columns so stated; and so read Grandmother Brady a few days afterward. So also read George Benedict, but it meant nothing to him.

When he received the note, his mind was almost as much excited as when he saw the little brown girl and the little brown horse vanishing behind the little brown station on the prairie. He went to the telephone, and reflected that he knew no names. He called up his automobile, and tore up to Flora Street; but in his bewilderment of the night before he had not noticed which block the house was in, nor which number. He thought he knew where to find it, but in broad daylight the houses were all alike for three blocks, and for the life of him he could not remember whether he had turned up to the right or the left when he came to Flora Street. He tried both, but saw no sign of the people he had but casually noticed at Willow Grove.

He could not ask where she lived, for he did not know her name. Nothing but Elizabeth, and they had called her Bessie. He could not go from house to house asking for a girl named Bessie. They would think him a fool, as he was, for not finding out her name, her precious name, at once. How could he let her slip from him again when he had just found her?

At last he hit upon a bright idea. He asked some children along the street whether they knew of any young woman named Bessie or Elizabeth living there, but they all with one accord shook their heads, though one volunteered the information that "Lizzie Smith lives there." It was most distracting and unsatisfying. There was nothing for it but for him to go home and wait in patience for her return. She would come back sometime probably. She had not said so, but she had not said she would not. He had found her once; he might find her again. And he could pray. She had found comfort in that; so would he. He would learn what her secret was. He would get acquainted with her "best Friend." Diligently did he study that little book, and then he went and hunted up the man of God who had written it, and who had been the one to lead Elizabeth into the path of light by his earnest preaching every Sabbath, though this fact he did not know.

The days passed, and the Saturday came. Elizabeth, heavy-hearted, stood on the deck of the Deutschland, and watched her native land disappear from view. So again George Benedict had lost her from sight.

It struck Elizabeth, as she stood straining her eyes to see the last of the shore through tears that would burn to the surface and fall down her white cheeks, that again she was running away from a man, only this time not of her own free will. She was being taken away. But perhaps it was better.

And it never once entered her mind that, if she had told her grandmother who the friend in Montana was, and where he lived in Philadelphia, it would have made all the difference in the world.

From the first of the voyage Grandmother Bailey grew steadily worse, and when they landed on the other side they went from one place to another seeking health. Carlsbad waters did not agree with her, and they went to the south of France to try the climate. At each move the little old lady grew weaker and more querulous. She finally made no further resistance, and gave up to the rôle of invalid. Then Elizabeth must be in constant attendance. Madam Bailey demanded reading, and no voice was so soothing as Elizabeth's.

Gradually Elizabeth substituted books of her own choice as her grandmother seemed not to mind, and now and then she would read a page of some book that told of the best Friend. At first because it was written by the dear pastor at home it commanded her attention, and finally because some dormant chord in her heart had been touched, she allowed Elizabeth to speak of these things. But it was not until they had been away from home for three months, and she had been growing daily weaker and weaker, that she allowed Elizabeth to read in the Bible.

The girl chose the fourteenth chapter of John, and over and over again, whenever the restless nerves tormented their victim, she would read those words, "Let not your heart be troubled" until the selfish soul, who had lived all her life to please the world and do her own pleasure, came at last to hear the words, and feel that perhaps she did believe in God, and might accept that invitation, "Believe also in me."

One day Elizabeth had been reading a psalm, and thought her grandmother was asleep. She was sitting back with weary heart, thinking what would happen if her grandmother should not get well. The old lady opened her eyes.

"Elizabeth," she said abruptly, just as when she was well, "you've been a good girl. I'm glad you came. I couldn't have died right without you. I never thought much about these things before, but it really is worth while. In my Father's house. He is my Father, Elizabeth."

She went to sleep then, and Elizabeth tiptoed out and left her with the nurse. By and by Marie came crying in, and told her that the Madam was dead.

Elizabeth was used to having people die. She was not shocked; only it seemed lonely again to find herself facing the world, in a foreign land. And when she came to face the arrangements that had to be made, which, after all, money and servants made easy, she found herself dreading her own land. What must she do after her grandmother was laid to rest? She could not live in the great house in Rittenhouse Square, and neither could she very well go and live in Flora Street. O, well, her Father would hide her. She need not plan; He would plan for her. The mansions on the earth were His too, as well as those in heaven.

And so resting she passed through the weary voyage and the day when the body was laid to rest in the Bailey lot in the cemetery, and she went back to the empty house alone. It was not until after the funeral that she went to see Grandmother Brady. She had not thought it wise or fitting to invite the hostile grandmother to the other one's funeral. She had thought Grandmother Bailey would not like it.

She rode to Flora Street in the carriage. She felt too weary to walk or go in the trolley. She was taking account of stock in the way of friends, thinking over whom she cared to see. One of the first bits of news she had heard on arriving in this country had been that Miss Loring's wedding was to come off in a few days. It seemed to strike her like a thunderbolt, and she was trying to arraign herself for this as she rode along. It was therefore not helpful to her state of mind to have her grandmother remark grimly:

"That feller o' yours 'n his oughtymobble has been goin' up an' down this street, day in, day out, this whole blessed summer. Ain't been a day he didn't pass, sometimes once, sometimes twicet. I felt sorry fer him sometimes. Ef he hadn't been so high an' mighty stuck up that he couldn't recognize me, I'd 'a' spoke to him. It was plain ez the nose on your face he was lookin' fer you. Don't he know where you live?"

"I don't believe he does," said Elizabeth languidly. "Say, grandmother, would you care to come up to Rittenhouse Square and live?"

"Me? In Rittenhouse Square? Fer the land sakes, child, no. That's flat. I've lived me days out in me own sp'ere, and I don't intend to change now at me time o' life. Ef you want to do somethin' nice fer me, child, now you've got all that money, I'd like real well to live in a house that hed white marble steps. It's been me one aim all me life. There's some round on the next street that don't come high. There'd be plenty room fer us all, an' a nice place fer Lizzie to get married when the time comes. The parlor's real big, and you would send her some roses, couldn't you?"

"All right, grandmother. You shall have it," said Elizabeth with a relieved sigh, and in a few minutes she went home. Some day pretty soon she must think what to do, but there was no immediate hurry. She was glad that Grandmother Brady did not want to come to Rittenhouse Square. Things would be more congenial without her.

But the house seemed great and empty when she entered, and she was glad to hear the friendly telephone bell ringing. It was the wife of her pastor, asking her to come to them for a quiet dinner.

This was the one home in the great city where she felt like going in her loneliness. There would be no form nor ceremony. Just a friend with them. It was good. The doctor would give her some helpful words. She was glad they had asked her.

CHAPTER XVII

A FINAL FLIGHT AND PURSUIT

"George," said Mrs. Vincent Benedict, "I want you to do something for me."

"Certainly, mother, anything I can."

"Well, it's only to go to dinner with me to-night. Our pastor's wife has telephoned me that she wants us very much. She especially emphasized you. She said she absolutely needed you. It was a case of charity, and she would be so grateful to you if you would come. She has a young friend with her who is very sad, and she wants to cheer her up. Now don't frown. I won't bother you again this week. I know you hate dinners and girls. But really, George, this is an unusual case. The girl is just home from Europe, and buried her grandmother yesterday. She hasn't a soul in the world belonging to her that can be with her, and the pastor's wife has asked her over to dinner quietly. Of course she isn't going out. She must be in mourning. And you know you're fond of the doctor."

"Yes, I'm fond of the doctor," said George, frowning discouragedly; "but I'd rather take him alone, and not with a girl flung at me everlastingly. I'm tired of it. I didn't think it of Christian people, though; I thought she was above such things."

"Now, George," said his mother severely, "that's a real insult to the girl, and to our friend too. She hasn't an idea of doing any such thing. It seems this girl is quite unusual, very religious, and our friend thought you would be just the one to cheer her. She apologized several times for presuming to ask you to help her. You really will have to go."

"Well, who is this paragon, anyway? Any one I know? I s'pose I've got to go."

"Why, she's a Miss Bailey," said the mother, relieved. "Mrs. Wilton Merrill Bailey's granddaughter. Did you ever happen to meet her? I never did."

"Never heard of her," growled George. "Wish I hadn't now."

"George!"

"Well, mother, go on. I'll be good. What does she do? Dance, and play bridge, and sing?"

"I haven't heard anything that she does," said his mother, laughing.

"Well, of course she's a paragon; they all are, mother. I'll be ready in half an hour. Let's go and get it done. We can come home early, can't we?"

Mrs. Benedict sighed. If only George would settle down on some suitable girl of good family! But he was so queer and restless. She was afraid for him. Ever since she had taken him away to Europe, when she was so ill, she had been afraid for him. He seemed so moody and absent-minded then and afterwards. Now this Miss Bailey was said to be as beautiful as she was good. If only George would take a notion to her!

Elizabeth was sitting in a great arm-chair by the open fire when he entered the room. He had not expected to find any one there. He heard voices up-stairs, and supposed Miss Bailey was talking with her hostess. His mother followed the servant to remove her wraps, and he entered the drawing-room alone. She stirred, looked up, and saw him.

"Elizabeth!" he said, and came forward to grasp her hand. "I have found you again. How came you here?"

But she had no opportunity to answer, for the ladies entered almost at once, and there stood the two smiling at each other.

"Why, you have met before!" exclaimed the hostess. "How delighted I am! I knew you two would enjoy meeting. Elizabeth, child, you never told me you knew George."

George Benedict kept looking around for Miss Bailey to enter the room; but to his relief she did not come, and, when they went out to the dining-room, there was no place set for her. She must have preferred to remain at home. He forgot her, and settled down to the joy of having Elizabeth by his side. His mother, opposite, watched his face blossom into the old-time joy as he handed this new girl the olives, and had eyes for no one else.

It was to Elizabeth a blessed evening. They held sweet converse one with another as children of the King. For a little time under the old influence of the restful, helpful talk she forgot "the lady," and all the perplexing questions that had vexed her soul. She knew only that she had entered into an atmosphere of peace and love and joy.

It was not until the evening was over, and the guests were about to leave, that Mrs. Benedict addressed Elizabeth as Miss Bailey. Up to that moment it had not entered her son's mind that Miss Bailey was present at all. He turned with a start, and looked into Elizabeth's eyes; and she smiled back to him as if to acknowledge the name. Could she read his thoughts? he wondered.

It was only a few steps across the Square, and Mrs. Benedict and her son walked to Elizabeth's door with her. He had no opportunity to speak to Elizabeth alone, but he said as he bade her good-night, "I shall see you to-morrow, then, in the morning?"

The inflection was almost a question; but Elizabeth only said, "Good night," and vanished into the house.

"Then you have met her before, George?" asked his mother wonderingly.

"Yes," he answered hurriedly, as if to stop her further question. "Yes, I have met her before. She is very beautiful, mother."

And because the mother was afraid she might say too much she assented, and held her peace. It was the first time in years that George had called a girl beautiful.

Meantime Elizabeth had gone to her own room and locked the door. She hardly knew what to think, her heart was so happy. Yet beneath it all was the troubled thought of the lady, the haunting lady for whom they had prayed together on the prairie. And as if to add to the thought she found a bit of newspaper lying on the floor beside her dressing-table. Marie must have dropped it as she came in to turn up the lights. It was nothing but the corner torn from a newspaper, and should be consigned to the waste-basket; yet her eye caught the words in large head-lines

151

as she picked it up idly, "Miss Geraldine Loring's Wedding to Be an Elaborate Affair." There was nothing more readable. The paper was torn in a zigzag line just beneath. Yet that was enough. It reminded her of her duty.

Down beside the bed she knelt, and prayed: "O my Father, hide me now; hide me! I am in trouble; hide me!" Over and over she prayed till her heart grew calm and she could think.

Then she sat down quietly, and put the matter before her.

This man whom she loved with her whole soul was to be married in a few days. The world of society would be at the wedding. He was pledged to another, and he was not hers. Yet he was her old friend, and was coming to see her. If he came and looked into her face with those clear eyes of his, he might read in hers that she loved him. How dreadful that would be!

Yes, she must search yet deeper. She had heard the glad ring in his voice when he met her, and said, "Elizabeth!" She had seen his eyes. He was in danger himself. She knew it; she might not hide it from herself. She must help him to be true to the woman to whom he was pledged, whom now he would have to marry.

She must go away from it all. She would run away, now at once. It seemed that she was always running away from some one. She would go back to the mountains where she had started. She was not afraid now of the man from whom she had fled. Culture and education had done their work. Religion had set her upon a rock. She could go back with the protection that her money would put about her, with the companionship of some good, elderly woman, and be safe from harm in that way; but she could not stay here and meet George Benedict in the morning, nor face Geraldine Loring on her wedding-day. It would be all the same the facing whether she were in the wedding-party or not. Her days of mourning for her grandmother would of course protect her from this public facing. It was the thought she could not bear. She must get away from it all forever.

Her lawyers should arrange the business. They would purchase the house that Grandmother Brady desired, and then give her her money to build a church. She would go back, and teach among the lonely wastes of mountain and prairie what Jesus Christ longed to be to the people made in His image. She would go back and place above the graves of her father and mother and brothers stones that should bear the words of life to all who should pass by in that desolate region. And that should be her excuse to the world for going, if she needed any excuse—she had gone to see about placing a monument over her father's grave. But the monument should be a church somewhere where it was most needed. She was resolved upon that.

That was a busy night. Marie was called upon to pack a few things for a hurried journey. The telephone rang, and the sleepy night-operator answered crossly. But Elizabeth found out all she wanted to know about the early Chicago trains, and then lay down to rest.

Early the next morning George Benedict telephoned for some flowers from the florist; and, when they arrived, he pleased himself by taking them to Elizabeth's door.

He did not expect to find her up, but it would be a pleasure to have them reach her by his own hand. They would be sent up to her room, and she would know in her first waking thought that he remembered her. He smiled as he touched the bell and stood waiting.

The old butler opened the door. He looked as if he had not fully finished his night's sleep. He listened mechanically to the message, "For Miss Bailey with Mr. Benedict's good-morning," and then his face took on a deprecatory expression.

"I'm sorry, Mr. Benedict," he said, as if in the matter he were personally to blame; "but she's just gone. Miss Elizabeth's mighty quick in her ways, and last night after she come home she decided to go to Chicago on the early train. She's just gone to the station not ten minutes ago. They was late, and had to hurry. I'm expecting the footman back every minute."

"Gone?" said George Benedict, standing blankly on the door-step and looking down the street as if that should bring her. "Gone? To Chicago, did you say?"

"Yes, sir, she's gone to Chicago. That is, she's going further, but she took the Chicago Limited. She's gone to see about a monument for Madam's son John, Miss 'Lizabuth's father. She said she must go at once, and she went."

"What time does that train leave?" asked the young man. It was a thread of hope. He was stung into a superhuman effort as he had been on the prairie when he had caught the flying vision of the girl and horse, and he had shouted, and she would not stop for him.

"Nine-fifty, sir," said the butler. He wished this excited young man would go after her. She needed some one. His heart had often stirred against fate that this pearl among young mistresses should have no intimate friend or lover now in her loneliness.

"Nine-fifty!" He looked at his watch. No chance! "Broad Street?" he asked sharply.

"Yes, sir."

Would there be a chance if he had his automobile? Possibly, but hardly unless the train was late. There would be a trifle more chance of catching the train at West Philadelphia. O for his automobile! He turned to the butler in despair.

"Telephone her!" he said. "Stop her if you possibly can on board the train, and I will try to get there. I must see her. It is important." He started down the steps, his mind in a whirl of trouble. How should he go? The trolley would be the only available way, and yet the trolley would be useless; it would take too long. Nevertheless, he sped down toward Chestnut Street blindly, and now in his despair his new habit came to him. "O my Father, help me! Help me! Save her for me!"

Up Walnut Street at a breakneck pace came a flaming red automobile, sounding its taunting menace, "Honk-honk! Honk-honk!" but George Benedict stopped not for automobiles. Straight into the jaws of death he rushed, and was saved only by the timely grasp of a policeman, who rolled him over on the ground. The machine came to a halt, and a familiar voice shouted: "Conscience alive, George, is that you? What are you trying to do? Say, but that was a close shave! Where you going in such a hurry, anyway? Hustle in, and I'll take you there."

The young man sprang into the seat, and gasped: "West Philadelphia station, Chicago Limited! Hurry! Train leaves Broad Street station at nine-fifty. Get me there if you can, Billy. I'll be your friend forever."

By this time they were speeding fast. Neither of the two had time to consider which station was the easier to make; and, as the machine was headed toward West Philadelphia, on they went, regardless of laws or vainly shouting policemen.

George Benedict sprang from the car before it had stopped, and nearly fell again. His nerves were not steady from his other fall yet. He tore into the station and out through the passageway past the beckoning hand of the ticket-man who sat in the booth at the staircase, and strode up three steps at a time. The guard shouted: "Hurry! You may get it; she's just starting!" and a friendly hand reached out, and hauled him up on the platform of the last car.

For an instant after he was safely in the car he was too dazed to think. It seemed as if he must keep on blindly rushing through that train all the way to Chicago, or she would get away from him. He sat down in an empty seat for a minute to get his senses. He was actually on the train! It had not gone without him!

Now the next question was, Was she on it herself, or had she in some way slipped from his grasp even yet? The old butler might have caught her by telephone. He doubted it. He knew her stubborn determination, and all at once he began to suspect that she was with intention running away from him, and perhaps had been doing so before! It was an astonishing thought and a grave one, yet, if it were true, what had meant that welcoming smile in her eyes that had been like dear sunshine to his heart?

But there was no time to consider such questions now. He had started on this quest, and he must continue it until he found her. Then she should be made to explain once and for all most fully. He would live through no more torturing agonies of separation without a full understanding of the matter. He got upon his shaking feet, and started to hunt for Elizabeth.

Then all at once he became aware that he was still carrying the box of flowers. Battered and out of shape it was, but he was holding it as if it held the very hope of life for him. He smiled grimly as he tottered shakily down the aisle, grasping his floral offering with determination. This was not exactly the morning call he had planned, nor the way he had expected to present his flowers; but it seemed to be the best he could do. Then, at last, in the very furthest car from the end, in the drawing-room he found her, sitting gray and sorrowful, looking at the fast-flying landscape.

"Elizabeth!" He stood in the open door and called to her; and she started as from a deep sleep, her face blazing into glad sunshine at sight of him. She put her hand to her heart, and smiled.

"I have brought you some flowers," he said grimly. "I am afraid there isn't much left of them now; but, such as they are, they are here. I hope you will accept them."

"Oh!" gasped Elizabeth, reaching out for the poor crushed roses as if they had been a little child in danger. She drew them from the battered box and to her arms with a delicious movement of caressing, as if she would make up to them for all they had come through. He watched her, half pleased, half savagely. Why should all that tenderness be wasted on mere fading flowers?

At last he spoke, interrupting her brooding over his roses.

"You are running away from me!" he charged.

"Well, and what if I am?" She looked at him with a loving defiance in her eyes.

"Don't you know I love you?" he asked, sitting down beside her and talking low and almost fiercely. "Don't you know I've been torn away from you, or you from me, twice before now, and that I cannot stand it any more? Say, don't you know it? Answer, please," The demand was kind, but peremptory.

"I was afraid so," she murmured with drooping eyes, and cheeks from which all color had fled.

"Well, why do you do it? Why did you run away? Don't you care for me? Tell me that. If you can't ever love me, you are excusable; but I must know it all now."

"Yes, I care as much as you," she faltered, "but——"

"But what?" sharply.

"But you are going to be married this week," she said in desperation, raising her miserable eyes to his.

He looked at her in astonishment.

"Am I?" said he. "Well, that's news to me; but it's the best news I've heard in a long time. When does the ceremony come off? I wish it was this morning. Make it this morning, will you? Let's stop this blessed old train and go back to the Doctor. He'll fix it so we can't ever run away from each other again. Elizabeth, look at me!"

But Elizabeth hid her eyes now. They were full of tears.

"But the lady——" she gasped out, struggling with the sobs. She was so weary, and the thought of what he had suggested was so precious.

"What lady? There is no lady but you, Elizabeth, and never has been. Haven't you known that for a long time? I have. That was all a hallucination of my foolish brain. I had to go out on the plains to get rid of it, but I left it there forever. She was nothing to me after I saw you."

"But—but people said—and it was in the paper, I saw it. You cannot desert her now; it would be dishonorable."

"Thunder!" ejaculated the distracted young man. "In the paper! What lady?"

"Why, Miss Loring! Geraldine Loring. I saw that the preparations were all made for her wedding, and I was told she was to marry you."

In sheer relief he began to laugh.

At last he stopped, as the old hurt look spread over her face.

"Excuse me, dear," he said gently, "There was a little acquaintance between Miss Loring and myself. It only amounted to a flirtation on her part, one of many. It was a great distress to my mother, and I went out West, as you know, to get away from her. I knew she would only bring me unhappiness, and she was not willing to give up some of her ways that were impossible. I am glad and thankful that God saved me from her. I believe she is going to marry a distant relative of mine by the name of Benedict, but I thank the kind Father that I am not going to marry her. There is only one woman in the whole wide world that I am willing to marry, or ever will be; and she is sitting beside me now."

The train was going rapidly now. It would not be long before the conductor would reach them. The man leaned over, and clasped the little gloved hand that lay in the girl's lap; and Elizabeth felt the great joy that had tantalized her for these three years in dreams and visions settle down about her in beautiful reality. She was his now forever. She need never run away again.

The conductor was not long in coming to them, and the matter-of-fact world had to be faced once more. The young man produced his card, and said a few words to the conductor, mentioning the name of his uncle, who, by the way, happened to be a director of the road; and then he explained the situation. It was very necessary that the young lady be recalled at once to her home because of a change in the circumstances. He had caught the train at West Philadelphia by automobile, coming as he was in his morning clothes, without baggage and with little money. Would the conductor be so kind as to put them off that they might return to the city by the shortest possible route?

The conductor glared and scolded, and said people "didn't know their own minds," and "wanted to move the earth." Then he eyed Elizabeth, and she smiled. He let a grim glimmer of what might have been a sour smile years ago peep out for an instant, and—he let them off.

They wandered delightedly about from one trolley to another until they found an automobile garage, and soon were speeding back to Philadelphia.

They waited for no ceremony, these two who had met and loved by the way in the wilderness. They went straight to Mrs. Benedict for her blessing, and then to the minister to arrange for his services; and within the week a quiet wedding-party entered the arched doors of the placid brown church with the lofty spire, and Elizabeth Bailey and George Benedict were united in the sacred bonds of matrimony.

There were present Mrs. Benedict and one or two intimate friends of the family, besides Grandmother Brady, Aunt Nan, and Lizzie.

Lizzie brought a dozen bread-and-butter-plates from the ten-cent store. They were adorned with cupids and roses and much gilt. But Lizzie was disappointed. No display, no pomp and ceremony. Just a simple white dress and white veil. Lizzie did not understand that the veil had been in the Bailey family for generations, and that the dress was an heirloom also. It was worn because Grandmother Bailey had given it to her, and told her she wanted her to wear it on her wedding-day. Sweet and beautiful she looked as she turned to walk down the aisle on her husband's arm, and she smiled at Grandmother Brady in a way that filled the grandmother's heart with pride and triumph. Elizabeth was not ashamed of the Bradys even among her fine friends. But Lizzie grumbled all the way home at the plainness of the ceremony, and the lack of bridesmaids and fuss and feathers.

The social column of the daily papers stated that young Mr. and Mrs. George Benedict were spending their honeymoon in an extended tour of the West, and Grandmother Brady so read it aloud at the breakfast table to the admiring family. Only Lizzie looked discontented:

"She just wore a dark blue tricotine one-piece dress and a little plain dark hat. She ain't got a bit of taste. Oh*Boy*! If I just had her pocket book wouldn't I show the world? But anyhow I'm glad she went in a private car. There was a *little* class to her, though if t'had been mine I'd uv preferred ridin' in the parlor coach an' havin' folks see me and my fine husband. He's some looker, George Benedict is! Everybody turns to watch 'em as they go by, and they just sail along and never seem to notice. It's all perfectly throwed away on 'em. Gosh! I'd hate to be such a nut!"

"Now, Lizzie, you know you hadn't oughtta talk like that!" reproved her grandmother, "After her giving you all that money fer your own wedding. A thousand dollars just to spend as you please on your cloes and a blow out, and house linens. Jest because she don't care for gewgaws like you do, you think she's a fool. But she's no fool. She's got a good head on her, and she'll get more in the long run out of life than you will. She's been real loving and kind to us all, and she didn't have any reason to neither. We never did much fer her. And look at how nice and common she's been with us all, not a bit high headed. I declare, Lizzie, I should think you'd be ashamed!"

"Oh, well," said Lizzie shrugging her shoulders indifferently, "She's all right in her way, only 'taint my way. And I'm thankful t'goodness that I had the nerve to speak up when she offered to give me my trousseau. She askt me would I druther hav her buy it for me, or have the money and pick it out m'self, and I spoke up right quick and says, 'Oh, cousin Bessie, I wouldn't *think* of givin' ya all that trouble. I'd take the *money* ef it's all the same t'you,' and she jest smiled and said all right, she expected I knew what I wanted better'n she did. So yes'teddy when I went down to the station to see her off she handed me a bank book. And—Oh, say, I fergot! She said there was a good-bye note inside. I ain't had time to look at it since. I went right to the movies on the dead run to get there 'fore the first show begun, and it's in my coat pocket. Wait 'till I get it. I spose it's some of her old *religion*! She's always preaching at me. It ain't that she says so much as that she's always *meanin'* it underneath, everything, that gets my goat! It's sorta like having a piece of God round with you all the time watching you. You kinda hate to be enjoyin' yerself fer fear she won't think yer doin' it accordin' to the Bible."

Lizzie hurtled into the hall and brought back her coat, fumbling in the pocket.

"Yes, here 'tis ma! Wanta see the figgers? You never had a whole thousand dollars in the bank t'woncet yerself, did ya?"

Mrs. Brady put on her spectacles and reached for the book, while Lizzie's mother got up and came behind her mother's chair to look over at the magic figures. Lizzie stooped for the little white note that had fluttered to her feet as she opened the book, but she had little interest to see what it said. She was more intent upon the new bank book.

It was Grandmother Brady that discovered it:

"Why, Lizzie! It ain't *one* thousand, it's *five* thousand, the book says! You don't 'spose she's made a mistake, do you?"

Lizzie seized the book and gazed, her jaw dropping open in amaze. "Let me have it!" demanded Lizzie's mother, reaching for the book.

"Where's yer note, Lizzie, mebbe it'll explain," said the excited Grandmother.

Lizzie recovered the note which again had fluttered to the floor in the confusion and opening it began to read:

"*Dear Lizzie*," it read

"I've made it five thousand so you will have some over for furnishing your home, and if you still think you want the little bungalow out on the Pike you will find the deed at my lawyer's, all made out in your name. It's my wedding gift to you, so you can go to work and buy your furniture at once, and not wait till Dan gets a raise. And here's wishing you a great deal of happiness,

"Your   loving   cousin,
ELIZABETH."

"There!" said Grandmother Brady sitting back with satisfaction and holding her hands composedly, "Whadd' I tell ya?"

"Mercy!" said Lizzie's mother, "Let me see that note! The idea of her *giving* all that money when she didn't have to!"

But Lizzie's face was a picture of joy. For once she lost her hard little worldly screwed-up expression and was wreathed in smiles of genuine eagerness:

"Oh *Boy*!" she exclaimed delightedly, dancing around the room, "Now we can have a victrola, an' a player-piano, and Dan'll get a Ford, one o' those limousine-kind! Won't I be some swell? What'll the girls at the store think now?"

"H'm! You'd much better get a washing machine and a 'lectric iron!" grumbled Grandmother Brady practically.

"Well, all I got to say about it is, she was an awful fool to trust *you* with so much money," said Lizzie's mother discontentedly, albeit with a pleased pride as she watched her giddy daughter fling on hat and coat to go down and tell Dan.

"I sh'll work in the store fer the rest of the week, jest to 'commodate 'em," she announced putting her head back in the door as she went out, "but not a day longer. I got a lot t'do. Say, won't I be some lady in the five-an'-ten the rest o' the week? Oh *Boy! I'll tell the world!*"

Meantime in their own private car the bride and groom were whirled on their way to the west, but they saw little of the scenery, being engaged in the all-absorbing story of each other's lives since they had parted.

And one bright morning, they stepped down from the train at Malta and gazed about them.

The sun was shining clear and wonderful, and the little brown station stood drearily against the brightness of the day like a picture that has long hung on the wall of one's memory and is suddenly brought out and the dust wiped away.

They purchased a couple of horses, and with camp accoutrements following began their real wedding trip, over the road they had come together when they first met. Elizabeth had to show her husband where she had hidden while the men went by, and he drew her close in his arms and thanked God that she had escaped so miraculously.

It seemed so wonderful to be in the same places again, for nothing out here in the wilderness seemed much to have changed, and yet they two were so changed that the people they met did not seem to recognize them as ever having been that way before.

They dined sumptuously in the same coulee, and recalled little things they had said and done, and Elizabeth now worldly wise, laughed at her own former ignorance as her husband reminded her of some questions she had asked him on that memorable journey. And ever through the beautiful journey he was telling her how wonderful she seemed to him, both then and now.

Not however, till they reached the old ranchhouse, where the woman had tried to persuade her to stay, did they stop for long.

Elizabeth had a tender feeling in her heart for that motherly woman who had sought to protect her, and felt a longing to let her know how safely she had been kept through the long journey and how good the Lord had been to her through the years. Also they both desired to reward these kind people for their hospitality in the time of need. So, in the early evening they rode up just as they did before to the little old log house. But no friendly door flung open wide as they came near, and at first they thought the cabin deserted, till a candle flare suddenly shone forth in the bedroom, and then Benedict dismounted and knocked.

After some waiting the old man came to the door holding a candle high above his head. His face was haggard and worn, and the whole place looked dishevelled. His eyes had a weary look as he peered into the night and it was evident that he had no thought of ever having seen them before:

"I can't do much fer ya, strangers," he said, his voice sounding tired and discouraged. "If it's a woman ye have with ye, ye better ride on to the next ranch. My woman is sick. Very sick. There's nobody here with her but me, and I have all I can tend to. The house ain't kept very tidy. It's six weeks since she took to bed."

Elizabeth had sprung lightly to the ground and was now at the threshold:

"Oh, is she sick? I'm so sorry? Couldn't I do something for her? She was good to me once several years ago!"

The old man peered at her blinkingly, noting her slender beauty, the exquisite eager face, the dress that showed her of another world—and shook his head:

"I guess you made a mistake, lady. I don't remember ever seeing you before—"

"But I remember you," she said eagerly stepping into the room, "Won't you please let me go to her?"

"Why, shore, lady, go right in ef you want to. She's layin' there in the bed. She ain't likely to get out of it again' I'm feared. The doctor says nothin' but a 'noperation will ever get her up, and we can't pay fer 'noperations. It's a long ways to the hospital in Chicago where he wants her sent, and M'ria and I, we ain't allowin' to part. It can't be many years—"

But Elizabeth was not waiting to hear. She had slipped into the old bedroom that she remembered now so well and was kneeling beside the bed talking to the white faced woman on the thin pillow:

"Don't you remember me," she asked, "I'm the girl you tried to get to stay with you once. The girl that came here with a man she had met in the wilderness. You told me things that I didn't know, and you were kind and wanted me to stay here with you? Don't you remember me? I'm Elizabeth!"

The woman reached out a bony hand and touched the fair young face that she could see but dimly in the flare of the candle that the old man now brought into the room:

"Why, yes, I remember," the woman said, her voice sounded alive yet in spite of her illness, "Yes, I remember you. You were a dear little girl, and I was so worried about you. I would have kept you for my own—but you wouldn't stay. And he was a nice looking young man, but I was afraid for you—You can't always tell about them—You *mostly* can't—!"

"But he was all right Mother!" Elizabeth's voice rang joyously through the cabin, "He took care of me and got me safely started toward my people, and now he's my husband. I want you to see him. George come here!"

The old woman half raised herself from the pillow and looked toward the young man in the doorway:

"You don't say! He's your *husband*! Well, now isn't that grand! Well, I certainly am glad! I was that worried—!"

They sat around the bed talking, Elizabeth telling briefly of her own experiences and her wedding trip which they were taking back over the old trail, and the old man and woman speaking of their trouble, the woman's breakdown and how the doctor at Malta said there was a chance she could get well if she went to a great doctor in Chicago, but how they had no money unless they sold the ranch and that nobody wanted to buy it.

"Oh, but we have money," laughed Elizabeth joyously, "and it is our turn now to help you. You helped us when we were in trouble. How soon can you start? I'm going to play you are my own father and mother. We can send them both, can't we George?"

It was a long time before they settled themselves to sleep that night because there was so much planning to be done, and then Elizabeth and her husband had to get out their stores and cook a good supper for the two old people who had been living mostly on corn meal mush, for several weeks.

And after the others were all asleep the old woman lay praying and thanking God for the two angels who had dropped down to help them in their distress.

The next morning George Benedict with one of the men who looked after their camping outfit went to Malta and got in touch with the Chicago doctor and hospital, and before he came back to the ranch that night everything was arranged for the immediate start of the two old people He had even planned for an automobile and the Malta doctor to be in attendance in a couple of days to get the invalid to the station.

Meantime Elizabeth had been going over the old woman's wardrobe which was scanty and coarse, and selecting garments from her own baggage that would do for the journey.

The old woman looked glorified as she touched the delicate white garments with their embroidery and ribbons:

"Oh, dear child! Why, I couldn't wear a thing like that on my old worn-out body. Those look like angels' clothes." She put a work-worn finger on the delicate tracery of embroidery and smoothed a pink satin ribbon bow.

But Elizabeth overruled her. It was nothing but a plain little garment she had bought for the trip. If the friend thought it was pretty she was glad, but nothing was too pretty for the woman who had taken her in in her distress and tried to help her and keep her safe.

The invalid was thin with her illness, and it was found that she could easily wear the girl's simple dress of dark blue with a white collar, and little dark hat, and Elizabeth donned a khaki skirt and brown cap and sweater herself and gladly arrayed her old friend in her own bridal travelling gown for her journey. She had not brought a lot of things for her journey because she did not want to be bothered, but she could easily get more when she got to a large city, and what was money for but to cloth the naked and feed the hungry? She rejoiced in her ability to help this woman of the wilderness.

On the third day, garbed in Elizabeth's clothes, her husband fitted out for the east in some of George Benedict's extra things, they started. They carried a bag containing some necessary changes, and some wonderful toilet accessories with silver monograms, enough to puzzle the most snobbish nurse, also there was a luscious silk kimona of Elizabeth's in the bag. The two old people were settled in the Benedict private car, and in due time hitched on to the Chicago express and hurried on their way. Before the younger pair went back to their pilgrimage they sent a series of telegrams arranging for every detail of the journey for the old couple, so that they would be met with cars and nurses and looked after most carefully.

And the thanksgiving and praise of the old people seemed to follow them like music as they rode happily on their way.

They paused at the little old school house where they had attended the Christian Endeavor meeting, and Elizabeth looked half fearfully up the road where her evil pursuers had ridden by, and rode closer to her husband's side. So they passed on the way as nearly as Elizabeth could remember every step back as she had come, telling her husband all the details of the journey.

That night they camped in the little shelter where Benedict had come upon the girl that first time they met, and under the clear stars that seemed so near they knelt together and thanked God for His leading.

They went to the lonely cabin on the mountain, shut up and going to ruin now, and Benedict gazing at the surroundings and then looking at the delicate face of his lovely wife was reminded of a white flower he had once seen growing out of the blackness down in a coal mine, pure and clean without a smirch of soil.

They visited the seven graves in the wilderness, and standing reverently beside the sand-blown mounds she told him much of her early life that she had not told him before, and introduced him to her family, telling a bit about each that would make him see the loveable side of them. And then they planned for seven simple white stones to be set up, bearing words from the book they both loved. Over the care worn mother was to be written "Come unto me all ye that labor and are heavy laden and I will give you rest."

It was on that trip that they planned what came to pass in due time. The little cabin was made over into a simple, pretty home, with vines planted about the garden, and a garage with a sturdy little car; and not far away a church nestled into the side of the hill, built out of the stones that were native, with many sunny windows and a belfry in which bells rang out to the whole region round.

At first it had seemed impractical to put a church out there away from the town, but Elizabeth said that it was centrally located, and high up where it could be seen from the settlements in the valleys, and was moreover on a main trail that was much travelled. She longed to have some such spot in the wilderness that could be a refuge for any who longed for better things.

When they went back they sent out two consecrated missionaries to occupy the new house and use the sturdy little car. They were to ring the bells, preach the gospel and play the organ and piano in the little church.

Over the pulpit there was a beautiful window bearing a picture of Christ, the Good Shepherd, and in clear letters above were the words: "And thou shalt remember all the way which the Lord thy God led thee these forty years in the wilderness, to humble thee, and to prove thee, to know what was in thine heart, whether thou wouldst keep his commandments, or no."

And underneath the picture were the words:

"'In the time of trouble He shall hide me in His pavilion; in the secret of his tabernacle shall he hide me.' In memory of His hidings,

"George and Elizabeth Benedict."

But in the beautiful home in Philadelphia, in an inner intimate room these words are exquisitely graven on the wall, "Let not your heart be troubled."

A Voice in the Wilderness

CHAPTER I

With a lurch the train came to a dead stop and Margaret Earle, hastily gathering up her belongings, hurried down the aisle and got out into the night.

It occurred to her, as she swung her heavy suit-case down the rather long step to the ground, and then carefully swung herself after it, that it was strange that neither conductor, brakeman, nor porter had come to help her off the train, when all three had taken the trouble to tell her that hers was the next station; but she could hear voices up ahead. Perhaps something was the matter with the engine that detained them and they had forgotten her for the moment.

The ground was rough where she stood, and there seemed no sign of a platform. Did they not have platforms in this wild Western land, or was the train so long that her car had stopped before reaching it?

She strained her eyes into the darkness, and tried to make out things from the two or three specks of light that danced about like fireflies in the distance. She could dimly see moving figures away up near the engine, and each one evidently carried a lantern. The train was tremendously long. A sudden feeling of isolation took possession of her. Perhaps she ought not to have got out until some one came to help her. Perhaps the train had not pulled into the station yet and she ought to get back on it and wait. Yet if the train started before she found the conductor she might be carried on somewhere and be justly blame her for a fool.

There did not seem to be any building on that side of the track. It was probably on the other, but she was standing too near the cars to see over. She tried to move back to look, but the ground sloped and she slipped and fell in the cinders, bruising her knee and cutting her wrist.

In sudden panic she arose. She would get back into the train, no matter what the consequences. They had no right to put her out here, away off from the station, at night, in a strange country. If the train started before she could find the conductor she would tell him that he must back it up again and let her off. He certainly could not expect her to get out like this.

She lifted the heavy suit-case up the high step that was even farther from the ground than it had been when she came down, because her fall had loosened some of the earth and caused it to slide away from the track. Then, reaching to the rail of the step, she tried to pull herself up, but as she did so the engine gave a long snort and the whole train, as if it were in league against her, lurched forward crazily, shaking off her hold. She slipped to her knees again, the suit-case, toppled from the lower step, descending upon her, and together they slid and rolled down the short bank, while the train, like an irresponsible nurse who had slapped her charge and left it to its fate, ran giddily off into the night.

The horror of being deserted helped the girl to rise in spite of bruises and shock. She lifted imploring hands to the unresponsive cars as they hurried by her—one, two, three, with bright windows, each showing a passenger, comfortable and safe inside, unconscious of her need.

A moment of useless screaming, running, trying to attract some one's attention, a sickening sense of terror and failure, and the last car slatted itself past with a mocking clatter, as if it enjoyed her discomfort.

Margaret stood dazed, reaching out helpless hands, then dropped them at her sides and gazed after the fast-retreating train, the light on its last car swinging tauntingly, blinking now and then with a leer in its eye, rapidly vanishing from her sight into the depth of the night.

She gasped and looked about her for the station that but a short moment before had been so real to her mind; and, lo! on this side and on that there was none!

The night was wide like a great floor shut in by a low, vast dome of curving blue set with the largest, most wonderful stars she had ever seen. Heavy shadows of purple-green, smoke-like, hovered over earth darker and more intense than the unfathomable blue of the night sky. It seemed like the secret nesting-place of mysteries wherein no human foot might dare intrude. It was incredible that such could be but common sage-brush, sand, and greasewood wrapped about with the beauty of the lonely night.

No building broke the inky outlines of the plain, nor friendly light streamed out to cheer her heart. Not even a tree was in sight, except on the far horizon, where a heavy line of deeper darkness might mean a forest. Nothing, absolutely nothing, in the blue, deep, starry dome above and the bluer darkness of the earth below save one sharp shaft ahead like a black mast throwing out a dark arm across the track.

As soon as she sighted it she picked up her baggage and made her painful way toward it, for her knees and wrist were bruised and her baggage was heavy.

A soft drip, drip greeted her as she drew nearer; something plashing down among the cinders by the track. Then she saw the tall column with its arm outstretched, and looming darker among the sage-brush the outlines of a water-tank. It was so she recognized the engine's drinking-tank, and knew that she had mistaken a pause to water the engine for a regular stop at a station.

Her soul sank within her as she came up to the dripping water and laid her hand upon the dark upright, as if in some way it could help her. She dropped her baggage and stood, trembling, gazing around upon the beautiful, lonely scene in horror; and then, like a mirage against the distance, there melted on her frightened eyes a vision of her father and mother sitting around the library lamp at home, as they sat every evening. They were probably reading and talking at this very minute, and trying not to miss her on this her first venture away from the home into the great world to teach. What would they say if they could see their beloved daughter, whom they had sheltered all these years and let go forth so reluctantly now, in all her confidence of youth, bound by almost absurd promises to be careful and not run any risks.

Yet here she was, standing alone beside a water-tank in the midst of an Arizona plain, no knowing how many miles from anywhere, at somewhere between nine and ten o'clock at night! It seemed incredible that it had really happened! Perhaps she was dreaming! A few moments before in the bright car, surrounded by drowsy fellow-travelers, almost at her journey's end, as she supposed; and now, having merely done as she thought right, she was stranded here!

She rubbed her eyes and looked again up the track, half expecting to see the train come back for her. Surely, surely the conductor, or the porter who had been so kind, would discover that she was gone, and do something about it. They couldn't leave her here alone on the prairie! It would be too dreadful!

That vision of her father and mother off against the purple-green distance, how it shook her! The lamp looked bright and cheerful, and she could see her father's head with its heavy white hair. He turned to look at her mother to tell her of something he read in the paper. They were sitting there, feeling contented and almost happy about her, and she, their little girl—all her dignity as school-teacher dropped from her like a garment now—she was standing in this empty space alone, with only an engine's water-tank to keep her from dying, and only the barren, desolate track to connect her with the world of men and women. She dropped her head upon her breast and the tears came, sobbing, choking, raining down. Then off in the distance she heard a low, rising howl of some snarling, angry beast, and she lifted her head and stood in trembling terror, clinging to the tank.

That sound was coyotes or wolves howling. She had read about them, but had not expected to experience them in such a situation. How confidently had she accepted the position which offered her the opening she had sought for the splendid career that she hoped was to follow! How fearless had she been! Coyotes, nor Indians, nor wild cowboy students—nothing had daunted her courage. Besides, she told her mother it was very different going to a town from what it would be if she were a missionary going to the wilds. It was an important school she was to teach, where her Latin and German and mathematical achievements had won her the place above several other applicants, and where her well-known tact was expected to work wonders. But what were Latin and German and mathematics now? Could they show her how to climb a water-tank? Would tact avail with a hungry wolf?

The howl in the distance seemed to come nearer. She cast frightened eyes to the unresponsive water-tanklooming high and dark above her. She must get up there somehow. It was not safe to stand here a minute. Besides, from that height she might be able to see farther, and perhaps there would be a light somewhere and she might cry for help.

Investigation showed a set of rude spikes by which the trainmen were wont to climb up, and Margaret prepared to ascend them. She set her suit-case dubiously down at the foot. Would it be safe to leave it there? She had read how coyotes carried off a hatchet from a camping-party, just to get the leather thong which was bound about the handle. She could not afford to lose her things. Yet how could she climb and carry that heavy burden with her? A sudden thought came.

Her simple traveling-gown was finished with a silken girdle, soft and long, wound twice about her waist and falling in tasseled ends. Swiftly she untied it and knotted one end firmly to the handle of her suit-case, tying the other end securely to her wrist. Then slowly, cautiously, with many a look upward, she began to climb.

It seemed miles, though in reality it was but a short distance. The howling beasts in the distance sounded nearer now and continually, making her heart beat wildly. She was stiff and bruised from her falls, and weak with fright. The spikes were far apart, and each step of progress was painful and difficult. It was good at last to rise high enough to see over the water-tank and feel a certain confidence in her defense.

But she had risen already beyond the short length of her silken tether, and the suit-case was dragging painfully on her arm. She was obliged to steady herself where she stood and pull it up before she could go on. Then she managed to get it swung up to the top of the tank in a comparatively safe place. One more long spike step and she was beside it.

The tank was partly roofed over, so that she had room enough to sit on the edge without danger of falling in and drowning. For a few minutes she could only sit still and be thankful and try to get her breath back again after the climb; but presently the beauty of the night began to cast its spell over her. That wonderful blue of the sky! It hadn't ever before impressed her that skies were blue at night. She would have said they were black or gray. As a matter of fact, she didn't remember to have ever seen so much sky at once before, nor to have noticed skies in general until now.

This sky was so deeply, wonderfully blue, the stars so real, alive and sparkling, that all other stars she had ever seen paled before them into mere imitations. The spot looked like one of Taylor's pictures of the Holy Land. She half expected to see a shepherd with his crook and sheep approaching her out of the dim shadows, or a turbaned, white-robed David with his lifted hands of prayer standing off among the depths of purple darkness. It would not have been out of keeping if a walled city with housetops should be hidden behind the clumps of sage-brush farther on. 'Twas such a night and such a scene as this, perhaps, when the wise men started to follow the star!

But one cannot sit on the edge of a water-tank in the desert night alone and muse long on art and history. It was cold up there, and the howling seemed nearer than before. There was no sign of a light or a house anywhere, and not even a freight-train sent its welcome clatter down the track. All was still and wide and lonely, save that terrifying sound of the beasts; such stillness as she had not ever thought could be—a fearful silence as a setting for the awful voices of the wilds.

The bruises and scratches she had acquired set up a fine stinging, and the cold seemed to sweep down and take possession of her on her high, narrow seat. She was growing stiff and cramped, yet dared not move much. Would there be no train, nor any help? Would she have to sit there all night? It looked so very near to the ground now. Could wild beasts climb, she wondered?

Then in the interval of silence that came between the calling of those wild creatures there stole a sound. She could not tell at first what it was. A slow, regular, plodding sound, and quite far away. She looked to find it, and thought she saw a shape move out of the sage-brush on the other side of the track, but she could not be sure. It might be but a figment of her brain, a foolish fancy from looking so long at the huddled bushes on the dark plain. Yet something prompted her to cry out, and when she heard her own voice she cried again and louder, wondering why she had not cried before.

"Help! Help!" she called; and again: "Help! Help!"

The dark shape paused and turned toward her. She was sure now. What if it were a beast instead of a human! Terrible fear took possession of her; then, to her infinite relief, a nasal voice sounded out:

"Who's thar?"

But when she opened her lips to answer, nothing but a sob would come to them for a minute, and then she could only cry, pitifully:

"Help! Help!"

"Whar be you?" twanged the voice; and now she could see a horse and rider like a shadow moving toward her down the track.

CHAPTER II

The horse came to a standstill a little way from the track, and his rider let forth a stream of strange profanity. The girl shuddered and began to think a wild beast might be preferable to some men. However, these remarks seemed to be a mere formality. He paused and addressed her:

"Heow'd yeh git up thar? D'j'yeh drap er climb?"

He was a little, wiry man with a bristly, protruding chin. She could see that, even in the starlight. There was something about the point of that stubby chin that she shrank from inexpressibly. He was not a pleasant man to look upon, and even his voice was unprepossessing. She began to think that even the night with its loneliness and unknown perils was preferable to this man's company.

"I got off the train by mistake, thinking it was my station, and before I discovered it the train had gone and left me," Margaret explained, with dignity.

"Yeh didn't 'xpect it t' sit reound on th' plain while you was gallivantin' up water-tanks, did yeh?"

Cold horror froze Margaret's veins. She was dumb for a second. "I am on my way to Ashland station. Can you tell me how far it is from here and how I can get there?" Her tone was like icicles.

"It's a little matter o' twenty miles, more 'r less," said the man protruding his offensive chin. "The walkin's good. I don't know no other way from this p'int at this time o' night. Yeh might set still till th' mornin' freight goes by an' drap atop o' one of the kyars."

"Sir!" said Margaret, remembering her dignity as a teacher.

The man wheeled his horse clear around and looked up at her impudently. She could smell bad whisky on his breath.

"Say, you must be some young highbrow, ain't yeh? Is thet all yeh want o' me? 'Cause ef 'tis I got t' git on t' camp. It's a good five mile yet, an' I 'ain't hed no grub sence noon."

The tears suddenly rushed to the girl's eyes as the horror of being alone in the night again took possession of her. This dreadful man frightened her, but the thought of the loneliness filled her with dismay.

"Oh!" she cried, forgetting her insulted dignity, "you're not going to leave me up here alone, are you? Isn't there some place near here where I could stay overnight?"

"Thur ain't no palace hotel round these diggin's, ef that's what you mean," the man leered at her. "You c'n come along t' camp 'ith me ef you ain't too stuck up."

"To camp!" faltered Margaret in dismay, wondering what her mother would say. "Are there any ladies there?"

A loud guffaw greeted her question. "Wal, my woman's thar, sech es she is; but she ain't no highflier like you. We mostly don't hev ladies to camp, But I got t' git on. Ef you want to go too, you better light down pretty speedy, fer I can't wait."

In fear and trembling Margaret descended her rude ladder step by step, primitive man seated calmly on his horse, making no attempt whatever to assist her.

"This ain't no baggage-car," he grumbled, as he saw the suit-case in her hand. "Well, h'ist yerself up thar; I reckon we c'n pull through somehow. Gimme the luggage."

Margaret stood appalled beside the bony horse and his uncouth rider. Did he actually expect her to ride with him? "Couldn't I walk?" she faltered, hoping he would offer to do so.

"'T's up t' you," the man replied, indifferently. "Try 't an' see!"

He spoke to the horse, and it started forward eagerly, while the girl in horror struggled on behind. Over rough, uneven ground, between greasewood, sage-brush, and cactus, back into the trail. The man, oblivious of her presence, rode contentedly on, a silent shadow on a dark horse wending a silent way between the purple-green clumps of other shadows, until, bewildered, the girl almost lost sight of them. Her breath came short, her ankle turned, and she fell with both hands in a stinging bed of cactus. She cried out then and begged him to stop.

"L'arned yer lesson, hev yeh, sweety?" he jeered at her, foolishly. "Well, get in yer box, then."

He let her struggle up to a seat behind himself with very little assistance, but when she was seated and started on her way she began to wish she had stayed behind and taken any perils of the way rather than trust herself in proximity to this creature.

From time to time he took a bottle from his pocket and swallowed a portion of its contents, becoming fluent in his language as they proceeded on their way. Margaret remained silent, growing more and more frightened every time the bottle came out. At last he offered it to her. She declined it with cold politeness, which seemed to irritate the little man, for he turned suddenly fierce.

"Oh, yer too fine to take a drap fer good comp'ny, are yeh? Wal, I'll show yeh a thing er two, my pretty lady. You'll give me a kiss with yer two cherry lips before we go another step. D'yeh hear, my sweetie?" And he turned with a silly leer to enforce his command; but with a cry of horror Margaret slid to the ground and ran back down the trail as hard as she could go, till she stumbled and fell in the shelter of a great sage-bush, and lay sobbing on the sand.

The man turned bleared eyes toward her and watched until she disappeared. Then sticking his chin out wickedly, he slung her suit-case after her and called:

"All right, my pretty lady; go yer own gait an' l'arn yer own lesson." He started on again, singing a drunken song.

Under the blue, starry dome alone sat Margaret again, this time with no friendly water-tank for her defense, and took counsel with herself. The howling coyotes seemed to be silenced for the time; at least they had become a minor quantity in her equation of troubles. She felt now that man was her greatest menace, and to get away safely from him back to that friendly water-tank and the dear old railroad track she would have pledged her next year's salary. She stole softly to the place where she had heard the suit-case fall, and, picking it up, started on the weary road back to the tank. Could she ever find the way? The trail seemed so intangible a thing, her sense of direction so confused. Yet there was nothing else to do. She shuddered whenever she thought of the man who had been her companion on horseback.

When the man reached camp he set his horse loose and stumbled into the door of the log bunk-house, calling loudly for something to eat.

The men were sitting around the room on the rough benches and bunks, smoking their pipes or stolidly staring into the dying fire. Two smoky kerosene-lanterns that hung from spikes driven high in the logs cast a weird light over the company, eight men in all, rough and hardened with exposure to stormy life and weather. They were men with unkempt beards and uncombed hair, their coarse cotton shirts open at the neck, their brawny arms bare above the elbow, with crimes and sorrows and hard living written large across their faces.

There was one, a boy in looks, with smooth face and white skin healthily flushed in places like a baby's. His face, too, was hard and set in sternness like a mask, as if life had used him badly; but behind it was a fineness of feature and spirit that could not be utterly hidden. They called him the Kid, and thought it was his youth that made him different from them all, for he was only twenty-four, and not one of the rest was under forty. They were doing their best to help him get over that innate fineness that was his natural inheritance, but although he stopped at nothing, and played his part always with the ease of one old in the ways of the world, yet he kept a quiet reserve about him, a kind of charm beyond which they had not been able to go.

He was playing cards with three others at the table when the man came in, and did not look up at the entrance.

The woman, white and hopeless, appeared at the door of the shed-room when the man came, and obediently set about getting his supper; but her lifeless face never changed expression.

"Brung a gal 'long of me part way," boasted the man, as he flung himself into a seat by the table. "Thought you fellers might like t' see 'er, but she got too high an' mighty fer me, wouldn't take a pull at th' bottle 'ith me, 'n' shrieked like a catamount when I kissed 'er. Found 'er hangin' on th' water-tank. Got off 't th' wrong place. One o' yer highbrows out o' th' parlor car! Good lesson fer 'er!"

The Boy looked up from his cards sternly, his keen eyes boring through the man. "Where is she now?" he asked, quietly; and all the men in the room looked up uneasily. There was that tone and accent again that made the Boy alien from them. What was it?

The man felt it and snarled his answer angrily. "Dropped 'er on th' trail, an' threw her fine-lady b'longin's after 'er. 'Ain't got no use fer thet kind. Wonder what they was created fer? Ain't no good to nobody, not even 'emselves." And he laughed a harsh cackle that was not pleasant to hear.

The Boy threw down his cards and went out, shutting the door. In a few minutes the men heard two horses pass the end of the bunk-house toward the trail, but no one looked up nor spoke. You could not have told by the flicker of an eyelash that they knew where the Boy had gone.

She was sitting in the deep shadow of a sage-bush that lay on the edge of the trail like a great blot, her suit-case beside her, her breath coming short with exertion and excitement, when she heard a cheery whistle in the distance. Just an old love-song dating back some years and discarded now as hackneyed even by the street pianos at home; but oh, how good it sounded!

From the desert I come to thee!

The ground was cold, and struck a chill through her garments as she sat there alone in the night. On came the clear, musical whistle, and she peered out of the shadow with eager eyes and frightened heart. Dared she risk it again? Should she call, or should she hold her breath and keep still, hoping he would pass her by unnoticed? Before she could decide two horses stopped almost in front of her and a rider swung himself down. He stood before her as if it were day and he could see her quite plainly.

"You needn't be afraid," he explained, calmly. "I thought I had better look you up after the old man got home and gave his report. He was pretty well tanked up and not exactly a fit escort for ladies. What's the trouble?"

Like an angel of deliverance he looked to her as he stood in the starlight, outlined in silhouette against the wide, wonderful sky: broad shoulders, well-set head, close-cropped curls, handsome contour even in the darkness. There was about him an air of quiet strength which gave her confidence.

"Oh, thank you!" she gasped, with a quick little relieved sob in her voice. "I am so glad you have come. I was— just a little—frightened, I think." She attempted to rise, but her foot caught in her skirt and she sank wearily back to the sand again.

The Boy stooped over and lifted her to her feet. "You certainly are some plucky girl!" he commented, looking down at her slender height as she stood beside him. "A 'little frightened,' were you? Well, I should say you had a right to be."

"Well, not exactly frightened, you know," said Margaret, taking a deep breath and trying to steady her voice. "I think perhaps I was more mortified than frightened, to think I made such a blunder as to get off the train before I reached my station. You see, I'd made up my mind not to be frightened, but when I heard that awful howl of some beast—And then that terrible man!" She shuddered and put her hands suddenly over her eyes as if to shut out all memory of it.

"More than one kind of beasts!" commented the Boy, briefly. "Well, you needn't worry about him; he's having his supper and he'll be sound asleep by the time we get back."

"Oh, have we got to go where he is?" gasped Margaret. "Isn't there some other place? Is Ashland very far away? That is where I am going."

"No other place where you could go to-night. Ashland's a good twenty-five miles from here. But you'll be all right. Mom Wallis 'll look out for you. She isn't much of a looker, but she has a kind heart. She pulled me through once when I was just about flickering out. Come on. You'll be pretty tired. We better be getting back. Mom Wallis 'll make you comfortable, and then you can get off good and early in the morning."

Without an apology, and as if it were the common courtesy of the desert, he stooped and lifted her easily to the saddle of the second horse, placed the bridle in her hands, then swung the suit-case up on his own horse and sprang into the saddle.

CHAPTER III

He turned the horses about and took charge of her just as if he were accustomed to managing stray ladies in the wilderness every day of his life and understood the situation perfectly; and Margaret settled wearily into her saddle and looked about her with content.

Suddenly, again, the wide wonder of the night possessed her. Involuntarily she breathed a soft little exclamation of awe and delight. Her companion turned to her questioningly:

"Does it always seem so big here—so—limitless?" she asked in explanation. "It is so far to everywhere it takes one's breath away, and yet the stars hang close, like a protection. It gives one the feeling of being alone in the great universe with God. Does it always seem so out here?"

He looked at her curiously, her pure profile turned up to the wide dome of luminous blue above. His voice was strangely low and wondering as he answered, after a moment's silence:

"No, it is not always so," he said. "I have seen it when it was more like being alone in the great universe with the devil."

There was a tremendous earnestness in his tone that the girl felt meant more than was on the surface. She turned to look at the fine young face beside her. In the starlight she could not make out the bitter hardness of lines that were beginning to be carved about his sensitive mouth. But there was so much sadness in his voice that her heart went out to him in pity.

"Oh," she said, gently, "it would be awful that way. Yes, I can understand. I felt so, a little, while that terrible man was with me." And she shuddered again at the remembrance.

Again he gave her that curious look. "There are worse things than Pop Wallis out here," he said, gravely. "But I'll grant you there's some class to the skies. It's a case of 'Where every prospect pleases and only man is vile.'" And with the words his tone grew almost flippant. It hurt her sensitive nature, and without knowing it she half drew away a little farther from him and murmured, sadly:

"Oh!" as if he had classed himself with the "man" he had been describing. Instantly he felt her withdrawal and grew grave again, as if he would atone.

"Wait till you see this sky at the dawn," he said. "It will burn red fire off there in the east like a hearth in a palace, and all this dome will glow like a great pink jewel set in gold. If you want a classy sky, there you have it! Nothing like it in the East!"

There was a strange mingling of culture and roughness in his speech. The girl could not make him out; yet there had been a palpitating earnestness in his description that showed he had felt the dawn in his very soul.

"You are—a—poet, perhaps?" she asked, half shyly. "Or an artist?" she hazarded.

He laughed roughly and seemed embarrassed. "No, I'm just a—bum! A sort of roughneck out of a job."

She was silent, watching him against the starlight, a kind of embarrassment upon her after his last remark. "You—have been here long?" she asked, at last.

"Three years." He said it almost curtly and turned his head away, as if there were something in his face he would hide.

She knew there was something unhappy in his life. Unconsciously her tone took on a sympathetic sound. "And do you get homesick and want to go back, ever?" she asked.

His tone was fairly savage now. "No!"

The silence which followed became almost oppressive before the Boy finally turned and in his kindly tone began to question her about the happenings which had stranded her in the desert alone at night.

So she came to tell him briefly and frankly about herself, as he questioned—how she came to be in Arizona all alone.

"My father is a minister in a small town in New York State. When I finished college I had to do something, and I had an offer of this Ashland school through a friend of ours who had a brother out here. Father and mother would rather have kept me nearer home, of course, but everybody says the best opportunities are in the West, and this was a good opening, so they finally consented. They would send post-haste for me to come back if they knew what a mess I have made of things right at the start—getting out of the train in the desert."

"But you're not discouraged?" said her companion, half wonderingly. "Some nerve you have with you. I guess you'll manage to hit it off in Ashland. It's the limit as far as discipline is concerned, I understand, but I guess you'll put one over on them. I'll bank on you after to-night, sure thing!"

She turned a laughing face toward him. "Thank you!" she said. "But I don't see how you know all that. I'm sure I didn't do anything particularly nervy. There wasn't anything else to do but what I did, if I'd tried."

"Most girls would have fainted and screamed, and fainted again when they were rescued," stated the Boy, out of a vast experience.

"I never fainted in my life," said Margaret Earle, with disdain. "I don't think I should care to faint out in the vast universe like this. It would be rather inopportune, I should think."

Then, because she suddenly realized that she was growing very chummy with this stranger in the dark, she asked the first question that came into her head.

"What was your college?"

That he had not been to college never entered her head. There was something in his speech and manner that made it a foregone conclusion.

It was as if she had struck him forcibly in his face, so sudden and sharp a silence ensued for a second. Then he answered, gruffly, "Yale," and plunged into an elaborate account of Arizona in its early ages, including a detailed description of the cliff-dwellers and their homes, which were still to be seen high in the rocks of the cañons not many miles to the west of where they were riding.

Margaret was keen to hear it all, and asked many questions, declaring her intention of visiting those cliff-caves at her earliest opportunity. It was so wonderful to her to be actually out here where were all sorts of queer things about which she had read and wondered. It did not occur to her, until the next day, to realize that her companion had of intention led her off the topic of himself and kept her from asking any more personal questions.

He told her of the petrified forest just over some low hills off to the left; acres and acres of agatized chips and trunks of great trees all turned to eternal stone, called by the Indians "Yeitso's bones," after the great giant of that name whom an ancient Indian hero killed. He described the coloring of the brilliant days in Arizona, where you stand on the edge of some flat-topped mesa and look off through the clear air to mountains that seem quite near by, but are in reality more than two hundred miles away. He pictured the strange colors and lights of the place; ledges of rock, yellow, white and green, drab and maroon, and tumbled piles of red boulders, shadowy buttes in the distance, serrated cliffs against the horizon, not blue, but rosy pink in the heated haze of the air, and perhaps a great, lonely eagle poised above the silent, brilliant waste.

He told it not in book language, with turn of phrase and smoothly flowing sentences, but in simple, frank words, as a boy might describe a picture to one he knew would appreciate it—for her sake, and not because he loved to put it into words; but in a new, stumbling way letting out the beauty that had somehow crept into his heart in spite of all the rough attempts to keep all gentle things out of his nature.

The girl, as she listened, marveled more and more what manner of youth this might be who had come to her out of the desert night.

She forgot her weariness as she listened, in the thrill of wonder over the new mysterious country to which she had come. She forgot that she was riding through the great darkness with an utter stranger, to a place she knew not, and to experiences most dubious. Her fears had fled and she was actually enjoying herself, and responding to the wonderful story of the place with soft-murmured exclamations of delight and wonder.

From time to time in the distance there sounded forth those awful blood-curdling howls of wild beasts that she had heard when she sat alone by the water-tank, and each time she heard a shudder passed through her and instinctively she swerved a trifle toward her companion, then straightened up again and tried to seem not to notice. The Boy saw and watched her brave attempts at self-control with deep appreciation. But suddenly, as they rode and talked, a dark form appeared across their way a little ahead, lithe and stealthy and furry, and two awful eyes like green lamps glared for an instant, then disappeared silently among the mesquite bushes.

She did not cry out nor start. Her very veins seemed frozen with horror, and she could not have spoken if she tried. It was all over in a second and the creature gone, so that she almost doubted her senses and wondered if she had seen aright. Then one hand went swiftly to her throat and she shrank toward her companion.

"There is nothing to fear," he said, reassuringly, and laid a strong hand comfortingly across the neck of her horse. "The pussy-cat was as unwilling for our company as we for hers. Besides, look here!"—and he raised his hand and shot into the air. "She'll not come near us now."

"I am not afraid!" said the girl, bravely. "At least, I don't think I am—very! But it's all so new and unexpected, you know. Do people around here always shoot in that—well—unpremeditated fashion?"

They laughed together.

"Excuse me," he said. "I didn't realize the shot might startle you even more than the wildcat. It seems I'm not fit to have charge of a lady. I told you I was a roughneck."

"You're taking care of me beautifully," said Margaret Earle, loyally, "and I'm glad to get used to shots if that's the thing to be expected often."

Just then they came to the top of the low, rolling hill, and ahead in the darkness there gleamed a tiny, wizened light set in a blotch of blackness. Under the great white stars it burned a sickly red and seemed out of harmony with the night.

"There we are!" said the Boy, pointing toward it. "That's the bunk-house. You needn't be afraid. Pop Wallis 'll be snoring by this time, and we'll come away before he's about in the morning. He always sleeps late after he's been off on a bout. He's been gone three days, selling some cattle, and he'll have a pretty good top on."

The girl caught her breath, gave one wistful look up at the wide, starry sky, a furtive glance at the strong face of her protector, and submitted to being lifted down to the ground.

Before her loomed the bunk-house, small and mean, built of logs, with only one window in which the flicker of the lanterns menaced, with unknown trials and possible perils for her to meet.

CHAPTER IV

When Margaret Earle dawned upon that bunk-room the men sat up with one accord, ran their rough, red hands through their rough, tousled hair, smoothed their beards, took down their feet from the benches where they were resting. That was as far as their etiquette led them. Most of them continued to smoke their pipes, and all of them stared at her unreservedly. Such a sight of exquisite feminine beauty had not come to their eyes in many a long day. Even in the dim light of the smoky lanterns, and with the dust and weariness of travel upon her, Margaret Earle was a beautiful girl.

"That's what's the matter, father," said her mother, when the subject of Margaret's going West to teach had first been mentioned. "She's too beautiful. Far too beautiful to go among savages! If she were homely and old, now, she might be safe. That would be a different matter."

Yet Margaret had prevailed, and was here in the wild country. Now, standing on the threshold of the log cabin, she read, in the unveiled admiration that startled from the eyes of the men, the meaning of her mother's fears.

Yet withal it was a kindly admiration not unmixed with awe. For there was about her beauty a touch of the spiritual which set her above the common run of women, making men feel her purity and sweetness, and inclining their hearts to worship rather than be bold.

The Boy had been right. Pop Wallis was asleep and out of the way. From a little shed room at one end his snoring marked time in the silence that the advent of the girl made in the place.

In the doorway of the kitchen offset Mom Wallis stood with her passionless face—a face from which all emotions had long ago been burned by cruel fires—and looked at the girl, whose expression was vivid with her opening life all haloed in a rosy glow.

A kind of wistful contortion passed over Mom Wallis's hopeless countenance, as if she saw before her in all its possibility of perfection the life that she herself had lost. Perhaps it was no longer possible for her features to show tenderness, but a glow of something like it burned in her eyes, though she only turned away with the same old apathetic air, and without a word went about preparing a meal for the stranger.

Margaret looked wildly, fearfully, around the rough assemblage when she first entered the long, low room, but instantly the boy introduced her as "the new teacher for the Ridge School beyond the Junction," and these were Long Bill, Big Jim, the Fiddling Boss, Jasper Kemp, Fade-away Forbes, Stocky, Croaker, and Fudge. An inspiration fell upon the frightened girl, and she acknowledged the introduction by a radiant smile, followed by the offering of her small gloved hand. Each man in dumb bewilderment instantly became her slave, and accepted the offered hand with more or less pleasure and embarrassment. The girl proved her right to be called tactful, and, seeing her advantage, followed it up quickly by a few bright words. These men were of an utterly different type from any she had ever met before, but they had in their eyes a kind of homage which Pop Wallis had not shown and they were not repulsive to her. Besides, the Boy was in the background, and her nerve had returned. The Boy knew how a lady should be treated. She was quite ready to "play up" to his lead.

It was the Boy who brought the only chair the bunk-house afforded, a rude, home-made affair, and helped her off with her coat and hat in his easy, friendly way, as if he had known her all his life; while the men, to whom such gallant ways were foreign, sat awkwardly by and watched in wonder and amaze.

Most of all they were astonished at "the Kid," that he could fall so naturally into intimate talk with this delicate, beautiful woman. She was another of his kind, a creature not made in the same mold as theirs. They saw it now, and watched the fairy play with almost childish interest. Just to hear her call him "Mr. Gardley"!—Lance Gardley, that was what he had told them was his name the day he came among them. They had not heard it since. The Kid! Mr. Gardley!

There it was, the difference between them! They looked at the girl half jealously, yet proudly at the Boy. He was theirs—yes, in a way he was theirs—had they not found him in the wilderness, sick and nigh to death, and nursed him back to life again? He was theirs; but he knew how to drop into her world, too, and not be ashamed. They were glad that he could, even while it struck them with a pang that some day he would go back to the world to which he belonged—and where they could never be at home.

It was a marvel to watch her eat the coarse corn-bread and pork that Mom Wallis brought her. It might have been a banquet, the pleasant way she seemed to look at it. Just like a bird she tasted it daintily, and smiled, showing her white teeth. There was nothing of the idea of greediness that each man knew he himself felt after a fast. It was all beautiful, the way she handled the two-tined fork and the old steel knife. They watched and dropped their eyes abashed as at a lovely sacrament. They had not felt before that eating could be an art. They did not know what art meant.

Such strange talk, too! But the Kid seemed to understand. About the sky—their old, common sky, with stars that they saw every night—making such a fuss about that, with words like "wide," "infinite," "azure," and "gems." Each man went furtively out that night before he slept and took a new look at the sky to see if he could understand.

The Boy was planning so the night would be but brief. He knew the girl was afraid. He kept the talk going enthusiastically, drawing in one or two of the men now and again. Long Bill forgot himself and laughed out a hoarse guffaw, then stopped as if he had been choked. Stocky, red in the face, told a funny story when commanded by the Boy, and then dissolved in mortification over his blunders. The Fiddling Boss obediently got down his fiddle from the smoky corner beside the fireplace and played a weird old tune or two, and then they sang. First the men, with hoarse, quavering approach and final roar of wild sweetness; then Margaret and the Boy in duet, and finally Margaret alone, with a few bashful chords on the fiddle, feeling their way as accompaniment.

Mom Wallis had long ago stopped her work and was sitting huddled in the doorway on a nail-keg with weary, folded hands and a strange wistfulness on her apathetic face. A fine silence had settled over the group as the girl, recognizing her power, and the pleasure she was giving, sang on. Now and then the Boy, when he knew the song, would join in with his rich tenor.

It was a strange night, and when she finally lay down to rest on a hard cot with a questionable-looking blanket for covering and Mom Wallis as her room-mate, Margaret Earle could not help wondering what her mother and father would think now if they could see her. Would they not, perhaps, almost prefer the water-tank and the lonely desert for her to her present surroundings?

Nevertheless, she slept soundly after her terrible excitement, and woke with a start of wonder in the early morning, to hear the men outside splashing water and humming or whistling bits of the tunes she had sung to them the night before.

Mom Wallis was standing over her, looking down with a hunger in her eyes at the bright waves of Margaret's hair and the soft, sleep-flushed cheeks.

"You got dretful purty hair," said Mom Wallis, wistfully.

Margaret looked up and smiled in acknowledgment of the compliment.

"You wouldn't b'lieve it, but I was young an' purty oncet. Beats all how much it counts to be young—an' purty! But land! It don't last long. Make the most of it while you got it."

Browning's immortal words came to Margaret's lips—

Grow old along with me,
The best is yet to be,
The last of life for which the first was made—

but she checked them just in time and could only smile mutely. How could she speak such thoughts amid these intolerable surroundings? Then with sudden impulse she reached up to the astonished woman and, drawing her down, kissed her sallow cheek.

"Oh!" said Mom Wallis, starting back and laying her bony hands upon the place where she had been kissed, as if it hurt her, while a dull red stole up from her neck over her cheeks and high forehead to the roots of her hay-colored hair. All at once she turned her back upon her visitor and the tears of the years streamed down her impassive face.

"Don't mind me," she choked, after a minute. "I liked it real good, only it kind of give me a turn." Then, after a second: "It's time t' eat. You c'n wash outside after the men is done."

That, thought Margaret, had been the scheme of this woman's whole life—"After the men is done!"

So, after all, the night was passed in safety, and a wonderful dawning had come. The blue of the morning, so different from the blue of the night sky, was, nevertheless, just as unfathomable; the air seemed filled with straying star-beams, so sparkling was the clearness of the light.

But now a mountain rose in the distance with heliotrope-and-purple bounds to stand across the vision and dispel the illusion of the night that the sky came down to the earth all around like a close-fitting dome. There were mountains on all sides, and a slender, dark line of mesquite set off the more delicate colorings of the plain.

Into the morning they rode, Margaret and the Boy, before Pop Wallis was yet awake, while all the other men stood round and watched, eager, jealous for the handshake and the parting smile. They told her they hoped she would come again and sing for them, and each one had an awkward word of parting. Whatever Margaret Earle might do with her school, she had won seven loyal friends in the camp, and she rode away amid their admiring glances, which lingered, too, on the broad shoulders and wide sombrero of her escort riding by her side.

"Wal, that's the end o' him, I 'spose," drawled Long Bill, with a deep sigh, as the riders passed into the valley out of their sight.

"H'm!" said Jasper Kemp, hungrily. "I reck'n *he* thinks it's jes' th' beginnin'!"

"Maybe so! Maybe so!" said Big Jim, dreamily.

The morning was full of wonder for the girl who had come straight from an Eastern city. The view from the top of the mesa, or the cool, dim entrance of a cañon where great ferns fringed and feathered its walls, and strange caves hollowed out in the rocks far above, made real the stories she had read of the cave-dwellers. It was a new world.

The Boy was charming. She could not have picked out among her city acquaintances a man who would have done the honors of the desert more delightfully than he. She had thought him handsome in the starlight and in the lantern-light the night before, but now that the morning shone upon him she could not keep from looking at him. His fresh color, which no wind and weather could quite subdue, his gray-blue eyes with that mixture of thoughtfulness and reverence and daring, his crisp, brown curls glinting with gold in the sunlight—all made him good to look upon. There was something about the firm set of his lips and chin that made her feel a hidden strength about him.

When they camped a little while for lunch he showed the thoughtfulness and care for her comfort that many an older man might not have had. Even his talk was a mixture of boyishness and experience and he seemed to know her thoughts before she had them fully spoken.

"I do not understand it," she said, looking him frankly in the eyes at last. "How ever in the world did one like*you* get landed among all those dreadful men! Of course, in their way, some of them are not so bad; but they are not like you, not in the least, and never could be."

They were riding out upon the plain now in the full afternoon light, and a short time would bring them to her destination.

A sad, set look came quickly into the Boy's eyes and his face grew almost hard.

"It's an old story. I suppose you've heard it before," he said, and his voice tried to take on a careless note, but failed. "I didn't make good back there"—he waved his hand sharply toward the East—"so I came out here to begin again. But I guess I haven't made good here, either—not in the way I meant when I came."

"You can't, you know," said Margaret. "Not here."

"Why?" He looked at her earnestly, as if he felt the answer might help him.

"Because you have to go back where you didn't make good and pick up the lost opportunities. You can't really make good till you do that *right where you left off*."

"But suppose it's too late?"

"It's never too late if we're in earnest and not too proud."

There was a long silence then, while the Boy looked thoughtfully off at the mountains, and when he spoke again it was to call attention to the beauty of a silver cloud that floated lazily on the horizon. But Margaret Earle had seen the look in his gray eyes and was not deceived.

A few minutes later they crossed another mesa and descended to the enterprising little town where the girl was to begin her winter's work. The very houses and streets seemed to rise briskly and hasten to meet them those last few minutes of their ride.

Now that the experience was almost over, the girl realized that she had enjoyed it intensely, and that she dreaded inexpressibly that she must bid good-by to this friend of a few hours and face an unknown world. It had been a wonderful day, and now it was almost done. The two looked at each other and realized that their meeting had been an epoch in their lives that neither would soon forget—that neither wanted to forget.

CHAPTER V

Slower the horses walked, and slower. The voices of the Boy and girl were low when they spoke about the common things by the wayside. Once their eyes met, and they smiled with something both sad and glad in them.

Margaret was watching the young man by her side and wondering at herself. He was different from any man whose life had come near to hers before. He was wild and worldly, she could see that, and unrestrained by many of the things that were vital principles with her, and yet she felt strangely drawn to him and wonderfully at home in his company. She could not understand herself nor him. It was as if his real soul had looked out of his eyes and spoken, untrammeled by the circumstances of birth or breeding or habit, and she knew him for a kindred spirit. And yet he was far from being one in whom she would have expected even to find a friend. Where was her confidence of yesterday? Why was it that she dreaded to have this strong young protector leave her to meet alone a world of strangers, whom yesterday at this time she would have gladly welcomed?

Now, when his face grew thoughtful and sad, she saw the hard, bitter lines that were beginning to be graven about his lips, and her heart ached over what he had said about not making good. She wondered if there was anything else she could say to help him, but no words came to her, and the sad, set look about his lips warned her that perhaps she had said enough. He was not one who needed a long dissertation to bring a thought home to his consciousness.

Gravely they rode to the station to see about Margaret's trunks and make inquiries for the school and the house where she had arranged to board. Then Margaret sent a telegram to her mother to say that she had arrived safely, and so, when all was done and there was no longer an excuse for lingering, the Boy realized that he must leave her.

They stood alone for just a moment while the voluble landlady went to attend to something that was boiling over on the stove. It was an ugly little parlor that was to be her reception-room for the next year at least, with red-and-green ingrain carpet of ancient pattern, hideous chromos on the walls, and frantically common furniture setting up in its shining varnish to be pretentious; but the girl had not seen it yet. She was filled with a great homesickness that had not possessed her even when she said good-by to her dear ones at home. She suddenly realized that the people with whom she was to be thrown were of another world from hers, and this one friend whom she had found in the desert was leaving her.

She tried to shake hands formally and tell him how grateful she was to him for rescuing her from the perils of the night, but somehow words seemed so inadequate, and tears kept crowding their way into her throat and eyes. Absurd it was, and he a stranger twenty hours before, and a man of other ways than hers, besides. Yet he was her friend and rescuer.

She spoke her thanks as well as she could, and then looked up, a swift, timid glance, and found his eyes upon her earnestly and troubled.

"Don't thank me," he said, huskily. "I guess it was the best thing I ever did, finding you. I sha'n't forget, even if you never let me see you again—and—I hope you will." His eyes searched hers wistfully.

"Of course," she said. "Why not?"

"I thank you," he said in quaint, courtly fashion, bending low over her hand. "I shall try to be worthy of the honor."

And so saying, he left her and, mounting his horse, rode away into the lengthening shadows of the afternoon.

She stood in the forlorn little room staring out of the window after her late companion, a sense of utter desolation upon her. For the moment all her brave hopes of the future had fled, and if she could have slipped unobserved out of the front door, down to the station, and boarded some waiting express to her home, she would gladly have done it then and there.

Try as she would to summon her former reasons for coming to this wild, she could not think of one of them, and her eyes were very near to tears.

But Margaret Earle was not given to tears, and as she felt them smart beneath her lids she turned in a panic to prevent them. She could not afford to cry now. Mrs. Tanner would be returning, and she must not find the "new schoolma'am" weeping.

With a glance she swept the meager, pretentious room, and then, suddenly, became aware of other presences. In the doorway stood a man and a dog, both regarding her intently with open surprise, not unmixed with open appraisement and a marked degree of admiration.

The man was of medium height, slight, with a putty complexion; cold, pale-blue eyes; pale, straw-colored hair, and a look of self-indulgence around his rather weak mouth. He was dressed in a city business suit of the latest cut, however, and looked as much out of place in that crude little house as did Margaret Earle herself in her simple gown of dark-blue crêpe and her undeniable air of style and good taste.

His eyes, as they regarded her, had in them a smile that the girl instinctively resented. Was it a shade too possessive and complacently sure for a stranger?

The dog, a large collie, had great, liquid, brown eyes, menacing or loyal, as circumstances dictated, and regarded her with an air of brief indecision. She felt she was being weighed in the balance by both pairs of eyes. Of the two the girl preferred the dog.

Perhaps the dog understood, for he came a pace nearer and waved his plumy tail tentatively. For the dog she felt a glow of friendliness at once, but for the man she suddenly, and most unreasonably, of course, conceived one of her violent and unexpected dislikes.

Into this tableau bustled Mrs. Tanner. "Well, now, I didn't go to leave you by your lonesome all this time," she apologized, wiping her hands on her apron, "but them beans boiled clean over, and I hed to put 'em in a bigger kettle. You see, I put in more beans 'count o' you bein' here, an' I ain't uset to calca'latin' on two extry." She looked happily from the man to the girl and back again.

"Mr. West, I 'spose, o' course, you interjuced yerself? Bein' a preacher, you don't hev to stan' on ceremony like the rest of mankind. You 'ain't? Well, let me hev the pleasure of interjucin' our new school-teacher, Miss Margaret Earle. I 'spect you two 'll be awful chummy right at the start, both bein' from the East that way, an' both hevin' ben to college."

Margaret Earle acknowledged the bow with a cool little inclination of her head. She wondered why she didn't hate the garrulous woman who rattled on in this happy, take-it-for-granted way; but there was something so innocently pleased in her manner that she couldn't help putting all her wrath on the smiling man who came forward instantly with a low bow and a voice of fulsome flattery.

"Indeed, Miss Earle, I assure you I am happily surprised. I am sure Mrs. Tanner's prophecy will come true and we shall be the best of friends. When they told me the new teacher was to board here I really hesitated. I have seen something of these Western teachers in my time, and scarcely thought I should find you congenial; but I can see at a glance that you are the exception to the rule."

He presented a soft, unmanly white hand, and there was nothing to do but take it or seem rude to her hostess; but her manner was like icicles, and she was thankful she had not yet removed her gloves.

If the reverend gentleman thought he was to enjoy a lingering hand-clasp he was mistaken, for the gloved finger-tips merely touched his hand and were withdrawn, and the girl turned to her hostess with a smile of finality as if he were dismissed. He did not seem disposed to take the hint and withdraw, however, until on a sudden the great dog came and stood between them with open-mouthed welcome and joyous greeting in the plumy, wagging tail. He pushed close to her and looked up into her face insistently, his hanging pink tongue and wide, smiling countenance proclaiming that he was satisfied with his investigation.

Margaret looked down at him, and then stooped and put her arms about his neck. Something in his kindly dog expression made her feel suddenly as if she had a real friend.

It seemed the man, however, did not like the situation. He kicked gingerly at the dog's hind legs, and said in a harsh voice:

"Get out of the way, sir. You're annoying the lady. Get out, I say!"

The dog, however, uttered a low growl and merely showed the whites of his menacing eyes at the man, turning his body slightly so that he stood across the lady's way protectingly, as if to keep the man from her.

Margaret smiled at the dog and laid her hand on his head, as if to signify her acceptance of the friendship he had offered her, and he waved his plume once more and attended her from the room, neither of them giving further attention to the man.

"Confound that dog!" said Rev. Frederick West, in a most unpreacher-like tone, as he walked to the window and looked out. Then to himself he mused: "A pretty girl. A *very pretty* girl. I really think it'll be worth my while to stay a month at least."

Up in her room the "very pretty girl" was unpacking her suit-case and struggling with the tears. Not since she was a wee little girl and went to school all alone for the first time had she felt so very forlorn, and it was the little bare bedroom that had done it. At least that had been the final straw that had made too great the burden of keeping down those threatening tears.

It was only a bare, plain room with unfinished walls, rough woodwork, a cheap wooden bed, a bureau with a warped looking-glass, and on the floor was a braided rug of rags. A little wooden rocker, another small, straight wooden chair, a hanging wall-pocket decorated with purple roses, a hanging bookshelf composed of three thin boards strung together with maroon picture cord, a violently colored picture-card of "Moses in the Bulrushes" framed in straws and red worsted, and bright-blue paper shades at the windows. That was the room!

How different from her room at home, simply and sweetly finished anew for her home-coming from college! It rose before her homesick vision now. Soft gray walls, rose-colored ceiling, blended by a wreath of exquisite wild roses, whose pattern was repeated in the border of the simple curtains and chair cushions, white-enamel furniture, pretty brass bed soft as down in its luxurious mattress, spotless and inviting always. She glanced at the humpy bed with its fringed gray spread and lumpy-looking pillows in dismay. She had not thought of little discomforts like that, yet how they loomed upon her weary vision now!

The tiny wooden stand with its thick, white crockery seemed ill substitute for the dainty white bath-room at home. She had known she would not have her home luxuries, of course, but she had not realized until set down amid these barren surroundings what a difference they would make.

Going to the window and looking out, she saw for the first tune the one luxury the little room possessed—a view! And such a view! Wide and wonderful and far it stretched, in colors unmatched by painter's brush, a purple mountain topped by rosy clouds in the distance. For the second time in Arizona her soul was lifted suddenly out of itself and its dismay by a vision of the things that God has made and the largeness of it all.

For some time she stood and gazed, marveling at the beauty and recalling some of the things her companion of the afternoon had said about his impressions of the place; then suddenly there loomed a dark speck in the near foreground of her meditation, and, looking down annoyed, she discovered the minister like a gnat between the eye and a grand spectacle, his face turned admiringly up to her window, his hand lifted in familiar greeting.

Vexed at his familiarity, she turned quickly and jerked down the shade; then throwing herself on the bed, she had a good cry. Her nerves were terribly wrought up. Things seemed twisted in her mind, and she felt that she had reached the limit of her endurance. Here was she, Margaret Earle, newly elected teacher to the Ashland Ridge School, lying on her bed in tears, when she ought to be getting settled and planning her new life; when the situation demanded her best attention she was wrought up over a foolish little personal dislike. Why did she have to dislike a minister, anyway, and then take to a wild young fellow whose life thus far had been anything but satisfactory even to himself? Was it her perverse nature that caused her to remember the look in the eyes of the Boy who had rescued her from a night in the wilderness, and to feel there was far more manliness in his face than in the face of the man whose profession surely would lead one to suppose he was more worthy of her respect and interest? Well, she was tired. Perhaps things would assume their normal relation to one another in the morning. And so, after a few minutes, she bathed her face in the little, heavy, iron-stone wash-bowl, combed her hair, and freshened the collar and ruffles in her sleeves preparatory to going down for the evening meal. Then, with a swift thought, she searched through her suit-case for every available article wherewith to brighten that forlorn room.

The dainty dressing-case of Dresden silk with rosy ribbons that her girl friends at home had given as a parting gift covered a generous portion of the pine bureau, and when she had spread it out and bestowed its silver-mounted brushes, combs, hand-glass, and pretty sachet, things seemed to brighten up a bit. She hung up a cobweb of a lace boudoir cap with its rose-colored ribbons over the bleary mirror, threw her kimono of flowered challis over the back of the rocker, arranged her soap and toothbrush, her own wash-rag and a towel brought from home on the wash-stand, and somehow felt better and more as if she belonged. Last she ranged her precious photographs of father and mother and the dear vine-covered church and manse across in front of the mirror. When her trunks came there would be other things, and she could bear it, perhaps, when she had this room buried deep in the home belongings. But this would have to do for to-night, for the trunk might not come till morning, and, anyhow, she was too weary to unpack.

She ventured one more look out of her window, peering carefully at first to make sure her fellow-boarder was not still standing down below on the grass. A pang of compunction shot through her conscience. What would her dear father think of her feeling this way toward a minister, and before she knew the first thing about him, too? It was dreadful! She must shake it off. Of course he was a good man or he wouldn't be in the ministry, and she had doubtless mistaken mere friendliness for forwardness. She would forget it and try to go down and behave to him the way her father would want her to behave toward a fellow-minister.

Cautiously she raised the shade again and looked out. The mountain was bathed in a wonderful ruby light fading into amethyst, and all the path between was many-colored like a pavement of jewels set in filigree. While she looked the picture changed, glowed, softened, and changed again, making her think of the chapter about the Holy City in Revelation.

She started at last when some one knocked hesitatingly on the door, for the wonderful sunset light had made her forget for the moment where she was, and it seemed a desecration to have mere mortals step in and announce supper, although the odor of pork and cabbage had been proclaiming it dumbly for some time.

She went to the door, and, opening it, found a dark figure standing in the hall. For a minute she half feared it was the minister, until a shy, reluctant backwardness in the whole stocky figure and the stirring of a large furry creature just behind him made her sure it was not.

"Ma says you're to come to supper," said a gruff, untamed voice; and Margaret perceived that the person in the gathering gloom of the hall was a boy.

"Oh!" said Margaret, with relief in her voice. "Thank you for coming to tell me. I meant to come down and not give that trouble, but I got to looking at the wonderful sunset. Have you been watching it?" She pointed across the room to the window. "Look! Isn't that a great color there on the tip of the mountain? I never saw anything like that at home. I suppose you're used to it, though."

The boy came a step nearer the door and looked blankly, half wonderingly, across at the window, as if he expected to see some phenomenon. "Oh! *That!*" he exclaimed, carelessly. "Sure! We have them all the time."

"But that wonderful silver light pouring down just in that one tiny spot!" exclaimed Margaret. "It makes the mountain seem alive and smiling!"

The boy turned and looked at her curiously. "Gee!" said he, "I c'n show you plenty like that!" But he turned and looked at it a long, lingering minute again.

"But we mustn't keep your mother waiting," said Margaret, remembering and turning reluctantly toward the door. "Is this your dog? Isn't he a beauty? He made me feel really as if he were glad to see me." She stooped and laid her hand on the dog's head and smiled brightly up at his master.

The boy's face lit with a smile, and he turned a keen, appreciative look at the new teacher, for the first time genuinely interested in her. "Cap's a good old scout," he admitted.

"So his name is Cap. Is that short for anything?"

"Cap'n."

"Captain. What a good name for him. He looks as if he were a captain, and he waves that tail grandly, almost as if it might be a badge of office. But who are you? You haven't told me your name yet. Are you Mrs. Tanner's son?"

The boy nodded. "I'm just Bud Tanner."

"Then you are one of my pupils, aren't you? We must shake hands on that." She put out her hand, but she was forced to go out after Bud's reluctant red fist, take it by force in a strange grasp, and do all the shaking; for Bud had never had that experience before in his life, and he emerged from it with a very red face and a feeling as if his right arm had been somehow lifted out of the same class with the rest of his body. It was rather awful, too, that it happened just in the open dining-room door, and that "preacher-boarder" watched the whole performance. Bud put on an extra-deep frown and shuffled away from the teacher, making a great show of putting Cap out of the dining-room, though he always sat behind his master's chair at meals, much to the discomfiture of the male boarder, who was slightly in awe of his dogship, not having been admitted into friendship as the lady had been.

Mr. West stood back of his chair, awaiting the arrival of the new boarder, an expectant smile on his face, and rubbing his hands together with much the same effect as a wolf licking his lips in anticipation of a victim. In spite of her resolves to like the man, Margaret was again struck with aversion as she saw him standing there, and was intensely relieved when she found that the seat assigned to her was on the opposite side of the table from him, and beside Bud. West, however, did not seem to be pleased with the arrangement, and, stepping around the table, said to his landlady:

"Did you mean me to sit over here?" and he placed a possessive hand on the back of the chair that was meant for Bud.

"No, Mister West, you jest set where you ben settin'," responded Mrs. Tanner. She had thought the matter all out and decided that the minister could converse with the teacher to the better advantage of the whole table if he sat across from her. Mrs. Tanner was a born match-maker. This she felt was an opportunity not to be despised, even if it sometime robbed the Ridge School of a desirable teacher.

But West did not immediately return to his place at the other side of the table. To Margaret's extreme annoyance he drew her chair and waited for her to sit down. The situation, however, was somewhat relieved of its intimacy by a sudden interference from Cap, who darted away from his frowning master and stepped up authoritatively to the minister's side with a low growl, as if to say:

"Hands off that chair! That doesn't belong to you!"

West suddenly released his hold on the chair without waiting to shove it up to the table, and precipitately retired to his own place. "That dog's a nuisance!" he said, testily, and was answered with a glare from Bud's dark eyes.

Bud came to his seat with his eyes still set savagely on the minister, and Cap settled down protectingly behind Margaret's chair.

Mrs. Tanner bustled in with the coffee-pot, and Mr. Tanner came last, having just finished his rather elaborate hair-comb at the kitchen glass with the kitchen comb, in full view of the assembled multitude. He was a little, thin, wiry, weather-beaten man, with skin like leather and sparse hair. Some of his teeth were missing, leaving deep hollows in his cheeks, and his kindly protruding chin was covered with scraggy gray whiskers, which stuck out ahead of him like a cow-catcher. He was in his shirt-sleeves and collarless, but looked neat and clean, and he greeted the new guest heartily before he sat down, and nodded to the minister:

"Naow, Brother West, I reckon we're ready fer your part o' the performance. You'll please to say grace."

Mr. West bowed his sleek, yellow head and muttered a formal blessing with an offhand manner, as if it were a mere ceremony. Bud stared contemptuously at him the while, and Cap uttered a low rumble as of a distant growl. Margaret felt a sudden desire to laugh, and tried to control herself, wondering what her father would feel about it all.

The genial clatter of knives and forks broke the stiffness after the blessing. Mrs. Tanner bustled back and forth from the stove to the table, talking clamorously the while. Mr. Tanner joined in with his flat, nasal twang, responding, and the minister, with an air of utter contempt for them both, endeavored to set up a separate and altogether private conversation with Margaret across the narrow table; but Margaret innocently had begun a conversation with Bud about the school, and had to be addressed by name each time before Mr. West could get her attention. Bud, with a boy's keenness, noticed her aversion, and put aside his own backwardness, entering into the contest with remarkably voluble replies. The minister, if he would be in the talk at all, was forced to join in with theirs, and found himself worsted and contradicted by the boy at every turn.

Strange to say, however, this state of things only served to make the man more eager to talk with the lady. She was not anxious for his attention. Ah! She was coy, and the acquaintance was to have the zest of being no lightly won friendship. All the better. He watched her as she talked, noted every charm of lash and lid and curving lip; stared so continually that she finally gave up looking his way at all, even when she was obliged to answer his questions.

Thus, at last, the first meal in the new home was concluded, and Margaret, pleading excessive weariness, went to her room. She felt as if she could not endure another half-hour of contact with her present world until she had had some rest. If the world had been just Bud and the dog she could have stayed below stairs and found out a little more about the new life; but with that oily-mouthed minister continually butting in her soul was in a tumult.

When she had prepared for rest she put out her light and drew up the shade. There before her spread the wide wonder of the heavens again, with the soft purple of the mountain under stars; and she was carried back to the experience of the night before with a vivid memory of her companion. Why, just *why* couldn't she be as interested in the minister down there as in the wild young man? Well, she was too tired to-night to analyze it all, and she knelt beside her window in the starlight to pray. As she prayed her thoughts were on Lance Gardley once more, and she felt her heart go out in longing for him, that he might find a way to "make good," whatever his trouble had been.

As she rose to retire she heard a step below, and, looking down, saw the minister stalking back and forth in the yard, his hands clasped behind, his head thrown back raptly. He could not see her in her dark room, but she pulled the shade down softly and fled to her hard little bed. Was that man going to obsess her vision everywhere, and must she try to like him just because he was a minister?

So at last she fell asleep.

CHAPTER VII

The next day was filled with unpacking and with writing letters home. By dint of being very busy Margaret managed to forget the minister, who seemed to obtrude himself at every possible turn of the day, and would have monopolized her if she had given him half a chance.

The trunks, two delightful steamer ones, and a big packing-box with her books, arrived the next morning and caused great excitement in the household. Not since they moved into the new house had they seen so many things arrive. Bud helped carry them up-stairs, while Cap ran wildly back and forth, giving sharp barks, and the minister stood by the front door and gave ineffectual and unpractical advice to the man who had brought them. Margaret heard the man and Bud exchanging their opinion of West in low growls in the hall as they entered her door, and she couldn't help feeling that she agreed with them, though she might not have expressed her opinion in the same terms.

The minister tapped at her door a little later and offered his services in opening her box and unstrapping her trunks; but she told him Bud had already performed that service for her, and thanked him with a finality that forbade him to linger. She half hoped he heard the vicious little click with which she locked the door after him, and then wondered if she were wicked to feel that way. But all such compunctions were presently forgotten in the work of making over her room.

The trunks, after they were unpacked and repacked with the things she would not need at once, were disposed in front of the two windows with which the ugly little room was blessed. She covered them with two Bagdad rugs, relics of her college days, and piled several college pillows from the packing-box on each, which made the room instantly assume a homelike air. Then out of the box came other things. Framed pictures of home scenes, college friends and places, pennants, and flags from football, baseball, and basket-ball games she had attended; photographs; a few prints of rare paintings simply framed; a roll of rose-bordered white scrim like her curtains at home, wherewith she transformed the blue-shaded windows and the stiff little wooden rocker, and even made a valance and bed-cover over pink cambric for her bed. The bureau and wash-stand were given pink and white covers, and the ugly walls literally disappeared beneath pictures, pennants, banners, and symbols.

When Bud came up to call her to dinner she flung the door open, and he paused in wide-eyed amazement over the transformation. His eyes kindled at a pair of golf-sticks, a hockey-stick, a tennis-racket, and a big basket-ball in the corner; and his whole look of surprise was so ridiculous that she had to laugh. He looked as if a miracle had been performed on the room, and actually stepped back into the hall to get his breath and be sure he was still in his father's house.

"I want you to come in and see all my pictures and get acquainted with my friends when you have time," she said. "I wonder if you could make some more shelves for my books and help me unpack and set them up?"

"Sure!" gasped Bud, heartily, albeit with awe. She hadn't asked the minister; she had asked *him—Bud!* Just a boy! He looked around the room with anticipation. What wonder and delight he would have looking at all those things!

Then Cap stepped into the middle of the room as if he belonged, mouth open, tongue lolling, smiling and panting a hearty approval, as he looked about at the strangeness for all the world as a human being might have done. It was plain he was pleased with the change.

There was a proprietary air about Bud during dinner that was pleasant to Margaret and most annoying to West. It was plain that West looked on the boy as an upstart whom Miss Earle was using for the present to block his approach, and he was growing most impatient over the delay. He suggested that perhaps she would like his escort to see something of her surroundings that afternoon; but she smilingly told him that she would be very busy all the afternoon getting settled, and when he offered again to help her she cast a dazzling smile on Bud and said she didn't think she would need any more help, that Bud was going to do a few things for her, and that was all that was necessary.

Bud straightened up and became two inches taller. He passed the bread, suggested two pieces of pie, and filled her glass of water as if she were his partner. Mr. Tanner beamed to see his son in high favor, but Mrs. Tanner looked a little troubled for the minister. She thought things weren't just progressing as fast as they ought to between him and the teacher.

Bud, with Margaret's instructions, managed to make a very creditable bookcase out of the packing-box sawed in half, the pieces set side by side. She covered them deftly with green burlap left over from college days, like her other supplies, and then the two arranged the books. Bud was delighted over the prospect of reading some of the books, for they were not all school-books, by any means, and she had brought plenty of them to keep her from being lonesome on days when she longed to fly back to her home.

At last the work was done, and they stood back to survey it. The books filled up every speck of space and overflowed to the three little hanging shelves over them; but they were all squeezed in at last except a pile of school-books that were saved out to take to the school-house. Margaret set a tiny vase on the top of one part of the packing-case and a small brass bowl on the top of the other, and Bud, after a knowing glance, scurried away for a few minutes and brought back a handful of gorgeous cactus blossoms to give the final touch.

"Gee!" he said, admiringly, looking around the room. "Gee! You wouldn't know it fer the same place!"

That evening after supper Margaret sat down to write a long letter home. She had written a brief letter, of course, the night before, but had been too weary to go into detail. The letter read:

DEAR MOTHER AND FATHER,—I'm unpacked and settled at last in my room, and now I can't stand it another minute till I talk to you.

Last night, of course, I was pretty homesick, things all looked so strange and new and different. I had known they would, but then I didn't realize at all how different they would be. But I'm not getting homesick already; don't think it. I'm not a bit sorry I came, or at least I sha'n't be when I get started in school. One of the scholars is Mrs. Tanner's son, and I like him. He's crude, of course, but he has a brain, and he's been helping me this afternoon. We made a bookcase for my books, and it looks fine. I wish you could see it. I covered it with the green burlap, and the books look real happy in smiling rows over on the other side of the room. Bud Tanner got me some wonderful cactus blossoms for my brass bowl. I wish I could send you some. They are gorgeous!

But you will want me to tell about my arrival. Well, to begin with, I was late getting here Margaret had decided to leave out the incident of the desert altogether, for she knew by experience that her mother would suffer terrors all during her absence if she once heard of that wild adventure, which accounts for the lateness of the telegram I sent you. I hope its delay didn't make you worry any.

A very nice young man named Mr. Gardley piloted me to Mrs. Tanner's house and looked after my trunks for me. He is from the East. It was fortunate for me that he happened along, for he was most kind and gentlemanly and helpful. Tell Jane not to worry lest I'll fall in love with him; he doesn't live here. He belongs to a ranch or camp or something twenty-five miles away. She was so afraid I'd fall in love with an Arizona man and not come back home.

Mrs. Tanner is very kind and motherly according to her lights. She has given me the best room in the house, and she talks a blue streak. She has thin, brown hair turning gray, and she wears it in a funny little knob on the tip-top of her round head to correspond with the funny little tuft of hair on her husband's protruding chin. Her head is set on her neck like a clothes-pin, only she is squattier than a clothes-pin. She always wears her sleeves rolled up (at least so far she has) and she always bustles around noisily and apologizes for everything in the jolliest sort of way. I would like her, I guess, if it wasn't for the other boarder; but she has quite made up her mind that I shall like him, and I don't, of course, so she is a bit disappointed in me so far.

Mr. Tanner is very kind and funny, and looks something like a jack-knife with the blades half-open. He never disagrees with Mrs. Tanner, and I really believe he's in love with her yet, though they must have been married a good while. He calls her "Ma," and seems restless unless she's in the room. When she goes out to the kitchen to get some more soup or hash or bring in the pie, he shouts remarks at her all the time she's gone, and she answers, utterly regardless of the conversation the rest of the family are carrying on. It's like a phonograph wound up for the day.

Bud Tanner is about fourteen, and I like him. He's well developed, strong, and almost handsome; at least he would be if he were fixed up a little. He has fine, dark eyes and a great shock of dark hair. He and I are friends already. And so is the dog. The dog is a peach! Excuse me, mother, but I just must use a little of the dear old college slang somewhere, and your letters are the only safety-valve, for I'm a schoolmarm now and must talk "good and proper" all the time, you know.

The dog's name is Captain, and he looks the part. He has constituted himself my bodyguard, and it's going to be very nice having him. He's perfectly devoted already. He's a great, big, fluffy fellow with keen, intelligent eyes, sensitive ears, and a tail like a spreading plume. You'd love him, I know. He has a smile like the morning sunshine.

And now I come to the only other member of the family, the boarder, and I hesitate to approach the topic, because I have taken one of my violent and naughty dislikes to him, and—awful thought—mother! father! *he's a minister!* Yes, he's a *Presbyterian minister*! I know it will make you feel dreadfully, and I thought some of not telling you, but my conscience hurt me so I had to. I just can't *bear* him, so there! Of course, I may get over it, but I don't see how ever, for I can't think of anything that's more like him than *soft soap*! Oh yes, there is one other word. Grandmother used to use it about men she hadn't any use for, and that was "squash." Mother, I can't help it, but he does seem something like a squash. One of that crook-necked, yellow kind with warts all over it, and a great, big, splurgy vine behind it to account for its being there at all. Insipid and thready when it's cooked, you know, and has to have a lot of salt and pepper and butter to make it go down at all. Now I've told you the worst, and I'll try to describe him and see what you think I'd better do about it. Oh, he isn't the regular minister here, or missionary—I guess they call him. He's located quite a distance off, and only comes once a month to preach here, and, anyhow, *he's* gone East now to take his wife to a hospital for an operation, and won't be back for a couple of months, perhaps, and this man isn't even taking his place. He's just here for his health or for fun or something, I guess. He says he had a large suburban church near New York, and had a nervous breakdown; but I've been wondering if he didn't make a mistake, and it wasn't the church had the nervous breakdown instead. He isn't very big nor very little; he's just insignificant. His hair is like wet straw, and his eyes like a fish's. His hand feels like a dead toad when you have to shake hands, which I'm thankful doesn't have to be done but once. He looks at you with a flat, sickening grin. He has an acquired double chin, acquired to make him look pompous, and he dresses stylishly and speaks of the inhabitants of this country with contempt. He wants to be very affable, and offers to take me to all sorts of places, but so far I've avoided him. I can't think how they ever came to let him be a minister—I really can't! And yet, I suppose it's all my horrid old prejudice, and father will be grieved and you will think I am perverse. But, really, I'm sure he's not one bit like father was when he was young. I never saw a minister like him. Perhaps I'll get over it. I do sometimes, you know, so don't begin to worry yet. I'll try real hard. I suppose he'll preach Sunday, and then, perhaps, his sermon will be grand and I'll forget how soft-soapy he looks and think only of his great thoughts.

But I know it will be a sort of comfort to you to know that there is a Presbyterian minister in the house with me, and I'll really try to like him if I can.

There's nothing to complain of in the board. It isn't luxurious, of course, but I didn't expect that. Everything is very plain, but Mrs. Tanner manages to make it taste good. She makes fine corn-bread, almost as good as yours—not quite.

My room is all lovely, now that I have covered its bareness with my own things, but it has one great thing that can't compare with anything at home, and that is its view. It is wonderful! I wish I could make you see it. There is a mountain at the end of it that has as many different garments as a queen. To-night, when sunset came, it grew filmy as if a gauze of many colors had dropped upon it and melted into it, and glowed and melted until it turned to slate blue under the wide, starred blue of the wonderful night sky, and all the dark about was velvet. Last night my mountain was all pink and silver, and I have seen it purple and rose. But you can't think the wideness of the sky, and I couldn't paint it for you with words. You must see it to understand. A great, wide, dark sapphire floor just simply ravished with stars like big jewels!

But I must stop and go to bed, for I find the air of this country makes me very sleepy, and my wicked little kerosene-lamp is smoking. I guess you would better send me my student-lamp, after all, for I'm surely going to need it.

Now I must turn out the light and say good night to my mountain, and then I will go to sleep thinking of you. Don't worry about the minister. I'm very polite to him, but I shall never—*no, never*—fall in love with *him*—tell Jane.

Your loving little girl,
MARGARET

CHAPTER VIII

Margaret had arranged with Bud to take her to the school-house the next morning, and he had promised to have a horse hitched up and ready at ten o'clock, as it seemed the school was a magnificent distance from her boarding-place. In fact, everything seemed to be located with a view to being as far from everywhere else as possible. Even the town was scattering and widespread and sparse.

When she came down to breakfast she was disappointed to find that Bud was not there, and she was obliged to suffer a breakfast tête-à-tête with West. By dint, however, of asking him questions instead of allowing him to take the initiative, she hurried through her breakfast quite successfully, acquiring a superficial knowledge of her fellow-boarder quite distant and satisfactory. She knew where he spent his college days and at what theological seminary he had prepared for the ministry. He had served three years in a prosperous church of a fat little suburb of New York, and was taking a winter off from his severe, strenuous pastoral labors to recuperate his strength, get a new stock of sermons ready, and possibly to write a book of some of his experiences. He flattened his weak, pink chin learnedly as he said this, and tried to look at her impressively. He said that he should probably take a large city church as his next pastorate when his health was fully recuperated. He had come out to study the West and enjoy its freedom, as he understood it was a good place to rest and do as you please unhampered by what people thought. He wanted to get as far away from churches and things clerical as possible. He felt it was due himself and his work that he should. He spoke of the people he had met in Arizona as a kind of tamed savages, and Mrs. Tanner, sitting behind her coffee-pot for a moment between bustles, heard his comments meekly and looked at him with awe. What a great man he must be, and how fortunate for the new teacher that he should be there when she came!

Margaret drew a breath of relief as she hurried away from the breakfast-table to her room. She was really anticipating the ride to the school with Bud. She liked boys, and Bud had taken her fancy. But when she came down-stairs with her hat and sweater on she found West standing out in front, holding the horse.

"Bud had to go in another direction, Miss Earle," he said, touching his hat gracefully, "and he has delegated to me the pleasant task of driving you to the school."

Dismay filled Margaret's soul, and rage with young Bud. He had deserted her and left her in the hands of the enemy! And she had thought he understood! Well, there was nothing for it but to go with this man, much as she disliked it. Her father's daughter could not be rude to a minister.

She climbed into the buckboard quickly to get the ceremony over, for her escort was inclined to be too officious about helping her in, and somehow she couldn't bear to have him touch her. Why was it that she felt so about him? Of course he must be a good man.

West made a serious mistake at the very outset of that ride. He took it for granted that all girls like flattery, and he proceeded to try it on Margaret. But Margaret did not enjoy being told how delighted he was to find that instead of the loud, bold "old maid" he had expected, she had turned out to be "so beautiful and young and altogether congenial"; and, coolly ignoring his compliments, she began a fire of questions again.

She asked about the country, because that was the most obvious topic of conversation. What plants were those that grew by the wayside? She found he knew greasewood from sage-brush, and that was about all. To some of her questions he hazarded answers that were absurd in the light of the explanations given her by Gardley two days before. However, she reflected that he had been in the country but a short time, and that he was by nature a man not interested in such topics. She tried religious matters, thinking that here at least they must have common interests. She asked him what he thought of Christianity in the West as compared with the East. Did he find these Western people more alive and awake to the things of the Kingdom?

West gave a startled look at the clear profile of the young woman beside him, thought he perceived that she was testing him on his clerical side, flattened his chin in his most learned, self-conscious manner, cleared his throat, and put on wisdom.

"Well, now, Miss Earle," he began, condescendingly, "I really don't know that I have thought much about the matter. Ah—you know I have been resting absolutely, and I really haven't had opportunity to study the situation out here in detail; but, on the whole, I should say that everything was decidedly primitive; yes—ah—I might say—ah—well, crude. Yes, *crude* in the extreme! Why, take it in this mission district. The missionary who is in charge seems to be teaching the most absurd of the old dogmas such as our forefathers used to teach. I haven't met him, of course. He is in the East with his wife for a time. I am told she had to go under some kind of an operation. I have never met him, and really don't care to do so; but to judge from all I hear, he is a most unfit man for a position of the kind. For example, he is teaching such exploded doctrines as the old view of the atonement, the infallibility of the Scriptures, the deity of Christ, belief in miracles, and the like. Of course, in one sense it really matters very little what the poor Indians believe, or what such people as the Tanners are taught. They have but little mind, and would scarcely know the difference; but you can readily see that with such a primitive, unenlightened man at the head of religious affairs, there could scarcely be much broadening and real religious growth. Ignorance, of course, holds sway out here. I fancy you will find that to be the case soon enough. What in the world ever led you to come to a field like this to labor? Surely there must have been many more congenial places open to such as you." He leaned forward and cast a sentimental glance at her, his eyes looking more "fishy" than ever.

"I came out here because I wanted to get acquainted with this great country, and because I thought there was an opportunity to do good," said Margaret, coldly. She did not care to discuss her own affairs with this man. "But, Mr. West, I don't know that I altogether understand you. Didn't you tell me that you were a Presbyterian minister?"

"I certainly did," he answered, complacently, as though he were honoring the whole great body of Presbyterians by making the statement.

"Well, then, what in the world did you mean? All Presbyterians, of course, believe in the infallibility of the Scriptures and the deity of Jesus—and the atonement!"

"Not necessarily," answered the young man, loftily. "You will find, my dear young lady, that there is a wide, growing feeling in our church in favor of a broader view. The younger men, and the great student body of our church, have thrown to the winds all their former beliefs and are ready to accept new light with open minds. The findings of science have opened up a vast store of knowledge, and all thinking men must acknowledge that the old dogmas are rapidly vanishing away. Your father doubtless still holds to the old faith, perhaps, and we must be lenient with the older men who have done the best they could with the light they had; but all younger, broad-minded men are coming to the new way of looking at things. We have had enough of the days of preaching hell-fire and damnation. We need a religion of love to man, and good works. You should read some of the books that have been written on this subject if you care to understand. I really think it would be worth your while. You look to me like a young woman with a mind. I have a few of the latest with me. I shall be glad to read and discuss them with you if you are interested."

"Thank you, Mr. West," said Margaret, coolly, though her eyes burned with battle. "I think I have probably read most of those books and discussed them with my father. He may be old, but he is not without 'light,' as you call it, and he always believed in knowing all that the other side was saying. He brought me up to look into these things for myself. And, anyhow, I should not care to read and discuss any of these subjects with a man who denies the deity of my Saviour and does not believe in the infallibility of the Bible. It seems to me you have nothing left—"

"Ah! Well—now—my dear young lady—you mustn't misjudge me! I should be sorry indeed to shake your faith, for an innocent faith is, of course, a most beautiful thing, even though it may be unfounded."

"Indeed, Mr. West, that would not be possible. You could not shake my faith in my Christ, because *I know Him.* If I had not ever felt His presence, nor been guided by His leading, such words might possibly trouble me, but having seen 'Him that is invisible,' *I know.*" Margaret's voice was steady and gentle. It was impossible for even that man not to be impressed by her words.

"Well, let us not quarrel about it," he said, indulgently, as to a little child. "I'm sure you have a very charming way of stating it, and I'm not sure that it is not a relief to find a woman of the old-fashioned type now and then. It really is man's place to look into these deeper questions, anyway. It is woman's sphere to live and love and make a happy home—"

His voice took on a sentimental purr, and Margaret was fairly boiling with rage at him; but she would not let her temper give way, especially when she was talking on the sacred theme of the Christ. She felt as if she must scream or jump out over the wheel and run away from this obnoxious man, but she knew she would do neither. She knew she would sit calmly through the expedition and somehow control that conversation. There was one relief, anyway. Her father would no longer expect respect and honor and liking toward a minister who denied the very life and foundation of his faith.

"It can't be possible that the school-house is so far from the town," she said, suddenly looking around at the widening desert in front of them. "Haven't you made some mistake?"

"Why, I thought we should have the pleasure of a little drive first," said West, with a cunning smile. "I was sure you would enjoy seeing the country before you get down to work, and I was not averse myself to a drive in such delightful company."

"I would like to go back to the school-house at once, please," said Margaret, decidedly, and there was that in her voice that caused the man to turn the horse around and head it toward the village.

"Why, yes, of course, if you prefer to see the school-house first, we can go back and look it over, and then, perhaps, you will like to ride a little farther," he said. "We have plenty of time. In fact, Mrs. Tanner told me she would not expect us home to dinner, and she put a very promising-looking basket of lunch under the seat for us in case we got hungry before we came back."

"Thank you," said Margaret, quite freezingly now. "I really do not care to drive this morning. I would like to see the school-house, and then I must return to the house at once. I have a great many things to do this morning."

Her manner at last penetrated even the thick skin of the self-centered man, and he realized that he had gone a step too far in his attentions. He set himself to undo the mischief, hoping perhaps to melt her yet to take the all-day drive with him. But she sat silent during the return to the village, answering his volubility only by yes or no when absolutely necessary. She let him babble away about college life and tell incidents of his late pastorate, at some of which he laughed immoderately; but he could not even bring a smile to her dignified lips.

He hoped she would change her mind when they got to the school building, and he even stooped to praise it in a kind of contemptuous way as they drew up in front of the large adobe building.

"I suppose you will want to go through the building," he said, affably, producing the key from his pocket and putting on a pleasant anticipatory smile, but Margaret shook her head. She simply would not go into the building with that man.

"It is not necessary," she said again, coldly. "I think I will go home now, please." And he was forced to turn the horse toward the Tanner house, crestfallen, and wonder why this beautiful girl was so extremely hard to win. He flattered himself that he had always been able to interest any girl he chose. It was really quite a bewildering type. But he would win her yet.

He set her down silently at the Tanner door and drove off, lunch-basket and all, into the wilderness, vexed that she was so stubbornly unfriendly, and pondering how he might break down the dignity wherewith she had surrounded herself. There would be a way and he would find it. There was a stubbornness about that weak chin of his, when one observed it, and an ugliness in his pale-blue eye; or perhaps you would call it a hardness.

CHAPTER IX

She watched him furtively from her bedroom window, whither she had fled from Mrs. Tanner's exclamations. He wore his stylish derby tilted down over his left eye and slightly to one side in a most unministerial manner, showing too much of his straw-colored back hair, which rose in a cowlick at the point of contact with the hat, and he looked a small, mean creature as he drove off into the vast beauty of the plain. Margaret, in her indignation, could not help comparing him with the young man who had ridden away from the house two days before.

And he to set up to be a minister of Christ's gospel and talk like that about the Bible and Christ! Oh, what was the church of Christ coming to, to have ministers like that? How ever did he get into the ministry, anyway? Of course, she knew there were young men with honest doubts who sometimes slid through nowadays, but a mean little silly man like that? How ever did he get in? What a lot of ridiculous things he had said! He was one of those described in the Bible who "darken counsel with words." He was not worth noticing. And yet, what a lot of harm he could do in an unlearned community. Just see how Mrs. Tanner hung upon his words, as though they were law and gospel! How *could* she?

Margaret found herself trembling yet over the words he had spoken about Christ, the atonement, and the faith. They meant so much to her and to her mother and father. They were not mere empty words of tradition that she believed because she had been taught. She had lived her faith and proved it; and she could not help feeling it like a personal insult to have him speak so of her Saviour. She turned away and took her Bible to try and get a bit of calmness.

She fluttered the leaves for something—she could not just tell what—and her eye caught some of the verses that her father had marked for her before she left home for college, in the days when he was troubled for her going forth into the world of unbelief.

As ye have therefore received Christ Jesus the Lord, so walk ye in him: Rooted and built up in him, and established in the faith, as ye have been taught, abounding therein with thanksgiving. Beware lest any man spoil you through philosophy and vain deceit, after the tradition of men, after the rudiments of the world, and not after Christ. For in him dwelleth all the fullness of the Godhead bodily....

How the verses crowded upon one another, standing out clearly from the pages as she turned them, marked with her father's own hand in clear ink underlinings. It almost seemed as if God had looked ahead to these times and set these words down just for the encouragement of his troubled servants who couldn't understand why faith was growing dim. God knew about it, had known it would be, all this doubt, and had put words here just for troubled hearts to be comforted thereby.

For I know whom I have believed How her heart echoed to that statement!, and am persuaded that he is able to keep that which I have committed unto him against that day.

And on a little further:

Nevertheless the foundation of God standeth sure, having this seal, The Lord knoweth them that are his.

There was a triumphant look to the words as she read them.

Then over in Ephesians her eye caught a verse that just seemed to fit that poor blind minister:

Having the understanding darkened, being alienated from the life of God through the ignorance that is in them, because of the blindness of their heart.

And yet he was set to guide the feet of the blind into the way of life! And he had looked on her as one of the ignorant. Poor fellow! He couldn't know the Christ who was her Saviour or he never would have spoken in that way about Him. What could such a man preach? What was there left to preach, but empty words, when one rejected all these doctrines? Would she have to listen to a man like that Sunday after Sunday? Did the scholars in her school, and their parents, and the young man out at the camp, and his rough, simple-hearted companions have to listen to preaching from that man, when they listened to any? Her heart grew sick within her, and she knelt beside her bed for a strengthening word with the Christ who since her little childhood had been a very real presence in her life.

When she arose from her knees she heard the kitchen door slam down-stairs and the voice of Bud calling his mother. She went to her door and opened it, listening a moment, and then called the boy.

There was a dead silence for an instant after her voice was heard, and then Bud appeared at the foot of the stairs, very frowning as to brow, and very surly as to tone:

"What d'ye want?"

It was plain that Bud was "sore."

"Bud,"—Margaret's voice was sweet and a bit cool as she leaned over the railing and surveyed the boy; she hadn't yet got over her compulsory ride with that minister—"I wanted to ask you, please, next time you can't keep an appointment with me don't ask anybody else to take your place. I prefer to pick out my own companions. It was all right, of course, if you had to go somewhere else, but I could easily have gone alone or waited until another time. I'd rather not have you ask Mr. West to go anywhere with me again."

Bud's face was a study. It cleared suddenly and his jaw dropped in surprise; his eyes fairly danced with dawning comprehension and pleasure, and then his brow drew down ominously.

"I never ast him," he declared, vehemently. "He told me you wanted him to go, and fer me to get out of the way 'cause you didn't want to hurt my feelings. Didn't you say nothing to him about it at all this morning?"

"No, indeed!" said Margaret, with flashing eyes.

"Well, I just thought he was that kind of a guy. I told ma he was lying, but she said I didn't understand young ladies, and, of course, you didn't want me when there was a man, and especially a preacher, round. Some preacher he is! This 's the second time I've caught him lying. I think he's the limit. I just wish you'd see our missionary. If he was here he'd beat the dust out o' that poor stew. *He's* some man, he is. He's a regular white man, *our missionary*! Just you wait till *he* gets back."

Margaret drew a breath of relief. Then the missionary was a real man, after all. Oh, for his return!

"Well, I'm certainly very glad it wasn't your fault, Bud. I didn't feel very happy to be turned off that way," said the teacher, smiling down upon the rough head of the boy.

"You bet it wasn't my fault!" said the boy, vigorously. "I was sore's a pup at you, after you'd made a date and all, to do like that; but I thought if you wanted to go with that guy it was up to you."

"Well, I didn't and I don't. You'll please understand hereafter that I'd always rather have your company than his. How about going down to the school-house some time to-day? Have you time?"

"Didn't you go yet?" The boy's face looked as if he had received a kingdom, and his voice had a ring of triumph.

"We drove down there, but I didn't care to go in without you, so we came back."

"Wanta go now?" The boy's face fairly shone.

"I'd love to. I'll be ready in three minutes. Could we carry some books down?"

"Sure! Oh—gee! That guy's got the buckboard. We'll have to walk. Doggone him!"

"I shall enjoy a walk. I want to find out just how far it is, for I shall have to walk every day, you know."

"No, you won't, neither, 'nless you wanta. I c'n always hitch up."

"That'll be very nice sometimes, but I'm afraid I'd get spoiled if you babied me all the time that way. I'll be right down."

They went out together into the sunshine and wideness of the morning, and it seemed a new day had been created since she got back from her ride with the minister. She looked at the sturdy, honest-eyed boy beside her, and was glad to have him for a companion.

Just in front of the school-house Margaret paused. "Oh, I forgot! The key! Mr. West has the key in his pocket! We can't get in, can we?"

"Aw, we don't need a key," said her escort. "Just you wait!" And he whisked around to the back of the building, and in about three minutes his shock head appeared at the window. He threw the sash open and dropped out a wooden box. "There!" he said, triumphantly, "you c'n climb up on that, cantcha? Here, I'll holdya steady. Take holta my hand."

And so it was through the front window that the new teacher of the Ridge School first appeared on her future scene of action and surveyed her little kingdom.

Bud threw open the shutters, letting the view of the plains and the sunshine into the big, dusty room, and showed her the new blackboard with great pride.

"There's a whole box o' chalk up on the desk, too; 'ain't never been opened yet. Dad said that was your property. Want I should open it?"

"Why, yes, you might, and then we'll try the blackboard, won't we?"

Bud went to work gravely opening the chalk-box as if it were a small treasure-chest, and finally produced a long, smooth stick of chalk and handed it to her with shining eyes.

"You try it first, Bud," said the teacher, seeing his eagerness; and the boy went forward awesomely, as if it were a sacred precinct and he unworthy to intrude.

Shyly, awkwardly, with infinite painstaking, he wrote in a cramped hand, "William Budlong Tanner," and then, growing bolder, "Ashland, Arizona," with a big flourish underneath.

"Some class!" he said, standing back and regarding his handiwork with pride. "Say, I like the sound the chalk makes on it, don't you?"

"Yes, I do," said Margaret, heartily, "so smooth and business-like, isn't it? You'll enjoy doing examples in algebra on it, won't you?"

"Good night! Algebra! Me? No chance. I can't never get through the arithmetic. The last teacher said if he'd come back twenty years from now he'd still find me working compound interest."

"Well, we'll prove to that man that he wasn't much of a judge of boys," said Margaret, with a tilt of her chin and a glint of her teacher-mettle showing in her eyes. "If you're not in algebra before two months are over I'll miss my guess. We'll get at it right away and show him."

Bud watched her, charmed. He was beginning to believe that almost anything she tried would come true.

"Now, Bud, suppose we get to work. I'd like to get acquainted with my class a little before Monday. Isn't it Monday school opens? I thought so. Well, suppose you give me the names of the scholars and I'll write them down, and that will help me to remember them. Where will you begin? Here, suppose you sit down in the front seat and tell me who sits there and a little bit about him, and I'll write the name down; and then you move to the next seat and tell me about the next one, and so on. Will you?"

"Sure!" said Bud, entering into the new game. "But it ain't a 'he' sits there. It's Susie Johnson. She's Bill Johnson's smallest girl. She has to sit front 'cause she giggles so much. She has yellow curls and she ducks her head down and snickers right out this way when anything funny happens in school." And Bud proceeded to duck and wriggle in perfect imitation of the small Susie.

Margaret saw the boy's power of imitation was remarkable, and laughed heartily at his burlesque. Then she turned and wrote "Susie Johnson" on the board in beautiful script.

Bud watched with admiration, saying softly under his breath; "Gee! that's great, that blackboard, ain't it?"

Amelia Schwartz came next. She was long and lank, with the buttons off the back of her dress, and hands and feet too large for her garments. Margaret could not help but see her in the clever pantomime the boy carried on. Next was Rosa Rogers, daughter of a wealthy cattleman, the pink-cheeked, blue-eyed beauty of the school, with all the boys at her feet and a perfect knowledge of her power over them. Bud didn't, of course, state it that way, but Margaret gathered as much from his simpering smile and the coy way he looked out of the corner of his eyes as he described her.

Down the long list of scholars he went, row after row, and when he came to the seats where the boys sat his tone changed. She could tell by the shading of his voice which boys were the ones to look out for.

Jed Brower, it appeared, was a name to conjure with. He could ride any horse that ever stood on four legs, he could outshoot most of the boys in the neighborhood, and he never allowed any teacher to tell him what to do. He was Texas Brower's only boy, and always had his own way. His father was on the school board. Jed Brower was held in awe, even while his methods were despised, by some of the younger boys. He was big and powerful, and nobody dared fool with him. Bud did not exactly warn Margaret that she must keep on the right side of Jed Brower, but he conveyed that impression without words. Margaret understood. She knew also that Tad Brooks, Larry Parker, Jim Long, and Dake Foster were merely henchmen of the worthy Jed, and not negligible quantities when taken by themselves. But over the name of Timothy Forbes—"Delicate Forbes," Bud explained was his nickname—the boy lingered with that loving inflection of admiration that a younger boy will sometimes have for a husky, courageous older lad. The second time Bud spoke of him he called him "Forbeszy," and Margaret perceived that here was Bud's model of manhood. Delicate Forbes could outshoot and outride even Jed Brower when he chose, and his courage with cattle was that of a man. Moreover, he was good to the younger boys and wasn't above pitching baseball with them when he had nothing better afoot. It became evident from the general description that Delicate Forbes was not called so from any lack of inches to his stature. He had a record of having licked every man teacher in the school, and beaten by guile every woman teacher they had had in six years. Bud was loyal to his admiration, yet it could be plainly seen that he felt Margaret's greatest hindrance in the school would be Delicate Forbes.

Margaret mentally underlined the names in her memory that belonged to the back seats in the first and second rows of desks, and went home praying that she might have wisdom and patience to deal with Jed Brower and Timothy Forbes, and through them to manage the rest of her school.

She surprised Bud at the dinner-table by handing him a neat diagram of the school-room desks with the correct names of all but three or four of the scholars written on them. Such a feat of memory raised her several notches in his estimation.

"Say, that's going some! Guess you won't forget nothing, no matter how much they try to make you."

CHAPTER X

The minister did not appear until late in the evening, after Margaret had gone to her room, for which she was sincerely thankful. She could hear his voice, fretful and complaining, as he called loudly for Bud to take the horse. It appeared he had lost his way and wandered many miles out of the trail. He blamed the country for having no better trails, and the horse for not being able to find his way better. Mr. Tanner had gone to bed, but Mrs. Tanner bustled about and tried to comfort him.

"Now that's too bad! Dearie me! Bud oughta hev gone with you, so he ought. Bud! *Oh*, Bud, you 'ain't gonta sleep yet, hev you? Wake up and come down and take this horse to the barn."

But Bud declined to descend. He shouted some sleepy directions from his loft where he slept, and said the minister could look after his own horse, he "wasn'ta gonta!" There was "plentya corn in the bin."

The minister grumbled his way to the barn, highly incensed at Bud, and disturbed the calm of the evening view of Margaret's mountain by his complaints when he returned. He wasn't accustomed to handling horses, and he thought Bud might have stayed up and attended to it himself. Bud chuckled in his loft and stole down the back kitchen roof while the minister ate his late supper. Bud would never leave the old horse to that amateur's tender mercies, but he didn't intend to make it easy for the amateur. Margaret, from her window-seat watching the night in the darkness, saw Bud slip off the kitchen roof and run to the barn, and she smiled to herself. She liked that boy. He was going to be a good comrade.

The Sabbath morning dawned brilliantly, and to the homesick girl there suddenly came a sense of desolation on waking. A strange land was this, without church-bells or sense of Sabbath fitness. The mountain, it is true, greeted her with a holy light of gladness, but mountains are not dependent upon humankind for being in the spirit on the Lord's day. They are "continually praising Him." Margaret wondered how she was to get through this day, this dreary first Sabbath away from her home and her Sabbath-school class, and her dear old church with father preaching. She had been away, of course, a great many times before, but never to a churchless community. It was beginning to dawn upon her that that was what Ashland was—a churchless community. As she recalled the walk to the school and the ride through the village she had seen nothing that looked like a church, and all the talk had been of the missionary. They must have services of some sort, of course, and probably that flabby, fish-eyed man, her fellow-boarder, was to preach; but her heart turned sick at thought of listening to a man who had confessed to the unbeliefs that he had. Of course, he would likely know enough to keep such doubts to himself; but he had told her, and nothing he could say now would help or uplift her in the least.

She drew a deep sigh and looked at her watch. It was late. At home the early Sabbath-school bells would be ringing, and little girls in white, with bunches of late fall flowers for their teachers, and holding hands with their little brothers, would be hurrying down the street. Father was in his study, going over his morning sermon, and mother putting her little pearl pin in her collar, getting ready to go to her Bible class. Margaret decided it was time to get up and stop thinking of it all.

She put on a little white dress that she wore to church at home and hurried down to discover what the family plans were for the day, but found, to her dismay, that the atmosphere below-stairs was just like that of other days. Mr. Tanner sat tilted back in a dining-room chair, reading the weekly paper, Mrs. Tanner was bustling in with hot corn-bread, Bud was on the front-door steps teasing the dog, and the minister came in with an air of weariness upon him, as if he quite intended taking it out on his companions that he had experienced a trying time on Saturday. He did not look in the least like a man who expected to preach in a few minutes. He declined to eat his egg because it was cooked too hard, and poor Mrs. Tanner had to try it twice before she succeeded in producing a soft-boiled egg to suit him. Only the radiant outline of the great mountain, which Margaret could see over the minister's head, looked peaceful and Sabbath-like.

"What time do you have service?" Margaret asked, as she rose from the table.

"Service?" It was Mr. Tanner who echoed her question as if he did not quite know what she meant.

Mrs. Tanner raised her eyes from her belated breakfast with a worried look, like a hen stretching her neck about to see what she ought to do next for the comfort of the chickens under her care. It was apparent that she had no comprehension of what the question meant. It was the minister who answered, condescendingly:

"Um! Ah! There is no church edifice here, you know, Miss Earle. The mission station is located some miles distant."

"I know," said Margaret, "but they surely have some religious service?"

"I really don't know," said the minister, loftily, as if it were something wholly beneath his notice.

"Then you are not going to preach this morning?" In spite of herself there was relief in her tone.

"Most certainly not," he replied, stiffly. "I came out here to rest, and I selected this place largely because it was so far from a church. I wanted to be where I should not be annoyed by requests to preach. Of course, ministers from the East would be a curiosity in these Western towns, and I should really get no rest at all if I had gone where my services would have been in constant demand. When I came out here I was in much the condition of our friend the minister of whom you have doubtless heard. He was starting on his vacation, and he said to a brother minister, with a smile of joy and relief, 'No preaching, no praying, no reading of the Bible for six whole weeks!'"

"Indeed!" said Margaret, freezingly. "No, I am not familiar with ministers of that sort." She turned with dismissal in her manner and appealed to Mrs. Tanner. "Then you really have no Sabbath service of any sort whatever in town?" There was something almost tragic in her face. She stood aghast at the prospect before her.

Mrs. Tanner's neck stretched up a little longer, and her lips dropped apart in her attempt to understand the situation. One would scarcely have been surprised to hear her say, "Cut-cut-cut-ca-daw-cut?" so fluttered did she seem.

Then up spoke Bud. "We gotta Sunday-school, ma!" There was pride of possession in Bud's tone, and a kind of triumph over the minister, albeit Bud had adjured Sunday-school since his early infancy. He was ready now, however, to be offered on the altar of Sunday-school, even, if that would please the new teacher—and spite the minister. "I'll take you ef you wanta go." He looked defiantly at the minister as he said it.

But at last Mrs. Tanner seemed to grasp what was the matter. "Why!—why!—why! You mean preaching service!" she clucked out. "Why, yes, Mr. West, wouldn't that be fine? You could preach for us. We could have it posted up at the saloon and the crossings, and out a ways on both trails, and you'd have quite a crowd. They'd come from over to the camp, and up the cañon way, and roundabouts. They'd do you credit, they surely would, Mr. West. And you could have the school-house for a meeting-house. Pa, there, is one of the school board. There wouldn't be a bit of trouble—"

"Um! Ah! Mrs. Tanner, I assure you it's quite out of the question. I told you I was here for absolute rest. I couldn't think of preaching. Besides, it's against my principles to preach without remuneration. It's a wrong idea. The workman is worthy of his hire, you know, Mrs. Tanner, the Good Book says." Mr. West's tone took on a self-righteous inflection.

"Oh! Ef that's all, that 'u'd be all right!" she said, with relief. "You could take up a collection. The boys would be real generous. They always are when any show comes along. They'd appreciate it, you know, and I'd like fer Miss Earle here to hear you preach. It 'u'd be a real treat to her, her being a preacher's daughter and all." She turned to Margaret for support, but that young woman was talking to Bud. She had promptly closed with his offer to take her to Sunday-school, and now she hurried away to get ready, leaving Mrs. Tanner to make her clerical arrangements without aid.

The minister, meantime, looked after her doubtfully. Perhaps, after all, it would have been a good move to have preached. He might have impressed that difficult young woman better that way than any other, seeing she posed as being so interested in religious matters. He turned to Mrs. Tanner and began to ask questions about the feasibility of a church service. The word "collection" sounded good to him. He was not averse to replenishing his somewhat depleted treasury if it could be done so easily as that.

Meantime Margaret, up in her room, was wondering again how such a man as Mr. West ever got into the Christian ministry.

West was still endeavoring to impress the Tanners with the importance of his late charge in the East as Margaret came down-stairs. His pompous tones, raised to favor the deafness that he took for granted in Mr. Tanner, easily reached her ears.

"I couldn't, of course, think of doing it every Sunday, you understand. It wouldn't be fair to myself nor my work which I have just left; but, of course, if there were sufficient inducement I might consent to preach some Sunday before I leave."

Mrs. Tanner's little satisfied cluck was quite audible as the girl closed the front door and went out to the waiting Bud.

The Sunday-school was a desolate affair, presided over by an elderly and very illiterate man, who nursed his elbows and rubbed his chin meditatively between the slow questions which he read out of the lesson-leaf. The woman who usually taught the children was called away to nurse a sick neighbor, and the children were huddled together in a restless group. The singing was poor, and the whole of the exercises dreary, including the prayer. The few women present sat and stared in a kind of awe at the visitor, half belligerently, as if she were an intruder. Bud lingered outside the door and finally disappeared altogether, reappearing when the last hymn was sung. Altogether the new teacher felt exceedingly homesick as she wended her way back to the Tanners' beside Bud.

"What do you do with yourself on Sunday afternoons, Bud?" she asked, as soon as they were out of hearing of the rest of the group.

The boy turned wondering eyes toward her. "Do?" he repeated, puzzled. "Why, we pass the time away, like 'most any day. There ain't much difference."

A great desolation possessed her. No church! Worse than no minister! No Sabbath! What kind of a land was this to which she had come?

The boy beside her smelled of tobacco smoke. He had been off somewhere smoking while she was in the dreary little Sunday-school. She looked at his careless boy-face furtively as they walked along. He smoked, of course, like most boys of his age, probably, and he did a lot of other things he ought not to do. He had no interest in God or righteousness, and he did not take it for granted that the Sabbath was different from any other day. A sudden heart-sinking came upon her. What was the use of trying to do anything for such as he? Why not give it up now and go back where there was more promising material to work upon and where she would be welcome indeed? Of course, she had known things would be discouraging, but somehow it had seemed different from a distance. It all looked utterly hopeless now, and herself crazy to have thought she could do any good in a place like this.

And yet the place needed somebody! That pitiful little Sunday-school! How forlorn it all was! She was almost sorry she had gone. It gave her an unhappy feeling for the morrow, which was to be her first day of school.

Then, all suddenly, just as they were nearing the Tanner house, there came one riding down the street with all the glory of the radiant morning in his face, and a light in his eyes at seeing her that lifted away her desolation, for here at last was a friend!

She wondered at herself. An unknown stranger, and a self-confessed failure so far in his young life, and yet he seemed so good a sight to her amid these uncongenial surroundings!

CHAPTER XI

This stranger of royal bearing, riding a rough Western pony as if it were decked with golden trappings, with his bright hair gleaming like Roman gold in the sun, and his blue-gray eyes looking into hers with the gladness of his youth; this one who had come to her out of the night-shadows of the wilderness and led her into safety! Yes, she was glad to see him.

He dismounted and greeted her, his wide hat in his hand, his eyes upon her face, and Bud stepped back, watching them in pleased surprise. This was the man who had shot all the lights out the night of the big riot in the saloon. He had also risked his life in a number of foolish ways at recent festal carouses. Bud would not have been a boy had he not admired the young man beyond measure; and his boy worship of the teacher yielded her to a fitting rival. He stepped behind and walked beside the pony, who was following his master meekly, as though he, too, were under the young man's charm.

"Oh, and this is my friend, William Tanner," spoke Margaret, turning toward the boy loyally, (Whatever good angel made her call him William? Bud's soul swelled with new dignity as he blushed and acknowledged the introduction by a grin.)

"Glad to know you, Will," said the new-comer, extending his hand in a hearty shake that warmed the boy's heart in a trice. "I'm glad Miss Earle has so good a protector. You'll have to look out for her. She's pretty plucky and is apt to stray around the wilderness by herself. It isn't safe, you know, boy, for such as her. Look after her, will you?"

"Right I will," said Bud, accepting the commission as if it were Heaven-sent, and thereafter walked behind the two with his head in the clouds. He felt that he understood this great hero of the plains and was one with him at heart. There could be no higher honor than to be the servitor of this man's lady. Bud did not stop to question how the new teacher became acquainted with the young rider of the plains. It was enough that both were young and handsome and seemed to belong together. He felt they were fitting friends.

The little procession walked down the road slowly, glad to prolong the way. The young man had brought her handkerchief, a filmy trifle of an excuse that she had dropped behind her chair at the bunk-house, where it had lain unnoticed till she was gone. He produced it from his inner pocket, as though it had been too precious to carry anywhere but over his heart, yet there was in his manner nothing presuming, not a hint of any intimacy other than their chance acquaintance of the wilderness would warrant. He did not look at her with any such look as West had given every time he spoke to her. She felt no desire to resent his glance when it rested upon her almost worshipfully, for there was respect and utmost humility in his look.

The men had sent gifts: some arrow-heads and a curiously fashioned vessel from the cañon of the cave-dwellers; some chips from the petrified forest; a fern with wonderful fronds, root and all; and a sheaf of strange, beautiful blossoms carefully wrapped in wet paper, and all fastened to the saddle.

Margaret's face kindled with interest as he showed them to her one by one, and told her the history of each and a little message from the man who had sent it. Mom Wallis, too, had baked a queer little cake and sent it. The young man's face was tender as he spoke of it. The girl saw that he knew what her coming had meant to Mom Wallis. Her memory went quickly back to those few words the morning she had wakened in the bunk-house and found the withered old woman watching her with tears in her eyes. Poor Mom Wallis, with her pretty girlhood all behind her and such a blank, dull future ahead! Poor, tired, ill-used, worn-out Mom Wallis! Margaret's heart went out to her.

"They want to know," said the young man, half hesitatingly, "if some time, when you get settled and have time, you would come to them again and sing? I tried to make them understand, of course, that you would be busy, your time taken with other friends and your work, and you would not want to come; but they wanted me to tell you they never enjoyed anything so much in years as your singing. Why, I heard Long Jim singing 'Old Folks at Home' this morning when he was saddling his horse. And it's made a difference. The men sort of want to straighten up the bunk-room. Jasper made a new chair yesterday. He said it would do when you came again." Gardley laughed diffidently, as if he knew their hopes were all in vain.

But Margaret looked up with sympathy in her face, "I'll come! Of course I'll come some time," she said, eagerly. "I'll come as soon as I can arrange it. You tell them we'll have more than one concert yet."

The young man's face lit up with a quick appreciation, and the flash of his eyes as he looked at her would have told any onlooker that he felt here was a girl in a thousand, a girl with an angel spirit, if ever such a one walked the earth.

Now it happened that Rev. Frederick West was walking impatiently up and down in front of the Tanner residence, looking down the road about that time. He had spent the morning in looking over the small bundle of "show sermons" he had brought with him in case of emergency, and had about decided to accede to Mrs. Tanner's request and preach in Ashland before he left. This decision had put him in so self-satisfied a mood that he was eager to announce it before his fellow-boarder. Moreover, he was hungry, and he could not understand why that impudent boy and that coquettish young woman should remain away at Sunday-school such an interminable time.

Mrs. Tanner was frying chicken. He could smell it every time he took a turn toward the house. It really was ridiculous that they should keep dinner waiting this way. He took one more turn and began to think over the sermon he had decided to preach. He was just recalling a particularly eloquent passage when he happened to look down the road once more, and there they were, almost upon him! But Bud was no longer walking with the maiden. She had acquired a new escort, a man of broad shoulders and fine height. Where had he seen that fellow before? He watched them as they came up, his small, pale eyes narrowing under their yellow lashes with a glint of slyness, like some mean little animal that meant to take advantage of its prey. It was wonderful how many different things that man could look like for a person as insignificant as he really was!

Well, he saw the look between the man and maiden; the look of sympathy and admiration and a fine kind of trust that is not founded on mere outward show, but has found some hidden fineness of the soul. Not that the reverend gentleman understood that, however. He had no fineness of soul himself. His mind had been too thoroughly taken up with himself all his life for him to have cultivated any.

Simultaneous with the look came his recognition of the man or, at least, of where he had last seen him, and his little soul rejoiced at the advantage he instantly recognized.

He drew himself up importantly, flattened his chin upward until his lower lip protruded in a pink roll across his mouth, drew down his yellow brows in a frown of displeasure, and came forward mentor-like to meet the little party as it neared the house. He had the air of coming to investigate and possibly oust the stranger, and he looked at him keenly, critically, offensively, as if he had the right to protect the lady. They might have been a pair of naughty children come back from a forbidden frolic, from the way he surveyed them. But the beauty of it was that neither of them saw him, being occupied with each other, until they were fairly upon him. Then, there he stood offensively, as if he were a great power to be reckoned with.

"Well, well, well, Miss Margaret, you have got home at last!" he said, pompously and condescendingly, and then he looked into the eyes of her companion as if demanding an explanation of *his* presence there.

Margaret drew herself up haughtily. His use of her Christian name in that familiar tone annoyed her exceedingly. Her eyes flashed indignantly, but the whole of it was lost unless Bud saw it, for Gardley had faced his would-be adversary with a keen, surprised scrutiny, and was looking him over coolly. There was that in the young man's eye that made the eye of Frederick West quail before him. It was only an instant the two stood challenging each other, but in that short time each knew and marked the other for an enemy. Only a brief instant and then Gardley turned to Margaret, and before she had time to think what to say, he asked:

"Is this man a friend of yours, Miss *Earle*?" with marked emphasis on the last word.

"No," said Margaret, coolly, "not a friend—a boarder in the house." Then most formally, "Mr. West, my *friend* Mr. Gardley."

If the minister had not been possessed of the skin of a rhinoceros he would have understood himself to be dismissed at that; but he was not a man accustomed to accepting dismissal, as his recent church in New York State might have testified. He stood his ground, his chin flatter than ever, his little eyes mere slits of condemnation. He did not acknowledge the introduction by so much as the inclination of his head. His hands were clasped behind his back, and his whole attitude was one of righteous belligerence.

Gardley gazed steadily at him for a moment, a look of mingled contempt and amusement gradually growing upon his face. Then he turned away as if the man were too small to notice.

"You will come in and take dinner with me?" asked Margaret, eagerly. "I want to send a small package to Mrs. Wallis if you will be so good as to take it with you."

"I'm sorry I can't stay to dinner, but I have an errand in another direction and at some distance. I am returning this way, however, and, if I may, will call and get the package toward evening."

Margaret's eyes spoke her welcome, and with a few formal words the young man sprang on his horse, said, "So long, Will!" to Bud, and, ignoring the minister, rode away.

They watched him for an instant, for, indeed, he was a goodly sight upon a horse, riding as if he and the horse were utterly one in spirit; then Margaret turned quickly to go into the house.

"Um! Ah! Miss Margaret!" began the minister, with a commandatory gesture for her to stop.

Margaret was the picture of haughtiness as she turned and said, "Miss *Earle*, if you please!"

"Um! Ah! Why, certainly, Miss—ah—*Earle*, if you wish it. Will you kindly remain here for a moment? I wish to speak with you. Bud, you may go on."

"I'll go when I like, and it's none of your business!" muttered Bud, ominously, under his breath. He looked at Margaret to see if she wished him to go. He had an idea that this might be one of the times when he was to look after her.

She smiled at him understandingly. "William may remain, Mr. West," she said, sweetly. "Anything you have to say to me can surely be said in his presence," and she laid her hand lightly on Bud's sleeve.

Bud looked down at the hand proudly and grew inches taller enjoying the minister's frown.

"Um! Ah!" said West, unabashed. "Well, I merely wished to warn you concerning the character of that person who has just left us. He is really not a proper companion for you. Indeed, I may say he is quite the contrary, and that to my personal knowledge—"

"He's as good as you are and better!" growled Bud, ominously.

"Be quiet, boy! I wasn't speaking to you!" said West, as if he were addressing a slave. "If I hear another word from your lips I shall report it to your father!"

"Go 's far 's you like and see how much I care!" taunted Bud, but was stopped by Margaret's gentle pressure on his arm.

"Mr. West, I thought I made you understand that Mr. Gardley is my friend."

"Um! Ah! Miss Earle, then all I have to say is that you have formed a most unwise friendship, and should let it proceed no further. Why, my dear young lady, if you knew all there is to know about him you would not think of speaking to that young man."

"Indeed! Mr. West, I suppose that might be true of a good many people, might it not, *if we knew all there is to know about them*? Nobody but God could very well get along with some of us."

"But, my dear young lady, you don't understand. This young person is nothing but a common ruffian, a gambler, in fact, and an habitué at the saloons. I have seen him myself sitting in a saloon at a very late hour playing with a vile, dirty pack of cards, and in the company of a lot of low-down creatures—"

"May I ask how you came to be in a saloon at that hour, Mr. West?" There was a gleam of mischief in the girl's eyes, and her mouth looked as if she were going to laugh, but she controlled it.

The minister turned very red indeed. "Well, I—ah—I had been called from my bed by shouts and the report of a pistol. There was a fight going on in the room adjoining the bar, and I didn't know but my assistance might be needed!" (At this juncture Bud uttered a sort of snort and, placing his hands over his heart, ducked down as if a sudden pain had seized him.) "But imagine my pain and astonishment when I was informed that the drunken brawl I was witnessing was but a nightly and common occurrence. I may say I remained for a few minutes, partly out of curiosity, as I wished to see all kinds of life in this new world for the sake of a book I am thinking of

185

writing. I therefore took careful note of the persons present, and was thus able to identify the person who has just ridden away as one of the chief factors in that evening's entertainment. He was, in fact, the man who, when he had pocketed all the money on the gaming-table, arose and, taking out his pistol, shot out the lights in the room, a most dangerous and irregular proceeding—"

"Yes, and you came within an ace of being shot, pa says. The Kid's a dead shot, he is, and you were right in the way. Served you right for going where you had no business!"

"I did not remain longer in that place, as you may imagine," went on West, ignoring Bud, "for I found it was no place for a—for—a—ah—minister of the gospel; but I remained long enough to hear from the lips of this person with whom you have just been walking some of the most terrible language my ears have ever been permitted to—ah—witness!"

But Margaret had heard all that she intended to listen to on that subject. With decided tone she interrupted the voluble speaker, who was evidently enjoying his own eloquence.

"Mr. West, I think you have said all that it is necessary to say. There are still some things about Mr. Gardley that you evidently do not know, but I think you are in a fair way to learn them if you stay in this part of the country long. William, isn't that your mother calling us to dinner? Let us go in; I'm hungry."

Bud followed her up the walk with a triumphant wink at the discomfited minister, and they disappeared into the house; but when Margaret went up to her room and took off her hat in front of the little warped looking-glass there were angry tears in her eyes. She never felt more like crying in her life. Chagrin and anger and disappointment were all struggling in her soul, yet she must not cry, for dinner would be ready and she must go down. Never should that mean little meddling man see that his words had pierced her soul.

For, angry as she was at the minister, much as she loathed his petty, jealous nature and saw through his tale-bearing, something yet told her that his picture of young Gardley's wildness was probably true, and her soul sank within her at the thought. It was just what had come in shadowy, instinctive fear to her heart when he had hinted at his being a "roughneck," yet to have it put baldly into words by an enemy hurt her deeply, and she looked at herself in the glass half frightened. "Margaret Earle, have you come out to the wilderness to lose your heart to the first handsome sower of wild oats that you meet?" her true eyes asked her face in the glass, and Margaret Earle's heart turned sad at the question and shrank back. Then she dropped upon her knees beside her gay little rocking-chair and buried her face in its flowered cushions and cried to her Father in heaven:

"Oh, my Father, let me not be weak, but with all my heart I cry to Thee to save this young, strong, courageous life and not let it be a failure. Help him to find Thee and serve Thee, and if his life has been all wrong—and I suppose it has—oh, make it right for Jesus' sake! If there is anything that I can do to help, show me how, and don't let me make mistakes. Oh, Jesus, Thy power is great. Let this young man feel it and yield himself to it."

She remained silently praying for a moment more, putting her whole soul into the prayer and knowing that she had been called thus to pray for him until her prayer was answered.

She came down to dinner a few minutes later with a calm, serene face, on which was no hint of her recent emotion, and she managed to keep the table conversation wholly in her own hands, telling Mr. Tanner about her home town and her father and mother. When the meal was finished the minister had no excuse to think that the new teacher was careless about her friends and associates, and he was well informed about the high principles of her family.

But West had retired into a sulky mood and uttered not a word except to ask for more chicken and coffee and a second helping of pie. It was, perhaps, during that dinner that he decided it would be best for him to preach in Ashland on the following Sunday. The young lady could be properly impressed with his dignity in no other way.

CHAPTER XII

When Lance Gardley came back to the Tanners' the sun was preparing the glory of its evening setting, and the mountain was robed in all its rosiest veils.

Margaret was waiting for him, with the dog Captain beside her, wandering back and forth in the unfenced dooryard and watching her mountain. It was a relief to her to find that the minister occupied a room on the first floor in a kind of ell on the opposite side of the house from her own room and her mountain. He had not been visible that afternoon, and with Captain by her side and Bud on the front-door step reading *The Sky Pilot* she felt comparatively safe. She had read to Bud for an hour and a half, and he was thoroughly interested in the story; but she was sure he would keep the minister away at all costs. As for Captain, he and the minister were sworn enemies by this time. He growled every time West came near or spoke to her.

She made a picture standing with her hand on Captain's shaggy, noble head, the lace of her sleeve falling back from the white arm, her other hand raised to shade her face as she looked away to the glorified mountain, a slim, white figure looking wistfully off at the sunset. The young man took off his hat and rode his horse more softly, as if in the presence of the holy.

The dog lifted one ear, and a tremor passed through his frame as the rider drew near; otherwise he did not stir from his position; but it was enough. The girl turned, on the alert at once, and met him with a smile, and the young man looked at her as if an angel had deigned to smile upon him. There was a humility in his fine face that sat well with the courage written there, and smoothed away all hardness for the time, so that the girl, looking at him in the light of the revelations of the morning, could hardly believe it had been true, yet an inner fineness of perception taught her that it was.

The young man dismounted and left his horse standing quietly by the roadside. He would not stay, he said, yet lingered by her side, talking for a few minutes, watching the sunset and pointing out its changes.

She gave him the little package for Mom Wallis. There was a simple lace collar in a little white box, and a tiny leather-bound book done in russet suède with gold lettering.

"Tell her to wear the collar and think of me whenever she dresses up."

"I'm afraid that'll never be, then," said the young man, with a pitying smile. "Mom Wallis never dresses up."

"Tell her I said she must dress up evenings for supper, and I'll make her another one to change with that and bring it when I come."

He smiled upon her again, that wondering, almost worshipful smile, as if he wondered if she were real, after all, so different did she seem from his idea of girls.

"And the little book," she went on, apologetically; "I suppose it was foolish to send it, but something she said made me think of some of the lines in the poem. I've marked them for her. She reads, doesn't she?"

"A little, I think. I see her now and then read the papers that Pop brings home with him. I don't fancy her literary range is very wide, however."

"Of course, I suppose it is ridiculous! And maybe she'll not understand any of it; but tell her I sent her a message. She must see if she can find it in the poem. Perhaps you can explain it to her. It's Browning's 'Rabbi Ben Ezra.' You know it, don't you?"

"I'm afraid not. I was intent on other things about the time when I was supposed to be giving my attention to Browning, or I wouldn't be what I am to-day, I suppose. But I'll do my best with what wits I have. What's it about? Couldn't you give me a pointer or two?"

"It's the one beginning:

"Grow old along with me!
The best is yet to be,
The last of life, for which the first was made:
Our times are in His hand
Who saith, 'A whole I planned,
Youth shows but half; trust God: see all, nor be afraid!'"

He looked down at her still with that wondering smile. "Grow old along with you!" he said, gravely, and then sighed. "You don't look as if you ever would grow old."

"That's it," she said, eagerly. "That's the whole idea. We don't ever grow old and get done with it all, we just go on to bigger things, wiser and better and more beautiful, till we come to understand and be a part of the whole great plan of God!"

He did not attempt an answer, nor did he smile now, but just looked at her with that deeply quizzical, grave look as if his soul were turning over the matter seriously. She held her peace and waited, unable to find the right word to speak. Then he turned and looked off, an infinite regret growing in his face.

"That makes living a different thing from the way most people take it," he said, at last, and his tone showed that he was considering it deeply.

"Does it?" she said, softly, and looked with him toward the sunset, still half seeing his quiet profile against the light. At last it came to her that she must speak. Half fearfully she began: "I've been thinking about what you said on the ride. You said you didn't make good. I—wish you would. I—I'm sure you could—"

She looked up wistfully and saw the gentleness come into his face as if the fountain of his soul, long sealed, had broken up, and as if he saw a possibility before him for the first time through the words she had spoken.

At last he turned to her with that wondering smile again. "Why should you care?" he asked. The words would have sounded harsh if his tone had not been so gentle.

Margaret hesitated for an answer. "I don't know how to tell it," she said, slowly. "There's another verse, a few lines more in that poem, perhaps you know them?—

'All I never could be, All, men ignored in me,

This I was worth to God, whose wheel the pitcher shaped.'

I want it because—well, perhaps because I feel you are worth all that to God. I would like to see you be that."

He looked down at her again, and was still so long that she felt she had failed miserably.

"I hope you will excuse my speaking," she added. "I—It seems there are so many grand possibilities in life, and for you—I couldn't bear to have you say you hadn't made good, as if it were all over."

"I'm glad you spoke," he said, quickly. "I guess perhaps I have been all kinds of a fool. You have made me feel how many kinds I have been."

"Oh no!" she protested.

"You don't know what I have been," he said, sadly, and then with sudden conviction, as if he read her thoughts: "You *do* know! That prig of a parson has told you! Well, it's just as well you should know. It's right!"

A wave of misery passed over his face and erased all its brightness and hope. Even the gentleness was gone. He looked haggard and drawn with hopelessness all in a moment.

"Do you think it would matter to me—*anything* that man would say?" she protested, all her woman's heart going out in pity.

"But it was true, all he said, probably, and more—"

"It doesn't matter," she said, eagerly. "The other is true, too. Just as the poem says, 'All that man ignores in you, just that you are worth to God!' And you *can* be what He meant you to be. I have been praying all the afternoon that He would help you to be."

"Have you?" he said, and his eyes lit up again as if the altar-fires of hope were burning once more. "Have you? I thank you."

"You came to me when I was lost in the wilderness," she said, shyly. "I wanted to help *you* back—if—I might."

"You will help—you have!" he said, earnestly. "And I was far enough off the trail, too, but if there's any way to get back I'll get there." He grasped her hand and held it for a second. "Keep up that praying," he said. "I'll see what can be done."

Margaret looked up. "Oh, I'm so glad, so glad!"

He looked reverently into her eyes, all the manhood in him stirred to higher, better things. Then, suddenly, as they stood together, a sound smote their ears as from another world.

"Um! Ah!—"

The minister stood within the doorway, barred by Bud in scowling defiance, and guarded by Cap, who gave an answering growl.

Gardley and Margaret looked at each other and smiled, then turned and walked slowly down to where the pony stood. They did not wish to talk here in that alien presence. Indeed, it seemed that more words were not needed— they would be a desecration.

So he rode away into the sunset once more with just another look and a hand-clasp, and she turned, strangely happy at heart, to go back to her dull surroundings and her uncongenial company.

"Come, William, let's have a praise service," she said, brightly, pausing at the doorway, but ignoring the scowling minister.

"A praise service! What's a praise service?" asked the wondering Bud, shoving over to let her sit down beside him.

She sat with her back to West, and Cap came and lay at her feet with the white of one eye on the minister and a growl ready to gleam between his teeth any minute. There was just no way for the minister to get out unless he jumped over them or went out the back door; but the people in the doorway had the advantage of not having to look at him, and he couldn't very well dominate the conversation standing so behind them.

"Why, a praise service is a service of song and gladness, of course. You sing, don't you? Of course. Well, what shall we sing? Do you know this?" And she broke softly into song:

"When peace like a river attendeth my way;
When sorrows like sea-billows roll;
Whatever my lot Thou hast taught me to say,
It is well, it is well with my soul."

Bud did not know the song, but he did not intend to be balked with the minister standing right behind him, ready, no doubt, to jump in and take the precedence; so he growled away at a note in the bass, turning it over and over and trying to make it fit, like a dog gnawing at a bare bone; but he managed to keep time and make it sound a little like singing.

The dusk was falling fast as they finished the last verse, Margaret singing the words clear and distinct, Bud growling unintelligibly and snatching at words he had never heard before. Once more Margaret sang:

"Abide with me; fast falls the eventide;
The darkness deepens; Lord, with me abide!
When other refuge fails and comforts flee,
Help of the helpless, oh, abide with me!"

188

Out on the lonely trail wending his way toward the purple mountain—the silent way to the bunk-house at the camp—in that clear air where sound travels a long distance the traveler heard the song, and something thrilled his soul. A chord that never had been touched in him before was vibrating, and its echoes would be heard through all his life.

On and on sang Margaret, just because she could not bear to stop and hear the commonplace talk which would be about her. Song after song thrilled through the night's wideness. The stars came out in thick clusters. Father Tanner had long ago dropped his weekly paper and tilted his chair back against the wall, with his eyes half closed to listen, and his wife had settled down comfortably on the carpet sofa, with her hands nicely folded in her lap, as if she were at church. The minister, after silently surveying the situation for a song or two, attempted to join his voice to the chorus. He had a voice like a cross-cut saw, but he didn't do much harm in the background that way, though Cap did growl now and then, as if it put his nerves on edge. And by and by Mr. Tanner quavered in with a note or two.

Finally Margaret sang:

> "Sun of my soul, Thou Saviour dear,
> It is not night if Thou art near,
> Oh, may no earth-born cloud arise
> To hide Thee from Thy servant's eyes."

During this hymn the minister had slipped out the back door and gone around to the front of the house. He could not stand being in the background any longer; but as the last note died away Margaret arose and, bidding Bud good night, slipped up to her room.

There, presently, beside her darkened window, with her face toward the mountain, she knelt to pray for the wanderer who was trying to find his way out of the wilderness.

CHAPTER XIII

Monday morning found Margaret at the school-house nerved for her new task.

One by one the scholars trooped in, shyly or half defiantly, hung their hats on the hooks, put their dinner-pails on the shelf, looked furtively at her, and sank into their accustomed seats; that is, the seats they had occupied during the last term of school. The big boys remained outside until Bud, acting under instructions from Margaret—after she had been carefully taught the ways of the school by Bud himself—rang the big bell. Even then they entered reluctantly and as if it were a great condescension that they came at all, Jed and "Delicate" coming in last, with scarcely a casual glance toward the teacher's desk, as if she were a mere fraction in the scheme of the school. She did not need to be told which was Timothy and which was Jed. Bud's description had been perfect. Her heart, by the way, instantly went out to Timothy. Jed was another proposition. He had thick, overhanging eyebrows, and a mouth that loved to make trouble and laugh over it. He was going to be hard to conquer. She wasn't sure the conquering would be interesting, either.

Margaret stood by the desk, watching them all with a pleasant smile. She did not frown at the unnecessary shuffling of feet nor the loud remarks of the boys as they settled into their seats. She just stood and watched them interestedly, as though her time had not yet come.

Jed and Timothy were carrying on a rumbling conversation. Even after they took their seats they kept it up. It was no part of their plan to let the teacher suppose they saw her or minded her in the least. They were the dominating influences in that school, and they wanted her to know it, right at the start; then a lot of trouble would be saved. If they didn't like her and couldn't manage her they didn't intend she should stay, and she might as well understand that at once.

Margaret understood it fully. Yet she stood quietly and watched them with a look of deep interest on her face and a light almost of mischief in her eyes, while Bud grew redder and redder over the way his two idols were treating the new teacher. One by one the school became aware of the twinkle in the teacher's eyes, and grew silent to watch, and one by one they began to smile over the coming scene when Jed and Timothy should discover it, and, worst of all, find out that it was actually directed against them. They would expect severity, or fear, or a desire to placate; but a twinkle—it was more than the school could decide what would happen under such circumstances. No one in that room would ever dare to laugh at either of those two boys. But the teacher was almost laughing now, and the twinkle had taken the rest of the room into the secret, while she waited amusedly until the two should finish the conversation.

The room grew suddenly deathly still, except for the whispered growls of Jed and Timothy, and still the silence deepened, until the two young giants themselves perceived that it was time to look up and take account of stock.

The perspiration by this time was rolling down the back of Bud's neck. He was about the only one in the room who was not on a broad grin, and he was wretched. What a fearful mistake the new teacher was making right at the start! She was antagonizing the two boys who held the whole school in their hands. There was no telling what they wouldn't do to her now. And he would have to stand up for her. Yes, no matter what they did, he would stand up for her! Even though he lost his best friends, he must be loyal to her; but the strain was terrible! He did not dare to look at them, but fastened his eyes upon Margaret, as if keeping them glued there was his only hope. Then suddenly he saw her face break into one of the sweetest, merriest smiles he ever witnessed, with not one single hint of reproach or offended dignity in it, just a smile of comradeship, understanding, and pleasure in the meeting; and it was directed to the two seats where Jed and Timothy sat.

With wonder he turned toward the two big boys, and saw, to his amazement, an answering smile upon their faces; reluctant, 'tis true, half sheepish at first, but a smile with lifted eyebrows of astonishment and real enjoyment of the joke.

A little ripple of approval went round in half-breathed syllables, but Margaret gave no time for any restlessness to start. She spoke at once, in her pleasantest partnership tone, such as she had used to Bud when she asked him to help her build her bookcase. So she spoke now to that school, and each one felt she was speaking just to him especially, and felt a leaping response in his soul. Here, at least, was something new and interesting, a new kind of teacher. They kept silence to listen.

"Oh, I'm not going to make a speech now," she said, and her voice sounded glad to them all. "I'll wait till we know one another before I do that. I just want to say how do you do to you, and tell you how glad I am to be here. I hope we shall like one another immensely and have a great many good times together. But we've got to get acquainted first, of course, and perhaps we'd better give most of the time to that to-day. First, suppose we sing something. What shall it be? What do you sing?"

Little Susan Johnson, by virtue of having seen the teacher at Sunday-school, made bold to raise her hand and suggest, "Thar-thpangle Banner, pleath!" And so they tried it; but when Margaret found that only a few seemed to know the words, she said, "Wait!" Lifting her arm with a pretty, imperative gesture, and taking a piece of chalk from the box on her desk, she went to the new blackboard that stretched its shining black length around the room.

The school was breathlessly watching the graceful movement of the beautiful hand and arm over the smooth surface, leaving behind it the clear, perfect script. Such wonderful writing they had never seen; such perfect, easy curves and twirls. Every eye in the room was fastened on her, every breath was held as they watched and spelled out the words one by one. "Gee!" said Bud, softly, under his breath, nor knew that he had spoken, but no one else moved.

"Now," she said, "let us sing," and when they started off again Margaret's strong, clear soprano leading, every voice in the room growled out the words and tried to get in step with the tune.

They had gone thus through two verses when Jed seemed to think it was about time to start something. Things were going altogether too smoothly for an untried teacher, if she *was* handsome and unabashed. If they went on like this the scholars would lose all respect for him. So, being quite able to sing a clear tenor, he nevertheless puckered his lips impertinently, drew his brows in an ominous frown, and began to whistle a somewhat erratic accompaniment to the song. He watched the teacher closely, expecting to see the color flame in her cheeks, the anger flash in her eyes; he had tried this trick on other teachers and it always worked. He gave the wink to Timothy, and he too left off his glorious bass and began to whistle.

But instead of the anger and annoyance they expected, Margaret turned appreciative eyes toward the two back seats, nodding her head a trifle and smiling with her eyes as she sang; and when the verse was done she held up her hand for silence and said:

"Why, boys, that's beautiful! Let's try that verse once more, and you two whistle the accompaniment a little stronger in the chorus; or how would it do if you just came in on the chorus? I believe that would be more effective. Let's try the first verse that way; you boys sing during the verse and then whistle the chorus just as you did now. We really need your voices in the verse part, they are so strong and splendid. Let's try it now." And she started off again, the two big astonished fellows meekly doing as they were told, and really the effect was beautiful. What was their surprise when the whole song was finished to have her say, "Now everybody whistle the chorus softly," and then pucker up her own soft lips to join in. That completely finished the whistling stunt. Jed realized that it would never work again, not while she was here, for she had turned the joke into beauty and made them all enjoy it. It hadn't annoyed her in the least.

Somehow by that time they were all ready for anything she had to suggest, and they watched again breathlessly as she wrote another song on the blackboard, taking the other side of the room for it, and this time a hymn—"I Need Thee Every Hour."

When they began to sing it, however, Margaret found the tune went slowly, uncertainly.

"Oh, how we need a piano!" she exclaimed. "I wonder if we can't get up an entertainment and raise money to buy one. How many will help?"

Every hand in the place went up, Jed's and Timothy's last and only a little way, but she noted with triumph that they went up.

"All right; we'll do it! Now let's sing that verse correctly." And she began to sing again, while they all joined anxiously in, really trying to do their best.

The instant the last verse died away, Margaret's voice took their attention.

"Two years ago in Boston two young men, who belonged to a little group of Christian workers who were going around from place to place holding meetings, sat talking together in their room in the hotel one evening."

There was instant quiet, a kind of a breathless quiet. This was not like the beginning of any lesson any other teacher had ever given them. Every eye was fixed on her.

"They had been talking over the work of the day, and finally one of them suggested that they choose a Bible verse for the whole year—"

There was a movement of impatience from one back seat, as if Jed had scented an incipient sermon, but the teacher's voice went steadily on:

"They talked it over, and at last they settled on II Timothy ii:15. They made up their minds to use it on every possible occasion. It was time to go to bed, so the man whose room adjoined got up and, instead of saying good night, he said, 'Well, II Timothy ii:15,' and went to his room. Pretty soon, when he put out his light, he knocked on the wall and shouted 'II Timothy ii:15,' and the other man responded, heartily, 'All right, II Timothy ii:15.' The next morning when they wrote their letters each of them wrote 'II Timothy ii:15' on the lower left-hand corner of the envelope, and sent out a great handful of letters to all parts of the world. Those letters passed through the Boston post-office, and some of the clerks who sorted them saw that queer legend written down in the lower left-hand corner of the envelope, and they wondered at it, and one or two wrote it down, to look it up afterward. The letters reached other cities and were put into the hands of mail-carriers to distribute, and they saw the queer little sentence, 'II Timothy ii:15,' and they wondered, and some of them looked it up."

By this time the entire attention of the school was upon the story, for they perceived that it was a story.

"The men left Boston and went across the ocean to hold meetings in other cities, and one day at a little railway station in Europe a group of people were gathered, waiting for a train, and those two men were among them. Pretty soon the train came, and one of the men got on the back end of the last car, while the other stayed on the platform, and as the train moved off the man on the last car took off his hat and said, in a good, loud, clear tone, 'Well, take care of yourself, II Timothy ii:15,' and the other one smiled and waved his hat and answered, 'Yes, II Timothy ii:15.' The man on the train, which was moving fast now, shouted back, 'II Timothy ii:15,' and the man on the platform responded still louder, waving his hat, 'II Timothy ii:15,' and back and forth the queer sentence was flung until the train was too far away for them to hear each other's voices. In the mean time all the people on the platform had been standing there listening and wondering what in the world such a strange salutation could mean. Some of them recognized what it was, but many did not know, and yet the sentence was said over so many times that they could not help remembering it; and some went away to recall it and ask their friends what it meant. A young man from America was on that platform and heard it, and he knew it stood for a passage in the Bible, and his curiosity was so great that he went back to his boarding-house and hunted up the Bible his mother had packed in his trunk when he came away from home, and he hunted through the Bible until he found the place, 'II Timothy ii:15,' and read it; and it made him think about his life and decide that he wasn't doing as he ought to do. I can't tell you all the story about that queer Bible verse, how it went here and there and what a great work it did in people's hearts; but one day those Christian workers went to Australia to hold some meetings, and one night, when the great auditorium was crowded, a man who was leading the meeting got up and told the story of this verse, how it had been chosen, and how it had gone over the world in strange ways, even told about the morning at the little railway station when the two men said good-by. Just as he got to that place in his story a man in the audience stood up and said: 'Brother, just let me say a word, please. I never knew anything about all this before, but I was at that railway station, and I heard those two men shout that strange good-by, and I went home and read that verse, and it's made a great difference in my life.'

"There was a great deal more to the story, how some Chicago policemen got to be good men through reading that verse, and how the story of the Australia meetings was printed in an Australian paper and sent to a lady in America who sent it to a friend in England to read about the meetings. And this friend in England had a son in the army in India, to whom she was sending a package, and she wrapped it around something in that package, and the young man read all about it, and it helped to change his life. Well, I thought of that story this morning when I was trying to decide what to read for our opening chapter, and it occurred to me that perhaps you would be interested to take that verse for our school verse this term, and so if you would like it I will put it on the blackboard. Would you like it, I wonder?"

She paused wistfully, as if she expected an answer, and there was a low, almost inaudible growl of assent; a keen listener might almost have said it had an impatient quality in it, as if they were in a hurry to find out what the verse was that had made such a stir in the world.

"Very well," said Margaret, turning to the board; "then I'll put it where we all can see it, and while I write it will you please say over where it is, so that you will remember it and hunt it up for yourselves in your Bibles at home?"

There was a sort of snicker at that, for there were probably not half a dozen Bibles, if there were so many, represented in that school; but they took her hint as she wrote, and chanted, "II Timothy ii:15, II Timothy ii:15," and then spelled out after her rapid crayon, "Study to show thyself approved unto God, a workman that needeth not to be ashamed."

They read it together at her bidding, with a wondering, half-serious look in their faces, and then she said, "Now, shall we pray?"

The former teacher had not opened her school with prayer. It had never been even suggested in that school. It might have been a dangerous experiment if Margaret had attempted it sooner in her program. As it was, there was a shuffling of feet in the back seats at her first word; but the room, grew quiet again, perhaps out of curiosity to hear a woman's voice in prayer:

"Our Heavenly Father, we want to ask Thee to bless us in our work together, and to help us to be such workmen that we shall not need to be ashamed to show our work to Thee at the close of the day. For Christ's sake we ask it. Amen."

They did not have time to resent that prayer before she had them interested in something else. In fact, she had planned her whole first day out so that there should not be a minute for misbehavior. She had argued that if she could just get time to become acquainted with them she might prevent a lot of trouble before it ever started. Her first business was to win her scholars. After that she could teach them easily if they were once willing to learn.

She had a set of mental arithmetic problems ready which she propounded to them next, some of them difficult and some easy enough for the youngest child who could think, and she timed their answers and wrote on the board the names of those who raised their hands first and had the correct answers. The questions were put in a fascinating way, many of them having curious little catches in them for the scholars who were not on the alert, and Timothy presently discovered this and set himself to get every one, coming off victorious at the end. Even Jed roused himself and was interested, and some of the girls quite distinguished themselves.

When a half-hour of this was over she put the word "TRANSFIGURATION" on the blackboard, and set them to playing a regular game out of it. If some of the school-board had come in just then they might have lifted up hands of horror at the idea of the new teacher setting the whole school to playing a game. But they certainly would have been delightfully surprised to see a quiet and orderly room with bent heads and knit brows, all intent upon papers and pencils. Never before in the annals of that school had the first day held a full period of quiet or orderliness. It was expected to be a day of battle; a day of trying out the soul of the teacher and proving whether he or she were worthy to cope with the active minds and bodies of the young bullies of Ashland. But the expected battle had been forgotten. Every mind was busy with the matter in hand.

Margaret had given them three minutes to write as many words as they could think of, of three letters or more, beginning with T, and using only the letters in the word she had put on the board. When time was called there was a breathless rush to write a last word, and then each scholar had to tell how many words he had, and each was called upon to read his list. Some had only two or three, some had ten or eleven. They were allowed to mark their words, counting one for each person present who did not have that word and doubling if it were two syllables, and so on. Excitement ran high when it was discovered that some had actually made a count of thirty or forty, and when they started writing words beginning with R every head was bent intently from the minute time was started.

Never had three minutes seemed so short to those unused brains, and Jed yelled out: "Aw, gee! I only got three!" when time was called next.

It was recess-time when they finally finished every letter in that word, and, adding all up, found that Timothy had won the game. Was that school? Why, a barbecue couldn't be named beside it for fun! They rushed out to the school-yard with a shout, and the boys played leap-frog loudly for the first few minutes. Margaret, leaning her tired head in her hands, elbows on the window-seat, closing her eyes and gathering strength for the after-recess session, heard one boy say: "Wal, how d'ye like 'er?" And the answer came: "Gee! I didn't think she'd be that kind of a guy! I thought she'd be some stiff old Ike! Ain't she a peach, though?" She lifted up her head and laughed triumphantly to herself, her eyes alight, herself now strengthened for the fray. She wasn't wholly failing, then?

After recess there was a spelling-match, choosing sides, of course, "Because this is only the first day, and we must get acquainted before we can do real work, you know," she explained.

The spelling-match proved an exciting affair also, with new features that Ashland had never seen before. Here the girls began to shine into prominence, but there were very few good spellers, and they were presently reduced to two girls—Rosa Rogers, the beauty of the school, and Amanda Bounds, a stolid, homely girl with deep eyes and a broad brow.

"I'm going to give this as a prize to the one who stands up the longest," said Margaret, with sudden inspiration as she saw the boys in their seats getting restless; and she unpinned a tiny blue-silk bow that fastened her white collar.

The girls all said "Oh-h-h!" and immediately every one in the room straightened up. The next few minutes those two girls spelled for dear life, each with her eye fixed upon the tiny blue bow in the teacher's white hands. To own that bow, that wonderful, strange bow of the heavenly blue, with the graceful twist to the tie! What delight! The girl who won that would be the admired of all the school. Even the boys sat up and took notice, each secretly thinking that Rosa, the beauty, would get it, of course.

But she didn't; she slipped up on the word "receive," after all, putting the i before the e; and her stolid companion, catching her breath awesomely, slowly spelled it right and received the blue prize, pinned gracefully at the throat of her old brown gingham by the teacher's own soft, white fingers, while the school looked on admiringly and the blood rolled hotly up the back of her neck and spread over her face and forehead. Rosa, the beauty, went crestfallen to her seat.

It was at noon, while they ate their lunch, that Margaret tried to get acquainted with the girls, calling most of them by name, to their great surprise, and hinting of delightful possibilities in the winter's work. Then she slipped out among the boys and watched their sports, laughing and applauding when some one made a particularly fine play, as if she thoroughly understood and appreciated.

She managed to stand near Jed and Timothy just before Bud rang the bell. "I've heard you are great sportsmen," she said to them, confidingly. "And I've been wondering if you'll teach me some things I want to learn? I want to know how to ride and shoot. Do you suppose I could learn?"

"Sure!" they chorused, eagerly, their embarrassment forgotten. "Sure, you could learn fine! Sure, *we'll learn* you!"

And then the bell rang and they all went in.

The afternoon was a rather informal arrangement of classes and schedule for the next day, Margaret giving out slips of paper with questions for each to answer, that she might find out just where to place them; and while they wrote she went from one to another, getting acquainted, advising, and suggesting about what they wanted to study. It was all so new and wonderful to them! They had not been used to caring what they were to study. Now it almost seemed interesting.

But when the day was done, the school-house locked, and Bud and Margaret started for home, she realized that she was weary. Yet it was a weariness of success and not of failure, and she felt happy in looking forward to the morrow.

CHAPTER XIV

The minister had decided to preach in Ashland, and on the following Sabbath. It became apparent that if he wished to have any notice at all from the haughty new teacher he must do something at once to establish his superiority in her eyes. He had carefully gone over his store of sermons that he always carried with him, and decided to preach on "The Dynamics of Altruism."

Notices had been posted up in saloons and stores and post-office. He had made them himself after completely tabooing Mr. Tanner's kindly and blundering attempt, and they gave full information concerning "the Rev. Frederick West, Ph.D., of the vicinity of New York City, who had kindly consented to preach in the school-house on 'The Dynamics of Altruism.'"

Several of these elaborately printed announcements had been posted up on big trees along the trails, and in other conspicuous places, and there was no doubt but that the coming Sabbath services were more talked of than anything else in that neighborhood for miles around, except the new teacher and her extraordinary way of making all the scholars fall in love with her. It is quite possible that the Reverend Frederick might not have been so flattered at the size of his audience when the day came if he could have known how many of them came principally because they thought it would be a good opportunity to see the new teacher.

However, the announcements were read, and the preacher became an object of deep interest to the community when he went abroad. Under this attention he swelled, grew pleased, bland, and condescending, wearing an oily smile and bowing most conceitedly whenever anybody noticed him. He even began to drop his severity and silence at the table, toward the end of the week, and expanded into dignified conversation, mainly addressed to Mr. Tanner about the political situation in the State of Arizona. He was trying to impress the teacher with the fact that he looked upon her as a most insignificant mortal who had forfeited her right to his smiles by her headstrong and unseemly conduct when he had warned her about "that young ruffian."

Out on the trail Long Bill and Jasper Kemp paused before a tree that bore the Reverend Frederick's church notice, and read in silence while the wide wonder of the desert spread about them.

"What d'ye make out o' them cuss words, Jap?" asked Long Bill, at length. "D'ye figger the parson's goin' to preach on swearin' ur gunpowder?"

"Blowed ef I know," answered Jasper, eying the sign ungraciously; "but by the looks of him he can't say much to suit me on neither one. He resembles a yaller cactus bloom out in a rain-storm as to head, an' his smile is like some of them prickles on the plant. He can't be no 'sky-pilot' to me, not just yet."

"You don't allow he b'longs in any way to *her*?" asked Long Bill, anxiously, after they had been on their way for a half-hour.

"B'long to *her*? Meanin' the schoolmarm?"

"Yes; he ain't sweet on her nor nothin'?"

"Wal, I guess not," said Jasper, contentedly. "She's got eyes sharp's a needle. You don't size her up so small she's goin' to take to a sickly parson with yaller hair an' sleek ways when she's seen the Kid, do you?"

"Wal, no, it don't seem noways reasonable, but you never can tell. Women gets notions."

"She ain't that kind! You mark my words, *she ain't that kind*. I'd lay she'd punch the breeze like a coyote ef he'd make up to her. Just you wait till you see him. He's the most no-'count, measleyest little thing that ever called himself a man. My word! I'd like to see him try to ride that colt o' mine. I really would. It would be some sight for sore eyes, it sure would."

"Mebbe he's got a intellec'," suggested Long Bill, after another mile. "That goes a long ways with women-folks with a education."

"No chance!" said Jasper, confidently. "'Ain't got room fer one under his yaller thatch. You wait till you set your lamps on him once before you go to gettin' excited. Why, he ain't one-two-three with our missionary! Gosh! I wish *he'd* come back an' see to such goin's-on—I certainly do."

"Was you figgerin' to go to that gatherin' Sunday?"

"I sure was," said Jasper. "I want to see the show, an', besides, we might be needed ef things got too high-soundin'. It ain't good to have a creature at large that thinks he knows all there is to know. I heard him talk down to the post-office the day after that little party we had when the Kid shot out the lights to save Bunchy from killin' Crapster, an' it's my opinion he needs a good spankin'; but I'm agoin' to give him a fair show. I ain't much on religion myself, but I do like to see a square deal, especially in a parson. I've sized it up he needs a lesson."

"I'm with ye, Jap," said Long Bill, and the two rode on their way in silence.

Margaret was so busy and so happy with her school all the week that she quite forgot her annoyance at the minister. She really saw very little of him, for he was always late to breakfast, and she took hers early. She went to her room immediately after supper, and he had little opportunity for pursuing her acquaintance. Perhaps he judged that it would be wise to let her alone until after he had made his grand impression on Sunday, and let her "make up" to him.

It was not until Sunday morning that she suddenly recalled that he was to preach that day. She had indeed seen the notices, for a very large and elaborate one was posted in front of the school-house, and some anonymous artist had produced a fine caricature of the preacher in red clay underneath his name. Margaret had been obliged to remain after school Friday and remove as much of this portrait as she was able, not having been willing to make it a matter of discipline to discover the artist. In fact, it was so true to the model that the young teacher felt a growing sympathy for the one who had perpetrated it.

Margaret started to the school-house early Sunday morning, attended by the faithful Bud. Not that he had any more intention of going to Sunday-school than he had the week before, but it was pleasant to be the chosen escort of so popular a teacher. Even Jed and Timothy had walked home with her twice during the week. He did not intend to lose his place as nearest to her. There was only one to whom he would surrender that, and he was too far away to claim it often.

Margaret had promised to help in the Sunday-school that morning, for the woman who taught the little ones was still away with her sick neighbor, and on the way she persuaded Bud to help her.

"You'll be secretary for me, won't you, William?" she asked, brightly. "I'm going to take the left-front corner of the room for the children, and seat them on the recitation-benches, and that will leave all the back part of the room for the older people. Then I can use the blackboard and not disturb the rest."

"Secretary?" asked the astonished Bud. He was, so to speak, growing accustomed to surprises. "Secretary" did not sound like being "a nice little Sunday-school boy."

"Why, yes! take up the collection, and see who is absent, and so on. I don't know all the names, perhaps, and, anyhow, I don't like to do that when I have to teach!"

Artful Margaret! She had no mind to leave Bud floating around outside the school-house, and though she had ostensibly prepared her lesson and her blackboard illustration for the little children, she had hidden in it a truth for Bud—poor, neglected, devoted Bud!

The inefficient old man who taught the older people that day gathered his forces together and, seated with his back to the platform, his spectacles extended upon his long nose, he proceeded with the questions on the lesson-leaf, as usual, being more than ordinarily unfamiliar with them; but before he was half through he perceived by the long pauses between the questions and answers that he did not have the attention of his class. He turned slowly around to see what they were all looking at, and became so engaged in listening to the lesson the new teacher was drawing on the blackboard that he completely forgot to go on, until Bud, very important in his new position, rang the tiny desk-bell for the close of school, and Margaret, looking up, saw in dismay that she had been teaching the whole school.

While they were singing a closing hymn the room began to fill up, and presently came the minister, walking importantly beside Mr. Tanner, his chin flattened upward as usual, but bent in till it made a double roll over his collar, his eyes rolling importantly, showing much of their whites, his sermon, in an elaborate leather cover, carried conspicuously under his arm, and the severest of clerical coats and collars setting out his insignificant face.

Walking behind him in single file, measured step, just so far apart, came the eight men from the bunk-house— Long Bill, Big Jim, Fiddling Boss, Jasper Kemp, Fade-away Forbes, Stocky, Croaker, and Fudge; and behind them, looking like a scared rabbit, Mom Wallis scuttled into the back seat and sank out of sight. The eight men, however, ranged themselves across the front of the room on the recitation-bench, directly in front of the platform, removing a few small children for that purpose.

They had been lined up in a scowling row along the path as the minister entered, looking at them askance under his aristocratic yellow eyebrows, and as he neared the door the last man followed in his wake, then the next, and so on.

Margaret, in her seat half-way back at the side of the school-house near a window, saw through the trees a wide sombrero over a pair of broad shoulders; but, though she kept close watch, she did not see her friend of the wilderness enter the school-house. If he had really come to meeting, he was staying outside.

The minister was rather nonplussed at first that there were no hymn-books. It almost seemed that he did not know how to go on with divine service without hymn-books, but at last he compromised on the long-meter Doxology, pronounced with deliberate unction. Then, looking about for a possible pipe-organ and choir, he finally started it himself; but it is doubtful whether any one would have recognized the tune enough to help it on if Margaret had not for very shame's sake taken it up and carried it along, and so they came to the prayer and Bible-reading.

These were performed with a formal, perfunctory style calculated to impress the audience with the importance of the preacher rather than the words he was speaking. The audience was very quiet, having the air of reserving judgment for the sermon.

Margaret could not just remember afterward how it was she missed the text. She had turned her eyes away from the minister, because it somehow made her feel homesick to compare him with her dear, dignified father. Her mind had wandered, perhaps, to the sombrero she had glimpsed outside, and she was wondering how its owner was coming on with his resolves, and just what change they would mean in his life, anyway. Then suddenly she awoke to the fact that the sermon had begun.

CHAPTER XV

"Considered in the world of physics," began the lordly tones of the Reverend Frederick, "dynamics is that branch of mechanics that treats of the effects of forces in producing motion, and of the laws of motion thus produced; sometimes called kinetics, opposed to statics. It is the science that treats of the laws of force, whether producing equilibrium or motion; in this sense including both statics and kinetics. It is also applied to the forces producing or governing activity or movement of any kind; also the methods of such activity."

The big words rolled out magnificently over the awed gathering, and the minister flattened his chin and rolled his eyes up at the people in his most impressive way.

Margaret's gaze hastily sought the row of rough men on the front seat, sitting with folded arms in an attitude of attention, each man with a pair of intelligent eyes under his shaggy brows regarding the preacher as they might have regarded an animal in a zoo. Did they understand what had been said? It was impossible to tell from their serious faces.

"Philanthropy has been called the dynamics of Christianity; that is to say, it is Christianity in action," went on the preacher. "It is my purpose this morning to speak upon the dynamics of altruism. Now altruism is the theory that inculcates benevolence to others in subordination to self-interest; interested benevolence as opposed to disinterested; also, the practice of this theory."

He lifted his eyes to the audience once more and nodded his head slightly, as if to emphasize the deep truth he had just given them, and the battery of keen eyes before him never flinched from his face. They were searching him through and through. Margaret wondered if he had no sense of the ridiculous, that he could, to such an audience, pour forth such a string of technical definitions. They sounded strangely like dictionary language. She wondered if anybody present besides herself knew what the man meant or got any inkling of what his subject was. Surely he would drop to simpler language, now that he had laid out his plan.

It never occurred to her that the man was trying to impress *her* with his wonderful fluency of language and his marvelous store of wisdom. On and on he went in much the same trend he had begun, with now and then a flowery sentence or whole paragraph of meaningless eloquence about the "brotherhood of man"—with a roll to the r's in brotherhood.

Fifteen minutes of this profitless oratory those men of the wilderness endured, stolidly and with fixed attention; then, suddenly, a sentence of unusual simplicity struck them and an almost visible thrill went down the front seat.

"For years the church has preached a dead faith, without works, my friends, and the time has come to stop preaching faith! I repeat it—fellow-men. I repeat it. The time has come *to stop preaching faith* and begin to do good works!" He thumped the desk vehemently. "Men don't need a superstitious belief in a Saviour to save them from their sins; they need to go to work and save themselves! As if a man dying two thousand years ago on a cross could do any good to you and me to-day!"

It was then that the thrill passed down that front line, and Long Bill, sitting at their head, leaned slightly forward and looked full and frowning into the face of Jasper Kemp; and the latter, frowning back, solemnly winked one eye. Margaret sat where she could see the whole thing.

Immediately, still with studied gravity, Long Bill cleared his throat impressively, arose, and, giving the minister a full look in the eye, of the nature almost of a challenge, he turned and walked slowly, noisily down the aisle and out the front door.

The minister was visibly annoyed, and for the moment a trifle flustered; but, concluding his remarks had been too deep for the rough creature, he gathered up the thread of his argument and proceeded:

"We need to get to work at our duty toward our fellow-men. We need to down trusts and give the laboring-man a chance. We need to stop insisting that men shall believe in the inspiration of the entire Bible and get to work at something practical!"

The impressive pause after this sentence was interrupted by a sharp, rasping sound of Big Jim clearing his throat and shuffling to his feet. He, too, looked the minister full in the face with a searching gaze, shook his head sadly, and walked leisurely down the aisle and out of the door. The minister paused again and frowned. This was becoming annoying.

Margaret sat in startled wonder. Could it be possible that these rough men were objecting to the sermon from a theological point of view, or was it just a happening that they had gone out at such pointed moments. She sat back after a minute, telling herself that of course the men must just have been weary of the long sentences, which no doubt they could not understand. She began to hope that Gardley was not within hearing. It was not probable that many others understood enough to get harm from the sermon, but her soul boiled with indignation that a man could go forth and call himself a minister of an evangelical church and yet talk such terrible heresy.

Big Jim's steps died slowly away on the clay path outside, and the preacher resumed his discourse.

"We have preached long enough of hell and torment. It is time for a gospel of love to our brothers. Hell is a superstition of the Dark Ages. *There is no hell!*"

Fiddling Boss turned sharply toward Jasper Kemp, as if waiting for a signal, and Jasper gave a slight, almost imperceptible nod. Whereupon Fiddling Boss cleared his throat loudly and arose, faced the minister, and marched down the aisle, while Jasper Kemp remained quietly seated as if nothing had happened, a vacancy each side of him.

By this time the color began to rise in the minister's cheeks. He looked at the retreating back of Fiddling Boss, and then suspiciously down at the row of men, but every one of them sat with folded arms and eyes intent upon the sermon, as if their comrades had not left them. The minister thought he must have been mistaken and took up the broken thread once more, or tried to, but he had hopelessly lost the place in his manuscript, and the only clue that offered was a quotation of a poem about the devil; to be sure, the connection was somewhat abrupt, but he clutched it with his eye gratefully and began reading it dramatically:

"'Men don't believe in the devil now
As their fathers used to do—'"

But he had got no further when a whole clearing-house of throats sounded, and Fade-away Forbes stumbled to his feet frantically, bolting down the aisle as if he had been sent for. He had not quite reached the door when Stocky clumped after him, followed at intervals by Croaker and Fudge, and each just as the minister had begun:

"Um! Ah! To resume—"

And now only Jasper Kemp remained of the front-seaters, his fine gray eyes boring through and through the minister as he floundered through the remaining portion of his manuscript up to the point where it began, "And finally—" which opened with another poem:

"'I need no Christ to die for me.'"

196

The sturdy, gray-haired Scotchman suddenly lowered his folded arms, slapping a hand resoundingly on each knee, bent his shoulders the better to pull himself to his feet, pressing his weight on his hands till his elbows were akimbo, uttered a deep sigh and a, "Yes—well—*ah*!"

With that he got to his feet and dragged them slowly out of the school-house.

By this time the minister was ready to burst with indignation. Never before in all the bombastic days of his egotism had he been so grossly insulted, and by such rude creatures! And yet there was really nothing that could be said or done. These men appeared to be simple creatures who had wandered in idly, perhaps for a few moments' amusement, and, finding the discourse above their caliber, had innocently wandered out again. That was the way it had been made to appear. But his plans had been cruelly upset by such actions, and he was mortified in the extreme. His face was purple with his emotions, and he struggled and spluttered for a way out of his trying dilemma. At last he spoke, and his voice was absurdly dignified:

"Is there—ah—any other—ah—auditor—ah—who is desirous of withdrawing before the close of service? If so he may do so now, or—ah—" He paused for a suitable ending, and familiar words rushed to his lips without consciousness for the moment of their meaning—"or forever after hold their peace—ah!"

There was a deathly silence in the school-house. No one offered to go out, and Margaret suddenly turned her head and looked out of the window. Her emotions were almost beyond her control.

Thus the closing eloquence proceeded to its finish, and at last the service was over. Margaret looked about for Mom Wallis, but she had disappeared. She signed to Bud, and together they hastened out; but a quiet Sabbath peace reigned about the door of the school-house, and not a man from the camp was in sight; no, nor even the horses upon which they had come.

And yet, when the minister had finished shaking hands with the worshipful women and a few men and children, and came with Mr. Tanner to the door of the school-house, those eight men stood in a solemn row, four on each side of the walk, each holding his chin in his right hand, his right elbow in his left hand, and all eyes on Jasper Kemp, who kept his eyes thoughtfully up in the sky.

"H'w aire yeh, Tanner? Pleasant 'casion. Mind steppin' on a bit? We men wanta have a word with the parson."

Mr. Tanner stepped on hurriedly, and the minister was left standing nonplussed and alone in the doorway of the school-house.

CHAPTER XVI

"Um! Ah!" began the minister, trying to summon his best clerical manner to meet—what? He did not know. It was best to assume they were a penitent band of inquirers for the truth. But the memory of their recent exodus from the service was rather too clearly in his mind for his pleasantest expression to be uppermost toward these rough creatures. Insolent fellows! He ought to give them a good lesson in behavior!

"Um! Ah!" he began again, but found to his surprise that his remarks thus far had had no effect whatever on the eight stolid countenances before him. In fact, they seemed to have grown grim and menacing even in their quiet attitude, and their eyes were fulfilling the promise of the look they had given him when they left the service.

"What does all this mean, anyway?" he burst forth, suddenly.

"Calm yourself, elder! Calm yourself," spoke up Long Bill. "There ain't any occasion to get excited."

"I'm not an elder; I'm a minister of the gospel," exploded West, in his most pompous tones. "I should like to know who you are and what all this means?"

"Yes, parson, we understand who you are. We understand quite well, an' we're agoin' to tell you who we are. We're a band of al-tru-ists! That's what we are. We're *altruists*!" It was Jasper Kemp of the keen eyes and sturdy countenance who spoke. "And we've come here in brotherly love to exercise a little of that dynamic force of altruism you was talkin' about. We just thought we'd begin on you so's you could see that we got some works to go 'long with our faith."

"What do you mean, sir?" said West, looking from one grim countenance to another. "I—I don't quite understand." The minister was beginning to be frightened, he couldn't exactly tell why. He wished he had kept Brother Tanner with him. It was the first time he had ever thought of Mr. Tanner as "brother."

"We mean just this, parson; you been talkin' a lot of lies in there about there bein' no Saviour an' no hell, ner no devil, an' while we ain't much credit to God ourselves, bein' just common men, we know all that stuff you said ain't true about the Bible an' the devil bein' superstitions, an' we thought we better exercise a little of that there altruism you was talkin' about an' teach you better. You see, it's real brotherly kindness, parson. An' now we're goin' to give you a sample of that dynamics you spoke about. Are you ready, boys?"

"All ready," they cried as one man.

There seemed to be no concerted motion, nor was there warning. Swifter than the weaver's shuttle, sudden as the lightning's flash, the minister was caught from where he stood pompously in that doorway, hat in hand, all grandly as he was attired, and hurled from man to man. Across the walk and back; across and back; across and back; until it seemed to him it was a thousand miles all in a minute of time. He had no opportunity to prepare for the onslaught. He jammed his high silk hat, wherewith he had thought to overawe the community, upon his sleek head, and grasped his precious sermon-case to his breast; the sermon, as it well deserved, was flung to the four winds of heaven and fortunately was no more—that is, existing as a whole. The time came when each of those eight men recovered and retained a portion of that learned oration, and Mom Wallis, not quite understanding, pinned up and used as a sort of shrine the portion about doubting the devil; but as a sermon the parts were never assembled on this earth, nor could be, for some of it was ground to powder under eight pairs of ponderous heels. But the minister at that trying moment was too much otherwise engaged to notice that the child of his brain lay scattered on the ground.

Seven times he made the round up and down, up and down that merciless group, tossed like a thistle-down from man to man. And at last, when his breath was gone, when the world had grown black before him, and he felt smaller and more inadequate than he had ever felt in his whole conceited life before, he found himself bound, helplessly bound, and cast ignominiously into a wagon. And it was a strange thing that, though seemingly but five short minutes before the place had been swarming with worshipful admirers thanking him for his sermon, now there did not seem to be a creature within hearing, for he called and cried aloud and roared with his raucous voice until it would seem that all the surrounding States might have heard that cry from Arizona, yet none came to his relief.

They carried him away somewhere, he did not know where; it was a lonely spot and near a water-hole. When he protested and loudly blamed them, threatening all the law in the land upon them, they regarded him as one might a naughty child who needed chastisement, leniently and with sorrow, but also with determination.

They took him down by the water's side and stood him up among them. He began to tremble with fear as he looked from one to another, for he was not a man of courage, and he had heard strange tales of this wild, free land, where every man was a law unto himself. Were they going to drown him then and there? Then up spoke Jasper Kemp:

"Mr. Parson," he said, and his voice was kind but firm; one might almost say there was a hint of humor in it, and there surely was a twinkle in his eye; but the sternness of his lips belied it, and the minister was in no state to appreciate humor—"Mr. Parson, we've brought you here to do you good, an' you oughtn't to complain. This is altruism, an' we're but actin' out what you been preachin'. You're our brother an' we're tryin' to do you good; an' now we're about to show you what a dynamic force we are. You see, Mr. Parson, I was brought up by a good Scotch grandmother, an' I know a lie when I hear it, an' when I hear a man preach error I know it's time to set him straight; so now we're agoin' to set you straight. I don't know where you come from, nor who brang you up, nor what church set you afloat, but I know enough by all my grandmother taught me—even if I hadn't been a-listenin' off and on for two years back to Mr. Brownleigh, our missionary—to know you're a dangerous man to have at large. I'd as soon have a mad dog let loose. Why, what you preach ain't the gospel, an' it ain't the truth, and the time has come for you to know it, an' own it and recant. Recant! That's what they call it. That's what we're here to see 't you do, or we'll know the reason why. That's the *dynamics* of it. See?"

The minister saw. He saw the deep, muddy water-hole. He saw nothing more.

"Folks are all too ready to believe them there things you was gettin' off without havin' 'em *preached* to justify 'em in their evil ways. We gotta think of those poor ignorant brothers of ours that might listen to you. See? That's the *altruism* of it!"

"What do you want me to do?" The wretched man's tone was not merely humble—it was abject. His grand Prince Albert coat was torn in three places; one tail hung down dejectedly over his hip; one sleeve was ripped half-way out. His collar was unbuttoned and the ends rode up hilariously over his cheeks. His necktie was gone. His sleek hair stuck out in damp wisps about his frightened eyes, and his hat had been "stove in" and jammed down as far as it would go until his ample ears stuck out like sails at half-mast. His feet were imbedded in the heavy mud on the margin of the water-hole, and his fine silk socks, which had showed at onetime above the erstwhile neat tyings, were torn and covered with mud.

"Well, in the first place," said Jasper Kemp, with a slow wink around at the company, "that little matter about hell needs adjustin'. Hell ain't no superstition. I ain't dictatin' what kind of a hell there is; you can make it fire or water or anything else you like, but *there is a hell*, an' *you believe in it*. D'ye understand? We'd just like to have you make that statement publicly right here an' now."

"But how can I say what I don't believe?" whined West, almost ready to cry. He had come proudly through a trial by Presbytery on these very same points, and had posed as being a man who had the courage of his convictions. He could not thus easily surrender his pride of original thought and broad-mindedness. He had received congratulations from a number of noble martyrs who had left their chosen church for just such reasons, congratulating him on his brave stand. It had been the first notice from big men he had ever been able to attract to himself, and it had gone to his head like wine. Give that up for a few miserable cowboys! It might get into the papers and go back East. He must think of his reputation.

"That's just where the dynamics of the thing comes in, brother," said Jasper Kemp, patronizingly. "We're here to *make* you believe in a hell. We're the force that will bring you back into the right way of thinkin' again. Are you ready, boys?"

The quiet utterance brought goose-flesh up to West's very ears, and his eyes bulged with horror.

"Oh, that isn't necessary! I believe—yes, I believe in hell!" he shouted, as they seized him.

But it was too late. The Rev. Frederick West was plunged into the water-hole, from whose sheep-muddied waters he came up spluttering, "Yes, I believe in *hell*!" and for the first time in his life, perhaps, he really did believe in it, and thought that he was in it.

The men were standing knee-deep in the water and holding their captive lightly by his arms and legs, their eyes upon their leader, waiting now.

Jasper Kemp stood in the water, also, looking down benevolently upon his victim, his chin in his hand, his elbow in his other hand, an attitude which carried a feeling of hopelessness to the frightened minister.

"An' now there's that little matter of the devil," said Jasper Kemp, reflectively. "We'll just fix that up next while we're near his place of residence. You believe in the devil, Mr. Parson, from now on? If you'd ever tried resistin' him I figger you'd have b'lieved in him long ago. But *you believe in him* from *now on*, an' you *don't preach against him any more*! We're not goin' to have our Arizona men gettin' off their guard an' thinkin' their enemy is dead. There *is* a devil, parson, and you believe in him! Duck him, boys!"

Down went the minister into the water again, and came up spluttering, "Yes, I—I—I—believe—in-the—devil." Even in this strait he was loath to surrender his pet theme—no devil.

"Very well, so far as it goes," said Jasper Kemp, thoughtfully. "But now, boys, we're comin' to the most important of all, and you better put him under about three times, for there mustn't be no mistake about this matter. You believe in the Bible, parson—*the whole Bible*?"

"Yes!" gasped West, as he went down the first time and got a mouthful of the bitter water, "I believe—" The voice was fairly anguished. Down he went again. Another mouthful of water. "*I believe in the whole Bible!*" he screamed, and went down the third time. His voice was growing weaker, but he came up and reiterated it without request, and was lifted out upon the mud for a brief respite. The men of the bunk-house were succeeding better than the Presbytery back in the East had been able to do. The conceit was no longer visible in the face of the Reverend Frederick. His teeth were chattering, and he was beginning to see one really needed to believe in something when one came as near to his end as this.

"There's just one more thing to reckon with," said Jasper Kemp, thoughtfully. "That line of talk you was handin' out about a man dyin' on a cross two thousand years ago bein' nothin' to you. You said you *an' me*, but you can speak for *yourself*. We may not be much to look at, but we ain't goin' to stand for no such slander as that. Our missionary preaches all about that Man on the Cross, an' if you don't need Him before you get through this little campaign of life I'll miss my guess. Mebbe we haven't been all we might have been, but we ain't agoin' to let you ner no one else go back on that there Cross!"

Jasper Kemp's tone was tender and solemn. As the minister lay panting upon his back in the mud he was forced to acknowledge that at only two other times in his life had a tone of voice so arrested his attention and filled him with awe; once when as a boy he had been caught copying off another's paper at examination-time, and he had been sent to the principal's office; and again on the occasion of his mother's funeral, as he sat in the dim church a few years ago and listened to the old minister. For a moment now he was impressed with the wonder of the Cross, and it suddenly seemed as if he were being arraigned before the eyes of Him with Whom we all have to do. A kind of shame stole into his pale, flabby face, all the smugness and complacence gone, and he a poor wretch in the hands of his accusers. Jasper Kemp, standing over him on the bank, looking down grimly upon him, seemed like the emissary of God sent to condemn him, and his little, self-centered soul quailed within him.

"Along near the end of that discourse of yours you mentioned that sin was only misplaced energy. Well, if that's so there's a heap of your energy gone astray this mornin', an' the time has come for you to pay up. Speak up now an' say what you believe or whether you want another duckin'—an' it'll be seven times this time!"

The man on the ground shut his eyes and gasped. The silence was very solemn. There seemed no hint of the ridiculous in the situation. It was serious business now to all those men. Their eyes were on their leader.

"Do you solemnly declare before God—I s'pose you still believe in a God, as you didn't say nothin' to the contrary—that from now on you'll stand for that there Cross and for Him that hung on it?"

The minister opened his eyes and looked up into the wide brightness of the sky, as if he half expected to see horses and chariots of fire standing about to do battle with him then and there, and his voice was awed and frightened as he said:

"I do!"

There was silence, and the men stood with half-bowed heads, as if some solemn service were being performed that they did not quite understand, but in which they fully sympathized. Then Jasper Kemp said, softly:

"Amen!" And after a pause: "I ain't any sort of a Christian myself, but I just can't stand it to see a parson floatin' round that don't even know the name of the firm he's workin' for. Now, parson, there's just one more requirement, an' then you can go home."

The minister opened his eyes and looked around with a frightened appeal, but no one moved, and Jasper Kemp went on:

"You say you had a church in New York. What was the name and address of your workin'-boss up there?"

"What do you mean? I hadn't any boss."

"Why, him that hired you an' paid you. The chief elder or whatever you called him."

"Oh!" The minister's tone expressed lack of interest in the subject, but he answered, languidly, "Ezekiel Newbold, Hazelton."

"Very good. Now, parson, you'll just kindly write two copies of a letter to Mr. Ezekiel Newbold statin' what you've just said to us concernin' your change of faith, sign your name, address one to Mr. Newbold, an' give the duplicate to me. We just want this little matter put on record so you can't change your mind any in future. Do you get my idea?"

"Yes," said the minister, dispiritedly.

"Will you do it?"

"Yes," apathetically.

"Well, now I got a piece of advice for you. It would be just as well for your health for you to leave Arizona about as quick as you can find it convenient to pack, but you won't be allowed to leave this town, day or night, cars or afoot, until them there letters are all O.K. Do you get me?"

"Yes," pathetically.

"I might add, by way of explainin', that if you had come to Arizona an' minded your own business you wouldn't have been interfered with. You mighta preached whatever bosh you darned pleased so far as we was concerned, only you wouldn't have had no sorta audience after the first try of that stuff you give to-day. But when you come to Arizona an' put your fingers in other folks' pie, when you tried to 'squeal' on the young gentleman who was keen enough to shoot out the lights to save a man's life, why, we 'ain't no further use for you. In the first place, you was all wrong. You thought the Kid shot out the lights to steal the gamin'-money; but he didn't. He put it all in the hands of the sheriff some hours before your 'private information' reached him through the mail. You thought you were awful sharp, you little sneak! But I wasn't the only man present who saw you put your foot out an' cover a gold piece that rolled on the floor just when the fight began. You thought nobody was a-lookin', but you'll favor us, please, with that identical gold piece along with the letter before you leave. Well, boys, that'll be about all, then. Untie him!"

In silence and with a kind of contemptuous pity in their faces the strong men stooped and unbound him; then, without another word, they left him, tramping solemnly away single file to their horses, standing at a little distance.

Jasper Kemp lingered for a moment, looking down at the wretched man. "Would you care to have us carry you back to the house?" he asked, reflectively.

"No!" said the minister, bitterly. "No!" And without another word Jasper Kemp left him.

Into the mesquite-bushes crept the minister, his glory all departed, and hid his misery from the light, groaning in bitterness of spirit. He who had made the hearts of a score of old ministers to sorrow for Zion, who had split in two a pleasantly united congregation, disrupted a session, and brought about a scandalous trial in Presbytery was at last conquered. The Rev. Frederick West had recanted!

CHAPTER XVII

When Margaret left the school-house with Bud she had walked but a few steps when she remembered Mom Wallis and turned back to search for her; but nowhere could she find a trace of her, and the front of the school-house was as empty of any people from the camp as if they had not been there that morning. The curtain had not yet risen for the scene of the undoing of West.

"I suppose she must have gone home with them," said the girl, wistfully. "I'm sorry not to have spoken with her. She was good to me."

"You mean Mom Wallis?" said the boy. "No, she ain't gone home. She's hiking 'long to our house to see you. The Kid went along of her. See, there—down by those cottonwood-trees? That's them."

Margaret turned with eagerness and hurried along with Bud now. She knew who it was they called the Kid in that tone of voice. It was the way the men had spoken of and to him, a mingling of respect and gentling that showed how much beloved he was. Her cheeks wore a heightened color, and her heart gave a pleasant flutter of interest.

They walked rapidly and caught up with their guests before they had reached the Tanner house, and Margaret had the pleasure of seeing Mom Wallis's face flush with shy delight when she caught her softly round the waist, stealing quietly up behind, and greeted her with a kiss. There had not been many kisses for Mom Wallis in the later years, and the two that were to Margaret Earle's account seemed very sweet to her. Mom Wallis's eyes shone as if she had been a young girl as she turned with a smothered "Oh!" She was a woman not given to expressing herself; indeed, it might be said that the last twenty years of her life had been mainly of self-repression. She gave that one little gasp of recognition and pleasure, and then she relapsed into embarrassed silence beside the two young people who found pleasure in their own greetings. Bud, boy-like, was after a cottontail, along with Cap, who had appeared from no one knew where and was attending the party joyously.

Mom Wallis, in her big, rough shoes, on the heels of which her scant brown calico gown was lifted as she walked, trudged shyly along between the two young people, as carefully watched and helped over the humps and bumps of the way as if she had been a princess. Margaret noticed with a happy approval how Gardley's hand was ready under the old woman's elbow to assist her as politely as he might have done for her own mother had she been walking by his side.

Presently Bud and Cap returned, and Bud, with observant eye, soon timed his step to Margaret's on her other side and touched her elbow lightly to help her over the next rut. This was his second lesson in manners from Gardley. He had his first the Sunday before, watching the two while he and Cap walked behind. Bud was learning. He had keen eyes and an alert brain. Margaret smiled understandingly at him, and his face grew deep red with pleasure.

"He was bringin' me to see where you was livin'," explained Mom Wallis, suddenly, nodding toward Gardley as if he had been a king. "We wasn't hopin' to see you, except mebbe just as you come by goin' in."

"Oh, then I'm so glad I caught up with you in time. I wouldn't have missed you for anything. I went back to look for you. Now you're coming in to dinner with me, both of you," declared Margaret, joyfully. "William, your mother will have enough dinner for us all, won't she?"

"Sure!" said Bud, with that assurance born of his life acquaintance with his mother, who had never failed him in a trying situation so far as things to eat were concerned.

Margaret looked happily from one of her invited guests to the other, and Gardley forgot to answer for himself in watching the brightness of her face, and wondering why it was so different from the faces of all other girls he knew anywhere.

But Mom Wallis was overwhelmed. A wave of red rolled dully up from her withered neck in its gala collar over her leathery face to the roots of her thin, gray hair.

"Me! Stay to dinner! Oh, I couldn't do that nohow! Not in these here clo'es. 'Course I got that pretty collar you give me, but I couldn't never go out to dinner in this old dress an' these shoes. I know what folks ought to look like an' I ain't goin' to shame you."

"Shame me? Nonsense! Your dress is all right, and who is going to see your shoes? Besides, I've just set my heart on it. I want to take you up to my room and show you the pictures of my father and mother and home and the church where I was christened, and everything."

Mom Wallis looked at her with wistful eyes, but still shook her head. "Oh, I'd like to mighty well. It's good of you to ast me. But I couldn't. I just couldn't. 'Sides, I gotta go home an' git the men's grub ready."

"Oh, can't she stay this time, Mr. Gardley?" appealed Margaret. "The men won't mind for once, will they?"

Gardley looked into her true eyes and saw she really meant the invitation. He turned to the withered old woman by his side. "Mom, we're going to stay," he declared, joyously. "She wants us, and we have to do whatever she says. The men will rub along. They all know how to cook. Mom, *we're going to stay.*"

"That's beautiful!" declared Margaret. "It's so nice to have some company of my own." Then her face suddenly sobered. "Mr. Wallis won't mind, will he?" And she looked with troubled eyes from one of her guests to the other. She did not want to prepare trouble for poor Mom Wallis when she went back.

Mom Wallis turned startled eyes toward her. There was contempt in her face and outraged womanhood. "Pop's gone off," she said, significantly. "He went yist'day. But he 'ain't got no call t' mind. I ben waitin' on Pop nigh on to twenty year, an' I guess I'm goin' to a dinner-party, now 't I'm invited. Pop 'd better *not* mind, I guess!"

And Margaret suddenly saw how much, how very much, her invitation had been to the starved old soul. Margaret took her guests into the stiff little parlor and slipped out to interview her landlady. She found Mrs. Tanner, as she had expected, a large-minded woman who was quite pleased to have more guests to sit down to her generous dinner, particularly as her delightful boarder had hinted of ample recompense in the way of board money; and she fluttered about, sending Tanner after another jar of pickles, some more apple-butter, and added another pie to the menu.

Well pleased, Margaret left Mrs. Tanner and slipped back to her guests. She found Gardley making arrangements with Bud to run back to the church and tell the men to leave the buckboard for them, as they would not be home for dinner. While this was going on she took Mom Wallis up to her room to remove her bonnet and smooth her hair.

It is doubtful whether Mom Wallis ever did see such a room in her life; for when Margaret swung open the door the poor little woman stopped short on the threshold, abashed, and caught her breath, looking around with wondering eyes and putting out a trembling hand to steady herself against the door-frame. She wasn't quite sure whether things in that room were real, or whether she might not by chance have caught a glimpse into heaven, so beautiful did it seem to her. It was not till her eyes, in the roving, suddenly rested on the great mountain framed in the open window that she felt anchored and sure that this was a tangible place. Then she ventured to step her heavy shoe inside the door. Even then she drew her ugly calico back apologetically, as if it were a desecration to the lovely room.

But Margaret seized her and drew her into the room, placing her gently in the rose-ruffled rocking-chair as if it were a throne and she a queen, and the poor little woman sat entranced, with tears springing to her eyes and trickling down her cheeks.

Perhaps it was an impossibility for Margaret to conceive what the vision of that room meant to Mom Wallis. The realization of all the dreams of a starved soul concentrated into a small space; the actual, tangible proof that there might be a heaven some day—who knew?—since beauties and comforts like these could be real in Arizona.

Margaret brought the pictures of her father and mother, of her dear home and the dear old church. She took her about the room and showed her the various pictures and reminders of her college days, and when she saw that the poor creature was overwhelmed and speechless she turned her about and showed her the great mountain again, like an anchorage for her soul.

Mom Wallis looked at everything speechlessly, gasping as her attention was turned from one object to another, as if she were unable to rise beyond her excitement; but when she saw the mountain again her tongue was loosed, and she turned and looked back at the girl wonderingly.

"Now, ain't it strange! Even that old mounting looks diffrunt—it do look diffrunt from a room like this. Why, it looks like it got its hair combed an' its best collar on!" And Mom Wallis looked down with pride and patted the simple net ruffle about her withered throat. "Why, it looks like a picter painted an' hung up on this yere wall, that's what that mounting looks like! It kinda ain't no mounting any more; it's jest a picter in your room!"

Margaret smiled. "It is a picture, isn't it? Just look at that silver light over the purple place. Isn't it wonderful? I like to think it's mine—my mountain. And yet the beautiful thing about it is that it's just as much yours, too. It will make a picture of itself framed in your bunk-house window if you let it. Try it. You just need to let it."

Mom Wallis looked at her wonderingly. "Do you mean," she said, studying the girl's lovely face, "that ef I should wash them there bunk-house winders, an' string up some posy caliker, an' stuff a chair, an' have a pin-cushion, I could make that there mounting come in an' set fer me like a picter the way it does here fer you?"

"Yes, that's what I mean," said Margaret, softly, marveling how the uncouth woman had caught the thought. "That's exactly what I mean. God's gifts will be as much to us as we will let them, always. Try it and see."

Mom Wallis stood for some minutes looking out reflectively at the mountain. "Wal, mebbe I'll try it!" she said, and turned back to survey the room again.

And now the mirror caught her eye, and she saw herself, a strange self in a soft white collar, and went up to get a nearer view, laying a toil-worn finger on the lace and looking half embarrassed at sight of her own face.

"It's a real purty collar," she said, softly, with a choke in her voice. "It's too purty fer me. I told him so, but he said as how you wanted I should dress up every night fer supper in it. It's 'most as strange as havin' a mounting come an' live with you, to wear a collar like that—me!"

Margaret's eyes were suddenly bright with tears. Who would have suspected Mom Wallis of having poetry in her nature? Then, as if her thoughts anticipated the question in Margaret's mind, Mom Wallis went on:

"He brang me your little book," she said. "I ain't goin' to say thank yeh, it ain't a big-'nuf word. An' he read me the poetry words it says. I got it wropped in a hankercher on the top o' the beam over my bed. I'm goin' to have it buried with me when I die. Oh, I *read* it. I couldn't make much out of it, but I read the words thorough. An' then *he* read 'em—the Kid did. He reads just beautiful. He's got education, he has. He read it, and he talked a lot about it. Was this what you mean? Was it that we ain't really growin' old at all, we're jest goin' on,*gettin'* there, if we go right? Did you mean you think Him as planned it all wanted some old woman right thar in the bunk-house, an' it's *me*? Did you mean there was agoin' to be a chanct fer me to be young an' beautiful somewheres in creation yit, 'fore I git through?"

The old woman had turned around from looking into the mirror and was facing her hostess. Her eyes were very bright; her cheeks had taken on an excited flush, and her knotted hands were clutching the bureau. She looked into Margaret's eyes earnestly, as though her very life depended upon the answer; and Margaret, with a great leap of her heart, smiled and answered:

"Yes, Mrs. Wallis, yes, that is just what I meant. Listen, these are God's own words about it: 'For I reckon that the sufferings of this present time are not worthy to be compared with the glory that shall be revealed in us.'"

A kind of glory shone in the withered old face now. "Did you say them was God's words?" she asked in an awed voice.

"Yes," said Margaret; "they are in the Bible."

"But you couldn't be sure it meant *me*?" she asked, eagerly. "They wouldn't go to put *me* in the Bible, o' course."

"Oh yes, you could be quite sure, Mrs. Wallis," said Margaret, gently. "Because if God was making you and had a plan for you, as the poem says, He would be sure to put down something in His book about it, don't you think? He would want you to know."

"It does sound reasonable-like now, don't it?" said the woman, wistfully. "Say them glory words again, won't you?"

Margaret repeated the text slowly and distinctly.

"Glory!" repeated Mom Wallis, wonderingly. "Glory! Me!" and turned incredulously toward the glass. She looked a long tune wistfully at herself, as if she could not believe it, and pulled reproachfully at the tight hair drawn away from her weather-beaten face. "I useta have purty hair onct," she said, sadly.

"Why, you have pretty hair now!" said Margaret, eagerly. "It just wants a chance to show its beauty, Here, let me fix it for dinner, will you?"

She whisked the bewildered old woman into a chair and began unwinding the hard, tight knot of hair at the back of her head and shaking it out. The hair was thin and gray now, but it showed signs of having been fine and thick once.

"It's easy to keep your hair looking pretty," said the girl, as she worked. "I'm going to give you a little box of my nice sweet-smelling soap-powder that I use to shampoo my hair. You take it home and wash your hair with it every two or three weeks and you'll see it will make a difference in a little while. You just haven't taken time to take care of it, that's all. Do you mind if I wave the front here a little? I'd like to fix your hair the way my mother wears hers."

Now nothing could have been further apart than this little weather-beaten old woman and Margaret's gentle, dove-like mother, with her abundant soft gray hair, her cameo features, and her pretty, gray dresses; but Margaret had a vision of what glory might bring to Mom Wallis, and she wanted to help it along. She believed that heavenly glory can be hastened a good deal on earth if one only tries, and so she set to work. Glancing out the window, she saw with relief that Gardley was talking interestedly with Mr. Tanner and seemed entirely content with their absence.

Mom Wallis hadn't any idea what "waving" her hair meant, but she readily consented to anything this wonderful girl proposed, and she sat entranced, looking at her mountain and thrilling with every touch of Margaret's satin fingers against her leathery old temples. And so, Sunday though it was, Margaret lighted her little alcohol-lamp and heated a tiny curling-iron which she kept for emergencies. In a few minutes' time Mom Wallis's astonished old gray locks lay soft and fluffy about her face, and pinned in a smooth coil behind, instead of the tight knot, making the most wonderful difference in the world in her old, tired face.

"Now look!" said Margaret, and turned her about to the mirror. "If there's anything at all you don't like about it I can change it, you know. You don't have to wear it so if you don't like it."

The old woman looked, and then looked back at Margaret with frightened eyes, and back to the vision in the mirror again.

"My soul!" she exclaimed in an awed voice. "My soul! It's come a'ready! Glory! I didn't think I could look like that! I wonder what Pop 'd say! My land! Would you mind ef I kep' it on a while an' wore it back to camp this way? Pop might uv come home an' I'd like to see ef he'd take notice to it. I used to be purty onct, but I never expected no sech thing like this again on earth. Glory! Glory! Mebbe I *could* get some glory, *too*."

"'The glory that shall be revealed' is a great deal more wonderful than this," said Margaret, gently. "This was here all the time, only you didn't let it come out. Wear it home that way, of course, and wear it so all the time. It's very little trouble, and you'll find your family will like it. Men always like to see a woman looking her best, even when she's working. It helps to make them good. Before you go home I'll show you how to fix it. It's quite simple. Come, now, shall we go down-stairs? We don't want to leave Mr. Gardley alone too long, and, besides, I smell the dinner. I think they'll be waiting for us pretty soon. I'm going to take a few of these pictures down to show Mr. Gardley."

She hastily gathered a few photographs together and led the bewildered little woman down-stairs again, and out in the yard, where Gardley was walking up and down now, looking off at the mountain. It came to Margaret, suddenly, that the minister would be returning to the house soon, and she wished he wouldn't come. He would be a false note in the pleasant harmony of the little company. He would be disagreeable to manage, and perhaps hurt poor Mom Wallis's feelings. Perhaps he had already come. She looked furtively around as she came out the door, but no minister was in sight, and then she forgot him utterly in the look of bewildered astonishment with which Gardley was regarding Mom Wallis.

He had stopped short in his walk across the little yard, and was staring at Mom Wallis, recognition gradually growing in his gaze. When he was fully convinced he turned his eyes to Margaret, as if to ask: "How did you do it? Wonderful woman!" and a look of deep reverence for her came over his face.

Then suddenly he noticed the shy embarrassment on the old woman's face, and swiftly came toward her, his hands outstretched, and, taking her bony hands in his, bowed low over them as a courtier might do.

"Mom Wallis, you are beautiful. Did you know it?" he said, gently, and led her to a little stumpy rocking-chair with a gay red-and-blue rag cushion that Mrs. Tanner always kept sitting by the front door in pleasant weather. Then he stood off and surveyed her, while the red stole into her cheeks becomingly. "What has Miss Earle been doing to glorify you?" he asked, again looking at her earnestly.

The old woman looked at him in awed silence. There was that word again—glory! He had said the girl had glorified her. There was then some glory in her, and it had been brought out by so simple a thing as the arrangement of her hair. It frightened her, and tears came and stood in her tired old eyes.

It was well for Mom Wallis's equilibrium that Mr. Tanner came out just then with the paper he had gone after, for the stolidity of her lifetime was about breaking up. But, as he turned, Gardley gave her one of the rarest smiles of sympathy and understanding that a young man can give to an old woman; and Margaret, watching, loved him for it. It seemed to her one of the most beautiful things a young man had ever done.

They had discussed the article in the paper thoroughly, and had looked at the photographs that Margaret had brought down; and Mrs. Tanner had come to the door numberless times, looking out in a troubled way down the road, only to trot back again, look in the oven, peep in the kettle, sigh, and trot out to the door again. At last she came and stood, arms akimbo, and looked down the road once more.

"Pa, I don't just see how I can keep the dinner waitin' a minute longer, The potatoes 'll be sp'iled. I don't see what's keepin' that preacher-man. He musta been invited out, though I don't see why he didn't send me word."

"That's it, likely, Ma," said Tanner. He was growing hungry. "I saw Mis' Bacon talkin' to him. She's likely invited him there. She's always tryin' to get ahead o' you, Ma, you know, 'cause you got the prize fer your marble cake."

Mrs. Tanner blushed and looked down apologetically at her guests. "Well, then, ef you'll just come in and set down, I'll dish up. My land! Ain't that Bud comin' down the road, Pa? He's likely sent word by Bud. I'll hurry in an' dish up."

Bud slid into his seat hurriedly after a brief ablution in the kitchen, and his mother questioned him sharply.

"Bud, wher you be'n? Did the minister get invited out?"

The boy grinned and slowly winked one eye at Gardley. "Yes, he's invited out, all right," he said, meaningly. "You don't need to wait fer him. He won't be home fer some time, I don't reckon."

Gardley looked keenly, steadily, at the boy's dancing eyes, and resolved to have a fuller understanding later, and his own eyes met the boy's in a gleam of mischief and sympathy.

It was the first time in twenty years that Mom Wallis had eaten anything which she had not prepared herself, and now, with fried chicken and company preserves before her, she could scarcely swallow a mouthful. To be seated beside Gardley and waited on like a queen! To be smiled at by the beautiful young girl across the table, and deferred to by Mr. and Mrs. Tanner as "Mrs. Wallis," and asked to have more pickles and another helping of jelly, and did she take cream and sugar in her coffee! It was too much, and Mom Wallis was struggling with the tears. Even Bud's round, blue eyes regarded her with approval and interest. She couldn't help thinking, if her own baby boy had lived, would he ever have been like Bud? And once she smiled at him, and Bud smiled back, a real boy-like, frank, hearty grin. It was all like taking dinner in the Kingdom of Heaven to Mom Wallis, and getting glory aforetime.

It was a wonderful afternoon, and seemed to go on swift wings. Gardley went back to the school-house, where the horses had been left, and Bud went with him to give further particulars about that wink at the dinner-table. Mom Wallis went up to the rose-garlanded room and learned how to wash her hair, and received a roll of flowered scrim wherewith to make curtains for the bunk-house. Margaret had originally intended it for the school-house windows in case it proved necessary to make that place habitable, but the school-room could wait.

And there in the rose-room, with the new curtains in her trembling hands, and the great old mountain in full view, Mom Wallis knelt beside the little gay rocking-chair, while Margaret knelt beside her and prayed that the Heavenly Father would show Mom Wallis how to let the glory be revealed in her now on the earth.

Then Mom Wallis wiped the furtive tears away with her calico sleeve, tied on her funny old bonnet, and rode away with her handsome young escort into the silence of the desert, with the glory beginning to be revealed already in her countenance.

Quite late that evening the minister returned.

He came in slowly and wearily, as if every step were a pain to him, and he avoided the light. His coat was torn and his garments were mud-covered. He murmured of a "slight accident" to Mrs. Tanner, who met him solicitously in a flowered dressing-gown with a candle in her hand. He accepted greedily the half a pie, with cheese and cold chicken and other articles, she proffered on a plate at his door, and in the reply to her query as to where he had been for dinner, and if he had a pleasant time, he said:

"Very pleasant, indeed, thank you! The name? Um—ah—I disremember! I really didn't ask—That is—"

The minister did not get up to breakfast, In fact, he remained in bed for several days, professing to be suffering with an attack of rheumatism. He was solicitously watched over and fed by the anxious Mrs. Tanner, who was much disconcerted at the state of affairs, and couldn't understand why she could not get the school-teacher more interested in the invalid.

On the fourth day, however, the Reverend Frederick crept forth, white and shaken, with his sleek hair elaborately combed to cover a long scratch on his forehead, and announced his intention of departing from the State of Arizona that evening.

He crept forth cautiously to the station as the shades of evening drew on, but found Long Bill awaiting him, and Jasper Kemp not far away. He had the two letters ready in his pocket, with the gold piece, though he had entertained hopes of escaping without forfeiting them, but he was obliged to wait patiently until Jasper Kemp had read both letters through twice, with the train in momentary danger of departing without him, before he was finally allowed to get on board. Jasper Kemp's parting word to him was:

"Watch your steps spry, parson. I'm agoin' to see that you're shadowed wherever you go. You needn't think you can get shy on the Bible again. It won't pay."

There was menace in the dry remark, and the Reverend Frederick's professional egotism withered before it. He bowed his head, climbed on board the train, and vanished from the scene of his recent discomfiture. But the bitterest thing about it all was that he had gone without capturing the heart or even the attention of that haughty little school-teacher. "And she was such a pretty girl," he said, regretfully, to himself. "Such a *very*pretty girl!" He sighed deeply to himself as he watched Arizona speed by the window. "Still," he reflected, comfortably, after a moment, "there are always plenty more! What was that remarkably witty saying I heard just before I left home? 'Never run after a street-car or a woman. There'll be another one along in a minute.' Um—ah—yes—very true—there'll be another one along in a minute."

CHAPTER XVIII

School had settled down to real work by the opening of the new week. Margaret knew her scholars and had gained a personal hold on most of them already. There was enough novelty in her teaching to keep the entire school in a pleasant state of excitement and wonder as to what she would do next, and the word had gone out through all the country round about that the new teacher had taken the school by storm. It was not infrequent for men to turn out of their way on the trail to get a glimpse of the school as they were passing, just to make sure the reports were true. Rumor stated that the teacher was exceedingly pretty; that she would take no nonsense, not even from the big boys; that she never threatened nor punished, but that every one of the boys was her devoted slave. There had been no uprising, and it almost seemed as if that popular excitement was to be omitted this season, and school was to sail along in an orderly and proper manner. In fact, the entire school as well as the surrounding population were eagerly talking about the new piano, which seemed really to be a coming fact. Not that there had been anything done toward it yet, but the teacher had promised that just as soon as every one was really studying hard and doing his best, she was going to begin to get them ready for an entertainment to raise money for that piano. They couldn't begin until everybody was in good working order, because they didn't want to take the interest away from the real business of school; but it was going to be a Shakespeare play, whatever that was, and therefore of grave import. Some people talked learnedly about Shakespeare and hinted of poetry; but the main part of the community spoke the name joyously and familiarly and without awe, as if it were milk and honey in their mouths. Why should they reverence Shakespeare more than any one else?

Margaret had grown used to seeing a head appear suddenly at one of the school-room windows and look long and frowningly first at her, then at the school, and then back to her again, as if it were a nine days' wonder. Whoever the visitor was, he would stand quietly, watching the process of the hour as if he were at a play, and Margaret would turn and smile pleasantly, then go right on with her work. The visitor would generally take off a wide hat and wave it cordially, smile back a curious, softened smile, and by and by he would mount his horse and pass on reflectively down the trail, wishing he could be a boy and go back again to school—such a school!

Oh, it was not all smooth, the way that Margaret walked. There were hitches, and unpleasant days when nothing went right, and when some of the girls got silly and rebellious, and the boys followed in their lead. She had her trials like any teacher, skilful as she was, and not the least of them became Rosa Rogers, the petted beauty, who presently manifested a childish jealousy of her in her influence over the boys. Noting this, Margaret went out of her way to win Rosa, but found it a difficult matter.

Rosa was proud, selfish, and unprincipled. She never forgave any one who frustrated her plans. She resented being made to study like the rest. She had always compelled the teacher to let her do as she pleased and still give her a good report. This she found she could not do with Margaret, and for the first time in her career she was compelled to work or fall behind. It presently became not a question of how the new teacher was to manage the big boys and the bad boys of the Ashland Ridge School, but how she was to prevent Rosa Rogers and a few girls who followed her from upsetting all her plans. The trouble was, Rosa was pretty and knew her power over the boys. If she chose she could put them all in a state of insubordination, and this she chose very often during those first few weeks.

But there was one visitor who did not confine himself to looking in at the window.

One morning a fine black horse came galloping up to the school-house at recess-time, and a well-set-up young man in wide sombrero and jaunty leather trappings sprang off and came into the building. His shining spurs caught the sunlight and flashed as he moved. He walked with the air of one who regards himself of far more importance than all who may be watching him. The boys in the yard stopped their ball-game, and the girls huddled close in whispering groups and drew near to the door. He was a young man from a ranch near the fort some thirty miles away, and he had brought an invitation for the new school-teacher to come over to dinner on Friday evening and stay until the following Monday morning. The invitation was from his sister, the wife of a wealthy cattleman whose home and hospitality were noted for miles around. She had heard of the coming of the beautiful young teacher, and wanted to attach her to her social circle.

The young man was deference itself to Margaret, openly admiring her as he talked, and said the most gracious things to her; and then, while she was answering the note, he smiled over at Rosa Rogers, who had slipped into her seat and was studiously preparing her algebra with the book upside down.

Margaret, looking up, caught Rosa's smiling glance and the tail end of a look from the young man's eyes, and felt a passing wonder whether he had ever met the girl before. Something in the boldness of his look made her feel that he had not. Yet he was all smiles and deference to herself, and his open admiration and pleasure that she was to come to help brighten this lonely country, and that she was going to accept the invitation, was really pleasant to the girl, for it was desolate being tied down to only the Tanner household and the school, and she welcomed any bit of social life.

The young man had light hair, combed very smooth, and light-blue eyes. They were bolder and handsomer than the minister's, but the girl had a feeling that they were the very same cold color. She wondered at her comparison, for she liked the handsome young man, and in spite of herself was a little flattered at the nice things he had said to her. Nevertheless, when she remembered him afterward it was always with that uncomfortable feeling that if he hadn't been so handsome and polished in his appearance he would have seemed just a little bit like that minister, and she couldn't for the life of her tell why.

After he was gone she looked back at Rosa, and there was a narrowing of the girl's eyes and a frown of hate on her brows. Margaret turned with a sigh back to her school problem—what to do with Rosa Rogers?

But Rosa did not stay in the school-house. She slipped out and walked arm in arm with Amanda Bounds down the road.

Margaret went to the door and watched. Presently she saw the rider wheel and come galloping back to the door. He had forgotten to tell her that an escort would be sent to bring her as early on Friday afternoon as she would be ready to leave the school, and he intimated that he hoped he might be detailed for that pleasant duty.

Margaret looked into his face and warmed to his pleasant smile. How could she have thought him like West? He touched his hat and rode away, and a moment later she saw him draw rein beside Rosa and Amanda, and presently dismount.

Bud rang the bell just then, and Margaret went back to her desk with a lingering look at the three figures in the distance. It was full half an hour before Rosa came in, with Amanda looking scared behind her; and troubled Margaret watched the sly look in the girl's eyes and wondered what she ought to do about it. As Rosa was passing out of the door after school she called her to the desk.

"You were late in coming in after recess, Rosa," said Margaret, gently. "Have you any excuse?"

"I was talking to a friend," said Rosa, with a toss of her head which said, as plainly as words could have done, "I don't intend to give an excuse."

"Were you talking to the gentleman who was here?"

"Well, if I was, what is that to you, Miss Earle?" said Rosa, haughtily. "Did you think you could have all the men and boys to yourself?"

"Rosa," said Margaret, trying to speak calmly, but her voice trembling with suppressed indignation, "don't talk that way to me. Child, did you ever meet Mr. Forsythe before?"

"I'm not a child, and it's none of your business!" flouted Rosa, angrily, and she twitched away and flung herself out of the school-house.

Margaret, trembling from the disagreeable encounter, stood at the window and watched the girl going down the road, and felt for the moment that she would rather give up her school and go back home than face the situation. She knew in her heart that this girl, once an enemy, would be a bitter one, and this her last move had been a most unfortunate one, coming out, as it did, with Rosa in the lead. She could, of course, complain to Rosa's family, or to the school-board, but such was not the policy she had chosen. She wanted to be able to settle her own difficulties. It seemed strange that she could not reach this one girl—who was in a way the key to the situation. Perhaps the play would be able to help her. She spent a long time that evening going over the different plays in her library, and finally, with a look of apology toward a little photographed head of Shakespeare, she decided on "Midsummer-Night's Dream." What if it was away above the heads of them all, wouldn't a few get something from it? And wasn't it better to take a great thing and try to make her scholars and a few of the community understand it, rather than to take a silly little play that would not amount to anything in the end? Of course, they couldn't do it well; that went without saying. Of course it would be away beyond them all, but at least it would be a study of something great for her pupils, and she could meantime teach them a little about Shakespeare and perhaps help some of them to learn to love his plays and study them.

The play she had selected was one in which she herself had acted the part of Puck, and she knew it by heart. She felt reasonably sure that she could help some of the more adaptable scholars to interpret their parts, and, at least, it would be good for them just as a study in literature. As for the audience, they would not be critics. Perhaps they would not even be able to comprehend the meaning of the play, but they would come and they would listen, and the experiment was one worth trying.

Carefully she went over the parts, trying to find the one which she thought would best fit Rosa Rogers, and please her as well, because it gave her opportunity to display her beauty and charm. She really was a pretty girl, and would do well. Margaret wondered whether she were altogether right in attempting to win the girl through her vanity, and yet what other weak place was there in which to storm the silly little citadel of her soul?

And so the work of assigning parts and learning them began that very week, though no one was allowed a part until his work for the day had all been handed in.

At noon Margaret made one more attempt with Rosa Rogers. She drew her to a seat beside her and put aside as much as possible her own remembrance of the girl's disagreeable actions and impudent words.

"Rosa," she said, and her voice was very gentle, "I want to have a little talk with you. You seem to feel that you and I are enemies, and I don't want you to have that attitude. I hoped we'd be the best of friends. You see, there isn't any other way for us to work well together. And I want to explain why I spoke to you as I did yesterday. It was not, as you hinted, that I want to keep all my acquaintances to myself. I have no desire to do that. It was because I feel responsible for the girls and boys in my care, and I was troubled lest perhaps you had been foolish—"

Margaret paused. She could see by the bright hardness of the girl's eyes that she was accomplishing nothing. Rosa evidently did not believe her.

"Well, Rosa," she said, suddenly, putting an impulsive, kindly hand on the girl's arm, "suppose we forget it this time, put it all away, and be friends. Let's learn to understand each other if we can, but in the mean time I want to talk to you about the play."

And then, indeed, Rosa's hard manner broke, and she looked up with interest, albeit there was some suspicion in the glance. She wanted to be in that play with all her heart; she wanted the very showiest part in it, too; and she meant to have it, although she had a strong suspicion that the teacher would want to keep that part for herself, whatever it was.

But Margaret had been wise. She had decided to take time and explain the play to her, and then let her choose her own part. She wisely judged that Rosa would do better in the part in which her interest centered, and perhaps the choice would help her to understand her pupil better.

And so for an hour she patiently stayed after school and went over the play, explaining it carefully, and it seemed at one time as though Rosa was about to choose to be Puck, because with quick perception she caught the importance of that character; but when she learned that the costume must be a quiet hood and skirt of green and brown she scorned it, and chose, at last, to be Titania, queen of the fairies. So, with a sigh of relief, and a keen insight into the shallow nature, Margaret began to teach the girl some of the fairy steps, and found her quick and eager to learn. In the first lesson Rosa forgot for a little while her animosity and became almost as one of the other pupils. The play was going to prove a great means of bringing them all together.

Before Friday afternoon came the parts had all been assigned and the plans for the entertainment were well under way.

Jed and Timothy had been as good as their word about giving the teacher riding-lessons, each vying with the other to bring a horse and make her ride at noon hour, and she had already had several good lessons and a long ride or two in company with both her teachers.

The thirty-mile ride for Friday, then, was not such an undertaking as it might otherwise have been, and Margaret looked forward to it with eagerness.

CHAPTER XIX

The little party of escort arrived before school was closed on Friday afternoon, and came down to the school-house in full force to take her away with them. The young man Forsythe, with his sister, the hostess herself, and a young army officer from the fort, comprised the party. Margaret dismissed school ten minutes early and went back with them to the Tanners' to make a hurried change in her dress and pick up her suit-case, which was already packed. As they rode away from the school-house Margaret looked back and saw Rosa Rogers posing in one of her sprite dances in the school-yard, saw her kiss her hand laughingly toward their party, and saw the flutter of a handkerchief in young Forsythe's hand. It was all very general and elusive, a passing bit of fun, but it left an uncomfortable impression on the teacher's mind. She looked keenly at the young man as he rode up smiling beside her, and once more experienced that strange, sudden change of feeling about him.

She took opportunity during that long ride to find out if the young man had known Rosa Rogers before; but he frankly told her that he had just come West to visit his sister, was bored to death because he didn't know a soul in the whole State, and until he had seen her had not laid eyes on one whom he cared to know. Yet while she could not help enjoying the gay badinage, she carried a sense of uneasiness whenever she thought of the young girl Rosa in her pretty fairy pose, with her fluttering pink fingers and her saucy, smiling eyes. There was something untrustworthy, too, in the handsome face of the man beside her.

There was just one shadow over this bit of a holiday. Margaret had a little feeling that possibly some one from the camp might come down on Saturday or Sunday, and she would miss him. Yet nothing had been said about it, and she had no way of sending word that she would be away. She had meant to send Mom Wallis a letter by the next messenger that came that way. It was all written and lying on her bureau, but no one had been down all the week. She was, therefore, greatly pleased when an approaching rider in the distance proved to be Gardley, and with a joyful little greeting she drew rein and hailed him, giving him a message for Mom Wallis.

Only Gardley's eyes told what this meeting was to him. His demeanor was grave and dignified. He acknowledged the introductions to the rest of the party gracefully, touched his hat with the ease of one to the manner born, and rode away, flashing her one gleam of a smile that told her he was glad of the meeting; but throughout the brief interview there had been an air of question and hostility between the two men, Forsythe and Gardley. Forsythe surveyed Gardley rudely, almost insolently, as if his position beside the lady gave him rights beyond the other, and he resented the coming of the stranger. Gardley's gaze was cold, too, as he met the look, and his eyes searched Forsythe's face keenly, as though they would find out what manner of man was riding with his friend.

When he was gone Margaret had the feeling that he was somehow disappointed, and once she turned in the saddle and looked wistfully after him; but he was riding furiously into the distance, sitting his horse as straight as an arrow and already far away upon the desert.

"Your friend is a reckless rider," said Forsythe, with a sneer in his voice that Margaret did not like, as they watched the speck in the distance clear a steep descent from the mesa at a bound and disappear from sight in the mesquite beyond.

"Isn't he fine-looking? Where did you find him, Miss Earle?" asked Mrs. Temple, eagerly. "I wish I'd asked him to join us. He left so suddenly I didn't realize he was going."

Margaret felt a wondering and pleasant sense of possession and pride in Gardley as she watched, but she quietly explained that the young stranger was from the East, and that he was engaged in some kind of cattle business at a distance from Ashland. Her manner was reserved, and the matter dropped. She naturally felt a reluctance to tell how her acquaintance with Gardley began. It seemed something between themselves. She could fancy the gushing Mrs. Temple saying, "How romantic!" She was that kind of a woman. It was evident that she was romantically inclined herself, for she used her fine eyes with effect on the young officer who rode with her, and Margaret found herself wondering what kind of a husband she had and what her mother would think of a woman like this.

There was no denying that the luxury of the ranch was a happy relief from the simplicity of life at the Tanners'. Iced drinks and cushions and easy-chairs, feasting and music and laughter! There were books, too, and magazines, and all the little things that go to make up a cultured life; and yet they were not people of Margaret's world, and when Saturday evening was over she sat alone in the room they had given her and, facing herself in the glass, confessed to herself that she looked back with more pleasure to the Sabbath spent with Mom Wallis than she could look forward to a Sabbath here. The morning proved her forebodings well founded.

Breakfast was a late, informal affair, filled with hilarious gaiety. There was no mention of any church service, and Margaret found it was quite too late to suggest such a thing when breakfast was over, even if she had been sure there was any service.

After breakfast was over there were various forms of amusement proposed for her pleasure, and she really felt very much embarrassed for a few moments to know how to avoid what to her was pure Sabbath-breaking. Yet she did not wish to be rude to these people who were really trying to be kind to her. She managed at last to get them interested in music, and, grouping them around the piano after a few preliminary performances by herself at their earnest solicitation, coaxed them into singing hymns.

After all, they really seemed to enjoy it, though they had to get along with one hymn-book for the whole company; but Margaret knew how to make hymn-singing interesting, and her exquisite voice was never more at its best than when she led off with "My Jesus, as Thou Wilt," or "Jesus, Saviour, Pilot Me."

"You would be the delight of Mr. Brownleigh's heart," said the hostess, gushingly, at last, after Margaret had finished singing "Abide With Me" with wonderful feeling.

"And who is Mr. Brownleigh?" asked Margaret. "Why should I delight his heart?"

"Why, he is our missionary—that is, the missionary for this region—and you would delight his heart because you are so religious and sing so well," said the superficial little woman. "Mr. Brownleigh is really a very cultured man. Of course, he's narrow. All clergymen are narrow, don't you think? They have to be to a certain extent. He's really *quite* narrow. Why, he believes in the Bible *literally*, the whale and Jonah, and the Flood, and making bread out of stones, and all that sort of thing, you know. Imagine it! But he does. He's sincere! Perfectly sincere. I suppose he has to be. It's his business. But sometimes one feels it a pity that he can't relax a little, just among us here, you know. We'd never tell. Why, he won't even play a little game of poker! And he doesn't smoke! *Imagine* it—*not even when he's by himself*, and *no one would know*! Isn't that odd? But he can preach. He's really very interesting; only a little too Utopian in his ideas. He thinks everybody ought to be good, you know, and all that sort of thing. He really thinks it's possible, and he lives that way himself. He really does. But he is a wonderful person; only I feel sorry for his wife sometimes. She's quite a cultured person. Has been wealthy, you know. She was a New York society girl. Just imagine it; out in these wilds taking gruel to the dirty little Indians! How she ever came to do it! Of course she adores him, but I can't really believe she is happy. No woman could be quite blind enough to give up everything in the world for one man, no matter how good he was. Do you think she could? It wasn't as if she didn't have plenty of other chances. She gave them all up to come out and marry him. She's a pretty good sport, too; she never lets you know she isn't perfectly happy."

"She *is* happy; mother, she's happier than *anybody* I ever saw," declared the fourteen-year-old daughter of the house, who was home from boarding-school for a brief visit during an epidemic of measles in the school.

"Oh yes, she manages to make people think she's happy," said her mother, indulgently; "but you can't make me believe she's satisfied to give up her house on Fifth Avenue and live in a two-roomed log cabin in the desert, with no society."

"Mother, you don't know! Why, *any* woman would be satisfied if her husband adored her the way Mr. Brownleigh does her."

"Well, Ada, you're a romantic girl, and Mr. Brownleigh is a handsome man. You've got a few things to learn yet. Mark my words, I don't believe you'll see Mrs. Brownleigh coming back next month with her husband. This operation was all well enough to talk about, but I'll not be surprised to hear that he has come back alone or else that he has accepted a call to some big city church. And he's equal to the city church, too; that's the wonder of it. He comes of a fine family himself, I've heard. Oh, people can't keep up the pose of saints forever, even though they do adore each other. But Mr. Brownleigh *certainly is* a good man!"

The vapid little woman sat looking reflectively out of the window for a whole minute after this deliverance. Yes, certainly Mr. Brownleigh was a good man. He was the one man of culture, education, refinement, who had come her way in many a year who had patiently and persistently and gloriously refused her advances at a mild flirtation, and refused to understand them, yet remained her friend and reverenced hero. He was a good man, and she knew it, for she was a very pretty woman and understood her art well.

Before the day was over Margaret had reason to feel that a Sabbath in Arizona was a very hard thing to find. The singing could not last all day, and her friends seemed to find more amusements on Sunday that did not come into Margaret's code of Sabbath-keeping than one knew how to say no to. Neither could they understand her feeling, and she found it hard not to be rude in gently declining one plan after another.

She drew the children into a wide, cozy corner after dinner and began a Bible story in the guise of a fairy-tale, while the hostess slipped away to take a nap. However, several other guests lingered about, and Mr. Temple strayed in. They sat with newspapers before their faces and got into the story, too, seeming to be deeply interested, so that, after all, Margaret did not have an unprofitable Sabbath.

But altogether, though she had a gay and somewhat frivolous time, a good deal of admiration and many invitations to return as often as possible, Margaret was not sorry when she said good night to know that she was to return in the early morning to her work.

Mr. Temple himself was going part way with them, accompanied by his niece, Forsythe, and the young officer who came over with them. Margaret rode beside Mr. Temple until his way parted from theirs, and had a delightful talk about Arizona. He was a kindly old fellow who adored his frivolous little wife and let her go her own gait, seeming not to mind how much she flirted.

The morning was pink and silver, gold and azure, a wonderful specimen of an Arizona sunrise for Margaret's benefit, and a glorious beginning for her day's work in spite of the extremely early hour. The company was gay and blithe, and the Eastern girl felt as if she were passing through a wonderful experience.

They loitered a little on the way to show Margaret the wonders of a fern-plumed cañon, and it was almost school-time when they came up the street, so that Margaret rode straight to the school-house instead of stopping at Tanners'. On the way to the school they passed a group of girls, of whom Rosa Rogers was the center. A certain something in Rosa's narrowed eyelids as she said good morning caused Margaret to look back uneasily, and she distinctly saw the girl give a signal to young Forsythe, who, for answer, only tipped his hat and gave her a peculiar smile.

In a moment more they had said good-by, and Margaret was left at the school-house door with a cluster of eager children about her, and several shy boys in the background, ready to welcome her back as if she had been gone a month.

In the flutter of opening school Margaret failed to notice that Rosa Rogers did not appear. It was not until the roll was called that she noticed her absence, and she looked uneasily toward the door many times during the morning, but Rosa did not come until after recess, when she stole smilingly in, as if it were quite the thing to come to school late. When questioned about her tardiness she said she had torn her dress and had to go home and change it. Margaret knew by the look in her eyes that the girl was not telling the truth, but what was she to do? It troubled her all the morning and went with her to a sleepless pillow that night. She was beginning to see that life as a school-teacher in the far West was not all she had imagined it to be. Her father had been right. There would likely be more thorns than roses on her way.

CHAPTER XX

The first time Lance Gardley met Rosa Rogers riding with Archie Forsythe he thought little of it. He knew the girl by sight, because he knew her father in a business way. That she was very young and one of Margaret's pupils was all he knew about her. For the young man he had conceived a strong dislike, but as there was no reason whatever for it he put it out of his mind as quickly as possible.

The second time he met them it was toward evening and they were so wholly absorbed in each other's society that they did not see him until he was close upon them. Forsythe looked up with a frown and a quick hand to his hip, where gleamed a weapon.

He scarcely returned the slight salute given by Gardley, and the two young people touched up their horses and were soon out of sight in the mesquite. But something in the frightened look of the girl's eyes caused Gardley to turn and look after the two.

Where could they be going at that hour of the evening? It was not a trail usually chosen for rides. It was lonely and unfrequented, and led out of the way of travelers. Gardley himself had been a far errand for Jasper Kemp, and had taken this short trail back because it cut off several miles and he was weary. Also, he was anxious to stop in Ashland and leave Mom Wallis's request that Margaret would spend the next Sabbath at the camp and see the new curtains. He was thinking what he should say to her when he saw her in a little while now, and this interruption to his thoughts was unwelcome. Nevertheless, he could not get away from that frightened look in the girl's eyes. Where could they have been going? That fellow was a new-comer in the region; perhaps he had lost his way. Perhaps he did not know that the road he was taking the girl led into a region of outlaws, and that the only habitation along the way was a cabin belonging to an old woman of weird reputation, where wild orgies were sometimes celebrated, and where men went who loved darkness rather than light, because their deeds were evil.

Twice Gardley turned in his saddle and scanned the desert. The sky was darkening, and one or two pale stars were impatiently shadowing forth their presence. And now he could see the two riders again. They had come up out of the mesquite to the top of the mesa, and were outlined against the sky sharply. They were still on the trail to old Ouida's cabin!

With a quick jerk Gardley reined in his horse and wheeled about, watching the riders for a moment; and then, setting spurs to his beast, he was off down the trail after them on one of his wild, reckless rides. Down through the mesquite he plunged, through the darkening grove, out, and up to the top of the mesa. He had lost sight of his quarry for the time, but now he could see them again riding more slowly in the valley below, their horses close together, and even as he watched the sky took on its wide night look and the stars blazed forth.

Suddenly Gardley turned sharply from the trail and made a detour through a grove of trees, riding with reckless speed, his head down to escape low branches; and in a minute or two he came with unerring instinct back to the trail some distance ahead of Forsythe and Rosa. Then he wheeled his horse and stopped stock-still, awaiting their coming.

By this time the great full moon was risen and, strangely enough, was at Gardley's back, making a silhouette of man and horse as the two riders came on toward him.

They rode out from the cover of the grove, and there he was across their path. Rosa gave a scream, drawing nearer her companion, and her horse swerved and reared; but Gardley's black stood like an image carved in ebony against the silver of the moon, and Gardley's quiet voice was in strong contrast to the quick, unguarded exclamation of Forsythe, as he sharply drew rein and put his hand hastily to his hip for his weapon.

"I beg your pardon, Mr. Forsythe"—Gardley had an excellent memory for names—"but I thought you might not be aware, being a new-comer in these parts, that the trail you are taking leads to a place where ladies do not like to go."

"Really! You don't say so!" answered the young man, insolently. "It is very kind of you, I'm sure, but you might have saved yourself the trouble. I know perfectly where I am going, and so does the lady, and we choose to go this way. Move out of the way, please. You are detaining us."

But Gardley did not move out of the way. "I am sure the lady does not know where she is going," he said, firmly. "I am sure that she does not know that it is a place of bad reputation, even in this unconventional land. At least, if she knows, I am sure that *her father* does not know, and I am well acquainted with her father."

"Get out of the way, sir," said Forsythe, hotly. "It certainly is none of your business, anyway, whoever knows what. Get out of the way or I shall shoot. This lady and I intend to ride where we please."

"Then I shall have to say you *cannot*," said Gardley; and his voice still had that calm that made his opponent think him easy to conquer.

"Just how do you propose to stop us?" sneered Forsythe, pulling out his pistol.

"This way," said Gardley, lifting a tiny silver whistle to his lips and sending forth a peculiar, shrilling blast. "And this way," went on Gardley, calmly lifting both hands and showing a weapon in each, wherewith he covered the two.

Rosa screamed and covered her face with her hands, cowering in her saddle.

Forsythe lifted his weapon, but looked around nervously. "Dead men tell no tales," he said, angrily.

"It depends upon the man," said Gardley, meaningly, "especially if he were found on this road. I fancy a few tales could be told if you happened to be the man. Turn your horses around at once and take this lady back to her home. My men are not far off, and if you do not wish the whole story to be known among your friends and hers you would better make haste."

Forsythe dropped his weapon and obeyed. He decidedly did not wish his escapade to be known among his friends. There were financial reasons why he did not care to have it come to the ears of his brother-in-law just now.

Silently in the moonlight the little procession took its way down the trail, the girl and the man side by side, their captor close behind, and when the girl summoned courage to glance fearsomely behind her she saw three more men riding like three grim shadows yet behind. They had fallen into the trail so quietly that she had not heard them when they came. They were Jasper Kemp, Long Bill, and Big Jim. They had been out for other purposes, but without question followed the call of the signal.

It was a long ride back to Rogers's ranch, and Forsythe glanced nervously behind now and then. It seemed to him that the company was growing larger all the time. He half expected to see a regiment each time he turned. He tried hurrying his horse, but when he did so the followers were just as close without any seeming effort. He tried to laugh it all off.

Once he turned and tried to placate Gardley with a few shakily jovial words:

"Look here, old fellow, aren't you the man I met on the trail the day Miss Earle went over to the fort? I guess you've made a mistake in your calculations. I was merely out on a pleasure ride with Miss Rogers. We weren't going anywhere in particular, you know. Miss Rogers chose this way, and I wanted to please her. No man likes to have his pleasure interfered with, you know. I guess you didn't recognize me?"

"I recognized you," said Gardley. "It would be well for you to be careful where you ride with ladies, especially at night. The matter, however, is one that you would better settle with Mr. Rogers. My duty will be done when I have put it into his hands."

"Now, my good fellow," said Forsythe, patronizingly, "you surely don't intend to make a great fuss about this and go telling tales to Mr. Rogers about a trifling matter—"

"I intend to do my duty, Mr. Forsythe," said Gardley; and Forsythe noticed that the young man still held his weapons. "I was set this night to guard Mr. Rogers's property. That I did not expect his daughter would be a part of the evening's guarding has nothing to do with the matter. I shall certainly put the matter into Mr. Rogers's hands."

Rosa began to cry softly.

"Well, if you want to be a fool, of course," laughed Forsythe, disagreeably; "but you will soon see Mr. Rogers will accept my explanation."

"That is for Mr. Rogers to decide," answered Gardley, and said no more.

The reflections of Forsythe during the rest of that silent ride were not pleasant, and Rosa's intermittent crying did not tend to make him more comfortable.

The silent procession at last turned in at the great ranch gate and rode up to the house. Just as they stopped and the door of the house swung open, letting out a flood of light, Rosa leaned toward Gardley and whispered:

"Please, Mr. Gardley, don't tell papa. I'll do *anything* in the world for you if you won't tell papa."

He looked at the pretty, pitiful child in the moonlight. "I'm sorry, Miss Rosa," he said, firmly. "But you don't understand. I must do my duty."

"Then I shall hate you!" she hissed. "Do you hear? I shall *hate* you forever, and you don't know what that means. It means I'll take my *revenge* on you and on *everybody you like*."

He looked at her half pityingly as he swung off his horse and went up the steps to meet Mr. Rogers, who had come out and was standing on the top step of the ranch-house in the square of light that flickered from a great fire on the hearth of the wide fireplace. He was looking from one to another of the silent group, and as his eyes rested on his daughter he said, sternly:

"Why, Rosa, what does this mean? You told me you were going to bed with a headache!"

Gardley drew his employer aside and told what had happened in a few low-toned sentences; and then stepped down and back into the shadow, his horse by his side, the three men from the camp grouped behind him. He had the delicacy to withdraw after his duty was done.

Mr. Rogers, his face stern with sudden anger and alarm, stepped down and stood beside his daughter. "Rosa, you may get down and go into the house to your own room. I will talk with you later," he said. And then to the young man, "You, sir, will step into my office. I wish to have a plain talk with you."

A half-hour later Forsythe came out of the Rogers house and mounted his horse, while Mr. Rogers stood silently and watched him.

"I will bid you good evening, sir," he said, formally, as the young man mounted his horse and silently rode away. His back had a defiant look in the moonlight as he passed the group of men in the shadow; but they did not turn to watch him.

"That will be all to-night, Gardley, and I thank you very much," called the clear voice of Mr. Rogers from his front steps.

The four men mounted their horses silently and rode down a little distance behind the young man, who wondered in his heart just how much or how little Gardley had told Rosa's father.

The interview to which young Forsythe had just been subjected had been chastening in character, of a kind to baffle curiosity concerning the father's knowledge of details, and to discourage any further romantic rides with Miss Rosa. It had been left in abeyance whether or not the Temples should be made acquainted with the episode, dependent upon the future conduct of both young people. It had not been satisfactory from Forsythe's point of view; that is, he had not been so easily able to disabuse the father's mind of suspicion, nor to establish his own guileless character as he had hoped; and some of the remarks Rogers made led Forsythe to think that the father understood just how unpleasant it might become for him if his brother-in-law found out about the escapade.

This is why Archie Forsythe feared Lance Gardley, although there was nothing in the least triumphant about the set of that young man's shoulders as he rode away in the moonlight on the trail toward Ashland. And this is how it came about that Rosa Rogers hated Lance Gardley, handsome and daring though he was; and because of him hated her teacher, Margaret Earle.

An hour later Lance Gardley stood in the little dim Tanner parlor, talking to Margaret.

"You look tired," said the girl, compassionately, as she saw the haggard shadows on the young face, showing in spite of the light of pleasure in his eyes. "You look *very* tired. What in the world have you been doing?"

"I went out to catch cattle-thieves," he said, with a sigh, "but I found there were other kinds of thieves abroad. It's all in the day's work. I'm not tired now." And he smiled at her with beautiful reverence.

Margaret, as she watched him, could not help thinking that the lines in his face had softened and strengthened since she had first seen him, and her eyes let him know that she was glad he had come.

"And so you will really come to us, and it isn't going to be asking too much?" he said, wistfully. "You can't think what it's going to be to the men—to *us*! And Mom Wallis is so excited she can hardly get her work done. If you had said no I would be almost afraid to go back." He laughed, but she could see there was deep earnestness under his tone.

"Indeed I will come," said Margaret. "I'm just looking forward to it. I'm going to bring Mom Wallis a new bonnet like one I made for mother; and I'm going to teach her how to make corn gems and steamed apple dumplings. I'm bringing some songs and some music for the violin; and I've got something for you to help me do, too, if you will?"

He smiled tenderly down on her. What a wonderful girl she was, to be willing to come out to the old shack among a lot of rough men and one uncultured old woman and make them happy, when she was fit for the finest in the land!

"You're *wonderful*!" he said, taking her hand with a quick pressure for good-by. "You make every one want to do his best."

He hurried out to his horse and rode away in the moonlight. Margaret went up to her "mountain window" and watched him far out on the trail, her heart swelling with an unnamed gladness over his last words.

"Oh, God, keep him, and help him to make good!" she prayed.

CHAPTER XXI

The visit to the camp was a time to be remembered long by all the inhabitants of the bunk-house, and even by Margaret herself. Margaret wondered Friday evening, as she sat up late, working away braiding a lovely gray bonnet out of folds of malines, and fashioning it into form for Mom Wallis, why she was looking forward to the visit with so much more real pleasure than she had done to the one the week before at the Temples'. And so subtle is the heart of a maid that she never fathomed the real reason.

The Temples', of course, was interesting and delightful as being something utterly new in her experience. It was comparatively luxurious, and there were pleasant, cultured people there, more from her own social class in life. But it was going to be such fun to surprise Mom Wallis with that bonnet and see her old face light up when she saw herself in the little folding three-leaved mirror she was taking along with her and meant to leave for Mom Wallis's log boudoir. She was quite excited over selecting some little thing for each one of the men—books, pictures, a piece of music, a bright cushion, and a pile of picture magazines. It made a big bundle when she had them together, and she was dubious if she ought to try to carry them all; but Bud, whom she consulted on the subject, said, loftily, it "wasn't a flea-bite for the Kid; he could carry anything on a horse."

Bud was just a little jealous to have his beloved teacher away from home so much, and rejoiced greatly when Gardley, Friday afternoon, suggested that he come along, too. He made quick time to his home, and secured a hasty permission and wardrobe, appearing like a footman on his father's old horse when they were half a mile down the trail.

Mom Wallis was out at the door to greet her guest when she arrived, for Margaret had chosen to make her visit last from Friday afternoon after school, until Monday morning. It was the generosity of her nature that she gave to her utmost when she gave.

The one fear she had entertained about coming had been set at rest on the way when Gardley told her that Pop Wallis was off on one of his long trips, selling cattle, and would probably not return for a week. Margaret, much as she trusted Gardley and the men, could not help dreading to meet Pop Wallis again.

There was a new trimness about the old bunk-house. The clearing had been cleaned up and made neat, the grass cut, some vines set out and trained up limply about the door, and the windows shone with Mom Wallis's washing.

Mom Wallis herself was wearing her best white apron, stiff with starch, her lace collar, and her hair in her best imitation of the way Margaret had fixed it, although it must be confessed she hadn't quite caught the knack of arrangement yet. But the one great difference Margaret noticed in the old woman was the illuminating smile on her face. Mom Wallis had learned how to let the glory gleam through all the hard sordidness of her life, and make earth brighter for those about her.

The curtains certainly made a great difference in the looks of the bunk-house, together with a few other changes. The men had made some chairs—three of them, one out of a barrel; and together they had upholstered them roughly. The cots around the walls were blazing with their red blankets folded smoothly and neatly over them, and on the floor in front of the hearth, which had been scrubbed, Gardley had spread a Navajo blanket he had bought of an Indian.

The fireplace was piled with logs ready for the lighting at night, and from somewhere a lamp had been rigged up and polished till it shone in the setting sun that slanted long rays in at the shining windows.

The men were washed and combed, and had been huddled at the back of the bunk-house for an hour, watching the road, and now they came forward awkwardly to greet their guest, their horny hands scrubbed to an unbelievable whiteness. They did not say much, but they looked their pleasure, and Margaret greeted every one as if he were an old friend, the charming part about it all to the men being that she remembered every one's name and used it.

Bud hovered in the background and watched with starry eyes. Bud was having the time of his life. He preferred the teacher's visiting the camp rather than the fort. The "Howdy, sonny!" which he had received from the men, and the "Make yourself at home, Bill" from Gardley, had given him great joy; and the whole thing seemed somehow to link him to the teacher in a most distinguishing manner.

Supper was ready almost immediately, and Mom Wallis had done her best to make it appetizing. There was a lamb stew with potatoes, and fresh corn bread with coffee. The men ate with relish, and watched their guest of honor as if she had been an angel come down to abide with them for a season. There was a tablecloth on the old table, too—a *white* tablecloth. It looked remarkably like an old sheet, to be sure, with a seam through the middle where it had been worn and turned and sewed together; but it was a tablecloth now, and a marvel to the men. And the wonder about Margaret was that she could eat at such a table and make it seem as though that tablecloth were the finest damask, and the two-tined forks the heaviest of silver.

After the supper was cleared away and the lamp lighted, the gifts were brought out. A book of Scotch poetry for Jasper Kemp, bound in tartan covers of the Campbell clan; a small illustrated pamphlet of Niagara Falls for Big Jim, because he had said he wanted to see the place and never could manage it; a little pictured folder of Washington City for Big Jim; a book of old ballad music for Fiddling Boss; a book of jokes for Fade-away Forbes; a framed picture of a beautiful shepherd dog for Stocky; a big, red, ruffled denim pillow for Croaker, because when she was there before he was always complaining about the seats being hard; a great blazing crimson pennant bearing the name HARVARD in big letters for Fudge, because she had remembered he was from Boston; and for Mom Wallis a framed text beautifully painted in water-colors, done in rustic letters twined with stray forget-me-nots, the words, "Come unto Me, all ye that labor and are heavy laden, and I will give you rest." Margaret had made that during the week and framed it in a simple raffia braid of brown and green.

It was marvelous how these men liked their presents; and while they were examining them and laughing about them and putting their pictures and Mom Wallis's text on the walls, and the pillow on a bunk, and the pennant over the fireplace, Margaret shyly held out a tiny box to Gardley.

"I thought perhaps you would let me give you this," she said. "It isn't much; it isn't even new, and it has some marks in it; but I thought it might help with your new undertaking."

Gardley took it with a lighting of his face and opened the box. In it was a little, soft, leather-bound Testament, showing the marks of usage, yet not worn. It was a tiny thing, very thin, easily fitting in a vest-pocket, and not a burden to carry. He took the little book in his hand, removed the silken rubber band that bound it, and turned the leaves reverently in his fingers, noting that there were pencil-marks here and there. His face was all emotion as he looked up at the giver.

"I thank you," he said, in a low tone, glancing about to see that no one was noticing them. "I shall prize it greatly. It surely will help. I will read it every day. Was that what you wanted? And I will carry it with me always."

His voice was very earnest, and he looked at her as though she had given him a fortune. With another glance about at the preoccupied room—even Bud was busy studying Jasper Kemp's oldest gun—he snapped the band on the book again and put it carefully in his inner breast-pocket. The book would henceforth travel next his heart and be his guide. She thought he meant her to understand that, as he put out his hand unobtrusively and pressed her fingers gently with a quick, low "Thank you!"

Then Mom Wallis's bonnet was brought out and tied on her, and the poor old woman blushed like a girl when she stood with meek hands folded at her waist and looked primly about on the family for their approval at Margaret's request. But that was nothing to the way she stared when Margaret got out the threefold mirror and showed her herself in the new headgear. She trotted away at last, the wonderful bonnet in one hand, the box in the other, a look of awe on her face, and Margaret heard her murmur as she put it away: "Glory! *Me!* Glory!"

Then Margaret had to read one or two of the poems for Jasper Kemp, while they all sat and listened to her Scotch and marveled at her. A woman like that condescending to come to visit them!

She gave a lesson in note-reading to the Fiddling Boss, pointing one by one with her white fingers to the notes until he was able to creep along and pick out "Suwanee River" and "Old Folks at Home" to the intense delight of the audience.

Margaret never knew just how it was that she came to be telling the men a story, one she had read not long before in a magazine, a story with a thrilling national interest and a keen personal touch that searched the hearts of men; but they listened as they had never listened to anything in their lives before.

And then there was singing, more singing, until it bade fair to be morning before they slept, and the little teacher was weary indeed when she lay down on the cot in Mom Wallis's room, after having knelt beside the old woman and prayed.

The next day there was a wonderful ride with Gardley and Bud to the cañon of the cave-dwellers, and a coming home to the apple dumplings she had taught Mom Wallis to make before she went away. All day Gardley and she, with Bud for delighted audience, had talked over the play she was getting up at the school, Gardley suggesting about costumes and tree boughs for scenery, and promising to help in any way she wanted. Then after supper there were jokes and songs around the big fire, and some popcorn one of the men had gone a long ride that day to get. They called for another story, too, and it was forthcoming.

It was Sunday morning after breakfast, however, that Margaret suddenly wondered how she was going to make the day helpful and different from the other days.

She stood for a moment looking out of the clear little window thoughtfully, with just the shadow of a sigh on her lips, and as she turned back to the room she met Gardley's questioning glance.

"Are you homesick?" he asked, with a sorry smile. "This must all be very different from what you are accustomed to."

"Oh no, it isn't that." She smiled, brightly. "I'm not a baby for home, but I do get a bit homesick about church-time. Sunday is such a strange day to me without a service."

"Why not have one, then?" he suggested, eagerly. "We can sing and—you could—do the rest!"

Her eyes lighted at the suggestion, and she cast a quick glance at the men. Would they stand for that sort of thing?

Gardley followed her glance and caught her meaning. "Let them answer for themselves," he said quickly in a low tone, and then, raising his voice: "Speak up, men. Do you want to have church? Miss Earle here is homesick for a service, and I suggest that we have one, and she conduct it."

"Sure!" said Jasper Kemp, his face lighting. "I'll miss my guess if she can't do better than the parson we had last Sunday. Get into your seats, boys; we're goin' to church."

Margaret's face was a study of embarrassment and delight as she saw the alacrity with which the men moved to get ready for "church." Her quick brain turned over the possibility of what she could read or say to help this strange congregation thus suddenly thrust upon her.

It was a testimony to her upbringing by a father whose great business of life was to preach the gospel that she never thought once of hesitating or declining the opportunity, but welcomed it as an opportunity, and only deprecated her unreadiness for the work.

The men stirred about, donned their coats, furtively brushing their hair, and Long Bill insisted that Mom Wallis put on her new bonnet; which she obligingly did, and sat down carefully in the barrel-chair, her hands neatly crossed in her lap, supremely happy. It really was wonderful what a difference that bonnet made in Mom Wallis.

Gardley arranged a comfortable seat for Margaret at the table and put in front of her one of the hymn-books she had brought. Then, after she was seated, he took the chair beside her and brought out the little Testament from his breast-pocket, gravely laying it on the hymn-book.

Margaret met his eyes with a look of quick appreciation. It was wonderful the way these two were growing to understand each other. It gave the girl a thrill of wonder and delight to have him do this simple little thing for her, and the smile that passed between them was beautiful to see. Long Bill turned away his head and looked out of the window with an improvised sneeze to excuse the sudden mist that came into his eyes.

Margaret chose "My Faith looks up to Thee" for the first hymn, because Fiddling Boss could play it, and while he was tuning up his fiddle she hastily wrote out two more copies of the words. And so the queer service started with a quaver of the old fiddle and the clear, sweet voices of Margaret and Gardley leading off, while the men growled on their way behind, and Mom Wallis, in her new gray bonnet, with her hair all fluffed softly gray under it, sat with eyes shining like a girl's.

So absorbed in the song were they all that they failed to hear the sound of a horse coming into the clearing. But just as the last words of the final verse died away the door of the bunk-house swung open, and there in the doorway stood Pop Wallis!

The men sprang to their feet with one accord, ominous frowns on their brows, and poor old Mom Wallis sat petrified where she was, the smile of relaxation frozen on her face, a look of fear growing in her tired old eyes.

Now Pop Wallis, through an unusual combination of circumstances, had been for some hours without liquor and was comparatively sober. He stood for a moment staring amazedly at the group around his fireside. Perhaps because he had been so long without his usual stimulant his mind was weakened and things appeared as a strange vision to him. At any rate, he stood and stared, and as he looked from one to another of the men, at the beautiful stranger, and across to the strangely unfamiliar face of his wife in her new bonnet, his eyes took on a frightened look. He slowly took his hand from the door-frame and passed it over his eyes, then looked again, from one to another, and back to his glorified wife.

Margaret had half risen at her end of the table, and Gardley stood beside her as if to reassure her; but Pop Wallis was not looking at any of them any more. His eyes were on his wife. He passed his hand once more over his eyes and took one step gropingly into the room, a hand reached out in front of him, as if he were not sure but he might run into something on the way, the other hand on his forehead, a dazed look in his face.

"Why, Mom—that ain't really—*you*, now, *is* it?" he said, in a gentle, insinuating voice like one long unaccustomed making a hasty prayer.

The tone made a swift change in the old woman. She gripped her bony hands tight and a look of beatific joy came into her wrinkled face.

"Yes, it's really *me*, Pop!" she said, with a kind of triumphant ring to her voice.

"But—but—you're right *here*, ain't you? You ain't *dead*, an'—an'—gone to—gl-oo-ry, be you? You're right*here*?"

"Yes, I'm right *here*, Pop. I ain't dead! Pop—glory's *come to me*!"

"Glory?" repeated the man, dazedly. "Glory?" And he gazed around the room and took in the new curtains, the pictures on the wall, the cushions and chairs, and the bright, shining windows. "You don't mean it's*heav'n*, do you, Mom? 'Cause I better go back—*I* don't belong in heav'n. Why, Mom, it can't be glory, 'cause it's the same old bunk-house outside, anyhow."

"Yes, it's the same old bunk-house, and it ain't heaven, but it's *goin'* to be. The glory's come all right. You sit down, Pop; we're goin' to have church, and this is my new bonnet. *She* brang it. This is the new school-teacher, Miss Earle, and she's goin' to have church. She done it *all*! You sit down and listen."

Pop Wallis took a few hesitating steps into the room and dropped into the nearest chair. He looked at Margaret as if she might be an angel holding open the portal to a kingdom in the sky. He looked and wondered and admired, and then he looked back to his glorified old wife again in wonder.

Jasper Kemp shut the door, and the company dropped back into their places. Margaret, because of her deep embarrassment, and a kind of inward trembling that had taken possession of her, announced another hymn.

It was a solemn little service, quite unique, with a brief, simple prayer and an expository reading of the story of the blind man from the sixth chapter of John. The men sat attentively, their eyes upon her face as she read; but Pop Wallis sat staring at his wife, an awed light upon his scared old face, the wickedness and cunning all faded out, and only fear and wonder written there.

In the early dawning of the pink-and-silver morning Margaret went back to her work, Gardley riding by her side, and Bud riding at a discreet distance behind, now and then going off at a tangent after a stray cottontail. It was wonderful what good sense Bud seemed to have on occasion.

The horse that Margaret rode, a sturdy little Western pony, with nerve and grit and a gentle common sense for humans, was to remain with her in Ashland, a gift from the men of the bunk-house. During the week that followed Archie Forsythe came riding over with a beautiful shining saddle-horse for her use during her stay in the West; but when he went riding back to the ranch the shining saddle-horse was still in his train, riderless, for Margaret told him that she already had a horse of her own. Neither had Margaret accepted the invitation to the Temples' for the next week-end. She had other plans for the Sabbath, and that week there appeared on all the trees and posts about the town, and on the trails, a little notice of a Bible class and vesper-service to be held in the school-house on the following Sabbath afternoon; and so Margaret, true daughter of her minister-father, took up her mission in Ashland for the Sabbaths that were to follow; for the school-board had agreed with alacrity to such use of the school-house.

CHAPTER XXII

Now when it became noised abroad that the new teacher wanted above all things to purchase a piano, and that to that end she was getting up a wonderful Shakespeare play in which the scholars were to act upon a stage set with tree boughs after the manner of some new kind of players, the whole community round about began to be excited.

Mrs. Tanner talked much about it. Was not Bud to be a prominent character? Mr. Tanner talked about it everywhere he went. The mothers and fathers and sisters talked about it, and the work of preparing the play went on.

Margaret had discovered that one of the men at the bunk-house played a flute, and she was working hard to teach him and Fiddling Boss and Croaker to play a portion of the elfin dance to accompany the players. The work of making costumes and training the actors became more and more strenuous, and in this Gardley proved a fine assistant. He undertook to train some of the older boys for their parts, and did it so well that he was presently in the forefront of the battle of preparation and working almost as hard as Margaret herself.

The beauty of the whole thing was that every boy in the school adored him, even Jed and Timothy, and life took on a different aspect to them in company with this high-born college-bred, Eastern young man who yet could ride and shoot with the daringest among the Westerners.

Far and wide went forth the fame of the play that was to be. The news of it reached to the fort and the ranches, and brought offers of assistance and costumes and orders for tickets. Margaret purchased a small duplicator and set her school to printing tickets and selling them, and before the play was half ready to be acted tickets enough were sold for two performances, and people were planning to come from fifty miles around. The young teacher began to quake at the thought of her big audience and her poor little amateur players; and yet for children they were doing wonderfully well, and were growing quite Shakespearian in their manner of conversation.

"What say you, sweet Amanda?" would be a form of frequent address to that stolid maiden Amanda Bounds; and Jed, instead of shouting for "Delicate" at recess, as in former times, would say, "My good Timothy, I swear to thee by Cupid's strongest bow; by his best arrow with the golden head"—until all the school-yard rang with classic phrases; and the whole country round was being addressed in phrases of another century by the younger members of their households.

Then Rosa Rogers's father one day stopped at the Tanners' and left a contribution with the teacher of fifty dollars toward the new piano; and after that it was rumored that the teacher said the piano could be sent for in time to be used at the play. Then other contributions of smaller amounts came in, and before the date of the play had been set there was money enough to make a first payment on the piano. That day the English exercise for the whole school was to compose the letter to the Eastern piano firm where the piano was to be purchased, ordering it to be sent on at once. Weeks before this Margaret had sent for a number of piano catalogues beautifully illustrated, showing by cuts how the whole instruments were made, with full illustrations of the factories where they were manufactured, and she had discussed the selection with the scholars, showing them what points were to be considered in selecting a good piano. At last the order was sent out, the actual selection itself to be made by a musical friend of Margaret's in New York, and the school waited in anxious suspense to hear that it had started on its way.

The piano arrived at last, three weeks before the time set for the play, which was coming on finely now and seemed to the eager scholars quite ready for public performance. Not so to Margaret and Gardley, as daily they pruned, trained, and patiently went over and over again each part, drawing all the while nearer to the ideal they had set. It could not be done perfectly, of course, and when they had done all they could there would yet be many crudities; but Margaret's hope was to bring out the meaning of the play and give both audience and performers the true idea of what Shakespeare meant when he wrote it.

The arrival of the piano was naturally a great event in the school. For three days in succession the entire school marched in procession down to the incoming Eastern train to see if their expected treasure had arrived, and when at last it was lifted from the freight-car and set upon the station platform the school stood awe-struck and silent, with half-bowed heads and bated breath, as though at the arrival of some great and honorable guest.

They attended it on the roadside as it was carted by the biggest wagon in town to the school-house door; they stood in silent rows while the great box was peeled off and the instrument taken out and carried into the school-room; then they filed in soulfully and took their accustomed seats without being told, touching shyly the shining case as they passed. By common consent they waited to hear its voice for the first time. Margaret took the little key from the envelope tied to the frame, unlocked the cover, and, sitting down, began to play. The rough men who had brought it stood in awesome adoration around the platform; the silence that spread over that room would have done honor to Paderewski or Josef Hoffman.

Margaret played and played, and they could not hear enough. They would have stayed all night listening, perhaps, so wonderful was it to them. And then the teacher called each one and let him or her touch a few chords, just to say they had played on it. After which she locked the instrument and sent them all home. That was the only afternoon during that term that the play was forgotten for a while.

After the arrival of the piano the play went forward with great strides, for now Margaret accompanied some of the parts with the music, and the flute and violin were also practised in their elfin dance with much better effect. It was about this time that Archie Forsythe discovered the rehearsals and offered his assistance, and, although it was declined, he frequently managed to ride over about rehearsal time, finding ways to make himself useful in spite of Margaret's polite refusals. Margaret always felt annoyed when he came, because Rosa Rogers instantly became another creature on his arrival, and because Gardley simply froze into a polite statue, never speaking except when spoken to. As for Forsythe, his attitude toward Gardley was that of a contemptuous master toward a slave, and yet he took care to cover it always with a form of courtesy, so that Margaret could say or do nothing to show her displeasure, except to be grave and dignified. At such times Rosa Rogers's eyes would be upon her with a gleam of hatred, and the teacher felt that the scholar was taking advantage of the situation. Altogether it was a trying time for Margaret when Forsythe came to the school-house. Also, he discovered to them that he played the violin, and offered to assist in the orchestral parts. Margaret really could think of no reason to decline this offer, but she was sadly upset by the whole thing. His manner to her was too pronounced, and she felt continually uncomfortable under it, what with Rosa Rogers's jealous eyes upon her and Gardley's eyes turned haughtily away.

She planned a number of special rehearsals in the evenings, when it was difficult for Forsythe to get there, and managed in this way to avoid his presence; but the whole matter became a source of much vexation, and Margaret even shed a few tears wearily into her pillow one night when things had gone particularly hard and Forsythe had hurt the feelings of Fiddling Boss with his insolent directions about playing. She could not say or do anything much in the matter, because the Temples had been very kind in helping to get the piano, and Mr. Temple seemed to think he was doing the greatest possible kindness to her in letting Forsythe off duty so much to help with the play. The matter became more and more of a distress to Margaret, and the Sabbath was the only day of real delight.

The first Sunday after the arrival of the piano was a great day. Everybody in the neighborhood turned out to the Sunday-afternoon class and vesper service, which had been growing more and more in popularity, until now the school-room was crowded. Every man from the bunk-house came regularly, often including Pop Wallis, who had not yet recovered fully from the effect of his wife's new bonnet and fluffy arrangement of hair, but treated her like a lady visitor and deferred to her absolutely when he was at home. He wasn't quite sure even yet but he had strayed by mistake into the outermost courts of heaven and ought to get shooed out. He always looked at the rose-wreathed curtains with a mingling of pride and awe.

Margaret had put several hymns on the blackboard in clear, bold printing, and the singing that day was wonderful. Not the least part of the service was her own playing over of the hymns before the singing began, which was listened to with reverence as if it had been the music of an angel playing on a heavenly harp.

Gardley always came to the Sunday services, and helped her with the singing, and often they two sang duets together.

The service was not always of set form. Usually Margaret taught a short Bible lesson, beginning with the general outline of the Bible, its books, their form, substance, authors, etc.—all very brief and exceedingly simple, putting a wide space of music between this and the vesper service, into which she wove songs, bits of poems, passages from the Bible, and often a story which she told dramatically, illustrating the scripture read.

But the very Sunday before the play, just the time Margaret had looked forward to as being her rest from all the perplexities of the week, a company from the fort, including the Temples, arrived at the school-house right in the midst of the Bible lesson.

The ladies were daintily dressed, and settled their frills and ribbons amusedly as they watched the embarrassed young teacher trying to forget that there was company present. They were in a distinct sense "company," for they had the air, as they entered, of having come to look on and be amused, not to partake in the worship with the rest.

Margaret found herself trembling inwardly as she saw the supercilious smile on the lips of Mrs. Temple and the amused stares of the other ladies of the party. They did not take any notice of the other people present any more than if they had been so many puppets set up to show off the teacher; their air of superiority was offensive. Not until Rosa Rogers entered with her father, a little later, did they condescend to bow in recognition, and then with that pretty little atmosphere as if they would say, "Oh, you've come, too, to be amused."

Gardley was sitting up in front, listening to her talk, and she thought he had not noticed the strangers. Suddenly it came to her to try to keep her nerve and let him see that they were nothing to her; and with a strong effort and a swift prayer for help she called for a hymn. She sat coolly down at the piano, touching the keys with a tender chord or two and beginning to sing almost at once. She had sent home for some old hymn-books from the Christian Endeavor Society in her father's church, so the congregation were supplied with the notes and words now, and everybody took part eagerly, even the people from the fort condescendingly joining in.

But Gardley was too much alive to every expression on that vivid face of Margaret's to miss knowing that she was annoyed and upset. He did not need to turn and look back to immediately discover the cause. He was a young person of keen intuition. It suddenly gave him great satisfaction to see that look of consternation on Margaret's face. It settled for him a question he had been in great and anxious doubt about, and his soul was lifted up with peace within him. When, presently, according to arrangement, he rose to sing a duet with Margaret, no one could have possibly told by so much as the lifting of an eyelash that he knew there was an enemy of his in the back of the room. He sang, as did Margaret, to the immediate audience in front of him, those admiring children and adoring men in the forefront who felt the school-house had become for them the gate of heaven for the time being; and he sang with marvelous feeling and sympathy, letting out his voice at its best.

"Really," said Mrs. Temple, in a loud whisper to the wife of one of the officers, "that young man has a fine voice, and he isn't bad-looking, either. I think he'd be worth cultivating. We must have him up and try him out."

But when she repeated this remark in another stage whisper to Forsythe he frowned haughtily.

The one glimpse Margaret caught of Forsythe during that afternoon's service was when he was smiling meaningly at Rosa Rogers; and she had to resolutely put the memory of their look from her mind or the story which she was about to tell would have fled.

It was the hunger in Jasper Kemp's eyes that finally anchored Margaret's thoughts and helped her to forget the company at the back of the room. She told her story, and she told it wonderfully and with power, interpreting it now and then for the row of men who sat in the center of the room drinking in her every word; and when the simple service was concluded with another song, in which Gardley's voice rang forth with peculiar tenderness and strength, the men filed forth silently, solemnly, with bowed heads and thoughtful eyes. But the company from the fort flowed up around Margaret like flood-tide let loose and gushed upon her.

"Oh, my dear!" said Mrs. Temple. "How beautifully you do it! And such attention as they give you! No wonder you are willing to forego all other amusements to stay here and preach! But it was perfectly sweet the way you made them listen and the way you told that story. I don't see how you do it. I'd be scared to death!"

They babbled about her awhile, much to her annoyance, for there were several people to whom she had wanted to speak, who drew away and disappeared when the new-comers took possession of her. At last, however, they mounted and rode away, to her great relief. Forsythe, it is true, tried to make her go home with them; tried to escort her to the Tanners'; tried to remain in the school-house with her awhile when she told him she had something to do there; but she would not let him, and he rode away half sulky at the last, a look of injured pride upon his face.

Margaret went to the door finally, and looked down the road. He was gone, and she was alone. A shade of sadness came over her face. She was sorry that Gardley had not waited. She had wanted to tell him how much she liked his singing, what a pleasure it was to sing with him, and how glad she was that he came up to her need so well with the strangers there and helped to make it easy. But Gardley had melted away as soon as the service was over, and had probably gone home with the rest of the men. It was disappointing, for she had come to consider their little time together on Sunday as a very pleasant hour, this few minutes after the service when they would talk about real living and the vital things of existence. But he was gone!

She turned, and there he was, quite near the door, coming toward her. Her face lighted up with a joy that was unmistakable, and his own smile in answer was a revelation of his deeper self.

"Oh, I'm so glad you are not gone!" she said, eagerly. "I wanted to tell you—" And then she stopped, and the color flooded her face rosily, for she saw in his eyes how glad he was and forgot to finish her sentence.

He came up gravely, after all, and, standing just a minute so beside the door, took both her hands in both his. It was only for a second that he stood so, looking down into her eyes. I doubt if either of them knew till afterward that they had been holding hands. It seemed the right and natural thing to do, and meant so much to each of them. Both were glad beyond their own understanding over that moment and its tenderness.

It was all very decorous, and over in a second, but it meant much to remember afterward, that look and hand-clasp.

"I wanted to tell you," he said, tenderly, "how much that story did for me. It was wonderful, and it helped me to decide something I have been perplexed over—"

"Oh, I am glad!" she said, half breathlessly.

So, talking in low, broken sentences, they went back to the piano and tried over several songs for the next Sunday, lingering together, just happy to be there with each other, and not half knowing the significance of it all. As the purple lights on the school-room wall grew long and rose-edged, they walked slowly to the Tanner house and said good night.

There was a beauty about the young man as he stood for a moment looking down upon the girl in parting, the kind of beauty there is in any strong, wild thing made tame and tender for a great love by a great uplift. Gardley had that look of self-surrender, and power made subservient to right, that crowns a man with strength and more than physical beauty. In his fine face there glowed high purpose, and deep devotion to the one who had taught it to him. Margaret, looking up at him, felt her heart go out with that great love, half maiden, half divine, that comes to some favored women even here on earth, and she watched him down the road toward the mountain in the evening light and marveled how her trust had grown since first she met him; marveled and reflected that she had not told her mother and father much about him yet. It was growing time to do so; yes—*it was growing time*! Her cheeks grew pink in the darkness and she turned and fled to her room.

That was the last time she saw him before the play.

CHAPTER XXIII

The play was set for Tuesday. Monday afternoon and evening were to be the final rehearsals, but Gardley did not come to them. Fiddling Boss came late and said the men had been off all day and had not yet returned. He himself found it hard to come at all. They had important work on. But there was no word from Gardley.

Margaret was disappointed. She couldn't get away from it. Of course they could go on with the rehearsal without him. He had done his work well, and there was no real reason why he had to be there. He knew every part by heart, and could take any boy's place if any one failed in any way. There was nothing further really for him to do until the performance, as far as that was concerned, except be there and encourage her. But she missed him, and an uneasiness grew in her mind. She had so looked forward to seeing him, and now to have no word! He might at least have sent her a note when he found he could not come.

Still she knew this was unreasonable. His work, whatever it was—he had never explained it very thoroughly to her, perhaps because she had never asked—must, of course, have kept him. She must excuse him without question and go on with the business of the hour.

Her hands were full enough, for Forsythe came presently and was more trying than usual. She had to be very decided and put her foot down about one or two things, or some of her actors would have gone home in the sulks, and Fiddling Boss, whose part in the program meant much to him, would have given it up entirely.

She hurried everything through as soon as possible, knowing she was weary, and longing to get to her room and rest. Gardley would come and explain to-morrow, likely in the morning on his way somewhere.

But the morning came and no word. Afternoon came and he had not sent a sign yet. Some of the little things that he had promised to do about the setting of the stage would have to remain undone, for it was too late now to do it herself, and there was no one else to call upon.

Into the midst of her perplexity and anxiety came the news that Jed on his way home had been thrown from his horse, which was a young and vicious one, and had broken his leg. Jed was to act the part of Nick Bottom that evening, and he did it well! Now what in the world was she to do? If only Gardley would come!

Just at this moment Forsythe arrived.

"Oh, it is you, Mr. Forsythe!" And her tone showed plainly her disappointment. "Haven't you seen Mr. Gardley to-day? I don't know what I shall do without him."

"I certainly have seen Gardley," said Forsythe, a spice of vindictiveness and satisfaction in his tone. "I saw him not two hours ago, drunk as a fish, out at a place called Old Ouida's Cabin, as I was passing. He's in for a regular spree. You'll not see him for several days, I fancy. He's utterly helpless for the present, and out of the question. What is there I can do for you? Present your request. It's yours—to the half of my kingdom."

Margaret's heart grew cold as ice and then like fire. Her blood seemed to stop utterly and then to go pounding through her veins in leaps and torrents. Her eyes grew dark, and things swam before her. She reached out to a desk and caught at it for support, and her white face looked at him a moment as if she had not heard. But when in a second she spoke, she said, quite steadily:

"I thank you, Mr. Forsythe; there is nothing just at present—or, yes, there is, if you wouldn't mind helping Timothy put up those curtains. Now, I think I'll go home and rest a few minutes; I am very tired."

It wasn't exactly the job Forsythe coveted, to stay in the school-house and fuss over those curtains; but she made him do it, then disappeared, and he didn't like the memory of her white face. He hadn't thought she would take it that way. He had expected to have her exclaim with horror and disgust. He watched her out of the door, and then turned impatiently to the waiting Timothy.

Margaret went outside the school-house to call Bud, who had been sent to gather sage-brush for filling in the background, but Bud was already out of sight far on the trail toward the camp on Forsythe's horse, riding for dear life. Bud had come near to the school-house door with his armful of sage-brush just in time to hear Forsythe's flippant speech about Gardley and see Margaret's white face. Bud had gone for help!

But Margaret did not go home to rest. She did not even get half-way home. When she had gone a very short distance outside the school-house she saw some one coming toward her, and in her distress of mind she could not tell who it was. Her eyes were blinded with tears, her breath was constricted, and it seemed to her that a demon unseen was gripping her heart. She had not yet taken her bearings to know what she thought. She had only just come dazed from the shock of Forsythe's words, and had not the power to think. Over and over to herself, as she walked along, she kept repeating the words: "I *do not* believe it! It is *not* true!" but her inner consciousness had not had time to analyze her soul and be sure that she believed the words wherewith she was comforting herself.

So now, when she saw some one coming, she felt the necessity of bringing her telltale face to order and getting ready to answer whoever she was to meet. As she drew nearer she became suddenly aware that it was Rosa Rogers coming with her arms full of bundles and more piled up in front of her on her pony. Margaret knew at once that Rosa must have seen Forsythe go by her house, and had returned promptly to the school-house on some pretext or other. It would not do to let her go there alone with the young man; she must go back and stay with them. She could not be sure that if she sent Rosa home with orders to rest she would be obeyed. Doubtless the girl would take another way around and return to the school again. There was nothing for it but to go back and stay as long as Rosa did.

Margaret stooped and, hastily plucking a great armful of sage-brush, turned around and retraced her steps, her heart like lead, her feet suddenly grown heavy. How could she go back and hear them laugh and chatter, answer their many silly, unnecessary questions, and stand it all? How could she, with that great weight at her heart?

She went back with a wonderful self-control. Forsythe's face lighted, and his reluctant hand grew suddenly eager as he worked. Rosa came presently, and others, and the laughing chatter went on quite as Margaret had known it would. And she—so great is the power of human will under pressure—went calmly about and directed here and there; planned and executed; put little, dainty, wholly unnecessary touches to the stage; and never let any one know that her heart was being crushed with the weight of a great, awful fear, and yet steadily upborne by the rising of a great, deep trust. As she worked and smiled and ordered, she was praying: "Oh, God, don't let it be true! Keep him! Save him! Bring him! Make him true! I *know* he is true! Oh, God, bring him safely *soon*!"

Meantime there was nothing she could do. She could not send Forsythe after him. She could not speak of the matter to one of those present, and Bud—where was Bud? It was the first time since she came to Arizona that Bud had failed her. She might not leave the school-house, with Forsythe and Rosa there, to go and find him, and she might not do anything else. There was nothing to do but work on feverishly and pray as she had never prayed before.

By and by one of the smaller boys came, and she sent him back to the Tanners' to find Bud, but he returned with the message that Bud had not been home since morning; and so the last hours before the evening, that would otherwise have been so brief for all there was to be done, dragged their weary length away and Margaret worked on.

She did not even go back for supper at the last, but sent one of the girls to her room for a few things she needed, and declined even the nice little chicken sandwich that thoughtful Mrs. Tanner sent back along with the things. And then, at last, the audience began to gather.

By this time her anxiety was so great for Gardley that all thought of how she was to supply the place of the absent Jed had gone from her mind, which was in a whirl. Gardley! Gardley! If only Gardley would come! That was her one thought. What should she do if he didn't come at all? How should she explain things to herself afterward? What if it had been true? What if he were the kind of man Forsythe had suggested? How terrible life would look to her! But it was not true. No, it was not true! She trusted him! With her soul she trusted him! He would come back some time and he would explain all. She could not remember his last look at her on Sunday and not trust him. He was true! He would come!

Somehow she managed to get through the terrible interval, to slip into the dressing-room and make herself sweet and comely in the little white gown she had sent for, with its delicate blue ribbons and soft lace ruffles. Somehow she managed the expected smiles as one and another of the audience came around to the platform to speak to her. There were dark hollows under her eyes, and her mouth was drawn and weary, but they laid that to the excitement. Two bright-red spots glowed on her cheeks; but she smiled and talked with her usual gaiety. People looked at her and said how beautiful she was, and how bright and untiring; and how wonderful it was that Ashland School had drawn such a prize of a teacher. The seats filled, the noise and the clatter went on. Still no sign of Gardley or any one from the camp, and still Bud had not returned! What could it mean?

But the minutes were rushing rapidly now. It was more than time to begin. The girls were in a flutter in one cloak-room at the right of the stage, asking more questions in a minute than one could answer in an hour; the boys in the other cloak-room wanted all sorts of help; and three or four of the actors were attacked with stage-fright as they peered through a hole in the curtain and saw some friend or relative arrive and sit down in the audience. It was all a mad whirl of seemingly useless noise and excitement, and she could not, no, she *could not*, go on and do the necessary things to start that awful play. Why, oh, *why* had she ever been left to think of getting up a play?

Forsythe, up behind the piano, whispered to her that it was time to begin. The house was full. There was not room for another soul. Margaret explained that Fiddling Boss had not yet arrived, and caught a glimpse of the cunning designs of Forsythe in the shifty turning away of his eyes as he answered that they could not wait all night for him; that if he wanted to get into it he ought to have come early. But even as she turned away she saw the little, bobbing, eager faces of Pop and Mom Wallis away back by the door, and the grim, towering figure of the Boss, his fiddle held high, making his way to the front amid the crowd.

She sat down and touched the keys, her eyes watching eagerly for a chance to speak to the Boss and see if he knew anything of Gardley; but Forsythe was close beside her all the time, and there was no opportunity. She struck the opening chords of the overture they were to attempt to play, and somehow got through it. Of course, the audience was not a critical one, and there were few real judges of music present; but it may be that the truly wonderful effect she produced upon the listeners was due to the fact that she was playing a prayer with her heart as her fingers touched the keys, and that instead of a preliminary to a fairy revel the music told the story of a great soul struggle, and reached hearts as it tinkled and rolled and swelled on to the end. It may be, too, that Fiddling Boss was more in sympathy that night with his accompanist than was the other violinist, and that was why his old fiddle brought forth such weird and tender tones.

Almost to the end, with her heart sobbing its trouble to the keys, Margaret looked up sadly, and there, straight before her through a hole in the curtain made by some rash youth to glimpse the audience, or perhaps even put there by the owner of the nose itself, she saw the little, freckled, turned-up member belonging to Bud's face. A second more and a big, bright eye appeared and solemnly winked at her twice, as if to say, "Don't you worry; it's all right!"

She almost started from the stool, but kept her head enough to finish the chords, and as they died away she heard a hoarse whisper in Bud's familiar voice:

"Whoop her up, Miss Earle. We're all ready. Raise the curtain there, you guy. Let her rip. Everything's O. K."

With a leap of light into her eyes Margaret turned the leaves of the music and went on playing as she should have done if nothing had been the matter. Bud was there, anyway, and that somehow cheered her heart. Perhaps Gardley had come or Bud had heard of him—and yet, Bud didn't know he had been missing, for Bud had been away himself.

Nevertheless, she summoned courage to go on playing. Nick Bottom wasn't in this first scene, anyway, and this would have to be gone through with somehow. By this time she was in a state of daze that only thought from moment to moment. The end of the evening seemed now to her as far off as the end of a hale old age seems at the beginning of a lifetime. Somehow she must walk through it; but she could only see a step at a time.

Once she turned half sideways to the audience and gave a hurried glance about, catching sight of Fudge's round, near-sighted face, and that gave her encouragement. Perhaps the others were somewhere present. If only she could get a chance to whisper to some one from the camp and ask when they had seen Gardley last! But there was no chance, of course!

The curtain was rapidly raised and the opening scene of the play began, the actors going through their parts with marvelous ease and dexterity, and the audience silent and charmed, watching those strangers in queer costumes that were their own children, marching around there at their ease and talking weird language that was not used in any class of society they had ever come across on sea or land before.

But Margaret, watching her music as best she could, and playing mechanically rather than with her mind, could not tell if they were doing well or ill, so loudly did her heart pound out her fears—so stoutly did her heart proclaim her trust.

And thus, without a flaw or mistake in the execution of the work she had struggled so hard to teach them, the first scene of the first act drew to its close, and Margaret struck the final chords of the music and felt that in another minute she must reel and fall from that piano-stool. And yet she sat and watched the curtain fall with a face as controlled as if nothing at all were the matter.

A second later she suddenly knew that to sit in that place calmly another second was a physical impossibility. She must get somewhere to the air at once or her senses would desert her.

With a movement so quick that no one could have anticipated it, she slipped from her piano-stool, under the curtain to the stage, and was gone before the rest of the orchestra had noticed her intention.

CHAPTER XXIV

Since the day that he had given Margaret his promise to make good, Gardley had been regularly employed by Mr. Rogers, looking after important matters of his ranch. Before that he had lived a free and easy life, working a little now and then when it seemed desirable to him, having no set interest in life, and only endeavoring from day to day to put as far as possible from his mind the life he had left behind him. Now, however, all things became different. He brought to his service the keen mind and ready ability that had made him easily a winner at any game, a brave rider, and a never-failing shot. Within a few days Rogers saw what material was in him, and as the weeks went by grew to depend more and more upon his advice in matters.

There had been much trouble with cattle thieves, and so far no method of stopping the loss or catching the thieves had been successful. Rogers finally put the matter into Gardley's hands to carry out his own ideas, with the men of the camp at his command to help him, the camp itself being only a part of Rogers's outlying possessions, one of several such centers from which he worked his growing interests.

Gardley had formulated a scheme by which he hoped eventually to get hold of the thieves and put a stop to the trouble, and he was pretty sure he was on the right track; but his plan required slow and cautious work, that the enemy might not suspect and take to cover. He had for several weeks suspected that the thieves made their headquarters in the region of Old Ouida's Cabin, and made their raids from that direction. It was for this reason that of late the woods and trails in the vicinity of Ouida's had been secretly patrolled day and night, and every passer-by taken note of, until Gardley knew just who were the frequenters of that way and mostly what was their business. This work was done alternately by the men of the Wallis camp and two other camps, Gardley being the head of all and carrying all responsibility; and not the least of that young man's offenses in the eyes of Rosa Rogers was that he was so constantly at her father's house and yet never lifted an eye in admiration of her pretty face. She longed to humiliate him, and through him to humiliate Margaret, who presumed to interfere with her flirtations, for it was a bitter thing to Rosa that Forsythe had no eyes for her when Margaret was about.

When the party from the fort rode homeward that Sunday after the service at the school-house, Forsythe lingered behind to talk to Margaret, and then rode around by the Rogers place, where Rosa and he had long ago established a trysting-place.

Rosa was watching for his passing, and he stopped a half-hour or so to talk to her. During this time she casually disclosed to Forsythe some of the plans she had overheard Gardley laying before her father. Rosa had very little idea of the importance of Gardley's work to her father, or perhaps she would not have so readily prattled of his affairs. Her main idea was to pay back Gardley for his part in her humiliation with Forsythe. She suggested that it would be a great thing if Gardley could be prevented from being at the play Tuesday evening, and told what she had overheard him saying to her father merely to show Forsythe how easy it would be to have Gardley detained on Tuesday. Forsythe questioned Rosa keenly. Did she know whom they suspected? Did she know what they were planning to do to catch them, and when?

Rosa innocently enough disclosed all she knew, little thinking how dishonorable to her father it was, and perhaps caring as little, for Rosa had ever been a spoiled child, accustomed to subordinating everything within reach to her own uses. As for Forsythe, he was nothing loath to get rid of Gardley, and he saw more possibilities in Rosa's suggestion than she had seen herself. When at last he bade Rosa good night and rode unobtrusively back to the trail he was already formulating a plan.

It was, therefore, quite in keeping with his wishes that he should meet a dark-browed rider a few miles farther up the trail whose identity he had happened to learn a few days before.

Now Forsythe would, perhaps, not have dared to enter into any compact against Gardley with men of such ill-repute had it been a matter of money and bribery, but, armed as he was with information valuable to the criminals, he could so word his suggestion about Gardley's detention as to make the hunted men think it to their advantage to catch Gardley some time the next day when he passed their way and imprison him for a while. This would appear to be but a friendly bit of advice from a disinterested party deserving a good turn some time in the future and not get Forsythe into any trouble. As such it was received by the wretch, who clutched at the information with ill-concealed delight and rode away into the twilight like a serpent threading his secret, gliding way among the darkest places, scarcely rippling the air, so stealthily did he pass.

As for Forsythe, he rode blithely to the Temple ranch, with no thought of the forces he had set going, his life as yet one round of trying to please himself at others' expense, if need be, but please himself, *anyway*, with whatever amusement the hour afforded.

At home in the East, where his early life had been spent, a splendid girl awaited his dilatory letters and set herself patiently to endure the months of separation until he should have attained a home and a living and be ready for her to come to him.

In the South, where he had idled six months before he went West, another lovely girl cherished mementoes of his tarrying and wrote him loving letters in reply to his occasional erratic epistles.

Out on the Californian shore a girl with whom he had traveled West in her uncle's luxurious private car, with a gay party of friends and relatives, cherished fond hopes of a visit he had promised to make her during the winter.

Innumerable maidens of this world, wise in the wisdom that crushes hearts, remembered him with a sigh now and then, but held no illusions concerning his kind.

Pretty little Rosa Rogers cried her eyes out every time he cast a languishing look at her teacher, and several of the ladies of the fort sighed that the glance of his eye and the gentle pressure of his hand could only be a passing joy. But the gay Lothario passed on his way as yet without a scratch on the hard enamel of his heart, till one wondered if it were a heart, indeed, or perhaps only a metal imitation. But girls like Margaret Earle, though they sometimes were attracted by him, invariably distrusted him. He was like a beautiful spotted snake that was often caught menacing something precious, but you could put him down anywhere after punishment or imprisonment and he would slide on his same slippery way and still be a spotted, deadly snake.

When Gardley left the camp that Monday morning following the walk home with Margaret from the Sabbath service, he fully intended to be back at the school-house Monday by the time the afternoon rehearsal began. His plans were so laid that he thought relays from other camps were to guard the suspected ground for the next three days and he could be free. It had been a part of the information that Forsythe had given the stranger that Gardley would likely pass a certain lonely crossing of the trail at about three o'clock that afternoon, and, had that arrangement been carried out, the men who lay in wait for him would doubtless have been pleased to have their plans mature so easily; but they would not have been pleased long, for Gardley's men were so near at hand at that time, watching that very spot with eyes and ears and long-distance glasses, that their chief would soon have been rescued and the captors be themselves the captured.

But the men from the farther camp, called "Lone Fox" men, did not arrive on time, perhaps through some misunderstanding, and Gardley and Kemp and their men had to do double time. At last, later in the afternoon, Gardley volunteered to go to Lone Fox and bring back the men.

As he rode his thoughts were of Margaret, and he was seeing again the look of gladness in her eyes when she found he had not gone yesterday; feeling again the thrill of her hands in his, the trust of her smile! It was incredible, wonderful, that God had sent a veritable angel into the wilderness to bring him to himself; and now he was wondering, could it be that there was really hope that he could ever make good enough to dare to ask her to marry him. The sky and the air were rare, but his thoughts were rarer still, and his soul was lifted up with joy. He was earning good wages now. In two more weeks he would have enough to pay back the paltry sum for the lack of which he had fled from his old home and come to the wilderness. He would go back, of course, and straighten out the old score. Then what? Should he stay in the East and go back to the old business wherewith he had hoped to make his name honored and gain wealth, or should he return to this wild, free land again and start anew?

His mother was dead. Perhaps if she had lived and cared he would have made good in the first place. His sisters were both married to wealthy men and not deeply interested in him. He had disappointed and mortified them; their lives were filled with social duties; they had never missed him. His father had been dead many years. As for his uncle, his mother's brother, whose heir he was to have been before he got himself into disgrace, he decided not to go near him. He would stay as long as he must to undo the wrong he had done. He would call on his sisters and then come back; come back and let Margaret decide what she wanted him to do—that is, if she would consent to link her life with one who had been once a failure. Margaret! How wonderful she was! If Margaret said he ought to go back and be a lawyer, he would go—yes, even if he had to enter his uncle's office as an underling to do it. His soul loathed the idea, but he would do it for Margaret, if she thought it best. And so he mused as he rode!

When the Lone Fox camp was reached and the men sent out on their belated task, Gardley decided not to go with them back to meet Kemp and the other men, but sent word to Kemp that he had gone the short cut to Ashland, hoping to get to a part of the evening rehearsal yet.

Now that short cut led him to the lonely crossing of the trail much sooner than Kemp and the others could reach it from the rendezvous; and there in cramped positions, and with much unnecessary cursing and impatience, four strong masked men had been concealed for four long hours.

Through the stillness of the twilight rode Gardley, thinking of Margaret, and for once utterly off his guard. His long day's work was done, and though he had not been able to get back when he planned, he was free now, free until the day after to-morrow. He would go at once to her and see if there was anything she wanted him to do.

Then, as if to help along his enemies, he began to hum a song, his clear, high voice reaching keenly to the ears of the men in ambush:

"'Oh, the time is long, mavourneen,

Till I come again, O mavourneen—'"

"And the toime 'll be longer thun iver, oim thinkin', ma purty little voorneen!" said an unmistakable voice of Erin through the gathering dusk.

Gardley's horse stopped and Gardley's hand went to his revolver, while his other hand lifted the silver whistle to his lips; but four guns bristled at him in the twilight, the whistle was knocked from his lips before his breath had even reached it, some one caught his arms from behind, and his own weapon was wrenched from his hand as it went off. The cry which he at once sent forth was stifled in its first whisper in a great muffling garment flung over his head and drawn tightly about his neck. He was in a fair way to strangle, and his vigorous efforts at escape were useless in the hands of so many. He might have been plunged at once into a great abyss of limitless, soundless depths, so futile did any resistance seem. And so, as it was useless to struggle, he lay like one dead and put all his powers into listening. But neither could he hear much, muffled as he was, and bound hand and foot now, with a gag in his mouth and little care taken whether he could even breathe.

They were leading him off the trail and up over rough ground; so much he knew, for the horse stumbled and jolted and strained to carry him. To keep his whirling senses alive and alert he tried to think where they might be leading him; but the darkness and the suffocation dulled his powers. He wondered idly if his men would miss him and come back when they got home to search for him, and then remembered with a pang that they would think him safely in Ashland, helping Margaret. They would not be alarmed if he did not return that night, for they would suppose he had stopped at Rogers's on the way and perhaps stayed all night, as he had done once or twice before. *Margaret!* When should he see Margaret now? What would she think?

And then he swooned away.

When he came somewhat to himself he was in a close, stifling room where candle-light from a distance threw weird shadows over the adobe walls. The witch-like voices of a woman and a girl in harsh, cackling laughter, half suppressed, were not far away, and some one, whose face was covered, was holding a glass to his lips. The smell was sickening, and he remembered that he hated the thought of liquor. It did not fit with those who companied with Margaret. He had never cared for it, and had resolved never to taste it again. But whether he chose or not, the liquor was poured down his throat. Huge hands held him and forced it, and he was still bound and too weak to resist, even if he had realized the necessity.

The liquid burned its way down his throat and seethed into his brain, and a great darkness, mingled with men's wrangling voices and much cursing, swirled about him like some furious torrent of angry waters that finally submerged his consciousness. Then came deeper darkness and a blank relief from pain.

Hours passed. He heard sounds sometimes, and dreamed dreams which he could not tell from reality. He saw his friends with terror written on their faces, while he lay apathetically and could not stir. He saw tears on Margaret's face; and once he was sure he heard Forsythe's voice in contempt: "Well, he seems to be well occupied for the present! No danger of his waking up for a while!" and then the voices all grew dim and far away again, and only an old crone and the harsh girl's whisper over him; and then Margaret's tears—tears that fell on his heart from far above, and seemed to melt out all his early sins and flood him with their horror. Tears and the consciousness that he ought to be doing something for Margaret now and could not. Tears—and more darkness!

CHAPTER XXV

When Margaret arrived behind the curtain she was aware of many cries and questions hurled at her like an avalanche, but, ignoring them all, she sprang past the noisy, excited group of young people, darted through the dressing-room to the right and out into the night and coolness. Her head was swimming, and things went black before her eyes. She felt that her breath was going, going, and she must get to the air.

But when she passed the hot wave of the school-room, and the sharp air of the night struck her face, consciousness seemed to turn and come back into her again; for there over her head was the wideness of the vast, starry Arizona night, and there, before her, in Nick Bottom's somber costume, eating one of the chicken sandwiches that Mrs. Tanner had sent down to her, stood Gardley! He was pale and shaken from his recent experience; but he was undaunted, and when he saw Margaret coming toward him through the doorway with her soul in her eyes and her spirit all aflame with joy and relief, he came to meet her under the stars, and, forgetting everything else, just folded her gently in his arms!

It was a most astonishing thing to do, of course, right there outside the dressing-room door, with the curtain just about to rise on the scene and Gardley's wig was not on yet. He had not even asked nor obtained permission. But the soul sometimes grows impatient waiting for the lips to speak, and Margaret felt her trust had been justified and her heart had found its home. Right there behind the school-house, out in the great wide night, while the crowded, clamoring audience waited for them, and the young actors grew frantic, they plighted their troth, his lips upon hers, and with not a word spoken.

Voices from the dressing-room roused them. "Come in quick, Mr. Gardley; it's time for the curtain to rise, and everybody is ready. Where on earth has Miss Earle vanished? Miss Earle! Oh, Miss Earle!"

There was a rush to the dressing-room to find the missing ones; but Bud, as ever, present where was the most need, stood with his back to the outside world in the door of the dressing-room and called loudly:

"They're comin', all right. Go on! Get to your places. Miss Earle says to get to your places."

The two in the darkness groped for each other's hands as they stood suddenly apart, and with one quick pressure and a glance hurried in. There was not any need for words. They understood, these two, and trusted.

With her cheeks glowing now, and her eyes like two stars, Margaret fled across the stage and took her place at the piano again, just as the curtain began to be drawn; and Forsythe, who had been slightly uneasy at the look on her face as she left them, wondered now and leaned forward to tell her how well she was looking.

He kept his honeyed phrase to himself, however, for she was not heeding him. Her eyes were on the rising curtain, and Forsythe suddenly remembered that this was the scene in which Jed was to have appeared—and Jed had a broken leg! What had Margaret done about it? It was scarcely a part that could be left out. Why hadn't he thought of it sooner and offered to take it? He could have bluffed it out somehow—he had heard it so much— made up words where he couldn't remember them all, and it would have been a splendid opportunity to do some real love-making with Rosa. Why hadn't he thought of it? Why hadn't Rosa? Perhaps she hadn't heard about Jed soon enough to suggest it.

The curtain was fully open now, and Bud's voice as Peter Quince, a trifle high and cracked with excitement, broke the stillness, while the awed audience gazed upon this new, strange world presented to them.

"Is all our company here?" lilted out Bud, excitedly, and Nick Bottom replied with Gardley's voice:

"You were best to call them generally, man by man, according to the scrip."

Forsythe turned deadly white. Jasper Kemp, whose keen eye was upon him, saw it through the tan, saw his lips go pale and purple points of fear start in his eyes, as he looked and looked again, and could not believe his senses.

Furtively he darted a glance around, like one about to steal away; then, seeing Jasper Kemp's eyes upon him, settled back with a strained look upon his face. Once he stole a look at Margaret and caught her face all transfigured with great joy; looked again and felt rebuked somehow by the pureness of her maiden joy and trust.

Not once had she turned her eyes to his. He was forgotten, and somehow he knew the look he would get if she should see him. It would be contempt and scorn that would burn his very soul. It is only a maid now and then to whom it is given thus to pierce and bruise the soul of a man who plays with love and trust and womanhood for selfishness. Such a woman never knows her power. She punishes all unconscious to herself. It was so that Margaret Earle, without being herself aware, and by her very indifference and contempt, showed the little soul of this puppet man to himself.

He stole away at last when he thought no one was looking, and reached the back of the school-house at the open door of the girls' dressing-room, where he knew Titania would be posing in between the acts. He beckoned her to his side and began to question her in quick, eager, almost angry tones, as if the failure of their plans were her fault. Had her father been at home all day? Had anything happened—any one been there? Did Gardley come? Had there been any report from the men? Had that short, thick-set Scotchman with the ugly grin been there? She must remember that she was the one to suggest the scheme in the first place, and it was her business to keep a watch. There was no telling now what might happen. He turned, and there stood Jasper Kemp close to his elbow, his short stature drawn to its full, his thick-set shoulders squaring themselves, his ugly grin standing out in bold relief, menacingly, in the night.

The young man let forth some words not in a gentleman's code, and turned to leave the frightened girl, who by this time was almost crying; but Jasper Kemp kept pace with Forsythe as he walked.

"Was you addressing me?" he asked, politely; "because I could tell you a few things a sight more appropriate for you than what you just handed to me."

Forsythe hurried around to the front of the school-house, making no reply.

"Nice, pleasant evening to be *free*," went on Jasper Kemp, looking up at the stars. "Rather onpleasant for some folks that have to be shut up in jail."

Forsythe wheeled upon him. "What do you mean?" he demanded, angrily, albeit he was white with fear.

"Oh, nothing much," drawled Jasper, affably. "I was just thinking how much pleasanter it was to be a free man than shut up in prison on a night like this. It's so much healthier, you know."

Forsythe looked at him a moment, a kind of panic of intelligence growing in his face; then he turned and went toward the back of the school-house, where he had left his horse some hours before.

"Where are you going?" demanded Jasper. "It's 'most time you went back to your fiddling, ain't it?"

But Forsythe answered him not a word. He was mounting his horse hurriedly—his horse, which, all unknown to him, had been many miles since he last rode him.

"You think you have to go, then?" said Jasper, deprecatingly. "Well, now, that's a pity, seeing you was fiddling so nice an' all. Shall I tell them you've gone for your health?"

Thus recalled, Forsythe stared at his tormentor wildly for a second. "Tell her—tell her"—he muttered, hoarsely—"tell her I've been taken suddenly ill." And he was off on a wild gallop toward the fort.

"I'll tell her you've gone for your health!" called Jasper Kemp, with his hands to his mouth like a megaphone. "I reckon he won't return again very soon, either," he chuckled. "This country's better off without such pests as him an' that measley parson." Then, turning, he beheld Titania, the queen of the fairies, white and frightened, staring wildly into the starry darkness after the departed rider. "Poor little fool!" he muttered under his breath as he looked at the girl and turned away. "Poor, pretty little fool!" Suddenly he stepped up to her side and touched her white-clad shoulder gently. "Don't you go for to care, lassie," he said in a tender tone. "He ain't worth a tear from your pretty eye. He ain't fit to wipe your feet on—your pretty wee feet!"

But Rosa turned angrily and stamped her foot.

"Go away! You bad old man!" she shrieked. "Go away! I shall tell my father!" And she flouted herself into the school-house.

Jasper stood looking ruefully after her, shaking his head. "The little de'il!" he said aloud; "the poor, pretty little de'il. She'll get her dues aplenty afore she's done." And Jasper went back to the play.

Meantime, inside the school-house, the play went gloriously on to the finish, and Gardley as Nick Bottom took the house by storm. Poor absent Jed's father, sent by the sufferer to report it all, stood at the back of the house while tears of pride and disappointment rolled down his cheeks—pride that Jed had been so well represented, disappointment that it couldn't have been his son up there play-acting like that.

The hour was late when the play was over, and Margaret stood at last in front of the stage to receive the congratulations of the entire countryside, while the young actors posed and laughed and chattered excitedly, then went away by two and threes, their tired, happy voices sounding back along the road. The people from the fort had been the first to surge around Margaret with their eager congratulations and gushing sentiments: "So sweet, my dear! So perfectly wonderful! You really have got some dandy actors!" And, "Why don't you try something lighter—something simpler, don't you know. Something really popular that these poor people could understand and appreciate? A little farce! I could help you pick one out!"

And all the while they gushed Jasper Kemp and his men, grim and forbidding, stood like a cordon drawn about her to protect her, with Gardley in the center, just behind her, as though he had a right there and meant to stay; till at last the fort people hurried away and the school-house grew suddenly empty with just those two and the eight men behind; and by the door Bud, talking to Pop and Mom Wallis in the buckboard outside.

Amid this admiring bodyguard at last Gardley took Margaret home. Perhaps she wondered a little that they all went along, but she laid it to their pride in the play and their desire to talk it over.

They had sent Mom and Pop Wallis home horseback, after all, and put Margaret and Gardley in the buckboard, Margaret never dreaming that it was because Gardley was not fit to walk. Indeed, he did not realize himself why they all stuck so closely to him. He had lived through so much since Jasper and his men had burst into his prison and freed him, bringing him in hot haste to the school-house, with Bud wildly riding ahead. But it was enough for him to sit beside Margaret in the sweet night and remember how she had come out to him under the stars. Her hand lay beside him on the seat, and without intending it his own brushed it. Then he laid his gently, reverently, down upon hers with a quiet pressure, and her smaller fingers thrilled and nestled in his grasp.

In the shadow of a big tree beside the house he bade her good-by, the men busying themselves with turning about the buckboard noisily, and Bud discreetly taking himself to the back door to get one of the men a drink of water.

"You have been suffering in some way," said Margaret, with sudden intuition, as she looked up into Gardley's face. "You have been in peril, somehow—"

"A little," he answered, lightly. "I'll tell you about it to-morrow. I mustn't keep the men waiting now. I shall have a great deal to tell you to-morrow—if you will let me. Good night, *Margaret*!" Their hands lingered in a clasp, and then he rode away with his bodyguard.

But Margaret did not have to wait until the morrow to hear the story, for Bud was just fairly bursting.

Mrs. Tanner had prepared a nice little supper—more cold chicken, pie, doughnuts, coffee, some of her famous marble cake, and preserves—and she insisted on Margaret's coming into the dining-room and eating it, though the girl would much rather have gone with her happy heart up to her own room by herself.

Bud did not wait on ceremony. He began at once when Margaret was seated, even before his mother could get her properly waited on.

"Well, we had *some ride*, we sure did! The Kid's a great old scout."

Margaret perceived that this was a leader. "Why, that's so, what became of you, William? I hunted everywhere for you. Things were pretty strenuous there for a while, and I needed you dreadfully."

"Well, I know," Bud apologized. "I'd oughta let you know before I went, but there wasn't time. You see, I had to pinch that guy's horse to go, and I knew it was just a chance if we could get back, anyway; but I had to take it. You see, if I could 'a' gone right to the cabin it would have been a dead cinch, but I had to ride to camp for the men, and then, taking the short trail across, it was some ride to Ouida's Cabin!"

Mrs. Tanner stepped aghast as she was cutting a piece of dried-apple pie for Margaret. "Now, Buddie—mother's boy—you don't mean to tell me *you* went to *Ouida's Cabin*? Why, sonnie, that's an *awful place*! Don't you know your pa told you he'd whip you if you ever went on that trail?"

"I should worry, Ma! I *had* to go. They had Mr. Gardley tied up there, and we had to go and get him rescued."

"*You* had to go, Buddie—now what could *you* do in that awful place?" Mrs. Tanner was almost reduced to tears. She saw her offspring at the edge of perdition at once.

But Bud ignored his mother and went on with his tale. "You jest oughta seen Jap Kemp's face when I told him what that guy said to you! Some face, b'lieve me! He saw right through the whole thing, too. I could see that! He ner the men hadn't had a bite o' supper yet; they'd just got back from somewheres. They thought the Kid was over here all day helping you. He said yesterday when he left 'em here's where he's a-comin'"—Bud's mouth was so full he could hardly articulate—"an' when I told 'em, he jest blew his little whistle—like what they all carry— three times, and those men every one jest stopped right where they was, whatever they was doin'. Long Bill had the comb in the air gettin' ready to comb his hair, an' he left it there and come away, and Big Jim never stopped to wipe his face on the roller-towel, he just let the wind dry it; and they all hustled on their horses fast as ever they could and beat it after Jap Kemp. Jap, he rode alongside o' me and asked me questions. He made me tell all what the guy from the fort said over again, three or four times, and then he ast what time he got to the school-house, and whether the Kid had been there at all yest'iday ur t'day; and a lot of other questions, and then he rode alongside each man and told him in just a few words where we was goin' and what the guy from the fort had said. Gee! but you'd oughta heard what the men said when he told 'em! Gee! but they was some mad! Bimeby we came to the woods round the cabin, and Jap Kemp made me stick alongside Long Bill, and he sent the men off in different directions all in a *big* circle, and waited till each man was in his place, and then we all rode hard as we could and came softly up round that cabin just as the sun was goin' down. Gee! but you'd oughta seen the scairt look on them women's faces; there was two of 'em—an old un an' a skinny-looking long-drink-o'-pump-water. I guess she was a girl. I don't know. Her eyes looked real old. There was only three men in the cabin; the rest was off somewheres. They wasn't looking for anybody to come that time o' day, I guess. One of the men was sick on a bunk in the corner. He had his head tied up, and his arm, like he'd been shot, and the other two men came jumping up to the door with their guns, but when they saw how many men *we* had they looked awful scairt. *We* all had *our* guns out, too!—Jap Kemp gave me one to carry—" Bud tried not to swagger as he told this, but it was almost too much for him. "Two of our men held the horses, and all the rest of us got down and went into the cabin. Jap Kemp, sounded his whistle and all our men done the same just as they went in the door—some kind of signals they have for the Lone Fox Camp! The two men in the doorway aimed straight at Jap Kemp and fired, but Jap was onto 'em and jumped one side and our men fired, too, and we soon had 'em tied up and went in—that is, Jap and me and Long Bill went in, the rest stayed by the door—and it wasn't long 'fore their other men came riding back hot haste; they'd heard the shots, you know—and some more of *our* men—why, most twenty or thirty there was, I guess, altogether; some from Lone Fox Camp that was watching off in the woods came and when we got outside again there they all were, like a big army. Most of the men belonging to the cabin was tied and harmless by that time, for our men took 'em one at a time as they came riding in. Two of 'em got away, but Jap Kemp said they couldn't go far without being caught, 'cause there was a watch out for 'em—they'd been stealing cattle long back something terrible. Well, so Jap Kemp and Long Bill and I went into the cabin after the two men that shot was tied with ropes we'd brung along, and handcuffs, and we went hunting for the Kid. At first we couldn't find him at all. Gee! It was something fierce! And the old woman kep' a-crying and saying we'd kill her sick son, and she didn't know nothing about the man we was hunting for. But pretty soon I spied the Kid's foot stickin' out from under the cot where the sick man was, and when I told Jap Kemp that sick man pulled out a gun he had under the blanket and aimed it right at me!"

"Oh, mother's little Buddie!" whimpered Mrs. Tanner, with her apron to her eyes.

"*Aw, Ma*, cut it out! *he* didn't *hurt* me! The gun just went off crooked, and grazed Jap Kemp's hand a little, not much. Jap knocked it out of the sick man's hand just as he was pullin' the trigger. Say, Ma, ain't you got any more of those cucumber pickles? It makes a man mighty hungry to do all that riding and shooting. Well, it certainly was something fierce—Say, Miss Earle, you take that last piece o' pie. Oh, g'wan! *Take* it! *You* worked hard. No, I don't want it, really! Well, if you won't take it *anyway*, I might eat it just to save it. Got any more coffee, Ma?"

But Margaret was not eating. Her face was pale and her eyes were starry with unshed tears, and she waited in patient but breathless suspense for the vagaries of the story to work out to the finish.

"Yes, it certainly was something fierce, that cabin," went on the narrator. "Why, Ma, it looked as if it had never been swept under that cot when we hauled the Kid out. He was tied all up in knots, and great heavy ropes wound tight from his shoulders down to his ankles. Why, they were bound so tight they made great heavy welts in his wrists and shoulders and round his ankles when we took 'em off; and they had a great big rag stuffed into his mouth so he couldn't yell. Gee! It was something fierce! He was 'most dippy, too; but Jap Kemp brought him round pretty quick and got him outside in the air. That was the worst place I ever was in myself. You couldn't breathe, and the dirt was something fierce. It was like a pigpen. I sure was glad to get outdoors again. And then— well, the Kid came around all right and they got him on a horse and gave him something out of a bottle Jap Kemp had, and pretty soon he could ride again. Why, you'd oughta seen his nerve. He just sat up there as straight, his lips all white yet and his eyes looked some queer; but he straightened up and he looked those rascals right in the eye, and told 'em a few things, and he gave orders to the other men from Lone Fox Camp what to do with 'em; and he had the two women disarmed—they had guns, too—and carried away, and the cabin nailed up, and a notice put on the door, and every one of those men were handcuffed—the sick one and all—and he told 'em to bring a wagon and put the sick one's cot in and take 'em over to Ashland to the jail, and he sent word to Mr. Rogers. Then we rode home and got to the school-house just when you was playing the last chords of the ov'rtcher. Gee! It was some fierce ride and some *close shave*! The Kid he hadn't had a thing to eat since Monday noon, and he was some hungry! I found a sandwich on the window of the dressing-room, and he ate it while he got togged up—'course I told him 'bout Jed soon's we left the cabin, and Jap Kemp said he'd oughta go right home to camp after all he had been through; but he wouldn't; he said he was goin' to *act*. So 'course he had his way! But, gee! You could see it wasn't any cinch game for him! He 'most fell over every time after the curtain fell. You see, they gave him some kind of drugged whisky up there at the cabin that made his head feel queer. Say, he thinks that guy from the fort came in and looked at him once while he was asleep. He says it was only a dream, but I bet he did. Say, Ma, ain't you gonta give me another doughnut?"

In the quiet of her chamber at last, Margaret knelt before her window toward the purple, shadowy mountain under the starry dome, and gave thanks for the deliverance of Gardley; while Bud, in his comfortable loft, lay down to his well-earned rest and dreamed of pirates and angels and a hero who looked like the Kid.

CHAPTER XXVI

The Sunday before Lance Gardley started East on his journey of reparation two strangers slipped quietly into the back of the school-house during the singing of the first hymn and sat down in the shadow by the door.

Margaret was playing the piano when they came in, and did not see them, and when she turned back to her Scripture lesson she had time for but the briefest of glances. She supposed they must be some visitors from the fort, as they were speaking to the captain's wife——who came over occasionally to the Sunday service, perhaps because it afforded an opportunity for a ride with one of the young officers. These occasional visitors who came for amusement and curiosity had ceased to trouble Margaret. Her real work was with the men and women and children who loved the services for their own sake, and she tried as much as possible to forget outsiders. So, that day everything went on just as usual, Margaret putting her heart into the prayer, the simple, storylike reading of the Scripture, and the other story-sermon which followed it. Gardley sang unusually well at the close, a wonderful bit from an oratorio that he and Margaret had been practising.

But when toward the close of the little vesper service Margaret gave opportunity, as she often did, for others to take part in sentence prayers, one of the strangers from the back of the room stood up and began to pray. And such a prayer! Heaven seemed to bend low, and earth to kneel and beseech as the stranger-man, with a face like an archangel, and a body of an athlete clothed in a brown-flannel shirt and khakis, besought the Lord of heaven for a blessing on this gathering and on the leader of this little company who had so wonderfully led them to see the Christ and their need of salvation through the lesson of the day. And it did not need Bud's low-breathed whisper, "The missionary!" to tell Margaret who he was. His face told her. His prayer thrilled her, and his strong, young, true voice made her sure that here was a man of God in truth.

When the prayer was over and Margaret stood once more shyly facing her audience, she could scarcely keep the tremble out of her voice:

"Oh," said she, casting aside ceremony, "if I had known the missionary was here I should not have dared to try and lead this meeting to-day. Won't you please come up here and talk to us for a little while now, Mr. Brownleigh?"

At once he came forward eagerly, as if each opportunity were a pleasure. "Why, surely, I want to speak a word to you, just to say how glad I am to see you all, and to experience what a wonderful teacher you have found since I went away; but I wouldn't have missed this meeting to-day for all the sermons I ever wrote or preached. You don't need any more sermon than the remarkable story you've just been listening to, and I've only one word to add; and that is, that I've found since I went away that Jesus Christ, the only-begotten Son of God, is just the same Jesus to me to-day that He was the last time I spoke to you. He is just as ready to forgive your sin, to comfort you in sorrow, to help you in temptation, to raise your body in the resurrection, and to take you home to a mansion in His Father's house as He was the day He hung upon the cross to save your soul from death. I've found I can rest just as securely upon the Bible as the word of God as when I first tested its promises. Heaven and earth may pass away, but His word shall *never* pass away."

"*Go to it!*" said Jasper Kemp under his breath in the tone some men say "Amen!" and his brows were drawn as if he were watching a battle. Margaret couldn't help wondering if he were thinking of the Rev. Frederick West just then.

When the service was over the missionary brought his wife forward to Margaret, and they loved each other at once. Just another sweet girl like Margaret. She was lovely, with a delicacy of feature that betokened the high-born and high-bred, but dressed in a dainty khaki riding costume, if that uncompromising fabric could ever be called dainty. Margaret, remembering it afterward, wondered what it had been that gave it that unique individuality, and decided it was perhaps a combination of cut and finish and little dainty accessories. A bit of creamy lace at the throat of the rolling collar, a touch of golden-brown velvet in a golden clasp, the flash of a wonderful jewel on her finger, the modeling of the small, brown cap with its two eagle quills—all set the little woman apart and made her fit to enter any well-dressed company of riders in some great city park or fashionable drive. Yet here in the wilderness she was not overdressed.

The eight men from the camp stood in solemn row, waiting to be recognized, and behind them, abashed and grinning with embarrassment, stood Pop and Mom Wallis, Mom with her new gray bonnet glorifying her old face till the missionary's wife had to look twice to be sure who she was.

"And now, surely, Hazel, we must have these dear people come over and help us with the singing sometimes. Can't we try something right now?" said the missionary, looking first at his wife and then at Margaret and Gardley. "This man is a new-comer since I went away, but I'm mighty sure he is the right kind, and I'm glad to welcome him—or perhaps I would better ask if he will welcome me?" And with his rare smile the missionary put out his hand to Gardley, who took it with an eager grasp. The two men stood looking at each other for a moment, as rare men, rarely met, sometimes do even on a sinful earth; and after that clasp and that look they turned away, brothers for life.

That was a most interesting song rehearsal that followed. It would be rare to find four voices like those even in a cultivated musical center, and they blended as if they had been made for one another. The men from the bunk-house and a lot of other people silently dropped again into their seats to listen as the four sang on. The missionary took the bass, and his wife the alto, and the four made music worth listening to. The rare and lovely thing about it was that they sang to souls, not alone for ears, and so their music, classical though it was and of the highest order, appealed keenly to the hearts of these rough men, and made them feel that heaven had opened for them, as once before for untaught shepherds, and let down a ladder of angelic voices.

"I shall feel better about leaving you out here while I am gone, since they have come," said Gardley that night when he was bidding Margaret good night. "I couldn't bear to think there were none of your own kind about you. The others are devoted and would do for you with their lives if need be, as far as they know; but I like you to have *real friends*—real *Christian* friends. This man is what I call a Christian. I'm not sure but he is the first minister that I have ever come close to who has impressed me as believing what he preaches, and living it. I suppose there are others. I haven't known many. That man West that was here when you came was a mistake!"

"He didn't even preach much," smiled Margaret, "so how could he live it? This man is real. And there are others. Oh, I have known a lot of them that are living lives of sacrifice and loving service and are yet just as strong and happy and delightful as if they were millionaires. But they are the men who have not thrown away their Bibles and their Christ. They believe every promise in God's word, and rest on them day by day, testing them and proving them over and over. I wish you knew my father!"

"I am going to," said Gardley, proudly. "*I* am going to him just as soon as I have finished my business and straightened out my affairs; and I am going to tell him *everything*—with your permission, Margaret!"

"Oh, how beautiful!" cried Margaret, with happy tears in her eyes. "To think you are going to see father and mother. I have wanted them to know the real you. I couldn't half *tell* you, the real you, in a letter!"

"Perhaps they won't look on me with your sweet blindness, dear," he said, smiling tenderly down on her. "Perhaps they will see only my dark, past life—for I mean to tell your father everything. I'm not going to have any skeletons in the closet to cause pain hereafter. Perhaps your father and mother will not feel like giving their daughter to me after they know. Remember, I realize just what a rare prize she is."

"No, father is not like that, Lance," said Margaret, with her rare smile lighting up her happy eyes. "Father and mother will understand."

"But if they should not?" There was the shadow of sadness in Gardley's eyes as he asked the question.

"I belong to you, dear, anyway," she said, with sweet surrender. "I trust you though the whole world were against you!"

For answer Gardley took her in his arms, a look of awe upon his face, and, stooping, laid his lips upon hers in tender reverence.

"Margaret—you wonderful Margaret!" he said. "God has blessed me more than other men in sending you to me! With His help I will be worthy of you!"

Three days more and Margaret was alone with her school work, her two missionary friends thirty miles away, her eager watching for the mail to come, her faithful attendant Bud, and for comfort the purple mountain with its changing glory in the distance.

A few days before Gardley left for the East he had been offered a position by Rogers as general manager of his estate at a fine salary, and after consultation with Margaret he decided to accept it, but the question of their marriage they had left by common consent unsettled until Gardley should return and be able to offer his future wife a record made as fair and clean as human effort could make it after human mistakes had unmade it. As Margaret worked and waited, wrote her charming letters to father and mother and lover, and thought her happy thoughts with only the mountain for confidant, she did not plan for the future except in a dim and dreamy way. She would make those plans with Gardley when he returned. Probably they must wait some time before they could be married. Gardley would have to earn some money, and she must earn, too. She must keep the Ashland School for another year. It had been rather understood, when she came out, that if at all possible she would remain two years at least. It was hard to think of not going home for the summer vacation; but the trip cost a great deal and was not to be thought of. There was already a plan suggested to have a summer session of the school, and if that went through, of course she must stay right in Ashland. It was hard to think of not seeing her father and mother for another long year, but perhaps Gardley would be returning before the summer was over, and then it would not be so hard. However, she tried to put these thoughts out of her mind and do her work happily. It was incredible that Arizona should have become suddenly so blank and uninteresting since the departure of a man whom she had not known a few short months before.

Margaret had long since written to her father and mother about Gardley's first finding her in the desert. The thing had become history and was not likely to alarm them. She had been in Arizona long enough to be acquainted with things, and they would not be always thinking of her as sitting on stray water-tanks in the desert; so she told them about it, for she wanted them to know Gardley as he had been to her. The letters that had traveled back and forth between New York and Arizona had been full of Gardley; and still Margaret had not told her parents how it was between them. Gardley had asked that he might do that. Yet it had been a blind father and mother who had not long ago read between the lines of those letters and understood. Margaret fancied she detected a certain sense of relief in her mother's letters after she knew that Gardley had gone East. Were they worrying about him, she wondered, or was it just the natural dread of a mother to lose her child?

So Margaret settled down to school routine, and more and more made a confidant of Bud concerning little matters of the school. If it had not been for Bud at that time Margaret would have been lonely indeed.

Two or three times since Gardley left, the Brownleighs had ridden over to Sunday service, and once had stopped for a few minutes during the week on their way to visit some distant need. These occasions were a delight to Margaret, for Hazel Brownleigh was a kindred spirit. She was looking forward with pleasure to the visit she was to make them at the mission station as soon as school closed. She had been there once with Gardley before he left, but the ride was too long to go often, and the only escort available was Bud. Besides, she could not get away from school and the Sunday service at present; but it was pleasant to have something to look forward to.

Meantime the spring Commencement was coming on and Margaret had her hands full. She had undertaken to inaugurate a real Commencement with class day and as much form and ceremony as she could introduce in order to create a good school spirit; but such things are not done with the turn of a hand, and the young teacher sadly missed Gardley in all these preparations.

At this time Rosa Rogers was Margaret's particular thorn in the flesh.

Since the night that Forsythe had quit the play and ridden forth into the darkness Rosa had regarded her teacher with baleful eyes. Gardley, too, she hated, and was only waiting with smoldering wrath until her wild, ungoverned soul could take its revenge. She felt that but for those two Forsythe would still have been with her.

Margaret, realizing the passionate, untaught nature of the motherless girl and her great need of a friend to guide her, made attempt after attempt to reach and befriend her; but every attempt was met with repulse and the sharp word of scorn. Rosa had been too long the petted darling of a father who was utterly blind to her faults to be other than spoiled. Her own way was the one thing that ruled her. By her will she had ruled every nurse and servant about the place, and wheedled her father into letting her do anything the whim prompted. Twice her father, through the advice of friends, had tried the experiment of sending her away to school, once to an Eastern finishing school, and once to a convent on the Pacific coast, only to have her return shortly by request of the school, more wilful than when she had gone away. And now she ruled supreme in her father's home, disliked by most of the servants save those whom she chose to favor because they could be made to serve her purposes. Her father, engrossed in his business and away much of the time, was bound up in her and saw few of her faults. It is true that when a fault of hers did come to his notice, however, he dealt with it most severely, and grieved over it in secret, for the girl was much like the mother whose loss had emptied the world of its joy for him. But Rosa knew well how to manage her father and wheedle him, and also how to hide her own doings from his knowledge.

Rosa's eyes, dimples, pink cheeks, and coquettish little mouth were not idle in these days. She knew how to have every pupil at her feet and ready to obey her slightest wish. She wielded her power to its fullest extent as the summer drew near, and day after day saw a slow torture for Margaret. Some days the menacing air of insurrection fairly bristled in the room, and Margaret could not understand how some of her most devoted followers seemed to be in the forefront of battle, until one day she looked up quickly and caught the lynx-eyed glance of Rosa as she turned from smiling at the boys in the back seat. Then she understood. Rosa had cast her spell upon the boys, and they were acting under it and not of their own clear judgment. It was the world-old battle of sex, of woman against woman for the winning of the man to do her will. Margaret, using all the charm of her lovely personality to uphold standards of right, truth, purity, high living, and earnest thinking; Rosa striving with her impish beauty to lure them into *any* mischief so it foiled the other's purposes. And one day Margaret faced the girl alone, looking steadily into her eyes with sad, searching gaze, and almost a yearning to try to lead the pretty child to finer things.

"Rosa, why do you always act as if I were your enemy?" she said, sadly.

"Because you are!" said Rosa, with a toss of her independent head.

"Indeed I'm not, dear child," she said, putting out her hand to lay it on the girl's shoulder kindly. "I want to be your friend."

"I'm not a child!" snapped Rosa, jerking her shoulder angrily away; "and you can *never* be my friend, because I *hate* you!"

"Rosa, look here!" said Margaret, following the girl toward the door, the color rising in her cheeks and a desire growing in her heart to conquer this poor, passionate creature and win her for better things. "Rosa, I cannot have you say such things. Tell me why you hate me? What have I done that you should feel that way? I'm sure if we should talk it over we might come to some better understanding."

Rosa stood defiant in the doorway. "We could never come to any better understanding, Miss Earle," she declared in a cold, hard tone, "because I understand you now and I hate you. You tried your best to get my friend away from me, but you couldn't do it; and you would like to keep me from having any boy friends at all, but you can't do that, either. You think you are very popular, but you'll find out I always do what I like, and you needn't try to stop me. I don't have to come to school unless I choose, and as long as I don't break your rules you have no complaint coming; but you needn't think you can pull the wool over my eyes the way you do the others by pretending to be friends. I won't be friends! I hate you!" And Rosa turned grandly and marched out of the school-house.

Margaret stood gazing sadly after her and wondering if her failure here were her fault—if there was anything else she ought to have done—if she had let her personal dislike of the girl influence her conduct. She sat for some time at her desk, her chin in her hands, her eyes fixed on vacancy with a hopeless, discouraged expression in them, before she became aware of another presence in the room. Looking around quickly, she saw that Bud was sitting motionless at his desk, his forehead wrinkled in a fierce frown, his jaw set belligerently, and a look of such, unutterable pity and devotion in his eyes that her heart warmed to him at once and a smile of comradeship broke over her face.

"Oh, William! Were you here? Did you hear all that? What do you suppose is the matter? Where have I failed?"

"You 'ain't failed anywhere! You should worry 'bout her! She's a nut! If she was a boy I'd punch her head for her! But seeing she's only a girl, *you should worry*! She always was the limit!"

Bud's tone was forcible. He was the only one of all the boys who never yielded to Rosa's charms, but sat in glowering silence when she exercised her powers on the school and created pandemonium for the teacher. Bud's attitude was comforting. It had a touch of manliness and gentleness about it quite unwonted for him. It suggested beautiful possibilities for the future of his character, and Margaret smiled tenderly.

"Thank you, dear boy!" she said, gently. "You certainly are a comfort. If every one was as splendid as you are we should have a model school. But I do wish I could help Rosa. I can't see why she should hate me so! I must have made some big mistake with her in the first place to antagonize her."

"Naw!" said Bud, roughly. "No chance! She's just a *nut*, that's all. She's got a case on that Forsythe guy, the worst kind, and she's afraid somebody 'll get him away from her, the poor stew, as if anybody would get a case on a tough guy like that! Gee! You should worry! Come on, let's take a ride over t' camp!"

With a sigh and a smile Margaret accepted Bud's consolations and went on her way, trying to find some manner of showing Rosa what a real friend she was willing to be. But Rosa continued obdurate and hateful, regarding her teacher with haughty indifference except when she was called upon to recite, which she did sometimes with scornful condescension, sometimes with pert perfection, and sometimes with saucy humor which convulsed the whole room. Margaret's patience was almost ceasing to be a virtue, and she meditated often whether she ought not to request that the girl be withdrawn from the school. Yet she reflected that it was a very short time now until Commencement, and that Rosa had not openly defied any rules. It was merely a personal antagonism. Then, too, if Rosa were taken from the school there was really no other good influence in the girl's life at present. Day by day Margaret prayed about the matter and hoped that something would develop to make plain her way.

After much thought in the matter she decided to go on with her plans, letting Rosa have her place in the Commencement program and her part in the class-day doings as if nothing were the matter. Certainly there was nothing laid down in the rules of a public school that proscribed a scholar who did not love her teacher. Why should the fact that one had incurred the hate of a pupil unfit that pupil for her place in her class so long as she did her duties? And Rosa did hers promptly and deftly, with a certain piquant originality that Margaret could not help but admire.

Sometimes, as the teacher cast a furtive look at the pretty girl working away at her desk, she wondered what was going on behind the lovely mask. But the look in Rosa's eyes, when she raised them, was both deep and sly.

Rosa's hatred was indeed deep rooted. Whatever heart she had not frivoled away in wilfulness had been caught and won by Forsythe, the first grown man who had ever dared to make real love to her. Her jealousy of Margaret was the most intense thing that had ever come into her life. To think of him looking at Margaret, talking to Margaret, smiling at Margaret, walking or riding with Margaret, was enough to send her writhing upon her bed in the darkness of a wakeful night. She would clench her pretty hands until the nails dug into the flesh and brought the blood. She would bite the pillow or the blankets with an almost fiendish clenching of her teeth upon them and mutter, as she did so: "I hate her! I *hate* her! I could *kill* her!"

The day her first letter came from Forsythe, Rosa held her head high and went about the school as if she were a princess royal and Margaret were the dust under her feet. Triumph sat upon her like a crown and looked forth regally from her eyes. She laid her hand upon her heart and felt the crackle of his letter inside her blouse. She dreamed with her eyes upon the distant mountain and thought of the tender names he had called her: "Little wild Rose of his heart," "No rose in all the world until you came," and a lot of other meaningful sentences. A real love-letter all her own! No sharing him with any hateful teachers! He had implied in herletter that she was the only one of all the people in that region to whom he cared to write. He had said he was coming back some day to get her. Her young, wild heart throbbed exultantly, and her eyes looked forth their triumph malignantly. When he did come she would take care that he stayed close by her. No conceited teacher from the East should lure him from her side. She would prepare her guiles and smile her sweetest. She would wear fine garments from abroad, and show him she could far outshine that quiet, common Miss Earle, with all her airs. Yet to this end she studied hard. It was no part of her plan to be left behind at graduating-time. She would please her father by taking a prominent part in things and outdoing all the others. Then he would give her what she liked—jewels and silk dresses, and all the things a girl should have who had won a lover like hers.

The last busy days before Commencement were especially trying for Margaret. It seemed as if the children were possessed with the very spirit of mischief, and she could not help but see that it was Rosa who, sitting demurely in her desk, was the center of it all. Only Bud's steady, frowning countenance of all that rollicking, roistering crowd kept loyalty with the really beloved teacher. For, indeed, they loved her, every one but Rosa, and would have stood by her to a man and girl when it really came to the pinch, but in a matter like a little bit of fun in these last few days of school, and when challenged to it by the school beauty who did not usually condescend to any but a few of the older boys, where was the harm? They were so flattered by Rosa's smiles that they failed to see Margaret's worn, weary wistfulness.

Bud, coming into the school-house late one afternoon in search of her after the other scholars had gone, found Margaret with her head down upon the desk and her shoulders shaken with soundless sobs. He stood for a second silent in the doorway, gazing helplessly at her grief, then with the delicacy of one boy for another he slipped back outside the door and stood in the shadow, grinding his teeth.

"Gee!" he said, under his breath. "Oh, gee! I'd like to punch her fool head. I don't care if she is a girl! She needs it. Gee! if she was a boy wouldn't I settle her, the little darned mean sneak!"

His remarks, it is needless to say, did not have reference to his beloved teacher.

It was in the atmosphere everywhere that something was bound to happen if this strain kept up. Margaret knew it and felt utterly inadequate to meet it. Rosa knew it and was awaiting her opportunity. Bud knew it and could only stand and watch where the blow was to strike first and be ready to ward it off. In these days he wished fervently for Gardley's return. He did not know just what Gardley could do about "that little fool," as he called Rosa, but it would be a relief to be able to tell some one all about it. If he only dared leave he would go over and tell Jasper Kemp about it, just to share his burden with somebody. But as it was he must stick to the job for the present and bear his great responsibility, and so the days hastened by to the last Sunday before Commencement, which was to be on Monday.

CHAPTER XXVII

Margaret had spent Saturday in rehearsals, so that there had been no rest for her. Sunday morning she slept late, and awoke from a troubled dream, unrested. She almost meditated whether she would not ask some one to read a sermon at the afternoon service and let her go on sleeping. Then a memory of the lonely old woman at the camp, and the men, who came so regularly to the service, roused her to effort once more, and she arose and tried to prepare a little something for them.

She came into the school-house at the hour, looking fagged, with dark circles under her eyes; and the loving eyes of Mom Wallis already in her front seat watched her keenly.

"It's time for *him* to come back," she said, in her heart. "She's gettin' peeked! I wisht he'd come!"

Margaret had hoped that Rosa would not come. The girl was not always there, but of late she had been quite regular, coming in late with her father just a little after the story had begun, and attracting attention by her smiles and bows and giggling whispers, which sometimes were so audible as to create quite a diversion from the speaker.

But Rosa came in early to-day and took a seat directly in front of Margaret, in about the middle of the house, fixing her eyes on her teacher with a kind of settled intention that made Margaret shrink as if from a danger she was not able to meet. There was something bright and hard and daring in Rosa's eyes as she stared unwinkingly, as if she had come to search out a weak spot for her evil purposes, and Margaret was so tired she wanted to lay her head down on her desk and cry. She drew some comfort from the reflection that if she should do so childish a thing she would be at once surrounded by a strong battalion of friends from the camp, who would shield her with their lives if necessary.

It was silly, of course, and she must control this choking in her throat, only how was she ever going to talk, with Rosa looking at her that way? It was like a nightmare pursuing her. She turned to the piano and kept them all singing for a while, so that she might pray in her heart and grow calm; and when, after her brief, earnest prayer, she lifted her eyes to the audience, she saw with intense relief that the Brownleighs were in the audience.

She started a hymn that they all knew, and when they were well in the midst of the first verse she slipped from the piano-stool and walked swiftly down the aisle to Brownleigh's side.

"Would you please talk to them a little while?" she pleaded, wistfully. "I am so tired I feel as if I just couldn't, to-day."

Instantly Brownleigh followed her back to the desk and took her place, pulling out his little, worn Bible and opening it with familiar fingers to a beloved passage:

"'Come unto me, all ye that labor and are heavy laden, and I will give you rest.'"

The words fell on Margaret's tired heart like balm, and she rested her head back against the wall and closed her eyes to listen. Sitting so away from Rosa's stare, she could forget for a while the absurd burdens that had got on her nerves, and could rest down hard upon her Saviour. Every word that the man of God spoke seemed meant just for her, and brought strength, courage, and new trust to her heart. She forgot the little crowd of other listeners and took the message to herself, drinking it in eagerly as one who has been a long time ministering accepts a much-needed ministry. When she moved to the piano again for the closing hymn she felt new strength within her to bear the trials of the week that were before her. She turned, smiling and brave, to speak to those who always crowded around to shake hands and have a word before leaving.

Hazel, putting a loving arm around her as soon as she could get up to the front, began to speak soothingly: "You poor, tired child!" she said; "you are almost worn to a frazzle. You need a big change, and I'm going to plan it for you just as soon as I possibly can. How would you like to go with us on our trip among the Indians? Wouldn't it be great? It'll be several days, depending on how far we go, but John wants to visit the Hopi reservation, if possible, and it'll be so interesting. They are a most strange people. We'll have a delightful trip, sleeping out under the stars, you know. Don't you just love it? I do. I wouldn't miss it for the world. I can't be sure, for a few days yet, when we can go, for John has to make a journey in the other direction first, and he isn't sure when he can return; but it might be this week. How soon can you come to us? How I wish we could take you right home with us to-night. You need to get away and rest. But your Commencement is to-morrow, isn't it? I'm so sorry we can't be here, but this other matter is important, and John has to go early in the morning. Some one very sick who wants to see him before he dies—an old Indian who didn't know a thing about Jesus till John found him one day. I suppose you haven't anybody who could bring you over to us after your work is done here to-morrow night or Tuesday, have you? Well, we'll see if we can't find some one to send for you soon. There's an old Indian who often comes this way, but he's away buying cattle. Maybe John can think of a way we could send for you early in the week. Then you would be ready to go with us on the trip. You would like to go, wouldn't you?"

"Oh, so much!" said Margaret, with a sigh of wistfulness. "I can't think of anything pleasanter!"

Margaret turned suddenly, and there, just behind her, almost touching her, stood Rosa, that strange, baleful gleam in her eyes like a serpent who was biding her time, drawing nearer and nearer, knowing she had her victim where she could not move before she struck.

It was a strange fancy, of course, and one that was caused by sick nerves, but Margaret drew back and almost cried out, as if for some one to protect her. Then her strong common sense came to the rescue and she rallied and smiled at Rosa a faint little sorry smile. It was hard to smile at the bright, baleful face with the menace in the eyes.

Hazel was watching her. "You poor child! You're quite worn out! I'm afraid you're going to be sick."

"Oh no," said Margaret, trying to speak cheerfully; "things have just got on my nerves, that's all. It's been a particularly trying time. I shall be all right when to-morrow night is over."

"Well, we're going to send for you very soon, so be ready!" and Hazel followed her husband, waving her hand in gay parting.

Rosa was still standing just behind her when Margaret turned back to her desk, and the younger girl gave her one last dagger look, a glitter in her eyes so sinister and vindictive that Margaret felt a shudder run through her whole body, and was glad that just then Rosa's father called to her that they must be starting home. Only one more day now of Rosa, and she would be done with her, perhaps forever. The girl was through the school course and was graduating. It was not likely she would return another year. Her opportunity was over to help her. She had failed. Why, she couldn't tell, but she had strangely failed, and all she asked now was not to have to endure the hard, cold, young presence any longer.

"Sick nerves, Margaret!" she said to herself. "Go home and go to bed. You'll be all right to-morrow!" And she locked the school-house door and walked quietly home with the faithful Bud.

The past month had been a trying time also for Rosa. Young, wild, and motherless, passionate, wilful and impetuous, she was finding life tremendously exciting just now. With no one to restrain her or warn her she was playing with forces that she did not understand.

She had subjugated easily all the boys in school, keeping them exactly where she wanted them for her purpose, and using methods that would have done credit to a woman of the world. But by far the greatest force in her life was her infatuation for Forsythe.

The letters had traveled back and forth many times between them since Forsythe wrote that first love-letter. He found a whimsical pleasure in her deep devotion and naïve readiness to follow as far as he cared to lead her. He realized that, young as she was, she was no innocent, which made the acquaintance all the more interesting. He, meantime, idled away a few months on the Pacific coast, making mild love to a rich California girl and considering whether or not he was ready yet to settle down.

In the mean time his correspondence with Rosa took on such a nature that his volatile, impulsive nature was stirred with a desire to see her again. It was not often that once out of sight he looked back to a victim, but Rosa had shown a daring and a spirit in her letters that sent a challenge to his sated senses. Moreover, the California heiress was going on a journey; besides, an old enemy of his who knew altogether too much of his past had appeared on the scene; and as Gardley had been removed from the Ashland vicinity for a time, Forsythe felt it might be safe to venture back again. There was always that pretty, spirited little teacher if Rosa failed to charm. But why should Rosa not charm? And why should he not yield? Rosa's father was a good sort and had all kinds of property. Rosa was her father's only heir. On the whole, Forsythe decided that the best move he could make next would be to return to Arizona. If things turned out well he might even think of marrying Rosa.

This was somewhat the train of thought that led Forsythe at last to write to Rosa that he was coming, throwing Rosa into a panic of joy and alarm. For Rosa's father had been most explicit about her ever going out with Forsythe again. It had been the most relentless command he had ever laid upon her, spoken in a tone she hardly ever disobeyed. Moreover, Rosa was fearfully jealous of Margaret. If Forsythe should come and begin to hang around the teacher Rosa felt she would go wild, or do something terrible, perhaps even kill somebody. She shut her sharp little white teeth fiercely down into her red under lip and vowed with flashing eyes that he should never see Margaret again if power of hers could prevent it.

The letter from Forsythe had reached her on Saturday evening, and she had come to the Sunday service with the distinct idea of trying to plan how she might get rid of Margaret. It would be hard enough to evade her father's vigilance if he once found out the young man had returned; but to have him begin to go and see Margaret again was a thing she could not and would not stand.

The idea obsessed her to the exclusion of all others, and made her watch her teacher as if by her very concentration of thought upon her some way out of the difficulty might be evolved; as if Margaret herself might give forth a hint of weakness somewhere that would show her how to plan.

To that intent she had come close in the group with the others around the teacher at the close of meeting, and, so standing, had overheard all that the Brownleighs had said. The lightning flash of triumph that she cast at Margaret as she left the school-house was her own signal that she had found a way at last. Her opportunity had come, and just in time. Forsythe was to arrive in Arizona some time on Tuesday, and wanted Rosa to meet him at one of their old trysting-places, out some distance from her father's house. He knew that school would just be over, for she had written him about Commencement, and so he understood that she would be free. But he did not know that the place he had selected to meet her was on one of Margaret's favorite trails where she and Bud often rode in the late afternoons, and that above all things Rosa wished to avoid any danger of meeting her teacher; for she not only feared that Forsythe's attention would be drawn away from her, but also that Margaret might feel it her duty to report to her father about her clandestine meeting.

Rosa's heart beat high as she rode demurely home with her father, answering his pleasantries with smiles and dimples and a coaxing word, just as he loved to have her. But she was not thinking of her father, though she kept well her mask of interest in what he had to say. She was trying to plan how she might use what she had heard to get rid of Margaret Earle. If only Mrs. Brownleigh would do as she had hinted and send some one Tuesday morning to escort Miss Earle over to her home, all would be clear sailing for Rosa; but she dared not trust to such a possibility. There were not many escorts coming their way from Ganado, and Rosa happened to know that the old Indian who frequently escorted parties was off in another direction. She could not rest on any such hope. When she reached home she went at once to her room and sat beside her window, gazing off at the purple mountains in deep thought. Then she lighted a candle and went in search of a certain little Testament, long since neglected and covered with dust. She found it at last on the top of a pile of books in a dark closet, and dragged it forth, eagerly turning the pages. Yes, there it was, and in it a small envelope directed to "Miss Rosa Rogers" in a fine angular handwriting. The letter was from the missionary's wife to the little girl who had recited her texts so beautifully as to earn the Testament.

Rosa carried it to her desk, secured a good light, and sat down to read it over carefully.

No thought of her innocent childish exultation over that letter came to her now. She was intent on one thing—the handwriting. Could she seize the secret of it and reproduce it? She had before often done so with great success. She could imitate Miss Earle's writing so perfectly that she often took an impish pleasure in changing words in the questions on the blackboard and making them read absurdly for the benefit of the school. It was such good sport to see the amazement on Margaret's face when her attention would be called to it by a hilarious class, and to watch her troubled brow when she read what she supposed she had written.

When Rosa was but a little child she used to boast that she could write her father's name in perfect imitation of his signature; and often signed some trifling receipt for him just for amusement. A dangerous gift in the hands of a conscienceless girl! Yet this was the first time that Rosa had really planned to use her art in any serious way. Perhaps it never occurred to her that she was doing wrong. At present her heart was too full of hate and fear and jealous love to care for right or wrong or anything else. It is doubtful if she would have hesitated a second even if the thing she was planning had suddenly appeared to her in the light of a great crime. She seemed sometimes almost like a creature without moral sense, so swayed was she by her own desires and feelings. She was blind now to everything but her great desire to get Margaret out of the way and have Forsythe to herself.

Long after her father and the servants were asleep Rosa's light burned while she bent over her desk, writing. Page after page she covered with careful copies of Mrs. Brownleigh's letter written to herself almost three years before. Finally she wrote out the alphabet, bit by bit as she picked it from the words, learning just how each letter was habitually formed, the small letters and the capitals, with the peculiarities of connection and ending. At last, when she lay down to rest, she felt herself capable of writing a pretty fair letter in Mrs. Brownleigh's handwriting. The next thing was to make her plan and compose her letter. She lay staring into the darkness and trying to think just what she could do.

In the first place, she settled it that Margaret must be gotten to Walpi at least. It would not do to send her to Ganado, where the mission station was, for that was a comparatively short journey, and she could easily go in a day. When the fraud was discovered, as of course it would be when Mrs. Brownleigh heard of it, Margaret would perhaps return to find out who had done it. No, she must be sent all the way to Walpi if possible. That would take at least two nights and the most of two days to get there. Forsythe had said his stay was to be short. By the time Margaret got back from Walpi Forsythe would be gone.

But how manage to get her to Walpi without her suspicions being aroused? She might word the note so that Margaret would be told to come half-way, expecting to meet the missionaries, say at Keams. There was a trail straight up from Ashland to Keams, cutting off quite a distance and leaving Ganado off at the right. Keams was nearly forty miles west of Ganado. That would do nicely. Then if she could manage to have another note left at Keams, saying they could not wait and had gone on, Margaret would suspect nothing and go all the way to Walpi. That would be fine and would give the school-teacher an interesting experience which wouldn't hurt her in the least. Rosa thought it might be rather interesting than otherwise. She had no compunctions whatever about how Margaret might feel when she arrived in that strange Indian town and found no friends awaiting her. Her only worry was where she was to find a suitable escort, for she felt assured that Margaret would not start out alone with one man servant on an expedition that would keep her out overnight. And where in all that region could she find a woman whom she could trust to send on the errand? It almost looked as though the thing were an impossibility. She lay tossing and puzzling over it till gray dawn stole into the room. She mentally reviewed every servant on the place on whom she could rely to do her bidding and keep her secret, but there was some reason why each one would not do. She scanned the country, even considering old Ouida, who had been living in a shack over beyond the fort ever since her cabin had been raided; but old Ouida was too notorious. Mrs. Tanner would keep Margaret from going with her, even if Margaret herself did not know the old woman's reputation. Rosa considered if there were any way of wheedling Mom Wallis into the affair, and gave that up, remembering the suspicious little twinkling eyes of Jasper Kemp. At last she fell asleep, with her plan still unformed but her determination to carry it through just as strong as ever. If worst came to worst she would send the half-breed cook from the ranch kitchen and put something in the note about his expecting to meet his sister an hour's ride out on the trail. The half-breed would do anything in the world for money, and Rosa had no trouble in getting all she wanted of that commodity. But the half-breed was an evil-looking fellow, and she feared lest Margaret would not like to go with him. However, he should be a last resort. She would not be balked in her purpose.

CHAPTER XXVIII

Rosa awoke very early, for her sleep had been light and troubled. She dressed hastily and sat down to compose a note which could be altered slightly in case she found some one better than the half-breed; but before she was half through the phrasing she heard a slight disturbance below her window and a muttering in guttural tones from a strange voice. Glancing hastily out, she saw some Indians below, talking with one of the men, who was shaking his head and motioning to them that they must go on, that this was no place for them to stop. The Indian motioned to his squaw, sitting on a dilapidated little moth-eaten burro with a small papoose in her arms and looking both dirty and miserable. He muttered as though he were pleading for something.

We believe that God's angels follow the feet of little children and needy ones to protect them; does the devil also send his angels to lead unwary ones astray, and to protect the plan's of the erring ones? If so then he must have sent these Indians that morning to further Rosa's plans, and instantly she recognized her opportunity. She leaned out of her window and spoke in a clear, reproving voice:

"James, what does he want? Breakfast? You know father wouldn't want any hungry person to be turned away. Let them sit down on the bench there and tell Dorset I said to give them a good hot breakfast, and get some milk for the baby. Be quick about it, too!"

James started and frowned at the clear, commanding voice. The squaw turned grateful animal eyes up to the little beauty in the window, muttering some inarticulate thanks, while the stolid Indian's eyes glittered hopefully, though the muscles of his mask-like countenance changed not an atom.

Rosa smiled radiantly and ran down to see that her orders were obeyed. She tried to talk a little with the squaw, but found she understood very little English. The Indian spoke better and gave her their brief story. They were on their way to the Navajo reservation to the far north. They had been unfortunate enough to lose their last scanty provisions by prowling coyotes during the night, and were in need of food. Rosa gave them a place to sit down and a plentiful breakfast, and ordered that a small store of provisions should be prepared for their journey after they had rested. Then she hurried up to her room to finish her letter. She had her plan well fixed now. These strangers should be her willing messengers. Now and then, as she wrote she lifted her head and gazed out of the window, where she could see the squaw busy with her little one, and her eyes fairly glittered with satisfaction. Nothing could have been better planned than this.

She wrote her note carefully:

DEAR MARGARET she had heard Hazel call Margaret by her first name, and rightly judged that their new friendship was already strong enough to justify this intimacy,—I have found just the opportunity I wanted for you to come to us. These Indians are thoroughly trustworthy and are coming in just the direction to bring you to a point where we will meet you. We have decided to go on to Walpi at once, and will probably meet you near Keams, or a little farther on. The Indian knows the way, and you need not be afraid. I trust him perfectly. Start at once, please, so that you will meet us in time. John has to go on as fast as possible. I know you will enjoy the trip, and am so glad you are coming.

Lovingly,
HAZEL RADCLIFFE BROWNLEIGH.

Rosa read it over, comparing it carefully with the little yellow note from her Testament, and decided that it was a very good imitation. She could almost hear Mrs. Brownleigh saying what she had written. Rosa really was quite clever. She had done it well.

She hastily sealed and addressed her letter, and then hurried down to talk with the Indians again.

The place she had ordered for them to rest was at some distance from the kitchen door, a sort of outshed for the shelter of certain implements used about the ranch. A long bench ran in front of it, and a big tree made a goodly shade. The Indians had found their temporary camp quite inviting.

Rosa made a detour of the shed, satisfied herself that no one was within hearing, and then sat down on the bench, ostensibly playing with the papoose, dangling a red ball on a ribbon before his dazzled, bead-like eyes and bringing forth a gurgle of delight from the dusky little mummy. While she played she talked idly with the Indians. Had they money enough for their journey? Would they like to earn some? Would they act as guide to a lady who wanted to go to Walpi? At least she wanted to go as far as Keams, where she might meet friends, missionaries, who were going on with her to Walpi to visit the Indians. If they didn't meet her she wanted to be guided all the way to Walpi? Would they undertake it? It would pay them well. They would get money enough for their journey and have some left when they got to the reservation. And Rosa displayed two gold pieces temptingly in her small palms.

The Indian uttered a guttural sort of gasp at sight of so much money, and sat upright. He gasped again, indicating by a solemn nod that he was agreeable to the task before him, and the girl went gaily on with her instructions:

"You will have to take some things along to make the lady comfortable. I will see that those are got ready. Then you can have the things for your own when you leave the lady at Walpi. You will have to take a letter to the lady and tell her you are going this afternoon, and she must be ready to start at once or she will not meet the missionary. Tell her you can only wait until three o'clock to start. You will find the lady at the school-house at noon. You must not come till noon—" Rosa pointed to the sun and then straight overhead. The Indian watched her keenly and nodded.

"You must ask for Miss Earle and give her this letter. She is the school-teacher."

The Indian grunted and looked at the white missive in Rosa's hand, noting once more the gleam of the gold pieces.

"You must wait till the teacher goes to her boarding-house and packs her things and eats her dinner. If anybody asks where you came from you must say the missionary's wife from Ganado sent you. Don't tell anybody anything else. Do you understand? More money if you don't say anything?" Rosa clinked the gold pieces softly.

The strange, sphinx-like gaze of the Indian narrowed comprehensively. He understood. His native cunning was being bought for this girl's own purposes. He looked greedily at the money. Rosa had put her hand in her pocket and brought out yet another gold piece.

"See! I give you this one now"—she laid one gold piece in the Indian's hand—"and these two I put in an envelope and pack with some provisions and blankets on another horse. I will leave the horse tied to a tree up where the big trail crosses this big trail out that way. You know?"

Rosa pointed in the direction she meant, and the Indian looked and grunted, his eyes returning to the two gold pieces in her hand. It was a great deal of money for the little lady to give. Was she trying to cheat him? He looked down at the gold he already held. It was good money. He was sure of that. He looked at her keenly.

"I shall be watching and I shall know whether you have the lady or not," went on the girl, sharply. "If you do not bring the lady with you there will be no money and no provisions waiting for you. But if you bring the lady you can untie the horse and take him with you. You will need the horse to carry the things. When you get to Walpi you can set him free. He is branded and he will likely come back. We shall find him. See, I will put the gold pieces in this tin can."

She picked up a sardine-tin that lay at her feet, slipped the gold pieces in an envelope from her pocket, stuffed it in the tin, bent down the cover, and held it up.

"This can will be packed on the top of the other provisions, and you can open it and take the money out when you untie the horse. Then hurry on as fast as you can and get as far along the trail as possible to-night before you camp. Do you understand?"

The Indian nodded once more, and Rosa felt that she had a confederate worthy of her need.

She stayed a few minutes more, going carefully over her directions, telling the Indian to be sure his squaw was kind to the lady, and that on no account he should let the lady get uneasy or have cause to complain of her treatment, or trouble would surely come to him. At last she felt sure she had made him understand, and she hurried away to slip into her pretty white dress and rose-colored ribbons and ride to school. Before she left her room she glanced out of the window at the Indians, and saw them sitting motionless, like a group of bronze. Once the Indian stirred and, putting his hand in his bosom, drew forth the white letter she had given him, gazed at it a moment, and hid it in his breast again. She nodded her satisfaction as she turned from the window. The next thing was to get to school and play her own part in the Commencement exercises.

The morning was bright, and the school-house was already filled to overflowing when Rosa arrived. Her coming, as always, made a little stir among admiring groups, for even those who feared her admired her from afar. She fluttered into the school-house and up the aisle with the air of a princess who knew she had been waited for and was condescending to come at all.

Rosa was in everything—the drills, the march, the choruses, and the crowning oration. She went through it all with the perfection of a bright mind and an adaptable nature. One would never have dreamed, to look at her pretty dimpling face and her sparkling eyes, what diabolical things were moving in her mind, nor how those eyes, lynx-soft with lurking sweetness and treachery, were watching all the time furtively for the appearance of the old Indian.

At last she saw him, standing in a group just outside the window near the platform, his tall form and stern countenance marking him among the crowd of familiar faces. She was receiving her diploma from the hand of Margaret when she caught his eye, and her hand trembled just a quiver as she took the dainty roll tied with blue and white ribbons. That he recognized her she was sure; that he knew she did not wish him to make known his connection with her she felt equally convinced he understood. His eye had that comprehending look of withdrawal. She did not look up directly at him again. Her eyes were daintily downward. Nevertheless, she missed not a turn of his head, not a glance from that stern eye, and she knew the moment when he stood at the front door of the school-house with the letter in his hand, stolid and indifferent, yet a great force to be reckoned with.

Some one looked at the letter, pointed to Margaret, called her, and she came. Rosa was not far away all the time, talking with Jed; her eyes downcast, her cheeks dimpling, missing nothing that could be heard or seen.

Margaret read the letter. Rosa watched her, knew every curve of every letter and syllable as she read, held her breath, and watched Margaret's expression. Did she suspect? No. A look of intense relief and pleasure had come into her eyes. She was glad to have found a way to go. She turned to Mrs. Tanner.

"What do you think of this, Mrs. Tanner? I'm to go with Mrs. Brownleigh on a trip to Walpi. Isn't that delicious? I'm to start at once. Do you suppose I could have a bite to eat? I won't need much. I'm too tired to eat and too anxious to be off. If you give me a cup of tea and a sandwich I'll be all right. I've got things about ready to go, for Mrs. Brownleigh told me she would send some one for me."

"H'm!" said Mrs. Tanner, disapprovingly. "Who you goin' with? Just *him*? I don't much like *his* looks!"

She spoke in a low tone so the Indian would not hear, and it was almost in Rosa's very ear, who stood just behind. Rosa's heart stopped a beat and she frowned at the toe of her slipper. Was this common little Tanner woman going to be the one to balk her plans?

Margaret raised her head now for her first good look at the Indian, and it must be admitted a chill came into her heart. Then, as if he comprehended what was at stake, the Indian turned slightly and pointed down the path toward the road. By common consent the few who were standing about the door stepped back and made a vista for Margaret to see the squaw sitting statue-like on her scraggy little pony, gazing off at the mountain in the distance, as if she were sitting for her picture, her solemn little papoose strapped to her back.

Margaret's troubled eyes cleared. The family aspect made things all right again. "You see, he has his wife and child," she said. "It's all right. Mrs. Brownleigh says she trusts him perfectly, and I'm to meet them on the way. Read the letter."

She thrust the letter into Mrs. Tanner's hand, and Rosa trembled for her scheme once more. Surely, surely Mrs. Tanner would not be able to detect the forgery!

"H'm! Well, I s'pose it's all right if she says so, but I'm sure I don't relish them pesky Injuns, and I don't think that squaw wife of his looks any great shakes, either. They look to me like they needed a good scrub with Bristol brick. But then, if you're set on going, you'll go, 'course. I jest wish Bud hadn't 'a' gone home with that Jasper Kemp. He might 'a' gone along, an' you'd 'a' had somebody to speak English to."

"Yes, it would have been nice to have William along," said Margaret; "but I think I'll be all right. Mrs. Brownleigh wouldn't send anybody that wasn't nice."

"H'm! I dun'no'! She's an awful crank. She just loves them Injuns, they say. But I, fer one, draw the line at holdin' 'em in my lap. I don't b'lieve in mixin' folks up that way. Preach to 'em if you like, but let 'em keep their distance, I say."

Margaret laughed and went off to pick up her things. Rosa stood smiling and talking to Jed until she saw Margaret and Mrs. Tanner go off together, the Indians riding slowly along behind.

Rosa waited until the Indians had turned off the road down toward the Tanners', and then she mounted her own pony and rode swiftly home.

She rushed up to her room and took off her fine apparel, arraying herself quickly in a plain little gown, and went down to prepare the provisions. There was none too much time, and she must work rapidly. It was well for her plans that she was all-powerful with the servants and could send them about at will to get them out of her way. She invented a duty for each now that would take them for a few minutes well out of sight and sound; then she hurried together the provisions in a basket, making two trips to get them to the shelter where she had told the Indian he would find the horse tied. She had to make a third trip to bring the blankets and a few other things she knew would be indispensable, but the whole outfit was really but carelessly gotten together, and it was just by chance that some things got in at all.

It was not difficult to find the old cayuse she intended using for a pack-horse. He was browsing around in the corral, and she soon had a halter over his head, for she had been quite used to horses from her babyhood.

She packed the canned things, tinned meats, vegetables, and fruit into a couple of large sacks, adding some fodder for the horses, a box of matches, some corn bread, of which there was always plenty on hand in the house, some salt pork, and a few tin dishes. These she slung pack fashion over the old horse, fastened the sardine-tin containing the gold pieces where it would be easily found, tied the horse to a tree, and retired behind a shelter of sage-brush to watch.

It was not long before the little caravan came, the Indians riding ahead single file, like two graven images, moving not a muscle of their faces, and Margaret a little way behind on her own pony, her face as happy and relieved as if she were a child let out from a hard task to play.

The Indian stopped beside the horse, a glitter of satisfaction in his eyes as he saw that the little lady had fulfilled her part of the bargain. He indicated to the squaw and the lady that they might move on down the trail, and he would catch up with them; and then dismounted, pouncing warily upon the sardine-tin at once. He looked furtively about, then took out the money and tested it with his teeth to make sure it was genuine.

He grunted his further satisfaction, looked over the pack-horse, made more secure the fastenings of the load, and, taking the halter, mounted and rode stolidly away toward the north.

Rosa waited in her covert until they were far out of sight, then made her way hurriedly back to the house and climbed to a window where she could watch the trail for several miles. There, with a field-glass, she kept watch until the procession had filed across the plains, down into a valley, up over a hill, and dropped to a farther valley out of sight. She looked at the sun and drew a breath of satisfaction. She had done it at last! She had got Margaret away before Forsythe came! There was no likelihood that the fraud would be discovered until her rival was far enough away to be safe. A kind of reaction came upon Rosa's overwrought nerves. She laughed out harshly, and her voice had a cruel ring to it. Then she threw herself upon the bed and burst into a passionate fit of weeping, and so, by and by, fell asleep. She dreamed that Margaret had returned like a shining, fiery angel, a two-edged sword in her hand and all the Wallis camp at her heels, with vengeance in their wake. That hateful little boy, Bud Tanner, danced around and made faces at her, while Forsythe had forgotten her to gaze at Margaret's face.

CHAPTER XXIX

To Margaret the day was very fair, and the omens all auspicious. She carried with her close to her heart two precious letters received that morning and scarcely glanced at as yet, one from Gardley and one from her mother. She had had only time to open them and be sure that all was well with her dear ones, and had left the rest to read on the way.

She was dressed in the khaki riding-habit she always wore when she went on horseback; and in the bag strapped on behind she carried a couple of fresh white blouses, a thin, white dress, a little soft dark silk gown that folded away almost into a cobweb, and a few other necessities. She had also slipped in a new book her mother had sent her, into which she had had as yet no time to look, and her chessmen and board, besides writing materials. She prided herself on having got so many necessaries into so small a compass. She would need the extra clothing if she stayed at Ganado with the missionaries for a week on her return from the trip, and the book and chessmen would amuse them all by the way. She had heard Brownleigh say he loved to play chess.

Margaret rode on the familiar trail, and for the first hour just let herself be glad that school was over and she could rest and have no responsibility. The sun shimmered down brilliantly on the white, hot sand and gray-green of the greasewood and sage-brush. Tall spikes of cactus like lonely spires shot up now and again to vary the scene. It was all familiar ground to Margaret around here, for she had taken many rides with Gardley and Bud, and for the first part of the way every turn and bit of view was fraught with pleasant memories that brought a smile to her eyes as she recalled some quotation of Gardley's or some prank of Bud's. Here was where they first sighted the little cottontail the day she took her initial ride on her own pony. Off there was the mountain where they saw the sun drawing silver water above a frowning storm. Yonder was the group of cedars where they had stopped to eat their lunch once, and this water-hole they were approaching was the one where Gardley had given her a drink from his hat.

She was almost glad that Bud was not along, for she was too tired to talk and liked to be alone with her thoughts for this few minutes. Poor Bud! He would be disappointed when he got back to find her gone, but then he had expected she was going in a few days, anyway, and she had promised to take long rides with him when she returned. She had left a little note for him, asking him to read a certain book in her bookcase while she was gone, and be ready to discuss it with her when she got back, and Bud would be fascinated with it, she knew. Bud had been dear and faithful, and she would miss him, but just for this little while she was glad to have the great out-of-doors to herself.

She was practically alone. The two sphinx-like figures riding ahead of her made no sign, but stolidly rode on hour after hour, nor turned their heads even to see if she were coming. She knew that Indians were this way; still, as the time went by she began to feel an uneasy sense of being alone in the universe with a couple of bronze statues. Even the papoose had erased itself in sleep, and when it awoke partook so fully of its racial peculiarities as to hold its little peace and make no fuss. Margaret began to feel the baby was hardly human, more like a little brown doll set up in a missionary meeting to teach white children what a papoose was like.

By and by she got out her letters and read them over carefully, dreaming and smiling over them, and getting precious bits by heart. Gardley hinted that he might be able very soon to visit her parents, as it looked as though he might have to make a trip on business in their direction before he could go further with what he was doing in his old home. He gave no hint of soon returning to the West. He said he was awaiting the return of one man who might soon be coming from abroad. Margaret sighed and wondered how many weary months it would be before she would see him. Perhaps, after all, she ought to have gone home and stayed them out with her mother and father. If the school-board could be made to see that it would be better to have no summer session, perhaps she would even yet go when she returned from the Brownleighs'. She would see. She would decide nothing until she was rested.

Suddenly she felt herself overwhelmingly weary, and wished that the Indians would stop and rest for a while; but when she stirred up her sleepy pony and spurred ahead to broach the matter to her guide he shook his solemn head and pointed to the sun:

"No get Keams good time. No meet Aneshodi."

"Aneshodi," she knew, was the Indians' name for the missionary, and she smiled her acquiescence. Of course they must meet the Brownleighs and not detain them. What was it Hazel had said about having to hurry? She searched her pocket for the letter, and then remembered she had left it with Mrs. Tanner. What a pity she had not brought it! Perhaps there was some caution or advice in it that she had not taken note of. But then the Indian likely knew all about it, and she could trust to him. She glanced at his stolid face and wished she could make him smile. She cast a sunny smile at him and said something pleasant about the beautiful day, but he only looked her through as if she were not there, and after one or two more attempts she fell back and tried to talk to the squaw; but the squaw only looked stolid, too, and shook her head. She did not seem friendly. Margaret drew back into her old position and feasted her eyes upon the distant hills.

The road was growing unfamiliar now. They were crossing rough ridges with cliffs of red sandstone, and every step of the way was interesting. Yet Margaret felt more and more how much she wanted to lie down and sleep, and when at last in the dusk the Indians halted not far from a little pool of rainwater and indicated that here they would camp for the night, Margaret was too weary to question the decision. It had not occurred to her that she would be on the way overnight before she met her friends. Her knowledge of the way, and of distances, was but vague. It is doubtful if she would have ventured had she known that she must pass the night thus in the company of two strange savage creatures. Yet, now that she was here and it was inevitable, she would not shrink, but make the best of it. She tried to be friendly once more, and offered to look out for the baby while the squaw gathered wood and made a fire. The Indian was off looking after the horses, evidently expecting his wife to do all the work.

Margaret watched a few minutes, while pretending to play with the baby, who was both sleepy and hungry, yet held his emotions as stolidly as if he were a grown person. Then she decided to take a hand in the supper. She was hungry and could not bear that those dusky, dirty hands should set forth her food, so she went to work cheerfully, giving directions as if the Indian woman understood her, though she very soon discovered that all her talk was as mere babbling to the other, and she might as well hold her peace. The woman set a kettle of water over the fire, and Margaret forestalled her next movement by cutting some pork and putting it to cook in a little skillet she found among the provisions. The woman watched her solemnly, not seeming to care; and so, silently, each went about her own preparations.

The supper was a silent affair, and when it was over the squaw handed Margaret a blanket. Suddenly she understood that this, and this alone, was to be her bed for the night. The earth was there for a mattress, and the sage-brush lent a partial shelter, the canopy of stars was overhead.

A kind of panic took possession of her. She stared at the squaw and found herself longing to cry out for help. It seemed as if she could not bear this awful silence of the mortals who were her only company. Yet her common sense came to her aid, and she realized that there was nothing for it but to make the best of things. So she took the blanket and, spreading it out, sat down upon it and wrapped it about her shoulders and feet. She would not lie down until she saw what the rest did. Somehow she shrank from asking the bronze man how to fold a blanket for a bed on the ground. She tried to remember what Gardley had told her about folding the blanket bed so as best to keep out snakes and ants. She shuddered at the thought of snakes. Would she dare call for help from those stolid companions of hers if a snake should attempt to molest her in the night? And would she ever dare to go to sleep?

She remembered her first night in Arizona out among the stars, alone on the water-tank, and her first frenzy of loneliness. Was this as bad? No, for these Indians were trustworthy and well known by her dear friends. It might be unpleasant, but this, too, would pass and the morrow would soon be here.

The dusk dropped down and the stars loomed out. All the world grew wonderful, like a blue jeweled dome of a palace with the lights turned low. The fire burned brightly as the man threw sticks upon it, and the two Indians moved stealthily about in the darkness, passing silhouetted before the fire this way and that, and then at last lying down wrapped in their blankets to sleep.

It was very quiet about her. The air was so still she could hear the hobbled horses munching away in the distance, and moving now and then with the halting gait a hobble gives a horse. Off in the farther distance the blood-curdling howl of the coyotes rose, but Margaret was used to them, and knew they would not come near a fire.

She was growing very weary, and at last wrapped her blanket closer and lay down, her head pillowed on one corner of it. Committing herself to her Heavenly Father, and breathing a prayer for father, mother, and lover, she fell asleep.

It was still almost dark when she awoke. For a moment she thought it was still night and the sunset was not gone yet, the clouds were so rosy tinted.

The squaw was standing by her, touching her shoulder roughly and grunting something. She perceived, as she rubbed her eyes and tried to summon back her senses, that she was expected to get up and eat breakfast. There was a smell of pork and coffee in the air, and there was scorched corn bread beside the fire on a pan.

Margaret got up quickly and ran down to the water-hole to get some water, dashing it in her face and over her arms and hands, the squaw meanwhile standing at a little distance, watching her curiously, as if she thought this some kind of an oblation paid to the white woman's god before she ate. Margaret pulled the hair-pins out of her hair, letting it down and combing it with one of her side combs; twisted it up again in its soft, fluffy waves; straightened her collar, set on her hat, and was ready for the day. The squaw looked at her with both awe and contempt for a moment, then turned and stalked back to her papoose and began preparing it for the journey.

Margaret made a hurried meal and was scarcely done before she found her guides were waiting like two pillars of the desert, but watching keenly, impatiently, her every mouthful, and anxious to be off.

The sky was still pink-tinted with the semblance of a sunset, and Margaret felt, as she mounted her pony and followed her companions, as if the day was all turned upside down. She almost wondered whether she hadn't slept through a whole twenty-four hours, and it were not, after all, evening again, till by and by the sun rose clear and the wonder of the cloud-tinting melted into day.

The road lay through sage-brush and old barren cedar-trees, with rabbits darting now and then between the rocks. Suddenly from the top of a little hill they came out to a spot where they could see far over the desert. Forty miles away three square, flat hills, or mesas, looked like a gigantic train of cars, and the clear air gave everything a strange vastness. Farther on beyond the mesas dimly dawned the Black Mountains. One could even see the shadowed head of "Round Rock," almost a hundred miles away. Before them and around was a great plain of sage-brush, and here and there was a small bush that the Indians call "the weed that was not scared." Margaret had learned all these things during her winter in Arizona, and keenly enjoyed the vast, splendid view spread before her.

They passed several little mud-plastered hogans that Margaret knew for Indian dwellings. A fine band of ponies off in the distance made an interesting spot on the landscape, and twice they passed bands of sheep. She had a feeling of great isolation from everything she had ever known, and seemed going farther and farther from life and all she loved. Once she ventured to ask the Indian what time he expected to meet her friends, the missionaries, but he only shook his head and murmured something unintelligible about "Keams" and pointed to the sun. She dropped behind again, vaguely uneasy, she could not tell why. There seemed something so altogether sly and wary and unfriendly in the faces of the two that she almost wished she had not come. Yet the way was beautiful enough and nothing very unpleasant was happening to her. Once she dropped the envelope of her mother's letter and was about to dismount and recover it. Then some strange impulse made her leave it on the sand of the desert. What if they should be lost and that paper should guide them back? The notion stayed by her, and once in a while she dropped other bits of paper by the way.

About noon the trail dropped off into a cañon, with high, yellow-rock walls on either side, and stifling heat, so that she felt as if she could scarcely stand it. She was glad when they emerged once more and climbed to higher ground. The noon camp was a hasty affair, for the Indian seemed in a hurry. He scanned the horizon far and wide and seemed searching keenly for some one or something. Once they met a lonely Indian, and he held a muttered conversation with him, pointing off ahead and gesticulating angrily. But the words were unintelligible to Margaret. Her feeling of uneasiness was growing, and yet she could not for the life of her tell why, and laid it down to her tired nerves. She was beginning to think she had been very foolish to start on such a long trip before she had had a chance to get rested from her last days of school. She longed to lie down under a tree and sleep for days.

Toward night they sighted a great blue mesa about fifty miles south, and at sunset they could just see the San Francisco peaks more than a hundred and twenty-five miles away. Margaret, as she stopped her horse and gazed, felt a choking in her heart and throat and a great desire to cry. The glory and awe of the mountains, mingled with her own weariness and nervous fear, were almost too much for her. She was glad to get down and eat a little supper and go to sleep again. As she fell asleep she comforted herself with repeating over a few precious words from her Bible:

"The angel of the Lord encampeth round about them that fear Him and delivereth them. Thou wilt keep him in perfect peace whose mind is stayed on Thee because he trusteth in Thee. I will both lay me down in peace and sleep, for Thou Lord only makest me to dwell in safety...."

The voice of the coyotes, now far, now near, boomed out on the night; great stars shot dartling pathways across the heavens; the fire snapped and crackled, died down and flickered feebly; but Margaret slept, tired out, and dreamed the angels kept close vigil around her lowly couch.

She did not know what time the stars disappeared and the rain began to fall. She was too tired to notice the drops that fell upon her face. Too tired to hear the coyotes coming nearer, nearer, yet in the morning there lay one dead, stretched not thirty feet from where she lay. The Indian had shot him through the heart.

Somehow things looked very dismal that morning, in spite of the brightness of the sun after the rain. She was stiff and sore with lying in the dampness. Her hair was wet, her blanket was wet, and she woke without feeling rested. Almost the trip seemed more than she could bear. If she could have wished herself back that morning and have stayed at Tanners' all summer she certainly would have done it rather than to be where and how she was.

The Indians seemed excited—the man grim and forbidding, the woman appealing, frightened, anxious. They were near to Keams Cañon. "Aneshodi" would be somewhere about. The Indian hoped to be rid of his burden then and travel on his interrupted journey. He was growing impatient. He felt he had earned his money.

But when they tried to go down Keam's Cañon they found the road all washed away by flood, and must needs go a long way around. This made the Indian surly. His countenance was more forbidding than ever. Margaret, as she watched him with sinking heart, altered her ideas of the Indian as a whole to suit the situation. She had always felt pity for the poor Indian, whose land had been seized and whose kindred had been slaughtered. But this Indian was not an object of pity. He was the most disagreeable, cruel-looking Indian Margaret had ever laid eyes on. She had felt it innately the first time she saw him, but now, as the situation began to bring him out, she knew that she was dreadfully afraid of him. She had a feeling that he might scalp her if he got tired of her. She began to alter her opinion of Hazel Brownleigh's judgment as regarded Indians. She did not feel that she would ever send this Indian to any one for a guide and say he was perfectly trustworthy. He hadn't done anything very dreadful yet, but she felt he was going to.

He had a number of angry confabs with his wife that morning. At least, he did the confabbing and the squaw protested. Margaret gathered after a while that it was something about herself. The furtive, frightened glances that the squaw cast in her direction sometimes, when the man was not looking, made her think so. She tried to say it was all imagination, and that her nerves were getting the upper hand of her, but in spite of her she shuddered sometimes, just as she had done when Rosa looked at her. She decided that she must be going to have a fit of sickness, and that just as soon as she got in the neighborhood of Mrs. Tanner's again she would pack her trunk and go home to her mother. If she was going to be sick she wanted her mother.

About noon things came to a climax. They halted on the top of the mesa, and the Indians had another altercation, which ended in the man descending the trail a fearfully steep way, down four hundred feet to the trading-post in the cañon. Margaret looked down and gasped and thanked a kind Providence that had not made it necessary for her to make that descent; but the squaw stood at the top with her baby and looked down in silent sorrow—agony perhaps would be a better name. Her face was terrible to look upon.

Margaret could not understand it, and she went to the woman and put her hand out sympathetically, asking, gently: "What is the matter, you poor little thing? Oh, what is it?"

Perhaps the woman understood the tenderness in the tone, for she suddenly turned and rested her forehead against Margaret's shoulder, giving one great, gasping sob, then lifted her dry, miserable eyes to the girl's face as if to thank her for her kindness.

Margaret's heart was touched. She threw her arms around the poor woman and drew her, papoose and all, comfortingly toward her, patting her shoulder and saying gentle, soothing words as she would to a little child. And by and by the woman lifted her head again, the tears coursing down her face, and tried to explain, muttering her queer gutturals and making eloquent gestures until Margaret felt she understood. She gathered that the man had gone down to the trading-post to find the "Aneshodi," and that the squaw feared that he would somehow procure firewater either from the trader or from some Indian he might meet, and would come back angrier than he had gone, and without his money.

If Margaret also suspected that the Indian had desired to get rid of her by leaving her at that desolate little trading-station down in the cañon until such time as her friends should call for her, she resolutely put the thought out of her mind and set herself to cheer the poor Indian woman.

She took a bright, soft, rosy silk tie from her own neck and knotted it about the astonished woman's dusky throat, and then she put a silver dollar in her hand, and was thrilled with wonder to see what a change came over the poor, dark face. It reminded her of Mom Wallis when she got on her new bonnet, and once again she felt the thrill of knowing the whole world kin.

The squaw cheered up after a little, got sticks and made a fire, and together they had quite a pleasant meal. Margaret exerted herself to make the poor woman laugh, and finally succeeded by dangling a bright-red knight from her chessmen in front of the delighted baby's eyes till he gurgled out a real baby crow of joy.

It was the middle of the afternoon before the Indian returned, sitting crazily his struggling beast as he climbed the trail once more. Margaret, watching, caught her breath and prayed. Was this the trustworthy man, this drunken, reeling creature, clubbing his horse and pouring forth a torrent of indistinguishable gutturals? It was evident that his wife's worst fears were verified. He had found the firewater.

The frightened squaw set to work putting things together as fast as she could. She well knew what to expect, and when the man reached the top of the mesa he found his party packed and mounted, waiting fearsomely to take the trail.

Silently, timorously, they rode behind him, west across the great wide plain.

In the distance gradually there appeared dim mesas like great fingers stretching out against the sky; miles away they seemed, and nothing intervening but a stretch of varying color where sage-brush melted into sand, and sage-brush and greasewood grew again, with tall cactus startling here and there like bayonets at rest but bristling with menace.

The Indian had grown silent and sullen. His eyes were like deep fires of burning volcanoes. One shrank from looking at them. His massive, cruel profile stood out like bronze against the evening sky. It was growing night again, and still they had not come to anywhere or anything, and still her friends seemed just as far away.

Since they had left the top of Keams Cañon Margaret had been sure all was not right. Aside from the fact that the guide was drunk at present, she was convinced that there had been something wrong with him all along. He did not act like the Indians around Ashland. He did not act like a trusted guide that her friends would send for her. She wished once more that she had kept Hazel Brownleigh's letter. She wondered how her friends would find her if they came after her. It was then she began in earnest to systematically plan to leave a trail behind her all the rest of the way. If she had only done it thoroughly when she first began to be uneasy. But now she was so far away, so many miles from anywhere! Oh, if she had not come at all!

And first she dropped her handkerchief, because she happened to have it in her hand—a dainty thing with lace on the edge and her name written in tiny script by her mother's careful hand on the narrow hem. And then after a little, as soon as she could scrawl it without being noticed, she wrote a note which she twisted around the neck of a red chessman, and left behind her. After that scraps of paper, as she could reach them out of the bag tied on behind her saddle; then a stocking, a bedroom slipper, more chessmen, and so, when they halted at dusk and prepared to strike camp, she had quite a good little trail blazed behind her over that wide, empty plain. She shuddered as she looked into the gathering darkness ahead, where those long, dark lines of mesas looked like barriers in the way. Then, suddenly, the Indian pointed ahead to the first mesa and uttered one word—"Walpi!" So that was the Indian village to which she was bound? What was before her on the morrow? After eating a pretense of supper she lay down. The Indian had more firewater with him. He drank, he uttered cruel gutturals at his squaw, and even kicked the feet of the sleeping papoose as he passed by till it awoke and cried sharply, which made him more angry, so he struck the squaw.

It seemed hours before all was quiet. Margaret's nerves were strained to such a pitch she scarcely dared to breathe, but at last, when the fire had almost died down, the man lay quiet, and she could relax and close her eyes.

Not to sleep. She must not go to sleep. The fire was almost gone and the coyotes would be around. She must wake and watch!

That was the last thought she remembered—that and a prayer that the angels would keep watch once again.

When she awoke it was broad daylight and far into the morning, for the sun was high overhead and the mesas in the distance were clear and distinct against the sky.

She sat up and looked about her, bewildered, not knowing at first where she was. It was so still and wide and lonely.

She turned to find the Indians, but there was no trace of them anywhere. The fire lay smoldering in its place, a thin trickle of smoke curling away from a dying stick, but that was all. A tin cup half full of coffee was beside the stick, and a piece of blackened corn bread. She turned frightened eyes to east, to west, to north, to south, but there was no one in sight, and out over the distant mesa there poised a great eagle alone in the vast sky keeping watch over the brilliant, silent waste.

CHAPTER XXX

When Margaret was a very little girl her father and mother had left her alone for an hour with a stranger while they went out to make a call in a strange city through which they were passing on a summer trip. The stranger was kind, and gave to the child a large green box of bits of old black lace and purple ribbons to play with, but she turned sorrowfully from the somber array of finery, which was the only thing in the way of a plaything the woman had at hand, and stood looking drearily out of the window on the strange, new town, a feeling of utter loneliness upon her. Her little heart was almost choked with the awfulness of the thought that she was a human atom drifted apart from every other atom she had ever known, that she had a personality and a responsibility of her own, and that she must face this thought of herself and her aloneness for evermore. It was the child's first realization that she was a separate being apart from her father and mother, and she was almost consumed with the terror of it.

As she rose now from her bed on the ground and looked out across that vast waste, in which the only other living creature was that sinister, watching eagle, the same feeling returned to her and made her tremble like the little child who had turned from her box of ancient finery to realize her own little self and its terrible aloneness.

For an instant even her realization of God, which had from early childhood been present with her, seemed to have departed. She could not grasp anything save the vast empty silence that loomed about her so awfully. She was alone, and about as far from anywhere or anything as she could possibly be in the State of Arizona. Would she ever get back to human habitations? Would her friends ever be able to find her?

Then her heart flew back to its habitual refuge, and she spoke aloud and said, "God is here!" and the thought seemed to comfort her. She looked about once more on the bright waste, and now it did not seem so dreary.

"God is here!" she repeated, and tried to realize that this was a part of His habitation. She could not be lost where God was. He knew the way out. She had only to trust. So she dropped upon her knees in the sand and prayed for trust and courage.

When she rose again she walked steadily to a height a little above the camp-fire, and, shading her eyes, looked carefully in every direction. No, there was not a sign of her recent companions. They must have stolen away in the night quite soon after she fell asleep, and have gone fast and far, so that they were now beyond the reach of her eyes, and not anywhere was there sign of living thing, save that eagle still sweeping in great curves and poising again above the distant mesa.

Where was her horse? Had the Indians taken that, too? She searched the valley, but saw no horse at first. With sinking heart she went back to where her things were and sat down by the dying fire to think, putting a few loose twigs and sticks together to keep the embers bright while she could. She reflected that she had no matches, and this was probably the last fire she would have until somebody came to her rescue or she got somewhere by herself. What was she to do? Stay right where she was or start out on foot? And should she go backward or forward? Surely, surely the Brownleighs would miss her pretty soon and send out a search-party for her. How could it be that they trusted an Indian who had done such a cruel thing as to leave a woman unprotected in the desert? And yet, perhaps, they did not know his temptation to drink. Perhaps they had thought he could not get any firewater. Perhaps he would return when he came to himself and realized what he had done.

And now she noticed what she had not seen at first—a small bottle of water on a stone beside the blackened bread. Realizing that she was very hungry and that this was the only food at hand, she sat down beside the fire to eat the dry bread and drink the miserable coffee. She must have strength to do whatever was before her. She tried not to think how her mother would feel if she never came back, how anxious they would be as they waited day by day for her letters that did not come. She reflected with a sinking heart that she had, just before leaving, written a hasty note to her mother telling her not to expect anything for several days, perhaps even as much as two weeks, as she was going out of civilization for a little while. How had she unwittingly sealed her fate by that! For now not even by way of her alarmed home could help come to her.

She put the last bit of hard corn bread in her pocket for a further time of need, and began to look about her again. Then she spied with delight a moving object far below her in the valley, and decided it was a horse, perhaps her own. He was a mile away, at least, but he was there, and she cried out with sudden joy and relief.

She went over to her blanket and bags, which had been beside her during the night, and stood a moment trying to think what to do. Should she carry the things to the horse or risk leaving them here while she went after the horse and brought him to the things? No, that would not be safe. Some one might come along and take them, or she might not be able to find her way back again in this strange, wild waste. Besides, she might not get the horse, after all, and would lose everything. She must carry her things to the horse. She stooped to gather them up, and something bright beside her bag attracted her. It was the sun shining on the silver dollar she had given to the Indian woman. A sudden rush of tears came to her eyes. The poor creature had tried to make all the reparation she could for thus hastily leaving the white woman in the desert. She had given back the money—all she had that was valuable! Beside the dollar rippled a little chain of beads curiously wrought, an inanimate appeal for forgiveness and a grateful return for the kindness shown her. Margaret smiled as she stooped again to pick up her things. There had been a heart, after all, behind that stolid countenance, and some sense of righteousness and justice. Margaret decided that Indians were not all treacherous. Poor woman! What a life was hers—to follow her grim lord whither he would lead, even as her white sister must sometimes, sorrowing, rebelling, crying out, but following! She wondered if into the heart of this dark sister there ever crept any of the rebellion which led some of her white sisters to cry aloud for "rights" and "emancipation."

But it was all a passing thought to be remembered and turned over at a more propitious time. Margaret's whole thoughts now were bent on her present predicament.

The packing was short work. She stuffed everything into the two bags that were usually hung across the horse, and settled them carefully across her shoulders. Then she rolled the blanket, took it in her arms, and started. It was a heavy burden to carry, but she could not make up her mind to part with any of her things until she had at least made an effort to save them. If she should be left alone in the desert for the night the blanket was indispensable, and her clothes would at least do to drop as a trail by which her friends might find her. She must carry them as far as possible. So she started.

It was already high day, and the sun was intolerably hot. Her heavy burden was not only cumbersome, but very warm, and she felt her strength going from her as she went; but her nerve was up and her courage was strong. Moreover, she prayed as she walked, and she felt now the presence of her Guide and was not afraid. As she walked she faced a number of possibilities in the immediate future which were startling, and to say the least, undesirable. There were wild animals in this land, not so much in the daylight, but what of the night? She had heard that a woman was always safe in that wild Western land; but what of the prowling Indians? What of a possible exception to the Western rule of chivalry toward a decent woman? One small piece of corn bread and less than a pint of water were small provision on which to withstand a siege. How far was it to anywhere?

It was then she remembered for the first time that one word—"Walpi!" uttered by the Indian as he came to a halt the night before and pointed far to the mesa—"Walpi." She lifted her eyes now and scanned the dark mesa. It loomed like a great battlement of rock against the sky. Could it be possible there were people dwelling there? She had heard, of course, about the curious Hopi villages, each village a gigantic house of many rooms, called pueblos, built upon the lofty crags, sometimes five or six hundred feet above the desert.

Could it be that that great castle-looking outline against the sky before her, standing out on the end of the mesa like a promontory above the sea, was Walpi? And if it was, how was she to get up there? The rock rose sheer and steep from the desert floor. The narrow neck of land behind it looked like a slender thread. Her heart sank at thought of trying to storm and enter, single-handed, such an impregnable fortress. And yet, if her friends were there, perhaps they would see her when she drew near and come to show her the way. Strange that they should have gone on and left her with those treacherous Indians! Strange that they should have trusted them so, in the first place! Her own instincts had been against trusting the man from the beginning. It must be confessed that during her reflections at this point her opinion of the wisdom and judgment of the Brownleighs was lowered several notches. Then she began to berate herself for having so easily been satisfied about her escort. She should have read the letter more carefully. She should have asked the Indians more questions. She should, perhaps, have asked Jasper Kemp's advice, or got him to talk to the Indian. She wished with all her heart for Bud, now. If Bud were along he would be saying some comical boy-thing, and be finding a way out of the difficulty. Dear, faithful Bud!

The sun rose higher and the morning grew hotter. As she descended to the valley her burdens grew intolerable, and several times she almost cast them aside. Once she lost sight of her pony among the sage-brush, and it was two hours before she came to him and was able to capture him and strap on her burdens. She was almost too exhausted to climb into the saddle when all was ready; but she managed to mount at last and started out toward the rugged crag ahead of her.

The pony had a long, hot climb out of the valley to a hill where she could see very far again, but still that vast emptiness reigned. Even the eagle had disappeared, and she fancied he must be resting like a great emblem of freedom on one of the points of the castle-like battlement against the sky. It seemed as if the end of the world had come, and she was the only one left in the universe, forgotten, riding on her weary horse across an endless desert in search of a home she would never see again.

Below the hill there stretched a wide, white strip of sand, perhaps two miles in extent, but shimmering in the sun and seeming to recede ahead of her as she advanced. Beyond was soft greenness—something growing—not near enough to be discerned as cornfields. The girl drooped her tired head upon her horse's mane and wept, her courage going from her with her tears. In all that wide universe there seemed no way to go, and she was so very tired, hungry, hot, and discouraged! There was always that bit of bread in her pocket and that muddy-looking, warm water for a last resort; but she must save them as long as possible, for there was no telling how long it would be before she had more.

There was no trail now to follow. She had started from the spot where she had found the horse, and her inexperienced eyes could not have searched out a trail if she had tried. She was going toward that distant castle on the crag as to a goal, but when she reached it, if she ever did, would she find anything there but crags and lonesomeness and the eagle?

Drying her tears at last, she started the horse on down the hill, and perhaps her tears blinded her, or because she was dizzy with hunger and the long stretch of anxiety and fatigue she was not looking closely. There was a steep place, a sharp falling away of the ground unexpectedly as they emerged from a thicket of sage-brush, and the horse plunged several feet down, striking sharply on some loose rocks, and slipping to his knees; snorting, scrambling, making brave effort, but slipping, half rolling, at last he was brought down with his frightened rider, and lay upon his side with her foot under him and a sensation like a red-hot knife running through her ankle.

Margaret caught her breath in quick gasps as they fell, lifting a prayer in her heart for help. Then came the crash and the sharp pain, and with a quick conviction that all was over she dropped back unconscious on the sand, a blessed oblivion of darkness rushing over her.

When she came to herself once more the hot sun was pouring down upon her unprotected face, and she was conscious of intense pain and suffering in every part of her body. She opened her eyes wildly and looked around. There was sage-brush up above, waving over the crag down which they had fallen, its gray-greenness shimmering hotly in the sun; the sky was mercilessly blue without a cloud. The great beast, heavy and quivering, lay solidly against her, half pinning her to earth, and the helplessness of her position was like an awful nightmare from which she felt she might waken if she could only cry out. But when at last she raised her voice its empty echo frightened her, and there, above her, with wide-spread wings, circling for an instant, then poised in motionless survey of her, with cruel eyes upon her, loomed that eagle—so large, so fearful, so suggestive in its curious stare, the monarch of the desert come to see who had invaded his precincts and fallen into one of his snares.

With sudden frenzy burning in her veins Margaret struggled and tried to get free, but she could only move the slightest bit each time, and every motion was an agony to the hurt ankle.

It seemed hours before she writhed herself free from that great, motionless horse, whose labored breath only showed that he was still alive. Something terrible must have happened to the horse or he would have tried to rise, for she had coaxed, patted, cajoled, tried in every way to rouse him. When at last she crawled free from the hot, horrible body and crept with pained progress around in front of him, she saw that both his forelegs lay limp and helpless. He must have broken them in falling. Poor fellow! He, too, was suffering and she had nothing to give him! There was nothing she could do for him!

Then she thought of the bottle of water, but, searching for it, found that her good intention of dividing it with him was useless, for the bottle was broken and the water already soaked into the sand. Only a damp spot on the saddle-bag showed where it had departed.

Then indeed did Margaret sink down in the sand in despair and begin to pray as she had never prayed before.

CHAPTER XXXI

The morning after Margaret's departure Rosa awoke with no feelings of self-reproach, but rather a great exultation at the way in which she had been able to get rid of her rival.

She lay for a few minutes thinking of Forsythe, and trying to decide what she would wear when she went forth to meet him, for she wanted to charm him as she had never charmed any one before.

She spent some time arraying herself in different costumes, but at last decided on her Commencement gown of fine white organdie, hand-embroidered and frilled with filmy lace, the product of a famous house of gowns in the Eastern city where she had attended school for a while and acquired expensive tastes.

Daintily slippered, beribboned with coral-silk girdle, and with a rose from the vine over her window in her hair, she sallied forth at last to the trysting-place.

Forsythe was a whole hour late, as became a languid gentleman who had traveled the day before and idled at his sister's house over a late breakfast until nearly noon. Already his fluttering fancy was apathetic about Rosa, and he wondered, as he rode along, what had become of the interesting young teacher who had charmed him for more than a passing moment. Would he dare to call upon her, now that Gardley was out of the way? Was she still in Ashland or had she gone home for vacation? He must ask Rosa about her.

Then he came in sight of Rosa sitting picturesquely in the shade of an old cedar, reading poetry, a little lady in the wilderness, and he forgot everything else in his delight over the change in her. For Rosa had changed. There was no mistake about it. She had bloomed out into maturity in those few short months of his absence. Her soft figure had rounded and developed, her bewitching curls were put up on her head, with only a stray tendril here and there to emphasize a dainty ear or call attention to a smooth, round neck; and when she raised her lovely head and lifted limpid eyes to his there was about her a demureness, a coolness and charm that he had fancied only ladies of the city could attain. Oh, Rosa knew her charms, and had practised many a day before her mirror till she had appraised the value of every curving eyelash, every hidden dimple, every cupid's curve of lip. Rosa had watched well and learned from all with whom she had come in contact. No woman's guile was left untried by her.

And Rosa was very sweet and charming. She knew just when to lift up innocent eyes of wonder; when to not understand suggestions; when to exclaim softly with delight or shrink with shyness that nevertheless did not repulse.

Forsythe studied her with wonder and delight. No maiden of the city had ever charmed him more, and withal she seemed so innocent and young, so altogether pliable in his hands. His pulses beat high, his heart was inflamed, and passion came and sat within his handsome eyes.

It was easy to persuade her, after her first seemingly shy reserve was overcome, and before an hour was passed she had promised to go away with him. He had very little money, but what of that? When he spoke of that feature Rosa declared she could easily get some. Her father gave her free access to his safe, and kept her plentifully supplied for the household use. It was nothing to her—a passing incident. What should it matter whose money took them on their way?

When she went demurely back to the ranch a little before sunset she thought she was very happy, poor little silly sinner! She met her father with her most alluring but most furtive smile. She was charming at supper, and blushed as her mother used to do when he praised her new gown and told her how well she looked in it. But she professed to be weary yet from the last days of school—to have a headache—and so she went early to her room and asked that the servants keep the house quiet in the morning, that she might sleep late and get really rested. Her father kissed her tenderly and thought what a dear child she was and what a comfort to his ripening years; and the house settled down into quiet.

Rosa packed a bag with some of her most elaborate garments, arrayed herself in a charming little outfit of silk for the journey, dropped her baggage out of the window; and when the moon rose and the household were quietly sleeping she paid a visit to her father's safe, and then stole forth, taking her shadowy way to the trail by a winding route known well to herself and secure from the watch of vigilant servants who were ever on the lookout for cattle thieves.

Thus she left her father's house and went forth to put her trust in a man whose promises were as ropes of sand and whose fancy was like a wave of the sea, tossed to and fro by every breath that blew. Long ere the sun rose the next morning the guarded, beloved child was as far from her safe home and her father's sheltering love as if alone she had started for the mouth of the bottomless pit. Two days later, while Margaret lay unconscious beneath the sage-brush, with a hovering eagle for watch, Rosa in the streets of a great city suddenly realized that she was more alone in the universe than ever she could have been in a wide desert, and her plight was far worse than the girl's with whose fate she had so lightly played.

Quite early on the morning after Rosa left, while the household was still keeping quiet for the supposed sleeper, Gardley rode into the inclosure about the house and asked for Rogers.

Gardley had been traveling night and day to get back. Matters had suddenly arranged themselves so that he could finish up his business at his old home and go on to see Margaret's father and mother, and he had made his visit there and hurried back to Arizona, hoping to reach Ashland in time for Commencement. A delay on account of a washout on the road had brought him back two days late for Commencement. He had ridden to camp from a junction forty miles away to get there the sooner, and this morning had ridden straight to the Tanners' to surprise Margaret. It was, therefore, a deep disappointment to find her gone and only Mrs. Tanner's voluble explanations for comfort. Mrs. Tanner exhausted her vocabulary in trying to describe the "Injuns," her own feeling of protest against them, and Mrs. Brownleigh's foolishness in making so much of them; and then she bustled in to the old pine desk in the dining-room and produced the letter that had started Margaret off as soon as commencement was over.

Gardley took the letter eagerly, as though it were something to connect him with Margaret, and read it through carefully to make sure just how matters stood. He had looked troubled when Mrs. Tanner told how tired Margaret was, and how worried she seemed about her school and glad to get away from it all; and he agreed that the trip was probably a good thing.

"I wish Bud could have gone along, though," he said, thoughtfully, as he turned away from the door. "I don't like her to go with just Indians, though I suppose it is all right. You say he had his wife and child along? Of course Mrs. Brownleigh wouldn't send anybody that wasn't perfectly all right. Well, I suppose the trip will be a rest for her. I'm sorry I didn't get home a few days sooner. I might have looked out for her myself."

He rode away from the Tanners', promising to return later with a gift he had brought for Bud that he wanted to present himself, and Mrs. Tanner bustled back to her work again.

"Well, I'm glad he's got home, anyway," she remarked, aloud, to herself as she hung her dish-cloth tidily over the upturned dish-pan and took up her broom. "I 'ain't felt noways easy 'bout her sence she left, though I do suppose there ain't any sense to it. But I'm *glad he's back*!"

Meantime Gardley was riding toward Rogers's ranch, meditating whether he should venture to follow the expedition and enjoy at least the return trip with Margaret, or whether he ought to remain patiently until she came back and go to work at once. There was nothing really important demanding his attention immediately, for Rogers had arranged to keep the present overseer of affairs until he was ready to undertake the work. He was on his way now to report on a small business matter which he had been attending to in New York for Rogers. When that was over he would be free to do as he pleased for a few days more if he liked, and the temptation was great to go at once to Margaret.

As he stood waiting beside his horse in front of the house while the servant went to call Rogers, he looked about with delight on the beauty of the day. How glad he was to be back in Arizona again! Was it the charm of the place or because Margaret was there, he wondered, that he felt so happy? By all means he must follow her. Why should he not?

He looked at the clambering rose-vine that covered one end of the house, and noticed how it crept close to the window casement and caressed the white curtain as it blew. Margaret must have such a vine at her window in the house he would build for her. It might be but a modest house that he could give her now, but it should have a rose-vine just like that; and he would train it round her window where she could smell the fragrance from it every morning when she awoke, and where it would breathe upon her as she slept.

Margaret! How impatient he was to see her again! To look upon her dear face and know that she was his! That her father and mother had been satisfied about him and sent their blessing, and he might tell her so. It was wonderful! His heart thrilled with the thought of it. Of course he would go to her at once. He would start as soon as Rogers was through with him. He would go to Ganado. No, Keams. Which was it? He drew the letter out of his pocket and read it again, then replaced it.

The fluttering curtain up at the window blew out and in, and when it blew out again it brought with it a flurry of papers like white leaves. The curtain had knocked over a paper-weight or vase or something that held them and set the papers free. The breeze caught them and flung them about erratically, tossing one almost at his feet. He stooped to pick it up, thinking it might be of value to some one, and caught the name "Margaret" and "Dear Margaret" written several times on the sheet, with "Walpi, Walpi, Walpi," filling the lower half of the page, as if some one had been practising it.

And because these two words were just now keenly in his mind he reached for the second paper just a foot or two away and found more sentences and words. A third paper contained an exact reproduction of the letter which Mrs. Tanner had given him purporting to come from Mrs. Brownleigh to Margaret. What could it possibly mean?

In great astonishment he pulled out the other letter and compared them. They were almost identical save for a word here and there crossed out and rewritten. He stood looking mutely at the papers and then up at the window, as though an explanation might somehow be wafted down to him, not knowing what to think, his mind filled with vague alarm.

Just at that moment the servant appeared.

"Mr. Rogers says would you mind coming down to the corral. Miss Rosa has a headache, and we're keeping the house still for her to sleep. That's her window up there—" And he indicated the rose-bowered window with the fluttering curtain.

Dazed and half suspicious of something, Gardley folded the two letters together and crushed them into his pocket, wondering what he ought to do about it. The thought of it troubled him so that he only half gave attention to the business in hand; but he gave his report and handed over certain documents. He was thinking that perhaps he ought to see Miss Rosa and find out what she knew of Margaret's going and ask how she came in possession of this other letter.

"Now," said Rogers, as the matter was concluded, "I owe you some money. If you'll just step up to the house with me I'll give it to you. I'd like to settle matters up at once."

"Oh, let it go till I come again," said Gardley, impatient to be off. He wanted to get by himself and think out a solution of the two letters. He was more than uneasy about Margaret without being able to give any suitable explanation of why he should be. His main desire now was to ride to Ganado and find out if the missionaries had left home, which way they had gone, and whether they had met Margaret as planned.

"No, step right up to the house with me," insisted Rogers. "It won't take long, and I have the money in my safe."

Gardley saw that the quickest way was to please Rogers, and he did not wish to arouse any questions, because he supposed, of course, his alarm was mere foolishness. So they went together into Rogers's private office, where his desk and safe were the principal furniture, and where no servants ventured to come without orders.

Rogers shoved a chair for Gardley and went over to his safe, turning the little nickel knob this way and that with the skill of one long accustomed, and in a moment the thick door swung open and Rogers drew out a japanned cash-box and unlocked it. But when he threw the cover back he uttered an exclamation of angry surprise. The box was empty!

CHAPTER XXXII

Mr. Rogers strode to the door, forgetful of his sleeping daughter overhead, and thundered out his call for James. The servant appeared at once, but he knew nothing about the safe, and had not been in the office that morning. Other servants were summoned and put through a rigid examination. Then Rogers turned to the woman who had answered the door for Gardley and sent her up to call Rosa.

But the woman returned presently with word that Miss Rosa was not in her room, and there was no sign that her bed had been slept in during the night. The woman's face was sullen. She did not like Rosa, but was afraid of her. This to her was only another of Miss Rosa's pranks, and very likely her doting father would manage to blame the servants with the affair.

Mr. Rogers's face grew stern. His eyes flashed angrily as he turned and strode up the stairs to his daughter's room, but when he came down again he was holding a note in his trembling hand and his face was ashen white.

"Read that, Gardley," he said, thrusting the note into Gardley's hands and motioning at the same time for the servants to go away.

Gardley took the note, yet even as he read he noticed that the paper was the same as those he carried in his pocket. There was a peculiar watermark that made it noticeable.

The note was a flippant little affair from Rosa, telling her father she had gone away to be married and that she would let him know where she was as soon as they were located. She added that he had forced her to this step by being so severe with her and not allowing her lover to come to see her. If he had been reasonable she would have stayed at home and let him give her a grand wedding; but as it was she had only this way of seeking her happiness. She added that she knew he would forgive her, and she hoped he would come to see that her way had been best, and Forsythe was all that he could desire as a son-in-law.

Gardley uttered an exclamation of dismay as he read, and, looking up, found the miserable eyes of the stricken father upon him. For the moment his own alarm concerning Margaret and his perplexity about the letters was forgotten in the grief of the man who had been his friend.

"When did she go?" asked Gardley, quickly looking up.

"She took supper with me and then went to her room, complaining of a headache," said the father, his voice showing his utter hopelessness. "She may have gone early in the evening, perhaps, for we all turned in about nine o'clock to keep the house quiet on her account."

"Have you any idea which way they went, east or west?" Gardley was the keen adviser in a crisis now, his every sense on the alert.

The old man shook his head. "It is too late now," he said, still in that colorless voice. "They will have reached the railroad somewhere. They will have been married by this time. See, it is after ten o'clock!"

"Yes, if he marries her," said Gardley, fiercely. He had no faith in Forsythe.

"You think—you don't think he would *dare*!" The old man straightened up and fairly blazed in his righteous wrath.

"I think he would dare anything if he thought he would not be caught. He is a coward, of course."

"What can we do?"

"Telegraph to detectives at all points where they would be likely to arrive and have them shadowed. Come, we will ride to the station at once; but, first, could I go up in her room and look around? There might be some clue."

"Certainly," said Rogers, pointing hopelessly up the stairs; "the first door to the left. But you'll find nothing. I looked everywhere. She wouldn't have left a clue. While you're up there I'll interview the servants. Then we'll go."

As he went up-stairs Gardley was wondering whether he ought to tell Rogers of the circumstance of the two letters. What possible connection could there be between Margaret Earle's trip to Walpi with the Brownleighs and Rosa Rogers's elopement? When you come to think of it, what possible explanation was there for a copy of Mrs. Brownleigh's letter to blow out of Rosa Rogers's bedroom window? How could it have got there?

Rosa's room was in beautiful order, the roses nodding in at the window, the curtain blowing back and forth in the breeze and rippling open the leaves of a tiny Testament lying on her desk, as if it had been recently read. There was nothing to show that the owner of the room had taken a hasty flight. On the desk lay several sheets of note-paper with the peculiar watermark. These caught his attention, and he took them up and compared them with the papers in his pocket. It was a strange thing that that letter which had sent Margaret off into the wilderness with an unknown Indian should be written on the same kind of paper as this; and yet, perhaps, it was not so strange, after all. It probably was the only note-paper to be had in that region, and must all have been purchased at the same place.

The rippling leaves of the Testament fluttered open at the fly-leaf and revealed Rosa's name and a date with Mrs. Brownleigh's name written below, and Gardley took it up, startled again to find Hazel Brownleigh mixed up with the Rogers. He had not known that they had anything to do with each other. And yet, of course, they would, being the missionaries of the region.

The almost empty waste-basket next caught his eye, and here again were several sheets of paper written over with words and phrases, words which at once he recognized as part of the letter Mrs. Tanner had given him. He emptied the waste-basket out on the desk, thinking perhaps there might be something there that would give a clue to where the elopers had gone; but there was not much else in it except a little yellowed note with the signature "Hazel Brownleigh" at the bottom. He glanced through the brief note, gathered its purport, and then spread it out deliberately on the desk and compared the writing with the others, a wild fear clutching at his heart. Yet he could not in any way explain why he was so uneasy. What possible reason could Rosa Rogers have for forging a letter to Margaret from Hazel Brownleigh?

Suddenly Rogers stood behind him looking over his shoulder. "What is it, Gardley? What have you found? Any clue?"

"No clue," said Gardley, uneasily, "but something strange I cannot understand. I don't suppose it can possibly have anything to do with your daughter, and yet it seems almost uncanny. This morning I stopped at the Tanners' to let Miss Earle know I had returned, and was told she had gone yesterday with a couple of Indians as guide to meet the Brownleighs at Keams or somewhere near there, and take a trip with them to Walpi to see the Hopi Indians. Mrs. Tanner gave me this letter from Mrs. Brownleigh, which Miss Earle had left behind. But when I reached here and was waiting for you some papers blew out of your daughter's window. When I picked them up I was startled to find that one of them was an exact copy of the letter I had in my pocket. See! Here they are! I don't suppose there is anything to it, but in spite of me I am a trifle uneasy about Miss Earle. I just can't understand how that copy of the letter came to be here."

Rogers was leaning over, looking at the papers. "What's this?" he asked, picking up the note that came with the Testament. He read each paper carefully, took in the little Testament with its fluttering fly-leaf and inscription, studied the pages of words and alphabet, then suddenly turned away and groaned, hiding his face in his hands.

"What is it?" asked Gardley, awed with the awful sorrow in the strong man's attitude.

"My poor baby!" groaned the father. "My poor little baby girl! I've always been afraid of that fatal gift of hers. Gardley, she could copy any handwriting in the world perfectly. She could write my name so it could not be told from my own signature. She's evidently written that letter. Why, I don't know, unless she wanted to get Miss Earle out of the way so it would be easier for her to carry out her plans."

"It can't be!" said Gardley, shaking his head. "I can't see what her object would be. Besides, where would she find the Indians? Mrs. Tanner saw the Indians. They came to the school after her with the letter, and waited for her. Mrs. Tanner saw them ride off together."

"There were a couple of strange Indians here yesterday, begging something to eat," said Rogers, settling down on a chair and resting his head against the desk as if he had suddenly lost the strength to stand.

"This won't do!" said Gardley. "We've got to get down to the telegraph-office, you and I. Now try to brace up. Are the horses ready? Then we'll go right away."

"You better question the servants about those Indians first," said Rogers; and Gardley, as he hurried down the stairs, heard groan after groan from Rosa's room, where her father lingered in agony.

Gardley got all the information he could about the Indians, and then the two men started away on a gallop to the station. As they passed the Tanner house Gardley drew rein to call to Bud, who hurried out joyfully to greet his friend, his face lighting with pleasure.

"Bill, get on your horse in double-quick time and beat it out to camp for me, will you?" said Gardley, as he reached down and gripped Bud's rough young paw. "Tell Jasper Kemp to come back with you and meet me at the station as quick as he can. Tell him to have the men where he can signal them. We may have to hustle out on a long hunt; and, Bill, keep your head steady and get back yourself right away. Perhaps I'll want you to help me. I'm a little anxious about Miss Earle, but you needn't tell anybody that but old Jasper. Tell him to hurry for all he's worth."

Bud, with his eyes large with loyalty and trouble, nodded understandingly, returned the grip of the young man's hand with a clumsy squeeze, and sprang away to get his horse and do Gardley's bidding. Gardley knew he would ride as for his life, now that he knew Margaret's safety was at stake.

Then Gardley rode on to the station and was indefatigable for two hours hunting out addresses, writing telegrams, and calling up long-distance telephones.

When all had been done that was possible Rogers turned a haggard face to the young man. "I've been thinking, Gardley, that rash little girl of mine may have got Miss Earle into some kind of a dangerousposition. You ought to look after her. What can we do?"

"I'm going to, sir," said Gardley, "just as soon as I've done everything I can for you. I've already sent for Jasper Kemp, and we'll make a plan between us and find out if Miss Earle is all right. Can you spare Jasper or will you need him?"

"By all means! Take all the men you need. I sha'n't rest easy till I know Miss Earle is safe."

He sank down on a truck that stood on the station platform, his shoulders slumping, his whole attitude as of one who was fatally stricken. It came over Gardley how suddenly old he looked, and haggard and gray! What a thing for the selfish child to have done to her father! Poor, silly child, whose fate with Forsythe would in all probability be anything but enviable!

But there was no time for sorrowful reflections. Jasper Kemp, stern, alert, anxious, came riding furiously down the street, Bud keeping even pace with him.

CHAPTER XXXIII

While Gardley briefly told his tale to Jasper Kemp, and the Scotchman was hastily scanning the papers with his keen, bright eyes, Bud stood frowning and listening intently.

"Gee!" he burst forth. "That girl's a mess! 'Course she did it! You oughta seen what all she didn't do the last six weeks of school. Miss Mar'get got so she shivered every time that girl came near her or looked at her. She sure had her goat! Some nights after school, when she thought she's all alone, she just cried, she did. Why, Rosa had every one of those guys in the back seat acting like the devil, and nobody knew what was the matter. She wrote things on the blackboard right in the questions, so's it looked like Miss Mar'get's writing; fierce things, sometimes; and Miss Mar'get didn't know who did it. And she was as jealous as a cat of Miss Mar'get. You all know what a case she had on that guy from over by the fort; and she didn't like to have him even look at Miss Mar'get. Well, she didn't forget how he went away that night of the play. I caught her looking at her like she would like to murder her. *Good night!* Some look! The guy had a case on Miss Mar'get, all right, too, only she was onto him and wouldn't look at him nor let him spoon nor nothing. But Rosa saw it all, and she just hated Miss Mar'get. Then once Miss Mar'get stopped her from going out to meet that guy, too. Oh, she hated her, all right! And you can bet she wrote the letter! Sure she did! She wanted to get her away when that guy came back. He was back yesterday. I saw him over by the run on that trail that crosses the trail to the old cabin. He didn't see me. I got my eye on him first, and I chucked behind some sage-brush, but he was here, all right, and he didn't mean any good. I follahed him awhile till he stopped and fixed up a place to camp. I guess he must 'a' stayed out last night—"

A heavy hand was suddenly laid from behind on Bud's shoulder, and Rogers stood over him, his dark eyes on fire, his lips trembling.

"Boy, can you show me where that was?" he asked, and there was an intensity in his voice that showed Bud that something serious was the matter. Boylike he dropped his eyes indifferently before this great emotion.

"Sure!"

"Best take Long Bill with you, Mr. Rogers," advised Jasper Kemp, keenly alive to the whole situation. "I reckon we'll all have to work together. My men ain't far off," and he lifted his whistle to his lips and blew the signal blasts. "The Kid here 'll want to ride to Keams to see if the lady is all safe and has met her friends. I reckon mebbe I better go straight to Ganado and find out if them mission folks really got started, and put 'em wise to what's been going on. They'll mebbe know who them Injuns was. I have my suspicions they weren't any friendlies. I didn't like that Injun the minute I set eyes on him hanging round the school-house, but I wouldn't have stirred a step toward camp if I'd 'a' suspected he was come fur the lady. 'Spose you take Bud and Long Bill and go find that camping-place and see if you find any trail showing which way they took. If you do, you fire three shots, and the men 'll be with you. If you want the Kid, fire four shots. He can't be so fur away by that time that he can't hear. He's got to get provisioned 'fore he starts. Lead him out, Bud. We 'ain't got no time to lose."

Bud gave one despairing look at Gardley and turned to obey.

"That's all right, Bud," said Gardley, with an understanding glance. "You tell Mr. Rogers all you know and show him the place, and then when Long Bill comes you can take the cross-cut to the Long Trail and go with me. I'll just stop at the house as I go by and tell your mother I need you."

Bud gave one radiant, grateful look and sprang upon his horse, and Rogers had hard work to keep up with him at first, till Bud got interested in giving him a detailed account of Forsythe's looks and acts.

In less than an hour the relief expedition had started. Before night had fallen Jasper Kemp, riding hard, arrived at the mission, told his story, procured a fresh horse, and after a couple of hours, rest started with Brownleigh and his wife for Keams Cañon.

Gardley and Bud, riding for all they were worth, said little by the way. Now and then the boy stole glances at the man's face, and the dead weight of sorrow settled like lead, the heavier, upon his heart. Too well he knew the dangers of the desert. He could almost read Gardley's fears in the white, drawn look about his lips, the ashen circles under his eyes, the tense, strained pose of his whole figure. Gardley's mind was urging ahead of his steed, and his body could not relax. He was anxious to go a little faster, yet his judgment knew it would not do, for his horse would play out before he could get another. They ate their corn bread in the saddle, and only turned aside from the trail once to drink at a water-hole and fill their cans. They rode late into the night, with only the stars and their wits to guide them. When they stopped to rest they did not wait to make a fire, but hobbled the horses where they might feed, and, rolling quickly in their blankets, lay down upon the ground.

Bud, with the fatigue of healthy youth, would have slept till morning in spite of his fears, but Gardley woke him in a couple of hours, made him drink some water and eat a bite of food, and they went on their way again. When morning broke they were almost to the entrance of Keams Cañon and both looked haggard and worn. Bud seemed to have aged in the night, and Gardley looked at him almost tenderly.

"Are you all in, kid?" he asked.

"Naw!" answered Bud, promptly, with an assumed cheerfulness. "Feeling like a four-year-old. Get on to that sky? Guess we're going to have some day! Pretty as a red wagon!"

Gardley smiled sadly. What would that day bring forth for the two who went in search of her they loved? His great anxiety was to get to Keams Cañon and inquire. They would surely know at the trading-post whether the missionary and his party had gone that way.

The road was still almost impassable from the flood; the two dauntless riders picked their way slowly down the trail to the post.

But the trader could tell them nothing comforting. The missionary had not been that way in two months, and there had been no party and no lady there that week. A single strange Indian had come down the trail above the day before, stayed awhile, picked a quarrel with some men who were there, and then ridden back up the steep trail again. He might have had a party with him up on the mesa, waiting. He had said something about his squaw. The trader admitted that he might have been drunk, but he frowned as he spoke of him. He called him a "bad Indian." Something unpleasant had evidently happened.

The trader gave them a good, hot dinner, of which they stood sorely in need, and because they realized that they must keep up their strength they took the time to eat it. Then, procuring fresh horses, they climbed the steep trail in the direction the trader said the Indian had taken. It was a slender clue, but it was all they had, and they must follow it. And now the travelers were very silent, as if they felt they were drawing near to some knowledge that would settle the question for them one way or the other. As they reached the top at last, where they could see out across the plain, each drew a long breath like a gasp and looked about, half fearing what he might see.

Yes, there was the sign of a recent camp-fire, and a few tin cans and bits of refuse, nothing more. Gardley got down and searched carefully. Bud even crept about upon his hands and knees, but a single tiny blue bead like a grain of sand was all that rewarded his efforts. Some Indian had doubtless camped here. That was all the evidence. Standing thus in hopeless uncertainty what to do next, they suddenly heard voices. Something familiar once or twice made Gardley lift his whistle and blow a blast. Instantly a silvery answer came ringing from the mesa a mile or so away and woke the echoes in the cañon. Jasper Kemp and his party had taken the longer way around instead of going down the cañon, and were just arriving at the spot where Margaret and the squaw had waited two days before for their drunken guide. But Jasper Kemp's whistle rang out again, and he shot three times into the air, their signal to wait for some important news.

Breathlessly and in silence the two waited till the coming of the rest of the party, and cast themselves down on the ground, feeling the sudden need of support. Now that there was a possibility of some news, they felt hardly able to bear it, and the waiting for it was intolerable, to such a point of anxious tension were they strained.

But when the party from Ganado came in sight their faces wore no brightness of good news. Their greetings were quiet, sad, anxious, and Jasper Kemp held out to Gardley an envelope. It was the one from Margaret's mother's letter that she had dropped upon the trail.

"We found it on the way from Ganado, just as we entered Steamboat Cañon," explained Jasper.

"And didn't you search for a trail off in any other direction?" asked Gardley, almost sharply. "They have not been here. At least only one Indian has been down to the trader's."

"There was no other trail. We looked," said Jasper, sadly. "There was a camp-fire twice, and signs of a camp. We felt sure they had come this way."

Gardley shook his head and a look of abject despair came over his face. "There is no sign here," he said. "They must have gone some other way. Perhaps the Indian has carried her off. Are the other men following?"

"No, Rogers sent them in the other direction after his girl. They found the camp all right. Bud tell you? We made sure we had found our trail and would not need them."

Gardley dropped his head and almost groaned.

Meanwhile the missionary had been riding around in radiating circles from the dead camp-fire, searching every step of the way; and Bud, taking his cue from him, looked off toward the mesa a minute, then struck out in a straight line for it and rode off like mad. Suddenly there was heard a shout loud and long, and Bud came riding back, waving something small and white above his head.

They gathered in a little knot, waiting for the boy, not speaking; and when he halted in their midst he fluttered down the handkerchief to Gardley.

"It's hers, all right. Gotter name all written out on the edge!" he declared, radiantly.

The sky grew brighter to them all now. Eagerly Gardley sprang into his saddle, no longer weary, but alert and eager for the trail.

"You folks better go down to the trader's and get some dinner. You'll need it! Bud and I'll go on. Mrs. Brownleigh looks all in."

"No," declared Hazel, decidedly. "We'll just snatch a bite here and follow you at once. I couldn't enjoy a dinner till I know she is safe." And so, though both Jasper Kemp and her husband urged her otherwise, she would take a hasty meal by the way and hurry on.

But Bud and Gardley waited not for others. They plunged wildly ahead.

It seemed a long way to the eager hunters, from the place where Bud had found the handkerchief to the little note twisted around the red chessman. It was perhaps nearly a mile, and both the riders had searched in all directions for some time before Gardley spied it. Eagerly he seized upon the note, recognizing the little red manikin with which he had whiled away an hour with Margaret during one of her visits at the camp.

The note was written large and clear upon a sheet of writing-paper:

"I am Margaret Earle, school-teacher at Ashland. I am supposed to be traveling to Walpi, by way of Keams, to meet Mr. and Mrs. Brownleigh of Ganado. I am with an Indian, his squaw and papoose. The Indian said he was sent to guide me, but he is drunk now and I am frightened. He has acted strangely all the way. I do not know where I am. Please come and help me."

Bud, sitting anxious like a statue upon his horse, read Gardley's face as Gardley read the note. Then Gardley read it aloud to Bud, and before the last word was fairly out of his mouth both man and boy started as if they had heard Margaret's beloved voice calling them. It was not long before Bud found another scrap of paper a half-mile farther on, and then another and another, scattered at great distances along the way. The only way they had of being sure she had dropped them was that they seemed to be the same kind of paper as that upon which the note was written.

How that note with its brave, frightened appeal wrung the heart of Gardley as he thought of Margaret, unprotected, in terror and perhaps in peril, riding on she knew not where. What trials and fears had she not already passed through! What might she not be experiencing even now while he searched for her?

It was perhaps two hours before he found the little white stocking dropped where the trail divided, showing which way she had taken. Gardley folded it reverently and put it in his pocket. An hour later Bud pounced upon the bedroom slipper and carried it gleefully to Gardley; and so by slow degrees, finding here and there a chessman or more paper, they came at last to the camp where the Indians had abandoned their trust and fled, leaving Margaret alone in the wilderness.

It was then that Gardley searched in vain for any further clue, and, riding wide in every direction, stopped and called her name again and again, while the sun grew lower and lower and shadows crept in lurking-places waiting for the swift-coming night. It was then that Bud, flying frantically from one spot to another, got down upon his

253

knees behind a sage-bush when Gardley was not looking and mumbled a rough, hasty prayer for help. He felt like the old woman who, on being told that nothing but God could save the ship, exclaimed, "And has it come to that?" Bud had felt all his life that there was a remote time in every life when one might need to believe in prayer. The time had come for Bud.

Margaret, on her knees in the sand of the desert praying for help, remembered the promise, "Before they call I will answer, and while they are yet speaking I will hear," and knew not that her deliverers were on the way.

The sun had been hot as it beat down upon the whiteness of the sand, and the girl had crept under a sage-bush for shelter from it. The pain in her ankle was sickening. She had removed her shoe and bound the ankle about with a handkerchief soaked with half of her bottle of witch-hazel, and so, lying quiet, had fallen asleep, too exhausted with pain and anxiety to stay awake any longer.

When she awoke again the softness of evening was hovering over everything, and she started up and listened. Surely, surely, she had heard a voice calling her! She sat up sharply and listened. Ah! There it was again, a faint echo in the distance. Was it a voice, or was it only her dreams mingling with her fancies?

Travelers in deserts, she had read, took all sorts of fancies, saw mirages, heard sounds that were not. But she had not been out long enough to have caught such a desert fever. Perhaps she was going to be sick. Still that faint echo made her heart beat wildly. She dragged herself to her knees, then to her feet, standing painfully with the weight on her well foot.

The suffering horse turned his anguished eyes and whinnied. Her heart ached for him, yet there was no way she could assuage his pain or put him out of his misery. But she must make sure if she had heard a voice. Could she possibly scale that rock down which she and her horse had fallen? For then she might look out farther and see if there were any one in sight.

Painfully she crawled and crept, up and up, inch by inch, until at last she gained the little height and could look afar.

There was no living thing in sight. The air was very clear. The eagle had found his evening rest somewhere in a quiet crag. The long corn waved on the distant plain, and all was deathly still once more. There was a hint of coming sunset in the sky. Her heart sank, and she was about to give up hope entirely, when, rich and clear, there it came again! A voice in the wilderness calling her name: "Margaret! Margaret!"

The tears rushed to her eyes and crowded in her throat. She could not answer, she was so overwhelmed; and though she tried twice to call out, she could make no sound. But the call kept coming again and again: "Margaret! Margaret!" and it was Gardley's voice. Impossible! For Gardley was far away and could not know her need. Yet it was his voice. Had she died, or was she in delirium that she seemed to hear him calling her name?

But the call came clearer now: "Margaret! Margaret! I am coming!" and like a flash her mind went back to the first night in Arizona when she heard him singing, "From the Desert I Come to Thee!"

Now she struggled to her feet again and shouted, inarticulately and gladly through her tears. She could see him. It was Gardley. He was riding fast toward her, and he shot three shots into the air above him as he rode, and three shrill blasts of his whistle rang out on the still evening air.

She tore the scarf from her neck that she had tied about it to keep the sun from blistering her, and waved it wildly in the air now, shouting in happy, choking sobs.

And so he came to her across the desert!

He sprang down before the horse had fairly reached her side, and, rushing to her, took her in his arms.

"Margaret! My darling! I have found you at last!"

She swayed and would have fallen but for his arms, and then he saw her white face and knew she must be suffering.

"You are hurt!" he cried. "Oh, what have they done to you?" And he laid her gently down upon the sand and dropped on his knees beside her.

"Oh no," she gasped, joyously, with white lips. "I'm all right now. Only my ankle hurts a little. We had a fall, the horse and I. Oh, go to him at once and put him out of his pain. I'm sure his legs are broken."

For answer Gardley put the whistle to his lips and blew a blast. He would not leave her for an instant. He was not sure yet that she was not more hurt than she had said. He set about discovering at once, for he had brought with him supplies for all emergencies.

It was Bud who came riding madly across the mesa in answer to the call, reaching Gardley before any one else. Bud with his eyes shining, his cheeks blazing with excitement, his hair wildly flying in the breeze, his young, boyish face suddenly grown old with lines of anxiety. But you wouldn't have known from his greeting that it was anything more than a pleasure excursion he had been on the past two days.

"Good work, Kid! Whatcha want me t' do?"

It was Bud who arranged the camp and went back to tell the other detachments that Margaret was found; Bud who led the pack-horse up, unpacked the provisions, and gathered wood to start a fire. Bud was everywhere, with a smudged face, a weary, gray look around his eyes, and his hair sticking "seven ways for Sunday." Yet once, when his labors led him near to where Margaret lay weak and happy on a couch of blankets, he gave her an unwonted pat on her shoulder and said in a low tone: "Hello, Gang! See you kept your nerve with you!" and then he gave her a grin all across his dirty, tired face, and moved away as if he were half ashamed of his emotion. But it was Bud again who came and talked with her to divert her so that she wouldn't notice when they shot her horse. He talked loudly about a coyote they shot the night before, and a cottontail they saw at Keams, and when he saw that she understood what the shot meant, and there were tears in her eyes, he gave her hand a rough, bear squeeze and said, gruffly: "You should worry! He's better off now!" And when Gardley came back he took himself thoughtfully to a distance and busied himself opening tins of meat and soup.

In another hour the Brownleighs arrived, having heard the signals, and they had a supper around the camp-fire, everybody so rejoiced that there were still quivers in their voices; and when any one laughed it sounded like the echo of a sob, so great had been the strain of their anxiety.

Gardley, sitting beside Margaret in the starlight afterward, her hand in his, listened to the story of her journey, the strong, tender pressure of his fingers telling her how deeply it affected him to know the peril through which she had passed. Later, when the others were telling gay stories about the fire, and Bud lying full length in their midst had fallen fast asleep, these two, a little apart from the rest, were murmuring their innermost thoughts in low tones to each other, and rejoicing that they were together once more.

CHAPTER XXXIV

They talked it over the next morning at breakfast as they sat around the fire. Jasper Kemp thought he ought to get right back to attend to things. Mr. Rogers was all broken up, and might even need him to search for Rosa if they had not found out her whereabouts yet. He and Fiddling Boss, who had come along, would start back at once. They had had a good night's rest and had found their dear lady. What more did they need? Besides, there were not provisions for an indefinite stay for such a large party, and there were none too many sources of supply in this region.

The missionary thought that, now he was here, he ought to go on to Walpi. It was not more than two hours' ride there, and Hazel could stay with the camp while Margaret's ankle had a chance to rest and let the swelling subside under treatment.

Margaret, however, rebelled. She did not wish to be an invalid, and was very sure she could ride without injury to her ankle. She wanted to see Walpi and the queer Hopi Indians, now she was so near. So a compromise was agreed upon. They would all wait in camp a couple of days, and then if Margaret felt well enough they would go on, visit the Hopis, and so go home together.

Bud pleaded to be allowed to stay with them, and Jasper Kemp promised to make it all right with his parents.

So for two whole, long, lovely days the little party of five camped on the mesa and enjoyed sweet converse. It is safe to say that never in all Bud's life will he forget or get away from the influences of that day in such company.

Gardley and the missionary proved to be the best of physicians, and Margaret's ankle improved hourly under their united treatment of compresses, lotions, and rest. About noon on Saturday they broke camp, mounted their horses, and rode away across the stretch of white sand, through tall cornfields growing right up out of the sand, closer and closer to the great mesa with the castle-like pueblos five hundred feet above them on the top. It seemed to Margaret like suddenly being dropped into Egypt or the Holy Land, or some of the Babylonian excavations, so curious and primitive and altogether different from anything else she had ever seen did it all appear. She listened, fascinated, while Brownleigh told about this strange Hopi land, the strangest spot in America. Spanish explorers found them away back years before the Pilgrims landed, and called the country Tuscayan. They built their homes up high for protection from their enemies. They lived on the corn, pumpkins, peaches, and melons which they raised in the valley, planting the seeds with their hands. It is supposed they got their seeds first from the Spaniards years ago. They make pottery, cloth, and baskets, and are a busy people.

There are seven villages built on three mesas in the northern desert. One of the largest, Orabi, has a thousand inhabitants. Walpi numbers about two hundred and thirty people, all living in this one great building of many rooms. They are divided into brotherhoods, or phratries, and each brotherhood has several large families. They are ruled by a speaker chief and a war chief elected by a council of clan elders.

Margaret learned with wonder that all the water these people used had to be carried by the women in jars on their backs five hundred feet up the steep trail.

Presently, as they drew nearer, a curious man with his hair "banged" like a child's, and garments much like those usually worn by scarecrows—a shapeless kind of shirt and trousers—appeared along the steep and showed them the way up. Margaret and the missionary's wife exclaimed in horror over the little children playing along the very edge of the cliffs above as carelessly as birds in trees.

High up on the mesa at last, how strange and weird it seemed! Far below the yellow sand of the valley; fifteen miles away a second mesa stretching dark; to the southwest, a hundred miles distant, the dim outlines of the San Francisco peaks. Some little children on burros crossing the sand below looked as if they were part of a curious moving-picture, not as if they were little living beings taking life as seriously as other children do. The great, wide desert stretching far! The bare, solid rocks beneath their feet! The curious houses behind them! It all seemed unreal to Margaret, like a great picture-book spread out for her to see. She turned from gazing and found Gardley's eyes upon her adoringly, a tender understanding of her mood in his glance. She thrilled with pleasure to be here with him; a soft flush spread over her cheeks and a light came into her eyes.

They found the Indians preparing for one of their most famous ceremonies, the snake dance, which was to take place in a few days. For almost a week the snake priests had been busy hunting rattlesnakes, building altars, drawing figures in the sand, and singing weird songs. On the ninth day the snakes are washed in a pool and driven near a pile of sand. The priests, arrayed in paint, feathers, and charms, come out in line and, taking the live snakes in their mouths, parade up and down the rocks, while the people crowd the roofs and terraces of the pueblos to watch. There are helpers to whip the snakes and keep them from biting, and catchers to see that none get away. In a little while the priests take the snakes down on the desert and set them free, sending them north, south, east, and west, where it is supposed they will take the people's prayers for rain to the water serpent in the underworld, who is in some way connected with the god of the rain-clouds.

It was a strange experience, that night in Walpi: the primitive accommodations; the picturesque, uncivilized people; the shy glances from dark, eager eyes. To watch two girls grinding corn between two stones, and a little farther off their mother rolling out her dough with an ear of corn, and cooking over an open fire, her pot slung from a crude crane over the blaze—it was all too unreal to be true.

But the most interesting thing about it was to watch the "Aneshodi" going about among them, his face alight with warm, human love; his hearty laugh ringing out in a joke that the Hopis seemed to understand, making himself one with them. It came to Margaret suddenly to remember the pompous little figure of the Rev. Frederick West, and to fancy him going about among these people and trying to do them good. Before she knew what she was doing she laughed aloud at the thought. Then, of course, she had to explain to Bud and Gardley, who looked at her inquiringly.

"Aw! Gee! *Him? He* wasn't a minister! He was a *mistake*! Fergit him, the poor simp!" growled Bud, sympathetically. Then his eyes softened as he watched Brownleigh playing with three little Indian maids, having a fine romp. "Gee! he certainly is a peach, isn't he?" he murmured, his whole face kindling appreciatively. "Gee! I bet that kid never forgets that!"

The Sunday was a wonderful day, when the missionary gathered the people together and spoke to them in simple words of God—their god who made the sky, the stars, the mountains, and the sun, whom they call by different names, but whom He called God. He spoke of the Book of Heaven that told about God and His great love for men, so great that He sent His son to save them from their sin. It was not a long sermon, but a very beautiful one; and, listening to the simple, wonderful words of life that fell from the missionary's earnest lips and were translated by his faithful Indian interpreter, who always went with him on his expeditions, watchingthe faces of the dark, strange people as they took in the marvelous meaning, the little company of visitors was strangely moved. Even Bud, awed beyond his wont, said, shyly, to Margaret:

"Gee! It's something fierce not to be born a Christian and know all that, ain't it?"

Margaret and Gardley walked a little way down the narrow path that led out over the neck of rock less than a rod wide that connects the great promontory with the mesa. The sun was setting in majesty over the desert, and the scene was one of breathless beauty. One might fancy it might look so to stand on the hills of God and look out over creation when all things have been made new.

They stood for a while in silence. Then Margaret looked down at the narrow path worn more than a foot deep in the solid rock by the ten generations of feet that had been passing over it.

"Just think," she said, "of all the feet, little and big, that have walked here in all the years, and of all the souls that have stood and looked out over this wonderful sight! It must be that somehow in spite of their darkness they have reached out to the God who made this, and have found a way to His heart. They couldn't look at this and not feel Him, could they? It seems to me that perhaps some of those poor creatures who have stood here and reached up blindly after the Creator of their souls have, perhaps, been as pleasing to Him as those who have known about Him from childhood."

Gardley was used to her talking this way. He had not been in her Sunday meetings for nothing. He understood and sympathized, and now his hand reached softly for hers and held it tenderly. After a moment of silence he said:

"I surely think if God could reach and find me in the desert of my life, He must have found them. I sometimes think I was a greater heathen than all these, because I knew and would not see."

Margaret nestled her hand in his and looked up joyfully into his face. "I'm so glad you know Him now!" she murmured, happily.

They stood for some time looking out over the changing scene, till the crimson faded into rose, the silver into gray; till the stars bloomed out one by one, and down in the valley across the desert a light twinkled faintly here and there from the camps of the Hopi shepherds.

They started home at daybreak the next morning, the whole company of Indians standing on the rocks to send them royally on their way, pressing simple, homely gifts upon them and begging them to return soon again and tell the blessed story.

A wonderful ride they had back to Ganado, where Gardley left Margaret for a short visit, promising to return for her in a few days when she was rested, and hastened back to Ashland to his work; for his soul was happy now and at ease, and he felt he must get to work at once. Rogers would need him. Poor Rogers! Had he found his daughter yet? Poor, silly child-prodigal!

But when Gardley reached Ashland he found among his mail awaiting him a telegram. His uncle was dead, and the fortune which he had been brought up to believe was his, and which he had idly tossed away in a moment of recklessness, had been restored to him by the uncle's last will, made since Gardley's recent visit home. The fortune was his again!

Gardley sat in his office on the Rogers ranch and stared hard at the adobe wall opposite his desk. That fortune would be great! He could do such wonderful things for Margaret now. They could work out their dreams together for the people they loved. He could see the shadows of those dreams—a beautiful home for Margaret out on the trail she loved, where wildness and beauty and the mountain she called hers were not far away; horses in plenty and a luxurious car when they wanted to take a trip; journeys East as often as they wished; some of the ideal appliances for the school that Margaret loved; a church for the missionary and convenient halls where he could speak at his outlying districts; a trip to the city for Mom Wallis, where she might see a real picture-gallery, her one expressed desire this side of heaven, now that she had taken to reading Browning and had some of it explained to her. Oh, and a lot of wonderful things! These all hung in the dream-picture before Gardley's eyes as he sat at his desk with that bit of yellow paper in his hand.

He thought of what that money had represented to him in the past. Reckless days and nights of folly as a boy and young man at college; ruthless waste of time, money, youth; shriveling of soul, till Margaret came and found and rescued him! How wonderful that he had been rescued! That he had come to his senses at last, and was here in a man's position, doing a man's work in the world! Now, with all that money, there was no need for him to work and earn more. He could live idly all his days and just have a good time—make others happy, too. But still he would not have this exhilarating feeling that he was supplying his own and Margaret's necessities by the labor of hand and brain. The little telegram in his hand seemed somehow to be trying to snatch from him all this material prosperity that was the symbol of that spiritual regeneration which had become so dear to him.

He put his head down on his clasped hands upon the desk then and prayed. Perhaps it was the first great prayer of his life.

"O God, let me be strong enough to stand this that has come upon me. Help me to be a man in spite of money! Don't let me lose my manhood and my right to work. Help me to use the money in the right way and not to dwarf myself, nor spoil our lives with it." It was a great prayer for a man such as Gardley had been, and the answer came swiftly in his conviction.

He lifted up his head with purpose in his expression, and, folding the telegram, put it safely back into his pocket. He would not tell Margaret of it—not just yet. He would think it out—just the right way—and he did not believe he meant to give up his position with Rogers. He had accepted it for a year in good faith, and it was his business to fulfil the contract. Meantime, this money would perhaps make possible his marriage with Margaret sooner than he had hoped.

Five minutes later Rogers telephoned to the office.

"I've decided to take that shipment of cattle and try that new stock, provided you will go out and look at them and see that everything is all O. K. I couldn't go myself now. Don't feel like going anywhere, you know. You wouldn't need to go for a couple of weeks. I've just had a letter from the man, and he says he won't be ready sooner. Say, why don't you and Miss Earle get married and make this a wedding-trip? She could go to the Pacific coast with you. It would be a nice trip. Then I could spare you for a month or six weeks when you got back if you wanted to take her East for a little visit."

Why not? Gardley stumbled out his thanks and hung up the receiver, his face full of the light of a great joy. How were the blessings pouring down upon his head these days? Was it a sign that God was pleased with his action in making good what he could where he had failed? And Rogers! How kind he was! Poor Rogers, with his broken heart and his stricken home! For Rosa had come home again a sadder, wiser child; and her father seemed crushed with the disgrace of it all.

Gardley went to Margaret that very afternoon. He told her only that he had had some money left him by his uncle, which would make it possible for him to marry at once and keep her comfortably now. He was to be sent to California on a business trip. Would she be married and go with him?

Margaret studied the telegram in wonder. She had never asked Gardley much about his circumstances. The telegram merely stated that his uncle's estate was left to him. To her simple mind an estate might be a few hundred dollars, enough to furnish a plain little home; and her face lighted with joy over it. She asked no questions, and Gardley said no more about the money. He had forgotten that question, comparatively, in the greater possibility of joy.

Would she be married in ten days and go with him?

Her eyes met his with an answering joy, and yet he could see that there was a trouble hiding somewhere. He presently saw what it was without needing to be told. Her father and mother! Of course, they would be disappointed! They would want her to be married at home!

"But Rogers said we could go and visit them for several weeks on our return," he said; and Margaret's face lighted up.

"Oh, that would be beautiful," she said, wistfully; "and perhaps they won't mind so much—though I always expected father would marry me if I was ever married; still, if we can go home so soon and for so long—and Mr. Brownleigh would be next best, of course."

"But, of course, your father must marry you," said Gardley, determinedly. "Perhaps we could persuade him to come, and your mother, too."

"Oh no, they couldn't possibly," said Margaret, quickly, a shade of sadness in her eyes. "You know it costs a lot to come out here, and ministers are never rich."

It was then that Gardley's eyes lighted with joy. His money could take this bugbear away, at least. However, he said nothing about the money.

"Suppose we write to your father and mother and put the matter before them. See what they say. We'll send the letters to-night. You write your mother and I'll write your father."

Margaret agreed and sat down at once to write her letter, while Gardley, on the other side of the room, wrote his, scratching away contentedly with his fountain-pen and looking furtively now and then toward the bowed head over at the desk.

Gardley did not read his letter to Margaret. She wondered a little at this, but did not ask, and the letters were mailed, with special-delivery stamps on them. Gardley awaited their replies with great impatience.

He filled in the days of waiting with business. There were letters to write connected with his fortune, and there were arrangements to be made for his trip. But the thing that occupied the most of his time and thought was the purchase and refitting of a roomy old ranch-house in a charming location, not more than three miles from Ashland, on the road to the camp.

It had been vacant for a couple of years past, the owner having gone abroad permanently and the place having been offered for sale. Margaret had often admired it in her trips to and from the camp, and Gardley thought of it at once when it became possible for him to think of purchasing a home in the West.

There was a great stone fireplace, and the beams of the ceilings and pillars of the porch and wide, hospitable rooms were of tree-trunks with the bark on them. With a little work it could be made roughly but artistically habitable. Gardley had it cleaned up, not disturbing the tangle of vines and shrubbery that had had their way since the last owner had left them and which had made a perfect screen from the road for the house.

Behind this screen the men worked—most of them the men from the bunk-house, whom Gardley took into his confidence.

The floors were carefully scrubbed under the direction of Mom Wallis, and the windows made shining. Then the men spent a day bringing great loads of tree-boughs and filling the place with green fragrance, until the big living-room looked like a woodland bower. Gardley made a raid upon some Indian friends of his and came back with several fine Navajo rugs and blankets, which he spread about the room luxuriously on the floor and over the rude benches which the men had constructed. They piled the fireplace with big logs, and Gardley took over some of his own personal possessions that he had brought back from the East with him to give the place a livable look. Then he stood back satisfied. The place was fit to bring his bride and her friends to. Not that it was as it should be. That would be for Margaret to do, but it would serve as a temporary stopping-place if there came need. If no need came, why, the place was there, anyway, hers and his. A tender light grew in his eyes as he looked it over in the dying light of the afternoon. Then he went out and rode swiftly to the telegraph-office and found these two telegrams, according to the request in his own letter to Mr. Earle.

Gardley's telegram read:

Congratulations. Will come as you desire. We await your advice. Have written.—FATHER.

He saddled his horse and hurried to Margaret with hers, and together they read:

Dear child! So glad for you. Of course you will go. I am sending you some things. Don't take a thought for us. We shall look forward to your visit. Our love to you both.—MOTHER.

Margaret, folded in her lover's arms, cried out her sorrow and her joy, and lifted up her face with happiness. Then Gardley, with great joy, thought of the surprise he had in store for her and laid his face against hers to hide the telltale smile in his eyes.

For Gardley, in his letter to his future father-in-law, had written of his newly inherited fortune, and had not only inclosed a check for a good sum to cover all extra expense of the journey, but had said that a private car would be at their disposal, not only for themselves, but for any of Margaret's friends and relatives whom they might choose to invite. As he had written this letter he was filled with deep thanksgiving that it was in his power to do this thing for his dear girl-bride.

The morning after the telegrams arrived Gardley spent several hours writing telegrams and receiving them from a big department store in the nearest great city, and before noon a big shipment of goods was on its way to Ashland. Beds, bureaus, wash-stands, chairs, tables, dishes, kitchen utensils, and all kinds of bedding, even to sheets and pillow-cases, he ordered with lavish hand. After all, he must furnish the house himself, and let Margaret weed it out or give it away afterward, if she did not like it. He was going to have a house party and he must be ready. When all was done and he was just about to mount his horse again he turned back and sent another message, ordering a piano.

"Why, it's *great*!" he said to himself, as he rode back to his office. "It's simply great to be able to do things just when I need them! I never knew what fun money was before. But then I never had Margaret to spend it for, and she's worth the whole of it at once!"

The next thing he ordered was a great easy carriage with plenty of room to convey Mother Earle and her friends from the train to the house.

The days went by rapidly enough, and Margaret was so busy that she had little time to wonder and worry why her mother did not write her the long, loving, motherly good-by letter to her little girlhood that she had expected to get. Not until three days before the wedding did it come over her that she had had but three brief, scrappy letters from her mother, and they not a whole page apiece. What could be the matter with mother? She was almost on the point of panic when Gardley came and bundled her on to her horse for a ride.

Strangely enough, he directed their way through Ashland and down to the station, and it was just about the time of the arrival of the evening train.

Gardley excused himself for a moment, saying something about an errand, and went into the station. Margaret sat on her horse, watching the oncoming train, the great connecting link between East and West, and wondered if it would bring a letter from mother.

The train rushed to a halt, and behold some passengers were getting off from a private car! Margaret watched them idly, thinking more about an expected letter than about the people. Then suddenly she awoke to the fact that Gardley was greeting them. Who could they be?

There were five of them, and one of them looked like Jane! Dear Jane! She had forgotten to write her about this hurried wedding. How different it all was going to be from what she and Jane had planned for each other in their dear old school-day dreams! And that young man that Gardley was shaking hands with now looked like Cousin Dick! She hadn't seen him for three years, but he must look like that now; and the younger girl beside him might be Cousin Emily! But, oh, who were the others? *Father!* And MOTHER!

Margaret sprang from her horse with a bound and rushed into her mother's arms. The interested passengers craned their necks and looked their fill with smiles of appreciation as the train took up its way again, having dropped the private car on the side track.

Dick and Emily rode the ponies to the house, while Margaret nestled in the back seat of the carriage between her father and mother, and Jane got acquainted with Gardley in the front seat of the carriage. Margaret never even noticed where they were going until the carriage turned in and stopped before the door of the new house, and Mrs. Tanner, furtively casting behind her the checked apron she had worn, came out to shake hands with the company and tell them supper was all ready, before she went back to her deserted boarding-house. Even Bud was going to stay at the new house that night, in some cooked-up capacity or other, and all the men from the bunk-house were hiding out among the trees to see Margaret's father and mother and shake hands if the opportunity offered.

The wonder and delight of Margaret when she saw the house inside and knew that it was hers, the tears she shed and smiles that grew almost into hysterics when she saw some of the incongruous furnishings, are all past describing. Margaret was too happy to think. She rushed from one room to another. She hugged her mother and linked her arm in her father's for a walk across the long piazza; she talked to Emily and Dick and Jane; and then rushed out to find Gardley and thank him again. And all this time she could not understand how Gardley had done it, for she had not yet comprehended his fortune.

Gardley had asked his sisters to come to the wedding, not much expecting they would accept, but they had telegraphed at the last minute they would be there. They arrived an hour or so before the ceremony; gushed over

Margaret; told Gardley she was a "sweet thing"; said the house was "dandy for a house party if one had plenty of servants, but they should think it would be dull in winter"; gave Margaret a diamond sunburst pin, a string of pearls, and an emerald bracelet set in diamond chips; and departed immediately after the ceremony. They had thought they were the chief guests, but the relief that overspread the faces of those guests who were best beloved by both bride and groom was at once visible on their departure. Jasper Kemp drew a long breath and declared to Long Bill that he was glad the air was growing pure again. Then all those old friends from the bunk-house filed in to the great tables heavily loaded with good things, the abundant gift of the neighborhood, and sat down to the wedding supper, heartily glad that the "city lady and her gals"—as Mom Wallis called them in a suppressed whisper—had chosen not to stay over a train.

The wedding had been in the school-house, embowered in foliage and all the flowers the land afforded, decorated by the loving hands of Margaret's pupils, old and young. She was attended by the entire school marching double file before her, strewing flowers in her way. The missionary's wife played the wedding-march, and the missionary assisted the bride's father with the ceremony. Margaret's dress was a simple white muslin, with a little real lace and embroidery handed down from former generations, the whole called into being by Margaret's mother. Even Gardley's sisters had said it was "perfectly dear." The whole neighborhood was at the wedding.

And when the bountiful wedding-supper was eaten the entire company of favored guests stood about the new piano and sang "Blest Be the Tie that Binds"—with Margaret playing for them.

Then there was a little hurry at the last, Margaret getting into the pretty traveling dress and hat her mother had brought, and kissing her mother good-by—though happily not for long this time.

Mother and father and the rest of the home party were to wait until morning, and the missionary and his wife were to stay with them that night and see them to their car the next day.

So, waving and throwing kisses back to the others, they rode away to the station, Bud pridefully driving the team from the front seat.

Gardley had arranged for a private apartment on the train, and nothing could have been more luxurious in traveling than the place where he led his bride. Bud, scuttling behind with a suit-case, looked around him with all his eyes before he said a hurried good-by, and murmured under his breath: "Gee! Wisht I was goin' all the way!"

Bud hustled off as the train got under way, and Margaret and Gardley went out to the observation platform to wave a last farewell.

The few little blurring lights of Ashland died soon in the distance, and the desert took on its vast wideness beneath a starry dome; but off in the East a purple shadow loomed, mighty and majestic, and rising slowly over its crest a great silver disk appeared, brightening as it came and pouring a silver mist over the purple peak.

"My mountain!" said Margaret, softly.

And Gardley, drawing her close to him, stooped to lay his lips upon hers.

"My darling!" he answered.

THE END

Exit Betty
CHAPTER I

THE crowd gave way and the car glided smoothly up to the curb at the canopied entrance to the church. The blackness of the wet November night was upon the street. It had rained at intervals all day.

The pavements shone wetly like new paint in the glimmer of the street lights, and rude shadows gloomed in every cranny of the great stone building.

Betty, alone in the midst of her bridal finery, shrank back from the gaze of the curious onlookers, seeming very small like a thing of the air caught in a mesh of the earth.

She had longed all day for this brief respite from everyone, but it had passed before she could concentrate her thoughts. She started forward, a flame of rose for an instant in her white cheeks, but gone as quickly. Her eyes reminded one of the stars among the far-away clouds on a night of fitful storm with only glimpses of their beauty in breaks of the overcast sky. Her small hands gripped one another excitedly, and the sweet lips were quivering.

A white-gloved hand reached out to open the car door, and other hands caught and cared for the billow of satin and costly lace with which she was surrounded, as if it, and not she, were the important one.

They led her up the curtained way, where envious eyes peeped through a furtive rip in the canvas, or craned around an opening to catch a better glimpse of her loveliness, one little dark-eyed foreigner even reached out a grimy, wondering finger to the silver whiteness of her train; but she, all unknowing, trod the carpeted path as in a dream.

The wedding march was just beginning. She caught the distant notes, felt the hush as she approached the audience, and wondered why the ordeal seemed so much greater now that she was actually come to the moment. If she had known it would be like this—! Oh, why had she given in!

The guests had risen and were stretching their necks for the first vision of her. The chaplet of costly blossoms sat upon her brow and bound her wedding veil floating mistily behind, but the lovely head was bowed, not lifted proudly as a bride's should be, and the little white glove that rested on the arm of the large florid cousin trembled visibly. The cousin was almost unknown until a few hours before. His importance overpowered her. She drooped her eyes and tried not to wish for the quiet, gray-haired cousin of her own mother. It was so strange for him to have failed her at the last moment, when he had promised long ago to let nothing hinder him from giving her away if she should ever be married. His telegram, "Unavoidably detained," had been received but an hour before. He seemed the only one of her kind, and now she was all alone. All the rest were like enemies, although they professed deep concern for her welfare; for they were leagued together against all her dearest wishes, until she had grown weary in the combat.

She gave a frightened glance behind as if some intangible thing were following her. Was it a hounding dread that after all she would not be free after marriage?

With measured tread she passed the long white-ribboned way, under arches that she never noticed, through a sea of faces that she never saw, to the altar smothered in flowers and tropical ferns. It seemed interminable. Would it never end? They paused at last, and she lifted frightened eyes to the florid cousin, and then to the face of her bridegroom!

It was a breathless moment, and but for the deep tones of the organ now hushing for the ceremony, one of almost audible silence. No lovelier bride had trod those aisles in many a long year; so exquisite, so small, so young—and so exceeding rich! The guests were entranced, and every eye was greedily upon her as the white-robed minister advanced with his open book.

"Beloved, we are met together to-night to join this man——!"

At that word they saw the bride suddenly, softly sink before them, a little white heap at the altar, with the white face turned upward, the white eyelids closed, the long dark lashes sweeping the pretty cheek, the wedding veil trailing mistily about her down the aisle, and her big bouquet of white roses and maiden-hair ferns clasped listlessly in the white-gloved hands.

For a moment no one stirred, so sudden, so unexpected it was. It all seemed an astonishing part of the charming spectacle. The gaping throng with startled faces stood and stared. Above the huddled little bride stood the bridegroom, tall and dark and frowning, an angry red surging through his handsome face. The white-haired minister, with two red spots on his fine scholarly cheeks, stood grave with troubled dignity, as though somehow he meant to hold the little still bride responsible for this unseemly break in his beautiful service. The organ died away with a soft crash of the keys and pedals as if they too leaped up to see; the scent of the lilies swept sickeningly up in a great wave on the top of the silence.

In a moment all was confusion. The minister stooped, the best man sprang into the aisle and lifted the flower-like head. Some one produced a fan, and one of the ushers hurried for a glass of water. A physician struggled from his pew across the sittings of three stout dowagers, and knelt, with practiced finger on the little fluttering pulse. The bride's stepmother roused to solicitous and anxious attention. The organ came smartly up again in a hopeless tangle of chords and modulations, trying to get its poise once more. People climbed upon their seats to see, or crowded out in the aisle curiously and unwisely kind, and in the way. Then the minister asked the congregation to be seated; and amid the rustle of wedding finery into seats suddenly grown too narrow and too low, the ushers gathered up the little inert bride and carried her behind the palms across a hall and into the vestry room. The stepmother and a group of friends hurried after, and the minister requested the people to remain quietly seated for a few minutes. The organ by this time had recovered its poise and was playing soft tender melodies, but the excited audience was not listening:

"I thought she looked ghastly when she came in," declared the mother of three frowsy daughters. "It's strange she didn't put on some rouge."

"Um-mm! What a pity! I suppose she isn't strong! What did her own mother die of?" murmured another speculatively, preparing to put forth a theory before any one else got ahead of her.

"Oh! The poor child!" sympathized a romantic friend. "They've been letting her do too much! Didn't they make a handsome couple? I'm crazy to see them come marching down the aisle. They surely wouldn't put off the wedding just for a faint, would they?"

And all over the church some woman began to tell how her sister's child, or her brother's niece, or her nephew's aunt had fainted just before her wedding or during it, till it began to seem quite a common performance, and one furnishing a unique and interesting part of the program for a wedding ceremony.

Meanwhile on a couch in the big gloomy vestry room lay Betty with a group of attendants about her. Her eyes were closed, and she made no move. She swallowed the aromatic ammonia that some one produced, and she drew her breath a little less feebly, but she did not open her eyes, nor respond when they spoke to her.

Her stepmother stooped over finally and spoke in her ear:

"Elizabeth Stanhope! sit up and control yourself!" she said sharply in a low tone. "You are making a spectacle of yourself that you can never get over. Your father would be ashamed of you if he were here!"

It was the one argument that had been held a successful lash over her poor little quivering heart for the last five years, and Betty flashed open her sorrowful eyes and looked around on them with a troubled concentration as if she were just taking in what had happened:

"I'm so tired!" she said in a little weary voice. "Won't you just let me get my breath a minute?"

The physician nodded emphatically toward the door and motioned them out:

"She'll be all right in just a minute. Step outside and give her a chance to get calm. She's only worn out with excitement."

She opened her eyes and looked furtively about the room. There was no one there, and the door was closed. She could hear them murmuring in low tones just beyond it. She looked wildly about her with a frantic thought of escape. The two windows were deeply curtained, giving a narrow glimpse of blank wall. She sprang softly to her feet and looked out. There was a stone pavement far below. She turned silently and tried a door. It opened into a closet overflowing with musty hymn-books. She closed it quickly and slipped back to her couch just in time as the door opened and the doctor came back. She could catch a glimpse of the others through the half open door, anxiously peering in. She gathered all her self-control and spoke:

"I'm all right now, Doctor," she said quite calmly. "Would you just ask them to send Bessemer here a minute?"

"Certainly." The doctor turned courteously and went back to the door, half closing it and making her request in a low tone. Then her stepmother's excited sibilant whisper:

"Bessemer! Why, he isn't here! He went down to the shore last night."

"Sh-h-h!" came another voice, and the door was shut smartly.

Betty's eyes grew wide with horror as she lay staring at the closed door, and a cold numbness seemed to envelop her, clutching at her throat, her heart and threatening to overwhelm her.

Bessemer not here! What could it mean? Her mind seemed unable to grasp and analyze the nameless fear that awaited her outside that door. In a moment more they would all swarm in and surround her, and begin to clamor for her to go back into that awful church—and *she could not*—EVER! She would far rather die!

She sprang to her feet again and glided noiselessly to the only remaining uninvestigated door in the room. If this was another closet she would shut herself inside and stay till she died. She had read tales of people dying in a small space from lack of air. At least, if she did not die she could stay here till she had time to think. There was a key in the lock. Her fingers closed around it and drew it stealthily from the keyhole, as she slid through the door, drawing her rich draperies ruthlessly after. Her fingers were trembling so that she scarcely could fit the key in the lock again and turn it, and every click of the metal, every creak of the door, sounded like a gong in her ears. Her heart was fluttering wildly and the blood seemed to be pouring in torrents behind her ear-drums. She could not be sure whether there were noises in the room she had just left or not. She put her hand over her heart, turned with a sickening dread to look about her prison, and behold, it was not a closet at all, but a dark landing to a narrow flight of stone steps that wound down out of sight into the shadows. With a shudder she gathered her white impediment about her and crept down the murky way, frightened, yet glad to creep within the friendly darkness.

There were unmistakable sounds of footsteps overhead now, and sharp exclamations. A hand tried the door above and rattled it violently. For an instant her heart beat frightfully in her throat at the thought that perhaps after all she had not succeeded in quite locking it, but the door held, and she flew on blindly down the stairs, caring little where they led only so that she might hide quickly before they found the janitor and pried that door open.

The stairs ended in a little hall and a glass door. She fumbled wildly with the knob. It was locked, but there was a key! It was a large one and stuck, and gave a great deal of trouble in turning. Her fingers seemed so weak!

Above the noises grew louder. She fancied the door was open and the whole churchful of people were after her. She threw her full weight with fear in the balance, and the key turned. She wrenched it out of the rusty keyhole, slid out shutting the door after her, and stooping, fitted in the key again. With one more Herculean effort she locked it and stood up, trembling so that she could scarcely keep her balance. At least she was safe for a moment and could get her breath. But where could she go? She looked about her. High walls arose on either hand, with a murky sky above. A stone walk filled the space between and ran down the length of the church to a big iron gate. The lights of the street glistened fitfully on the puddles of wet in the depressions of the paving-stones. The street looked quiet, and only one or two people were passing. Was that gate locked also, and if so could she ever climb it, or break through? Somehow she must! She shuddered at the thought of what would happen if she did not get away at once. She strained at the buttons on her soft white gloves and pulled the fingers off, slipping her hands out and letting the glove hands hang limp at her wrists. Then with a quick glance backward at a flicker of light that appeared wavering beyond the glass door, she gathered her draperies again and fled down the long stone walk. Silently, lightly as a ghost she passed, and crouched at the gate as she heard footsteps, her heart beating so loudly it seemed like a bell calling attention to her. An old man was shuffling past, and she shrank against the wall, yet mindful of the awful glass door back at the end of the narrow passage. If they should come now she could not hope to elude them!

She stooped and studied the gate latch. Yes, it was a spring lock, and had no key in it. Stealthily she tried it and found to her relief that it swung open. She stepped around it and peered out. The gateway was not more than a hundred feet from the brightly lighted corner of the main avenue where rows of automobiles were lined up waiting for the wedding ceremony to be over. She could see the chauffeurs walking back and forth and chatting together. She could hear the desultory wandering of the organ, too, from the partly open window near by. A faint sickening waft of lily sweetness swept out, mingled with a dash of drops from the maple tree on the sidewalk. In a panic she stepped forth and drew back again, suddenly realizing for the first time what it would be to go forth into the streets clad in her wedding garments? How could she do it and get away? It could not be done!

Down the street, with a backward, wistful glance at the church, hurried a large woman with a market basket. Her curious eyes shone in the evening light and darkness of the street. There was something about her face that made Betty know instantly that this woman would love to tell how she had seen her, would gather a crowd in no time and pursue her. She shrank farther back, and then waited in awful fear and tried to listen again. Was that a rattling at the glass door? She must get away no matter what happened! Where? Was there an alleyway or anything across the block? Could she hope to cross the street between the shadows unnoticed?

She looked out fearfully once more. A girl of her own age was approaching around the corner, paddling along in rubbers, and a long coat. She was chewing gum. Betty could see the outline of a strong good-natured jaw working contentedly as she was silhouetted against the light. She had her hands in her pockets, and a little dark hat worn boyishly on the back of her head, and she was humming a popular song. Betty had slipped behind the half open gate again and was watching her approach, her desperation driving her to thoughts that never would have entered her mind at another time. Suddenly, as the girl passed directly in front of the gate, Betty leaned forward and plucked at her sleeve:

"Wait!" she said sharply; and then, with a pitiful pleading in her voice, "Won't you help me just a minute, please?"

CHAPTER II

THE girl came to a standstill abruptly and faced about, drawing away just a hair's-breadth from the detaining hand, and surveying her steadily, the boyish expression in her eyes changing to an amused calculation such as one would fancy a cowboy held up on his native plains by a stray lamb might have worn.

"What's the little old idea!" asked the girl coldly, her eyes narrowing as she studied the other girl in detail and attempted to classify her into the known and unknown quantities of her world. Her face was absolutely expressionless as far as any sign of interest or sympathy was concerned. It was like a house with the door still closed and a well-trained butler in attendance.

"I've got to get away from here at once before anybody sees me," whispered Betty excitedly, with a fearful glance behind her.

"Do you want me to call a cab for you?" sneered the girl on the sidewalk, with an envious glance at the white satin slippers.

"Oh, no! Never!" cried Betty, wringing her hands in desperation. "I want you to show me somewhere to go out of sight, and if you will I'd like you to walk a block or so with me so I won't be so—so conspicuous! I'm so frightened I don't know which way to go."

"What do you want to go at all for?" asked the girl bluntly, with the look of an inquisitor, and the intolerance of the young for its contemporary of another social class.

"Because I *must!*" said Betty with terror in her voice. "They're coming! Listen! Oh, help me quick! I can't wait to explain!"

Betty dashed out of the gate and would have started up the street but that a strong young arm came out like a flash and a firm young fist gripped her arm like a vise. The girl's keen ears had caught a sound of turning key and excited voices, and her quick eyes pierced the darkness of the narrow court and measured the distance back.

"Here! You can't go togged out like that!" she ordered in quite a different tone. She flung off her own long coat and threw it around the shrinking little white figure, then knelt and deftly turned up the long satin draperies out of sight and fixed them firmly with a pin extracted from somewhere about her person. Quickly she stood up and pulled off her rubbers, her eye on the long dark passageway whence came now the decided sound of a forcibly opened door and footsteps.

"Put these on, quick!" she whispered, lifting first one slippered foot and then the other and supporting the trembling Betty in her strong young arms, while she snapped on the rubbers.

Lastly, she jerked the rakish hat from her own head, crammed it down hard over the orange-wreathed brow and gave her strange protégée a hasty shove.

"Now beat it around that corner and wait till I come!" she whispered, and turning planted herself in an idle attitude just under the church window, craning her neck and apparently listening to the music. A second later an excited usher, preceded by the janitor, came clattering down the passageway.

"Have you seen any one go out of this gate recently?" asked the usher.

The girl, hatless and coatless in the chill November night, turned nonchalantly at the question, surveyed the usher coolly from the point of his patent leather shoes to the white gardenia in his buttonhole, gave his features a cursory glance, and then shook her head.

"There might have been an old woman come out a while back. Dressed in black, was she? I wasn't paying much attention. I think she went down the avenoo," she said, and stretched her neck again, standing on her tiptoes to view the wedding guests. Her interest suddenly became real, for she spied a young man standing in the church, in full view of the window, back against the wall with his arms folded, a fine handsome young man with pleasant eyes and a head like that of a young nobleman, and she wanted to make sure of his identity. He looked very much like the young lawyer whose office boy was her "gentleman friend." Just to make sure she gave a little spring from the sidewalk that brought her eyes almost on a level with the window and gave her a brief glimpse, enough to see his face quite clearly; then she turned with satisfaction to see that the janitor and the usher had gone back up the passageway, having slammed the gate shut. Without more ado the girl wheeled and hurried down the street toward the corner where Betty crouched behind a tree trunk, watching fearfully for her coming.

"Aw! You don't need to be that scared!" said the girl, coming up. "They've gone back. I threw 'em off the scent. Come on! We'll go to my room and see what to do. Don't talk! Somebody might recognize your voice. Here, we'll cut through this alley and get to the next block. It's further away and not so many folks passing."

Silently they hurried through the dark alley and down the next street, Betty holding the long cloak close that no gleam of her white satin might shine out and give away her secret, her heart beating like a trip hammer in her breast, her eyes filled with unshed tears, the last words of her stepmother ringing in her ears. Was she making her father ashamed? Her dear dead father! Was she doing the wrong thing? So long that thought had held her! But she could not go back now. She had taken an irrevocable step.

Her guide turned another corner abruptly and led her up some stone steps to the door of a tall, dingy brick house, to which she applied a latchkey.

The air of the gloomy hall was not pleasant. The red wall-paper was soiled and torn, and weird shadows flickered from the small gas taper that blinked from the ceiling. There were suggestions of old dinners, stale fried potatoes and pork in all the corners, and one moving toward the stairs seemed to stir them up and set them going again like old memories.

The stairs were bare and worn by many feet, and not particularly clean. Betty paused in dismay then hurried on after her hostess, who was mounting up, one, two, three flights, to a tiny hall bedroom at the back. A fleeting fear that perhaps the place was not respectable shot through her heart, but her other troubles were so great that it found no lodgment. Panting and trembling she arrived at the top and stood looking about her in the dark, while the other girl found a match and lighted another wicked little flickering gas-burner.

Then her hostess drew her into the room and closed and locked the door. As a further precaution she climbed upon a chair and pushed the transom shut.

"Now," she said with a sigh of evident relief, "we're safe! No one can hear you here, and you can say what you please. But first we'll get this coat and hat off and see what's the damage."

As gently as if she were undressing a baby the girl removed the hat and coat from her guest, and shook out the wonderful shining folds of satin. It would have been a study for an artist to have watched her face as she worked, smoothing out wrinkles, shaking the lace down and uncrushing it, straightening a bruised orange-blossom, and putting everything in place. It was as if she herself were an artist restoring a great masterpiece, so silently and absorbedly she worked, her eyes full of a glad wonder that it had come to her once to be near and handle anything so rare and costly. The very touch of the lace and satin evidently thrilled her; the breath of the exotic blossoms was nectar as she drew it in.

Betty was still panting from her climb, still trembling from her flight, and she stood obedient and meek while the other girl pulled and shook and brushed and patted her into shape again. When all was orderly and adjusted about the crumpled bride, the girl stood back as far as the limits of the tiny room allowed and surveyed the finished picture.

"There now! You certainly do look great! That there band of flowers round your forehead makes you look like some queen. 'Coronet'—ain't that what they call it? I read that once in a story at the Public Library. Say! Just to think I should pick that up in the street! Good night! I'm glad I came along just then instead o' somebody else! This certainly is some picnic! Well, now, give us your dope. It must've been pretty stiff to make you cut and run from a show like the one they got up for you! Come, tune up and let's hear the tale. I rather guess I'm entitled to know before the curtain goes up again on this little old stage!"

The two tears that had been struggling with Betty for a long time suddenly appeared in her eyes and drowned them out, and in dismay she brought out a faint little sorry giggle of apology and amusement and dropped on the tiny bed, which filled up a good two-thirds of the room.

"Good night!" exclaimed the hostess in alarm, springing to catch her. "Don't drop down that way in those glad rags! You'll finish 'em! Come, stand up and we'll get 'em off. You look all in. I'd oughta known you would be!" She lifted Betty tenderly and began to remove her veil and unfasten the wonderful gown. It seemed to her much like helping an angel remove her wings for a nap. Her eyes shone with genuine pleasure as she handled the hooks deftly.

"But I've nothing else to put on!" gurgled Betty helplessly.

"I have!" said the other girl.

"Oh!" said Betty with a sudden thought. "I wonder! Would you be willing to exchange clothes? Have you perhaps got some things you don't need that I could have, and I'll give you mine for them? I don't suppose perhaps a wedding dress would be very useful unless you're thinking of getting married soon, but you could make it over and use it for the foundation of an evening dress——"

The other girl was carefully folding the white satin skirt at the moment, but she stopped with it in her arms and sat down weakly on the foot of the bed with it all spread out in her lap and looked at her guest in wonder:

"You don't mean you *wantta give it up!*" she said in an awed tone. "You don't mean you would be willing to take some of my old togs for it?"

"I certainly would!" cried Betty eagerly. "I never want to see these things again! *I hate* them! And besides, I want to get away somewhere. I can't go in white satin! You know that! But I don't like to take anything of yours that you might need. Do you think these things would be worth anything to you? You weren't thinking of getting married yourself some time soon, were you?"

"Well, I might," said the other girl, looking self-conscious. "I got a gentleman friend. But I wasn't expectin' to get in on any trooso like this!" She let her finger move softly over the satin hem as if she had been offered a plume of the angel's wing. "Sure, I'll take it off you if I've got anything you're satisfied to have in exchange. I wouldn't mind havin' it to keep jest to look at now and then and know it's mine. It'd be somethin' to live for, jest to know you had that dress in the house!"

Suddenly Betty, without any warning even to herself, dropped upon her knees beside the diminutive bed and began to weep. It seemed somehow so touching that a thing like a mere dress could make a girl glad like that. All the troubles of the days that were past went over her in a great wave of agony, and overwhelmed her soul. In soft silk and lace petticoat and camisole with her pretty white arms and shoulders shaking with great sobs she buried her face in the old patchwork quilt that her hostess had brought from her village home, and gave way to a grief that had been long in growing. The other girl now thoroughly alarmed, laid the satin on a chair and went over to the little stranger, gathering her up in a strong embrace, and gradually lifting her to the bed.

"You poor little Kid, you! I oughtta known better! You're just all in! You ben gettin' ready to be married, and something big's been troubling you, and I bet they never gave you any lunch—er else you wouldn't eat it,—and you're jest natcheraly all in. Now you lie right here an' I'll make you some supper. My name's Jane Carson, and I've got a good mother out to Ohio, and a nice home if I'd had sense enough to stay in it; only I got a chance to make big money in a fact'ry. But I know what 'tis to be lonesome, an' I ain't hard-hearted, if I do know how to take care of misself. There! There!"

She smoothed back the lovely hair that curled in golden tendrils where the tears had wet it.

"Say, now, you needn't be afraid! Nobody'll getcha here! I know how to bluff 'em. Even if a policeman should come after yeh, I'd get around him somehow, and I don't care what you've done or ain't done, I'll stand by yeh. I'm not one to turn against anybody in distress. My mother always taught me that. After you've et a bite and had a cup of my nice tea with cream and sugar in it you'll feel better, and we'll have a real chin-fest and hear all about it. Now, you just shut your eyes and wait till I make that tea."

Jane Carson thumped up the pillow scientifically to make as many of the feathers as possible and shifted the little flower-head upon it. Then she hurried to her small washstand and took a little iron contrivance from the drawer, fastening it on the sickly gas-jet. She filled a tiny kettle with water from a faucet in the hall and set it to boil. From behind a curtain in a little box nailed to the wall she drew a loaf of bread, a paper of tea and a sugar-bowl. A cup and saucer and other dishes appeared from a pasteboard box under the washstand. A small shelf outside the tiny window yielded a plate of butter, a pint bottle of milk, and two eggs. She drew a chair up to the bed, put a clean handkerchief on it, and spread forth her table. In a few minutes the fragrance of tea and toast pervaded the room, and water was bubbling happily for the eggs. As cosily as if she had a chum to dine with her she sat down on the edge of the bed and invited her guest to supper. As she poured the tea she wondered what her co-laborers at the factory would think if they knew she had a real society lady visiting her. It wasn't every working girl that had a white satin bride thrust upon her suddenly this way. It was like a fairy story, having a strange bride lying on her bed, and everything a perfect mystery about her. She eyed the white silk ankles and dainty slippers with satisfaction. Think of wearing underclothes made of silk and real lace!

It seemed to Betty as if never before in all her life had she tasted anything so delicious as that tea and toast and soft boiled egg cooked by this wonderful girl on a gaslight and served on a chair. She wanted to cry again over her gladness at being here. It didn't seem real after all the trouble she had been through. It couldn't last! Oh, of course it couldn't last!

This thought came as she swallowed the last bite of toast, and she sat up suddenly!

"I ought to be doing something quick!" she said in sudden panic. "It is getting late and I must get away. They'll be watching the trains, perhaps. I ought to have gone at once. But I don't know where I can go. Give me some old things, please. I must get dressed at once."

"Lie down first and tell me who you are and what it's all about. I can't do a thing for you till I know. I've got to go into this with my eyes open or I won't stir one step," she declared stubbornly.

Betty looked at her with wide eyes of trouble and doubt. Then the doubt suddenly cleared away, and trust broke through.

"I can trust you, I'm sure! You've been so good to me! But it seems dreadful to tell things about my family, even to one who has been so kind. My father would be so hurt——"

"Your father? Where is your father? Why didn't he take care of you and keep you from getting into such big trouble, I'd like to know?"

The blue eyes clouded with tears again.

"My father died five years ago," she said, "but I've always tried to do as he would want to have me do. Only—this—I *couldn't*."

"H'm!" said Jane Carson. "Then he prob'ly wouldn't of wanted you to. Suppose you take the rest of those togs off. I'll find you a warm nightgown and we'll get to bed. It's turning cold here. They take the heat off somewhere about six o'clock in the evening, and it gets like ice up here sometimes."

Jane shivered and went to her small trunk, from which she produced a coarse but clean flanellete nightgown, and Betty, who had never worn anything but a dainty lingerie one before in all her life, crept into it thankfully and cuddled down with a warm feeling that she had found a real friend. It was curious why she did not shrink from this poor girl, but she did not, and everything looked clean and nice. Besides, this was a wonderful haven of refuge in her dire necessity.

CHAPTER III

MEANWHILE, in the stately mansion that Betty had called home, a small regiment of servants hastened with the last tasks in preparation for the guests that were soon expected to arrive. The great rooms had become a dream of paradise, with silver rain and white lilies in a mist of soft green depending from the high ceilings. In the midst of all, a fairy bower of roses and tropical ferns created a nook of retirement where everyone might catch a glimpse of the bride and groom from any angle in any room. The spacious vistas stretched away from an equally spacious hallway, where a wide and graceful staircase curved up to a low gallery, smothered in flowers and palms and vines; and even so early the musicians were taking their places and tuning their instruments. On the floor above, where room after room shone in beauty, with costly furnishings, and perfect harmonies, white-capped maids flitted about, putting last touches to dressing tables and pausing to gossip as they passed one another:

"Well, 'twill all be over soon," sighed one, a wan-faced girl with discontented eyes. "Ain't it kind of a pity, all this fuss just for a few minutes?"

"Yes, an' glad I'll be!" declared another, a fresh young Irish girl with a faint, pretty brogue. "I don't like the look of my Lady Betty. A pretty fuss Candace her old nurse would be makin' if she was here the night! I guess the madam knew what she was about when she give her her walkin' ticket! Candace never could bear them two bys, and *him* was the worse of the two, she always said."

"Well, a sight of good it would do for old Candace to make a fuss!" said the discontented one. "And anyhow, he's as handsome as the devil, and she's got money enough, so she oughtn't complain."

"Money ain't everything!" sniffed Aileen. "I wouldn't marry a king if I wasn't crazy about him!"

"Oh, you're young!" sneered Marie with disdain. "Wait till your looks go! You don't know what you'd take up with!"

"Well I'd never take up with the likes of *him!*" returned the Irish girl grandly, "and what's more he knows it!" She tossed her head meaningfully and was about to sail away on her own business when a stir below stairs attracted their attention. A stout, elderly woman, dressed in a stiff new black silk and an apoplectic hat, came panting up the stairs looking furtively from side to side, as if she wished to escape before anyone recognized her:

"It's Candace!" exclaimed Aileen. "As I live! Now what d'ye wantta know about that! Poor soul! Poor soul! Candy! Oh!—Candy! What iver brought ye here the night? This is no place for the loikes of you. You better beat it while the beatin' is good if ye know which side yer bread's buthered!"

But the old nurse came puffing on, her face red and excited:

"Is she here? Has she come, yet, my poor wee Betty?" she besought them eagerly.

"Miss Betty's at the church now gettin' married!" announced Marie uppishly, "and you'd best be gettin' out of here right away, for the wedding party's due to arrive any minute now and madam'll be very angry to have a servant as doesn't belong snoopin' round at such a time!"

"Be still, Marie! For shame!" cried Aileen. "You've no need to talk like that to a self-respectin' woman as has been in this house more years than you have been weeks! Come along, Candace, and I'll slip you in my room and tell you all about it when I can get away long enough. You see, Miss Betty's being married——"

"But she's *not!*" cried Candace wildly. "I was at the church myself. Miss Betty sent me the word to be sure and come, and where to sit and all, so she'd see me; and I went, and she come up the aisle as white as a lily and dropped right there before the poolpit, just like a little white lamb that couldn't move another step, all of a heap in her pretty things! And they stopped the ceremony and everybody got up, and they took her away, and we waited till bime-by the minister said the bride wasn't well enough to proceed with the ceremony and would they all go home, and I just slipped out before the folks got their wraps on and took a side street with wings to my feet and got up here! Haven't they brought her home yet, the poor wee thing? I been thinkin' they might need me yet, for many's the time I've brought her round by my nursin'."

The two maids looked wildly at one another, their glances growing into incredulity, the eyebrows of Marie moving toward her well-dressed hair with a lofty disapproval.

"Well, you'd better come with me, Candy," said Aileen drawing the excited old servant along the hall to the back corridor gently. "I guess there's some mistake somewheres; anyway, you better stay in my room till you see what happens. We haven't heard anything yet, and they'd likely send word pretty soon if there's to be any change in the program. You say she fell——?"

But just then sounds of excitement came distantly up to them and Aileen hastened back to the gallery to listen. It was the voice of Madam Stanhope angrily speaking to her youngest son:

"You must get Bessemer on the 'phone at once and order him home! I told you it was a great mistake sending him away. If he had been standing there, where she could see him, everything would have gone through just as we planned it——"

"Aw! Rot! Mother. Can't you shut up? I know what I'm about and I'm going to call up another detective. Bessemer may go to the devil for all I care! How do you know but he has, and taken her with him? The first thing to do is to get that girl back! You ought to have had more sense than to show your whole hand to my brother. You might have known he'd take advantage——"

Herbert Hutton slammed into the telephone booth under the stairs and Madam Stanhope was almost immediately aware of the staring servants who were trying not to seem to have listened.

Mrs. Stanhope stood in the midst of the beautiful empty rooms and suddenly realized her position. Her face froze into the haughty lines with which her menage was familiar, and she was as coldly beautiful in her exquisite heliotrope gown of brocaded velvet and chiffon with the glitter of jewels about her smooth plump neck, and in her carefully marcelled black hair as if she were quietly awaiting the bridal party instead of facing defeat and mortification:

"Aileen, you may get Miss Betty's room ready to receive her. She has been taken ill and will be brought home as soon as she is able to be moved," she announced, without turning an eyelash. "Put away her things, and get the bed ready!" One could see that she was thinking rapidly. She was a woman who had all her life been equal to an emergency, but never had quite such a tragic emergency been thrust upon her to camouflage before.

"James!" catching the eye of the butler, "there will be no reception to-night, of course, and you will see that the hired people take their things away as soon as possible, and say that I will agree to whatever arrangements they see fit to make, within reason, of course. Just use your judgment, James, and by the way, there will be telephone calls, of course, from our friends. Say that Miss Betty is somewhat better, and the doctor hopes to avert a serious nervous breakdown, but that she needs entire rest and absolute quiet for a few days. Say that and nothing more, do you understand, James?"

The butler bowed his thorough understanding and Madam Stanhope sailed nobly up the flower-garlanded staircase, past the huddled musicians, to her own apartment. Aileen, with a frightened glance, scuttled past the door as she was closing it:

"Aileen, ask Mr. Herbert to come to my room at once when he has finished telephoning, and when Mr. Bessemer arrives send him to me at once!" Then the door closed and the woman was alone with her defeat, and the placid enameled features melted into an angry snarl like an animal at bay. In a moment more Herbert stormed in.

"It's all your fault, mother!" he began, with an oath. "If you hadn't dragged Bessemer into this thing I'd have had her fixed. I had her just about where I wanted her, and another day would have broken her in. She's scared to death of insane asylums, and I told her long ago that it would be dead easy to put a woman in one for life. If I had just hinted at such a thing she'd have married me as meek as a lamb!"

"Now look here, Bertie," flared his mother excitedly, "you've got to stop blaming me! Haven't I given in to you all your life, and now you say it's all my fault the least little thing that happens! It was for your sake that I stopped you; you know it was. You couldn't carry out any such crazy scheme. Betty's almost of age, and if those trustees should find out what you had threatened, you would be in jail for life, and goodness knows what would become of me."

"Trustees! How would the trustees find it out?"

"Betty might tell them."

"Betty might *not* tell them, not if she was *my wife!*" He bawled out the words in a way that boded no blissful future to the one who should have the misfortune to become his wife. "I think I'd have her better trained than that. As for you, Mother, you're all off, as usual! What do you think could possibly happen to *you?* You're always saying you do everything for me, but when it comes right down to brass tacks I notice you're pretty much of a selfish coward on your own account."

For a moment the baffled woman faced her angry uncontrolled son in speechless rage, then gathered command of the situation once more, an inscrutable expression on her hard-lined face. Her voice took on an almost pitiful reproach as she spoke in a low, even tone that could hardly fail to bring the instant attention of her spoiled son:

"Bertie, you don't know what you're talking about!" she said, and there was a strained white look of fear about her mouth and eyes as she spoke. "I'm going to tell you, in this great crisis, what I did for you, what I risked that you might enjoy the luxury which you have had for the last five years. Listen! The day before Mr. Stanhope died he wrote a letter to the trustees of Betty's fortune giving very explicit directions about her money and her guardianship, tying things up so that not one cent belonging to her should pass through my hands, which would have left us with just my income as the will provided, and would have meant comparative poverty for us all except as Betty chose to be benevolent. I kept a strict watch on all his movements those last few days, of course, and when I found he had given Candace a letter to mail, I told her I would look after it, and I brought it up to my room and read it, for I suspected just some such thing as he had done. He was very fussy about Betty and her rights, you remember, and he had always insisted that this was Betty's house, her mother's wedding present from the grandfather, and therefore not ours at all, except through Betty's bounty. I was determined that we should not be turned out of here, and that you should not have to go without the things you wanted while that child had everything and far more than she needed. So I burned the letter! Now, do you see what the mother you have been blaming has done for you?"

But the son looked back with hard glittering eyes and a sneer on his handsome lustful lips:

"I guess you did it about as much for your own sake as mine, didn't you?" he snarled. "And I don't see what that's got to do with it, anyway. Those trustees don't know what they missed if they never got the letter, and you've always kept in with them, you say, and made them think you were crazy about the girl. They pay you Betty's allowance till she's of age, don't they? They can't lay a finger on you. You're a fool to waste my time talking about a little thing like that when we ought to be planning a way to get hold of that girl before the trustees find out about it. If we don't get her fixed before she's of age we shall be in the soup as far as the property is concerned. Isn't that so? Well, then, we've got to get her good and married——"

"If you only had let her marry Bessemer quietly," whimpered his mother, "and not have brought in all this deception. It will look so terrible if it ever comes out. I shall never be able to hold up my head in society again———!"

"There you are again! Thinking of yourself——!" sneered the dutiful son, getting up and stamping about her room like a wild man. "I tell you, Mother, that girl is *mine*, and I won't have Bessemer or anybody else putting in a finger. *She's mine!* I told her so a long time ago, and she knows it! She can't get away from me, and it's going to go the harder with her because she's tried. I'm never going to forgive her making a fool out of me before all those people! I'll get her yet! Little fool!"

Herbert was well on his way into one of those fits of uncontrollable fury that had always held his mother in obedience to his slightest whim since the days when he used to lie on the floor and scream himself black in the face and hold his breath till she gave in; and the poor woman, wrought to the highest pitch of excitement already by the tragic events of the evening, which were only the climax of long weeks of agitation, anxiety and plotting, dropped suddenly into her boudoir chair and began to weep.

But this new manifestation on the part of his usually pliable mother only seemed to infuriate the young man. He walked up to her, and seizing her by the shoulder, shook her roughly:

"Cut that out!" he said hoarsely. "This is no time to cry. We've got to make some kind of a plan. Don't you see we'll have the hounds of the press at our heels in a few hours? Don't you see we've got to make a plan and stick to it?"

His mother looked up, regardless for once of the devastation those few tears had made of her carefully groomed face, a new terror growing in her eyes:

"I've told James to answer all telephone calls and say that Betty is doing as well as could be expected, but that the doctor says she must have perfect quiet to save her from a nervous breakdown——" she answered him coldly. "I'm not quite a fool if you do think so——"

"Well, that's all right for to-night, but what'll we say to-morrow if we don't find her——"

"Oh! She'll come back," said the stepmother confidently. "She can't help it. Why, where would she go? She hasn't a place on earth since she's lost confidence in that cousin of her mother's because he didn't come to her wedding. She hasn't an idea that he never got her note asking him to give her away. Thank heaven I got hold of that before it reached the postman! If that old granny had been here we should have had trouble indeed. I had an experience with him once just before I married Betty's father, and I never want to repeat it. But we must look out what gets in the papers!"

"It's rather late for that, I suspect. The bloodhounds 'ill be around before many minutes and you better think up what you want said. But I'm not so sure she wouldn't go there, and we better tell the detectives that. What's the old guy's address? I'll call him up long distance and say she was on a motoring trip and intended to stop there if she had time. I'll ask if she's reached there yet."

"That's a good idea, although I'm sure she was too hurt about it to go to him. She cried all the afternoon. It's a wonder she didn't look frightful! But that's Betty! Cry all day and come out looking like a star without any paint either. It's a pity somebody that would have appreciated it couldn't have had her complexion."

"That's you all over, Mother, talking about frivolous things when everything's happening at once. You're the limit! I say, you'd better be getting down to business! I've thought of another thing. How about that old nurse, Candace? Betty used to be crazy about her? What became of her?"

Mrs. Stanhope's face hardened, and anxiety grew in her eyes.

"She might have gone to her, although I don't believe she knows where she is. I'm sure I don't. I sent her away just before we began to get ready for the wedding. I didn't dare have her here. She knows too much and takes too much upon herself. I wouldn't have kept her so long, only she knew I took the trustee's letter, and she was very impudent about it once or twice, so that I didn't really dare to let her go until just a few days ago. I thought things would all be over here before she could do any harm, and Betty would be of age and have her money in her own right, and being your wife, of course there wouldn't be any more trouble about it."

"Well, you better find out what's become of her!" said the young man with darkening face. "*She* ought to be locked up somewhere! She's liable to make no end of trouble! You can't tell what she's stirred up already! Ring for a servant and find out if they know where she is. Ten to one that's where Betty is."

Mrs. Stanhope, with startled face, stepped to the bell and summoned Aileen:

"Aileen, have you any idea where we could find Miss Betty's old nurse, Candace?" she asked in a soothing tone, studying the maid's countenance. "I think it might be well to send for her in case Miss Betty needs her. She was so much attached to her!"

Aileen lifted startled eyes to her mistress' face. There was reserve and suspicion in her glance:

"Why, she was here a few minutes ago," she said guardedly. "It seems Miss Betty sent her an invitation, and when Miss Betty took sick she was that scared she ran out of the church and come here to find out how she was. She might not have gone yet. I could go see."

"Here! Was she here?" Mrs. Stanhope turned her head to her son and her eyes said: "That's strange!" but she kept her face well under control.

"Yes, you might go and see if you can find her, Aileen, and if you do, tell her I would like to see her a moment."

Aileen went away on her errand and Mrs. Stanhope turned to her son:

"Betty can't have gone to her unless there was some collusion. But in any case I think we had better keep her here until we know something."

Quick trotting steps were heard hurrying along the hall and a little jerky knock announced unmistakably the presence of Candace.

Mrs. Stanhope surveyed the little red-faced creature coolly and sharply:

"Candace, you have broken one of my express commands in returning here without permission from me, but seeing it was done in kindness I will overlook it this time and let you stay. You may be useful if they bring my daughter home to-night and I presume she will be very glad to see you. Just now she is—umm——" she glanced furtively at her son, and lifting her voice a trifle, as if to make her statement more emphatic—"she is at a private hospital near the church where they took her till she should be able to come home. It will depend on her condition whether they bring her to-night or to-morrow or in a few days. Meantime, if you like you may go up to your old room and wait until I send for you. I shall have news soon and will let you know. Don't go down to the servant's quarters, I wish to have you where I can call you at a moment's notice."

Candace gave her ex-mistress a long, keen suspicious stare, pinned her with a glance as steely as her own for an instant, in search of a possible ulterior motive, and then turning on her little fat heel, vanished like a small fast racer in the direction of her old room.

"Now," said Mrs. Stanhope, turning with a sigh of relief, "she's safe! I'll set Marie to watch her and if there's anything going on between those two Marie will find it out."

But Herbert Hutton was already sitting at his mother's desk with the telephone book and calling up Long Distance.

All the long hours when he had expected to have been standing under the rose bower downstairs in triumph with his bride, Herbert Hutton sat at that telephone in his mother's boudoir alternately raging at his mother and shouting futile messages over the 'phone. The ancient cousin of Betty's mother was discovered to be seriously ill in a hospital and unable to converse even through the medium of his nurse, so there was nothing to be gained there. Messages to the public functionaries in his town developed no news. Late into the night, or rather far toward the morning, Bessemer was discovered at a cabaret where his persistent mother and brother had traced him, too much befuddled with his evening's carouse to talk connectedly. He declared Betty was a good old girl, but she might go to thunder for all he cared; he knew a girl "worth twice of her."

His mother turned with disgust from his babbling voice, convinced that he knew nothing of Betty's whereabouts. Nevertheless, by means of a financial system of threats and rewards which she had used on him successfully for a number of years, she succeeded in impressing upon him the necessity of coming home at once, and just as the pink was beginning to dawn in the gray of the morning, Bessemer drove up in a hired car, and stumbled noisily into the house, demanding to know where the wedding was. He wanted to kiss the bride.

Candace, still in her stiff black silk, stood in the shadowy hall, as near as she dared venture, and listened, with her head thoughtfully on one side. Betty in her note about the wedding had said she was going to be married to Bessemer. But Bessemer didn't sound like a bridegroom. Had Bessemer run away then, or what? But some things looked queer. She remembered that Aileen had spoken as if Herbert was the bridegroom, but she had taken it for a mere slip of the tongue and thought nothing of it. When Aileen next came that way, she asked her if she happened to have got hold of one of the invitations, and Aileen, with her finger on her lips, nodded, and presently returned with something under her apron:

"I slipped it from the waste-basket," she said, "and Miss Betty got a holt of it, and there was a tremenjus fuss about something, I couldn't make out what; but I heard the missus say it was all a mistake as she gave the order over the 'phone, and she must have misspoke herself, but anyhow she thought she'd destroyed them all and given a rush order and they would be all right and sent out in plenty of time. So she sticks this back in the waste-basket and orders me to take the basket down and burn it, but I keeps this out and hides it well. I couldn't see nothin' the matter with it, can you?"

"There's *all* the matter with it!" declared the angry nurse as she glared at the name of Herbert Hutton thoughtfully, and read between the lines more than she cared to tell.

CHAPTER IV

NOT two miles away, Betty lay safe and warm in the flanellette nightgown, and watched Jane Carson turn out the light and open the window. A light leaped up from the street and made a friendly spot of brightness on the opposite wall, and Betty had a sense of cosiness that she had not felt since she was in boarding school with a roommate.

"Now," said Jane, climbing into bed and pulling up the covers carefully lest she should let the cold in on her guest, "let's hear!—You warm enough?"

There was a curious tenderness in her voice as if she had brought home a young princess and must guard her carefully.

"Oh, perfectly!" said Betty, giving a little nervous shiver. "And I'm so glad to be here safe away from them all! Oh, I've needed some one to advise with *so* much! I haven't had a soul since they sent my old nurse away because she dared to take my part sometimes."

Suddenly Betty buried her face in the pillow and began to sob and Jane reached out quick gentle arms and gathered her in a close comforting embrace. In a moment more Betty had gained control of herself and began to explain:

"You see," she said, catching her breath bravely, "they were determined I should marry a man I can't *endure*, and when I wouldn't they tried to *trick* me into it anyway. I never suspected until I got into the church and looked around and couldn't see Bessemer anywhere; only the other one with his evil eyes gloating over me, and then I knew! They thought they would get me there before all that church full of people and I wouldn't dare do anything. But when I realized it, I just dropped right down in the aisle. I couldn't stand up, I was so frightened."

"But I don't understand," said Jane. "Were there *two* men?"

"Oh, yes," sighed Betty, "there were two."

"Well, where was the other one, the one you *wanted* to marry?"

"I don't know——" said Betty with a half sob in her voice. "That's just what frightened me. You see they were my stepmother's two sons, and it was my father's dying wish that I should marry one of them. I didn't really *want* to marry Bessemer, but I simply *loathed* Herbert, the younger one, who was so determined to marryme. I was terribly afraid of him. He had been frightfully cruel to me when I was a child and when he grew up he was always tormenting me; and then when he tried to make love to me he was so repulsive that I couldn't bear to look at him. It really made me sick to think of ever marrying him. Oh—I *couldn't*—no matter who asked me. So Bessemer and I decided to get married to stop the trouble. They were always nagging him, too, and I was kind of sorry for him."

"But why should you marry anybody you didn't want to, I'd like to know!" exclaimed Jane in horror. "This is a free country and nobody ever makes people marry anybody they don't like any more. Why didn't you just beat it?"

"I thought about that a good many times," said Betty, pressing her tired eyes with her cold little fingers, "but I couldn't quite bring myself to do it. In the first place, I didn't know where to go, nor what to do. They never would let me learn to do anything useful, so I couldn't have got any work; and anyhow I had a feeling that it wouldn't be possible to get away where Herbert couldn't find me if he wanted to. He's that way. He always gets what he wants, no matter whom it hurts. He's *awful*—Jane—really!"

There was a pitiful note in her voice that appealed to the mother in Jane, and she stooped over her guest and patted her comfortingly on the shoulder:

"You poor little kid," she said tenderly, "you must have been worried something awful, but still I don't get you; what was the idea in sticking around and thinking you *had* to marry somebody you didn't like? You coulda gone to some one and claimed pertection. You could uv appealed to the p'lice if worst came to worst——!"

"Oh! But Jane I couldn't! That would have brought our family into disgrace, and father would have felt so*dreadfully* about it if he had been alive! I couldn't quite bring myself, either, to go against his dying request. We had always been so much to each other, Daddy and I. Besides, I didn't mind *Bessemer* so *much*—he was always kind—though we never had much to do with each other——"

"Well, I don't think I'd have stopped around long to please a father that didn't care any more for me than to want me to marry somebody I felt that way about!" said Jane, indignantly. "I haven't much use for a father like that!"

"Oh, but he wasn't like that!" said Betty, rising up in her eagerness and looking at Jane through her shining curls that were falling all about her eager, troubled young face, "and he did love me, Jane, he loved me better than anything else in the whole world! That was why I was willing to sacrifice almost anything to please him."

"Well, I'll be darned!" said Jane Carson, sitting up squarely in bed and staring at the spot of light on the wall. "That gets my goat! How could a man love you and yet want to torment you?"

"Well, you see, Jane, he hadn't been very fond of them when they were boys"—she spoke it with dignity and a little gasp as if she were committing a breach of loyalty to explain, but realized that it was necessary—"and he felt when he was dying that he wanted to make reparation, so he thought if I should marry one of them it would show them that he had forgiven them——"

"It—may—be—so," drawled Jane slowly, nodding her head deliberately with each word, "but—I don't see it that *way!* What kind of a man was this father of yours, anyway?"

"Oh, a wonderful man, Jane!" Betty eagerly hastened to explain. "He was all the world to me, and he used to come up to school week-ends and take me on beautiful trips and we had the best times together, and he would tell me about my own dear mother——"

Betty's hand grasped Jane's convulsively and her voice died out, in a sudden sob. Jane's hand went quickly to the bright head on the pillow:

"There! there!" she whispered tenderly, "don't take on so, I didn't mean anything. I was just trying to dope it out; get it through my bean what in thunder——! Say! Did *he* TELL *you* he wanted you to marry those guys?"

"Oh, no, he left word—it was his dying request."

"Who'd he request it to?"

"My stepmother."

"H'm! I thought so! How'd you know he did? How'd you know but she was lyin'?"

"No," said Betty sorrowfully, "she wasn't lying, she showed me the paper it was written on. There couldn't be any mistake. And his name was signed to it, his dear hand-writing, just as he always wrote it with the little quirl to the S that wasn't like anybody else. It went through me just like a knife when I saw it, that my dear father should have asked me to do what was so very very hard for me to think of. It was so much harder to have it come that way. If he had only asked me himself and we could have talked it over, perhaps he would have helped me to be strong enough to do it, but to have *her* have to *tell me!* She felt that herself. She tried to be kind, I think. She said she wanted to have him wake me up and tell me himself, but she saw his strength was going and he was so anxious to have her write it down quick and let him sign it that she did as he asked——"

"Well, you may depend on it he never wrote it at all—or anyhow, never knew what he was signing. Like as not she dragged it out of him some way while he was out of his mind or so near dying he didn't know what he was about. Besides, they mightta some of 'em forged his name. It's easy to copy signatures. Lotsa people do it real good. If I was you I wouldn't think another mite about it. If he was a man like you say he is, he couldn'ta done a thing like that to his own little girl, not on his life! It ain't like real fathers and mothers to. I know, fer I've got a mother that's a peach and no mistake! No, you may depend on it, he never knew a thing about that, and marrying a guy like that is the last thing on earth he'd want you to do."

"Oh, do you really think so? Oh, are you *sure?*" cried Betty, clinging to Jane eagerly, the tears raining down her white cheeks. "I've thought so a thousand times, but I didn't dare trust myself to decide."

"Yes, I'm sure!" said Jane, gathering her in her arms and hugging her tight, just as she would have done with a little sister who had waked up in the night with a bad dream. "Now, look here, you stop crying and don't you worry another bit. Just tell me the rest if there's any rest, so I'll know what to bank on. Who is the other guy, the one you didn't mind marryin'? What became of him?"

"Why, that's the queer part," said Betty, troubled again. "He didn't seem to be anywhere, and when they carried me into the room back of the church and fanned me and got water to bathe my face, a doctor came and gave me some medicine and sent them all out, and I asked him to send Bessemer to me. I wanted to find out why he hadn't been standing up there by the minister the way I expected. I heard the doctor go out and ask for Bessemer and I heard my stepmother's voice say, 'Why Bessemer isn't here! He's gone down to the shore!' and then somebody said, 'Hush,' and they shut the door, and I was so frightened that I got up and tried all the doors till I found one that led down some stairs, and I locked it behind me and ran and found you!"

"You poor little kid!" cried Jane, cuddling her again. "I sure am glad I was on the job! But now, tell me, what's your idea? Will they make a big noise and come huntin' you?"

"Oh, yes!" said Betty wearily. "I suppose they will. I *know* they will, in fact. Herbert won't be balked in anything he wants——Bessemer won't count. He never counts. I'm sort of sorry for him, though I don't like him much. You see they had been making an awful fuss with him, too, about some actress down at the shore that he was sending flowers to, and I knew he didn't have a very easy time. So when he came in one day and asked me why I didn't marry *him* and settle the whole thing that way, I was horrified at first, but I finally thought perhaps that would be the best thing to do. He said he wouldn't bother me any, if I wouldn't bother him; and we thought perhaps the others would let us alone then. But I might have known Herbert wouldn't give in! Bessemer is easily led—Herbert could have hired him to go away to-night—or they may have *made* him ask me to marry him. He's like that," sadly. "You can't depend on him. I don't know. You see, it was kind of queer about the invitations. They came with Herbert's name in them first, and my stepmother tried to keep me from seeing them. She said they were late and she had them all sent off; but I found one, and when I went to my stepmother with it she said it was a mistake. She hadn't meant me to be annoyed by seeing it; and she didn't know how it happened; she must have misspoken herself—but it had been corrected and they would rush it through and send them right from the store this time so there wouldn't be any delay. I tried to think it was all right, but it troubled me, for I saw that Herbert hadn't given up at all—though he pretended to go away, and I hoped I wouldn't have any more trouble—but I might have known! Herbert never gave up anything in his life, not even when father was living. He always managed to get his way, somehow——"

"Did he love you so much?" Jane asked awesomely.

Betty shuddered:

"Oh, I don't know whether it was love or hate! It was all the same. I hate to think about him—he is—*unbearable*, Jane! Why, Jane, once he told me if he ever got me in his power he'd break my will or kill me in the attempt!"

"Well, now, there, Kid! Don't you think another bit about him, the old brute! You just lie down and sleep as easy as if you was miles away. They won't any of 'em ever find you here with me, and I've pulled the washstand in front of the door, so you needn't be dreaming of anybody coming in and finding you. Now go to sleep, and to-morrow I'll sneak you away to a place where they can't ever find you. Good night, Kid!" and Jane leaned down and kissed the soft hair on the pillow beside her. Betty flung her arms about her new-found friend and kissed her tenderly:

"Oh, you've been so good to me! What should I ever have done if I hadn't found you. You were like an angel. I think surely God must have sent you to help me."

"I shouldn't wonder if he did!" said Jane thoughtfully. "An angel in a mackintosh! Some angel!"

Jane Carson with her eyes wide open lay staring into the darkness and thinking it all over. She did not waste much time marvelling over the wonder that it had all happened to her. That would do for afterward when there was nothing else to be done about it. Now there must be some plans made and she was the one to make them. It was quite plain that the wonderful and beautiful Elizabeth Stanhope, the plans for whose wedding had been blazoned in the papers for days beforehand, was not at present capable of making or carrying out anything effective. Jane was. She knew it. She was a born leader and promoter. She liked nothing better than to work out a difficult situation. But this was the most difficult proposition that she had ever come up against. When her father died and her mother was left with the little house and the three younger children to support in a small country village, and only plain sewing and now and then a boarder to eke out a living for them all, she had sought and found, through a summer visitor who had taught her Sunday school class for a few weeks, a good position in this big Eastern city. She had made good and been promoted until her wages not only kept herself with strict economy, but justified her in looking forward to the time when she might send for her next younger sister. Her deft fingers kept her meagre wardrobe in neatness—and a tolerable deference to fashion, so that she had been able to annex the "gentleman friend" and take a little outing with him now and then at a moving picture theatre or a Sunday evening service. She had met and vanquished the devil on more than one battlefield in the course of her experience with different department heads; and she was wise beyond her years in the ways of the world. But this situation was different. Here was a girl who had been brought up "by hand," as she would have said with a sneer a few hours before, and she would have despised her for it. She raised up on one elbow and leaned over once more to watch the delicate profile of this gentle maiden, in the dim fitful light of the city night that came through the one little window. There had been something appealing in the beauty and frankness of the girl bride, something appalling in the situation she had found herself in. Jane Carson didn't know whether she was doing right or not to help this stray bride. It made her catch her breath to think how she might be bringing all the power of the law and of money upon her reckless young head, but she meant to do it, just the same.

Elizabeth Stanhope! What a beautiful name! It fitted right in with all the romance Jane had ever dreamed. If she only could write scenarios, what a thriller this would make!

Then she lay down and fell to planning.

CHAPTER V

THE morning dawned, and still no word from the missing bride. But the brief guarded sentences which Herbert Hutton had telephoned to the newspapers had been somehow sidetracked, and in their place a ghastly story had leaked out which some poor, hard-pressed reporter had gleaned from the gossip in the church and hurried off to put into type before there was time for it to be denied. Hot foot the story had run, and great headlines proclaimed the escape of Betty even while the family were carefully paving the way for the report of a protracted illness and absence, if need be, till they could find trace of her. The sun rose brightly and made weird gleaming of the silver wire on which the dying roses hung. The air was heavy with their breath, and the rooms in the early garish light looked out of place as if some fairy wand had failed to break the incantation at the right hour and left a piece of Magicland behind. The parlor maid went about uncertainly, scarcely knowing what to do and what to leave undone, and the milk cars, and newsboys, and early laborers began to make a clatter of every day on the streets. The morning paper, flung across the steps with Betty's picture, where Betty's reluctant feet had gone a few hours before, seemed to mock at life, and upstairs the man that Betty thought she went out to marry, lay in a heavy stupor of sleep. Happy Betty, to be resting beneath the coarse sheet of the kindly working girl, sleeping the sleep of exhaustion and youth in safety, two miles from the rose-bowered rooms!

Long before day had really started in the great city Jane Carson was up and at work. She dressed swiftly and silently, then went to her little trunk, and from it selected a simple wardrobe of coarse clean garments. One needed mending and two buttons were off. She sat by the dingy window and strained her eyes in the dawn to make the necessary repairs. She hesitated long over the pasteboard suit-box that she drew from under the bed. It contained a new dark blue serge dress for which she had saved a long time and in which she had intended to appear at church next Sabbath. She was divided between her desire to robe the exquisite little guest in its pristine folds and her longing to wear it herself. There was a sense of justice also which entered into the matter. If that elegant wedding dress was to be hers, and all those wonderful silk underclothes, which very likely she would never allow herself to wear, for they would be out of place on a poor working girl, it was not fair to repay their donor in old clothes. She decided to give the runaway bride her new blue serge. With just a regretful bit of a sigh she laid it out on the foot of the bed, and carefully spread out the tissue papers and folded the white satin garments away out of sight, finishing the bundle with a thick wrapping of old newspapers from a pile behind the door and tying it securely. She added a few pins to make the matter more sure, and got out a stub of a pencil and labeled it in large letters, "My summer dresses," then shoved it far back under the bed. If any seeking detective came he would not be likely to bother with that, and he might search her trunk in vain for white satin slippers and wedding veils.

Breakfast was next, and she put on her cloak and hurried out for supplies for the larder had been heavily depleted the night before to provide for her guest. With a tender glance toward the sleeper she slipped the key from the lock and placed it in the outside of the door, silently locking her guest within. Now there would be no danger of any one spiriting her away while she was gone, and no danger that the girl might wake up and depart in her absence.

She stopped a newsboy on his way to the subway and bought a paper, thrilling at the thought that there might be something in it about the girl who lay asleep in her little hall bedroom.

While she waited for her bundles she stole a glance at her paper, and there on the front page in big letters ran the heading:

STANHOPE WEDDING
HELD UP AT ALTAR BY
UNCONSCIOUS BRIDE

Relatives Seek Runaway Girl Who is
Thought to be Insane

She caught her breath and rolled the paper in a little wad, stuffing it carelessly into her pocket. She could not read any more of that in public. She hastened back to her room.

Betty was still sleeping. Jane stood watching her for a full minute with awe in her face. She could not but recognize the difference between herself and this fine sweet product of civilization and wealth. With the gold curls tossed back like a ripple of sunshine, and a pathetic little droop at the corners of her sweet mouth, nothing lovelier could be. Jane hurried to the window and turned her back on the bed while she perused the paper, herrage rising at the theories put forth. It was even hinted that her mother had been insane. Jane turned again and looked hard at the young sleeper, and the idea crossed her mind that even she might be deceived. Still, she was willing to trust her judgment that this girl was entirely sane, and anyhow she meant to help her! She stuffed the paper down behind the trunk and began to get breakfast. When it was almost ready she gently awoke the sleeper.

Betty started at the light touch on her shoulder and looked wildly around at the strange room and stranger face of the other girl. In the dim light of the evening she had scarcely got to know Jane's face. But in a moment all the happenings of the day before came back, and she sat up excitedly.

"I ought to have got away before it was light," she said gripping her hands together. "I wonder where I could go, Jane?" It was pleasant to call this girl by her first name. Betty felt that she was a tower of strength, and so kind.

"I have this ring," she said, slipping off an exquisite diamond and holding it out. "Do you suppose there would be any way I could get money enough to travel somewhere with this? If I can't I'll have to walk, and I can't get far in a day that way."

Betty was almost light-hearted, and smiling. The night had passed and no one had come. Perhaps after all she was going to get away without being stopped.

Jane's face set grimly.

"I guess there won't be any walking for you. You'll have to travel regular. It wouldn't be safe. And you don't want no rich jewelry along either. Was that your wedding ring?"

"Oh, no; father gave it to me. It was mother's, but I guess they'd want me to use it now. I haven't anything else."

"Of course," said Jane shortly to hide the emotion in her voice. "Now eat this while I talk," thrusting a plate of buttered toast and a glass of orange marmalade at her, and hastening to pour an inviting cup of coffee.

"Now, I been thinking," she said sitting down on the edge of the bed and eating bits of the piece of toast she had burned—Betty's was toasted beautifully—"I got a plan. I think you better go to Ma. She's got room enough for you for a while, and I want my sister to come over and take a place I can get fer her. If you was there she could leave. Mebbe you could help Ma with the kids. Of course we're poor and you ain't used to common things like we have them, but I guess you ain't got much choice in your fix. I got a paper this morning. They're huntin' fer you hot foot. They say you was temperary insane, an' 'f I was you I'd keep out o' their way a while. You lay low an' I'll keep my eye out and let you know, I've got a little money under the mattrass I can let you have till that ring gets sold. You can leave it with me an' I'll do the best I can if you think you can trust me. Of course I'm a stranger, but then, land! So are you! We just *gotta* trust each other. And I'm sending you to my mother if you'll go!"

"Oh!" said Betty, springing up and hugging her impulsively, "you're so good! To think I should find somebody just like that right in the street when I needed you so. I almost think God did it!"

"Well, mebbe!" said Jane, in her embarrassment turning to hang up a skirt that had fallen from its hook. "That's what they say sometimes in Chrishun Deavor meetin'. Ever go to Chrishun Deavor? Better go when you get out home. They have awful good socials an' ice cream, and you'll meet some real nice folks. We've got a peach of a minister, and his wife is perfec'ly dandy. I tell you I missed 'em when I came to the city! They was always doing something nice fer the young folks."

"How interesting!" said Betty, wondering if she might really be going to live like other girls. Then the shadow of her danger fell over her once more, and her cheek paled.

"If I can only get there safely," she shuddered. "Oh, Jane! You can't understand what it would be to have to go back!"

"Well, you're not going back. You're going to Tinsdale, and nobody's going to find you ever, unless you want 'em to! See? Now, listen! We haven't any time to waste. You oughtta get off on the ten o'clock train. I put out some clothes there for yeh. They ain't like yours, but it won't do fer you to go dressed like a millionairess. Folks out to Tinsdale would suspect yeh right off the bat. You gotta go plain like me, and it's this way: You're a friend I picked up in the city whose mother is dead and you need country air a while, see? So I sent you home to stay with Ma till you got strong again. I'm wirin' Ma. She'll understand. She always does. I kinda run Ma anyhow. She thinks the sun rises an' sets in me, so she'll do just what I say."

"I'm afraid I oughtn't to intrude," said Betty soberly, taking up the coarse, elaborately trimmed lingerie with a curious look, and trying not to seem to notice that it was different from any she had ever worn before.

"Say! Looka here!" said Jane Carson, facing round from her coffee cup on the washstand. "I'm sorry to criticize, but if you could just talk a little slang or something. Folks'll never think you belong to me. *'Intrude!'* Now, that sounds stuck up! You oughtta say 'be in the way,' or something natural like that. See?"

"I'm afraid I don't," said Betty dubiously, "but I'll try."

"You're all right, Kid," said Jane with compunction in her voice. "Just let yourself down a little like I do, and remember you don't wear silk onderclothes now. I'm afraid those stockings won't feel very good after yours, but you gotta be careful. An' 'f I was you I'd cut my hair off, I really would. It's an awful pity, it's so pretty, but it'll grow again. How old are you?"

"Almost twenty-one," said Betty thoughtfully. "Just three months more and I'll be twenty-one."

"H'm! Of age!" said Jane with a sharp significant look at her, as if a new thought had occurred. "Well, you don't look it! You could pass for fifteen, especially if you had your hair bobbed. I can do it for you if you say so."

"All right," said Betty promptly without a qualm. "I always wanted it short. It's an awful nuisance to comb."

275

"That's the talk!" said Jane. "Say 'awful' a lot, and you'll kinda get into the hang of it. It sounds more— well,*natural*, you know; not like society talk. Here, sit down and I'll do it quick before you get cold feet. I sure do hate to drop them curls, but I guess it's best."

The scissors snipped, snipped, and the lovely strands of bright hair fell on the paper Jane had spread for them. Betty sat cropped like a sweet young boy. Jane stood back and surveyed the effect through her lashes approvingly. She knew the exact angle at which the hair should splash out on the cheek to be stylish. She had often contemplated cutting her own, only that her mother had begged her not to, and she realized that her hair was straight as a die and would never submit to being tortured into that alluring wave over the ear and out toward the cheekbone. But this sweet young thing was a darling! She felt that the daring deed had been a success.

"I got a bottle of stuff to make your hair dark," she remarked. "I guess we better put it on. That hair of yours is kinda conspicuous, you know, even when it's cut off. It won't do you any harm. It washes off soon." And she dashed something on the yellow hair. Betty sat with closed eyes and submitted. Then her mentor burnt a cork and put a touch to the eyebrows that made a different Betty out of her. A soft smudge of dark under her eyes and a touch of talcum powder gave her a sickly complexion and when Betty stood up and looked in the glass she did not know herself. Jane finished the toilet by a smart though somewhat shabby black hat pulled well down over Betty's eyes, and a pair of gray cotton gloves, somewhat worn at the fingers. The high-laced boots she put upon the girl's feet were two sizes too large, and wobbled frightfully, but they did well enough, and there seemed nothing more to be desired.

"Now," said Jane as she pinned on her own hat, "you've gotta have a name to go by. I guess you better be Lizzie Hope. It kinda belongs to yeh, and yet nobody'd recognize it. You don't need to tell Ma anything you don't want to, and you can tell her I'll write a letter to-night all about it. Now come on! We gotta go on the trolley a piece. I don't see havin' you leave from the General Station. We'll go up to the Junction and get the train there."

With an odd feeling that she was bidding good-by to herself forever and was about to become somebody else, Betty gave one more glance at the slim boylike creature in the little mirror over the washstand and followed Jane out of the room, shuffling along in the big high-heeled boots, quite unlike the Betty that she was.

CHAPTER VI

WARREN REYBURN laid down his pen and shoved back his office chair impatiently, stretching out his long muscular limbs nervously and rubbing his hands over his eyes as if to clear them from annoying visions.

James Ryan, his office boy and stenographer, watched him furtively from one corner of his eye, while his fingers whirled the typewriter on through the letter he was typing. James wanted to take his girl to the movies that evening and he hadn't had a chance to see her the day before. He was wondering if Mr. Reyburn would go out in time for him to call her up at her noon hour. He was a very temperamental stenographer and understood the moods and tenses of his most temperamental employer fully. It was all in knowing how to manage him. James was most deferential, and knew when to keep still and not ask questions. This was one of the mornings when he went to the dictionary himself when he wasn't sure of a word rather than break the ominous silence. Not that Mr. Reyburn was a hard master, quite the contrary, but this was James's first place straight from his brief course at business school, and he was making a big bluff of being an old experienced hand.

There was not much business to be done. This was Warren Reyburn's "first place" also in the world of business since finishing his law course, and he was making a big bluff at being very busy, to cover up a sore heart and an anxious mind. It was being borne in upon him gradually that he was not a shouting success in business so far. The rosy dreams that had floated near all through his days of hard study had one by one left him, until his path was now leading through a murky gray way with little hope ahead. Nothing but sheer grit kept him at it, and he began to wonder how long he could stick it out if nothing turned up.

True, he might have accepted an offer that even now lay open on his desk; a tempting offer, too, from a big corporation who recognized the influence of his old family upon their particular line of business; but it was a line that his father and his grandfather had scorned to touch, and he had grown up with an honest contempt for it. He just could not bring himself to wrest the living from the poor and needy, and plunder the unsuspecting, and he knew that was what it would be if he closed with this offer. Not yet had he been reduced to such depths, he told himself, shutting his fine lips in a firm curve. "No, not if he starved!"

That was the legitimate worry that ruffled his handsome brow as he sat before his desk frowning at that letter. He meant to begin dictation on its answer in another five minutes or so, but meantime he was forcing himself to go over every point and make it strong and clear to himself, so that he should say, "No!" strongly and clearly to the corporation. It might do harm to make his reason for declining so plain, but he owed it to his self-respect to give it nevertheless, and he meant to do so. After all, he had no business so far to harm, so what did it matter? If nothing turned up pretty soon to give him a start he would have to change his whole plan of life and take up something else where one did not have to wait for a reputation before he could have a chance to show what was in him.

But underneath the legitimate reason for his annoyance this morning there ran a most foolish little fretting, a haunting discomfort.

He had taken his cousin to a wedding the night before because her husband had been called away on business, and she had no one to escort her. They had been late and the church was crowded. He had had to stand, and as he idly looked over the audience he suddenly looked full into the great sad eyes of the sweetest little bride he had ever seen. He had not been a young man to spend his time over pretty faces, although there were one or two nice girls in whom he was mildly interested. He had even gone so far as to wonder now and then which of them he would be willing to see sitting at his table day after day the rest of his life, and he had not yet come to a satisfactory conclusion. His cousin often rallied him about getting married, but he always told her it would be time enough to think about that when he had an income to offer her.

But when he saw that flower-face, his attention was held at once. Somehow he felt as if he had not known there was a face like that in all the world, so like a child's, with frank yet modest droop to the head, and the simplicity of an angel, yet the sadness of a sacrificial offering. Unbidden, a great desire sprang up to lift for her whatever burden she was bearing, and bring light into those sad eyes. Of course it was a passing sensation, but his eyes had traveled involuntarily to the front of the church to inspect the handsome forbidding face of the bridegroom, and with instant dissatisfaction he looked back to the girl once more and watched her come up to the altar, speculating as those who love to study humanity are wont to do when they find an interesting subject. How had those two types ever happened to come together? The man's part in it was plain. He was the kind who go about seeking whom they may devour, thought Warren Reyburn. But the woman! How could a wise-eyed child like that have been deceived by a handsome face? Well, it was all speculation of course, and he had nothing to do with any of them. They were strangers to him and probably always would be. But he had no conception at that time what a small world he lived in, nor how near the big experiences of life lie all about us.

He watched the lovely bride as all the audience watched her until he saw her fall, and then he started forward without in the least realizing what he was doing. He found himself half way up the side aisle to the altar before he came to himself and forced his feet back to where his cousin was sitting. Of course he had no right up there, and what could he do when there were so many of her friends and relatives about her?

His position near the side door through which they carried her made it quite possible for him to look down into her still face as they took her to the vestry room, and he found a great satisfaction in seeing that she was even more beautiful at close hand than at a distance. He wondered afterward why his mind had laid so much stress upon the fact that her skin was lovely like a baby's without any sign of cosmetics. He told himself that it was merely his delight to learn that there was such a type, and that it ran true.

He was therefore not a little disappointed that the minister, after the congregation had waited an unconscionable time for the return of the bride, came out and announced that owing to her continued collapse the ceremony would have to be postponed. The clatter of polite wonder and gossip annoyed him beyond measure, and he was actually cross with his cousin on the way home when she ranted on about the way girls nowadays were brought up, coddled, so that a breath would blow them away. Somehow she had not looked like that kind of a girl.

But when the morning papers came out with sensational headlines proclaiming that the bride had run away, and suggesting all sorts of unpleasant things about her, he felt a secret exultation that she had been brave enough to do so. It was as if he had found that her spirit was as wise and beautiful as her face had been. His interest in the matter exceeded all common sense and he was annoyed and impatient with himself more than he cared to own. Never before had a face lured his thoughts like this one. He told himself that his business was getting on his nerves, and that as soon as he could be sure about one or two little matters that he hoped would fall into his hands to transact, he would take a few days off and run down to the shore.

Again and again the little white bride came across his vision and thoughts, and hindered the courteous but stinging phrases with which he had intended to illumine his letter. At last he gave it up and taking his hat went out in the keen November air for a walk to clear his brain.

This was James Ryan's opportunity. It was almost twelve o'clock and no harm in calling the "forelady" in the cotton blouse department of the big factory. He swung to the telephone with alacrity.

"I want to speak with Miss Carson, please. Yes, Miss J. Carson. Is that Miss Carson? Oh, hello, Jane, is that you?"

"Yes, it is *Mister* Ryan," answered Jane sweetly.

"Jane!"

"Well, didn't you 'Miss Carson' me?"

"Give it up, Jane. You win. Say, Jane!"

"Well, Jimmie?"

"That's my girl, say how about that wedding veil? Been thinking any more about it?"

There was silence for a moment, then a conscious giggle, the full significance of which James Ryan was not in a position to figure out.

"Say, Jimmie, quit your kiddin'! You mustn't say things like that over the 'phone."

"Why not?"

"'Cause. Folks might listen."

"I should worry! Well, since you say so. How about seein' a show together to-night?"

"Fine an' dandy, Jimmie! I'll be ready at the usual time. I gotta go now, the boss is comin'. So long, Jimmie!"

"So long, darling!"

But the receiver at the other end hung up with a click, while Jane with a smile on her lips thought of the pasteboard box under her bed and wondered what Jimmie would say if he could know. For Jane had fully made up her mind that Jimmie was not to know. Not at present, anyhow. Some time she might tell him if things turned out all right, but she knew just what lordly masculine advice and criticism would lie upon James Ryan's lips if she attempted to tell him about her strange and wonderful guest of the night before. Maybe she was a fool to have trusted a stranger that way. Maybe the girl would turn out to be insane or wrong somehow, and trouble come, but she didn't believe it; and anyhow, she was going to wait, until she saw what happened next before she got Jimmie mixed up in it. Besides, the secret wasn't hers to tell. She had promised Betty, and she always kept her promises. That was one reason why she was so slow in promising to think about a wedding veil in response to James Ryan's oft repeated question.

That evening on the way to the movies Jane instituted an investigation.

"Jimmie, what kind of a man is your boss?"

"White man!" said Jimmie promptly.

"Aw! Cut it out, James Ryan! I don't mean how'd s'e look, or what color is he; I mean what kind of a *man* is he?"

"Well, that's the answer. White man! What's the matter of that? I said it and I meant it. He's white if there ever was one!"

"Oh, that!" said Miss Carson in scorn. "Of course I know he's a peach. If he wasn't you wouldn't be workin' for him. What I mean, is he a *snob?*"

"No chance!"

"Well, I saw him *with* 'em last night. I was passin' that big church up Spruce Street and I saw him standin' with his arms folded so——" she paused on the sidewalk and indicated his pose. "It was a swell weddin' and the place was full up. He had a big white front an' a clawhammer coat. I know it was him 'cause I took a good look at him that time you pointed him out at church that evenin'. I wondered was he *in with* them swells?"

Her tone expressed scorn and not a little anxiety, as if she had asked whether he frequented places of low reputation.

"Oh, if you mean, *could* he be, why that's a diffrunt thing!" said James the wise. "*Sure*, he could be if he wanted, I guess. He's got a good family. His uncle's some high muckymuck, and you often see his aunts' and cousins' names in the paper giving teas and receptions and going places. But he don't seem to go much. I often hear folks ask him why he wasn't some place last night, or 'phone to know if he won't come, and he always says he can't spare the time, or he can't afford it, or something like that."

"Ain't he rich, Jimmie?"

"Well, no, not exactly. He may have some money put away, or left him by some one. If he don't have I can't fer the life of me see how he lives. But he certainly don't get it in fees. I often wonder where my salary comes from, but it always does, regular as the clock."

"Jimmie, doesn't he have *any* business at all?"

"Oh, yes he has business, but it ain't the paying kind. Fer instance, there was a man in to-day trying to get his house back that another man took away from him, and my boss *took the case!* He took it *right off the bat* without waiting to see whether the man could pay him anything or not! He can't! He's only a poor laboring man, and a rich man stole his house. Just out an' out stole it, you know. It's how he got rich. Like as not we'll lose it, too, those rich men have so many ways of crawling out of a thing and making it look nice to the world. Oh, he'll get a fee, of course—twenty-five dollars, perhaps—but what's twenty-five dollars, and like as not never get even the whole of that, or have to wait for it? Why, it wouldn't keep *me* in his office long! Then there was a girl trying to get hold of the money her own father left her, and her uncle frittered away and pertends it cost him all that, and *he's* been supporting *her!* Well, we took that, too, and we won't get much out of that even if we do win. Then there come along one of these here rich guys with a pocket full of money and a nice slick tongue wanting to be protected from the law in some devilment, and *him we turned down flat!* That's how it goes in our office. I can't just figger out how it's coming out! But he's a good guy, a white man if there ever was one!"

"I should say!" responded Jane with shining eyes. "Say, Jimmie, what's the matter of us throwin' a little business in his way—real, payin' business, I mean?"

"Fat chance!" said Jimmie dryly.

"You never can tell!" answered Jane dreamily. "I'm goin' to think about it. Our fact'ry has lawyers sometimes. I might speak to the boss."

"Do!" said Jimmie sarcastically! "And have yer labor for yer pains! We'll prob'ly turn *them* down. Fact'ries are *always* doing things they hadn't ought to."

But Jane was silent and thoughtful, and they were presently lost in the charms of Mary Pickford.

The evening papers came out with pictures of Elizabeth Stanhope and her bridegroom that was to have been. Jane cut away the bridegroom and pasted the bride's picture in the flyleaf of her Bible, then hid it away in the bottom of her trunk.

CHAPTER VII

WHEN Betty found herself seated on the day coach of a way train, jogging along toward a town she had never seen and away from the scenes and people of her childhood, she found herself trembling violently. It was as if she had suddenly been placed in an airplane all by herself and started off to the moon without any knowledge of her motor power or destination. It both frightened and exhilarated her. She wanted to cry and she wanted to laugh, but she did neither. Instead she sat demurely for the first hour and a half looking out of the window like any traveler, scarcely turning her head nor looking at anything in the car. It seemed to her that there might be a detective in every seat just waiting for her to lift her eyes that he might recognize her. But gradually as the time dragged by and the landscape grew monotonous she began to feel a little more at her ease. Furtively she studied her neighbors. She had seldom traveled in a common car, and it was new to her to study all types as she could see them here. She smiled at a dirty baby and wished she had something to give it. She studied the careworn man and the woman in black who wept behind her veil and would not smile no matter how hard the man tried to make her. It was a revelation to her that any man would try as hard as that to make a woman smile. She watched the Italian family with five children and nine bundles, and counted the colors on a smart young woman who got in at a way station. Every minute of the day was interesting. Every mile of dreary November landscape that whirled by gave her more freedom.

She opened the little shabby handbag that Jane had given her and got out the bit of mirror one inch by an inch and a half backed with pasteboard on which lingered particles of the original green taffeta lining and studied her own strange face, trying to get used to her new self and her new name. Jane had written it, Lizzie Hope, on the back of the envelope containing the address of Mrs. Carson. It seemed somehow an identification card. She studied it curiously and wondered if Lizzie Hope was going to be any happier than Betty Stanhope had been. And then she fell to thinking over the strange experiences of the last twenty-four hours and wondering whether she had done right or not, and whether her father would have been disappointed in her, "ashamed of her," as her stepmother had said. Somehow Jane had made her feel that he would not, and she was more light-hearted than she had been for many a day.

Late in the afternoon she began to wonder what Tinsdale would be like. In the shabby handbag was her ticket to Tinsdale and eight dollars and a half in change. It made her feel richer than she had ever felt in her life, although she had never been stinted as to pocket money. But this was her very own, for her needs, and nobody but herself to say how she should spend either it or her time.

Little towns came in sight and passed, each one with one or two churches, a schoolhouse, a lot of tiny houses. Would Tinsdale look this way? How safe these places seemed, yet lonely, too! Still, no one would ever think of looking for her in a lonely little village.

They passed a big brick institution, and she made out the words, "State Asylum," and shuddered inwardly as she thought of what Jane had told her about the morning paper. Suppose they should hunt her up and *put her in an insane asylum,* just to show the world that it had not been their fault that she had run away from her wedding! The thought was appalling. She dropped her head on her hand with her face toward the window and tried to pretend she was asleep and hide the tears that would come, but presently a boy came in at the station with a big basket and she bought a ham sandwich and an apple. It tasted good. She had not expected that it would. She decided that she must have been pretty hungry and then fell to counting her money, aghast that the meager supper had made such a hole in her capital. She must be very careful. This might be all the money she would have for a very long time, and there was no telling what kind of an impossible place she was going to. She might have to get away as eagerly as she had come. Jane was all right, but that was not saying that her mother and sisters would be.

It was growing dark, and the lights were lit in the car. All the little Italian babies had been given drinks of water, and strange things to eat, and tumbled to sleep across laps and on seats, anywhere they would stick. They looked so funny and dirty and pitiful with their faces all streaked with soot and molasses candy that somebody had given them. The mother looked tired and greasy and the father was fat and dark, with unpleasant black eyes that seemed to roll a great deal. Yet he was kind to the babies and his wife seemed to like him. She wondered what kind of a home they had, and what relation the young fellow with the shiny dark curls bore to them. He seemed to take as much care of the babies as did their father and mother.

The lights were flickering out in the villages now and gave a friendly inhabited look to the houses. Sometimes when the train paused at stations Betty could see people moving back and forth at what seemed to be kitchen tables and little children bringing dishes out, all working together. It looked pleasant and she wondered if it would be like that where she was going. A big lump of loneliness was growing in her throat. It was one thing to run away from something that you hated, but it was another to jump into a new life where one neither knew nor was known. Betty began to shrink inexpressibly from it all. Not that she wanted to go back! Oh, no; far from it! But once when they passed a little white cemetery with tall dark fir trees waving guardingly above the white stones she looked out almost wistfully. If she were lying in one of those beside her father and mother how safe and rested she would be. She wouldn't have to worry any more. What was it like where father and mother had gone? Was it a real place? Or was that just the end when one died? Well, if she were sure it was all she would not care. She would be willing to just go out and not be. But somehow that didn't seem to be the commonly accepted belief. There was always a beyond in most people's minds, and a fear of just what Betty didn't know. She was a good deal of a heathen, though she did not know that either.

Then, just as she was floundering into a lot of theological mysteries of her own discovery the nasal voice of the conductor called out: "Tinsdale! Tinsdale!" and she hurried to her feet in something of a panic, conscious of her short hair and queer clothes.

Down on the platform she stood a minute trying to get used to her feet, they felt so numb and empty from long sitting. Her head swam just a little, too, and the lights on the station and in the houses near by seemed to dance around her weirdly. She had a feeling that she would rather wait until the train was gone before she began to search for her new home, and then when the wheels ground and began to turn and the conductor shouted "All aboard!" and swung himself up the step as she had seen him do a hundred times that afternoon, a queer sinking feeling of loneliness possessed her, and she almost wanted to catch the rail and swing back on again as the next pair of car steps flung by her.

Then a voice that sounded a little like Jane's said pleasantly in her ear: "Is this Lizzie Hope?" and Betty turned with a thrill of actual fright to face Nellie Carson and her little sister Emily.

"Bobbie'll be here in a minute to carry your suitcase," said Nellie efficiently; "he just went over to see if he could borrow Jake Peter's wheelbarrow in case you had a trunk. You didn't bring your trunk? O, but you're going to stay, aren't you? I'm goin' up to the city to take a p'sition, and Mother'd be awful lonesome. Sometime of course we'll send fer them to come, but now the children's little an' the country's better fer them. They gotta go to school awhile. You'll stay, won't you?"

"How do you know you'll want me?" laughed Betty, at her ease in this unexpected air of welcome.

"Why, of course we'd want you. Jane sent you. Jane wouldn't of sent you if you hadn't been a good scout. Jane knows. Besides, I've got two eyes, haven't I? I guess I can tell right off."

Emily's shy little hand stole into Betty's and the little girl looked up:

"I'm awful glad you come! I think you're awful pretty!"

"Thank you!" said Betty, warmly squeezing the little confiding hand. It was the first time in her life that a little child had come close to her in this confiding way. Her life had not been among children.

Then Bob whirled up, bareheaded, freckled, whistling, efficient, and about twelve years old. He grabbed the suitcase, eyed the stranger with a pleasant grin, and stamped off into the darkness ahead of them.

It was a new experience to Betty to be walking down a village street with little houses on each side and lights and warmth and heads bobbing through the windows. It stirred some memory of long ago, before she could scarcely remember. She wondered, had her own mother ever lived in a small village?

"That's our church," confided Emily, as they passed a large frame building with pointed steeple and belfry. "They're goin' to have a entertainment t'morra night, an' we're all goin' and Ma said you cud go too."

"Isn't that lovely!" said Betty, feeling a sudden lump like tears in her throat. It was just like living out a fairy story. She hadn't expected to be taken right in to family life this way.

"But how did you know I was coming on that train?" she asked the older girl suddenly. "Jane said she was going to telegraph, but I expected to have to hunt around to find the house."

"Oh, we just came down to every train after the telegram came. This is the last train to-night, and we were awful scared for fear you wouldn't come till morning, an' have to stay on the train all night. Ma says it isn't nice for a girl to have to travel alone at night. Ma always makes Jane and me go daytimes."

"It was just lovely of you," said Betty, wondering if she was talking "natural" enough to please Jane.

"Did you bob you hair 'cause you had a fever?" asked Nellie enviously.

"No," said Betty, "that is, I haven't been very well, and I thought it might be good for me," she finished, wondering how many questions like that it was going to be hard for her to answer without telling a lie. A lie was something that her father had made her feel would hurt him more deeply than anything else she could do.

"I just love it," said Nellie enthusiastically. "I wanted to cut mine, an' so did Jane, but Ma wouldn't let us. She says God gave us our hair, an' we oughtta take care of it."

"That's true, too," said Betty. "I never thought about that. But I guess mine will grow again after a while. I think it will be less trouble this way. But it's very dirty with traveling. I think I'll have to wash it before I put it on a pillow."

That had troubled Betty greatly. She didn't know how to get rid of that hair dye before Jane's family got used to having it dark.

"Sure, you can wash it, if you ain't 'fraid of takin' cold. There's lots of hot water. Ma thought you'd maybe want to take a bath. We've got a big tin bath-tub out in the back shed. Ma bought it off the Joneses when they got their porcelain one put into their house. We don't have no runnin' water but we have an awful good well. Here's our house. I guess Bob's got there first. See, Ma's out on the steps waitin' fer us."

The house was a square wooden affair, long wanting paint, and trimmed with little scrollwork around the diminutive front porch. The color was indescribable, blending well into the surroundings either day or night. It had a cheerful, decent look, but very tiny. There was a small yard about it with a picket fence, and a leafless lilac bush. A cheerful barberry bush flanked the gate on either side. The front door was open into a tiny hall and beyond the light streamed forth from a glass lamp set on a pleasant dining-room table covered with a red cloth. Betty stepped inside the gate and found herself enveloped in two motherly arms, and then led into the light and warmth of the family dining-room.

CHAPTER VIII

THERE was a kettle of stew on the stove in the kitchen, kept hot from supper for Betty, with fresh dumplings just mixed before the train came in, and bread and butter with apple sauce and cookies. They made her sit right down and eat, before she even took her hat off, and they all sat around her and talked while she ate. It made her feel very much at home as if somehow she was a real relative.

It came over her once how different all this was from the house which she had called home all her life. The fine napery, the cut glass and silver, the stately butler! And here was she eating off a stone china plate thick enough for a table top, with a steel knife and fork and a spoon with the silver worn off the bowl. She could not help wondering what her stepmother would have said to the red and white tablecloth, and the green shades at the windows. There was an old sofa covered with carpet in the room, with a flannel patchwork pillow, and a cat cuddled up cosily beside it purring away like a tea-kettle boiling. Somehow, poor as it was, it seemed infinitely more attractive than any room she had ever seen before, and she was charmed with the whole family. Bobbie sat at the other end of the table with his elbows on the table and his round eyes on her. When she smiled at him he winked one eye and grinned and then wriggled down under the table out of sight.

The mother had tired kind eyes and a firm cheerful mouth like Jane's. She took Betty right in as if she had been her sister's child.

"Come, now, get back there, Emily. Don't hang on Lizzie. She'll be tired to death of you right at the start. Give her a little peace while she eats her supper. How long have you and Jane been friends, Lizzie?" she asked, eager for news of her own daughter.

Betty's cheeks flushed and her eyes grew troubled. She was very much afraid that being Lizzie was going to be hard work:

"Why, not so very long," she said hesitatingly.

"Are you one of the girls in her factory?"

"Oh, no!" said Betty wildly, wondering what would come next. "We—just met—that is—why—*out one evening!*" she finished desperately.

"Oh, I see!" said the mother. "Yes, she wrote about going out sometimes, mostly to the movies. And to church. My children always make it a point to go to church wherever they are. I brought 'em up that way. I hope you go to church."

"I shall love to," said Betty eagerly.

"Is your mother living?" was the next question.

"No," answered Betty. "Mother and father are both dead and I've been having rather a hard time. Jane was kind to me when I was in trouble."

"I'll warrant you! That's Jane!" beamed her mother happily. "Jane always was a good girl, if I do say so. I knew Jane was at her tricks again when she sent me that telegram."

"Ma's got you a place already!" burst out Nellie eagerly.

"Now, Nellie, you said you'd let Ma tell that!" reproached Bob. "You never can keep your mouth shut."

"There! There! Bob, don't spoil the evening with anything unkind," warned the mother. "Yes, Lizzie, I got you a position. It just happened I had the chance, and I took it, though I don't really b'lieve that anythin' in this world just happens, of course. But it did seem providential. Mrs. Hathaway wanted somebody to look after her little girl. She's only three years old and she is possessed to run away every chance she gets. Course I s'pose she's spoiled. Most rich children are. Now, my children wouldn't have run away. They always thought too much of what I said to make me trouble. But that's neither here nor there. She does it, and besides her Ma is an invalid. She had an operation, so she has to lie still a good bit, and can't be bothered. She wants somebody just to take the little girl out walking and keep her happy in the house, an' all."

"How lovely!" exclaimed Betty. "I shall enjoy it, I know."

"She's awful pretty!" declared Emily eagerly. "Got gold curls and blue eyes just like you, and she has ever an' ever so many little dresses, and wears pink shoes and blue shoes, an' rides a tricycle."

"How interesting!" said Betty.

"You'll get good wages," said the mother. "She said she'd give you six dollars a week, an' mebbe more, an' you'd get some of your meals."

"Then I can pay my board to you," cried Betty.

"Don't worry about that, child. We'll fix that up somehow. We're awful glad to have you come, and I guess we shall like each other real well. Now, children, it's awful late. Get to bed. Scat! Lizzie can have her bath an' get to bed, too. Come, mornin's half way here already!"

The children said good night and Betty was introduced to the tin bath tub and improvised bathroom—a neat little addition to the kitchen evidently intended originally for a laundry. She wanted to laugh when she saw the primitive makeshifts, but instead the tears came into her eyes to think how many luxuries she had taken all her life as a matter of course and never realized how hard it was for people who had none. In fact it had never really entered her head before that there were people who had no bathrooms.

Betty was not exactly accustomed to washing her own hair, and with the added problem of the dye it was quite a task; but she managed it at last, using all the hot water, to get it so that the rinsing water was clear, and her hair felt soft. Then, attired in the same warm nightgown she had worn the night before, which Jane had thoughtfully put in the suitcase—otherwise filled with old garments she wished to send home—Betty pattered upstairs to the little room with the sloping roof and the dormer window and crept into bed with Nellie. That young woman had purposely stayed awake, and kept Betty as long as she could talk, telling all the wonderful things she wanted to know about city life, and Betty found herself in deep water sometimes because the city life she knew about was so very different from the city life that Jane would know. But at last sleep won, and Nellie had to give up because her last question was answered with silence. The guest was deep in slumber.

The next morning the children took her over the house, out in the yard, showing her everything. Then they had to take her down to the village and explain all about the little town and its people. They were crazy about Betty's beautiful hair and much disappointed when she would insist on wearing her hat. It was a bright sunny morning, not very cold, and they told her that nobody wore a hat except to church or to go on the train, but Betty had a feeling that her hair might attract attention, and in her first waking hours a great shadow of horror had settled upon her when she realized that her people would leave no stone unturned to find her. It was most important that she should do or be nothing whereby she might be recognized. She even thought of getting a cap and apron to wear when attending her small charge, but Nellie told her they didn't do that in the country and she would be thought stuck up, so she desisted. But she drew the blue serge skirt up as high above her waistband as possible when she dressed in the morning so that she might look like a little girl and no one would suspect her of being a runaway bride. Also she had a consultation with herself in the small hours of the morning while Nellie was still fast asleep, and settled with her conscience just what she would tell about her past and what she would keep to herself. There was a certain reserve that any one might have, and if she was frank about a few facts no one would be likely to question further.

So next morning she told Mrs. Carson that since her parents' death she had lived with a woman who knew her father well, but lately things had been growing very unpleasant and she found she had to leave. She had left under such conditions that she could not bring away anything that belonged to her, so she would have to work and earn some more clothes.

Mrs. Carson looked into her sweet eyes and agreed that it was the best thing she could do; they might follow her up and make all sorts of trouble for her in her new home if she wrote for her things; and so the matter dropped. They were simple folks, who took things at their face value and were not over inquisitive.

On the third day there arrived a long letter from Jane in which she gave certain suggestions concerning the new member of the family, and ended: "Ma, she's got a story, but don't make her tell any more of it than she wants. She's awful sensitive about it, and trust me, she's all right! She's been through a lot. Just make her feel she's got some folks that loves and trusts her."

Ma, wise beyond her generation and experience, said no more, and took the little new daughter into her heart. She took the opportunity to inform the village gossips that a friend of Jane's had come to rest up and get a year's country air, boarding with them; and so the amalgamation of Betty Stanhope into the life of the little town began.

The "job" proved to be for only part of the day, so that Betty was free most of the mornings to help around the house and take almost a daughter's place. That she was a rare girl is proved by the way she entered into her new life. It was almost as if she had been born again, and entered into a new universe, so widely was her path diverging from everything which had been familiar in the old life. So deep had been her distress before she came into it that this new existence, despite its hard and unaccustomed work, seemed almost like heaven.

It is true there was much bad grammar and slang, but that did not trouble Betty. She had been brought up to speak correctly, and it was second nature to her, but no one had ever drummed it into her what a crime against culture an illiterate way of speaking could be. She never got into the way of speaking that way herself, but it seemed a part of these people she had come to know and admire so thoroughly, as much as for a rose to have thorns, and so she did not mind it. Her other world had been so all-wrong for years that the hardships of this one were nothing. She watched them patch and sacrifice cheerfully to buy their few little plain coarse new things. She marveled at their sweetness and content, where those of her world would have thought they could not exist under the circumstances.

She learned to make that good stew with carrots and celery and parsley and potatoes and the smallest possible amount of meat, that had tasted so delicious the night she arrived. She learned the charms of the common little bean, and was proud indeed the day she set upon the table a luscious pan of her own baking, rich and sweet and brown with their coating of molasses well baked through them. She even learned to make bread and never let any one guess that she had always supposed it something mysterious.

During the week that Nellie was preparing to go to the city, Betty had lessons in sewing. Nellie would bring down an old garment, so faded and worn that it would seem only fit for the rag-bag. She would rip and wash, dye with a mysterious little package of stuff, press, and behold, there would come forth pretty breadths of cloth, blue or brown or green, or whatever color was desired. It seemed like magic. And then a box of paper-patterns would be brought out, and the whole evening would be spent in contriving how to get out a dress, with the help of trimmings or sleeves of another material. Betty would watch and gradually try to help, but she found there were so many strange things to be considered. There, for instance, was the up and down of a thing and the right and wrong of it. It was exactly like life. And one had to plan not to have both sleeves for one arm, and to have the nap of the goods running down always. It was as complicated as learning a new language. But at the end of the week there came forth two pretty dresses and a blouse. Betty, as she sat sewing plain seams and trying to help all she could, kept thinking of the many beautiful frocks she had thrown aside in the years gone by, and of the rich store of pretty things that she had left when she fled. If only Nellie and Jane and little Emily could have them! Ah, and if only she herself might have them now! How she needed them! For a girl who had always had all she wanted it was a great change to get along with this one coarse serge and aprons.

But the sewing and other work had not occupied them so fully that they had not had time to introduce Betty into their little world. The very next evening after she arrived she had been taken to that wonderful church entertainment that the girls had told her about on the way from the station, and there she had met the minister's wife and been invited to her Sabbath school class.

Betty would not have thought of going if Nellie and her mother had not insisted. In fact, she shrank unspeakably from going out into the little village world. But it was plain that this was expected of her, and if she remained here she must do as they wanted her to do. It was the least return she could make to these kind people.

The question of whether or not she should remain began to come to her insistently now. The children clamored every day for her to bind herself for the winter, and Jane's mother had made her most welcome. She saw that they really wanted her; why should she not stay? And yet it did seem queer to arrange deliberately to spend a whole year in a poor uncultured family. Still, where could she go and hope to remain unknown if she attempted to get back into her own class? It was impossible. Her mother had just the one elderly cousin whom she had always secretly looked to to help her in any time of need, but his failing her and sending that telegram without even a good wish in it, just at the last minute, too, made her feel it was of no use to appeal to him. Besides, that was the first place her stepmother would seek for her. She had many good society friends, but none who would stand by her in trouble. No one with whom she had ever been intimate enough to confide in. She had been kept strangely alone in her little world after all, hedged in by servants everywhere. And now that she was suddenly on her own responsibility, she felt a great timidity in taking any step alone. Sometimes at night when she thought what she had done she was so frightened that her heart would beat wildly as if she were running away from them all yet. It was like a nightmare that pursued her.

Mrs. Hathaway had sent for her and made arrangements for her to begin her work with the little Elise the following week when the present governess should leave, and Betty felt that this might prove a very pleasant way to earn her living. The Hathaways lived in a great brick house away back from the street in grounds that occupied what in the city would have been a whole block. There was a high hedge about the place so that one could not see the road, and there were flower-beds, a great fountain, and a rustic summerhouse. Betty did not see why days passed in such a pleasant place would not be delightful in summertime. She was not altogether sure whether she would like to have to be a sort of servant in the house—and of course these cold fall days she would have to be much in the house—but the nursery had a big fireplace in it, a long chest under the window where toys were kept, and many comfortable chairs. That ought to be pleasant, too. Besides, she was not just out looking for pleasant things on this trip. She was trying to get away from unbearable ones, and she ought to be very thankful indeed to have fallen on such comfort as she had.

There was another element in the Carson home that drew her strongly, although she was shy about even thinking of it, and that was the frank, outspoken Christianity. "Ma" tempered all her talk with it, adjusted all her life to God and what He would think about her actions, spoke constantly of what was right and wrong. Betty had never lived in an atmosphere where right and wrong mattered. Something sweet and pure like an instinct in her own soul had held her always from many of the ways of those about her, perhaps the spirit of her sweet mother allowed to be one of those who "bear them up, lest at any time they dash their feet against a stone." Or it might have been some memory of the teachings of her father, whom she adored, and who in his last days often talked with her alone about how he and her own mother would want her to live. But now, safe and quiet in this shelter of a real home, poor though it was, the God-instinct stirred within her, caused her to wonder what He was, why she was alive, and if He cared? One could not live with Mrs. Carson without thinking something about her God, for He was an ever-present help in all her times of need, and she never hesitated to give God the glory for all she had achieved, and for all the blessings she had received.

The very first Sabbath in the little white church stirred still deeper her awakening interest in spiritual things. The minister's wife was a sweet-faced woman who called her "my dear" and invited her to come and see her, and when she began to teach the lesson Betty found to her amazement that it was interesting. She spoke of God in much the same familiar way that "Ma" had done, only with a gentler refinement, and made the girls very sure that whatever anybody else believed, Mrs. Thornley was a very intimate friend of Jesus Christ. Betty loved her at once, but so shy was she that the minister's wife never dreamed it, and remarked to her husband Sunday night after church, when they were having their little, quiet Sabbath talk together, that she was afraid she was going to have a hard time winning that little new girl that had come to live with Mrs. Carson.

"Somehow I can't get away from the thought that she comes from aristocracy somewhere," she added. "It's the way she turns her head, or lifts her eyes or the quiet assurance with which she answers. And she smiles, Charles, never grins like the rest. She is delicious, but somehow I find myself wondering if I have remembered to black my shoes and whether my hat is on straight, when she looks at me."

"Well, maybe she's the daughter of some black sheep who has gone down a peg, and our Father has sent her here for you to help her back again," said her husband with an adorable look at his helper. "If anyone can do it you can."

"I'm not so sure," she said, shaking her head. "She maybe doesn't need me. She has Mrs. Carson, remember, and she is a host in herself. If anybody can lead her to Christ she can, plain as she is."

"Undoubtedly you were meant to help, too, dear, or she would not have been sent to you."

His wife smiled brilliantly a look of thorough understanding: "Oh, I know. I'm not going to shirk any but I wish I knew more about her. She is so sad and quiet, I can't seem to get at her."

Even at that moment Betty lay in her little cot bed under the roof thinking about the minister's wife and what she had said about Christ being always near, ready to show what to do, if one had the listening heart and the ready spirit. Would Christ tell her what to do, she wondered, now right here, if she were to ask him? Would He show her whether to stay in this place or seek further to hide herself from the world? Would He show her how to earn her living and make her life right and sweet as it ought to be.

Then she closed her eyes and whispered softly under the sheltering bedclothes, "O Christ, if you are here, please show me somehow and teach me to understand."

CHAPTER IX

WHEN Betty had been in Tinsdale about a month it was discovered that she could play the piano. It happened on a rainy Sunday in Sunday school, and the regular pianist was late. The superintendent looked about helplessly and asked if there was anybody present who could play, although he knew the musical ability of everybody in the village. The minister's wife had already pleaded a cut finger which was well wrapped up in a bandage, and he was about to ask some one to start the tune without the piano when Mrs. Thornton leaned over with a sudden inspiration to Betty and asked:

"My dear, you couldn't play for us, could you?"

Betty smiled assent, and without any ado went to the instrument, not realizing until after she had done so that it would have been better policy for her to have remained as much in the background as possible, and not to have shown any accomplishments lest people should suspect her position. However, she was too new at acting a part to always think of these little things, and she played the hymns so well that they gathered about her after the hour was over and openly rejoiced that there was another pianist in town. The leader of Christian Endeavor asked her to play in their meeting sometimes, and Betty found herself quite popular. The tallest girl in their class, who had not noticed her before, smiled at her and patronized her after she came back from playing the first hymn, and asked her where she learned to play so well.

"Oh, I used to take lessons before my father died," she said, realizing that she must be careful.

Emily and Bob came home in high feather and told their mother, who had not been able to get out that morning, and she beamed on Betty with as warm a smile as if she had been her own daughter:

"Now, ain't that great!" she said, and her voice sounded boyish just like Jane's. "Why, we'll have to get a pianna. I heard you could get 'em cheap in the cities sometimes—old-fashioned ones, you know. I heard they have so many old-fashioned ones that they have to burn 'em to get rid of 'em, and they even give 'em away sometimes. I wonder, could we find out and get hold of one?"

"I guess 'twould cost too much to get it here," said Bob practically. "My! I wisht we had one. Say, Lizzie, 'f we had a pianna would you show me how to read notes?"

"Of course," said Betty.

"Well, we'll get one somehow! We always do when we need anything awfully. Look at the bathtub! Good-night! I'm goin' to earn one myself!" declared Bob.

"Mrs. Crosby's gotta get a new one. P'raps she'll sell us her old one cheap."

That was the way the music idea started, and nothing else was talked of at the table for days but how to get a piano. Then one day Emily came rushing home from school all out of breath, her eyes as bright as stars, and her cheeks like roses. "Mrs. Barlow came to our school to-day and talked to the teacher, and I heard her say she was going away for the winter. She's going to store her goods in the Service Company barn, but she wants to get somebody to take care of her piano. I stepped right up and told her my mother was looking for a piano, and we'd be real careful of it, and she's just delighted; and—it's coming to-morrow morning at nine o'clock! The man's going to bring it!"

She gasped it out so incoherently that they had to make her tell it over twice to get any sense out of it; but when Bob finally understood he caught his little sister in his arms and hugged her with a big smacking kiss:

"You sure are a little peach, Em'ly!" he shouted. "You're a pippin of the pippins! I didn't know you had that much nerve, you kid, you! I sure am proud of you! My! Think of havin' a pianna! Say, Betty, I can play the base of chopsticks now!"

The next evening when Betty got home from the Hathaways there was the piano standing in the big space opposite the windows in the dining-room. Ma had elected to have it there rather than in the front room, because it might often be too cold in the front room for the children to practice, and besides it wouldn't be good for the piano. So the piano became a beloved member of the family, and Betty began to give instructions in music, wondering at herself that she knew how, for her own music had been most desultory, and nobody had ever cared whether she practiced or not. She had been allowed to ramble among the great masters for the most part unconducted, with the meagerest technique, and her own interpretation. She could read well and her sense of time and rhythm were natural, else she would have made worse work of it than she did. But she forthwith set herself to practicing, realizing that it might yet stand her in good stead since she had to earn her living.

Little Emily and Bob stood one on either side and watched her as she played, with wondering admiration, and when Betty went to help their mother Bob would sit down and try to imitate what she had done. Failing, he would fall headlong into the inevitable chopsticks, beating it out with the air of a master.

It was the piano that brought to Betty's realization the first real meaning of the Sabbath day. Bob came down early and went at the piano as usual banging out chopsticks, and a one-fingered arrangement of "The Long, Long Trail," while his mother was getting breakfast. Betty was making the coffee, proud of the fact that she had learned how. But Bob had accomplished only a brief hint of his regular program when the music stopped suddenly and Betty glanced through the kitchen door to see Ma standing with her hand on her son's shoulder and a look on her face she had not seen before: It was quite gentle, but it was decided:

"No, Bob! We won't have that kinda music on Sunday," she said. "This is God's day, an' we'll have all we can rightly do to keep it holy without luggin' in week-day music to make us forget it. You just get t' work an' learn 'Safely Through Another Week,' an' if you can't play it right you get Lizzie to teach you."

Bob pouted:

"There ain't nothin' wrong with chopsticks, Ma. 'Tain't got words to it."

"Don't make any diffrence. It b'longs to weekdays an' fun, an' anyhow it makes you think of other things, an' you can't keep your mind on God. That's what Sunday was made fer, to kinda tone us up to God, so's we won't get so far away in the week that we won't be any kind of ready for heaven some time. An' anyhow, 'tisn't seemly. You better go learn your Golden Text, Bob. The minister'll be disappointed if you don't have it fine."

Betty stood by the window thoughtfully looking out. Was that what Sunday was made for, or was it only a quaint idea of this original woman? She wished she knew. Perhaps some time she would know the minister's wife well enough to ask. She would have liked to ask Ma more about it, but somehow felt shy. But Ma herself was started now, and when she came back to the kitchen, as if she felt some explanation was due the new inmate of the family, she said:

"I don't know how you feel about it. I know city folks don't always hold to the old ways. But it always seemed to me God meant us to stick to Sunday, and make it diff'rent from other days. I never would let my children go visitin', nor play ball an' we always tried to have something good for supper fixed the night before. I heard somebody say a long time ago that it says somewhere in the Bible that Sunday was meant to be a sign forever between God and folks. The ones that keeps it are his'n, an' them as don't aren't. Anyhow, that's the only day we have got to kinda find out what's wanted of us. You wouldn't mind just playin' hymns and Sunday things t'day, would you?"

"Oh, no," said Betty, interested. "I like it. It sounds so kind of safe, and as if God cared. I never thought much about it before. You think God really thinks about us and knows what we're doing then, don't you?"

"Why, sure, child. I don't just think, I *know* He does. Hadn't you never got onto that? Why, you poor little ducky, you! O' course He does."

"I'd like to feel sure that He was looking out for me," breathed Betty wistfully.

"Well, you can!" said Ma, hurrying back to see that her bacon didn't burn. "It's easy as rollin' off a log."

"What would I have to do?"

"Why, just b'lieve."

"Believe?" asked Betty utterly puzzled. "Believe what?"

"Why, believe that He'll do it. He said 'Come unto me, an' I will give you rest,' an' He said, 'Cast your burden on the Lord,' an' He said 'Castin' all yer care 'pon Him, fer He careth fer you,' an' a whole lot more such things, an' you just got to take it fer straight, an' act on it."

"But how could I?" asked Betty.

"Just run right up to your room now, while you're feelin' that way, an' kneel down by your bed an' tell Him what you just told me," said Mrs. Carson, stirring the fried potatoes with her knife to keep them from burning. "It won't take you long, an' I'll tend the coffee. Just you tell Him you want Him to take care of you, an' you'll believe what I told you He said. It's all in the Bible, an' you can read it for yourself, but I wouldn't take the time now. Just run along an' speak it out with Him, and, then come down to breakfast."

Betty was standing by the kitchen door, her hand on her heart, as if about to do some great wonderful thing that frightened her:

"But, Mrs. Carson, suppose, maybe, He might not be pleased with me. Suppose I've done something that He doesn't like, something that makes Him ashamed of me."

"Oh, why, didn't you know He fixed for all that when He sent His Son to be the Saviour of the world? We all do wrong things, an' everybody has sinned. But ef we're rightly sorry, He'll fergive us, and make us His children."

Betty suddenly sat down in a chair near the door:

"But, Mrs. Carson, I'm not sure I *am* sorry—at least I know I'm *not*. I'm afraid I'd do it all over again if I got in the same situation."

Mrs. Carson stood back from the stove and surveyed her thoughtfully a moment:

"Well, then, like's not it wasn't wrong at all, and if it wasn't He ain't displeased. You can bank on that. You better go talk it out to Him. Just get it off your mind. I'll hold up breakfast a minute while you roll it on Him and depend on it he'll show you in plenty of time for the next move."

Betty with her cheeks very red and her eyes shining went up to her little cot, and with locked door knelt and tried to talk to God for the first time in her life. It seemed queer to her, but when she arose and hurried back to her duties she had a sense of having a real Friend who knew all about her and could look after things a great deal better than she could.

That night she went with Bob and Emily to the young people's meeting and heard them talk about Christ familiarly as if they knew Him. It was all strange and new and wonderful to Betty, and she sat listening and wondering. The old question of whether she was pleasing her earthly father was merging itself into the desire to please her Heavenly Father.

There were of course many hard and unpleasant things about her new life. There were so many things to learn, and she was so awkward at work of all kinds! Her hands seemed so small and inadequate when she tried to wring clothes or scrub a dirty step. Then, too, her young charge, Elise Hathaway, was spoiled and hard to please, and she was daily tried by the necessity of inventing ways of discipline for the poor little neglected girl which yet would not bring down a protest from her even more undisciplined mother. If she had been independent she would not have remained with Mrs. Hathaway, for sometimes the child was unbearable in her naughty tantrums, and it took all her nerve and strength to control her. She would come back to the little gray house too weary even to smile, and the keen eye of Ma would look at her wisely and wonder if something ought not to be done about it.

Betty felt that she must keep this place, of course, because it was necessary for her to be able to pay some board. She could not be beholden to the Carsons. And they had been so kind, and were teaching her so many things, that it seemed the best and safest place she could be in. So the days settled down into weeks, and a pleasant life grew up about her, so different from the old one that more and more the hallucination was with her that she had become another creature, and the old life had gone out forever.

Of course as striking-looking a girl as Betty could not enter into the life of a little town even as humbly as through the Carson home, without causing some comment and speculation. People began to notice her. The church ladies looked after her and remarked on her hair, her complexion, and her graceful carriage, and some shook their heads and said they should think Mrs. Hathaway would want to know a little more about her before she put her only child in her entire charge; and they told weird stories about girls they had known or heard of.

Down at the fire-house, which was the real clearing-house of Tinsdale for all the gossip that came along and went the rounds, they took up the matter in full session several evenings in succession. Some of the younger members made crude remarks about Betty's looks, and some of the older ones allowed that she was entirely too pretty to be without a history. They took great liberties with their surmises. The only two, the youngest of them all, who might have defended her, had been unconsciously snubbed by her when they tried to be what Bobbie called "fresh" with her, and so she was at their mercy. But if she had known it she probably would have been little disturbed. They seemed so far removed from her two worlds, so utterly apart from herself. It would not have occurred to her that they could do her any harm.

One night the fire-house gang had all assembled save one, a little shrimp of a good-for-nothing, nearly hairless, toothless, cunning-eyed, and given to drink when he could lay lips on any. He had a wide loose mouth with a tendency to droop crookedly, and his hands were always clammy and limp. He ordinarily sat tilted back against the wall to the right of the engine, sucking an old clay pipe. He had a way of often turning the conversation to imply some deep mystery known only to himself behind the life of almost any one discussed. He often added choice embellishments to whatever tale went forth as authentic to go the rounds of the village, and he acted the part of a collector of themes and details for the evening conversations.

His name was Abijah Gage.

"Bi not come yet?" asked the fire chief settling a straw comfortably between his teeth and looking around on the group. "Must be somepin' doin'. Don't know when Bi's been away."

"He went up to town this mornin' early," volunteered Dunc Withers. "Reckon he was thirsty. Guess he'll be back on the evenin' train. That's her comin' in now."

"Bars all closed in the city," chuckled the chief. "Won't get much comfort there."

"You bet Bi knows some place to get it. He won't come home thirsty, that's sure."

"I donno, they say the lid's down pretty tight."

"Aw, shucks!" sneered Dunc. "Bet I could get all I wanted."

Just then the door opened and Abijah Gage walked in, with a toothless grin all around.

"Hello, Bi, get tanked up, did yeh?" greeted the chief.

"Well, naow, an' ef I did, what's that to you?" responded Bi, slapping the chief's broad shoulder with a folded newspaper he carried. "You don't 'spose I'm goin' to tell, an' get my frien's in trouble?"

"Le's see yer paper, Bi," said Dunc, snatching at it as Bi passed to his regular seat.

Bi surrendered his paper with the air of one granting a high favor and sank to his chair and his pipe.

"How's crops in the city?" asked Hank Fielder, and Bi's tale was set a-going. Bi could talk; that was one thing that always made him welcome.

Dunc was deep in the paper. Presently he turned it over:

"Whew!" he said speculatively. "If that don't look like that little lollypop over to Carson's I'll eat my hat! What's her name?"

They all drew around the paper and leaned over Dunc's shoulder squinting at the picture, all but Bi, who was lighting his pipe:

"They're as like as two peas!" said one.

"It sure must be her sister!" declared another.

"Don't see no resemblance 'tall," declared the chief, flinging back to his comfortable chair. "She's got short hair, an she's only a kid. This one's growed up!"

"She might a cut her hair," suggested one.

Bi pricked up his ears, narrowed his cunning eyes, and slouched over to the paper, looking at the picture keenly: "Read it out, Dunc!" he commanded.

"Five thousand dollars reward for information concerning Elizabeth Stanhope!"

There followed a description in detail of her size, height, coloring, etc.

An inscrutable look overspread Bi's face and hid the cunning in his eyes. He slouched to his seat during the reading and tilted back comfortably smoking, but he narrowed his eyes to a slit and spoke little during the remainder of the evening. They discussed the picture and the possibility of the girl in the paper being a relative of the girl at Carson's, but as Bi did not come forward with information the subject languished. Some one said he had heard the Carson kid call her Lizzie, he thought, but he wasn't sure. Ordinarily Bi would have known the full name, but Bi seemed to be dozing, and so the matter was finally dropped. But the hounds were out and on the scent, and it was well for Betty sleeping quietly in her little cot beneath the roof of the humble Carson home, that she had committed her all to her heavenly Father before she slept.

CHAPTER X

"WELL, he gave me notice t'day," said James Ryan sadly as Jane and he rounded the corner from her boarding-house and turned toward their favorite movie theater. "I been expectin' it, an' now it's come!"

Jane stopped short on the sidewalk appalled:

"He gave you notice!" she exclaimed, as if she could not believe it was true. "Now, Jimmie! You don't mean it? Did he find any fault? He'd better not! B'leeve me, if he did he gets a piece of *my* mind, even if I am a poor workin' girl!"

"Oh, no, he didn't find any fault," said Jimmie cheerfully. "He was awful nice! He said he'd recommend me away up high. He's gonta give me time every day to hunt a new place, an' he's gonta recommend me to some of his rich friends."

"But what's the matter of him keepin' you? Did you ast him that?"

"Oh, he told me right out that things wasn't working the way he hoped when he started; the war and all had upset his prospects, and he couldn't afford to keep me. He's gonta take an office way down town and do his own letters. He says if he ever succeeds in business and I'm free to come to him he'll take me back. Oh, he's pleased with me all right! He's a peach! He certainly is."

"Jimmie, what d'you tell him?"

"Tell him? There wasn't much for me to tell him, only I was sorry, and I thanked him, and I told him I was gonta stick by him as long as I didn't have a place. Of course I can't live on air, but seeing he's willing I should go out and hunt a place every day, why I ain't that mean that I can't write a few letters for him now and then. He don't have that many, and it keeps me in practice. I s'pose I've got to get another place but I haven't tried yet. I can't somehow bring myself to give him up. I kind of wanted to stick in my first place a long time. It doesn't'look well to be changing."

"Well, if it ain't your fault, you know, when you can't help it," advised Jane.

They were seated in the theater by this time, and the screen claimed their attention. It was just at the end of the funny reel, and both forgot more serious matters in following the adventures of a dog and a bear who were chasing each other through endless halls and rooms, to say nothing of bathtubs, and wash boilers, and dining tables, and anything that came in their way, with a shock to the people who happened to be around when they passed. But suddenly the film ended and the announcements for the next week began to flash on the screen.

"We must go to that, sure!" said Jimmie, nudging Jane, as the Mary Pickford announcement was put on.

Then immediately afterward came the photograph of a beautiful girl, and underneath in great letters:

FIVE THOUSAND DOLLARS' REWARD FOR ACCURATE
INFORMATION AS TO THE PRESENT WHEREABOUTS
OF ELIZABETH STANHOPE

There followed further particulars and an address and the showing stayed on the screen for a full minute.

Jane sat gripping the arms of the seat and trying to still the wild excitement that possessed her, while her eyes looked straight into the eyes of the little bride whom she had helped to escape on the night of her wedding.

Jimmie took out his pencil and wrote down the address in shorthand, but Jane did not notice. She was busy thinking what she ought to do.

"What do you s'pose they want her for?" she asked in a breathless whisper, as a new feature film began to dawn on the screen.

"Oh, she's mebbe eloped," said the wise young man, "or there might be some trouble about property. There mostly is."

Jane said no more, and the pictures began again, but her mind was not following them. She was very quiet on the way home, and when Jimmie asked her if she had a grouch on she shivered and said, no, she guessed she was tired. Then she suddenly asked him what time he was going out to hunt for another job. He told her he couldn't be sure. He would call her up about noon and let her know. Could she manage to get out a while and meet him? She wasn't sure either, but would see when he called her up. And so they parted for the night.

The next morning when Reyburn entered his office Jimmie was already seated at his typewriter. On Reyburn's desk lay a neatly typed copy of the announcement that had been put on the screen the night before.

"What's this, Ryan?" he questioned as he took his seat and drew the paper toward him.

"Something I saw last night on the screen at the movies, sir. I thought it might be of interest."

"Were you thinking of trying for the reward?" asked Reyburn with a comical smile. "What is it, anyway?" And he began to read.

"Oh, no sir!" said Jimmie. "*I* couldn't, of course; but I thought mebbe *you'd* be able to find out something about her and get all that money. That would help you through until you got started in your own business."

"H'm! That's kind of you, Ryan," said the young lawyer, reading the paper with a troubled frown. "I'm afraid it's hardly in my line, however. I'm not a detective, you know." He laid the paper down and looked thoughtfully out of the window.

"Oh, of course not, sir!" Jimmie hastened to apologize. "Only you know a lot of society folks in the city, and I thought you might think of some way of finding out where she is. I know it isn't up to what you ought to be doing, sir, but it wouldn't do any harm. You could work it through me, you know, and nobody need ever know 'twas you got the reward. I'd be glad to help you out doing all I could, but of course it would take your brains to get the information, sir. You see, it would be to my interest, because then you could afford to keep me, and—I like you, Mr. Reyburn, I certainly do. I would hate to leave you."

"Well, now, I appreciate that, Ryan. It's very thoughtful of you. I scarcely think there would be any possibility of my finding out anything about this girl, but I certainly appreciate your thoughtfulness. I'll make a note of it, and if anything turns up I'll let you know. I don't believe, however, that I would care to go after a reward even through someone else. You know, I was at that wedding, Ryan!" His eyes were dreamily watching the smoke from a distant funnel over the roof-tops in line with his desk.

"You were!" said Jimmie, watching his employer with rapt admiration. He had no higher ambition than to look like Warren Reyburn and have an office of his own.

"Yes, I was there," said Reyburn again, but his tone was so far off that Jimmie dared approach no nearer, and resumed the letter he was typing.

About noon Jimmie called up the factory while Reyburn was out to lunch and told Jane that he expected to go out at two o'clock. Could she meet him and walk a little way with him? Jane said no, she couldn't, but she would try and see him the next day, then he could tell her how he had "made out."

At exactly five minutes after two, Jane, having watched from a telephone booth in a drug store until Jimmie went by, hurried up to Reyburn's office and tapped on the door, her heart in her mouth lest he should be occupied with some one else and not be able to see her before her few minutes of leave which she had obtained from the factory should have expired.

Reyburn himself opened the door to her, and treated her as if she had been a lady every inch, handing her a chair and speaking quite as if she were attired in sealskin and diamonds.

She looked him over with bright eyes of approval. Jane was a born sentimentalist, fed on the movies. Not for anything would she have had a knight rescue her lady fair who did not look the part. She was entirely satisfied with this one. In fact, she was almost tongue-tied with admiration for the moment.

Then she rallied to the speech she had prepared:

"Mr. Reyburn," she said, "I came to see you about a matter of very great importance. I heard you was a great lawyer, and I've got a friend that's in trouble. I thought mebbe you could do something about it. But first, I want to ast you a question, an' I want you to consider it perfectly confidential!"

Jane took great credit to herself that she had assembled all these words and memorized them so perfectly.

"Certainly!" said Reyburn gravely, wondering what kind of a customer he had now.

"I don't want you to think I can't pay for it," said Jane, laying down a five-dollar bill grandly. "I know you can't afford to waste your valuable time even to answer a question."

"Oh, that's all right," said Reyburn heartily. "Let me hear what the question is first. There may be no charge."

"No," said Jane hastily, laying the bill firmly on the desk before him. "I shan't feel right astin' unless I know it's to be paid for."

"Oh, very well," said Reyburn, taking the bill and laying it to one side. "Now, what is the question?"

"Well, Mr. Reyburn, will you please tell me what would anybody want to offer a reward, a big reward, like a thousand dollars—or several of them,—for information about any one? Could you think of any reason?"

Reyburn started. Reward again! This was uncanny. Probably this girl had been to the movies and seen the same picture that Ryan had told him about. But he smiled gravely and answered, watching her quizzically the while:

"Well, they might love the person that had disappeared," he suggested at random.

"Oh, no!" said Jane decidedly. "They didn't! I know that fer a fac'! What else could it be?"

"Well, they might have a responsibility!" he said thoughtfully.

"No chance!" said Jane scornfully.

"Couldn't they be anxious, don't you think?"

"Not so's you'd notice it."

"Well, there might be some property to be divided, perhaps."

"I'd thought of that," said Jane, her face growing practical. "It would have to be a good deal of property to make them offer a big reward, wouldn't it?"

"I should think so," answered Reyburn politely, watching her plain eager face amusedly. He could not quite get at her idea in coming to him.

"Would her coming of age have anything to do with it?" put Jane, referring to a much folded paper she carried in her hand, as if she had a written catechism which she must go through.

"It might." Reyburn was growing interested. This queer visitor evidently had thought something out, and was being very cautious.

"I really can't answer very definitely without knowing more of the circumstances," he said with sudden alarm lest the girl might take some random answer and let serious matters hinge on his word.

"Well, there's just one more," she said, looking down at her paper. "If a man was trying to make a girl marry him when she just hated him, could anybody make her do it, and would anybody have a right to put her in an insane 'sylum or anythin' ef she wouldn't?"

"Why, no, of course not! Where did you ever get such a ridiculous idea?" He sat up suddenly, annoyed beyond expression over disturbing suggestions that seemed to rise like a bevy of black bats all around the borders of his mind.

"See here," he said, sitting up very straight. "I really can't answer any more blind questions. I've got to know what I'm talking about. Why, I may be saying the most impossible things without knowing it."

"I know," said Jane, looking at him gravely. "I've thought of that, but you've said just the things I thought you would. Well, say, if I tell you about it can you promise on yer honor you won't ever breathe a word of it? Not to nobody? Whether you take the case or not?"

"Why, certainly, you can trust me to look out for any confidence you may put in me. If you can't I should prefer that you say nothing more."

"Oh, I c'n trust you all right," said Jane smiling. "I just mean, would you be 'lowed to keep it under yer hat?"

"Would I be allowed? What do you mean?"

"I mean would the law let you? You wouldn't *have* to go an' tell where she was or nothin' an' give her away? You'd be 'lowed to keep it on the q. t. an' take care of her?"

"You mean would it be right and honorable for me to protect my client? Why, certainly."

"Well, I mean you wouldn't get into no trouble if you did."

"Of course not."

"Well, then I'll tell you."

CHAPTER XI

JANE opened a small shabby handbag, and took out a folded newspaper, opening it up and spreading it on the desk before him. "There!" she said, and then watched his face critically.

Reyburn looked, and found himself looking into Betty's eyes. Only a newspaper cut, and poor at that, but wonderfully real and mournful, as they had struck him when she lifted them for that swift glance before she sank in the church aisle.

"Where did you get this?" he asked, his voice suddenly husky.

"Out o' the mornin' paper." Her tone was low and excited. "Were you wanting to try for the reward?" Reyburn asked.

There was a covert sneer in the question from which the girl shrank perceptibly. She sprang to her feet, her eyes flashing:

"If that's what you take me for, I better be goin'!" she snapped and reached out her hand for the paper. But Reyburn's hand covered the paper, and his tone was respectful and apologetic as he said:

"Excuse me, I didn't quite understand, I see. Sit down, please. You and I must understand each other or there is no use in our talking. You can trust me to keep this conversation entirely to myself, whatever the outcome. Will you tell me what it is you want of me?"

Jane subsided into a chair, tears of excitement springing into her eyes.

"Well, you see, it's pretty serious business," she said, making a dab at the corner of one eye. "I thought I could trust you, or I wouldn't a come. But you gotta take me on trust, too."

"Of course," said Reyburn. "Now, what have you to do with this girl? Do you know where she is?"

"I certainly do!" said Jane, "but I ain't a-goin' ta tell until you say if there's anything you can do fer her. 'Cause you see, if you can't find a way to help her, I've gotta do it myself, an' it might get you into trouble somehow fer you to know what you ain't supposed to know."

"I see," said Reyburn, meekly. "Well, what are you going to tell me? Am I allowed to ask that?"

Jane grinned.

"Say, you're kiddin' me! I guess you are all right. Well, I'll just tell you all about it. One night last November,— you can see the date there in the paper, I was goin' home to my boardin' house in Camac Street, an' I was passin' the side of that church on 18th an' Spruce, where the weddin' was—you know, fer you was there!"

Reyburn looked at her astonished.

"How did you know I was there?"

"I saw you through the window, over against the wall to the street side of the altar," said Jane calmly.

"How did you know me?"

"Oh, somebody I know pointed you out once an' said you was goin' to be one of the risin' lawyers of the day," she answered nonchalantly, her face quite serious.

A flicker of amusement passed like a ray of light through his eyes, but his face was entirely grave as he ignored the compliment.

"Go on!"

"I saw there was a weddin' an' I stopped to watch a minute, 'cause I expect to get married myself some day, an' I wanted to see how they did things. But I couldn't get near the door, an' the windows were all high up. I could only see folks who were standing up like you were. So I thought I'd go on. I turned the corner and went long-side the church listenin' to the music, an' just as I passed a big iron gate at the back end of the church somebody grabbed me an' begged me to help 'em. I looked round, an' there was the bride, all in her white togs, with the prettiest white satin slippers, in the wet an' mud! I tried to get her line, but she cried out somebody was comin' back in the passageway, so I slipped off my coat an' hat and whisked her into 'em an' clapped my rubbers over her satin shoes, and we beat it round the corner. I took her to my room, an' gave her some supper. She was all in. Then I put her to bed, an' she told me a little bit about it. She didn't tell me much. Only that they had been tryin' fer a long time back to make her marry a man she hated, an' now they'd almost tricked her into it, an' she'd die if she had to do it. She wanted to exchange clothes with me, cause, of course, she couldn't get anywhere togged out that way, so we changed things, an' I fixed her up. In the mornin' I ran out an' got a paper, an' found they was sayin' she was temporary insane, an' stuff like that, an' so I saw their game was tryin' to get her in a 'sylum till they could make her do what they wanted. I fixed her up an' got her off to a place I know where she'd be safe. An' she's got a job an' doin' real well. But now they've got this here reward business out everywhere in the papers an' the movies, she ain't safe nowhere. An' I want somebody that's wiser'n me to take a holt an' do somethin'. I can't pay much, but I'll pay a little every month as long's I live ef it takes that long to pay yer bill, an' I have a notion she may have some money herself, though she didn't say nothin' about it. But there's a ring she left with me to sell, to pay fer what I gave her. It oughtta be worth somethin'. It looks real. I ain't sold it. I couldn't. I thought she might want it sometime——"

But Reyburn interrupted her excitedly.

"Do you mean to say that Miss Stanhope is in the city and you know where she is?"

"Now, don't get excited," warned Jane coolly. "I didn't say she was in this city, did I? I didn't say where she was, did I? I said she was safe."

"But are you aware that you have told me a very strange story? What proof can you give me that it is true?"

Jane looked at him indignantly.

"Say, I thought you was goin' to trust me? I have to trust you, don't I? Course you don't know who I am, an' I haven't told you, but I've got a good p'sition myself, an' I don't go round tellin' privarications! An' there's the weddin' dress, an' veil and fixin's! I got them. You can see 'em if you like,—that is pervided I know what you're up to! I ain't taking any chances till I see what you mean to do."

"I beg your pardon," said Reyburn, trying to smile assurance once more. "You certainly must own this whole thing is enough to make anybody doubt."

"Yes, it is," said Jane. "I was some upset myself, havin' a thing like that happen to me, a real millionairess bride drop herself down on my hands just like that, an' I 'spose it *is* hard to b'lieve. But I can't waste much more time now. I gotta get back to my job. Is there anything can be done to keep 'em from gettin' her again?"

"I should most certainly think so," said Reyburn, "but I would have to know her side of the story, the whole of it, before I could say just what!"

"Well, s'pose you found there wasn't anythin' you could do to help her, would you go an' tell on her?"

Reyburn leaned back in his chair and smiled at his unique client:

"I shall have to quote your own language. 'What do you take me for?'"

"A white man!" said Jane suddenly, and showed all her fine teeth in an engaging smile. "Say, you're all right. Now, I gotta go. When will you tell me what you can do?" She glanced anxiously at her little leather-bound wrist watch. It was almost time for Jimmie to return. Jimmie mustn't find her here. He wouldn't understand, and what Jimmie didn't know wouldn't hurt him.

"Well, this ought to be attended to, at once, if anything is to be done," he said eagerly. "Let me see. I have an engagement at five. How would seven o'clock do? Could I call at your boarding-house? Would there be any place where we could talk uninterrupted?"

"Sure," said Jane, rising. "I'll get my landlady to let me have her settin' room fer an hour."

"Meantime, I'll think it over and try to plan something."

Jane started down the long flights of stairs, not daring to trust to the elevator, lest she should come face to face with Jimmie and have to explain.

Reyburn stood with his back to the room, his hands in his pockets, frowning and looking out the window, when Jimmie entered a moment later.

"I hope I'm not late, sir?" he said anxiously, as he hung up his hat and sat down at his typewriter. "I had to wait. The man was out."

"Oh, that's all right, Ryan," said his employer, obviously not listening to his explanation. "I'm going out now, Ryan. I may not be back this afternoon. Just see that everything is all right."

"Very well, sir."

Reyburn went out, then opened the door and put his head back in the room.

"I may have to go out of town to-night, Ryan. I'm not sure. Something has come up. If I'm not in to-morrow, could you—would you mind just staying here all day and looking after things? I may need you. Of course you'll lock up and leave the card out when you go to lunch."

"Very well, sir."

"I'll keep in touch with you in case I'm delayed," and Reyburn was off again. When the elevator had clanked down to the next floor Jimmie went to the window and looked dreamily out over the roofs of the city:

"Aw!" he breathed joyously. "Now I'll bet he's going to do something about that reward!"

Reyburn hurried down the street to the office of an old friend where he had a bit of business as an excuse, and asked a few casual questions when he was done. Then he went on to a telephone booth and called up a friend of his mother's, with whom he had a brief gossip, ostensibly to give a message from his mother, contained in her last letter to him. None of the questions that he asked were noticeable. He merely led the conversation into certain grooves. The lady was an old resident and well known in the higher social circles. She knew all there was to know about everybody and she loved to tell it. She never dreamed that he had any motive in leading her on.

He dropped into a bank and asked a few questions, called up an address they gave him and made another inquiry, then dropped around to his cousin's home for a few minutes, where he allowed her to tell all she knew about the Stanhope wedding they had attended together, and the different theories concerning the escaped bride. Quite casually he asked if she knew whether the bride had property of her own, if so who were her guardians. His cousin thought she knew a lot, but, sifting it down, he discovered that it was nearly all hearsay or surmise.

When he reached Jane Carson's boarding house he found that young woman ensconced in a tiny room, nine by twelve, a faded ingrain carpet on the floor, a depressed looking bed lounge against the bleary wall-paper, beneath crayon portraits of the landlady's dead husband and sons. There was a rocking-chair, a trunk, a cane-seat chair, and an oil stove turned up to smoking point in honor of the caller, but there was little room left for the caller. On the top of the trunk reposed a large pasteboard box securely tied.

Jane, after a shy greeting, untied the strings and opened the cover, having first carefully slipped the bolt of the door.

"You can't be too careful," she said. "You never can tell."

Reyburn stood beside her and looked in a kind of awe at the glistening white, recognized the thick texture of the satin, the rare quality of the rose-point lace with which it was adorned, caught the faint fragrance of faded orange blossoms wafting from the filmy mist of the veil as Jane lifted it tenderly; then leaned over and touched a finger to the pile of whiteness, reverently, as though he were paying a tribute at a lovely shrine.

Jane even unwrapped the little slippers, one at a time, and folded them away again, and they said no word until it was all tied back in its papers, Reyburn assisting with the strings.

"Now, ef you don't mind waitin' a minute I guess it would be safer to put it away now," she said as she slipped the bolt and ran upstairs.

She was back in a minute and sat down opposite to him, drawing out from the neck of her blouse a ribbon with a heavy glittering circlet at its end.

"Here's the ring." She laid it in his palm. He took it, wondering, a kind of awe still upon him that he should be thus handling the intimate belongings of that little unknown bride whom he had seen lying unconscious in a strange church a few short months before. How strange that all this should have come to him when many wiser, more nearly related, were trying their best to get some clue to the mystery!

He lifted the ring toward the insufficient gas jet to make out the initials inside, and copied them down in his note-book.

"Take good care of that. It is valuable," he said as he handed it back to her.

"Mebbe I better give it to you," she half hesitated.

"You've taken pretty good care of it so far," he said. "I guess you've a better right to it than I. Only don't let anybody know you've got it. Now, I've been making inquiries, and I've found out a few things, but I've about come to the conclusion that I can't do much without seeing the lady. Do you suppose she would see me? Is she very far away?"

"When do you want to go?" asked Jane.

"At once," he answered decidedly. "There's no time to waste if she is really in danger, as you think."

Jane's eyes glittered with satisfaction.

"There's a train at ten-thirty. You'll get there in the morning. I've written it all down here on a paper so you can't make any mistakes. I've written her a letter so she'll understand and tell you everythin'. I'll wire Ma, too, so she'll let you see her. Ma might not size you up right."

Reyburn wondered at the way he accepted his orders from this coolly impudent girl, but he liked her in spite of himself.

In a few minutes more he was out in the street again, hurrying to his own apartment, where he put together a few necessities in a bag and went to the train.

CHAPTER XII

IT was one of those little ironies of fate that are spoken about so much, that when Warren Reyburn alighted from the train in Tinsdale Abijah Gage should be supporting one corner of the station, and contributing a quid now and then to the accumulations of the week scattered all about his feet.

He spotted the stranger at once and turned his cunning little eyes upon him, making it obvious that he was bulging with information. It was, therefore, quite natural, when Reyburn paused to take his bearings, that Bi should speak up and inquire if he was looking for some one. Reyburn shook his head and passed on, but Bi was not to be headed off so easily as that. He shuffled after him:

"Say!" he said, pointing to a shackley horse and buckboard that stood near, belonging to a pal over at the freight house. "Ef you want a lift I'll take you along."

"Thank you, no," said Reyburn, smiling; "I'm not going far."

"Say!" said Bi again as he saw his quarry about to disappear. "You name ain't Bains, is it?"

"No!" said Reyburn, quite annoyed by the persistent old fellow.

"From New York?" he hazarded cheerfully.

"No," answered Reyburn, turning to go. "You must excuse me. I'm in a hurry."

"That's all right," said Bi contentedly. "I'll walk a piece with you. I was lookin' fer a doctor to take down to see a sick child. A doctor from New York. You ain't by any chance a doctor, are you?" Bi eyed the big leather bag inquiringly.

"No," said Reyburn, laughing in spite of his annoyance. "I'm only a lawyer." And with a bound he cleared the curb and hurried off down the street, having now recognized the direction described in Jane's diagram of Tinsdale.

Abijah Gage looked after him with twinkling eyes of dry mirth, and slowly sauntered after him, watching him until he entered the little unpainted gate of the Carson house and tapped at the old gray door. Then Bi lunged across the street and entered a path that ran along the railroad track for a few rods, curving suddenly into a stretch of vacant lots. On a convenient fence rail with a good outlook toward the west end of the village he ensconced himself and set about whittling a whistle from some willow stalks. He waited until he saw Bobbie Carson hurry off toward Hathaway's house and return with Lizzie Hope; waited hopefully until the stranger finally came out of the house again, touching his hat gracefully to the girl as she stood at the open door. Then he hurried back to the station again, and was comfortably settled on a tub of butter just arrived by freight, when Reyburn reached there. He was much occupied with his whistle, and never seemed to notice, but not a movement of the stranger escaped him, and when the Philadelphia express came by, and the stranger got aboard the parlor car, old Bi Gage swung his lumbering length up on the back platform of the last car. The hounds were hot on the trail now.

It was several years since Bi Gage had been on so long a journey, but he managed to enjoy the trip, and kept in pretty good touch with the parlor car, although he was never in evidence. If anybody had told Warren Reyburn as he let himself into his apartment late that night that he was being followed, he would have laughed and told them it was an impossibility. When he came out to the street the next morning and swung himself into a car that would land him at his office, he did not see the lank flabby figure of the toothless Bi standing just across the block, and keeping tab on him from the back platform, nor notice that he slid into the office building behind him and took the same elevator up, crowding in behind two fat men and effacing himself against the wall of the cage. Reyburn was reading his paper, and did not look up. The figure slid out of the elevator after him and slithered into a shadow, watching him, slipping softly after, until sure which door he took, then waited silently until sure that the door was shut. No one heard the slouching footsteps come down the marble hall. Bi Gage always wore rubbers when he went anywhere in particular. He had them on that morning. He took careful note of the name on the door: "*Warren Reyburn*, Attorney-at-Law," and the number. Then he slid down the stairs as unobserved as he had come, and made his way to a name and number on a bit of paper from his pocket which he consulted in the shelter of a doorway.

When Warren Reyburn started on his first trip to Tinsdale his mind was filled with varying emotions. He had never been able to quite get away from the impression made upon him by that little white bride lying so still amid her bridal finery, and the glowering bridegroom above her. It epitomized for him all the unhappy marriages of the world, and he felt like starting out somehow in hot pursuit of that bridegroom and making him answer for the sadness of his bride. Whenever the matter had been brought to his memory he had always been conscious of the first gladness he had felt when he knew she had escaped. It could not seem to him anything but a happy escape, little as he knew about any of the people who played the principal parts in the little tragedy he had witnessed.

Hour after hour as he sat in the train and tried to sleep or tried to think he kept wondering at himself that he was going on this "wild goose chase," as he called it in his innermost thoughts. Yet he knew he had to go. In fact, he had known it from the moment James Ryan had shown him the advertisement. Not that he had ever had any idea of trying for that horrible reward. Simply that his soul had been stirred to its most knightly depths to try somehow to protect her in her hiding. Of course, it had been a mere crazy thought then, with no way of fulfilment, but when the chance had offered of really finding her and asking if there was anything she would like done, he knew from the instant it was suggested that he was going to do it, even if he lost every other business chance he ever had or expected to have, even if it took all his time and every cent he could borrow. He knew he had to try to find that girl! The thought that the only shelter between her and the great awful world lay in the word of an untaught girl like Jane Carson filled him with terror for her. If that was true, the sooner some one of responsibility and sense got to her the better. The questions he had asked of various people that afternoon had revealed more than he had already guessed of the character of the bridegroom to whom he had taken such a strong dislike on first sight.

Thus he argued the long night through between the fitful naps he caught when he was not wondering if he should find her, and whether he would know her from that one brief sight of her in church. How did he know but this was some game put up on him to get him into a mix-up? He must go cautiously, and on no account do anything rash or make any promises until he had first found out all about her.

When morning dawned he was in a state of perturbation quite unusual for the son and grandson of renowned lawyers noted for their calmness and poise under all circumstances. This perhaps was why the little incident with Abijah Gage at the station annoyed him so extremely. He felt he was doing a questionable thing in taking this journey at all. He certainly did not intend to reveal his identity or business to this curious old man.

The little gray house looked exactly as Jane had described it, and as he opened the gate and heard the rusty chain that held it clank he had a sense of having been there before.

He was pleasantly surprised, however, when the door was opened by Emily, who smiled at him out of shy blue eyes, and stood waiting to see what he wanted. It was like expecting a viper and finding a flower. Somehow he had not anticipated anything flower-like in Jane's family. The mother, too, was a surprise when she came from her ironing, and, pushing her wavy gray hair back from a furrowed brow lifted intelligent eyes that reminded him of Jane, to search his face. Ma did not appear flustered. She seemed to be taking account of him and deciding whether or not she would be cordial to him.

"Yes, I had a telegram from Jane this morning," she was scanning his eyes once more to see whether there was a shadow of what she called "shiftiness" in them. "Come in," she added grudgingly.

He was not led into the dining-room, but seated on one of the best varnished chairs in the "parlor," as they called the little unused front room. He felt strangely ill at ease and began to be convinced that he was on the very wildest of wild goose chases. To think of expecting to find Elizabeth Stanhope in a place like this! If she ever had been here she certainly must have flown faster than she had from the church on her wedding night.

So, instead of beginning as he had planned, to put a list of logically prepared keen questions to a floundering and suspecting victim, he found the clear eyes of Ma looking into his unwaveringly and the wise tongue of Ma putting him through a regular orgy of catechism before she would so much as admit that she had ever heard of a girl named Lizzie Hope. Then he bethought him of her daughter's letter and handed it over for her to read.

"Well," she admitted at last, half satisfied, "she isn't here at present. I sent her away when I found you was comin'. I wasn't sure I'd let you see her at all if I didn't like your looks."

"That's right, Mrs. Carson," he said heartily, with real admiration in his voice. "I'm glad she has some one so careful to look out for her. Your daughter said she was in a good safe place, and I begin to see she knew what she was talking about."

Then the strong look around Ma's lips settled into the sweeter one, and she sent Bob after the girl.

"Are you a friend of hers?" she asked, watching him keenly.

"No," said Reyburn. "I've never seen her but once. She doesn't know me at all."

"Are you a friend of her—family?"

"Oh, no!"

"Or any of her friends or relations?" Ma meant to be comprehensive.

"No. I'm sorry I am not. I am a rather recent comer to the city where she made her home, I understand."

Ma looked at him thoughtfully for a moment. It wouldn't have been called a stare, it was too kindly for that, but Reyburn thought to himself that he would not have liked to have borne her scrutiny if he had anything to conceal, for he felt as if she might read the truth in his eyes.

"Are you—please excuse me for askin'—but are you a member of any church?"

Reyburn flushed, and wanted to laugh, but was embarrassed in spite of himself:

"Why, yes—I'm a member," he said slowly, then with a frank lifting of his eyes to her troubled gaze, "I united with the church when I was a mere kid, but I'm afraid I'm not much of a member. I really am not what you'd call 'working' at it much nowadays. I go to morning service sometimes, but that's about all. I don't want to be a hypocrite."

He wondered as he spoke why he took the trouble to answer the woman so fully. Her question was in a way impertinent, much like the way her daughter talked. Yet she seemed wholly unconscious of it.

"I know," she assented sorrowfully. "There's lots of them in the church. We have 'em, too, even in our little village. But still, after all, you can't help havin' confidence more in them that has 'named the name' than in them that has not."

Reyburn looked at her curiously and felt a sudden infusion of respect for her. She was putting the test of her faith to him, and he knew by the little stifled sigh that he had been found wanting.

"I s'pose lawyers don't have much time to think about being Christians," she apologized for him.

He felt impelled to be frank with her:

"I'm afraid I can't urge that excuse. Unfortunately I have a good deal of time on my hands now. I've just opened my office and I'm waiting for clients."

"Where were you before that? You did not just get through studying?"

He saw she was wondering whether he was wise enough to help her protege.

"No, I spent the last three years in France."

"Up at the front?" The pupils of her eyes dilated eagerly.

"Yes, in every drive," he answered, wondering that a woman of this sort should be so interested now that the war was over.

"And you came back safe!" she said slowly, looking at him with a kind of wistful sorrow in her eyes. "My boy was shot the first day he went over the top."

"Oh, I'm sorry," said Reyburn gently, a sudden tightness in his throat.

"But it was all right." She flashed a dazzling smile at him through the tears that came into her eyes. "It wasn't as if he wasn't ready. Johnny was always a good boy, an' he joined church when he was fourteen, an' always kep' his promises. He used to pray every night just as faithful, an' read his Bible. I've got the little Testament he carried all through. His chaplain sent it to me. It's got a bullet hole through it, and blood-marks, but it's good to me to look at, 'cause I know Johnny's with his Saviour. He wasn't afraid to die. He said to me before he left, he says: 'Ma, if anythin' happens to me it's all right. You know, Ma, I ain't forgettin' what you taught me, an' I ain't forgettin' Christ is with me.'"

Mrs. Carson wiped her eyes furtively, and tried to look cheerful. Reyburn wished he knew how to comfort her.

"It makes a man feel mean," he said at last, trying to fit his toe into the pattern of the ingrain carpet, "to come home alive and whole when so many poor fellows had to give their lives. I've often wondered how I happened to get through."

She looked at him tenderly:

"Perhaps your Heavenly Father brought you back to give you more chance to do things for Him, an' get ready to die when your time comes."

There was something startling to this self-composed city chap in hearing a thing like this from the lips of the mother whose beloved son was gone forever beyond her teaching but had "been ready." Reyburn looked at her steadily, soberly, and then with a queer constriction in his throat he looked down at the floor thoughtfully and said:

"Perhaps He did."

"Well, I can't help bein' glad you're a church member, anyhow," said Mrs. Carson, rising to look out of the window. "She needs a Christian to help her, an' I'd sooner trust a Christian. If you really meant it when you joined church you've got somethin' to fall back on anyhow. Here she comes. I'll just go an' tell her you're in here."

CHAPTER XIII

BETTY, her eyes wide with fear, her face white as a lily, appeared like a wraith at the parlor door and looked at him. It gave Reyburn a queer sensation, as if a picture one had been looking at in a story book should suddenly become alive and move and stare at one. As he rose and came forward he still seemed to see like a dissolving view between them the little huddled bride on the floor of the church. Then he suddenly realized that she was trembling.

"Please don't be afraid of me, Miss Stanhope," he said gently. "I have only come to help you, and if after you have talked with me you feel that you would rather I should have nothing to do with your affairs I will go away and no one in the world shall be the wiser for it. I give you my word of honor."

"Oh!" said Betty, toppling into a chair near by. "I—guess—I'm not afraid of you. I just didn't know who you might be——!" She stopped, caught her breath and tried to laugh, but it ended sorrily, almost in a sob.

"Well, I don't wonder," said Reyburn, trying to find something reassuring to say. "The truth is, I was rather upset about you. I didn't quite know who you might turn out to be, you see!"

"Oh!" Betty's hand slipped up to her throat, and her lips quivered as she tried to smile.

"Please don't feel that way," he said, "or I'll go away at once." He was summoning all his courage and hoping she wasn't going to break down and cry. How little she was, and sweet! Her eyes pleaded, just as they did in that one look in the church. How could anybody be unkind to her?

"I'm quite all right," said Betty with a forced smile, siting up very straight.

"Perhaps I'd better introduce myself," he said, trying to speak in a very commonplace tone. "I'm just a lawyer that your friend Miss Jane Carson sent out to see if I could be of any service to you. It may possibly make things a little easier for you if I explain that while I never had heard of you before, and have no possible connection with your family or friends, I happened to be at your wedding!"

"Oh!" said Betty with a little agonized breath.

"Do you know Mrs. Bryce Cochrane?" he asked.

Betty could not have got any whiter, but her eyes seemed to blanch a trifle.

"A little," she said in a very small voice.

"Well, she is my cousin."

"Oh!" said Betty again.

"Her husband was unable to accompany her to the wedding, and so I went in his place to escort Isabel. I knew nothing of your affairs either before or after the wedding, until this announcement was brought to my notice, and Miss Carson called on me."

Betty took the paper in her trembling fingers, and looked into her own pictured eyes. Then everything seemed to swim before her for a moment. She pressed her hand against her throat and set her white lips firmly, looking up at the stranger with a sudden terror and comprehension.

"You want to get that five thousand dollars!" she said, speaking the words in a daze of trouble. "Oh, I haven't got five thousand dollars! Not now! But perhaps I could manage to get it if you would be good enough to wait just a little, till I can find a way. Oh, if you knew what it means to me!"

Warren Reyburn sprang to his feet in horror, a flame of anger leaping into his eyes.

"Five thousand dollars be hanged!" he said fiercely. "Do I look like that kind of a fellow? It may seem awfully queer to you for an utter stranger to be butting into your affairs like this unless I did have some ulterior motive, but I swear to you that I have none. I came out here solely because I saw that you were in great likelihood of being found by the people from whom you had evidently run away. Miss Stanhope, I stood where I could watch your face when you came up the aisle at your wedding, and something in your eyes just before you dropped made me wish I could knock that bridegroom down and take care of you somehow until you got that hurt look out of your face. I know it was rather ridiculous for an utter stranger to presume so far, but when I saw that the sleuths were out after you, and when the knowledge of your whereabouts was put into my hands without the seeking, I wouldn't have been a man if I hadn't come and offered my services. I'm not a very great lawyer, nor even a very rising one, as your Miss Carson seems to think, but I'm a man with a soul to protect a woman who is in danger, and if that's you, I'm at your service. If not, you've only to say so and I'll take the next train home and keep my mouth shut!"

He took his watch out and looked at it hastily, although he had not the slightest idea what it registered, nor what time the next train for home left. He looked very tall and strong and commanding as he stood in his dignity waiting for her answer, and Betty looked up like a little child and trusted him.

"Oh! Please forgive me!" she cried. "I've been so frightened ever since Bob came after me. I couldn't think you had come for any good, because I didn't know any one in the world who would want to help me."

"Certainly!" said Warren Reyburn with a lump in his throat, sitting down quickly to hide his emotion. "Please consider me a friend, and command me."

"Thank you," said Betty taking a deep breath and trying to crowd back the tears. "I'm afraid there isn't any way to help me, but I'm glad to have a friend, and I'm sorry I was so rude."

"You weren't rude, and that was a perfectly natural conclusion from my blundering beginning," he protested, looking at the adorable waves of hair that framed her soft cheeks. "But there is always a way to help people when they are in trouble, and I'm here to find out what it is. Do you think you could trust me enough to tell me what it's all about? Miss Carson didn't seem to know much or else she didn't feel free to say."

"I didn't tell her much," said Betty, lifting her sea-blue eyes. "She was a stranger, too, you know."

"Well, she's a mighty good friend of yours, I'll say, and she's acted in a very wise manner. She took more precautions than an old detective would have done. She told me only that some one was trying to make you marry a man you did not wish to marry. Is that correct?"

Betty shivered involuntarily and a wave of color went over her white face.

"It sounds queer," she said, "as if I hadn't any character or force myself, but you don't understand. No one would understand unless they knew it all, and had been through it for years. At first I didn't quite understand it myself. I'd better tell you the story. I thought I never could tell any one, because they were my father's family, and I know he would shrink so from having it known, but I'm sure he wouldn't blame me now."

"He certainly would not blame you, Miss Stanhope. I have heard that your father was a wonderful man, with high principles. I feel sure he would justify you in appealing to some one who was willing to advise you in a strait like this. You know no woman need ever marry any man against her will."

"Not if it were her father's dying wish?"

"Certainly not. Miss Stanhope, did your father love you?"

"Oh, I'm sure he did. He was the most wonderful father! I've often thought that he would never have asked it of me if he had realized——"

"Did he ever during his lifetime seem to wish you to be unhappy?"

"Never! That was the strange part of it. But you see he didn't know how I felt. I think I'd better tell you all about it."

"That would be the better way, if it won't be too hard for you."

Betty clasped her small hands together tightly and began:

"My own mother died when I was quite a little girl, so father and I were a great deal to each other. He used to look after my lessons himself, and was always very careful what kind of teachers I had. He was mother and father both to me. When I was ten years old my governess died suddenly while father was away on a business trip, and one of our neighbors was very kind to me, coming in and looking after the servants and everything and keeping me over at her house for a few days till father got back. She had a widowed sister visiting her, a rather young woman who was very beautiful. At least I thought she was beautiful then, and she made a great pet of me, so that I grew fond of her, although I had not liked her at first.

297

"After father came home she used to slip over every day to see me while he was at his business, and he was grateful to her for making me happy. Then he found out that she was in trouble, had lost her money or something, and wanted to get a position teaching. He arranged to have her teach me, and so she came to our house to stay.

"Somehow after that I never seemed to see so much of my father as I used to do, for she was always there, but at first I didn't care, because she was nice to me, and always getting up things to keep me busy and happy. She would make my father buy expensive toys and books and games for me, and fine clothes, and so of course I was pleased. In about a year my father married her, and at first it seemed very beautiful to me to have a real mother, but little by little I began to see that she preferred to be alone with my father and did not want me around so much. It was very hard to give up the companionship of my father, but my stepmother kept me busy with other things, so that I really didn't think much about it while it was first happening.

"But one day there came a letter. I remember it came while we were at breakfast, and my father got very white and stern when he read it, and handed it over to my mother and asked whether it was true, and then she began to cry and sent me from the table. I found out a few days after that that my stepmother had two sons, both older than myself, and that she had not told my father. It was through some trouble they had got into at school which required quite a large sum of money to cover damages that my father discovered it, and he was terribly hurt that she should have concealed it from him. I learned all this from the servants, who talked when they thought I was not within hearing. There were days and days when my father scarcely spoke at the table, and when he looked at me it made a pain go through my heart, he looked so stern and sad. My stepmother stayed a great deal in her room and looked as if she had been crying. But after a few weeks things settled down a good deal as they had been, only that my father never lost that sad troubled look. There was some trouble about my stepmother's sons, too, for there was a great deal of argument between her and my father, of which I only heard snatches, and then one day they came home to stay with us. Something had happened at the school where they were that they could not stay any longer. I can remember distinctly the first night they ate dinner with us. It seemed to me that it was like a terrific thunderstorm that never quite broke. Everybody was trying to be nice and polite, but underneath it all there was a kind of lightning of all kinds of feelings, hurt feelings and wrong ones and right ones all mixed up.

"Only the two boys didn't seem to feel it much. They sort of took things for granted, as if that had always been their home, and they didn't act very polite. It seemed to trouble my father, who looked at them so severely that it almost choked me, and I couldn't go on eating my dinner. He didn't seem like my dear father when he looked like that. I always used to watch my father, and he seemed to make the day for me. If he was sad, then I was sad; and if he was glad then I was happy all over, until one day my stepmother noticed me and said: 'See, dear little Elizabeth is trembling. You ought not to speak that way before her, Charles.' And then father looked at me, and all suddenly I learned to smile when I didn't feel like it. I smiled back to him just to let him know it didn't matter what he did, I would love him anyhow!"

During the recital Reyburn had sat with courteous averted gaze as though he would not trouble her with more of his presence than was absolutely necessary. Now he gave her a swift glance.

Betty's eyes were off on distance, and she was talking from the depths of her heart, great tears welling into her eyes. All at once she remembered the stranger:

"I beg your pardon," she said, and brushed her hand across her eyes. "I haven't gone over it to any one ever, and I forgot you would not be interested in details."

"Please don't mind me. I am interested in every detail you are good enough to give me. It all makes the background of the truth, you know, and that is what I am after," said Reyburn, deeply touched. "I think you are wonderful to tell me all this. I shall regard it most sacredly."

Betty flashed a look of gratitude at him, and noticed the sympathy in his face. It almost unnerved her, but she went on:

"The oldest boy was named Bessemer, and he wasn't very good-looking. He was very tall and awkward, and always falling over things. He had little pale eyes, and hardly any chin. His teeth projected, too, and his hair was light and very straight and thin. His mother didn't seem to love him very much, even when he was a little boy. She bullied him and found fault with him continually, and quite often I felt very sorry for him, although I wasn't naturally attracted to him. He wasn't really unpleasant to me. We got along very nicely, although I never had much to do with him. There wasn't much to him.

"The other brother, Herbert, was handsome like his mother, only dark, with black curly hair, black wicked eyes, and a big, loose, cruel mouth. His mother just idolized him, and he knew it. He could make her do anything on earth. He used to force Bessemer into doing wrong things, too, things that he was afraid to do himself, because he knew father would not be so hard on Bessemer as on him. For father had taken a great dislike to Herbert, and it was no wonder. He seemed to have no idea at all that he was not owner of the house. He took anything he pleased for his own use, even father's most sacred possessions, and broke them in a fit of anger, too, sometimes, without ever saying he was sorry. He talked very disrespectfully of father and to him, and acted so to the servants that they gave notice and left. Every few days there would be a terrible time over something Herbert had done. Once I remember he went to the safe and got some money out that belonged to father and went off and spent it in some dreadful way that made father very angry. Of course I was still only a little girl, and I did not know all that went on. Father was very careful that I should not know. He guarded me more than ever, but he always looked sad when he came to kiss me good-night.

"Herbert took especial delight in tormenting me," she went on with a sad far-away look in her eyes as if she were recalling unpleasant memories. She did not see the set look on Reyburn's face nor notice his low exclamation of anger. She went steadily on: "He found out that I did not like June-bugs, and once he caught hundreds of them and locked me into a room with them with all the lights turned on. I was almost frightened to death, but it cured me of being afraid of June-bugs." A little smile trembled out on Betty's lips. "Just because I wouldn't give him the satisfaction of letting him hear me scream." She finished. "Then he caught a snake and put it in my room, and he put a lot of burdocks in my hat so they would get in my hair. Foolish things those were, of course, but he was a constant nightmare to me. Sometimes he would tie a wire across the passages in the upper hall where I had to pass to my room, and when I fell my hands went down against a lot of slimy toads in the dark, for he always somehow managed to have the light go out just as I fell. There were hundreds of things like that, but I needn't multiply them. That's the kind of boy he was. And because he discovered that my father loved me very much, and because he knew my father disliked him, he spent much time in trying to torment me in secret. I couldn't tell my father, because he always looked so sad whenever there was trouble, and there was sure to be trouble between him and my stepmother if my father found out that Herbert had done anything wrong. One day my father came upon us just as Herbert had caught me and was trying to cut my curls off. I didn't care about the curls, but I knew my father did. I began to scream. Herbert gripped me so I thought I would die with the pain, putting his big strong fingers around my throat and choking me so I could not make any noise."

Reyburn clenched his hands until the knuckles went white and uttered an exclamation, but Betty did not notice:

"There was a terrible time then, and I was sent away to a school, a good many miles from home, where I stayed for several years. Father always came up to see me every week end, for a few hours at least, and we had wonderful times together. Sometimes in vacation he would bring my stepmother along and she would bring me beautiful presents and smile and pet me, and say she missed me so much and she wished I would ask my father to let me come back and go to school in the city. But I never did, because I was afraid of Herbert. As I grew older I used to have an awful horror of him. But finally one vacation father and mother both came up and said they wanted me at home. My stepmother went to my room with me and told me I needn't be afraid of Herbert any more, that he was quite grown up and changed and would be good to me, and that it would please my father to have all his family together happily again. I believed her and I told father I would like to go. He looked very happy, and so I went home. Herbert had been away at school himself most of the time, and so had Bessemer, although they had been in trouble a good many times, so the servants told me, and had to change to new schools. They were both away when I got home. I had a very happy time for three weeks, only that I never saw father alone once. My stepmother was always there. But she was kind and I tried not to mind. Then all of a sudden one night I woke up and heard voices, and I knew that the boys were back from the camp to which they had been sent. I didn't sleep much the rest of the night, but in the morning I made up my mind that it was only a little while before I could go back to school, and I would be nice to the boys and maybe they wouldn't trouble me.

"I found that it was quite true that Herbert had grown up and changed. He didn't want to torment me any more, he wanted to make love to me, and I was only a child yet. I wasn't quite fifteen. It filled me with horror, and after he had caught me in the dark—he always loved to get people in the dark—and tried to kiss me, I asked father to let me go back to school at once. I can remember how sad he looked at me as if I had cut him to the heart when I asked him."

During this part of the tale Reyburn sat with stern countenance, his fingers clenched around the arms of the chair in which he sat, but he held himself quiet and listened with compressed lips, watching every expression that flitted across the sweet pale face.

"That was the last time I was at home with my father," she said, trying to control her quivering lips. "He took me back to school, and he came three times to see me, though not so often as before. The last time he said beautiful things to me about trying to live a right life and being kind to those about me, and he asked me to forgive him if he had ever done anything to hurt me in any way. Of course I said he hadn't. And then he said he hoped I wouldn't feel too hard at him for marrying again and bringing those boys into my life. I told him it was all right, that some day they would grow up and go away and he and I would live together again! And he said some awful words about them under his breath. But he asked me to forgive him again and kissed me and went away.

"He was taken very sick when he got home, and they never let me know until he was dead. Of course I went home to the funeral, but I didn't stay; I couldn't. I went back to school alone. My stepmother had been very kind, but she said she knew it was my father's wish that I should finish my school year. When vacation came she was traveling for her health. She wrote me a beautiful letter telling me how she missed me, and how much she needed me now in her bereavement, and how she hoped another summer would see us together; but she stayed abroad two years and the third year she went to California. I was sent to another school, and because I was not asked about it and there didn't seem anything else to do, I went. Every time I would suggest doing something else my stepmother would write and say how sorry she was she could not give her consent, but my father had left very explicit directions about me and she was only trying to carry out his wishes. She knew me well enough to be sure I would want to do anything he wished for me. And I did, of course."

Reyburn gave her a look of sympathy and getting up began to pace the little room.

CHAPTER XIV

"IT was not until last spring that she sent for me to come home," went on Betty, "and was very effusive about how much she needed me and how she was so much better, and meant to be a real mother to me now, helping me see the world and have a good time. She took me from one summer resort to another. Of course it was pleasant after having been shut up in school all those years, but she kept me close with her all the time, and I met only the people she chose to have me meet. All the time she kept talking about 'dear Herbert' and telling how wonderful he was and how he had grown to be 'such a dear boy.' Finally he arrived and began the very first evening he was with us to coax me to marry him. At first he was very courteous and waited upon me whenever I stirred, and I almost thought his mother was right about his being changed. But when I told him that I did not love him and could not ever marry him I caught a look on his face like an angry snarl, and I heard him tell his mother I was a crazy little fool, and that he would break my neck for me after he got me good and married. Then his mother began to come to me and cry and tell me how dear Herbert was almost heart-broken, that he would never lift up his head again, and that I would send him to ruin. It was simply awful, and I didn't know how to endure it. I began to wonder where I could go. Of course I had never been brought up to do anything, so I could not very well expect to go out into the world and make my living."

"Didn't you have any money at all?" interrupted Reyburn suddenly.

"Oh, yes," she said, looking up as if she had just remembered his presence. "I had always plenty of spending money, but if I went away where they couldn't find me, why, of course, I would have to give that up."

"Why, where did your money come from? Was it an allowance from your stepmother, or did your father leave it to you, or what?"

"I'm not just sure," said Betty, with troubled brow. "I never really knew much about the money affairs. When I asked, they always put me off and said that I was too young to be bothered with business yet, I would be told all about it when I came of age. My stepmother harped a great deal on keeping me young as long as possible. She said it was my father's wish that I should be relieved of all care until I came of age. But there were some trustees in Boston. I know that, because I had to write to them, about once or twice a year. My stepmother was most particular about that. I think they were old friends of my own mother, though I don't know when I learned that. Father told me once that mother had left me enough to keep me comfortably even without what he would leave me, so I'm sure I shall have enough to repay you if I could once get it."

"Don't worry about me!" he exclaimed. "It seems so terrible for you to have been alone in a situation like that! Wasn't there any one you could appeal to for help?"

"No, not any one whom I thought it would be right to tell. You see, in a way it was my father's honor. She was his wife, and I'm sure he loved her—at least at first—and she really was very good to me, except when it was a question of her son."

"I'm afraid I can't agree with you there!" he said sternly. "I think she was a clever actress. But excuse me. Go on, please."

"At last, when things had got so bad that I thought I must run away somewhere, my stepmother came into my room one morning and locked the door. She had been weeping, and she looked very sweet and pitiful. She said she had something to tell me. She had tried not to have to do it, for she was afraid it would grieve me and might make me have hard feelings against my father. I told her that was impossible. Then she told me that my father on his deathbed had called her to him and told her that it was his wish that I should marry one of her sons, and he wanted her to tell me. He felt that he had wronged them by hating them for my sake and he felt that I could make it all right by marrying one of them. My stepmother said that when she saw how infatuated dear Herbert was with me she hoped that she would be spared having to tell me, but now that I was treating him so she felt bound to deliver the message. Then she handed me a paper which said virtually the same thing which she had told me, and was signed by my father in his own handwriting."

"Was the paper written or printed?" interrupted Reyburn.

"I think it was typewritten, but the signature was papa's. There could be no mistake about that, and he wouldn't have signed something he didn't mean." Betty sighed as if it were a subject she had worn into her heart by much sorrowful thought.

"It might be quite possible for him to have done that under influence or delirium, or when he was too sick to realize."

"Oh, do you think so?" Betty caught at the hope. "It seems so awful to go against papa's last request."

"There is nothing awful but the idea of your being tied to that—beast!" said Reyburn with unexpected fervor. Betty looked at him gratefully and went on:

"I was simply appalled. I couldn't think, and I made my stepmother go away and leave me for a little while, but things got blacker and blacker and I thought I was going crazy. I couldn't marry Herbert even to please my father. The next day Bessemer arrived. He had been worrying his mother a lot about money, and when he arrived I couldn't help hearing what they said to him. They charged him with all sort of dreadful things. They called him a disgrace, and threatened to let him be arrested, and a great many more such things. Finally his mother ended up by telling him she never had loved him and that if he made any more trouble about money she would cut him off without a cent. I was sitting upstairs in my room with my windows open, and all their talk floated right up to me. It made me feel sick, and yet I felt sorry for Bessemer, for lately whenever he had been around he had been kind to me, and sometimes I had stayed near him to get rid of Herbert. We often talked over our troubles together and sympathized with one another. He felt sorry for me, but he was weak himself and couldn't see any way out for either of us.

"They had pretty stormy times all that day. Late in the afternoon Herbert and Bessemer went to their mother's room and were closeted with her for two hours, after which Herbert went away in the car with his suitcase and bags as if he were not coming back soon. I watched him from my window, and in great relief went down to take a little walk, for I had stayed closely in my room all day trying to plan what to do. One thing that held me from running away was that it would be such a disgrace to the family, and I knew my father would have felt it so keenly. That was always the great trouble when the boys got into scrapes at college, my father would groan and say he felt disgraced to be so conspicuous before the world. So I hesitated to do what would have been a sorrow to him had he been alive.

"Half an hour later I was sitting alone in the twilight on one of the porches, and Bessemer came out and sat down beside me.

"He looked so sort of homely and lonesome that I put my hand on his arm and told him I was awfully sorry for him, and suddenly he turned around and said:

"'Say, Betty, why don't you marry *me?* Then they can't say a word to either of us. Your father's wishes will be carried out and Herb'll have to whistle.'

"At first I was horrified, but we talked a long time about it, and he told me how lonely he had always been, and how nobody had ever loved him, and he knew he wasn't attractive, and all that; and then he said that if I married him we would go away and live by ourselves and he would let me do just as I wanted to. He wouldn't bother me about anything. If I didn't love him he would keep out of my sight, and things like that, till I got very sorry for him, and began to think that perhaps after all it was the best thing that would ever come for either of us. So I said I would.

"It surprised me a little that my stepmother took it so calmly when we told her. She cried a little, but did it very prettily, and kissed Bessemer, and told him he was fortunate. Then she kissed me and said I was a darling, and that she would be so happy if it only weren't for poor dear Herbert.

"But after that they began to rush things for a grand wedding, and I let them do it because I didn't see anything else in the world for me."

Betty raised her eyes and encountered the clear grave gaze of Reyburn fixed on her, and the color flew into her cheeks:

"I know you think I'm dreadful," she said, shrinking. "I've thought so myself a thousand times, but truly I didn't realize then what an awful thing it would be to marry a man I didn't love. I only wanted to hurry up and get it done before Herbert came home. They said he had been called away by important business and might be at home any day. I gave my consent to everything they wanted to do, and they fixed it all just as they pleased. One thing that happened upset me terribly. When the wedding invitations came home my stepmother carried them off to her room. I was too sad to pay much attention anyway. But the next morning I happened to be down in the kitchen looking over the papers that the maid had taken down from the waste baskets to search for a missing letter and there in the pile I found one of the invitations partly addressed and flung aside, and the invitation was still in the envelope. I pulled it out with a ghastly kind of curiosity to see how I looked on paper, and there it read, Mrs. Charles Garland Stanhope invites you to be present at the marriage of her daughter Elizabeth to *Mr. Herbert Hutton!*

"My heart just stood still. With the paper in my hand I rushed up to my stepmother's room and demanded to know what that meant. She smiled and said she was so sorry I had been annoyed that way, that that was a mistake, the invitations had come wrongly engraved and she had had to send them back and have them done over again. She was afraid I might be superstitious about it, so she hadn't told me. She was very gentle and sweet and tried to soothe me, and called me 'Betty,' the name my father always had for me, and at last I went back to my room feeling quite comfortable. She had said she always felt troubled for poor Bessemer, that nobody could love him right, he was so homely, and now I was going to make everything right by marrying him. She was going to try to forget what I had done to poor dear Herbert, and just be happy about Bessemer. She talked so nicely that I kissed her, a thing I hadn't done in years, not since she was first married to father. But somehow the shock of seeing Herbert's name on the invitation stayed with me, and I began to feel gloomier about it all and to wonder if perhaps I had done right. The last day I was terribly depressed and when I got to the church that night it suddenly came to me that perhaps after all I was not going to be free at all as I had hoped, but was just tying myself up to them all for life. I was thinking that as I walked up the aisle, and my throat had a big lump in it the way it always does when I am frightened, and then I looked up hoping a glimpse of poor Bessemer's face would steady me and he wasn't there at all! And right over me, waiting beside the minister, to marry me stood *Herbert!* My knees just gave way under me, and everything got black so I couldn't go on another step, nor even stand up. I had to drop. I wasn't unconscious as you all thought—I heard everything that went on, but I couldn't do anything about it.

"After they had carried me into the other room and given me things to drink, and I could get my breath again I saw it all clearly. Herbert hadn't given up at all. He meant to marry me anyway. He had had the invitations printed with his name on purpose and they probably hadn't been changed at all. Everybody in that great church out there was *expecting* me to marry Herbert Hutton, and I *was not going to do it!* I didn't quite know how I was going to stop it, but I knew I had to! You see I was brought up to think a great deal about what people would think of me if I did anything out of the usual, and it seemed to me I had disgraced myself forever by dropping down in the aisle. I knew Herbert well enough to be sure he would carry that wedding through now if he had to hold me up in his arms till the ceremony was over, and I was desperate. I would have given everything I had in the world if the floor had opened and swallowed me up then, but of course I knew wild thoughts like that wouldn't get me anywhere, so I just shut my eyes and tried to think of a way; and then I asked them all to go out a minute and let me be quiet. The doctor who had come out of the church told them to go. I shall always bless that man, whoever he was! Then when they were gone I opened a door that had a key in it, and I locked it behind me and ran away down some stairs and out a passage that led to the street. That girl, Jane Carson, was passing and she put her own coat on me and took me to her room and sent me here. Oh, it's been so good to get here! Do you think they can take me away against my will?"

"Certainly not!" said the young man. "Not without some foul play, but I don't intend to give them any chance for that. By the way, when do you come of age?"

"In three weeks," said Betty, looking troubled. "Why, would I be safe after I was of age?"

"You certainly would not be under their guardianship any longer," said the young lawyer, "and they would have no right to control your actions, unless of course you were incapacitated somehow and unfit to manage your own affairs."

Betty looked troubled.

"I've thought sometimes, ever since I saw that paper in which they hinted that I was temporarily insane, that they might try to shut me up in an insane asylum. Herbert wouldn't stop at anything. Could he do that?"

"They would have to get a doctor to swear that you were mentally unsound," said Reyburn, looking troubled. "Does he really love you, do you think or does he only want to get you in his power for some reason?"

"It is more like that," said Betty sorrowfully, "he couldn't really love anybody but himself."

"Well, don't you worry. I'm going at the case at once, and I'll put those people where they'll have to walk a chalk line before many hours are over. The first thing I must do is to see those trustees of yours. Can you give me the names and addresses?"

He got out his fountain pen, and Betty told him all he wanted to know, that is, all she knew herself, and then suddenly it was train time and he hurried away. On the steps he paused and said in a low tone:

"Are you perfectly comfortable with these people for a few days until I can get you better accommodations where you will be safe?"

"Entirely," said Betty eagerly. "I wouldn't want to go elsewhere."

"But it must be very hard for one like you to be thrown constantly with illiterate, uncultured people."

Betty smiled dreamily:

"I don't think they are exactly uncultured," she said slowly. "They—well, you see, they make a friend of God, and somehow I think that makes a difference. Don't you think it would?"

"I should think it would," said Warren Reyburn reverently with a light in his eyes. "I think, perhaps, if you don't mind my saying it, that you, too, have been making a friend of God."

"I've been trying to," said Betty softly, with a shy glow on her face that he remembered all the way back to the city.

CHAPTER XV

CANDACE CAMERON paced her little gabled room restively, with face growing redder and more excited at every step. For several weeks now she had been virtually a prisoner—albeit a willing enough one—in the house of Stanhope. But the time had come when she felt that she must do something.

She had gone quietly enough about a proscribed part of the house, doing little helpful things, making herself most useful to the madam, slipping here and there with incredible catlike tread for so plump a body, managing to overhear important conversations, and melting away like a wraith before her presence was discovered. She had made herself so unobtrusive as to be almost forgotten by all save the maid Marie, who had been set to watch her; and she had learned that if she went to bed quite early in the evening, Marie relaxed her watch and went down to the servants' quarters, or even sometimes went out with a lover for a while, that is, if the madam herself happened to be out also. On several such occasions she had made valuable tours of investigation through the madam's desk and private papers.

That she was overstepping her privileges as a servant in the house went without saying, but she silenced her Scotch conscience, which until this period of her existence had always kept her strictly from meddling with other people's affairs, by declaring over and over again to herself that she was doing perfectly right because she was doing it for the sake of "that poor wee thing that was being cheated of her rights."

Several weeks had passed since her sudden re-establishment in the family, and the reports of Betty, so hastily readjusted and refurbished to harmonize with the newspaper reports, had not been any more satisfying. Mrs. Stanhope had explained to the servants the day after the excitement that Miss Betty had become temporarily deranged, and later that she had escaped from the private hospital where she had been taken, and they were doing all in their power to find her. In reply to Candace's gimlet-like questions she had given the name of a hospital where she said Betty had been taken at first, and everything seemed altogether plausible. But as the days went by and the horror of her absence grew into the soul of the lonely woman whose care Betty had been for years, Candace became more and more restive and suspicious. It was these suspicions which sent her on her investigations, and made her uncannily wise to pry open secret locks and cover all trace of her absence after she had gleaned what knowledge she sought.

On this particular evening her excitement was due to having come across some correspondence bearing the signature of a man to whom a certain letter had been addressed, which had been entrusted to her charge by Betty's dying father and taken from her by his wife. For years she had been worried about that, and yet she had no absolute reason to doubt that the madam had not sent it to its destination, except as she knew its contents and read Mrs. Stanhope's character beneath the excellent camouflage. But to-night, even the briefest glance through the bundle of letters showed plainly that those men in Boston never knew the master's wishes, or at least, if they knew them, they were utterly disregarding them.

Aroused on one point, her suspicions began to extend further. Where was Betty? Did her stepmother know, and was she somewhere suffering, alone, perhaps being neglected because she had not done as they wanted her to do? If the stepmother was capable of destroying a letter, was she perhaps not also capable of putting Betty out of the way? There were points of detail which of course did not harmonize with any such theory as this. Candace was no logician, but she was keen enough to feel that something was wrong. As for that theory of Betty's insanity she scouted it with a harsh laugh whenever it was mentioned in her hearing. Betty—keen, sweet, trusting little Betty *insane!* Nonsense! It was unthinkable. If she was in an asylum anywhere she was there without warrant, and it behoved her faithful old nurse to find a way out for her. This she meant to do against all odds, for she was thoroughly aroused now.

She went to the window and looked down into the lighted street. Over there not four blocks away rose the steeple of the church where Betty had gone to be married! Around the corner was the great brick pile of the hospital where her stepmother said she had been taken from the church, and from which she was believed by the other servants to have escaped.

Standing thus looking out into the light-starred city, Candace began to form a plan, her plump tightly garmented chest rising and falling excitedly as she thought it all out. It was up to her to find out what had become of Betty. But how was she to get away without being suspected? Somehow she must do it. She knew perfectly the address that had been on that letter. She had written it down carefully from memory as soon as it had been taken away from her. She must go to Boston and find that man to whom it had been written, and discover whether he had ever received it. But she could not go until she found out certainly whether or not Betty had ever really escaped from the hospital. Who knew but that she was shut up there yet, and the madam telling this tale all about and advertising with a five thousand dollar reward! In the movies, too! Such a disgrace on the family! How the master would have writhed at the publicity of his beloved daughter—"poor wee thing!"

Candace turned from the window with her lips set, and tiptoeing to the door, listened. Yes, it was Aileen who was coming lightly up the stairs, singing in a low tone. It was Aileen's evening out. That meant that Marie would be more than usually active on the upper floor. She must manage it before Aileen left and Marie was called upstairs, or there would be no opportunity to get away without Marie seeing her.

Hastily she gathered her silk dress, her cloak and her apoplectic hat into a bundle with her purse and her gloves, and tied them into an old apron, with the strings hanging free. Then stealthily opening the window, she dropped them out into the kitchen area below, close to the region of the ash cans. It was a risk, of course, but one must take some chances, and the servants would all be in the kitchen just now, laughing and talking. They would scarcely have heard it fall.

She listened a tense instant, then closed the window, and possessing herself of a few little things, gathered hastily about the room, which she could stuff in her pockets, she opened her door softly, closed it behind her, and trotted off down the stairs just as if she were going about her ordinary duty. Listening a minute outside the kitchen door she slipped stealthily down the cellar stairs, and tiptoed over to the area door where the ashman took out the ashes. Softly slipping the bolt she opened the door and drew in her bundle. Then standing within, she quickly slipped the black silk over her housemaid's gown, donned her coat and hat and gloves, and sallied forth. A moment more and she was in the next street with the consciousness that she "might have done the like any time sooner, if she'd wanted, in spite of that little spy-cat Marie."

"If I want to go back I'll just say I went after my insurance book," she chuckled to herself as she sped down the street in the direction of the hospital.

Arrived at the big building she asked to see the list of patients taken in on the day of Betty's wedding, and succeeded in getting a pretty accurate description of each one, sufficient at least to satisfy her that Betty was not among them. Then she asked a few more bold questions, and came away fully convinced that Betty had never been in that hospital.

By this time it was nine o'clock, and she meant to take the evening train for Boston, which left, she was sure, somewhere near midnight. She took a trolley to her old lodgings where she had been since Mrs. Stanhope had sent her away the first time, and hastily packed a small hand bag with a few necessities, made a few changes in her garments, then went to see a fellow lodger whom she knew well, and where she felt sure she could easily get a check cashed, for she had a tidy little bank account of her own, and was well known to be reliable.

Having procured the necessary funds, she made her way to the station and found that she had still an hour to spare before the Boston train left.

Settled down at last in the back seat of a common car, she made herself as comfortable as her surroundings would allow, and gave herself up to planning the campaign that was before her.

Canny Candace did not go at once to the office of the brothers, James and George McIntyre, though she looked them up in the telephone book the very first thing when the train arrived in Boston even before she had had a bite to eat, and her cup of tea which meant more to her than the "bite." She reasoned that they would be busy in the early hours and not be able to give her their undivided attention. She had not lived out all her life for nothing. She knew the ways of the world, and she had very strict ideas about the best ways of doing everything. So it happened that when she was at last shown into the office of the McIntyres, Warren Reyburn who had traveled to Boston on the sleeper of the same train that she had taken the night before, was just arising from an earnest conference with the two men. With her first glance, as the three emerged from the inner office, Candace saw that the two elder gentlemen were much disturbed and it flitted through her mind that she had come at an inopportune moment. Then her quick eye took in the younger man and her little alert head cocked to one side with a questioning attitude. Where had she seen him before? Candace had the kind of a mind that kept people and events card-indexed even to the minutest detail, and it didn't take many seconds for her to place Warren Reyburn back in the church at the wedding, standing against the wall with his arms folded. She had noticed him particularly because he was so courteous to a little old lady who came in too late to get a seat. She had studied him as he stood there, waiting for the wedding march, and she had thought how handsome he looked and how fine it would have been if her wee Betty had been getting a man like that in place of the weak-faced Bessemer Hutton. She had watched to see who he was with, and felt deep satisfaction when she noticed him lean over and speak to Mrs. Bryce Cochrane as if he belonged to her. He wasn't her husband, because she knew Mr. Cochrane, who had been a favorite with Mr. Stanhope and much at the house. This man might be Mrs. Cochrane's brother "or the likes," and she had pleased herself watching him till Betty arrived and took all her thoughts. So now she stood with her little round head in its hectic hat tilted interestedly to one side, watching, ears on the keen to catch any word, for all the world like a "bit brown sparrow" saucily perched on another man's window, where it really had no right to be.

At last one of the McIntyre's shook hands gravely with the younger man, and the other one attended him to the door, talking in low tones. The McIntyre thus set at liberty, turned questioningly toward the stranger, who was not slow in getting to her feet and coming forward.

"You will maybe be Mr. James McIntyre?" she asked, lifting her sea-blue eyes set in her apple-red face, and fixing her firm little lips in dignity. Candace was a servant and knew her place, but she felt the importance of her mission, and meant to have no disrespect done to it.

"I am Mr. George McIntyre," the gentleman replied, and, indicating the man at the door, "Mr. James McIntyre will be at liberty in a moment, but perhaps I will do as well?"

Candace cocked a glance toward the elderly back at the door; and then returned her look to Mr. George:

"You'll maybe be knowing Mr. Charles Stanhope?" she propounded, as if she were giving him a riddle, and her blue eyes looked him through and through:

"Oh, surely, surely! He was a very close friend! You—knew him?"

"I was Miss Betty's nurse who cooked the griddle cakes for you the morning after the funeral——" she said, and waited with breathless dignity to see how he would take it.

"Oh! Is that so!" He beamed on her kindly. "Yes, yes, I remember those cakes. They were delicious! And what can I do for you? Just sit down. Why, bless me, I don't know but that your coming may be very opportune! Can you tell me anything of Miss Betty?"

Candace pressed her lips together with a knowing smile as much as to say she might tell volumes if it were wise, and she cast a glance at the other brother who was shaking hands now with his visitor and promising to meet him a little later:

"Yon man'll be knowing a bit, too, I'll be thinking," she hazarded nodding toward Reyburn as he left. "He was at the wedding, I'm most sure——!"

The elder McIntyre gave her a quick glance and signalled to his brother to come near:

"This is Miss Stanhope's nurse, the one who cooked breakfast for us at the time of the funeral," he said, and to Candace, "This is Mr. James McIntyre."

Candace fixed him with another of her inquisitive little glances:

"I've some bit papers put by that I thought ye might like to see," she said with a cautious air. "I've kept them fer long because I thought they might be wanted sometime, yet I've never dared bring them to your notice before lest I would be considered meddlin', and indeed I wasn't sure but you had them already. Will you please to look over them papers and see if you've ever seen them before?" She drew forth an envelope from her bag and handed it to them. "It's a bit letter that Mr. Stanhope wrote the day he was dyin' an' then copied and give to me to mail, and his lady took it away, sayin' she would attend to it. What I want to know is, did ye ever get the letter? If ye did it's all right and none of my business further, an' I'll go on my way back home again and think no more about it; but if ye didn't then there it is, an' you ought to see it, that's sure!"

The two men drew eagerly together and studied the trembling lines:

"It's his writing all right," murmured one, under his breath, and the brother nodded gravely:

"You say that this was the original of a letter that was given to you to mail to us?"

Candace nodded.

"It's what he wrote first, and got ink on it, an' then wrote it over. I can't say what changes he made, as I didn't read it, but this he gave to me to burn, and before I gets it burned my lady comes in and takes the letter from me while he was sleepin'; and so I hid the bit papers, thinkin' they might be a help to wee Betty sometime. And oh, can ye tell me anything of my little Lady Betty? Is she safe? Did she come to you for refuge? You needn't be afraid to tell me. I'll never breathe a word——!"

The two brothers exchanged quick glances of warning and the elder man spoke:

"My good woman, we appreciate your coming, and these papers may prove very useful to us. We hope to be able to clear up this matter of Miss Stanhope's disappearance very soon. She did not come to us, however, and she is not here. But if you will step into the room just beyond and wait for a little while we may be able to talk this matter over with you."

Very courteously he ushered the plump, apprehensive little woman into the next room and established her in an easy leather chair with a quantity of magazines and newspapers about her, but she kept her little head cocked anxiously on one side, and watched the door like a dog whose master has gone in and shut the way behind him; and she never sat back in her chair nor relaxed one iota during the whole of the two hours that she had to wait before she was called at last to the inner office where she found the handsome young man whom she remembered seeing at the wedding.

She presently found that Reyburn was as keen as he was handsome, but if she hadn't remembered him at the wedding as a friend of that nice Mrs. Cochrane, she never would have made it as easy as she did for him to find out things from her, for she could be canny herself on occasion if she tried, and she did not trust everybody.

CHAPTER XVI

THE mysterious disappearance of Candace from the Stanhope house caused nothing short of a panic. Herbert and his mother held hourly wrangles, and frantically tried one thing and then another. Day after day the responses came in from the advertisements they had caused to be put forth. Everyone was hot-foot for the reward, but so far little of encouragement had been brought out. More and more the young man was fixing his mind on the idea that Candace had something to do with Betty's disappearance, so he was leaving no stone unturned to find the nurse as well as the girl. To this end he insisted on seeing personally and cross-examining every person who came claiming to have a clue to the lost girl.

That morning, at about the same hour when Candace walked into the office of the McIntyre Brothers in Boston, James, the butler, much against his dignity, was ushering a curious person into the presence of the son of the house. James showed by every line of his noble figure that he considered this duty beneath his dignity, and that it was only because the occasion was unusual that he tolerated it for a moment, but the man who ambled observantly behind him, stretching his neck to see everything that was to be seen in this part of the great house, that he might tell about it at the fire-house, failed to get the effect. He was wondering why in thunder such rich people as these seemed to be, couldn't afford carpets big enough to cover their whole floors, instead of just having skimpy little bits of pieces dropped around here and there, that made you liable to skid all over the place if you stepped on one of them biasly.

Herbert Hutton lifted his head and watched Abijah Gage slouch into the room. He measured him keenly and remained silent while Abijah opened up. There had been many other applicants for that reward that day, with stories cunningly woven, and facts, substantiated by witnesses, in one case a whole family brought along to swear to the fabrication; but as yet Herbert had not found a promising clue to his missing bride, and the time was going by. In a few days it would be too late, and his undisciplined spirit raged within him. It was not only his bride he wanted, it was her fortune, which was worth any trouble he might take; and every day, every hour, every minute now, it was slipping, slipping, slipping from his eager grasp.

Abijah was a little overawed in the presence of this insolent man of the world, but he felt he had, for almost the first time in his life, Truth on his side, and he was strong in the power of it. With a cunning equal to the one that matched him he dealt out his information bit by bit, giving only enough at a time to make his victim sure it was the real thing this time; and then he halted stubbornly and would say no more until that five thousand dollars was signed and sealed over to him. They had a long argument, but in the end Bi won, and was given certain documents which he was satisfied would stand in court. A little later the telephone in Reyburn's office rang sharply, and when Jimmie Ryan responded a voice that he had never heard before asked for Mr. Warren Reyburn.

"He's out of town," Jimmie replied.

"How soon will he be back?" The voice was like a snarl.

"I'm not quite sure. He's called to Boston on business," swelled Jimmie loyally.

An oath ripped over the wire, and Jimmie raged within and quailed. Was his idol then losing a great case?

"He might be back in a few hours," insinuated Jimmie. "Who shall I say called up if he should have me over long distance?"

"You needn't say anybody! I'll call up again," growled the voice, and the man hung up.

Jimmie sat for a long time in blissful reverie. "He's getting there!" he whispered to himself. "He'll get the big cases yet, and I can keep my first place. I must see Jane to-night and tell her."

Meanwhile, back at Tinsdale improvements had been going on at the Carsons'. Bob, always handy with tools, had been putting in a tank over the bathtub. They had one at the house on the hill, only it was run by a windmill. Bob had a friend who was a plumber's son, and from him had obtained some lengths of second-hand water-pipe and an old faucet. He had conceived the idea of a tank on the roof, and his first plan had been only a rainwater tank, but gradually as his vision widened he included a force pump in the outfit of desires. He hung around the plumber's until they unearthed an old force pump somewhat out of repair, and for a few days' assisting the plumber Bob acquired it, together with after-hour help to put it into operation. The next object was a tank, which seemed at first to represent the impossible; but the grocer at last offered a suggestion in the shape of several large empty hogsheads which he readily accepted at the price of four Saturdays' work in the store.

All Bob's extra time was put into these improvements, and he was as excited every night when it grew dark and he was forced to come to supper because he couldn't see any longer to work, as if he had been building an airship.

The day the hogsheads were marshaled and connected and the force pump sent its first stream into them was a great occasion. The family assembled in the yard, with Elise Hathaway, who had been allowed to come over for a few minutes with Betty. Bob and his plumber friend pumped, and Emily climbed to the attic window, which overlooked the row of hogsheads, ranged so that the water would flow from one to the other, and acted as pilot to the new enterprise. As the first stream from the force pump, which Bob had lavishly painted red, crept its way up the pipes and began to wet the bottom of the first and highest hogshead Emily gave a little squeal of delight and shouted "It's come! It's come! The water's come!" and the family below fairly held their breath with the wonder of it. Not that such a thing could be, but that their own freckled, grinning Bob should have been able to achieve it.

There was an elaborate system of tin conductors which conveyed the waste water from the bathtub out through a hole in the wall of the little laundry bathroom, and distributed it along the garden beds wherever its controller desired to irrigate. Thus the system became practical as well as a luxury. There was also an arrangement of gutter pipes for carrying off any surplus water from the hogsheads, so saving the Carson house from possible inundation at any time of heavy storms.

After the plumbing was finished Bob painted the laundry neatly inside with beautiful white paint and robin's-egg blue for the ceiling, and Betty told him it almost made one think of going swimming in the ocean. Next he began to talk about a shower bath. Betty told him what one was like and he began to spend more days down at the plumber's asking questions and picking up odd bits of pipe, making measurements, and doing queer things to an old colander for experiment's sake. The day that Warren Reyburn came for the first time Bob had the shower part finished and ready to erect, and the next day saw it complete with a rod for the rubber curtain that Betty had promised to make for him. He and she were planning how they would make further improvements on the house before Jane and Nellie should come home for their summer vacation week. Betty had thoroughly entered into the life of the little household now, and was a part of it. She saved her own small wages, and grudged all she had to spend for necessary clothes, that she might contribute further to the comfort and beauty of the general home.

After Warren Reyburn's visit the last barrier between Betty and Ma seemed to be broken down. As soon as she had closed the door she flew into the other room and flung her arms around Ma's neck, bursting into soft weeping on her motherly shoulder. Ma had done a rapid turning act when she heard her coming, for in truth she had been peeping behind the green window-shade to watch the handsome stranger go down the street, but she would have dropped the iron on her foot and pretended to be picking it up rather than let Betty suspect her interest in the visitor.

"Oh, mother," she murmured in Mrs. Carson's willing ear, "I have been so frightened——"

"I know, dearie!" soothed the mother, quite as if she had been her own. "I know!"

"But he was very kind," she said lifting her head with an April effect of tears. "He's going to try to fix things for me so that I don't need ever to be afraid of any one making trouble for me any more. You see, I sort of ran away. There was somebody I was afraid of who troubled me a great deal."

"Yes, dearie, I thought as much," said Ma. "Jane kind of gave me to understand there was something like that. I'm real glad there's somebody goin' to look into your affairs an' fix things right for you. I knew you was restless an' worried. Now it'll get all straightened out. He's got a nice face. I trusted him first off. He's a church member, an' that's somethin'. They ain't all spiritual, but they're mostly clean an' just an' kindly, when they're anythin' at all but just plain hypocrites, which, thank the Lord, there ain't so many as some would have us believe. Now wash your face, dearie, an' run back to your place so you can come home early, for we're goin' to have the old hen with dumplin's for supper to celebrate."

That was one charming thing about that household: they celebrated every blessed little trifle that came into their lives, so that living with them was like a procession of beautiful thanksgivings.

It was while Betty was eating the gala "hen," delicious in its festive gravy and dumplings, that she looked off across the little dining-room to the dark window with its twinkling village lights in the distance and thought of the stranger. A dark fear flashed across her sweet face and sparkled in the depths of her eyes for just an instant. Was it perhaps the distant bay of the hounds on her trail, coming nearer every moment? Then she remembered the heavenly Father and her new-found faith, and turned back to the cheery little room and the children's pleasant clatter, resolved to forget the fear and to trust all to Him who cared for her. Perhaps he had sent the pleasant stranger, and the thought brought a quiet little smile to settle about her lips. She laughed with Bob and Emily at how they had got wet with a sudden unexpected shower from the new bath while they were arranging the curtain on the rod, and Emily had turned the faucet on without knowing it. The patient-eyed mother watched them all and was satisfied.

How good it is that we cannot hear all the noises of the earth at the same time, nor know of every danger that lurks near as we are passing by! We grumble a great deal that God does not send us as much as we think he might, but we give scarce a thought to our escape from the many perils, lying close as our very breath, of which we never even dream.

At that moment, as they sat quietly eating their happy meal, a deadly particular peril was headed straight for Tinsdale.

Abijah Gage and Herbert Hutton boarded the evening train for Tinsdale together and entered the sleeper. Abijah shuffled behind, carrying the bags, a most extraordinary and humiliating position for him. He had never been known to carry anything, not even himself if he could help it, since the day his mother died and ceased to force him to carry in wood and water for her at the end of a hickory switch. He glanced uneasily round with a slight cackle of dismay as he arrived in the unaccustomed plush surroundings and tried to find some place to dump his load. But the well-groomed Herbert strode down the long aisle unnoticing and took possession of the section he had secured as if he owned the road.

"You can sit there!" he ordered Bi with a condescending motion, dropping into his own seat and opening a newspaper.

Bi sat down on the edge of the seat, and held on to the arm in a gingerly way as if he were afraid to trust himself to anything so different. He looked furtively up and down the car, eyed the porter, who ignored him contemptuously and finally came back and demanded his sleeper ticket with a lordliness that Bi did not feel he could take from a negro. But somehow the ticket got tangled in his pocket, and Bi had a hard time finding it, which deepened his indignation at the porter.

"I ain't takin' no sass from no one. My seat's paid fer all right," he said distinctly for the enlightenment of the other passengers, and Herbert Hutton reached out a discreet arm and dropped something in the porter's hand which sent him on his way and left Bi snorting audibly after him.

"You'd better shut up!" growled the dictator to Bi. "We don't want to be conspicuous, you know. If you can't hold your tongue and act as if you had ever traveled before, I'll get off this train at the next station and you can whistle for your reward. Do you understand?"

Bi dropped his toothless lower jaw a trifle and his little eyes grew narrow. This was no way to manage affable Bi. He loved a good visit, and he had counted on one all the way to Tinsdale. He had no idea of sitting silent.

"I understand," he drawled, "an' I'll be gormed ef I'll agree. I ain't told you yet where we get off, an' I don't have to ef I don't wantta. Ef you can't treat me like a gen'l'man you know where you can get off, an' I ain't havin' to state it."

Herbert Hutton drew his arrogant brows in a frown of annoyance, and whirled around to placate his guide:

"Now see here, you old popinjay, what's got into you?"

"No, sir, I ain't nobody's papa," babbled Bi, seeing he had scored a point. "I have enough to do to support myself without any family."

"That's all right, have it your own way, only shut up or we'll have somebody listening. Have a cigar. Take two. But you can't smoke 'em in here, you'll have to go to the smoking-room. Wait! I'll see if we can get the drawing-room."

The porter appeared and the change was effected, to the great disappointment of Bi, who kept continually poking his head out to get a glimpse of the fine ladies. He would much have preferred staying out in the main car and getting acquainted with people. His cunning had departed with the need. He had put things in the hands of this surly companion, and now he meant to have a good time and something to tell the gang about when he got home.

About midnight the train drew into a station and Herbert Hutton roused himself and looked out of the window. Bi, whose cunning had returned, followed his example. Suddenly he leaned forward excitedly and tapped the glass with a long finger:

"That's him! That's the guy," he whispered excitedly as another train drew in and passengers began to hurry down the platform and across to the waiting sleeper.

"Are you sure?"

"Sartin!"

"You mean the one with the coat over his arm, and the two men behind?" He stopped short with an exclamation.

Bi looked up cunningly. Now what was up? He saw a thunder-cloud on the face of his companion.

With embellishments Herbert Hutton asked if Bi had ever seen the two tall gray-haired men who were walking with their prey.

Bi narrowed his eyes and denied any knowledge, but perceived there were more sides than two to the enigma. Now, what could he figure out of those two guys? Were there more rewards to be offered? If so, he was a candidate. He wondered what chance there was of getting away from H. H. and sauntering through the train. He found, however, a sudden willingness on the part of his companion to vanish and let him do the scout work for the rest of the night.

With a sense of being on a vacation and a chance at catching big fish Bi swung out through the train. Bumping down among the now curtained berths, adjusting his long form to the motion of the express, lurching to right and to left as they went round a curve, falling over an occasional pair of shoes and bringing down lofty reproaches from the sleepy porter, he penetrated to the day coaches and at last located his quarry.

They were sitting in a double seat, the younger man facing the two older ones, and had evidently been unable to get sleepers. Bi hung around the water-cooler at the far end of the car until he had laid out his plans; then he sauntered up to the vacant seat behind the three men and dropped noiselessly into its depths, drawing his hat down well over his face, and apparently falling into instant slumber, with a fair sample of Tinsdale snoring brought in at moderate distances.

The conversation was earnest, in well-modulated voices, and hard to follow connectedly, for the men knew how to talk without seeming to the outside world to be saying anything intelligible. Occasionally a sentence would come out clear cut in an interval of the rhythm of the train, but for the most part Bi could make little or nothing of it.

"In all the years we've been trustees of that estate we haven't seen her but twice," said one of the older men; "once at her father's second marriage, and again at his funeral. Then we only saw her at a distance. Her stepmother said she was too grief-stricken to speak with any one, and it was by the utmost effort she could be present at the service."

"She looked very frail and young," said the other old man; "and her hair—I remember her hair!"

Bi changed his position cautiously and tried to peer over the back of his seat, but the voices were crowded together now, and the younger man was talking earnestly. He could not catch a syllable. "Trustees!" That word stayed with him. "Estate" was another promising one, and the fact that her hair had been remembered. He nodded his old head sagaciously, and later when the three men settled back in their seats more comfortably with their eyes closed he slid back to the water-cooler and so on through the sleeper to the drawing-room.

Hutton was sleeping the sleep of the unjust, which means that he woke at the slightest breath, and Bi's breath was something to wake a heavier sleeper. So they sat and planned as the train rushed on through the night. Now and again Bi took a pilgrimage up to the day coach and back to report the three travelers still asleep.

About six o'clock in the morning the train slowed down, and finally came to a thrashing halt, waking the sleepers uncomfortably and making them conscious of crunching feet in the cinders outside, and consulting voices of trainmen busy with a hammer underneath the car somewhere. Then they drowsed off to sleep again and the voices and hammering blended comfortably into their dreams.

The passengers in the day coach roused, looked at their watches, stretched their cramped limbs, squinted out to see if anything serious was the matter, and settled into a new position to sleep once more.

Bi, stretched for the nonce upon the long couch of the drawing-room while his superior occupied the more comfortable berth, roused to instant action, slipped out to the platform and took his bearings. He had lived in that part of the country all his life and he knew where they ought to be by that time. Yes, there was the old saw mill down by Hague's Crossing, and the steeple over by the soft maple grove just beyond Fox Glove. It would not be a long walk, and they had a garage at Fox Glove!

He sauntered along the cinder path; discovered that the trouble with the engine was somewhat serious, requiring to wait for help, took a glimpse into the day coach ahead to assure himself that the three men were still safely asleep, and sauntered back to the drawing-room.

His entrance roused the sleeper, who was on the alert instantly.

"Say, we got a hot box an' a broken engyne!" Bi announced. "It'll take us some time. We ain't fur from Fox Glove. We could santer over an' git a car an' beat 'em to it!"

"We could?" said Hutton. "You sure? No chances, mind you!"

"Do it easy. Those guys are asleep. They won't get to the Junction 'fore ten o'clock, mebbe later, an' they can't possibly get to our place 'fore 'leven."

"Lead the way!" ordered Hutton, cramming himself into his coat and hat.

"Better slide down on the other side," whispered Bi as they reached the platform. "We kin go back round the train an' nobody'll notice."

As if they were only come out to see what was the matter they idled along the length of the train around out of sight, slid down the bank, took a shortcut across a meadow to a road, and were soon well on their way to Fox Glove in the early cool of the spring morning, a strangely mated couple bent on mischief.

Back on the cinder track the express waited, dreamily indifferent, with a flagman ahead and behind to guard its safety, and while men slept the enemy took wings and flew down the white morning road to Tinsdale, but no one ran ahead with a little red flag to the gray cottage where slept Betty, to warn her, though perchance an angel with a flaming sword stood invisibly to guard the way.

CHAPTER XVII

BOB had just finished feeding the chickens when the automobile drew up at the door, and he hurried around the house to see who it might be. He was rather looking for the return of that nice lawyer again. He felt the family expected him some time soon. Perhaps he would be to breakfast and mother would want some fresh eggs.

They had dropped Bi at the edge of the village and there were only Hutton and the driver who had brought them. Bi had no mind to get mixed up in this affair too openly. He valued his standing in his home town, and did not wish to lose it. He had an instinct that what he was doing might make him unpopular if it became known. Besides, he had another ax to grind.

Bob did not like the looks of the strange dark man who got out of the car and came into the yard with the air of a thrashing machine bolting into whatever came in his way. He stood sturdily and waited until he was asked who lived there, and admitted with a stingy "yes" that it was Mrs. Carson's house. A thundering knock on the front door followed, and the other man in the car got out and came into the yard behind the first.

"Well, you needn't take the door down," snapped Bob, and scuttled around the house to warn his mother, aware that he had been rude, and glad of it.

It was Betty who came to the door, for Ma was frying bacon and eggs for breakfast, and Bob hadn't been quite soon enough. She started back with a scream, and eluding the hand that reached for her arm, fairly flew back to the kitchen, taking refuge behind Mrs. Carson, with her eyes wild with fear and her hand on her heart, while Hutton strode after her.

Mrs. Carson wheeled around with her knife in her hand and faced him:

"What do you mean by coming into my house this way, I'd like to know?" she demanded angrily, putting her arm around Betty.

"I beg your pardon," said Hutton, a poor apology for courtesy slipping into his manner. "I don't suppose you know it, but that is my wife you are harboring there, and she ran away from home several months ago! I have just discovered her whereabouts and have come to take her away!"

Ma straightened up with the air of a queen and a judge, while Betty stifled a scream and in a small voice full of terror cried: "It isn't true, Mrs. Carson, it isn't true! Oh, *mother*, don't let him take me!"

Mrs. Carson pushed Betty behind her, the knife still in her other hand, and answered with dignity:

"You've made a big mistake, Mr. Herbert Hutton; this isn't your wife at all. I know all about you."

Hutton put on a look of instant suavity.

"Oh, of course, madam, she has told you that, but I'm sorry to have to tell you that she is not in her right mind. She made her escape from the insane asylum."

"Oh, rats!" shouted Bob, and vanished out the kitchen door, slamming it behind him.

Emily, frightened and white, stood just outside, and he nearly knocked her over in his flight. He pulled her along with him, whispering in her ear excitedly:

"You beat it down to the fire gong and hit it for all you're worth! Quick!"

Emily gave him one frightened look and sprang to action. Her little feet sped down the path to the lot where hung the big fire gong, like two wild rabbits running for their life, and in a moment more the loud whang of alarm rang through the little town, arousing the "gang" and greatly disconcerting Bi, who was craning his neck at the station and watching the fast-growing speck down the railroad track. That sure was the train coming already. How had they made it so soon?

But Bob was on his stomach in the road scuttling the ship that was to have carried away the princess. The chauffeur was fully occupied in the house, for he had been ordered to follow and be ready to assist in carrying away an insane person, and he had no thought for his car at present. It was an ugly job, and one that he didn't like, but he was getting big pay, and such things had to be done.

Bob's knife was sharp. He always kept it in good condition. It did many of the chores about the house, and was cunning in its skill. It cut beautiful long punctures in the four tires, until there was no chance at all of that car's going on its way for some time to come. Then he squirmed his way out on the opposite side from the house, slid along by the fence to the side door, around to the back like a flash and without an instant's hesitation hauled up his elaborate system of drainage. He stuck the longest conductor pipe through the open window of the old laundry, clutched at the sill and swung inside, drawing the pipe in after him.

The altercation in the kitchen had reached white heat. Hutton's suavity was fast disappearing behind a loud angry tone. He had about sized up Ma and decided to use force.

It was a tense moment when Bob, his hasty arrangements made, silently swung open the laundry door in full range of the uninvited guests and waited for the psychological moment. Mrs. Carson had dropped her knife and seized the smoking hot frying-pan of bacon as a weapon. She was cool and collected, but one could see in her eyes the little devil of battle that sometimes sat in Bob's eyes as she swung the frying-pan back for a blow. Suddenly out flashed a cold steel eye, menacing, unanswerable, looking straight into her own.

At that instant, unannounced and unobserved, through the laundry door lumbered a long ugly tin conductor pipe, and the deluge began. Straight into the eyes of the would-be husband it gushed, battering swashingly down on the cocked revolver, sending it harmlessly to the floor, where it added to the confusion by going off with a loud report, and sending the chauffeur to the shelter of the parlor. Bob never knew how near he came to killing some one by his hasty service, and Ma never had the heart to suggest it. Instead she acted promptly and secured the weapon before the enemy had time to recover from his shock.

Bob, in the laundry, standing on a chair mounted on a board across the bathtub, sturdily held his wobbling conductor pipe and aimed it straight to the mark. Of course he knew that even a well-filled phalanx of hogsheads could not hold the enemy forever, but he was counting on the fire company to arrive in time to save the day.

Gasping, clawing the air, ducking, diving here and there to escape the stream, Herbert Hutton presented a spectacle most amusing and satisfying to Bob's boy mind.

"Beat it, Lizzie, beat it! Beat it!" he shouted above the noise of the pouring waters. But Betty, white with horror, seemed to have frozen to the spot. She could not have moved if she had tried, and her brain refused to order her to try. She felt as if the end of everything had come and she were paralyzed.

Down the street with dash and flourish, licking up excitement like a good meal, dashed the gang, the fire chief ostentatiously arraying himself in rubber coat and helmet as he stood on the side of the engine, while the hysterical little engine bell banged away, blending with the sound of the bell of the incoming train at the station. Bi, with his mouth stretched wide, and one foot holding him for the train while the other urged toward the fire and excitement, vibrated on the platform, a wild figure of uncertainty. Where Duty and Inclination both called, Cupidity still had the upper hand.

For once Bi did not have to act a part as he stood watching the three travelers descend from the train. The excitement in his face was real and his gestures were quite natural, even the ones made by his one and only long waving top-lock of gray hair that escaped all bounds as his hat blew off with the suction of the train. Bi rushed up to the three men wildly:

"Say, was you goin' down to Carson's house after that Hope girl?" he demanded loudly.

The three men surveyed him coldly, and the young one gave him a decided shove:

"That will do, my friend," he said firmly. "We don't need any of your assistance."

"But I got a line on this thing you'll want to know," he insisted, hurrying alongside. "There's a guy down there in a car goin' to take her away. He ain't been gone long, but you won't find her 'thout my help. He's goin' to take her to a insane institution. I let on I was helpin' him an' I found out all about it."

"What's all this?" said Reyburn, wheeling about and fixing the old fellow with a muscular young shake that made his toothless jaws chatter. "How long ago did he go? What kind of a looking man was he?"

"Lemme go!" whined Bi, playing to make time, one cunning eye down the road. "I ain't as young as I used to be, an' I can't stand gettin' excited. I got a rig here a purpose, an' I'll take you all right down, an' then ef he's gone, an' I s'pose he must be, 'cause your train was late, why, we'll foller."

"Well, quick, then!" said Reyburn, climbing into the shackley spring wagon that Bi indicated, the only vehicle in view. The two trustees climbed stiffly and uncertainly into the back seat as if they felt they were risking their lives, and Bi lumbered rheumatically into the driver's place and took up the lines. It appeared that the only living thing in Tinsdale that wasn't awake and keen to go to the fire was that horse, and Bi had to do quite a little urging with the stump of an old whip. So, reluctantly, they joined the procession toward the Carson house.

As the stream from the hogshead gurgled smaller, and the victim writhed out of its reach and began to get his bearings, suddenly the outside kitchen door burst open and a crew of rubber-coated citizens sprang in, preceded by a generous stream of chemicals which an ardent young member of the company set free indiscriminately in his excitement. It struck the right man squarely in the middle and sent him sprawling on the floor.

Bob dropped the conductor pipe in exhausted relief and flew to the scene of action. It had been fearful to be held from more active service so long. Emily, outside, could be seen dancing up and down excitedly and directing the procession, with frightened shouts, "In there! In the kitchen! Quick!" as the neighbors and townsmen crowded in and filled the little kitchen demanding to know where the fire was.

Mrs. Carson with dignity stepped forward to explain:

"There ain't any fire, friends, an' I don't know how you all come to get here, but I reckon the Lord sent you. You couldn't a-come at a better moment. We certainly was in some trouble, an' I'll be obliged to you all if you'll just fasten that man up so't he can't do any more harm. He came walkin' in here tryin' to take away a member of my family by force, an' he pointed this at me!"

She lifted the incriminating weapon high where they could all see.

Herbert Hutton, struggling to his feet in the crowd, began to understand that this was no place for him, and looked about for an exit, but none presented itself. The chauffeur had vanished and was trying to make out what had happened to his car.

Hutton, brought to bay, turned on the crowd like a snarling animal, although the effect was slightly spoiled by his drabbled appearance, and roared out insolently:

"The woman doesn't know what she's talking about, men; she's only frightened. I came here after my wife, and I intend to take her away with me! She escaped from an insane asylum some time ago, and we've been looking for her ever since. This woman is doing a very foolish and useless thing in resisting me, for the law can take hold of her, of course."

The crowd wavered and looked uncertainly at Mrs. Carson and at Betty cowering horrified behind her, and Hutton saw his advantage:

"Men," he went on, "there is one of your own townsmen who knows me and can vouch for me. A Mr. Gage. Abijah Gage. If you will just look him up—he was down at the station a few minutes ago. He knows that all I am saying is true!"

A low sound like a rumble went over the little audience and they seemed to bunch together and look at one another while some kind of an understanding traveled from eye to eye. An articulate syllable, "Bi!" breathed in astonishment, and then again "Bi!" in contempt. Public opinion, like a panther crouching, was forming itself ready to spring, when suddenly a new presence was felt in the room. Three strangers had appeared and somehow quietly gotten into the doorway. Behind them, stretching his neck and unable to be cautious any longer, appeared Bi's slouching form. Crouching Public Opinion caught sight of him and showed its teeth, but was diverted by the strangers.

Then suddenly, from the corner behind Ma, slipped Betty with outstretched hands, like a lost thing flying to its refuge, straight to the side of the handsome young stranger.

He put out his hands and drew her to his side with a protecting motion, and she whispered:

"Tell, them, please; oh, make them understand."

Then Reyburn, with her hand still protectingly in his, spoke:

"What that man has just said is a lie!"

Hutton looked up, went deadly white and reeled as he saw the two elderly men.

The crowd drew a united breath and stood straighter, looking relieved. Bi blanched, but did not budge. Whatever happened he was in with both crowds. Reyburn continued:

"I carry papers in my pocket which give authority to arrest him. If the sheriff is present will he please take charge of him. His name is Herbert Hutton, and he is charged with trying to make this lady marry him under false pretenses in order to get control of her property. She is not his wife, for she escaped before the ceremony was performed. I know, for I was present. These two gentlemen with me are the trustees of her estate."

Estate!

The neighbors looked at Betty respectfully.

Bi dropped his jaw perceptibly and tried to figure out how that would affect him. The sheriff stepped forward to magnify his office, and the silence was impressive, almost reverent. In the midst of it broke Bob's practical suggestion:

"Shut him in the coal shed. It's got a padlock an' is good an' strong. He can't kick it down."

Then the law began to take its course, the fire gang stepped out, and Mrs. Carson set to work to clean up. In the midst of it all Reyburn looked down at Betty, and Betty looked up at Reyburn, and they discovered in some happy confusion that they still had hold of hands. They tried to cover their embarrassment by laughing, but something had been established between them that neither could forget.

CHAPTER XVIII

THE days that followed were full of bliss and peace to Betty. With Hutton safely confined in the distant city, and a comfortable sum of her accumulated allowance in the Tinsdale bank, with a thorough understanding between herself and her trustees and the knowledge that her estate was large enough to do almost anything in reason that she wished to do with it, and would be hers in three weeks, life began to take on a different look to the poor storm-tossed child. The days in the Carson home were all Thanksgivings now, and every member of the family was as excited and happy as every other member. There were arguments long and earnest between Betty and her benefactor as to how much she might in reason be allowed to do for the family now that she had plenty of money, but in the end Betty won out, declaring that she had wished herself on this family in her distress, and they took her as a man does when he marries, for better for worse. Now that the worse had passed by she was theirs for the better, and she intended to exercise the privilege of a daughter of the house for the rest of her natural life.

Bi Gage was worried. He was still trying to get something out of the estate for his part in the exercises, and he vibrated between Tinsdale and Warren Reyburn's office working up his case. The five-thousand-dollar reward was as yet unpaid, and the papers he held didn't seem to impress the functionaries nearly so much as he had expected. It began to look as though Bi had missed his chances in life once more, and when he took his old seat in the fire-house and smoked, he said very little. Popular Opinion was still crouching with her eye in his direction and it behooved him to walk cautiously and do nothing to offend. So while he smoked he cogitated in his cunning little brain, and hatched out a plan by which he might get in with the heiress later, perhaps, when things had quieted down a little and she had her money.

Betty received a pitiful letter from her stepmother, trying to explain away her part in the affair and professing to be so relieved at the news that Betty was still alive and well that she cared nothing about anything else, not even the fact that poor dear Herbert was landed in jail, or that the fortune which she had schemed so long to keep in her own power was wrested from her so ignominiously. She begged Betty to come back to their home and "be happy again together."

But Betty was so happy where she was that she could afford to be generous and try to forget her wrongs. She wrote a decent little note gently but firmly declining to come "home" ever again, making it quite plain that she was no longer deceived by honeyed phrases, and closing with a request that if in future any communication might be necessary it should be made through her lawyer, Mr. Warren Reyburn.

This same Warren Reyburn had returned to his city office in a very much exalted state of mind. He could not get away from that little hand of Betty's that had been laid so tremblingly and confidingly in his; and yet how could he, a poverty-stricken lawyer with absolutely no prospects at all, ever dare to think of her, a lady of vast estates. Still, there was some comfort in the fact that he had still some business to transact for her, and would have to return to Tinsdale again. He might at least see her once more. So he solaced himself on his return trip, feeling that he had done some good work, and that he would have a pleasant report to give to Jane Carson when he called upon her, as he meant to do the next day.

He arrived at home to find James Ryan in a great state of excitement. A pile of mail had arrived, and he had memorized the return addresses on the outside of all the envelopes. One was from a big corporation, and another bore a name widely spoken of in the circles of the world of finance, Jimmie in close council with Jane Carson, had decided that it must be from that person who called up twice on the 'phone and swore such terrible oaths when he found that Reyburn was away.

Jimmie hovered nervously about, putting things to rights, while Reyburn read his mail. He had come to the smallest envelope of all, a plain government envelope now, and nothing had developed. Jimmie saw his first place fast slipping away from him and his heart grew heavy with fear. Perhaps after all nothing good had turned up yet.

Suddenly Reyburn sprang up and came toward him with an open letter, holding out his hand in a joyous greeting:

"Read that, Ryan! We're made at last, and I shan't have to let you go after all!"

Ryan read, the letters dancing before his delighted eyes, every one wearing an orange blossom on its brow. It was from an old established and influential firm, asking Reyburn to take full charge of all their law business, and saying they had been referred to him by two old friends in Boston, who by the way were Betty's two trustees.

"Come on, Ryan, come out to lunch with me! We've got to celebrate," said Reyburn. "I have a hunch somehow that you have been the one that brought me this good luck. You and a Miss Jane Carson. You both share alike, I guess, but you were the first with your five-thousand-dollar reward story."

"Jane Carson!" said Jimmie mystified. "Why, *she's* my *girl!*"

"Your girl?" said Reyburn, a queer look coming in his eyes. "You don't say! Well, you're in some luck, boy, with a girl like that! And, by the way, next time you see her, ask her to show you her wedding dress!"

And not another word would Reyburn tell him, though he recurred frequently to the subject during the very excellent lunch which they had together in friendly companionship.

They spent the afternoon composing the brief and comprehensive letter in response to the momentous one of the morning, and in the evening together they sought out Jane Carson, Reyburn staying only long enough to outline the ending of the Elizabeth Stanhope story, while Jimmie remained to hear the beginning, and get a glimpse of the wedding gown, which Reyburn assured Jane he was sure she need never return. He said he thought if the owner of it was married ever in the future she would be likely to want a gown that had no unpleasant associations.

Great excitement prevailed in Tinsdale as the weeks went by. Betty had bought the lots either side of the Carson house, and wonderful improvements were in progress. A windmill was being erected and water pipes laid scientifically. Workmen arrived, some of them from the village, some from the city. Extensive excavations went on about the old house, and stone arrived. It began to be whispered about that "Miss Stanhope," as Betty was now called, was going to build the house all over and all of stone.

The work went forward rapidly as work can go when there is money enough behind it, and the family, living in the little old part of the house, and still using the faithful tin bath-tub and shower of Bob's manufacture, now looked forward to real bathrooms on the bedroom floor, with tiled floors and porcelain fittings. Large windows cropped out on the new walls that were going up, a wide stone chimney and porches. A charming little stone affair in the back yard that went up so quietly it was hardly noticed until it was done suddenly became the home of a big gray car that arrived in town one morning. Betty gave up her position at the Hathaways so that she could have more time to superintend the work and see that it was just as she wanted it, and she and Bob spent hours going over the plans together, he making many wise suggestions. Mrs. Hathaway called her "Miss Stanhope" with elaborate ceremony, and made Elise kiss her whenever she met her.

313

Betty went to a near-by town and bought some pretty clothes, and a lot of things for Ma and Emily and Bob. A beautiful new piano came by express and took the place of Mrs. Barlow's tinpanny one.

Then Betty went up to the city and bought more things, furniture and silver and curtains and rugs, and brought Jane back with her to take a rest and see the little old house once more before it became the big new house, and stay until she was ready to be married; for Betty was determined to have the house ready for Jane's wedding.

When all the new beautiful things began to arrive Betty told Ma that she had taken her in when she was poor and homeless and absolutely penniless, and now all these things were her reward, and Betty couldn't do enough ever to thank her for what she had done for her. They had offered a five-thousand-dollar reward for news of her, and Ma had done more than ten thousand and thousands of thousands of dollars' worth of holding back news about her, and she was never going to get done giving her her reward.

Of course Betty brought Nellie home, too, and established her in a lovely new room just fit for a young girl, and began to pet her and fix her up with pretty things as any loving sister might do if she had money of her own.

All this time Reyburn had much business to transact in Tinsdale, for Betty had asked him to look after all the little details about the building for her, and he had to come down every week-end and look things over to see that she was not being cheated. And once he brought Jimmie down with him for Ma to look over and approve and they had a wonderful time with the two best hens in the hen-coop for dinner. Ryan incidentally gave his approval to Betty.

During these visits Reyburn was making great strides in the wisdom and the knowledge of the love of God. One could not be in that family over Sunday and not feel the atmosphere of a Christian home. Even Jimmie felt it and said he liked it; that he wanted his house to be that way when he had one. He went obediently to church with Jane, and marveled at the way social classes were getting all muddled up in his world.

The Christmas time was coming on when the house finally got itself completed and was ready for living, and with holly and mistletoe and laurel they made it gay for the wedding. Betty spent several days with Jane in New York picking out Jane's "trooso" things, and then a few more days doing some shopping of her own, and at last the wedding day arrived.

Nobody thought it queer, though Jimmie felt just the least bit shy when the two trustees of Betty's estate arrived the night before from Boston and incorporated themselves into the wedding party. Ma seemed to think it was all right, so nobody said anything about it.

But after the ceremony when Jane and Jimmie were happily married, Jane looking very young and pretty indeed in Betty's old wedding gown, veil and slippers and all, and standing under the holly bell in the laurel arch to be congratulated just as it had been arranged, there suddenly came a hush over everybody. Jane noticed for the first time that Betty was not anywhere in the room. Then everybody's eyes went to the wide staircase, and here came Betty trailing down the stairs on the arm of Reyburn, wearing still the little white organdie she had worn a few minutes before as a bridesmaid, only she had thrown aside the rose-colored sash and put over her brow a simple tulle veil, and her arms were full of little pink rosebuds and lilies of the valley.

Up they walked in front of the minister just where the others had stood, and were married with the same sweet simple service, and everybody was so surprised and delighted and excited and breathless that Bob simply couldn't stand it. He slipped into the little music room where the piano had been installed, turned a handspring on the floor, and then sat down and played chopsticks on the piano with all the pedals on, till Ma had to send Emily in to stop him.

Cloudy Jewel

CHAPTER I

"Well, all I've got to say, then, is, you're a very foolish woman!"

Ellen Robinson buttoned her long cloak forcefully, and arose with a haughty air from the rocking-chair where she had pointed her remarks for the last half-hour by swaying noisily back and forth and touching the toes of her new high-heeled shoes with a click each time to the floor.

Julia Cloud said nothing. She stood at the front window, looking out across the sodden lawn to the road and the gray sky in the distance. She did not turn around to face her arrogant sister.

"What I'd like to know is what you do propose to do, then, if you don't accept our offer and come to live with us? Were you expecting to keep on living in this great barn of a house?" Ellen Robinson's voice was loud and strident with a crude kind of pain. She could not understand her sister, in fact, never had. She had thought her proposition that Julia come to live in her home and earn her board by looking after the four children and being useful about the house was most generous. She had admired the open-handedness of Herbert, her husband, for suggesting it. Some husbands wouldn't have wanted a poor relative about. Of course Julia always had been a hard worker; and it would relieve Ellen, and make it possible for her to go around with her husband more. It would save the wages of a servant, too, for Julia had always been a wonder at economy. It certainly was vexing to have Julia act in this way, calmly putting aside the proposition as if it were nothing and saying she hadn't decided what she was going to do yet, for all the world as if she were a millionaire!

"I don't know, Ellen. I haven't had time to think. There have been so many things to think about since the funeral I haven't got used yet to the idea that mother's really gone." Julia's voice was quiet and controlled, in sharp contrast with Ellen's high-pitched, nervous tones.

"That's it!" snapped Ellen. "When you do, you'll go all to pieces, staying here alone in this great barn. That's why I want you to decide now. I think you ought to lock up and come home with me to-night. I've spent just as much time away from home as I can spare the last three weeks, and I've got to get back to my house. I can't stay with you any more."

"Of course not, Ellen. I quite understand that," said Julia, turning around pleasantly. "I hadn't expected you to stay. It isn't in the least necessary. You know I'm not at all afraid."

"But it isn't decent to leave you here alone, when you've got folks that can take care of you. What will people think? It places us in an awfully awkward position."

"They will simply think that I have chosen to remain in my own house, Ellen. I don't see anything strange or indecent about that."

Julia Cloud had turned about, and was facing her sister calmly now. Her quiet voice seemed to irritate Ellen.

"What nonsense!" she said sharply. "How exceedingly childish, letting yourself be ruled by whims, when common sense must show you that you are wrong. I wonder if you aren't ever going to be a *woman*."

Ellen said this word "woman" as if her sister had already passed into the antique class and ought to realize it. It was one of the things that hurt Julia Cloud to realize that she was growing old apparently without the dignity that belonged to her years, for they all talked to her yet as if she were a little child and needed to be managed. She opened her lips to speak, but thought better of it, and shut them again, turning back to the window and the gray, sodden landscape.

"Well, as I said before, you're a very foolish woman; and you'll soon find it out. I shall have to go and leave you to the consequences of your folly. I'm sure I don't know what Herbert will say when he finds out how you've scorned his kindness. It isn't every brother-in-law would offer—yes, *offer*, Julia, for I never even suggested it—to take on extra expense in his family. But you won't see your ingratitude if I stand here and talk till doomsday; so I'm going back to my children. If you come to your senses, you can ride out with Boyce Bains to-morrow afternoon. Good-by, and I'm sure I hope you won't regret this all your life."

Julia walked to the door with her sister, and stood watching her sadly while she climbed into her smart little Ford and skillfully steered it out of the yard and down the road. The very set of her shoulders as she sailed away toward home was disapproving.

With a sigh of relief Julia Cloud shut the door and went back to her window and the dreary landscape. It was time for a sunset, but the sky was leaden. There Would be nothing but grayness to look at, grayness in front of her, grayness behind in the dim, silent room. It was like her life, her long, gray life, behind and ahead. All her life she had had to serve, and see others happy. First as a child, the oldest child. There had been the other children, three brothers and Ellen. She had brought them all up, as it were, for the mother had always been delicate and ailing. She had washed their faces, kissed their bruises, and taken them to school. She had watched their love-affairs and sent them out into the world one by one. Two of the brothers had come home to die, and she had nursed them through long months. The third brother married a wealthy girl in California, and never came home again except on flying visits. He was dead now, too, killed in action in France during the first year of the Great War. Then her father had been thrown from his horse and killed; and she had borne the burden for her mother, settled up the estate, and made both ends meet somehow, taking upon herself the burden of the mother, now a chronic invalid. From time to time her young nieces and nephews had been thrust upon her to care for in some home stress, and always she had done her duty by them all through long days of mischief and long nights of illness. She had done it cheerfully and patiently, and had never complained even to herself. Always there had been so much to be done that there had been no time to think how the years were going by, her youth passing from her forever without even a glimpse of the rose-color that she supposed was meant to come into every life for at least a little while.

She hadn't realized it fully, she had been so busy. But now, with the last service over, an empty house about her, an empty heart within her, she was looking with startled eyes into the future and facing facts.

It was Ellen's attempt to saddle her with a new responsibility and fit her out to drudge on to the end of her days that had suddenly brought the whole thing out in its true light. She was tired. Too tired to begin all over again and raise those children for Ellen. They were nice, healthy children and well behaved; but they were Ellen's children, and always would be. If she went out to live with the Robinsons, she would be Ellen's handmaid, at her beck and call, always feeling that she must do whatever she was asked, whether she was able or not, because she was a dependent. Never anything for love. Oh, Ellen loved her in a way, of course, and she loved Ellen; but they had never understood each other, and Ellen's children had been brought up to laugh and joke at her expense as if she were somehow mentally lacking.

"O Aunt *Ju*lia!" they would say in a tone of pity and scorn, as if she were too ignorant to understand even their sneers.

Perhaps it was pride, but Julia Cloud felt she would rather die than face a future like that. It was respectable, of course, and entirely reliable. She would be fed and clothed, and nursed when she was ill. She would be buried respectably when she died, and the neighbors would say the Robinsons had been kind and done the right thing by her; but Julia Cloud shuddered as she looked down the long, dull vista of that future which was offered her, and drew back for the first time in her life. Not that she had anything better in view, only that she shrank from taking the step that would bring inevitable and irrevocable grayness to the end of her days. She was not above cooking and nursing and toiling forever if there were independence to be had. She would have given her life if love beckoned her. She would have gone to France as a nurse in a moment if she had not been needed at her mother's bedside. Little children drew her powerfully, but to be a drudge for children who did not love her, in a home where love was the only condition that would make dependence possible, looked intolerable.

Julia Cloud had loved everybody that would let her, and had received very little love in return. Back in the years when she was twelve and went to school a boy of fifteen or sixteen had been her comrade and companion. They had played together whenever Julia had time to play, and had roamed the woods and waded the creeks in company. Then his people moved away, and he had kissed her good-by and told her that some day he was coming back to get her. It was a childish affection, but it was the only kiss of that kind she had to remember.

The boy had written to her for a whole year, when one day there came a letter from his grandmother telling how he was drowned in saving the life of a little child; and Julia Cloud had put the memory of that kiss away as the only bright thing in her life that belonged wholly to herself, and plodded patiently on. The tears that she shed in secret were never allowed to trouble her family, and gradually the pain had grown into a great calm. No one ever came her way to touch her heart again. Only little children brought the wistful look to her eyes, and a wonder whether people had it made up to them in heaven when they had failed of the natural things of this life.

Julia Cloud was not one to pity herself. She was sane, healthy, and not naturally morbid; but to-night, for some reason, the gray sky, and the gray, sodden earth, and the gray road of the future had got her in their clutches, and she could not get away from them. With straining eyes she searched the little bit of west between the orchard tree that always showed a sunset if there was one; but no streak of orange, rose, or gold broke the sullen clouds.

Well, what was she going to do, anyway? Ellen's question seemed to ring on stridently in her ears; she tried to face it looking down the gray road into the gray sky.

She had the house, but there were taxes to pay, and there would be repairs every little while to eat up the infinitesimal income which was left her, when all the expenses of her mother's long illness and death were paid. They had been spending their principal. It could not have been helped. In all, she knew, she had something like two hundred dollars a year remaining. Not enough to board her if she tried to board anywhere, to say nothing of clothing. All this had been fully and exhaustively commented upon by Ellen Robinson during the afternoon.

The house might be rented, of course—though it was too antiquated and shabby-looking to bring much—if Julia was not "so ridiculously sentimental about it." Julia had really very little sentiment connected with the house, but Ellen had chosen to think she had; so it amounted to the same thing as far as the argument went. Julia knew in her own heart that the only thing that held her to the dreary old house with its sad memories and its haunting emptiness was the fact that it was hers and that here she could be independent and do as she pleased. If she pleased to starve, no one else need know it. The big ache that was in her heart was the fact that there was nobody really to care if she did starve. Even Ellen's solicitations were largely from duty and a fear of what the neighbors would say if she did not look after her sister.

Julia was lonely and idle for the first time in her busy, dull life, and her heart had just discovered its love-hunger, and was crying out in desolation. She wanted something to love and be loved by. She missed even the peevish, childish invalid whose last five years had been little else than a living death, with a mind so vague and hazy as seldom to know the faithful daughter who cared for her night and day. She missed the heart and soul out of life, the bit of color that would glorify all living and make it beautiful.

Well, to come back to sordid things, what was there that she could do to eke out her pitiful little living? For live she must, since she was here in this bleak world and it seemed to be expected of her. Keep boarders? Yes, if there were any to keep; but in this town there were few who boarded. There was nothing to draw strangers, and the old inhabitants mostly owned their own houses.

She could sew, but there were already more sewing women in the community than could be supported by the work there was to be done, for most of the women in Sterling did their own sewing. There were two things which she knew she could do well, which everybody knew she could do, and for which she knew Ellen was anxious to have her services. She was the best nurse in town and a fine cook. But again the women of Sterling, most of them, did their own cooking, and there was comparatively little nursing where a trained nurse would not be hired. In short, the few things she could do were not in demand in this neighborhood.

Nevertheless, she knew in her heart that she intended trying to live by her own meagre efforts, going out for a few days nursing, or to care for some children while their mothers went out to dinner or to the city, to the theatre or shopping. There would be but little of that, but perhaps by and by she could manage to make it the fashion.

As she looked into the future, she saw herself trudging gloomily down the sunset way into a leaden sky, caring for the Brown twins all day while their mother was shopping; while they slept, mending stockings out of the big round basket that Mrs. Brown always kept by her sewing-chair; coming home at night to a cheerless house and a solitary meal for which she had no appetite; getting up in the night to go to Grandma Fergus taken down suddenly with one of her attacks; helping Mrs. Smith out with her sewing and spring cleaning. Menial, monotonous tasks many of them. Not that she minded that, if they only got somewhere and gave her something from life besides the mere fighting for existence.

She looked clear down to the end of her loveless life, and saw the neighbors coming virtuously to perform the last rites, and wondered why it all had to be. She was unaware of all her years of sacrifice, glorious patience, loving toil. Her life seemed to have been so without point, so useless heretofore; and all that could yet be, how useless and dreary it looked! Her spirit was at its lowest ebb. Her soul was weary unto death. She looked vainly for a break in that solid wall of cloud at the end of the road, and looked so hard that the tears came and fell plashing on the window-seat and on her thin, tired hands. It was because of the tears that she did not see the boy on a bicycle coming down the road, until he vaulted off at the front gate, left his wheel by the curb, and came whistling up the path, pulling a little book and pencil out of his pocket in a business-like way.

With a start she brushed the tears away, pushed back the gray hair from her forehead, and made ready to go to the door. It was Johnny Knox, the little boy from the telegraph office. He had made a mistake, of course. There would be no telegram for her. It would likely be for the Cramers next door. Johnny Knox had not been long in the village, and did not know.

But Johnny did know.

"Telegram for Miss Julia Cloud!" he announced smartly, flourishing the yellow envelope at her and putting the pencil in her hand. "Sign 'ere!" indicating a line in the book.

Julia Cloud looked hard at the envelope. Yes, there was her name, though it was against all reason. She could not think of a disaster in life of which it might possibly be the forerunner. Telegrams of course meant death or trouble. They had never brought anything else to her.

She signed her name with a vague wonder that there was nothing to pay. There had been so many things to pay during the last two painful weeks, and her little funds were almost gone.

She stood with the telegram in her hand, watching the boy go whistling back to his wheel and riding off with a careless whirl out into the evening. His whistle lingered far behind, and her ears strained to hear it. Now if a whistle like that were coming home to her! Some one who would be glad to see her and want something she could do for him! Why, even little snub-nosed, impudent Johnny Knox would be a comfort if he were all her own. Her arms suddenly felt empty and her hands idle because there was nothing left for her to do. Involuntarily she stretched them out to the gray dusk with a wistful motion. Then she turned, and went back to the window to read her telegram.

"DEAR CLOUDY JEWEL: Leslie and I are on our way East for a visit, and will stop over Wednesday night to see you. Please make us some caraway cookies if not too much trouble.

"Your loving nephew,
"ALLISON CLOUD."

A glad smile crept into Julia Cloud's lonely eyes. Leslie and Allison were her California brother's children, who had spent three happy months with her when they were five and seven while their father and mother went abroad. "Cloudy Jewel" was the pet name they had made up for her. That was twelve long years ago, and they had not forgotten! They were coming to see her, and wanted some caraway cookies! A glad light leaped into her face, and she lifted her eyes to the gray distance. Lo! the leaden clouds had broken and a streak of pale golden-rose was glowing through the bars of gray.

CHAPTER II

Leslie and Allison!

Julia Cloud stood gazing out into the west, while the whole sky lightened and sank away into dusk with a burning ruby on its breast. The gloom of her spirit glowed into brightness, and joy flooded her soul.

Leslie and Allison! What round little warm bodies they had, and what delicate, refined faces! They had not seemed like Ellen's blowsy, obstreperous youngsters, practical and grasping to the last extreme after the model of their father. They had starry eyes and hair like tangled sunbeams. Their laughter rippled like brooks in summer, and their hands were like bands that bound the heart. Cookies and stories and long walks and picnics! Those had made up the beautiful days that they spent with her, roaming the woods and meadows, picking dandelions and violets, and playing fairy stories. It had been like a brief return of her old childish days with her boy comrade. She remembered the heartache and the empty days after they had gone back to their Western home, and the little printed childish letters that came for a few months till she was forgotten.

But not really forgotten, after all. For some link of tenderness must still remain that they should think of her now after all these years of separation, and want to visit her. They remembered the cookies! She smiled reminiscently. What a batch of delectable cookies she would make in the morning! Why, to-morrow would be Wednesday! They would be here to-morrow night! And there was a great deal to be done!

She turned from the belated sunset unregretting, and hastened to begin her preparations. There were the two front rooms up-stairs to be prepared. She would open the windows at once, and let the air sweep through all night. They had been shut up a long time, for she had brought the invalid down-stairs to the little sitting-room the last few months to save steps and be always within hearing. The second story had been practically unused except when Ellen or the children were over for a day or two.

She hurried up-stairs, and lit the gas in the two rooms, throwing wide the windows, hunting out fresh sheets and counterpanes. She could dust and run the carpet-sweeper over the rooms right away, and have them in order; and that would save time for to-morrow. Oh, it was good to have something cheerful to do once more. Just supposing she had yielded—as once that afternoon she almost had—to Ellen's persistent urgings, and had gone home with her to-night! Why, the telegram might not have reached her till after the children had come, and found the house empty, and gone again!

Julia bustled around happily, putting the rooms into charming order, hunting up a little picture of the child Samuel kneeling in the temple, that Allison used to like, going to the bottom of an old hair trunk for the rag doll she had made for Leslie to cuddle when she went to sleep at night.

Mrs. Ambrose Perkins across the way looked uneasily out of her bedroom window at half-past nine, and said to her husband:

"Seems like Julia Cloud is staying up awful late to-night. She's got a light in both front rooms, too. There can't be company. I s'pose Ellen and some of her children have stayed down after all. Poor Ellen! She told me she simply couldn't spare the time away from home any longer, but Julia was set on staying there. I never thought Julia was selfish; but I s'pose she doesn't realize how hard it is for Ellen, living that way between two houses. Julia'll go to live with Ellen now, of course. It's real good of Herbert Robinson to ask her. Julia ought to appreciate having relatives like that."

"Relatives nothing!" said Mr. Ambrose, pulling off his coat and hanging it over a chair. "She'll be a fool if she goes! She's slaved all her life, and she deserves a little rest now. If she goes out to Herbert Robinson's, she won't be allowed to call her eyelashes her own; you mark my words!"

"Well, what else can she do?" said his wife. "She hasn't any husband or children, and I think she'll be mighty well off to get a good home. Men are awful hard on each other, Ambrose. I always knew that."

Julia Cloud meanwhile, with a last look at the neat rooms, put out her lights, and went to bed, but not to sleep. She was so excited that the darkness seemed luminous about her. She was trying to think how those two children would look grown up. Allison was nineteen and Leslie nearly seventeen now. Their mother had been dead five years, and they had been in boarding-schools. Their guardian was an old gentleman, a friend of their mother's. That was about all she knew concerning them. Would they seem like strangers, she wondered, or would there be enough resemblance to recall the dear girl and boy of the years that were gone? How she clung to those cookies with hope! There was some remembrance left, or they would not have put cookies in a telegram. How impetuous and just like Allison, the boy, that telegram had sounded!

It was scarcely daylight when Julia Cloud arose and went down to the kitchen to bake the cookies; and the preparations she made for baking pies and doughnuts and other toothsome dainties would lead one to suppose that she was expecting to feed a regiment for a week at least.

She filled the day with hard work, as she had been wont to do, and never once thought of gray sunsets or dreary futures. Not even the thought of her sister Ellen came to trouble her as she put the house in order, filled her pantry with good things to eat, and set the table for three with all the best things the house afforded.

At evening she stood once more beside the front window, looking out sunsetward. There was nothing gray about either sky or road or landscape now. There had been brilliant sunshine all day long, and the sky lay mellow and yellow behind the orchard, with a clear, transparent greenish-blue above and a hint of rosy light in the long rays that reached their fingers along the ground between the apple-trees. In a few minutes the evening train would be in, and there would be rose in the sunset. She knew the signs, and the sky would be glorious to-night. They would see it as they came from the train. In fifteen minutes it would be time for her to put on her hat and go down to meet them! How her heart throbbed with anticipation!

Forebodings came to shadow her brightness. Suppose they should not come! Suppose they were delayed, or had changed their minds and should send another telegram saying so! She drew a deep breath, and tried to brace herself for the shock of the thought. She looked fearfully down the road for a possible Johnny Knox speeding along with another telegram, and was relieved to see only Ambrose Perkins ambling home for supper followed by his tall, smiling Airedale.

There was a shadow, too, that stood behind her, though she ignored it utterly; it was the thought of the afterwards, when the two bright young things had been and gone, and she would have to face the gray in her life again without the rose. But that would be afterwards, and this was now! Ten minutes more, and she would go to the station!

At that minute a great blue automobile shot up to the front gate, and stopped. A big lump flew into Julia Cloud's throat, and her hand went to her heart. Had it then come, that telegram, saying they had changed their minds? She stood trembling by the window, unable to move.

But out from the front seat and the back as if ejected from a catapult shot two figures, and flew together up the front walk, a tall boy and a little girl, just as the sun dropped low and swung a deep red light into the sky, flooding the front yard with glory, and staining the heavens far up into the blue.

They had come! They had come before it was yet train-time!

Julia Cloud got herself to her front door in a tremor of delight, and instantly four strong young arms encircled her, and nearly smothered the life out of her.

"O you dear Cloudy Jewel! You look just the same. I knew you would. Only your hair is white and pretty," Leslie gurgled.

"Sure, she is just the same! What did I tell you?" cried Allison, lifting them both and carrying them inside.

"Now, who on earth can that be?" said Mrs. Ambrose Perkins, flying to her parlor window at the first sound of the automobile. "It isn't any of them folks from the city that were out to the funeral, for there wasn't a car like that there, I'm certain! I mean to run over and borrow a spoonful of soda pretty soon, just to find out. It couldn't be any of Tom's folks from out West, for they couldn't come all that way in a car. It must be some of her father's relations from over in Maryland, though I never heard they were that well off. A chauffeur in livery! The idea of all that style coming to see Julia Cloud!"

"No, we didn't come on the train," explained Leslie eagerly. "We came in Allison's new car. Mr. Luddington— that's our guardian—was coming East, and he said we might come with him. We've been dying to come for ages. And he'd been promising Allison he might get this new car; so we stopped in the city and bought it, and Allison drove it down. Of course Mr. Luddington made his man come along. He wouldn't let us come alone. He's gone up to Boston for three days; and, when he comes back, he's coming down here to see you."

Leslie was talking as fast as an express train, and Julia Cloud stood and admired her in wonder.

She was slim and delicately pretty as ever, with the same mop of goldy-brown curls, done up in a knot now and making her look quaintly like the little five-year-old on a hot day with her curls twisted on the top of her head for comfort. She wore a simple little straight frock of some dark silk stuff, with beaded pockets and marvellous pleats and belts and straps in unexpected places, such as one sees in fashion-books, but not on young girls in the town of Sterling; and her hat was a queer little cap with a knob of bright beads, wonderfully becoming, but quite different from anything that Julia Cloud had ever seen before. Her movements were darting and quick like a humming-bird's; and she wore long soft suède gloves and tiny high suède boots. The older woman watched her, fascinated.

"And you're sure we're not being an inconvenience, dropping down upon you in this unexpected way?" asked Allison in a quite grown-up man's voice, and looking so tall and handsome and responsible that Julia Cloud wanted to take him in her arms and hug him to make sure he was the same little boy she used to tuck into bed at night.

"So soon after Grandma's death, too," put in Allison. "We didn't know, of course, till we got about a mile from Sterling and stopped to ask the way to the house, and a man told us about the funeral being Monday. We weren't sure then but it would be an intrusion. You see we left California about two weeks ago, and none of our mail has reached us yet; so we hadn't heard. You're sure we won't bother you a bit, you dear?"

Their aunt assured them rapturously that their coming was the most blessed thing that could have been just at this time.

"Oh! then I'm relieved," said Leslie, throwing off her hat and dropping into the nearest chair. "Allison, tell that man to put the car somewhere in a garage and get back to the city. They said there was a train back about this time. The man who directed us told us so. No, dear, he doesn't need any dinner. He's not used to it till seven, and he'll be in the city by that time. He's in a hurry to get back. Cookies? Well, yes, you might give him a cooky or two if you're sure there'll be enough left for us. I've just dreamed of those cookies all these years. I'm so anxious to see if they'll taste as they did when I was a child. May I come with you and see if I remember where the cooky-jar is? Oh, joy, Allison! Just look! A whole crock and a platter full! Isn't this peachy? Allison, do hustle up and get that man off so we can begin our visit!"

It was like having a couple of dolls suddenly come alive and begin to talk.

They talked so fast and they took everything so delightfully for granted that Julia Cloud was in a tremble of joy. It seemed the most beautiful thing in the world that these two strong, handsome, vivid young things should have dropped into her life and taken her into their hearts in this way as if she really belonged, as if they loved her! She was too excited to talk. She hardly knew what to do first. But they did not wait for her initiative. Allison was off with his car and his man, munching cookies as he went, and promising to return in fifteen minutes hungry as a bear.

"Now let's go up-stairs, you dear Cloudy Jewel, and I'll smooth my hair for dinner. I'm crazy to see if I remember things. There was a little red chair that I used to sit in——"

"It's here, in your room, dear, and the old rag doll, Betsey; do you remember her?"

"Well, I should say I did! Is Betsey alive yet? Dear old Betsey! How ducky of you to have kept her for me all these years! Oh, isn't it perfectly peachy that we could come? That we're really here at last, and you want us? You do, don't you, Cloudy, dear? You're sure you do?" Lesley's tone was anxious, and her bright brown eyes studied the older woman's face eagerly; but what she saw there was fully satisfactory, for she smiled, and rattled joyfully on in the old babbling-brook voice that reminded one so of years ago.

"I'm not to tell you what we've really come for till Allison comes, because I've promised; and anyway he's the man, and he wants to tell you himself; but it's the dandiest reason, perfectly peachy! It's really a plan. And say, Cloudy, dear, won't you promise me right here and now that you will say 'Yes' to what he asks you if you possibly, *possibly* can?"

Julia Cloud promised in a maze of delight.

She stood in hovering wonder, and watched the mass of curls come down and go up again with the swift manipulation of the slim white fingers, remembering how she used to comb those tangled curls with the plump little body leaning sturdily against her knee. It seemed to be the first time since she was a child that youth and beauty had come to linger before her. All her experience had been of sickness and suffering and death, not life and happiness.

There was stewed chicken and little biscuits with gravy for supper. It was a dish the children used to love. It was all dished up and everything ready when Allison came back. He reported that the car was housed but a block away, and the man had gone to his train, tickled to death with his cookies. Allison was so glad to be back that he had to take his aunt in his arms again and give her a regular bear-hug till she pleaded for mercy, but there was a happy light in her eyes and a bright color in her cheeks when he released her that made her a very good-looking aunt indeed to sit down at the table with two such handsome children.

Just at that moment Ellen Robinson in her own home was pouring her husband's second cup of coffee.

"Don't you think I'd better take the car and run down for Julia before dark?" she said. "I think she'll be about ready to come back with me by this time, and I need her early in the morning if I'm going to begin cleaning house."

"Better wait one more night," said Herbert stolidly. "Let her get her fill of staying alone nights. It'll do her good. We don't want her to be high and mighty when she gets here. I'm boss here, and she's got to understand that. She's so mighty independent, you know, it's important she should find that out right at the start. I'm not going to have her get bossy with these children, either. They aren't her children."

Four pairs of keen little Robinson eyes took in this saying with quick intelligence, and four stolid sets of shoulders straightened up importantly with four uplifted saucy chins. They would store these remarks away for future reference when the aunt in question arrived on the scene. They would come in well, they knew, for they had had experience with her in times past.

"Aunt Jule ain't goin' to boss me," swaggered the youngest.

"Ner me, neither!"

"Ner me!"

"I guess she wouldn't *dast* try it on *me*!" boasted the eldest.

CHAPTER III

"You haven't asked us what we came for," opened up Allison as soon as everybody was served with chicken, mashed potato, succotash, stewed tomatoes, biscuits, pickles, and apple-sauce.

"I thought you came for cookies," said Julia Cloud, with a mischievous twinkle in her gray eyes.

"Hung one on me, didn't you?" said Allison, laughing. "But that wasn't all. Guess again."

"Perhaps you came to see me," she suggested shyly.

"Right you are! But that's not all, either. That wouldn't last much longer than the cookies. Guess again."

"Oh, I couldn't!" said Julia Cloud, growing suddenly stricken with the thought of their going. "I give it up."

"Well, then I'll tell you. You see we've come East to college, both of us. Of course I've had my freshman year, but the Kid's just entering. We haven't decided which college it's to be yet, but it's to be co-ed, we know that much, because we're tired of being separated. When one hasn't but two in the family and has been apart for five years, one appreciates a home, I tell you that. And so we've decided we want a home. We're not just going to college to live there in the usual way; we're going to take a house, live like real folks, and go to school every day. We want a fireplace and a cooky-jar of our own; a place to bring our friends and have good times. But most of all we want a mother, and we've come all this way to coax you to come and live with us, play house, you know, as you used to do down on the mossy rocks with broken bits of china for dishes and acorns for cups and saucers. Play house and you be mother. Will you do it, Cloudy Jewel? It means a whole lot to us, and we'll try to play fair and make you have a good time."

Julia Cloud put her hand on her heart, and lifted her bewildered eyes to the boy's eager face.

"Me!" she said wonderingly. "You want *me*!"

"We sure do!" said Allison.

"Indeed we do, Cloudy, dear! That's just what we do want!" cried Leslie, jumping up and running around to her aunt's chair to embrace her excitedly. "And you promised, you know, that you would do what we wanted if you possibly, *possibly* could."

"You see, we put it up to our guardian about the house," went on Allison, "and he said the difficulty would be to get the right kind of a housekeeper that he could trust us with. Of course he's way off in California, and he has to be fussy. He's built that way. But we told him we didn't want any housekeeper at all, we wanted a mother. He said you couldn't pick mothers off trees, but we told him we knew where there was one if we could only get her. So he let us come and ask; and, if you say you'll do it, he's coming down to see you and fix it up about the money part. He said you'd have to have a regular salary or he wouldn't consider it, because there were things he'd have to insist upon that he had promised mother; and, if there wasn't a business arrangement about it, he wouldn't know what to do. Besides, he said it was worth a lot to run a couple of rough-necks like Les and me, and he'd make the salary all right so you could afford to leave whatever you were doing and just give your time to mothering us. Now it's up to you, Cloudy Jewel, to help us out with our proposition or spoil everything, because we simply won't have a housekeeper, and we don't know another real mother in the whole world that hasn't a family of her own."

They both left their delicious dinner, and got around her, coaxing and wheedling exactly as if she had already declined, when the truth was she was too dazed with joy to open her lips, even if they had given her opportunity to speak.

It was some time before the excitement quieted down and they gave her a chance to say she would go. Even then she spoke the words with fear and trembling as one might step off a commonplace threshold into a fairy palace, not sure but it might be stepping into space.

Outside the sky was still flooded with after-sunset glory, but there was so much glory in the hearts of the three inside the dining-room that they never noticed it at all. It might have been raining or hailing, and they would not have known, they were so happy.

Both the guests donned long gingham aprons and wiped the dishes when the meal was over, both talking with all their might, recalling the days of their childhood when they had had towels pinned around them and been allowed to dry the cups and pans; then suddenly jumping ahead and planning what they would do in the dear new home of the future. They were all three as excited about it as if they had been a bridal couple planning for their honeymoon.

"We shall want five bedrooms," said Leslie decidedly. "I've thought that all out, one for each of us and two guest-rooms, so we can have a boy and a girl home for overnight with us as often as we want to. And there simply must be a fireplace, or we won't take the house. If there isn't the right kind of a house in town, we'll choose some other college. There are plenty of colleges, but you can have only one home, and it must be the right kind. Then of course we want a big kitchen where we can make fudge as often as we choose in the evenings, and a dining-room with a bay-window, with seats and flowers and a canary. Cloudy Jewel, you don't mind cats, do you? I want two at least. I've been crazy for a kitten all the time I was in school, and Al wants a big collie. You won't mind, will you?"

Suddenly Julia Cloud discovered that latent in her heart all these years there had also lain a desire for a cat and a dog; and she lifted guilty eyes, and confessed it. She felt a pang of remembrance as she recalled how her mother used so often to tell her she was nothing but an "old child."

"Perhaps your guardian will not think me a proper person to chaperon you," she suggested in sudden alarm.

"Well, he'd just better not!" declared Allison, bristling up. "I'd like to know where he could find a better."

"I've never been in society," said Julia Cloud thoughtfully. "I don't know social ways much, and I've never been considered to have any dignity or good judgment."

"That's just why we like you," chorused the children. "You've never grown up and got dull and stiff and poky like most grown folks."

"We were so afraid," began Leslie, putting a loving arm about her aunt's waist, "that you would have changed since we were children. We talked it all over on the way here. We had a kind of eyebrow code by which we could let each other know what we thought about it without your seeing us. We were to lift one eyebrow, the right one, if we were favorably impressed, and draw down the left if we were disappointed. But in case we were sure both eyebrows were to go up. And of course we were sure you were just the same dear the minute we laid eyes on you, and all four of our eyebrows went high as they'd go the first instant. Didn't you notice Allison? His eyebrows were almost up to his hair, and they pulled his eyes so wide open they were perfectly round like saucers. As for me I think mine went way up under my hair. I'm not sure if they've got back to their natural place even yet!" And Leslie laid a rosy finger over her brow, and felt anxiously along the delicate velvety line.

"I shall go out and telegraph Mr. Luddington that you are willing," announced Allison as he hung up the dish-towel. "He'll get it in the morning when he reaches Boston, and then he needn't fuss and fume any longer about what he's going to do with us. Besides, I like to have the bargain clinched somehow, and a telegram will do it." Allison slammed out of the house noisily to the extreme confusion of Mrs. Ambrose Perkins, who hadn't been able to eat her supper properly for watching the house to see what would happen next. Who could that young man be?

She simply couldn't get a clew; for, when she went over for the soda, though she knocked several times, and heard voices up-stairs, and altogether unseemly laughter for a house where there had just been a funeral, not a soul came to the door! Could it be that Julia Cloud heard her and stayed up-stairs on purpose? She felt that as the nearest neighbor and a great friend, of Ellen's it would be rather expected of her to find out what was going on. She resolutely refrained from lighting the parlor lamp, and took up her station at the dark window to watch; but, although she sat there until after ten o'clock, she was utterly unable to find out anything except that the household across the way stayed up very late and there were lights in both front rooms again. She felt that if nothing developed by morning she would just have to get Ambrose to hitch, up and drive out to Ellen's. Ellen ought to know.

But Julia Cloud was serenely unconscious of this espionage. She had entered an Eden of bliss, and was too happy to care about anything else.

Seated on the big old couch in the parlor with a child on either side of her, a hand in each of hers, often a head on each shoulder nestling down, they talked. Planned and talked. Now the brother would break in with some tale of his school-days; now the sister would add a bit of reminiscence, just as if they had been storing it all up to tell her. The joyous happiness of them all seemed like heaven dropped down to earth. It was as she had sometimes dreamed mothers might talk with their own children. And God had granted this unspeakable gift to her! Was it real? Would it last? Or was she only dreaming? Once it vaguely passed through her mind that she would not be sure of the reality of the whole thing until she had seen Ellen. If she could talk with Ellen about it, tell her what she was going to do, show her the children, and then come back and find it all the same, it would last. But somehow she shrank unspeakably from seeing Ellen. She could not get away from the feeling that Ellen would dispel it all; that someway, somehow, she would succeed in breaking up all the bright plans and scattering them like soap-bubbles in the wind.

Nevertheless, it was a very beautiful illusion, if illusion it was; and one to be prolonged as late as possible.

She was horrified when at last she heard the rebuking strokes of the town clock, ten! eleven! *twelve!*

She started to her feet ashamed.

And even then they would not let her go to bed at once. She must turn out the lights, and sit in the hall between their rooms as she did long ago, and tell the story of "The Little Rid Hin" just as she had told it night after night when they were children.

It was characteristic of the unfailing youth of the woman that she entered into the play with zest. Attired in a long kimono, with her beautiful white hair in two long silver braids down over her shoulders, she sat in the dark and told the story with the same vivid language; and then she stole on tiptoe first to the sister's bedside, to tuck her in and kiss her softly, and then to the brother's; and at each bedside a young, strong arm reached out and drew her face down, whispering "Good-night" with a kiss and "I love you, Cloudy Jewel," in tender, thrilling tones.

The two big children were asleep at last, and Julia Cloud stole to her own bed to lie in a tumult of wonder and joy, and finally sink into a light slumber, wherein she dreamed that she had fallen heir to a rose-garden, and all the roses were alive and could talk; until Ellen came driving up in her Ford and ran right over them, crushing them down and cutting their heads off with a long, sharp whip she carried that somehow turned out to be made of words strung together with biting sarcasm.

She awoke in the broad morning sunlight to find both children done up in bath-robes and slippers, sitting one each side of her on the bed, laughing at her and tickling her chin with a feather from the seam of the pillow.

"Now, Cloudy Jewel, you've just got to begin to make plans!" announced Leslie, curling up in a ball at her feet and looking very business-like with her fluffy curls around her face like a golden fleece. "There isn't much time, and Guardy Lud will be down upon us by to-morrow or the next day at least."

"Guardy Lud!" exclaimed Julia Cloud bewildered. "Who is that?"

"That's our pet name for Mr. Luddington," explained Leslie, wrinkling up her nose in a grin of merriment. "Isn't it cute? Wait till you see him, and you'll see how it fits. He's round and bald with a shiny red nose, and spectacles; and he doesn't mind our kidding at all. He'd have made a lovely father if he wasn't married, but he has a horrid wife. We don't like her at all. She's like a frilly piece of French china with too much decoration; and she's always sick and nervous; and she jumps, and says 'Oh, mercy!' every time we do the least little thing. She doesn't like us any better than we like her. Her name is Alida, and Allison says we're always trying to 'elude' her. The only good thing she ever did was to advise Guardy Lud to let us come East to college. She wanted to get us as far away from her as possible. And it certainly was mutual."

"There, now, Leslie, you're chattering again," broke in Allison, looking very tall and efficient in his blue bath-robe. "You said you would talk business, and not bleat."

"Well, so I am," pouted Leslie. "I guess Cloudy has got to understand about our family."

"Well, now let's get down to business," said her brother. "Cloudy, what have you got to do before you leave? You know it isn't very long before the colleges open, and we've got to start out and hunt a home right away. Do you have to pack up here or anything?"

"Oh, I don't know!" gasped Julia Cloud, looking around half frightened. "I suppose I ought to ask Ellen. She will be very much opposed to anything I do, but I suppose she ought to be told first."

Allison frowned.

"Gee whiz! I don't see why Aunt Ellen has to butt into our affairs. She's got her own home and family, and she never did like us very much. I remember hearing her tell Grandma that we were a regular nuisance, and she would be glad when we were gone back to California."

"That was because you hid behind the sofa when Uncle Herbert was courting her, and kidded them," giggled Leslie.

A stray little twinkle of a dimple peeped out by the corner of Julia Cloud's mouth. It hadn't been out for a number of years, and she knew she ought not to laugh at such pranks now; but it was so funny to think of Herbert Robinson being kidded in the midst of his courting!

The dimple started the lights dancing in Leslie's eyes.

"There! now you dear old Jewel, you know you don't want to talk to Aunt Ellen about us. She'll just mess things all up. Let's just *do* things, and get 'em all fixed up, and then tell her when it's too late for her to make a fuss," gurgled Leslie down close to Julia's ear, finishing up with a delicious bear-hug.

"I suppose she'll be mortally offended," murmured Julia Cloud in troubled hesitancy.

"Well, suppose she is; she'll get over it, won't she?" growled Allison. "And anyhow you're old enough to manage your own affairs, Cloudy Jewel. I guess you're older than she is, aren't you? I guess you've got a right to do as you please, haven't you? And you *do* want to go with us, don't you?" His voice was anxious.

"I certainly do, dear boy," said Julia Cloud eagerly; "but you know your guardian may not approve at all when he sees what a foolish 'young' aunt I am, allowing you to sit up late and talk fairy stories all the time."

They smothered her in kisses, compliments, and assurances; and it was some time before the conversation swung around again to the important subject of the morning.

"You don't have to do anything to the house but just shut it up, do you?" asked Allison, looking anxiously about in a helpless, mannish way. "Because, if you do, we ought to be getting to work."

"There's a man over at Harmony Village that wanted to rent a house here," said Julia Cloud thoughtfully. "I might write a letter to him. I don't know whether he's found anything or not. He's the new superintendent of the high school. But it's time we got dressed and had breakfast."

"Write to him nothing!" said Allison eagerly. "I'll get the car, and we'll drive over to Harmony in no time, and get the thing fixed up. Hustle there, Leslie, and get yourself togged up. We don't need to wait for breakfast; we can eat cookies. Hurry everybody!" And he slammed over to his own room and began to stir about noisily.

Julia Cloud arose and made a hasty toilet, with a bright spot of excitement on each cheek; but she had no time to think what Ellen would say, for she meant that these children should have a real old-time breakfast before they began the day; and now that she was up her little round black clock on the bureau told her that it was high time the day had begun. She looked fearfully out of the window, half expecting to see Ellen's Ford bobbing down the hill already, and then hurried down to the kitchen. Allison soon came down, calling out to her to be ready when he came back with the car; but the delicious odors that had already begun to float out from the old kitchen made him lenient toward the idea of breakfast; and, when he came back with the full cut-out roaring the announcement of his arrival to the Perkinses, he was quite ready to wait a few minutes and eat some of Julia Cloud's flapjacks and sausages with maple-syrup and apple-sauce.

Julia Cloud herself ate little. She was in a tremor of delightful uncertainty and dread. Ought she to go ahead this way and manage her own affairs, leaving her own sister out of the question? But then, if she consulted with Ellen that meant consulting with Herbert; for Herbert ran his wife most thoroughly, and Herbert could make things very unpleasant when he took the trouble.

So, when the children, unable at last to eat any more, pleaded with her to leave the dishes and go to see the man about the house at once, she gave one swift, apprehensive glance about, and assented. If Ellen should come to the house while they were away, and should look in at the window and see the breakfast dishes standing! It would be appalling! But, as the children said, why worry? Somehow she felt like a little schoolgirl playing hookey as she carefully drew down the dining-room and kitchen window-shades that looked on the back porch, and locked the front door behind her. Well, perhaps she had earned the right to take this bit of a holiday, and wash her dishes when she liked. Anyhow, hadn't God sent these blessed children to her in answer to her earnest prayer that He would show her what to do and save her if possible from having to spend the remainder of her days under Herbert Robinson's roof? Well, then she would just accept it that way and be grateful, at least until He showed her otherwise. So she drew a long breath of delight, and climbed into the luxurious back seat of the great blue car, utterly oblivious of the prying eyes behind the parlor shade across the way.

CHAPTER IV

Down the little village street, past the station, and across the railroad toward Harmony swept the great blue car, with the villagers turning to stare at Miss Cloud taking a ride so early in the morning in so gaudy a car, so soon after the funeral, and even without a veil!

A few minutes later Ellen in her Ford rattled up to the door and got out with the air of one who had come to do things. She walked confidently up to the front door and tried it, rattled it, knocked, and then went angrily around to the back, trying all the doors and windows. Mrs. Perkins from her parlor window watched a minute; and, when she saw Ellen come around to the front again and look up at the second story, she threw a shawl around her shoulders and ran across the street to impart faithfully her story.

"For the land's sake!" said Ellen indignantly. "What can Julia be about? Mother always said she never would grow up, and I believe it. I was afraid when I went away she had some scheme in her mind. She's always getting up fool ideas. I remember that time when Mrs. Marsh died she wanted to adopt the twins and bring them up. The idea! When there was a county poorhouse and no reason why they shouldn't go to it! But she'll have to come down off her independence and be sensible. Herbert says we can't have any of her foolishness. It's us that would have to suffer if she got into trouble and lost what little she's got, and I suppose I've got to have it out with her once and for all and get this thing settled. It's getting on all our nerves, and I've got the fall house-cleaning and jelly to do, and I can't fool around any longer. Well, I suppose I better try to get into this house. Have you got any keys that might fit?"

Mrs. Perkins hurried over for all her keys, including trunk-keys; and soon they had tried every door and every key with no effect, and had to call in the youngest Perkins and boost him up to the upper-hall window.

Under the guise of looking after Julia Cloud the two good ladies invaded her home and proceeded to investigate. The parlor and the hall gave forth no secrets except for a couple of handsome raincoats slung carelessly upon chairs. But the dining-room, oh, the dining-room! If Julia Cloud could have seen their faces as they swung open that carefully closed door and stood upon the threshold aghast, looking at the wreck of the breakfast, she would have cringed and shivered even on her way to Harmony.

But Julia Cloud could not see; she was safely over the bridge and out on the highway where she would not be likely to be followed, and the wine of the morning was rising in her veins. Such wonderful air, such clear blue sky and flying clouds! She felt like a flying cloud herself as she sped along in the great blue car with the chatter of the children in her ears and the silvery laughter of Leslie by her side. How could she help smiling and letting her cheeks grow pink and her eyes grow bright? Too soon after a funeral? The thought did come to her. But she knew by the thrill of her heart that her mother in heaven was gladder now than she had been for years of her bedridden life on earth, and, if she could look down to see, would no doubt be happy that some joy was coming to her hard-worked daughter at last. Julia would just enjoy this day and this delight to the full while it lasted. If it was not meant to last longer than the day, at least she would have this wonderful ride to remember always, this bird-like motion as if she were floating through a panorama! Not a thought of Ellen poking through her half-cleared house, finding unswept hearth and unmade beds and unwashed dishes, came to trouble her joy. It was as if the childhood of her life, long held in abeyance, had come back to her, and would not be denied.

Ellen and Mrs. Perkins in their inspection of the house came at last to the upper story and the guests' room strewn with brushes bearing silver monograms and elaborate appointments of travel that kept them guessing their use and exclaiming in wonder and horror that any one would spend so much on little details. Leslie's charming silk negligée and her frilly little nightgown with its lace and floating ribbons came in for a large amount of contempt, and it was some time before the good ladies arrived at Julia Cloud's room and found the open telegram on her bureau that gave the key to the mystery of the two visitors.

"H'm!" said Ellen. "So that's it! Well, I thought she had some bee in her bonnet. She must have written to them or they never would have come. Now, I suppose she means to keep them all winter, perhaps, and feed them, and baby them up; and, when she has spent all she has, she'll come back on us. Well, she'll find out she's much mistaken; and, when she gets back, I'll just tell her plainly that she can bundle up her company and send them home and come out to us now, to-day or to-morrow, or the offer is withdrawn, and she needn't think she can fall back on Herbert, either, when she's spent everything. Herbert is not a man to be put upon."

"I should say not!" said Mrs. Perkins sympathetically, looking over her friend's shoulder at the telegram. "So those were your brother's two children! He must 'uv been pretty well off for them to have a car like that. I must say I think it's a harm to children to be brought up wealthy."

"Their mother was rich," said Ellen sourly. It had always been a thorn in her flesh. "She was a snob, too, and her children'll likely be the limit by this time. But Julia is such a fool!"

They sat in Julia Cloud's parlor, one at each window, discussing the probabilities until half-past eleven. Then Ellen said she must go. She positively couldn't wait another minute; but she would return, in the afternoon, and Mrs. Perkins must tell her sister that she was coming and wanted her to remain at home. That it was very important.

"I'll settle her!" she said with her thin lips set in a hard line. Then she stooped to crank her Ford.

Mrs. Perkins watched her away, then hurried to her own neglected work; and ten minutes later the big blue car sailed noiselessly up to the place. It was not until the Perkins children discovered it and told their mother that she knew it had arrived. This was very annoying. She had wanted to catch them quite casually on their arrival, and now she would have to make a special errand over, and as likely as not have them not come to the door again. Besides, she was getting dinner, and things were likely to burn. Nevertheless, she dared not wait with that big blue car standing so capably at the door, ready to spirit them away again at any moment. She wiped her hands on her apron, grabbed a teacup for an excuse, and ran over to borrow that soda once more.

Peals of laughter were echoing through the old house when she knocked at the door, and a regular rush and scramble was going on, so unseemly just after a funeral! The door was on the latch, too, as if they did not care who heard; and to save her life she couldn't help pushing it a little with her foot, just enough to see in. And there was Julia Cloud, her white hair awry, and her face rosy with mirth, an ear of corn in one hand and a knife in the other, being carried—yes, actually *carried*—across the dining-room in the arms of a tall young man and deposited firmly on the big old couch.

"There, Cloudy Jewel! You'll lie right there and rest while Leslie and I get lunch. You're all tired out; I can see it in your eyes; and we can't afford to let you stay so. No, we don't need any succotash for lunch or dinner, either. I know it's good; but we haven't time now, and we aren't going to let you work," announced the young man joyously as he towered above her lying quiescent and weak with laughter.

"No, nor you aren't going to wash the dishes, either," gurgled the young girl who danced behind the young man; "Allison and I will wash them all while you take a nap, and then we're going to ride again."

Julia Cloud, her eyes bright with the joy of all this loving playfulness, tried to protest; but suddenly into the midst of this tumult came Mrs. Perkins's raucous assertion:

"H'm-m!"

The two young people whirled around alertly, and Julia Cloud sat up with a wild attempt to bring her hair into subjection as she recognized her neighbor. The color flooded into her sweet face, but she rose with gentle dignity.

"O Mrs. Perkins, we must have been making such a noise that we didn't hear your knock," she said.

As a matter of fact Mrs. Perkins hadn't knocked. She had been led on by curiosity until she stood in the open dining-room door, rank disapproval written on her face.

"It did seem a good bit of noise for a house of mourning," said Mrs. Perkins dryly.

Julia Cloud's sweet eyes suddenly lost their smile, and she drew herself up ever so little. There was just a ripple of a quiver of her gentle lips, and she said quite quietly and with a dignity that could not help impressing her caller:

"This is not a house of mourning, Mrs. Perkins. I don't think my dear mother would want us to mourn because she was released from a bed of pain where she had lain for nine long years, and gone to heaven where she could

325

be young and free and happy. I'm glad for her, just as glad as I can be; and I know she would want me to be. But won't you sit down? Mrs. Perkins, this is my niece and nephew, Leslie and Allison Cloud from California. I guess you remember them when they were little children. Or no; you hadn't moved here yet when they were here——"

Mrs. Perkins with pursed lips acknowledged the introduction distantly, one might almost say insolently, and turned her back on them as if they had been little children.

"Your sister's been here all morning waiting for you!" she said accusingly. She gave a significant glance at the unwashed breakfast dishes, only part of which had been removed to the kitchen. "She couldn't imagine where you'd gone at that hour an' left your beds and your dishes."

A wave of indignation swept over Julia Cloud's sweet face.

"So you have been in my house during my absence!" she said quietly. "That seems strange since Ellen has no key!"

There was nothing in her voice to indicate rebuke, but Mrs. Perkins got very red.

"I s'pose your own sister has a right to get into the house where she was born," she snapped.

"Oh, of course," said Julia Cloud pleasantly. "And Ellen used to be a good climber before she got so fat. I suppose she climbed in the second-story window, although I hadn't realized she could. However, it doesn't matter. I suppose you have had to leave your dishes and beds once in a while when you were called away on business. You have a cup there; did you want to borrow something?"

Mrs. Perkins was one of those people who are never quite aware of it when they are in a corner; but she felt most uncomfortable, especially as she caught a stifled giggle from Allison, who bolted into the parlor hastily and began noisily to turn over the pages of a book on the table; but she managed to ask for her soda and get herself out of the house.

"Thank you for bringing my sister's message," called Julia Cloud after her. She never could quite bear to be unpleasant even to a prying neighbor, and Mrs. Perkins through the years had managed to make herself unpleasant many times.

"The old cat!" said Leslie in a clear, carrying voice. "Why did you thank her, Auntie Jewel? She didn't deserve it."

"Hush, Leslie, dear! She will hear you!" said Julia Cloud, hastily closing the door on the last words.

"I hope she did," said Leslie comfortably. "I *meant* she should."

"But, deary, that isn't right! It isn't—Christian!" said her aunt in distress.

"Then I'm no Christian," chanted Leslie mischievously. "Why isn't it right, I'd like to know? Isn't she an old cat?"

"But you hurt her feelings, dear. I'm afraid I was to blame, too; I didn't answer her any too sweetly myself."

"Well, didn't she hurt yours first? *Sweet!* Why, you were honey itself, Cloudy, dear, thanking her for her old prying!"

"I hope it's the kind of honey that gets bitter after you swallow it!" growled Allison, coming out of the parlor. "If she'd said much more, I'd just have put her out of the house, talking to you like that, as if you were a little child, Cloudy!"

"Why, children! That didn't really hurt me any; it just stirred up my temper a little; but I'm ashamed that I let it, and I don't want you to talk like that. It isn't a bit right. It distresses me to have you think it's right to answer back that way and take vengeance on people."

"Well, there, Cloudy, let's lay that subject on the table for some of our night talks; and you can scold us all you like. We have a lot of work to do now, and let's forget the old pry. Now you lie down on that couch where I put you, and Leslie and I'll wash these dishes."

Julia Cloud lay obediently on the couch, but her mind was not at rest. She was in a tumult of indignation at her prying neighbor and an uncertainty of anxiety about Ellen and what she might do next. But beneath it all was a vague fear about these her dear children who were about to become her responsibility. Could she do it? Dared she do it? How differently they had been brought up from all the traditions which had controlled her life!

Take, for instance, that matter of Christianity. How would they feel about it? Would they be in sympathy with her ideas and ideals of right and wrong? They were no longer little children to obey her. They would have ideas of their own, yes, and ideals. Would there be constant clashing? Would she be haunted with a feeling that she was not doing her duty by them? There were so many such questions, amusements, and Sabbath, and churchgoing, and how to treat other people. And doubtless she was old-fashioned, and they would chafe under her rule.

Take the little matter of Leslie's calling Mrs. Perkins a cat. She *was* a cat, but Leslie ought not to have told her so. It wasn't polite, and it wasn't Christian. And yet how could she, plain Julia Cloud, who had never been anywhere much outside of her home town, who had had no opportunity for study or wide reading, and who had only worked quietly all her life, and thought her plain little thoughts of love to God and to her neighbors, be able to explain all those things to this pair of lovable, uncontrolled children, who had always had their own way, and whose ideals were the ideals of the great wide unchristian world?

A little pucker grew between her brows, and a tired, troubled tear stole softly between her lashes. When the children, tiptoeing about and whispering, came to peek in at the door and see whether she was asleep, they discovered her expression at once, and, drawing near, sighted the tear. Then they went down upon their knees beside her couch, and noisily demanded the cause thereof.

Little by little they drew her fears from her.

"Why, Cloudy, dear! We'll do what you want. We'll let all the old cats in the community walk over you if that will make you happy," declared Leslie, patting her face.

"No, we won't!" put in Allison; "we'll keep 'em away from her, but we won't let 'em know how we despise 'em. Won't that do, Cloudy? And as for all those other things you are afraid about, why couldn't you just wait till we come to them? We're anything but angels, I admit, but we're going to try to do what you want us to if it busts the eye-teeth out of us, because we want you. And you always have been such a good scout. As for the church dope and all that, why, it's like that guy in the Bible you used to tell us about when we were children—or was she a lady? It's a case of 'Thy people shall be my people, and thy God my God,' or words to that effect. If we don't agree on our own account, we'll do it because you want it. Isn't that about the idea? Wouldn't that fill the bill?"

"You dear children!" said Julia Cloud, her eyes full of smiles and tears now as she gathered them both into a loving embrace. "I don't know how anybody could promise more than that. I wasn't afraid of you; it was myself. You know I'm not at all wise, and it's pretty late in life for me to begin to bring up children."

"Well, you're all right, anyhow, Cloudy; and you're the only person in the world we'll let bring us up; so it's up to you to do it the best you can, or it won't get done. Come on now; we've got lunch ready. There's cold chicken and bread and milk and pie and cake, and I've got the teakettle boiling like a house afire, so if you want any tea or anything you can have it."

So they had a merry meal, and Julia Cloud ate and laughed with them, and thought she never had been so happy since she was a little girl. Then, mindful of her prying neighbor and her imminent sister, she insisted on putting the house in order to the last bed and dish before she was ready for the afternoon.

"And now we're going to call on Aunt Ellen!" announced Allison as Julia Cloud hung up the clean dish-towels steaming from their scalding bath, and washed her hands at the sink.

"Why, she's coming here!" said his aunt, whirling around with a troubled look. "And, as she's left word she was coming, I suppose we'll have to wait for her. It's too bad, for she won't be here till three, and it's only a quarter of two. I'm sorry, because you wanted to go out in the car, didn't you?"

"We're going!" said Allison, again with a commanding twinkle in his eye. "We can't waste all that time; and, besides, don't you see if she comes here, she'll likely stay all the afternoon and argue? If we go there, we can come away when we like; and she'll feel we're more polite to come to her, anyhow, won't she, Cloudy?"

Julia Cloud looked into the boy's convincing eyes, and her trouble cleared away. Perhaps he was right. Anyhow, why should they spoil a whole day to conciliate Ellen? Ellen would be disagreeable about it, however they did; and they might as well rise above it, and just be pleasant, and let it go at that.

It was the first time in her long life of self-sacrifice that Julia Cloud had been able to rise above her anxiety about her sister's tantrums and go calmly on her way. It is scarcely likely that she would have managed it now if it hadn't been that she felt that Allison and Leslie ought not to be sacrificed.

She never did anything just for herself. It was not in her.

"All right," she said briskly, glancing at the clock; "then we must go at once, or we shall miss her. I'll be ready in five minutes. How about you, Leslie?"

"Oh, I'm ready now," said the girl, patting her curly hair into shape before the old mahogany-framed mirror in the hall.

In five minutes more they were stowed away in the big blue car again, speeding down the road, with Mrs. Perkins indignantly and openly watching them from her front porch.

"We put one over on Mrs. Pry, didn't we, Cloudy?" said Allison, turning around to wink a naughty eye back toward the Perkins house. "She thinks you've dared to run away after she gave you orders to stay at home."

Julia Cloud could not suppress a smile of enjoyment, and wondered whether she was getting childish that she should be so happy with these children.

CHAPTER V

The air was fine; the sky was clear without a cloud; and the spice of autumn flavored everything. Along the roadside blackberry vines were turning scarlet, and here and there in the distance a flaming branch proclaimed the approach of a frosty wooing. One could not ask anything better on such a day than to be speeding along this white velvet road in the great blue car with two beloved children.

But all too soon Herbert Robinson's ornate house loomed up, stark and green, with very white trimmings, and regular flower-beds each side of the gravel walk. It was the home of a prosperous man, and as such asserted itself. There had never been anything attractive about it to Julia Cloud. She preferred the ugly old house in which she had always lived, with its scaling gray paint and no pretensions to fineness. At least it was softened by age, and had a look of experience which saved its ugliness from being crude, and gave it the dignity of time.

And now Julia Cloud's heart began to beat rapidly. All at once she felt that she had done a most foolish thing in allowing the children to overrule her and bring her here. Ellen would not be dressed up nor have the children ready for inspection, and she would be angry at her sister for not having given warning of their coming. She leaned forward breathlessly to suggest turning back; but Allison, perhaps anticipating her feeling, said:

"Now don't you get cold feet, Cloudy Jewel. If Aunt Ellen is sore, just you talk up to her, and smile a lot, and we'll back you up. Remember everything's, going fine, and the whole thing's settled. It's too late to change it now. Is this the place? We'll turn right in, shall we?" And with the words he swept up under the elaborate wooden porte-cochère, and, swinging down, flung the door open for Julia Cloud to alight.

Leslie gave a quick, disdainful glance about, fluttered out beside her aunt, and, catching the look of apprehension on her face, tripped up the steps and rang the bell, poising bird-like on the threshold and calling in a sweet, flute-like voice:

"Aunt Ellen! O Aunt Ellen! Where are you? Don't you know you've got company all the way from California?"

It was just like taking the bull by the horns, and Julia Cloud paused on the upper step in wonder. How winning a child she was! and how she had known by intuition just how to mollify her unpleasant relative!

What would Ellen say? How would she take it?

Ellen Robinson bustled frowning into the hall, whetting her sharp tongue for an encounter. She had seen the big blue car turn in at the gate, and knew from Mrs. Perkins's description who it must be. Julia Cloud had well judged her state of mind, for her four children could not have been caught in a worse plight so far as untidiness was concerned, and there had barely been time to marshal them all up the back stairs with orders to scrub and dress or not to come down till the visitors were gone. They were even now creeping shufflingly about overhead on their bare feet, hunting for their respective best shoes and stockings and other garments, and scrapping in loud whispers.

But Leslie, little diplomat that she was, wasted no time in taking stock of her aunt. She flung her arms joyously around that astonished woman, and fairly took her by storm, talking volubly and continuously until they were all in the house and seated in Ellen's best satin brocatelle parlor chairs, surrounded by crayon portraits of Herbert Robinson's ancestors and descendants. Allison too caught on to his sister's game, and talked a good deal about how nice it was to get East again after all the years, and how glad they were to have some relatives of their own. Julia Cloud sat quietly and proudly listening; and Ellen forgot her anger, and ceased to frown. After all, it was something to have such good-looking relatives. For the first few minutes the well-prepared speech wherewith she had intended to dress down poor Julia lay idle on her lips, and a few sentences of grudging welcome even, managed to slip by. Then suddenly she turned to her sister, and the sight of the adoration for the visitors in Julia's transparent face kindled her anger. Never had such a look as this glowed in Julia Cloud's face for any little Robinson, save perhaps in the first few days of their tiny lives before the Robinson had begun to crop out in them.

"Where were you this morning, Jule? It certainly seems queer for you to be gadding around having a good time so soon after poor mother's death. And the dishes not washed, either! Upon my word, you have lost your head! You weren't brought up that way. I stood up-stairs and looked around on those unmade beds, and thought what poor mother would have said if she could see them. Such goings-on! I certainly was ashamed to have Mrs. Perkins see it."

Two rosy spots bloomed out on Julia Cloud's cheeks, and a tremble came in her lips, though one could see she was making a great effort to control herself; and the two long breaths that Leslie and Allison drew simultaneously were heavily threatening, much like the distant rumble of thunder.

"I'm sure I don't see what occasion Mrs. Perkins had to see it," she answered steadily.

"Well, she was there!" said her sister dryly. She seemed to have forgotten the presence of the two young people, who, if they had been in the foreground, might have been noticed doing things with their eyebrows to their mutual understanding and agreement.

"Yes, so she told me," said Julia Cloud significantly. "But that was not what I came over to talk about, Ellen; I wanted to let you know that I've rented the house, and the tenant wants possession next week. I thought you might like to pick out some of mother's things to bring over here before I pack up. You spoke about wishing you had another couch for the sitting-room, and you might just as well have the dining-room one as not. Then I thought perhaps you could use mother's bedroom suit."

"You've rented the house!" screamed Ellen as soon as she got breath from her astonishment to interrupt. "You've rented the house without consulting me? Who to, I'd like to know? I had a tenant already for that house, I told you."

"Why, I had no time to consult you, Ellen; and, besides, why should I? The house is mine, and I knew you didn't want it. You have your own home."

"Well, you certainly are blossoming out and getting independent! I should think mere decency would have made you consult us before you did anything. What do you know about business? Herbert will be mad as anything when I tell him; and like as not you'll get into no end of trouble with a strange tenant, and we'll have to help you out. Herbert always says women make all the trouble they can for him before they call on him for assistance."

Julia smiled.

"I shall not be obliged to call on Herbert for assistance, Ellen. Everything is arranged. The contract was signed this morning, and I have promised to vacate as soon as possible. The tenant is the new school superintendent, and he wants to come at once. I just heard last evening that he had been disappointed in getting the Harvey house. It's sold to the foreman of the mill. So I went over to Harmony to see him at once."

The news was so overwhelming and so unquestionably satisfactory from a business point of view that Ellen was speechless with astonishment. Allison gave Leslie a grave wink, and turned to look out of the window to prevent an outburst of giggles from his sister.

"Well, I think you might have let me know," Ellen resumed with almost her usual poise. "It's rather mortifying not to know what's going on in your own family when the neighbors ask. Here was I without any knowledge of the arrival of my own niece and nephew! Had to be told by Mrs. Perkins."

Then Allison and Leslie did laugh, but they veiled their mirth by talking about the two white chickens out in the yard which were contending for a worm. Suddenly Leslie exclaimed:

"O Allison! I hear the children coming down-stairs, and I forgot their presents! Run out to the car, and bring me that box."

Allison was off at once, and the entrance of the soapy and embarrassed children created a further diversion.

For a few minutes even Ellen Robinson was absorbed in the presents. There was a camera for Junior, a gold chain and locket for Elaine, a beautiful doll for Dorothy, and a small train of cars that would wind up and run on a miniature track for Bertie; so of course everything had to be looked at and tried. Elaine put on her chain, and preened herself before the glass; Junior had to understand at once just how to take a picture; everybody had to watch the doll open and shut its eyes, and to try to unbutton and button its coat and dress; and then the railroad track had to be set up and the train started off on its rounds. Ellen Robinson really looked almost motherly while she watched her happy children; and Julia Cloud relaxed, and let the smile come around her lips once more.

But all things come to an end, and Ellen Robinson was not one to forget her own affairs for long at a time. She sat back from starting the engine on its third round, and fixed her eyes on her sister with that air of commander-general that was so intolerable.

"Well, then, I suppose you won't be over here till next week," she frowned thoughtfully. "I needed you to help with the crabapple jelly. That makes it inconvenient. But perhaps I can hold off the fruit a little longer; I'll see. You ought to be able to get all your packing done this week, I should think. When do they go?" She nodded toward the niece and nephew quite indifferently as though they were deaf.

Julia Cloud's sensitive face flushed with annoyance, but the two pairs of bright eyes that lifted and fixed themselves upon their aunt held nothing but enjoyment of the situation.

"Why, we're not going until Aunt Jewel is ready to go with us, Aunt Ellen," announced Leslie, looking up from the doll she was reclothing. "You know we're all going to college together, Auntie, too!"

Ellen Robinson lifted an indignant chin. She had no sense of humor, and did not enjoy jokes, especially those practised upon herself.

"Going to college! At her age!" she snorted. "Well, I always knew she was childish, but I never expected her to want to go back to kindergarten!"

Leslie rose up straight as a rush, her strong young arms down at her sides, her fingers in their soft suède gloves working restively as if she wanted to rush at her aunt and administer corporal punishment. Her pretty red lips were pursed angrily, and her blue eyes fairly blazed righteous wrath. Julia Cloud caught her breath, and wondered how she was to control this young fury; but before she could say a word Allison stepped in front of her, and spoke coolly.

"That's the reason she's such a good scout, Aunt Ellen. That's why we want her to come and take care of us. Because she knows how to stay young."

He suddenly seemed to have grown very tall and quite mature as he spoke, and there was something about his manly bearing that held Ellen Robinson's tongue in check as he looked at his watch with a polite "Excuse me," and then turned to Julia Cloud. "Aunt Jewel, if we are to meet my guardian on that train, I think we shall have to hurry. It's quite a run into the city, you know." Julia Cloud arose with a breath of relief.

"The city!" gasped Ellen. "You're not going into the city this late in the afternoon, I hope! Do you know how long it takes?"

Allison glanced out to his high-powered machine confidently.

"We made it in an hour and a half coming over. I guess we shall have plenty of time to meet the five-o'clock train if we go at once. I've got a peach of a car, Aunt Ellen. I'll have to come round and take you and the kids a ride to-morrow or the next day if Aunt Jewel can spare me."

"Thank you! I have a car of my own!" snapped his aunt disagreeably.

"Oh! I beg your pardon! Well, Aunt Jewel, we really must go if we are to meet Mr. Luddington. Good-by, Aunt Ellen! Good-by, cousins! We'll see you again before we leave town, of course. Come on, Aunt Jewel!" And he took Julia Cloud lightly, protectingly by the elbow, and steered her out of the room, down the steps, and into the car, while Leslie danced gayly after, chattering away about how nice it was to get back East and meet real relatives.

But Ellen Robinson was not listening to Leslie. She hurried after her departing guests regardless of a noisy struggle that was going on between her two youngest over the railway train, and stood on her front steps, fairly snorting with indignation.

"Julia Cloud, what does all this mean? You shan't go away until you explain. Have you taken leave of your senses? What is this nonsense about going to college?"

Allison with his hand on the starter gave his aunt a swift, reassuring smile; and Julia Cloud from the safe vantage of the back seat leaned forward, smiling.

"Why, it's the children that are going to college, Ellen, not I. I'm only going along to keep house and play mother for them. Isn't it lovely? I'll tell you all about it to-morrow when you come down to pick out your things. Be sure to come early, because I want to get started packing the first thing in the morning. Mr. Luddington, the children's guardian, is coming to-night to complete the arrangements, and we expect to get away just as soon as I can get packed up. So come early."

The engine purred softly for a rhythmical second, and the car slid quickly away from the door.

"But—the very idea!" snorted Aunt Ellen. "Julia Cloud!" she fairly shouted. "Stop! You had no right in the world to go ahead and make plans without consulting me!"

But the car was beyond ear-shot now, and Leslie was waving a pretty, tantalizing hand from the back seat.

"The very idea!" Ellen Robinson gasped to the autumn landscape as she stood alone and watched the car, a mere speck down the road, on its way to town. "The idea!" And then as if for self-justification: "Poor mother! What would she think if she could know? Well, I wash my hands of her."

But Ellen Robinson did not wash her hands of her sister. Instead, she found that it was going to be very hard indeed to wash her hands of her own affairs without her sister's help. She had, in fact, been counting on that help for the last several years, after her mother became an invalid and she knew that it was only a matter of time before Julia's hands would be set free for other labor. It was quite too disconcerting now, after having got along all these years on the strength of the help that was to come, to find her capable sister snatched away from her by two young things in this ridiculous way.

They talked it over at supper, and Herbert was almost savage about it, as if in some way his wife had misrepresented the possibilities, and led him to expect the assistance that would come from her sister and save him from paying wages to a servant.

"Well, she'll be good and sick of it inside of three months, mark my words; and then she'll come whining back and want us to take her in;—be glad enough to get a home. So don't you worry. But what I want understood is this: *She's not going to find it so easy to get back.* See? You make her thoroughly understand that. You better go down to-morrow and pick out everything you want. Take plenty. You can't tell but something may happen to the house, and the furniture burn up. We might as well have it as anybody. And you make it good and sure that she understands right here and now that if she goes she doesn't come back. Of course, I'm not saying she can't come back if she comes to her senses, and is real humble; but you needn't let her know that. Just give her to understand it is her last chance, that I can't be monkeyed with this way. I've offered her a very generous thing, and she knows it, and she's a fool, that's what she is, a *fool* I say!" He brought his big fist down heavily on the table, and jarred the dishes; and the children looked up in premature comprehension, storing up the epithet for future use. "She's no end of a fool, going off with those crazy kids. Some one ought to warn their guardian about her. Why, she has no more idea of how to take care of two high and mighty good-for-nothings like that than an infant in arms!"

Meantime the subject of their discussion was seated serenely at a table in one of the best hotels of the great city, having the time of her life. In the years that were to come there might be many more delightful suppers, even more elegantly served, perhaps; but none would ever rival this first time in her existence when she had sat among the wealthy and great of the land and been treated like one of them.

Mr. Luddington was a typical business man, elderly and kind, with wise eyes and a great smile. He turned his eyes keenly on Julia Cloud for an instant at their first meeting, then let his full smile envelop her, and she was somehow made aware of the fact that he had set his seal of approval to the contract already made by his two enthusiastic wards. All the forebodings she had entertained in the little intervals when Leslie and Allison allowed her to think at all were swept aside by his kind look and big, serious tone when he first took her hand and scanned her true face. "I'm glad they've picked such a woman!" he said. "You'll have your hands full, for they're a pair! But it's worth it!"

And, when they all rode home through the moonlight, Julia Cloud nestled under the soft, thick robes of the car, and listened to the pleasant talk between the young people and their guardian with a sense of peace. If this strong, wise business man thought the arrangement was all right, why, then she need not fear any longer. It was real, and not a dream, and she might rely upon the wisdom of her decision. And with that sense of being upheld by something wiser than her own wish she fell asleep that night, haunted by no dreams of her domineering sister.

CHAPTER VI

The pleasant aromas of coffee and sausages were mingling in the air when "Guardy Lud" woke up and looked about the old-fashioned room with a sense of satisfaction. The very pictures on the walls rested him, they reminded him so much of the rooms in his boyhood home. He had a feeling that old-fashioned things were best, and in spite of the fact that he owned a house most different from this one himself and knew that his wife would not for a minute have tolerated any old-fashioned things about unless they were so old-fashioned that they had become the latest rage, he could not help feeling that a woman brought up amid such simple surroundings would be the very best kind to mother these orphan children who had been left on his helpless hands. He would have loved to take them to his heart and his home; but his wife was not so minded, and that ended it. But it rolled a great burden from his shoulders to feel that he might leave them in such capable hands.

They had a rollicking time at breakfast, for Guardy Lud was delighted with the crisp brown sausages, fried potatoes, and buckwheats with real maple-syrup; and he laughed, and ate, and told stories with the children, and kept the old dining-room walls ringing with joy as they had not resounded within the memory of Julia Cloud. Then suddenly the door opened, and there stood Ellen Robinson, disapproval and hauteur written in every line of her unpleasant face! One could hardly imagine how those two, Julia and Ellen, could possibly be sisters.

Dismay filled Julia Cloud's heart for an instant, and brought a pallor to her cheek. How had she forgotten Ellen? What a fool she had been to tell Ellen to come early in the morning! But she had not realized that Mr. Luddington would be willing to come out to her humble home and stay all night. She had supposed that the arrangements would be made in the city. However, it could not be helped now; and a glance at the kind, strong face of the white-haired man gave her courage. Ellen could not really spoil their plans with him there. He felt that the arrangement was good, and with him to back her she felt she could stand out against any arguments her sister might bring forth.

So she rose with a natural ease, and introduced her. "My sister Mrs. Robinson, Mr. Luddington"; and Ellen stiffly and still disapprovingly acknowledged the introduction.

"I won't interrupt," she said disagreeably. "I'm just going up to look over some of my mother's things." And she turned to the back stairway, and went up, closing the door behind her.

Mr. Luddington gazed after her a second; and then, taking his glasses off and wiping them energetically, he remarked:

"Well, well, bless my soul! It must be getting late! We've had such a good time I didn't realize. Those certainly were good buckwheats, Miss Cloud. I shan't forget them very soon. And now I suppose we'd better get down to business. Could we just go into the other room there, and close the door for a few minutes, not to be interrupted?" and he cast an anxious glance toward the stair-door again.

Julia Cloud smiled understandingly, and ushered them into the little parlor ablaze with fall sunshine, its windows wreathed about with crimsoning woodbine; and, as she caught the glow and glint from the window, she remembered the gray evening when she had looked out across into her future as she supposed it would be. How beautiful and wonderful that the gray had changed to glow! As she sat down to enter into the contract that was to bind her to a new and wonderful life with great responsibilities and large possibilities, her heart, accustomed to look upward, sent a whisper of thanksgiving heavenward.

The details did not take long, after all; for Mr. Luddington was a keen business man, and he had gone over the whole proposition, and had the plan in writing for her to sign, telling just what were her duties and responsibilities with regard to his wards, just how much money she would have for housekeeping and servants and other expenses, and the salary she would receive herself for accepting this care.

"You're practically in a position of mother to them, you know," he said, beaming at her genially; "and I declare I never laid eyes on a woman that I thought could fill the part better!"

Julia Cloud was quite overwhelmed. But the matter of the salary troubled her.

"I think it should not be a matter of money," she demurred. "I would rather do it for love, you know."

"Love's all right!" said the old man, smiling; "but this thing has got to be on a business basis, or the terms of the will will not allow me to agree to it. You see what you are going to undertake means work, and it means sticking to it; and you deserve pay for it, and we're not going to accept several of the best years out of your life for nothing. Besides, you've got to feel free to give up the job if it proves too burdensome for you."

"And you to dismiss me if I do not prove capable for the position," suggested Julia Cloud, lifting meek and honest eyes to meet his gaze.

"Well, well, well, I can see there won't be any need of that!" sputtered the old gentleman pleasantly. "But, however that is, this is the contract I've made out. And I'm quite satisfied. So are the children. Are you willing to sign it? Of course there's a clause in there about reasonable notice if there is dissatisfaction on either side; that lets you out at any time you get tired of it. Only give me a chance to look after these youngsters properly."

Julia Cloud took the pen eagerly, tremblingly, a sense of wonder in her pounding heart, and signed her name just as Ellen's heavy footsteps could be heard pounding down the back stairs. Leslie seized Julia, and gave her a great hug as the last letter was finished, and then threw open the parlor door in the nick of time to save her Aunt Ellen from seeming to be deserted.

Ellen Robinson appeared on the scene just in time to witness the hearty hand-shake that Guardy Lud gave Julia Cloud as he picked up the papers and went up-stairs for his suitcase while Allison went after the car to take him to the train.

"Is that man married? Because, if he isn't, I don't think it's respectable for you to go and live near him!" declared Ellen in a penetrating voice to the intense distress of Julia Cloud, who was happily hurrying the dishes from the breakfast table.

But Leslie came to the rescue.

"Oh, indeed, Aunt Ellen, he's very much married! Altogether too much married for comfort. He would be a dear if it wasn't for his silly little old bossy wife! But he doesn't intend to live anywhere near us. His home is off in California, and he's going back next week. He's only waiting to see us settled somewhere before he goes back; so you needn't worry about Aunt Jewel's morals. We'll take good care of her. But isn't he a dear? He was my Grandfather Leslie's best friend."

Leslie chattered on gayly till the visitor's footsteps could be heard coming down-stairs again, and Ellen Robinson could only shut her lips tight and go into the kitchen, from which her sister beat immediately a hasty retreat lest more unpleasant remarks should be forthcoming.

Julia Cloud bade Mr. Luddington good-by, standing on her own front steps, and then waited a moment, looking off toward the hills which had shut in her vision all her life. The two young people had rushed down to the car, and were pulling their guardian joyously inside. They seemed to do everything joyously, like two young creatures let out of prison into the sunshine. Julia Cloud smiled at the thought of them, but her soul was not watching them just then. She was looking off to the hills that had been her strength all the years through so many trials, and gathering strength now to go in and meet her sister in final combat. She knew that there would be a scene; that was inevitable. That she might maintain her calmness and say nothing unkind or regrettable she was praying earnestly now as her eyes sought the hills.

Across the road behind her parlor curtains Mrs. Perkins was keeping lookout, and remarking to a neighbor who had run in:

"Yes, I thought as much. There's always a man in the case when a woman acts queer! Now, doesn't that beat all? Do you suppose he's a long-lost lover or something, come back now he knows she's free? Seems to me I did hear there was somebody died or something before we came here to live, but she must have been awful young."

The car moved noisily away, and the old gentleman leaned out with a courteous lift of his hat toward Julia Cloud. She acknowledged it with a bow and a smile which Mrs. Perkins pounced on and analyzed audibly.

"Well, there's no fool like an old fool, as the saying is! Just watch her smirk! I'm mighty glad Ellen Robinson's there to relieve me of the responsibility. She'll be over after a while, and then we'll know who he is. There goes Julia in. She watched him out o' sight! Well, I wonder what her mother would think."

Julia Cloud went slowly back to the dining-room, where Ellen was seated on the couch, waiting like a visitor. Julia's smile was utterly lost on her glum countenance, which resembled an embattled tower under siege.

"Well!" she said as Julia began to gather up more dishes from the breakfast table. "I suppose you think you've done something smart now, don't you, getting that old snob here and fixing things all up without consulting any of your relatives?"

"Really, Ellen, this has all been so sudden that I had no opportunity," said Julia gently. "But it did not seem likely that you would object, for you suggested yourself that I rent the house, and you said you did not want me to stay here alone. This seemed quite providential."

"Providential!" sniffed Ellen. "Providential to take you away from your own home and your own people, and send you out into a world where nobody really cares for you, and where all they want of you is to make a drudge of you! You call that providential, do you? Well, I *don't*! And when I object, and try to save you from yourself, and offer you a good home where you will be cared for all the rest of your days, right among your own, where mother would have wanted to see you, you will probably get high-headed, and say I am interfering with your rights. But I can't help it. I've got to speak. I can't see you put the halter around your neck to hang yourself without doing everything I can to stop it. My own sister!"

"Why, Ellen, dear!" said Julia Cloud eagerly, sitting down beside her sister. "You don't understand. It isn't in the least that way. I'm sorry I had to spring it on you so suddenly and give you such a wrong impression. You know I couldn't think of coming to live on you and Herbert. It was kind of you to suggest it, and I am grateful and all that; but I know how it would be to have some one else, even a sister, come into the home, and I couldn't think of it. I have always resolved that I would never be dependent on my relatives while I had my health."

Ellen sat up bristling.

"And yet you are willing to go away to some strange place where nobody knows you, and slave for a couple of little snobs!"

"O Ellen!" said Julia pleadingly. "You don't understand. I am not going to slave. I'm just going to be a sort of mother to them. And you oughtn't to call them snobs. They are your own brother's children."

"Own brother's children, nothing!" sneered Ellen. "He's been away so many years he was just like a stranger when he came back the last time, and as for the children they are just like his stuck-up wife and her family. Yet you'll leave the children that were born and raised close beside you, and go and slave for them. Mother! fiddlesticks! You'll slave all right. I know you. In six weeks you'll be a drudge for them the way you've been all your life! I know how it is, and you may not believe it; but I have feelings for my sister, and I don't like to see her put upon."

Ellen fumbled for her handkerchief, and managed a comely tear or two that quite touched Julia's heart. Affection between them even when Ellen was a child had been quite one-sided; for Ellen had always been a selfish, spoiled little thing, and Julia had looked in vain for any signs of tenderness. Now her heart warmed toward her younger sister in this long-delayed thoughtfulness, and her tone grew gentler.

"That's dear of you, Ellen, and I appreciate it; but I haven't been able to make you understand yet, I see. I'm not to be a worker, nor even a housekeeper. I'm to be just a sort of mother, or aunt, if you please, to see that the house runs all right, to be with the children and have a happy time with them and their young friends, and to see that they are cared for in every way necessary; just a housemother, you understand. I am to have servants to do the work, although I'm sure one servant will be all that I shall want in a little household like that. But Mr. Luddington quite insisted there should be servants, and that no work of any sort should fall upon me. He said that as their nearest relative I was to be in the position of mother and guardian to them, and to preside over their home."

"That's ridiculous!" put in Ellen. "Why don't they go to college and board like any other reasonable young folks if they must go to college at all? I think it's all nonsense for 'em to go. What do they do it for? They've got money, and don't have to teach or anything. What do they need of learning? They've got enough now to get along. That girl thinks she's too smart to live. I call her impudent, for my part!"

"They want a home," said Julia, waiving the subject of higher education; "and they have chosen me, and I mean to do my best."

There was a quiet finality in her tone that impressed her sister. She looked at her angrily.

"Well, if you will, you will, I suppose. Nobody can stop you. But I see just what will come of it. You'll fool away a little while there, and find out how mistaken you were; and then you'll come back to Herbert to be taken care of. And you don't realize how offended Herbert is going to be by your actions, and how he'll feel about letting you come back after you have gone away in such high feather. You haven't anything to speak of to support yourself, of course, and how on earth do you expect to live anyway after these children get through their college and get married or something? They won't want you then."

Julia arose and went to the window to get calmed. She was more angry than she had been for years. The thought of Herbert's having to take care of her ever was intolerable. But she was able to hold her tongue until she could get her eyes on those hills out of the window. "I will lift up mine eyes unto the hills, from whence cometh my help." That had been the verse which she had read from her little Bible before leaving her room in the early morning and she was grappling it close to her heart, for she had known it would be a hard day.

Ellen was watching her silently. Almost she thought she had made an impression. Perhaps this was the time to repeat Herbert's threat.

"Herbert feels," she began, "that if you refuse his offer now he can't promise to keep it open. He can't be responsible for you if you take this step. He said he wanted you to understand thoroughly."

Julia Cloud turned and walked with swift step to the little parlor where lay the paper she and Mr. Luddington had just signed, and a copy of which he had taken with him. She returned to her astonished sister with the paper in her hand.

"Perhaps it would be just as well for you to read this," she said with dignity, and put the paper into Ellen's hands, going back to her clearing of the table.

There was silence in the dining-room while Ellen read, Julia moving on quiet feet about the table, putting things to rights. She had finished her part of the argument. She was resolutely putting out of her mind the things her sister had just said, and refusing altogether to think of Herbert. She knew in her heart just how Herbert had looked

333

when he had said those things, even to the snarl at the corner of his nose. She knew, too, that Ellen had probably not reported the message even so disagreeably as the original, and she knew that it would be better to forget.

"Well," said Ellen, rising after a long perusal, laying the paper on the table, "that sounds all very well in writing. The thing is to see how it comes out. The proof of the pudding is in the eating, and you needn't tell me that any man in his senses will pay all that salary merely for a 'chaperon,' as he calls it. If he does, he's a fool; that's all I've got to say. But I suppose nothing short of getting caught in a trap will make you see it; so I better save my breath. I'm sure I hope you won't go to the poorhouse through your stubbornness. I've done all I could to keep you from it, and it's pretty hard to have my only sister leave me—so soo-oo-on after mother's—death."

"Well, Ellen," said Julia Cloud, looking at her speculatively, "I'm sure I never dreamed you cared about having me away from here. You've never shown much interest in being with me. But I'm sorry if you feel it that way, and I'm sure I'll write to you and try to do little things for the children often, now that I shall have something to do with." But her kindly feeling was cut short by Ellen interrupting her.

"Oh, you needn't trouble yourself! We can look after the children ourselves. You better save what you get to look after yourself when those two get over this whim!"

And then to her great relief Julia Cloud heard the car returning from the station, and the two young people rushing into the hall.

CHAPTER VII

"I'm going up-stairs to put on that calico wrapper you loaned me, Aunt Jewel," shouted Leslie, putting a rosy face into the dining-room for an instant and then vanishing.

"I bought a pair of overalls at the store, as you suggested, Cloudy," put in Allison, waving a pair of blue jeans at her and vanishing also.

Ellen Robinson stood mopping her eyes and staring out from the dining-room window—not at the hills—and sniffing.

"I should think you'd stop them calling you that ridiculous name!" she snorted. "It isn't respectful. It sounds like making fun of the family."

Poor Ellen Robinson! She had her good points, but a sense of humor wasn't one of them. Also it went against the grain to give up her own way, and she couldn't remember when she hadn't planned for the freedom she would have when Julia came to live with her. Having an entirely different temperament from Julia's and no spiritual outlook whatever on life, she was unable to understand what thraldom she had been preparing and planning for her patient elder sister. A little of this perhaps penetrated to Julia Cloud's disturbed consciousness as she watched her sister's irate back; for, when she spoke again, it was in a gentle, soothing tone.

"There now, Ellen, let's forget it all, and just put it away. I shall be coming back to see you now and then, perhaps, and you can come and see me. That'll be something new to look forward to. Suppose now we just get to work and see what's to be done. Have you decided what you want to have taken over to the house?"

It is doubtful whether Ellen would have succumbed so easily, had not the two young people returned just then and demanded that they have something to do.

As quietly as if she were used to packing and moving every year of her life, Julia Cloud gave them each a pile of newspapers, and set them to wrapping and packing dishes in a big barrel; and Ellen was forced to join in and say what she wanted to have of her mother's things.

Without a word Julia set aside anything Ellen asked for, even when it was something she would have liked to keep herself; and Ellen, her lips pursed and her eyes bright with defeat, went from room to room, picking and choosing as if she were at an auction.

Allison still in overalls rushed out in the car, and got a man with a moving-wagon; and before twelve o'clock Ellen Robinson saw a goodly load of household furniture start for her own home; and, being somewhat anxious as to how it would be disposed on its arrival, she took the car, and sped away to placate Herbert. She really felt quite triumphant at the ease with which she had secured several valuable pieces of mahogany which she knew had always been favorites with Julia.

"Gee!" said Allison as the car vanished out of sight, "isn't Aunt Ellen some depressor? Was she always so awfully grown up? I say, Cloudy, you won't get that way, will you when we get you off in our house? If you do, take poison, or get married, or something. Say, Cloudy Jewel, you're twenty years younger than she is, do you know it? Now what'll I do next? That closet is all empty. Shall I begin on this one? You want this barrel up in the attic, you say? All right; here goes! No, I won't hurt my back; I'm strong as a horse. I know how to lift things without hurting myself. Open that door, Leslie, and move that chair out of my way. Which corner shall I stow it, Cloudy? Southwest? All right!" and he vanished up the stairs with his barrel.

At half-past twelve a man and a woman arrived whom Julia Cloud had hired to help; and the house was like a busy hive, not a drone among them. It really was wonderful how short a time it took to dismantle a home that had been running for years. But the hands were wonderfully eager that took hold of the work, and they went at things with a will. Moreover, Julia Cloud's domain was always in perfect order, which made a big difference.

They ate their lunch from the pantry shelf, because Ellen had taken the dining-room table. But it was a good lunch, bread and butter, apple butter, cookies, half a custard pie, and glasses of rich, foamy milk. Then they went to work again. The children were smudged with dust and tumbled and happy. They were doing real things for the first time in their lives, and they liked it. Moreover, they were bringing to pass a beloved plan that had seemed at first impossible; and they wanted to hustle it through before anything spoiled or delayed it. There was Aunt Ellen. There was no telling what she might not do to hinder, and Julia Cloud was easily troubled by her sister, they could see that, wise children that they were; so they worked with all their might and main.

Two more men were requisitioned, and the furniture began a steady march up to the attic, where it was to be stored.

Leslie developed a talent for finding the place where she was most needed and getting to work. She put the sideboard drawers in order, and then went to packing away garments from the closets in drawers and trunks and chests, until by four o'clock a great many little nooks and corners in the house were absolutely clear and empty, ready for the cleaning before the new tenants arrived, although, to tell the truth, there was scarcely a spot in Julia Cloud's house that needed much cleaning, because it had always been kept immaculate.

When Ellen Robinson in her car arrived in sight of the house at half-past four she identified the parlor and dining-room carpets hanging on a line strung across the back yard, and two bedroom carpets being beaten in the side yard. Mrs. Perkins from her patient watch-tower had also identified them, and hurried out to greet her friend and get more accurate information; but Ellen was in too much of a hurry to get inside and secure several other articles, which she had thought of and desired to have, to spend much time in gossip. Besides, if Julia was really going, it was just as well to make as much of it as possible; so she greeted Mrs. Perkins as one too busy with important affairs to tell details, and hurried into the house. Standing within the old hallway, she gazed about, startled. How on earth had Julia managed to tear up things in such a hurry? The pictures had all vanished from the walls. The books were gone from the old book-case; the furniture itself was being carried away, the marble-topped table being the last piece left. The woman was washing the parlor floor, slopping on the soapy water with that air of finality that made Ellen Robinson realize that the old home was broken up at last. Grimly she walked into the dining-room, and saw immaculate empty closets and cleanly shining window-panes. As far as the work had progressed it had been done thoroughly.

Up-stairs a cheery chatter came from the rooms, and Ellen Robinson experienced a pang of real jealousy of these two young things who had swept in and carried her neglected sister by storm. Somehow it seemed to her that they had taken something that belonged to her, and she began to feel bereft. Julia ought to love her better than these two young strangers; why didn't she? Why didn't those two children make such a fuss over her as they did over Julia? It certainly was strange! Perhaps some gleam of perception that it might all be her own fault began to filter to Ellen Robinson's consciousness as she stood there on the stairs and listened to the pleasant chatter.

"O Cloudy, dear! Is this really Daddy's picture when he was a little boy? What a funny collar and necktie! But wasn't he a darling? I love the way his hair curls around his face. I can remember Daddy quite well. Mother used to say he was a wonderful man. I think he must have been a good deal like you. Our old nurse used to say that families went in streaks. I guess you and Daddy were off the same streak, weren't you? I hope Allison and I will be, too. Say, Cloudy, can't I have this picture of Daddy to hang in my room in our new house? I love it."

Ellen Robinson wondered whether they had classified her as another "streak," and somehow the thought was unpleasant. It was like one of those little rare mirrors that flash us a look now and then in which we "see oursel's as ithers see us," and are warned to take account of stock. As she climbed the old stairs, Ellen Robinson took account of herself, as it were, and resolved to show a better side to these children than she had shown heretofore; and so, when she appeared among them, she put aside her grim aspect for a while, and spoke in quite an affable tone:

"Well, you certainly can work!"

The contrast was so great that both the young people blinked at her in wonder, and a smile broke out on Leslie's lovely face. Somehow it warmed Aunt Ellen's heart, and she went on:

"But you all must be tired. You better come up to our house for supper to-night. You won't have any chance to get it here."

"Oh, we don't mind picnicking," said Leslie hastily. Then she caught a glimpse of her aunt's face, and her natural kindliness came to the front. "But of course that would be lovely if it won't be too much trouble for you," she added pleasantly with one of her brilliant smiles, although she could see Allison making violent motions and shaking his head at her from the other room, where he was out of his Aunt Ellen's sight. Leslie really had a lovely nature, and was always quick to discern it when she had hurt any one. Ellen Robinson looked at her suspiciously, alert for the insult always, but yielded suddenly and unexpectedly to the girl's loveliness. Was it something in Leslie's eyes that reminded Ellen of her big brother who used to come home now and then, and tease her, and bring her lovely gifts? She watched Leslie a moment wistfully, and then with a sigh turned away. She wished one of her little girls could look like that.

"Well, I'd better go right home and get supper ready," she said alertly; and there was a note of almost pleased eagerness in her voice that she was included in this function of packing and moving that seemed somehow to have turned into a delightful game in which weariness and care were forgotten.

"I'll have supper ready to dish up by seven o'clock," she admonished her astonished sister as she swept past the bedroom where she was at work putting away blankets and pillows in camphor. "You won't be ready much before that; but don't you be a minute later, or the supper will be spoiled."

By which admonition Julia Cloud became aware that Ellen was going to favor them with some of her famous chicken potpie. She stood still for a whole minute with a light in her eyes and a smile on her face, listening to Ellen's retreating footsteps down the stairs; then, as the Ford set up its churning clatter, she turned back to her task, and murmured softly, "Poor Ellen!"

The supper passed off very well. Herbert was a trifle gruff and silent; but it was plain that Allison's stories amused him, for now and then a half-smile crept into his stolid countenance. Julia Cloud was so glad that she could have cried. She hated scenes, and she dreaded being at outs with her relatives. So she ate her chicken potpie and fresh pumpkin-pie thankfully, and forgot how weary she was. After supper Leslie sat down at the piano, and rattled off rag-time; and she and Allison sang song after song, while the children stood about admiringly, and even Herbert sat by as at a social function and listened. The atmosphere was really quite clear when at last they prepared to leave, and Julia Cloud had an inkling that the big blue car had something to do with it.

"That's some car you've got," said Herbert patronizingly as he held a lantern for them to get down the steps. "Get it this year? What do you have to pay for that make now? I'm thinking of getting a new one myself pretty soon."

Down upon their knees in the lantern-light went the two men of the party, examining this and that point of interest, their noses turned to the mysterious inner workings of the wonderful mechanism, while Julia Cloud sat and marveled that here at last was something which Herbert Robinson respected.

And Ellen stood upon the steps, really smiling and saying how nice it had been to have them, for all the world as if they were company, all the hard lines of her rapidly maturing face softened by kindliness! It seemed like a miracle. Julia Cloud settled back into the deep cushions, and lifted her eyes to the dark line of the hills against the sky. "From whence cometh my help," trailed the words through her tired brain; and her heart murmured, "God, I thank Thee!"

CHAPTER VIII

They all slept very late the next morning, being utterly worn out from the unaccustomed work; and, when they finally got down-stairs, they took a sort of a lunch-breakfast off the pantry shelves again. It was strange how good even shredded-wheat biscuit and milk can taste when one has been working hard and has a young appetite, although Leslie and Allison had been known to scorn all cereals. Still, there were cookies and wonderful apples from the big tree in the back yard for dessert.

"When are those men coming back to finish up?" suddenly demanded Leslie, poising a glass of milk and a cooky in one hand and taking a great bite from her apple.

"Not till to-morrow," said Julia Cloud, looking around the empty kitchen speculatively, and wondering how in the world she was going to cook with all the cooking-utensils packed in the attic.

"We ought to have left the kitchen till last," she added with a troubled look. "You crazy children! Didn't you know we had to eat? I told that man not to take any of those things on the kitchen-table, that they were to stay down until the very last thing, and now he has taken the table even! I went up-stairs to see if I could get at things, and I find he has put them away at the back, and piled all the chairs and some bed-springs in front of them. I'm afraid we shall have to get some things out again. I don't see how we can get along."

"Not a bit of it, Cloudy!" said Leslie, giving a spring and perching herself on the drain-board of the sink, where she sat swinging her dainty little pumps as nonchalantly as if she were sitting on a velvet sofa. "See! Here's my plan. I woke up early, and thought it all out. Let's see," consulting her wee wrist-watch, "it's nine o'clock. That isn't bad. Now we'll work till twelve; that's long enough for to-day, because you got too tired yesterday; and, besides, we've got some other things to attend to. Then we'll hustle into the car, and get to town, and do some shopping ready for our trip. That will rest you. We'll get lunch at a tea-room, and shop all the afternoon. We'll go to a hotel for dinner, and stay all night. Then in the morning we can get up early, have our breakfast, and drive back here in time before the men come. Now isn't that perfectly spick-and-span for a plan?"

"Leslie! But, dear, that would cost a lot! And, besides, it isn't in the least necessary."

"Cost has nothing to do with it. Look!" and Leslie flourished a handful of bills. "See what Guardy Lud gave me! And Allison has another just like it. He said particularly that we were not to let you get all worked out and get sick so you couldn't go with us, and he particularly told us about a lot of things he wanted us to buy to make things easy on the way. After he leaves us and goes back to California we're in your charge, I know; but just now you're in ours, you dear, unselfish darling; and we're going to run you. Oh, we're going to run you to beat the band!" laughed Leslie, and jumped down from her perch to hug and squeeze the breath out of Julia Cloud.

"But child! Dear!" said that good woman when she could get her breath to speak. "You mustn't begin in that extravagant way!"

But they put their hands over her lips, and laughed away her protests until she had to give up for laughing with them.

"Well, then," she said at last, when they had subsided from a regular rough-house frolic for all the world as if they were children, "we'll have to get to work in good earnest; only it doesn't seem right to let you work so hard when you are visiting me."

"Visiting, nothing!" declared Allison; "we're having the time of our lives. I haven't been in a place where I could do as I pleased since I was eight years old. This is real work, and I like it. Come now, don't let's waste any time. What can I do first? Wouldn't you like to have me take down all the pictures on the second floor, stack them in the attic, and sweep down the walls the way we did down here yesterday?"

"Yes," said their aunt with an affectionate homage in her eyes for this dear, capable boy who was so eager over everything as if it were his own.

"And those big bookcases. What are you going to do with the books? Do you want any of them to go with you, or are they to be packed away?"

"No, I won't take any of those books. They'll need to be dusted and put in boxes. There are a lot of boxes in the cellar, and there's a pile of papers to use for lining the boxes. But you'll have your hands full with the pictures, I think. Let the books go till to-morrow."

Allison went whistling up-stairs, and began taking down the pictures; but anybody could see by the set of his shoulders that he meant to get the books out of the way too before noon.

"Now, what can I do?" said Leslie, whirling around from wiping the last cup and plate they had used. "There's one more bureau besides yours. Does it need emptying out?"

"No, dear. That has your grandmother's things in it, and is in perfect order. She had me fix up the things several months ago. Everything is tied up and labelled. I don't think we need to disturb it. The men can move it up as it is. But we need to get the rest of the bed-clothes out on the line for an airing before I pack them away in the chest up-stairs. You might do that."

So Leslie went back and forth, carrying blankets and quilts, and hanging them on the line, till Mrs. Perkins had to come over to see what was going on. She came with a cup in her hand to ask for some baking-powder, and Julia Cloud gave her the whole box.

"No, you needn't return it," she said, smiling. "I shall not need it. I've rented the house, and am going away for a while." Mrs. Perkins was so astonished that she actually went home without finding out where Julia Cloud was going, and had to come back to see whether there was anything she could do to help, in order to get a chance to ask.

It was really quite astonishing what a lot could be done in three hours. When twelve o'clock came, the two children descended upon their aunt with insistence that she wash her hands and put on her hat. The rooms had assumed that cleared-up, ready look that rests the tired worker just to look around and see what has been accomplished. With a conviction that she was being quite a child to run away this way when there was still a lot to be done, but with an overwhelming desire to yield to the pressure, Julia Cloud surrendered.

When she came down-stairs five minutes later in her neat black suit and small black hat with the mourning veil about it that Ellen had insisted upon for the funeral, the car was already at the door, and she felt almost guilty as she locked the door and went down the path. But the beauty of the day intoxicated her at once, and she forgot immediately everything but the joy of riding out into the world.

Leslie was a bit quiet as they glided down the road out of town, and kept eyeing her aunt silently. At last, as Julia Cloud was calling attention to a wonderful red woodbine that had twined itself about an old dead tree and was setting the roadside ablaze with splendor, Leslie caught her eye.

"What is it, dear? Does something trouble you? Is anything wrong with me?" asked Julia Cloud, putting up a prospecting hand to her hair and hat.

Leslie's cheeks went rosy red.

"O Cloudy, dear," said Leslie, "I was just wondering. But I'm afraid to say it. Maybe it will make you feel bad."

"Not a bit, deary; what is it?"

"Well, then, Cloudy, do you think Grandmother would care very much if you didn't wear black? Do you like it yourself, or feel it wouldn't be right not to wear it? I don't mean any disrespect to Grandmother; but oh, you would look so sweet in gray, gray and lavender and soft pink, or just gray now for a while. Are you very mad at me for saying it?"

Julia Cloud reached over and patted the young hand that lay near her on the seat.

"Why, no, dear! I'm not mad, and I don't care for black myself. I don't believe in wearing black for the people who have left us and gone to heaven. It seems to me white would be a great deal better. But I put on these things to please Ellen. She thought it would be showing great disrespect to mother if I didn't, and rather than argue about it I did as she wanted me to. But I don't intend to darken the place around me by dressing in mourning, child; and I'm glad you don't want me to. I like bright, happy things. And, besides, Leslie, dear, your grandmother was a bright, happy woman herself once when she was young, before she was sick and had trouble; and I like to remember her that way, because I'm sure that is the way she looks now in heaven."

"Oh, I'm so glad!" sighed Leslie. "That makes the day just perfect."

"I think I'll wait until I get away to change, however," said Julia Cloud thoughtfully. "It would just annoy Ellen to do it now, and might make such people as Mrs. Perkins say disagreeable things that would make it unpleasant for your aunt."

"Of course!" said Leslie, nestling closer, her eyes dancing with some secret plans of her own. "That's all right, Cloudy. How dear and sort of 'understanding' you are, just like a real mother."

And somehow Julia Cloud felt as if she was entering into a new world.

Allison seemed to know by intuition just where to find the right kind of tea-room. He ushered them into the place, and found a table in a secluded nook, with a fountain playing nearby over ferns, and ivy climbing over a mimic pergola. There were not many people eating, for it was past one o'clock. There were little round tables with high-backed chairs that seemed to shut them off in a corner by themselves.

"This is nice!" he sighed. "We're a real family now, aren't we?" and he looked over at Julia Cloud with that fine homage that now and then a boy just entering manhood renders to an older woman.

"Creamed chicken on toast, fruit-salad, toasted muffins, and ice-cream with hot chocolate sauce," ordered Allison after studying the menu-card for a moment. "You like all those, don't you, Cloudy?"

"Oh, but my dear! You mustn't order all that. A sandwich is all I need. Just a tongue sandwich. You must not begin by being extravagant."

"This is my party, Cloudy. This goes under the head of expenses. If you can't find enough you like among what I order, why, I'll get you a tongue sandwich, too; but you've been feeding us out of the cooky-jar, and I guess I'll get the finest I can find to pay you back. I told you this was my time. When we get settled, you can order things; but now I'm going to see that you get enough to eat while you're working so hard."

Leslie's eyes danced with her dimples as Julia Cloud appealed to her to stop this extravagance.

"That's all right, Cloudy. I heard Guardy Lud tell Al not to spare any expense to make things comfortable for you while you were moving."

So Julia Cloud settled down to the pleasure of a new and delicious combination of foods, and thoroughly enjoyed it all.

"Now," said Leslie as the meal drew to a close, "we must get to work. It's half-past two, and the stores close at half-past five. I've a lot of shopping to do. How about you, Cloudy?"

"I must buy a trunk," said Julia Cloud thoughtfully, "and a hand-bag and some gloves. I ought to get a new warm coat, but that will do later."

Leslie eyed her thoughtfully, and raised one brow intensively at her brother as she rose from the table.

Allison landed them at a big department store, and guided his aunt to the trunk department with instructions to stay there until he and Leslie came back. Then they went off with great glee and many whisperings.

It is a curious thing how easily and quickly young people can shop provided they have plenty of money and no older person by to hamper them. Allison and Leslie were back within the time they had set, looking very meek and satisfied. Leslie carried a small package, which she laid in Julia Cloud's lap.

"You said you needed a hand-bag," she said; "and I came on a place where they were having a sale. I thought this was a peach; so I bought it. If you don't like it, we can give it to Aunt Ellen or some one."

Julia Cloud's cheeks grew pink with pleasure, and she felt like a very young, happy child as she opened the parcel to find a lovely gray suède hand-bag with silver clasp and fittings, containing quite a little outfit of toilet articles and brushes in neat, compact form. She caught her breath with delight as she touched the soft white leather lining, and noticed the perfection and finish of the whole. It seemed fit for a queen, yet was plain and quiet enough on the outside for a dove to carry. She looked up to see the two pairs of eager eyes upon her, and could hardly refrain from throwing her arms about the children right there in the store; but she stopped in time and let her eyes do the caressing, as she said with a tremble in her low, sweet voice:

"O you dear children! How you are going to spoil me! I see I must get settled quickly so that I shall have the power to restrain you."

They rollicked forth then, and bought several things, a big steamer rug for the car, a pair of long gray mocha gloves to match the hand-bag, a silk umbrella, and for Aunt Ellen a shiny black hand-bag with a number of conveniences in it, and a pair of new black gloves with long, warm wrists tucked inside of it. Then Allison thoughtfully suggested a handsome leather wallet for Uncle Herbert, and Julia Cloud lingered by the handkerchief-counter, and selected half a dozen new fine handkerchiefs. It all seemed just like a play to her, it was

338

so very long since she had been shopping herself. Ellen had bought everything for her for years, because she was always too busy or too burdened to get away.

When they were out in the street again, it was still too early to think of going to the hotel for dinner.

"How about a movie, Cloudy?" asked Allison shyly. "There's a pippin down the street a ways. I saw it as we came by. Or don't you like movies? Perhaps you'd rather go to the hotel and lie down. I suppose you are maybe worn out. I ought to have thought of that."

"Not a bit of it!" said the game little woman. "I should love to go. Maybe you won't believe it, but I never went to a movie in my life, and I've been wanting to know what they were like for a long time."

"Never went to a movie in your life! Why, Cloudy, you poor dear!" said Allison, who had been fairly fed on movies. "Why, how did it happen? Don't they have moving pictures in your town?"

"Yes, they have them now, though only a year or so ago. But you know I've never been able to get away, even if they had been all about me. Besides, I suppose I should have been considered crazy if I had gone, me, an oldish woman! If there had been children to take, it would have been different. I suppose it is a childish desire, but I always loved pictures."

"Well, we're going," said Allison. "Get in quick, and I'll have you there before you say Jack Robinson!"

And so in the restful cool of a flower-laden atmosphere in one of the finest moving-picture places in the city Julia Cloud sat with her two children and saw her first moving picture, holding her breath in wonder and delight as the people on the screen lived and moved before her.

"I'm afraid I'm having too good a time," she said quietly as she settled back in the car again, and was whirled away to the hotel. "I feel as if I were a child again. If this keeps on, I won't have dignity enough left to chaperon you properly."

"Oh, but Cloudy, dear, that's just why we want you, because you know how to be young and play with us," clamored both of them together.

Then after a good dinner they went up to their rooms, and there was Julia Cloud's shining new trunk that had to be looked over; and there on the floor beside it stood two packages, big boxes, both of them.

"This must be a mistake," said Julia Cloud, looking at them curiously. "Allison, you better call the boy and have him take them away to the right room."

Allison picked up the top package, a big, square box.

"Why, this is your name, Cloudy Jewel!" he exclaimed. "It must be yours. Open it!"

"But how could it be?" said Julia Cloud perplexedly.

"Open it, Cloudy. I want to see what's in it."

Julia Cloud was bending over the long pasteboard box on the floor and finding her name on that, too.

"It's very strange," she said, her cheeks beginning to grow pink like those of a child on her first Christmas morning. "I suppose it's some more of your extravagant capers. I don't know what I shall do with you!"

But her eager fingers untied the string, while Leslie and Allison executed little silent dances around the room and tried to stifle their mirth.

The cover fell off at last, and the tissue-paper blew up in a great fluff; and out of it rolled a beautiful long, soft, thick gray cloak of finest texture and silken lining, with a great puffy collar and cuffs of deep, soft silver-gray fox.

"Oh-h!" was all Julia Cloud could say as the wonderful garment slipped out and spread about over the box and floor. And then the two children caught it up, and enveloped her in it, buttoning it down the front and turning the collar around her ears.

"It's yours, Cloudy, to keep you warm on the journey!" cried Leslie, dancing around and clapping her hands. "Doesn't she look lovely in it, Allison? Oh, isn't she dear?" and Leslie caught her and whirled her around the room.

Then Allison brought the big square box, and demanded that it be opened; and out of it came a small gray hat in soft silky beaver, with a close gray feather curled quietly about it, that settled down on Julia Cloud's lovely white hair as if it had been made for her.

"You don't mind, do you, Cloudy, dear? You don't think I'm officious or impertinent?" begged Leslie anxiously. "It was Allison's idea to get the hat to match the coat, and it was such a dear we couldn't help taking it; but, if there is anything about them you don't like, we got special permission for you to exchange them to-morrow morning."

"Like them!"

Julia Cloud settled down in a chair, and looked at herself in helpless joy and admiration. Like them!

"But O children! You oughtn't to have got such wonderful, expensive things for me. I'm just a plain, simple woman, you know, and it's not fitting."

Then there arose a great clamor about her. Why was it not fitting? She who had given her life for others, why should she not have some of the beautiful, comfortable things of earth? It wasn't sensible for her to talk that way. That was being too humble. And, besides, weren't these things quite sensible and practical? Weren't they warm, and wouldn't they be convenient and comfortable and neat? Well, then, "Good-night," finished Allison.

And so at last they said "Good-night," and went to their beds; but long after the children were asleep Julia Cloud lay awake and thought it out. God had been good to her, and was leading her into green pastures beside quiet waters; but there were things He was expecting of her, and was she going to be able to fulfil them? These two young souls were hers to guide. Would she have the grace to guide them into the knowledge of God in Christ? And then she lay praying for strength for this great work until the peace of God's sleep dropped down upon her.

CHAPTER IX

The next two days were busy ones. There were a great many last little things to be done, and Julia Cloud would have worked herself out, had not the children interfered and carried her off for a ride every little while. The intervening Sabbath was spent at Ellen Robinson's. The handsome hand-bag and wallet served to keep Ellen from being very disagreeable. In fact, at the last, when she began to realize that Julia was really going away, and would not be down at the old house any more for her to burden and torment, she really revealed a gleam of affection for her, and quite worried poor Julia with thinking that perhaps, after all, she ought not to go away so far from her only sister. When Ellen sat down on the bare stairs in the old hall Monday morning, and gave vent to a real sob at parting, Julia had a swift vision of her little sister years ago sitting on that same stair weeping from a fall, and herself comforting her; and she put her arms around Ellen, and kissed her for the first time in many reticent years.

But at last they were off, having handed over the keys to the new tenant, and Julia Cloud leaned back on the luxurious cushions and laughed. Not from mirth, for there were tears in her eyes; and not from nervousness, for she was never subject to hysteria; but just from sheer excitement and joy to think that she was really going out in the world at last to see things and live a life of her own.

The two young people felt it, and laughed with her, until the blackbirds, swirling in a rustling chorus overhead on their way south, seemed to be joining in, and a little squirrel whisked across the road and sat up inquiringly on a log framed in scarlet leaves.

They went straight to the city, for Mr. Luddington had promised to meet them there and confer with them further about their plans. But, when they reached the hotel, they found only a telegram from him saying that business had held him longer than he expected and that he should have to arrange to meet them farther along in their journey. He suggested three colleges, either one of which he should favor, and outlined their journey to take in a stop at each. He promised to communicate with them later, and gave his own address in case they decided to remain at either the first or the second place visited.

"Now," said Julia Cloud after the telegram was disposed of, "I want to get a new dress and a few things before we go any farther. I know you children don't like these old black things, and we might as well start out right. It won't take me long, and I shall be ready to go on my way right after lunch."

Leslie was delighted, and the two spent two hours of happiness in shopping, while Allison drove to a garage to have his car looked over thoroughly, and laid in a supply of good things for the journey. He also spent a profitable half-hour studying a road-map and asking questions concerning the journey.

They tried to make Julia Cloud take a nap before they started, but she declared she would rather rest in the car; and so they started off, feeling like three children going to find the end of the rainbow.

It was a wonderful afternoon. The air was like wine, and the autumn foliage was in all its glory. As they flew along, it seemed as if they were leaving all care behind. A soft pink color grew in Julia Cloud's cheeks, and she sat with her hands folded and her eyes bright with the beauty of the day.

"Oh, but you're a beauty, Cloudy, dear!" exclaimed Leslie suddenly. "See her, Allison! Just look at her. Isn't she great? She was all right in those black things, of course, but she's wonderful in the gray things!"

For Julia Cloud had laid aside in the very bottom of her new trunk the prim black serge that Ellen had bought, and the black funeral gloves and coat and hat; and she was wearing a lovely soft gray wool jersey dress with white collar and cuffs. The big gray coat was nestled by her side ready for use when the wind grew colder, and she was wearing the new gray hat and gloves, and looked a lady every inch. Allison turned slowly, and gave her a look that made her blush like a girl.

"I should say she *is* great! She's a peach!" he agreed. "That hat is a cracker jack! It looks like a pigeon's wing. I like it; don't you, Cloudy? But say, Leslie, she's something more than a beauty. She's a good scout. That's what she is. Do you realize she hasn't opened her lips about the car once? 'Member the time I took Mrs. Luddington down to the office for Guardy, how she squeaked every time another car went by, and cautioned me to be careful and go slow, and asked me how many times I had ever driven before, and if I wasn't exceeding the speed-limit, and no end of things? But Cloudy hasn't batted an eye. She just sits there as if she was riding a cloud and enjoyed it."

"Well, I do," said Julia Cloud, laughing; "and I never thought of being afraid. I didn't know enough to. Ought I to? Because I'm having such a good time that I'm afraid I'd forget to be frightened."

"That's what I said. You're a good sport. I believe you like to go fast."

Julia Cloud admitted shamedly that she did.

"He's a splendid driver, and so am I," Leslie explained earnestly. "Guardy had us taught ages ago, and we're driven a lot; only of course we didn't have our own car. We just had the regular car that belongs to the house. But we made that work some. And Allison took a full course in cars. He knows how to repair them, and put them together, and everything."

"Shall I let her go, Cloudy?" asked Allison eagerly. "Will you be afraid?"

"I should love it," said Julia Cloud eagerly, and then with a sober look at the boy: "Don't do anything crazy, dear! Don't do anything that you oughtn't to do."

"Of course not!" said Allison gravely, sitting up with a manly look in his handsome young face. And by the look he gave her she knew that she had put him upon his honor, and she knew that he would take no risks now that she had trusted him. If she had been a squealing, hectoring kind of woman, he might have been challenged into taking risks, but not here, when she trusted him and the responsibility was all his.

Julia Cloud, as she drew a long breath and prepared, to enjoy the flight down the white ribbon of road, up a hill and down another, registered the thought that here was a clew to this boy's character. Trust him, and he would be faithful. Distrust him, and you wouldn't be anywhere. It did not come to her in words that way, but rather as a subconscious fact that was incorporated into her soul, and gave her a solid and sure feeling about her boy. She had seen all that in his eyes.

He turned around presently, and told her how fast they had been going; and her eyes were shining as brightly as Leslie's.

"You're a pretty good pard, Cloudy," he said. "We'll make you a member of the gang and take you everywhere. See! You're being initiated now, and you're making good right along. I knew we did a good thing when we came after you. Didn't we, Les?"

And Leslie turned and flung herself into Julia Cloud's arms with one of her enthusiastic hugs.

It was just evening when they entered the little town about twenty miles from a larger city, where was located a seat of learning, co-educational, which had been highly recommended to Mr. Luddington, and which seemed to him to have a great many good points in its favor.

The sign-posts warned them of their approach; and the three sat silently watching, judging the place from the outskirts. Big square houses and lawns multiplied as they progressed. Some streets had fences. Substantial churches rose here and there, and the college grounds became visible as they neared the centre of the town. The buildings were spacious and attractive, with tall old elms and maples shading the broad walks. There was an ideal chapel of dark-red stone with arches and a wonderful belfry, and one could easily imagine young men and maidens flitting here and there.

The two young people studied the scene as the car drove slowly by, and said nothing. Allison went on to the other end of town till the houses grew farther apart, and nothing had been said. Then Leslie drew a big sigh.

"Turn around, brother, and let's go back past there again."

Allison turned around, and drove slowly by the college grounds again.

"There are tennis-courts at the back," said Leslie, "and that looks like a gym over there. Do you suppose that's the athletic field over at the back?"

They drove slowly around the block, and Julia Cloud sat silently, trying to think of herself in this strange environment, and feeling suddenly chilly and alone. There would be a lot of strange people to meet, and the children would be off at college all day. She hadn't thought of that.

"Try some of the side streets," ordered Leslie; "I haven't seen our house yet."

They came to the business part of the town, and found the stopping-place suggested in Mr. Luddington's directions.

"We can't tell much about it to-night," said Allison gravely. "I guess we better get some supper and let Cloudy Jewel get rested for a while. Then to-morrow we can look around."

They were wise words, and Julia Cloud assented at once; but it was quite plain that neither he nor Leslie was much elated at the place.

Allison slipped out for a walk through the college grounds after the others had gone to their rooms, and came back whistling gravely.

"He doesn't like it, Cloudy," whispered Leslie as the sound floated in through the transom. "He won't have anything to do with it. You see!"

"What makes you think so, dear? He's whistling. That sounds as if he liked it."

"Yes, but look what he's whistling. He always begins on 'The Long, Long Trail' if he isn't pleased or has to wait when he's in a hurry to get anywhere. Now, if he had been pleased, you would have heard 'One grasshopper hopped right over th' other grasshopper's back.' I can always tell. Well, I don't care; do you, Cloudy? There's plenty of other colleges, and I didn't see our house in any of the streets we went through, did you?"

Julia Cloud had to confess that she had not been in love with anything she had seen yet.

"Well, then, what's the use of going over the old college? I say let's beat it in the morning."

But Julia Cloud would not hear to that. She said they must be fair even to a college, and Mr. Luddington would want them to look the place over thoroughly while they were there. So after breakfast the two reluctant young people went with Julia Cloud to make investigation.

They went through the classrooms and the chapel and the library and gymnasiums. They visited the science halls and workshops. They even climbed up to the observatory, and took a squint at the big telescope, and then they came down and went with a real-estate dealer to see some houses. But at twelve o'clock they came back to their boarding-house with a sigh of relief, ate a good dinner, and, climbing into their car, shook the dust of the town, as it were, from their feet.

"It may be a very nice town, but it's not the town for me," chanted Leslie, nestling back among the cushions.

"Here, too!" said Allison, letting the car ride out under full power over the smooth country road. But, though Julia Cloud questioned several times, she could get no explanation except Allison's terse "Too provincial," whatever he meant by that. She doubted whether he knew himself. She wondered whether it were that they each felt the same homesick feeling that she had experienced.

They stayed that night at a little country inn, and started on their way again at early morning, for they had a long journey before them to reach the second place that Mr. Luddington had suggested. Late that afternoon they stopped in a small city, and decided to rest until morning; for the children wanted to stretch their limbs, and they felt that their aunt was very weary though she declared she was only sleepy.

The sun had quite gone down the next evening, and the twilight was beginning to settle over everything as they drove at last into the second college town of their tour, and the church bells were pealing for prayer meeting. Church bells! The thought of them sent a thrill through Julia Cloud's heart. There was somehow a familiar, home-like sound to them that made her think of the prayer meetings that had cheered her heart through many lonely days.

It had really been for many years her one outing to go to prayer meeting. Even after her mother had become bedridden she had always insisted on Julia's going off to prayer meeting, and a neighbor who was lame and sometimes stayed with her would come hobbling in and send her off. The old cracked church bell at home had always sounded sweet to her ears because it meant that this hour was her own quiet time to go away alone and rest. And it had been real heart-rest always, even though sometimes the meetings themselves had been wofully prosy. There had always been the pleasant little chat and the warm hand-shake afterwards, and then the going home again beneath the stars with a bit of the last hymn in one's soul to sing one to sleep with,

᾽ my

to

ıgh it b

ᴣth me;

and the burden had grown less, and her heart had grown light with the promise of her Father. Those meetings had been to Julia Cloud very real meetings with her Christ; and now, as the evening bells pealed out, her heart leaped to meet and answer the call.

"Oh! I'd like to go to prayer meeting!" she said impulsively as they passed the lighted church, and saw a few faithful going in at the door.

"Do you mean it?" asked Allison, bringing the car to a stop. "Do you *mean* it, Cloudy? Then let's go. We can size the people up, and see if we like their looks. I guess we can stand a prayer meeting unless you are too tired."

With the eagerness of a child Julia Cloud got out of the car and went into the house of the Lord. It was like a bit of heaven to her. She didn't realize what a bore it might be to her two companions.

It was a good little meeting as such meetings go. Very little enthusiasm, very few present, mostly elders and their wives, with an old saint or two almost at the journey's end, and a dignified white-haired minister, who said some good things in a drony, sleepy tone. The piano was played by a homely young woman who wore unfashionable clothes, and made frightful mistakes in the bass occasionally; but that did not seem to trouble the singers, who sang with the heart rather than with their voices.

Allison sat solemnly, and refrained from looking at his sister; but both stole occasional glances at their aunt, and admired her new clothes and the beautiful light on her face. For Julia Cloud felt as if she were glimpsing into heaven and seeing her Lord in this bit of communion with some of His saints; and, when she bowed her head in the closing prayer, she was thanking Him for all His mercies in bringing this wonderful change into her gray life, and giving her these two dear children to love her and be loved by her. As she rose to come out, her face was glorified by that vision on the mount.

The gentle-faced minister came and spoke to them, and welcomed them to the church, although Allison told him quite curtly that they were only passing through the town; but Julia Cloud trod the neat brown ingrain carpet of the aisle as if it were golden pavement.

"Of all the stupid places!" said Allison as they got into the car. "What do they have prayer meetings for, anyway? Did you manage to keep awake, Cloudy?"

And suddenly like a pall there fell upon Julia Cloud's bright soul the realization that these children did not, would not, feel as she did about such things. They had probably never been taught to love the house of God, and how was she ever to make them see? Perhaps it had been prosy and dull to one who did not hear the Lord's voice behind the Bible words. Perhaps the old minister had been long and tiresome, and the children were weary with the journey and sleepy; she ought not to have let them stop now; and she began to say how sorry she was. But, when they saw from her words that she had really enjoyed that dull little meeting, they were silent.

"Well, Cloudy, I'll hand it to you," said Allison at last. "If you could stand that meeting and enjoy it, you're some Christian! But I'm glad for one that we went if you liked it; and I guess, if you can go a football game now and then, I ought to be able to stand a prayer meeting. So now here goes for seeing the town. It's only nine o'clock, and I believe that's the college up there on the hill where all those lights are. Shall we drive up there?"

The car slipped through the pleasant evening streets, turning a corner, slowing up at a crossing to take a view of the town, and keeping all the time in view the clusters of lights on the hill, which Allison conceived to be the college. Suddenly Leslie leaned forward, and cried:

"O Allison, stop! Stop! There it is, just there on the right. And it's for sale, too! Oh, let's get right out and get the name of the agent, so we won't lose it again."

Allison stopped the car suddenly, and turned to look. There in the full blaze of an electric arc-light, nestled among shrubbery and tall trees, with a smooth terrace in front, was a beautiful little cottage of white stone, with a pink roof, and windows everywhere.

"Why, that's not the college, Les; what's the matter with you?" said Allison, putting his hand on the starter again. "Better wake up. Don't you know a college when you don't see one?"

"College nothing!" said his sister. "That's our house. That's our *home*, Allison. The very house I've dreamed of. It looks a little like the houses in California, and it is the very thing. Now, there's no use; you've got to get out and get that agent's name, or I'll jump out myself, and get lost, and walk the rest of the way!"

"It is lovely!" said Julia Cloud, leaning over to look. "But it looks expensive, and you wouldn't want to *buy* a house, you know, dear; for you might not stay."

"Oh, yes, we would if we liked it. And, besides, houses can be sold again when you get done with them, though I'd never want to sell that! It's a perfect little duck. Allison, will you get out or shall I?"

"Oh, I'm game," said Allison, getting out and jumping the hedge into the pretty yard.

He took out his pencil, and wrote down the address in his note-book, stepped up the terrace and glanced about, then went close to the street sign, and found out what corner it was near.

"It is a pippin, sure thing," he said as he sprang into the car again; "but, Leslie, for the love of Mike, don't find any more houses to-night! I'm hungry as a bear. That prayer meeting was one too many for me; I'm going to make for the nearest restaurant; and then, if you want to go house-hunting after that, all right; but I'm going to find the eats first."

They asked a group of boys where the restaurant was, and one pointed to an open door from which light was streaming forth.

"There's the pie-shop," they said, and the party descended hungry and happy with the delicious uncertainty of having found a dream of a house in the dark, and wondering what it would turn out to be in the daytime. They inquired the way to the inn, and decided to stop further investigations until morning.

CHAPTER X

They were all very weary, and slept well that night; but, strange to say, Allison, who was the sleepy-head, awoke first, and was out looking the town over before the others had thought of awaking. He came back to breakfast eager and impatient.

"We don't need to go any farther," he declared. "It's a peach of a place. There's a creek that reaches up in the woods for miles; and they have canoes and skating and a swimming-hole; and there are tennis-courts everywhere; and it's only eleven miles from the city. I say we just camp here, and not bother about going on to the other place. I'm satisfied. If that house is big enough, it's just the thing."

"But have you been to the college?"

"No, but I asked about it. They have intercollegiate games and frats, and I guess it's all right. It has a peach of a campus, too, and a Carnegie library with chimes——"

"Well, but, dear, you aren't going to college just for those things."

"Oh, the college'll be all right. Guardy wouldn't have suggested it if it wasn't. But we'll go up there this morning and look around."

"Now, children, don't get your heart set on it before you know all about it. You know that house may be quite impossible."

"Now, Cloudy!" put in Leslie. "You know Allison told you you were a good sport. You mustn't begin by preaching before you find out. If it isn't all right, why, of course we don't want it; so let's have the fun of thinking it is till we prove it isn't—or it is."

Julia Cloud looked into the laughing, happy eyes, and yielded with a smile.

"Of course," she said, "that's reasonable. I'm agreed to that. But there's one thing: you know we're bound to go on to the other college, because Mr. Luddington expects us; and we can come back here again if we like this better."

"Oh, we can wire him to come here," said Leslie. "Now, let's go! First to that house, please, because I'm so afraid somebody will buy it before we get the option on it. I've heard that houses are very scarce in the East just now, and people are snapping them up. I read that on the back of that old man's paper at the next table to ours this morning."

All three of them having the hearts of children, they went at once to hunt up the agent before ever they got even a glimpse of the halls of learning standing brave and fair on the hillside in the morning sunshine. "Because there are plenty more colleges," said Leslie; "but there is only one home for us, and I believe we've found it, if it looks half as pretty in the daylight as it did at night."

It took only a few minutes to find the agent and get the key of the house, and presently they were standing on the terrace gazing with delight at the house.

It was indeed a lovely little dwelling. It was built of stone, and then painted white, but the roof and gables were tiled with great pink tiles, giving an odd little foreign look to it, something like Anne Hathaway's cottage in general contour, Leslie declared.

The top of the terrace was pink-tiled, too, and all the porches were paved with tiles. The house itself seemed filled with windows all around. Allison unlocked the door, and they exclaimed with pleasure as he threw it wide open and they stepped in. The sunshine was flooding the great living-room from every direction, it seemed. To begin with, the room was very large, and gave the effect of being a sun-parlor because of its white panelled walls and its many windows. Straight across from the front door on the opposite side of the room opened a small hallway or passage with stairs leading up to a platform where more windows shed a beautiful light down the stairs on walls papered with strange tropical birds in delicate old-fashioned tracery.

To the right through a wide white arch from the living-room was a charming white dining-room with little, high, leaded-paned windows over the spot for the sideboard and long windows in front.

To the left was an enormous stone fireplace with high mantel-shelf of stone and the chimney above. The fire-opening was wide enough for an old Yule log, and on either side of it were double glass doors opening into a long porch room, which also had a fireplace on the opposite side of the chimney, and was completely shut in by long casement windows.

Up-stairs there were four large bedrooms and a little hall room that could be used for a sewing-room or den, or an extra bedroom, besides a neat little maid's room in a notch on the half-way landing, and two bathrooms, white-tiled and delightful, tucked away in between things. Then Leslie opened a glass door in the very prettiest room of all, which she and Allison immediately decided must belong to their aunt, and exclaimed in delight; for here nestled between the gables, with a tiled wall all about it, was a delightful housetop or uncovered porch, so situated among the trees that it was entirely shut in from the world.

It was perfect! They stood and looked at one another in delight, and for the time the college was forgotten. Then Allison dashed away, and came back eagerly almost immediately.

"There's a garage!" he said, "just behind the kitchen, a regular robin's nest of a one, white with pink tiles just like the house, and a pebbled drive. Say, it must be some fool of a guy that would sell this. Isn't it just a crackerjack?"

"My dear," put in Julia Cloud, "it can't help being very expensive——"

"Now, Cloudy, remember!" said Leslie, holding up her finger in mock rebuke. "Just wait and see! And, anyhow, you don't know Guardy Lud. If he could see us located in a peach of a home like this, he'd go back to his growley old dear of a wife with happy tears rolling down his nice old cheeks. Allison, you go talk to that agent, and you give him a hundred dollars if you've got it left—here, I guess I've got some, too—just to bind the bargain till Guardy gets here. And say, you go see if you can't get Guardy on the 'phone. I don't want to go a step farther. Couldn't you be happy here, Cloudy, with that fireplace, and that prayer meeting to go to? I wouldn't mind going with you sometimes when I didn't have to study."

Julia Cloud stooped, and kissed the eager face, and whispered, "Very happy, darling!"

And then they went to the agent again and the telephone.

"Guardy Lud" proved himself quite equal to the occasion by agreeing to come on at once and approve their choice, and promised to be there before evening.

"I knew he would," said Leslie happily, as they seated themselves in the car again for the pleasant run to the college.

They found the dean in his office, and Allison was taken with him at once.

"He isn't much like that musty little guy in the other college. He looked like a wet hen!" growled Allison in a low tone to his sister and aunt, while the dean was out in the hall talking to a student. "I like him, don't you?" and Julia Cloud sat wondering what the boy's standards could be that he could judge so suddenly and enthusiastically. Yet she had to admit herself that she liked this man, tall and grave with a pleasant twinkle hidden away in his wine-brown eyes and around the corners of his firm mouth. She felt satisfied that here was a man who would be both wise and just.

They made the rounds of the college buildings and campus with growing enthusiasm, and then drove back to the inn to lunch with hearty appetites.

"Let's go down to the house, and measure things, and look around once more," proposed Leslie. "Then we can come back and wait here for Guardy. We mustn't be away when he arrives, for he'll want to get everything fixed up and get away. I know him. Allison, did you get a time-table?"

Allison produced one from his coat-pocket, and they studied the trains, and decided that there was no possibility of the arrival of their guardian until three o'clock, and probably not until five.

"That's all right," said Leslie. "Cloudy and I'll stay here from three to five, and you can meet the trains; but first I want the dimensions of those rooms, so Cloudy and I can plan. We've got a whole lot to do before college opens, and we can't spare a minute. O Cloudy! I'm so happy! Isn't that house just a duck?"

They went to the village store, bought a foot-rule, a yardstick, and a tape-measure, and repaired to the house. Allison took the foot-rule by masculine right; Julia Cloud said she felt more at home with the tape-measure; and Leslie preferred the yardstick. With pencil and paper they went to work, making a diagram of each room, with spaces between windows and doors for furniture, taking it room by room.

"We've got to know about length of curtains, and whether furniture will fit in," declared Leslie wisely. "I've thought it all out nights in the sleeper on the way over here. Just think! Isn't it going to be fun furnishing the whole house? You know, Cloudy, I didn't have hardly anything sent, because it really wasn't worth while. We sort of wanted to leave the house at home just as it was when Mamma was living, to come back to sometimes; and so we let it to an old gentleman, a friend of Grandfather's and Guardy's, who has only himself and his wife and servants, and will take beautiful care of it. But I went around and picked out anything I wanted, rugs and pictures and some bric-à-brac, and a few bits of old mahogany that I love, just small things that would pack easily. Guardy said we might buy our own things. He set a limit on our spending, of course; but he said it would be good experience for us to learn how to buy wisely inside a certain sum."

Julia Cloud went around like one in a dream with her new tape-measure, setting down careful figures, and feeling like a child playing dolls again. It was almost three o'clock when they finally finished their measurements, and Allison hurried them back to the inn, and repaired to the station to meet trains.

Leslie made her aunt lie down on the bed, supposedly for a nap; but no one could have taken a nap even if he had wanted to—which Julia Cloud did not—with an eager, excited girl sitting beside the bed, just fluttering with ideas about couches and pillows and furniture and curtains.

"We'll have a great deep couch, with air-cushions on the seat and back, and put it in the middle of the living-room facing the fireplace, won't we, Cloudy? And what color do you think would be pretty for the cushions? I guess blue, deep, dark-blue brocaded velvet, or something soft that will tone well with the mahogany woodwork. I love mahogany in a white room, don't you, Cloudy? And I had a great big blue Chinese rug sent over that I think will do nicely for there. You like blue, don't you, Cloudy?" she finished anxiously. "Because I want to have you like it more even than we do."

"Oh, I love it!" gasped Julia Cloud, trying to set her mind to revel in extravagant desires without compunction. She was not used to considering life in terms of Chinese rugs or mahogany and brocade velvet.

"I'd like the curtains next the windows to be all alike all over the house, wouldn't you? Just sheer, soft, creamy white. And then inner curtains of Chinese silk or something like that. We'd want blue in the living-room, of course, if we had the blue rugs and couch, and oh! old rose, I guess, in the dining-room, or perhaps mahogany color or tan. Green for that sun-porch room! That's it, and lots of willow chairs and tables! And rush mats on the tiled floor! Oh! Aren't we having fun, Cloudy, dear? Now, I'll write out a list of things we have to buy while you take a nap."

And so it went on the whole afternoon, until the sound of a distant whistle warned them that the five-o'clock train was coming in and they must be prepared to meet Mr. Luddington.

According to programme they hurried into their wraps, and went down to the piazza, to wait for the car. None too soon, for Allison was already driving around the curve in front of the door, and Mr. Luddington sat beside him, radiating satisfaction. Anything that pleased his adorable wards pleased him, but this especially so, for he was in a hurry to respond to the many telegrams summoning him home to California, and the quicker this little household was settled, the sooner he might leave them.

They drove at once, of course, to the house, Allison and Leslie talking fast and eagerly every minute of the way, their eyes bright and their faces beautiful with enthusiasm; and Mr. Luddington could only sit and listen, and smile over their heads at Julia Cloud, who was smiling also, and who in her new silvery garments looked to him all the more a lady and fit to play mother to his wards.

"Well, now, now, now!" said Guardy Lud after they had gone carefully over every room and were coming down-stairs again. "This is great! This certainly is great. I couldn't have had it better if I'd made it to order, could I? And I certainly wish you were settled here, and I could stay long enough to take breakfast with you and enjoy some more of your excellent buckwheat cakes, Miss Cloud." He turned with a gallant bow to Julia. "I hope you'll teach my little girl here to bake them just like that, so she can make me some when she comes back to California to visit us again."

They rode him around the town, through the college grounds, and then back to the inn for dinner. That evening they spent in discussion and business plans for the winter. The next morning they took Mr. Luddington up to the college, where he made final arrangements for the young people to be entered as students, and afterwards drove to the city. Mr. Luddington had one or two friends there to whom he wished to introduce them, that they might have some one near at hand to call upon in a time of need. He also took them all to a bank, and arranged their bank accounts so that they might draw what they needed at any time. After lunch he went with them to several of the largest stores, and opened a charge account for them. Then, with a warm hand-shake for Julia Cloud and an emotional good-by for the young people, he left them to rush for his train.

"We might stay in town to-night, and be ready to shop early in the morning," proposed Leslie.

"No," said Allison decidedly. "Cloudy looks worn to a frazzle, and I'm sick to death of the city. Let's beat it back to where they have good air. We can go right to bed after dinner, and get up good and early, and be here as soon as the stores are open. They don't open till nine o'clock. I saw the signs on the doors everywhere."

So back they went for a good night's rest, and were up and at it early in the morning, scarcely noticing the way they rode, so interested were they in deciding how many chairs and beds and tables they needed to buy.

"Let's get the curtains first, and then we can have the windows washed, and put them right up," said Leslie, "and nobody can see in. I'm crazy to be shut into our own house, and feel that it belongs to us. We can select them while Allison's gone to see what's the matter with his engine."

But, when Julia Cloud heard the stupendous price that was asked for ready-made curtains or curtains made to order, with fixtures and installation, she exclaimed in horror:

"Leslie! This is foolish. We can easily make them ourselves, and put them up for less than half the price. If I had only brought my sewing-machine! But it was all out of repair."

"Could we really make them ourselves, Cloudy? Wouldn't that be fun? We'll get a sewing-machine, of course. We'll need it for other things, too, sometimes, won't we? Of course we'll get one. We'll buy that next. Now, how many yards of each of these do we need?"

In a few minutes the salesman had figured out how much was needed, counted the number of fixtures for doorways and windows, and arranged to send the package down to the car at a certain time later in the morning. Then they went at once and bought a sewing-machine, one that Julia Cloud knew all about and said was the best and lightest on the market. Leslie was as pleased with the idea of learning to run it as if it had been a new toy and she a child.

"We'll have it sent right to the little new house, and then we can go there evenings after we are through shopping, and sew. You can cut, and I can put in the hems, if you think I can do them well enough. We must get scissors and thread, a lot of it, and silk to match the colored curtains, too."

They took the rooms one at a time, and furnished them, Allison joining them, and taking as much interest in the design of the furniture as if he had been a young bridegroom just setting up housekeeping for himself.

They had set aside a certain sum for each room so that they would not overstep their guardian's limit, and with Julia Cloud to put on the brakes, and suggest simplicity, and decide what was in good taste for such a small village house, they easily came within the generous limit allowed them.

It was a great game for Julia Cloud to come out of her simple country life and plunge into this wholesale beautiful buying untroubled by a continual feeling that she must select the very cheapest without regard to taste or desire. It was wonderful; but it was wearying in spite of the delight, and so the little house was not all furnished in a day.

"Well, the living-room's done, anyway, and the willow set for the porch room!" sighed Leslie, leaning back with a fling of weariness. "Now to-morrow we'll do the dining-room."

"To-morrow's Sunday, Les; the stores aren't open. Use your bean a little, child."

"Sunday!"

Leslie's beautiful face drew itself into a snarl of impatience, the first, really, that Julia Cloud had seen.

"Oh, darn!" said Leslie's pretty lips. "Isn't that too horrid? I forgot all about it. I wonder what they have to have Sunday for, anyway. It's just a dull old bore!"

"O Leslie, darling!" said Julia Cloud, aghast, something in her heart growing suddenly heavy and sinking her down, down, so that she felt as if she could hardly hold her head up another minute.

"Well, Cloudy, dear, don't you think it's a bore yourself, truly? Come, now, own up. And I'm sure I don't see what's the use of it, do you? One can't do a thing that's nice. But I'll tell you what we can do!" her eyes growing bright with eagerness again. "We'll measure and cut all the curtains, and turn the hems up. And, Allison, you can put up the fixtures. If only the machine could have been sent up to-day, we could have had the curtains all done, couldn't we, Cloudy?"

But Julia Cloud's lips were white and trembling, and her sweet eyes had suddenly gone dark with trouble and apprehension.

"O Leslie, darling child!" she gasped again. "You don't mean you would work on the Sabbath day!"

"Why, why not, Cloudy, dear? Is there anything wrong about that?"

CHAPTER XI

Julia Cloud had a sudden feeling that everything was whirling beneath her—the very foundations of the earth. She drew a deep breath, and tried to steady herself, thinking in her heart that she must be very calm and not make any mistakes in this great crisis that had arisen. It flashed across her consciousness that she was a simple, old-fashioned woman, accustomed to old-fashioned ideas, living all her life in a little town where the line between the church and the world was strongly marked, where the traditions of Christianity were still held sacred in the hearts of many and where the customs of worldliness had not yet noticeably invaded. All the articles she had read in the religious press about the worldliness of the modern Sabbath, the terrible desecration of the day that had been dear and sacred to her all her life as being the time when she came closest to her Lord; all the struggle between the church and the world to keep the old laws rigidly; and all the sneers she had seen in the secular press against the fanatics who were trying to force the world back to Puritanism, came shivering to her mind in one great thrill of agony as she recognized that she was face to face with one of the biggest religious problems of the day, and must fight it out alone.

The beautiful life that had seemed to be opening out before her was not, then, to be all beauty. Behind the flowers of this new Eden there hid a serpent of temptation; and she, Julia Cloud, disciple of the Lord Christ, was to be tried out to see what faith there was in her. For a moment she faltered, and closed her eyes, shuddering. How could she face it, she, who knew so little what to say and how to tell her quiet heart-beliefs? Why had she been placed in such a position? Why was there not some one wiser than she to guide the feet of these children into the straight and narrow way?

But only a moment she shrank thus. The voice of her Master seemed to speak in her heart as the wind whirled by the car and stirred the loose hair on her forehead. The voice that had been her guide through life was requiring her now to witness to these two whom she loved, as no other could do it, be they ever so wise; just because she loved them and loved Him, and was not pretending to be wise, only following. Then she drew a deep breath, reminded herself once more that she must be careful not to antagonize, and sat up gravely.

"Dear, it is God's day, and I have always felt that He wanted us to make it holy for Him, keep worldly things out of it, you know. I wouldn't feel that I could work on that day. Of course I have no right to say you shall not. I'm only your adviser and friend, you know. But I'd rather you wouldn't, because I know God would rather you wouldn't."

Leslie pouted uneasily.

"How in the world could you know that?" she said almost crossly. She did love to carry out her projects, and hitherto Julia Cloud had put no hindrance in her way.

"Why, He said so in His book. He said, 'Thou shalt not do any work, thou, nor thy son, nor thy daughter——'"

"Oh, those are the old commandments, Cloudy, dear; and I've heard people, even ministers, say that they are out of date now. They don't have anything to do with us nowadays."

Julia Cloud looked still graver.

"God doesn't change, Leslie. He is the same yesterday and to-day and forever. And He said that whoever took away from the meaning of the words of His book would have some terrible punishment, so that it were better that a millstone were hanged about his neck and that he were drowned."

"Well, I think He'd be a perfectly horrid God to do that!" said Leslie. "I can't see how you can believe any such old thing. It isn't like you, Cloudy, dear; it's just some old thing you were taught. You don't like to be long-faced and unhappy one day in the week, you know you don't."

"Long-faced! Unhappy! Why, dear child, God doesn't want the Sabbath to be that. He wants it to be the happiest day of all the week. I'm never unhappy on Sunday. I like it best of all."

Suddenly Allison turned around, and looked at Julia Cloud, saw the white, strained look around her lips, the yearning light in her eyes, and had some swift man's intuition about the true woman's soul of her. For men, especially young men, do have these intuitions sometimes as well as women.

"Leslie," he said gently, as if he had suddenly grown much older than his sister, "can't you see you're hurting Cloudy? Cut it out! If Cloudy likes Sunday, she shall have it the way she wants it."

Leslie turned with sudden compunction.

"O Cloudy, dear, I didn't mean to hurt you; indeed I didn't! I never thought you'd care."

"It's all right, dear," said Julia Cloud with her gentle voice, and just the least mite of a gasp. "You see—I—Sunday has been always very dear to me; I hadn't realized you wouldn't feel the same."

She seemed to shrink into herself; and, though the smile still trembled on her lips, there was a hovering of distress over her fine brows.

"We *will* feel the same!" declared Allison. "If you feel that way so much, we'll manage somehow to be loyal to what you think. You always do it for us; and, if we can't be as big as you are, we haven't got the gang spirit. It's teamwork, Leslie. Cloudy goes to football games, and makes fudge for our friends; and we go to church and help her keep Sunday her way. See?"

"Why, of course! Sure!" said Leslie, half bewildered. "I didn't mean not to, of course, if Cloudy likes such things; only she'll have to teach me how, for I never did like those things."

"Well, I say, let's get Cloudy to spend the first Sunday telling us how she thinks Sunday ought to be kept, and why. Is that a bargain, Cloudy?"

"But I'm afraid I wouldn't be wise enough to explain," faltered Julia Cloud, distress in her voice. "I could maybe find something to read to you about it."

"Oh, preserve us, Cloudy! We don't want any old dissertations out of a book. If we can't have your own thoughts that make you live it the way you do, we haven't any use for any of it. See?"

Julia Cloud forced a trembling little smile, and said she saw, and would do her best; but her heart sank at the prospect. What a responsibility to be put upon her ignorant shoulders. The Lord's Sabbath in her bungling hands to make or to mar for these two young souls! She must pray. Oh, she must pray continually that she might be led!

And then there came swiftly to her mind one of the verses that had become dear and familiar to her through the years as she read and reread her Bible, "And when they bring you unto the synagogues, and unto magistrates, and powers, take ye no thought how or what thing ye shall answer, or what ye shall say; for the Holy Ghost shall teach you in the same hour what ye ought to say."

This was not exactly being brought before magistrates; but it was being challenged for a reason for the hope that was in her, and perhaps she could claim the promise. Surely, if the Lord wanted her to defend His Sabbath before these two, He would give her wise words in which to speak. Anyhow, she would just have to trust Him, for she had none of her own.

"Now see what you've done, Leslie!" said her brother sharply. "Cloudy hasn't looked that way once before. Next thing you know she'll be washing her hands of us and running off back to Sterling again."

"O Cloudy!" said the penitent Leslie, flinging herself into her aunt's arms and nestling there beseechingly. "You wouldn't do that, would you, Cloudy, dear? No matter how naughty I got? Because you would know I wouldn't mean it ever. Even if I was real bad."

"No, dear," said Julia Cloud, kissing her fair forehead. "But this is just one of those things that I meant when I was afraid to undertake it. You see there may be a great many things you will want to do on Sunday that I would not feel it right for me to do, and I may be a hindrance to you in lots of ways. I shouldn't like to get to be a sort of burden to you, and it isn't as if they were things that I could give up, you know. This is a matter of conscience."

"That's all right, Cloudy," put in Allison. "You have your say in things like that. We aren't so selfish as all that. And besides, if it's wrong for you, who knows but it's wrong for us, too? We'll look into it."

Julia Cloud went smiling through the rest of the evening, but underneath was a tugging of strange dread and fear at her heart. It was all so new, this having responsibility with souls. She had always so quietly trusted her Bible and tried to follow her Lord. She had never had to guide others. There had not been time for her even to take a class in Sunday school, and she knew her religion only as it applied to her one little narrow life, she thought, not realizing that, when one has applied a great faith to the circumstances of even a narrow life, and applied it thoroughly through a lifetime, one has learned more theology than one could get in years of a theological seminary. Theories, after all, are worth little unless they have been worked out in experience; and when one has patiently, even happily, given up much of the joy of living to serve, has learned to keep self under and love even the unlovable, has put to the test the promises of the Bible and found them hold true in time of need, and has found the Sabbath day an oasis in the desert of an otherwise dreary life, even an old theologian wouldn't have much more to go on in beginning a discussion on Sabbath-keeping.

Quite early the next morning, before Leslie had awakened, Julia Cloud had slipped softly to her knees by the bedside, and was communing with her heavenly Father concerning her need of guidance.

When Leslie awoke, her aunt was sitting by the window with her Bible on her knee and a sweet look of peace on her face, the morning sunlight resting on the silvery whiteness of her hair like a benediction. It was perhaps the soft turning of a leaf that brought the girl to wakefulness, and she lay for some time quietly watching her aunt and thinking the deep thoughts of youth. Perhaps nothing could have so well prepared her for the afternoon talk as that few minutes of watching Julia Cloud's face as she read her Bible, glancing now and then from the window thoughtfully, as if considering something she had read. Julia Cloud was reading over everything that her Bible said about the Sabbath, and with the help of her concordance she was being led through a very logical train of thought, although she did not know it. If you had asked her, she would have said that she had not been thinking about what she would say to the children; she had been deep in the meaning that God sent to her own soul.

But when Leslie finally stirred and greeted her, Julia Cloud looked up with a smile of peace; and there was no longer a little line of worry between her straight brows.

The peace lasted all through the morning, and went with her down to breakfast; and something of her enjoyment of the day seemed to pervade the atmosphere about her and extend to the two young people. They hovered about her, anxious to please, and a trifle ill at ease at first lest they should make some mistake about this day that seemed so holy to their aunt and had always been to them nothing but a bore to get through with in the jolliest way possible.

There was no question about going to church. They just went. Leslie and Allison had never made a practice of doing so since they had been left to themselves. It had not been necessary in the circle in which they moved. When they went to school, and had to go to church, they evaded the rule as often as possible. But somehow they felt without being told that if they tried to remain away now it would hurt their aunt more than anything else they could do; and, while they were usually outspoken and frank, they both felt that here was a time to be silent about their habits.

"We're going to church," said Allison in a low tone as he drew his sister's chair away from the breakfast-table. His tone had the quality of command.

"Of course," responded Leslie quietly.

It was so that Julia Cloud was spared the knowledge that her two dear young people did not consider it necessary to attend church every Sabbath, and her peace was not disturbed.

The sermon in the little stucco church where they had gone to prayer meeting that first night was not exceedingly enlivening nor uplifting. The minister was prosy with dignity, soaring into occasional flights of eloquence that reminded one of a generation ago. There was nothing about it to bring to mind the sweetness of a Sabbath communion with Christ, nothing to remind a young soul that Christ was ready to be Friend and Saviour. It was rather a dissertation on one of the epistles with a smack of modern higher criticism. The young people watched the preacher a while listlessly, and wished for the end; but a glance at the quiet, worshipful face of their aunt kept them thoughtful. Julia Cloud evidently had something that most other people did not have, they said to themselves, some inner light that shone through her face, some finer sight and keener ear that made her see and hear what was not given to common mortals to comprehend; and because she sat thus with the light of communion on her face they, too, sat with respectful hearts and tried to join lustily in the hymns with their fresh voices.

The minister came down and shook hands with them, welcoming them kindly. He seemed more human out of the pulpit, and asked quite interestedly where they were to live and whether he might call. He mentioned Sunday school and Christian Endeavor, and said he hoped they would "cast in their lot" among them; and the young people gave him cold little smiles and withdrew into themselves while their aunt did the talking. They were willing she should have her Sabbath, and they would do all in their power to make it what she wanted; but they were hostile toward this church and this minister and all that it had to do with. It simply did not interest them. Julia Cloud saw this in their eyes as she turned to go away, and sighed softly to herself. How much there was to teach them! Could she ever hope to make them feel differently? In two short weeks the college would open, and they would be swept away on a whirl of work and play and new friends and functions. Was she strong enough to stem the tide of worldliness that would ingulf them? No, not of herself. But she had read that very morning the promises of her Lord, "Surely I will be with thee," "I will help thee"; and she meant to lay hold on them closely. She could do nothing of herself, but she with her Lord helping could do anything He wanted done. That was enough.

Leslie turned longing eyes toward the winding creek and an alluring canoe that lolled idly at the bank down below the inn as she stood on the piazza after dinner waiting for her aunt; but Allison saw her glance, and shook his head.

"Better not suggest it," he said. "There are a lot of picnickers down there carrying on high. She would not like it, I'm sure. If it were all quiet and no one about, it would be different."

"Well, there are a lot of people around here on the piazzas," said Leslie disconsolately. "I don't see the difference."

But, when Julia Cloud came with her Bible slipped unobtrusively under her arm, she suggested a quiet spot in the woods; and so they wandered off through the trees with a big blanket from the car to sit on, and found a wonderful place, high above the water, where a great rift of rocks jutted out among drooping hemlocks, and was carpeted with pine-needles.

"It would please me very much," said Julia Cloud as she sat down on the blanket and opened her Bible, looking up wistfully at the two, "if you two would go to that Christian Endeavor meeting to-night. I hate to ask you to do anything like that right away, but that minister begged me to get you to come. He said they were having such a struggle to make it live and that they needed some fresh young workers. He asked me if you didn't sing, and he said singers were very much needed."

There was a heavy silence for a moment while the two young things looked at each other aghast across her, and Julia Cloud kept her eyes on the floating clouds above the hemlocks. She still had that softened look of being within a safe shelter where storms and troubles could not really trouble her; yet there was a dear, eager look in her eyes. Both children saw it, and with wonderful intuition interpreted it; and because their hearts were young and tender they yielded to its influence.

Leslie swooped down upon her aunt with an overwhelming kiss, and Allison dropped down beside her with a "Sure, we'll go, Cloudy, if that will do you any good. I can't say I'm keen about pleasing that stiff old parson guy, but anything *you* want is different. I don't know just what you're letting us in for, but I guess we can stand most anything once."

Julia Cloud put out a hand to grasp a hand of each; and, looking up, they saw that there were tears in her eyes.

"Are those happy tears, Cloudy, or the other kind? Tell us quick, or we'll jump in the creek and drown ourselves," laughed Leslie; and then two white handkerchiefs, one big and one little, came swiftly out and dabbed at her cheeks until there wasn't a sign of a tear to be seen.

"I think I'm almost too happy to talk," said Julia Cloud, resting back against the tree and looking up into its lacy green branches. "It seems as if I was just beginning my life over and being a child again."

For a few minutes they sat so, looking up into the changing autumn sky, listening to the soft tinkle of the water running below, the dip of an oar, the swirl of a blue heron's wing as it clove the air, the distant voices of the picnickers farther down the creek, the rustle of the yellow beech-leaves as they whispered of the time to go, and how they would drift down like little brown boats to the stream and glide away to the end. Now and then a nut would fall with a tiny crisp thud, and a squirrel would whisk from a limb overhead. They were very quiet, and let the beauty of the spot sink deep into their souls. Then at last Julia Cloud took up her Bible, and began to talk.

CHAPTER XII

There were tiny slips of paper in Julia Cloud's well-worn Bible, and she turned to the first one shyly. It was such new work to her to be talking about these things to any but her own worshipful soul.

The two young people settled back in comfortable attitudes on the blanket, and put their gaze upon the far sky overhead. They were embarrassed also, but they meant to carry this thing through.

"Thus the heavens and the earth were finished, and all the host of them," read Julia Cloud; and straightway the shining blue above them took on a personality, and became a witness in the day's proceedings. It was as if some one whom they had known all their lives, quite familiar in their daily life, should suddenly have stood up and declared himself to have been an eye-witness to most marvellous proceedings. The hazy blue with its floating clouds was no longer a diversion from the subject in hand. Their eyes were riveted with mysterious thoughts as they lay and listened, astonished, fascinated. It was the first time it had ever really entered into their consciousness that there had been a time when there was no blue, no firm earth, no anything. Whether it were true or not had not as yet become a question with them. They were near enough to their fairy-story days to accept a tale while it was being read, and revel in it.

The quiet voice went on:

"And on the seventh day God ended his work which he had made; and he rested on the seventh day from all his work which he had made. And God blessed the seventh day, and sanctified it: because that in it he had rested from all his work which God created and made."

"What did He have to rest for? A God wouldn't get tired, would He?" burst forth Leslie, turning big inquiring eyes on Julia Cloud.

"I don't know, unless He did it for our sakes to set us an example," she answered slowly, "although that might mean He rested in the sense of stopped doing it, you know. And that would imply that He had some reason for doing so. I'm not very wise, you know, and because I may not be able to answer your questions doesn't mean they can't be answered by some one who has studied it all out. I've often wished I could have gone to college and studied Greek and Hebrew, so I could have read the Bible in the original."

"H'm!" said Allison thoughtfully. "That would be interesting, wouldn't it? I always wondered why they did it, but I don't know but I'll study them myself. I think I'd enjoy it if there was a real reason besides just the discipline of it they are always talking about when you kick about mathematics and languages."

"Well," said Leslie, sitting up interestedly, "is that all there is to it? Did some one just up and say we had to keep Sunday because God did? I think that is a kind of superstition. I don't see that God would want to make us do everything He did. We couldn't. I *wouldn't* unless *He* said to, anyhow."

"O Les! You're way off," laughed her brother. "God did. He said, 'Remember the sabbath day to keep it holy. Six days shalt thou labor, and do all thy work, but the seventh day is the sabbath of the Lord thy God; in it thou shalt not do any work, thou, nor thy son, nor thy daughter, thy man servant nor thy maid servant——' Don't you remember the Ten Commandments? No, I guess you were too little to learn them. But I got a Testament for learning them once. Say, Cloudy, when did He give that command? Right away after He made Adam and Eve?"

"I'm not sure," said Julia Cloud, fluttering the leaves of her Bible over to the second slip of paper. "I don't find any reference to it in my concordance till way over here in Exodus, after the children of Israel had been in Egypt so many years, and Moses led them out through the wilderness, and they got fretful because they hadn't any bread such as they used to have in Egypt, so God sent them manna that fell every morning. But He told them not to leave any over for the next day because it would gather worms and smell bad, except on Saturday, when they were to gather enough for the Sabbath. Listen: 'And they gathered it every morning, every man according to his eating; and when the sun waxed hot, it melted. And it came to pass, that on the sixth day they gathered twice as much bread, two omers for one man; and all the rulers of the congregation came and told Moses. And he said unto them, This is that which the Lord hath said, To-morrow is the rest of the holy sabbath unto the Lord; bake that, which ye will bake to-day, and seethe that ye will seethe; and that which remaineth over lay up for you to be kept until the morning. And they laid it up till the morning, as Moses bade; and it did not stink, neither was there any worm therein. And Moses said, Eat that to-day; for to-day is a sabbath unto the Lord: to-day ye shall not find it in the field. Six days ye shall gather it; but on the seventh day, which is the sabbath, in it there shall be none. And it came to pass, that there went out some of the people on the seventh day for to gather, and they found none. And the Lord said unto Moses, How long refuse ye to keep my commandments and my laws? See, for that the Lord hath given you the sabbath, therefore he giveth you on the sixth day the bread of two days; abide ye every man in his place, let no man go out of his place on the seventh day. So the people rested on the seventh day.' It looks as though the people had been used to the Sabbath already, for the commandments given on the mount come three whole chapters later. It looks to me as if God established the Sabbath right at the beginning when He rested from His own work, and that's what it means when it says He sanctified it."

"What do you suppose He said, 'I have given *you* a sabbath' for? It looks as if it were meant for a benefit for the people and not for God, doesn't it?" said Allison, sitting up and looking over his aunt's shoulder. "Why, I always supposed God wanted the Sabbath for His own sake, so people would see how great He was."

Julia Cloud's cheeks grew red with a flash of distress as if he had said something against some one she loved very much.

"Oh, no!" she said earnestly. "God isn't like that. Why, He loves us! He wouldn't have given a Sabbath at all if it hadn't been quite necessary for our good. Besides, in the New Testament, Jesus said, 'The sabbath was made for man, and not man for the sabbath'! Oh, He made it for us, to be happy in, I'm sure. And perhaps He rested Himself so that we might understand He had set apart that time of leisure in order to be everything to us on the day when we had most time for Him. I have read somewhere that God had to teach those early people little by little just as we teach babies, a few things each year; and over in the New Testament it says that all these things that happened in the Old Testament to those children of Israel happened and were written down for an example to us who should live in the later part of the world. So, little by little, by pictures and stories He taught those people what He wanted all of us to know as a sort of inheritance. And He took the things first that were of the most importance. It would seem as if He considered this matter of the Sabbath very important, and as if He had it in mind right away at the first when He made the world, and intended to set apart this day out of every seven, because He stopped right off the very first week Himself to establish a precedent, and then He 'sanctified' it, which must mean He set it apart in such a way that all the world should understand."

"What is a precedent?" asked Leslie sharply.

"Oh, you know, Les, it's something you have to do just like because you always have done it that way," said Allison, waving her aside. "But, Cloudy, what I can't get at at all is why He wanted it in the first place if He didn't want it just entirely for His own glorification."

"Why, dear, I am not sure; but I think it was just so that He and we might have a sort of a trysting-time when we could be sure of having nothing to interfere between us. And He meant it, too, to be the sign between Himself and those who really loved Him and were His children, a sign that should show to the world who were His. He said so in several places. Listen to this." She turned the leaves quickly. "'And the Lord spake unto Moses, saying: Speak thou also unto the children of Israel, saying, Verily my sabbaths ye shall keep; for it is a sign between me and you throughout your generations; that ye may know that I am the Lord that doth sanctify you. Ye shall keep the sabbath therefore; for it is holy unto you; every one that defileth it shall surely be put to death; for whosoever doeth any work therein, that soul shall be cut off from among his people. Six days may work be done; but in the seventh is the sabbath of rest, holy to the Lord; whosoever doeth any work in the sabbath day, he shall surely be put to death. Wherefore the children of Israel shall keep the sabbath, to observe the sabbath throughout their generations, for a perpetual covenant. It is a sign between me and the children of Israel forever; for in six days the Lord made heaven and earth, and on the seventh day he rested, and was refreshed.'"

"There! Now!" said Leslie, sitting up. "That's just what I thought! That was only for the children of Israel. It hasn't the leastest bit to do with us. Those were Jews, and they keep it yet, on Saturday."

"Wait, dear!" Julia Cloud turned the leaves of her Bible rapidly to Corinthians.

"Listen! 'Moreover, brethren, I would not that ye should be ignorant, how that all our fathers were under the cloud, and all passed through the sea; and were all baptized unto Moses in the cloud and in the sea; and did all eat the same spiritual meat; and did all drink the same spiritual drink; for they drank of that spiritual Rock that followed them; and that Rock was Christ. But with many of them God was not well pleased; for they were overthrown in the wilderness. Now these things were our examples, to the intent we should not lust after evil things, as they also lusted. Neither, be ye idolators, as were some of them; as it is written, The people sat down to eat and drink, and rose up to play.... Neither let us tempt Christ, as some of them also tempted, and were destroyed of serpents. Neither murmur ye, as some of them also murmured, and were destroyed of the destroyer. Now all these things happened unto them for ensamples: and they are written for our admonition, upon whom the ends of the world are come. Wherefore let him that thinketh he standeth take heed lest he fall.' Doesn't that look as though God meant the Sabbath for us, too, Leslie?"

Leslie dropped back on her pillow of moss with a sigh. "I s'pose it does," she answered somewhat disconsolately. "But I never did like Sundays anyhow!" and she drew a deep breath of unrest.

"But, dear,"—Julia Cloud's hand rested on the bright head lovingly,—"there's a closer sense than that in which this belongs to us if we belong to Christ; we are Israel ourselves. I was reading about it just this morning, how all those who want to be Christ's chosen people, and are willing to accept Him as their Saviour, are Israel just as much as a born Jew. I think I can find it again. Yes, here it is in Romans: 'For they are not all Israel which are *of* Israel: neither, because they are the seed of Abraham, are they all children; but, In Isaac shall thy seed be called. That is, they which are children of the flesh, these are not the children of God: but the children of the promise are counted for the seed.' That means the promise that was given to Abraham that there should be a Messiah sometime in his family who would be the Saviour of the world, and the idea is that all who believe in that Messiah are the real chosen people. It was to the chosen people God gave these careful directions—commands, if you like to call them—to help them be what a chosen people ought to be. And the Sabbath rest and communion seems to be the basis of the whole idea of a people who were guided by God. It is the coming home to God after the toil of the week. They had to have a time when other things did not call them away from spending a whole day with Him and getting acquainted, from getting to know what He wanted and how to shape their lives, or they would just as surely get interested in the world and forget God."

"Well, I don't see why we have to go to church, anyway," declared Leslie discontentedly. "This is a great deal better out here under the trees, reading the Bible."

"Yes," said Allison. "Cloudy, that minister's dull. I know I wouldn't get anything out of hearing him chew the rag."

"O Allison, dear! Don't speak of God's minister that way!"

"Why not, Cloudy? Maybe he isn't God's minister. How did he get there, anyway? Just decided to be a minister, and studied, and got himself called to that church, didn't he?"

"Oh, no, dear! I trust not. That is terrible! Where ever did you get such an idea? There may be some unworthy men in the ministry. Of course there must be, for the Bible said there would be false leaders and wolves in sheep's clothing; but surely, *surely* you know that the most of the men in the pulpit are there because they believe that God has called them to give up everything else and spend their lives bringing the message of the gospel to the souls of men. The office is a holy office, and must be reverenced even if we do not fancy the man who occupies it. He may have a message if you listen for it, even though he may seem dull to you. If you knew him better, could look into his life and see the sacrifices he has made to be a minister, see the burdens of the people he has to bear!"

"O Cloudy, come now. Most of the ministers I ever saw have automobiles and fine houses, and about as good a time as anybody. They get big salaries, and don't bother themselves much about anything but church services and getting people to give money. Honestly, now, Cloudy Jewel, I think they're putting it over on you. I'll bet not half of them are sincere in that sacrifice stuff they put over. It may have been so long ago; but ministers have a pretty soft snap nowadays, in cities anyhow."

"Allison! Didn't you ever see any true, sincere ministers, child? There are so many, many of them!"

"To tell you the truth, Cloudy, I never saw but one that didn't have shifty eyes. He was a little missionary chap that worked in a slum settlement and would have taken his eye-teeth out for anybody. Oh, I don't mean that old guy to-day looked shifty. I should say he was just dull and uninteresting. He may have thought he had a call long ago, but he's been asleep so long he's forgotten about it." "O Allison! This is dreadful!"

Julia Cloud closed her Bible, and looked down in horror at the frank young face of the boy who minced no words in saying what he thought about these holy things that had always been so precious and sacred to her. She felt like putting her hands over her ears and running away screaming. Her very soul was in agony over the desecration. The children looked into her face, saw the white, scared look, and took warning.

"There now, Cloudy, don't worry!" said Allison, leaning over and patting her hand awkwardly. "I didn't mean to hurt you; honest I didn't. Perhaps I'm wrong. Of course I am if you say so. I don't really know any ministers, anyhow. I was just saying what is the general impression among the fellows. I didn't realize you would *care*."

"Do the young men all think that?" Julia Cloud's lips were white, and an agonized expression for the church of God had grown in her eyes. She searched the boy's face with a look he did not soon forget. It made an impression that stayed with him always. At least, there was something in religion if it could make her look like that to hear it lightly spoken of. At least this one woman was a sincere follower of Christ.

"There now, Cloudy! I tell you I'm sorry I said that; and just to prove it I'll go to that old Christian Endeavor to-night, and try to find something interesting. I will truly. And Les will go, too!"

"Of course!" said Leslie, nestling close. "Forget what he said, and tell us why we have to go to church, Cloudy, dear."

Julia Cloud tried to recall her troubled thoughts to the subject in hand.

"Well, God had them build the tabernacle for worship, you know, dear; told them how to make everything even to the minutest details, and established worship. That was to be part of the Sabbath day, a place to worship, and a promise that He would be there to meet any one who came. That promise holds good to-day. You needn't ever think about the minister. Just fancy you see Christ in the pulpit. He is there, come to meet His own, you know. He'll be in that Christian Endeavor to-night. He was in the tabernacle of old. There was a brightness in the cloud of His presence to show the people that God had come down to meet them. They were children, and had to be helped by a visible manifestation."

"Yes, that would be something like!" said Allison. "If we could see something to help us believe——"

"Those who truly believe with the heart will have the assurance," said Julia Cloud earnestly. "I *know*."

There was something in her tone and the look of her eye that added, "For I have experienced it." The young people looked at her, and were silent. There was a long, quiet pause in which the sounds of the falling nuts and the whispering of the hemlocks closed in about them, and made the day and hour a sacred time. At last Leslie broke the silence.

"Well, Cloudy, suppose we go to church and Christian Endeavor. What can we do the rest of the day? We don't have to go to church every minute, do we? I don't really see how it's going to do me any good. I don't, indeed."

Julia Cloud smiled at her wistfully. It was so wonderfully sweet to have this bright, beautiful young thing asking her these vital questions.

"Why, deary, it's just a day to spend with God and get to enjoy His company," she said. "Let me read you this verse in Isaiah: 'Blessed'—that means, 'O the happiness of': I'll read it so—'O the happiness of the man that doeth this, and the son of man that layeth hold on it; that keepeth the sabbath from polluting it, and keepeth his hand from doing any evil. Neither let the son of the stranger that hath joined himself to the Lord'—there, Leslie, that means us, or any Gentiles that want to be Christ's—'speak, saying, The Lord hath utterly separated us from his people.... For thus saith the Lord to' them 'that keep my sabbaths, and choose the things that please me, and take hold of my covenant; even unto them will I give in mine house and within my walls a place and a name better than of sons and of daughters; I will give them an everlasting name, that shall not be cut off. Also the sons of the stranger that join themselves to the Lord, to serve him, and to love the name of the Lord, to be his servants, every one that keepeth the sabbath from polluting it, and taketh hold of my covenant; even them will I bring to my holy mountain, and make them joyful in my house of prayer'—you see, Allison, there's a promise that will secure you from feeling the service dull and dry if you are willing to comply with its conditions—'their burnt offerings and their sacrifices shall be accepted upon mine altar; for mine house shall be called an house of prayer for all people.'"

She turned the leaves quickly again.

"And now I want to read you the verse that seems to me to tell how God likes us to keep the Sabbath. 'If thou turn away thy foot from the sabbath, from doing thy pleasure on my holy day; and call the sabbath a delight'—you see, Leslie, He doesn't want it to be a dull, poky day. He wants us to call it a delight. And yet we are to find our pleasure in Him, and not in the things that belong just to ourselves. Listen: 'a delight, the holy of the Lord, honorable; and shalt honor him, not doing thine own ways, nor finding thine own pleasure, nor speaking thine own words: then shalt thou delight thyself in the Lord; and I will cause thee to ride upon the high places of the earth, and feed thee with the heritage of Jacob thy father; for the mouth of the Lord hath spoken it.'"

Leslie suddenly threw her head in Julia Cloud's lap right over the Bible, and looked up into her face with an exquisite earnestness all her own.

"Cloudy Jewel, it sounds all different from anything I ever heard of, and I don't know how to do it; but something inside says it ought to be true, and I'm going to try it!" she said. "Anyhow, we've had a grand time this afternoon, and it hasn't been a bit dull. Do you suppose maybe we've been 'delighting' in Him this afternoon? But there goes the supper bell, and I'm hungry as a bear. How about that, Cloudy? Is it right to cook on Sunday? That place you read about the man who picked up sticks to make a fire in camp doesn't sound like it."

"Well, dear, you know in the old times we always got the Sunday cooking and baking done on Saturday, just as the Lord told the Israelites to do. I haven't any business to judge other people, and every one must decide for himself what is necessary and what is not, I suppose; but, as for me, I like to do as mother always did. I always have the cake-box and bread-box full of nice fresh things, and make a pie, perhaps, and cook a piece of meat, or have some salad in the ice-box; and then it is the work of but a few minutes to get the nicest kind of a meal on Sunday. It is easy to have a beefsteak to broil, or cold meat, or something to warm up in a minute if one cares enough to get it ready; and it really makes a lovely, restful time on Sunday to know all that work is done. Besides, it isn't any harder. I like it."

Allison gathered up the rug and books, and they walked slowly toward the inn, watching the wonderful colorings of the foliage they passed, and drinking in all the woodsy odors and gentle sounds of dying leaves and dropping nuts.

"Say, Cloudy," said Allison suddenly out of the midst of his thoughtfulness, "why don't the ministers preach about all this? I had to go to church a lot when I was in prep school, and I never yet heard a sermon on it. Or, if I did, it was so dull I didn't get the hang of it. But I should think if they preached about it just as you've done, made it plain so people could understand, that most folks, that is, the ones who wanted to do half right, would see to it that Sunday wasn't so rotten."

"Well, Allison," said Julia Cloud, a soft smile playing dreamfully about her lips, "perhaps they don't realize the need. Perhaps it's 'up to you,' as you say, to somehow wake them up and set them at it."

Allison drew a long whistle and grinned as they went into the house.

CHAPTER XIII

A few minutes later Julia Cloud watched them go off into the dusk to the Christian Endeavor meeting. She was to follow them in a little while and meet them for the evening service. She wondered as she saw them disappear into the shadows of the long maple-lined avenue whether perhaps she was not overdoing the matter a little in the way of meetings, and was almost sorry she had not suggested staying home from the evening service. It would not do to make them weary of it all on this first Sunday.

As they walked along together, the brother and sister were thinking deeply.

"Say, Allison, isn't this the very funniest thing we ever did, going off like this to a prayer meeting alone? What did we do it for?" asked the sister.

"Well, I guess just because Cloudy wanted it," replied the brother. "She's given up her home and everything for us; we ought to. But say, Les, there's a whole lot in what Cloudy was reading this afternoon. If it's all true, it's a wonder more people don't try it. I've often wondered why we were alive, anyway, haven't you? There doesn't seem much sense to it unless there's something like this." "Oh, I don't know, Allison; it's nice to be alive. But of course we never will feel quite as if this is the only place since Mother and Dad aren't here any more. Aren't things queer, anyway? I wish there was some way to be sure."

"Well, I s'pose the Bible claims to be sure. Perhaps we could find out a lot if we read it."

"We're likely to read it quite a good deal, don't you think?" asked the sister archly. "But really, now, it was interesting, and isn't Cloudy a dear? If Christians were all like that, I'd believe in them."

"Perhaps they are, real Christians. Perhaps the ones we mean aren't anything but shams."

"Well, there's a good many shams, then."

The big, noisy bell began to bang out a tardy summons now; but the two young people did not feel the same antipathy toward it that they had felt the night they heard it first. It seemed somehow to have a homely, friendly sound. As they neared the open door, they grew suddenly shy, however, and drew back, lingering on the corner, watching the few stragglers who walked into the pathway of light that streamed from the doorway.

"Some bunch!" growled Allison. "I should say they did need waking up, but I don't hanker for the job."

They slipped in, and followed the sound of voices, through a dimly-lighted hall, smelling of moldy ingrain carpet, into a wide, rather pleasant, chapel room. There were branches of autumn leaves about the walls, reminiscent of some recent festivity, and a bunch of golden-rod in a vase on the little table by the leader's chair.

Two girls were turning over the hymn-book, picking out hymns for the evening; and a tall, shy, girlish young fellow was making fancy letters on a blackboard up in front. Three more girls with their arms about one another had surrounded him, and were giggling and gurgling at him after the manner of that kind of girl. Another plain-faced, plainly-dressed young woman sat half-way up at one side, her hands folded and a look of quiet waiting on her face. That was all that were in the room.

Allison and Leslie found a seat half-way up on the other side from the plain-faced girl, and sat down. No one noticed them save for furtive glances, and no one came near them. The three giggling girls began to talk a little louder. One with her hair bobbed and a long view of vertebrae above her blue dress-collar began to prattle of a dance the night before.

"I thought I'd die!" she chortled. "Bob had me by the arm; and here was my dress caught on Archie's button, and he not knowing and whirling off in the other direction; and the georgette just ripped and tore to beat the band, and me trying to catch up with Archie, and Bob hanging on to me, honest.—You'd uv croaked if you could uv seen me. Oh, but Mother was mad when she saw my dress! She kept blaming me, for she knew I hated that dress and wanted a new one. But me, *I'm* glad. Now I'll get after Dad for a new one. Say, when's Mary's surprise? Is it true it's put off till next week?"

"I'm going to have a new dress for that and silver slippers," declared the girl next her, teetering back and forth on her little high-heeled pumps. "Say, Will, that letter's cock-eyed. What are you giving us? What's the old topic, anyway? I don't see any use in topics. They don't mean anything. I never can find a verse with the words in. I just always ask for a hymn, and half the time I give out any old number without knowing what it is, just to see what it'll turn out."

"Oh, say! Did you hear Chauncey Cramer singing last Sunday night?" broke out the third girl with a side glance at the strangers. "He was perfectly killing. He was twisting the words all around in every hymn. He had girls' names and fellers' all mixed up, and made it rhyme in the neatest way. I thought I'd choke laughing, and Dr. Tarrant was just coming in, and looked at me as if he'd eat me. Oh, my goodness! There he comes now. We better beat it, Hattie. Come on, Mabel. Let's sit back in the last row."

The three girls toppled down the aisle on their high-heeled pumps, and rustled into the back row just as the pastor entered and looked about the room. His eyes brightened when he saw the brother and sister, and with a pleasant "Good-evening" to the three whispering misses in the back seat he came over to shake hands with Allison and Leslie. But, when he expressed a most cordial hope that the two would come in and help in the young people's work, Allison was wary. He said they would have to see how much time they had to spare after college opened. It was altogether likely that they would be exceedingly busy with their college work.

The minister, watching their bright faces wistfully, and knowing their kind, sighed, and thought how little likelihood there was that his Christian Endeavor society would see much of them.

A few more people straggled in, and one of the girls who had been picking out hymns went and sat down at the piano. The other girl sat near her. The young man at the blackboard took his place at the little table in front of the desk, and the elaborate colored letters which he had just made were visible as a whole for the first time.

"The Great Companion: How to Live with Him."

There was something startling and solemn in the words as they stood out in blue and gold and crimson and white on the little blackboard. Allison and Leslie looked and turned wonderingly toward the young leader. He had corn-colored hair, light, ineffective blue eyes, and a noticeably weak chin. He did not look like a person who would be putting forth a topic of that sort and attempting to do anything about it. His face grew pink, and his eyelashes seemed whiter in contrast as he stood up to give out the first hymn. It was plain that he was painfully embarrassed. He glanced now and then deprecatingly toward the visitors with an anxious gasp as he announced that they would open the meeting by singing number twenty-nine. The two young strangers opened their hymn-books and found the place, marvelling how such a youth had ever been persuaded to get himself into such a trying situation. Allison found himself thinking that there must be some power greater than the ordinary influences of life that made him do it. He seemed so much out of his element, and so painfully shy.

"All to Jesus I surrender!" chirped the little gathering gayly. They had good voices, and the harmony was simple and pleasing. Allison and Leslie joined their beautiful voices in with the rest, and liked it, felt almost as if they were on the verge of doing something toward helping on the kingdom of heaven.

They sang another hymn, and more young people came in until there were twenty-four in the room. Then the leader called upon Tom Forbes to read the Scripture, and a boy about fourteen years old read in a clear voice the story of the walk to Emmaus. To the brother and sister whose Bible knowledge was limited to the days of their very young childhood, it was most interesting. They listened intently, but were surprised to notice a tendency to whisper on the part of some, especially the girls in the back seat, who had been joined by three young fellows of about their own age and caliber. Leslie, glancing over her shoulder at the whisperers, saw they had no thrill over the story, no interest save in their own voluble conversation. The story went on to the point where Jesus at the table blessed the bread, and the two men knew Him, and He vanished out of their sight, without an interruption in the whispering. The Great Companion had come into the room and gone, and they had not even known it.

The leader rose, and cleared his voice with courage; and then in a tone of diffidence he recited the few words he had learned for the occasion.

"Our topic to-night is 'The Great Companion: How to Live with Him.' It seems hard to realize that Christ is still on the earth. That He is with us all the time. We ought to realize this. We ought to try to realize it. It would make our lives different if we could realize that Christ is always with us. I expect some of us wouldn't always feel comfortable if we should find Him walking along with us, listening to our talk. We ought to try to live so we would feel all right if we should find Christ walking with us some day. And I heard a story once about a boy who had been a cripple, and he had been a great Christian; and, when he came to die, they asked him if he was afraid; and he said no, he wasn't afraid, that it was only going into another room with Jesus. And I think we ought to all live that way. We will now listen to a solo by Mame Beecher, after which the meeting will be open, and I hope that all will take part."

It was a crude little speech, haltingly spoken, and the speaker was evidently relieved when it was over. Yet there had been amazing truth in what he had said, and it came to the two visitors with the force of newness. As he mopped his perspiring brow with a large handkerchief and sat down, adjusting his collar and necktie nervously, they watched him, and marvelled again that he had been willing to be put in so trying a position. There had been a genuineness about him that brought conviction. This young man really believed in Christ and that He walked with men.

Allison, always ready to curl his lips over anything sissified, sat watching him gravely. Here was a new specimen. He didn't know where to place him. Did he *have* to lead a meeting? Was he a minister's son or something, or did he just do it because he wanted to, because it seemed his duty to do it? Allison could not decide. He knew that he himself could have made a much better speech on the subject, but he would not want to. He would hate it, talking about sacred things like that out to the world; yet he was frank enough to see that a better speech might not have been so acceptable to God as this halting one full of repetition and crudities.

The girl up by the piano was singing the solo. Why did she let herself be called "Mame" in that common way? She was a rather common-looking girl, with loud colors in her garments and plenty of powder in evidence on her otherwise pretty face; but she had a good voice, and sang the words distinctly.

secret of His presence how my soul deligh

precious are the lessons which I learn at Jes

The words were wonderful. They somehow held you through to the end. The girl named Mame had that quality of holding attention with her voice and carrying a message to a heart. There were two lines that seemed particularly impressive,

hene'er you leave the silence of that happy

mind and bear the image of the Master in you

Leslie found herself looking around the room to see whether any one present bore that image, and her eyes lingered longest on the quiet girl in the plain garments over on the other side of the room. She had a face that was almost beautiful in its repose, if it had not worn that air of utter reticence.

There was a long pause after the soloist was done, and much whispering from the back row, which at last terminated in a flutter of Bible leaves and the reading of three Bible verses containing the word "companion," without much reference to the topic, from the three girls on the back seat, passing the Bible in turn, with much ado to find their respective places. Another hymn followed, and a prayer from a solemn-looking boy in shell-rimmed spectacles. It was a good prayer, but the young man wore also that air of reticence that characterized the girl on the other side of the room, as if he were not a part of these young people, had nothing in common with them. Allison decided that they were all dead, and surely did need some one to wake them up; but the task was not to his liking. What had he in common with a bunch like that? In fact, what had any of them in common that they should presume to form themselves into a society? It was rank nonsense. You couldn't bring people together that had nothing in common and make them have a good time. These were his thoughts during another painful pause, during which the pastor in the back seat half rose, then sat down and looked questioningly toward the two visitors. The young leader seemed to understand the signal; for he grew very red, looked at Allison and Leslie several times, cleared his throat, turned over his hymn-book, and finally said with painful embarrassment:

"We should be glad to hear from our visitors to-night. We'd like to know how you conduct things in your society."

He lifted agonized eyes to Allison, and broke down in a choking cough.

Allison, chilled with amazement, filled with a sudden strange pity, looked around with growing horror to see whether it was really true that he had been called upon to speak in meeting. Then with the old nonchalance that nothing ever quite daunted he rose to his feet.

"Why, I," he began, looking around with a frank smile, "I never was in a Christian Endeavor meeting before in my life, and I don't know the first thing about it. My sister and I only came to-night because somebody wanted us to; so I can't very well tell about any other society. But I belong to a college frat, and I suppose it's a good deal the same thing in the long run. I've been reading that pledge up there on the wall. I suppose that's your line. You've got good dope all right. If you live up to that, you're going some.

"I remember when I first went to college the fellows began to rush me. I had bids from two or three different frats, and they had me going so hard I got bewildered. I didn't know which I wanted to join. Then one day one of the older fellows got hold of me, and he saw how it was with me; and he said: 'You want to look around and analyze things. Just you look the fellows over, and see how they size up in the different frats. Then you see what they stand for, and how they live up to it; and lastly you look up their alumni.' So I began to size things up, and I found that one frat was all for the social doings, dances, and dinners, and always having a good time; and another was pretty wild, had the name of always getting in bad with the faculty, and had the lowest marks in college; three fellows had been expelled the year before for drunkenness and disorderliness. Then another one was known as ranking highest in scholarship and having the most athletes in it. I looked over their alumni, too, for they used to come around a good bit and get in with us boys; and you could see just which were making good out in the world, and which were just in life for what they could get out of it; and I made my decision one day just because of one big man who had been out of college for ten years; but he had made good in the world, and was known all over as being a successful man and a wonderful man, and he used to come back to every game and everything that went on at the college, and sit around and talk with the fellows, and encourage them; and, if anybody was falling down on his job, he would show him where he was wrong and how to get into line again, and even help him financially if he got in a tight place. And so I thought with men like that back of it that frat was a pretty good thing to tie up to, and I joined it, and found it was even better than I expected.

"And I was thinking as I looked at the blackboard, and heard you talking about the Great Companion, it was something like that man. If all that's true that you've been reading and saying to-night, why, you've got pretty good things back of you. With an Alumnus like that"—nodding toward the blackboard—"and a line of talk like that pledge, you sure ought to have a drag with the world. All you've got to do is to make everybody believe that it is really so, and you'd have this room full; for, believe me, that's the kind of dope everybody wants, especially young people, whether they own it or not."

Allison sat down abruptly, suddenly realizing that he had just made a religious speech and had the interest of the meeting in his hands. His speech seemed to set loose something in the heart of the young leader; for he rose eagerly, alertly, his embarrassment departed, and began to speak:

"I'm glad our friend has spoken that way. I guess it's all true what he has just said. We've got the right dope; only we aren't using it. I guess it looks mighty like to the world as if we didn't really believe it all, the way we live; but believe me, I'm going to try to make things different in my life this week, and see if I can't make at least one person believe we have something here they want before next Sunday."

He seemed about to give out another hymn, but the plain girl spoke up and interrupted him. She was sitting forward in her chair, an almost radiant look upon her face that quite changed it; and she spoke rapidly, breathlessly, like a shy person who had a great message to convey. She was looking straight at Allison as if she had forgotten everyone else in the room.

"I've got to speak," she said earnestly. "It isn't right to keep still when I've had such a wonderful experience, and you spoke as if it might not all be true about Christ's being our companion every day." In spite of himself Allison met her eyes as though they were talking alone together, and waited for what she should tell.

"I've always been just a quiet Christian," she went on; "and I don't often speak here except to recite a Bible verse. I'm sort of a stranger myself. But you all ought to know what Christ has done for me. When my people died and everything in my life was changed, and troubles came very thick and fast, there wasn't anybody in the world I could turn to for every-day help and companionship but Jesus; and one day it came to me how my mother used to feel about Him, and I just went to Him, and asked Him to be my companion, as He used to be hers. I didn't half believe He would when I asked Him; but I was so hurt and alone I had to do something; and I found out it was all true! He helped me in so many little every-day ways, you wouldn't believe it, perhaps, unless you could have lived it out yourself. I guess you really have to live it out to know it, after all. But I found that I could go to Him just as if I could see Him, and I was so surprised the first day when He answered a prayer in a perfectly wonderful way. It all came over me, 'Why, He loves me!' And at first I thought it was just happening; but I tried it again and again, and every day wonderful things began to come into my life, and it got to be that I could talk with Him and feel His answer in my heart. If it were not for Him, I couldn't stand life sometimes. And I'm sure He'll talk with any one that way who wants Him enough to try and find Him," she finished; and then, suddenly conscious of herself, she sat back, white and shy again, with trembling lips.

The meeting closed then; but, while they were singing the last hymn Allison and Leslie were watching the face of the quiet girl with the holy, uplifted light on it.

"I think she is lovely, don't you?" whispered Leslie after the benediction, as they turned to go out. "I'd like to know her."

"H'm!" assented Allison. "Cloudy would like her, I guess."

"I mean to find out who she is," declared Leslie.

The minister came up just then with cordial greeting and urgent appeal that the young people would at once join their Christian Endeavor.

"That was a great talk you gave us to-night," he said with his hand resting admiringly on Allison's shoulder. "We need young blood. You are the very one to stir up this society."

"But I'm not a Christian," said Allison, half laughing. "I don't belong here."

"Oh, well," answered the smiling minister, "if you take hold of the Endeavor, perhaps you'll find you're more of a Christian than you think. Come, I want you to meet some of our young people."

The young people were all gathered in groups, looking toward the strangers, and came quite willingly to have a nearer glimpse of them. Last of all, and by herself, came the plain-faced girl; and the minister introduced her as Jane Bristol. He did not speak to her more than that, and it occurred to Allison that she seemed as if she came more at the instigation of some higher power than at the call of her pastor; for she passed quietly on again in a pleasant dignity, and did not stop to talk and joke with her pastor as some of the other young people had done.

"Who is she?" asked Allison, hardly aware that he was asking.

"Why, she is the daughter of a forger who died in prison. Her mother, I believe, died of a broken heart. Sad experience for so young a girl. She seems to be a good little thing. She is working at housework in town, I believe. I understand she has an idea of entering college in the fall. You are entering college here? That will be delightful. My wife and I will take pleasure in calling on you as soon as you are ready to receive visitors."

Leslie's eyes were on Jane Bristol as she moved slowly toward the door, lingering a moment in the hall. None of the other girls seemed to have anything to do with her. With her usual impulsiveness Leslie left Allison, and went swiftly down the aisle till she stood by Jane Bristol's side.

"We are going to meet my aunt and stay to church. Would you come and sit with us to-night?" she asked eagerly. "I'd like to get acquainted with you."

Jane Bristol shook her head with a wistful smile.

"I'm sorry," she said. "I wish I could. But I take care of a little girl evenings, and I only get off long enough for Christian Endeavor. It's dear of you to ask me."

"Well, you'll come and see me when I get settled in my new home, won't you?"

Jane looked at her thoughtfully, and then gave her a beautiful smile in answer to Leslie's brilliant one.

"Yes, if you find you want me when you get settled, I'll come," she answered, and, giving Leslie's little gloved hand an impulsive squeeze, she said, "Good-night," and went away.

Leslie looked after her a minute, half understanding, and then turned to find her brother beside her.

"She thinks I won't want her because she works!" she said. "But I do. I shall."

"Sure you will, kid," said her brother. "Just tell Cloudy about her. She'll fix things. That old party—I mean, the reverend gentleman——"

"Look out, Allison, that isn't any better; and there comes Cloudy. Don't make her feel bad again."

"Well, parson, then—doesn't seem to have much use for a person who's had the misfortune to have her father commit forgery and her mother die of a broken heart, or is it because she has to work her way through college? He may be all right, sister; but I'd bank on that girl's religion over against his any day in the week, Sundays included."

Then Julia Cloud came up the steps, and they went in to a rather dreary evening service with a sparse congregation and a bored-looking choir, who passed notes and giggled during the sermon. Allison and Leslie sat and wondered what kind of a shock it would be to them all if the Great Companion should suddenly become visible in the room. If all that about His being always present was true, it certainly was a startling thing.

CHAPTER XIV

The next morning dawned with a dull, dreary drizzle coming noisily down on the red and yellow leaves of the maple by the window; but the three rose joyously and their ardor was not damped.

"Six days shalt thou labor and do all thy work," quoted Allison at the breakfast-table. "Cloudy, we've got to hustle. Do you mind if it does rain? We've got our car."

But Julia Cloud smiled unconcernedly.

"I should worry," she said with a gay imitation of Leslie's inimitable toss of the head, and the two young people laughed so hilariously that the other staid couples already in the dining-room turned in amaze to see who was taking life so happily on a day like this.

They piled into the car, and hied themselves to town at once, chattering joyfully over their list as to which things they would buy first.

"Let's begin with the kitchen," said Leslie. "I'm crazy to learn how to make cookies. Cloudy, you'll teach me how so I can make some all myself, won't you?"

"And waffles!" said Allison from the front seat.

"Um-mmm-mmmm! I remember Cloudy's waffles. And buckwheat cakes."

"We're going to have everything for the kitchen to make things easy, so that when we can't get a maid Cloudy won't be always overdoing," said Leslie. "Guardy told me especially about that. He said we were to get every convenience to make things easy, so the cook wouldn't leave; for he'd rather pay any amount than have Cloudy work herself to death and have to break down and leave us."

So it was the house-furnishing department of the great store to which they first repaired, and there they hovered for two hours among tins and aluminum and wooden ware, discussing the relative charms of white-enamel refrigerators and gas-ranges, vacuum cleaners and dish-washers, the new ideas against the old. Julia Cloud was for careful buying and getting along with few things; the children were infatuated with the idea of a kitchen of their own, and wanted everything in sight. They went wild over a new kind of refrigerator that would freeze its own ice, making ice-cream in the bargain, and run by an electric motor; but here Julia Cloud held firm. No such expensive experiment was needed in their tiny kitchen. A small white, old-fashioned kind was good enough for them. So the children immediately threw their enthusiasm into selecting the best kind of ice-cream freezer.

When they finally went to the tea-room for lunch, everything on Julia Cloud's list was carefully checked off by Allison with its respective price; and, while they were waiting to be served, he added the column twice to make sure he was right.

"We're shy five dollars yet of what we planned to spend on our kitchen, Cloudy," he announced radiantly. "What did I tell you?"

"But where would you have been if I had let you get that refrigerator?" she retorted.

"Well, there were a lot of things we didn't really need," he answered.

"Such as what?"

"Oh, clothes-pins and—well, all those pans. Did you need so many?" he answered helplessly.

They laughed his masculine judgment out of countenance, and chatted away about what they should do next, until their order arrived.

They were like three children as they ate their lunch, recalling now and then some purchase which gave them particular pleasure.

Suddenly Julia Cloud lifted her hands in mock distress. "I know what we've forgotten! Dish-towels!" she said.

"Dish-towels! Why, sure. We have to have a lot so we can all wipe dishes when the cook goes out. Will five dollars buy them, Cloudy?" asked Leslie distressingly.

"Well, I certainly should hope so!" said Julia Cloud, laughing. "The idea! Five dollars' worth of dish-towels!"

"Well, we'll go and get them at once," said Leslie; "and after that we'll do the bedrooms."

Five o'clock found them wending their way homeward once more, tired but happy.

"Now, to-morrow," said Julia Cloud, leaning back on the soft cushions, "I think we had better stay at home and receive the things. The house must be cleaned at once, and then we can put things right where they are going to belong. Allison, you ought to be able to get a man to wash windows. I'll ask the chambermaid about a woman to help clean, and Leslie and I will make curtains while you put up the rods."

They were so interesting a trio at their table in the inn dining-room that night that people around began to ask who were those two charming young people and their beautiful mother. Little ripples of query went around the room as they entered, for they were indeed noticeable anywhere. The young people were bubbling over with life and spirits and kindliness, and Julia Cloud in her silvery robes and her white hair made a pleasant picture. But they were so wholly wrapped up in their own housekeeping plans that they were utterly unaware of the interest they excited in their fellow-boarders. Just at present they had no time to spare on other people. They were playing a game, just as they used to play house when they were little, with their aunt; and they wanted no interruption until they should have completed the home and were ready to move in and begin to live. After that other people might come in for their attention.

The next morning bright and early Allison was up and out, hunting his man, and announced triumphantly at the breakfast-table that he was found and would be down at the house and ready for work in half an hour. Breakfast became a brief ceremony after that. For Julia Cloud also had not been idle, and had procured the address of a good woman to clean the house. Allison rushed off after the car, and in a few minutes they were on their way, first to leave Julia Cloud and Leslie at the house to superintend the man, and then to hunt the woman. He presently returned with a large colored woman sitting imposingly in the back seat, her capable hands folded in her lap, a look of intense satisfaction on her ample countenance.

Julia Cloud had thoughtfully brought from home a large bundle of cleaning-rags, and a little canned-alcohol heater presently supplied hot water. Leslie made a voyage of discovery, and purchased soap and scouring-powder; and soon the whole little house was a hive of workers.

"Now," said Julia Cloud, opening the bundle of curtain material, "where shall we begin?"

"Right here," said Leslie, looking around the big white living-room with satisfaction. "I'm just longing to see this look like a home; and you must admit, Cloudy, that this room is the real heart of the house. We'll eat and sleep and work and study in the other rooms; but here we'll really live, right around that dear fireplace. I'm just crazy to see it made up and burning. Oh, won't it be great?"

Busy hands and shining scissors went to work, measuring, cutting, turning hems; and presently a neat pile of white curtains, the hems all turned ready for stitching, lay in the wide back window-seat. Then they went at the other rooms, the sun-porch room and the dining-room. But before that was quite finished a large furniture-truck arrived, and behold the sewing-machine had come! Leslie was so eager to get at it that she could hardly wait until the rest of the load was properly disposed.

She was not an experienced sewer, but she brought to her work an enthusiasm that stood loyally beside her aunt's experience, and soon some of the curtains were up.

They could not bear to stop and go back to the inn for lunch; so Allison ran down to the pie-shop with the car, and brought back buns cut into halves and buttered, with great slices of ham in them, a pail of hot sweetened coffee, a big cocoanut pie, a bag of cakes and a basket of grapes; and they made a picnic of it.

"Our first meal in our own house! Isn't it great?" cried Leslie, dancing around with a roll sandwich in one hand and a wedge of pie in the other.

By night every clean little window in that many-windowed house was curtained with white drapery, and in some rooms also with inner curtains of soft silk. The house began to look cozy in spite of its emptiness, and they could hardly bear to leave it when sunset warned them that it was getting near dinner-time and they must return to the inn to freshen up for the evening.

Another day at the little house completed the cleaning and curtaining, and by this time all the furniture so far purchased had arrived, and they had no need to be there to watch for anything else; so another day of shopping was agreed upon.

"And I move we pick out the piano first of all," said Leslie. "I'm just crazy to get my fingers on the keys again, and you don't know how well Allison can sing, Cloudy. You just ought to hear him. Oh, boy!"

Julia Cloud smiled adoringly at the two, and agreed that the piano was as good a place as any to begin.

That day was the best of all the wonderful shopping to Julia Cloud. To be actually picking out wonderful mahogany furniture such as she had seen occasionally in houses of the rich, such as she had admired in pictures and read of in magazine articles, seemed too wonderful to be true. For the first time in her life she was to live among beautiful things, and she felt as if she had stepped into at least the anteroom of heaven. It troubled her a little to be allowing the children to spend so much, even though their guardian had made it plain that they had plenty to spend; for it did not seem quite right to use so much on one's self when so many were in need; but gradually her viewpoint began to change. It was true that these things were only relative, and what seemed much to her was little to another. Perhaps coming directly from her exceedingly limited sphere she was no fit judge of what was right and necessary. And of course there was always the fact that good things lasted, and were continually beautiful if well chosen. Also much good might be done to a large circle of outsiders by a beautiful home.

So Julia Cloud, because the matter of expenditure was not, after all, in her hands, decided just to have a good time and enjoy picking out these wonderful things, interfering only where she thought the article the children selected was not worth buying, or was foolish and useless. But on the whole they got along beautifully, and agreed most marvellously about what fitted the little pink-and-white stone "villa," as Leslie had named it. "'Cloud Villa,' that's what we'll call it," she cried one day in sudden inspiration; and so it was called thereafter in loving jest.

Two days more of hard work, and their list was nearly finished. By this time they were almost weary of continually trying to decide which thing to get. A bewildering jumble of French gray bedsteads and mahogany tables and dining-room chairs swung around in their minds when they went to sleep at night, and smilingly met their waking thoughts. They were beginning to long for the time when they could sit down in the dining-room chairs, and get acquainted with their beds and tables, and feel at home.

"I wish we could get in by Sunday," grumbled Allison. "It's fierce hanging around this hotel with nothing to do."

"Well, why not?" assented Julia Cloud as she buttered her breakfast muffin. "The bedding was promised to come out this morning, and I don't see why we couldn't make up the beds and sleep there to-night, although I don't know whether we can get the gas-range connected in time to do much cooking."

"Oh, we can come back here for our meals till next week," declared Leslie. "Then we'll have time to get the dishes unpacked and washed and put in that lovely china-closet. Perhaps we'll be able to get at that to-day. The curtains are every blessed one up, inside and out, now; and, if we succeed in getting that maid that you heard of, why, we'll be all fixed for next week. I do wish those California things would arrive and we could get the rugs down. It doesn't look homey without rugs and pictures."

And, sure enough, they had not been at work ten minutes before the newly-acquired telephone bell rang, and the freight agent announced that their goods were at the station, and asked whether they wanted them sent up to-day, for he wanted to get the car out of his way.

In two hours more the goods arrived, and right in the midst of their unloading the delivery-wagons from the city brought a lot more articles; and so the little pink-and-white house was a scene of lively action for some time.

When the last truck had started away from the house, Allison drove the car up.

"Now, Cloudy, you jump in quick, and we're going back to the inn for lunch. Then you lie down and rest a whole hour, and sleep, or I won't let you come back," he announced. "I saw a tired look around your eyes, and it won't do. We are not going to have you worked out, not if we stay in that old inn for another month. So there!"

He packed them in, and whirled them away to the inn in spite of Julia Cloud's protest that she was not tired and wanted to work; but, when they came back at two o'clock, they all felt rested and fit for work again.

"Now, I'm the man, and I'm going to boss for a while," said Allison. "You two ladies go up-stairs, and make beds. Here, which are the blankets and sheets? I'll take the bundles right up there, and you won't have any running up and down to do. These? All of them? All right. Now come on up, and I'll be undoing the rugs and boxes from California. When you come down, they'll be all ready for you to say where they shall go."

Leslie and her aunt laughingly complied, and had a beautiful time unfolding and spreading the fine white sheets, plumping the new pillows into their cases, laying the soft, gay-bordered blankets and pretty white spreads, till each bed was fair and fit for a good night's sleep. And then at the foot of each was plumped, in a puff of beauty, the bright satin eiderdowns that Leslie had insisted upon. Rose-color for Julia Cloud's, robin's-egg blue for Leslie's, and orange and brown for Allison's, who had insisted upon mahogany and quiet colors for his room. Leslie's furniture was ivory-white, and Julia Cloud's room was furnished in French gray enamel, with insets of fine cane-work. She stood a moment in the open doorway, and looked about the place; soft gray walls, with a trellis of roses at the top, filmy white draperies with a touch of rose, a gray couch luxuriously upholstered, with many pillows, some rose, some gray, a thick, gray rug under her feet, and her own little gray desk drawn out conveniently when she wanted to write. Over all a flood of autumn sunshine, and on the wall a great water-color of a marvellous sunset that Leslie had insisted belonged in that room and must be bought or the furnishing would not be complete.

It filled Julia Cloud's eyes with tears of wonder and gratitude to think that such a princess's abode should have come to be her abiding-place after her long years of barren living in dreary surroundings. She lifted her eyes to the sunset picture on the wall, and it reminded her of the evening when she had stood at her own home window in her distress and sorrow, looking into the gray future, and had watched it break into rose-color before her eyes. For just an instant after Leslie had run down-stairs she closed her door, and dropped upon her knees beside the lovely bed to thank her Lord for this green and pleasant pasture where He had led her tired feet.

Allison had all the rugs spread out on the porch and lawn, and he and Leslie were hard at work giving them a good sweeping. They were wonderful rugs, just such as one would expect to come from a home of wealth where money had never been a consideration. Julia Cloud looked at them almost with awe, recognizing by instinct the priceless worth of them, and almost afraid at the idea of living a common, daily life on them. For Julia Cloud had read about rugs. She knew that in far lands poor peasant people, whole families, sometimes wove their history into them for a mere pittance; and they had come to mean something almost sacred in her thoughts.

But Allison and Leslie had no such reverence for them; and they swept away gayly, and slammed them about familiarly, in a happy hurry to get them in place. So presently the big blue Chinese rug covered the living-room, almost literally; for it was an immense one, and left very little margin around it. A handsome Kermanshah in old rose and old gold with pencillings of black was spread forth under the mahogany dining-table, and a rich dark-red and black Bokhara runner fitted the porch-room as if it had been bought for it. The smaller rugs were quickly disposed here and there, a lovely little rose-colored silk prayer rug being forced upon Julia Cloud for her bedroom as just the finishing touch it needed, and Leslie took possession of two or three smaller blue rugs for her room. Then they turned their attention to pictures, bits of jade and bronze, a few rare pieces of furniture, a wonderful old bronze lamp with a great dragon on a sea of wonderful blue enamel, with a shade that cast an amber light; brass andirons and fender, and a lot of other little things that go to make a lovely home.

"Now," said Allison, "when we get our books unpacked, and some magazines thrown around, it will look like living. Cloudy, can we sleep here to-night?"

"Why, surely," said Julia Cloud with a child-like delight in her eyes. "What's to hinder? I feel as if I was in a dream, and if I didn't go right on playing it was true I would wake up and find it all gone."

So they rode back to the inn for their supper, hurried their belongings into the trunk, and moved bag and baggage into the new house at nine o'clock on Saturday night.

While Leslie and her aunt were up-stairs putting away their clothes from the trunk into the new closets and bureau-drawers, Allison brought in a few kindlings, and made a bit of a fire on the hearth; and now he called them down.

"We've got to have a housewarming the first night, Cloudy," he called. "Come down and see how it all looks in the firelight."

So the two came down-stairs, and all three sat together on the deep-blue velvet settee in front of the fireplace, Julia Cloud in the middle and a child on either side.

They were all very tired and did not say much, just sat together happily, watching the wood blaze up and flicker and fall into embers. Presently both children nestled closer to her, and put down a head on each of her shoulders. So they sat for a long time quietly.

"Now," said Julia Cloud, as the fire died down and the room grew dusky with shadows, "it is time we went to bed. But there is something I wish we could do this first night in our new home. Don't you think we ought to dedicate it to God, or at least thank God for giving it to us? Would you be willing to kneel down with me, and— we might just all pray silently, if you don't feel like praying out loud. Would you be willing to do that?"

There was a tender silence for a moment while the children thought.

"Sure!" growled Allison huskily. "You pray out, Cloudy. We'd like it."

"Yes," whispered Leslie, nestling her hand in her aunt's.

And so, trembling, half fearful, her heart in her throat, but bravely, Julia Cloud knelt with a child on either side, hiding wondering, embarrassed, but loyal faces.

There was a tense silence while Julia Cloud struggled for words to break through her unwilling lips, and then quite softly she breathed:

"O dear Christ, come and dwell in this home, and bless it. Help us to live to please Thee. Help me to be a wise guide to these dear children——"

She paused, her voice suddenly giving way with a nervous choke in her throat, and two young hands instantly squeezed her hands in sympathy.

Then a gruff young voice burst out on one side,

"Help me to be good, and not hurt her or make it hard for her."

And Leslie gasped out, "And me, too, dear God!"

Then a moment more, and they all rose, tears on their faces. In the dying firelight they kissed Julia Cloud fervently, and said good-night.

CHAPTER XV

Leslie and Allison did not go to the Christian Endeavor meeting that second Sunday. They were tired out, and wanted to stay at home all the evening, and Julia Cloud felt that it would be unwise to urge them; so they sat around the fire and talked. Leslie sat down at the new piano, and played softly old hymns that Julia Cloud hummed; and they all went to bed early, having had a happy Sabbath in their new home.

But Monday evening quite early, just after they had come back from supper and were talking about reading a story aloud, there came a knock at the door. Their first caller! And behold, there stood the inefficient-looking young man who had led the Christian Endeavor meeting, the boy with the goggles who had prayed, and the two girls who had sat by the piano.

"We're a committee," announced the young man, quite embarrassed. "My name's Herricote, Joe Herricote. I'm president of our Christian Endeavor Society, and this is Roy Bryan; he's the secretary. This is Mame Beecher. I guess you remember her singing. She's chairman of our social committee, and Lila Cary's our pianist and chairman of the music committee. We've come to see if you won't help us."

"Come in," said Allison cordially, but with a growing disappointment. Now, here were these dull people coming to interrupt their pleasant evening, and there wouldn't be many of them, for college would soon begin, and they would be too busy then to read stories and just enjoy themselves.

Leslie, too, frowned, but came forward politely to be introduced. She knew at a glance that these were not people of the kind she cared to have for friends.

"We're a committee," repeated young Herricote, sitting down on the edge of a chair, and looking around most uncomfortably at the luxurious apartment. He had not realized it would be like this. He was beginning to feel like a fish out of water. As for the rest of the committee, they were overawed and dumb, all except the little fellow with the tortoise-rimmed glasses. He was not looking at anything but Allison, and was intent on his mission. When he saw that his superior had been struck dumb, he took up the story.

"They appointed us to come and interview you, and see if you wouldn't give us some new ideas how to run our society so it would be a success," he put in. "They all liked your speech so much the other night they felt you could help us out of the rut we've got into."

"Me?" asked Allison, laughing incredulously. "Why, I told you I didn't know the first thing about Christian Endeavor."

"But we've gotta have your help," said the young secretary earnestly. "This thing's gotta go! It's needed in our church, and it's the only thing in the town to help some of the young people. It's just *gotta* go!"

"Well, if you feel that way, you'll make it go, I'm sure," encouraged Allison. "You're just the kind of a fellow to make it go. You know all about it. Not I. I never heard of the thing till last week, except just in a casual way. Don't know much about it yet."

"Well, s'pose it was one of your frats, and it wasn't succeeding. What would you do? You saw what kind of a dead-and-alive meeting we had, only a few there, and nobody taking much interest. How would you pull up a frat that was that way?"

"Well," said Allison, speaking at random, "I'd look around, and find some of the right kind of fellows, and rush 'em. Get in some new blood."

"That's all right," said Bryan doggedly. "I'm rushin' you. How do you do it? I never went to college yet; so I don't know."

Allison laughed now. He rather liked this queer boy.

"He's a nut!" he said to himself, and entered into the talk in earnest.

"Why, you have parties, and rides, and good times generally, and invite a fellow, and make him feel at home, and make him want to belong. See?"

"I see," said Bryan, with a twinkling glance at the rest of his committee. "We have a party down at my house Friday night. Will you come?"

Allison saw that the joke was on him, and his reserve broke down entirely.

"Well, I guess it's up to me to come," he said. "Yes, I'm game. I'll come."

Bryan turned his big goggles on Leslie.

"Will you come?"

"Why, yes, if Allison does, I will," agreed Leslie, dimpling.

"That's all right," said Bryan, turning back to Allison. "Now, what do you do when you rush? You'll have to teach us how."

"Well," said Allison thoughtfully, "we generally pick out our best rushers, the ones that can talk best, and put them wise. We never let the fellow that's rushed know what we're doing. Oh, if he has brains, he always knows, of course; but you don't say you're rushing him in so many words. At college we meet a fellow at the train, and show him around the place, and put him onto all the little things that will make it easy for him; and we invite him to eat with us, and help him out in every way we can. We appoint some one to look after him specially, and a certain group have him in their charge so the other frats won't have a chance to rush him——"

"I see. The other frats being represented by the devil, I suppose," said the round-eyed boy keenly without a smile.

Allison stared at him, and then broke into a laugh again.

"Exactly," he cried; "you've got onto the idea. It's your society over against the other things that can draw them away from what you stand for. See? And then there's another thing. You want to have something ready to show them when you get them there. That's where our alumni come in. They often run down to college for a few days and help us out with money and influence and experience. If you've got good working alumni, you're right in it, you see. We generally appoint a committee to talk things over with the alumni."

"You mean," said Bryan, drawing his brows together in a comical way behind his goggles, "you mean—pray, I suppose."

"Why," said Allison, flushing, "I suppose that would be a good idea. I hadn't thought of it just in that way."

"You called Christ our alumnus the other night," reminded the literal youth solemnly.

"So I did," acknowledged Allison embarrassedly. "Well, I guess you're right. But I don't know much about that kind of line."

"I'm afraid there don't many of us," put in the bashful president. "I wouldn't hardly know who to appoint on such a committee. There's only two or three like to pray in our meetings. There's Bryan; we always ask him because he doesn't mind, and I—well, I do sometimes when there's no one else, but it comes hard; and there's old Miss Ferby, but she always prays so long, and gets in the president and all the missionary stations——"

"I should think you'd ask that Jane Bristol," spoke up Leslie earnestly. "I know she must be able to. She talked that way."

"I suppose she would," responded the president hesitatingly, looking toward the two ladies of the committee with a half apology. "What do you girls think about it?"

"Oh, I suppose she could *pray*," said the girl called Mame, with a shrug. "She does, you know, often in meeting."

Then with a giggle toward Leslie she added as if in explanation, "She works *out*, you know."

"It must be very hard for her," said Leslie, purposely ignoring the inference.

"Well, you know she isn't in our set. Nobody has much to do with her."

"Why not? I think she is very unusual," said Leslie with just the least bit of hauteur.

"Well, it wouldn't be wise to get her into things. It might keep some others out if we made her prominent," put in Lila Cary with some asperity. "We must have some social distinction, you know."

"In our frat one fellow is as good as another if he has the right kind of character," remarked Allison dryly. "That girl sounded to me as if she had some drag with your alumni. But of course you know her better than I."

"She is a good girl all right and real religious," hastened Lila to amend. "I suppose she'd be real good on a prayer committee, and would help to fill up there, as you haven't many."

"Well, I'll tell you one thing," said Allison, "if you really want to succeed, you've got to pull together, every member of you, or you won't get anywhere. And I should think that you'd have to be careful now at first whom you get in. Of course after you're pretty strong you can take in a few just to help them; but, if you get in too many of that lame kind, your society'll go bad. The weak kind will rule, and the mischief will be to pay. I shouldn't think it would help you any just now to get in any folks that would feel that way about a good girl just because she earns her living."

Mame Beecher and Lila Cary looked at each other in alarm, and hastened to affirm that they never felt that way about Jane Bristol. *They* thought she was a real good sort, and had always meant to get acquainted with her; only she always slipped out as soon as meeting was over.

Back in the dining-room behind the rose-lined blue-velvet hangings Julia Cloud lingered and smiled over the way her two children were developing opinions and character. How splendid of them to take this stand! And who was Jane Bristol? Assuredly she must be looked up and helped if that was the way the town felt about her, poor child!

"Well," said Bryan in a business-like tone, "I'm secretary. Joe, you call that prayer committee together Thursday night at your house at half-past seven, and I'll send a notice to each one. You make Jane Bristol chairman, and I'll be on the committee; and I'll go after her and take her home. Now, who else are you going to have on it?"

The president assented readily. He was one not used to taking the initiative, but he eagerly did as he was told when a good idea presented itself.

"We want you on it," he said, nodding to Allison and then, looking shyly at Leslie, added, "And you?"

"Oh!" said Leslie, flushing in fright, "what would we have to do? I never prayed before anybody in my life. I'm not sure I even know how to pray, only just to say 'Thank you' to God sometimes. I think you could find somebody better."

"We've got to have you this time," said the president, shaking his head. "You needn't pray if you don't want to, but you must come and help us through."

"But I couldn't go and be a—a sort of slacker!" said Leslie, her cheeks quite beautifully red.

"That's all right! You come!" said Bryan, looking solemnly at her.

When the visitors finally took themselves away, Allison, polite to the last, closed the door with a courteous "Good-night," and then stood frowning at the fire.

Julia Cloud came softly into the room, and went and stood beside him with loving question in her eyes. He met her gaze with a new kind of hardness.

"Now, you see what you let me in for, Cloudy, when you made me go to that little old dull Christian Endeavor! But I won't do it! That's all there is to it. You needn't think I'm going to. The idea! Why, what did we come here to college for? To run an asylum for sick Sunday schools, I'd like to know? As if I had time to monkey with their little old society! It's rank nonsense, anyhow! What good do they think they can do, a couple of sissies, and two or three kid vamps, setting up to lisp religion? It's ridiculous!"

He was working himself up into a fine frenzy. Julia Cloud stood and watched him, an amused smile growing on her sweet lips. He caught the amusement, and fired up at it.

"What are you looking like that at me for, Cloudy? You know it is. You know it's all foolishness. And you know I couldn't help them, anyhow. Come, now, don't you? *What* are you looking like that for, Cloudy? I believe you're laughing at me! You think I'll go and get into this thing, but I'll show you. I *won't*! And that's an end of it. Cloudy, I insist on knowing what you find to laugh at in this situation."

"Why, I was just thinking how much you reminded me of Moses," said Julia Cloud sweetly.

"Of *Moses*!" screamed Allison half angrily. "Why, he was a meek man, and I'm not meek. I'm mad! Out and out *mad*, Cloudy. What do you mean?"

"Oh, no, he wasn't always meek," said his aunt thoughtfully; "and he talked just as you are doing when God called on him first to lead the children of Israel out of Egypt. He said he couldn't and he wouldn't and he shouldn't, and made every excuse in the calendar; and finally God had to send along Aaron to help him, although God had said *He* would be with him and make him perfectly able alone to do what He wanted done."

"I suppose I'm Aaron," sighed Leslie, settling into a big chair by the fire. "But I don't like those girls one bit! And I don't care if they stay in seven Egypts."

"Now, look here, Cloudy Jewel," pleaded Allison. "You're not going to get me into any such corner as that. The idea that God would call me to do any of His work when I never had anything at all to do with the church in my life, and I don't want to. How should I know what to do? Why should He ever call me, I'd like to know, when I don't know the first thing about churches? You're all off, Cloudy. Think again. Why, I'm not even what you'd call a Christian. He surely wouldn't call people that haven't—well, what you'd call enlisted with Him, would He?"

"He might," answered Julia Cloud reflectively. She was sitting on the end of the big blue couch, and the firelight played over her white hair with silvery lights, and cast a lovely rose tint over her sweet face. "There were several instances where He called people who had never known Him at all, who, in fact, were worshipping idols and strange gods, and told them to go and do something for Him. There was Paul; he was actually against Him. And there was Abraham; he lived among regular idol-worshippers, and God called him to go into a strange land and founded a new family for him, the beginning of the peculiar people through whose line was to come Jesus, the Saviour of the world. And Abraham went."

"Oh, nonsense, Cloudy! That was in those times. Of course. There wasn't anybody else, I suppose; and He had to take some one. But now there are plenty of people who go to church all the time and like that sort of thing."

"How do you know, Allison? Perhaps you are the only one in this town, and God has sent you here just to do this special work."

"Well, I won't, and that's flat, Cloudy; so you can put the idea right out of your head. I won't, not even for you. Anything that has to do with your personal comfort I wouldn't say that about, of course; but this belongs entirely to that little old ratty church, and I haven't anything at all to do with it; and I want you to forget it, Cloudy, for *I'm not going to do it*!"

"Why, Allison, you're mistaken about me. It isn't my affair, and I don't intend to make it so. I didn't get this up. It's between you and God. If God really called you, you'll have to say no to Him, not to me. I don't intend to make excuses to God for you, child. You needn't think it. And, besides, there's another thing you're very much mistaken about, and that is that you haven't anything to do with the church. When you were a little baby six months old, your father and mother brought you home to our house; and the first Sunday they were there they took you to the old church where all the children and grandchildren had been christened for years, and they stood up and assented to the vows that gave you to God. And they promised for themselves that they would do their best to bring you up in the nurture and admonition of the Lord until you came to years and could finish the bond by giving yourself to the Lord. I shall never forget the sweet, serious look on the face of your lovely girl-mother when she bowed her head in answer to the minister's question, 'Do you thus promise?'"

Allison had stopped in his angry walk up and down the room, and was looking at her interestedly.

"Is that right, Cloudy? Was I baptized in the old Sterling church? I never knew that. Tell me about it," and he seated himself on the other end of the couch, while Leslie switched off the light and nestled down between them, scenting a story.

"Wasn't I, too, Cloudy?" she asked hungrily.

"No, dear, I think you were baptized in California in your mother's church, and I'm sorry to say I wasn't there to see; so I can't tell you about it; but I remember very distinctly all about Allison's christening, for we were all so happy to have it happen in the East, and he was the first grandchild, and we hadn't seen your father for over two years, nor ever seen his young wife before; so it was a great event. It was a beautiful bright October day, and I had the pleasure of making the dress you wore, Allison, every stitch by hand, hemstitching and embroidery and all. And right in the midst of the ceremony you looked over your father's shoulder, and saw me sitting in the front seat, and smiled the sweetest smile! Then you jumped up and down in your father's arms, and spatted your little pink hands together, and called out 'Ah-*Jah*!' That's what you used to call me then, and everybody all over the church smiled. How could they help it?"

"Gee! I must 'a' been some kid!" said Allison, slipping down into a comfortable position among the pillows. "Say, Cloudy, I knew a good thing when I saw it even then, didn't I?"

"You know, Allison, that ceremony wasn't just all on your father's and mother's part; it entailed some responsibility upon you. It was part of your heritage, and you've no right to waste it any more than if it were gold or bank stock or houses and lands. It was your title to a heavenly sonship, and it gave God the right to call upon you to do whatever He wants you to do. It's between you and God now, and you'll have to settle it yourself. It's not anything I could settle for you either way, much as I might want it, because it is you who must answer God, and you must answer Him from the heart either way; so nobody else has anything to do with it."

"Oh, good-*night*! Cloudy, you certainly can put things in an awkward way. Oh, hang it! Now this whole evening's spoiled. I wish I hadn't gone to the front door at all. I wish I'd turned out the lights and let 'em knock. And there was that story you were going to read, and now it's too late!"

"Why, no; it's not too late at all," said Julia Cloud, consulting her little watch in the firelight. "It's only quarter to nine, and I'm sure we can indulge ourselves a little to-night, and finish the story before we go to bed. Turn the light on, and get the magazine."

With an air of finality Julia Cloud put aside the debated question, and settled herself in the big willow chair by the lamp with her book. Leslie went back to her chair by the fire, and Allison flung himself down on the couch with a pillow half over his eyes; but anybody watching closely would have seen that his eyes were wide open and he was studying the calm, quiet profile of his aunt's sweet face as she read in a gentle, even tone, paragraph after paragraph without a flicker of disturbance on her brow. Allison was not more than half listening to the story. He was thinking hard. Those things Julia Cloud had said about obligations and Moses and Abraham and Paul stuck hard in his mind, and he couldn't get away from them.

CHAPTER XVI

Julia Cloud said nothing more to her boy about that Christian Endeavor Society, but she said much to her Lord, praying continually that he might be led to see his duty and want to do it, and that through it he might be led to know Christ.

In the meantime she went sunnily about setting the new home to rights and getting the right maid to fit into their household régime. Julia Cloud had never had a maid in her life, but she had always had ideas about one, and she put as much thought and almost as much care into preparing the little chamber the maid was to occupy as she had put upon the other rooms. To begin with, the room itself was admirably adapted to making the right maid feel at home and comfortable. It had three windows looking into gardens on the next block, and a blaze of salvia and cosmos and geraniums would greet her eyes the first time she looked out from her new room. Then it had a speck of a bathroom all its own, which Julia Cloud felt would go a long way toward making any maid the right maid, for there would be no excuse for her not being clean and no excuse for her keeping her tooth-brush down on the edge of the kitchen sink or taking a bath in the laundry tubs, as she had heard that some of her neighbors' maids had done at various times.

The windows were shrouded with white curtains of the same kind as those all over the house, and within were draperies with bright flower borders. The bureau was daintily fitted out, and the bed was spotless and inviting-looking. A cushioned rocking-chair stood beside a small table, with a dainty work-basket on the shelf below; and against the wall were some shelves with a few interesting books and magazines. A droplight with a pretty shade gave a home-like air, and the room was as attractive as any other in the house. Any maid might think her lines had fallen in pleasant places who was fortunate enough to occupy that room. As a last touch Julia Cloud laid a neat coarse-print Testament on the table, and then knelt beside the rocking-chair and asked God to make the unknown comer a blessing to their house, and help them all to be a blessing to her. Then she went down to the car, and let Allison take her out to the addresses that had been given her. As a result, by Wednesday the little gay chamber half-way up the stairs was occupied by a pleasant-faced, sturdy colored girl about eighteen years old, who rejoiced in the name of Cherry, and was at once adopted as part of the new household with the same spirit with which everything else had been done. Perhaps if every household would go about it in the same way it would go far toward settling the much-mooted servant question.

When Cherry was introduced into her bedchamber the look on her face was worth seeing. It was in the early evening when she arrived, riding on the front seat of the wagon that brought her trunk; and, when she was ushered in by Julia Cloud, with Leslie in the offing to see what the newcomer would say to it, the girl stepped in, gave a wild glance around, then backed off, and rolled her eyes at her new mistress.

"This ain't—you-all ain't puttin' me inta dis year fine bedroom!" she exclaimed in a kind of horror.

"Yes, this is your room," said Julia Cloud kindly, stepping in and moving a chair a little farther from the bed, that there might be room for the girl's trunk. "You can put your trunk right here, I should think; and here is your closet," swinging open the closet door and showing a plenitude of hooks and hangers, "and that is your bathroom." She pushed back the crash curtain that shut off the tiny bathroom, and stood back smiling. But the girl was not looking at her. She had cast one wild look around, and then her eyes had been riveted on the little vase on her bureau, containing a single late rose that Leslie had found blooming in the small garden at the rear, and put there for good luck, she said. Could it be that any one had cared to pick a flower for a servant's room? Her eyes filled with tears; she dropped her bundles on the floor, and came over to where her new mistress stood.

"Oh!" she said in a choked voice. "If you-all is goin' to treat me like comp'ny, I'se jest goin' to wuk my fingahs to de bone for youse!"

After the advent of Cherry things began to settle down into something like routine. The inn was abandoned entirely, and each meal was a festive occasion. Cherry took kindly to the cooking-lessons that Julia Cloud knew well how to give. Light, wonderful white bread came forth from the white-enamel gas-range oven, sweet, rich, nutty loaves of brown bread, even more delectable. Waffles and muffins and pancakes vied with one another to make one meal better than another; apple dumpling, cherry pie, and blackberry roly-poly varied with chocolate steamed pudding, lemon custard, and velvet whip made the desserts an eagerly awaited surprise.

Leslie hovered over everything new that was made, and wanted to have a hand in it. Each day she learned some new and wholesome fact about housekeeping, and seemed to take to the knowledge readily. Her first attempt at real cooking was learning to make bread; and, when she succeeded so well that Allison thought it was his aunt's baking, she declared her intention of making it once a week just to keep her hand in.

Allison had said no more about Christian Endeavor; and, when Thursday afternoon came, he asked his aunt to ride to the city after a few little articles that were still needed to make the house complete. They had a pleasant trip, and Julia Cloud entirely forgot that the young people had been asked to attend the committee meeting that evening. Perhaps Allison was waiting for her to speak about it; for he looked at his watch uneasily several times, and glanced back at his aunt suspiciously; but she sat serenely enjoying the ride, and said nothing. At last, just as they were nearing home he burst forth with, "Cloudy, do you really think we ought to go to that bl-looming thing to-night?"

Julia Cloud lifted quiet eyes and smiled.

"I didn't say you ought to go; did I, dear?"

"Well, yes, you sorta did, Cloudy."

Julia Cloud shook her head.

"I don't think I did. I said it wasn't a matter for me to meddle with."

"Well, don't you?"

"No, Allison, not unless you feel that God has called you and you are willing to do what He wants you to. If you just went because you thought I wanted you to go, I don't believe it would be worth while, because you wouldn't be working with the right spirit. But, as I said before, that is something you have got to account for to God, not to me."

Allison drew his brows in a frown, and said no more; but he was almost silent at supper, and ate with an abstracted air. At quarter to eight he flung down the magazine he had been reading, and got up.

"Well, I s'pose I've got to go to that bloomin' thing," he said half angrily. "Come on, kid; you going?"

Leslie hurried into her hat and cape, and they went off together, Allison grumbling in a low, half-pleasant voice all the time. Julia Cloud sat apparently reading, watching the little byplay, and praying that God would strengthen the young heart.

"Dear Moses!" she murmured with a smile on her lips as the front door banged behind the children and she was left reading alone.

Two hours later the two returned full of enthusiasm. Leslie was brimming over.

"O Cloudy, we're going to give this sleepy old town the surprise of a lifetime! We're going to have a grand time to-morrow night, just getting all the members together and doping it out what to do. And you ought to hear Allison talk! He's just like a man! He made a wonderful speech telling them how they ought to get together, and everybody do teamwork and all that, like they do in football; and they asked him to make it over again to-morrow night, and he's going to!"

Leslie's eyes were shining with pride, and she looked at her brother lovingly. He flushed embarrassedly.

"Well, what could you do, Cloudy? There they were sitting like a lot of boobs, and nobody knowing what to do except that Jane Bristol. She's the only sensible one of the bunch, and they don't listen to her. They made me mad, ignoring her suggestions the way they did; so I had to speak up and say she was right; and I guess I talked a lot more when I got started, because she really had the right dope, all right, and they ought to have had sense enough to know it. She's been in this work before, and been to big State conventions and things. Say, Cloudy, that Christian Endeavor stuff must be a pretty big thing. It seems to have members all over the world, and it's really a kind of international fraternity. I rather like their line. It's stiff all right, but that's the only way if you're going into a thing like that."

"And how did the praying go?" asked Julia Cloud, watching her boy's handsome, eager face as he talked.

"All right," he evaded reticently.

"*He* prayed, Cloudy!" announced Leslie proudly. "It was *regular*!"

"Well, what could a fellow do?" said Allison apologetically, as if he had done something he was half ashamed of. "That poor girl prayed something wonderful, and then they all sat and sat like a parcel of boobs until you could feel her cheeks getting red, and nobody opening their mouths; so I started in. I didn't know what to say, but I thought somebody ought to say something. I did the best I knew how."

"It was regular, Cloudy!" repeated Leslie with shining eyes.

"Well, it got 'em started, anyhow," said Allison. "That was all that mattered."

Julia Cloud with lips trembling joyously into a smile of thanksgiving listened, and felt her heart glad. Somehow she knew that her boy had yielded himself to the call of his God to lead this band of young people out of an Egypt into a promised land, and she saw as by faith how he himself would be led to talk with God on the mount before the great work was completed.

"It really was regular, Cloudy," reiterated Leslie. "I didn't know my brother could pray like that, or talk, either. After he prayed everybody prayed, just a sentence or two, even that little baby doll Lila that was here the other night. They didn't say much, but you could see they wanted to do the right thing and be right in it. But everybody was in earnest; they really were, Cloudy. That Jane Bristol is wonderful! The president had told her she was chairman, and all about the meeting; and she read some verses out of the Bible about Christ's being always in a meeting where there were just two or three, and about two or three agreeing to ask for something and always getting it. I never knew there were such verses in the Bible, did you? Well, and after that it seemed awfully solemn, just as if we had all come into God's reception-room and were waiting to ask Him as a big favor to help this little Christian Endeavor Society to be worth something in His kingdom. Those aren't my words, Cloudy; you needn't look surprised. That's the way Jane Bristol put it, and it made me feel queer all down my back when she said it, as it did the first time I went to hear some great music. And—why, after that you couldn't help praying just a little, so the promise would hold good. It wasn't square not to help them out, you see."

"And we're not going to have anybody to-morrow night but the regular members until we get them all to understand and be ready to help," went on Allison.

"Yes, they asked Allison to take charge and help plan it all out; and Allison is going to hunt up some of the big Christian Endeavor people in the city, and get them to come out one or two at a time to our meetings,"—Julia Cloud noted the pronoun "our" with satisfaction,—"and stir things up on Sundays; and we'll drive in and get them, and bring them to our house to supper, maybe, and put them wise to things so they'll know best how to help; and then we'll drive them home after church that night, see? And Allison suggested that we have pretty soon a series of parties or receptions, just for the young people to get together and bring new ones in one at a time, just as the boys in college have rushing-parties, you know. We'll have a reception, real formal, with regular eats from a caterer, and flowers and invitations and everything, for the first one; and a Hallowe'en party for the October meeting, and a banquet for the November meeting, just about Thanksgiving time, you know. Oh, it's going to be lots of fun. And, Cloudy, I told them we'd make a hundred sandwiches for to-morrow night; you don't mind, do you? We can buy the bread, and it won't take long to make them. I know how to cut them in pretty shapes, and I thought I'd tie them with ribbons to match the lemonade."

Julia Cloud with radiant face entered into the plans eagerly, and to have heard them talk one would never have imagined that twenty-four hours before these two young people had been exceedingly averse to having anything to do with that little dying Christian Endeavor Young People's Society.

"And, Cloudy, that Jane Bristol is real pretty. She had on a charming collar to-night, and her hair fixed all soft around her face. She has beautiful hair! I think they were all surprised at the easy way she talked; I don't believe she is a day older than I am, either. And she is going to college. I'm awfully glad, for I want to get to know her. We'll invite her down here sometimes, won't we? I want you to know her, Cloudy. You'll like her, I'm sure."

So Julia Cloud went to her pretty gray bed that night, and lay marvelling at the goodness of God to answer her prayers. As for the children, they could hardly settle down to sleep, so full of plans were they for the revivifying of that Christian Endeavor Society. They kept calling back and forth from room to room, and after everything had been quiet for a long time and Julia Cloud was just dropping off to sleep, Leslie woke them all up calling to know if it wouldn't be a good plan to have the Hallowe'en party there at the house and have everybody come in costume. Then they had to begin all over again, and decide what they would wear and who they would be. Allison declared he was going to be a firecracker; he had a "dandy" costume for it in California, and he would write to-morrow morning to the housekeeper to look it up.

Leslie wanted to have a candy-pull, with apples and nuts and raisins for refreshments. Julia Cloud began to wonder whether it was just as acceptable to God to have play mixed up with the religion as these children were doing it.

"You must look out that your festivities don't get ahead of your righteousness," she warned half laughingly; but Allison took her in earnest.

"You're right there, Cloudy. That's one of the things we have to look out for in frats. We have to see we don't have too many social things. If we do, the marks suffer; and right away we lose ground. We'll have to keep those Sunday meetings up to the mark—see, kid?—or the other things will only bring in a lot of dead-wood that won't count. They must come to the Sunday meetings, or they don't get invited to the parties. That's the way we'll fix 'em."

"There's no use saying 'must,'" said Leslie wisely. "If you don't have your meetings interesting, they won't come anyhow you fix it."

"That's a girl for you!" scorned Allison. "No loyalty in the whole bunch. They've got to like everything. Now, the real spirit is to come and make the meetings good, just because they're your meetings. See, kid?"

368

"Yes, I see," snapped Leslie; "but I won't come to your old meetings at all if you are going to talk that way about girls. I guess I've always been loyal to everything, especially you, and I won't stand for that!"

"Oh, I didn't mean you, kid; I was talking about girls in general," soothed the brother. "You're all right, of course. But those little fluffy-ruffles that sat in the back seat, now, you'll have to teach them what loyalty means. See?"

Finally the household settled to sleep.

The next day the little house saw little else done save the making of marvellous dainty sandwiches in various forms and shapes.

Even Cherry entered into the work with zest, and Julia Cloud proved herself rich in suggestion for different fillings, till great platters of the finished product reposed in the big white refrigerator, neatly tucked about with damp napkins to keep them from drying.

All that day Allison flew hither and yon in his car, carrying some member of the committee on errands connected with the evening social. Never had such a stir been made about a mere church social in all the annals of the society. Every remotest member was hunted out and persuaded to be present, and Allison agreed to go around in the evening and pick up at least a dozen who had professed their inability to get there alone. So the big blue car was enlisted in Christian Endeavor service, and the young people were as busy and as happy as ever they had been in getting their little new home settled. They drove away about seven o'clock after a hasty supper, with their platters of sandwiches safely guarded on the back seat; and Julia Cloud watched them, and smiled and was glad. She wondered whether this work would get such a hold upon them that it would last after they started their college work, and fervently hoped that it might, so that there would be another link to bind them to God's house and His work. She sighed to think how many things there would likely be to draw them away.

About ten o'clock Leslie telephoned. She wanted to bring Jane Bristol home for the night, as the people where Jane was living were away, and she would otherwise have to stay alone in a big house. Julia Cloud readily assented, and she and Cherry had a pleasant half-hour putting one of the guest-rooms in order. It was while she was doing this that she began to wonder seriously what Jane Bristol would be like. Who was brought intimately into their new home might mean so much to her two children. And in this room, too, after Cherry had gone to bed, she knelt and breathed a consecrating prayer. Then she went down-stairs to wait for the coming of her children, building up the fire and lighting the porch light so that all would be cheery and attractive for them and their guest. Only a little, lonesome child who did housework for her living, but it was good to be able to give her a pleasant welcome.

In a few minutes the car arrived, and the two girls came chattering in, while Allison put the car away. At least, Leslie was chattering.

"I think you look so lovely in that soft blue dress!" she was saying. "It is so graceful, and the color just fits your eyes."

"It's only some old accordion-pleated chiffon I had," answered the guest half ashamed. "I had to wash it and dye it and make it myself, and I wasn't sure the pleats would iron out, or that it would do at all. You know I don't have much use for evening dresses, and I really couldn't afford to get one. That's the reason I hesitated at your suggestion about having receptions and parties. But I guess you have to have them."

"You don't mean to say you made it all yourself! Why you're a wonder! Isn't she, Cloudy? Just take her in and look for yourself! She made that dress all herself out of old things that she washed and dyed. Why, it looks like an imported frock. Doesn't it look like one, Cloudy? And that girdle is darling, all shirred that way!"

That was Julia Cloud's introduction to the guest as she stood in the open door and watched the two trip along the brick terrace to the entrance.

Leslie snatched away the long, dark cloak that covered Jane Bristol's dress; and she stood forth embarrassed in the firelight, clad in soft, pale-blue chiffon in simple straight lines blending into the white throat in a little round neck, and draping the white girlish, arms. The firelight and lamplight glimmered and flickered over the softly waved brown hair, the sweet, serious brow, the delicate, refined face; and Jane Bristol lifted two earnest deep-blue eyes, and looked at Julia Cloud. Then between them flashed a look of understanding and sympathy, and each knew at once that she liked the other.

"Isn't she a dear, Cloudy Jewel?" demanded Leslie.

"She is!" responded Julia Cloud, and put her arms softly around the slender blue-clad shoulders. Then she looked up to see the eyes of Allison resting upon them with satisfaction.

They turned down the light and sat before the fire for a little while, telling about the success of the evening and talking of this and that, just getting acquainted; and, when they finally took Jane Bristol up to the pretty guest-room, it was with a sense that a new and lasting friendship had been well begun. Julia Cloud as she lay down to sleep found herself wondering whether her children would always show so much good sense in picking out their friends as they had done this time.

CHAPTER XVII

The day when college opened was a great day. The children could hardly eat any breakfast, and Allison gave Leslie a great many edifying instructions about registering.

"Now, kid, if you get stuck for anything, just you hunt me up. I'll see that you get straightened out. If you and Jane Bristol could only get together, you could help each other a lot. I'll get some dope from some of the last-year fellows. That's the advantage I get from finding a chapter of my frat here. They'll put me wise as to the best course-advisers, and you stick around near the entrance till I give you the right dope. It doesn't pay to get started wrong in college."

Leslie meekly accepted all these admonitions, and they started off together in the car with an abstracted wave of good-by to Julia Cloud, who somehow felt suddenly left out of the universe. To have her two newly-acquired children suddenly withdrawn by the power of a great educational institution and swept beyond her horizon was disconcerting. She had not imagined she would feel this way. She stood in the window watching them, and wiped away a furtive tear, and then laughed to herself.

"Old fool!" she said softly to the window-pane. "The trouble with you is, you'd like to be going to college yourself, and you know it! Now put this out of your mind, and go to work planning how to make home doubly attractive when they get back, so that they will want to spend every minute possible here instead of being drawn away from it. They love it. Now keep them loving it. That's your job."

When the two came back at noon, they were radiant and enthusiastic as usual, albeit they had many a growl to express. One would have thought to hear Allison that he had been running colleges for some fifty years the way he criticized the policy and told how things ought to be run. At first Julia Cloud was greatly distressed by it all, thinking that they surely had made a mistake in their selection of a college, but it gradually dawned upon her that this was a sort of superior attitude maintained by upper-class men toward all institutions of learning, particularly those in which they happened to be studying, that it was really only an indication of growing developing minds keen to see mistakes and trying to think out remedies, and as yet inexperienced enough to think they could remedy the whole sick world.

The opening days of college were turbulent days for Julia Cloud. Her children were so excited they could neither eat nor sleep. They were liable to turn up unexpectedly at almost any hour of the morning or afternoon, hungry as bears, and always in a hurry. They had so many new things to tell her about, and no time in which to talk. They mixed things terribly, and gave her impressions that took months to right; and they could not understand why she looked distressed at their flightiness. They were both taken up eagerly by the students and invited hither and yon by the various groups and societies, which frequently caused them to be absent from meals while they were being dined and lunched and breakfasted. Of course, Julia Cloud reflected, two such good-looking, well-dressed, easy-mannered young people, with a home in the town where they could invite people, a car in which to take friends out, and a free hand with money, would be popular anywhere. Her anxiety grew as the first week waxed toward its end and finished up Saturday night with invitations to two dances and one week-end party at a country house ten miles away.

Leslie rushed in breathless about six o'clock Saturday evening, and declared she was too much in a hurry to eat anything; she must get dressed at once, and put some things in her bag. She rattled on about the different social functions she was expected to attend that evening until Julia Cloud was in hopeless confusion, and could only stand and listen, and try to find the things that Leslie in her hurry had overlooked. Then Allison arrived, and wanted some supper. He talked with his mouth full about where he was going and what he was going to do, and at the end of an hour and a half Julia Cloud had a very indefinite idea of anything. She had a swift mental vision of church and Sabbath and Christian Endeavor all slipping slowly out of their calculation, and the WORLD in large letters taking the forefront of their vision.

"You are going to a dance!" she said in a white, stricken way she had when an anxiety first bewildered her. "To *two* dances! O my dear Leslie! You—*dance*, then? I—hadn't thought of that!"

"Sure I dance!" said Leslie gayly, drawing up the delicate silk stocking over her slim ankles and slipping on a silver slipper. "You ought to see me. And Allison can dance, too. We'll show you sometime. Don't you like dancing, Cloudy? Why, Cloudy! You couldn't mean you don't approve of dancing? Not *really*! But where would we be? *Everybody* dances! Why, there wouldn't be anything else to do when young people went out. Oh, do you suppose Cherry would press out this skirt a little bit? It's got horribly mussed in that drawer."

Julia Cloud had dropped into a chair with an all-gone feeling and a lightness in the top of her head. She felt as if the world, the flesh, and the devil had suddenly dropped down upon the house and were carrying off her children bodily, and she was powerless to prevent it. She could not keep the pain of it out of her eyes; yet she did not know what to say in this emergency. None of the things that had always seemed entirely convincing in forming her own opinions seemed adequate to the occasion. Leslie turned suddenly, and saw her stricken face.

"What's the matter, Cloudy? Is something wrong? Aren't you well? Don't you like me to go to a dance? Why, Cloudy! Do you really *object*?"

"I have no right to object, I suppose, dear," she said, trying to speak calmly; "but—Leslie, I can't bear to think of you dancing; it's not nice. It's too—too intimate! My little flower of a girl!"

"Oh, but we have to dance, Cloudy; that's ridiculous! And you aren't used to dances, or you wouldn't say so. Can't you trust me to be perfectly nice?"

Julia Cloud shuddered, and went to the head of the stairs to answer a question Allison was calling up to her; and, when, she came back, she said no more about it. The pain was too great, and she felt too bewildered for argument. Leslie was enveloped in rose-colored tulle, with touches of silver, and looked like a young goddess with straps of silver over her slim shoulders and a thread of pearls about her throat. The white neck and back that the wisp of rose-color made no attempt to conceal were very beautiful and quite childish, but they shocked the sweet soul of Julia Cloud inexpressibly. She stood aghast when Leslie whirled upon her and demanded to know how she liked the gown.

"O my dear!" gasped her aunt. "You're not going out before people—*men*—all undressed like that!"

Leslie gave her one glance of hurt dismay, whirled back to her glass, and examined herself critically.

"Why, Cloudy!" Her voice was almost trembling, and her cheeks were rosier than the tulle with disappointment. "Why, Cloudy, I thought it was lovely! It's just like everybody's else. I thought you would think I looked *nice*!" The child drooped, and Julia Cloud went up to her gently.

"It is beautiful, darling, and you are—exquisite! But, dear! It seems terrible for my little girl to go among young men so sort of nakedly. I'm sure if you understood life better, you wouldn't do it. You are tempting men to wrong thoughts, undressed that way, and you are putting on common view the intimate loveliness of the body God gave you to keep holy and pure. It is the way cheap women have of making many men love them in a careless, physical way. I don't know how to tell you, but it seems terrible to me. If you were my own little girl, I never, *never* would be willing to have you go out that way."

"You've said enough!" almost screamed Leslie with a sudden frenzy of rage, shame, and disappointment. "I feel as if I never could look anybody in the face again!" And with a cry she flung herself into the jumble of bright garments on her bed, and wept as if her heart would break. Julia Cloud stood over her in consternation, and tried to soothe her; but nothing did any good. The young storm had to have its way, and the slim pink shoulders shook in convulsive sobs, while the dismayed elder sat down beside the bed, with troubled eyes upon her, and waited, praying quietly.

In the midst of it all Allison appeared at the door.

"What in thunder is the matter? I've yelled my head off, and nobody answers. What is the matter with you, kid? It's time we started, and you doing the baby act! I never thought you'd get hystericky."

Leslie lifted a wet and smeary face out of her pillow and addressed her brother defiantly:

"I've good reason to cry!" she said. "Cloudy thinks I'm not decent to go out in this dress, and she won't believe everybody dresses this way; and I'm *not going*! I'm *never* going *anywhere* again; I'm *disgraced*!" And down went her head in the pillow again with another long, convulsive sob.

Her brother strode over to her, and lifted her up firmly but gently.

"There, kid, quit your crying and be sensible. Stand up and let's look at you."

He stood her upon her feet; and she swayed there, quivering, half ashamed, her hands to her tear-stained face, her pink shoulders heaving and her soft, pink chest quivering with sobs, while he surveyed her.

"Well, kid, I must say I agree with Cloudy," he said half reluctantly at last. "The dress is a peach, of course, and you look like an angel in it; but, if you could hear the rotten things the fellows say about the way the girls dress, you wouldn't want to go that way; and I don't want them to talk that way about my sister. Couldn't you stick in a towel or an apron or something, and make a little more waist to the thing? I'm sure you'd look just as pretty, and the fellows would think you a whole lot nicer girl. I don't want you to get the nickname of the Freshman Vamp. I couldn't stand for that."

Poor Leslie sank into a chair, and covered her face for another cry, declaring it was no use, it would utterly spoil the dress to do anything to it, and she couldn't go, and wouldn't go and wear it; but at last Julia Cloud came to the rescue with needle and thread and soft rose drapery made from a scarf of Leslie's that exactly matched the dress; and presently she stood meek and sweet, and quite modest, blooming prettily out of her pink, misty garments like an opening apple-blossom in spite of her recent tears.

"But when are you coming back?" asked Julia Cloud in sudden dismay, her troubles returning in full force as she watched them going out the door to the car, Allison carrying two bags and telling Leslie to hurry for all she was worth.

The two children turned then, and faced their aunt, with a swift, comprehending vision of what this expedition of theirs meant to her. It had not occurred to them before that they were deliberately planning to spend most of the night, Saturday night, in mirth, and stay over Sunday at a house-party where the Sabbath would be as a thing unknown. Nobody had ever talked to them about these things before. They had accepted it as a part of the world of society into which they had been born, and they had never questioned it. They were impatient now that their tried and true friend and comrade did not comprehend that this occasion was different from most, and that it must be an exception. They were willing to keep the Sabbath in general, but in this particular they felt they must not be hampered. The whole idea shone plainly in their faces, and the pain and disappointment and chagrin shone clearly, emphatically in Julia Cloud's eyes as she faced them and read the truth.

"Why, we don't know, just for sure, Cloudy," Allison tried to temporize. "You see, they usually dance to all hours. It's Saturday night, and no classes to-morrow, and this is an unusual occasion. It's a week-end party, you know——"

"Then—you won't be back to-night! You are not going to church to-morrow! You will spend the Sabbath at a party!"

She said these things as if she were telling them to herself so that she could better take in the facts and not cry out with the disappointment of it. There was no quality of fault-finding in her tone, but the pain of her voice cut to the heart the two young culprits. Therefore, according to the code of loving human nature, they got angry.

"Why, of course!" chirped Leslie. "Didn't you expect that? That's what week-end parties are!"

"Oh, cut this out, Leslie," cried Allison. "We've gotta beat it. We're way late now! Cloudy, you can expect us when we get here. Don't bother about anything. There's no need to. We'll telephone you later when we expect to come back. Nightie, nightie, Cloudy. You go rest yourself. You look tired."

He gave her a hurried, deprecatory kiss, and swept his sister out into the night. Julia Cloud heard the purring of the engine, saw the lights of the car glide away from the door down the street and out of sight. They were gone! She felt as though a piece of herself had been torn away from her and flung out for the world to trample upon. For a long time she stood staring from the window into the darkness, unshed tears burning behind her eyes and throat, trying to steady the beating of her heart and get used to the gnawing trouble that somehow made her feel faint and weak.

It came over her that she had been a fool to attempt to fill the place of mother to these two modern young things. Their own ideas were fully made up about all questions that seemed vital to her. She had been a fossil in a back-country place all her life, and of course they felt she did not know. Well, of course she did not know much about modern society and its ways, save to dread it, and to doubt it, and to wish to keep them away from it. She was prejudiced, perhaps. Yes, she had been reared that way, and the world would call her narrow. Would Christ the Lord feel that way about it? Did He like to have His children dressing like abandoned women and making free with one another under the guise of polite social customs? Did He want His children to spend their Sabbaths in play, however innocent the play might be? She turned with a sigh away from the window. No, she could not see it any other way. It was the way of the world, and that was all there was to it. Leslie had made it plain when she said they had to do it or be left out. And wasn't that just what it meant to be a "peculiar people" unto the Lord, to be willing to give up doubtful things that harmed people for the sake of keeping pure and unspotted from the world? "If ye were of the world, the world would love its own; but because I have chosen you out of the world, therefore the world hateth you," came the familiar old words. Well, and what should she do now? It wouldn't do to rave and fuss about things. That never did any good. She couldn't say she wouldn't stay if they danced and went away over the Sabbath. Those were things in which she might advise, but had no authority. They were old enough to decide such matters for themselves. She could only use her influence, and trust the rest with the Lord. Yes, there was one thing she could do. She could pray!

So Julia Cloud gave her quiet orders to Cherry, and went up to her rose-and-gray room to kneel by the bed and pray, agonizing for her beloved children through the long hours of that long, long evening.

It was a quiet face that she lifted at last from her vigil, for it bore the brightness of a face-to-face communion with her Lord; and she rose and went about her preparations for the night. Then, just as she had taken down her hair and was brushing it in a silver cloud about her shoulders, she heard a car drive up. A moment more a key turned in the latch, and some one came in.

Julia Cloud stood with the hair-brush poised half-way down a strand of hair, and listened. Yes, the car had gone on to the garage. What could have happened?

CHAPTER XVIII

It was all still below stairs, then a soft, stealthy silken movement, cautiously coming up the stairs. Julia Cloud went quickly to the hall door, and switched on the light. On the landing stood Leslie, lovely and flushed, with her hair slightly ruffled and her velvet evening cloak thrown back, showing the rosy mist of her dress. She stood with one silver slipper poised on the stairs, a sweet, guilty look on her face.

"O Cloudy! I thought you were asleep, and I didn't want to waken you," she said, penitently; "but you haven't gone to bed yet, have you? I'm glad. We wanted you to know we were home."

"Is anything the matter?" Julia Cloud asked with a stricture of emotion in her throat.

"No; only we got tired, and we didn't want to stay to their old party, anyway, and we'd rather be home." Leslie sprang up the stairs, and caught her aunt in her arms with one of her sweet, violent kisses.

"O my dear!" was all Julia Cloud could say. And then they heard Allison closing the door softly below, and creaking across the floor and up the stairs.

"Oh, you waked her up!" he said reproachfully as he caught sight of his sister in Julia Cloud's arms.

"No, you're wrong. She hadn't even gone to bed yet. I knew she wouldn't," said Leslie, nestling closer. "Say, Cloudy, we're not going to trouble you that way again. It isn't worth it. We don't like their old dancing, anyway. I couldn't forget the way you looked so hurt—and the things you said. Won't you please come down to the fire awhile? We want to tell you about it."

Down on the couch, with Allison stirring up the dying embers and Leslie nestled close to her, Julia Cloud heard bits about the evening.

"It wasn't bad, Cloudy, 'deed it wasn't. They dance a lot nicer in colleges than they do other places. I know, for I've been to lots of dances, and I never let men get too familiar. Allison taught me that when I was little. That's why what you said made me so mad. I've always been a lot carefuller than you'd think, and I never dance with anybody the second time if I don't like the way he does it the first time. And everybody was real nice and dignified to-night, Cloudy. The boys are all shy and bashful, anyway; only I couldn't forget what you had said about not liking to have me do it; and it made everything seem so—so—well, not nice; and I just felt uncomfortable; and one dance I sent the boy for a glass of water for me, and I just sat it out; and, when Allison saw me, he came over, and said, 'Let's beat it!' and so I slipped up to the dressing-room, and got my cloak, and we just ran away without telling anybody. Wasn't that perfectly dreadful? But I'll call the girl up after a while, and tell her we had to come home and we didn't want to spoil their fun telling them so."

They sat for an hour talking before the fire, the young people telling her all about their experiences of the last few days, and letting her into their lives again with the old sweet relation. Then they drifted back again to the subject of dancing.

"I don't give a whoop whether I dance or not, Cloudy," said Allison. "I never did care much about it, and I don't see having my sister dance with some fellows, either. Only it does cut you out of lots of fun, and you get in bad with everybody if you don't do it. I expected we'd have to have dances here at the house, too, sometimes; but, if you don't like it, we won't; and that's all there is to it."

"Well, dear, that's beautiful of you. Of course I couldn't allow you to let me upset your life and spoil all your pleasure; but I'm wondering if we couldn't try an experiment. It seems to me there ought to be things that people would enjoy as much as dancing, and why couldn't we find enough of them to fill up the evenings and make them forget about the dancing?"

"There'll be some that won't come, of course," said Leslie; "but we should worry! They won't be the kind we'll like, anyway. Jane Bristol doesn't dance. She told me so yesterday. She said her mother never did, and brought her up to feel that she didn't want to, either."

"She's some girl," said Allison irrelevantly. "She entered the sophomore class with credits she got for studying in the summer school and some night-work. Did you know that, kid? I was in the office when she came in for her card, and I heard the profs talking about her and saying she had some bean. Those chumps in the village will find out some day that the girl they despised is worth more than the whole lot of them put together."

Julia Cloud leaned forward, and touched lightly and affectionately the hair that waved back from the boy's forehead, and spoke tenderly.

"Dear boy, I'll not forget your leaving your friends and coming back to me and to the Sabbath and church and all that. It means a lot to me to have my children observe those things. I hope some day you'll do it because you feel you want to please God instead of me."

"Sure!" said Allison, trying not to look embarrassed. "I guess maybe I care about that, too, a little bit. To tell the truth, Cloudy, I couldn't see staying away from that Christian Endeavor meeting after I've worked hard all the week to get people to come to it. It didn't seem square."

The moment was tense with deep feeling, and Julia Cloud could not bring herself to break it by words. She brought the boy's hand up to her lips, and pressed it close; and then just as she was about to speak the telephone rang sharply again and again.

Allison sprang up, and went to answer.

"Hello. Yes. Oh! Miss Bristol! What? Are you sure? I'll be there at once. Lock yourself in your room till I get there."

He hung up the receiver excitedly.

"Call up the fire department quick, Leslie! Tell them to hurry. There's some one breaking into the Johnson house, and Jane Bristol is there alone with the children. It's Park Avenue, you know. Hustle!"

He was out the door before they could exclaim, and Leslie hastened to the telephone.

"He went without his overcoat," said Julia Cloud, hurrying to the closet for it. "It will be very cold riding. He ought to have it."

Leslie hung up the receiver, and flung her velvet cloak about her hurriedly, grabbing the overcoat.

"Give it to me, Cloudy; I'm going with him!" she cried, and dashed out the door as the car slid out of the garage.

"O Leslie! Child! You *oughtn't* to go!" she cried, rushing to the door; but Leslie was already climbing into the car, moving as it was.

"It's all right, Cloudy!" she called. "There's a revolver in the car, you know!" and the car whirled away down the street.

Julia Cloud stood gasping after them; the horrible thought of a revolver in the car did not cheer her as Leslie had evidently hoped it would. What children they were, after all, plunging her from one trouble into another, yet what dear, tender-hearted, loving children! She went in, and found a heavy cloak, and went out again to listen. Then it came to her that perhaps Leslie had not made the operator understand; so she went back to the telephone to try to find out whether any one had been sent. Suppose those children should try to face a burglar alone! There might be more than one for aught they knew. Oh, Leslie *should not* have gone! A terrible anxiety took possession of her, and she tried to pray as she worked the telephone hook up and down and waited for the operator. Then into the quiet of the night there came the loud clang of the fire-bell, and a moment later hurried calls and voices in the distance, sounding through the front door that Julia Cloud had left open. For an instant she was relieved, and then she reflected that this might be a fire somewhere else, and not the call for the Johnson house at all; so she kept on trying to call the operator. At last a snappy voice snarled into her ear. "We don't tell where the fire is; we're not allowed any more," and snap! The operator was gone again.

"But I don't want to know where the fire is!" called Julia Cloud in dismay. "I want to ask a question."

No answer came, and the dim buzz of the wire sounded emptily back to her anxious ear. At last she gave it up, and went out to the street to look up and down. If she only knew which way was Park Avenue! She could hear the engine now, clattering along with the hook and ladder behind; and dark, hurrying forms crossed the street just beyond the next corner, but no one came by. She hurried out to the corner, and called to a boy who was passing; and he yelled out: "Don't know, lady. Up Park Avenue somewhere." Then the street grew very quiet again, and all the noise centred away in the distance. A shot rang out, and voices shouted, and her heart beat so loud she could hear it. She hurried back to the house again, and tried to get the telephone operator; but nothing came of it, and for the next twenty minutes she vibrated between the street and the telephone, and wondered whether she ought not to wake up Cherry and do something else.

It seemed perfectly terrible to think of those two children handling a burglar alone—and yet what could she do?

Pretty soon, however, she heard the fire-engine returning, with the crowd, and she hurried down to the corner to find out.

"It wasn't no fire at all, lady," answered a boy whom she questioned. "It was just two men breakin' into a house, but they ketched 'em both an' are takin' 'em down to the lockup. No, lady, there wasn't nobody killed. There was some shootin', sure! A girl done it! Some college girl in a car. She see the guy comin' to make a get-away in her car, see? And she let go at him, and picked him off the first call, got him through the knee; an' by that time the fire comp'ny got there, and cinched 'em both. She's some girl, she is!"

Julia Cloud felt her head whirling, and hurried back to the house to sit down. She was trembling from head to foot. Was it Leslie who had shot the burglar? Leslie, her little pink-and-silver butterfly, who seemed so much like a baby yet in many ways? Oh, what a horrible danger she had escaped! If she had escaped. Perhaps the boy did not know. Oh, if they would but come! It seemed hours since they had left. The midnight train was just pulling into the station! How exasperating that the telephone did not respond! Something must be out of order with it. Hark! Was that the car? It surely was!

CHAPTER XIX

How welcome a sound was the churn of the engine as it came flying up the road and turned into the driveway!

Julia Cloud was at the door, waiting to receive them, straining her eyes into the darkness to be sure they were both there.

Leslie sprang out, and dashed into her arms.

"O Cloudy! You waited up, didn't you? We thought you must be asleep and didn't hear the telephone. We tried to call you up and explain. You see, Jane was there alone, and of course she didn't much enjoy staying after what had happened; so we waited till the Johnsons got back from the city. They had been to the theatre, and they just came on that midnight train. If I lived in a lonely place like that, I wouldn't leave three babies with a young girl all alone in the house. It seems the servants were all away, or left, or something. I guess they were pretty scared when they got back. I wanted to bring the children up here to stay all night with us, and let them *be* scared when they got home; but she wouldn't, of course; so we stayed with her."

Leslie tossed aside her velvet cloak as she talked.

"It was awfully exciting, Cloudy. I'm glad I went. There's no telling what might have happened to Allison if somebody hadn't been there. You see he shut down the motor as we came up to the house. We'd been going like a streak of lightning all the way, and we tried to sneak up so they wouldn't hear us and get away; but there was one man outside on the watch, and he gave the word; and just as Allison got out of the car he disappeared into the shadows. The other one came piling out of a window, and streaked it across the porch and down the lawn. Allison made for him; but he changed his course, and came straight toward the car. I guess they thought it was empty. And then the other one came flying out from behind the bushes, and made for Allison; so I just leaned out of the car and shot. I don't know how I ever had the nerve, for I was terribly frightened; but he would have got Allison in another minute, and Allison didn't see him coming. He had a big club in his hand. I saw it as he went across in front of the window, and I knew I must do something; so I aimed right in front of him, and I saw him go down on his knees and throw up his hands; and then I felt sick, and began to think what if I had killed him. I didn't, Cloudy; they say I only hit his knee; but wouldn't it have been awful all my life to have to think I had killed a man? I couldn't have stood it, Cloudy!" and with sudden breaking of the tension the high-strung child flung herself down in a little, brilliant heap at Julia Cloud's knees, buried her bright face in her aunt's lap, and burst into tears.

"You brave little darling!" Julia Cloud caressed her, and folded her arms about her.

"She's all of that, Cloudy! She saved my life!" It was Allison who spoke, standing tall and proud above his sister and looking down at her tenderly. "Come now, kiddie, don't give way when you've been such a trump. I knew you could shoot, but I didn't think you could keep your head like that. Cloudy, she was a little winner, the cool way she aimed at that man with the other one coming right toward her and meaning plainly to get in the car and run away in it. He'd have taken her, too, of course, and stopped at nothing to get away. But, when he saw the good shot she was, and heard his pal groaning, he threw up his hands, and turned sharp about for me. He knew it was his only chance, and that whoever was shooting wouldn't shoot at him while he was all tangled up with me; so he made a spring at me before I knew what he was doing, and threw me off my feet, and got a half Nelson on me, you know——"

"Yes, Cloudy, he was fiendish, and I couldn't do a thing, for fear of hitting Allison; and just then I heard a motor-cycle chugging by the car. I hadn't heard it before, there was so much going on; and a big, strong fellow with his hair all standing up in the wind jumped off, and ran toward them where they were rolling on the ground. Then I thought of the flash-light, and turned it on them; and that motor-cycle man saw just how things were, and he jumped in, and grabbed the burglar; and then all of a sudden the yard was full of men and boys and a terrible noise and clanging, and the fire-engine and hook and ladder came rushing up, Cloudy! You didn't tell them there was a fire, did you? I didn't. I told that telephone girl there was a burglar and to send a policeman. But somehow she got it that the house was on fire. And Jane Bristol was in the house, with the baby in her arms and the other little children asleep in their cribs; and she didn't know what was happening because she didn't dare to open the window."

Into the midst of the excitement and explanations there came a loud knock on the door, and Allison sprang up, and went to see who was there. A young man with dishevelled garments, hair standing on end, and face much streaked with mud and dust stood there. A motor-cycle leaned against the end of the porch.

"Pardon me," he said half shyly. "I saw the light, and thought some one was up yet. Did the lady drop this? I found it in the grass when I went back to hunt for my key-ring. It was right where she stood."

He held forth his hand, and there dropped from his fingers a slender white, gleaming thing.

Allison flashed on the porch-light, and looked at it.

"Leslie, is this yours?"

The motor-cycle man looked up, and there stood the princess, her rosy garments like the mist of dawn glowing in the light of fire and lamp, her tumbled golden curls, her eyes bright with recent tears, her cheeks pink with excitement. He had seen her dimly a little while before in a long velvet cloak and a little concealing head-scarf, standing in a motor-car shooting with a steady hand, and again coming with swift feet to her brother's side in the grass after he was released from the burglar's hold; but he had not caught the look of her face. Now he stood speechless, and stared at the lovely apparition. Was it possible that this lovely child had been the cool, brave girl in the car?

Leslie had put her hand to her throat with a quick cry, and found it bare.

"My string of pearls!" she said. "How careless of me not to have noticed they were gone! I'm so glad you found them! They are the ones that mamma used to have." Then, looking up for the first time, she said:

"Oh, you are the young man who saved my brother's life. Won't you please come in? I think you were perfectly splendid! I want my aunt to meet you, and we all want to thank you."

"Oh, I didn't do anything," said the stranger, turning as if to go. "It was you who saved his life. I got there just in time to watch you. You're some shot, I'll tell the world. I sure am proud to meet you. I didn't know any girl could shoot like that."

"Oh, that's nothing!" laughed Leslie. "Our guardian made us both learn. Please come in."

"Yes, we want to know you," urged Allison. "Come in. We can't let you go like that."

"It's very late," urged the young man.

But Allison put out a firm arm, and pulled him in, shutting the door behind him.

"Cloudy," he said, turning to his aunt, "this man came in the nick of time, and saved me just as I was getting woosey. That fellow sure had a grip on my throat, and something had hit my head and taken away all the sense I had, so I couldn't seem to get him off."

"That's all right. I noticed you were holding your own," put in the stranger. "It isn't every man would have tackled two unknown burglars alone." He spoke in a voice of deep admiration.

"Well, I noticed you were the only man on the spot till the parade was about over," said Allison, slapping him heartily on the shoulder. "Say, I think I've seen you before riding that motor-cycle; tell me your name, please. I want to know you next time I see you."

"Thanks, I'm not much to know, but I have an idea you are. My name's Howard Letchworth. I have a room over the garage, and take my meals at the pie-shop. My motor-cycle is all the family I have at present."

Allison laughed, and held out his hand with a warm grip of admiration.

"I'm Allison Cloud; and this is my sister, Leslie Cloud, and my aunt, Miss Cloud; and this house we call Cloudy Villa. You'll always be welcome whenever you are willing to come. You've saved my life and brought back my sister's pearls, and put us doubly in your debt. I'm sure no one in this town has a better right to be welcome here. Please sit down a minute, and tell us who you are. You don't belong to the church bunch, and I don't think I've seen you about the college."

"No," said Letchworth, "not this year. I'm a laboring man. I work over at the ship-building plant. If everything goes well with me this winter, I may get back to college next fall. I was a junior last year, but I couldn't quite make the financial part; so I had to go to work again."

There was a defiance in his tone as he told it, as if he had said, "Now perhaps you won't want to know me!" and he had not taken the offered chair, but was standing, as if he would not take their friendship under false pretences.

But trust Allison to say the graceful thing.

"I somehow felt you were my superior," he said with his eyes full of real friendship. "Sit down just a minute, so we can be sure you really mean to come again."

"Yes, do sit down," said Julia Cloud. "I was just going to get these children a bite to eat, and I'm sure they'd like to have you share it with them. It's a long time since supper, and you have been through a good deal. Aren't you hungry? The pie-shop won't be open this time of night."

She smiled that welcoming home smile that no young person could resist, and the young man sat down with a swift, furtive glance at Leslie. She seemed too bright and wonderful to be true. He let his eyes wander about the charming room; the fire, the couch, the lamplight on the books, the little home touches everywhere, and then he sank into the big cushions of the chair gratefully.

"Say, this is wonderful!" he said. "I haven't known what home was like for seven years."

"Well, it's almost that long since we had a real home, too," said Leslie gravely; "and we love this one."

"Yes," said Allison, "we've just got this home, and we sure do appreciate it. I hope, if you like it, you'll often share it with us."

"Well, I call that generous to an utter stranger!"

Then Julia Cloud entered with a tray, and Allison and Leslie both jumped up to help her. Leslie brought a plate with wonderful frosted cakes and little sandwiches, which somehow Julia Cloud always managed to have just ready to serve; Allison passed the cups of hot chocolate with billows of whipped cream on the top, and they all sat down before the fire to eat in the coziest way. Suddenly, right in the midst of their talk the big grandfather clock in the corner chimed softly out a single clear, reminding stroke.

"Why, Cloudy! It's one o'clock! Sunday morning, and here we are having a Sunday-morning party, after all, right at home!" laughed Leslie teasingly.

The stranger stood up with apology.

"Oh, please don't go for a minute," said Leslie. "I want you to do one more thing for me. Now, Allison, I can see it in your eyes that you mean to get ahead of me, but I have first chance. He's my find. Mr. Letchworth, you don't happen to belong to a Christian Endeavor Society anywhere, do you?"

The startled young man shook his head, a look of being on his guard suddenly coming into his eyes.

"Do I look like it?" he asked half comically, suddenly glancing down at his muddy, greasy garments and old torn sweater.

"Well, then I want you to come to the meeting to-morrow night—no, to-night, at seven o'clock, down at that little brick church on the next street. Everybody had to promise to bring some one who has never come before, and I didn't have anybody to ask because all the college people I know are off at a house-party; and I ran away from it, and came home; so I couldn't very well ask them. Will you go?"

The young man looked at the lovely girl with a smile on his lips that might easily have grown into a sneer and a curt refusal; but somehow the clear, true look in her eyes made refusal impossible. Against all his prejudices he hesitated, and then suddenly said:

"Yes, I'll go if you want me to. I'm not in the habit of going to such places, but—if you want me, I'll go."

She put her slim, cool hand into his, and thanked him sweetly; and he went out into the starlight feeling as if a princess had knighted him.

"There!" sighed Leslie as the sound of his motor-cycle died away in the distance. "I think he's a real man. It's queer; but he and Jane Bristol are the nicest people we've met in this town yet, and they both work for their living."

"I was just thinking that, too," said Allison, vigorously poking the fire into a shower of ruby sparks. "Don't you like him, Cloudy?"

"Yes," said Julia Cloud emphatically. "He looks as if he took life in earnest. But come, don't you think we better go to bed?"

So they all lay down to sleep at last, Julia Cloud too profoundly thankful for words in the prayer her heart fervently breathed.

CHAPTER XX

The routine of college classes became settled at last, and gradually the young people found bits of leisure for the family life which they craved and loved. Allison came in one day, and announced that he had bought a canoe.

"It's a peach, Cloudy, and I got it cheap from a fellow that has to leave college. His father has got a job out in California, and they are going to move, and want to transfer him to a Western college so he won't be so far away from them. I got it for fifteen dollars with all the outfit, and it's only been used one season. But he couldn't take it with him. There are three paddles and two cushions and some rugs belonging to it, and I've arranged to keep it down behind the inn so it won't be far for us to go to it. Now, I want you to be ready to take a trial trip this afternoon at three when Leslie and I get through our classes."

With much inward questioning but entire loyalty Julia Cloud yielded herself to the uncertainties of canoeing, but it needed but that first trip to make her an ardent admirer of that form of recreation. Re-creation it really seemed to her to be, as she sank among the pillows in the comfortable nest the children had prepared for her, and felt herself glide out upon the smooth bosom of the creek into the glow of the autumn afternoon. For in the shelter of the winding ravine where the creek wandered the frost had not yet completed its work, and the trees were still in glowing colors, blending brilliantly with the dark green of the hemlock. A few stark trunks were bare and bleak against the sky in unsheltered places, but for the most part the banks of the creek still set forth a most pleasing display to the nature-lover who chose to come and see. Winding dark and soft and still, with braided ripples here and there, and little floating brown leaves that slithered against the boat as they passed, the creek meandered between the hills, now turning almost upon itself around a mossy, grassy stretch of meadow-land, skirting a chestnut-grove, or slipping beneath great rocks that cropped out on the hillside, where moss had crept in a lovely carpet, and graceful hemlocks found a foothold and leaned over to dip in the water and brush the faces of those who passed. Up, up, and up, through the frantic little rapids that bubbled and fought and were conquered, into the stiller waters above, between banks all dark and green and quiet, most brilliantly and cunningly embroidered with exquisite squawberry vines and scarlet berries. It was most entrancing, and Julia Cloud was reluctant to come home. No need ever to coax her any more. She was ready always to go in that canoe, jealous of anything that prevented a chance to go.

Often she and Cherry, instead of getting a hot lunch at home, would put up the most delectable lunch in paper boxes, and when the children came home she would be ready to go right down to the canoe and spend two delightful hours floating up and down the creek and eating an unconscionable number of sandwiches and cakes. This happened most often on Wednesdays, when the children had no classes from eleven o'clock until three and there was time to take the noon hour in a leisurely way. Not even cool weather coming on could daunt them. Steamer-rugs and warm sweaters and gloves were requisitioned, and the open-air lunches went on just the same. One day they took a pot of hot soup and three small bowls and spoons. They landed at the great rocks, and, climbing up, built a fire and gave their soup another little touch of heat before they ate it. Such experiences welded their hearts more and more together, and Julia Cloud came to be more and more a part of the lives of these two young people who had taken her for their mother-in-love.

It was on these outings that they talked over serious problems: whether Leslie should join one of the girls' sororities, what they should do about the next Christian Endeavor meeting, why it was that Howard Letchworth and Jane Bristol were so much more interesting than any of their other friends, why Cloudy did not like to have Myrtle Villers come to the house, and what Allison was going to do in life when he got through with college. They were absolutely one in all their thoughts and wishes just at this time, and there was not anything that any one of them would not willingly talk over with the others. It was a beautiful relation, and one that Julia Cloud daily, tremblingly prayed might last, might find nothing to break it up.

By this time the young people had begun to bring their college mates to the house, and everybody up there was crazy for an invitation to the little lunches and dinners and pleasant evening gatherings that had begun to be so popular. There were not wanting the usual "boy-crazy" girls, who went eagerly trailing Allison, literally begging him for rides and attention, and making up to Julia Cloud and Leslie in the most sickening of silly girl fashions.

And of these Myrtle Villers was at once the most subtle and least attractive. Julia Cloud had an intuitive shrinking from her at the start, although she tried in her sweet, Christian way to overcome it and do as much for this girl as she was trying to do for all the others who came into their home. But Myrtle Villers was quick to understand, and played her part so well that it was impossible to shake her off as some might have been shaken. She studied Leslie like an artist, and learned how to play upon her frank, emotional, impulsive nature. She confided in her, telling the sorrows of an unloved life, and her longings for great and better things, and fell to attending Christian Endeavor most strenuously. She was always coming home with Leslie for overnight and being around in the way.

Allison did not like her in the least, and Julia Cloud barely tolerated her; but, as the weeks went by, Leslie began to champion her, to tell the others they were unfair to the girl, and that she really had a sincere heart and a lovely nature, which had been crushed by loneliness and sorrow. Allison always snorted angrily when Leslie got off anything like that, and habitually absented himself whenever he knew "the vamp," as he called her, was to be there.

It was one day quite late in the fall, almost their last balmy picnic before the cold weather set in, that they were sitting up on the rocks around a pleasant, resinous pine-needle fire they had made, discussing this. Allison was maintaining that it was not good for Leslie to go with a girl like that, that all the fellows despised; and Leslie was pouting and saying she didn't see why he had to be so prejudiced and unfair; and Julia Cloud was looking troubled and wondering whether her heart and her head were both on the wrong side, or what she ought to do about it, when a step behind them made them all turn around startled. It was the first time they had been interrupted by an intruder in this retreat, and it had come to seem all their own. Moreover, the cocoa on the fire was boiling, and the lunch was about to be served on the little paper plates.

There stood a tall man with a keen, care-worn face, a scholarly air, and an unmistakably wistful look in his eyes.

"Why, is this where you spend your nooning, Cloud? It certainly looks inviting," he said with a comprehensive glance at the wax-papered sandwiches and the little heap of cakes and fruit.

Allison arose with belated recognition.

"O Dr. Bowman," he said, "let me introduce you to my aunt, Miss Cloud, and my sister Leslie."

The scholarly gentleman bowed low in acknowledgment of the introduction, and fairly seemed to melt under the situation.

"Well, now, this certainly is delightful!" he said, still eying the generously spread rock table. "Quite an idea! Quite an idea! Is this some special occasion, some celebration or something?" He glanced genially round on the group.

"Oh, no, we often bring our lunch out here," said Julia Cloud in a matter-of-fact tone. "It keeps us out-of-doors, and makes a pleasant change." There was finality in her tone, and a sensitive-minded professor would have moved on at once, for the cocoa was boiling over, and had to be rescued, and he might have seen they did not want him; but he lingered affably.

"Well, that certainly is an original idea. Quite so. It really makes one quite hungry to think of it. That certainly looks like an attractive repast."

There was nothing for it but to invite him to partake, which Allison did as curtly as he dared, considering that the intruder was one of his major professors, and hoping sincerely that he would refuse. But Professor Bowman did not refuse. No such good chance, and quite to Julia Cloud's annoyance—for she wanted to have the talk out with her children—he sat himself down on the rock as if he were quite acclimated to picnics in November, and accepted so many sandwiches that Leslie, seated slightly behind and out of his sight, made mock signs of horror lest there should not be enough to go around.

It appeared that he had started out to search for his pocket-knife, which his young son had borrowed and lost somewhere in that region as nearly as he could remember, and thus had come upon the picnickers.

"Old pill!" growled Allison gruffly when at last the unwelcome guest had departed hastily to a class, with many praises for his dinner and a promise to call to see them in the near future. "Old pill! Now we'll never dare to come here again as long as he's around. Bother him. I wish I'd told him to go to thunder. We don't want him. He lives right up here over that bluff. His wife's dead, and his sister or aunt or something keeps house for him. She looks like a bottle of pickles! Say, Cloudy, we'll just be out evenings for a while till he forgets it."

But Dr. Bowman did not forget it as Allison had hoped. He came the very next week on a stormy night when no one in his senses would go out if he could help it; and there were the gay little household, with the addition of Jane Bristol and Howard Letchworth, down on their knees before the fire, roasting chestnuts, toasting marshmallows, and telling stories. His grim, angular presence descended upon the joyous gathering like a wet blanket; and the young people subsided into silence until Leslie, rising to the occasion, went to the piano and started them all singing. A wicked little spirit seemed to possess her, and she picked out the most jazzy rag-time she could find, hoping to freeze out the unwelcome guest, but he sat with patient set smile, and endured it, making what he seemed to think were little pleasantries to Julia Cloud, who sat by, busy with some embroidery. She, poor lady, was divided between a wicked delight at the daring of the children and a horror of reproach that they should be treating a college professor in this rude manner. She certainly gave him no encouragement; and, when he at last rose to go, saying he had spent a very pleasant and profitable evening getting acquainted with his students, and he thought he should soon repeat it, she did not ask him to return. But he was a man of the kind who needs no encouragement, and he did return many times and often, until he became a fixed institution, which taxed all their faculties inventing ways of escape from him. The winter went, and Dr. Bowman became the one fly in the pleasant ointment of Cloud Villa.

"We'll just have to send Cloudy away awhile, or put her to bed and pretend she is sick every time he comes, or something!" said Leslie one night, after his departure had made them free to express their feelings. "We've tried everything else. He just won't take a hint! What do you say, Cloudy; will you play sick?"

"My dear!" said Julia Cloud aghast, "he doesn't come to see me! What on earth put that in your head?" Her face was flaming scarlet, and distress showed in every feature.

The children fairly shouted.

"You dear, old, blind Cloudy, of course he does! Who on earth else would he come to see?"

"But," said Julia Cloud, tears coming into her eyes, "he mustn't. I don't want to see him! Mercy!"

"That's all right, Cloudy; you should worry! I'll go tell him so if you want me to."

"Allison! You wouldn't!" said Julia Cloud, aghast.

"No, of course not, Cloudy, but we'll find a way to get rid of the old pill if we have to move away for a while."

Nevertheless, the old pill continued to come early and often, and there seemed no escape; for he was continually stealing in on their privacy at the most unexpected times and acting as if he were sure of a welcome. The children froze him, and were rude, and Julia Cloud withdrew farther and farther; but nothing seemed to faze him.

"It's too bad to have so much sweetness wasted," mocked Leslie one night at the supper-table when their unwelcome visitor had been a subject of discussion. "Miss Detliff is eating her heart out for him. She's always noseying round in the hall when his class is out, and it's about time for hers to begin, just to get a word with him. She kept us waiting for our papers ten whole minutes the other day while she discussed better classroom ventilation with him. 'O Doctah, don't you think we might do something about this mattah of ventilation?'" she mimicked, convulsing Allison with her likeness to her English teacher.

"That's an idea!" said Allison suddenly. "No, don't ask me what it is. It would spoil things. Cloudy, may I bring a guest to dinner to-morrow night?"

"Certainly, anybody you please," replied Julia Cloud innocently; and the incorrigible Allison appeared the next afternoon with Miss Detliff, smiling and pleased, sitting up in the back seat of the car. Julia Cloud received her graciously, and never so much as suspected anything special was going on until later in the evening, when Dr. Bowman arrived and was ushered in to find his colaborer there before him. He did not look especially pleased, and Julia Cloud caught a glance of intelligence passing between Leslie and Allison, with a sudden revelation of a plot behind it all. During the entire evening she sat quietly, saying little, but her eyes dancing with the fun of it. What children they were, and how she loved them! yes, and what a child she was herself! for she couldn't help loving their pranks as well as they did.

However, though Dr. Bowman had to take Miss Detliff home, and got very little satisfaction out of his call that evening, it did not discourage him in the least, and Julia Cloud decided that extreme measures were necessary to rid them of his presence.

"We might go away during Thanksgiving week; only there's the Christian Endeavor banquet," said Leslie. "We couldn't be away from that. And then I wanted to have Jane to dinner. She's gone up to college this week to live. She's doing office work there, and she'll be alone on Thanksgiving Day."

"Yes, and there's Howard. I thought we'd have him here," put in Allison dubiously.

"Of course!" said Julia Cloud determinedly. "And we don't want to go away, anyway. You children run up to your rooms this evening and study. Stay there, I mean, no matter who comes. Do you understand?"

With a curious look at her they both obeyed; and a little later, when the knocker sounded through the house, they sat silently above, not daring to move, and heard their aunt open the door, heard Dr. Bowman's slow, scholarly voice and Julia Cloud's even tones, back and forth for a little while, and then heard the front door open and shut again, and slow steps go down the brick terrace and out to the sidewalk.

What passed in that interview no one ever knew. Julia Cloud came to the foot of the stairs, and called them down, and her eyes were shining and confident as she sat by the lamp and sewed while they studied and joked in front of the fire; but the unwelcome guest came no more, and whenever they met him in the street, or at receptions, or passing at a college game, he gave them a distant, pleasant bow; that was all. Julia Cloud had done the work well, however she had done it. The little Bowmans need not look to her to fill their mother's place, for she was not so minded.

Meantime, the winter had been going on, and the little pink-and-white house was becoming popular among the students at college as well as among the members of the Christian Endeavor Society of the little brick church. Many an evening specially picked groups of girls or boys or both spent before that fire, playing games, and talking, and singing. Sometimes the college glee-club came down and had dinner. Again it was the football team that was feasted. Another time Allison's frat came for his birthday, aided and abetted by his sister and aunt.

Jane Bristol became a frequent visitor, though not so frequent as they would have liked to have her, for her time was very much taken up with her work and her studies. Julia Cloud often wished she might lift the financial burden from the young shoulders and make things easier for her, both for her own sake and Leslie's, who would have liked to make her her constant companion; but Jane Bristol was too independent to let anybody help her, and there seemed no way to do anything about it. Meantime, Myrtle Villers improved each idle hour, and kept Leslie busy inventing excuses to get away from her, and Julia Cloud busy worrying. Leslie was so dear, but she was also self-willed. And she would go off with that wild girl in the car for long rides. Not that Julia Cloud worried about the driving; for Leslie was most careful, and handled a car as if she had been born with the knowledge, as indeed she did all things athletic; but her aunt distrusted the other girl.

And then one clear, cold afternoon in December Leslie went off for a ride in the car with Myrtle. Of course Julia Cloud did not know that the girl had pestered the life out of Leslie for the ride, and had finally promised that, if she would go, she would stop going with a certain wild boy in the village of whom Leslie disapproved. Neither did she know that Leslie had resolved never to go again without her aunt along. So she sat at the window through the short winter afternoon, and watched and waited in vain for the car to return; and Allison came back at half-past six after basket-ball practice, and still Leslie had not appeared.

CHAPTER XXI

There had been a little friction between Allison and Leslie about the use of the car. Allison had always been most generous with it until his sister took up this absurd intimacy with Myrtle Villers. It has been rather understood between them that Leslie should use the car afternoons when she wanted it, as Allison was busy with basket-ball and other things; but several times Allison had objected to his sister's taking her new friend out, and Leslie told him he was unfair. After a heated discussion they had left the question still unsettled. In fact, it did not seem that it could be settled, for Leslie was of such a nature that great opposition only made her more firm; and Julia Cloud advised her nephew to say nothing more for a time. Let Leslie find out for herself the character of the girl she had made her friend. It was really the only way she would learn not to be carried away by flattery and high-sounding words. Allison, grumbling a little, assented; but in his heart he still boiled with rage at the idea of that girl's winding his sister around her little finger just for the sake of using the car when she wanted it. It was not, perhaps, all happening that for two or three days Allison had left the switch-key where his sister could not find it, and a hot war of words ended in Leslie's quietly ordering a new switch-key so that such a happening would be impossible in future, She would have one of her own. A card had come that very morning from the express office, notifying Leslie that there was a package there waiting for her; so, when she started out with Myrtle, she stopped and got it. She tossed it carelessly into the car with a feeling of satisfaction that now Allison could not hamper her movements any longer by his carelessness.

"Which way shall we go?" she asked as she always did when taking her friends out, and Myrtle named a favorite pike where they often drove.

Out upon the smooth, white road they sped, rejoicing in the clear beauty of the day and in the freedom with which they flew through space. Myrtle had chosen to sit in the back seat, and lolled happily among rugs and wraps, keeping a keen eye out on the road ahead and chattering away like a magpie to Leslie, telling her what a darling she was—she pronounced it "dolling"—and how this ride was just the one thing she needed to recuperate from her violent study of the night before, incident to an examination that morning. Myrtle professed to be utterly overcome and exhausted by the physical effort of writing for three whole hours without a let-up. If Leslie could have seen her meagre paper, through which a much-tortured professor was at that moment wearily plodding, she would have been astonished. Leslie herself was keen and thorough in her class work, and had no slightest conception of what a lazy student could avoid when she set herself to do so.

Five miles from home two masculine figures came in sight ahead, strolling leisurely down the road. Any one watching might have seen Myrtle suddenly straighten up and cast a hasty glance at Leslie. But Leslie with bright cheeks and shining eyes was forging ahead, regardless of stray strollers.

At exactly the right moment Myrtle leaned forward, and clutched Leslie's shoulder excitedly:

"O Leslie! That's my cousin Fred Hicks! And that must be his friend, Bartram Laws! They're out for a hike. How lucky! Stop a minute, please; I want to speak to my cousin."

At the same moment the two young men turned, with a well-timed lifting of surprised hats in response to Myrtle's violent waving and shouting.

Leslie of course slowed down. She could not carry a girl past her own cousin when she asked to stop to speak to him; besides, it never occurred to her not to do so.

Myrtle went through the introductions glibly.

"Mr. Laws, meet my friend Miss Cloud; my cousin, Fred Hicks, Leslie. Pile in, boys! Isn't this great that we should meet? Out for a hike? We'll give you a lift. Which way are you going? Fred, you can sit in front with Leslie. I want Bart back here with me."

Leslie caught her breath in a troubled hesitancy. This wasn't the kind of thing she had bargained for. It was the sort of thing that her aunt and brother would object to most strenuously. Yet how could she object when her guest had asked them? Of course Myrtle didn't realize that it was not quite the thing for them to be off here in the country unchaperoned, with two strange young men, though of course they weren't strangers really, both of them friends of Myrtle's, and one her cousin. Myrtle could not be expected to think how it would seem to her.

But the young men were not waiting for Leslie's invitation. They seemed to feel that their company would be ample compensation for any objections that might be had. They scrambled in with alacrity.

The color flew into Leslie's cheeks. In her heart she said they were altogether too "fresh."

"Why, I suppose we can give you a lift for a little way," said Leslie, trying to sound patronizing. "How far are you going? We turn off here pretty soon."

"Oh, that's all right," said Cousin Fred easily; "any old road suits us so it's going in this direction. Want me to take the wheel?"

"No, thank you," said Leslie coldly, "I always drive myself. My brother doesn't care for me to let other people use the car."

"That's all right; I thought you might be tired, and I'm a great driver. People trust me that won't trust any one else."

"That's right, Leslie," chimed in Myrtle. "Fred can drive like a breeze. You ought to see him!"

Leslie said nothing, but dropped in the clutch, and drove on. She was not prepossessed in Fred Hicks's favor. She let him make all the remarks, and sat like a slim, straight, little offended goddess. But Fred Hicks was not disturbed in the least. He started in telling a story about a trip he took from Washington up to Harrisburg in an incredibly brief space of time, and he laughed uproariously at all his own jokes. Leslie was a girl of violent likes and dislikes, and she took one of them now. She fairly froze Cousin Fred, though he showed no outward sign of being aware of it.

"Here's a nice road off to the right," he indicated, reaching out a commanding hand to the wheel suddenly. "Turn here."

Leslie with set lips bore on past the suggested road at high speed.

"Please don't touch my wheel," was all she said, in a haughty little voice. She was very angry indeed.

They were nearing an old mansion, closed now for the winter, with a small artificial lake between the grounds and the highway.

Leslie felt a passing wish that she might dump her undesired cargo in that lake and fly away from them.

"I think you will have to get out at the next crossroads," she said with more dignity. "I have to go home now."

"Why, Leslie Cloud! You don't any such thing!" broke in Myrtle. "You told me you could be out till quarter of six. It's only half-past four! I thought you were a good sport."

"I've changed my mind," said Leslie coldly, bringing the car to a standstill. "I'm going back right now. Do you and your friend want to get out here, Mr. Hicks?"

Fred Hicks lolled back in the car, and leered at Leslie.

"Why, no, I can't say I'm particularly anxious to get out, but I think I'd like to change around a little. If you'll just step over here, I'll run the car for you, my dear. I don't think Myrtle is ready to go back yet. How 'bout it, Myrt?" He turned and deliberately winked at Myrtle, who leaned over with a light laugh, and patted Leslie on the shoulder.

"There, there, Leslie, don't get up in the air," she soothed, "I'll explain all about it if you'll just turn around and go up that road back there. It won't take you much longer, and we'll be back in plenty of time. The fact is, I had a little plan in the back of my head when I came out this afternoon; and I want you to help me out. Now be a good girl and let Fred run the car a little while. He won't do it any harm, and your brother will never know a thing about it."

Leslie's eyes were flashing, and her head was held haughtily; but she kept her hands firmly on the wheel.

"Your friends will have to get out, Myrtle," she said coldly. "I can't help you out in any scheme I don't understand. You'll have to go to some one else for that kind of help."

Myrtle pouted.

"I must say I don't think you're very nice, Leslie Cloud, speaking in that way before my friends; but of course you don't understand; I'll have to tell you. Bart Laws and I are engaged, and we're going to a town down in the next State to get married. Bart has the license and the minister, and it's all arranged nicely. His aunt will be there for a chaperon. If you behave yourself and do as we tell you, the whole thing will go off quietly and no one will know the difference. You and I will go back home before dark, and everything will be lovely. You see, dear, I've been engaged all this time; only I couldn't tell you, because my guardians don't approve of my getting married until I'm through college. You didn't understand why I had so much to do with Rich Price, but he was just a go-between for Bart and me. Now, do you understand why I wanted you to go this afternoon?"

Myrtle's voice was very soft and insinuating. She had tears always near the surface for ready use. "You never have been in love, Leslie; you don't know what it is to be separated from the one who is all the world to you. Come, now, Leslie; I'll do anything in the world for you if you'll only help me out now."

"And if I won't?" asked Leslie calmly, deliberately, as if she were really weighing the question.

"Well, if you won't," put in the person called Fred Hicks, "why, Bart and I will just fix you up perfectly harmlessly in the back seat there, where you can't do any damage"—and he put his hand in his pocket, and brought out the end of an ugly-looking rope—"and then we'll take charge of this expedition and go on our way. You can take it or leave it as you please. Shut up there, Myrt; we haven't any more time to waste. We're behind schedule now."

Leslie's mouth shut in a pretty little tight line, and her eyes got like two blue sparks, but her voice was cool and steady.

"Well, I *won't*!" she said tensely; and with a sudden motion she grabbed the switch-key and, springing to her feet, flung it far out across the road, across a little scuttled canoe that lay at the bank, and plunk into the water, before the other occupants of the car could realize what she was doing.

Fred Hicks saw just an instant too late, and sprang for her arm to stop it, then arose in his seat with curses on his lips, watching the exact location of the splash and calling to his mate to go out and fish for it.

Leslie sank back in her seat, tense and white, and both young men sprang out and rushed to the shore of the little lake, leaving a stream of unspeakable language behind them. Myrtle began to berate her friend.

"You little *fool*!" she said. "You think you've stopped us, don't you? But you'll suffer for this! If you make us late, I'll see that you don't get back to your blessed home for a whole week; and, when you do, you won't have such a pretty reputation to go on as you have now! It won't do a bit of good, either, for those two men can find that switch-key; or, if they can't, Fred knows how to start a car without one. You've only made a lot of trouble for yourself, and that's all the good it will do you. You thought you were smart, but you're nothing but an ignorant little kid!"

But the ignorant little kid was not listening. With trembling fingers she was pulling off the wrappings from a small package, and suddenly a warning whir cut short Myrtle's harangue. She lurched forward, and tried to pull Leslie's hands away from the wheel.

"Bart! Come quick! She's got another! Hurry, boys!"

CHAPTER XXII

The two young men had shoved the old canoe up on the bank, turned it over, emptied it, and put it back in the water. Fred Hicks was holding it at arm's length now in the water; and the would-be bridegroom had crawled out to the extreme end, and with rolled-up sleeves was pawing about in the water, which did not appear to be very deep. At the cry they turned; and Fred Hicks, forgetting the other man's plight, let go the boat, and dashed back to the road. Young Laws, arising too hastily, rolled into the water completely, and came splashing up the bank in a frothy state of mind. But suddenly, as they came, while Myrtle's best efforts were put forth to hinder Leslie's movements, something cold and gleaming flashed in her face that sent her crouching back in the corner of her seat and screaming. Leslie had slipped her hand into the little secret pocket of the car door and brought out her revolver, hoping fervently that it was still loaded, and that Allison had not chosen to shoot at a mark or anything with it the last time he was out.

"You'd better sit down and keep quiet," she said coolly. "I'm a good shot."

Then she put her foot on the clutch, and the car started just as Fred Hicks lit on the running-board.

Leslie's little revolver came promptly around to meet him, and he dropped away with a gasp of surprise as suddenly as he had lit. Suddenly Leslie became aware of the other young man dripping and breathless, but with a dangerous look in his eye, bearing down upon her from the lake side of the road; and she flashed around and sent a shot ringing out into the road, the bullet ploughing into the dust at his very feet. The car leaped forward to obey her touch, and in a second more they had left the two young men safely behind them.

Myrtle was crouched in the back seat, weeping; and Leslie, cool and brave in the front seat, was trembling from head to foot. This was a new road to her; at least, she had never been more than two or three miles on it, and she did not know where she would bring up. She began to wonder how long her gasoline would hold out, for she had been in such a hurry to get away with Myrtle before Allison should come home that she had forgotten to look to see if everything was all right; and she now remembered that Allison had had the car out late the night before. Everything seemed to be falling in chaos about her. The earth rose and fell in front of her excited gaze; the sun was going down; and the road ahead seemed endless, without a turning as far as she could see.

A great burying-ground stretched for what seemed like miles along one side of the road. The polished marble gleamed red and bleak in the setting sun. The sky had suddenly gone lead-color, and there was a chill in the air. Leslie longed for nothing so much as to hide her head in Julia Cloud's lap and weep. Yet she must go on and on and on till this awful road came to an end. Would it *ever* come to an end? Oh, it *must* somewhere! A great tower of bricks loomed ahead with a wide paved driveway leading to it through an arched gateway, and over the arch some words. Leslie got only one of them, "CREMATORY." She shuddered, and put on speed. It seemed that she had come to the place of death and desolation. It was lonely everywhere, and not a soul in sight. What horror if her gasoline should give out in a place like this, and they have to spend the night here, she and that poor, weak creature sobbing behind! What contempt she felt for her former friend! What contempt she felt for herself! Oh, she was well punished for her wilfulness! To think she should have presumed to hope she could help her to better ways, she, a little innocent, who never dreamed of such depths of duplicity as had been shown her that afternoon! Oh, to think of that loathsome Hicks person daring to touch her! To try to take her car away from her! and to *smile* at her in that disgusting way!

On and on went the car, and the road wound away into the dusk up a high hill and down again, up another, past an old farmhouse with one dim light in the back window and a great dog howling like one in some old classic tale she had read; on and on, till at last a cross-road came, and she knew not which way to take, to right or to left. There was a sign-board; but it was too dark to read, and she dared not get out and leave Myrtle. There was no telling but she might try to run off with the car. It was at the crematory that she began to pray, and, when she reached the crossing, her heart put up a second plea for guidance. "O God, if You will just help me home, I will try, *try*, TRY to be what You want me to be! Please, please, *please*!" It was the old vow of a heart bowed down and brought to the limit. It was the first time Leslie had ever realized that there could be a situation in which Leslie Cloud would not find some way out. It was the first time, too, perhaps, when she realized herself as being a sinner in the sense of having a will against God and having exercised it for her own pleasure rather than for His glory.

Down the road to the left the car sped, and after a mile and a half of growing darkness, with woods and scattered farmhouses, the lights of a village began to appear. But it was no village that Leslie knew, and nothing anywhere gave her a clew. A trolley line appeared, however; and after a little a car came along with a name that showed it was going cityward. Leslie decided to follow the trolley track.

In the meantime the girl in the back seat roused up, and began to look about her, evidently recognizing something familiar in the streets or town.

"You can put me out here, Leslie; I'm done with you," she said haughtily. "I don't care to go any farther with you. I'll go back on the train."

"No!" said Leslie sharply. "You'll go home with me. I took you away without knowing what you intended, but I mean to put you back where you were before I'm done. Then my responsibility for you will be over. I was a fool to let you deceive me that way, but I'm not a fool any longer."

"Well, I *won't* go home with you, so! and that's flat, Leslie Cloud. You needn't think you can frighten me into going, either. We're in a village now, and my aunt lives here. If you get out that revolver again, I'll scream and have you arrested, and tell them you're trying to murder me; so there!"

For answer Leslie turned sharply into a cross-road that led away from the settled portion of the town, and put on all speed, tearing away into the dusk like a wild creature. Myrtle screamed and stormed behind her, all to no purpose. Leslie Cloud had her mettle up, and meant to take her prisoner home. Out of the town she turned into another road that ran parallel to the trolley track, from which she could see the lights of the trolleys passing now and again, as it grew darker; and by and by when they came to another cross-road, Leslie got back to the trolley track, and followed it; but whenever they came into a town she kept to its outskirts.

Leslie had a pretty good general sense of direction, and she knew just where the sun went down. If it had not been for a river and some hills that turned up and bewildered her, she would have made a pretty direct course home; but, as it was, she went far out of her way, and was long delayed and much distressed besides, being continually harassed by the angry girl in the back seat. The gasoline was holding out. It was evident that Allison had looked after it. Blessed Allison, who always did everything when he ought to do it, and never put off things until the next day! How cross she had been with him for the last six weeks, and how good and kind he always was to her! How she had deceived dear Cloudy and troubled her by going off this afternoon! Oh, what would they think? Would they ever forgive her, and take her back into their hearts, and trust her again? The tears were blurring her eyes now as she stared ahead at the road. It seemed as if she had been tearing on through the night for hours like this. Her arms ached with the nervous strain; her back ached; her head ached. Perhaps they were going around the world, and would only stop when the gasoline gave out!

They swept around a curve. Could it be that those were the lights of the college ahead on the hill? Oh, joy at last! They were! Up this hill, over across two blocks, and the little pink-and-white house would be nestled among the hemlocks; and rest and home at last! But there was something to be done first. She turned toward the back seat, where sat her victim silent and angry.

"Well, you can let me out now, Leslie Cloud," said Myrtle scornfully. "I suppose you won't dare lord it over me any longer, and I'll take good care that the rest of the town understands what a dangerous little spitfire *you* are. You ought to be arrested for this night's work! That's all *I've* got to say."

"Well, I have one more thing to say," said Leslie slowly, as she swerved into her own street and her eyes hungrily sought for the lights of Cloudy Villa. "You're coming into the house with me first, before you go anywhere else, and you're going to tell this whole story to my Aunt Jewel. After that—*I should worry!*"

"Well, I rather guess I am not going into your old house and tell your old aunt anything! I'm going to get right out here this minute; and you're good and going to *let* me out, too, or I'll scream bloody murder, and tell it all over this town how you went out there to meet those boys. You haven't got any witnesses, and *I have*, remember!" said Myrtle, suddenly feeling courageous now that she was back among familiar streets.

But Leslie turned sharply into the little drive, and brought up the car in a flood of light at the end of the terrace.

"Now, get out!" she ordered, swinging the door open and flashing her little revolver about again at the angry girl.

"O Leslie!" pleaded the victim, quickly quelled by the sight of the cold steel, and thrilled with the memory of that shot whistling by her into the road a few hours before.

"Get out!" said Leslie coolly as the front door was flung open and Julia Cloud peered through the brightness of the porch light into the darkness.

"Get out!" Leslie held the cold steel nearer to Myrtle's face, and the girl shuddered, and got out.

"Now go into the house!" she ordered; and shuddering, shivering, with a frightened glance behind her and a fearful glance ahead, she walked straight into the wondering, shocked presence of Julia Cloud, who threw the door open wide and stepped aside to let them in. Leslie, with the revolver still raised, and pointed toward the other girl, came close behind Myrtle, who sidled hastily around to get behind Miss Cloud.

"Why, Leslie! What is the matter?" gasped Julia Cloud.

"Tell her!" ordered Leslie, the revolver still pointed straight at Myrtle.

"What shall I tell?" gasped the other girl, turning a white, miserable face toward Miss Cloud as if to appeal to her leniency. But there was a severity in Julia Cloud's face now after her long hours of anxiety that boded no good for the cause of all her alarm.

"Tell her the whole story!" ordered the fierce young voice of Leslie.

"Why, we went out to take a ride," began Myrtle, looking up with her old braggadocio. There had seldom been a time when Myrtle had not been able to get out of a situation by use of her wily tongue.

"Tell it all," said Leslie, looking across the barrel of her weapon. "Tell who wanted to go on that ride."

"Why, yes, I asked Leslie to take me. I—we—well, that is—I wanted to meet a friend."

"Tell it straight!" ordered Leslie.

"Why, of course I didn't tell Leslie I expected to meet them—him. I wasn't just sure he could make the arrangements. I meant to tell her when we got out. And when we met him—and my cousin—it was my cousin I was to meet—you see I'm—we—he——"

Myrtle was getting all tangled up with her glib tongue under the clear gaze of Julia Cloud's truth-compelling eyes. She looked up and down, and twisted the fringe on her sash, and turned red and white by turns, and seemed for the first time a very young, very silly child. But Leslie had suffered, and just now Leslie had no mercy. This girl had been a kind of idol to whom she had sacrificed much, and now that her idol had fallen she wanted to make the idol pay. Or no, was that it? Leslie afterwards searched her heart, and felt that she could truly say that her strongest motive in compelling this confession had been to get the burden of the knowledge of it off her own shrinking soul.

"Tell the rest!" came the relentless voice of Leslie, and Myrtle struggled on.

"Well, I'm engaged to Mr. Bartram Laws; and my guardian won't let us get married till I'm through college, and we fixed it up to get married to-day quietly. I knew it would be all right after he found out he couldn't help himself, and so——"

"Tell how you asked the boys to get in the car!" ordered the fierce voice again; and Myrtle, recalled from another attempt to pass it all off pleasantly, went step by step through the whole shameful story until it was complete.

Then Leslie with a sudden motion of finality flung the little weapon down upon the mahogany table, and dashed into Julia Cloud's arms in a storm of tears. "O Cloudy, I'll never, never do any such thing again! And I hate her! I *hate* her! I'll never forgive her! Can you ever forgive *me*?"

No one had heard a sudden, startled exclamation from the porch room as Leslie and Myrtle came into the house; but now Myrtle suddenly looked up, thinking the time had come for her to steal away unseen; and there in the two doorways that opened on either side of the fireplace stood, on one side Allison Cloud and the dean of the college, and on the other side two members of the student executive body, all looking straight at her! Moreover, she read it in their eyes that they had heard every word of her confession. Without a word she dropped white and stricken into a chair, and covered her face with her hands. For once her brazen wiles were gone.

CHAPTER XXIII

It happened that Miss Myrtle Villers had not confined her affections to Mr. Bartram Laws. She had been seen wandering about the campus with other youths at odd hours of the evening when young-lady students were supposed to be safely within college halls or properly chaperoned at some public gathering. The "student exec" had had her in tow for several weeks, and she had already received a number of reproofs and warnings. A daring escapade the evening before had brought matters to a head, and it was very possibly because of some suspicion that they might have found her out that Myrtle had made her plans to be absent on that afternoon. However that was, when the executive body in consultation with the dean sent for her, they traced her to the Clouds' house. At least, they came there about seven o'clock to inquire and hoping to take her unaware. They had found Allison in a great state of excitement, telephoning hither and yon to try to get some clew to his sister's whereabouts. They had remained to advise and suggest, greatly worried at the whole situation, the more so because it involved Leslie Cloud, whose bright presence had taken great hold upon everybody.

And now, without knowing it, Leslie Cloud had taken the one way to put the whole matter into the right hands and to exonerate herself. If she had known that any member of the faculty was in that room listening, if she had dreamed that even her brother was there, she would not have thought it right or honorable to put even an enemy in such a position, either for her own sake or for the girl's. She had only wanted some wise, true adviser to know the truth, so that the girl might learn what was right and have the responsibility taken from her own shoulders. She thought, too, that she had a right to be exonerated before her aunt. So now, while she wept out her contrition in Julia Cloud's arms, retribution was coming swiftly to Myrtle Villers; and her career in that college was sealed with finality. It was only too plain that such a girl was a menace to the other students, and needed to be removed.

Presently Leslie, feeling something strange in the atmosphere, lifted frightened, tear-filled eyes, and saw the grave faces of the dean and his companions! She held her breath with suspense. How terrible! How public and unseemly! She had brought all this upon herself and her family by her persistent friendship with this silly girl! And she fell to trembling and shuddering, all her fine, sweet nerve gone now that the strain was over.

Julia Cloud drew her down upon the couch, and soothed her, covering her with an afghan and trying to comfort her. Then the dean stepped over to the couch and spoke to Leslie.

"Miss Cloud, you must not feel so bad," he said gently, as if she had been his own child. "You have acted nobly, and no one will blame you. You have perhaps saved Miss Villers from great shame and sorrow, and you certainly have been brave and true. Don't worry, child," and he patted Leslie's heaving shoulder kindly.

Presently the dean and his committee were gone, taking the cowering Myrtle with them, and Leslie lay snuggled up on the couch, with Allison building up the fire and Cherry bringing a tray with a nice supper. Julia Cloud fixed a hot-water bag to warm the chilled hands and feet. It was so good to be at home! The tears rushed into her eyes again, and her throat filled with sobs.

"O Cloudy!" She caught her aunt's hands. "I'll never, never do anything again you don't want me to!" she sobbed out, and then burst into another paroxysm of tears.

"There! Now, kid! Don't cry any more!" pleaded Allison, springing to her side and kneeling by her, smoothing her hair roughly. "You were a little winner! You had every bit of your nerve with you. Why, you did a great thing, kid! Outwitting those two brutes and bringing that girl back in spite of herself. But the greatest thing of all was your making her confess. Now they've got something to go on. If you hadn't done that, it would have been her word against yours; and I imagine she's always managed to keep things where she could get around people with her wiles. Now she's got to face facts; and believe me, kid, it'll be better for her in the end. She was headed straight for a bad end, and no mistake. All the fellows knew it, and the faculty suspected it; and it was making no end of trouble. But now the girl may be saved, for that dean never lets a student go to destruction, they say, if he can help it. Oh, of course he'll fire her. She isn't fit to be around here. But he'll keep an eye on her, and he'll fire her in such a way that she'll have another chance to make good if she's willing to take it. Don't you worry about spoiling her life. She'd set out to spoil it in the first place, and the best thing that could possibly happen to her was to get stopped before she went too far. From all you say I shouldn't think a marriage with that fellow would have been any advantage to her."

"Oh, he was *awful*, Allison!" shuddered Leslie. "He smelled of liquor; and he had great, coarse lips and eyes; and he put his arms around her, and kissed her right there before us all; and they acted perfectly disgusting! I'm almost sure from things I heard them say that she hadn't been engaged to him at all, she hadn't even known him till last week. She met him in town—just picked him up on the street! And that Fred Hicks! I don't *believe* now he was her cousin at all."

"Probably not. But leave that all to the dean. He'll ferret it out. He went in there to the telephone before he left, and from what I heard I imagine he's got detectives out after those two guys, and they may sleep in the lockup to-night. They certainly deserve to. And I shall have a hand in settling with them, too. I can't have my sister treated that way and let it go easily. They've got to answer to me. There, kid!"

He stooped down, and kissed her gently on her hot, wet forehead; and Leslie caught his hand and nestled her own in it.

"O Allison! It's so good to be home!" she murmured, squeezing his hand appreciatively. "I'll never, never, *never* go with a girl again that you don't like. I'm just going to stick to Jane. She's the only one up there I really love, anyway."

Allison seemed quite satisfied with these sentiments, and they had a beautiful time eating their supper before the fire, for no one had had any appetite before; and Cherry was as pleased to have the anxiety over and wait upon them all as if Leslie had been her own sister.

Into the midst of their little family group broke a hurried, excited knock on the door, and there stood Howard Letchworth with anxious face.

"I heard that your sister and one of the college girls had gone off in a car and got lost. Is it true? I came right around to see if I could help."

Leslie sat up with her teary eyes bright and eager, and her cheeks rosy with pleasure, all her pretty hair in a tumble about her face and the firelight playing over her features in a most charming way.

"Oh, it's awfully good of you," she called eagerly. "But I'm perfectly all right and safe."

He came over to the couch, and took her offered hand most eagerly, expressing his delight, and saying he had been almost sure it was some town gossip, but he could not rest satisfied until he was positive.

But Allison would not let it go at that.

"I'm going to tell him, Leslie," he said. "He won't let any one be the wiser; and, if people are saying anything like that, he can help stop their mouths." So Allison told the whole story. When it came to the part about Fred Hicks and Bartram Laws, Howard's face grew dark, and he flashed a look that boded no good to the two young ruffians.

"I know who that Laws fellow is," he said gravely. "He's rotten! And I shouldn't wonder if I could locate his friend. I get around quite a bit on my motor-cycle. May I use your 'phone a minute? I have a friend who is a detective. They ought to be rounded up. Miss Leslie, would you tell me carefully just what roads you took, as nearly as you know?"

So Leslie told in detail of the wild ride once more. Julia Cloud watched the young man's face as he listened, and knew that Leslie had a faithful friend and champion, knew also that here was one whose friendship was well worth cultivating, a clean, fine, strong young soul, and was glad for her little girl. Something stirred in her memory as she watched his look, and she went back to her childish days and the boy friend who had kissed her when he went away never to return. There was the same look in Howard Letchworth's eyes when he looked at Leslie, the age-old beauty of a man's clean devotion to a sweet, pure woman soul.

Of course Leslie was a mere child yet, and was not thinking of such things; but there need be no fear that that fine, strong young man would be unwise enough to let the child in her be frightened away prematurely. They were friends now, beautiful friends; and that would be enough for them both for a long time. She was content.

She watched them all the evening, and listened to their talk about the Christian Endeavor Society. How beautiful it was that Leslie had been able to bring the boy to a degree of interest in that! Of course it was for her sake, but he was man enough to be interested on his own account now; and from their talk she could see that he had gone heart and soul with Allison into the plans for the winter work. He had a fine voice, and was to sing a solo at the next meeting. Presently Leslie so far recovered her nerves as to smooth out her hair and go to the piano to practise with him.

ıs, Thou ar
he fast-clo:

rang out the rich, sweet notes; and the tender, sympathetic voice brought out each word with an appeal. The boy could not sing like that and not feel it himself sometime. Julia Cloud found herself praying; praying, as if she whispered to a dear Companion sitting close beside her at the hearthside: "Dear Christ, show this boy. Teach him what Thou art. Make him Thy true disciple."

Suddenly the young fellow turned to Allison with a smile.

"I like the way you take your religion with you into college, Cloud. It makes it seem real. I haven't met many fellows that had any before, or perhaps I shouldn't have been such a heathen as I am. But I say, why don't you try to get some of your frat brothers to come down to the meeting? They ought to be willing to do that for you, and it would be great to have them sing. You've got a lot of the glee club in your crowd."

"That's so!" said Allison. "I don't know but I'll try it. I'd like to have them come the night you sing. Guess I'll have to hunt around and get a speaker. No, I won't either. Just the meeting itself is good enough now for anybody. They're a pretty good little bunch down there. They've been working like beavers. Jane Bristol gets the girls together, and coaches them for every meeting. She's some girl, do you know it?"

Howard Letchworth agreed that she was, but he cast a side glance down at the bright head of the girl, who was playing his accompaniment as if he felt there were others. Julia Cloud was watching her darling girl, wondering, hoping, praying that she might always stay so sweet and unspoiled.

But when the young man was gone home, and Leslie came back to the couch again, she suddenly drooped.

"Cloudy Jewel," she said wearily, "it isn't right. I don't deserve people to be so nice to me, the dean, and you all, and Howard and everybody. It was a lot my fault that all this happened. I thought I could make that girl over if I just stuck to her. She had promised me she would come to Christian Endeavor, and join; and I wanted to show you all what a power I had over her. I was just conceited; that was all there was about it. Now I see that she was only fooling me. I couldn't have done anything at all alone. I needed God. I didn't ask Him to help. You've talked a lot about that in our Sunday meetings, but it never went down into my heart until I was driving past that old crematory, and I felt as if I was all alone and Death all in black trailing robes was going along fast beside me. Then I knew God was the only one who could help, and I began to pray. I hope maybe I've learned my lesson, and I'll not be so swelled-headed next time. But you oughtn't to forgive me, Cloudy, not so easy. Cloudy, you're just like God!"

It was several days before Leslie recovered fully from the nervous strain she had been under. She slept long the next day, and Julia Cloud would not waken her. For a week there were dark circles under the bright eyes, and the rose of her cheek was pale. She went about meekly with downcast eyes, and the bright fervor of her spirit seemed dimmed. It was not until one afternoon when Allison suggested that they get Jane Bristol and Howard Letchworth and go for bittersweet-berry vines and hemlock-branches to decorate for the Christian Endeavor social that her spirits seemed to return, and the unwholesome experience was put away in the past at last.

Howard Letchworth had been most thoughtful about the matter in the village, and had managed so that the tragic had been taken out of the story that had started to roll about, and Leslie could go around and not feel that all eyes were upon her wondering about her escapade. Gradually the remembrance of it died out of her thoughts, although the wholesome lesson she had learned never faded.

More and more popular in the college grew the gatherings down at Cloudy Villa. Sometimes Leslie brought home three or four girls for Friday and Saturday, not often any on Sunday, unless it was Jane; for Sundays were their very own day for the little family, and they dreaded any who might seem like intruders.

"It is our time when we catch up in our loving for all the week," Leslie explained with a quaint smile to one girl who broadly hinted that she would not mind being asked for over Sunday. "And, besides, you mightn't like the way we keep Sunday. Everybody who comes has to go to church and Christian Endeavor with us, and enjoy our Bible-reading, singing hour around the fire; and I didn't think you would."

"Well, I like your nerve!" answered the girl; but she sat studying Leslie afterwards with a thoughtful gaze, and began to wonder whether, after all, a Sunday spent in that way might not be really interesting.

"She's a kind of a nut, isn't she?" she remarked to another friend of Leslie's.

"She's a pretty nice kind of a nut, then, Esther," was the response. "If that's a nut, we better grow a whole tree of them. I'm going down there all I can. I like 'em!"

Julia Cloud seemed to have a fertile brain for all kinds of lovely ways to while away a holiday. As the cold weather came on, winter picnics became the glory of the hour. Long walks with heavy shoes and warm sweaters and mittens were inaugurated. A kettle of hot soup straight from the fire, wrapped in a blanket and carried in a big basket, was a feature of the lunch. When the party reached a camping-spot, a fire would be built and the soup-kettle hung over an improvised crane to put on its finishing touches, while the rest of the eatables were set forth in paper plates, each portion neatly wrapped in waxed paper ready for easy handling. Sometimes big mince pies came along, and were stood on edge near the fire to get thawed out. Bean soup, corned-beef sandwiches, and hot mince pie made a hearty meal for people who had tramped ten or fifteen miles since breakfast.

Oh, how those college-fed boys and girls enjoyed these picnics, with Julia Cloud as a kind of hovering angel to minister with word or smile or in some more practical way, wherever there was need! They all called her "Cloudy Jewel" now whenever they dared, and envied those who got closest to her and told her their troubles. Many a lad or lassie brought her his or her perplexities; and often as they sat around the winter camp, perhaps on a rock brushed free from snow, she gave them sage advice wrapped up in pleasant stories that were brought in ever so incidentally. There was nothing ever like preaching about Julia Cloud; she did not feel that she knew enough to preach. And sometimes, as they walked homeward through the twilight of a long, happy afternoon, and the streaks of crimson were beginning to glow in the gray of the horizon, some one or two would lag behind and ask her deep, sweet questions about life and its meaning and its hereafter. Often they showed her their hearts as they had never shown them even to their own people, and often a word with her sent some student back to work harder and fight stronger against some subtle temptation. She became a wholesome antidote to the spirit of doubt and atheism that had crept stealthily into the college and was attacking so many and undermining what little faith in religion they had when they came there.

It came to be a great delight to many of the young college people to spend an evening around the hearth at Cloudy Villa. There never had been any trouble about that question of dancing, because they just did not do it; and there was always something else going on, some lively games, sometimes almost a "rough-house," as the boys called it, but never anything really unpleasant. Julia Cloud was "a good sport," the boys said; and the girls delighted in her. The evenings were filled with impromptu programmes thought out carefully by Julia Cloud, but proposed and exploited in the most casual manner.

"Allison, why wouldn't it be a good idea for you to act out that story we were reading the other day the next time you have some of the young people down? You and Leslie and Jane with the help of one or two others could do it, and there wouldn't be much to learn. If you all read it over once or twice more, you'd have it so you could easily extemporize. Do you know, I think there's a hidden lesson in that story that would do some of those boys and girls good if they could see it lived out, and perhaps set them to reading the book?"

Again they would be asked suddenly, soon after their arrival, each one to represent his favorite character in Shakespeare, or to reproduce some great public man so that they all could recognize him; and they would be sent up-stairs to select from a great pile of shawls, wraps, and all sorts of garments any which they needed for an improvised costume.

Another evening there would be brought forth a new game which nobody had seen, and which absorbed them all for perhaps two hours until some delicious and unique refreshments would be produced to conclude the festivities. At another time the round dining-table would be stretched to take in all its leaves, and the entire company would gather around it with uplifted thumbs and eager faces unroariously playing "up Jenkins" for an hour or two. Any little old game went well under that roof, though Julia Cloud kept a controlling mind on things, and always managed to change the game before anybody was weary of it.

Also there was much music in the little house. Allison played the violin well; two or three others who played a little at stringed and wind instruments were discovered; and often the whole company would break loose into song until people on the street halted and walked back and forth in front of the house to listen to the wild, sweet harmonies of the fresh young voices.

At the close of such an evening it was not an uncommon happening for a crowd of the frat boys to gather in a knot in front of the house and give the college yell, with a tiger at the end, and then "CLOUD! CLOUD! CLOUD!" The people living on that street got used to it, and opened their windows to listen, with eyes tender and thoughtful as they pondered on how easily this little family had caught the hearts of those college people, and were helping them to have a good time. Perhaps it entered into their minds that other people might do the same thing if they would only half try.

In return for all her kindness a number of the young people would often respond to Julia Cloud's wistful invitation to go to church, and more and more they were being drawn by twos and threes to come to the Christian Endeavor meetings in the village. It seemed as if they had but just discovered that there was such a thing, to the equal amazement of themselves and the original members of the Christian Endeavor Society, who had always responded to any such suggestions on the part of their pastor or elders with a hopeless "Oh, you can't get those college guys to do anything! They think they're it!" The feeling was gradually melting away, and a new brotherhood and sisterhood was springing up between them. It was not infrequent now for a college maiden to greet some village girl with a frank, pleasant smile, and accept invitations to lunch and dinner. And college boys were friendly and chummy with the village boys who were not fellow-students, and often took them up to their frat rooms to visit. So the two elements of the locality were coming nearer to each other, and their bond was the village Christian Endeavor Society.

So passed the first winter and spring in the little pink-and-white house. And with the first week of vacation there came visitors.

CHAPTER XXIV

"Guardy Lud" was the first visitor, just for a night and a day. He had come East for a flying business trip, and could not pass by his beloved wards without at least a glimpse. He dropped down into their midst quite unexpectedly the night before college closed, and found them with a bevy of young people at the supper-table, who opened their ranks right heartily, and took him in. He sat on the terrace in the moonlight with them afterwards, joking, telling them stories, and eating chocolates with the rest. When they gathered about the piano for a sing, he joined in with a good old tenor, surprising them all by knowing a lot of the songs they sang.

After the young people were gone he lingered, wiping his eyes, and saying, "Bless my soul!" thoughtfully. He told Julia Cloud over and over again how more than pleased he was with what she had done for his children, and insisted that her salary should be twice as large. He told her she was a big success, and should have more money at her command to do with as she pleased, and that he wanted the children to have a larger allowance during the coming year. Allison had spoken of his work among the young people of the church, and he felt that it would have been the wish of their father and mother both that the young people should give liberally toward church-work. He would see that a sum was set aside in the bank for their use in any such plans as they might have for their Christian Endeavor work.

They talked far into the night, for he had to hear all the stories of all their doings, and every minute or two one or the other of the children would break in to tell something about the other or to praise their dear Cloudy Jewel for her part in everything.

The next day they took him everywhere and showed him everything about the college and the place, introduced him to their favorite professors, at least those who were not already gone on their vacations, and took him for a long drive past their favorite haunts. Then he had to meet Jane Bristol and Howard Letchworth. Julia Cloud was greatly relieved and delighted when he set his approval upon both these young people as suitable friends for the children.

"They are both poor and earning their own living," said Julia Cloud, feeling that in view of the future and what it might contain she wanted to be entirely honest, that the weight of responsibility should not rest too heavily upon her.

"All the better for that, no doubt," said Guardy Lud thoughtfully, watching Jane Bristol's sweet smile as she talked over some committee plans with Allison. "I should say they were about as wholesome a couple of young people as could be found to match your two. Just keep 'em to that kind for a year or two more, and they'll choose that kind for life. I'm entirely satisfied with the work you're doing, Miss Cloud. I couldn't have found a better mother for 'em if I'd searched heaven, I'm sure."

And so Julia Cloud was well content to go on with her beloved work as home-maker.

But the day after Guardy Lud left, just as the three were sitting together over a great State map of roads, perfecting their plans for a wonderful vacation, which was to include a brief visit to Ellen Robinson at Sterling, a noisy Ford drew up at the door, and there was Ellen Robinson herself, with the entire family done up in linen dust-coats and peering curiously, half contemptuously, at the strange pink-and-white architecture of the many-windowed "villa."

Allison arose and went down the terrace to do the honors, showing his uncle where to drive in and put his car in the little garage, helping his aunt and the little cousins to alight.

"For mercy's sake, Julia, what a queer house you've got!" said Ellen the minute she arrived, gazing disapprovingly at the many windows and the brick terrace. "I should think 'twould take all your time to keep clean. What's the idea in making a sidewalk of your front porch? Looks as if some crazy person had built it. Couldn't you find anything better than this in the town? I saw some real pretty frame houses with gardens as we came through."

"We like this very well," said Julia Cloud with her old patient smile and the hurt flush that always accompanied her answers to her sister's contempt. "Cherry doesn't seem to mind washing windows. She likes to keep them bright. We find it very comfortable and light and airy. Come inside, and see how pretty it is."

Once inside, Ellen Robinson was somewhat awed with the strangeness of the rooms and the beauty of the furnishings, but all she said after a prolonged survey was: "Um! No paper on the wall! That's queer, isn't it? And the chimney right in the room! It looks as though they didn't have plaster enough to go around."

Leslie took the children up-stairs to wash their faces and freshen up, and Julia Cloud led her sister to the lovely guest-room that was always in perfect order.

"Well, you certainly have things well fixed," said Ellen grudgingly. "What easy little stairs! It's like child's play going up. I suppose that's one consolation for having such a little playhouse affair to live in; you don't have to climb up far. Well, we've come to stay two days if you want us. Herbert said he could spare that much time off, and we're going to stop in Thayerville on the way back and see his folks a couple of days; and that'll be a week. Now, if you don't want us, say so, and we'll go on to-night. It isn't as if we couldn't go when we like, you know."

But Julia Cloud was genuinely glad to see her sister, and said so heartily enough to satisfy even so jealous a nature as Ellen's; and so presently they were walking about the pretty rooms together, and Ellen was taking in all the beauties of the home.

"And this is your bedroom!" she paused in the middle of the rose-and-gray room, and looked about her, taking in every little detail with an eye that would put it away for remembrance long afterwards. "Well, they certainly have feathered your nest well!" she declared as her eyes rested on the luxury everywhere. "Though I don't like that painted furniture much myself," she said as she glanced at the French gray enamel of the bed; "but I suppose it's all right if that's the kind of thing you like. Was it some of their old furniture from California?"

"Oh, no," said Julia Cloud quickly, the pretty flush coming in her cheeks. "Everything was bought new except a few little bits of mahogany down-stairs. We had such fun choosing it, too. Don't you like my furniture? I love it. I hovered around it again and again; but I didn't dream of having it in my room, it was so expensive. It's real French enamel, you know, and happens to be a craze of fashion at present. I thought it was ridiculous to buy it, but Leslie insisted that it was the only thing for my room; and those crazy, extravagant children went and bought it when I had my head turned."

"You don't say!" said Ellen Robinson, putting a hard, investigating finger on the foot-board. "Well, it does seem sort of smooth. But I never thought my cane-seat chairs were much. Guess I'll have to get 'em out and varnish 'em. What's that out there, a porch?"

Julia Cloud led her out to the upper porch with its rush rugs, willow chairs, and table, and its stone wall crowned with blooming plants and trailing vines. She showed her the bird's nest in the tree overhead.

"Well," said Ellen half sourly, "I suppose there's no chance of your getting sick of it all and coming back, and I must say I don't blame you. It certainly is a contrast from the way you've lived up to now. But these children will grow up and get married, and then where will you be? I suppose you have chances here of getting married, haven't you?"

The color flamed into Julia Cloud's cheeks in good earnest now.

"I'm not looking for such chances, Ellen," she said decidedly. "I don't intend ever to marry. I'm happier as I am."

"Yes, but after these children are married what'll you do? Who'll support you?"

"Don't let that worry you, Ellen, There are other children, and I love to mother them. But as far as support is concerned I'm putting away money in the bank constantly, more than I ever expected to have all together in life; and I shall not trouble anybody for support. However, I hope to be able to work for a good many years yet, and what I'm doing now I love. Shall we go down-stairs?"

"Have Allison and Leslie got any sweethearts yet?" she asked pryingly as she followed her sister down the stairs. "I suppose they have by this time."

"They have a great many young friends, and we have beautiful times together. But you won't see many of them now. College closed last week."

For two long days Allison and Leslie devoted themselves religiously to their relatives, taking them here and there in the car, showing them over the college and the town, and trying in all the ways they knew to make them have a good time; but when at last the two days and two nights were over, and the Robinsons had piled into their car and started away with grudging thanks for the efforts in their behalf, Leslie sat on the terrace musingly; and at last quite shyly she said:

"Cloudy, dear, what makes such a difference in people? Why are some so much harder to make have a good time than others? Why, I feel as if I'd lived years since day before yesterday, and I don't feel as if they'd half enjoyed anything. I really wanted to make them happy, for I felt as if we'd taken so much from them when we took you; but I just seemed to fail, everything I did."

Julia Cloud smiled.

"I don't know what it is, dear, unless it is that some people have different ideals and standards from other people, and they can't find their pleasure the same way. Your Aunt Ellen always wanted to have a lot of people around, and liked to go to tea-parties and dress a great deal; and she never cared for reading or study or music. But I think you're mistaken about their not having had a good time. They appreciated your trying to do things for them, I know, for Aunt Ellen said to me that you were a very thoughtful girl. And the children enjoyed the victrola, especially the funny records. Herbert liked it that Allison let him drive his car when they went out. They enjoyed the eating, too, I know, even though Ellen did say she shouldn't care to have her meals cooked by a servant; she should want to be *sure* they were clean."

"Did she truly say that, Cloudy?" twinkled Leslie. "Isn't she funny?" They both broke down and laughed.

"But I'm glad they came, Cloudy. I truly am. It was nice to play with the children, and nice to have a home to show our relatives, and nicest of all to have them see you—how beautiful you are at the head of the house."

"Dear, flattering child!" said Julia Cloud lovingly. "It is so good to know you feel that way! But now here comes Allison, and we must finish up our plans for the trip and get ready to close the house for the summer."

They had a wonderful trip to mountains and lakes and seaside, staying as long as they pleased wherever they liked, and everywhere making friends and having good times; but toward the end of their trip the children began to get restless for the little pink-and-white cottage and home.

"We really ought to get back and see how the Christian Endeavor Society is getting along," said Allison one day as they glided through a little village that reminded them of home. "I don't see any place as nice as our town, do you, Cloudy? And I don't feel quite right anywhere but home on Sunday, do you? For, really, all the Christian Endeavor societies I've been to this summer acted as if their members were all away on vacations and they didn't care whether school kept or not."

And so they went home to begin another happy winter. But the very first day there came a rift in their happiness in the shape of the new professor of chemistry, a man about Julia Cloud's age, whom Ellen Robinson had met on her visit to Thayerville, and told about her sister. Ellen had suggested that maybe he could get her sister to take him to board!

To this day Julia Cloud has never decided whether Ellen really thought Julia would take a professor from the college to board, or whether she just sent him there as a joke. There was a third solution, which Julia Cloud kept in the back of her mind and only took out occasionally with an angry, troubled look when she was very much annoyed. It was that Ellen was still anxious to have her sister get married, and she had taken this way to get her acquainted with a man whom she thought a "good match". If Julia had been sure that this idea had entered into her sister's thoughts, she might have slammed the door in Professor Armitage's face that night when he had the audacity to come and ask to be taken into Cloudy Villa as a boarder.

"Why, the very idea!" said Leslie with snapping eyes. "As if we wanted a *man* always around! No, indeed! *Horrors!* Wouldn't that be *awful*?"

But Professor Armitage, like everybody else who came once to Cloudy Villa, liked it, and begged a thousand pardons for presuming, but came again and again, until even the children began to like him in a way, and did not in the least mind having him around.

But the day came at last, about the middle of the winter, or nearer to the spring, when Leslie and Allison began to realize that Professor Armitage came to see their Cloudy Jewel, and they met in solemn conclave to talk it over.

CHAPTER XXV

It was out on a lonely road in the car that they had chosen to go for their conference, where there was no chance of their being interrupted; and they whirled away through the town and out to the long stretch of whiteness in glum silence, the tears welling to overflow in Leslie's eyes.

At last they were past the bounds where they were likely to meet acquaintances, and Leslie broke forth.

"Do you really think it's true that we've got to give her up? Are you sure it has come to that, Allison? It seems perfectly preposterous!"

"Well, you know if she cares for him," said Allison gravely, "we've no right to hold on to her and spoil her life. You know it was different when it was old Pill Bowman. This is a real man."

"Care for him! How *could* she possibly care for him?" snapped Leslie. "Why, he has a wart on his nose, and he snuffs! I never thought of it before till last night, but he does; he snuffs every little while! Ugh!"

"Why, I thought you liked him, Leslie!"

"So I did until I thought he wanted Cloudy, but I can't see that! I hate him. I always thought he was about the nicest man in the faculty except the dean, and he's married; but since I got onto the idea that he wants Cloudy I can't bear the sight of him. I went way round the block to-day to keep from meeting him. He isn't nice enough for Cloudy, Allison."

"What's the matter with him? Warts and snuffing don't count if you love a person. I like him. I like him ever so much, and I think he's lonesome. He'd appreciate a home like ours. You know what a wonderful wife Cloudy would make."

Leslie fairly screamed.

"O Allison! To think you have come to it that you're *willing* to give up our lovely home, and have Cloudy go off, and we go the dear knows where, and have to board at the college or something."

"Some day we'll be getting married, too, I suppose," said Allison speculatively.

His sister flashed a wise, curious look up at him, and studied his face a minute. Then a shade came over her own once more.

"Yes, I s'pose *you* will, pretty soon. You're almost done college. But poor me! I'll have to board for two whole years more, and I'm not sure I'll ever get married. The man I like might not like me. And you may be very sure I'm not going to live on any sister-in-law, no matter how much I love her, so there!"

Allison smiled, and put his arm protectingly around his sister.

"There, kid, you needn't get excited yet awhile. It's me and thee always, no matter how many wives I have; and you won't ever have to board. But, kid, I'm not willing to give up our house and Cloudy and all; I'm just thinking that maybe we *ought* to, you know. I guess we're not pigs, are we? Cloudy has had a mighty hard life, and missed a lot of things out of it."

"Well, isn't she having 'em now, I'd like to know? I think Cloudy likes us, and wants to stay with us. I think she's just loved the house and everything about it."

"Yes, I think so, too; but this is something bigger than anything else in the world if she really cares. Don't you think we ought to give her the chance?"

"I s'pose so, if she really wants it; but how can we find out?"

"That's it; just give her the chance. When Armitage comes in, just sneak out and stay away, and let her have a little time alone with him. It isn't right, us kids always sticking around. We ought to go out or up-stairs or something."

Leslie was still for a long time; and then she heaved a big sigh, and said, "All right!" in a very small voice. As they sped on their way toward home, there was hardly a word more between them.

It was after supper that very night that Leslie, having almost frightened Julia Cloud out of her happy calm by refusing to eat much supper, went off to bed with a headache as soon as the professor came in. Allison, too, said he had to go up to the college for a book he had forgotten; and for the first time since his advent the professor had a clear evening ahead of him with Julia Cloud, without anybody else by.

But Julia Cloud was distraught, and gave him little attention at first, with an attitude of listening directed toward the floor above. Finally she gently excused herself for a moment, and hurried up to Leslie's room, where she found a very damp and tearful Leslie attempting to appear wonderfully calm.

"What is it, dear child? Has something happened?" she begged. "I know you must be sick, or you wouldn't have gone to bed so early. Please tell me what is the matter. I shall send for the doctor at once if you don't."

Then Leslie, knowing that her brother would blame her if she spoiled the test, sat up bravely, and tried to laugh, assuring her aunt that she was only tired from studying and a little stiff from playing hockey too long, and she thought it would be better to rest to-night so she could be all right in the morning.

Julia Cloud, only half reassured by this unprecedented carefulness for her health on the part of the usually careless Leslie, went down abstractedly to her professor, and wished he would go home. He was well into the midst of a most heartfelt and touching proposal of marriage before she realized what was coming.

His voice was low and pleading; and Leslie, lying breathless above, not deigning to try to listen, yet painfully aware of the change of tones, was in tortures. Then Julia Cloud's pained, gentle tones, firmly replying, and more entreaty, with brief, simple answers. Most unexpectedly, before an hour passed Leslie heard the front door open and the professor go out and pass slowly down the walk. Her heart was in her throat, beating painfully. What had happened? A quick intuition presented a possible solution. Cloudy would not leave them while they were in college, and had bid him wait, or perhaps turned him down altogether! How dear of her! And yet with quick revulsion of spirit she began to pity the poor, lonely man who could not have Cloudy when he loved her.

A moment later Julia Cloud came softly up the stairs and tiptoed into her own room, and, horror of horrors! Leslie could hear her catch her breath like soft sobbing! Did Cloudy care, then, and had she turned down a man she loved in order to stick to them and keep her promise to their guardian?

Quick as a flash she was out of bed and pattering barefoot into Julia Cloud's room.

"Cloudy! Cloudy! You are crying! What is the matter? Quick! Tell me, please!"

Julia Cloud drew the girl down beside her on the bed, and nestled her lovingly and close.

"It's nothing, dear. It's only that I had to hurt a good man. It always makes me sorry to have to hurt any one."

Leslie nestled closer, smoothed her aunt's hair, and tried to think what to say; but nothing came. She felt shy about it. Finally she put her lips up, and touched her aunt's cheek, and whispered, "Don't cry, Cloudy dear!" and just then she heard Allison's key in the lock. She sprang up, drew her bath-robe about her, and ran down to whisper to him on the stairs what had happened.

"Well, it's plain she cares," whispered Allison sadly, gravely, turning his face away from the light. "I say, Les, we ought to do something. We ought to tell her it's all right for her to go ahead."

"I can't, Allison; I'd break down and cry, I know I would. I tried up there just now, but the words wouldn't come."

"Well, then, let's write her a letter! And we'll both sign it."

"All right. You write it," choked Leslie. "I'll sign it."

They slipped over to the desk in the porch room, and Leslie cuddled into a big willow cushioned chair, and shivered and sniffed while Allison scratched away at a sheet of paper for a few minutes. Then he handed it to her to read and sign. This was what he had written:

"DEAR CLOUDY: We see just how it is, and we want you to know that we are willing. Of course it'll be awfully hard to lose you; but it's right, and we wouldn't be happy not to have you be happy; and we want you to go ahead and not think of us. We'll manage all right somehow, and we love you and want to see you happy."

Leslie dropped a great tear on the page when she signed it; but she took the soft, embroidered sleeve of her nightgown, and dabbled it dry, so that it didn't blur the writing; and then together they slipped up-stairs. Leslie went into her aunt's room in the dark, and in a queer little voice said, "Cloudy, dear, here's a note for you." Laying it in her hand, Leslie hurried into her own room, shut her door softly, and hid in the closet so that Julia Cloud would not hear her sob.

A moment later Julia Cloud came into the hall with a dear, glad ring in her voice, and called: "Children! Where are you? Come here quick, you darlings!" and they flocked into her arms like lost ducklings.

"You blessed darlings!" she said, laughing and crying at the same time. "Did you think I wanted to get married and go away from you forever? Well, you're all wrong. I'll never do that. You may get married and go away from me; but I'll never go away from you till you send me, and I won't ever get married to any one on this earth at any time! Do you understand? I don't want to get married, *ever*!"

They all went into Julia Cloud's room then, and sat down with her on her couch, one on either side of her.

"Do you really mean it, Cloudy Jewel?" asked Leslie happily. "You *don't want* to get married, not even to that nice Professor Armitage?"

"Look here! Leslie, you said he had a wart!" put in her brother.

"Now keep still, Allison. He was nice all the time; only I didn't like him to want our Cloudy. He didn't seem to be quite nice enough for her. He didn't quite fit her. But if she wanted him——"

"But I don't, Leslie," cried Julia Cloud in distress. "I *never* did!"

"Are you really true, Cloudy, dear? You're such a dear, unselfish Cloudy. How shall we ever quite be sure she isn't giving him up just for us, Allison?"

"Children, listen!" said Julia Cloud, suddenly putting a quieting hand on each young hand in her lap. "I'll tell you something I never told to a living soul."

There was that in her voice that thrilled them into silence. It was as if she suddenly opened the door of her soul and let them look in on her real self as only God saw her. Their fingers tightened in sympathy as she went on.

"A long time ago—a great many years ago—perhaps you would laugh and think me foolish if you knew how many——"

"Oh, no, Cloudy, never!" said Leslie softly; and Allison growled a dissenting note.

"Well—there was some one whom I loved—who died. That is all; only—I never could love anybody that way again. Marriage without a love like that is a desecration."

"O Cloudy! We never knew——" murmured Leslie.

"No one ever knew, dear. He was very young. We were both scarcely more than children. I was only fourteen——"

"O Cloudy! How beautiful! And you have kept it all these years! Won't you—tell us just a little about it? I think it is wonderful; don't you, Allison?"

"Yes, wonderful!" said Allison in that deep, full tone of his that revealed a man's soul growing in the boy's heart.

"There is very little to tell, dear. He was a neighbor's son. We went to school together, and sometimes took walks on Saturdays. He rode me on his sled, and helped me fasten on my skates, and carried my books; and we played together when we had time to play. Then his people moved away out West; and he kissed me good-by, and told me he was coming back for me some day. That was all there was to it except a few little letters. Then they stopped, and one day his grandmother wrote that he had been drowned saving the life of a little child. Can you understand why I want to wait and be ready for him over there where he is gone? I keep feeling God will let him come for me when my life down here is over."

There was a long silence during which the young hands gripped hers closely, and the young thoughts grew strangely wise with insight into human life and all its joys and sorrows. They were thinking out in detail just what their aunt had missed, the sweet things that every woman hopes for, and thinks about alone with God; of love, strong care, little children, and a home. She had missed it all; and yet she had its image in her heart, and had been true to her first thought of it all the years. Now, when it was offered her again, she would not give up the old love for a new, would not take what was left of life. She would wait till the morning broke and her boy met her on the other shore.

Suddenly, as they thought, strong young arms encircled her, and held her close in a dear embrace.

"Then you're ours, Cloudy, all ours, for the rest of down here, aren't you?" half whispered Leslie.

"Yes, dear, as long as you need me—*want* me," she finished.

"We shall want you always, Cloudy!" said Allison in a clear man's voice of decision. "Put that down forever, Cloudy Jewel. You are our mother from now on and we want you always."

"That is dear," said Julia Cloud; "but"—a resignation in her voice—"some day you will marry, and then you will not need me any more and I shall find something to do somewhere."

Two fierce young things rose up in arms at once.

"Put that right out of your head, Cloudy Jewel!" cried Leslie. "You shan't say it again! If I thought any man could be mean enough not to feel as I do about you, I would never marry him; so there! I would never marry anybody!"

"My wife will love you as much as I do!" said Allison with conviction. "I shall never love anybody that doesn't. You'll see!"

And so with loving arms about her and tender words of fierce assertion they convinced her at last, and the bond that held them was only strengthened by the little tension it had sustained.

Professor Armitage came no more to the little pink-and-white house; but Julia Cloud was happy with her children, and they were content together. The happy days moved on.

"I don't see how you get time for that Christian Endeavor Society of yours, Cloud," said one of the professors to Allison. "I hear you're the moving spirit in it; yet you never fall down on your class work. How do you manage it? I'd like to put some of my other students onto your ways of planning."

"Well, there's all of Sunday, you know, professor," answered Allison promptly. "I don't give so very much more time, except a half-hour here and there to a committee meeting, or now and then a social on Friday night, when I'd otherwise be fooling, anyway. My sister and I cut out the dances, and put these social parties in their place."

"But don't you have to study on Sundays?"

"*Never* do!" was the quick reply. "Made it a rule when I started in here at this college, and haven't broken it once, not even for examinations. I find I'm fresher for my work Monday morning when I make the Sabbath*real*."

The professor eyed him curiously.

"Well, that certainly is interesting," he said. "I'll have to try it. Though I don't see how I'd quite manage it. I usually have to spend the whole Sunday correcting papers."

"Save 'em up till early Monday morning, and come over to our Christian Endeavor meeting. See if it isn't worth while, and then see how much more you can do Monday morning at five o'clock, when you're really rested, than you could all day Sunday hacking at the same old job you've had all the week. I'll look for you next Sunday night. So-long!" And with a courteous wave he was off with a lacrosse stick, gliding down the campus like a wild thing. The professor stood and watched him a moment, and then turned thoughtfully up the asphalt path, pondering.

"They are a power in the college and in the community, that sister and brother," he said. "I wonder why."

Down at the church they wondered also as they came in crowds to the live Christian Endeavor meetings, and listened to the clear, ringing words of the young man who had been president before him; as they praises sounded by his admiring friends, especially the young man who had been president before him; as they saw the earnest spirit that went out to save, and had no social distinctions or classes to hinder the fraternal interest. The pastor wondered most of all, and thanked God, and told his wife that that Endeavor Society was making his church all over. He didn't know but it had converted him again, too. The session wondered as it listened to the earnest, simple gospel sermons that the pastor now preached, and saw his zeal for bringing men to the service of Christ.

Oh, they pointed out the four young people, the Clouds, Jane Bristol, and Howard Letchworth, as the moving spirits in the work; and they admitted, some of them, that prayer had made the transformation, for there were not many of the original bunch of young people who by this time had not been fully trained to understand that if you wanted anything in the spiritual world you must take time and give energy to getting acquainted with God. But, if they could have gone with some spirit guide to find out the true secret of all the wonderful spiritual growth and power of that young people's society, they must have looked in about Julia Cloud's fireplace on Sabbath afternoon, and seen the four earnest young people with their Bibles, and Julia Cloud in the midst, spending the long, beautiful hours in actual spiritual study of God's word, and then kneeling and communing with God for a little while, all of them on intimate terms with God. They were actually learning to delight themselves in the Lord. It was no wonder that other people, even outside the church and the Christian Endeavor Society, were beginning to notice the difference in the four, just as they noticed the shining of Moses's face when he came down from the mountain after communing with God.

Julia Cloud stood at the window of her rose-and-gray room one Sabbath evening after such an afternoon, watching the four children walk out into the sunset to their Christian Endeavor meeting, and smiled with a tender light in her eyes. She had come to call them her *four* children in her heart now, for they all seemed to love and need her alike; and for many a month, though they seemed not yet openly aware of it, they had been growing more and more all in all to one another; and she was glad.

She watched them as they walked. Allison ahead with Jane, earnestly discussing something. Jane's sweet, serious eyes looking up so trustfully to Allison, and he so tall and fine beside her; Leslie tripping along like a bird behind with Howard, and pointing out the colors in the sunset, which he watched only as they were reflected in her eyes.

CHAPTER XXVI

Howard Letchworth settled himself comfortably by an open window in the . express and spread out the evening paper, turning, like any true college man, first to the sporting page. He was anxious to know how his team had come out in the season's greatest contest with another larger college. He had hoped to be there to witness the game himself, and in fact the Clouds had invited him to go with them in their car, but unfortunately at the last minute a telegram came from a firm with whom he expected to be located during the summer, saying that their representative would be in the city that afternoon and would like to see him. Howard had been obliged to give up the day's pleasure and see his friends start off without him. Now, his business over, he was returning to college and having his first minute of leisure to see how the game came out.

The train was crowded, for it was just at closing time and every one was in a rush to get home. Engrossed in his paper, he noticed none of them until someone dropped, or rather sprawled, in the seat beside him, taking far more room than was really necessary, and making a lot of fuss pulling up his trousers and getting his patent leather feet adjusted to suit him around a very handsome sole-leather suitcase which he crowded unceremoniously over to Howard's side of the floor.

The intruder next addressed himself to the arrangement of a rich and striking necktie, and seemed to have no compunctions about annoying his neighbor during the process. Howard glanced up in surprise as a more strenuous knock than before jarred his paper out of focus. He saw a young fellow of about his own age with a face that would have been strikingly handsome if it had not also been bold and conceited. He had large dark eyes set off by long curling black lashes, black hair that crinkled close to his head in satiny sleek sheen, well-chiselled features, all save a loose-hung, insolent lip that gave the impression of great self-indulgence and selfishness. He was dressed with a careful regard to the fashion and with evidently no regard whatever for cost. He bore the mark at once of wealth and snobbishness. Howard, in spite of his newly-acquired desire to look upon all men as brothers, found himself disliking him with a vehemence that was out of all proportion to the occasion.

"Don't they have any pahlah cars on this road?"

The question was addressed to him in a calm, insolent tone as if he were a paid servitor of the road. He looked up amusedly and eyed the stranger pityingly:

"Not so as you'd notice it," he remarked crushingly as he turned back to his paper. "People on this road too busy to use 'em."

But the stranger did not crush easily:

"Live far out?" he asked, turning his big, bold eyes on his seatmate and calmly examining him from the toe of a well-worn shoe to the crown of a dusty old hat that Howard was trying to make last till the end of the season. When he had finished the survey his eyes travelled complacently back to his own immaculate attire, and his well-polished shoes fresh from the hands of the city station bootblack. With a well-manicured thumb and finger he flecked an imaginary bit of dust from the knee of his trousers.

Howard named the college town brusquely.

"Ah, indeed!" Another survey brief and significant this time. "I don't suppose you know any people at the college." It was scarcely a question, more like a statement of a deplorable fact. Howard was suddenly amused.

"Oh, a few," he said briefly. (He was just finishing his senior year rather brilliantly and his professors were more than proud of him.)

Another glance seemed to say: "In what capacity?" but the elegant youth finally decided to voice another question:

"Don't happen to know a fellah by the name of Cloud, I suppose? Al Cloud?"

"I've met him," said Howard with his eyes still on his paper.

"He's from my State!" announced the youth with a puff of importance. "We live next door in California. He's a regular guy, he is. Got all kinds of money coming to him. He'll be of age in a month or two now, and then you'll see him start something! He's some spender, *he* is."

Howard made no comment, but something in him revolted at the idea of talking over his friend in such company.

"I've got to hunt him up," went on the young man, not noticing that his auditor appeared uninterested. "I'm to stay with him to-night. I was to send a telegram, but didn't think of it till it was almost train time. Guess it won't make much difference. The Clouds always used to keep open house. I suppose they have a swell place out here?"

"Oh, it's quite comfortable, I believe," Howard turned over a page of the paper and fell to reading an article on the high price of sugar and the prospect of a fall.

"You ought to see their dump out in Cally. It's some mansion, believe me! There wasn't anything else in that part of the State to compare with it for miles around. And cahs! They had cahs to burn! The old man was just lousy with gold, you know; struck a rich mine years ago. His wife had a pile, too. Her father was all kinds of a millionaire and left every bit to her; and Al and his sister'll get everything. Seen anything of *her*? She ought to be a winner pretty soon. She was a peach when she was little. She's some speedy kid! We used to play together, you know, and our folks sorta fixed it up we were just made for each other and all that sorta thing, you know—but I don't know—I'm not going to be bound by any such nonsense, of course, unless I like. One doesn't want one's wife to be such an awfully good shot, fer instance, you know——!"

A great anger surged up in Howard's soul, and his jaw set with a fierce line that those who knew him well had learned to understand meant self-control under deep provocation. He would have liked nothing better than to surprise the insolent young snob with a well-directed blow in his pretty face that would have sent him sprawling in the aisle. His hands fairly twitched to give him the lesson that he needed, but he only replied with a slight inscrutable smile in one corner of his mouth:

"It *might* be inconvenient for *some people*." There an aloofness in his tone that did not encourage further remarks, but the young stranger was evidently not thin-skinned, or else he loved to hear himself babbling.

"I'm coming on heah, you know, to look this college ovah——!" he drawled. "If it suits me, I may come heah next yeah. Got fired from three institutions out West for larking, and father thought I better go East awhile. Any fun doing out this way?"

"I suppose those that go to college looking for it can find it," answered Howard noncommittally.

"Well—that's what I'm looking for. That's about all anybody goes to college for anyway, that and making a lot of friends. Believe me, it would be a beastly bore if it wasn't for that. Al Cloud used to be a lively one. I'll wager he's into everything. See much of the college people down in town—do you?" He eyed his companion patronizingly. "S'pose you get in on some of the spoahts now and then?"

"Oh, occasionally," said Howard with a twinkle in his eye. He was captain of the football team and forward in basket-ball, but it didn't seem to be necessary to mention it.

"Any fellows with any pep in them out here? I suppose there must be or Al wouldn't stay unless he's changed. He used to keep things pretty lively. That's one reason why I told dad I'd come out here. I like a place with plenty of ginger. It gets my goat to be among a lot of grinds and sissies! This is a co-ed college, isn't it? That suits me all right if the girls have any pep and aren't too straitlaced. Any place around here where you can go off and take a girl for a good dinner and a dash of life? I couldn't stand for any good-little-boy stuff. Know any place around here where you can get a drink of the real thing now and then, some place near enough to go joy-riding to, you know? I shall bring my cah of course——! One can get away with a lot more stuff if they have their own cah, you know—especially where there's girls. You can't pull off any devilment if you have to depend on hired cahs. You might get caught. I suppose they have some pretty spicy times down at the frat rooms, don't they? I understood the frats were mostly located down in the town."

Howard suddenly folded his paper, looking squarely in the limpid eyes of his seatmate for the first time, with a cold, searching, subduing gaze.

"I really couldn't say," he answered coldly.

"Oh, I s'pose you're not interested in that sort of thing, not being in college," said the other insolently. "But Al Cloud'll put me wise. He's no grind, I'll wager. He's always in for a good time, and he's such a good bluff he never gets found out. Now I, somehow, always get caught, even when I'm not the guilty one."

The boy laughed unroariously as if it were a good joke, and his weak chin seemed to grow weaker in the process.

Howard was growing angry and haughty, but it was his way to be calm when excited. He did not laugh with the stranger. Instead, he waited until the joke had lost its amusement and then he turned soberly to the youth with as patronizing an air as ever the other had worn:

"Son, you've got another guess coming to you about Allison Cloud. You'll have the surprise of your young life when you see him, I imagine. Why, he's been an A student ever since he came to this college, and he has the highest average this last semester of any man in his class. As for bluff, he's as clear as crystal, and a prince of a fellow; and if you're looking for a spot where you can bluff your way through college you better seek elsewhere. Bluff doesn't go down in *our* college. We have student government, and I happen to be chairman of the student exec. just now. You better change your tactics if you expect to remain here. Excuse me, I see a friend up at the front of the car!"

With which remarks Howard Letchworth strode across the sprawling legs of his fellow-traveller and departed up the aisle, leaving the elegant stranger to enjoy the whole seat and his own company.

Thus did Clive Terrence introduce himself to Howard Letchworth and bring dismay into the little clique of four young people who had been enjoying a most unusually perfect friendship. Howard Letchworth, as he stood the rest of the ride on the front platform of the car conversing with apparent interest with a fraternity brother, was nevertheless filled with a growing dismay. Now and then he glanced back and glared down the aisle at the elegant sprawling youth and wondered how it was that a being as insignificant as that could so upset his equilibrium. But the assured drawl of the stranger as he spoke of Leslie and called her a "speedy kid" had made him boil with rage. He carried the mood back to college with him, and sat gloomily at the table thinking the whole incident over, while the banter and chaffing went on about him unnoticed. Underneath it all there was a deep uneasiness that would not be set aside. The young man had said that the Clouds were very wealthy. That Leslie was especially so. That when she was of age she would have a vast inheritance. There had been no sign of great wealth or ostentation in their living but if that were so then there was an insuperable wall between him and her.

It was strange that the question of wealth had never come up between them. Howard had known that they were comfortably off, of course. They had a beautiful car and wore good clothes, and were always free with their entertaining, but they lived in a modest house, and never made any pretences. It had not occurred to him that they were any better off than he might be some day if he worked hard. They never talked about their circumstances. Of course, now he came to think about it, there were fine mahogany pieces of furniture in the little house and wonderful rugs and things, but they all fitted in so harmoniously with their surroundings that it never occurred to him that they might have cost a mint of money. They never cried out their price to those who saw them, they were simply the fitting thing in the fitting place, doing their service as all right-minded things both animate and inanimate in this world should do. It was the first serpent in the Eden of this wonderful friendship at Cloudy Villa and it stung the proud-spirited young man to the soul.

Alone in his room that night he finally gave up all pretence at study and faced the truth. He had been drifting in a delightful dream during the last two years, with only a vague and alluring idea of the future before him, a future in which there was no question but that Allison Cloud AND his sister Leslie should figure intimately. Now he was suddenly and roughly awakened to ask himself whether he had any right to count on all this. If these young people belonged to the favored few of the world who were rolling in wealth, wasn't it altogether likely that when they finished college they would pass out of this comradely atmosphere into a world of their own, with a new set of laws whereby to judge and choose their friends and life companions? He could not quite imagine Allison and Leslie as anything but the frank, friendly, enthusiastic comrades they had been since he had known them—and yet—he knew the world, knew what the love of money could do to a human soul, for he had seen it many times before in people he had come to love and trust who had grown selfish and forgetful as soon as money and power were put into their hands. He had to confess that it was possible. Also, his own pride forbade him to wish to force himself into a crowd where he could not hold his own and pay his part. They would simply not be in his class, at least not for many years to come, and his heart sank with desolation. It was then, and not till then, that the heart of the trouble came out and looked him in the face. It was not that he could not be in their class, that he could not keep pace with Allison Cloud and come and go in his company as freely as he had done; it was that he loved the bright-haired Leslie, the sweet-faced, eager, earnest, wonderful girl. She held his future happiness in her little rosy hand, and if she really were a rich girl he couldn't of course tell her now that he loved her, because he was a poor man. He didn't expect to stay poor always, of course, but it would be a great many years before he could ever hope to compete with anything like wealth, and during those years who might not take her from him? Was it conceivable that such a cad as that youth who had boasted himself a playmate of her childhood could possibly win her?

Howard went out and sat on the campus under a great shadowing tree. He watched a silver thread of a moon slip down between the branches and dip behind the hill, and while he sat there he went through all the desolation of a lonely life; the bitterness of having Leslie taken from him by one who was unworthy!—He persuaded himself that he loved her enough to be willing to step aside and give her up to a man who was better than himself—but this little whiffet—ugh!

The chimes on the library pealed out nine o'clock, reminding him of his work half done, yet the shadow of engulfing sorrow and loss hung over him. With a jerk he drew himself up and tried to grasp at common sense. How ridiculous of him to get up all this nightmare out of a few minutes' talk with a fellow who used to be the Clouds' old neighbor. He might not have been telling the truth. And anyhow it was a libel on friendship to distrust them all this way, as though riches were some kind of a disease like leprosy that set people apart. It wasn't his night to go down to the village, but just to dispel this nonsense and bring back his normal state of mind he would go and drop in on the Clouds for a few minutes. A sight of them all would reassure him and clear his brain for the work he must do before midnight. Leslie Cloud was very young yet, and much can happen in a year or two. He might even be in a fair way to make a fortune himself somewhere, who knew? And as for that little cad, it was nonsense to suppose he was anything to fear. Besides, it wasn't time yet to think about being married when he wasn't even out of college. He would forget it and work the harder. Of course he could never quite go back and forget that he had admitted to himself that he was in love with Leslie, but he would keep it like a precious jewel hid far in his heart, so carefully locked that not even for his own delight would he take it out to look at now at this time.

Having thus resolved, a weight seemed to have rolled from his shoulders and he sprang up and walked with a quick tread down to the village. There was a cheerful clang of victrolas, player-pianos and twanging guitars as he passed the fraternity rooms, and he went whistling on his way toward Cloudy Villa.

But as he neared the tall arched hedge, and looked eagerly for the welcome light, he saw that the big living-room windows were only lit by a soft play of firelight. Did that mean they were all sitting in the firelight around the hearth? A fearful thought of the stranger intruded just here upon his fine resolves, and to dispel it he knocked noisily on the little brass knocker.

It was very still inside, but a quick electric light responded to his knock and in a moment he could hear someone coming down-stairs to the door. His heart leaped. Could it be Leslie? Ah! He must not—yet how wonderful it was going to be to look at her this first time after really knowing his own heart in plain language. Could he keep the joy of her out of his eyes, and the wonder of her from his voice? Then the door opened and there stood Cherry in negligée of flaring rosy cotton crêpe embroidered with gorgeous peacocks, and her pigtails in eclipse behind an arrangement of cheap lace and pink ribbons.

"No, sir, Mister Howard, dey ain't none ob 'em heah! Dey got cumpney—some young fellah fum back to California way. Dey done tuk him out to see de town."

Howard's heart sank and he turned his heavy footsteps back to college. The worst fear had come to pass. Of course reason asserted itself, and he told himself that he was a fool, a perfect fool. Of course they had to be polite to an old neighbor whether they liked him or not. And what was he to presume to judge a stranger from a five-minute conversation, and turn him down so completely that he wasn't willing to have his old friends even like him? Well, he was worse than he had thought himself and something would have to be done about it.

What he did about it was to stay away from Cloudy Villa for almost a week, and when Leslie at last, after repeated efforts to get hold of him by telephone, called him up to say there was an important committee meeting at the church which he ought to attend, he excused his long absence by telling how busy he had been. Of course he had been busy, but Leslie knew that he had always been busy, and yet had found time to come in often. She was inclined to be hurt and just the least bit stand-offish. Of course if he didn't *want* to come he needn't! And she took Clive Terrence driving in the car and showed him all the wonders of the surrounding neighborhood with much more cordiality than she really felt. It was her way of bearing her hurt. At last she got Allison by himself and asked him quite casually why Howard hadn't been down. But Allison, in haste to keep an appointment with Jane, and knowing that Howard enjoyed being down as much as they wanted him, hadn't even noticed the absence yet.

"Oh, he's up to his eyes in work," responded Allison. "He's likely busy as a one-armed paper-hanger with fleas! He's a senior, you know. Wait till next year and you'll see me in the same boat!" and he hurried away whistling.

CHAPTER XXVII

Clive Terrence hung around. He calmly took it for granted that the Clouds wanted him as long as he condescended to stay. In fact, it wouldn't have troubled him whether they wanted him or not if he wanted to stay. He had discovered that Leslie was the very same kind of a "peach" which her younger days had promised her to be, and there was plenty of good fun, so he stayed. He said he wanted to see what the college was like before he made his decision, and day after day went by with apparently no plans whatever for leaving in the near future.

Julia Cloud didn't like him. She admitted that much to herself the very first evening, and for that reason she was twice as cordial to him as she might have been if she had liked him better. She reasoned that it was unfair to take a sudden dislike that way, and perhaps it was only a sign he needed a bit of their home all the more. So she made him welcome and treated him as she did any other boys who came. But more and more as the days slipped by she did not like him. At first she was a bit worried about his influence on Allison, till she saw that he merely annoyed Allison. Then she began to be annoyed by his constant attendance on Leslie. And finally she grew exceedingly restless and anxious as day succeeded day and Howard came no more. Finally, one evening just before dinner, she went to the 'phone and called up the college. It happened that she caught Howard just as he was going down to dinner. She told him they were homesick for him and there was roast lamb and green peas and strawberry shortcake for dinner, wouldn't he come? He came. Who could refuse Julia Cloud?

But the face of Clive Terrence was a study when, unannounced, Howard entered the living-room. Julia Cloud had seen him coming and quietly opened the door. Such a storm of delighted welcome as met him warmed his heart and dispelled the evil spirits that had haunted him during the week.

In the chatter of talk while they were being seated at the dinner table the visitor was almost forgotten, and he sat watching them glumly while Allison and Leslie eagerly discussed plans for some society in which they seemed to be interested. At last he grew weary of being ignored and in the first pause he languidly drawled:

"Leslie, I think you and I'll take the cah and go in town to a show this evening. I'm bored to death."

Leslie looked at him with flashing eyes and then extinguished him with her cool tone:

"Do you? Well, think again! I'm having a lovely time"—and went on talking to Howard about the senior play that was to come off the next week. It did not suit Clive in the least to be ignored, so he started in to tell about other senior plays in other colleges where he had been and quite made himself the centre of the stage, laughing at his own jokes and addressing all his remarks to Leslie until her cheeks grew hot with annoyance. She wanted so to hear what Howard and Allison were talking about in low, grave tones. She watched the strong, fine face of Howard Letchworth, and it suddenly came over her that he seemed very far away from her, like a friend who used to be, but had moved away. Something in her throat hurt, and a sinking feeling came in her heart. Like a flash it came to her that Howard Letchworth would be graduated in three more weeks, and perhaps would go away then and they would see him no more. She caught a word or two now and then as he talked to Allison that indicated that he was seriously contemplating such a possibility. Yet he had not said a word to her about it! And they had been such good friends! A grieved look began to grow around her expressive little cupid's bow of a mouth, and her big eyes grew sorrowful as she watched the two. She was not listening to Clive, who drawled on unaware of her inattention.

Suddenly Leslie became aware that Clive had risen and was standing over her with something in his hand which he had taken from his vest, something small and shining, and he was saying:

"Want to wear it, Les? Here, I'll put it on you, then everybody will think we are engaged——!"

It was his fraternity pin he was holding out with smiling assurance and the significance of his words came over her as a sentence read without comprehension will suddenly recall itself and pierce into the realization. With a stifled cry she sprang away from him.

"Mercy, no, Clive! I didn't know you were so silly. I never wear boys' fraternity pins. I think such things are too sacred to be trifled with!"

This was what she said, but she was miserably aware that Howard had turned away and picked up his hat just as Clive had leaned over her with the pin, and almost immediately he left. He had been so engrossed with his talk with Allison that he had not seemed to see her repulsion of Clive, and his manner toward her as he bade her good-night was cool and distant. All the pleasant intimacy of all the months together seemed suddenly wiped out, and Howard a grown-up stranger. She felt herself a miserably unhappy little girl.

Julia Cloud, from the advantage of the dining-room where she was doing little things, for the next day, watched the drama with a heavy heart. What had come between her children, and what could she do about it? The only comforting thing about it seemed to be that each was as unhappy as the other. Could it be that Howard Letchworth was jealous of this small-souled, spoiled son of fortune who was visiting them? Surely not. Yet what made him act in this ridiculous fashion? She felt like shaking him even while she pitied him. She half-meditated calling him back and trying to find out what was the matter, but gave it up. After all, what could she do?

Leslie, as the door closed behind Howard, turned with one dagger look at Clive, and dashed up-stairs to her room, where she locked herself in and cried till her eyes were too swollen for study; but she only told Julia Cloud, when she came up gently to inquire, that she had a bad headache and wanted to go to bed.

Julia Cloud, kneeling beside her gray couch a little later, laying all her troubles on the One who was her strength, found it hard not to emphasize her dislike even in prayer toward the useless little excuse for a young man who was lolling down-stairs reading a novel and smoking innumerable cigarettes in spite of her expressed wish to the contrary.

The first Sunday after young Terrence's arrival it rained and was very dismal and cold for spring. Howard had been asked to go to a nearby Reform School for the afternoon and speak to the boys, and Jane was caring for a little child whose mother was ill in the hospital. Leslie was unhappy and restless, wandering from window to window looking out. Their guest had chosen to remain in bed that morning, so relieving them from the necessity of trying to get him to go to church, but he was on hand for lunch in immaculate attire, apparently ready for a holiday. There was a cozy fire on the hearth, and he lolled luxuriously in an arm-chair seemingly well pleased with himself and all the world. Julia Cloud wondered just what she would better do about the afternoon hour with this uncongenial guest on hand, but Leslie and Allison, after a hasty whispered consultation in the dining-room with numerous dubious glances toward the guest, ending in wry faces, came and settled down with their Bibles as usual. There was a loyalty in the quiet act that almost brought the tears to Julia Cloud's eyes, and she rewarded them with a loving, understanding smile.

But when the guest was asked to join the little circle he only stared in amazement. He had no idea of trying to conform to their habits.

"Thanks! No! I hate reading aloud. Books always bore me anyway. The *Bible*! Oh *Heck*! NO! Count me out!"

And he swung one leg over the arm of his chair, and picked up the Sunday illustrated supplement which he had gone out and purchased, and which was now strewn all about the floor. He continued for sometime to rattle the paper and whistle in a low tone rudely while the reading went on, then he threw down his paper and lighted a cigarette. But that did not seem to soothe his nerves sufficiently, so he strolled over to the piano and began to drum bits of popular airs and sing in a high nasal tone that he was pleased to call "whiskey tenor." Julia Cloud, with a despairing glance at him, finally closed her book and suggested that they had read enough for that day, and the little audience drifted away unhappily to their rooms. Leslie did not come down again all the afternoon until just time for Christian Endeavor. Young Terrence by this time was reduced to almost affability, and looked up hopefully. He was about to propose a game of cards, but when he saw Leslie attired in raincoat and hat he stared:

"Great Scott! You don't have to go up to college to-night, do you? It's raining cats and dogs!"

"Allison and I are going to Christian Endeavor," answered Leslie quietly. "Would you like to go?" She had been trying to school herself to give this invitation because she thought she ought to, but she hoped sincerely it would not be accepted. It seemed as if she could not bear to have the whole day spoiled.

For answer young Terrence laughed extravagantly:

"Christian Endeavor! What's the little old idea?"

"Better come and find out," said Allison, coming down-stairs just then. "Ready, Leslie? We'll have to hustle. It's getting late."

In alarm at the idea of spending any more time alone the young man arose most unexpectedly.

"Oh, sure! I'll go! Anything for a little fun!" and he joined them in a moment more, clad in rubber coat and storm hat.

Leslie could scarcely keep back the tears as she walked beside him through the dark street, not listening to his boasting about riding the waves in Hawaii. Suppose Howard was at meeting! He would think—what would he think?

And of course Howard was at the meeting that night, for he happened to be the leader. Leslie's cheeks burned as she sat down and saw that Clive had manœuvred to sit beside her. She tried to catch Howard's eyes and fling a greeting to him, but he seemed not to see his old friends and to be utterly absorbed in hunting up hymns.

The first song had scarcely died away before Clive began a conversation with a low growl, making remarks of what he apparently considered a comic nature about everything and everybody in the room, with a distinctness that made them entirely audible to those seated around them. Leslie's cheeks flamed and her eyes flashed angrily, but he only seemed to enjoy it the more, and kept on with his running commentary.

"For pity's sake, Clive, keep still, can't you?" whispered Leslie anxiously. "They will think you never had any bringing up!"

"I should worry!" shrugged the amiable Clive comically with a motion of his handsome shoulders that sent two susceptible young things near him into a series of poorly suppressed giggles. Clive looked up and gravely winked at them, and the two bent down their heads in sudden hopeless mirth. Clive was delighted. He was having a grand time. He could see that the leader was annoyed and disgusted. This was balm to his bored soul. He made more remarks under cover of a bowed head during the prayer, and stole glances at the two giggling neighbors. Then he nudged Leslie and endeavored to get her to join in the mirth. Poor Leslie with her burning cheeks, her brimming eyes, and her angry heart! Her last vision of the leader as she bowed her head had been a haughty, annoyed glance in their direction as he said: "Let us pray." She felt that she could not stand another minute of this torture. Almost she felt she must get up and go out, and she made a hasty little movement to carry out the impulse, and then suddenly it came to her that if she went Clive would follow her, and it would look to Howard as if she had created the disturbance and they had gone off together to have a good time. So she settled down to endure the rest of the meeting, lifting miserable eyes of appeal to Allison as soon as the prayer was ended. If only there had been a seat vacant up front somewhere, a single seat with no other near it, where her tormentor could not follow, she would have gone to it swiftly, but the seats were all filled and there was nothing to do but sit still and frown her disapproval. Perhaps Allison might have done something to quiet the guest if he had noticed, but Allison was, at the moment of Leslie's appeal, deeply wrapped in setting down a few items which must be announced, and he almost immediately arose and went forward with his slip of paper and held a whispered converse with Howard Letchworth during the hymn that followed, afterwards taking a chair down from the platform and placing it beside the chairman of an important committee that he might consult with him about something. During this sudden move on the part of Allison, Clive Terrence did have his attention turned aside somewhat from his mischief-making, for he was watching Allison with an amazed expression. Not anything that he had seen since coming to the town had so astonished him as to see this young man of wealth and position and undoubted strength of will and purpose, get up in a church and go forward as if he had some business in the affair. He sat up, with his loose, handsome under lip half-dropped in surprise, and watched Allison, with a curious startled expression, and when a moment later the leader said quietly: "Our president has a message for us" and Allison arose and faced the crowded room with an eager, spirited, interested look on his face, and began to talk earnestly, outlining a plan for a deeper spiritual life among the members, his expression was one of utter bewilderment, as if he suddenly saw trees walking about the streets or inanimate objects beginning to show signs of intellect. He was thinking that

Allison Cloud certainly had changed, and was wondering what on earth had brought it about. It couldn't be any line that his guardian had on him, for he was a thousand miles away. Was it that little, quiet, insipid mouse of an aunt that had done it? She must be rich or something, the way the brother and sister seemed to be tied to her apron-string. Where did Al Cloud get that line of talk he was handing out, anyway? Why, he talked about God as if He were an intimate friend of his, and spoke of prayer and Bible reading in the way common, ordinary people talked of going to breakfast or eating candy, as if they were necessary and pleasurable acts. Why, it was inconceivable! What was he doing it for? There must be a reason.

For fully five minutes he sat quiet in puzzled thought, watching this strange gathering, gradually taking it in that they were all taking part in the proceedings and that they seemed interested and eager. Why, even those two giggling girls who had "fallen" so readily for his nonsense had sobered down and one read a verse from the Bible while the other repeated a verse of poetry! He turned and blinked at them in wonder. What had so influenced them that they all fell in line and performed their part as if it were being rehearsed for his benefit? What was the motive power? The query interested him to the point of good behavior all through the remainder of the meeting, and while he was standing waiting for Allison and Leslie at the close. It seemed that somehow there was a real interest, for they lingered as if there were vital matters to discuss, and Leslie was the centre of a group of quite common-looking girls. It must be some sort of social settlement work or other connected with the church and someone had induced these two who were to his thinking of a higher order of being by right of wealth and social position, to take an interest and "run" this society or whatever it was. He could not make it out at all. He was much disgusted that the young people insisted on staying to church and had a bad hour living through it, although he was surprised to find it as interesting as it was. The minister seemed quite human and they had a great deal of singing. Still it was all a bore, of course. He found a great many things in life to bore him.

As soon as he and Allison were out on the street he broached the subject:

"What's the little old idea, old man? Are you a sort of grand mogul or high priest or something to this mob? And what do you get out of it?"

Allison turned and looked solemnly at him through the dark, and answered with a kind of glow in his voice that seemed to lighten his face and puzzled the questioner more than all that had gone before:

"I'm just one of them, son, and it happens to be my turn just now to be presiding officer; but I get out of it more than I ever got out of anything in life before."

"Oh!" said Clive inanely, quite at a loss to know what he meant.

"I never knew before that people could know God personally, be His pal sort of, you know, and work with Him, and it's been GREAT!" added Allison.

"Oh!" said Clive once more, quite weakly, not knowing what else to say, and they walked on for almost a block without speaking another word. Clive was thinking that certainly Allison had changed, as that unmannerly chump on the train had said. Changed most perplexingly and peculiarly. But Allison had forgotten almost that Clive was there. He was thinking over some good news he had to tell Jane about a protégé of hers who had taken a shy part in the meeting, and wondering if he could get away for a few minutes to run up and tell her or if it would be better to call her up on the 'phone.

Howard Letchworth had not come home with them. He had whispered a hurried excuse to Allison about someone he had to see up at college before they left for the city, and hurried away at the close of the meeting, and Leslie with a choking feeling in her throat and burning tears held back from her eyes by mighty effort, announced to Allison that she wasn't coming home just now, she was going to stay for a little after prayer meeting the Lookout Committee were having. She would walk home with the Martins, who went right by their door. For Leslie was done with Clive Terrence and she wanted him to understand it. So Clive was landed at home with Julia Cloud for companion, who had not gone to church on account of staying to nurse Cherry, who had taken a bad cold and needed medicine. Allison hurried away to give Jane her message, and there was nothing for Clive to do but to go to bed and resolve never to spend another Sunday in such boredom. For he "couldn't see" hobnobbing with an "old woman," as he called Julia Cloud, the way the others seemed entirely willing to do. What was she anyway but some poor relation likely who was acting as housekeeper? But at least for once in his life Clive Terrence realized that there was such a thing in the world as a live religion and a few people who held to it and loved it and *enjoyed* it. He couldn't understand it, but he had to admit it, although he was convinced that behind it all there must be some ulterior motive or those people would never bother themselves to that extent.

But Leslie came home from the church with a heavy heart and crept up to her room with bravely cheerful smiles to deceive Julia Cloud; and then cried herself to sleep; while Julia Cloud, wise-eyed, kept her own counsel and carried her perplexities to the throne of God.

CHAPTER XXVIII

During the next three days there were stirring times, and Leslie, even with a heavy heart, was kept busy. Clive Terrence was ignored as utterly as if he had been a fly on the ceiling, and Leslie managed to keep every minute full. Moreover, her mind was so much occupied with other things that she had not time to realize how fully she was cutting their guest out of sight of her, nor how utterly amazed it made him. He was not accustomed to being ignored by young ladies, even though they were both beautiful and rich. He felt that he was quite ornamental himself, and had plenty of money, too, and he could not brook any such treatment. So he set himself to procure revenge by going hot-foot after the Freshman "vamp"—who, to tell the truth, was much more in his style than Leslie and quite, *quite* willing—though Leslie, dear child, was too absorbed to know it.

She came home at lunchtime a bit late and called Allison from the table to give him an excited account in a low tone of something that had happened that morning. Julia Cloud, from her vantage point at the head of the table, could see the flash in her eye and the brilliant flush of the soft cheeks as she talked and wondered what new trouble had come to the dear child. Then she noted the sudden stern set of Allison's jaw and the squaring of shoulder as he listened and questioned. Meanwhile she passed Clive Terrence the muffins and jam, and urged more iced-tea and a hot, stuffed potato, and kept up a pleasant hum of talk so that the excited words should not be heard in the dining-room.

"Jane's had a perfectly terrible time!" had been Leslie's opening sentence, "and we've got to do something about it! Those little *cats* in the AOU have done the meanest thing you can think of. Jane looked just *crushed*! They've hauled up that old stuff about her father being a forger and urged it as a reason that she shouldn't be made treasurer in place of Anne Dallas—who is leaving on account of the death of her father and she has to go home and take care of her little sisters—and JANE HEARD THEM!"

A low growl of indignation reached Julia Cloud's ears from Allison, who squared his shoulders into position for immediate action.

"They said——" went on Leslie in excited whisper. "They said that since we had such a large sum to look out for now that the subscriptions for the sorority house were coming in, we should put in a treasurer of tried and true integrity. Yes, they used just those words, *tried and true integrity*! Think of it! And OUR JANE! The idea! The catty little snobs! The jealous little—*cats*! No, it wasn't Eugenia Frazer who *said* it, it was Eunice Brice—but I'm certain she was at the bottom of it, for she sat with her nice smug little painted face as sweet and complacent as an angel, all the time it was going on, and she *seconded the motion*! Just like that! With aSMILE, too! She said she fully agreed with what Miss Brice had said. *Agreed!* H'm! As if every one didn't know she had started it, and got it all fixed up with enough girls to carry the motion before the rest of us got down from an exam. Yes, they had it thought out as carefully as that! They knew all the sophomore girls would be up in that exam. till almost twelve o'clock, for it's always as long as the moral law, anything with Professor Crabbs—and they counted up and had just enough to a name to carry their motion. They even got Marian Hobbs to cut a class to get there. They hadn't counted on my getting in in time to hear, I guess, or else they didn't care. Perhaps they wanted me to hear it all; I'm sure I don't know. I suppose that must have been it. They thought perhaps I'd tell *you* and that would stop you from going with Jane. You know Eugenia and Eunice are both crazy about you, especially Eugenia——!"

An impatient exclamation from Allison reached the dining-room thunderously:

"Where was Jane?" Julia Cloud caught that anxious question, and then Clive, who had evidently heard also, roused himself to ask a question:

"Who is this *Jane* person they talk so much about? I don't seem to have seen her! Where is she?"

"She is Miss Bristol," said Julia Cloud, stiffening just a little at the young fellow's tone of insolence. "She is in college and very busy, but has been unusually busy since you have been here because she is caring for a little child whose mother has been very ill."

"Oh!—You mean she's a sort of sehvant?"—He drawled the question most offensively, and Julia Cloud had a sudden ridiculous impulse to seize his sleek shoulder and shake him. Instead she only smiled and quoted a Bible verse: "I have seen servants upon horses, and princes walking as servants upon the earth."

Clive eyed her with a puzzled expression:

"I don't getcha!" he answered finally, but Julia Cloud made no further comment than to pass him a second cup of coffee. She could hear the soft excited whispers still going on in the living-room and she longed to fly in there and leave this ill-bred guest to his own devices, for she knew something must have happened to trouble her children, and that if this intruder were not present she would be at once taken into their confidence. Still she had to sit and smile and keep him from hearing them.

Leslie was talking more softly now, with cautious looks toward the dining-room.

"Jane had finished her exam. and hurried down because she thought there would be a lot of business and she wanted Emily Reeder to be put in treasurer and was trying to work it, and hadn't an idea Alice and I were working it to put *her* in. We didn't think she would get there and meant to have it all finished before she came, but someone turned around and gave a queer little cough just as Eunice finished her nasty speech, and we all turned quickly and there in the open door stood Jane, as white as a sheet, with her great, big blue eyes looking black as coals and such suffering I never saw in a human face—and she just stood and looked at them all, a hurt, loving, searching look, as if she was reading their souls, and no one spoke nor moved, only Eunice, who got very red, and

Eugenia, who straightened up and got haughty and hateful, looking as if she was glad Jane heard it all. She had a kind of glitter in her eyes, like triumph—and it was very still for a whole minute, and then Jane put out her hands in a little, quick, pleading motion and turned away quickly and was gone——"

"And what did you do?" Allison's tone had hope, threat, condemnation and praise all held in abeyance on her answer.

Leslie drew herself up eagerly, her eyes shining.

"I——? Oh—I wanted to run after her and comfort her, but I had something else to do. I jumped up and offered my resignation to the AOU, and said I wished to withdraw my subscription to the Sorority House, that I couldn't have anything to do with a bunch of girls that would stand for a thing as contemptible and mean as that."

"Of course!" said Allison with a proud look at his sister.

"And Phoebe Kemp jumped up and withdrew hers until they all apologized to Jane, and then Alice Lowe said she'd have to withdraw hers, too—she's given the highest amount subscribed, you know; she has slews of money all in her own right, because she's of age, you know—and then the girls began to get scared and Elsie Dare got right up and said she thought there had been some kind of a mistake—a blunder—they mustn't get excited—they must begin all over, and somebody must go after Jane and bring her back and explain—as if there was any way to explain a bold, bare insult like that!—and they sent a committee after her. They wanted me to go, but I declined to go in their name. I said I had handed in my resignation and I wasn't one of them any more, and they might send somebody who would better represent them, and they said they hadn't accepted my resignation and a lot of stuff, but they sent off a committee to find Jane, and they tried to think up something quickly to say to her, and they got Eunice Brice to crying and made Eugenia real mad so the powder came off her nose from rubbing it so much, and I came away. I've been hunting for Jane for half an hour, but I can't find her in any of the places she always is, and I thought I better come and tell you——"

"That's right. I'll find her——" Allison made one step to the hat-rack and took his hat, then raising his voice: "Cloudy, I've been called away on business suddenly. Don't bother keeping anything for me, I've had all I want——" and he was gone.

Julia Cloud gave a glance at Allison's plate and saw that he had scarcely touched his lunch, and she sighed as she heard Leslie run quickly up the stairs and shut the door of her own room. Was Leslie going to spend the afternoon in weeping?

But Leslie was down again in a moment and standing in the doorway, her curls tumbled, her eyes bright and anxious, an indignant little set of lips and chin giving her a worried expression.

"Jewel, dear, I've got to go; there's something important on—I'll tell you about it all when I get back. No, please, I couldn't eat now. You get Cherry to save me some strawberry shortcake." And she was off like a breeze and out of sight.

"Wait a minute, Leslie, I'll go up with you," called Clive with his mouth full of shortcake and cream, but Leslie was already whirling down the street like the wind. Allison had taken the car, so there was nothing left for Clive to do but finish his shortcake and think up some form of amusement with the Freshman vamp for the afternoon.

Allison, meantime, had made a straight dash for the college and sent a message up to Jane that he must see her at once on very important business. After what seemed to him an endless wait, word came down that Jane was not in her room and her roommate knew nothing of her whereabouts. Allison made a wild dive for his car and drove to every one of the places where Jane sometimes went to help out with the children when their mothers were particularly busy, but no Jane materialized. He drove madly back to the college, forgetting his usual cool philosophy of life and fancying all sorts of terrible things that might have happened to Jane. He swept past Eugenia Frazer without even seeing her and brought up in front of the office once more, intending to send up and see if Jane had yet returned, but on the steps stood Leslie waiting for him.

"She's gone to the woods up above the old quarry!" she said anxiously. "I've just found out. Benny, the kitchen boy, told me. He says he saw her go out between Chemistry Hall and the Boys' Gym. about an hour ago. She must have gone right after she left the meeting. Nobody seems to have seen her since. Nobody but Benny knows anything about her going to the woods and I gave him some money and told him not to say anything about it if anyone asked. I was just going to hunt her——"

"That's all right, kid! You take the car and follow up the road. I'll go through the woods and look for her——!" said Allison, springing out.

"You will be careful, won't you? You know that quarry is terribly deep——"

"I *know*!" said Allison, his tone showing his own anxiety. "And Jane hasn't scrambled around here as much as we have; she hasn't had the time. And there is so much undergrowth close up to the edge, one could come on it unaware—especially if one was excited, and not paying attention——! I better beat it! Jump in and drive me around college and I'll get off at the gym."

Leslie sprang in and Allison stood on the running-board. His sister cast a wistful glance at him as she started the car.

"Allison—I think maybe you needn't worry——" she said softly. "You know Jane is—REAL! She isn't weak like some people. She won't go all to pieces like—well, like I would. God means something to her, you know."

"I know!" said Allison gravely, gently. "Thank you, kid! Well. I get off here. Meet me at the top of the second hill in half an hour, and hang around there for a bit. I may whistle, see? So long."

He dashed off between the buildings and disappeared between the trees in the edge of the woods. Leslie whirled off down the drive to the street. As she passed the big stone gateway, ivy garlanded and sweet with climbing roses, three seniors turned into the drive, and the foremost of the three was Howard Letchworth. Her heart leaped up with joy that here was someone who would understand and sympathize, and she put her foot to the brake to slow down with a light of welcome in her eyes, but before she could stop he had lifted his hat and passed on with the others as if he were just anyone. Of course he had not seen her intention, did not realize that she wanted to speak with him, yet it hurt her. A week or two before she would have called after him, or even backed the car to catch him, but now something froze within her and with her heart beating wildly, and tears scorching her eyes, she put on speed and whirled away up the hill. It seemed to her that all her lovely world was breaking into pieces under her feet. If it had not been that she was worried about Jane, she would have been tempted to abandon everything and rush off in some wild way by herself, anywhere to be alone and face the ache in her heart. It was such a torrent of deep-mingled feelings, hurt pride and anger, humiliation, and pain—all these words rushed through her mind, but there was something else besides, something that ought to have been beautiful and wonderful, and was only shame and pain, and she had not yet come to the point where she was willing to call that something by name. She knew that soon she must face the truth and have it out with herself, and so her cheeks flamed and paled, and the tears scorched and hurt in her eyes and throat, and she tried to put it all away and think about Jane, poor hurt Jane. Jane gone into the woods to have it but with herself. But Jane was strong and Jane trusted in God. Her God was strong, too! Jane would come through only the sweeter. But what would become of her—little, fiery, tempestuous Leslie, who always did the wrong thing first and was sorry afterwards, and who forgot God when she needed Him most? These thoughts flitted like visions through her brain while she put on all speed and tore away up the hill at a much faster rate than she had any business to do. But the road was clear ahead of her and there was some relief in flying along through space this way. It seemed to clear the mists from her brain, and cool down her throbbing pulses. Yet just when she would think she had control of her thoughts, that stern, distant expression on Howard's face would come between her and the afternoon brightness, and back would roll the trouble with renewed vigor. What a world this was anyway and why did people have to live? Just trouble, trouble, trouble, everywhere! And who would have thought there would come trouble between her and Howard, such good friends as they had been now almost two years—two wonderful years! And again her weary brain would beat over the question, what had been the matter? What made Howard act that way? Surely nothing she could have done.

CHAPTER XXIX

Meantime Allison was dashing over fallen trees, climbing rocks, and pushing his way between tangled vines and close-grown laurel, up and up through the college woods, and across country in the direction of the quarry, a still, wonderful place like a cathedral, with a deep, dark pool at the bottom of the massive stone walls. There were over-arching pines, hemlocks, and oaks for vaulted roof with the fresco of sky and flying cloud between. It was a wonderful place. Once when they had climbed there together and stood for a long time in silence watching the shadows on the deep pool below, looking up to the arching green, and listening to the praisings of a song sparrow up above in some hidden choir, Jane had said that this was a place to come and worship—or to come when one was in trouble! A place where one might meet God! He had looked down at her sweet face upturned searching for the little thrilling singer, and had thought how sweet and wonderful she was, and how he wanted to tell her so, and would some day, but must not just yet. He hadn't thought much about what she was saying—but now it came back—and he knew that she must have gone here with her trouble.

He need not have worried about the quarry and the deep, dark pool. He kept telling himself all the way up that he need not, but when he reached the top and came in sight of her he knew it. Knew also that he had been *sure* of it all along.

She was sitting on a great fallen log, quietly, calmly, with her back against an old gnarled branch that rose in a convenient way, and her head was thrown back and up as if she were seeing wonderful visions somewhere among the green, and the blue and white above. It was as if she had reached a higher plane where earthly annoyances do not come, and felt it good to be there. There was almost a smile on her beautiful lips, a strong, sweet, wistful smile. She had not been looking down at the deep, treacherous pool at all. She had been looking *up* and her strength had come upon her so. For one long instant the young man paused and lifted his hat, watching her in a kind of awe. Her face almost seemed to shine as if she had been talking with God. He remembered dimly the story of Moses on the Mount talking with God. He hesitated almost to intrude upon a solitude so fine and wonderful. Then in relief and eagerness he spoke her name:

"Jane!"

She turned and looked at him and her face lit up with joy:

"Oh! It is you! Why—how did you happen——?"

"I came to find you, Jane. Leslie told me everything and I have hunted everywhere. But when you were not at college I somehow knew you would be here. I wanted to find you—and—enfold you, Jane—wrap you around somehow with my love and care if you will let me, so that nothing like that can ever hurt you again. I love you, Jane. I suppose I'm a little previous and all that, being only a kid, as it were, and neither of us out of college yet, but I shan't change, and I'll be hanged if I see why it isn't all right for me to have the right to protect you against such annoyances as this——"

He was beside her on the log now, his face burning eagerly with deep feeling, one arm protectingly behind her, the other hand laid strongly, possessively over the small folded hands in her lap.

"Perhaps I'm taking a whole lot for granted," he said humbly. "Perhaps you don't love me—can't even like me the way I hoped you do. Oh, Jane, speak quick, and tell me! Darling, can you ever love me enough? You haven't drawn your hands away! Look up and let me read your eyes, please——"

No, she had not drawn her hands away, and she did not shrink from his supporting arm—and she was the kind of girl who would not have allowed such familiarities *unless*—Ah! She had lifted her eyes and there was something blindingly beautiful in them, and tears—great wonderful tears, so sweet and misty that they made him glad with a thrill of beautiful pain! Her lips were trembling. He longed to kiss her, yet knew he must wait until he had her permission——

"Allison! Listen! You are dear—*wonderful*—but you don't know a thing about me!"

"I know all I want to know, and that is a great deal, you darling, you!" And now he did kiss her, and drew her close into his arms and would not let her go even when she struggled gently.

"Allison, listen. *Listen*—please! I must tell you! *Wait*——!"

She put her hands against his breast and pushed herself back away from him where she could look in his face.

"Please, you *must* let me go and listen to what I have to say!"

"I'll let you go when you tell me yes or no, Jane. Do you, can you love me? I must know that first. Then you shall have your way."

Jane's eyes did not falter. She looked at him, "You promised, you know——!"

"Yes, Allison—I love you—but—*NO!* You must *not* kiss me again. You must let me go, and listen—You promised, you know——!"

Allison's arms dropped away from her, but his eyes held her in a long look of joy.

"All right, darling, go to it"—he said with a joyous sound in his voice—"I can stand anything now, I know. It seems too good to be true and it's enough for me. But hurry! A fellow can't wait forever."

"No, Allison, you must sit back and be serious. It isn't really *happy*, you know—what I have to tell you——!"

Allison became grave at once.

"All right, Jane, only I can't imagine anything terrible enough to stop this happiness of mine unless you're already married—and have been concealing it from us all this time——!"

In spite of herself Jane laughed at that, and Allison breathed more freely now the tenseness was gone out of her voice. His hands went out and grasped hers.

"At least I can do this," he pleaded, and Jane lifted her eyes, now serious again, and smiled tenderly, letting her hands stay in his passively.

"Listen, Allison—my father!"

"I know, Jane, dear—I heard it long ago. Your father was a forger! What do you suppose I care? He probably had some overpowering temptation and yielded, never dreaming but he would be able to make it right. You can't make me believe that any parent of *yours* was actually bad! And besides, if he was, it wouldn't be *you*——"

"Allison! Listen!" broke in Jane gravely, stopping the torrent of words with which he was attempting to silence her. "It isn't what you think at all. My father *wasn't* a forger! He was a good man!"

"He wasn't!" exclaimed Allison joyously. "Then what in thunder? Why didn't you tell 'em so, Jane?" He tried to draw her to him, but she still resisted.

"That's just it, Allison, I can't. I *never* can——"

"Well, then *I* will! You shan't have a thing like that hanging over you——!"

"But that is just what you *must not do*. And you *can't* do it, either, if I don't tell you about it, for you wouldn't have a thing to say, nor any way to prove it. And I won't tell you, Allison, ever, unless you will promise——!"

Allison was sobered in an instant.

"Jane, don't you know me well enough to be sure I would not betray any confidence you put in me?"

"I thought so——" said Jane, smiling through her tears.

"Dear!" said Allison in a tone that was a caress, full of longing and sympathy.

Jane sat up bravely and began her story.

405

"When I was twelve years old my mother died. That left father and me alone, and we became very close comrades indeed. He was a wonderful father!"

Allison's fingers answered with a warm pressure of sympathy and interest.

"He was father and mother both to me. And more and more we grew to confide in one another. I was interested in all his business, and used to amuse myself asking him about things at the office when he came home, the way mother used to do when she was with us. He used to talk over all my school friends and interests and we had beautiful times together. My father had a friend—a man who had grown up with him, lived next door and went to school with him when he was a boy. He was younger than father, and—well, not so serious. Father didn't always approve of what he did and used to urge him to do differently. He lived in the same suburb with us, and his wife had been a friend of mother's. She was a sweet little child-like woman, very pretty, and an invalid. They had one daughter, a girl about my age, and when we were children we used to play together, but as we grew older mother didn't care for us to be together much. She thought—it was better for us not to—and as the years went by we didn't have much to do with one another. Her father was the only one who kept up the acquaintance, and sometimes I used to think he worried my father every time he came to the house. One day when I was about fourteen he came in the afternoon just after I got home from school and said he wanted to see father as soon as he came home. Couldn't I telephone father and ask him to come home at once, that there was someone there wanting to see him on important business? He finally called him up himself and when father got there they went into a room by themselves and talked until late into the night. When at last Mr.—that is—the *man*, went away, father did not go to bed but walked up and down the floor in his study all night long. Toward morning I could not stand it any longer. I knew my father was in trouble. So I went down to him, and when I saw him I was terribly frightened. His face was white and drawn and his eyes burned like coals of fire. He looked at me with a look that I never shall forget. He took me in his arms and lifted up my face, a way he often had when he was in earnest, and he seemed to be looking down into my very soul. 'Little girl,' he said, 'we're in deep trouble. I don't know whether I've done right or not.' There was something in his voice that made me tremble all over, and he saw I was frightened and tried to be calm himself. 'Janie,' he said—he always called me Janie when he was deeply moved— 'Janie, it may hit hardest on you, and oh, I meant your life to be so safe and happy!'

"I tried to tell him it didn't matter about me, and for him not to be troubled, but he went on telling about it. It seems the father of this man had once done a great deal for my father when he was in a very trying situation, and father always felt an obligation to look after the son. Indeed, he had promised when the old man was dying that he would be a brother to him no matter what happened. And now the son had been speculating and got deep into debt. He had formed some kind of stock company, something to do with Western land and mines. I never fully understood it all, but there had been a lot of fraudulent dealing, although father only suspected that at the time, but anyway, everything was going to fall through and the man was going to be brought up in disgrace before the world if somebody didn't help him out. And father felt obliged to stand by him. Of course, he did not know how bad it was, because the man had not told him all the truth, but father had taken over the obligations of the whole thing. He thought he might be able to pull the thing out of trouble by putting a good deal of his own money into it, and make it a fair and square proposition for all the stockholders without their ever finding out that everything had been on the verge of going to pieces. You see the man had put it up to father very eloquently that his wife was very ill in the hospital and, if anything should happen to him and he were arrested it could not be kept from her and she would die. It's true she was very critically ill, had just been through a severe operation, and was very frail indeed. Father felt it was up to him to shoulder the whole responsibility, although, of course, he felt that the man richly deserved the law to the full. Nevertheless, because of his promise he stood by him.

"That night the man was killed in an automobile accident soon after leaving our house, and when it developed that the business was built on a rotten foundation, and that father was in partnership—you see the man had been very wily and had his papers all fixed up so that it looked as if father had been a silent partner from the beginning—everything came back on father, and he found there were overwhelming debts that he had not been told about, although he supposed he had sifted the business to the foundation and understood it all before he made the agreement to help him. Perhaps if the man had lived he would have been able to carry his crooked dealings through and save the whole thing, with what help father had given him, and neither father nor the world would ever have found out—I don't know.—But anyway, his dying just then made the whole thing fall in ruins, and right on top of father. But even that we could have stood. We didn't care so much about money. Father was well off, and he found that if he put in everything he could satisfy the creditors, and pay off everything, and he had courage enough to be planning to start all over again. But suddenly it turned out that there had been a check forged for a large amount and it all looked as if father had done it. I can't go into the details now, but we were suddenly face to face with the fact that there was no evidence to prove that he had not been a hypocrite all these years except his own life. We thought for a few days that of course that would put him beyond suspicion—but do you know, the world is very hard. One of father's best friends—one he thought was a friend—came to him and offered to go bail for him for my sake if he would just tell him the whole truth and own up. There was only one way and that was to go to the man's wife and try to get certain papers which father knew were in existence because he had seen them, and which he had supposed were left in his own safe the night the man talked with him, but which could not be found. As the wife had just been brought back from the hospital and was still in a very critical condition, father would not do more than ask if he might go through the house and search. And that woman sent back a very indignant refusal, charging father with having been at the bottom of her husband's failure, and even the cause of his death, and telling him he had pauperized her and her little helpless daughter. And the daughter began treating me as a stranger whenever we chanced to meet——"

Allison's face darkened and his eyes looked stern and hard. He said something under his breath angrily. Jane couldn't catch the words, but he drew her close in his arms and held her tenderly:

"And were those papers never found, dear?" he asked after a moment:

"Yes," said Jane wearily, resting her head back against his shoulder, "I found them, after father died."

"You found them?"

"Yes, I found them slipped down behind the chest in the hall. It was a heavy oak chest, a great carved affair that had belonged in the family a long time, and it was seldom moved. It stood below the hat-rack in the alcove in the hall, and I figured it out that the man must have meant to keep those papers himself, so there would be no incriminating evidence in father's hands, and that he must have picked them up without father's noticing and started to carry them home; but that when he was going away, putting on his overcoat, he had somehow dropped some of them behind that chest without knowing it. Because they were not all there—two of them were missing. Father had described them to me, and three—the most important ones with the empty envelope—were found. The other two were probably larger, and looked like the whole bundle, which explains how he came to think he had them all. But the two he had and must have had about him when he was killed would not in themselves have been any evidence against him. So, my father was arrested——!"

The tears choked Jane's voice and suddenly rained into her sweet eyes as she struggled to recall the whole sorrowful experience.

"Oh, my darling!" cried Allison, tenderly holding her close.

"Father was very brave. He said it was sure to come out all right, but he wouldn't accept bail, though it was offered him by several loyal friends. He saw that they suspected him, and the papers all came out with big headlines, 'CHURCH ELDER ARRESTED.'"

Allison's voice was deep with loving sympathy as his lips swept her forehead softly and he murmured, "My poor little girl!" but Jane went bravely on.

"That was a hard time," she said with trembling lips, "but God was good; he didn't let it last long. There came an old friend back from abroad who had known father ever since he was a boy, and who happened to have been associated with him in business long enough to give certain proofs that cleared the whole thing up. In a week the case was dismissed so far as father was concerned, and he was back at home again, and restored to the full confidence of his business associates—that is, those who knew intimately about the matter. If father had lived I have no doubt everything would have been all right, and he would have been able to live down the whole thing, but the trouble had struck him hard, he was so terribly worried for my sake, you know. Then he took a little cold which we didn't think anything about, and suddenly, before we realized it, he was down with double pneumonia from which he never rallied. His vitality seemed to be gone. After he died, the papers said beautiful things about his bravery and courage and Christianity, and people tried to be nice, but when it was all over there were still people who looked at me curiously when I passed, and whispered noticeably together; and that man's wife and daughter openly called me a forger's daughter and said that my father had stolen their income, when all the time they were living on what he had given up to save them from disgrace. The daughter made it so unpleasant for me that I decided to go away where I was not known, although I had several dear beautiful homes opened to me if I had chosen to stay, where I might have been a daughter and treated as one of the other children. But I thought it was better to go away and make my own life——"

"But you had evidence. Did you never go and tell those two how wrong they were and how it was their father, not yours, who was the forger?"

"No, not exactly," said Jane, lifting clear untroubled eyes to his face. "You see that was part of father's obligation; it was a point of honor not to give that man's shame away to his wife—he had promised—and then, the man, was dead—he could not be brought to justice; what good would it do?"

"It would have done the good that those two women wouldn't have gone around snubbing you and telling lies about you——"

"Oh, well, after all, that didn't really hurt me——"

"And that brazen girl wouldn't have dared come here to the same college and make it hot for you——!"

"Allison! How did you *know*?" Jane sat up and looked into his eyes, startled.

"I knew from the first mention that it must have been Eugenia Frazer. No girl in her senses would have taken the trouble to do what she did to-day without some grievance——! Oh, that girl! She is beyond words! Think of anybody ever falling in love with her! I'd like the pleasure of informing her what her father was. Of course, though, it wasn't her fault. She couldn't help her father being what he was, but she could help what she is herself. I should certainly like to see her get what's coming to her——!"

"Don't Allison—please! It isn't the right spirit for us to have. Perhaps I'd be just like her if I were in her place——"

"I see you being like her—you angel!" And Allison leaned over again to look into the eyes of his beloved.

"Well, dear, we'll get the right spirit about it somehow, and forget her, but I mean she shall understand right where she gets off before this thing goes any farther. No, you needn't protest. I'm not going to give away your confidence. But I'm going to settle that girl where she won't dare to make any more trouble for you ever again. And the first thing we're going to do is to announce our engagement. I feel like going up to the college bulletin board right this minute and writing it out in great big letters!"

"Allison!" Jane sat up with shining eyes and her cheeks very red. Then they both broke down and laughed, Jane's merriment ending in a serious look.

"Allison, you really *want me*, now you know what people may think about my father?"

"Jane, I've known all that since I first saw you. Our beloved pastor kindly informed me of it the night he introduced us, so you see how little weight it had with any of us. I had no knowledge but that it was all true, although I couldn't for the life of me see how a man who was unworthy of you could have possibly been your father; but it was you, and not your father, I fell in love with the first night I saw you. I'm mighty glad for your sake that he wasn't that kind of man, because I know how you would feel about it, but as for what other people think about it, *I should worry*! And Jane, make up your mind right here and now that we're going to be married the day we both graduate, see? I won't wait a day longer to have the right to protect you——"

The tall trees whispered above their heads, and the birds looked down and dropped wonderful melodies about them, and Leslie stormily drove her car back and forth on the pike and sounded her klaxon loud and long, but it was almost an hour later that it suddenly occurred to Allison that Leslie was waiting for them, and still later before the two with blissful lingering finally wended their way out to the road and were taken up by the subdued and weary Leslie, who greeted them with relief and fell upon her new sister with eager enthusiasm and genuine delight.

An hour later Allison, after committing his future bride to the tender ministries of Julia Cloud, who had received her as a daughter, took his way collegeward. He sent up his card to Miss Frazer and Miss Brice and requested that he might see them both as soon as possible, and in a flutter of expectancy the two presently entered the reception-room. They were hoping he had come to take them out in his car, although each was disappointed to find that she was not the only one summoned.

Allison in that few minutes of waiting for them, seemed to have lost his care-free boyish air and have grown to man's estate. He greeted the two young women with utmost courtesy and gravity and proceeded at once to business:

"I have come to inform you," he said with a bow that might almost be called stately, so much had the tall, slender figure lost its boyishness, "that Miss Bristol is my fiancée, and as such it is my business to protect her. I must ask you both to publicly apologize before your sorority for what happened this morning."

Eunice Brice grew white and frightened, but Eugenia Frazer's face flamed angrily.

"Indeed, Allison Cloud, I'll do nothing of the kind. What in the world did you suppose I had to do with what happened this morning?"

"You had all to do with it. Miss Frazer, I happen to know all about the matter."

"Well, you certainly don't," flamed Eugenia, "or you wouldn't be engaged to that little Bristol hypocrite. Her father was a common——"

Allison took a step toward her, his face stern but controlled.

"Her father was *not a forger*, Miss Frazer, and I have reason to believe that you know that the report you are spreading about college is not true. But however that may be, Miss Frazer, if I should say that your father was a forger would that change *you* any? I have asked Miss Bristol to marry me because of what *she is herself*, and not because of what her father was. But there is ample evidence that her father was a noble and an upright man and so recognized by the law and by his fellow-townsmen, and I demand that you take back your words publicly, both of you, and that you, Miss Frazer, take upon yourself publicly the responsibility for starting this whole trouble. I fancy it may be rather unpleasant for you to remain in this college longer unless this matter is adjusted satisfactorily."

"Well, I certainly do not intend to be bullied into any such thing!" said Eugenia angrily. "I'll leave college first!"

Eunice Brice began to cry. She was the protégée of a rich woman and could not afford to be disgraced.

"I shall tell them all that you asked me to make that motion for you and promised to give me your pink evening dress if I did," reproached Eunice tearfully.

"Tell what you like," returned Eugenia grandly, "it will only prove you what you are, a little fool! I'm going up to pack. You needn't think you can hush me up, Allison Cloud, if you *are* rich. Money won't cover up the truth——"

"No," said Allison looking at her steadily, controlledly, with a memory of his promise to Jane. "No, but *Christianity* will—sometimes."

"Oh, yes, everybody knows you're a fanatic!" sneered Eugenia, and swept herself out of the room with high head, knowing that the wisest thing she could do was to depart while the going was good.

When Allison reached home a few minutes later Julia Cloud put into his hand a letter which his guardian had written her soon after his first visit, in which he stated that he had made it a point to look up both the young people with whom his wards were intimate, and he found their records and their family irreproachable. He especially went into details concerning Jane's father and the noble way in which he had acted, and the completeness with which his name had been cleared. He uncovered one or two facts which Jane apparently did not know, and which proved that time had revealed the true criminal to those most concerned and that only pity for his family, and the expressed wish of the man who had borne for a time his shame, had caused the matter to be hushed up.

Allison, after he had read it, went to find Jane and drew her into the little sun-parlor to read it with him, and together they rejoiced quietly.

Jane lifted a shining face to Allison after the reading.

"Then I'm glad we never said anything to Eugenia! Poor Eugenia! She is greatly to be pitied!"

Allison, a little shamefacedly, agreed, and then owned up that he had "fired" Eugenia, as he expressed it, from the college.

"O, Allison!" said Jane, half troubled, though laughing in spite of herself at the vision of Eugenia trying to be lofty in the face of the facts. "You ought not to have done it, dear. I have stood it so long, it didn't matter! Only for your sake—and Leslie's——!"

"For our sakes, nothing!" said Allison. "That girl needed somebody to tell her where to get off, and only a man could do it. She'll be more polite to people hereafter, I'm thinking. It won't do her any harm. Now, Jane darling, forget it, and let's be happy!"

"Be careful, Allison, some one is coming. I think it's that Mr. Terrence."

"Dog-gone his fool hide!" muttered Allison. "I wish he'd take himself home! I certainly would like to tell *him* where to get off. Leslie's as sick of him as I am, and as for Cloudy, she's about reached the limit."

"Why, Allison, isn't Leslie interested in him? He told Howard that they were as good as engaged."

"Leslie interested in that little cad? I should say not. If she was I'd disown her. You say he told Howard they were engaged! What a lie! So that's what's the matter with the old boy, is it? I thought something must be the matter that he got so busy all of a sudden. Well, I'll soon fix that! Come on up to Cloudy's porch, quick, while he's in his room. Cloudy won't mind. We'll be by ourselves there till dinner is ready!"

CHAPTER XXX

But matters came to a climax with Howard Letchworth before Allison had any opportunity to do any "fixing."

The next afternoon was Class Day and there were big doings at the college. Howard kept out of the way, for it was a day on which he had counted much, and during the winter once or twice he and Leslie had talked of it as a matter of course that they would be around together. His Class Day had seemed then to be of so much importance to her—and now—now she was going to attend it in Clive Terrence's company! Terrence had told him so, and there seemed no reason to doubt his word. She went everywhere with him, and he was their guest; why shouldn't she? So Howard went glumly about his duties, keeping as much as possible out of everyone's way. If he had not been a part of the order of exercises, and a moving spirit of the day, as it were, he would certainly have made up an excuse to absent himself. As it was, he meditated trying to get some one else to take his place, and was on his way to arrange it, just before the hour for the afternoon exercises to begin, when suddenly he saw, coming up the wide asphalt walk of the campus, young Terrence, and the girl who had come to be known among them as the "Freshman Vamp." His eyes hastily scanned the groups about, and searched the walk as far as he could see it, but nowhere could he discover Leslie.

With a sudden impulse he dashed over to Julia Cloud, and forgetful of his late estrangement spoke with much of his old eagerness; albeit trying his best to appear careless and matter-of-fact:

"Isn't Leslie hereabouts somewhere, Miss Cloud? I believe I promised to show her the ivy that our class is to plant."

It was the first excuse he could think of. But Julia Cloud was full of sympathy and understanding, and only too glad to hear the old ring of friendliness in his voice. She lowered her tone and spoke confidentially:

"She wouldn't come, Howard: I don't just know what has taken her. She said she would rather stay at home——"

"Is she down there now?"

Julia Cloud nodded.

"Perhaps you——"

"I *will*!" he said, and was off like a flash. On his way down the campus he thrust some papers into a classmate's hands.

"If I don't get back in time, give those to Halsted and tell him to look out for things. I'm called away."

Never in all his running days had he run as he did that day. He made the station in four minutes where it usually took him six, and was at the Cloud Villa in two more, all out of breath but radiant. Something jubilant had been let loose in his heart by the smile in Julia Cloud's eyes, utterly unreasonable, of course, but still it had come, and he was entertaining it royally. It was rather disheartening to find the front door locked and only Cherry to respond to his knock.

"Isn't Miss Leslie here?" he asked, a blank look coming into his eyes as Cherry appeared.

"Miss Leslie done jes' skittered acrost de back yahd wid a paddle in her han'. I reckum she's gone to de crick. Miss Jewel, she'll be powerful upset ef she comes back an' finds out. She don't like Miss Leslie go down to them canoes all by her lonesome."

"That's all right, Cherry," said Howard, cheering up; "I'll go down and find her. Got an extra paddle anywhere, or did she take them both?"

"No, sir, she only took de one. Here's t'other. I reckum she'll be right glad to see yeh, Mas'r Howard. We-all hes missed you mighty powerful lot. That there little fish-eyed lady-man wot is visitin' us ain't no kind of substoote 'tall fer you——"

Howard beamed on her silently and was off like a shot, forgetful of the chimes on the clock of the college, which were now striking the hour at which he was to have led the procession down the ivy walk to the scene of festivities.

Over two fences, across lots, down a steep, rocky hill, and he was at the little landing where the Cloud canoe usually anchored. But Leslie and her boat were gone. No glimpse of bright hair either up or down stream gave hint of which she had taken, no ripple in the water even to show where she had passed. But he knew pretty well her favorite haunts up-stream where the hemlocks bowed and bent to the water, and made dark shadows under which to slip. The silence and the beauty called her as they had always called him. He was sure he would find her there rather than down-stream where the crowds of inn people played around, and the tennis courts overflowed into canoes and dawdled about with ukeleles and cameras. He looked about for a means of transport. There was only one canoe, well-chained to its rest. He examined the padlock for a moment, then put forth his strong young arm and jerked up the rest from its firm setting in the earth. It was the work of a second to shoot the boat into the water, fling the chains, boat-rest and all into the bow, and spring after. Long, strong, steady strokes, and he shot out into the stream and away up beyond the willows; around the turn where the chestnut grove bloomed in good promise for the autumn; beyond the railroad bridge and the rocks; past the first dipping hemlocks; around the curve; below the old camp where they had had so many delightful picnics and watched the sunset from the rocks; and on, up above the rapids. The current was swift to-day. He wondered if Leslie had been able to pass them all alone, yet somehow he felt she had and he would find her up in the quiet haven where few ever came and where she would be undisturbed. Paddling "Indian" he came around the curve silently and was almost upon her, but was unprepared for the little huddled figure down in the bottom of the boat, one hand grasping the paddle which was wedged between some stones in the shallow stream bed to anchor the frail bark, the other arm curved about as a pillow for the face which was hidden, with only the bright hair gleaming in the stray rays of sunshine that crept through the young leaves overhead.

"Leslie, little girl—my darling—what is the matter?"

He scarcely knew what he was saying, so anxiously he watched her. Was she hurt or in trouble, and if so, what was the trouble? Did the vapid little guest and the Freshman Vamp have anything to do with it? Somehow he forgot all about himself now and his own grievance—he only wanted to comfort her whom he loved, and it never entered his head that just at that moment the anxious Halsted was inquiring of everyone: "Haven't you seen Letchworth? Class Day'll be a mess without him! Something must have happened to him!"

Leslie lifted a tear-stained face in startled amaze. His voice! Those precious words! Leslie heard them even if *he* took no cognizance of them himself.

"I—you—WELL, YOU ought to know——!" burst forth Leslie and then down went the bright head once more and the slender shoulders shook with long-suppressed sobs.

It certainly was a good thing that the creek was shallow at that point and the canoes quite used to all sorts of conditions. Howard Letchworth waited for no invitation. He arose and stepped into Leslie's boat, pinioned his own with a dextrous paddle, and gave attention to comforting the princess. It somehow needed no words for awhile, until at last Leslie lifted a woebegone face that already looked half-appeased and inquired sobbily:

"What made you act so perfectly horrid all this time?"

"Why—I—" began Howard lamely, wondering now just why he *had*—! "Why, you see, Leslie, you had company and—"

"Company! *That!* Now, Howard, you weren't jealous of that little excuse for a man, were you?"

Howard colored guiltily:

"Why, you see, Leslie, you are so far above me—"

"Oh, I was, was I? Well, if I was above *you*, where did you think that other ridiculous little simp belonged, I should like to know? *Not* with *me*, I hope?"

"But you see, Leslie—" somehow the great question that had loomed between them these weeks dwarfed and shrivelled when he tried to explain it to Leslie—

"Well—?"

"Well, I've just found out you are very rich—"

"Well?"

"Well, *I'm* POOR."

"But I thought you just said you *loved* me!" flashed Leslie indignantly. "If you do, I don't see what rich and poor matter. It'll all belong to us both, won't it?"

"I should *hope* not," said the young man, drawing himself up as much as was consistent with life in a canoe. "I would *never* let my wife support me."

"Well, perhaps you might be able to make enough to *support yourself*," twinkled Leslie with mischief in a dimple near her mouth.

"Leslie, now you're making fun! I mean this!"

"Well, what do you want me to do about it, give away my money?"

"Of course not. I was a cad and all that, but somehow it seemed as though I hadn't any business to be coming around you when you were so young and with plenty of chances of men worth more than I—"

"More what? More money?"

"Leslie, this is a serious matter with me—"

"Well, it is with me, too," said Leslie, suddenly grave. "You certainly have made me most unhappy for about three weeks. But I'm beginning to think you don't love me after all. What is money between people who love each other? Only something that they can have a good time spending for others, isn't it? And suppose *I* should say I wouldn't let *you support me*? I guess after all if you think so much of money you don't really care!"

"Leslie!" Their eyes met and his suddenly fell before her steady, beautiful gaze:

"Well, then, Howard Letchworth, if you are so awfully proud that you have to be the richest, I'll throw away or give away all my money and be a pauper, *so there*! Then will you be satisfied? What's money without the one you love, anyway?"

"I see, Leslie! I was a fool. You darling, wonderful princess. No, keep your money and I'll try to make some more and we'll have a wonderful time helping others with it. I suppose I knew I was a fool all the time, only I wanted to be told so, because you see that fellow told me you and he had been set apart for each other by your parents—!"

A sudden lurch of the canoe roused him to look at Leslie's face:

"Oh, that little—liar! Yes, he is! He is the meanest, conceitedest, most disagreeable little snob—!"

"There, there! We'll spare him—" laughed Howard. "I see I was wrong again, only, Leslie, little princess, there's one thing you must own is true, you're very young yet and you may change—"

"Now, *I like that*!" cried Leslie. "You don't even think I have the stability to be true to you. Well, if I'm as weak-looking as that you better go and find someone else—"

But he stopped her words with his face against her lips, and his arms about her, and at last she nestled against his shoulder and was at peace.

Chiming out above the notes of the wood-robin and the thrush there came the faint and distant notes of the quarter hour striking on the college library. It was Leslie who heard it. Howard was still too far upon the heights to think of earthly duties yet awhile.

"Howard! Isn't this your Class Day? And haven't you a part in the exercises? Why aren't you there?"

He turned with startled eyes, and rising color.

"I couldn't stay, Leslie. I was too miserable! I had to come after you. You promised to be with me to-day, you know—"

"But your Class Poem, Howard! Quick! It must be almost time to read it—!"

He took out his watch.

"Great Scott! I didn't know the time had gone like that!"

Leslie's fingers were already at work with the other canoe, tying its chain to the seat of her own.

"Now!" she turned and picked up her paddle swiftly, handing Howard the other one. "Go! For all your worth! You mustn't fail on this day anyway! Beat it with all your might!"

"It's too late!" said the man reluctantly, taking the paddle and moving to his right position.

"It's not too late. It *shan't* be too late! *Paddle*, I say, *now*, ONE—and—TWO—and——!"

And they settled to a rhythmic stroke.

"It was so wonderful back there, Leslie," said Howard wistfully. "We oughtn't to let anything interfere with this first hour together."

"This isn't interfering," said Leslie practically, "it's just duty, and that never interferes. Here, we'll land over there and you beat it up the hill! I'll padlock the boats by that old tree and follow, but *don't you dare* wait for me! I'll be there to hear the first word and they'll have waited for you, I know. A little to the right, there—*now*—step out and *beat it*!"

He obeyed her, and presently came panting to the audience room, with a fine color, and a great light in his eyes, just as Halsted was slipping down to inquire of Allison:

"Where in thunder is Letchworth? Seen him anywhere?"

"Heavens, man! Hasn't he showed up yet?" cried Allison startled. "Where could he be?"

Julia Cloud beside him leaned over and quietly drew their attention to the figure hastening up the aisle. Halsted hurried back to the platform, and Allison, relieved, settled once more in his seat. But Julia Cloud rested not in satisfaction until another figure breathlessly slipped in with eyes for none but the speaker.

Then into the eyes of Julia Cloud there came a vision as comes to one who watching the glorious setting of the sun sees not the regretful close of the day that is past, but the golden promise of the day that is to come.

The Mystery of Mary

I

He paused on the platform and glanced at his watch. The train on which he had just arrived was late. It hurried away from the station, and was swallowed up in the blackness of the tunnel, as if it knew its own shortcomings and wished to make up for them.

It was five minutes of six, and as the young man looked back at the long flight of steps that led to the bridge across the tracks, a delicate pencilling of electric light flashed into outline against the city's deepening dusk, emphasizing the lateness of the hour. He had a dinner engagement at seven, and it was yet some distance to his home, where a rapid toilet must be made if he were to arrive on time.

The stairway was long, and there were many people thronging it. A shorter cut led down along the tracks under the bridge, and up the grassy embankment. It would bring him a whole block nearer home, and a line of cabs was standing over at the corner just above the bridge. It was against the rules to walk beside the tracks—there was a large sign to that effect in front of him—but it would save five minutes. He scanned the platform hastily to see if any officials were in sight, then bolted down the darkening tracks.

Under the centre of the bridge a slight noise behind him, as of soft, hurrying footsteps, caught his attention, and a woman's voice broke upon his startled senses.

"Please don't stop, nor look around," it said, and the owner caught up with him now in the shadow. "But will you kindly let me walk beside you for a moment, till you can show me how to get out of this dreadful place? I am very much frightened, and I'm afraid I shall be followed. Will you tell me where I can go to hide?"

After an instant's astonished pause, he obeyed her and kept on, making room for her to walk beside him, while he took the place next to the tracks. He was aware, too, of the low rumble of a train, coming from the mouth of the tunnel.

His companion had gasped for breath, but began again in a tone of apology:

"I saw you were a gentleman, and I didn't know what to do. I thought you would help me to get somewhere quickly."

Just then the fiery eye of the oncoming train burst from the tunnel ahead. Instinctively, the young man caught his companion's arm and drew her forward to the embankment beyond the bridge, holding her, startled and trembling, as the screaming train tore past them.

The pent black smoke from the tunnel rolled in a thick cloud about them, stifling them. The girl, dazed with the roar and blinded by the smoke, could only cling to her protector. For an instant they felt as if they were about to be drawn into the awful power of the rushing monster. Then it had passed, and a roar of silence followed, as if they were suddenly plunged into a vacuum. Gradually the noises of the world began again: the rumble of a trolley-car on the bridge; the "honk-honk" of an automobile; the cry of a newsboy. Slowly their breath and their senses came back.

The man's first thought was to get out of the cut before another train should come. He grasped his companion's arm and started up the steep embankment, realizing as he did so that the wrist he held was slender, and that the sleeve which covered it was of the finest cloth.

They struggled up, scarcely pausing for breath. The steps at the side of the bridge, made for the convenience of railroad hands, were out of the question, for they were at a dizzy height, and hung unevenly over the yawning pit where trains shot constantly back and forth.

As they emerged from the dark, the man saw that his companion was a young and beautiful woman, and that she wore a light cloth gown, with neither hat nor gloves.

At the top of the embankment they paused, and the girl, with her hand at her throat, looked backward with a shudder. She seemed like a young bird that could scarcely tell which way to fly.

Without an instant's hesitation, the young man raised his hand and hailed a four-wheeler across the street.

"Come this way, quick!" he urged, helping her in. He gave the driver his home address and stepped in after her. Then, turning, he faced his companion, and was suddenly keenly aware of the strange situation in which he had placed himself.

"Can you tell me what is the matter," he asked, "and where you would like to go?"

The girl had scarcely recovered breath from the long climb and the fright, and she answered him in broken phrases.

"No, I cannot tell you what is the matter"—she paused and looked at him, with a sudden comprehension of what he might be thinking about her—"but—there is nothing—that is—I have done nothing wrong—" She paused again and looked up with eyes whose clear depths, he felt, could hide no guile.

"Of course," he murmured with decision, and then wondered why he felt so sure about it.

"Thank you," she said. Then, with frightened perplexity: "I don't know where to go. I never was in this city before. If you will kindly tell me how to get somewhere—suppose to a railroad station—and yet—no, I have no money—and"—then with a sudden little movement of dismay—"and I have no hat! Oh!"

The young man felt a strong desire to shield this girl so unexpectedly thrown on his mercy. Yet vague fears hovered about the margin of his judgment. Perhaps she was a thief or an adventuress. It might be that he ought to let her get out of the odd situation she appeared to be in, as best she might. Yet even as the thought flashed through his mind he seemed to hear an echo of her words, "I saw you were a gentleman," and he felt incapable of betraying her trust in him.

The girl was speaking again: "But I must not trouble you any more. You have been very kind to get me out of that dreadful place. If you will just stop the carriage and let me out, I am sure I can take care of myself."

"I could not think of letting you get out here alone. If you are in danger, I will help you." The warmth of his own words startled him. He knew he ought to be more cautious with a stranger, but impetuously he threw caution to the winds. "If you would just tell me a little bit about it, so that I should know what I ought to do for you——"

"Oh, I must not tell you! I couldn't!" said the girl, her hand fluttering up to her heart, as if to hold its wild beating from stifling her. "I am sorry to have involved you for a moment in this. Please let me out here. I am not frightened, now that I got away from that terrible tunnel. I was afraid I might have to go in there alone, for I didn't see any way to get up the bank, and I couldn't go back."

"I am glad I happened to be there," breathed the young man fervently. "It would have been dangerous for you to enter that tunnel. It runs an entire block. You would probably have been killed."

The girl shut her eyes and pressed her fingers to them. In the light of the street lamps, he saw that she was very white, and also that there were jewels flashing from the rings on her fingers. It was apparent that she was a lady of wealth and refinement. What could have brought her to this pass?

The carriage came to a sudden stop, and, looking out, he saw they had reached his home. A new alarm seized him as the girl moved as if to get out. His dignified mother and his fastidious sister were probably not in, but if by any chance they should not have left the house, what would they think if they saw a strange, hatless young woman descend from the carriage with him? Moreover, what would the butler think?

"Excuse me," he said, "but, really, there are reasons why I shouldn't like you to get out of the carriage just here. Suppose you sit still until I come out. I have a dinner engagement and must make a few changes in my dress, but it will take me only a few minutes. You are in no danger, and I will take you to some place of safety. I will try to think what to do while I am gone. On no account get out of the carriage. It would make the driver suspicious, you know. If you are really followed, he will let no one disturb you in the carriage, of course. Don't distress yourself. I'll hurry. Can you give me the address of any friend to whom I might 'phone or telegraph?"

She shook her head and there was a glitter of tears in her eyes as she replied:

"No, I know of no one in the city who could help me."

"I will help you, then," he said with sudden resolve, and in a tone that would be a comfort to any woman in distress.

His tone and the look of respectful kindliness he gave her kept the girl in the carriage until his return, although in her fear and sudden distrust of all the world, she thought more than once of attempting to slip away. Yet without money, and in a costume which could but lay her open to suspicion, what was she to do? Where was she to go?

As the young man let himself into his home with his latch-key, he heard the butler's well trained voice answering the telephone. "Yes, ma'am; this is Mrs. Dunham's residence.... No, ma'am, she is not at home.... No, ma'am, Miss Dunham is out also.... Mr. Dunham? Just wait a moment, please I think Mr. Dunham has just come in. Who shall I say wishes to speak to him?... Mrs. Parker Bowman?... Yes, ma'am; just wait a minute, please. I'll call Mr. Dunham."

The young man frowned. Another interruption! And Miss Bowman! It was at her house that he was to dine. What could the woman want? Surely it was not so late that she was looking him up. But perhaps something had happened, and she was calling off her dinner. What luck if she was! Then he would be free to attend the problem of the young woman whom fate, or Providence, had suddenly thrust upon his care.

He took the receiver, resolved to get out of going to the dinner if it were possible.

"Good evening, Mrs. Bowman."

"Oh, is that you, Mr. Dunham? How relieved I am! I am in a bit of difficulty about my dinner, and called up to see if your sister couldn't help me out. Miss Mayo has failed me. Her sister has had an accident, and she cannot leave her. She has just 'phoned me, and I don't know what to do. Isn't Cornelia at home? Couldn't you persuade her to come and help me out? She would have been invited in Miss Mayo's place if she had not told me that she expected to go to Boston this week. But she changed her plans, didn't she? Isn't she where you could reach her by 'phone and beg her to come and help me out? You see, it's a very particular dinner, and I've made all my arrangements."

"Well, now, that's too bad, Mrs. Bowman," began the young man, thinking he saw a way out of both their difficulties. "I'm sorry Cornelia isn't here. I'm sure she would do anything in her power to help you. But she and mother were to dine in Chestnut Hill to-night, and they must have left the house half an hour ago. I'm afraid she's out of the question. Suppose you leave me out? You won't have any trouble then except to take two plates off the table"—he laughed pleasantly—"and you would have even couples. You see," he hastened to add, as he heard Mrs. Parker Bowman's preliminary dissent—"you see, Mrs. Bowman, I'm in somewhat of a predicament myself. My train was late, and as I left the station I happened to meet a young woman—a—a friend." (He reflected rapidly on the old proverb, "A friend in need is a friend indeed." In that sense she was a friend.) "She is temporarily separated from her friends, and is a stranger in the city. In fact, I'm the only acquaintance or friend she has, and I feel rather under obligation to see her to her hotel and look up trains for her. She leaves the city to-night."

"Now, look here, Tryon Dunham, you're not going to leave me in the lurch for any young woman. I don't care how old an acquaintance she is! You simply bring her along. She'll make up my number and relieve me wonderfully. No, don't you say a word. Just tell her that she needn't stand on ceremony. Your mother and I are too old friends for that. Any friend of yours is a friend of mine, and my house is open to her. She won't mind. These girls who have travelled a great deal learn to step over the little formalities of calls and introductions. Tell her I'll call on her afterwards, if she'll only remain in town long enough, or I'll come and take dinner with her when I happen to be in her city. I suppose she's just returned from abroad—they all have—or else she's just going—and if she hasn't learned to accept things as she finds them, she probably will soon. Tell her what a plight I'm in, and that it will be a real blessing to me if she'll come. Besides—I didn't mean to tell you—I meant it for a surprise, but I may as well tell you now—Judge Blackwell is to be here, with his wife, and I especially want you to meet him. I've been trying to get you two together for a long time."

"Ah!" breathed the young man, with interest. "Judge Blackwell! I have wanted to meet him."

"Well, he has heard about you, too, and I think he wants to meet you. Did you know he was thinking of taking a partner into his office? He has always refused—but that's another story, and I haven't time to talk. You ought to be on your way here now. Tell your friend I will bless her forever for helping me out, and I won't take no for an answer. You said she'd just returned from abroad, didn't you? Of course she's musical. You must make her give us some music. She will, won't she? I was depending on Miss Mayo for that this evening."

"Well, you might be able to persuade her," murmured the distracted young man at the 'phone, as he struggled with one hand to untie his necktie and unfasten his collar, and mentally calculated how long it would take him to get into his dress suit.

"Yes, of course. You'd better not speak of it—it might make her decline. And don't let her stop to make any changes in her dress. Everybody will understand when I tell them she's just arrived—didn't you say?—from the other side, and we caught her on the wing. There's some one coming now. Do, for pity's sake, hurry, Tryon, for my cook is terribly cross when I hold up a dinner too long. Good-by. Oh, by the way, what did you say was her name?"

"Oh—ah!" He had almost succeeded in releasing his collar, and was about to hang up the receiver, when this new difficulty confronted him.

"Oh, yes, of course; her name—I had almost forgotten," he went on wildly, to make time, and searched about in his mind for a name—any name—that might help him. The telephone book lay open at the r's. He pounced upon it and took the first name his eye caught.

"Yes—why—Remington, Miss Remington."

"Remington!" came in a delighted scream over the phone. "Not Carolyn Remington? That would be too good luck!"

"No," he murmured distractedly; "no, not Carolyn. Why, I—ah—I think—Mary—Mary Remington."

"Oh, I'm afraid I haven't met her, but never mind. Do hurry up, Tryon. It is five minutes of seven. Where did you say she lives?" But the receiver was hung up with a click, and the young man tore up the steps to his room three at a bound. Dunham's mind was by no means at rest. He felt that he had done a tremendously daring thing, though, when he came to think of it, he had not suggested it himself; and he did not quite see how he could get out of it, either, for how was he to have time to help the girl if he did not take her with him?

Various plans floated through his head. He might bring her into the house, and make some sort of an explanation to the servants, but what would the explanation be? He could not tell them the truth about her, and how would he explain the matter to his mother and sister? For they might return before he did, and would be sure to ask innumerable questions.

And the girl—would she go with him? If not, what should he do with her? And about her dress? Was it such as his "friend" could wear to one of Mrs. Parker Bowman's exclusive dinners? To his memory, it seemed quiet and refined. Perhaps that was all that was required for a woman who was travelling. There it was again! But he had not said she was travelling, nor that she had just returned from abroad, nor that she was a musician. How could he answer such questions about an utter stranger, and yet how could he not answer them, under the circumstances?

And she wore no hat, nor cloak. That would be a strange way to arrive at a dinner How could she accept? He was settling his coat into place when a queer little bulge attracted his attention to an inside pocket. Impatiently he pulled out a pair of long white gloves. They were his sister's, and he now remembered she had given them to him to carry the night before, on the way home from a reception, she having removed them because it was raining. He looked at them with a sudden inspiration. Of course! Why had he not thought of that? He hurried into his sister's room to make a selection of a few necessities for the emergency—only to have his assurance desert him at the very threshold. The room was immaculate, with no feminine finery lying about. Cornelia Dunham's maid was well trained. The only article that seemed out of place was a hand-box on a chair near the door. It bore the name of a fashionable milliner, and across the lid was pencilled in Cornelia's large, angular hand, "To be returned to Madame Dollard's." He caught up the box and strode over to the closet. There was no time to lose, and this box doubtless contained a hat of some kind. If it was to be returned, Cornelia would think it had been called for, and no further inquiry would be made about the matter. He could call at Madame's and settle the bill without his sister's knowledge.

He poked back into the closet and discovered several wraps and evening cloaks of more or less elaborate style, but the thought came to him that perhaps one of these would be recognized as Cornelia's. He closed the door hurriedly and went down to a large closet under the stairs, from which he presently emerged with his mother's new black rain-coat. He patted his coat-pocket to be sure he had the gloves, seized his hat, and hurried back to the carriage, the hat-box in one hand and his mother's rain-coat dragging behind him. His only anxiety was to get out before the butler saw him.

As he closed the door, there flashed over him, the sudden possibility that the girl had gone. Well, perhaps that would be the best thing that could happen and would save him a lot of trouble; yet to his amazement he found that the thought filled him with a sense of disappointment. He did not want her to be gone. He peered anxiously into the carriage, and was relieved to find her still there, huddled into the shadow, her eyes looking large and frightened. She was seized with a fit of trembling, and it required all her strength to keep him from noticing it. She was half afraid of the man, now that she had waited for him. Perhaps he was not a gentleman, after all.

II

"I am afraid I have been a long time," he said apologetically, as he closed the door of the carriage, after giving Mrs. Parker Bowman's address to the driver. In the uncertain light of the distant arc-lamp, the girl looked small and appealing. He felt a strong desire to lift her burdens and carry them on his own broad shoulders.

"I've brought some things that I thought might help," he said. "Would you like to put on this coat? It may not be just what you would have selected, but it was the best I could find that would not be recognized. The air is growing chilly."

He shook out the coat and threw it around her.

"Oh, thank you," she murmured gratefully, slipping her arms into the sleeves.

"And this box has some kind of a hat, I hope," he went on. "I ought to have looked, but there really wasn't time." He unknotted the strings and produced a large picture hat with long black plumes. He was relieved to find it black. While he untied the strings, there had been a growing uneasiness lest the hat be one of those wild, queer combinations of colors that Cornelia frequently purchased and called "artistic."

The girl received the hat with a grateful relief that was entirely satisfactory to the young man.

"And now," said he, as he pulled out the gloves and laid them gravely in her lap, "we're invited out to dinner."

"Invited out to dinner!" gasped the girl.

"Yes. It's rather a providential thing to have happened, I think. The telephone was ringing as I opened the door, and Mrs. Parker Bowman, to whose house I was invited, was asking for my sister to fill the place of an absent guest. My sister is away, and I tried to beg off. I told her I had accidentally met—I hope you will pardon me—I called you a friend."

"Oh!" she said. "That was kind of you."

"I said you were a stranger in town, and as I was your only acquaintance, I felt that I should show you the courtesy of taking you to a hotel, and assisting to get you off on the night train; and I asked her to excuse me, as that would give her an even number. But it seems she had invited some one especially to meet me, and was greatly distressed not to have her full quota of guests, so she sent you a most cordial invitation to come to her at once, promising to take dinner with you some time if you would help her out now. Somehow, she gathered from my talk that you were travelling, had just returned from abroad, and were temporarily separated from your friends. She is also sure that you are musical, and means to ask you to help her out in that way this evening. I told her I was not sure whether you could be persuaded or not, and she mercifully refrained from asking whether you sang or played. I tell you all this so that you will be prepared for anything. Of course I didn't tell her all these things. I merely kept still when she inferred them. Your name, by the way, is Miss Remington—Mary Remington. She was greatly elated for a moment when she thought you might be Carolyn Remington—whoever she may be. I suppose she will speak of it. The name was the first one that my eye lit upon in the telephone-book. If you object to bearing it for the evening, it is easy to see how a name could be misunderstood over the 'phone. But perhaps you would better give me a few pointers, for I've never tried acting a part, and can't be sure how well I shall do it."

The girl had been silent from astonishment while the man talked.

"But I cannot possibly go there to dinner," she gasped, her hand going to her throat again, as if to pluck away the delicate lace about it and give more room, for breathing. "I must get away somewhere at once. I cannot trouble you in this way. I have already imposed upon your kindness. With this hat and coat and gloves, I shall be able to manage quite well, and I thank you so much! I will return them to you as soon as possible."

The cab began to go slowly, and Tryon Dunham noticed that another carriage, just ahead of theirs, was stopping before Mrs. Bowman's house. There was no time for halting decision.

"My friend," he said earnestly, "I cannot leave you alone, and I do not see a better way than for you to go in here with me for a little while, till I am free to go with you. No one can follow you here, or suspect that you had gone out to dinner at a stranger's house. Believe me, it is the very safest thing you could do. This is the house. Will you go in with me? If not, I must tell the driver to take us somewhere else."

"But what will she think of me," she said in trepidation, "and how can I do such a thing as to steal into a woman's house to a dinner in this way! Besides, I am not dressed for a formal occasion."

The carriage had stopped before the door now, and the driver was getting down from his seat.

"Indeed, she will think nothing about it," Dunham assured her, "except to be glad that she has the right number of guests. Her dinners are delightful affairs usually, and you have nothing to do but talk about impersonal matters for a little while and be entertaining. She was most insistent that you take no thought about the matter of dress. She said it would be perfectly understood that you were travelling, and that the invitation was unexpected. You can say that your trunk has not come, or has gone on ahead. Will you come?"

Then the driver opened the carriage door.

In an instant the girl assumed the self-contained manner she had worn when she had first spoken to him. She stepped quietly from the carriage, and only answered in a low voice, "I suppose I'd better, if you wish it."

Dunham paused for a moment to give the driver a direction about carrying the great pasteboard box to his club. This idea had come as a sudden inspiration. He had not thought of, the necessity of getting rid of that box before.

"If it becomes necessary, where shall I say you are going this evening?" he asked in a low tone, as they turned to go up the steps. She summoned a faint, flickering smile.

"When people have been travelling abroad and are stopping over in this city, they often go on to Washington, do they not?" she asked half shyly.

He smiled in response, and noted with pleasure that the black hat was intensely becoming. She was not ill-dressed for the part she had to play, for the black silk rain-coat gave the touch of the traveller to her costume.

The door swung open before they could say another word, and the young man remembered that he must introduce his new friend. As there was no further opportunity to ask her about her name, he must trust to luck.

The girl obeyed the motion of the servant and slipped up to the dressing-room as if she were a frequent guest in the house, but it was in some trepidation that Tryon Dunham removed his overcoat and arranged his necktie. He had caught a passing glimpse of the assembled company, and knew that Mr. Bowman was growing impatient for his dinner. His heart almost failed him now that the girl was out of sight. What if she should not prove to be accustomed to society, after all, and should show it? How embarrassing that would be! He had seen her only in a half-light as yet. How had he dared?

But it was too late now, for she was coming from the dressing-room, and Mrs. Bowman was approaching them with outstretched hands, and a welcome in her face.

"My dear Miss Remington, it is so good of you to help me out! I can see by the first glance that it is going to be a privilege to know you. I can't thank you enough for waiving formalities."

"It was very lovely of you to ask me," said the girl, with perfect composure, "a stranger——"

"Don't speak of it, my dear. Mr. Dunham's friends are not strangers, I assure you. Tryon, didn't you tell her how long we have known each other? I shall feel quite hurt if you have never mentioned me to her. Now, come, for my cook is in the last stages of despair over the dinner. Miss Remington, how do you manage to look so fresh and lovely after a long sea voyage? You must tell me your secret."

The young man looked down at the girl and saw that her dress was in perfect taste for the occasion, and also that she was very young and beautiful. He was watching her with a kind of proprietary pride as she moved forward to be introduced to the other guests, when he saw her sweep one quick glance about the room, and for just an instant hesitate and draw back. Her face grew white; then, with a supreme effort, she controlled her feelings, and went through her part with perfect ease.

When Judge Blackwell was introduced to the girl, he looked at her with what seemed to Dunham to be more than a passing interest; but the keen eyes were almost immediately transferred to his own face, and the young man had no further time to watch his protégé, as dinner was immediately announced.

Miss Remington was seated next to Dunham at the table, with the Judge on her other side. The young man was pleased with the arrangement, and sat furtively studying the delicate tinting of her face, the dainty line of cheek and chin and ear, the sweep of her dark lashes, and the ripple of her brown hair, as he tried to converse easily with her, as an old friend might.

At length the Judge turned to the girl and said:

"Miss Remington, you remind me strongly of a young woman who was in my office this afternoon."

The delicate color flickered out of the girl's face entirely, leaving even her lips white, but she lifted her dark eyes bravely to the kindly blue ones, and with sweet dignity baffled the questioned recognition in his look.

"Yes, you are so much like her that I would think you were—her sister perhaps, if it were not for the name," Judge Blackwell went on. "She was a most interesting and beautiful young lady." The old gentleman bestowed upon the girl a look that was like a benediction. "Excuse me for speaking of it, but her dress was something soft and beautiful, like yours, and seemed to suit her face. I was deeply interested in her, although until this afternoon she was a stranger. She came to me for a small matter of business, and after it was attended to, and before she received the papers, she disappeared! She had removed her hat and gloves, as she was obliged to wait some time for certain matters to be looked up, and these she left behind her. The hat is covered with long, handsome plumes of the color of rich cream in coffee."

Young Dunham glanced down at the cloth of the girl's gown, and was startled to find the same rich creamy-coffee tint in its silky folds; yet she did not show by so much as a flicker of an eyelash that she was passing under the keenest inspection. She toyed with the salted almonds beside her plate and held the heavy silver fork as firmly as if she were talking about the discovery of the north pole. Her voice was steady and natural as she asked, "How could she disappear?"

"Well, that is more than I can understand. There were three doors in the room where she sat, one opening into the inner office where I was at work, and two opening into a hall, one on the side and the other on the end opposite the freight elevator. We searched the entire building without finding a clew, and I am deeply troubled."

"Why should she want to disappear?" The question was asked coolly and with as much interest as a stranger would be likely to show.

"I cannot imagine," said the old man speculatively. "She apparently had health and happiness, if one may judge from her appearance, and she came to me of her own free will on a matter of business. Immediately after her disappearance, two well-dressed men entered my office and inquired for her. One had an intellectual head, but looked hard and cruel; the other was very handsome—and disagreeable. When he could not find the young lady, he laid claim to her hat, but I had it locked away. How could I know that man was her friend or her relative? I intend to keep that hat until the young woman herself claims it. I have not had anything happen that has so upset me in years."

"You don't think any harm has come to her?" questioned the girl.

"I cannot think what harm could, and yet—it is very strange. She was about the age of my dear daughter when she died, and I cannot get her out of my mind. When you first appeared in the doorway you gave me quite a start. I thought you were she. If I can find any trace of her, I mean to investigate this matter. I have a feeling that that girl needs a friend."

"I am sure she would be very happy to have a friend like you," said the girl, and there was something in the eyes that were raised to his that made the Judge's heart glow with admiration.

"Thank you," said he warmly. "That is most kind of you. But perhaps she has found a better friend by this time. I hope so."

"Or one as kind," she suggested in a low voice.

The conversation then became general, and the girl did not look up for several seconds; but the young man on her right, who had not missed a word of the previous tête-à-tête, could not give attention to the story Mrs. Blackwell was telling, for pondering what he had heard.

The ladies now left the table, and though this was the time that Dunham had counted upon for an acquaintance with the great judge who might hold a future career in his power, he could not but wish that he might follow them to the other room. He felt entire confidence in his new friend's ability to play her part to the end, but he wanted to watch her, to study her and understand her, if perchance he might solve the mystery that was ever growing more intense about her.

As she left the room, his eyes followed her. His hostess, in passing behind his chair, had whispered:

"I don't wonder you feel so about her. She is lovely. But please don't begrudge her to us for a few minutes. I promise you that you shall have your innings afterwards."

Then, without any warning and utterly against his will, this young man of much experience and self-control blushed furiously, and was glad enough when the door closed behind Mrs. Bowman.

Miss Remington walked into the drawing-room with a steady step, but with a rapidly beating heart. Her real ordeal had now come. She cast about in her mind for subjects of conversation which should forestall unsafe topics, and intuitively sought the protection of the Judge's wife. But immediately she saw her hostess making straight for the little Chippendale chair beside her.

"My dear, it is too lovely," she began. "So opportune! Do tell me how long you have known Tryon?"

The girl caught her breath and gathered her wits together. She looked up shyly into the pleasantly curious eyes of Mrs. Bowman, and a faint gleam of mischief came into her face.

"Why——" Her hesitation seemed only natural, and Mrs. Bowman decided that there must be something very special between these two. "Why, not so very long, Mrs. Bowman—not as long as you have known him." She finished with a smile which Mrs. Bowman decided was charming.

"Oh, you sly child!" she exclaimed, playfully tapping the round cheek with her fan. "Did you meet him when he was abroad this summer?"

"Oh, no, indeed!" said the girl, laughing now in spite of herself. "Oh, no; it was after his return."

"Then it must have been in the Adirondacks," went on the determined interlocutor. "Were you at——" But the girl interrupted her. She could not afford to discuss the Adirondacks, and the sight of the grand piano across the room had given her an idea.

"Mr. Dunham told me that you would like me to play something for you, as your musician friend has failed you. I shall be very glad to, if it will help you any. What do you care for? Something serious or something gay? Are you fond of Chopin, or Beethoven, or something more modern?"

Scenting a possible musical prodigy, and desiring most earnestly to give her guests a treat, Mrs. Bowman exclaimed in enthusiasm:

"Oh, how lovely of you! I hardly dared to ask, as Tryon was uncertain whether you would be willing. Suppose you give us something serious now, and later, when the men come in, we'll have the gay music. Make your own choice, though I'm very fond of Chopin, of course."

Without another word, the girl moved quietly over to the piano and took her seat. For just a moment her fingers wandered caressingly over the keys, as if they were old friends and she were having an understanding with them, then she began a Chopin Nocturne. Her touch was firm and velvety, and she brought out a bell-like tone from the instrument that made the little company of women realize that the player was mistress of her art. Her graceful figure and lovely head, with its simple ripples and waves of hair, were more noticeable than ever as she sat there, controlling the exquisite harmonies. Even Mrs. Blackwell stopped fanning and looked interested. Then she whispered to Mrs. Bowman: "A very sweet young girl. That's a pretty piece she's playing." Mrs. Blackwell was sweet and commonplace and old-fashioned.

Mrs. Parker Bowman sat up with a pink glow in her cheeks and a light in her eyes. She began to plan how she might keep this acquisition and exploit her among her friends. It was her delight to bring out new features in her entertainments.

"We shall simply keep you playing until you drop from weariness," she announced ecstatically, when the last wailing, sobbing, soothing chord had died away; and the other ladies murmured, "How delightful!" and whispered their approval.

The girl smiled and rippled into a Chopin Valse, under cover of which those who cared to could talk in low tones. Afterwards the musician dashed into the brilliant movement of a Beethoven Sonata.

It was just as she was beginning Rubinstein's exquisite tone portrait, Kamennoi-Ostrow, that the gentlemen came in.

Tryon Dunham had had his much desired talk with the famous judge, but it had not been about law.

They had been drawn together by mutual consent, each discovering that the other was watching the young stranger as she left the dining-room.

"She is charming," said the old man, smiling into the face of the younger. "Is she an intimate friend?"

"I—I hope so," stammered Dunham. "That is, I should like to have her consider me so."

"Ah!" said the old man, looking deep into the other's eyes with a kindly smile, as if he were recalling pleasant experiences of his own. "You are a fortunate fellow. I hope you may succeed in making her think so. Do you know, she interests me more than most young women, and in some way I cannot disconnect her with an occurrence which happened in my office this afternoon."

The young man showed a deep interest in the matter, and the Judge told the story again, this time more in detail.

They drew a little apart from the rest of the men. The host, who had been warned by his wife to give young Dunham an opportunity to talk with the Judge, saw that her plans were succeeding admirably.

When the music began in the other room the Judge paused a moment to listen, and then went on with his story.

"There is a freight elevator just opposite that left door of my office, and somehow I cannot but think it had something to do with the girl's disappearance, although the door was closed and the elevator was down on the cellar floor all the time, as nearly as I can find out."

The young man asked eager questions, feeling in his heart that the story might in some way explain the mystery of the young woman in the other room.

"Suppose you stop in the office to-morrow," said the Judge. "Perhaps you'll get a glimpse of her, and then bear me out in the statement that she's like your friend. By the way, who is making such exquisite music? Suppose we go and investigate. Mr. Bowman, will you excuse us if we follow the ladies? We are anxious to hear the music at closer range."

The other men rose and followed.

The girl did not pause or look up as they came in, but played on, while the company listened with the most rapt and wondering look. She was playing with an *empressement* which could not fail to command attention.

Tryon Dunham, standing just behind the Judge, was transfixed with amazement. That this delicate girl could bring forth such an entrancing volume of sound from the instrument was a great surprise. That she was so exquisite an artist filled him with a kind of intoxicating elation—it was as though she belonged to him.

At last she played Liszt's brilliant Hungarian Rhapsody, her slender hands taking the tremendous chords and octave runs with a precision and rapidity that seemed inspired. The final crash came in a shower of liquid jewels of sound, and then she turned to look at him, her one friend in that company of strangers.

He could see that she had been playing under a heavy strain. Her face looked weary and flushed, and her eyes were brilliant with feverish excitement. Those eyes seemed to be pleading with him now to set her free from the kindly scrutiny of these good-hearted, curious strangers. They gathered about her in delight, pouring their questions and praises upon her.

"Where did you study? With some great master, I am sure. Tell us all about yourself. We are dying to know, and will sit at your feet with great delight while you discourse."

Tryon Dunham interrupted these disquieting questions, by drawing his watch from his pocket with apparent hasty remembrance, and giving a well feigned exclamation of dismay.

"I'm sorry, Mrs. Bowman; it is too bad to interrupt this delightful evening," he apologized; "but I'm afraid if Miss Remington feels that she must take the next train, we shall have to make all possible speed. Miss Remington, can you get your wraps on in three minutes? Our carriage is probably at the door now."

With a look of relief, yet keeping up her part of dismay over the lateness of the hour, the girl sprang to her feet, and hurried away to get her wraps, in spite of her protesting hostess. Mrs. Bowman was held at bay with sweet expressions of gratitude for the pleasant entertainment. The great black picture hat was settled becomingly on the small head, the black cloak thrown over her gown, and the gloves fitted on hurriedly to hide the fact that they were too large.

"And whom did you say you studied with?" asked the keen hostess, determined to be able to tell how great a guest she had harbored for the evening.

"Oh, is Mr. Dunham calling me, Mrs. Bowman? You will excuse me for hurrying off, won't you? And it has been so lovely of you to ask me—perfectly delightful to find friends this way when I was a stranger."

She hurried toward the stairway and down the broad steps, and the hostess had no choice but to follow her.

The other guests crowded out into the hall to bid them good-by and to tell the girl how much they had enjoyed the music. Mrs. Blackwell insisted upon kissing the smooth cheek of the young musician, and whispered in her ear: "You play very nicely, my dear. I should like to hear you again some time." The kindness in her tone almost brought a rush of tears to the eyes of the weary, anxious girl.

III

Dunham hurried her off amid the goodbyes of the company, and in a moment more they were shut into the semi-darkness of the four-wheeler and whirled from the too hospitable door.

As soon as the door was shut, the girl began to tremble.

"Oh, we ought not to have done that!" she exclaimed with a shiver of recollection. "They were so very kind. It was dreadful to impose upon them. But—you were not to blame. It was my fault. It was very kind of you."

"We did not impose upon them!" he exclaimed peremptorily. "You are my friend, and that was all that we claimed. For the rest, you have certainly made good. Your wonderful music! How I wish I might hear more of it some time!"

The carriage paused to let a trolley pass, and a strong arc-light beat in upon the two. A passing stranger peered curiously at them, and the girl shrank back in fear. It was momentary, but the minds of the two were brought back to the immediate necessities of the occasion.

"Now, what may I do for you?" asked Dunham in a quiet, business-like tone, as if it were his privilege and right to do all that was to be done. "Have you thought where you would like to go?"

"I have not been able to do much thinking. It required all my wits to act with the present. But I know that I must not be any further trouble to you. You have done more already than any one could expect. If you can have the carriage stop in some quiet, out-of-the-way street where I shall not be noticed, I will get out and relieve you. If I hadn't been so frightened at first, I should have had more sense than to burden you this way. I hope some day I shall be able to repay your kindness, though I fear it is too great ever to repay."

"Please don't talk in that way," said he protestingly. "It has been a pleasure to do the little that I have done, and you have more than repaid it by the delight you have given me and my friends. I could not think of leaving you until you are out of your trouble, and if you will only give me a little hint of how to help, I will do my utmost for you. Are you quite sure you were followed? Don't you think you could trust me enough to tell me a little more about the matter?"

She shuddered visibly.

"Forgive me," he murmured. "I see it distresses you. Of course it is unpleasant to confide in an utter stranger. I will not ask you to tell me. I will try to think for you. Suppose we go to the station and get you a ticket to somewhere. Have you any preference? You can trust me not to tell any one where you have gone, can you not?" There was a kind rebuke in his tone, and her eyes, as she lifted them to his face, were full of tears.

"Oh, I do trust you!" she cried, distressed "You must not think that, but—you do not understand."

"Forgive me," he said again, holding out his hand in appeal. She laid her little gloved hand in his for an instant.

"You are so kind!" she murmured, as if it were the only thing she could think of. Then she added suddenly:

"But I cannot buy a ticket. I have no money with me, and I——"

"Don't think of that for an instant. I will gladly supply your need. A little loan should not distress you."

"But I do not know when I shall be able to repay it," she faltered, "unless"—she hastily drew off her glove and slipped a glittering ring from her finger—"unless you will let this pay for it. I do not like to trouble you so, but the stone is worth a good deal."

"Indeed," he protested, "I couldn't think of taking your ring. Let me do this. It is such a small thing. I shall never miss it. Let it rest until you are out of your trouble, at least."

"Please!" she insisted, holding out the ring. "I shall get right out of this carriage unless you do."

"But perhaps some one gave you the ring, and you are attached to it."

"My father," she answered briefly, "and he would want me to use it this way." She pressed the ring into his hand almost impatiently.

His fingers closed over the jewel impulsively. Somehow, it thrilled him to hold the little thing, yet warm from her fingers. He had forgotten that she was a stranger. His mind was filled with the thought of how best to help her.

"I will keep it until you want it again," he said kindly.

"You need not do that, for I shall not claim it," she declared. "You are at liberty to sell it. I know it is worth a good deal."

"I shall certainly keep it until I am sure you do not want it yourself," he repeated. "Now let us talk about this journey of yours. We are almost at the station. Have you any preference as to where you go? Have you friends to whom you could go?"

She shook her head.

"There are trains to New York every hour almost."

"Oh, no!" she gasped in a frightened tone.

"And to Washington often."

"I should rather not go to Washington," she breathed again.

"Pittsburg, Chicago?" he hazarded.

"Chicago will do," she asserted with relief. Then the carriage stopped before the great station, ablaze with light and throbbing with life. Policemen strolled about, and trolley-cars twinkled in every direction. The girl shrank back into the shadows of the carriage for an instant, as if she feared to come out from the sheltering darkness. Her escort half defined her hesitation.

"Don't feel nervous," he said in a low tone. "I will see that no one harms you. Just walk into the station as if you were my friend. You are, you know, a friend of long standing, for we have been to a dinner together. I might be escorting you home from a concert. No one will notice us. Besides, that hat and coat are disguise enough."

He hurried her through the station and up to the ladies' waiting-room, where he found a quiet corner and a large rocking-chair, in which he placed her so that she might look out of the great window upon the panorama of the evening street, and yet be thoroughly screened from all intruding glances by the big leather and brass screen of the "ladies' boot-black."

He was gone fifteen minutes, during which the girl sat quietly in her chair, yet alert, every nerve strained. At any moment the mass of faces she was watching might reveal one whom she dreaded to see, or a detective might place his hand upon her shoulder with a quiet "Come with me."

When Dunham came back, the nervous start she gave showed him how tense and anxious had been her mind. He studied her lovely face under the great hat, and noted the dark shadows beneath her eyes. He felt that he must do something to relieve her. It was unbearable to him that this young girl should be adrift, friendless, and apparently a victim to some terrible fear.

Drawing up a chair beside her, he began talking about her ticket.

"You must remember I was utterly at your mercy," she smiled sadly. "I simply had to let you help me."

"I should be glad to pay double for the pleasure you have given me in allowing me to help you," he said.

Just at that moment a boy in a blue uniform planted a sole-leather suit-case at his feet, and exclaimed: "Here you are, Mr. Dunham. Had a fierce time findin' you. Thought you said you would be by the elevator door."

"So I did," confessed the young man. "I didn't think you had time to get down yet. Well, you found me anyhow, Harkness."

The boy took the silver given him, touched his hat, and sauntered off.

"You see," explained Dunham, "it wasn't exactly the thing for you to be travelling without a bit of baggage. I thought it might help them to trace you if you really were being followed. So I took the liberty of 'phoning over to the club-house and telling the boy to bring down the suit-case that I left there yesterday. I don't exactly know what's in it. I had the man pack it and send it down to me, thinking I might stay all night at the club. Then I went home, after all, and forgot to take it along. It probably hasn't anything very appropriate for a lady's costume, but there may be a hair-brush and some soap and handkerchiefs. And, anyhow, if you'll accept it, it'll be something for you to hitch on to. One feels a little lost even for one night without a rag one can call one's own except a Pullman towel. I thought it might give you the appearance of a regular traveller, you know, and not a runaway."

He tried to make her laugh about it, but her face was deeply serious as she looked up at him.

"I think this is the kindest and most thoughtful thing you have done yet," she said. "I don't see how I can ever, ever thank you!"

"Don't try," he returned gaily. "There's your train being called. We'd better go right out and make you comfortable. You are beginning to be very tired."

She did not deny it, but rose to follow him, scanning the waiting-room with one quick, frightened look. An obsequious porter at the gate seized the suit-case and led them in state to the Pullman.

The girl found herself established in the little drawing-room compartment, and her eyes gave him thanks again. She knew the seclusion and the opportunity to lock the compartment door would give her relief from the constant fear that an unwelcome face might at any moment appear beside her.

"The conductor on this train is an old acquaintance of mine," he explained as that official came through the car. "I have taken this trip with him a number of times. Just sit down a minute. I am going to ask him to look out for you and see that no one annoys you."

The burly official looked grimly over his glasses at the sweet face under the big black hat, while Tryon Dunham explained, "She's a friend of mine. I hope you'll be good to her." In answer, he nodded grim assent with a smileless alacrity which was nevertheless satisfactory and comforting. Then the young man walked through the train to interview the porter and the newsboy, and in every way to arrange for a pleasant journey for one who three hours before had been unknown to him. As he went, he reflected that he would rather enjoy being conductor himself just for that night. He felt a strange reluctance toward giving up the oversight of the young woman whose destiny for a few brief hours had been thrust upon him, and who was about to pass out of his world again.

When he returned to her he found the shades closely drawn and the girl sitting in the sheltered corner of the section, where she could not be seen from the aisle, but where she could watch in the mirror the approach of any one. She welcomed him with a smile, but instantly urged him to leave the train, lest he be carried away.

He laughed at her fears, and told her there was plenty of time. Even after the train had given its preliminary shudder, he lingered to tell her that she must be sure to let him know by telegraph if she needed any further help; and at last swung himself from the platform after the train was in full motion.

Immediately he remembered that he had not given her any money. How could he have forgotten? And there was the North Side Station yet to be passed before she would be out of danger. Why had he not remained on the train until she was past that stop, and then returned on the next train from the little flag-station a few miles above, where he could have gotten the conductor to slow up for him? The swiftly moving cars asked the question as the long train flew by him. The last car was almost past when he made a daring dash and flung himself headlong upon the platform, to the horror of several trainmen who stood on the adjoining tracks.

"Gee!" said one, shaking his head. "What does that dude think he is made of, any way? Like to got his head busted that time, fer sure."

The brakeman, coming out of the car door with his lantern, dragged him to his feet, brushed him off, and scolded him vigorously. The young man hurried through the car, oblivious of the eloquent harangue, happy only to feel the floor jolting beneath his feet and to know that he was safe on board.

He found the girl sitting where he had left her, only she had flung up the shade of the window next her, and was gazing with wide, frightened eyes into the fast flying darkness. He touched her gently on the shoulder, and she turned with a cry.

"Oh, I thought you had fallen under the train!" she said in an awed voice. "It was going so fast! But you did not get off, after all, did you? Now, what can you do? It is too bad, and all on my account."

"Yes, I got off," he said doggedly, sitting down opposite her and pulling his tie straight. "I got off, but it wasn't altogether satisfactory, and so I got on again. There wasn't much time for getting on gracefully, but you'll have to excuse it. The fact is, I couldn't bear to leave you alone just yet. I couldn't rest until I knew you had passed the North Side Station. Besides, I had forgotten to give you any money."

"Oh, but you mustn't!" she protested, her eyes eloquent with feeling.

"Please don't say that," he went on eagerly. "I can get off later and take the down train, you know. Really, the fact is, I couldn't let you go right out of existence this way without knowing more about you."

"Oh!" she gasped, turning a little white about the lips, and drawing closer into her corner.

"Don't feel that way," he said. "I'm not going to bother you. You couldn't think that of me, surely. But isn't it only fair that you should show me a little consideration? Just give me an address, or something, where I could let you know if I heard of anything that concerned you. Of course it isn't likely I shall, but it seems to me you might at least let me know you are safe."

"I will promise you that," she said earnestly. "You know I'm going to send you back these things." She touched the cloak and the hat. "You might need them to keep you from having to explain their absence," she reminded him.

The moments fairly flew. They passed the North Side Station, and were nearing the flag station. After that there would be no more stops until past midnight. The young man knew he must get off.

"I have almost a mind to go on to Chicago and see that you are safely located," he said with sudden daring. "It seems too terrible to set you adrift in the world this way."

"Indeed, you must not," said the young woman, with a gentle dignity. "Have you stopped to think what people—what your mother, for instance—would think of me if she were ever to know I had permitted such a thing? You know you must not. Please don't speak of it again."

"I cannot help feeling that I ought to take care of you," he said, but half convinced.

"But I cannot permit it," she said firmly, lifting her trustful eyes to smile at him.

"Will you promise to let me know if you need anything?"

"No, I'm afraid I cannot promise even that," she answered, "because, while you have been a true friend to me, the immediate and awful necessity is, I hope, past."

"You will at least take this," he said, drawing from his pocket an inconspicuous purse of beautiful leather, and putting into it all the money his pockets contained. "I saw you had no pocketbook," he went on, "and I ventured to get this one in the drug-store below the station. Will you accept it from me? I have your ring, you know, and when you take the ring back you may, if you wish, return the purse. I wish it were a better one, but it was the most decent one they had. You will need it to carry your ticket. And I have put in the change. It would not do for you to be entirely without money. I'm sorry it isn't more. There are only nine dollars and seventy-five cents left. Do you think that will see you through? If there had been any place down-town here where I could cash a check at this time of night, I should have made it more."

He looked at her anxiously as he handed over the pocketbook. It seemed a ridiculously small sum with which to begin a journey alone, especially for a young woman of her apparent refinement. On the other hand, his friends would probably say he was a fool for having hazarded so much as he had upon an unknown woman, who was perhaps an adventuress. However, he had thrown discretion to the winds, and was undeniably interested in his new acquaintance.

"How thoughtful you are!" said the girl. "It would have been most embarrassing not to have a place to put my ticket, nor any money. This seems a fortune after being penniless"—she smiled ruefully. "Are you sure you have not reduced yourself to that condition? Have you saved enough to carry you home?"

"Oh, I have my mileage book with me," he said happily. It pleased him absurdly that she had not declined the pocketbook.

"Thank you so much. I shall return the price of the ticket and this money as soon as possible," said the girl earnestly.

"You must not think of that," he protested. "You know I have your ring. That is far more valuable than anything I have given you."

"Oh, but you said you were going to keep the ring, so that will not pay for this, I want to be sure that you lose nothing."

He suddenly became aware that the train was whistling and that the conductor was motioning him to go.

"But you have not told me your name," he cried in dismay.

"You have named me," she answered, smiling. "I am Mary Remington."

"But that is not your real name."

"You may call me Mary if you like," she said. "Now go, please, quick! I'm afraid you'll get hurt."

"You will remember that I am your friend?"

"Yes, thank you. Hurry, please!"

The train paused long enough for him to step in front of her window and wave his hat in salute. Then she passed on into the night, and only two twinkling lights, like diminishing red berries, marked the progress of the train until it disappeared in the cut. Nothing was left but the hollow echoes of its going, which the hills gave back.

Dunham listened as long as his ear could catch the sound, then a strange desolation settled down upon him. How was it that a few short hours ago he had known nothing, cared nothing, about this stranger? And now her going had left things blank enough! It was foolish, of course—just highly wrought nerves over this most extraordinary occurrence. Life had heretofore run in such smooth, conventional grooves as to have been almost prosaic; and now to be suddenly plunged into romance and mystery unbalanced him for the time. To-morrow, probably, he would again be able to look sane living in the face, and perhaps call himself a fool for his most unusual interest in this chance acquaintance; but just at this moment when he had parted from her, when the memory of her lovely face and pure eyes lingered with him, when her bravery and fear were both so fresh in his mind, and the very sound of her music was still in his brain, he simply could not without a pang turn back again to life which contained no solution of her mystery, no hope of another vision of her face.

The little station behind him was closed, though a light over the desk shone brightly through its front window and the telegraph sounder was clicking busily. The operator had gone over the hill with an important telegram, leaving the station door locked. The platform was windy and cheerless, with a view of a murky swamp, and the sound of deep-throated inhabitants croaking out a late fall concert. A rusty-throated cricket in a crack of the platform wailed a plaintive note now and then, and off beyond the swamp, in the edge of the wood, a screech-owl hooted.

Turning impatiently from the darkness, Dunham sought the bright window, in front of which lay a newspaper. He could read the large headlines of a column—no more, for the paper was upside down, and a bunch of bill-heads lay partly across it. It read:

MYSTERIOUS DISAPPEARANCE OF YOUNG AND PRETTY WOMAN

His heart stood still, and then went thudding on in dull, horrid blows. Vainly he tried to read further. He followed every visible word of that paper to discover its date and origin, but those miserable bill-heads frustrated his effort. He felt like dashing his hand through the glass, but reflected that the act might result in his being locked up in some miserable country jail. He tried the window and gave the door another vicious shake, but all to no purpose. Finally he turned on his heel and walked up and down for an hour, tramping the length of the shaky platform, back and forth, till the train rumbled up. As he took his seat in the car he saw the belated agent come running up the platform with a lighted lantern on his arm, and a package of letters, which he handed to the brakeman, but there was not time to beg the newspaper from him. Dunham's indignant mind continued to dwell upon the headlines, to the annoying accompaniment of screech-owl and frog and cricket. He resented the adjective "pretty." Why should any reporter dare to apply that word to a sweet and lovely woman? It seemed so superficial, so belittling, and—but then, of course, this headline did not apply to his new friend. It was some other poor creature, some one to whom perhaps the word "pretty" really applied; some one who was not really beautiful, only pretty.

At the first stop a man in front got out, leaving a newspaper in the seat. With eager hands, Dunham leaned forward and grasped it, searching its columns in vain for the tantalizing headlines. But there were others equally arrestive. This paper announced the mysterious disappearance of a young actress who was suspected of poisoning her husband. When seen last, she was boarding a train en route to Washington. She had not arrived there, however, so far as could be discovered. It was supposed that she was lingering in the vicinity of Philadelphia or Baltimore. There were added a few incriminating details concerning her relationship with her dead husband, and a brief sketch of her sensational life. The paragraph closed with the statement that she was an accomplished musician.

The young man frowned and, opening his window, flung the scandalous sheet to the breeze. He determined to forget what he had read, yet the lines kept coming before his eyes.

When he reached the city he went to the news-stand in the station, where was an agent who knew him, and procured a copy of every paper on sale. Then, instead of hurrying home, he found a seat in a secluded corner and proceeded to examine his purchases.

In large letters on the front page of a New York paper blazed:

HOUSE ROBBED OF JEWELS WORTH TEN THOUSAND DOLLARS BY BEAUTIFUL YOUNG ADVENTURESS MASQUERADING AS A PARLOR MAID

He ran his eye down the column and gathered that she was still at large, though the entire police force of New York was on her track. He shivered at the thought, and began to feel sympathy for all wrong-doers and truants from the law. It was horrible to have detectives out everywhere watching for beautiful young women, just when this one in whom his interest centred was trying to escape from something.

He turned to another paper, only to be met by the words:

and underneath:

Prison walls could not confine Miss Nancy Lee, who last week threw a lighted lamp at her mother, setting fire to the house, and then attempted suicide. The young woman seems to have recovered her senses, and professes to know nothing of what happened, but the physicians say she is liable to another attack of insanity, and deem it safe to keep her confined. She escaped during the night, leaving no clew to her whereabouts. How she managed to get open the window through which she left the asylum is still a mystery.

In disgust he flung the paper from him and took up another.

FOUL PLAY SUSPECTED! BEAUTIFUL YOUNG HEIRESS MISSING

His soul turned sick within him. He looked up and saw a little procession of late revellers rushing out to the last suburban train, the girls leaving a trail of orris perfume and a vision of dainty opera cloaks. One of the men was a city friend of his. Dunham half envied him his unperturbed mind. To be sure, he would not get back to the city till three in the morning, but he would have no visions of robberies and fair lunatics and hard pressed maidens unjustly pursued, to mar his rest.

Dunham buttoned his coat and turned up his collar as he started out into the street, for the night had turned cold, and his nerves made him chilly. As he walked, the blood began to race more healthily in his veins, and the horrors of the evening papers were dispelled. In their place came pleasant memories of the evening at Mrs. Bowman's, of the music, and of their ride and talk together. In his heart a hope began to rise that her dark days would pass, and that he might find her again and know her better.

His brief night's sleep was cut short by a sharp knock at his door the next morning. He awoke with a confused idea of being on a sleeping-car, and wondered if he had plenty of time to dress, but his sister's voice quickly dispelled the illusion.

"Tryon, aren't you almost ready to come down to breakfast? Do hurry, please. I've something awfully important to consult you about."

His sister's tone told him there was need for haste if he would keep in her good graces, so he made a hurried toilet and went down, to find his household in a state of subdued excitement.

"I'm just as worried as I can be," declared his mother. "I want to consult you, Tryon. I have put such implicit confidence in Norah, and I cannot bear to accuse her unjustly, but I have missed a number of little things lately. There was my gold link bag——"

"Mother, you know you said you were sure you left that at the Century Club."

"Don't interrupt, Cornelia. Of course it is possible I left it at the club rooms, but I begin to think now I didn't have it with me at all. Then there is my opal ring. To be sure, it isn't worth a great deal, but one who will take little things will take large ones."

"What's the matter, Mother? Norah been appropriating property not her own?"

"I'm very much afraid she has, Tryon. What would you do about it? It is so unpleasant to charge a person with stealing. It is such a vulgar thing to steal. Somehow I thought Norah was more refined."

"Why, I suppose there's nothing to do but just charge her with it, is there? Are you quite sure it is gone? What is it, any way? A ring, did you say?"

"No, it's a hat," said Cornelia shortly. "A sixty-dollar hat. I wish I'd kept it now, and then she wouldn't have dared. It had two beautiful willow ostrich plumes on it, but mother didn't think it was becoming. She wanted some color about it instead of all black. I left it in my room, and charged Norah to see that the man got it when he called, and now the man comes and says he wants the hat, and it is *gone*! Norah insists that when she last saw it, it was in my room. But of course that's absurd, for there was nobody else to take it but Thompson, and he's been in the family for so long."

"Nonsense!" said her brother sharply, dropping his fruit knife in his plate with a rattle that made the young woman jump. "Cornelia, I'm ashamed of you, thinking that poor, innocent girl has stolen your hat. Why, she wouldn't steal a pin, I am sure. You can tell she's honest by looking into her eyes. Girls with blue eyes like that don't lie and steal."

"Really!" Cornelia remarked haughtily. "You seem to know a great deal about her eyes. You may feel differently when I find the hat in her possession."

"Cornelia," interrupted Tryon, quite beside himself, "don't think of such a thing as speaking to that poor girl about that hat. I know she hasn't stolen it. The hat will probably be found, and then how will you feel?"

"But I tell you the hat cannot be found!" said the exasperated sister. "And I shall just have to pay for a hat that I can never wear."

"Mother, I appeal to you," said the son earnestly. "Don't allow Cornelia to speak of the hat to the girl. I wouldn't have such an injustice done in our house. The hat will turn up soon if you just go about the matter calmly. You'll find it quite naturally and unexpectedly, perhaps. Any way, if you don't, I'll pay for the hat, rather than have the girl suspected."

"But, Tryon," protested his mother, "if she isn't honest, you know we wouldn't want her about."

"Honest, Mother? She's as honest as the day is long. I am certain of that."

The mother rose reluctantly.

"Well, we might let it go another day," she consented. Then, looking up at the sky, she added, "I wonder if it is going to rain. I have a Reciprocity meeting on for to-day, and I'm a delegate to some little unheard-of place. It usually does rain when one goes into the country, I've noticed."

She went into the hall, and presently returned with a distressed look upon her face.

"Tryon, I'm afraid you're wrong," she said. "Now my rain-coat is missing. My new rain-coat! I hung it up in the hall-closet with my own hands, after it came from the store. I really think something ought to be done!"

"There! I hope you see!" said Cornelia severely. "I think it's high time something was done. I shall 'phone for a detective at once!"

"Cornelia, you'll do nothing of the kind," her brother protested, now thoroughly aroused. "I'll agree to pay for the hat and the rain-coat if they are not forthcoming before a fortnight passes, but you simply shall not ruin that poor girl's reputation. I insist, Mother, that you put a stop to such rash proceedings. I'll make myself personally responsible for that girl's honesty."

"Well, of course, Tryon, if you wish it——" said his mother, with anxious hesitation.

"I certainly do wish it, Mother. I shall take it as personal if anything is done in this matter without consulting me. Remember, Cornelia, I will not have any trifling. A girl's reputation is certainly worth more than several hats and rain-coats, and I *know* she has not taken them."

He walked from the dining-room and from the house in angry dignity, to the astonishment of his mother and sister, to whom he was usually courtesy itself. Consulting him about household matters was as a rule merely a form, for he almost never interfered. The two women looked at each other in startled bewilderment.

"Mother," said Cornelia, "you don't suppose he can have fallen in love with Norah, do you? Why, she's Irish and freckled! And Tryon has always been so fastidious!"

"Cornelia! How dare you suggest such a thing? Tryon is a *Dunham*. Whatever else a Dunham may or may not do, he never does anything low or unrefined."

The small, prim, stylish mother looked quite regal in her aristocratic rage.

"But, Mother, one reads such dreadful things in the papers now. Of course Tryon would never *marry* any one like that, but——"

"Cornelia!"—her mother's voice had almost reached a patrician scream—"I forbid you to mention the subject again. I cannot think where you learned to voice such thoughts."

"Well, my goodness, Mother, I don't mean anything, only I do wish I had my hat. I always did like all black. I can't imagine what ails Try, if it isn't that."

Tryon Dunham took his way to his office much perturbed in mind. Perplexities seemed to be thickening about him. With the dawn of the morning had come that sterner common-sense which told him he was a fool for having taken up with a strange young woman on the street, who was so evidently flying from justice. He had deceived not only his intimate friends by palming her off as a fit companion for them, but his mother and sister. He had practically stolen their garments, and had squandered more than fifty dollars of his own money. And what had he to show for all this? The memory of a sweet face, the lingering beauty of the name "Mary" when she bade him good-by, and a diamond ring. The cool morning light presented the view that the ring was probably valueless, and that he was a fool.

Ah, the ring! A sudden warm thrill shot through him, and his hand searched his vest pocket, where he had hastily put the jewel before leaving his room. That was something tangible. He could at least know what it was worth, and so make sure once for all whether he had been deceived. No, that would not be fair either, for her father might have made her think it was valuable, or he might even have been taken in himself, if he were not a judge of jewels.

Dunham examined it as he walked down the street, too perplexed with his own tumultuous thoughts to remember his usual trolley. He slipped the ring on his finger and let it catch the morning sunlight, now shining broad and clear in spite of the hovering rain-clouds in the distance. And gloriously did the sun illumine the diamond, burrowing into the great depths of its clear white heart, and causing it to break into a million fires of glory, flashing and glancing until it fairly dazzled him. The stone seemed to be of unusual beauty and purity, but he would step into the diamond shop as he passed and make sure. He had a friend there who could tell him all about it. His step quickened, and he covered the distance in a short time.

After the morning greeting, he handed over his ring.

"This belongs to a friend of mine," he said, trying to look unconcerned. "I should like to know if the stone is genuine, and about what it is worth."

His friend took the ring and retired behind a curious little instrument for the eye, presently emerging with a respectful look upon his face.

"Your friend is fortunate to have such a beautiful stone. It is unusually clear and white, and exquisitely cut. I should say it was worth at least"—he paused and then named a sum which startled Dunham, even accustomed as he was to counting values in high figures. He took the jewel back with a kind of awe. Where had his mysterious lady acquired this wondrous bauble which she had tossed to him for a trifle? In a tumult of feeling, he went on to his office more perplexed than ever. Suspicions of all sorts crowded thickly into his mind, but for every thought that shadowed the fair reputation of the lady, there came into his mind her clear eyes and cast out all doubts. Finally, after a bad hour of trying to work, he slipped the ring on his little finger, determined to wear it and thus prove to himself his belief in her, at least until he had absolute proof against her. Then he took up his hat and went out, deciding to accept Judge Blackwell's invitation to visit his office. He found a cordial reception, and the Judge talked business in a most satisfactory manner. His proposals bade fair to bring about some of the dearest wishes of the young man's heart, and yet as he left the building he was thinking more about the mysterious stranger who had disappeared from the Judge's office the day before than about the wonderful good luck that had come to him in a business way.

They had not talked much about her. The Judge had brought out her hat—a beautiful velvet one, with exquisite plumes—her gloves, a costly leather purse, and a fine hemstitched handkerchief, and as he put them sadly away on a closet shelf, he said no trace of her had as yet been found.

On his way toward his own office, Tryon Dunham pondered the remarkable coincidence which had made him the possessor of two parts of the same mystery—for he had no doubt that the hat belonged to the young woman who had claimed his help the evening before.

Meantime, the girl who was speeding along toward Chicago had not forgotten him. She could not if she would, for all about her were reminders of him. The conductor took charge of her ticket, telling her in his gruff, kind way what time they would arrive in the city. The porter was solicitous about her comfort, the newsboy brought the latest magazines and a box of chocolates and laid them at her shrine with a smile of admiration and the words, "Th' g'n'lmun sent 'em!" The suit-case lay on the seat opposite, the reflection of her face in the window-glass, as she gazed into the inky darkness outside, was crowned by the hat he had provided, and when she moved the silken rustle of the rain-coat reminded her of his kindness and forethought. She put her head back and closed her eyes, and for just an instant let her weary, overwrought mind think what it would mean if the man from whom she was fleeing had been such as this one seemed to be.

By and by, she opened the suit-case, half doubtfully, feeling that she was almost intruding upon another's possessions.

There were a dress-suit and a change of fine linen, handkerchiefs, neckties, a pair of gloves, a soft, black felt negligée hat folded, a large black silk muffler, a bath-robe, and the usual silver-mounted brushes, combs, and other toilet articles. She looked them over in a business-like way, trying to see how she could make use of them. Removing her hat, she covered it with the silk muffler, to protect it from dust. Then she took off her dress and wrapped herself in the soft bath-robe, wondering as she did so at her willingness to put on a stranger's garments. Somehow, in her brief acquaintance with this man, he had impressed her with his own pleasant fastidiousness, so that there was a kind of pleasure in using his things, as if they had been those of a valued friend.

She touched the electric button that controlled the lights in the little apartment, and lay down in the darkness to think out her problem of the new life that lay before her.

V

Beginning with the awful moment when she first realized her danger and the necessity for immediate flight, she lived over every perilous instant, her nerves straining, her breath bated as if she were experiencing it all once more. The horror of it! Her own hopeless, helpless condition! But finally, because her trouble was new and her body and mind, though worn with excitement, were healthy and young, she sank into a deep sleep, without having decided at all what she should do.

At last she woke from a terrible dream, in which the hand of her pursuer was upon her, and her preserver was in the dark distance. With that strange insistence which torments the victim of such dreams, she was obliged to lie still and imagine it out, again and again, until the face and voice of the young man grew very real in the darkness, and she longed inexpressibly for the comfort of his presence once more.

At length she shook off these pursuing thoughts and deliberately roused herself to plan her future.

The first necessity, she decided, was to change her appearance so far as possible, so that if news of her escape, with full description, had been telegraphed, she might evade notice. To that end, she arose in the early dawning of a gray and misty morning, and arranged her hair as she had never worn it before, in two braids and wound closely about her head. It was neat, and appropriate to the vocation which she had decided upon, and it made more difference in her appearance than any other thing she could have done. All the soft, fluffy fulness of rippling hair that had framed her face was drawn close to her head, and the smooth bands gave her the simplicity and severity of a saint in some old picture. She pinned up her gown until it did not show below the long black coat, and folded a white linen handkerchief about her throat over the delicate lace and garniture of the modish waist. Then she looked dubiously at the hat.

With a girl's instinct, her first thought was for her borrowed plumage. A fine mist was slanting down and had fretted the window-pane until there was nothing visible but dull gray shadows of a world that flew monotonously by. With sudden remembrance, she opened the suit-case and took out the folded black hat, shook it into shape, and put it on. It was mannish, of course, but girls often wore such hats.

As she surveyed herself in the long mirror of her door, the slow color stole into her cheeks. Yet the costume was not unbecoming, nor unusual. She looked like a simple schoolgirl, or a young business woman going to her day's work.

But she looked at the fashionable proportions of the other hat with something like alarm. How could she protect it? She did not for a moment think of abandoning it, for it was her earnest desire to return it at once, unharmed, to its kind purloiner.

She summoned the newsboy and purchased three thick newspapers. From these, with the aid of a few pins, she made a large package of the hat. To be sure, it did not look like a hat when it was done, but that was all the better. The feathers were upheld and packed softly about with bits of paper crushed together to make a springy cushion, and the whole built out and then covered over with paper. She reflected that girls who wore their hair wound about their heads and covered by plain felt hats would not be unlikely to carry large newspaper-wrapped packages through the city streets.

She decided to go barehanded, and put the white kid gloves in the suit-case, but she took off her beautiful rings, and hid them safely inside her dress.

When the porter came to announce that her breakfast was waiting in the dining-car, he looked at her almost with a start, but she answered his look with a pleasant, "Good morning. You see I'm fixed for a damp day."

"Yes, miss," said the man deferentially. "It's a nasty day outside. I 'spect Chicago'll be mighty wet. De wind's off de lake, and de rain's comin' from all way 'twoncet."

She sacrificed one of her precious quarters to get rid of the attentive porter, and started off with a brisk step down the long platform to the station. It was part of her plan to get out of the neighborhood as quickly as possible, so she followed the stream of people who instead of going into the waiting-room veered off to the street door and out into the great, wet, noisy world. With the same reasoning, she followed a group of people into a car, which presently brought her into the neighborhood of the large stores, as she had hoped it would. It was with relief that she recognized the name on one of the stores as being of world-wide reputation.

Well for her that she was an experienced shopper. She went straight to the millinery department and arranged to have the hat boxed and sent to the address Dunham had given her. Her gentle voice and handsome rain-coat proclaimed her a lady and commanded deference and respectful attention. As she walked away, she had an odd feeling of having communicated with her one friend and preserver.

It had cost less to express the hat than she had feared, yet her stock of money was woefully small. Some kind of a dress she must have, and a wrap, that she might be disguised, but what could she buy and yet have something left for food? There was no telling how long it would be before she could replenish her purse. Life must be reduced to its lowest terms. True, she had jewelry which might be sold, but that would scarcely be safe, for if she were watched, she might easily be identified by it. What did the very poor do, who were yet respectable?

The ready-made coats and skirts were entirely beyond her means, even those that had been marked down. With a hopeless feeling, she walked aimlessly down between the tables of goods. The suit-case weighed like lead, and she put it on the floor to rest her aching arms. Lifting her eyes, she saw a sign over a table—"Linene Skirts, 75 cts. and $1.00."

Here was a ray of hope. She turned eagerly to examine them. Piles of sombre skirts, blue and black and tan. They were stout and coarse and scant, and not of the latest cut, but what mattered it? She decided on a seventy-five cent black one. It seemed pitiful to have to economize in a matter of twenty-five cents, when she had been used to counting her money by dollars, yet there was a feeling of exultation at having gotten for that price any skirt at all that would do. A dim memory of what she had read about ten-cent lodging-houses, where human beings were herded like cattle, hovered over her.

Growing wise with experience, she discovered that she could get a black sateen shirt-waist for fifty cents. Rubbers and a cotton umbrella took another dollar and a half. She must save at least a dollar to send back the suit-case by express.

A bargain-table of odds and ends of woollen jackets, golf vests, and old fashioned blouse sweaters, selling off at a dollar apiece, solved the problem of a wrap. She selected a dark blouse, of an ugly, purply blue, but thick and warm. Then with her precious packages she asked a pleasant-faced saleswoman if there were any place near where she could slip on a walking skirt she had just bought to save her other skirt from the muddy streets. She was ushered into a little fitting-room near by. It was only about four feet square, with one chair and a tiny table, but it looked like a palace to the girl in her need, and as she fastened the door and looked at the bare painted walls that reached but a foot or so above her head and had no ceiling, she wished with all her heart that such a refuge as this might be her own somewhere in the great, wide, fearful world.

Rapidly she slipped off her fine, silk-lined cloth garments, and put on the stiff sateen waist and the coarse black skirt. Then she surveyed herself, and was not ill pleased. There was a striking lack of collar and belt. She sought out a black necktie and pinned it about her waist, and then, with a protesting frown, she deliberately tore a strip from the edge of one of the fine hem-stitched handkerchiefs, and folded it in about her neck in a turn-over collar. The result was quite startling and unfamiliar. The gown, the hair, the hat, and the neat collar gave her the look of a young nurse-girl or upper servant. On the whole, the disguise could not have been better. She added the blue woollen blouse, and felt certain that even her most intimate friends would not recognize her. She folded the rain-coat, and placed it smoothly in the suit-case, then with dismay remembered that she had nothing in which to put her own cloth dress, save the few inadequate paper wrappings that had come about her simple purchases. Vainly she tried to reduce the dress to a bundle that would be covered by the papers. It was of no use. She looked down at the suit-case. There was room for the dress in there, but she wanted to send Mr. Dunham's property back at once. She might leave the dress in the store, but some detective with an accurate description of that dress might be watching, find it, and trace her. Besides, she shrank from leaving her garments about in public places. If there had been any bridge near at hand where she might unobserved throw the dress into a dark river, or a consuming fire where she might dispose of it, she would have done it. But whatever she was to do with it must be done at once. Her destiny must be settled before the darkness came down. She folded the dress smoothly and laid it in the suit-case, under the rain-coat.

She sat down at a writing-desk, in the waiting-room, and wrote: "I am safe, and I thank you." Then she paused an instant, and with nervous haste wrote "Mary" underneath. She opened the suit-case and pinned the paper to the lapel of the evening coat. Just three dollars and sixty-seven cents she had left in her pocket-book after paying the expressage on the suit-case.

She felt doubtful whether she might not have done wrong about thus sending her dress back, but what else could she have done? If she had bought a box in which to put it, she would have had to carry it with her, and perhaps the dress might have been found during her absence from her room, and she suspected because of it. At any rate, it was too late now, and she felt sure the young man would understand. She hoped it would not inconvenience him especially to get rid of it. Surely he could give it to some charitable organization without much trouble.

At her first waking, in the early gray hours of the morning, she had looked her predicament calmly in the face. It was entirely likely that it would continue indefinitely; it might be, throughout her whole life. She could now see no way of help for herself. Time might, perhaps, give her a friend who would assist her, or a way might open back into her old life in some unthought-of manner, but for a time there must be hiding and a way found to earn her living.

She had gone carefully over her own accomplishments. Her musical attainments, which would naturally have been the first thought, were out of the question. Her skill as a musician was so great, and so well known by her enemy, that she would probably be traced by it at once. As she looked back at the hour spent at Mrs. Bowman's piano, she shuddered at the realization that it might have been her undoing, had it chanced that her enemy passed the house, with a suspicion that she was inside. She would never dare to seek a position as accompanist, and she knew how futile it would be for her to attempt to teach music in an unknown city, among strangers. She might starve to death before a single pupil appeared. Besides, that too would put her in a position where she would be more easily found. The same arguments were true if she were to attempt to take a position as teacher or governess, although she was thoroughly competent to do so. Rapidly rejecting all the natural resources which under ordinary circumstances she would have used to maintain herself, she determined to change her station entirely, at least for the present. She would have chosen to do something in a little, quiet hired room somewhere, sewing or decorating or something of the sort, but that too would be hopelessly out of her reach, without friends to aid her. A servant's place in some one's home was the only thing possible that presented itself to her mind. She could not cook, nor do general housework, but she thought she could fill the place of waitress.

With a brave face, but a shrinking heart, she stepped into a drug-store and looked up in the directory the addresses of several employment agencies.

VI

It was half past eleven when she stepped into the first agency on her list, and business was in full tide.

While she stood shrinking by the door the eyes of a dozen women fastened upon her, each with keen scrutiny. The sensitive color stole into her delicate cheeks. As the proprietress of the office began to question her, she felt her courage failing.

"You wish a position?" The woman had a nose like a hawk, and eyes that held no sympathy. "What do you want? General housework?"

"I should like a position as waitress." Her voice was low and sounded frightened to herself.

The hawk nose went up contemptuously.

"Better take general housework. There are too many waitresses already."

"I understand the work of a waitress, but I never have done general housework," she answered with the voice of a gentlewoman, which somehow angered the hawk, who had trained herself to get the advantage over people and keep it or else know the reason why.

"Very well, do as you please, of course, but you bite your own nose off. Let me see your references."

The girl was ready for this.

"I am sorry, but I cannot give you any. I have lived only in one home, where I had entire charge of the table and dining-room, and that home was broken up when the people went abroad three years ago. I could show you letters written by the mistress of that home if I had my trunk here, but it is in another city, and I do not know when I shall be able to send for it."

"No references!" screamed the hawk, then raising her voice, although it was utterly unnecessary: "Ladies, here is a girl who has no references. Do any of you want to venture?" The contemptuous laugh that followed had the effect of a warning to every woman in the room. "And this girl scorns general housework, and presumes to dictate for a place as waitress," went on the hawk.

"I want a waitress badly," said a troubled woman in a subdued whisper, "but I really wouldn't dare take a girl without references. She might be a thief, you know, and then—really, she doesn't look as if she was used to houses like mine. I must have a neat, stylish-looking girl. No self-respecting waitress nowadays would go out in the street dressed like that."

All the eyes in the room seemed boring through the poor girl as she stood trembling, humiliated, her cheeks burning, while horrified tears demanded to be let up into her eyes. She held her dainty head proudly, and turned away with dignity.

"However, if you care to try," called out the hawk, "you can register at the desk and leave two dollars, and if in the meantime you can think of anybody who'll give us a reference, we'll look it up. But we never guarantee girls without references."

The tears were too near the surface now for her even to acknowledge this information flung at her in an unpleasant voice. She went out of the office, and immediately,—surreptitiously,—two women hurried after her.

One was flabby, large, and overdressed, with a pasty complexion and eyes like a fish, in which was a lack of all moral sense. She hurried after the girl and took her by the shoulder just as she reached the top of the stairs that led down into the street.

The other was a small, timid woman, with anxiety and indecision written all over her, and a last year's street suit with the sleeves remodelled. When she saw who had stopped the girl, she lingered behind in the hall and pretended there was something wrong with the braid on her skirt. While she lingered she listened.

"Wait a minute, Miss," said the flashy woman. "You needn't feel bad about having references. Everybody isn't so particular. You come with me, and I'll put you in the way of earning more than you can ever get as a waitress. You weren't cut out for work, any way, with that face and voice. I've been watching you. You were meant for a lady. You need to be dressed up, and you'll be a real pretty girl——"

As she talked, she had come nearer, and now she leaned over and whispered so that the timid woman, who was beginning dimly to perceive what manner of creature this other woman was, could not hear.

But the girl stepped back with sudden energy and flashing eyes, shaking off the be-ringed hand that had grasped her shoulder.

"Don't you dare to speak to me!" she said in a loud, clear voice. "Don't you dare to touch me! You are a wicked woman! If you touch me again, I will go in there and tell all those women how you have insulted me!"

"Oh, well, if you're a saint, starve!" hissed the woman.

"I should rather starve ten thousand times than take help from you," said the girl, and her clear, horrified eyes seemed to burn into the woman's evil face. She turned and slid away, like the wily old serpent that she was.

Down the stairs like lightning sped the girl, her head up in pride and horror, her eyes still flashing. And down the stairs after her sped the little, anxious woman, panting and breathless, determined to keep her in sight till she could decide whether it was safe to take a girl without a character—yet who had just shown a bit of her character unaware.

Two blocks from the employment office the girl paused, to realize that she was walking blindly, without any destination. She was trembling so with terror that she was not sure whether she had the courage to enter another office, and a long vista of undreamed-of fears arose in her imagination.

The little woman paused, too, eying the girl cautiously, then began in an eager voice:

"I've been following you."

The girl started nervously, a cold chill of fear coming over her. Was this a woman detective?

"I heard what that awful woman said to you, and I saw how you acted. You must be a good girl, or you wouldn't have talked to her that way. I suppose I'm doing a dangerous thing, but I can't help it. I believe you're all right, and I'm going to try you, if you'll take general housework. I need somebody right away, for I'm going to have a dinner party to-morrow night, and my girl left me this morning."

The kind tone in the midst of her troubles brought tears to the girl's eyes.

"Oh, thank you!" she said as she brushed the tears away. "I'm a stranger here, and I have never before been among strangers this way. I'd like to come and work for you, but I couldn't do general housework, I'm sure. I never did it, and I wouldn't know how."

"Can't you cook a little? I could teach you my ways."

"I don't know the least thing about cooking. I never cooked a thing in my life."

"What a pity! What was your mother thinking about? Every girl ought to be brought up to know a little about cooking, even if she does have some other employment."

"My mother has been dead a good many years." The tears brimmed over now, but the girl tried to smile. "I could help you with your dinner party," she went on. "That is, I know all about setting the tables and arranging the flowers and favors. I could paint the place-cards, too—I've done it many a time. And I could wait on the table. But I couldn't cook even an oyster."

"Oh, place-cards!" said the little woman, her eyes brightening. She caught at the word as though she had descried a new star in the firmament. "I wish I could have them. They cost so much to buy. I might have my washerwoman come and help with the cooking. She cooks pretty well, and I could help her beforehand, but she couldn't wait on table, to save her life. I wonder if you know much about menus. Could you help me fix out the courses and say what you think I ought to have, or don't you know about that? You see, I have this very particular company coming, and I want to have things nice. I don't know them very well. My husband has business relations with them and wants them invited, and of all times for Betty to leave this was the worst!" She had unconsciously fallen into a tone of equality with the strange girl.

"I should like to help you," said the girl, "but I must find somewhere to stay before night, and if I find a place I must take it. I just came to the city this morning, and have nowhere to stay overnight."

The troubled look flitted across the woman's face for a moment, but her desire got the better of her.

"I suppose my husband would think I was crazy to do it," she said aloud, "but I just can't help trusting you. Suppose you come and stay with me to-day and to-morrow, and help me out with this dinner party, and you can stay overnight at my house and sleep in the cook's room. If I like your work, I'll give you a recommendation as waitress. You can't get a good place anywhere without it, not from the offices, I'm sure. A recommendation ought to be worth a couple of days' work to you. I'd pay you something besides, but I really can't afford it, for the washerwoman charges a dollar and a half a day when she goes out to cook; but if you get your board and lodging and a reference, that ought to pay you."

"You are very kind," said the girl. "I shall be glad to do that."

"When will you come? Can you go with me now, or have you got to go after your things?"

"I haven't any things but these," she said simply, "and perhaps you will not think I am fine enough for your dinner party. I have a little money. I could buy a white apron. My trunk is a good many miles away, and I was in desperate straits and had to leave it."

"H'm! A stepmother, probably," thought the kindly little woman. "Poor child! She doesn't look as if she was used to roughing it. If I could only hold on to her and train her, she might be a treasure, but there's no telling what John will say. I won't tell him anything about her, if I can help it, till the dinner is over."

Aloud she said: "Oh, that won't be necessary. I've got a white apron I'll lend you—perhaps I'll give it to you if you do your work well. Then we can fix up some kind of a waitress's cap out of a lace-edged handkerchief, and you'll look fine. I'd rather do that and have you come right along home with me, for everything is at sixes at sevens. Betty went off without washing the breakfast dishes. You can wash dishes, any way."

"Why, I can try," laughed the girl, the ridiculousness of her present situation suddenly getting the better of other emotions.

And so they got into a car and were whirled away into a pretty suburb. The woman, whose name was Mrs. Hart, lived in a common little house filled with imitation oriental rugs and cheap furniture.

The two went to work at once, bringing order out of the confusion that reigned in the tiny kitchen. In the afternoon the would-be waitress sat down with a box of water-colors to paint dinner-cards, and as her skilful brush brought into being dainty landscapes, lovely flowers, and little brown birds, she pondered the strangeness of her lot.

The table the next night was laid with exquisite care, the scant supply of flowers having been used to best advantage, and everything showing the touch of a skilled hand. The long hours that Mrs. Hart had spent puckering her brow over the household department of fashion magazines helped her to recognize the fact that in her new maid she had what she was pleased to call "the real thing."

She sighed regretfully when the guest of honor, Mrs. Rhinehart, spoke of the deftness and pleasant appearance of her hostess's waitress.

"Yes," Mrs. Hart said, swelling with pride, "she is a treasure. I only wish I could keep her."

"She's going to get married, I suppose. They all do when they're good," sympathized the guest.

"No, but she simply won't do cooking, and I really haven't work enough for two servants in this little house."

The guest sat up and took notice.

"You don't mean to tell me that you are letting a girl like that slip through your fingers? I wish I had known about her. I have spent three days in intelligence offices. Is there any chance for me, do you think?"

Then did the little woman prove that she should have had an *e* in her name, for she burst into a most voluble account of the virtues of her new maid, until the other woman was ready to hire her on the spot. The result of it all was that "Mary" was summoned to an interview with Mrs. Rhinehart in the dining-room, and engaged at four dollars a week, with every other Sunday afternoon and every other Thursday out, and her uniforms furnished.

The next morning Mr. Hart gave her a dollar-bill and told her that he appreciated the help she had given them, and wanted to pay her something for it.

She thanked him graciously and took the money with a kind of awe. Her first earnings! It seemed so strange to think that she had really earned some money, she who had always had all she wanted without lifting a finger.

She went to a store and bought a hair-brush and a few little things that she felt were necessities, with a fifty-cent straw telescope in which to put them. Thus, with her modest baggage, she entered the home of Mrs. Rhinehart, and ascended to a tiny room on the fourth floor, in which were a cot and a washstand, a cracked mirror, one chair, and one window. Mrs. Rhinehart had planned that the waitress should room with the cook, but the girl had insisted that she must have a room alone, no matter how small, and they had compromised on this unused, ill-furnished spot.

As she took off the felt hat, she wondered what its owner would think if he could see her now, and she brushed a fleck of dust gently from the felt, as if in apology for its humble surroundings. Then she smoothed her hair, put on the apron Mrs. Hart had given her, and descended to her new duties as maid in a fashionable home.

VII

Three days later Tryon Dunham entered the office of Judge Blackwell by appointment. After the business was completed the Judge said with a smile, "Well, our mystery is solved. The little girl is all safe. She telephoned me just after you had left the other day, and sent her maid after her hat. It seems that while she stood by the window, looking down into the street, she saw an automobile containing some of her friends. It stopped at the next building. Being desirous of speaking with a girl friend who was seated in the auto, she hurried out to the elevator, hoping to catch them. The elevator boy who took her down-stairs went off duty immediately, which accounts for our not finding any trace of her, and he was kept at home by illness the next morning. The young woman caught her friends, and they insisted that she should get in and ride to the station with one of them who was leaving the city at once. They loaned her a veil and a wrap, and promised to bring her right back for her papers and other possessions, but the train was late, and when they returned the building was closed. The two men who called for her were her brother and a friend of his, it seems. I must say they were not so attractive as she is. However, the mystery is solved, and I got well laughed at by my wife for my fears."

But the young man was puzzling how this all could be if the hat belonged to the girl he knew—to "Mary." When he left the Judge's office, he went to his club, determined to have a little quiet for thinking it over.

Matters at home had not been going pleasantly. There had been an ominous cloud over the breakfast table. The bill for the hat had arrived from Madame Dollard's, and Cornelia had laid it impressively by his plate. Even his mother had looked at him with a glance that spoke volumes as she remarked that it would be necessary for her to have a new rain-coat before another storm came.

There had been a distinct coolness between Tryon Dunham and his mother and sister ever since the morning when the loss of the hat and rain-coat was announced. Or did it date from the evening of that day when both mother and sister had noticed the beautiful ring which he wore? They had exclaimed over the flash of the diamond, and its peculiar pureness and brilliancy, and Cornelia had been quite disagreeable when he refused to take it off for her to examine. He had replied to his mother's question by saying that the ring belonged to a friend of his. He knew his mother was hurt by the answer, but what more could he do at present? True, he might have taken the ring off and prevented further comment, but it had come to him to mean loyalty to and belief in the girl whom he had so strangely been permitted to help. It was therefore in deep perplexity that he betook himself to his club and sat down in a far corner to meditate. He was annoyed when the office-boy appeared to tell him, there were some packages awaiting him in the office. "Bring them to me here, Henry."

The boy hustled away, and soon came back, bearing two hat-boxes—one of them in a crate—and the heavy leather suit-case.

With a start of surprise, Dunham sat up in his comfortable chair.

"Say, Henry, those things ought not to come in here." He glanced anxiously about, and was relieved to find that there was only one old gentleman in the room, and that he was asleep. "Suppose we go up to a private room with them. Take them out to the elevator, and I'll come in a moment."

"All right, sah."

"And say, Henry, suppose you remove that crate from the box. Then it won't be so heavy to carry."

"All right, sah. I'll be thah in jest a minute."

The young man hurried out to the elevator, and he and Henry made a quick ascent to a private room. He gave the boy a round fee, and was left in quiet to examine his property.

As he fumbled with the strings of the first box his heart beat wildly, and he felt the blood mounting to his face. Was he about to solve the mystery which had surrounded the girl in whom his interest had now grown so deep that he could scarcely get her out of his mind for a few minutes at a time?

But the box was empty, save for some crumpled white tissue-paper. He took up the cover in perplexity and saw his own name written by himself. Then he remembered. This was the box he had sent down to the club by the cabman, to get it out of his way. He felt disappointed, and turned quickly to the other box and cut the cord. This time he was rewarded by seeing the great black hat, beautiful and unhurt in spite of its journey to Chicago. The day was saved, and also the reputation of his mother's maid. But was there no word from the beautiful stranger? He searched hurriedly through the wrappings, pulled out the hat quite unceremoniously, and turned the box upside down, but nothing else could he find. Then he went at the suit-case. Yes, there was the rain-coat. He took it out triumphantly, for now his mother could say nothing, and, moreover, was not his trust in the fair stranger justified? He had done well to believe in her. He began to take out the other garments, curious to see what had been there for her use.

A long, golden brown hair nestling on the collar of the bathrobe gleamed in a chance ray of sunlight. He looked at it reverently, and laid the garment down carefully, that it might not be disturbed. As he lifted the coat, he saw the little note pinned to the lapel, and seized it eagerly. Surely this would tell him something!

But no, there was only the message that she had arrived safely, and her thanks. Stay, she had signed her name "Mary." She had told him he might call her that. Could it be that it was her real name, and that she had meant to trust him with so much of her true story?

He pondered the delicate writing of the note, thinking how like her it seemed, then he put the note in an inner pocket and thoughtfully lifted out the evening clothes. It was then that he touched the silken lined cloth of her dress, and he drew back almost as if he had ventured roughly upon something sacred. Startled, awed, he looked upon it, and then with gentle fingers lifted it and laid it upon his knee. Her dress! The one she had worn to the dinner with him! What did it all mean? Why was it here, and where was she?

He spread it out across his lap and looked at it almost as if it hid her presence. He touched with curious, wistful fingers the lace and delicate garniture about the waist, as if he would appeal to it to tell the story of her who had worn it.

What did its presence here mean? Did it bear some message? He searched carefully, but found nothing further. Had she reached a place of safety where she did not need the dress? No, for in that case, why should she have sent it to him? Had she been desperate perhaps, and——? But no, he would not think such things of her.

Gradually, as he looked, the gown told its own story, as she had thought it would: how she had been obliged to put on a disguise, and this was the only way to hide her own dress. Gradually he came to feel a great pleasure in the fact that she had trusted him with it. She had known he would understand, and perhaps had not had time to make further explanation. But if she had need of a disguise, she was still in danger! Oh, why had she not given him some clue? He dropped his head upon his hand in troubled perplexity.

A faint perfume of violets stole upon his senses from the dress lying across his knee. He touched it tenderly, and then half shamefacedly laid his cheek against it, breathing in the perfume. But he put it down quickly, looking quite foolish, and reminded himself that the girl was still a stranger, and that she might belong to another.

Then he thought again of the story the Judge had told him, and of his own first conviction that the two young women were identical. Could that be? Why could he not discover who the other girl was, and get some one to introduce him? He resolved to interview the Judge about it at their next meeting. In the meantime, he must wait and hope for further word from Mary. Surely she would write him again, and claim her ring perhaps, and, as she had been so thoughtful about returning the hat and coat at once, she would probably return the money he had loaned her. At least, he would hear from her in that way. There was nothing to do but be patient.

Yes, there was the immediate problem of how he should restore his sister's hat and his mother's coat to their places, unsuspected.

With a sigh, he carefully folded up the cloth gown, wrapped it in folds of tissue paper from the empty hat-box, and placed it in his suit-case. Then he transferred the hat to its original box, rang the bell, and ordered the boy to care for the box and suit-case until he called for them.

During the afternoon he took occasion to run into the Judge's office about some unimportant detail of the business they were transacting, and as he was leaving he said:

"By the way, Judge, who was your young woman who gave you such a fright by her sudden disappearance? You never told me her name. Is she one of my acquaintances, I wonder?"

"Oh, her name is Mary Weston," said the Judge, smiling. "I don't believe you know her, for she was from California, and was visiting here only for a few days. She sailed for Europe the next day."

That closed the incident, and, so far as the mystery was concerned, only added perplexity to it.

Dunham purposely remained down-town, merely having a clerk telephone home for him that he had gone out of the city and would not be home until late, so they need not wait up. He did this because he did not wish to have his mother or his sister ask him any more questions about the missing hat and coat. Then he took a twenty-mile trolley ride into the suburbs and back, to make good his word that he had gone out of town; and all the way he kept turning over and over the mystery of the beautiful young woman, until it began to seem to him that he had been crazy to let her drift out into the world alone and practically penniless. The dress had told its tale. He saw, of course, that if she were afraid of detection, she must have found it necessary to buy other clothing, and how could she have bought it with only nine dollars and seventy-five cents? He now felt convinced that he should have found some way to cash a check and thus supply her with what she needed. It was terrible. True, she had those other beautiful rings, which were probably valuable, but would she dare to sell them? Perhaps, though, she had found some one else as ready as he had been to help her. But, to his surprise, that thought was distasteful to him. During his long, cold ride in solitude he discovered that the thing he wanted most in life was to find that girl again and take care of her.

Of course he reasoned with himself most earnestly from one end of the trolley line to the other, and called himself all kinds of a fool, but it did not the slightest particle of good. Underneath all the reasoning, he knew he was glad that he had found her once, and he determined to find her again, and to unravel the mystery. Then he sat looking long and earnestly into the depths of the beautiful white stone she had given to him, as if he might there read the way to find her.

A little after midnight he arrived at the club-house, secured his suit-case and the hat-box, and took a cab to his home. He left the vehicle at the corner, lest the sound of it waken his mother or sister.

He let himself silently into the house with his latch-key, and tiptoed up to his room. The light was burning low. He put the hat-box in the farthest corner of his closet, then he took out the rain-coat, and, slipping off his shoes, went softly down to the hall closet.

In utter darkness he felt around and finally hung the coat on a hook under another long cloak, then gently released the hanging loop and let the garment slip softly down in an inconspicuous heap on the floor. He stole upstairs as guiltily as if he had been a naughty boy stealing sugar. When he reached his room, he turned up his light, and, pulling out the hat-box, surveyed it thoughtfully. This was a problem which he had not yet been able to solve. How should he dispose of the hat so that it would be discovered in such a way as to cast no further suspicion upon the maid? How would it do to place the hat in the hall-closet, back among the coats? No, it might excite suspicion to find them together. Could he put it in his own closet and profess to have found it there? No, for that might lead to unpleasant questioning, and perhaps involve the servants again. If he could only put it back where he had found it! But Cornelia, of course, would know it had not been there in her room all this week. It would be better to wait until the coast was clear and hide it in Cornelia's closet, where it might have been put by mistake and forgotten. It was going to be hard to explain, but that was the best plan he could evolve.

He took the hat out and held it on his hand, looking at it from different angles and trying to remember just how the girl had looked out at him from under its drooping plumes. Then with a sigh he laid it carefully in its box again and went to bed.

The morning brought clearer thought, and when the summons to breakfast pealed through the hall he took the box boldly in his hand and descended to the dining-room, where he presented the hat to his astonished sister.

"I am afraid I am the criminal, Cornelia," he said in his pleasantest manner. "I'm sorry I can't explain just how this thing got on my closet-shelf. I must have put it there myself through some unaccountable mix-up. It's too bad I couldn't have found it before and so saved you a lot of worry. But you are one hat the richer for it, for I paid the bill yesterday. Please accept it with my compliments."

Cornelia exclaimed with delight over the recovered hat.

"But how in the world could it have got into your closet, Tryon? It was impossible. I left it my room, I know I did, for I spoke to Norah about it before I left. How do you account for it?"

"Oh, I don't attempt to account for it," he said, with a gay wave of his hand. "I've been so taken up with other things this past week, I may have done almost anything. By the way, Mother, I'm sure you'll be glad to hear that Judge Blackwell has made me a most generous offer of business relations, and that I have decided to accept it."

Amid the exclamations of delight over this bit of news, the hat was forgotten for a time, and when the mother and sister finally reverted to it and began to discuss how it could have gotten on the closet shelf, he broke in upon their questions with a suggestion.

"I should advise, Mother, that you make a thorough search for your rain-coat. I am sure now that you must have overlooked it. Such things often happen. We were so excited the morning Cornelia missed the hat that I suppose no one looked thoroughly."

"But that is impossible, Tryon," said his mother, with dignity. "I had that closet searched most carefully."

"Nevertheless, Mother, please me by looking again. That closet is dark, and I would suggest a light."

"Of course, if you wish it," said his mother stiffly. "You might look, yourself."

"I'm afraid I shall not have time this morning," professed the coward. "But suppose you look in your own closets, too, Mother. I'm sure you'll find it somewhere. It couldn't get out of the house of itself, and Norah is no thief. The idea is preposterous. Please have it attended to carefully to-day. Good-by. I shall have to hurry down-town, and I can't tell just what time I shall get back this evening. 'Phone me if you find the coat anywhere. If you don't find it, I'll buy you another this afternoon."

"I shall *not* find the rain-coat," said his mother sternly, "but of course I will look to satisfy you. I *know* it is not in this house."

He beat a hasty retreat, for he did not care to be present at the finding of the rain-coat.

"There is something strange about this," said Mrs. Dunham, as with ruffled dignity she emerged from the hall closet, holding her lost rain-coat at arm's length. "You don't suppose your brother could be playing some kind of a joke on us, do you, Cornie? I never did understand jokes."

"Of course not," said practical Cornelia, with a sniff. "It's my opinion that Norah knows all about the matter, and Tryon has been helping her out with a few suggestions."

"Now, Cornelia, what do you mean by that? You surely don't suppose your brother would try to deceive us—his mother and sister?"

"I didn't say that, Mother," answered Cornelia, with her head in the air. "You've got your rain-coat back, but you'd better watch the rest of your wardrobe. I don't intend to let Norah have free range in my room any more."

VIII

Meantime, the girl in Chicago was walking in a new and hard way. She brought to her task a disciplined mind, a fine artistic taste, a delicate but healthy body, and a pair of willing, if unskilled, hands. To her surprise, she discovered that the work for which she had so often lightly given orders was beyond her strength. Try as she would, she could not accomplish the task of washing and ironing table napkins and delicate embroidered linen pieces in the way she knew they should be done. Will power can accomplish a good deal, but it cannot always make up for ignorance, and the girl who had mastered difficult subjects in college, and astonished music masters in the old world with her talent, found that she could not wash a window even to her own satisfaction, much less to that of her new mistress. That these tasks were expected of her was a surprise. Yet with her ready adaptability and her strong good sense, she saw that if she was to be a success in this new field she had chosen, she must be ready for any emergency. Nevertheless, as the weary days succeeded each other into weeks, she found that while her skill in table-setting and waiting was much prized, it was more than offset by her discrepancies in other lines, and so it came about that with mutual consent she and Mrs. Rhinehart parted company.

This time, with her reference, she did not find it so hard to get another place, and, after trying several, she learned to demand certain things, which put her finally into a home where her ability was appreciated, and where she was not required to do things in which she was unskilled.

She was growing more secure in her new life now, and less afraid to venture into the streets lest some one should be on the watch for her. But night after night, as she climbed to her cheerless room and crept to her scantily-covered, uncomfortable couch, she shrank from all that life could now hold out to her. Imprisoned she was, to a narrow round of toil, with no escape, and no one to know or care.

And who knew but that any day an enemy might trace her?

Then the son of the house came home from college in disgrace, and began to make violent love to her, until her case seemed almost desperate. She dreaded inexpressibly to make another change, for in some ways her work was not so hard as it had been in other places, and her wages were better; but from day to day she felt she could scarcely bear the hourly annoyances. The other servants, too, were not only utterly uncompanionable, but deeply jealous of her, resenting her gentle breeding, her careful speech, her dainty personal ways, her room to herself, her loyalty to her mistress.

Sometimes in the cold and darkness of the night-vigils she would remember the man who had helped her, who had promised to be her friend, and had begged her to let him know if she ever needed help. Her hungry heart cried out for sympathy and counsel. In her dreams she saw him coming to her across interminable plains, hastening with his kindly sympathy, but she always awoke before he reached her.

It was about this time that the firm of Blackwell, Hanover & Dunham had a difficult case to work out which involved the gathering of evidence from Chicago and thereabouts, and it was with pleasure that Judge Blackwell accepted the eager proposal from the junior member of the firm that he should go out and attend to it.

As Tryon Dunham entered the sleeper, and placed his suit-case beside him on the seat, he was reminded of the night when he had taken this train with the girl who had come to occupy a great part of his thoughts in these days. He had begun to feel that if he could ever hope to shake off his anxiety and get back to his normal state of mind, he must find her and unravel the mystery about her. If she were safe and had friends, so that he was not needed, perhaps he would be able to put her out of his thoughts, but if she were not safe——He did not quite finish the sentence even in his thoughts, but his heart beat quicker always, and he knew that if she needed him he was ready to help her, even at the sacrifice of his life.

All during the journey he planned a campaign for finding her, until he came to know in his heart that this was the real mission for which he had come to Chicago, although he intended to perform the other business thoroughly and conscientiously.

Upon his arrival in Chicago, he inserted a number of advertisements in the daily papers, having laid various plans by which she might safely communicate with him without running the risk of detection by her enemy.

If M.R. is in Chicago, will she kindly communicate with T. Dunham, General Delivery? Important.

Mrs. Bowman's friend has something of importance to say to the lady who dined with her October 8th. Kindly send address to T.D., Box 7 *Inter-Ocean* office.

"Mary," let me know where and when I can speak with you about a matter of importance. Tryon D., *Record-Herald* L.

These and others appeared in the different papers, but when he began to get communications from all sorts of poor creatures, every one demanding money, and when he found himself running wild-goose chases after different Marys and M.R.s, he abandoned all hope of personal columns in the newspapers. Then he began a systematic search for music teachers and musicians, for it seemed to him that this would be her natural way of earning her living, if she were so hard pressed that this was necessary.

In the course of his experiments he came upon many objects of pity, and his heart was stirred with the sorrow and the misery of the human race as it had never been stirred in all his happy, well-groomed life. Many a poor soul was helped and strengthened and put into the way of doing better because of this brief contact with him. But always as he saw new miseries he was troubled over what might have become of her—"Mary." It came to pass that whenever he looked upon the face of a young woman, no matter how pinched and worn with poverty, he dreaded lest *she* might have come to this pass, and be in actual need. As these thoughts went on day by day, he came to feel that she was his by a God-given right, his to find, his to care for. If she was in peril, he must save her. If she had done wrong—but this he could never believe. Her face was too pure and lovely for that. So the burden of her weighed upon his heart all the days while he went about the difficult business of gathering evidence link by link in the important law case that had brought him to Chicago.

Dunham had set apart working hours, and he seemed to labor with double vigor then because of the other task he had set himself. When at last he finished the legal business he had come for, and might go home, he lingered yet a day, and then another, devoting himself with almost feverish activity to the search for his unknown friend.

It was the evening of the third day after his law work was finished that with a sad heart he went toward the hotel where he had been stopping. He was obliged at last to face the fact that his search had been in vain.

He had almost reached the hotel when he met a business acquaintance, who welcomed him warmly, for far and wide among legal men the firm of which Judge Blackwell was the senior member commanded respect.

"Well, well!" said the older man. "Is this you, Dunham? I thought you were booked for home two days ago. Suppose you come home to dinner with me. I've a matter I'd like to talk over with you before you leave. I shall count this a most fortunate meeting if you will."

Just because he caught at any straw to keep him longer in Chicago, Dunham accepted the invitation. Just as the cab door was flung open in front of the handsome house where he was to be a guest, two men passed slowly by, like shadows out of place, and there floated to his ears one sentence voiced in broadest Irish: "She goes by th' name of Mary, ye says? All roight, sorr. I'll keep a sharp lookout."

Tryon Dunham turned and caught a glimpse of silver changing hands. One man was slight and fashionably dressed, and the light that was cast from the neighboring window showed his face to be dark and handsome. The other was short and stout, and clad in a faded Prince Albert coat that bagged at shoulders and elbows. He wore rubbers over his shoes, and his footsteps sounded like those of a heavy dog. The two passed around the corner, and Dunham and his host entered the house.

They were presently seated at a well appointed table, where an elaborate dinner was served. The talk was of pleasant things that go to make up the world of refinement; but the mind of the guest was troubled, and constantly kept hearing that sentence, "She goes by the name of Mary."

Then, suddenly, he looked up and met her eyes!

She was standing just back of her mistress's chair, with quiet, watchful attitude, but her eyes had been unconsciously upon the guest, until he looked up and caught her glance.

She turned away, but the color rose in her cheeks, and she knew that he was watching her.

Her look had startled him. He had never thought of looking for her in a menial position, and at first he had noticed only the likeness to her for whom he was searching. But he watched her furtively, until he became more and more startled with the resemblance.

She did not look at him again, but he noticed that her cheeks were scarlet, and that the long lashes drooped as if she were trying to hide her eyes. She went now and again from the room on her silent, deft errands, bringing and taking dishes, filling the glasses with ice water, seeming to know at a glance just what was needed. Whenever she went from the room he tried to persuade himself that it was not she, and then became feverishly impatient for her return that he might anew convince himself that it *was*. He felt a helpless rage at the son of the house for the familiar way in which he said: "Mary, fill my glass," and could not keep from frowning. Then he was startled at the similarity of names. Mary! The men on the street had used the name, too! Could it be that her enemy had tracked her? Perhaps he, Dunham, had appeared just in time to help her!

His busy brain scarcely heard the questions with which his host was plying him, and his replies were distraught and monosyllabic. At last he broke in upon the conversation:

"Excuse me, but I wonder if I may interrupt you for a moment. I have thought of something that I ought to attend to at once. I wonder if the waitress would be kind enough to send a 'phone message for me. I am afraid it will be too late if I wait."

"Why, certainly," said the host, all anxiety. "Would you like to go to the 'phone yourself, or can I attend to it for you? Just feel perfectly at home."

Already the young man was hastily writing a line or two on a card he had taken from his pocket, and he handed it to the waitress, who at his question had moved silently behind his chair to do his bidding.

"Just call up that number, please, and give the message below. They will understand, and then you will write down their answer?"

He handed her the pencil and turned again to his dessert, saying with a relieved air:

"Thank you. I am sorry for the interruption. Now will you finish that story?" Apparently his entire attention was devoted to his host and his ice, but in reality he was listening to the click of the telephone and the low, gentle voice in an adjoining room. It came after only a moment's pause, and he wondered at the calmness with which the usual formula of the telephone was carried on. He could not hear what she said, but his ears were alert to the pause, just long enough for a few words to be written, and then to her footsteps coming quietly back.

His heart was beating wildly. It seemed to him that his host must see the strained look in his face, but he tried to fasten his interest upon the conversation and keep calm.

He had applied the test. There was no number upon the card, and he knew that if the girl were not the one of whom he was in search, she would return for an explanation.

If you are "Mary Remington," tell me where and when I can talk with you. Immediately important to us both!

This was what he had written on the card. His fingers trembled as he took it from the silver tray which she presented to him demurely. He picked it up and eagerly read the delicate writing—hers—the same that had expressed her thanks and told of her safe arrival in Chicago. He could scarcely refrain from leaping from his chair and shouting aloud in his gladness.

The message she had written was simple. No stranger reading it would have thought twice about it. If the guest had read it aloud, it would have aroused no suspicion.

Y.W.C.A. Building, small parlor, three to-morrow.

He knew the massive building, for he had passed it many times, but never had he supposed it could have any interest for him. Now suddenly his heart warmed to the great organization of Christian women who had established these havens for homeless ones in the heart of the great cities.

He looked up at the girl as she was passing the coffee on the other side of the table, but not a flicker of an eyelash showed she recognized him. She went through her duties and withdrew from the room, but though they lingered long over the coffee, she did not return. When they went into the other room, his interest in the family grew less and less. The daughter of the house sat down at the piano, after leading him up to ask her to sing, and chirped through several sentimental songs, tinkling out a shallow accompaniment with her plump, manicured fingers. His soul revolted at the thought that she should be here entertaining the company, while that other one whose music would have thrilled them all stayed humbly in the kitchen, doing some menial task.

He took his leave early in the evening and hurried back to his hotel. As he crossed the street to hail a cab, he thought he saw a short, baggy figure shambling along in the shadow on the other side, looking up at the house.

He had professed to have business to attend to, but when he reached his room he could do nothing but sit down and think. That he had found her for whom he had so long sought filled him with a deeper joy than any he had ever known before. That he had found her in such a position deepened the mystery and filled him with a nameless dread. Then out of the shadow of his thoughts shambled the baggy man in the rubbers, and he could not rest, but took his hat and walked out again into the great rumbling whirl of the city night, walking on and on, until he again reached the house where he had dined.

He passed in front of the building, and found lights still burning everywhere. Down the side street, he saw the windows were brightly lighted in the servants' quarters, and loud laughter was sounding. Was she in there enduring such company? No, for there high in the fourth story gleamed a little light, and a shadow moved about across the curtain. Something told him that it was her room. He paced back and forth until the light went out, and then reverently, with lifted hat, turned and found his way back to the main avenue and a car line. As he passed the area gate a bright light shot out from the back door, there was a peal of laughter, an Irish goodnight, and a short man in baggy coat and rubbers shambled out and scuttled noiselessly down to the back street.

X

Dunham slept very little that night. His soul was hovering between joy and anxiety. Almost he was inclined to find some way to send her word about the man he had seen lingering about the place, and yet perhaps it was foolish. He had doubtless been to call on the cook, and there might be no connection whatever between what Dunham had heard and seen and the lonely girl.

Next day, with careful hands, the girl made herself neat and trim with the few materials she had at hand. Her own fine garments that had lain carefully wrapped and hidden ever since she had gone into service were brought forth, and the coarse ones with which she had provided herself against suspicion were laid aside. If any one came into her room while she was gone, he would find no fine French embroidery to tell tales. Also, she wished to feel as much like herself as possible, and she never could feel quite that in her cheap outfit. True, she had no finer outer garments than a cheap black flannel skirt and coat which she had bought with the first money she could spare, but they were warm, and answered for what she had needed. She had not bought a hat, and had nothing now to wear upon her head but the black felt that belonged to the man she was going to meet. She looked at herself pityingly in the tiny mirror, and wondered if the young man would understand and forgive? It was all she had, any way, and there would be no time to go to the store and buy another before the appointed hour, for the family had brought unexpected company to a late lunch and kept her far beyond her hour for going out.

She looked down dubiously at her shabby shoes, their delicate kid now cracked and worn. Her hands were covered by a pair of cheap black silk gloves. It was the first time that she had noticed these things so keenly, but now it seemed to her most embarrassing to go thus to meet the man who had helped her.

She gathered her little hoard of money to take with her, and cast one look back over the cheerless room, with a great longing to bid it farewell forever, and go back to the world where she belonged; yet she realized that it was a quiet refuge for her from the world that she must hereafter face. Then she closed her door, went down the stairs and out into the street, like any other servant on her afternoon out, walking away to meet whatever crisis might arise. She had not dared to speculate much about the subject of the coming interview. It was likely he wanted to inquire about her comfort, and perhaps offer material aid. She would not accept it, of course, but it would be a comfort to know that some one cared. She longed inexpressibly for this interview, just because he had been kind, and because he belonged to that world from which she had come. He would keep her secret. He had true eyes. She did not notice soft, padded feet that came wobbling down the street after her, and she only drew a little further out toward the curbing when a blear-eyed, red face peered into hers as she stood waiting for the car. She did not notice the shabby man who boarded the car after she was seated.

Tryon Dunham stood in the great stone doorway, watching keenly the passing throng. He saw the girl at once as she got out of the car, but he did not notice the man in the baggy coat, who lumbered after her and watched with wondering scrutiny as Dunham came forward, lifted his hat, and took her hand respectfully. Here was an element he did not understand. He stood staring, puzzled, as they disappeared into the great building; then planted himself in a convenient place to watch until his charge should come out again. This was perhaps a gentleman who had come to engage her to work for him. She might be thinking of changing her place. He must be on the alert.

Dunham placed two chairs in the far corner of the inner parlor, where they were practically alone, save for an occasional passer through the hall. He put the girl into the most comfortable one, and then went to draw down the shade, to shut a sharp ray of afternoon sunlight from her eyes. She sat there and looked down upon her shabby shoes, her cheap gloves, her coarse garments, and honored him for the honor he was giving her in this attire. She had learned by sharp experience that such respect to one in her station was not common. As he came back, he stood a moment looking down upon her. She saw his eye rest with recognition upon the hat she wore, and her pale cheeks turned pink.

"I don't know what you will think of my keeping this," she said shyly, putting her hand to the hat, "but it seemed really necessary at the time, and I haven't dared spend the money for a new one yet. I thought perhaps you would forgive me, and let me pay you for it some time later."

"Don't speak of it," he broke in, in a low voice. "I am so glad you could use it at all. It would have been a comfort to me if I had known where it was. I had not even missed it, because at this time of year I have very little use for it. It is my travelling hat."

He looked at her again as though the sight of her was good to him, and his gaze made her quite forget the words she had planned to say.

"I am so glad I have found you!" he went on. "You have not been out of my thoughts since I left you that night on the train. I have blamed myself over and over again for having gone then. I should have found some way to stand by you. I have not had one easy moment since I saw you last."

His tone was so intense that she could not interrupt him; she could only sit and listen in wonder, half trembling, to the low-spoken torrent of feeling that he expressed. She tried to protest, but the look in his face stopped her. He went on with an earnestness that would not be turned aside from its purpose.

"I came to Chicago that I might search for you. I could not stand the suspense any longer. I have been looking for you in every way I could think of, without openly searching, for that I dared not do lest I might jeopardize your safety. I was almost in despair when I went to dine with Mr. Phillips last evening. I felt I could not go home without knowing at least that you were safe, and now that I have found you, I cannot leave you until I know at least that you have no further need for help."

She summoned her courage now, and spoke in a voice full of feeling:

"Oh, you must not feel that way. You helped me just when I did not know what to do, and put me in the way of helping myself. I shall never cease to thank you for your kindness to an utter stranger. And now I am doing very well." She tried to smile, but the tears came unbidden instead.

"You poor child!" His tone was full of something deeper than compassion, and his eyes spoke volumes. "Do you suppose I think you are doing well when I see you wearing the garb of a menial and working for people to whom you are far superior—people who by all the rights of education and refinement ought to be in the kitchen serving you?"

"It was the safest thing I could do, and really the only thing I could get to do at once," she tried to explain. "I'm doing it better every day."

"I have no doubt. You can be an artist at serving as well as anything else, if you try. But now that is all over. I am going to take care of you. There is no use in protesting. If I may not do it in one way, I will in another. There is one question I must ask first, and I hope you will trust me enough to answer it. Is there any other—any other man who has the right to care for you, and is unable or unwilling to do it?"

She looked up at him, her large eyes still shining with tears, and shuddered slightly.

"Oh, no!" she said. "Oh, no, I thank God there is not! My dear uncle has been dead for four years, and there has never been any one else who cared since Father died."

He looked at her, a great light beginning to come into his face; but she did not understand and turned her head to hide the tears.

"Then I am going to tell you something," he said, his tone growing lower, yet clear enough for her to hear every word distinctly.

A tall, oldish girl with a discontented upper lip stalked through the hall, glanced in at the door, and sniffed significantly, but they did not see her. A short, baggy-coated man outside hovered anxiously around the building and passed the very window of that room, but the shade opposite them was down, and they did not know. The low, pleasant voice went on:

"I have come to care a great deal for you since I first saw you, and I want you to give me the right to care for you always and protect you against the whole world."

She looked up, wondering.

"What do you mean?"

"I mean that I love you, and I want to make you my wife. Then I can defy the whole world if need be, and put you where you ought to be."

"Oh!" she breathed softly.

"Wait, please," he pleaded, laying his hand gently on her little, trembling one. "Don't say anything until I have finished. I know of course that this will be startling to you. You have been brought up to feel that such things must be more carefully and deliberately done. I do not want you to feel that this is the only way I can help you, either. If you are not willing to be my wife, I will find some other plan. But this is the best way, if it isn't too hard on you, for I love you as I never dreamed that I could love a woman. The only question is, whether you can put up with me until I can teach you to love me a little."

She lifted eloquent eyes to his face.

"Oh, it is not that," she stammered, a rosy light flooding cheek and brow. "It is not that at all. But you know nothing about me. If you knew, you would very likely think as others do, and——"

"Then do not tell me anything about yourself, if it will trouble you. I do not care what others think. If you have poisoned a husband, I should know that he needed poisoning, and any way I should love you and stand by you."

"I have not done anything wrong," she said gravely.

"Then if you have done nothing wrong, we will prove it to the world, or, if we cannot prove it, we will fly to some desert island and live there in peace and love. That is the way I feel about you. I know that you are good and true and lovely! Any one might as well try to prove to me that you were crazy as that you had done wrong in any way."

Her face grew strangely white.

"Well, suppose I was crazy?"

"Then I would take you and cherish you and try to cure you, and if that could not be done, I should help you to bear it."

"Oh, you are wonderful!" she breathed, the light of a great love growing in her eyes.

The bare, prosaic walls stood stolidly about them, indifferent to romance or tragedy that was being wrought out within its walls. The whirl and hum of the city without, the grime and soil of the city within, were alike forgotten by these two as their hearts throbbed in the harmony of a great passion.

"Do you think you could learn to love me?" said the man's voice, with the sweetness of the love song of the ages in its tone.

"I love you now," said the girl's low voice. "I think I have loved you from the beginning, though I never dared to think of it in that way. But it would not be right for me to become your wife when you know practically nothing about me."

"Have you forgotten that you know nothing of me?"

"Oh, I do know something about you," she said shyly. "Remember that I have dined with your friends. I could not help seeing that they were good people, especially that delightful old man, the Judge. He looked startlingly like my dear father. I saw how they all honored and loved you. And then what you have done for me, and the way that you treated an utterly defenceless stranger, were equal to years of mere acquaintance. I feel that I know a great deal about you."

He smiled. "Thank you," he said, "but I have not forgotten that something more is due you than that slight knowledge of me, and before I came out here I went to the pastor of the church of which my mother is a member, and which I have always attended and asked him to write me a letter. He is so widely known that I felt it would be an introduction for me."

He laid an open letter in her lap, and, glancing down, she saw that it was signed by the name of one of the best known pulpit orators in the land, and that it spoke in highest terms of the young man whom it named as "my well-loved friend."

"It is also your right to know that I have always tried to live a pure and honorable life. I have never told any woman but you that I loved her—except an elderly cousin with whom I thought I was in love when I was nineteen. She cured me of it by laughing at me, and I have been heart-whole ever since."

She raised her eyes from reading the letter.

"You have all these, and I have nothing." She spread out her hands helplessly. "It must seem strange to you that I am in this situation. It does to me. It is awful."

She put her hands over her eyes and shuddered.

"It is to save you from it all that I have come." He leaned over and spoke tenderly, "Darling!"

"Oh, wait!" She caught her breath as if it hurt her, and put out her hand to stop him, "Wait! You must not say any more until I have told you all about it. Perhaps when I have told you, you will think about me as others do, and I shall have to run from you."

"Can you not trust me?" he reproached her.

"Oh, yes, I can trust you, but you may no longer trust me, and that I cannot bear."

"I promise you solemnly that I will believe every word you say."

"Ah, but you will think I do not know, and that it is your duty to give me into the hands of my enemies."

"That I most solemnly vow I will never do," he said earnestly. "You need not fear to tell me anything. But listen, tell me this one thing: in the eyes of God, is there any reason, physical, mental, or spiritual, why you should not become my wife?"

She looked him clearly in the eyes.

"None at all."

"Then I am satisfied to take you without hearing your story until afterwards."

"But I am not satisfied. If I am to see distrust come into your eyes, it must be now, not afterwards."

"Then tell it quickly."

He put out his hand and took hers firmly into his own, as if to help her in her story.

"My father died when I was only a young girl. We had not much money, and my mother's older brother took us to his home to live. My mother was his youngest sister, and he loved her more than any one else living. There was another sister, a half-sister, much older than my mother, and she had one son. He was a sulky, handsome boy, with a selfish, cruel nature. He seemed to be happy only when he was tormenting some one. He used to come to Uncle's to visit when I was there, and he delighted in annoying me. He stretched barbed wire where he knew I was going to pass in the dark, to throw me down and tear my clothes. He threw a quantity of burrs in my hair, and once he led me into a hornet's nest. After we went to live at my uncle's, Richard was not there so much. He had displeased my uncle, and he sent him away to school; but at vacation times he came again, and kept the house in discomfort. He seemed always to have a special spite against me. Once he broke a rare Dresden vase that Uncle prized, and told him I had done it.

"Mother did not live long after Father died, and after she was gone, I had no one to stand between me and Richard. Sometimes I had to tell my uncle, but oftener I tried to bear it, because I knew Richard was already a great distress to him.

"At last Richard was expelled from college, and Uncle was so angry with him that he told him he would do nothing more for him. He must go to work. Richard's father and mother had not much money, and there were other children to support. Richard threatened me with all sorts of awful things if I did not coax Uncle to take him back into his good graces again. I told him I would not say a word to Uncle. He was very angry and swore at me. When I tried to leave the room he locked the door and would not let me go until I screamed for help. Then he almost choked me, but when he heard Uncle coming he jumped out of the window. The next day he forged a check in my uncle's name, and tried to throw suspicion on me, but he was discovered, and my uncle disinherited him. Uncle had intended to educate Richard and start him well in life, but now he would have nothing further to do with him. It seemed to work upon my uncle's health, all the disgrace to the family name, although no one ever thought of my uncle in connection with blame. As he paid Richard's debts, it was not known what the boy had done, except by the banker, who was a personal friend.

"We went abroad then, and everywhere Uncle amused himself by putting me under the best music masters, and giving me all possible advantages in languages, literature, and art. Three years ago he died at Carlsbad, and after his death I went back to my music studies, following his wishes in the matter, and staying with a dear old lady in Vienna, who had been kind to us when we were there before.

"As soon as my uncle's death was known at home, Richard wrote the most pathetic letter to me, professing deep contrition, and saying he could never forgive himself for having quarrelled with his dear uncle. He had a sad tale of how the business that he had started had failed and left him with debts. If he had only a few hundred dollars, he could go on with it and pay off everything. He said I had inherited all that would have been his if he had done right, and he recognized the justice of it, but begged that I would lend him a small sum until he could get on his feet, when he would repay me.

"I had little faith in his reformation, but felt as if I could not refuse him when I was enjoying what might have been his, so I sent him all the money I had at hand. As I was not yet of age, I could not control all the property, but my allowance was liberal. Richard continued to send me voluminous letters, telling of his changed life, and finally asked me to marry him. I declined emphatically, but he continued to write for money, always ending with a statement of his undying affection. In disgust, I at last offered to send him a certain sum of money regularly if he would stop writing to me on this subject, and finally succeeded in reducing our correspondence to a check account. This has been going on for three years, except that he has been constantly asking for larger sums, and whenever I would say that I could not spare more just then he would begin telling me how much he cared for me, and how hard it was for him to be separated from me. I began to feel desperate about him, and made up my mind that when I received the inheritance I should ask the lawyers to make some arrangement with him by which I should no longer be annoyed.

"It was necessary for me to return to America when I came of age, in order to sign certain papers and take full charge of the property. Richard knew this. He seems to have had some way of finding out everything my uncle did.

"He wrote telling me of a dear friend of his mother, who was soon to pass through Vienna, and who by some misfortune had been deprived of a position as companion and chaperon to a young girl who was travelling. He said it had occurred to him that perhaps he could serve us both by suggesting to me that she be my travelling companion on the voyage. He knew I would not want to travel alone, and he sent her address and all sorts of credentials, with a message from his mother that she would feel perfectly safe about me if I went in this woman's guardianship.

"I really did need a travelling companion, of course, having failed to get my dear old lady to undertake the voyage, so I thought it could do no harm. I went to see her, and found her pretty and frail and sad. She made a piteous appeal to me, and though I was not greatly taken with her, I decided she would do as well as any one for a companion.

"She did not bother me during the voyage, but fluttered about and was quite popular on board, especially with a tall, disagreeable man with a cruel jaw and small eyes, who always made me feel as if he would gloat over any one in his power. I found out that he was a physician, a specialist in mental diseases, so Mrs. Chambray told me, and she talked a great deal about his skill and insight into such maladies.

"At New York my cousin Richard met us and literally took possession of us. Without my knowledge, the cruel-looking doctor was included in the party. I did not discover it until we were on the train, bound, as I supposed, for my old home just beyond Buffalo. It was some time since I had been in New York, and I naturally did not notice much which way we were going. The fact was, every plan was anticipated, and I was told that all arrangements had been made. Mrs. Chambray began to treat me like a little child and say: 'You see we are going to take good care of you, dear, so don't worry about a thing.'

"I had taken the drawing-room compartment, not so much because I had a headache, as I told them, as because I wanted to get away from their society. My cousin's marked devotion became painful to me. Then, too, the attentions and constant watchfulness of the disagreeable doctor became most distasteful.

"We had been sitting on the observation platform, and it was late in the afternoon, when I said I was going to lie down, and the two men got up to go into the smoker. In spite of my protests, Mrs. Chambray insisted upon following me in, to see that I was perfectly comfortable. She fussed around me, covering me up and offering smelling salts and eau de cologne for my head. I let her fuss, thinking that was the quickest way to get rid of her. I closed my eyes, and she said she would go out to the observation platform. I lay still for awhile, thinking about her and how much I wanted to get rid of her. She acted as if she had been engaged to stay with me forever, and it suddenly became very plain to me that I ought to have a talk with her and tell her that I should need her services no longer after this journey was over. It might make a difference to her if she knew it at once, and perhaps now would be as good a time to talk as any, for she was probably alone out on the platform. I got up and made a few little changes in my dress, for it would soon be time to go into the dining-car. Then I went out to the observation platform, but she was not there. The chairs were all empty, so I chose the one next to the railing, away from the car door, and sat down to wait for her, thinking she would soon be back.

"We were going very fast, through a pretty bit of country. It was dusky and restful out there, so I leaned back and closed my eyes. Presently I heard voices approaching, above the rumble of the train, and, peeping around the doorway, I saw Mrs. Chambray, Richard, and the doctor coming from the other car. I kept quiet, hoping they would not come out, and they did not. They settled down near the door, and ordered the porter to put up a table for them to play cards.

"The train began to slow down, and finally came to a halt for a longer time on a sidetrack, waiting for another train to pass. I heard Richard ask where I was. Mrs. Chambray said laughingly that I was safely asleep. Then, before I realized it, they began to talk about me. It happened there were no other passengers in the car. Richard asked Mrs. Chambray if she thought I had any suspicion that I was not on the right train, and she said, 'Not the slightest,' and then by degrees there floated to me through the open door the most diabolical plot I had ever heard of. I gathered from it that we were on the way to Philadelphia, would reach there in a little while, and would then proceed to a place near Washington, where the doctor had a private insane asylum, and where I was to be shut up. They were going to administer some drug that would make me unconscious when I was taken off the train. If they could not get me to take it for the headache I had talked about, Mrs. Chambray was to manage to get it into my food or give it to me when asleep. Mrs. Chambray, it seems, had not known the entire plot before leaving Europe, and this was their first chance of telling her. They thought I was safely in my compartment, asleep, and she had gone into the other car to give the signal as soon as she thought she had me where I would not get up again for a while.

"They had arranged every detail. Richard had been using as models the letters I had written him for the last three years, and had constructed a set of love letters from me to him, in perfect imitation of my handwriting. They compared the letters and read snatches of the sentences aloud. The letters referred constantly to our being married as soon as I should return from abroad, and some of them spoke of the money as belonging to us both, and that now it would come to its own without any further trouble.

"They even exhibited a marriage certificate, which, from what they said, must have been made out with our names, and Mrs. Chambray and the doctor signed their names as witnesses. As nearly as I could make out, they were going to use this as evidence that Richard was my husband, and that he had the right to administer my estate during the time that I was incapable. They had even arranged that a young woman who was hopelessly insane should take my place when the executors of the estate came to see me, if they took the trouble to do that. As it was some years since either of them had seen me, they could easily have been deceived. And for their help Mrs. Chambray and the doctor were to receive a handsome sum.

"I could scarcely believe my ears at first. It seemed to me that I must be mistaken, that they could not be talking about me. But my name was mentioned again and again, and as each link in the horrible plot was made plain to me, my terror grew so great that I was on the verge of rushing into the car and calling for the conductor and porter to help me. But something held me still, and I heard Richard say that he had just informed the trainmen that I was insane, and that they need not be surprised if I had to be restrained. He had told them that I was comparatively harmless, but he had no doubt that the conductor had whispered it to our fellow-passengers in the car, which explained their prolonged absence in the smoker. Then they all laughed, and it seemed to me that the cover to the bottomless pit was open and that I was falling in.

"I sat still, hardly daring to breathe. Then I began to go over the story bit by bit, and to put together little things that had happened since we landed, and even before I had left Vienna; and I saw that I was caught in a trap. It would be no use to appeal to any one, for no one would believe me. I looked wildly out at the ground and had desperate thoughts of climbing over the rail and jumping from the train. Death would be better than what I should soon have to face. My persecutors had even told how they had deceived my friends at home by sending telegrams of my mental condition, and of the necessity for putting me into an asylum. There would be no hope of appealing to them for help. The only witnesses to my sanity were far away in Vienna, and how could I reach them if I were in Richard's power?

"I watched the names of the stations as they flew by, but it gradually grew dark, and I could hardly make them out. I thought one looked like the name of a Philadelphia suburb, but I could not be sure.

"I was freezing with horror and with cold, but did not dare to move, lest I attract their attention.

"We began to rush past rows of houses, and I knew we were approaching a city. Then, suddenly, the train slowed down and stopped, with very little warning, as if it intended to halt only a second and then hurry on.

"There was a platform on one side of the train, but we were out beyond the car-shed, for our train was long. I could not climb over the rail to the platform, for I was sitting on the side away from the station, and would have had to pass the car door in order to do so. I should be sure to be seen.

"On the other side were a great many tracks separated by strong picket fences as high as the car platform and close to the trains, and they reached as far as I could see in either direction. I had no time to think, and there was nothing I could do but climb over the rail and get across those tracks and fences somehow.

"My hands were so cold and trembling that I could scarcely hold on to the rail as I jumped over.

"I cannot remember how I got across. Twice I had to cling to a fence while an express train rushed by, and the shock and noise almost stunned me. It was a miracle that I was not killed, but I did not think of that until afterwards. I was conscious only of the train I had left standing by the station. I glanced back once, and thought I saw Richard come to the door of the car. Then I stumbled on blindly. I don't remember any more until I found myself hurrying along that dark passage under the bridge and saw you just ahead. I was afraid to speak to you, but I did not know what else to do, and you were so good to me——!" Her voice broke in a little sob.

All the time she had been talking, he had held her hand firmly. She had forgotten that any one might be watching; he did not care.

The tall girl with the discontented upper lip went to the matron and told her that she thought the man and the woman in the parlor ought to be made to go. She believed the man was trying to coax the girl to do something she didn't want to do. The matron started on a voyage of discovery up the hall and down again, with penetrating glances into the room, but the two did not see her.

"Oh, my poor dear little girl!" breathed the man. "And you have passed through all this awful experience alone! Why did you not tell me about it? I could have helped you. I am a lawyer."

"I thought you would be on your guard at once and watch for evidences of my insanity. I thought perhaps you would believe it true, and would feel it necessary to return me to my friends. I think I should have been tempted to do that, perhaps, if any one had come to me with such a story."

"One could not do that after seeing and talking with you. I never could have believed it. Surely no reputable physician would lend his influence to put you in an asylum, yet I know such things have been done. Your cousin must be a desperate character. I shall not feel safe until you belong to me. I saw two men hanging about Mr. Phillips's house last evening as I went in. They were looking up at the windows and talking about keeping a close watch on some one named Mary. One of the men was tall and slight and handsome, with dark hair and eyes; the other was Irish, and wore a coat too large for him, and rubbers. I went back later in the evening, and the Irishman was hovering about the house."

The girl looked up with frightened eyes and grasped the arms of her chair excitedly.

"Will you go with me now to a church not far away, where a friend of mine is the pastor, and be married? Then we can defy all the cousins in creation. Can't you trust me?" he pleaded.

"Oh, yes, but——"

"Is it that you do not love me?"

"No," she said, and her eyes drooped shyly. "It seems strange that I dare to say it to you when I have known you so little." She lifted her eyes, full of a wonderful love light, and she was glorified to him, all meanly dressed though she was. The smooth Madonna braids around the shapely head, covered by the soft felt hat, seemed more beautiful to him than all the elaborate head-dresses of modern times.

"Where is the 'but' then, dear? Shall we go now?"

"How can I go in this dress?" She looked down at her shabby shoes, rough black gown, and cheap gloves in dismay, and a soft pink stole into her face.

"You need not. Your own gown is out in the office in my suit-case. I brought it with me, thinking you might need it—*hoping* you might, I mean;" and he smiled. "I have kept it always near me; partly because I wanted the comfort of it, partly because I was afraid some one else might find it, and desecrate our secret with their common-place wondering."

It was at this moment that the matron of the building stepped up to the absorbed couple, resolved to do her duty. Her lips were pursed to their thinnest, and displeasure was in her face.

The young man arose and asked in a grave tone:

"Excuse me, but can you tell me whether this lady can get a room here to rest for a short time, while I go out and attend to a matter of business?"

The matron noticed his refined face and true eyes, and she accepted with a good grace the ten-dollar bill he handed to her.

"We charge only fifty cents a night for a room," she said, glancing at the humble garments of the man's companion. She thought the girl must be a poor dependent or a country relative.

"That's all right," said the young man. "Just let the change help the good work along."

That made a distinct change in the atmosphere. The matron smiled, and retired to snub the girl with the discontented upper lip. Then she sent the elevator boy to carry the girl's suit-case. As the matron came back to the office, a baggy man with cushioned tires hustled out of the open door into the street, having first cast back a keen, furtive glance that searched every corner of the place.

"Now," said Dunham reassuringly, as the matron disappeared, "you can go up to your room and get ready, and I will look after a few little matters. I called on my friend, the minister, this morning, and I have looked up the legal part of this affair. I can see that everything is all right in a few minutes. Is there anything you would like me to do for you?"

"No," she answered, looking up half frightened; "but I am afraid I ought not to let you do this. You scarcely know me."

"Now, dear, no more of that. We have no time to lose. How long will it take you to get dressed? Will half an hour do? It is getting late."

"Oh, it will not take long." She caught her breath with gladness. Her companion's voice was so strong and comforting, his face so filled with a wonderful love, that she felt dazed with the sudden joy of it all.

The elevator boy appeared in the doorway with the familiar suit-case.

"Don't be afraid, dear heart," whispered the young man, as he attended her to the elevator. "I'll soon be back again, and then, *then*, we shall be together!"

It was a large front room to which the boy took her. The ten-dollar bill had proven effective. It was not a "fifty-cents-a-night" room. Some one—some guest or kindly patron—had put a small illuminated text upon the wall in a neat frame. It met her eye as she entered—"Rejoice and be glad." Just a common little picture card, it was, with a phrase that has become trite to many, yet it seemed a message to her, and her heart leaped to obey. She went to the window to catch a glimpse of the man who would soon be her husband, but he was not there, and the hurrying people reminded her that she must hasten. Across the street a slouching figure in a baggy coat looked fixedly up and caught her glance. She trembled and drew back out of the sunshine, remembering what Dunham had told her about the Irishman of the night before. With a quick instinct, she drew down the shade, and locked her door.

XII

The rubbered feet across the way hurried their owner into the cigar-store in front of which he had been standing, and where he had a good view of the Y.W.C.A. Building. He flung down some change and demanded the use of the telephone. Then, with one eye on the opposite doorway, he called up a number and delivered his message.

"Oi've treed me bird. She's in a room all roight at the Y.W.C.A. place, fer I seed her at the winder. She come with a foine gintlemin, but he's gahn now, an' she's loike to stay a spell. You'd best come at once.... All roight. Hurry up!" He hung up the telephone-receiver and hurried back to his post in front of the big entrance. Meanwhile the bride-elect upstairs, with happy heart and trembling fingers, was putting on her own beautiful garments once more, and arranging the waves of lovely hair in their old accustomed way.

Tryon Dunham's plans were well laid. He first called up his friend the minister and told him to be ready; then a florist not far from the church; then a large department store where he had spent some time that morning. "Is that Mr. Hunter, head of the fur department? Mr. Hunter, this is Mr. Dunham. You remember our conversation this morning? Kindly send the coat and hat I selected to the Y.W.C.A. Building at once. Yes, just send them to the office. You remember it was to be C.O.D., and I showed you my certified check this morning. It's all right, is it? How long will it take you to get it there?... All right. Have the boy wait if I'm not there. Good-by."

His next move was to order a carriage, and have it stop at the florist's on the way. That done, he consulted his watch. Seventeen minutes of his precious half-hour were gone. With nervous haste he went into a telephone booth and called up his own home on the long-distance.

To his relief, his mother answered.

"Is that you, Mother? This is Tryon. Are you all well? That's good. Yes, I'm in Chicago, but will soon be home. Mother, I've something to tell you that may startle you, though there is nothing to make you sad. You have known that there was something on my mind for some time." He paused for the murmur of assent.

He knew how his mother was looking, even though he could not see her—that set look of being ready for anything. He wanted to spare her as much as possible, so he hastened on:

"You remember speaking to me about the ring I wore?"

"Tryon! Are you engaged?" There was a sharp anxiety in the tone as it came through the hundreds of miles of space.

"One better, Mother. I'm just about to be married!"

"My son! What have you done? Don't forget the honorable name you bear!"

"No, Mother, I don't forget. She's fine and beautiful and sweet. You will love her, and our world will fall at her feet!"

"But who is she? You must remember that love is very blind. Tryon, you must come home at once. I shall die if you disgrace us all. Don't do anything to spoil our lives. I know it is something dreadful, or you would not do it in such haste."

"Nothing of the kind, Mother. Can't you trust me? Let me explain. She is alone, and legal circumstances which it would take too long for me to explain over the 'phone have made it desirable for her to have my immediate protection. We are going at once to Edwin Twinell's church, and he will marry us. It is all arranged, but I felt that you ought to be told beforehand. We shall probably take the night express for home. Tell Cornelia that I shall expect congratulations telegraphed to the hotel here inside of two hours."

"But, Tryon, what will our friends think? It is most extraordinary! How can you manage about announcements?"

"Bother the red tape, Mother! What difference does that make? Put it in the society column if you want to."

"But, Tryon, we do not want to be conspicuous!"

"Well, Mother, I'm not going to put off my wedding at the last minute for a matter of some bits of pasteboard. I'll do any reasonable thing to please you, but not that."

"Couldn't you get a chaperon for her, and bring her on to me? Then we could plan the wedding at our leisure."

"Impossible, Mother! In the first place, she never would consent. Really, I cannot talk any more about it. I must go at once, or I shall be late. Tell me you will love her for my sake, until you love her for her own."

"Tryon, you always were unreasonable. Suppose you have the cards engraved at once, and I will telegraph our list to the engraver if you will give me his address. If you prefer, you can get them engraved and sent out from there. That will keep tongues still."

"All right, I'll do it. I'll have the engraver telegraph his address to you within two hours. Have your list ready. And, Mother, don't worry. She's all right. You couldn't have chosen better yourself. Say you will love her, Mother dear."

"Oh, I suppose I'll try," sighed the wires disconsolately; "but I never thought you would be married in such a way. Why, you haven't even told me who she is."

"She's all right, Mother—good family and all. I really must hurry——"

"But what is her name, Tryon?"

"Say, Mother, I really must go. Ask Mrs. Parker Bowman what she thinks of her. Good-by! Cheer up, it'll be all right."

"But, Tryon, her name——"

The receiver was hung up with a click, and Dunham looked at his watch nervously. In two minutes his half-hour would be up, yet he must let Judge Blackwell know. Perhaps he could still catch him at the office. He sometimes stayed down-town late. Dunham rang up the office. The Judge was still there, and in a moment his cheery voice was heard ringing out, "Hello!"

"Hello, Judge! Is that you?... This is Dunham.... Chicago. Yes, the business is all done, and I'm ready to come home, but I want to give you a bit of news. Do you remember the young woman who dined with us at Mrs. Bowman's and played the piano so well?... Yes, the night I met you.... Well, you half guessed that night how it was with us, I think. And now she is here, and we are to be married at once, before I return. I am just about to go to the church, but I wanted your blessing first."

"Blessings and congratulations on you both!" came in a hearty voice over the phone. "Tell her she shall be at once taken into the firm as chief consultant on condition that she plays for me whenever I ask her."

A great gladness entered the young man's heart as he again hung up the receiver, at this glimpse into the bright vista of future possibilities. He hurried into the street, forgetful of engravers. The half-hour was up and one minute over.

In the meantime, the girl had slipped into her own garments once more with a relief and joy she could scarcely believe were her own. Had it all been an ugly dream, this life she had been living for the past few months, and was she going back now to rest and peace and real life? Nay, not going back, but going forward. The sweet color came into her beautiful face at thought of the one who, though not knowing her, yet had loved her enough to take her as she was, and lift her out of her trouble. It was like the most romantic of fairy tales, this unexpected lover and the joy that had come to her. How had it happened to her quiet, conventional life? Ah, it was good and dear, whatever it was! She pressed her happy eyes with her fluttering, nervous fingers, to keep the glad tears back, and laughed out to herself a joyful ripple such as she had not uttered since her uncle's death.

A knock at the door brought her back to realities again. Her heart throbbed wildly. Had he come back to her already? Or had her enemy found her out at last?

Tryon Dunham hurried up the steps of the Y.W.C.A. Building, nearly knocking over a baggy individual in rubbers, who was lurking in the entrance. The young man had seen a boy in uniform, laden with two enormous boxes, run up the steps as he turned the last corner. Hastily writing a few lines on one of his cards and slipping it into the largest box, he sent them both up to the girl's room. Then he sauntered to the door to see if the carriage had come. It was there. He glanced inside to see if his orders about flowers had been fulfilled, and spoke a few words of direction to the driver. Turning back to the door, he found the small, red eyes of the baggy Irishman fixed upon him. Something in the slouch of the figure reminded Dunham strongly now of the man he had noticed the night before, and as he went back into the building he looked the man over well and determined to watch him. As he sat in the office waiting, twice he saw the bleary eyes of the baggy man applied to the glass panes in the front door and as suddenly withdrawn. It irritated him, and finally he strode to the door and asked the man if he were looking for some one.

"Just waitin' fer me sweetheart," whined the man, with a cringing attitude. "She has a room in here, an' I saw her go in a while back."

"Well, you'd better move on. They don't care to have people hanging around here."

The man slunk away with a vindictive glance, and Tryon Dunham went back to the office, more perturbed at the little incident than he could understand.

Upstairs the girl had dared to open her door and had been relieved to find the elevator boy there with the two boxes.

"The gentleman's below, an' he says he'll wait, an' he sent these up," said the boy, depositing his burden and hurrying away.

She locked her door once more, for somehow a great fear had stolen over her now that she was again dressed in her own garments and could easily be recognized.

She opened the large box and read the card lying on the top:

These are my wedding gifts to you, dear. Put them on and come as soon as possible to the one who loves you better than anything else in life.

TRYON

Her eyes shone brightly and her cheeks grew rosy red as she lifted out from its tissue-paper wrappings a long, rich coat of Alaska seal, with exquisite brocade lining. She put it on and stood a moment looking at herself in the glass. She felt like one who had for a long time lost her identity, and has suddenly had it restored. Such garments had been ordinary comforts of her former life. She had not been warm enough in the coarse black coat.

The other box contained a beautiful hat of fur to match the coat. It was simply trimmed with one long, beautiful black plume, and in shape and general appearance was like the hat he had borrowed for her use in the fall. She smiled happily as she set it upon her head, and then laughed outright as she remembered her shabby silk gloves. Never mind. She could take them off when she reached the church.

She packed the little black dress into the suit-case, folded the felt hat on the top with a tender pat, and, putting on her gloves, hurried down to the one who waited for her.

The matron had gone upstairs to the linen closet and left the girl with the discontented upper lip in charge in the office. The latter watched the elegant lady in the rich furs come down the hall from the elevator, and wondered who she was and why she had been upstairs. Probably to visit some poor protégée, she thought. The girl caught the love-light in the eyes of Tryon Dunham as he rose to meet his bride, and she recognized him as the same man who had been in close converse with the cheaply dressed girl in the parlor an hour before, and sneered as she wondered what the fine lady in furs would think if she knew about the other girl. Then they went out to the carriage, past the baggy, rubbered man, who shrank back suddenly behind a stone column and watched them.

As Dunham shut the door, he looked back just in time to see a slight man, with dark eyes and hair, hurry up and touch the baggy man on the shoulder. The latter pointed toward their carriage.

"See!" said Dunham. "I believe those are the men who were hovering around the house last night."

The girl leaned forward to look, and then drew back with an exclamation of horror as the carriage started.

"Oh, that man is my cousin Richard," she cried.

"Are you sure?" he asked, and a look of determination settled into his face.

"Perfectly," she answered, looking out again. "Do you suppose he has seen me?"

"I suppose he has, but we'll soon turn the tables." He leaned out and spoke a word to the driver, who drew up around the next corner in front of a telephone pay-station.

"Come with me for just a minute, dear. I'll telephone to a detective bureau where they know me and have that man watched. He is unsafe to have at large." He helped her out and drew her arm firmly within his own. "Don't be afraid any more. I will take care of you."

He telephoned a careful description of the two men and their whereabouts, and before he had hung up the receiver a man had started post-haste for the Y.W.C.A. Building.

Then Tryon Dunham put the girl tenderly into the carriage, and to divert her attention he opened the box of flowers and put a great sheaf of white roses and lilies-of-the-valley into the little gloved hands. Then, taking her in his arms for the first time, he kissed her. He noticed the shabby gloves, and, putting his hand in his breast pocket, drew out the white gloves she had worn before, saying, "See! I have carried them there ever since you sent them back! My sister never asked for them. I kept them for your sake."

The color had come back into her cheeks when they reached the church, and he thought her a beautiful bride as he led her into the dim aisle. Some one up in the choir loft was playing the wedding march, and the minister's wife and young daughter sat waiting to witness the ceremony.

The minister met them at the door with a welcoming smile and hand-shake, and led them forward. As the music hushed for the words of the ceremony, he leaned forward to the young man and whispered:

"I neglected to ask you her name, Tryon."

"Oh, yes." The young man paused in his dilemma and looked for an instant at the sweet face of the girl beside him. But he could not let his friend see that he did not know the name of his wife-to-be, and with quick thought he answered, "Mary!"

The ceremony proceeded, and the minister's voice sounded out solemnly in the empty church: "Do you, Tryon, take this woman whom you hold by the hand to be your lawful wedded wife?"

The young man's fingers held the timid hand of the woman firmly as he answered, "I do."

"Do you, Mary, take this man?" came the next question, and the girl looked up with clear eyes and said, "I do."

Then the minister's wife, who knew and prized Tryon Dunham's friendship, said to herself: "It's all right. She loves him."

When the solemn words were spoken that bound them together through life, and they had thanked their kind friends and were once more out in the carriage, Tryon said:

"Do you know you haven't told me your real name yet?"

She laughed happily as the carriage started on its way, and answered, "Why, it is Mary!"

As the carriage rounded the first corner beyond the church, two breathless individuals hurried up from the other direction. One was short and baggy, and the sole of one rubber flopped dismally as he struggled to keep up with the alert strides of the other man, who was slim and angry. They had been detained by an altercation with the matron of the Y.W.C.A. Building, and puzzled by the story of the plainly dressed girl who had taken the room, and the fine lady who had left the building in company with a gentleman, until it was settled by the elevator boy, who declared the two women to be one and the same.

A moment later a man in citizen's clothing, who had keen eyes, and who was riding a motor-cycle, rounded the corner and puffed placidly along near the two. He appeared to be looking at the numbers on the other side of the street, but he heard every word that they said as they caught sight of the disappearing carriage and hurried after it. He had been standing in the entrance of the Y.W.C.A. Building, an apparently careless observer, while the elevator boy gave his evidence.

The motor-cycle shot ahead a few rods, passed the carriage, and discovered by a keen glance who were the occupants. Then it rounded the block and came almost up to the two pursuers again.

When the carriage stopped at the side entrance of a hotel the man on the motor-cycle was ahead of the pursuers and discovered it first, long enough to see the two get out and go up the marble steps. The carriage was driving away when the thin man came in sight, with the baggy man struggling along half a block behind, his padded feet coming down in heavy, dragging thuds, like a St. Bernard dog in bedroom slippers.

One glimpse the pursuers had of their prey as the elevator shot upward. They managed to evade the hotel authorities and get up the wide staircase without observation. By keeping on the alert, they discovered that the elevator had stopped at the second floor, so the people they were tracking must have apartments there. Lurking in the shadowy parts of the hall, they watched, and soon were rewarded by seeing Dunham come out of a room and hurry to the elevator. He had remembered his promise to his mother about the engravers. As soon as he was gone, they presented themselves boldly at the door.

Filled with the joy that had come to her and feeling entirely safe now in the protection of her husband, Mary Dunham opened the door. She supposed, of course, it was the bell-boy with a pitcher of ice-water, for which she had just rung.

"Ah, here you are at last, my pretty cousin!" It was the voice of Richard that menaced her, with all the stored-up wrath of his long-baffled search.

At that moment the man from the motor-cycle stepped softly up the top stair and slid unseen into the shadows of the hall.

For an instant it seemed to Mary Dunham that she was going to faint, and in one swift flash of thought she saw herself overpowered and carried into hiding before her husband should return. But with a supreme effort she controlled herself, and faced her tormentor with unflinching gaze. Though her strength had deserted her at first, every faculty was now keen and collected. As if nothing unusual were happening, she put out her cold, trembling fingers, and laid them firmly over the electric button on the wall. Then with new strength coming from the certainty that some one would soon come to her aid, she opened her lips to speak.

"What are you doing here, Richard?"

"I've come after you, my lady. A nice chase you've led me, but you shall pay for it now."

The cruelty in his face eclipsed any lines of beauty which might have been there. The girl's heart froze within her as she looked once more into those eyes, which had always seemed to her like sword-points.

"I shall never go anywhere with you," she answered steadily.

He seized her delicate wrist roughly, twisting it with the old wrench with which he had tormented her in their childhood days. None of them saw the stranger who was quietly walking down the hall toward them.

"Will you go peaceably, or shall I have to gag and bind you?" said Richard. "Choose quickly. I'm in no mood to trifle with you any longer."

Although he hurt her wrist cruelly, she threw herself back from him and with her other hand pressed still harder against the electric button. The bell was ringing furiously down in the office, but the walls were thick and the halls lofty. It could not be heard above.

"Catch that other hand, Mike," commanded Richard, "and stuff this in her mouth, while I tie her hands behind her back."

It was then that Mary screamed. The man in the shadow stepped up behind and said in a low voice:

"What does all this mean?"

The two men, startled, dropped the girl's hands for the instant. Then Richard, white with anger at this interference, answered insolently: "It means that this girl's an escaped lunatic, and we're sent to take her back. She's dangerous, so you'd better keep out of the way."

Then Mary Dunham's voice, clear and penetrating, rang through the halls:

"Tryon, Tryon! Come quick! Help! Help!"

As if in answer to her call, the elevator shot up to the second floor, and Tryon Dunham stepped out in time to see the two men snatch Mary's hands again and attempt to bind them behind her back.

In an instant he had seized Richard by the collar and landed him on the hall carpet, while a well directed blow sent the flabby Irishman sprawling at the feet of the detective, who promptly sat on him and pinioned his arms behind him.

"How dare you lay a finger upon this lady?" said Tryon Dunham, as he stepped to the side of his wife and put a strong arm about her, where she stood white and frightened in the doorway.

No one had noticed that the bell-boy had come to the head of the stairs and received a quiet order from the detective.

In sudden fear, the discomfited Richard arose and attempted to bluff the stranger who had so unwarrantly interfered just as his fingers were about to close over the golden treasure of his cousin's fortune.

"Indeed, sir, you wholly misunderstand the situation," he said to Dunham, with an air of injured innocence, "though perhaps you can scarcely be blamed. This girl is an escaped lunatic. We have been searching for her for days, and have just traced her. It is our business to take her back at once. Her friends are in great distress about her. Moreover, she is dangerous and a menace to every guest in this house. She has several times attempted murder——"

"Stop!" roared Dunham, in a thunderous voice of righteous anger. "She is my wife. And you are her cousin. I know all about your plot to shut her up in an insane asylum and steal her fortune. I have found you sooner than I expected, and I intend to see that the law takes its full course with you."

Two policemen now arrived on the scene, with a number of eager bell-boys and porters in their wake, ready to take part in the excitement.

Richard had turned deadly white at the words, "She is my wife!" It was the death-knell of his hopes of securing the fortune for which he had not hesitated to sacrifice every particle of moral principle. When he turned and saw impending retribution in the shape of the two stalwart representatives of the law, a look of cunning came into his face, and with one swift motion he turned to flee up the staircase close at hand.

"Not much you don't," said an enterprising bell-boy, flinging himself in the way and tripping up the scoundrel in his flight.

The policemen were upon him and had him handcuffed in an instant. The Irishman now began to protest that he was but an innocent tool, hired to help discover the whereabouts of an escaped lunatic, as he supposed. He was walked off to the patrol wagon without further ceremony.

It was all over in a few minutes. The elevator carried off the detective, the policemen, and their two prisoners. The door closed behind Dunham and his bride, and the curious guests who had peered out, alarmed by the uproar, saw nothing but a few bell-boys standing in the hall, describing to one another the scene as they had witnessed it.

"He stood here and I stood right there," said one, "and the policeman, he come——"

The guests could not find out just what had happened, but supposed there had been an attempted robbery, and retired behind locked doors to see that their jewels were safely hidden.

Dunham drew the trembling girl into his arms and tried to soothe her. The tears rained down the white cheeks as her head lay upon his breast, and he kissed them away.

"Oh!" she sobbed, shuddering. "If you had not come! It was terrible, *terrible*! I believe he would have killed me rather than have let me go again."

Gradually his tender ministrations calmed her, but she turned troubled eyes to his face.

"You do not know yet that I am all I say. You have nothing to prove it. Of course, by and by, when I can get to my guardians, and with your help perhaps make them understand, you will know, but I don't see how you can trust me till then."

For answer he brought his hand up in front of her face and turned the flashing diamond—her diamond—so that its glory caught the single ray of setting sun that filtered into the hotel window.

"See, darling," he said. "It is your ring. I have worn it ever since as an outward sign that I trusted you."

"You are taking me on trust, though, in spite of all you say, and it is beautiful."

He laid his lips against hers. "Yes," he said; "it is beautiful, and it is best."

It was very still in the room for a moment while she nestled close to him and his eyes drank in the sweetness of her face.

"See," said he, taking a tiny velvet case from his pocket and touching the spring that opened it. "I have amused myself finding a mate to your stone. I thought perhaps you would let me wear your ring always, while you wear mine."

He lifted the jewel from its white velvet bed and showed her the inscription inside: "Mary, from Tryon." Then he slipped it on her finger to guard the wedding ring he had given her at the church. His arm that encircled her clasped her left wrist, and the two diamonds flashed side by side. The last gleam of the setting sun, ere it vanished behind the tall buildings on the west, glanced in and blazed the gems into tangled beams of glory, darting out in many colored prisms to light the vision of the future of the man and the woman. He bent and kissed her again, and their eyes met like other jewels, in which gleamed the glory of their love and trust.

THE END.

Marcia Schuyler
CHAPTER I

The sun was already up and the grass blades were twinkling with sparkles of dew, as Marcia stepped from the kitchen door.

She wore a chocolate calico with little sprigs of red and white scattered over it, her hair was in smooth brown braids down her back, and there was a flush on her round cheeks that might have been but the reflection of the rosy light in the East. Her face was as untroubled as the summer morning, in its freshness, and her eyes as dreamy as the soft clouds that hovered upon the horizon uncertain where they were to be sent for the day.

Marcia walked lightly through the grass, and the way behind her sparkled again like that of the girl in the fairy-tale who left jewels wherever she passed.

A rail fence stopped her, which she mounted as though it had been a steed to carry her onward, and sat a moment looking at the beauty of the morning, her eyes taking on that far-away look that annoyed her stepmother when she wanted her to hurry with the dishes, or finish a long seam before it was time to get supper.

She loitered but a moment, for her mind was full of business, and she wished to accomplish much before the day was done. Swinging easily down to the other side of the fence she moved on through the meadow, over another fence, and another meadow, skirting the edge of a cool little strip of woods which lured her with its green mysterious shadows, its whispering leaves, and twittering birds. One wistful glance she gave into the sweet silence, seeing a clump of maiden-hair ferns rippling their feathery locks in the breeze. Then resolutely turning away she sped on to the slope of Blackberry Hill.

It was not a long climb to where the blackberries grew, and she was soon at work, the great luscious berries dropping into her pail almost with a touch. But while she worked the vision of the hills, the sheep meadow below, the river winding between the neighboring farms, melted away, and she did not even see the ripe fruit before her, because she was planning the new frock she was to buy with these berries she had come to pick.

Pink and white it was to be; she had seen it in the store the last time she went for sugar and spice. There were dainty sprigs of pink over the white ground, and every berry that dropped into her bright pail was no longer a berry but a sprig of pink chintz. While she worked she went over her plans for the day.

There had been busy times at the old house during the past weeks. Kate, her elder sister, was to be married. It was only a few days now to the wedding.

There had been a whole year of preparation: spinning and weaving and fine sewing. The smooth white linen lay ready, packed between rose leaves and lavender. There had been yards and yards of tatting and embroidery made by the two girls for the trousseau, and the village dressmaker had spent days at the house, cutting, fitting, shirring, till now there was a goodly array of gorgeous apparel piled high upon bed, and chairs, and hanging in the closets of the great spare bedroom. The outfit was as fine as that made for Patience Hartrandt six months before, and Mr. Hartrandt had given his one daughter all she had asked for in the way of a "setting out." Kate had seen to it that her things were as fine as Patience's,—but, they were all for Kate!

Of course, that was right! Kate was to be married, not Marcia, and everything must make way for that. Marcia was scarcely more than a child as yet, barely seventeen. No one thought of anything new for her just then, and she did not expect it. But into her heart there had stolen a longing for a new frock herself amid all this finery for Kate. She had her best one of course. That was good, and pretty, and quite nice enough to wear to the wedding, and her stepmother had taken much relief in the thought that Marcia would need nothing during the rush of getting Kate ready.

But there were people coming to the house every day, especially in the afternoons, friends of Kate, and of her stepmother, to be shown Kate's wardrobe, and to talk things over curiously. Marcia could not wear her best dress all the time. And *he* was coming! That was the way Marcia always denominated the prospective bridegroom in her mind.

His name was David Spafford, and Kate often called him Dave, but Marcia, even to herself, could never bring herself to breathe the name so familiarly. She held him in great awe. He was so fine and strong and good, with a face like a young saint in some old picture, she thought. She often wondered how her wild, sparkling sister Kate dared to be so familiar with him. She had ventured the thought once when she watched Kate dressing to go out with some young people and preening herself like a bird of Paradise before the glass. It all came over her, the vanity and frivolousness of the life that Kate loved, and she spoke out with conviction:

"Kate, you'll have to be very different when you're married." Kate had faced about amusedly and asked why.

"Because *he* is so good," Marcia had replied, unable to explain further.

"Oh, is that all?" said the daring sister, wheeling back to the glass. "Don't you worry; I'll soon take that out of him."

But Kate's indifference had never lessened her young sister's awe of her prospective brother-in-law. She had listened to his conversations with her father during the brief visits he had made, and she had watched his face at church while he and Kate sang together as the minister lined it out: "Rock of Ages cleft for me, Let me hide myself in Thee," a new song which had just been written. And she had mused upon the charmed life Kate would lead. It was wonderful to be a woman and be loved as Kate was loved, thought Marcia.

So in all the hurry no one seemed to think much about Marcia, and she was not satisfied with her brown delaine afternoon dress. Truth to tell, it needed letting down, and there was no more left to let down. It made her feel like last year to go about in it with her slender ankles so plainly revealed. So she set her heart upon the new chintz.

Now, with Marcia, to decide was to do. She did not speak to her stepmother about it, for she knew it would be useless; neither did she think it worth while to go to her father, for she knew that both his wife and Kate would find it out and charge her with useless expense just now when there were so many other uses for money, and they were anxious to have it all flow their way. She had an independent spirit, so she took the time that belonged to herself, and went to the blackberry patch which belonged to everybody.

Marcia's fingers were nimble and accustomed, and the sun was not very high in the heavens when she had finished her task and turned happily toward the village. The pails would not hold another berry.

Her cheeks were glowing with the sun and exercise, and little wisps of wavy curls had escaped about her brow, damp with perspiration. Her eyes were shining with her purpose, half fulfilled, as she hastened down the hill.

Crossing a field she met Hanford Weston with a rake over his shoulder and a wide-brimmed straw hat like a small shed over him. He was on his way to the South meadow. He blushed and greeted her as she passed shyly by. When she had passed he paused and looked admiringly after her. They had been in the same classes at school all winter, the girl at the head, the boy at the foot. But Hanford Weston's father owned the largest farm in all the country round about, and he felt that did not so much matter. He would rather see Marcia at the head anyway, though there never had been the slightest danger that he would take her place. He felt a sudden desire now to follow her. It would be a pleasure to carry those pails that she bore as if they were mere featherweights.

He watched her long, elastic step for a moment, considered the sun in the sky, and his father's command about the South meadow, and then strode after her.

It did not take long to reach her side, swiftly as she had gone.

As well as he could, with the sudden hotness in his face and the tremor in his throat, he made out to ask if he might carry her burden for her. Marcia stopped annoyed. She had forgotten all about him, though he was an attractive fellow, sometimes called by the girls "handsome Hanford."

She had been planning exactly how that pink sprigged chintz was to be made, and which parts she would cut first in order to save time and material. She did not wish to be interrupted. The importance of the matter was too great to be marred by the appearance of just a schoolmate whom she might meet every day, and whom she could so easily "spell down." She summoned her thoughts from the details of mutton-leg sleeves and looked the boy over, to his great confusion. She did not want him along, and she was considering how best to get rid of him.

"Weren't you going somewhere else?" she asked sweetly. "Wasn't there a rake over your shoulder? What have you done with it?"

The culprit blushed deeper.

"Where were you going?" she demanded.

"To the South meadow," he stammered out.

"Oh, well, then you must go back. I shall do quite well, thank you. Your father will not be pleased to have you neglect your work for me, though I'm much obliged I'm sure."

Was there some foreshadowing of her womanhood in the decided way she spoke, and the quaint, prim set of her head as she bowed him good morning and went on her way once more? The boy did not understand. He only felt abashed, and half angry that she had ordered him back to work; and, too, in a tone that forbade him to take her memory with him as he went. Nevertheless her image lingered by the way, and haunted the South meadow all day long as he worked.

Marcia, unconscious of the admiration she had stirred in the boyish heart, went her way on fleet feet, her spirit one with the sunny morning, her body light with anticipation, for a new frock of her own choice was yet an event in her life.

She had thought many times, as she spent long hours putting delicate stitches into her sister's wedding garments, how it would seem if they were being made for her. She had whiled away many a dreary seam by thinking out, in a sort of dream-story, how she would put on this or that at will if it were her own, and go here or there, and have people love and admire her as they did Kate. It would never come true, of course. She never expected to be admired and loved like Kate. Kate was beautiful, bright and gay. Everybody loved her, no matter how she treated them. It was a matter of course for Kate to have everything she wanted. Marcia felt that she never could attain to such heights. In the first place she considered her own sweet serious face with its pure brown eyes as exceedingly plain. She could not catch the lights that played at hide and seek in her eyes when she talked with animation. Indeed few saw her at her best, because she seldom talked freely. It was only with certain people that she could forget herself.

She did not envy Kate. She was proud of her sister, and loved her, though there was an element of anxiety in the love. But she never thought of her many faults. She felt that they were excusable because Kate was Kate. It was as if you should find fault with a wild rose because it carried a thorn. Kate was set about with many a thorn, but amid them all she bloomed, her fragrant pink self, as apparently unconscious of the many pricks she gave, and as unconcerned, as the flower itself.

So Marcia never thought to be jealous that Kate had so many lovely things, and was going out into the world to do just as she pleased, and lead a charmed life with a man who was greater in the eyes of this girl than any prince that ever walked in fairy-tale. But she saw no harm in playing a delightful little dream-game of "pretend" now and then, and letting her imagination make herself the beautiful, admired, elder sister instead of the plain younger one.

But this morning on her way to the village store with her berries she thought no more of her sister's things, for her mind was upon her own little frock which she would purchase with the price of the berries, and then go home and make.

A whole long day she had to herself, for Kate and her stepmother were gone up to the neighboring town on the packet to make a few last purchases.

She had told no one of her plans, and was awake betimes in the morning to see the travellers off, eager to have them gone that she might begin to carry out her plan.

Just at the edge of the village Marcia put down the pails of berries by a large flat stone and sat down for a moment to tidy herself. The lacing of one shoe had come untied, and her hair was rumpled by exercise. But she could not sit long to rest, and taking up her burdens was soon upon the way again.

Mary Ann Fothergill stepped from her own gate lingering till Marcia should come up, and the two girls walked along side by side. Mary Ann had stiff, straight, light hair, and high cheek bones. Her eyes were light and her eyelashes almost white. They did not show up well beneath her checked sunbonnet. Her complexion was dull and tanned. She was a contrast to Marcia with her clear red and white skin. She was tall and awkward and wore a linsey-woolsey frock as though it were a meal sack temporarily appropriated. She had the air of always trying to hide her feet and hands. Mary Ann had some fine qualities, but beauty was not one of them. Beside her Marcia's delicate features showed clear-cut like a cameo, and her every movement spoke of patrician blood.

Mary Ann regarded Marcia's smooth brown braids enviously. Her own sparse hair barely reached to her shoulders, and straggled about her neck helplessly and hopelessly, in spite of her constant efforts.

"It must be lots of fun at your house these days," said Mary Ann wistfully. "Are you most ready for the wedding?"

Marcia nodded. Her eyes were bright. She could see the sign of the village store just ahead and knew the bolts of new chintz were displaying their charms in the window.

"My, but your cheeks do look pretty," admired Mary Ann impulsively. "Say, how many of each has your sister got?"

"Two dozens," said Marcia conscious of a little swelling of pride in her breast. It was not every girl that had such a setting out as her sister.

"My!" sighed Mary Ann. "And outside things, too. I 'spose she's got one of every color. What are her frocks? Tell me about them. I've been up to Dutchess county and just got back last night, but Ma wrote Aunt Tilly that Mis' Hotchkiss said her frocks was the prettiest Miss Hancock's ever sewed on."

"We think they are pretty," admitted Marcia modestly. "There's a sprigged chin—" here she caught herself, remembering, and laughed. "I mean muslin-de-laine, and a blue delaine, and a blue silk——"

"My! silk!" breathed Mary Ann in an ecstasy of wonder. "And what's she going to be married in?"

"White," answered Marcia, "white satin. And the veil was mother's—our own mother's, you know."

Marcia spoke it reverently, her eyes shining with something far away that made Mary Ann think she looked like an angel.

"Oh, my! Don't you just envy her?"

"No," said Marcia slowly; "I think not. At least—I hope not. It wouldn't be right, you know. And then she's my sister and I love her dearly, and it's nearly as nice to have one's sister have nice things and a good time as to have them one's self."

"You're good," said Mary Ann decidedly as if that were a foregone conclusion. "But I should envy her, I just should. Mis' Hotchkiss told Ma there wa'nt many lots in life so all honey-and-dew-prepared like your sister's. All the money she wanted to spend on clo'es, and a nice set out, and a man as handsome as you'll find anywhere, and he's well off too, ain't he? Ma said she heard he kept a horse and lived right in the village too, not as how he needed to keep one to get anywhere, either. That's what I call luxury—a horse to ride around with. And then Mr. What's-his-name? I can't remember. Oh, yes, Spafford. He's good, and everybody says he won't make a bit of fuss if Kate does go around and have a good time. He'll just let her do as she pleases. Only old Grandma Doolittle says she doesn't believe it. She thinks every man, no matter how good he is, wants to manage his wife, just for the name of it. She says your sister'll have to change her ways or else there'll be trouble. But that's Grandma!

Everybody knows her. She croaks! Ma says Kate's got her nest feathered well if ever a girl had. My! I only wish I had the same chance!"

Marcia held her head a trifle high when Mary Ann touched upon her sister's personal character, but they were nearing the store, and everybody knew Mary Ann was blunt. Poor Mary Ann! She meant no harm. She was but repeating the village gossip. Besides, Marcia must give her mind to sprigged chintz. There was no time for discussions if she would accomplish her purpose before the folks came home that night.

"Mary Ann," she said in her sweet, prim way that always made the other girl stand a little in awe of her, "you mustn't listen to gossip. It isn't worth while. I'm sure my sister Kate will be very happy. I'm going in the store now, are you?" And the conversation was suddenly concluded.

Mary Ann followed meekly watching with wonder and envy as Marcia made her bargain with the kindly merchant, and selected her chintz. What a delicious swish the scissors made as they went through the width of cloth, and how delightfully the paper crackled as the bundle was being wrapped! Mary Ann did not know whether Kate or Marcia was more to be envied.

"Did you say you were going to make it up yourself?" asked Mary Ann.

Marcia nodded.

"Oh, my! Ain't you afraid? I would be. It's the prettiest I ever saw. Don't you go and cut both sleeves for one arm. That's what I did the only time Ma ever let me try." And Mary Ann touched the package under Marcia's arm with wistful fingers.

They had reached the turn of the road and Mary Ann hoped that Marcia would ask her out to "help," but Marcia had no such purpose.

"Well, good-bye! Will you wear it next Sunday?" she asked.

"Perhaps," answered Marcia breathlessly, and sped on her homeward way, her cheeks bright with excitement.

In her own room she spread the chintz out upon the bed and with trembling fingers set about her task. The bright shears clipped the edge and tore off the lengths exultantly as if in league with the girl. The bees hummed outside in the clover, and now and again buzzed between the muslin curtains of the open window, looked in and grumbled out again. The birds sang across the meadows and the sun mounted to the zenith and began its downward march, but still the busy fingers worked on. Well for Marcia's scheme that the fashion of the day was simple, wherein were few puckers and plaits and tucks, and little trimming required, else her task would have been impossible.

Her heart beat high as she tried it on at last, the new chintz that she had made. She went into the spare room and stood before the long mirror in its wide gilt frame that rested on two gilt knobs standing out from the wall like giant rosettes. She had dared to make the skirt a little longer than that of her best frock. It was almost as long as Kate's, and for a moment she lingered, sweeping backward and forward before the glass and admiring herself in the long graceful folds. She caught up her braids in the fashion that Kate wore her hair and smiled at the reflection of herself in the mirror. How funny it seemed to think she would soon be a woman like Kate. When Kate was gone they would begin to call her "Miss" sometimes. Somehow she did not care to look ahead. The present seemed enough. She had so wrapped her thoughts in her sister's new life that her own seemed flat and stale in comparison.

The sound of a distant hay wagon on the road reminded her that the sun was near to setting. The family carryall would soon be coming up the lane from the evening packet. She must hurry and take off her frock and be dressed before they arrived.

Marcia was so tired that night after supper that she was glad to slip away to bed, without waiting to hear Kate's voluble account of her day in town, the beauties she had seen and the friends she had met.

She lay down and dreamed of the morrow, and of the next day, and the next. In strange bewilderment she awoke in the night and found the moonlight streaming full into her face. Then she laughed and rubbed her eyes and tried to go to sleep again; but she could not, for she had dreamed that she was the bride herself, and the words of Mary Ann kept going over and over in her mind. "Oh, don't you envy her?" *Did* she envy her sister? But that was wicked. It troubled her to think of it, and she tried to banish the dream, but it would come again and again with a strange sweet pleasure.

She lay wondering if such a time of joy would ever come to her as had come to Kate, and whether the spare bed would ever be piled high with clothes and fittings for her new life. What a wonderful thing it was anyway to be a woman and be loved!

Then her dreams blended again with the soft perfume of the honeysuckle at the window, and the hooting of a young owl.

The moon dropped lower, the bright stars paled, dawn stole up through the edges of the woods far away and awakened a day that was to bring a strange transformation over Marcia's life.

CHAPTER II

As a natural consequence of her hard work and her midnight awakening, Marcia overslept the next morning. Her stepmother called her sharply and she dressed in haste, not even taking time to glance toward the new folds of chintz that drew her thoughts closetward. She dared not say anything about it yet. There was much to be done, and not even Kate had time for an idle word with her. Marcia was called upon to run errands, to do odds and ends of things, to fill in vacant places, to sew on lost buttons, to do everything for which nobody else had time. The household had suddenly become aware that there was now but one more intervening day between them and the wedding.

It was not until late in the afternoon that Marcia ventured to put on her frock. Even then she felt shy about appearing in it.

Madam Schuyler was busy in the parlor with callers, and Kate was locked in her own room whither she had gone to rest. There was no one to notice if Marcia should "dress up," and it was not unlikely that she might escape much notice even at the supper table, as everybody was so absorbed in other things.

She lingered before her own little glass looking wistfully at herself. She was pleased with the frock she had made and liked her appearance in it, but yet there was something disappointing about it. It had none of the style of her sister's garments, newly come from the hand of the village mantua-maker. It was girlish, and showed her slip of a form prettily in the fashion of the day, but she felt too young. She wanted to look older. She searched her drawer and found a bit of black velvet which she pinned about her throat with a pin containing the miniature of her mother, then with a second thought she drew the long braids up in loops and fastened them about her head in older fashion. It suited her well, and the change it made astonished her. She decided to wear them so and see if others would notice. Surely, some day she would be a young woman, and perhaps then she would be allowed to have a will of her own occasionally.

She drew a quick breath as she descended the stairs and found her stepmother and the visitor just coming into the hall from the parlor.

They both involuntarily ceased their talk and looked at her in surprise. Over Madam Schuyler's face there came a look as if she had received a revelation. Marcia was no longer a child, but had suddenly blossomed into young womanhood. It was not the time she would have chosen for such an event. There was enough going on, and Marcia was still in school. She had no desire to steer another young soul through the various dangers and follies that beset a pretty girl from the time she puts up her hair until she is safely married to the right man—or the wrong one. She had just begun to look forward with relief to having Kate well settled in life. Kate had been a hard one to manage. She had too much will of her own and a pretty way of always having it. She had no deep sense of reverence for old, staid manners and customs. Many a long lecture had Madam Schuyler delivered to Kate upon her unseemly ways. It did not please her to think of having to go through it all so soon again, therefore upon her usually complacent brow there came a look of dismay.

"Why!" exclaimed the visitor, "is this the bride? How tall she looks! No! Bless me! it isn't, is it? Yes,—Well! I'll declare. It's just Marsh! What have you got on, child? How old you look!"

Marcia flushed. It was not pleasant to have her young womanhood questioned, and in a tone so familiar and patronizing. She disliked the name of "Marsh" exceedingly, especially upon the lips of this woman, a sort of second cousin of her stepmother's. She would rather have chosen the new frock to pass under inspection of her stepmother without witnesses, but it was too late to turn back now. She must face it.

Though Madam Schuyler's equilibrium was a trifle disturbed, she was not one to show it before a visitor. Instantly she recovered her balance, and perhaps Marcia's ordeal was less trying than if there had been no third person present.

"That looks very well, child!" she said critically with a shade of complacence in her voice. It is true that Marcia had gone beyond orders in purchasing and making garments unknown to her, yet the neatness and fit could but reflect well upon her training. It did no harm for cousin Maria to see what a child of her training could do. It was, on the whole, a very creditable piece of work, and Madam Schuyler grew more reconciled to it as Marcia came down toward them.

"Make it herself?" asked cousin Maria. "Why, Marsh, you did real well. My Matilda does all her own clothes now. It's time you were learning. It's a trifle longish to what you've been wearing them, isn't it? But you'll grow into it, I dare say. Got your hair a new way too. I thought you were Kate when you first started down stairs. You'll make a good-looking young lady when you grow up; only don't be in too much hurry. Take your girlhood while you've got it, is what I always tell Matilda."

Matilda was well on to thirty and showed no signs of taking anything else.

Madam Schuyler smoothed an imaginary pucker across the shoulders and again pronounced the work good.

"I picked berries and got the cloth," confessed Marcia.

Madam Schuyler smiled benevolently and patted Marcia's cheek.

"You needn't have done that, child. Why didn't you come to me for money? You needed something new, and that is a very good purchase, a little light, perhaps, but very pretty. We've been so busy with Kate's things you have been neglected."

Marcia smiled with pleasure and passed into the dining room wondering what power the visitor had over her stepmother to make her pass over this digression from her rules so sweetly,—nay, even with praise.

At supper they all rallied Marcia upon her changed appearance. Her father jokingly said that when the bridegroom arrived he would hardly know which sister to choose, and he looked from one comely daughter to the other with fatherly pride. He praised Marcia for doing the work so neatly, and inwardly admired the courage and independence that prompted her to get the money by her own unaided efforts rather than to ask for it, and later, as he passed through the room where she was helping to remove the dishes from the table, he paused and handed her a crisp five-dollar note. It had occurred to him that one daughter was getting all the good things and the other was having nothing. There was a pleasant tenderness in his eyes, a recognition of her rights as a young woman, that made Marcia's heart exceedingly light. There was something strange about the influence this little new frock seemed to have upon people.

Even Kate had taken a new tone with her. Much of the time at supper she had sat staring at her sister. Marcia wondered about it as she walked down toward the gate after her work was done. Kate had never seemed so quiet. Was she just beginning to realize that she was leaving home forever, and was she thinking how the home would be after she had left it? How she, Marcia, would take the place of elder sister, with only little Harriet and the boys, their stepsister and brothers, left? Was Kate sad over the thought of going so far away from them, or was she feeling suddenly the responsibility of the new position she was to occupy and the duties that would be hers? No, that could not be it, for surely that would bring a softening of expression, a sweetness of anticipation, and Kate's expression had been wondering, perplexed, almost troubled. If she had not been her own sister Marcia would have added, "hard," but she stopped short at that.

It was a lovely evening. The twilight was not yet over as she stepped from the low piazza that ran the length of the house bearing another above it on great white pillars. A drapery of wistaria in full bloom festooned across one end and half over the front. Marcia stepped back across the stone flagging and driveway to look up the purple clusters of graceful fairy-like shape that embowered the house, and thought how beautiful it would look when the wedding guests should arrive the day after the morrow. Then she turned into the little gravel path, box-bordered, that led to the gate. Here and there on either side luxuriant blooms of dahlias, peonies and roses leaned over into the night and peered at her. The yard had never looked so pretty. The flowers truly had done their best for the occasion, and they seemed to be asking some word of commendation from her.

They nodded their dewy heads sleepily as she went on.

To-morrow the children would be coming back from Aunt Eliza's, where they had been sent safely out of the way for a few days, and the last things would arrive,—and *he* would come. Not later than three in the afternoon he ought to arrive, Kate had said, though there was a possibility that he might come in the morning, but Kate was not counting upon it. He was to drive from his home to Schenectady and, leaving his own horse there to rest, come on by coach. Then he and Kate would go back in fine style to Schenectady in a coach and pair, with a colored coachman, and at Schenectady take their own horse and drive on to their home, a long beautiful ride, so thought Marcia half enviously. How beautiful it would be! What endless delightful talks they might have about the trees and birds and things they saw in passing only Kate did not love to talk about such things. But then she would be with David, and he talked beautifully about nature or anything else. Kate would learn to love it if she loved him. Did Kate love David? Of course she must or why should she marry him? Marcia resented the thought that Kate might have other objects in view, such as Mary Ann Fothergill had suggested for instance. Of course Kate would never marry any man unless she loved him. That would be a dreadful thing to do. Love was the greatest thing in the world. Marcia looked up to the stars, her young soul thrilling with awe and reverence for the great mysteries of life. She wondered again if life would open sometime for her in some such great way, and if she would ever know better than now what it meant. Would some one come and love her? Some one whom she could love in return with all the fervor of her nature?

She had dreamed such dreams before many times, as girls will, while lovers and future are all in one dreamy, sweet blending of rosy tints and joyous mystery, but never had they come to her with such vividness as that night. Perhaps it was because the household had recognized the woman in her for the first time that evening. Perhaps because the vision she had seen reflected in her mirror before she left her room that afternoon had opened the door of the future a little wider than it had ever opened before.

She stood by the gate where the syringa and lilac bushes leaned over and arched the way, and the honeysuckle climbed about the fence in a wild pretty way of its own and flung sweetness on the air in vivid, erratic whiffs.

The sidewalk outside was brick, and whenever she heard footsteps coming she stepped back into the shadow of the syringa and was hidden from view. She was in no mood to talk with any one.

She could look out into the dusty road and see dimly the horses and carryalls as they passed, and recognize an occasional laughing voice of some village maiden out with her best young man for a ride. Others strolled along

455

the sidewalk, and fragments of talk floated back. Almost every one had a word to say about the wedding as they neared the gate, and if Marcia had been in another mood it would have been interesting and gratifying to her pride. Every one had a good word for Kate, though many disapproved of her in a general way for principle's sake.

Hanford Weston passed, with long, slouching gait, hands in his trousers pockets, and a frightened, hasty, sideways glance toward the lights of the house beyond. He would have gone in boldly to call if he had dared, and told Marcia that he had done her bidding and now wanted a reward, but John Middleton had joined him at the corner and he dared not make the attempt. John would have done it in a minute if he had wished. He was brazen by nature, but Hanford knew that he would as readily laugh at another for doing it. Hanford shrank from a laugh more than from the cannon's mouth, so he slouched on, not knowing that his goddess held her breath behind a lilac bush not three feet away, her heart beating in annoyed taps to be again interrupted by him in her pleasant thoughts.

Merry, laughing voices mingling with many footsteps came sounding down the street and paused beside the gate. Marcia knew the voices and again slid behind the shrubbery that bordered all the way to the house, and not even a gleam of her light frock was visible. They trooped in, three or four girl friends of Kate's and a couple of young men.

Marcia watched them pass up the box-bordered path from her shadowy retreat, and thought how they would miss Kate, and wondered if the young men who had been coming there so constantly to see her had no pangs of heart that their friend and leader was about to leave them. Then she smiled at herself in the dark. She seemed to be doing the retrospect for Kate, taking leave of all the old friends, home, and life, in Kate's place. It was not her life anyway, and why should she bother herself and sigh and feel this sadness creeping over her for some one else? Was it that she was going to lose her sister? No, for Kate had never been much of a companion to her. She had always put her down as a little girl and made distinct and clear the difference in their ages. Marcia had been the little maid to fetch and carry, the errand girl, and unselfish, devoted slave in Kate's life. There had been nothing protective and elder-sisterly in her manner toward Marcia. At times Marcia had felt this keenly, but no expression of this lack had ever crossed her lips, and afterwards her devotion to her sister had been the greater, to in a measure compensate for this reproachful thought.

But Marcia could not shake the sadness off. She stole in further among the trees to think about it till the callers should go away. She felt no desire to meet any of them.

She began again to wonder how she would feel if day after to-morrow were her wedding day, and she were going away from home and friends and all the scenes with which she had been familiar since babyhood. Would she mind very much leaving them all? Father? Yes, father had been good to her, and loved her and was proud of her in a way. But one does not lose one's father no matter how far one goes. A father is a father always; and Mr. Schuyler was not a demonstrative man. Marcia felt that her father would not miss her deeply, and she was not sure she would miss him so very much. She had read to him a great deal and talked politics with him whenever he had no one better by, but aside from that her life had been lived much apart from him. Her stepmother? Yes, she would miss her as one misses a perfect mentor and guide. She had been used to looking to her for direction. She was thoroughly conscious that she had a will of her own and would like a chance to exercise it, still, she knew that in many cases without her stepmother she would be like a rudderless ship, a guideless traveller. And she loved her stepmother too, as a young girl can love a good woman who has been her guide and helper, even though there never has been great tenderness between them. Yes, she would miss her stepmother, but she would not feel so very sad over it. Harriet and the little brothers? Oh, yes, she would miss them, they were dear little things and devoted to her.

Then there were the neighbors, and the schoolmates, and the people of the village. She would miss the minister,—the dear old minister and his wife. Many a time she had gone with her arms full of flowers to the parsonage down the street, and spent the afternoon with the minister's wife. Her smooth white hair under its muslin cap, and her soft wrinkled cheek were very dear to the young girl. She had talked to this friend more freely about her innermost thoughts than she had ever spoken to any living being. Oh, she would miss the minister's wife very much if she were to go away.

The names of her schoolmates came to her. Harriet Woodgate, Eliza Buchanan, Margaret Fletcher, three girls who were her intimates. She would miss them, of course, but how much? She could scarcely tell. Margaret Fletcher more than the other two. Mary Ann Fothergill? She almost laughed at the thought of anybody missing Mary Ann. John Middleton? Hanford Weston? There was not a boy in the school she would miss for an instant, she told herself with conviction. Not one of them realized her ideal. There was much pairing off of boy and girl in school, but Marcia, like the heroine of "Comin' thro' the Rye," was good friends with all the boys and intimate with none. They all counted it an honor to wait upon her, and she cared not a farthing for any. She felt herself too young, of course, to think of such things, but when she dreamed her day dreams the lover and prince who figured in them bore no familiar form or feature. He was a prince and these were only schoolboys.

The merry chatter of the young people in the house floated through the open windows, and Marcia could hear her sister's voice above them all. Chameleon-like she was all gaiety and laughter now, since her gravity at supper.

They were coming out the front door and down the walk. Kate was with them. Marcia could catch glimpses of the girls' white frocks as they came nearer. She saw that her sister was walking with Captain Leavenworth. He was a handsome young man who made a fine appearance in his uniform. He and Kate had been intimate for two years, and it might have been more than friendship had not Kate's father interfered between them. He did not think so well of the handsome young captain as did either his daughter Kate or the United States Navy who had given him his position. Squire Schuyler required deep integrity and strength of moral character in the man who aspired to be his son-in-law. The captain did not number much of either among his virtues.

There had been a short, sharp contest which had ended in the departure of young Leavenworth from the town some three years before, and the temporary plunging of Kate Schuyler into a season of tears and pouting. But it had not been long before her gay laughter was ringing again, and her father thought she had forgotten. About that time David Spafford had appeared and promptly fallen in love with the beautiful girl, and the Schuyler mind was relieved. So it came about that, upon the reappearance of the handsome young captain wearing the insignia of his first honors, the Squire received him graciously. He even felt that he might be more lenient about his moral character, and told himself that perhaps he was not so bad after all, he must have something in him or the United States government would not have seen fit to honor him. It was easier to think so, now Kate was safe.

Marcia watched her sister and the captain go laughing down to the gate, and out into the street. She wondered that Kate could care to go out to-night when it was to be almost her last evening at home; wondered, too, that Kate would walk with Captain Leavenworth when she belonged to David now. She might have managed it to go with one of the girls. But that was Kate's way. Kate's ways were not Marcia's ways.

Marcia wondered if she would miss Kate, and was obliged to acknowledge to herself that in many ways her sister's absence would be a relief to her. While she recognized the power of her sister's beauty and will over her, she felt oppressed sometimes by the strain she was under to please, and wearied of the constant, half-fretful, half playful fault-finding.

The gay footsteps and voices died away down the village street, and Marcia ventured forth from her retreat. The moon was just rising and came up a glorious burnished disk, silhouetting her face as she stood a moment listening to the stirring of a bird among the branches. It was her will to-night to be alone and let her fancies wander where they would. The beauty and the mystery of a wedding was upon her, touching all her deeper feelings, and she wished to dream it out and wonder over it. Again it came to her what if the day after the morrow were her wedding day and she stood alone thinking about it. She would not have gone off down the street with a lot of giggling girls nor walked with another young man. She would have stood here, or down by the gate—and she moved on toward her favorite arch of lilac and syringa—yes, down by the gate in the darkness looking out and thinking how it would be when he should come. She felt sure if it had been herself who expected David she would have begun to watch for him a week before the time he had set for coming, heralding it again and again to her heart in joyous thrills of happiness, for who knew but he might come sooner and surprise her? She would have rejoiced that to-night she was alone, and would have excused herself from everything else to come down there in the stillness and watch for him, and think how it would be when he would really get there. She would hear his step echoing down the street and would recognize it as his. She would lean far over the gate to listen and watch, and it would come nearer and nearer, and her heart would beat faster and faster, and her breath come quicker, until he was at last by her side, his beautiful surprise for her in his eyes. But now, if David should really try to surprise Kate by coming that way to-night he would not find her waiting nor thinking of him at all, but off with Captain Leavenworth.

With a passing pity for David she went back to her own dream. With one elbow on the gate and her cheek in her hand she thought it all over. The delayed evening coach rumbled up to the tavern not far away and halted. Real footsteps came up the street, but Marcia did not notice them only as they made more vivid her thoughts.

Her dream went on and the steps drew nearer until suddenly they halted and some one appeared out of the shadow. Her heart stood still, for form and face in the darkness seemed unreal, and the dreams had been most vivid. Then with tender masterfulness two strong arms were flung about her and her face was drawn close to his across the vine-twined gate until her lips touched his. One long clinging kiss of tenderness he gave her and held her head close against his breast for just a moment while he murmured: "My darling! My precious, precious Kate, I have you at last!"

The spell was broken! Marcia's dream was shattered. Her mind awoke. With a scream she sprang from him, horror and a wild but holy joy mingling with her perplexity. She put her hand upon her heart, marvelling over the sweetness that lingered upon her lips, trying to recover her senses as she faced the eager lover who opened the little gate and came quickly toward her, as yet unaware that it was not Kate to whom he had been talking.

CHAPTER III

Marcia stood quivering, trembling. She comprehended all in an instant. David Spafford had come a day earlier than he had been expected, to surprise Kate, and Kate was off having a good time with some one else. He had mistaken her for Kate. Her long dress and her put-up hair had deceived him in the moonlight. She tried to summon some womanly courage, and in her earnestness to make things right she forgot her natural timidity.

"It is not Kate," she said gently; "it is only Marcia. Kate did not know you were coming to-night. She did not expect you till to-morrow. She had to go out,—that is—she has gone with—" the truthful, youthful, troubled sister paused. To her mind it was a calamity that Kate was not present to meet her lover. She should at least have been in the house ready for a surprise like this. Would David not feel the omission keenly? She must keep it from him if she could about Captain Leavenworth. There was no reason why he should feel badly about it, of course, and yet it might annoy him. But he stepped back laughing at his mistake.

"Why! Marcia, is it you, child? How you have grown! I never should have known you!" said the young man pleasantly. He had always a grave tenderness for this little sister of his love. "Of course your sister did not know I was coming," he went on, "and doubtless she has many things to attend to. I did not expect her to be out here watching for me, though for a moment I did think she was at the gate. You say she is gone out? Then we will go up to the house and I will be there to surprise her when she comes."

Marcia turned with relief. He had not asked where Kate was gone, nor with whom.

The Squire and Madam Schuyler greeted the arrival with elaborate welcome. The Squire like Marcia seemed much annoyed that Kate had gone out. He kept fuming back and forth from the window to the door and asking:"What did she go out for to-night? She ought to have stayed at home!"

But Madam Schuyler wore ample satisfaction upon her smooth brow. The bridegroom had arrived. There could be no further hitch in the ceremonies. He had arrived a day before the time, it is true; but he had not found *her* unprepared. So far as she was concerned, with a few extra touches the wedding might proceed at once. She was always ready for everything in time. No one could find a screw loose in the machinery of her household.

She bustled about, giving orders and laying a bountiful supper before the young man, while the Squire sat and talked with him, and Marcia hovered watchfully, waiting upon the table, noticing with admiring eyes the beautiful wave of his abundant hair, tossed back from his forehead. She took a kind of pride of possession in his handsome face,—the far-removed possession of a sister-in-law. There was his sunny smile, that seemed as though it could bring joy out of the gloom of a bleak December day, and there were the two dimples—not real dimples, of course, men never had dimples—but hints, suggestions of dimples, that caught themselves when he smiled, here and there like hidden mischief well kept under control, but still merrily ready to come to the surface. His hands were white and firm, the fingers long and shapely, the hands of a brain worker. The vision of Hanford Weston's hands, red and bony, came up to her in contrast. She had not known that she looked at them that day when he had stood awkwardly asking if he might walk with her. Poor Hanford! He would ill compare with this cultured scholarly man who was his senior by ten years, though it is possible that with the ten years added he would have been quite worthy of the admiration of any of the village girls.

The fruit cake and raspberry preserves and doughnuts and all the various viands that Madam Schuyler had ordered set out for the delectation of her guest had been partaken of, and David and the Squire sat talking of the news of the day, touching on politics, with a bit of laughter from the Squire at the man who thought he had invented a machine to draw carriages by steam in place of horses.

"There's a good deal in it, I believe," said the younger man. "His theory is all right if he can get some one to help him carry it out."

"Well, maybe, maybe," said the Squire shaking his head dubiously, "but it seems to me a very fanciful scheme. Horses are good enough for me. I shouldn't like to trust myself to an unknown quantity like steam, but time will tell."

"Yes, and the world is progressing. Something of the sort is sure to come. It has come in England. It would make a vast change in our country, binding city to city and practically eradicating space."

"Visionary schemes, David, visionary schemes, that's what I call them. You and I'll never see them in our day, I'm sure of that. Remember this is a new country and must go slow." The Squire was half laughing, half in earnest.

Amid the talk Marcia had quietly slipped out. It had occurred to her that perhaps the captain might return with her sister.

She must watch for Kate and warn her. Like a shadow in the moonlight she stepped softly down the gravel path once more and waited at the gate. Did not that sacred kiss placed upon her lips all by mistake bind her to this solemn duty? Had it not been given to her to see as in a revelation, by that kiss, the love of one man for one woman, deep and tender and true?

In the fragrant darkness her soul stood still and wondered over Love, the marvellous. With an insight such as few have who have not tasted years of wedded joy, Marcia comprehended the possibility and joy of sacrifice that made even sad things bright because of Love. She saw like a flash how Kate could give up her gay life, her home, her friends, everything that life had heretofore held dear for her, that she might be by the side of the man who loved her so. But with this knowledge of David's love for Kate came a troubled doubt. Did Kate love David that way? If Kate had been the one who received that kiss would she have returned it with the same tenderness and warmth with which it was given? Marcia dared not try to answer this. It was Kate's question, not hers, and she must never let it enter her mind again. Of course she must love him that way or she would never marry him.

The night crept slowly for the anxious little watcher at the gate. Had she been sure where to look for her sister, and not afraid of the tongues of a few interested neighbors who had watched everything at the house for days that no item about the wedding should escape them, she would have started on a search at once. She knew if she just ran into old Miss Pemberton's, whose house stood out upon the street with two straight-backed little, high, white seats each side of the stoop, a most delightful post of observation, she could discover at once in which direction Kate had gone, and perhaps a good deal more of hints and suggestions besides. But Marcia had no mind to make gossip. She must wait as patiently as she could for Kate. Moreover Kate might be walking even now in some secluded, rose-lined lane arm in arm with the captain, saying a pleasant farewell. It was Kate's way and no one might gainsay her.

Marcia's dreams came back once more, the thoughts that had been hers as she stood there an hour before. She thought how the kiss had fitted into the dream. Then all at once conscience told her it was Kate's lover, not her own, whose arms had encircled her. And now there was a strange unwillingness to go back to the dreams at all, a lingering longing for the joys into whose glory she had been for a moment permitted to look. She drew back from all thoughts and tried to close the door upon them. They seemed too sacred to enter. Her maidenhood was but just begun and she had much yet to learn of life. She was glad, glad for Kate that such wonderfulness was coming to her. Kate would be sweeter, softer in her ways now. She could not help it with a love like that enfolding her life.

At last there were footsteps! Hark! Two people—only two! Just what Marcia had expected. The other girls and boys had dropped into other streets or gone home. Kate and her former lover were coming home alone. And, furthermore, Kate would not be glad to see her sister at the gate. This last thought came with sudden conviction, but Marcia did not falter.

"Kate, David has come!" Marcia said it in low, almost accusing tones, at least so it sounded to Kate, before the two had hardly reached the gate. They had been loitering along talking in low tones, and the young captain's head was bent over his companion in an earnest, pleading attitude. Marcia could not bear to look, and did not wish to see more, so she had spoken.

Kate, startled, sprang away from her companion, a white angry look in her face.

"How you scared me, Marsh!" she exclaimed pettishly. "What if he has come? That's nothing. I guess he can wait a few minutes. He had no business to come to-night anyway. He knew we wouldn't be ready for him till to-morrow."

Kate was recovering her self-possession in proportion as she realized the situation. That she was vexed over her bridegroom's arrival neither of the two witnesses could doubt. It stung her sister with a deep pity for David. He was not getting as much in Kate as he was giving. But there was no time for such thoughts, besides Marcia was trembling from head to foot, partly with her own daring, partly with wrath at her sister's words.

"For shame, Kate!" she cried. "How can you talk so, even in fun! David came to surprise you, and I think he had a right to expect to find you here so near to the time of your marriage."

There was a flash in the young eyes as she said it, and a delicate lifting of her chin with the conviction of the truth she was speaking, that gave her a new dignity even in the moonlight. Captain Leavenworth looked at her in lazy admiration and said:

"Why, Marsh, you're developing into quite a spitfire. What have you got on to-night that makes you look so tall and handsome? Why didn't you stay in and talk to your fine gentleman? I'm sure he would have been just as well satisfied with you as your sister."

Marcia gave one withering glance at the young man and then turned her back full upon him. He was not worth noticing. Besides he was to be pitied, for he evidently cared still for Kate.

But Kate was fairly white with anger. Perhaps her own accusing conscience helped it on. Her voice was imperious and cold. She drew herself up haughtily and pointed toward the house.

"Marcia Schuyler," she said coldly, facing her sister, "go into the house and attend to your own affairs. You'll find that you'll get into serious trouble if you attempt to meddle with mine. You're nothing but a child yet and ought to be punished for your impudence. Go! I tell you!" she stamped her foot, "I will come in when I get ready."

Marcia went. Not proudly as she might have gone the moment before, but covered with confusion and shame, her head drooping like some crushed lily on a bleeding stalk. Through her soul rushed indignation, mighty and forceful; indignation and shame, for her sister, for David, for herself. She did not stop to analyze her various feelings, nor did she stop to speak further with those in the house. She fled to her own room, and burying her face in the pillow she wept until she fell asleep.

The moon-shadows grew longer about the arbored gateway where the two she had left stood talking in low tones, looking furtively now and then toward the house, and withdrawing into the covert of the bushes by the walk. But Kate dared not linger long. She could see her father's profile by the candle light in the dining room. She did not wish to receive further rebuke, and so in a very few minutes the two parted and Kate ran up the box-edged path, beginning to hum a sweet old love song in a gay light voice, as she tripped by the dining-room windows, and thus announced her arrival. She guessed that Marcia would have gone straight to her room and told nothing. Kate intended to be fully surprised. She paused in the hall to hang up the light shawl she had worn, calling good-night to her stepmother and saying she was very tired and was going straight to bed to be ready for to-morrow. Then she ran lightly across the hall to the stairs.

She knew they would call her back, and that they would all come into the hall with David to see the effect of his surprise upon her. She had planned to a nicety just which stair she could reach before they got there, and where she would pause and turn and poise, and what pose she would take with her round white arm stretched to the handrail, the sleeve turned carelessly back. She had ready her countenances, a sleepy indifference, then a pleased surprise, and a climax of delight. She carried it all out, this little bit of impromptu acting, as well as though she had rehearsed it for a month.

They called her, and she turned deliberately, one dainty, slippered foot, with its crossed black ribbons about the slender ankle, just leaving the stair below, and showing the arch of the aristocratic instep. Her gown was blue and she held it back just enough for the stiff white frill of her petticoat to peep below. Well she read the admiration in the eyes below her. Admiration was Kate's life: she thrived upon it. She could not do without it.

David stood still, his love in his eyes, looking upon the vision of his bride, and his heart swelled within him that so great a treasure should be his. Then straightway they all forgot to question where she had been or to rebuke her that she had been at all. She had known they would. She ever possessed the power to make others forget her wrong doings when it was worth her while to try.

The next morning things were astir even earlier than usual. There was the sound of the beating of eggs, the stirring of cakes, the clatter of pots and pans from the wide, stone-flagged kitchen.

Marcia, fresh as a flower from its morning dew in spite of her cry the night before, had arisen to new opportunities for service. She was glad with the joyous forgetfulness of youth when she looked at David's happy face, and she thought no more of Kate's treatment of herself.

David followed Kate with a true lover's eyes and was never for more than a few moments out of her sight, though it seemed to Marcia that Kate did not try very hard to stay with him. When afternoon came she dismissed him for what she called her "beauty nap." Marcia was passing through the hall at the time and she caught the tender look upon his face as he touched her brow with reverent fingers and told her she had no need for that. Her eyes met Kate's as they were going up the stairs, and in spite of what Kate had said the night before Marcia could not refrain from saying: "Oh, Kate! how could you when he loves you so? You know you never take a nap in the daytime!"

"You silly girl!" said Kate pleasantly enough, "don't you know the less a man sees of one the more he thinks of her?" With this remark she closed and fastened her door after her.

Marcia pondered these words of wisdom for some time, wondering whether Kate had really done it for that reason, or whether she did not care for the company of her lover. And why should it be so that a man loved you less because he saw you more? In her straightforward code the more you loved persons the more you desired to be in their company.

Kate had issued from her "beauty nap" with a feverish restlessness in her eyes, an averted face, and ink upon one finger. At supper she scarcely spoke, and when she did she laughed excitedly over little things. Her lover watched her with eyes of pride and ever increasing wonder over her beauty, and Marcia, seeing the light in his face, watched for its answer in her sister's, and finding it not was troubled.

She watched them from her bedroom window as they walked down the path where she had gone the evening before, decorously side by side, Kate holding her light muslin frock back from the dew on the hedges. She wondered if it was because Kate had more respect for David than for Captain Leavenworth that she never seemed to treat him with as much familiarity. She did not take possession of him in the same sweet imperious way.

Marcia had not lighted her candle. The moon gave light enough and she was very weary, so she undressed in the dim chamber and pondered upon the ways of the great world. Out there in the moonlight were those two who to-morrow would be one, and here was she, alone. The world seemed all circling about that white chamber of hers, and echoing with her own consciousness of self, and a loneliness she had never felt before. She wondered what it might be. Was it all sadness at parting with Kate, or was it the sadness over inevitable partings of all human relationships, and the all-aloneness of every living spirit?

She stood for a moment, white-robed, beside her window, looking up into the full round moon, and wondering if God knew the ache of loneliness in His little human creatures' souls that He had made, and whether He had ready something wherewith to satisfy. Then her meek soul bowed before the faith that was in her and she knelt for her shy but reverent evening prayer.

She heard the two lovers come in early and go upstairs, and she heard her father fastening up the doors and windows for the night. Then stillness gradually settled down and she fell asleep. Later, in her dreams, there echoed the sound of hastening hoofs far down the deserted street and over the old covered bridge, but she took no note of any sound, and the weary household slept on.

CHAPTER IV

The wedding was set for ten o'clock in the morning, after which there was to be a wedding breakfast and the married couple were to start immediately for their new home.

David had driven the day before with his own horse and chaise to a town some twenty miles away, and there left his horse at a tavern to rest for the return trip, for Kate would have it that they must leave the house in high style. So the finest equipage the town afforded had been secured to bear them on the first stage of their journey, with a portly negro driver and everything according to the custom of the greatest of the land. Nothing that Kate desired about the arrangements had been left undone.

The household was fully astir by half past four, for the family breakfast was to be at six promptly, that all might be cleared away and in readiness for the early arrival of the various aunts and uncles and cousins and friends who would "drive over" from the country round about. It would have been something Madam Schuyler would never have been able to get over if aught had been awry when a single uncle or aunt appeared upon the scene, or if there seemed to be the least evidence of fluster and nervousness.

The rosy sunlight in the east was mixing the morning with fresher air, and new odors for the new day that was dawning, when Marcia awoke. The sharp click of spoons and dishes, the voices of the maids, the sizzle, sputter, odor of frying ham and eggs, mingled with the early chorus of the birds, and calling to life of all living creatures, like an intrusion upon nature. It seemed not right to steal the morning's "quiet hour" thus rudely. The thought flitted through the girl's mind, and in an instant more the whole panorama of the day's excitement was before her, and she sprang from her bed. As if it had been her own wedding day instead of her sister's, she performed her dainty toilet, for though there was need for haste, she knew she would have no further time beyond a moment to slip on her best gown and smooth her hair.

Marcia hurried downstairs just as the bell rang for breakfast, and David, coming down smiling behind her, patted her cheek and greeted her with, "Well, little sister, you look as rested as if you had not done a thing all day yesterday."

She smiled shyly back at him, and her heart filled with pleasure over his new name for her. It sounded pleasantly from his happy lips. She was conscious of a gladness that he was to be so nearly related to her. She fancied how it would seem to say to Mary Ann: "My brother-in-law says so and so." It would be grand to call such a man "brother."

They were all seated at the table but Kate, and Squire Schuyler waited with pleasantly frowning brows to ask the blessing on the morning food. Kate was often late. She was the only member of the family who dared to be late to breakfast, and being the bride and the centre of the occasion more leniency was granted her this morning than ever before. Madam Schuyler waited until every one at the table was served to ham and eggs, coffee and bread-and-butter, and steaming griddle cakes, before she said, looking anxiously at the tall clock: "Marcia, perhaps you better go up and see if your sister needs any help. She ought to be down by now. Uncle Joab and Aunt Polly will be sure to be here by eight. She must have overslept, but we made so much noise she is surely awake by this time."

Marcia left her half-eaten breakfast and went slowly upstairs. She knew her sister would not welcome her, for she had often been sent on like errands before, and the brunt of Kate's anger had fallen upon the hapless messenger, wearing itself out there so that she might descend all smiles to greet father and mother and smooth off the situation in a most harmonious manner.

Marcia paused before the door to listen. Perhaps Kate was nearly ready and her distasteful errand need not be performed. But though she held her breath to listen, no sound came from the closed door. Very softly she tried to lift the latch and peep in. Kate must still be asleep. It was not the first time Marcia had found that to be the case when sent to bring her sister.

But the latch would not lift. The catch was firmly down from the inside. Marcia applied her eye to the keyhole, but could get no vision save a dim outline of the window on the other side of the room. She tapped gently once or twice and waited again, then called softly: "Kate, Kate! Wake up. Breakfast is ready and everybody is eating. Aunt Polly and Uncle Joab will soon be here."

She repeated her tapping and calling, growing louder as she received no answer. Kate would often keep still to tease her thus. Surely though she would not do so upon her wedding morning!

She called and called and shook the door, not daring, however, to make much of an uproar lest David should hear. She could not bear he should know the shortcomings of his bride.

But at last she grew alarmed. Perhaps Kate was ill. At any rate, whatever it was, it was time she was up. She worked for some minutes trying to loosen the catch that held the latch, but all to no purpose. She was forced to go down stairs and whisper to her stepmother the state of the case.

Madam Schuyler, excusing herself from the table, went upstairs, purposeful decision in every line of her substantial body, determination in every sound of her footfall. Bride though she be, Kate would have meted out to her just dues this time. Company and a lover and the nearness of the wedding hour were things not to be trifled with even by a charming Kate.

But Madam Schuyler returned in a short space of time, puffing and panting, somewhat short of breath, and color in her face. She looked troubled, and she interrupted the Squire without waiting for him to finish his sentence to David.

"I cannot understand what is the matter with Kate," she said, looking at her husband. "She does not seem to be awake, and I cannot get her door open. She sleeps soundly, and I suppose the unusual excitement has made her very tired. But I should think she ought to hear my voice. Perhaps you better see if you can open the door."

There was studied calm in her voice, but her face belied her words. She was anxious lest Kate was playing one of her pranks. She knew Kate's careless, fun-loving ways. It was more to her that all things should move decently and in order than that Kate should even be perfectly well. But Marcia's white face behind her stepmother's ample shoulder showed a dread of something worse than a mere indisposition. David Spafford took alarm at once. He put down the silver syrup jug from which he had been pouring golden maple syrup on his cakes, and pushed his chair back with a click.

"Perhaps she has fainted!" he said, and Marcia saw how deeply he was concerned. Father and lover both started up stairs, the father angry, the lover alarmed. The Squire grumbled all the way up that Kate should sleep so late, but David said nothing. He waited anxiously behind while the Squire worked with the door. Madam Schuyler and Marcia had followed them, and halting curiously just behind came the two maids. They all loved Miss Kate and were deeply interested in the day's doings. They did not want anything to interfere with the well-planned pageant.

The Squire fumbled nervously with the latch, all the time calling upon his daughter to open the door; then wrathfully placed his solid shoulder and knee in just the right place, and with a groan and wrench the latch gave way, and the solid oak door swung open, precipitating the anxious group somewhat suddenly into the room.

Almost immediately they all became aware that there was no one there. David had stood with averted eyes at first, but that second sense which makes us aware without sight when others are near or absent, brought with it an unnamed anxiety. He looked wildly about.

The bed had not been slept in; that they all saw at once. The room was in confusion, but perhaps not more than might have been expected when the occupant was about to leave on the morrow. There were pieces of paper and string upon the floor and one or two garments lying about as if carelessly cast off in a hurry. David recognized the purple muslin frock Kate had worn the night before, and put out his hand to touch it as it lay across the foot of the bed, vainly reaching after her who was not there.

They stood in silence, father, mother, sister, and lover, and took in every detail of the deserted room, then looked blankly into one another's white faces, and in the eyes of each a terrible question began to dawn. Where was she?

Madam Schuyler recovered her senses first. With her sharp practical system she endeavored to find out the exact situation.

"Who saw her last?" she asked sharply looking from one to the other. "Who saw her last? Has she been down stairs this morning?" she looked straight at Marcia this time, but the girl shook her head.

"I went to bed last night before they came in," she said, looking questioningly at David, but a sudden remembrance and fear seized her heart. She turned away to the window to face it where they could not look at her.

"We came in early," said David, trying to keep the anxiety out of his voice, as he remembered his well-beloved's good-night. Surely, surely, nothing very dreadful could have happened just over night, and in her father's own house. He looked about again to see the natural, every-day, little things that would help him drive away the thoughts of possible tragedy.

"Kate was tired. She said she was going to get up very early this morning and wash her face in the dew on the grass." He braved a smile and looked about on the troubled group. "She must be out somewhere upon the place," he continued, gathering courage with the thought; "she told me it was an old superstition. She has maybe wandered further than she intended, and perhaps got into some trouble. I'd better go and search for her. Is there any place near here where she would be likely to be?" He turned to Marcia for help.

"But Kate would never delay so long I'm sure," said the stepmother severely. "She's not such a fool as to go traipsing through the wet grass before daylight for any nonsense. If it were Marcia now, you might expect anything, but Kate would be satisfied with the dew on the grass by the kitchen pump. I know Kate."

Marcia's face crimsoned at her stepmother's words, but she turned her troubled eyes to David and tried to answer him.

"There are plenty of places, but Kate has never cared to go to them. I could go out and look everywhere." She started to go down, but as she passed the wide mahogany bureau she saw a bit of folded paper lying under the corner of the pincushion. With a smothered exclamation she went over and picked it up. It was addressed to David in Kate's handwriting, fine and even like copperplate. Without a word Marcia handed it to him, and then stood back where the wide draperies of the window would shadow her.

Madam Schuyler, with sudden keen prescience, took alarm. Noticing the two maids standing wide-mouthed in the hallway, she summoned her most commandatory tone, stepped into the hall, half closing the door behind her, and cowed the two handmaidens under her glance.

"It is all right!" she said calmly. "Miss Kate has left a note, and will soon return. Go down and keep her breakfast warm, and not a word to a soul! Dolly, Debby, do you understand? Not a word of this! Now hurry and do all that I told you before breakfast."

They went with downcast eyes and disappointed droops to their mouths, but she knew that not a word would pass their lips. They knew that if they disobeyed that command they need never hope for favor more from madam. Madam's word was law. She would be obeyed. Therefore with remarkable discretion they masked their wondering looks and did as they were bidden. So while the family stood in solemn conclave in Kate's room the preparations for the wedding moved steadily forward below stairs, and only two solemn maids, of all the helpers that morning, knew that a tragedy was hovering in the air and might burst about them.

David had grasped for the letter eagerly, and fumbled it open with trembling hand, but as he read, the smile of expectation froze upon his lips and his face grew ashen. He tottered and grasped for the mantel shelf to steady himself as he read further, but he did not seem to take in the meaning of what he read. The others waited breathless, a reasonable length of time, Madam Schuyler impatiently patient. She felt that long delay would be perilous to her arrangements. She ought to know the whole truth at once and be put in command of the situation. Marcia with sorrowful face and drooping eyelashes stood quiet behind the curtain, while over and over the echo of a horse's hoofs in a silent street and over a bridge sounded in her brain. She did not need to be told, she knew intuitively what had happened, and she dared not look at David.

"Well, what has she done with herself?" said the Squire impatiently. He had not finished his plate of cakes, and now that there was word he wanted to know it at once and go back to his breakfast. The sight of his daughter's handwriting relieved and reassured him. Some crazy thing she had done of course, but then Kate had always done queer things, and probably would to the end of time. She was a hussy to frighten them so, and he meant to tell her so when she returned, if it was her wedding day. But then, Kate would be Kate, and his breakfast was getting cold. He had the horses to look after and orders to give to the hands before the early guests arrived.

But David did not answer, and the sight of him was alarming. He stood as one stricken dumb all in a moment. He raised his eyes to the Squire's—pleading, pitiful. His face had grown strained and haggard.

"Speak out, man, doesn't the letter tell?" said the Squire imperiously. "Where is the girl?"

And this time David managed to say brokenly: "She's gone!" and then his head dropped forward on his cold hand that rested on the mantel. Great beads of perspiration stood out upon his white forehead, and the letter fluttered gayly, coquettishly to the floor, a reminder of the uncertain ways of its writer.

The Squire reached for it impatiently, and wiping his spectacles laboriously put them on and drew near to the window to read, his heavy brows lowering in a frown. But his wife did not need to read the letter, for she, like Marcia, had divined its purport, and already her able faculties were marshalled to face the predicament.

The Squire with deepening frown was studying his elder daughter's letter, scarce able to believe the evidence of his senses that a girl of his could be so heartless.

"DEAR DAVID," the letter ran,—written as though in a hurry, done at the last moment,—which indeed it was:—

"I want you to forgive me for what I am doing. I know you will feel bad about it, but really I never was the right one for you. I'm sure you thought me all too good, and I never could have stayed in a strait-jacket, it would have killed me. I shall always consider you the best man in the world, and I like you better than anyone else except Captain Leavenworth. I can't help it, you know, that I care more for him than anyone else, though I've tried. So I am going away to-night and when you read this we shall have been married. You are so very good that I know you will forgive me, and be glad I am happy. Don't think hardly of me for I always did care a great deal for you.

"Your loving
"KATE."

It was characteristic of Kate that she demanded the love and loyalty of her betrayed lover to the bitter end, false and heartless though she had been. The coquette in her played with him even now in the midst of the bitter pain she must have known she was inflicting. No word of contrition spoke she, but took her deed as one of her prerogatives, just as she had always taken everything she chose. She did not even spare him the loving salutation that had been her custom in her letters to him, but wrote herself down as she would have done the day before when all was fair and dear between them. She did not hint at any better day for David, or give him permission to forget her, but held him for all time as her own, as she had known she would by those words of hers, "I like you better than anyone else except!—" Ah! That fatal "except!" Could any knife cut deeper and more ways? They sank into the young man's heart as he stood there those first few minutes and faced his trouble, his head bowed upon the mantel-piece.

Meantime Madam Schuyler's keen vision had spied another folded paper beside the pincushion. Smaller it was than the other, and evidently intended to be placed further out of sight. It was addressed to Kate's father, and her stepmother opened it and read with hard pressure of her thin lips, slanted down at the corners, and a steely look in her eyes. Was it possible that the girl, even in the midst of her treachery, had enjoyed with a sort of malicious glee the thought of her stepmother reading that note and facing the horror of a wedding party with no bride? Knowing her stepmother's vast resources did she not think that at last she had brought her to a situation to which she was unequal? There had always been this unseen, unspoken struggle for supremacy between them; though it had been a friendly one, a sort of testing on the girl's part of the powers and expedients of the woman, with a kind of vast admiration, mingled with amusement, but no fear for the stepmother who had been uniformly kind and loving toward her, and for whom she cared, perhaps as much as she could have cared for her own mother. The other note read:

"DEAR FATHER:—I am going away to-night to marry Captain Leavenworth. You wouldn't let me have him in the right way, so I had to take this. I tried very hard to forget him and get interested in David, but it was no use. You couldn't stop it. So now I hope you will see it the way we do and forgive us. We are going to Washington and you can write us there and say you forgive us, and then we will come home. I know you will forgive us, Daddy dear. You know you always loved your little Kate and you couldn't really want me to be unhappy. Please send my trunks to Washington. I've tacked the card with the address on the ends.

"Your loving little girl,

"KATE."

There was a terrible stillness in the room, broken only by the crackling of paper as the notes were turned in the hands of their readers. Marcia felt as if centuries were passing. David's soul was pierced by one awful thought. He had no room for others. She was gone! Life was a blank for him! stretching out into interminable years. Of her treachery and false-heartedness in doing what she had done in the way she had done it, he had no time to take account. That would come later. Now he was trying to understand this one awful fact.

Madam Schuyler handed the second note to her husband, and with set lips quickly skimmed through the other one. As she read, indignation rose within her, and a great desire to outwit everybody. If it had been possible to bring the erring girl back and make her face her disgraced wedding alone, Madam Schuyler would have been glad to do it. She knew that upon her would likely rest all the re-arrangements, and her ready brain was already taking account of her servants and the number of messages that would have to be sent out to stop the guests from arriving. She waited impatiently for her husband to finish reading that she might consult with him as to the best message to send, but she was scarcely prepared for the burst of anger that came with the finish of the letters. The old man crushed his daughter's note in his hand and flung it from him. He had great respect and love for David, and the sight of him broken in grief, the deed of his daughter, roused in him a mighty indignation. His voice shook, but there was a deep note of command in it that made Madam Schuyler step aside and wait. The Squire had arisen to the situation, and she recognized her lord and master.

"She must be brought back at once at all costs!" he exclaimed. "That rascal shall not outwit us. Fool that I was to trust him in the house! Tell the men to saddle the horses. They cannot have gone far yet, and there are not so many roads to Washington. We may yet overtake them, and married or unmarried the hussy shall be here for her wedding!"

But David raised his head from the mantel-shelf and steadied his voice:

"No, no, you must not do that—father—" the appellative came from his lips almost tenderly, as if he had long considered the use of it with pleasure, and now he spoke it as a tender bond meant to comfort.

The older man started and his face softened. A flash of understanding and love passed between the two men.

"Remember, she has said she loves some one else. She could never be mine now."

There was terrible sadness in the words as David spoke them, and his voice broke. Madam Schuyler turned away and took out her handkerchief, an article of apparel for which she seldom had use except as it belonged to every well ordered toilet.

The father stood looking hopelessly at David and taking in the thought. Then he too bowed his head and groaned.

"And my daughter, *my little Kate* has done it!" Marcia covered her face with the curtains and her tears fell fast.

David went and stood beside the Squire and touched his arm.

"Don't!" he said pleadingly. "You could not help it. It was not your fault. Do not take it so to heart!"

"But it is my disgrace. I have brought up a child who could do it. I cannot escape from that. It is the most dishonorable thing a woman can do. And look how she has done it, brought shame upon us all! Here we have a wedding on our hands, and little or no time to do anything! I have lived in honor all my life, and now to be disgraced by my own daughter!"

Marcia shuddered at her father's agony. She could not bear it longer. With a soft cry she went to him, and nestled her head against his breast unnoticed.

"Father, father, don't!" she cried.

But her father went on without seeming to see her.

"To be disgraced and deserted and dishonored by my own child! Something must be done. Send the servants! Let the wedding be stopped!"

He looked at Madam and she started toward the door to carry out his bidding, but he recalled her immediately.

"No, stay!" he cried. "It is too late to stop them all. Let them come. Let them be told! Let the disgrace rest upon the one to whom it belongs!"

Madam stopped in consternation! A wedding without a bride! Yet she knew it was a serious thing to try to dispute with her husband in that mood. She paused to consider.

"Oh, father!" exclaimed Marcia, "we couldn't! Think of David."

Her words seemed to touch the right chord, for he turned toward the young man, intense, tender pity in his face.

"Yes, David! We are forgetting David! We must do all we can to make it easier for you. You will be wanting to get away from us as quickly as possible. How can we manage it for you? And where will you go? You will not want to go home just yet?"

He paused, a new agony of the knowledge of David's part coming to him.

"No, I cannot go home," said David hopelessly, a look of keen pain darting across his face, "for the house will be all ready for her, and the table set. The friends will be coming in, and we are invited to dinner and tea everywhere. They will all be coming to the house, my friends, to welcome us. No, I cannot go home." Then he passed his hand over his forehead blindly, and added, in a stupefied tone, "and yet I must—sometime—I must—go—home!"

CHAPTER V

The room was very still as he spoke. Madam Schuyler forgot the coming guests and the preparations, in consternation over the thought of David and his sorrow. Marcia sobbed softly upon her father's breast, and her father involuntarily placed his arm about her as he stood in painful thought.

"It is terrible!" he murmured, "terrible! How could she bear to inflict such sorrow! She might have saved us the scorn of all of our friends. David, you must not go back alone. It must not be. You must not bear that. There are lovely girls in plenty elsewhere. Find another one and marry her. Take your bride home with you, and no one in your home need be the wiser. Don't sorrow for that cruel girl of mine. Give her not the satisfaction of feeling that your life is broken. Take another. Any girl might be proud to go with you for the asking. Had I a dozen other daughters you should have your pick of them, and one should go with you, if you would condescend to choose another from the home where you have been so treacherously dealt with. But I have only this one little girl. She is but a child as yet and cannot compare with what you thought you had. I blame you not if you do not wish to wed another Schuyler, but if you will she is yours. And she is a good girl. David, though she is but a child. Speak up, child, and say if you will make amends for the wrong your sister has done!"

The room was so still one could almost hear the heartbeats. David had raised his head once more and was looking at Marcia. Sad and searching was his gaze, as if he fain would find the features of Kate in her face, yet it seemed to Marcia, as she raised wide tear-filled eyes from her father's breast where her head still lay, that he saw her not. He was looking beyond her and facing the home-going alone, and the empty life that would follow.

Her thoughts the last few days had matured her wonderfully. She understood and pitied, and her woman-nature longed to give comfort, yet she shrunk from going unasked. It was all terrible, this sudden situation thrust upon her, yet she felt a willing sacrifice if she but felt sure it was his wish.

But David did not seem to know that he must speak. He waited, looking earnestly at her, through her, beyond her, to see if Heaven would grant this small relief to his sufferings. At last Marcia summoned her voice:

"If David wishes I will go."

She spoke the words solemnly, her eyes lifted slightly above him as if she were speaking to Another One higher than he. It was like an answer to a call from God. It had come to Marcia this way. It seemed to leave her no room for drawing back, if indeed she had wished to do so. Other considerations were not present. There was just the one great desire in her heart to make amends in some measure for the wrong that had been done. She felt almost responsible for it, a family responsibility. She seemed to feel the shame and pain as her father was feeling it. She would step into the empty place that Kate had left and fill it as far as she could. Her only fear was that she was not acceptable, not worthy to fill so high a place. She trembled over it, yet she could not hold back from the high calling. It was so she stood in a kind of sorrowful exaltation waiting for David. Her eyes lowered again, looking at him through the lashes and pleading for recognition. She did not feel that she was pleading for anything for herself, only for the chance to help him.

Her voice had broken the spell. David looked down upon her kindly, a pleasant light of gratitude flashing through the sternness and sorrow in his face. Here was comradeship in trouble, and his voice recognized it as he said:

"Child, you are good to me, and I thank you. I will try to make you happy if you will go with me, and I am sure your going will be a comfort in many ways, but I would not have you go unwillingly."

There was a dull ache in Marcia's heart, its cause she could not understand, but she was conscious of a gladness that she was not counted unworthy to be accepted, young though she was, and child though he called her. His tone had been kindness itself, the gentle kindliness that had won her childish sisterly love when first he began to visit her sister. She had that answer of his to remember for many a long day, and to live upon, when questionings and loneliness came upon her. But she raised her face to her father now, and said: "I will go, father!"

The Squire stooped and kissed his little girl for the last time. Perhaps he realized that from this time forth she would be a little girl no longer, and that he would never look into those child-eyes of hers again, unclouded with the sorrows of life, and filled only with the wonder-pictures of a rosy future. She seemed to him and to herself to be renouncing her own life forever, and to be taking up one of sacrificial penitence for her sister's wrong doing.

The father then took Marcia's hand and placed it in David's, and the betrothal was complete.

Madam Schuyler, whose reign for the time was set aside, stood silent, half disapproving, yet not interfering. Her conscience told her that this wholesale disposal of Marcia was against nature. The new arrangement was a relief to her in many ways, and would make the solution of the day less trying for every one. But she was a woman and knew a woman's heart. Marcia was not having her chance in life as her sister had had, as every woman had a right to have. Then her face hardened. How had Kate used her chances? Perhaps it was better for Marcia to be well placed in life before she grew headstrong enough to make a fool of herself as Kate had done. David would be good to her, that was certain. One could not look at the strong, pleasant lines of his well cut mouth and chin and not be sure of that. Perhaps it was all for the best. At least it was not her doing. And it was only the night before that she had been looking at Marcia and worrying because she was growing into a woman so fast. Now she would be relieved of that care, and could take her ease and enjoy life until her own children were grown up. But the voice of her husband aroused her to the present.

"Let the wedding go on as planned, Sarah, and no one need know until the ceremony is over except the minister. I myself will go and tell the minister. There will need to be but a change of names."

"But," said the Madam, with housewifely alarm, as the suddenness of the whole thing flashed over her, "Marcia is not ready. She has no suitable clothes for her wedding."

"Not ready! No clothes!" said the Squire, now thoroughly irritated over this trivial objection, as a fly will sometimes ruffle the temper of a man who has kept calm under fire of an enemy. "And where are all the clothes that have been making these weeks and months past? What more preparation does she need? Did the hussy take her wedding things with her? What's in this trunk?"

"But those are Kate's things, father," said Marcia in gentle explanation. "Kate would be very angry if I took her things. They were made for her, you know."

"And what if they were made for her?" answered the father, very angry now at Kate. "You are near of a size. What will do for one is good enough for the other, and Kate may be angry and get over it, for not one rag of it all will she get, nor a penny of my money will ever go to her again. She is no daughter of mine from henceforth. That rascal has beaten me and stolen my daughter, but he gets a dowerless lass. Not a penny will ever go from the Schuyler estate into his pocket, and no trunk will ever travel from here to Washington for that heartless girl. I forbid it. Let her feel some of the sorrow she has inflicted upon others more innocent. I forbid it, do you hear?" He brought his fist down upon the solid mahogany bureau until the prisms on a candle-stand in front of the mirror jangled discordantly.

"Oh, father!" gasped Marcia, and turned with terror to her stepmother. But David stood with his back toward the rest looking out of the window. He had forgotten them all.

Madam Schuyler was now in command again. For once the Squire had anticipated his wife, and the next move had been planned without her help, but it was as she would have it. Her face had lost its consternation and beamed with satisfaction beneath its mask of grave perplexity. She could not help it that she was glad to have the terrible ordeal of a wedding without a bride changed into something less formidable.

At least the country round about could not pity, for who was to say but that David was as well suited with one sister as with the other? And Marcia was a good girl; doubtless she would grow into a good wife. Far more suitable for so good and steady a man as David than pretty, imperious Kate.

Madam Schuyler took her place of command once more and began to issue her orders.

"Come, then, Marcia, we have no time to waste. It is all right, as your father has said. Kate's things will fit you nicely and you must go at once and put everything in readiness. You will want all your time to dress, and pack a few things, and get calm. Go to your room right away and pick up anything you will want to take with you, and I'll go down and see that Phoebe takes your place and then come back."

David and the Squire went out like two men who had suddenly grown old, and had not the strength to walk rapidly. No one thought any more of breakfast. It was half-past seven by the old tall clock that stood upon the stair-landing. It would not be long before Aunt Polly and Uncle Joab would be driving up to the door.

Straight ahead went the preparations, just as if nothing had happened, and if Mistress Kate Leavenworth could have looked into her old room an hour after the discovery of her flight she would have been astonished beyond measure.

Up in her own room stood poor bewildered Marcia. She looked about upon her little white bed, and thought she would never likely sleep in it again. She looked out of the small-paned window with its view of distant hill and river, and thought she was bidding it good-bye forever. She went toward her closet and put out her hand to choose what she would take with her, and her heart sank. There hung the faded old ginghams short and scant, and scorned but yesterday, yet her heart wildly clung to them. Almost would she have put one on and gone back to her happy care-free school life. The thought of the new life frightened her. She must give up her girlhood all at once. She might not keep a vestige of it, for that would betray David. She must be Kate from morning to evening. Like a sword thrust came the remembrance that she had envied Kate, and God had given her the punishment of being Kate in very truth. Only there was this great difference. She was not the chosen one, and Kate had been. She must bear about forever in her heart the thought of Kate's sin.

The voice of her stepmother drew nearer and warned her that her time alone was almost over, and out on the lawn she could hear the voices of Uncle Joab and Aunt Polly who had just arrived.

She dropped upon her knees for one brief moment and let her young soul pour itself out in one great cry of distress to God, a cry without words borne only on the breath of a sob. Then she arose, hastily dashed cold water in her face, and dried away the traces of tears. There was no more time to think. With hurried hand she began to gather a few trifles together from closet and drawer.

One last lingering look she took about her room as she left it, her arms filled with the things she had hastily culled from among her own. Then she shut the door quickly and went down the hall to her sister's room to enter upon her new life. She was literally putting off herself and putting on a new being as far as it was possible to do so outwardly.

There on the bed lay the bridal outfit. Madam Schuyler had just brought it from the spare room that there might be no more going back and forth through the halls to excite suspicion. She was determined that there should be no excitement or demonstration or opportunity for gossip among the guests at least until the ceremony was over. She had satisfied herself that not a soul outside the family save the two maids suspected that aught was the matter, and she felt sure of their silence.

Kate had taken very little with her, evidently fearing to excite suspicion, and having no doubt that her father would relent and send all her trousseau as she had requested in her letter. For once Mistress Kate had forgotten her fineries and made good her escape with but two frocks and a few other necessaries in a small hand-bag.

Madam Schuyler was relieved to the point of genuine cheerfulness, over this, despite the cloud of tragedy that hung over the day. She began to talk to Marcia as if she had been Kate, as she smoothed down this and that article and laid them back in the trunk, telling how the blue gown would be the best for church and the green silk for going out to very fine places, to tea-drinkings and the like, and how she must always be sure to wear the cream undersleeves with the Irish point lace with her silk gown as they set it off to perfection. She recalled, too, how little experience Marcia had had in the ways of the world, and all the while the girl was being dressed in the dainty bridal garments she gave her careful instructions in the art of being a success in society, until Marcia felt that the green fields and the fences and trees to climb and the excursions after blackberries, and all the joyful merry-makings of the boys and girls were receding far from her. She could even welcome Hanford Weston as a playfellow in her new future, if thereby a little fresh air and freedom of her girlhood might be left. Nevertheless there gradually came over her an elation of excitement. The feel of the dainty garments, the delicate embroidery, the excitement lest the white slippers would not fit her, the difficulty of making her hair stay up in just Kate's style—for her stepmother insisted that she must dress it exactly like Kate's and make herself look as nearly as possible as Kate would have looked,—all drove sadness from her mind and she began to taste a little delight in the pretty clothes, the great occasion, and her own importance. The vision in the looking-glass, too, told her that her own face was winsome, and the new array not unbecoming. Something of this she had seen the night before when she put on her new chintz; now the change was complete, as she stood in the white satin and lace with the string of seed pearls that had been her mother's tied about her soft white throat. She thought about the tradition of the pearls that Kate's girl friends had laughingly reminded her of a few days before when they were looking at the bridal garments. They had said that each pearl a bride wore meant a tear she would shed. She wondered if Kate had escaped the tears with the pearls, and left them for her.

She was ready at last, even to the veil that had been her mother's, and her mother's mother's before her. It fell in its rich folds, yellowed by age, from her head to her feet, with its creamy frost-work of rarest handiwork, transforming the girl into a woman and a bride.

Madam Schuyler arranged and rearranged the folds, and finally stood back to look with half-closed eyes at the effect, deciding that very few would notice that the bride was other than they had expected until the ceremony was over and the veil thrown back. The sisters had never looked alike, yet there was a general family resemblance that was now accentuated by the dress; perhaps only those nearest would notice that it was Marcia instead of Kate. At least the guests would have the good grace to keep their wonderment to themselves until the ceremony was over.

Then Marcia was left to herself with trembling hands and wildly throbbing heart. What would Mary Ann think! What would all the girls and boys think? Some of them would be there, and others would be standing along the shady streets to watch the progress of the carriage as it drove away. And they would see her going away instead of Kate. Perhaps they would think it all a great joke and that she had been going to be married all the time and not Kate. But no; the truth would soon come out. People would not be astonished at anything Kate did. They would only say it was just what they had all along expected of her, and pity her father, and pity her perhaps. But they would look at her and admire her and for once she would be the centre of attraction. The pink of pride swelled up into her cheeks, and then realizing what she was thinking she crushed the feeling down. How could she think of such things when Kate had done such a dreadful thing, and David was suffering so terribly? Here was she actually enjoying, and delighting in the thought of being in Kate's place. Oh, she was wicked, wicked! She must not be happy for a moment in what was Kate's shame and David's sorrow. Of her future with David she did not now think. It was of the pageant of the day that her thoughts were full. If the days and weeks and months that were to follow came into her mind at all between the other things it was always that she was to care for David and to help him, and that she would have to grow up quickly; and remember all the hard housewifely things her stepmother had taught her; and try to order his house well. But that troubled her not at all at present. She was more concerned with the ceremony, and the many eyes that would be turned upon her. It was a relief when a tap came on the door and the dear old minister entered.

CHAPTER VI

He stood a moment by the door looking at her, half startled. Then he came over beside her, put his hands upon her shoulders, looking down into her upturned, veiled face.

"My child!" he said tenderly, "my little Marcia, is this you? I did not know you in all this beautiful dress. You look as your own mother looked when she was married. I remember perfectly as if it were but yesterday, her face as she stood by your father's side. I was but a young man then, you know, and it was my first wedding in my new church, so you see I could not forget it. Your mother was a beautiful woman, Marcia, and you are like her both in face and life."

The tears came into Marcia's eyes and her lips trembled.

"Are you sure, child," went on the gentle voice of the old man, "that you understand what a solemn thing you are doing? It is not a light thing to give yourself in marriage to any man. You are so young yet! Are you doing this thing quite willingly, little girl? Are you sure? Your father is a good man, and a dear old friend of mine, but I know what has happened has been a terrible blow to him, and a great humiliation. It has perhaps unnerved his judgment for the time. No one should have brought pressure to bear upon a child like you to make you marry against your will. Are you sure it is all right, dear?"

"Oh, yes, sir!" Marcia raised her tear-filled eyes. "I am doing it quite of myself. No one has made me. I was glad I might. It was so dreadful for David!"

"But child, do you love him?" the old minister said, searching her face closely.

Marcia's eyes shone out radiant and child-like through her tears.

"Oh, yes, sir! I love him of course. No one could help loving David."

There was a tap at the door and the Squire entered. With a sigh the minister turned away, but there was trouble in his heart. The love of the girl had been all too frankly confessed. It was not as he would have had things for a daughter of his, but it could not be helped of course, and he had no right to interfere. He would like to speak to David, but David had not come out of his room yet. When he did there was but a moment for them alone and all he had opportunity to say was:

"Mr. Spafford, you will be good to the little girl, and remember she is but a child. She has been dear to us all."

David looked at him wonderingly, earnestly, in reply:

"I will do all in my power to make her happy," he said.

The hour had come, and all things, just as Madam Schuyler had planned, were ready. The minister took his place, and the impatient bridesmaids were in a flutter, wondering why Kate did not call them in to see her. Slowly, with measured step, as if she had practised many times, Marcia, the maiden, walked down the hall on her father's arm. He was bowed with his trouble and his face bore marks of the sudden calamity that had befallen his house, but the watching guests thought it was for sorrow at giving up his lovely Kate, and they said one to another, "How much he loved her!"

The girl's face drooped with gentle gravity. She scarcely felt the presence of the guests she had so much dreaded, for to her the ceremony was holy. She was giving herself as a sacrifice for the sin of her sister. She was too young and inexperienced to know all that would be thought and said as soon as the company understood. She also felt secure behind that film of lace. It seemed impossible that they could know her, so softly and so mistily it shut her in from the world. It was like a kind of moving house about her, a protection from all eyes. So sheltered she might go through the ceremony with composure. As yet she had not begun to dread the afterward. The hall was wide through which she passed, and the day was bright, but the windows were so shadowed by the waiting bridesmaids that the light did not fall in full glare upon her, and it was not strange they did not know her at once. She heard their smothered exclamations of wonder and admiration, and one, Kate's dearest friend, whispered softly behind her: "Oh, Kate, why did you keep us waiting, you sly girl! How lovely you are! You look like an angel straight from heaven."

There were other whispered words which Marcia heard sadly. They gave her no pleasure. The words were for Kate, not her. What would they say when they knew all?

There was David in the distance waiting for her. How fine he looked in his wedding clothes! How proud Kate might have been of him! How pitiful was his white face! He had summoned his courage and put on a mask of happiness for the eyes of those who saw him, but it could not deceive the heart of Marcia. Surely not since the days when Jacob served seven years for Rachel and then lifted the bridal veil to look upon the face of her sister Leah, walked there sadder bridegroom on this earth than David Spafford walked that day.

Down the stairs and through the wide hall they came, Marcia not daring to look up, yet seeing familiar glimpses as she passed. That green plaid silk lap at one side of the parlor door, in which lay two nervous little hands and a neatly folded pocket handkerchief, belonged to Sabrina Bates, she knew; and the round lace collar a little farther on, fastened by the brooch with a colored daguerreotype encircled by a braid of faded brown hair under glass, must be about the neck of Aunt Polly. There was not another brooch like that in New York state, Marcia felt sure. Beyond were Uncle Joab's small meek Sunday boots, toeing in, and next were little feet covered by white stockings and slippers fastened with crossed black ribbons, some child's, not Harriet—Marcia dared not raise her eyes to identify them now. She must fix her mind upon the great things before her. She wondered at herself for noticing such trivial things when she was walking up to the presence of the great God, and there before her stood the minister with his open book!

Now, at last, with the most of the audience behind her, shut in by the film of lace, she could raise her eyes to the minister's familiar face, take David's arm without letting her hand tremble much, and listen to the solemn words read out to her. For her alone they seemed to be read. David's heart she knew was crushed, and it was only a form for him. She must take double vows upon her for the sake of the wrong done to him. So she listened:

"Dearly beloved, we are gathered together"—how the words thrilled her!—"in the sight of God and in the presence of this company to join together this man and woman in the bonds of holy matrimony;"—a deathly stillness rested upon the room and the painful throbbing of her heart was all the little bride could hear. She was glad she might look straight into the dear face of the old minister. Had her mother felt this way when she was being married? Did her stepmother understand it? Yes, she must, in part at least, for she had bent and kissed her most tenderly upon the brow just before leaving her, a most unusually sentimental thing for her to do. It touched Marcia deeply, though she was fond of her stepmother at all times.

She waited breathless with drooped eyes while the minister demanded, "If any man can show just cause why they may not be lawfully joined together, let him now declare it, or else hereafter forever hold his peace." What if some one should recognize her and, thinking she had usurped Kate's place, speak out and stop the marriage! How would David feel? And she? She would sink to the floor. Oh, did they any of them know? How she wished she dared raise her eyes to look about and see. But she must not. She must listen. She must shake off these worldly thoughts. She was not hearing for idle thinking. It was a solemn, holy vow she was taking upon herself for life. She brought herself sharply back to the ceremony. It was to David the minister was talking now:

"Wilt thou love her, comfort her, honor and keep her, in sickness and in health, and forsaking all other, keep thee only unto her, so long as ye both shall live?"

It was hard to make David promise that when his heart belonged to Kate. She wondered that his voice could be so steady when it said, "I will," and the white glove of Kate's which was just a trifle large for her, trembled on David's arm as the minister next turned to her:

"Wilt thou, Marcia"—Ah! It was out now! and the sharp rustle of silk and stiff linen showed that all the company were aware at last who was the bride; but the minister went steadily on. He cared not what the listening assembly thought. He was talking earnestly to his little friend, Marcia,—"have this man to be thy wedded husband, to live together after God's ordinance in the holy estate of matrimony? Wilt thou obey him, and serve him, love, honor, and keep him, in sickness and in health"—the words of the pledge went on. It was not hard. The girl felt she could do all that. She was relieved to find it no more terrible, and to know that she was no longer acting a lie. They all knew who she was now. She held up her flower-like head and answered in her clear voice, that made her few schoolmates present gasp with admiration:

"I will!"

And the dear old minister's wife, sitting sweet and dove-like in her soft grey poplin, fine white kerchief, and cap of book muslin, smiled to herself at the music in Marcia's voice and nodded approval. She felt that all was well with her little friend.

They waited, those astonished people, till the ceremony was concluded and the prayer over, and then they broke forth. There had been lifted brows and looks passing from one to another, of question, of disclaiming any knowledge in the matter, and just as soon as the minister turned and took the bride's hand to congratulate her the heads bent together behind fans and the soft buzz of whispers began.

What does it mean? Where is Kate? She isn't in the room! Did he change his mind at the last minute? How old is Marcia? Mercy me! Nothing but a child! Are you sure? Why, my Mary Ann is older than that by three months, and she's no more able to become mistress of a home than a nine-days-old kitten. Are you sure it's Marcia? Didn't the minister make a mistake in the name? It looked to me like Kate. Look again. She's put her veil back. No, it can't be! Yes, it is! No, it looks like Kate! Her hair's done the same, but, no, Kate never had such a sweet innocent look as that. Why, when she was a child her face always had a sharpness to it. Look at Marcia's eyes, poor lamb! I don't see how her father could bear it, and she so young. But Kate! Where can she be? What has happened? You don't say! Yes, I did see that captain about again last week or so. Do you believe it? Surely she never would. Who told you? Was he sure? But Maria and Janet are bridesmaids and they didn't see any signs of anything. They were over here yesterday. Yes, Kate showed them everything and planned how they would all walk in. No, she didn't do anything queer, for Janet would have mentioned it. Janet always sees everything. Well, they say he's a good man and Marcia'll be well provided for. Madam Schuyler'll be relieved about that. Marcia can't ever lead her the dance Kate has among the young men. How white he looks! Do you suppose he loves her? What on earth can it all mean? Do you s'pose Kate feels bad? Where is she anyway? Wouldn't she come down? Well, if 'twas his choosing it serves her right. She's too much of a flirt for a good man and maybe he found her out. She's probably got just what she deserves, and *I* think Marcia'll make a good little wife. She always was a quiet, grown-up child and Madam Schuyler has trained her well! But what will Kate do now? Hush! They are coming this way. How do you suppose we can find out? Go ask Cousin Janet, perhaps they've told her, or Aunt Polly. Surely she knows.

But Aunt Polly sat with pursed lips of disapproval. She had not been told, and it was her prerogative to know everything. She always made a point of being on hand early at all funerals and weddings, especially in the family circle, and learning the utmost details, which she dispensed at her discretion to late comers in fine sepulchral whispers.

Now she sat silent, disgraced, unable to explain a thing. It was unhandsome of Sarah Schuyler, she felt, though no more than she might have expected of her, she told herself. She had never liked her. Well, wait until her opportunity came. If they did not wish her to say the truth she must say something. She could at least tell what she thought. And what more natural than to let it be known that Sarah Schuyler had always held a dislike for Marcia, and to suggest that it was likely she was glad to get her off her hands. Aunt Polly meant to find a trail somewhere, no matter how many times they threw her off the scent.

Meantime for Marcia the sun seemed to have shined out once more with something of its old brightness. The terrible deed of self-renunciation was over, and familiar faces actually were smiling upon her and wishing her joy. She felt the flutter of her heart in her throat beneath the string of pearls, and wondered if after all she might hope for a little happiness of her own. She could climb no more fences nor wade in gurgling brooks, but might there not be other happy things as good? A little touch of the pride of life had settled upon her. The relatives were coming with pleasant words and kisses. The blushes upon her cheeks were growing deeper. She almost forgot David in the pretty excitement. A few of her girl friends ventured shyly near, as one might look at a mate suddenly and unexpectedly translated into eternal bliss. They put out cold fingers in salute with distant, stiff phrases belonging to a grown-up world. Not one of them save Mary Ann dared recognize their former bond of playmates. Mary Ann leaned down and whispered with a giggle: "Say, you didn't need to envy Kate, did you? My! Ain't you in clover! Say, Marsh," wistfully, "do invite me fer a visit sometime, won't you?"

Now Mary Ann was not quite on a par with the Schuylers socially, and had it not been for a distant mutual relative she would not have been asked to the wedding. Marcia never liked her very much, but now, with the uncertain, dim future it seemed pleasant and home-like to think of a visit from Mary Ann and she nodded and said childishly: "Sometime, Mary Ann, if I can."

Mary Ann squeezed her hand, kissed her, blushed and giggled herself out of the way of the next comer.

They went out to the dining room and sat around the long table. It was Marcia's timid hand that cut the bridecake, and all the room full watched her. Seeing the pretty color come and go in her excited cheeks, they wondered that they had never noticed before how beautiful Marcia was growing. A handsome couple they would make! And they looked from Marcia to David and back again, wondering and trying to fathom the mystery.

It was gradually stealing about the company, the truth about Kate and Captain Leavenworth. The minister had told it in his sad and gentle way. Just the facts. No gossip. Naturally every one was bristling with questions, but not much could be got from the minister.

"I really do not know," he would say in his courteous, old-worldly way, and few dared ask further. Perhaps the minister, wise by reason of much experience, had taken care to ask as few questions as possible himself, and not to know too much before undertaking this task for his old friend the Squire.

And so Kate's marriage went into the annals of the village, at least so far as that morning was concerned, quietly, and with little exclamation before the family. The Squire and his wife controlled their faces wonderfully. There was an austerity about the Squire as he talked with his friends that was new to his pleasant face, but Madam conversed with her usual placid self-poise, and never gave cause for conjecture as to her true feelings.

There were some who dared to offer their surprised condolences. To such the stepmother replied that of course the outcome of events had been a sore trial to the Squire, and all of them, but they were delighted at the happy arrangement that had been made. She glanced contentedly toward the child-bride.

It was a revelation to the whole village that Marcia had grown up and was so handsome.

Dismay filled the breasts of the village gossips. They had been defrauded. Here was a fine scandal which they had failed to discover in time and spread abroad in its due course.

Everybody was shy of speaking to the bride. She sat in her lovely finery like some wild rose caught as a sacrifice. Yet every one admitted that she might have done far worse. David was a good man, with prospects far beyond most young men of his time. Moreover he was known to have a brilliant mind, and the career he had chosen, that of journalism, in which he was already making his mark, was one that promised to be lucrative as well as influential.

It was all very hurried at the last. Madam Schuyler and Dolly the maid helped her off with the satin and lace finery, and she was soon out of her bridal attire and struggling with the intricacies of Kate's travelling costume.

Marcia was not Marcia any longer, but Mrs. David Spafford. She had been made to feel the new name almost at once, and it gave her a sense of masquerading pleasant enough for the time being, but with a dim foreboding of nameless dread and emptiness for the future, like all masquerading which must end sometime. And when the mask is taken off how sad if one is not to find one's real self again: or worse still if one may never remove the mask, but must grow to it and be it from the soul.

All this Marcia felt but dimly of course, for she was young and light hearted naturally, and the excitement and pretty things about her could not but be pleasant.

To have Kate's friends stand about her, half shyly trying to joke with her as they might have done with Kate, to feel their admiring glances, and half envious references to her handsome husband, almost intoxicated her for the moment. Her cheeks grew rosier as she tied on Kate's pretty poke bonnet whose nodding blue flowers had been brought over from Paris by a friend of Kate's. It seemed a shame that Kate should not have her things after all. The pleasure died out of Marcia's eyes as she carefully looped the soft blue ribbons under her round chin and drew on Kate's long gloves. There was no denying the fact that Kate's outfit was becoming to Marcia, for she had that complexion that looks well with any color under the sun, though in blue she was not at her best.

When Marcia was ready she stood back from the little looking-glass, with a frightened, half-childish gaze about the room.

Now that the last minute was come, there was no one to understand Marcia's feelings nor help her. Even the girls were merely standing there waiting to say the last formal farewell that they might be free to burst into an astonished chatter of exclamations over Kate's romantic disappearance. They were Kate's friends, not Marcia's, and they were bidding Kate's clothes good-bye for want of the original bride. Marcia's friends were too young and too shy to do more than stand back in awe and gaze at their mate so suddenly promoted to a life which but yesterday had seemed years away for any of them.

So Marcia walked alone down the hall—yet, no, not all the way alone. A little wrinkled hand was laid upon her gloved one, and a little old lady, her true friend, the minister's wife, walked down the stairs with the bride arm in arm. Marcia's heart fluttered back to warmth again and was glad for her friend, yet all she had said was: "My dear!" but there was that in her touch and the tone of her gentle voice that comforted Marcia.

She stood at the edge of the steps, with her white hair shining in the morning, her kind-faced husband just behind her during all the farewell, and Marcia felt happier because of her motherly presence.

The guests were all out on the piazza in the gorgeousness of the summer morning. David stood on the flagging below the step beside the open coach door, a carriage lap-robe over his arm and his hat on, ready. He was talking with the Squire. Every one was looking at them, and they were entirely conscious of the fact. They laughed and talked with studied pleasantness, though there seemed to be an undertone of sadness that the most obtuse guest could not fail to detect.

471

Harriet, as a small flower-girl, stood upon the broad low step ready to fling posies before the bride as she stepped into the coach.

The little boys, to whom a wedding merely meant a delightful increase of opportunities, stood behind a pillar munching cake, more of which protruded from their bulging pockets.

Marcia, with a lump in her throat that threatened tears, slipped behind the people, caught the two little step-brothers in her arms and smothered them with kisses, amid their loud protestations and the laughter of those who stood about. But the little skirmish had served to hide the tears, and the bride came back most decorously to where her stepmother stood awaiting her with a smile of complacent—almost completed—duty upon her face. She wore the sense of having carried off a trying situation in a most creditable manner, and she knew she had won the respect and awe of every matron present thereby. That was a great deal to Madam Schuyler.

The stepmother's arms were around her and Marcia remembered how kindly they had felt when they first clasped her little body years ago, and she had been kissed, and told to be a good little girl. She had always liked her stepmother. And now, as she came to say good-bye to the only mother she had ever known, who had been a true mother to her in many ways, her young heart almost gave way, and she longed to hide in that ample bosom and stay under the wing of one who had so ably led her thus far along the path of life.

Perhaps Madam Schuyler felt the clinging of the girl's arms about her, and perchance her heart rebuked her that she had let so young and inexperienced a girl go out to the cares of life all of a sudden in this way. At least she stooped and kissed Marcia again and whispered: "You have been a good girl, Marcia."

Afterwards, Marcia cherished that sentence among memory's dearest treasures. It seemed as though it meant that she had fulfilled her stepmother's first command, given on the night when her father brought home their new mother.

Then the flowers were thrown upon the pavement, to make it bright for the bride. She was handed into the coach behind the white-haired negro coachman, and by his side Kate's fine new hair trunk. Ah! That was a bitter touch! Kate's trunk! Kate's things! Kate's husband! If it had only been her own little moth-eaten trunk that had belonged to her mother, and filled with her own things—and if he had only been her own husband! Yet she wanted no other than David—only if he could have been *her* David!

Then Madam Schuyler, her heart still troubled about Marcia, stepped down and whispered:

"David, you will remember she is young. You will deal gently with her?"

Gravely David bent his head and answered:

"I will remember. She shall not be troubled. I will care for her as I would care for my own sister." And Madam Schuyler turned away half satisfied. After all, was that what woman wanted? Would she have been satisfied to have been cared for as a sister?

Then gravely, with his eyes half unseeing her, the father kissed his daughter good-bye, David got into the coach, the door was slammed shut, and the white horses arched their necks and stepped away, amid a shower of rice and slippers.

CHAPTER VII

For some distance the way was lined with people they knew, servants and negroes, standing about the driveway and outside the fence, people of the village grouped along the sidewalk, everybody out upon their doorsteps to watch the coach go by, and to all the face of the bride was a puzzle and a surprise. They half expected to see another coach coming with the other bride behind.

Marcia nodded brightly to those she knew, and threw flowers from the great nosegay that had been put upon her lap by Harriet. She felt for a few minutes like a girl in a fairy-tale riding in this fine coach in grand attire. She stole a look at David. He certainly looked like a prince, but gravity was already settling about his mouth. Would he always look so now, she wondered, would he never laugh and joke again as he used to do? Could she manage to make him happy sometimes for a little while and help him to forget?

Down through the village they passed, in front of the store and post-office where Marcia had bought her frock but three days before, and they turned up the road she had come with Mary Ann. How long ago that seemed! How light her heart was then, and how young! All life was before her with its delightful possibilities. Now it seemed to have closed for her and she was some one else. A great ache came upon her heart. For a moment she longed to jump down and run away from the coach and David and the new clothes that were not hers. Away from the new life that had been planned for some one else which she must live now. She must always be a woman, never a girl any more.

Out past Granny McVane's they drove, the old lady sitting upon her front porch knitting endless stockings. She stared mildly, unrecognizingly at Marcia and paused in her rocking to crane her neck after the coach.

The tall corn rustled and waved green arms to them as they passed, and the cows looked up munching from the pasture in mild surprise at the turnout. The little coach dog stepped aside from the road to give them a bark as he passed, and then pattered and pattered his tiny feet to catch up. The old school house came in sight with its worn playground and dejected summer air, and Marcia's eyes searched out the window where she used to sit to eat her lunch in winters, and the tree under which she used to sit in summers, and the path by which she and Mary Ann used to wander down to the brook, or go in search of butternuts, even the old door knob that her hand would probably never grasp again. She searched them all out and bade them good-bye with her eyes. Then once she turned a little to see if she could catch a glimpse of the old blackboard through the window where she and Susanna Brown and Miller Thompson used to do arithmetic examples. The dust of the coach, or the bees in the sunshine, or something in her eyes blurred her vision. She could only see a long slant ray of a sunbeam crossing the wall where she knew it must be. Then the road wound around through a maple grove and the school was lost to view.

They passed the South meadow belonging to the Westons, and Hanford was plowing. Marcia could see him stop to wipe the perspiration from his brow, and her heart warmed even to this boy admirer now that she was going from him forever.

Hanford had caught sight of the coach and he turned to watch it thinking to see Kate sitting in the bride's place. He wondered if the bride would notice him, and turned a deeper red under his heavy coat of tan.

And the bride did notice him. She smiled the sweetest smile the boy had ever seen upon her face, the smile he had dreamed of as he thought of her, at night standing under the stars all alone by his father's gate post whittling the cross bar of the gate. For a moment he forgot that it was the bridal party passing, forgot the stern-faced bridegroom, and saw only Marcia—his girl love. His heart stood still, and a bright light of response filled his eyes. He took off his wide straw hat and bowed her reverence. He would have called to her, and tried three times, but his dry throat gave forth no utterance, and when he looked again the coach was passed and only the flutter of a white handkerchief came back to him and told him the beginning of the truth.

Then the poor boy's face grew white, yes, white and stricken under the tan, and he tottered to the roadside and sat down with his face in his hands to try and comprehend what it might mean, while the old horse dragged the plow whither he would in search of a bite of tender grass.

What could it mean? And why did Marcia occupy that place beside the stranger, obviously the bridegroom? Was she going on a visit? He had heard of no such plan. Where was her sister? Would there be another coach presently, and was this man then not the bridegroom but merely a friend of the family? Of course, that must be it. He got up and staggered to the fence to look down the road, but no one came by save the jogging old gray and carryall, with Aunt Polly grim and offended and Uncle Joab meek and depressed beside her. Could he have missed the bridal carriage when he was at the other end of the lot? Could they have gone another way? He had a half a mind to call to Uncle Joab to enquire only he was a timid boy and shrank back until it was too late.

But why had Marcia as she rode away wafted that strange farewell that had in it the familiarity of the final? And why did he feel so strange and weak in his knees?

Marcia was to help his mother next week at the quilting bee. She had not gone away to stay, of course. He got up and tried to whistle and turn the furrows evenly as before, but his heart was heavy, and, try as he would, he could not understand the feeling that kept telling him Marcia was gone out of his life forever.

At last his day's work was done and he could hasten to the house. Without waiting for his supper, he "slicked up," as he called it, and went at once to the village, where he learned the bitter truth.

It was Mary Ann who told him.

Mary Ann, the plain, the awkward, who secretly admired Hanford Weston as she might have admired an angel, and who as little expected him to speak to her as if he had been one. Mary Ann stood by her front gate in the dusk of the summer evening, the halo of her unusual wedding finery upon her, for she had taken advantage of being dressed up to make two or three visits since the wedding, and so prolong the holiday. The light of the sunset softened her plain features, and gave her a gentler look than was her wont. Was it that, and an air of lonesomeness akin to his own, that made Hanford stop and speak to her?

And then she told him. She could not keep it in long. It was the wonder of her life, and it filled her so that her thought had no room for anything else. To think of Marcia taken in a day, gone from their midst forever, gone to be a grown-up woman in a new world! It was as strange as sudden death, and almost as terrible and beautiful.

There were tears in her eyes, and in the eyes of the boy as they spoke about the one who was gone, and the kind dusk hid the sight so that neither knew, but each felt a subtle sympathy with the other, and before Hanford started upon his desolate way home under the burden of his first sorrow he took Mary Ann's slim bony hand in his and said quite stiffly: "Well, good night, Miss Mary Ann. I'm glad you told me," and Mary Ann responded, with a deep blush under her freckles in the dark, "Good night, Mr. Weston, and—call again!"

Something of the sympathy lingered with the boy as he went on his way and he was not without a certain sort of comfort, while Mary Ann climbed to her little chamber in the loft with a new wonder to dream over.

Meanwhile the coach drove on, and Marcia passed from her childhood's home into the great world of men and women, changes, heartbreakings, sorrows and joys.

David spoke to her kindly now and then; asked if she was comfortable; if she would prefer to change seats with him; if the cushions were right; and if she had forgotten anything. He seemed nervous, and anxious to have this part of the journey over and asked the coachman frequent questions about the horses and the speed they could make. Marcia thought she understood that he was longing to get away from the painful reminder of what he had expected to be a joyful trip, and her young heart pitied him, while yet it felt an undertone of hurt for herself. She found so much unadulterated joy in this charming ride with the beautiful horses, in this luxurious coach, that she could not bear to have it spoiled by the thought that only David's sadness and pain had made it possible for her.

Constantly as the scene changed, and new sights came upon her view, she had to restrain herself from crying out with happiness over the beauty and calling David's attention. Once she did point out a bird just leaving a stalk of goldenrod, its light touch making the spray to bow and bend. David had looked with unseeing eyes, and smiled with uncomprehending assent. Marcia felt she might as well have been talking to herself. He was not even the old friend and brother he used to be. She drew a gentle little sigh and wished this might have been only a happy ride with the ending at home, and a longer girlhood uncrossed by this wall of trouble that Kate had put up in a night for them all.

The coach came at last to the town where they were to stop for dinner and a change of horses.

Marcia looked about with interest at the houses, streets, and people. There were two girls of about her own age with long hair braided down their backs. They were walking with arms about each other as she and Mary Ann had often done. She wondered if any such sudden changes might be coming to them as had come into her life. They turned and looked at her curiously, enviously it seemed, as the coach drew up to the tavern and she was helped out with ceremony. Doubtless they thought of her as she had thought of Kate but last week.

She was shown into the dim parlor of the tavern and seated in a stiff hair-cloth chair. It was all new and strange and delightful.

Before a high gilt mirror set on great glass knobs like rosettes, she smoothed her wind-blown hair, and looked back at the reflection of her strange self with startled eyes. Even her face seemed changed. She knew the bonnet and arrangement of hair were becoming, but she felt unacquainted with them, and wished for her own modest braids and plain bonnet. Even a sunbonnet would have been welcome and have made her feel more like herself.

David did not see how pretty she looked when he came to take her to the dining room ten minutes later. His eyes were looking into the hard future, and he was steeling himself against the glances of others. He must be the model bridegroom in the sight of all who knew him. His pride bore him out in this. He had acquaintances all along the way home.

They were expecting the bridal party, for David had arranged that a fine dinner should be ready for his bride. Fine it was, with the best cooking and table service the mistress of the tavern could command, and with many a little touch new and strange to Marcia, and therefore interesting. It was all a lovely play till she looked at David.

David ate but little, and Marcia felt she must hurry through the meal for his sake. Then when the carryall was ready he put her in and they drove away.

Marcia's keen intuition told her how many little things had been thought of and planned for, for the comfort of the one who was to have taken this journey with David. Gradually the thought of how terrible it was for him, and how dreadful of Kate to have brought this sorrow upon him, overcame all other thoughts.

Sitting thus quietly, with her hands folded tight in the faded bunch of roses little Harriet had given her at parting, the last remaining of the flowers she had carried with her, Marcia let the tears come. Silently they flowed in gentle rain, and had not David been borne down with the thought of his own sorrow he must have noticed long before he did the sadness of the sweet young face beside him. But she turned away from him as much as possible that he might not see, and so they must have driven for half an hour through a dim sweet wood before he happened to catch a sight of the tear-wet face, and knew suddenly that there were other troubles in the world beside his own.

"Why, child, what is the matter?" he said, turning to her with grave concern. "Are you so tired? I'm afraid I have been very dull company," with a sigh. "You must forgive me—child, to-day."

"Oh, David, don't," said Marcia putting her face down into her hands and crying now regardless of the roses. "I do not want you to think of me. It is dreadful, dreadful for you. I am so sorry for you. I wish I could do something."

"Dear child!" he said, putting his hand upon hers. "Bless you for that. But do not let your heart be troubled about me. Try to forget me and be happy. It is not for you to bear, this trouble."

"But I must bear it," said Marcia, sitting up and trying to stop crying. "She was my sister and she did an awful thing. I cannot forget it. How could she, how *could* she do it? How could she leave a man like you that—"Marcia stopped, her brown eyes flashing fiercely as she thought of Captain Leavenworth's hateful look at her that night in the moonlight. She shuddered and hid her face in her hands once more and cried with all the fervor of her young and undisciplined soul.

David did not know what to do with a young woman in tears. Had it been Kate his alarm would have vied with a delicious sense of his own power to comfort, but even the thought of comforting any one but Kate was now a bitter thing. Was it always going to be so? Would he always have to start and shrink with sudden remembrance of his pain at every turn of his way? He drew a deep sigh and looked helplessly at his companion. Then he did a hard thing. He tried to justify Kate, just as he had been trying all the morning to justify her to himself. The odd thing about it all was that the very deepest sting of his sorrow was that Kate could have done this thing! His peerless Kate!

"She cared for him," he breathed the words as if they hurt him.

"She should have told you so before then. She should not have let you think she cared for you—*ever!*" said Marcia fiercely. Strangely enough the plain truth was bitter to the man to hear, although he had been feeling it in his soul ever since they had discovered the flight of the bride.

"Perhaps there was too much pressure brought to bear upon her," he said lamely. "Looking back I can see times when she did not second me with regard to hurrying the marriage, so warmly as I could have wished. I laid it to her shyness. Yet she seemed happy when we met. Did you—did she—have you any idea she had been planning this for long, or was it sudden?"

The words were out now, the thing he longed to know. It had been writing its fiery way through his soul. Had she meant to torture him this way all along, or was it the yielding to a sudden impulse that perhaps she had already repented? He looked at Marcia with piteous, almost pleading eyes, and her tortured young soul would have given anything to have been able to tell him what he wanted to know. Yet she could not help him. She knew no more than he. She steadied her own nerves and tried to tell all she knew or surmised, tried her best to reveal Kate in her true character before him. Not that she wished to speak ill of her sister, only that she would be true and give this lover a chance to escape some of the pain if possible, by seeing the real Kate as she was at home without varnish or furbelows. Yet she reflected that those who knew Kate's shallowness well, still loved her in spite of it, and always bowed to her wishes.

Gradually their talk subsided into deep silence once more, broken only by the jog-trot of the horse or the stray note of some bird.

The road wound into the woods with its fragrant scents of hemlock, spruce and wintergreen, and out into a broad, hot, sunny way.

The bees hummed in the flowers, and the grasshoppers sang hotly along the side of the dusty road. Over the whole earth there seemed to be the sound of a soft simmering, as if nature were boiling down her sweets, the better to keep them during the winter.

The strain of the day's excitement and hurry and the weariness of sorrow were beginning to tell upon the two travellers. The road was heavy with dust and the horse plodded monotonously through it. With the drone of the insects and the glare of the afternoon sun, it was not strange that little by little a great drowsiness came over Marcia and her head began to droop like a poor wilted flower until she was fast asleep.

David noticed that she slept, and drew her head against his shoulder that she might rest more comfortably. Then he settled back to his own pain, a deeper pang coming as he thought how different it would have been if the head resting against his shoulder had been golden instead of brown. Then soon he too fell asleep, and the old horse, going slow, and yet more slowly, finding no urging voice behind her and seeing no need to hurry herself, came at last on the way to the shade of an apple tree, and halted, finding it a pleasant place to remain and think until the heat of the afternoon was passed. Awhile she ate the tender grass that grew beneath the generous shade, and nipped daintily at an apple or two that hung within tempting reach. Then she too drooped her white lashes, and nodded and drooped, and took an afternoon nap.

A farmer, trundling by in his empty hay wagon, found them so, looked curiously at them, then drew up his team and came and prodded David in the chest with his long hickory stick.

"Wake up, there, stranger, and move on," he called, as he jumped back into his wagon and took up the reins. "We don't want no tipsy folks around these parts," and with a loud clatter he rode on.

David, whose strong temperance principles had made him somewhat marked in his own neighborhood, roused and flushed over the insinuation, and started up the lazy horse, which flung out guiltily upon the way as if to make up for lost time. The driver, however, was soon lost in his own troubles, which returned upon him with redoubled sharpness as new sorrow always does after brief sleep.

But Marcia slept on.

CHAPTER VIII

Owing to the horse's nap by the roadside, it was quite late in the evening when they reached the town and David saw the lights of his own neighborhood gleaming in the distance. He was glad it was late, for now there would be no one to meet them that night. His friends would think, perhaps, that they had changed their plans and stopped over night on the way, or met with some detention.

Marcia still slept.

David as he drew near the house began to feel that perhaps he had made a mistake in carrying out his marriage just as if nothing had happened and everything was all right. It would be too great a strain upon him to live there in that house without Kate, and come home every night just as he had planned it, and not to find her there to greet him as he had hoped. Oh, if he might turn even now and flee from it, out into the wilderness somewhere and hide himself from human kind, where no one would know, and no one ever ask him about his wife!

He groaned in spirit as the horse drew up to the door, and the heavy head of the sweet girl who was his wife reminded him that he could not go away, but must stay and face the responsibilities of life which he had taken upon himself, and bear the pain that was his. It was not the fault of the girl he had married. She sorrowed for him truly, and he felt deeply grateful for the great thing she had done to save his pride.

He leaned over and touched her shoulder gently to rouse her, but her sleep was deep and healthy, the sleep of exhausted youth. She did not rouse nor even open her eyes, but murmured half audibly; "David has come, Kate, hurry!"

Half guessing what had passed the night he arrived, David stooped and tenderly gathered her up in his arms. He felt a bond of kindliness far deeper than brotherly love. It was a bond of common suffering, and by her own choice she had made herself his comrade in his trouble. He would at least save her what suffering he could.

She did not waken as he carried her into the house, nor when he took her upstairs and laid her gently upon the white bed that had been prepared for the bridal chamber.

The moonlight stole in at the small-paned windows and fell across the floor, showing every object in the room plainly. David lighted a candle and set it upon the high mahogany chest of drawers. The light flickered and played over the sweet face and Marcia slept on.

David went downstairs and put up the horse, and then returned, but Marcia had not stirred. He stood a moment looking at her helplessly. It did not seem right to leave her this way, and yet it was a pity to disturb her sleep, she seemed so weary. It had been a long ride and the day had been filled with unwonted excitement. He felt it himself, and what must it be for her? She was a woman.

David had the old-fashioned gallant idea of woman.

Clumsily he untied the gay blue ribbons and pulled the jaunty poke bonnet out of her way. The luxuriant hair, unused to the confinement of combs, fell rich about her sleep-flushed face. Contentedly she nestled down, the bonnet out of her way, her red lips parted the least bit with a half smile, the black lashes lying long upon her rosy cheek, one childish hand upon which gleamed the new wedding ring—that was not hers,—lying relaxed and appealing upon her breast, rising and falling with her breath. A lovely bride!

David, stern, true, pained and appreciative, suddenly awakened to what a dreadful thing he had done.

Here was this lovely woman, her womanhood not yet unfolded from the bud, but lovely in promise even as her sister had been in truth, her charms, her dreams, her woman's ways, her love, her very life, taken by him as ruthlessly and as thoughtlessly as though she had been but a wax doll, and put into a home where she could not possibly be what she ought to be, because the place belonged to another. Thrown away upon a man without a heart! That was what she was! A sacrifice to his pride! There was no other way to put it.

It fairly frightened him to think of the promises he had made. "Love, honor, cherish," yes, all those he had promised, and in a way he could perform, but not in the sense that the wedding ceremony had meant, not in the way in which he would have performed them had the bride been Kate, the choice of his love. Oh, why, why had this awful thing come upon him!

And now his conscience told him he had done wrong to take this girl away from the possibilities of joy in the life that might have been hers, and sacrifice her for the sake of saving his own sufferings, and to keep his friends from knowing that the girl he was to marry had jilted him.

As he stood before the lovely, defenceless girl her very beauty and innocence arraigned him. He felt that God would hold him accountable for the act he had so thoughtlessly committed that day, and a burden of responsibility settled upon his weight of sorrow that made him groan aloud. For a moment his soul cried out against it in rebellion. Why could he not have loved this sweet self-sacrificing girl instead of her fickle sister? Why? Why? She might perhaps have loved him in return, but now nothing could ever be! Earth was filled with a black sorrow, and life henceforth meant renunciation and one long struggle to hide his trouble from the world.

But the girl whom he had selfishly drawn into the darkness of his sorrow with him, she must not be made to suffer more than he could help. He must try to make her happy, and keep her as much as possible from knowing what she had missed by coming with him! His lips set in stern resolve, and a purpose, half prayer, went up on record before God, that he would save her as much as he knew how.

Lying helpless so, she appealed to him. Asking nothing she yet demanded all from him in the name of true chivalry. How readily had she given up all for him! How sweetly she had said she would fill the place left vacant by her sister, just to save him pain and humiliation!

A desire to stoop and kiss the fair face came to him, not for affection's sake, but reverently, as if to render to her before God some fitting sign that he knew and understood her act of self sacrifice, and would not presume upon it.

Slowly, as though he were performing a religious ceremony, a sacred duty laid upon him on high, David stooped over her, bringing his face to the gentle sleeping one. Her sweet breath fanned his cheek like the almost imperceptible fragrance of a bud not fully opened yet to give forth its sweetness to the world. His soul, awake and keen through the thoughts that had just come to him, gave homage to her sweetness, sadly, wistfully, half wishing his spirit free to gather this sweetness for his own.

And so he brought his lips to hers, and kissed her, his bride, yet not his bride. Kissed her for the second time. That thought came to him with the touch of the warm lips and startled him. Had there been something significant in the fact that he had met Marcia first and kissed her instead of Kate by mistake?

It seemed as though the sleeping lips clung to his lingeringly, and half responded to the kiss, as Marcia in her dreams lived over again the kiss she had received by her father's gate in the moonlight. Only the dream lover was her own and not another's. David, as he lifted up his head and looked at her gravely, saw a half smile illuminating her lips as if the sleeping soul within had felt the touch and answered to the call.

With a deep sigh he turned away, blew out the candle, and left her with the moonbeams in her chamber. He walked sadly to a rear room of the house and lay down upon the bed, his whole soul crying out in agony at his miserable state.

Kate, the careless one, who had made all this heart-break and misery, had quarreled with her husband already because he did not further some expensive whim of hers. She had told him she was sorry she had not stayed where she was and carried on her marriage with David as she had planned to do. Now she sat sulkily in her room alone, too angry to sleep; while her husband smoked sullenly in the barroom below, and drank frequent glasses of brandy to fortify himself against Kate's moods.

Kate was considering whether or not she had been a fool in marrying the captain instead of David, though she called herself by a much milder word than that. The romance was already worn away. She wished for her trunk and her pretty furbelows. Her father's word of reconciliation would doubtless come in a few days, also the trunks.

After all there was intense satisfaction to Kate in having broken all bounds and done as she pleased. Of course it would have been a bit more comfortable if David had not been so absurdly in earnest, and believed in her so thoroughly. But it was nice to have some one believe in you no matter what you did, and David would always do that. It began to look doubtful if the captain would. But David would never marry, she was sure, and perhaps, by and by, when everything had been forgotten and forgiven, she might establish a pleasant relationship with him again. It would be charming to coquet with him. He made love so earnestly, and his great eyes were so handsome when he looked at one with his whole soul in them. Yes, she certainly must keep in with him, for it would be good to have a friend like that when her husband was off at sea with his ship. Now that she was a married woman she would be free from all such childish trammels as being guarded at home and never going anywhere alone. She could go to New York, and she would let David know where she was and he would come up on business and perhaps take her to the theatre. To be sure, she had heard David express views against theatre-going, and she knew he was as much of a church man, almost, as her father, but she was sure she could coax him to do anything for her, and she had always wanted to go to the theatre. His scruples might be strong, but she knew his love for her, and thought it was stronger. She had read in his eyes that it would never fail her. Yes, she thought, she would begin at once to make a friend of David. She would write him a letter asking forgiveness, and then she would keep him under her influence. There was no telling what might happen with her husband off at sea so much. It was well to be foresighted, besides, it would be wholesome for the captain to know she had another friend. He might be less stubborn. What a nuisance that the marriage vows had to be taken for life! It would be much nicer if they could be put off as easily as they were put on. Rather hard on some women perhaps, but she could keep any man as long as she chose, and then—she snapped her pretty thumb and finger in the air to express her utter disdain for the man whom she chose to cast off.

It seemed that Kate, in running away from her father's house and her betrothed bridegroom, and breaking the laws of respectable society, had with that act given over all attempt at any principle.

So she set herself down to write her letter, with a pout here and a dimple there, and as much pretty gentleness as if she had been talking with her own bewitching face and eyes quite near to his. She knew she could bewitch him if she chose, and she was in the mood just now to choose very much, for she was deeply angry with her husband.

She had ever been utterly heartless when she pleased, knowing that it needed but her returning smile, sweet as a May morning, to bring her much abused subjects fondly to her feet once more. It did not strike her that this time she had sinned not only against her friends, but against heaven, and God-given love, and that a time of reckoning must come to her,—had come, indeed.

She had never believed they would be angry with her, her father least of all. She had no thought they would do anything desperate. She had expected the wedding would be put off indefinitely, that the servants would be sent out hither and yon in hot haste to unbid the guests, upon some pretext of accident or illness, and that it would be left to rest until the village had ceased to wonder and her real marriage with Captain Leavenworth could be announced.

She had counted upon David to stand up for her. She had not understood how her father's righteous soul would be stirred to the depths of shame and utter disgrace over her wanton action. Not that she would have been in the least deterred from doing as she pleased had she understood, only that she counted upon too great power with all of them.

When the letter was written it sounded quite pathetic and penitent, putting all the blame of her action upon her husband, and making herself out a poor, helpless, sweet thing, bewildered by so much love put upon her, and suggesting, just in a hint, that perhaps after all she had made a mistake not to have kept David's love instead of the wilder, fiercer one. She ended by begging David to be her friend forever, and leaving an impression with him, though it was but slight, that already shadows had crossed her path that made her feel his friendship might be needed some day.

It was a letter calculated to drive such a lover as David had been, half mad with anguish, even without the fact of his hasty marriage added to the situation.

And in due time, by coach, the letter came to David.

CHAPTER IX

The morning sunbeams fell across the floor when Marcia awoke suddenly to a sense of her new surroundings. For a moment she could not think where she was nor how she came there. She looked about the unfamiliar walls, covered with paper decorated in landscapes—a hill in the distance with a tall castle among the trees, a blue lake in the foreground and two maidens sitting pensively upon a green bank with their arms about one another. Marcia liked it. She felt there was a story in it. She would like to imagine about the lives of those two girls when she had more time.

There were no pictures in the room to mar those upon the paper, but the walls did not look bare. Everything was new and stiff and needed a woman's hand to bring the little homey touches, but the newness was a delight to the girl. It was as good as the time when she was a little girl and played house with Mary Ann down on the old flat stone in the pasture, with acorns for cups and saucers, and bits of broken china carefully treasured upon the mossy shelves in among the roots of the old elm tree that arched over the stone.

She was stiff from the long ride, but her sleep had wonderfully refreshed her, and now she was ready to go to work. She wondered as she rose how she got upon that bed, how the blue bonnet got untied and laid upon the chair beside her. Surely she could not have done it herself and have no memory of it. Had she walked upstairs herself, or did some one carry her? Did David perhaps? Good kind David! A bird hopped upon the window seat and trilled a song, perked his head knowingly at her and flitted away. Marcia went to the window to look after him, and was held by the new sights that met her gaze. She could catch glimpses of houses through bowers of vines, and smoke rising from chimneys. She wondered who lived near, and if there were girls who would prove pleasant companions. Then she suddenly remembered that she was a girl no longer and must associate with married women hereafter.

But suddenly the clock on the church steeple across the way warned her that it was late, and with a sense of deserving reprimand she hurried downstairs.

The fire was already lighted and David had brought in fresh water. So much his intuition had told him was necessary. He had been brought up by three maiden aunts who thought that a man in the kitchen was out of his sphere, so the kitchen was an unknown quantity to him.

Marcia entered the room as if she were not quite certain of her welcome. She was coming into a kingdom she only half understood.

"Good morning," she said shyly, and a lovely color stole into her cheeks. Once more David's conscience smote him as her waking beauty intensified the impression made the night before.

"Good morning," he said gravely, studying her face as he might have studied some poor waif whom he had unknowingly run over in the night and picked up to resuscitate. "Are you rested? You were very tired last night."

"What a baby I was!" said Marcia deprecatingly, with a soft little gurgle of a laugh like a merry brook. David was amazed to find she had two dimples located about as Kate's were, only deeper, and more gentle in their expression.

"Did I sleep all the afternoon after we left the canal? And did you have hard work to get me into the house and upstairs?"

"You slept most soundly," said David, smiling in spite of his heavy heart. "It seemed a pity to waken you, so I did the next best thing and put you to bed as well as I knew how."

"It was very good of you," said Marcia, coming over to him with her hands clasped earnestly, "and I don't know how to thank you."

There was something quaint and old-fashioned in her way of speaking, and it struck David pitifully that she should be thanking her husband, the man who had pledged himself to care for her all his life. It seemed that everywhere he turned his conscience would be continually reproaching him.

It was a dainty breakfast to which they presently sat down. There was plenty of bread and fresh butter just from the hands of the best butter-maker in the county; the eggs had been laid the day before, and the bacon was browned just right. Marcia well knew how to make coffee, there was cream rich and yellow as ever came from the cows at home and there were blackberries as large and fine every bit as those Marcia picked but a few days before for the purchase of her pink sprigged chintz.

David watched her deft movements and all at once keen smiting conscience came to remind him that Marcia was defrauded of all the loving interchange of mirth that would have been if Kate had been here. Also, keener still the thought that Kate had not wanted it: that she had preferred the love of another man to his, and that these joys had not been held in dear anticipation with her as they had with him. He had been a fool. All these months of waiting for his marriage he had thought that he and Kate held feelings in common, joys and hopes and tender thoughts of one another; and, behold, he was having these feelings all to himself, fool and blind that he was! A bitter sigh came to his lips, and Marcia, eager in the excitement of getting her first breakfast upon her own responsibility, heard and forgot to smile over the completed work. She could hardly eat what she had prepared, her heart felt David's sadness so keenly.

Shyly she poured the amber coffee and passed it to David. She was pleased that he drank it eagerly and passed his cup back for more. He ate but little, but seemed to approve of all she had done.

After breakfast David went down to the office. He had told Marcia that he would step over and tell his aunts of their arrival, and they would probably come over in the course of the day to greet her. He would be back to dinner at twelve. He suggested that she spend her time in resting, as she must be weary yet. Then hesitating, he went out and closed the door behind him. He waited again on the door stone outside and opened the door to ask:

"You won't be lonesome, will you, child?" He had the feeling of troubled responsibility upon him.

"Oh, no!" said Marcia brightly, smiling back. She thought it so kind of him to take the trouble to think of her. She was quite anticipating a trip of investigation over her new domain, and the pleasure of feeling that she was mistress and might do as she pleased. Yet she stood by the window after he was gone and watched his easy strides down the street with a feeling of mingled pride and disappointment. It was a very nice play she was going through, and David was handsome, and her young heart swelled with pride to belong to him, but after all there was something left out. A great lack, a great unknown longing unsatisfied. What was it? What made it? Was it David's sorrow?

She turned with a sigh as he disappeared around a curve in the sidewalk and was lost to view. Then casting aside the troubles which were trying to settle upon her, she gave herself up to a morning of pure delight.

She flew about the kitchen putting things to rights, washing the delicate sprigged china with its lavender sprays and buff bands, and putting it tenderly upon the shelves behind the glass doors; shoving the table back against the wall demurely with dropped leaves. It did not take long.

There was no need to worry about the dinner. There was a leg of lamb beautifully cooked, half a dozen pies, their flaky crusts bearing witness to the culinary skill of the aunts, a fruit cake, a pound cake, a jar of delectable cookies and another of fat sugary doughnuts, three loaves of bread, and a sheet of puffy rusks with their shining tops dusted with sugar. Besides the preserve closet was rich in all kinds of preserves, jellies and pickles. No, it would not take long to get dinner.

It was into the great parlor that Marcia peeped first. It had been toward that room that her hopes and fears had turned while she washed the dishes.

The Schuylers were one of the few families in those days that possessed a musical instrument, and it had been the delight of Marcia's heart. She seemed to have a natural talent for music, and many an hour she spent at the old spinet drawing tender tones from the yellowed keys. The spinet had been in the family for a number of years and very proud had the Schuyler girls been of it. Kate could rattle off gay waltzes and merry, rollicking tunes that fairly made the feet of the sedate village maidens flutter in time to their melody, but Marcia's music had always been more tender and spiritual. Dear old hymns, she loved, and some of the old classics. "Stupid old things without any tune," Kate called them. But Marcia persevered in playing them until she could bring out the beautiful passages in a way that at least satisfied herself. Her one great desire had been to take lessons of a real musician and be able to play the wonderful things that the old masters had composed. It is true that very few of these had come in her way. One somewhat mutilated copy of Handel's "Creation," a copy of Haydn's "Messiah," and a few fragments of an old book of Bach's Fugues and Preludes. Many of these she could not play at all, but others she had managed to pick out. A visit from a cousin who lived in Boston and told of the concerts given there by the Handel and Haydn Society had served to strengthen her deeper interest in music. The one question that had been going over in her mind ever since she awoke had been whether there was a musical instrument in the house. She felt that if there was not she would miss the old spinet in her father's house more than any other thing about her childhood's home.

So with fear and trepidation she entered the darkened room, where the careful aunts had drawn the thick green shades. The furniture stood about in shadowed corners, and every footfall seemed a fearsome thing.

Marcia's bright eyes hurried furtively about, noting the great glass knobs that held the lace curtains with heavy silk cords, the round mahogany table, with its china vase of "everlastings," the high, stiff-backed chairs all decked in elaborate antimacassars of intricate pattern. Then, in the furthest corner, shrouded in dark coverings she found what she was searching for. With a cry she sprang to it, touched its polished wood with gentle fingers, and lovingly felt for the keyboard. It was closed. Marcia pushed up the shade to see better, and opened the instrument cautiously.

It was a pianoforte of the latest pattern, and with exclamations of delight she sat down and began to strike chords, softly at first, as if half afraid, then more boldly. The tone was sweeter than the old spinet, or the harpsichord owned by Squire Hartrandt. Marcia marvelled at the volume of sound. It filled the room and seemed to echo through the empty halls.

She played soft little airs from memory, and her soul was filled with joy. Now she knew she would never be lonely in the new life, for she would always have this wonderful instrument to flee to when she felt homesick.

Across the hall were two square rooms, the front one furnished as a library. Here were rows of books behind glass doors. Marcia looked at them with awe. Might she read them all? She resolved to cultivate her mind that she might be a fit companion for David. She knew he was wise beyond his years for she had heard her father say so. She went nearer and scanned the titles, and at once there looked out to her from the rows of bindings a few familiar faces of books she had read and re-read. "Thaddeus of Warsaw," "The Scottish Chiefs,""Mysteries of Udolpho," "Romance of the Forest," "Baker's Livy," "Rollin's History," "Pilgrim's Progress,"and a whole row of Sir Walter Scott's novels. She caught her breath with delight. What pleasure was opening before her! All of Scott! And she had read but one!

It was with difficulty she tore herself away from the tempting shelves and went on to the rest of the house.

Back of David's library was a sunny sitting room, or breakfast room,—or "dining room" as it would be called at the present time. In Marcia's time the family ate most of their meals in one end of the large bright kitchen, that end furnished with a comfortable lounge, a few bookshelves, a thick ingrain carpet, and a blooming geranium in the wide window seat. But there was always the other room for company, for "high days and holidays."

Out of this morning room the pantry opened with its spicy odors of preserves and fruit cake.

Marcia looked about her well pleased. The house itself was a part of David's inheritance, his mother's family homestead. Things were all on a grand scale for a bride. Most brides began in a very simple way and climbed up year by year. How Kate would have liked it all! David must have had in mind her fastidious tastes, and spent a great deal of money in trying to please her. That piano must have been very expensive. Once more Marcia felt how David had loved Kate and a pang went through her as she wondered however he was to live without her. Her young soul had not yet awakened to the question of how *she* was to live *with* him, while his heart went continually mourning for one who was lost to him forever.

The rooms upstairs were all pleasant, spacious, and comfortably furnished. There was no suggestion of bareness or anything left unfinished. Much of the furniture was old, having belonged to David's mother, and was in a state of fine preservation, a possession of which to be justly proud.

There were four rooms besides the one in which Marcia had slept: a front and back on the opposite side of the hall, a room just back of her own, and one at the end of the hall over the large kitchen.

She entered them all and looked about. The three beside her own in the front part of the house were all large and airy, furnished with high four-posted bedsteads, and pretty chintz hangings. Each was immaculate in its appointments. Cautiously she lifted the latch of the back room. David had not slept in any of the others, for the bedcoverings and pillows were plump and undisturbed. Ah! It was here in the back room that he had carried his heavy heart, as far away from the rest of the house as possible!

The bed was rumpled as if some one had thrown himself heavily down without stopping to undress. There was water in the washbowl and a towel lay carelessly across a chair as if it had been hastily used. There was a newspaper on the bureau and a handkerchief on the floor. Marcia looked sadly about at these signs of occupancy, her eyes dwelling upon each detail. It was here that David had suffered, and her loving heart longed to help him in his suffering.

But there was nothing in the room to keep her, and remembering the fire she had left upon the hearth, which must be almost spent and need replenishing by this time, she turned to go downstairs.

Just at the door something caught her eye under the edge of the chintz valence round the bed. It was but the very tip of the corner of an old daguerreotype, but for some reason Marcia was moved to stoop and draw it from its concealment. Then she saw it was her sister's saucy, pretty face that laughed back at her in defiance from the picture.

As if she had touched something red hot Marcia dropped it, and pushed it with her foot far back under the bed. Then shutting the door quickly she went downstairs. Was it always to be thus? Would Kate ever blight all her joy from this time forth?

CHAPTER X

Marcia's cheeks were flushed when David came home to dinner, for at the last she had to hurry.

As he stood in the doorway of the wide kitchen and caught the odor of the steaming platter of green corn she was putting upon the table, David suddenly realized that he had eaten scarcely anything for breakfast.

Also, he felt a certain comfort from the sweet steady look of wistful sympathy in Marcia's eyes. Did he fancy it, or was there a new look upon her face, a more reserved bearing, less childish, more touched by sad knowledge of life and its bitterness? It was mere fancy of course, something he had just not noticed. He had seen so little of her before.

In the heart of the maiden there stirred a something which she did not quite understand, something brought to life by the sight of her sister's daguerreotype lying at the edge of the valence, where it must have fallen from David's pocket without his knowledge as he lay asleep. It had seemed to put into tangible form the solid wall of fact that hung between her and any hope of future happiness as a wife, and for the first time she too began to realize what she had sacrificed in thus impetuously throwing her young life into the breach that it might be healed. But she was not sorry,—not yet, anyway,—only frightened, and filled with dreary forebodings.

The meal was a pleasant one, though constrained. David roused himself to be cheerful for Marcia's sake, as he would have done with any other stranger, and the girl, suddenly grown sensitive, felt it, and appreciated it, yet did not understand why it made her unhappy.

She was anxious to please him, and kept asking if the potatoes were seasoned right and if his corn were tender, and if he wouldn't have another cup of coffee. Her cheeks were quite red with the effort at matronly dignity when David was finally through his dinner and gone back to the office, and two big tears came and sat in her eyes for a moment, but were persuaded with a determined effort to sink back again into those unfathomable wells that lie in the depths of a woman's eyes. She longed to get out of doors and run wild and free in the old south pasture for relief. She did not know how different it all was from the first dinner of the ordinary young married couple; so stiff and formal, with no gentle touches, no words of love, no glances that told more than words. And yet, child as she was, she felt it, a lack somewhere, she knew not what.

But training is a great thing. Marcia had been trained to be on the alert for the next duty and to do it before she gave herself time for any of her own thoughts. The dinner table was awaiting her attention, and there was company coming.

She glanced at the tall clock in the hall and found she had scarcely an hour before she might expect David's aunts, for David had brought her word that they would come and spend the afternoon and stay to tea.

She shrank from the ordeal and wished David had seen fit to stay and introduce her. It would have been a relief to have had him for a shelter. Somehow she knew that he would have stayed if it had been Kate, and that thought pained her, with a quick sharpness like the sting of an insect. She wondered if she were growing selfish, that it should hurt to find herself of so little account. And, yet, it was to be expected, and she must stop thinking about it. Of course, Kate was the one he had chosen and Kate would always be the only one to him.

It did not take her long to reduce the dinner table to order and put all things in readiness for tea time; and in doing her work Marcia's thoughts flew to pleasanter themes. She wondered what Dolly and Debby, the servants at home, would say if they could see her pretty china and the nice kitchen. They had always been fond of her, and naturally her new honors made her wish to have her old friends see her. What would Mary Ann say? What fun it would be to have Mary Ann there sometime. It would be almost like the days when they had played house under the old elm on the big flat stone, only this would be a real house with real sprigged china instead of bits of broken things. Then she fell into a song, one they sang in school,

"Sister, thou wast mild and lovely,

Gentle as the summer breeze,

Pleasant as the air of evening

When it floats among the trees."

But the first words set her to thinking of her own sister, and how little the song applied to her, and she thought with a sigh how much better it would have been, how much less bitter, if Kate had been that way and had lain down to die and they could have laid her away in the little hilly graveyard under the weeping willows, and felt about her as they did about the girl for whom that song was written.

The work was done, and Marcia arrayed in one of the simplest of Kate's afternoon frocks, when the brass knocker sounded through the house, startling her with its unfamiliar sound.

Breathlessly she hurried downstairs. The crucial moment had come when she must stand to meet her new relatives alone. With her hand trembling she opened the door, but there was only one person standing on the stoop, a girl of about her own age, perhaps a few months younger. Her hair was red, her face was freckled, and her blue eyes under the red lashes danced with repressed mischief. Her dress was plain and she wore a calico sunbonnet of chocolate color.

"Let me in quick before Grandma sees me," she demanded unceremoniously, entering at once before there was opportunity for invitation. "Grandma thinks I've gone to the store, so she won't expect me for a little while. I was jest crazy to see how you looked. I've ben watchin' out o' the window all the morning, but I couldn't ketch a glimpse of you. When David came out this morning I thought you'd sure be at the kitchen door to kiss him good-bye, but you wasn't, and I watched every chance I could get, but I couldn't see you till you run out in the garden fer corn. Then I saw you good, fer I was out hangin' up dish towels. You didn't have a sunbonnet on, so I could see real well. And when I saw how young you was I made up my mind I'd get acquainted in spite of Grandma. You don't mind my comin' over this way without bein' dressed up, do you? There wouldn't be any way to get here without Grandma seeing me, you know, if I put on my Sunday clo'es."

"I'm glad you came!" said Marcia impulsively, feeling a rush of something like tears in her throat at the relief of delay from the aunts. "Come in and sit down. Who are you, and why wouldn't your Grandmother like you to come?"

The strange girl laughed a mirthless laugh.

"Me? Oh, I'm Mirandy. Nobody ever calls me anything but Mirandy. My pa left ma when I was a baby an' never come back, an' ma died, and I live with Grandma Heath. An' Grandma's mad 'cause David didn't marry Hannah Heath. She wanted him to an' she did everything she could to make him pay 'tention to Hannah, give her fine silk frocks, two of 'em, and a real pink parasol, but David he never seemed to know the parasol was pink at all, fer he'd never offer to hold it over Hannah even when Grandma made him walk with her home from church ahead of us. So when it come out that David was really going to marry, and wouldn't take Hannah, Grandma got as mad as could be and said we never any of us should step over his door sill. But I've stepped, I have, and Grandma can't help herself."

"And who is Hannah Heath?" questioned the dazed young bride. It appeared there was more than a sister to be taken into account.

"Hannah? Oh, Hannah is my cousin, Uncle Jim's oldest daughter, and she's getting on toward thirty somewhere. She has whitey-yellow hair and light blue eyes and is tall and real pretty. She held her head high fer a good many years waitin' fer David, and I guess she feels she made a mistake now. I noticed she bowed real sweet to Hermon Worcester last Sunday and let him hold her parasol all the way to Grandma's gate. Hannah was mad as hops when she heard that you had gold hair and blue eyes, for it did seem hard to be beaten by a girl of the same kind? but you haven't, have you? Your hair is almost black and your eyes are brownie-brown. You're years younger than Hannah, too. My! Won't she be astonished when she sees you! But I don't understand how it got around about your having gold hair. It was a man that stopped at your father's house once told it——"

"It was my sister!" said Marcia, and then blushed crimson to think how near she had come to revealing the truth which must not be known.

"Your sister? Have you got a sister with gold hair?"

"Yes, he must have seen her," said Marcia confusedly. She was not used to evasion.

"How funny!" said Miranda. "Well, I'm glad he did, for it made Hannah so jealous it was funny. But I guess she'll get a set-back when she sees how young you are. You're not as pretty as I thought you would be, but I believe I like you better."

Miranda's frank speech reminded Marcia of Mary Ann and made her feel quite at home with her curious visitor. She did not mind being told she was not up to the mark of beauty. From her point of view she was not nearly so pretty as Kate, and her only fear was that her lack of beauty might reveal the secret and bring confusion to David. But she need not have feared: no one watching the two girls, as they sat in the large sunny room and faced each other, but would have smiled to think the homely crude girl could suggest that the other calm, cool bud of womanhood was not as near perfection of beauty as a bud could be expected to come. There was always something child-like about Marcia's face, especially her profile, something deep and other-world-like in her eyes, that gave her an appearance so distinguished from other girls that the word "pretty" did not apply, and surface observers might have passed her by when searching for prettiness, but not so those who saw soul beauties.

But Miranda's time was limited, and she wanted to make as much of it as possible.

"Say, I heard you making music this morning. Won't you do it for me? I'd just love to hear you."

Marcia's face lit up with responsive enthusiasm, and she led the way to the darkened parlor and folded back the covers of the precious piano. She played some tender little airs she loved as she would have played them for Mary Ann, and the two young things stood there together, children in thought and feeling, half a generation apart in position, and neither recognized the difference.

"My land!" said the visitor, "'f I could play like that I wouldn't care ef I had freckles and no father and red hair," and looking up Marcia saw tears in the light blue eyes, and knew she had a kindred feeling in her heart for Miranda.

They had been talking a minute or two when the knocker suddenly sounded through the long hall again making both girls start. Miranda boldly tiptoed over to the front window and peeped between the green slats of the Venetian blind to see who was at the door, while Marcia started guiltily and quickly closed the instrument.

"It's David's aunts," announced Miranda in a stage whisper hurriedly. "I might 'a' known they would come this afternoon. Well, I had first try at you anyway, and I like you real well. May I come again and hear you play? You go quick to the door, and I'll slip into the kitchen till they get in, and then I'll go out the kitchen door and round the house out the little gate so Grandma won't see me. I must hurry for I ought to have been back ten minutes ago."

"But you haven't been to the store," said Marcia in a dismayed whisper.

"Oh, well, that don't matter! I'll tell her they didn't have what she sent me for. Good-bye. You better hurry." So saying, she disappeared into the kitchen; and Marcia, startled by such easy morality, stood dazed until the knocker sounded forth again, this time a little more peremptorily, as the elder aunt took her turn at it.

And so at last Marcia was face to face with the Misses Spafford.

They came in, each with her knitting in a black silk bag on her slim arm, and greeted the flushed, perturbed Marcia with gentle, righteous, rigid inspection. She felt with the first glance that she was being tried in the fire, and that it was to be no easy ordeal through which she was to pass. They had come determined to sift her to the depths and know at once the worst of what their beloved nephew had brought upon himself. If they found aught wrong with her they meant to be kindly and loving with her, but they meant to take it out of her. This had been the unspoken understanding between them as they wended their dignified, determined way to David's house that afternoon, and this was what Marcia faced as she opened the door for them.

She gasped a little, as any girl overwhelmed thus might have done. She did not tilt her chin in defiance as Kate would have done. The thought of David came to support her, and she grasped for her own little part and tried to play it creditably. She did not know whether the aunts knew of her true identity or not, but she was not left long in doubt.

"My dear, we have long desired to know you, of whom we have heard so much," recited Miss Amelia, with slightly agitated mien, as she bestowed a cool kiss of duty upon Marcia's warm cheek. It chilled the girl, like the breath from a funeral flower.

"Yes, it is indeed a pleasure to us to at last look upon our dear nephew's wife," said Miss Hortense quite precisely, and laid the sister kiss upon the other cheek. In spite of her there flitted through Marcia's brain the verse, "Whosoever shall smite thee on thy right cheek, turn to him the other also." Then she was shocked at her own irreverence and tried to put away a hysterical desire to laugh.

The aunts, too, were somewhat taken aback. They had not looked for so girlish a wife. She was not at all what they had pictured. David had tried to describe Kate to them once, and this young, sweet, disarming thing did not in the least fit their preconceived ideas of her. What should they do? How could they carry on a campaign planned against a certain kind of enemy, when lo, as they came upon the field of action the supposed enemy had taken another and more bewildering form than the one for whom they had prepared. They were for the moment silent, gathering their thoughts, and trying to fit their intended tactics to the present situation.

During this operation Marcia helped them to remove their bonnets and silk capes and to lay them neatly on the parlor sofa. She gave them chairs, suggested palm-leaf fans, and looked about, for the moment forgetting that this was not her old home plentifully supplied with those gracious breeze wafters.

They watched her graceful movements, those two angular old ladies, and marvelled over her roundness and suppleness. They saw with appalled hearts what a power youth and beauty might have over a man. Perhaps she might be even worse than they had feared, though if you could have heard them talk about their nephew's coming bride to their neighbors for months beforehand, you would have supposed they knew her to be a model in every required direction. But their stately pride required that of them, an outward loyalty at least. Now that loyalty was to be tried, and Marcia had two old, narrow and well-fortified hearts to conquer ere her way would be entirely smooth.

Well might Madam Schuyler have been proud of her pupil as alone and unaided she faced the trying situation and mastered it in a sweet and unassuming way.

They began their inquisition at once, so soon as they were seated, and the preliminary sentences uttered. The gleaming knitting needles seemed to Marcia like so many swarming, vindictive bees, menacing her peace of mind.

"You look young, child, to have the care of so large a house as this," said Aunt Amelia, looking at Marcia over her spectacles as if she were expected to take the first bite out of her. "It's a great responsibility!" she shut her thin lips tightly and shook her head, as if she had said: "It's a great *impossibility*."

"Have you ever had the care of a house?" asked Miss Hortense, going in a little deeper. "David likes everything nice, you know, he has always been used to it."

There was something in the tone, and in the set of the bow on Aunt Hortense's purple-trimmed cap that roused the spirit in Marcia.

"I think I rather enjoy housework," she responded coolly. This unexpected statement somewhat mollified the aunts. They had heard to the contrary from some one who had lived in the same town with the Schuylers. Kate's reputation was widely known, as that of a spoiled beauty, who did not care to work, and would do whatever she pleased. The aunts had entertained many forebodings from the few stray hints an old neighbor of Kate's had dared to utter in their hearing.

The talk drifted at once into household matters, as though that were the first division of the examination the young bride was expected to undergo. Marcia took early opportunity to still further mollify her visitors by her warmest praise of the good things with which the pantry and store-closet had been filled. The expression that came upon the two old faces was that of receiving but what is due. If the praise had not been forthcoming they would have marked it down against her, but it counted for very little with them, warm as it was.

"Can you make good bread?"

The question was flung out by Aunt Hortense like a challenge, and the very set of her nostrils gave Marcia warning. But it was in a relieved voice that ended almost in a ripple of laugh that she answered quite assuredly:"Oh, yes, indeed. I can make beautiful bread. I just love to make it, too!"

"But how do you make it?" quickly questioned Aunt Amelia, like a repeating rifle. If the first shot had not struck home, the second was likely to. "Do you use hop yeast? Potatoes? I thought so. Don't know how to make salt-rising, do you? It's just what might have been expected."

"David has always been used to salt-rising bread," said Aunt Hortense with a grim set of her lips as though she were delivering a judgment. "He was raised on it."

"If David does not like my bread," said Marcia with a rising color and a nervous little laugh, "then I shall try to make some that he does like."

There was an assurance about the "if" that did not please the oracle.

"David was raised on salt-rising bread," said Aunt Hortense again as if that settled it. "We can send you down a loaf or two every time we bake until you learn how."

"I'm sure it's very kind of you," said Marcia, not at all pleased, "but I do not think that will be necessary. David has always seemed to like our bread when he visited at home. Indeed he often praised it."

"David would not be impolite," said Aunt Amelia, after a suitable pause in which Marcia felt disapprobation in the air. "It would be best for us to send it. David's health might suffer if he was not suitably nourished."

Marcia's cheeks grew redder. Bread had been one of her stepmother's strong points, well infused into her young pupil. Madam Schuyler had never been able to say enough to sufficiently express her scorn of people who made salt-rising bread.

"My stepmother made beautiful bread," she said quite childishly; "she did not think salt-rising was so healthy as that made from hop yeast. She disliked the odor in the house from salt-rising bread."

Now indeed the aunts exchanged glances of "On to the combat." Four red spots flamed giddily out in their four sallow cheeks, and eight shining knitting needles suddenly became idle. The moment was too momentous to work. It was as they feared, even the worst. For, be it known, salt-rising bread was one of their most tender points, and for it they would fight to the bitter end. They looked at her with four cold, forbidding, steely, spectacled eyes, and Marcia felt that their looks said volumes: "And she so young too! To be so out of the way!" was what they might have expressed to one another. Marcia felt she had been unwise in uttering her honest, indignant sentiments concerning salt-rising bread.

The pause was long and impressive, and the bride felt like a naughty little four-year-old.

At last Aunt Hortense took up her knitting again with the air that all was over and an unrevokable verdict was passed upon the culprit.

"People have never seemed to stay away from our house on that account," she said dryly. "I'm sure I hope it will not be so disagreeable that it will affect your coming to see us sometimes with David."

There was an iciness in her manner that seemed to suggest a long line of offended family portraits of ancestors frowning down upon her.

Marcia's cheeks flamed crimson and her heart fairly stopped beating.

"I beg your pardon," she said quickly, "I did not mean to say anything disagreeable. I am sure I shall be glad to come as often as you will let me." As she said it Marcia wondered if that were quite true. Would she ever be glad to go to the home of those two severe-looking aunts? There were three of them. Perhaps the other one would be even more withered and severe than these two. A slight shudder passed over Marcia, and a sudden realization of a side of married life that had never come into her thoughts before. For a moment she longed with all the intensity of a child for her father's house and the shelter of his loving protection, amply supported by her stepmother's capable, self-sufficient, comforting countenance. Her heart sank with the fear that she would never be able to do justice to the position of David's wife, and David would be disappointed in her and sorry he had accepted her sacrifice. She roused herself to do better, and bit her tongue to remind it that it must make no more blunders. She praised the garden, the house and the furnishings, in voluble, eager, girlish language until the thin lines of lips relaxed and the drawn muscles of the aunts' cheeks took on a less severe aspect. They liked to be appreciated, and they certainly had taken a great deal of pains with the house—for David's sake—not for hers. They did not care to have her deluded by the idea that they had done it for her sake. David was to them a young god, and with this one supreme idea of his supremacy they wished to impress his young wife. It was a foregone conclusion in their minds that no mere pretty young girl was capable of appreciating David, as could they, who had watched him from babyhood, and pampered and petted and been severe with him by turns, until if he had not had the temper of an angel he would surely have been spoiled.

"We did our best to make the house just as David would have wished to have it," said Aunt Amelia at last, a self-satisfied shadow of what answered for a smile with her, passing over her face for a moment.

"We did not at all approve of this big house, nor indeed of David's setting up in a separate establishment for himself," said Aunt Hortense, taking up her knitting again. "We thought it utterly unnecessary and uneconomical, when he might have brought his wife home to us, but he seemed to think you would want a house to yourself, so we did the best we could."

There was a martyr-like air in Aunt Hortense's words that made Marcia feel herself again a criminal, albeit she knew she was suffering vicariously. But in her heart she felt a sudden thankfulness that she was spared the trial of living daily under the scrutiny of these two, and she blest David for his thoughtfulness, even though it had not been meant for her. She went into pleased ecstasies once more over the house, and its furnishings, and ended by her pleasure over the piano.

There was grim stillness when she touched upon that subject. The aunts did not approve of that musical instrument, that was plain. Marcia wondered if they always paused so long before speaking when they disapproved, in order to show their displeasure. In fact, did they always disapprove of everything?

"You will want to be very careful of it," said Aunt Amelia, looking at the disputed article over her glasses, "it cost a good deal of money. It was the most foolish thing I ever knew David to do, buying that."

"Yes," said Aunt Hortense, "you will not want to use it much, it might get scratched. It has a fine polish. I'd keep it closed up only when I had company. You ought to be very proud to have a husband who could buy a thing like that. There's not many has them. When I was a girl my grandfather had a spinet, the only one for miles around, and it was taken great care of. The case hadn't a scratch on it."

Marcia had started toward the piano intending to open it and play for her new relatives, but she halted midway in the room and came back to her seat after that speech, feeling that she must just sit and hold her hands until it was time to get supper, while these dreadful aunts picked her to pieces, body, soul and spirit.

It was with great relief at last that she heard David's step and knew she might leave the room and put the tea things upon the table.

CHAPTER XI

They got through the supper without any trouble, and the aunts went home in the early twilight, each with her bonnet strings tied precisely, her lace mitts drawn smoothly over her bony hands, and her little knitting bag over her right arm. They walked decorously up the shaded, elm-domed street, each mindful of her aristocratic instep, and trying to walk erect as in the days when they were gazed upon with admiration, knowing that still an air of former greatness hovered about them wherever they went.

They had brightened considerably at the supper table, under the genial influence of David's presence. They came as near to worshiping David as one can possibly come to worshiping a human being. David, desirous above all things of blinding their keen, sure-to-say-"I-told-you-so" old eyes, roused to be his former gay self with them, and pleased them so that they did not notice how little lover-like reference he made to his bride, who was decidedly in the background for the time, the aunts, perhaps purposely, desiring to show her a wife's true place,— at least the true place of a wife of a David.

They had allowed her to bring their things and help them on with capes and bonnets, and, when they were ready to leave, Aunt Amelia put out a lifeless hand, that felt in its silk mitt like a dead fish in a net, and said to Marcia:

"Our sister Clarinda is desirous of seeing David's wife. She wished us most particularly to give you her love and say to you that she wishes you to come to her at the earliest possible moment. You know she is lame and cannot easily get about."

"Young folks should always be ready to wait upon their elders," said Aunt Hortense, grimly. "Come as soon as you can,—that is, if you think you can stand the smell of salt-rising."

Marcia's face flushed painfully, and she glanced quickly at David to see if he had noticed what his aunt had said, but David was already anticipating the moment when he would be free to lay aside his mask and bury his face in his hands and his thoughts in sadness.

Marcia's heart sank as she went about clearing off the supper things. Was life always to be thus? Would she be forever under the espionage of those two grim spectres of women, who seemed, to her girlish imagination, to have nothing about them warm or loving or woman-like?

She seemed to herself to be standing outside of a married life and looking on at it as one might gaze on a panorama. It was all new and painful, and she was one of the central figures expected to act on through all the pictures, taking another's place, yet doing it as if it were her own. She glanced over at David's pale, grave face, set in its sadness, and a sharp pain went through her heart. Would he ever get over it? Would life never be more cheerful than it now was?

He spoke to her occasionally, in a pleasant abstracted way, as to one who understood him and was kind not to trouble his sadness, and he lighted a candle for her when the work was done and said he hoped she would rest well, that she must still be weary from the long journey. And so she went up to her room again.

She did not go to bed at once, but sat down by the window looking out on the moonlit street. There had been some sort of a meeting at the church across the way, and the people were filing out and taking their various ways home, calling pleasant good nights, and speaking cheerily of the morrow. The moon, though beginning to wane, was bright and cast sharp shadows. Marcia longed to get out into the night. If she could have got downstairs without being heard she would have slipped out into the garden. But downstairs she could hear David pacing back and forth like some hurt, caged thing. Steadily, dully, he walked from the front hall back into the kitchen and back again. There was no possibility of escaping his notice. Marcia felt as if she might breathe freer in the open air, so she leaned far out of her window and looked up and down the street, and thought. Finally,—her heart swelled to bursting, as young hearts with their first little troubles will do,—she leaned down her dark head upon the window seat and wept and wept, alone.

It was the next morning at breakfast that David told her of the festivities that were planned in honor of their home coming. He spoke as if they were a great trial through which they both must pass in order to have any peace, and expressed his gratitude once more that she had been willing to come here with him and pass through it. Marcia had the impression, after he was done speaking and had gone away to the office, that he felt that she had come here merely for these few days of ceremony and after they were passed she was dismissed, her duty done, and she might go home. A great lump arose in her throat and she suddenly wished very much indeed that it were so. For if it were, how much, how very much she would enjoy queening it for a few days—except for David's sadness. But already, there had begun to be an element to her in that sadness which in spite of herself she resented. It was a heavy burden which she began dimly to see would be harder and harder to bear as the days went by. She had not yet begun to think of the time before her in years.

They were to go to the aunts' to tea that evening, and after tea a company of David's old friends—or rather the old friends of David's aunts—were coming in to meet them. This the aunts had planned: but it seemed they had not counted her worthy to be told of the plans, and had only divulged them to David. Marcia had not thought that a little thing could annoy her so much, but she found it vexed her more and more as she thought upon it going about her work.

There was not so much to be done in the house that morning after the breakfast things were cleared away. Dinners and suppers would not be much of a problem for some days to come, for the house was well stocked with good things.

The beds done and the rooms left in dainty order with the sweet summer breeze blowing the green tassels on the window shades, Marcia went softly down like some half guilty creature to the piano. She opened it and was forthwith lost in delight of the sounds her own fingers brought forth.

She had been playing perhaps half an hour when she became conscious of another presence in the room. She looked up with a start, feeling that some one had been there for some time, she could not tell just how long. Peering into the shadowy room lighted only from the window behind her, she made out a head looking in at the door, the face almost hidden by a capacious sunbonnet. She was not long in recognizing her visitor of the day before. It was like a sudden dropping from a lofty mountain height down into a valley of annoyance to hear Miranda's sharp metallic voice:

"Morning!" she courtesied, coming in as soon as she perceived that she was seen. "At it again? I ben listening sometime. It's as pretty as Silas Drew's harmonicker when he comes home evenings behind the cows."

Marcia drew her hands sharply from the keys as if she had been struck. Somehow Miranda and music were inharmonious. She scarcely knew what to say. She felt as if her morning were spoiled. But Miranda was too full of her own errand to notice the clouded face and cool welcome. "Say, you can't guess how I got over here. I'll tell you. You're going over to the Spafford house to-night, ain't you? and there's going to be a lot of folks there. Of course we all know all about it. It's been planned for months. And my cousin Hannah Heath has an invite. You can't think how fond Miss Amelia and Miss Hortense are of her. They tried their level best to make David pay attention to her, but it didn't work. Well, she was talking about what she'd wear. She's had three new frocks made last week, all frilled and fancy. You see she don't want to let folks think she is down in the mouth the least bit about David. She'll likely make up to you, to your face, a whole lot, and pretend she's the best friend you've got in the world. But I've just got this to say, don't you be too sure of her friendship. She's smooth as butter, but she can give you a slap in the face if you don't serve her purpose. I don't mind telling you for she's given me many a one," and the pale eyes snapped in unison with the color of her hair. "Well, you see I heard her talking to Grandma, and she said she'd give anything to know what you were going to wear to-night."

"How curious!" said Marcia surprised. "I'm sure I do not see why she should care!" There was the coolness born of utter indifference in her reply which filled the younger girl with admiration. Perhaps too there was the least mite of haughtiness in her manner, born of the knowledge that she belonged to an old and honored family, and that she had in her possession a trunk full of clothes that could vie with any that Hannah Heath could display. Miranda wished silently that she could convey that cool manner and that wide-eyed indifference to the sight of her cousin Hannah.

"H'm!" giggled Miranda. "Well, she does! If you were going to wear blue you'd see she'd put on her green. She's got one that'll kill any blue that's in the same room with it, no matter if it's on the other side. Its just sick'ning to see them together. And she looks real well in it too. So when she said she wanted to know so bad, Grandma said she'd send me over to know if you'd accept a jar of her fresh pickle-lily, and mebbe I could find out about your clothes. The pickle-lily's on the kitchen table. I left it when I came through. It's good, but there ain't any love in it." And Miranda laughed a hard mirthless laugh, and then settled down to her subject again.

"Now, you needn't be a mite afraid to tell me about it. I won't tell it straight, you know. I'd just like to see what you are going to wear so I could keep her out of her tricks for once. Is your frock blue?"

Now it is true that the trunk upstairs contained a goodly amount of the color blue, for Kate Schuyler had been her bonniest in blue, and the particular frock which had been made with reference to this very first significant gathering was blue. Marcia had accepted the fact as unalterable. The garment was made for a purpose, and its mission must be fulfilled however much she might wish to wear something else, but suddenly as Miranda spoke there came to her mind the thought of rebellion. Why should she be bound down to do exactly as Kate would do in her place? If she had accepted the sacrifice of living Kate's life for her, she might at least have the privilege of living it in the pleasantest possible way, and surely the matter of dress was one she might be allowed to settle for herself if she was old enough at all to be trusted away from home. Among the pretty things that Kate had made was a sweet rose-pink silk tissue. Madam Schuyler had frowned upon it as frivolous, and besides she did not think it becoming to Kate. She had a fixed theory that people with blue eyes and gold hair should never wear pink or red, but Kate as usual had her own way, and with her wild rose complexion had succeeded in looking like the wild rose itself in spite of blue eyes and golden hair. Marcia knew in her heart, in fact she had known from the minute the lovely pink thing had come into the house, that it was the very thing to set her off. Her dark eyes and hair made a charming contrast with the rose, and her complexion was even fresher than Kate's. Her heart grew suddenly eager to don this dainty, frilley thing and outshine Hannah Heath beyond any chance of further trying. There were other frocks, too, in the trunk. Why should she be confined to the stately blue one that had been marked out for this occasion? Marcia, with sudden inspiration, answered calmly, just as though all these tumultuous possibilities of clothes had not been whirling through her brain in that half second's hesitation:

"I have not quite decided what I shall wear. It is not an important matter, I'm sure. Let us go and see the piccalilli. I'm very much obliged to your grandmother, I'm sure. It was kind of her."

Somewhat awed, Miranda followed her hostess into the kitchen. She could not reconcile this girl's face with the stately little airs that she wore, but she liked her and forthwith she told her so.

"I like you," she said fervently. "You remind me of one of Grandma's sturtions, bright and independent and lively, with a spice and a color to 'em, and Hannah makes you think of one of them tall spikes of gladiolus all fixed up without any smell."

Marcia tried to smile over the doubtful compliment. Somehow there was something about Miranda that reminded her of Mary Ann. Poor Mary Ann! *Dear* Mary Ann! For suddenly she realized that everything that reminded her of the precious life of her childhood, left behind forever, was dear. If she could see Mary Ann at this moment she would throw her arms about her neck and call her "Dear Mary Ann," and say, "I love you," to her. Perhaps this feeling made her more gentle with the annoying Miranda than she might have been.

When Miranda was gone the precious play hour was gone too. Marcia had only time to steal hurriedly into the parlor, close the instrument, and then fly about getting her dinner ready. But as she worked she had other thoughts to occupy her mind. She was becoming adjusted to her new environment and she found many unexpected things to make it hard. Here, for instance, was Hannah Heath. Why did there have to be a Hannah Heath? And what was Hannah Heath to her? Kate might feel jealous, indeed, but not she, not the unloved, unreal, wife of David. She should rather pity Hannah that David had not loved her instead of Kate, or pity David that he had not. But somehow she did not, somehow she could not. Somehow Hannah Heath had become a living, breathing enemy to be met and conquered. Marcia felt her fighting blood rising, felt the Schuyler in her coming to the front. However little there was in her wifehood, its name at least was hers. The tale that Miranda had told was enough, if it were true, to put any woman, however young she might be, into battle array. Marcia was puzzling her mind over the question that has been more or less of a weary burden to every woman since the fatal day that Eve made her great mistake.

David was silent and abstracted at the dinner table, and Marcia absorbed in her own problems did not feel cut by it. She was trying to determine whether to blossom out in pink, or to be crushed and set aside into insignificance in blue, or to choose a happy medium and wear neither. She ventured a timid little question before David went away again: Did he, would he,—that is, was there any thing,—any word he would like to say to her? Would she have to do anything to-night?

David looked at her in surprise. Why, no! He knew of nothing. Just go and speak pleasantly to every one. He was sure she knew what to do. He had always thought her very well behaved. She had manners like any woman. She need not feel shy. No one knew of her peculiar position, and he felt reasonably sure that the story would not soon get around. Her position would be thoroughly established before it did, at least. She need not feel uncomfortable. He looked down at her thinking he had said all that could be expected of him, but somehow he felt the trouble in the girl's eyes and asked her gently if there was anything more.

"No," she said slowly, "unless, perhaps—I don't suppose you know what it would be proper for me to wear."

"Oh, that does not matter in the least," he replied promptly. "Anything. You always look nice. Why, I'll tell you, wear the frock you had on the night I came." Then he suddenly remembered the reason why that was a pleasant memory to him, and that it was not for her sake at all, but for the sake of one who was lost to him forever. His face contracted with sudden pain, and Marcia, cut to the heart, read the meaning, and felt sick and sore too.

"Oh, I could not wear that," she said sadly, "it is only chintz. It would not be nice enough, but thank you. I shall be all right. Don't trouble about me," and she forced a weak smile to light him from the house, and shut from his pained eyes the knowledge of how he had hurt her, for with those words of his had come the vision of herself that happy night as she stood at the gate in the stillness and moonlight looking from the portal of her maidenhood into the vista of her womanhood, which had seemed then so far away and bright, and was now upon her in sad reality. Oh, if she could but have caught that sentence of his about her little chintz frock to her heart with the joy of possession, and known that he said it because he too had a happy memory about her in it, as she had always felt the coming, misty, dream-expected lover would do!

She spread the available frocks out upon the bed after the other things were put neatly away in closet and drawer, and sat down to decide the matter. David's suggestion while impossible had given her an idea, and she proceeded to carry it out. There was a soft sheer white muslin, whereon Kate had expended her daintiest embroidering, edged with the finest of little lace frills. It was quaint and simple and girlish, the sweetest, most simple affair in all of Kate's elaborate wardrobe, and yet, perhaps, from an artistic point of view, the most elegant. Marcia soon made up her mind.

She dressed herself early, for David had said he would be home by four o'clock and they would start as soon after as he could get ready. His aunts wished to show her the old garden before dark.

When she came to the arrangement of her hair she paused. Somehow her soul rebelled at the style of Kate. It did not suit her face. It did not accord with her feeling. It made her seem unlike herself, or unlike the self she would ever wish to be. It suited Kate well, but not her. With sudden determination she pulled it all down again from the top of her head and loosened its rich waves about her face, then loosely twisted it behind, low on her neck, falling over her delicate ears, until her head looked like that of an old Greek statue. It was not fashion, it was pure instinct the child was following out, and there was enough conformity to one of the fashionable modes of the day to keep her from looking odd. It was lovely. Marcia could not help seeing herself that it was much more becoming than the way she had arranged it for her marriage, though then she had had the wedding veil to soften the tightly drawn outlines of her head. She put on the sheer white embroidered frock then, and as a last touch pinned the bit of black velvet about her throat with a single pearl that had been her mother's. It was the bit of black velvet she had worn the night David came. It gave her pleasure to think that in so far she was conforming to his suggestion.

She had just completed her toilet when she heard David's step coming up the walk.

David, coming in out of the sunshine and beholding this beautiful girl in the coolness and shadow of the hall awaiting him shyly, almost started back as he rubbed his eyes and looked at her again. She was beautiful. He had to admit it to himself, even in the midst of his sadness, and he smiled at her, and felt another pang of condemnation that he had taken this beauty from some other man's lot perhaps, and appropriated it to shield himself from the world's exclamation about his own lonely life.

"You have done it admirably. I do not see that there is anything left to be desired," he said in his pleasant voice that used to make her girl-heart flutter with pride that her new brother-to-be was pleased with her. It fluttered now, but there was a wider sweep to its wings, and a longer flight ahead of the thought.

Quite demurely the young wife accepted her compliment, and then she meekly folded her little white muslin cape with its dainty frills about her pretty shoulders, drew on the new lace mitts, and tied beneath her chin the white strings of a shirred gauze bonnet with tiny rosebuds nestling in the ruching of tulle about the face.

Once more the bride walked down the world the observed of all observers, the gazed at of the town, only this time it was brick pavement not oaken stairs she trod, and most of the eyes that looked upon her were sheltered behind green jalousies. None the less, however, was she conscious of them as she made her way to the house of solemn feasting with David by her side. Her eyes rested upon the ground, or glanced quietly at things in the distance, when they were not lifted for a moment in wifely humility to her husband's face at some word of his. Just as she imagined a hundred times in her girlish thoughts that her sister Kate would do, so did she, and after what seemed to her an interminable walk, though in reality it was but four village blocks, they arrived at the house of Spafford.

CHAPTER XII

"This is your Aunt Clarinda!"

There was challenge in the severely spoken pronoun Aunt Hortense used. It seemed to Marcia that she wished to remind her that all her old life and relations were passed away, and she had nothing now but David's, especially David's relatives. She shrank from lifting her eyes, expecting to find the third aunt, who was older, as much sourer and sharper in proportion to the other two, but she controlled herself and lifted her flower face to meet a gentle, meek, old face set in soft white frills of a cap, with white ribbons flying, and though the old lady leaned upon a crutch she managed to give the impression that she had fairly flown in her gladness to welcome her new niece. There was the lighting of a repressed nature let free in her kind old face as she looked with true pleasure upon the lovely young one, and Marcia felt herself folded in truly loving arms in an embrace which her own passionate, much repressed, loving nature returned with heartiness. At last she had found a friend!

She felt it every time she spoke, more and more. They walked out into the garden almost immediately, and Aunt Clarinda insisted upon hobbling along by Marcia's side, though her sisters both protested that it would be too hard for her that warm afternoon. Every time that Marcia spoke she felt the kind old eyes upon her, and she knew that at least one of the aunts was satisfied with her as a wife for David, for her eyes would travel from David to Marcia and back again to David, and when they met Marcia's there was not a shade of disparagement in them.

It was rather a tiresome walk through a tiresome old garden, laid out in the ways of the past generation, and bordered with much funereal box. The sisters, Amelia and Hortense, took the new member of the family, conscientiously, through every path, and faithfully told how each spot was associated with some happening in the family history. Occasionally there was a solemn pause for the purpose of properly impressing the new member of the house, and Amelia wiped her eyes with her carefully folded handkerchief. Marcia felt extremely like laughing. She was sure that if Kate had been obliged to pass through this ordeal she would have giggled out at once and said some shockingly funny thing that would have horrified the aunts beyond forgiveness. The thought of this nerved her to keep a sober face. She wondered what David thought of it all, but when she looked at him she wondered no longer, for David stood as one waiting for a certain ceremony to be over, a ceremony which he knew to be inevitable, but which was wholly and familiarly uninteresting. He did not even see how it must strike the girl who was going through it all for him, for David's thoughts were out on the flood-tide of sorrow, drifting against the rocks of the might-have-been.

They went in to tea presently, just when the garden was growing loveliest with a tinge of the setting sun, and Marcia longed to run up and down the little paths like a child and call to them all to catch her if they could. The house was dark and stately and gloomy.

"You are coming up to my room for a few minutes after supper," whispered Aunt Clarinda encouragingly as they passed into the dark hall. The supper table was alight with a fine old silver candelabra whose many wavering lights cast a solemn, grotesque shadow on the different faces.

Beside her plate the young bride saw an ostentatious plate of puffy soda biscuits, and involuntarily her eyes searched the table for the bread plate.

Aunt Clarinda almost immediately pounced upon the bread plate and passed it with a smile to Marcia, and as Marcia with an answering smile took a generous slice she heard the other two aunts exclaim in chorus, "Oh, don't pass her the bread, Clarinda; take it away sister, quick! She does not like salt-rising! It is unpleasant to her!"

Then with blazing cheeks the girl protested that she wished to keep the bread, that they were mistaken, she had not said it was obnoxious to her, but had merely given them her stepmother's opinion when they asked. They must excuse her for her seeming rudeness, for she had not intended to hurt them. She presumed salt-rising bread was very nice; it looked beautiful. This was a long speech for shy Marcia to make before so many strangers, but David's wondering, troubled eyes were upon her, questioning what it all might mean, and she felt she could do anything to save David from more suffering or annoyance of any kind.

David said little. He seemed to perceive that there had been an unpleasant prelude to this, and perhaps knew from former experience that the best way to do was to change the subject. He launched into a detailed account of their wedding journey. Marcia on her part was grateful to him, for when she took the first brave bite into the very puffy, very white slice of bread she had taken, she perceived that it was much worse than that which had been baked for their homecoming, and not only justified all her stepmother's execrations, but in addition it was sour. For an instant, perceiving down the horoscope of time whole calendars full of such suppers with the aunts, and this bread, her soul shuddered and shrank. Could she ever learn to like it? Impossible! Could she ever tolerate it? Could she? She doubted. Then she swallowed bravely and perceived that the impossible had been accomplished once. It could be again, but she must go slowly else she might have to eat two slices instead of one. David was kind. He had roused himself to help his helper. Perhaps something in her girlish beauty and helplessness, helpless here for his sake, appealed to him. At least his eyes sought hers often with a tender interest to see if she were comfortable, and once, when Aunt Amelia asked if they stopped nowhere for rest on their journey, his eyes sought Marcia's with a twinkling reminder of their roadside nap, and he answered, "Once, Aunt Amelia. No, it was not a regular inn. It was quieter than that. Not many people stopping there."

Marcia's merry laugh almost bubbled forth, but she suppressed it just in time, horrified to think what Aunt Hortense would say, but somehow after David had said that her heart felt a trifle lighter and she took a big bite from the salt-rising and smiled as she swallowed it. There were worse things in the world, after all, than salt-rising, and, when one could smother it in Aunt Amelia's peach preserves, it was quite bearable.

Aunt Clarinda slipped her off to her own room after supper, and left the other two sisters with their beloved idol, David. In their stately parlor lighted with many candles in honor of the occasion, they sat and talked in low tones with him, their voices suggesting condolence with his misfortune of having married out of the family, and disapproval with the married state in general. Poor souls! How their hard, loving hearts would have been wrung could they but have known the true state of the case! And, strange anomaly, how much deeper would have been their antagonism toward poor, self-sacrificing, loving Marcia! Just because she had dared to think herself fit for David, belonging as she did to her renegade sister Kate. But they did not know, and for this fact David was profoundly thankful. Those were not the days of rapid transit, of telegraph and telephone, nor even of much letter writing, else the story would probably have reached the aunts even before the bride and bridegroom arrived at home. As it was, David had some hope of keeping the tragedy of his life from the ears of his aunts forever. Patiently he answered their questions concerning the wedding, questions that were intended to bring out facts showing whether David had received his due amount of respect, and whether the family he had so greatly honored felt the burden of that honor sufficiently.

Upstairs in a quaint old-fashioned room Aunt Clarinda was taking Marcia's face in her two wrinkled hands and looking lovingly into her eyes; then she kissed her on each rosy cheek and said:

"Dear child! You look just as I did when I was young. You wouldn't think it from me now, would you? But it's true. I might not have grown to be such a dried-up old thing if I had had somebody like David. I'm so glad you've got David. He'll take good care of you. He's a dear boy. He's always been good to me. But you mustn't let the others crush those roses out of your cheeks. They crushed mine out. They wouldn't let me have my life the way I wanted it, and the pink in my cheeks all went back into my heart and burst it a good many years ago. But they can't spoil your life, for you've got David and that's worth everything."

Then she kissed her on the lips and cheeks and eyes and let her go. But that one moment had given Marcia a glimpse into another life-story and put her in touch forever with Aunt Clarinda, setting athrob the chord of loving sympathy.

When they came into the parlor the other two aunts looked up with a quick, suspicious glance from one to the other and then fastened disapproving eyes upon Marcia. They rather resented it that she was so pretty. Hannah had been their favorite, and Hannah was beautiful in their eyes. They wanted no other to outshine her. Albeit they would be proud enough before their neighbors to have it said that their nephew's wife was beautiful.

After a chilling pause in which David was wondering anew at Marcia's beauty, Aunt Hortense asked, as though it were an omission from the former examination, "Did you ever make a shirt?"

"Oh, plenty of them!" said Marcia, with a merry laugh, so relieved that she fairly bubbled. "I think I could make a shirt with my eyes shut."

Aunt Clarinda beamed on her with delight. A shirt was something she had never succeeded in making right. It was one of the things which her sisters had against her that she could not make good shirts. Any one who could not make a shirt was deficient. Clarinda was deficient. She could not make a shirt. Meekly had she tried year after year. Humbly had she ripped out gusset and seam and band, having put them on upside down or inside out. Never could she learn the ins and outs of a shirt. But her old heart trembled with delight that the new girl, who was going to take the place in her heart of her old dead self and live out all the beautiful things which had been lost to her, had mastered this one great accomplishment in which she had failed so supremely.

But Aunt Hortense was not pleased. True, it was one of the seven virtues in her mind which a young wife should possess, and she had carefully instructed Hannah Heath for a number of years back, while Hannah bungled out a couple for her father occasionally, but Aunt Hortense had been sure that if Hannah ever became David's wife she might still have the honor of making most of David's shirts. That had been her happy task ever since David had worn a shirt, and she hoped to hold the position of shirt-maker to David until she left this mortal clay.

Therefore Aunt Hortense was not pleased, even though David's wife was not lacking, and, too, even though she foreheard herself telling her neighbors next day how many shirts David's wife had made.

"Well, David will not need any for some time," she said grimly. "I made him a dozen just before he was married."

Marcia reflected that it seemed to be impossible to make any headway into the good graces of either Aunt Hortense or Aunt Amelia. Aunt Amelia then took her turn at a question.

"Hortense," said she, and there was an ominous inflection in the word as if the question were portentous, "have you asked our new niece by what name she desires us to call her?"

"I have not," said Miss Hortense solemnly, "but I intend to do so immediately," and then both pairs of steely eyes were leveled at the girl. Marcia suddenly was face to face with a question she had not considered, and David started upright from his position on the hair-cloth sofa. But if a thunderbolt had fallen from heaven and rendered him utterly unconscious David would not have been more helpless than he was for the time being. Marcia saw the mingled pain and perplexity in David's face, and her own courage gathered itself to brave it out in some way. The color flew to her cheeks, and rose slowly in David's, through heavy veins that swelled in his neck till he could feel their pulsation against his stock, but his smooth shaven lips were white. He felt that a moment had come which he could not bear to face.

Then with a hesitation that was but pardonable, and with a shy sweet look, Marcia answered; and though her voice trembled just the least bit, her true, dear eyes looked into the battalion of steel ones bravely.

"I would like you to call me Marcia, if you please."

"Marcia!" Miss Hortense snipped the word out as if with scissors of surprise.

But there was a distinct relaxation about Miss Amelia's mouth. She heaved a relieved sigh. Marcia was so much better than Kate, so much more classical, so much more to be compared with Hannah, for instance.

"Well, I'm glad!" she allowed herself to remark. "David has been calling you 'Kate' till it made me sick, such a frivolous name and no sense in it either. Marcia sounds quite sensible. I suppose Katharine is your middle name. Do you spell it with a K or a C?"

But the knocker sounded on the street door and Marcia was spared the torture of a reply. She dared not look at David's face, for she knew there must be pain and mortification mingling there, and she hoped that the trying subject would not come up again for discussion.

The guests began to arrive. Old Mrs. Heath and her daughter-in-law and grand-daughter came first.

Hannah's features were handsome and she knew exactly how to manage her shapely hands with their long white fingers. The soft delicate undersleeves fell away from arms white and well moulded, and she carried her height gracefully. Her hair was elaborately stowed upon the top of her head in many puffs, ending in little ringlets carelessly and coquettishly straying over temple, or ears, or gracefully curved neck. She wore a frock of green, and its color sent a pang through the bride's heart to realize that perhaps it had been worn with an unkindly purpose. Nevertheless Hannah Heath was beautiful and fascinated Marcia. She resolved to try to think the best of her, and to make her a friend if possible. Why, after all, should she be to blame for wanting David? Was he not a man to be admired and desired? It was unwomanly, of course, that she had let it be known, but perhaps her relatives were more to blame than herself. At least Marcia made up her mind to try and like her.

Hannah's frock was of silk, not a common material in those days, soft and shimmery and green enough to take away the heart from anything blue that was ever made, but Hannah was stately and her skin as white as the lily she resembled, in her bright leaf green.

Hannah chose to be effusive and condescending to the bride, giving the impression that she and David had been like brother and sister all their lives and that she might have been his choice if she had chosen, but as she had not chosen, she was glad that David had found some one wherewith to console himself. She did not say all this in so many words, but Marcia found that impression left after the evening was over.

With sweet dignity Marcia received her introductions, given in Miss Amelia's most commanding tone, "Our niece, Marcia!"

"Marshy! Marshy!" the bride heard old Mrs. Heath murmur to Miss Spafford. "Why, I thought 'twas to be Kate!"

"Her name is Marcia," said Miss Amelia in a most satisfied tone; "you must have misunderstood."

Marcia caught a look in Miss Heath's eyes, alert, keen, questioning, which flashed all over her like something searching and bright but not friendly.

She felt a painful shyness stealing over her and wished that David were by her side. She looked across the room at him. His face had recovered its usual calmness, though he looked pale. He was talking on his favorite theme with old Mr. Heath: the newly invented steam engine and its possibilities. He had forgotten everything else for the time, and his face lighted with animation as he tried to answer William Heath's arguments against it.

"Have you read what the Boston *Courier* said, David? 'Long in June it was I think," Marcia heard Mr. Heath ask. Indeed his voice was so large that it filled the room, and for the moment Marcia had been left to herself while some new people were being ushered in. "It says, David, that 'the project of a railroad from Bawston to Albany is impracticable as everybody knows who knows the simplest rule of arithmetic, and the expense would be little less than the market value of the whole territory of Massachusetts; and which, if practicable, every person of common sense knows would be as useless as a railroad from Bawston to the moon.' There, David, what do ye think o' that?" and William Heath slapped David on the knee with his broad, fat fist and laughed heartily, as though he had him in a tight corner.

Marcia would have given a good deal to slip in beside David on the sofa and listen to the discussion. She wanted with all her heart to know how he would answer this man who could be so insufferably wise, but there was other work for her, and her attention was brought back to her own uncomfortable part by Hannah Heath's voice:

"Come right ovah heah, Mistah Skinnah, if you want to meet the bride. You must speak verra nice to me or I sha'n't introduce you at all."

A tall lanky man with stiff sandy hair and a rubicund complexion was making his way around the room. He had a small mouth puckered a little as if he might be going to whistle, and his chin had the look of having been pushed back out of the way, a stiff fuzz of sandy whiskers made a hedge down either cheek, and but for that he was clean shaven. The skin over his high cheek bones was stretched smooth and tight as if it were a trifle too close a fit for the genial cushion beneath. He did not look brilliant, and he certainly was not handsome, but there was an inoffensive desire to please about him. He was introduced as Mr. Lemuel Skinner. He bowed low over Marcia's hand, said a few embarrassed, stiff sentences and turned to Hannah Heath with relief. It was evident that Hannah was in his eyes a great and shining light, to which he fluttered as naturally as does the moth to the candle. But Hannah did not scruple to singe his wings whenever she chose. Perhaps she knew, no matter how badly he was burned he would only flutter back again whenever she scintillated. She had turned her back upon him now, and left him to Marcia's tender mercies. Hannah was engaged in talking to a younger man. "Harry Temple, from New York," Lemuel explained to Marcia.

The young man, Harry Temple, had large lazy eyes and heavy dark hair. There was a discontented look in his face, and a looseness about the set of his lips that Marcia did not like, although she had to admit that he was handsome. Something about him reminded her of Captain Leavenworth, and she instinctively shrank from him. But Harry Temple had no mind to talk to any one but Marcia that evening, and he presently so managed it that he and she were ensconced in a corner of the room away from others. Marcia felt perturbed. She did not feel flattered by the man's attentions, and she wanted to be at the other end of the room listening to the conversation.

She listened as intently as she might between sentences, and her keen ears could catch a word or two of what David was saying. After all, it was not so much the new railroad project that she cared about, though that was strange and interesting enough, but she wanted to watch and listen to David.

Harry Temple said a great many pretty things to Marcia. She did not half hear some of them at first, but after a time she began to realize that she must have made a good impression, and the pretty flush in her cheeks grew deeper. She did little talking. Mr. Temple did it all. He told her of New York. He asked if she were not dreadfully bored with this little town and its doings, and bewailed her lot when he learned that she had not had much experience there. Then he asked if she had ever been to New York and began to tell of some of its attractions. Among other things he mentioned some concerts, and immediately Marcia was all attention. Her dark eyes glowed and her speaking face gave eager response to his words. Seeing he had interested her at last, he kept on, for he was possessor of a glib tongue, and what he did not know he could fabricate without the slightest compunction. He had been about the world and gathered up superficial knowledge enough to help him do this admirably, therefore he was able to use a few musical terms, and to bring before Marcia's vivid imagination the scene of the performance of Handel's great "Creation" given in Boston, and of certain musical events that were to be attempted soon in New York. He admitted that he could play a little upon the harpsichord, and, when he learned that Marcia could play also and that she was the possessor of a piano, one of the latest improved makes, he managed to invite himself to play upon it. Marcia found to her dismay that she actually seemed to have invited him to come some afternoon when her husband was away. She had only said politely that she would like to hear him play sometime, and expressed her great delight in music, and he had done the rest, but in her inexperience somehow it had happened and she did not know what to do.

It troubled her a good deal, and she turned again toward the other end of the room, where the attention of most of the company was riveted upon the group who were discussing the railroad, its pros and cons. David was the centre of that group.

"Let us go over and hear what they are saying," she said, turning to her companion eagerly.

"Oh, it is all stupid politics and arguments about that ridiculous fairy-tale of a railroad scheme. You would not enjoy it," answered the young man disappointedly. He saw in Marcia a beautiful young soul, the only one who had really attracted him since he had left New York, and he wished to become intimate enough with her to enjoy himself.

It mattered not to him that she was married to another man. He felt secure in his own attractions. He had ever been able to while away the time with whom he chose, why should a simple village maiden resist him? And this was an unusual one, the contour of her head was like a Greek statue.

Nevertheless he was obliged to stroll after her. Once she had spoken. She had suddenly become aware that they had been in their corner together a long time, and that Aunt Amelia's cold eyes were fastened upon her in disapproval.

"The farmers would be ruined, man alive!" Mr. Heath was saying. "Why, all the horses would have to be killed, because they would be wholly useless if this new fandango came in, and then where would be a market for the wheat and oats?"

"Yes, an' I've heard some say the hens wouldn't lay, on account of the noise," ventured Lemuel Skinner in his high voice. "And think of the fires from the sparks of the engine. I tell you it would be dangerous." He looked over at Hannah triumphantly, but Hannah was endeavoring to signal Harry Temple to her side and did not see nor hear.

"I tell you," put in Mr. Heath's heavy voice again, "I tell you, Dave, it can't be done. It's impractical. Why, no car could advance against the wind."

"They told Columbus he couldn't sail around the earth, but he did it!"

There was sudden stillness in the room, for it was Marcia's clear, grave voice that had answered Mr. Heath's excited tones, and she had not known she was going to speak aloud. It came before she realized it. She had been used to speak her mind sometimes with her father, but seldom when there were others by, and now she was covered with confusion to think what she had done. The aunts, Amelia and Hortense, were shocked. It was so unladylike. A woman should not speak on such subjects. She should be silent and leave such topics to her husband.

"Deah me, she's strong minded, isn't she?" giggled Hannah Heath to Lemuel, who had taken the signals to himself and come to her side.

"Quite so, quite so!" murmured Lemuel, his lips looking puffier and more cherry-fied than ever and his chin flattened itself back till he looked like a frustrated old hen who did not understand the perplexities of life and was clucking to find out, after having been startled half out of its senses.

But Marcia was not wholly without consolation, for David had flashed a look of approval at her and had made room for her to sit down by his side on the sofa. It was almost like belonging to him for a minute or two. Marcia felt her heart glow with something new and pleasant.

Mr. William Heath drew his heavy grey brows together and looked at her grimly over his spectacles, poking his bristly under-lip out in astonishment, bewildered that he should have been answered by a gentle, pretty woman, all frills and sparkle like his own daughter. He had been wont to look upon a woman as something like a kitten,—that is, a young woman,—and suddenly the kitten had lifted a velvet paw and struck him squarely in the face. He had felt there were claws in the blow, too, for there had been a truth behind her words that set the room a mocking him.

"Well, Dave, you've got your wife well trained already!" he laughed, concluding it was best to put a smiling front upon the defeat. "She knows just when to come in and help when your side's getting weak!"

They served cake and raspberry vinegar then, and a little while after everybody went home. It was later than the hours usually kept in the village, and the lights in most of the houses were out, or burning dimly in upper stories. The voices of the guests sounded subdued in the misty waning moonlight air. Marcia could hear Hannah Heath's voice ahead giggling affectedly to Harry Temple and Lemuel Skinner, as they walked one on either side of her, while her father and mother and grandmother came more slowly.

David drew Marcia's hand within his arm and walked with her quietly down the street, making their steps hushed instinctively that they might so seem more removed from the others. They were both tired with the unusual excitement and the strain they had been through, and each was glad of the silence of the other.

But when they reached their own doorstep David said: "You spoke well, child. You must have thought about these things."

Marcia felt a sob rising in a tide of joy into her throat. Then he was not angry with her, and he did not disapprove as the two aunts had done. Aunt Clarinda had kissed her good-night and murmured, "You are a bright little girl, Marcia, and you will make a good wife for David. You will come soon to see me, won't you?" and that had made her glad, but these words of David's were so good and so unexpected that Marcia could hardly hide her happy tears.

"I was afraid I had been forward," murmured Marcia in the shadow of the front stoop.

"Not at all, child, I like to hear a woman speak her mind,—that is, allowing she has any mind to speak. That can't be said of all women. There's Hannah Heath, for instance. I don't believe she would know a railroad project from an essay on ancient art."

After that the house seemed a pleasant place aglow as they entered it, and Marcia went up to her rest with a lighter heart.

But the child knew not that she had made a great impression that night upon all who saw her as being beautiful and wise.

The aunts would not express it even to each other,—for they felt in duty bound to discountenance her boldness in speaking out before the men and making herself so prominent, joining in their discussions,—but each in spite of her convictions felt a deep satisfaction that their neighbors had seen what a beautiful and bright wife David had selected. They even felt triumphant over their favorite Hannah, and thought secretly that Marcia compared well with her in every way, but they would not have told this even to themselves, no, not for worlds.

So the kindly gossipy town slept, and the young bride became a part of its daily life.

CHAPTER XIII

Life began to take on a more familiar and interesting aspect to Marcia after that. She had her daily round of pleasant household duties and she enjoyed them.

There were many other gatherings in honor of the bride and groom, tea-drinkings and evening calls, and a few called in to a neighbor's house to meet them. It was very pleasant to Marcia as she became better acquainted with the people and grew to like some of them, only there was the constant drawback of feeling that it was all a pain and weariness to David.

But Marcia was young, and it was only natural that she should enjoy her sudden promotion to the privileges of a matron, and the marked attention that was paid her. It was a mercy that her head was not turned, living as she did to herself, and with no one in whom she could confide. For David had shrunk within himself to such an extent that she did not like to trouble him with anything.

It was only two days after the evening at the old Spafford house that David came home to tea with ashen face, haggard eyes and white lips. He scarcely tasted his supper and said he would go and lie down, that his head ached. Marcia heard him sigh deeply as he went upstairs. It was that afternoon that the post had brought him Kate's letter.

Sadly Marcia put away the tea things, for she could not eat anything either, though it was an unusually inviting meal she had prepared. Slowly she went up to her room and sat looking out into the quiet, darkening summer night, wondering what additional sorrow had come to David.

David's face looked like death the next morning when he came down. He drank a cup of coffee feverishly, then took his hat as if he would go to the office, but paused at the door and came back saying he would not go if Marcia would not mind taking a message for him. His head felt badly. She need only tell the man to go on with things as they had planned and say he was detained. Marcia was ready at once to do his bidding with quiet sympathy in her manner.

She delivered her message with the frank straightforward look of a school girl, mingled with a touch of matronly dignity she was trying to assume, which added to her charm; and she smiled her open smile of comradeship, such as she would have dispensed about the old red school house at home, upon boys and girls alike, leaving the clerk and type-setters in a most subjected state, and ready to do anything in the service of their master's wife. It is to be feared that they almost envied David. They watched her as she moved gracefully down the street, and their eyes had a reverent look as they turned away from the window to their work, as though they had been looking upon something sacred.

Harry Temple watched her come out of the office.

She impressed him again as something fresh and different from the common run of maidens in the village. He lazily stepped from the store where he had been lounging and walked down the street to intercept her as she crossed and turned the corner.

"Good morning, Mrs. Spafford," he said, with a courtly grace that was certainly captivating, "are you going to your home? Then our ways lie together. May I walk beside you?"

Marcia smiled and tried to seem gracious, though she would rather have been alone just then, for she wanted to enjoy the day and not be bothered with talking.

Harry Temple mentioned having a letter from a friend in Boston who had lately heard a great chorus rendered. He could not be quite sure of the name of the composer because he had read the letter hurriedly and his friend was a blind-writer, but that made no difference to Harry. He could fill in facts enough about the grandeur of the music from his own imagination to make up for the lack of a little matter like the name of a composer. He was keen enough to see that Marcia was more interested in music than in anything he said, therefore he racked his brains for all the music talk he had ever heard, and made up what he did not know, which was not hard to do, for Marcia was very ignorant on the subject.

At the door they paused. Marcia was eager to get in. She began to wonder how David felt, and she longed to do something for him. Harry Temple looked at her admiringly, noted the dainty set of chin, the clear curve of cheek, the lovely sweep of eyelashes, and resolved to get better acquainted with this woman, so young and so lovely.

"I have not forgotten my promise to play for you," he said lightly, watching to see if the flush of rose would steal into her cheek, and that deep light into her expressive eyes. "How about this afternoon? Shall you be at home and disengaged?"

But welcome did not flash into Marcia's face as he had hoped. Instead a troubled look came into her eyes.

"I am afraid it will not be possible this afternoon," said Marcia, the trouble in her eyes creeping into her voice. "That is—I expect to be at home, but—I am not sure of being disengaged."

"Ah! I see!" he raised his eyebrows archly, looking her meanwhile straight in the eyes; "some one else more fortunate than I. Some one else coming?"

Although Marcia did not in the least understand his insinuation, the color flowed into her cheeks in a hurry now, for she instinctively felt that there was something unpleasant in his tone, something below her standard of morals or culture, she did not quite know what. But she felt she must protect herself at any cost. She drew up a little mantle of dignity.

"Oh, no," she said quickly, "I'm not expecting any one at all, but Mr. Spafford had a severe headache this morning, and I am not sure but the sound of the piano would make it worse. I think it would be better for you to come another time, although he may be better by that time."

"Oh, I see! Your husband's at home!" said the young man with relief. His manner implied that he had a perfect understanding of something that Marcia did not mean nor comprehend.

"I understand perfectly," he said, with another meaning smile as though he and she had a secret together; "I'll come some other time," and he took himself very quickly away, much to Marcia's relief. But the trouble did not go out of her eyes as she saw him turn the corner. Instead she went in and stood at the dining room window a long time looking out on the Heaths' hollyhocks beaming in the sun behind the picket fence, and wondered what he could have meant, and why he smiled in that hateful way. She decided she did not like him, and she hoped he would never come. She did not think she would care to hear him play. There was something about him that reminded her of Captain Leavenworth, and now that she saw it in him she would dislike to have him about.

With a sigh she turned to the getting of a dinner which she feared would not be eaten. Nevertheless, she put more dainty thought in it than usual, and when it was done and steaming upon the table she went gently up and tapped on David's door. A voice hoarse with emotion and weariness answered. Marcia scarcely heard the first time.

"Dinner is ready. Isn't your head any better,—David?" There was caressing in his name. It wrung David's heart. Oh, if it were but Kate, his Kate, his little bride that were calling him, how his heart would leap with joy! How his headache would disappear and he would be with her in an instant.

For Kate's letter had had its desired effect. All her wrongdoings, her crowning outrage of his noble intentions, had been forgotten in the one little plaintive appeal she had managed to breathe in a minor wail throughout that treacherous letter, treacherous alike to her husband and to her lover. Just as Kate had always been able to do with every one about her, she had blinded him to her faults, and managed to put herself in the light of an abused, troubled maiden, who was in a predicament through no fault of her own, and sat in sorrow and a baby-innocence that was bewilderingly sweet.

There had been times when David's anger had been hot enough to waft away this filmy mist of fancies that Kate had woven about herself and let him see the true Kate as she really was. At such times David would confess that she must be wholly heartless. That bright as she was it was impossible for her to have been so easily persuaded into running away with a man she did not love. He had never found it so easy to persuade her against her will. Did she love him? Had she truly loved him, and was she suffering now? His very soul writhed in agony to think of his bride the wife of another against her will. If he might but go and rescue her. If he might but kill that other man! Then his soul would be confronted with the thought of murder. Never before had he felt hate, such hate, for a human being. Then again his heart would soften toward him as he felt how the other must have loved her, Kate, his little wild rose! and there was a fellow feeling between them too, for had she not let him see that she did not half care aright for that other one? Then his mind would stop in a whirl of mingled feeling and he would pause, and pray for steadiness to think and know what was right.

Around and around through this maze of arguing he had gone through the long hours of the morning, always coming sharp against the thought that there was nothing he could possibly do in the matter but bear it, and that Kate, after all, the Kate he loved with his whole soul, had done it and must therefore be to blame. Then he would read her letter over, burning every word of it upon his brain, until the piteous minor appeal would torture him once more and he would begin again to try to get hold of some thread of thought that would unravel this snarl and bring peace.

Like a sound from another world came Marcia's sweet voice, its very sweetness reminding him of that other lost voice, whose tantalizing music floated about his imagination like a string of phantom silver bells that all but sounded and then vanished into silence.

And while all this was going on, this spiritual torture, his living, suffering, physical self was able to summon its thoughts, to answer gently that he did not want any dinner; that his head was no better; that he thanked her for her thought of him; and that he would take the tea she offered if it was not too much trouble.

Gladly, with hurried breath and fingers that almost trembled, Marcia hastened to the kitchen once more and prepared a dainty tray, not even glancing at the dinner table all so fine and ready for its guest, and back again she went to his door, an eager light in her eyes, as if she had obtained audience to a king.

He opened the door this time and took the tray from her with a smile. It was a smile of ashen hue, and fell like a pall upon Marcia's soul. It was as if she had been permitted for a moment to gaze upon a martyred soul upon the rack. Marcia fled from it and went to her own room, where she flung herself on her knees beside her bed and buried her face in the pillows. There she knelt, unmindful of the dinner waiting downstairs, unmindful of the bright day that was droning on its hours. Whether she prayed she knew not, whether she was weeping she could not have told. Her heart was crying out in one great longing to have this cloud of sorrow that had settled upon David lifted.

She might have knelt there until night had there not come the sound of a knock upon the front door. It startled her to her feet in an instant, and she hastily smoothed her rumpled hair, dashed some water on her eyes, and ran down.

It was the clerk from the office with a letter for her. The post chaise had brought it that afternoon, and he had thought perhaps she would like to have it at once as it was postmarked from her home. Would she tell Mr. Spafford when he returned—he seemed to take it for granted that David was out of town for the day—that everything had been going on all right at the office during his absence and the paper was ready to send to press. He took his departure with a series of bows and smiles, and Marcia flew up to her room to read her letter. It was in the round unformed hand of Mary Ann. Marcia tore it open eagerly. Never had Mary Ann's handwriting looked so pleasant as at that moment. A letter in those days was a rarity at all times, and this one to Marcia in her distress of mind seemed little short of a miracle. It began in Mary Ann's abrupt way, and opened up to her the world of home since she had left it. But a few short days had passed, scarcely yet numbering into weeks, since she left, yet it seemed half a lifetime to the girl promoted so suddenly into womanhood without the accompanying joy of love and close companionship that usually makes desolation impossible.

"DEAR MARSH,"—the letter ran:—

"I expect you think queer of me to write you so soon. I ain't much on writing you know, but something happened right after you leaving and has kept right on happening that made me feel I kinder like to tell you. Don't you mind the mistakes I make. I'm thankful to goodness you ain't the school teacher or I'd never write 'slong s' I'm living, but ennyhow I'm going to tell you all about it.

"The night you went away I was standing down by the gate under the old elm. I had on my best things yet from the wedding, and I hated to go in and have the day over and have to begin putting on my old calico to-morrow morning again, and washing dishes just the same. Seemed as if I couldn't bear to have the world just the same now you was gone away. Well, I heard someone coming down the street, and who do you think it was? Why, Hanford Weston. He came right up to the gate and stopped. I don't know's he ever spoke two words to me in my life except that time he stopped the big boys from snow-balling me and told me to run along quick and git in the school-house while he fit 'em. Well, he stopped and spoke, and he looked so sad, seemed like I knew just what he was feeling sad about, and I told him all about you getting married instead of your sister. He looked at me like he couldn't move for a while and his face was as white as that marble man in the cemetery over Squire Hancock's grave. He grabbed the gate real hard and I thought he was going to fall. He couldn't even move his lips for a while. I felt just awful sorry for him. Something came in my throat like a big stone and my eyes got all blurred with the moonlight. He looked real handsome. I just couldn't help thinking you ought to see him. Bimeby he got his voice back again, and we talked a lot about you. He told me how he used to watch you when you was a little girl wearing pantalettes. You used to sit in the church pew across from his father's and he could just see your big eyes over the top of the door. He says he always thought to himself he would marry you when he grew up. Then when you began to go to school and was so bright he tried hard to study and keep up just to have you think him good enough for you. He owned up he was a bad speller and he'd tried his level best to do better but it didn't seem to come natural, and he thought maybe ef he was a good farmer you wouldn't mind about the spelling. He hired out to his father for the summer and he was trying with all his might to get to be the kind of man t'would suit you, and then when he was plowing and planning all what kind of a house with big columns to the front he would build here comes the coach driving by and *you* in it! He said he thought the sky and fields was all mixed up and his heart was going out of him. He couldn't work any more and he started out after supper to see what it all meant.

"That wasn't just the exact way he told it, Marsh, it was more like poetry, that kind in our reader about "Lord Ullin's daughter"—you know. We used to recite it on examination exhibition. I didn't know Hanford could talk like that. His words were real pretty, kind of sorrowful you know. And it all come over me that you ought to know about it. You're married of course, and can't help it now, but 'taint every girl that has a boy care for her like that from the time she's a baby with a red hood on, and you ought to know 'bout it, fer it wasn't Hanford's fault he didn't have time to tell you. He's just been living fer you fer a number of years, and its kind of hard on him. 'Course you may not care, being you're married and have a fine house and lots of clo'es of your own and a good time, but it does seem hard for him. It seems as if somebody ought to comfort him. I'd like to try if you don't mind. He does seem to like to talk about you to me, and I feel so sorry for him I guess I could comfort him a little, for it seems as if it would be the nicest thing in the world to have some one like you that way for years, just as they do in books, only every time I think about being a comfort to him I think he belongs to you and it ain't right. So Marsh, you just speak out and say if your willing I should try to comfort him a little and make up to him fer what he lost in you, being as you're married and fixed so nice yourself.

"Of course I know I aint pretty like you, nor can't hold my head proud and step high as you always did, even when you was little, but I can feel, and perhaps that's something. Anyhow Hanford's been down three times to talk about you to me, and ef you don't mind I'm going to let him come some more. But if you mind the leastest little bit I want you should say so, for things are mixed in this world and I don't want to get to trampling on any other person's feelings, much less you who have always been my best friend and always will be as long as I live I guess. 'Member how we used to play house on the old flat stone in the orchard, and you give me all the prettiest pieces of china with sprigs on 'em? I aint forgot that, and never will. I shall always say you made the prettiest bride I ever saw, no matter how many more I see, and I hope you won't forget me. It's lonesome here without you. If it wasn't for comforting Hanford I shouldn't care much for anything. I can't think of you a grown up woman. Do you feel any different? I spose you wouldn't climb a fence nor run through the pasture lot for anything now. Have you got a lot of new friends? I wish I could see you. And now Marsh, I want you to write right off and tell me what to do about comforting Hanford, and if you've any message to send to him I think it would be real nice. I hope you've got a good husband and are happy.

"From your devoted and loving school mate,

"MARY ANN FOTHERGILL."

Marcia laid down the letter and buried her face in her hands. To her too had come a thrust which must search her life and change it. So while David wrestled with his sorrow Marcia entered upon the knowledge of her own heart.

There was something in this revelation by Mary Ann of Hanford Weston's feelings toward her that touched her immeasurably. Had it all happened before she left home, had Hanford come to her and told her of his love, she would have turned from him in dismay, almost disgust, and have told him that they were both but children, how could they talk of love. She could never have loved him. She would have felt it instantly, and her mocking laugh might have done a good deal toward saving him from sorrow. But now, with miles between them, with the wall of the solemn marriage vows to separate them forever, with her own youth locked up as she supposed until the day of eternity should perhaps set it free, with no hope of any bright dream of life such as girls have, could she turn from even a school boy's love without a passing tenderness, such as she would never have felt if she had not come away from it all? Told in Mary Ann's blunt way, with her crude attempts at pathos, it reached her as it could not otherwise. With her own new view of life she could sympathize better with another's disappointments. Perhaps her own loneliness gave her pity for another. Whatever it was, Marcia's heart suddenly turned toward Hanford Weston with a great throb of gratitude. She felt that she had been loved, even though it had been impossible for that love to be returned, and that whatever happened she would not go unloved down to the end of her days. Suddenly, out of the midst of the perplexity of her thoughts, there formed a distinct knowledge of what was lacking in her life, a lack she had never felt before, and probably would not have felt now had she not thus suddenly stepped into a place much beyond her years. It seemed to the girl as she sat in the great chintz chair and read and re-read that letter, as if she lived years that afternoon, and all her life was to be changed henceforth. It was not that she was sorry that she could not go back, and live out her girlhood and have it crowned with Hanford Weston's love. Not at all. She knew, as well now as she ever had known, that he could never be anything to her, but she knew also, or thought she knew, that he could have given her something, in his clumsy way, that now she could never have from any man, seeing she was David's and David could not love her that way, of course.

Having come to this conclusion, she arose and wrote a letter giving and bequeathing to Mary Ann Fothergill all right, title, and claim to the affections of Hanford Weston, past, present, and future—sending him a message calculated to smooth his ruffled feelings, with her pretty thanks for his youthful adoration; comfort his sorrow with the thought that it must have been a hallucination, that some day he would find his true ideal which he had only thought he had found in her; and send him on his way rejoicing with her blessings and good wishes for a happy life. As for Mary Ann, for once she received her meed of Marcia's love, for homesick Marcia felt more tenderness for her than she had ever been able to feel before; and Marcia's loving messages set Mary Ann in a flutter of delight, as she laid her plans for comforting Hanford Weston.

CHAPTER XIV

David slowly recovered his poise. Faced by that terrible, impenetrable wall of impossibility he stood helpless, his misery eating in upon his soul, but there still remained the fact that there was nothing, absolutely nothing, which he could possibly do. At times the truth rose to the surface, the wretched truth, that Kate was at fault, that having done the deed she should abide by it, and not try to keep a hold upon him, but it was not often he was able to think in this way. Most of the time he mourned over and for the lovely girl he had lost.

As for Marcia, she came and went unobtrusively, making quiet comfort for David which he scarcely noticed. At times he roused himself to be polite to her, and made a labored effort to do something to amuse her, just as if she had been visiting him as a favor and he felt in duty bound to make the time pass pleasantly, but she troubled him so little with herself, that nearly always he forgot her. Whenever there was any public function to which they were bidden he always told her apologetically, as though it must be as much of a bore to her as to him, and he regretted that it was necessary to go in order to carry out their mutual agreement. Marcia, hailing with delight every chance to go out in search of something which would keep her from thinking the new thoughts which had come to her, demurely covered her pleasure and dressed herself dutifully in the robes made for her sister, hating them secretly the while, and was always ready when he came for her. David had nothing to complain of in his wife, so far as outward duty was concerned, but he was too busy with his own heart's bitterness to even recognize it.

One afternoon, of a day when David had gone out of town not expecting to return until late in the evening, there came a knock at the door.

There was something womanish in the knock, Marcia thought, as she hastened to answer it, and she wondered, hurriedly smoothing her shining hair, if it could be the aunts come to make their fortnightly-afternoon penance visit. She gave a hasty glance into the parlor hoping all was right, and was relieved to make sure she had closed the piano. The aunts would consider it a great breach of housewifely decorum to allow a moment's dust to settle upon its sacred keys.

But it was not the aunts who stood upon the stoop, smiling and bowing with a handsome assurance of his own welcome. It was Harry Temple.

Marcia was not glad to see him. A sudden feeling of unreasoning alarm took possession of her.

"You're all alone this time, sweet lady, aren't you?" he asked with easy nonchalance, as he lounged into the hall without waiting her bidding.

"Sir!" said Marcia, half frightened, half wondering.

But he smiled reassuringly down upon her and took the door knob in his own hands to close the door.

"Your good man is out this time, isn't he?" he smiled again most delightfully. His face was very handsome when he smiled. He knew this fact well.

Marcia did not smile. Why did he speak as if he knew where David was, and seemed to be pleased that he was away?

"My husband is not in at present," she said guardedly, her innocent eyes searching his face, "did you wish to see him?"

She was beautiful as she stood there in the wide hall, with only the light from the high transom over the door, shedding an afternoon glow through its pleated Swiss oval. She looked more sweet and little-girlish than ever, and he felt a strong desire to take her in his arms and tell her so, only he feared, from something he saw in those wide, sweet eyes, that she might take alarm and run away too soon, so he only smiled and said that his business with her husband could wait until another time, and meantime he had called to fulfil his promise to play for her.

She took him into the darkened parlor, gave him the stiffest and stateliest hair-cloth chair; but he walked straight over to the instrument, and with not at all the reverence she liked to treat it, flung back the coverings, threw the lid open, and sat down.

He had white fingers, and he ran them over the keys with an air of being at home among them, light little airs dripping from his touch like dew from a glistening grass blade. Marcia felt there were butterflies in the air, and buzzing bees, and fairy flowers dancing on the slightest of stems, with a sky so blue it seemed to be filled with the sound of lily bells. The music he played was of the nature of what would be styled to-day "popular," for this man was master of nothing but having a good time. Quick music with a jingle he played, that to the puritanic-bred girl suggested nothing but a heart bubbling over with gladness, but he meant it should make her heart flutter and her foot beat time to the tripping measure. In his world feet were attuned to gay music. But Marcia stood with quiet dignity a little away from the instrument, her lips parted, her eyes bright with the pleasure of the melody, her hands clasped, and her breath coming quickly. She was all absorbed with the music. All unknowingly Marcia had placed herself where the light from the window fell full across her face, and every flitting expression as she followed the undulant sounds was visible. The young man gazed, almost as much pleased with the lovely face as Marcia was with the music.

At last he drew a chair quite near his own seat.

"Come and sit down," he said, "and I will sing to you. You did not know I could sing, too, did you? Oh, I can. But you must sit down for I couldn't sing right when you are standing."

He ended with his fascinating smile, and Marcia shyly sat down, though she drew the chair a bit back from where he had placed it and sat up quite straight and stiff with her shoulders erect and her head up. She had forgotten her distrust of the man in what seemed to her his wonderful music. It was all new and strange to her, and she could not know how little there really was to it. She had decided as he played that she liked the kind best that made her think of the birds and the sunny sky, rather than the wild whirly kind that seemed all a mad scramble. She meant to ask him to play over again what he played at the beginning, but he struck into a Scotch love ballad. The melody intoxicated her fancy, and her face shone with pleasure. She had not noticed the words particularly, save that they were of love, and she thought with pain of David and Kate, and how the pleading tenderness might have been his heart calling to hers not to forget his love for her. But Harry Temple mistook her expression for one of interest in himself. With his eyes still upon hers, as a cat might mesmerize a bird, he changed into a minor wail of heart-broken love, whose sadness brought great tears to Marcia's eyes, and deep color to her already burning cheeks, while the music throbbed out her own half-realized loneliness and sorrow. It was as if the sounds painted for her a picture of what she had missed out of love, and set her sorrow flowing tangibly.

The last note died away in an impressive diminuendo, and the young man turned toward her. His eyes were languishing, his voice gentle, persuasive, as though it had but been the song come a little nearer.

"And that is the way I feel toward you, dear," he said, and reached out his white hands to where hers lay forgotten in her lap.

But his hands had scarcely touched hers, before Marcia sprang back, in her haste knocking over the chair.

Erect, her hands snatched behind her, frightened, alert, she stood a moment bewildered, all her fears to the front.

Ah! but he was used to shy maidens. He was not to be baffled thus. A little coaxing, a little gentle persuasion, a little boldness—that was all he needed. He had conquered hearts before, why should he not this unsophisticated one?

"Don't be afraid, dear; there is no one about. And surely there is no harm in telling you I love you, and letting you comfort my poor broken heart to think that I have found you too late—"

He had arisen and with a passionate gesture put his arms about Marcia and before she could know what was coming had pressed a kiss upon her lips.

But she was aroused now. Every angry force within her was fully awake. Every sense of right and justice inherited and taught came flocking forward. Horror unspeakable filled her, and wrath, that such a dreadful thing should come to her. There was no time to think. She brought her two strong supple hands up and beat him in the face, mouth, cheeks, and eyes, with all her might, until he turned blinded; and then she struggled away crying, "You are a wicked man!" and fled from the room.

Out through the hall she sped to the kitchen, and flinging wide the door before her, the nearest one at hand, she fairly flew down the garden walk, past the nodding dahlias, past the basking pumpkins, past the whispering corn, down through the berry bushes, at the lower end of the lot, and behind the currant bushes. She crouched a moment looking back to see if she were pursued. Then imagining she heard a noise from the open door, she scrambled over the low back fence, the high comb with which her hair was fastened falling out unheeded behind her, and all her dark waves of hair coming about her shoulders in wild disarray.

She was in a field of wheat now, and the tall shocks were like waves all about her, thick and close, kissing her as she passed with their bended stalks. Ahead of her it looked like an endless sea to cross before she could reach another fence, and a bare field, and then another fence and the woods. She knew not that in her wake she left a track as clear as if she had set up signals all along the way. She felt that the kind wheat would flow back like real waves and hide the way she had passed over. She only sped on, to the woods. In all the wide world there seemed no refuge but the woods. The woods were home to her. She loved the tall shadows, the whispering music in the upper branches, the quiet places underneath, the hushed silence like a city of refuge with cool wings whereunder to hide. And to it, as her only friend, she was hastening. She went to the woods as she would have flown to the minister's wife at home, if she only had been near, and buried her face in her lap and sobbed out her horror and shame. Breathless she sped, without looking once behind her, now over the next fence and still another. They were nothing to her. She forgot that she was wearing Kate's special sprigged muslin, and that it might tear on the rough fences. She forgot that she was a matron and must not run wild through strange fields. She forgot that some one might be watching her. She forgot everything save that she must get away and hide her poor shamed face.

At last she reached the shelter of the woods, and, with one wild furtive look behind her to assure herself that she was not pursued, she flung herself into the lap of mother earth, and buried her face in the soft moss at the foot of a tree. There she sobbed out her horror and sorrow and loneliness, sobbed until it seemed to her that her heart had gone out with great shudders. Sobbed and sobbed and sobbed! For a time she could not even think clearly. Her brain was confused with the magnitude of what had come to her. She tried to go over the whole happening that afternoon and see if she might have prevented anything. She blamed herself most unmercifully for listening to the foolish music and, too, after her own suspicions had been aroused, though how could she dream any man in his senses would do a thing like that! Not even Captain Leavenworth would stoop to that, she thought. Poor child! She knew so little of the world, and her world had been kept so sweet and pure and free from contamination. She turned cold at the thought of her father's anger if he should hear about this strange young man. She felt sure he would blame her for allowing it. He had tried to teach his girls that they must exercise judgment and discretion, and surely, surely, she must have failed in both or this would not have happened. Oh, why had not the aunts come that afternoon! Why had they not arrived before this man came! And yet, oh, horror! if they had come after he was there! How disgusting he seemed to her with his smirky smile, and slim white fingers! How utterly unfit beside David did he seem to breathe the same air even. David, her David—no, Kate's David! Oh, pity! What a pain the world was!

There was nowhere to turn that she might find a trace of comfort. For what would David say, and how could she ever tell him? Would he find it out if she did not? What would he think of her? Would he blame her? Oh, the agony of it all! What would the aunts think of her! Ah! that was worse than all, for even now she could see the tilt of Aunt Hortense's head, and the purse of Aunt Amelia's lips. How dreadful if they should have to know of it. They would not believe her, unless perhaps Aunt Clarinda might. She did not look wise, but she seemed kind and loving. If it had not been for the other two she might have fled to Aunt Clarinda. Oh, if she might but flee home to her father's house! How could she ever go back to David's house! How could she ever play on that dreadful piano again? She would always see that hateful, smiling face sitting there and think how he had looked at her. Then she shuddered and sobbed harder than ever. And mother earth, true to all her children, received the poor child with open arms. There she lay upon the resinous pine needles, at the foot of the tall trees, and the trees looked down tenderly upon her and consulted in whispers with their heads bent together. The winds blew sweetness from the buckwheat fields in the valley about her, murmuring delicious music in the air above her, and even the birds hushed their loud voices and peeped curiously at the tired, sorrowful creature of another kind that had come among them.

Marcia's overwrought nerves were having their revenge. Tears had their way until she was worn out, and then the angel of sleep came down upon her. There upon the pine-needle bed, with tear-wet cheeks she lay, and slept like a tired child come home to its mother from the tumult of the world.

Harry Temple, recovering from his rebuff, and left alone in the parlor, looked about him with surprise. Never before in all his short and brilliant career as a heart breaker had he met with the like, and this from a mere child! He could not believe his senses! She must have been in play. He would sit still and presently she would come back with eyes full of mischief and beg his pardon. But even as he sat down to wait her coming, something told him he was mistaken and that she would not come. There had been something beside mischief in the smart raps whose tingle even now his cheeks and lips felt. The house, too, had grown strangely hushed as though no one else besides himself were in it. She must have gone out. Perhaps she had been really frightened and would tell somebody! How awkward if she should presently return with one of those grim aunts, or that solemn puritan-like husband of hers. Perhaps he had better decamp while the coast was still clear. She did not seem to be returning and there was no telling what the little fool might do.

With a deliberation which suddenly became feverish in his haste to be away, he compelled himself to walk slowly, nonchalantly out through the hall. Still as a thief he opened and closed the front door and got himself down the front steps, but not so still but that a quick ear caught the sound of the latch as it flew back into place, and the scrape of a boot on the path; and not so invisibly nor so quickly but that a pair of keen eyes saw him.

When Harry Temple had made his way toward the Spafford house that afternoon, with his dauntless front and conceited smile, Miranda had been sent out to pick raspberries along the fence that separated the Heath garden from the Spafford garden.

Harry Temple was too new in the town not to excite comment among the young girls wherever he might go, and Miranda was always having her eye out for anything new. Not for herself! Bless you! no! Miranda never expected anything from a young man for herself, but she was keenly interested in what befell other girls.

So Miranda, crouched behind the berry bushes, watched Harry Temple saunter down the street and saw with surprise that he stopped at the house of her new admiration. Now, although Marcia was a married woman, Miranda felt pleased that she should have the attention of others, and a feeling of pride in her idol, and of triumph over her cousin Hannah that he had not stopped to see her, swelled in her brown calico breast.

She managed to bring her picking as near to the region of the Spafford parlor windows as possible, and much did her ravished ear delight itself in the music that tinkled through the green shaded window, for Miranda had tastes that were greatly appealed to by the gay dance music. She fancied that her idol was the player. But then she heard a man's voice, and her picking stopped short insomuch that her grandmother's strident tones mingled with the liquid tenor of Mr. Temple, calling to Miranda to "be spry there or the sun'll catch you 'fore you get a quart." All at once the music ceased, and then in a minute or two Miranda heard the Spafford kitchen door thrown violently open and saw Marcia rush forth.

She gazed in astonishment, too surprised to call out to her, or to remember to keep on picking for a moment. She watched her as she fairly flew down between the rows of currant bushes, saw the comb fly from her hair, saw the glow of excitement on her cheek, and the fire in her eye, saw her mount the first fence. Then suddenly a feeling of protection arose within her, and, with a hasty glance toward her grandmother's window to satisfy herself that no one else saw the flying figure, she fell to picking with all her might, but what went into her pail, whether raspberries or green leaves or briars, she did not know. Her eyes were on the flying figure through the wheat, and she progressed in her picking very fast toward the lower end of the lot where nothing but runty old sour berries ever grew, if any at all. Once hidden behind the tall corn that grew between her and her grandmother's vigilant gaze, she hastened to the end of the lot and watched Marcia; watched her as she climbed the fences, held her breath at the daring leaps from the top rails, expecting to see the delicate muslin catch on the rough fence and send the flying figure to the ground senseless perhaps. It was like a theatre to Miranda, this watching the beautiful girl in her flight, the long dark hair in the wind, the graceful untrammeled bounds. Miranda watched with unveiled admiration until the dark of the green-blue wood had swallowed her up, then slowly her eyes traveled back over the path which Marcia had taken, back through the meadow and the wheat, to the kitchen door left standing wide. Slowly, painfully, Miranda set herself to understand it. Something had happened! That was flight with fear behind it, fear that left everything else forgotten. What had happened?

Miranda was wiser in her generation than Marcia. She began to put two and two together. Her brows darkened, and a look of cunning came into her honest blue eyes. Stealthily she crept with cat-like quickness along the fence near to the front, and there she stood like a red-haired Nemesis in a sunbonnet, with irate red face, confronting the unsuspecting man as he sauntered forth from the unwelcoming roof where he had whiled away a mistaken hour.

"What you ben sayin' to her?"

It was as if a serpent had stung him, so unexpected, so direct. He jumped aside and turned deadly pale. She knew her chance arrow had struck the truth. But he recovered himself almost immediately when he saw what a harmless looking creature had attacked him.

"Why, my dear girl," he said patronizingly, "you quite startled me! I'm sure you must have made some mistake!"

"I ain't your girl, thank goodness!" snapped Miranda, "and I guess by your looks there ain't anybody 'dear' to you but yourself. But I ain't made a mistake. It's you I was asking. *What you bin in there for?*" There was a blaze of defiance in Miranda's eyes, and her stubby forefinger pointed at him like a shotgun. Before her the bold black eyes quailed for an instant. The young man's hand sought his pocket, brought out a piece of money and extended it.

"Look here, my friend," he said trying another line, "you take this and say nothing more about it. That's a good girl. No harm's been done."

Miranda looked him in the face with noble scorn, and with a sudden motion of her brown hand sent the coin flying on the stone pavement.

"I tell you I'm not your friend, and I don't want your money. I wouldn't trust its goodness any more than your face. As fer keepin' still I'll do as I see fit about it. I intend to know what this means, and if you've made *her* any trouble you'd better leave this town, for I'll make it too unpleasant fer you to stay here!"

With a stealthy glance about him, cautious, concerned, the young man suddenly hurried down the street. He wanted no more parley with this loud-voiced avenging maiden. His fear came back upon him in double force, and he was seen to glance at his watch and quicken his pace almost to a run as though a forgotten engagement had suddenly come to mind. Miranda, scowling, stood and watched him disappear around the corner, then she turned back and began to pick raspberries with a diligence that would have astonished her grandmother had she not been for the last hour engaged with a calling neighbor in the room at the other side of the house, where they were overhauling the character of a fellow church member.

Miranda picked on, and thought on, and could not make up her mind what she ought to do. From time to time she glanced anxiously toward the woods, and then at the lowering sun in the West, and half meditated going after Marcia, but a wholesome fear of her grandmother held her hesitating.

At length she heard a firm step coming down the street. Could it be? Yes, it was David Spafford. How was it he happened to come home so soon? Miranda had heard in a round-about-way, as neighbors hear and know these things, that David had taken the stage that morning, presumably on business to New York, and was hardly expected to return for several days. She had wondered if Marcia would stay all night alone in the house or if she would go to the aunts. But now here was David!

Miranda looked again over the wheat, half expecting to see the flying figure returning in haste, but the parted wheat waved on and sang its song of the harvest, unmindful and alone, with only a fluttering butterfly to give life to the landscape. A little rusty-throated cricket piped a doleful sentence now and then between the silences.

David Spafford let himself in at his own door, and went in search of Marcia.

He wanted to find Marcia for a purpose. The business which had taken him away in the morning, and which he had hardly expected to accomplish before late that night, had been partly transacted at a little tavern where the coach horses had been changed that morning, and where he had met most unexpectedly the two men whom he had been going to see, who were coming straight to his town. So he turned him back with them and came home, and they were at this minute attending to some other business in the town, while he had come home to announce to Marcia that they would take supper with him and perhaps spend the night.

Marcia was nowhere to be found. He went upstairs and timidly knocked at her door, but no answer came. Then he thought she might be asleep and knocked louder, but only the humming-bird in the honeysuckle outside her window sent back a little humming answer through the latch-hole. Finally he ventured to open the door and peep in, but he saw that quiet loneliness reigned there.

He went downstairs again and searched in the pantry and kitchen and then stood still. The back door was stretched open as though it had been thrown back in haste. He followed its suggestion and went out, looking down the little brick path that led to the garden. Ah! what was that? Something gleamed in the sun with a spot of blue behind it. The bit of blue ribbon she had worn at her throat, with a tiny gold brooch unclasped sticking in.

Miranda caught sight of him coming, and crouched behind the currants.

David came on searching the path on every side. A bit of a branch had been torn from a succulent, tender plant that leaned over the path and was lying in the way. It seemed another blaze along the trail. Further down where the bushes almost met a single fragment of a thread waved on a thorn as though it had snatched for more in the passing and had caught only this. David hardly knew whether he was following these little things or not, but at any rate they were apparently not leading him anywhere for he stopped abruptly in front of the fence and looked both ways behind the bushes that grew along in front of it. Then he turned to go back again. Miranda held her breath. Something touched David's foot in turning, and, looking down, he saw Marcia's large shell comb lying there in the grass. Curiously he picked it up and examined it. It was like finding fragments of a wreck along the sand.

All at once Miranda arose from her hiding place and confronted him timidly. She was not the same Miranda who came down upon Harry Temple, however.

"She ain't in the house," she said hoarsely. "She's gone over there!"

David Spafford turned surprised.

"Is that you, Miranda? Oh, thank you! Where do you say she has gone? Where?"

"Through there, don't you see?" and again the stubby forefinger pointed to the rift in the wheat.

David gazed stupidly at the path in the wheat, but gradually it began to dawn upon him that there was a distinct line through it where some one must have gone.

"Yes, I see," he said thinking aloud, "but why should she have gone there? There is nothing over there."

"She went on further, she went to the woods," said Miranda, looking fearfully around lest even now her grandmother might be upon her, "and she was scared, I guess. She looked it. Her hair all come tumblin' down when she clum the fence, an' she just went flyin' over like some bird, didn't care a feather if she did fall, an' she never oncet looked behind her till she come to the woods."

David's bewilderment was growing uncomfortable. There was a shade of alarm in his face and of the embarrassment one feels when a neighbor divulges news about a member of one's own household.

"Why, surely, Miranda, you must be mistaken. Maybe it was some one else you saw. I do not think Mrs. Spafford would be likely to run over there that way, and what in the world would she have to be frightened at?"

"No, I ain't mistaken," said Miranda half sullenly, nettled at his unbelief. "It was her all right. She came flyin' out the kitchen door when I was picking raspberries, and down that path to the fence, and never stopped fer fence ner wheat, ner medder lot, but went into them woods there, right up to the left of them tall pines, and she,—she looked plum scared to death 's if a whole circus menagerie was after her, lions and 'nelefunts an' all. An' I guess she had plenty to be scared at ef I ain't mistaken. That dandy Temple feller went there to call on her, an' I heard him tinklin' that music box, and its my opinion he needs a wallupin'! You better go after her! It's gettin' late and you'll have hard times finding her in the dark. Just you foller her path in the wheat, and then make fer them pines. I'd a gone after her myself only grandma'd make sech a fuss, and hev to know it all. You needn't be afraid o' me. I'll keep still."

By this time David was thoroughly alive to the situation and much alarmed. He mounted the fence with alacrity, gave one glance with "thank you" at Miranda, and disappeared through the wheat, Miranda watched him till she was sure he was making for the right spot, then with a sigh of relief she hastened into the house with her now brimming pail of berries.

CHAPTER XV

As David made his way with rapid strides through the rippling wheat, he experienced a series of sensations. For the first time since his wedding day he was aroused to entirely forget himself and his pain. What did it mean? Marcia frightened! What at? Harry Temple at their house! What did he know of Harry Temple? Nothing beyond the mere fact that Hannah Heath had introduced him and that he was doing business in the town. But why had Mr. Temple visited the house? He could have no possible business with himself, David was sure; moreover he now remembered having seen the young man standing near the stable that morning when he took his seat in the coach, and knew that he must have heard his remark that he would not return till the late coach that night, or possibly not till the next day. He remembered as he said it that he had unconsciously studied Mr. Temple's face and noted its weak points. Did the young man then have a purpose in coming to the house during his absence? A great anger rose within him at the thought.

There was one strange thing about David's thoughts. For the first time he looked at himself in the light of Marcia's natural protector—her husband. He suddenly saw a duty from himself to her, aside from the mere feeding and clothing her. He felt a personal responsibility, and an actual interest in her. Out of the whole world, now, he was the only one she could look to for help.

It gave him a feeling of possession that was new, and almost seemed pleasant. He forgot entirely the errand that had made him come to search for Marcia in the first place, and the two men who were probably at that moment preparing to go to his house according to their invitation. He forgot everything but Marcia, and strode into the purply-blue shadows of the wood and stopped to listen.

The hush there seemed intense. There were no echoes lingering of flying feet down that pine-padded pathway of the aisle of the woods. It was long since he had had time to wander in the woods, and he wondered at their silence. So much whispering above, the sky so far away, the breeze so quiet, the bird notes so subdued, it seemed almost uncanny. He had not remembered that it was thus in the woods. It struck him in passing that here would be a good place to bring his pain some day when he had time to face it again, and wished to be alone with it.

He took his hat in his hand and stepped firmly into the vast solemnity as if he had entered a great church when the service was going on, on an errand of life and death that gave excuse for profaning the holy silence. He went a few paces and stopped again, listening. Was that a long-drawn sighing breath he heard, or only the wind soughing through the waving tassels overhead? He summoned his voice to call. It seemed a great effort, and sounded weak and feeble under the grandeur of the vaulted green dome. "Marcia!" he called,—and "Marcia!"realizing as he did so that it was the first time he had called her by her name, or sought after her in any way. He had always said "you" to her, or "child," or spoken of her in company as "Mrs. Spafford," a strange and far-off mythical person whose very intangibility had separated her from himself immeasurably.

He went further into the forest, called again, and yet again, and stood to listen. All was still about him, but in the far distance he heard the faint report of a gun. With a new thought of danger coming to mind he hurried further into the shadows. The gun sounded again more clearly. He shuddered involuntarily and looked about in all directions, hoping to see the gleam of her gown. It was not likely there were any wild beasts about these parts, so near the town and yet, they had been seen occasionally,—a stray fox, or even a bear,—and the sun was certainly very low. He glanced back, and the low line of the horizon gleamed the gold of intensified shining that is the sun's farewell for the night. The gun again! Stray shots had been known to kill people wandering in the forest. He was growing nervous as a woman now, and went this way and that calling, but still no answer came. He began to think he was not near the clump of pines of which Miranda spoke, and went a little to the right and then turned to look back to where he had entered the wood, and there, almost at his feet, she lay!

She slept as soundly as if she had been lying on a couch of velvet, one round white arm under her cheek. Her face was flushed with weeping, and her lashes still wet. Her tender, sensitive mouth still quivered slightly as she gave a long-drawn breath with a catch in it that seemed like a sob, and all her lovely dark hair floated about her as if it were spread upon a wave that upheld her. She was beautiful indeed as she lay there sleeping, and the man, thus suddenly come upon her, anxious and troubled and every nerve quivering, stopped, awed with the beauty of her as if she had been some heavenly being suddenly confronting him. He stepped softly to her side and bending down observed her, first anxiously, to make sure she was alive and safe, then searchingly, as though he would know every detail of the picture there before him because it was his, and he not only had a right but a duty to possess it, and to care for it.

She might have been a statue or a painting as he looked upon her and noted the lovely curve of her flushed cheek, but when his eyes reached the firm little brown hand and the slender finger on which gleamed the wedding ring that was not really hers, something pathetic in the tear-wet lashes, and the whole sorrowful, beautiful figure, touched him with a great tenderness, and he stooped down gently and put his arm about her.

"Marcia,—child!" he said in a low, almost crooning voice, as one might wake a baby from its sleep, "Marcia, open your eyes, child, and tell me if you are all right."

At first she only stirred uneasily and slept on, the sleep of utter exhaustion; but he raised her, and, sitting down beside her, put her head upon his shoulder, speaking gently. Then Marcia opened her eyes bewildered, and with a start, sprang back and looked at David, as though she would be sure it was he and not that other dreadful man from whom she had fled.

"Why, child! What's the matter?" said David, brushing her hair back from her face. Bewildered still, Marcia scarcely knew him, his voice was so strangely sweet and sympathetic. The tears were coming back, but she could not stop them. She made one effort to control herself and speak, but her lips quivered a moment, and then the flood-gates opened again, and she covered her face with her hands and shook with sobs. How could she tell David what a dreadful thing had happened, now, when he was kinder to her than he had ever thought of being before! He would grow grave and stern when she had told him, and she could not bear that. He would likely blame her too, and how could she endure more?

But he drew her to him again and laid her head against his coat, trying to smooth her hair with unaccustomed passes of his hand. By and by the tears subsided and she could control herself again. She hushed her sobs and drew back a little from the comforting rough coat where she had lain.

"Indeed, indeed, I could not help it, David,"—she faltered, trying to smile like a bit of rainbow through the rain.

"I know you couldn't, child." His answer was wonderfully kind and his eyes smiled at her as they had never done before. Her heart gave a leap of astonishment and fluttered with gladness over it. It was so good to have David care. She had not known how much she wanted him to speak to her as if he saw her and thought a little about her.

"And now what was it? Remember I do not know. Tell me quick, for it is growing late and damp, and you will take cold out here in the woods with that thin frock on. You are chilly already."

"I better go at once," she said reservedly, willing to put off the telling as long as possible, peradventure to avoid it altogether.

"No, child," he said firmly drawing her back again beside him, "you must rest a minute yet before taking that long walk. You are weary and excited, and besides it will do you good to tell me. What made you run off up here? Are you homesick?"

He scanned her face anxiously. He began to fear with sudden compunction that the sacrifice he had accepted so easily had been too much for the victim, and it suddenly began to be a great comfort to him to have Marcia with him, to help him hide his sorrow from the world. He did not know before that he cared.

"I was frightened," she said, with drooping lashes. She was trying to keep her lips and fingers from trembling, for she feared greatly to tell him all. But though the woods were growing dusky he saw the fluttering little fingers and gathered them firmly in his own.

"Now, child," he said in that tone that even his aunts obeyed, "tell me all. What frightened you, and why did you come up here away from everybody instead of calling for help?"

Brought to bay she lifted her beautiful eyes to his face and told him briefly the story, beginning with the night when she had first met Harry Temple. She said as little about music as possible, because she feared that the mention of the piano might be painful to David, but she made the whole matter quite plain in a few words, so that David could readily fill in between the lines.

"Scoundrel!" he murmured clenching his fists, "he ought to be strung up!" Then quite gently again, "Poor child! How frightened you must have been! You did right to run away, but it was a dangerous thing to run out here! Why, he might have followed you!"

"Oh!" said Marcia, turning pale, "I never thought of that. I only wanted to get away from everybody. It seemed so dreadful I did not want anybody to know. I did not want you to know. I wanted to run away and hide, and never come back!" She covered her face with her hands and shuddered. David thought the tears were coming back again.

"Child, child!" he said gently, "you must not talk that way. What would I do if you did that?" and he laid his hand softly upon the bowed head.

It was the first time that anything like a personal talk had passed between them, and Marcia felt a thrill of delight at his words. It was like heavenly comfort to her wounded spirit.

She stole a shy look at him under her lashes, and wished she dared say something, but no words came. They sat for a moment in silence, each feeling a sort of comforting sense of the other's presence, and each clasping the hand of the other with clinging pressure, yet neither fully aware of the fact.

The last rays of the sun which had been lying for a while at their feet upon the pine needles suddenly slipped away unperceived, and behold! the world was in gloom, and the place where the two sat was almost utterly dark. David became aware of it first, and with sudden remembrance of his expected guests he started in dismay.

"Child!" said he,—but he did not let go of her hand, nor forget to put the tenderness in his voice, "the sun has gone down, and here have I been forgetting what I came to tell you in the astonishment over what you had to tell me. We must hurry and get back. We have guests to-night to supper, two gentlemen, very distinguished in their lines of work. We have business together, and I must make haste. I doubt not they are at the house already, and what they think of me I cannot tell; let us hurry as fast as possible."

"Oh, David!" she said in dismay. "And you had to come out here after me, and have stayed so long! What a foolish girl I have been and what a mess I have made! They will perhaps be angry and go away, and I will be to blame. I am afraid you can never forgive me."

"Don't worry, child," he said pleasantly. "It couldn't be helped, you know, and is in no wise your fault. I am only sorry that these two gentlemen will delay me in the pleasure of hunting up that scoundrel of a Temple and suggesting that he leave town by the early morning stage. I should like to give him what Miranda suggested, a good 'wallupin',' but perhaps that would be undignified."

He laughed as he said it, a hearty laugh with a ring to it like his old self. Marcia felt happy at the sound. How wonderful it would be if he would be like that to her all the time! Her heart swelled with the great thought of it.

He helped her to her feet and taking her hand led her out to the open field where they could walk faster. As he walked he told her about Miranda waiting for him behind the currant bushes. They laughed together and made the way seem short.

It was quite dark now, with the faded moon trembling feebly in the West as though it meant to retire early, and wished they would hurry home while she held her light for them. David had drawn Marcia's arm within his, and then, noticing that her dress was thin, he pulled off his coat and put it firmly about her despite her protest that she did not need it, and so, warmed, comforted, and cheered Marcia's feet hurried back over the path she had taken in such sorrow and fright a few hours before.

When they could see the lights of the village twinkling close below them David began to tell her about the two men who were to be their guests, if they were still waiting, and so interesting was his brief story of each that Marcia hardly knew they were at home before David was helping her over their own back fence.

"Oh, David! There seems to be a light in the kitchen! Do you suppose they have gone in and are getting their own supper? What shall I do with my hair? I cannot go in with it this way. How did that light get there?"

"Here!" said David, fumbling in his pocket, "will this help you?" and he brought out the shell comb he had picked up in the garden.

By the light of the feeble old moon David watched her coil the long wavy hair and stood to pass his criticism upon the effect before they should go in. They were just back of the tall sunflowers, and talked in whispers. It was all so cheery, and comradey, and merry, that Marcia hated to go in and have it over, for she could not feel that this sweet evening hour could last. Then they took hold of hands and swiftly, cautiously, stole up to the kitchen window and looked in. The door still stood open as both had left it that afternoon, and there seemed to be no one in the kitchen. A candle was burning on the high little shelf over the table, and the tea kettle was singing on the crane by the hearth, but the room was without occupant. Cautiously, looking questioningly at one another, they stole into the kitchen, each dreading lest the aunts had come by chance and discovered their lapse. There was a light in the front part of the house and they could hear voices, two men were earnestly discussing politics. They listened longer, but no other presence was revealed.

David in pantomime outlined the course of action, and Marcia, understanding perfectly flew up the back stairs as noiselessly as a mouse, to make her toilet after her nap in the woods, while David with much show and to-do of opening and shutting the wide-open kitchen door walked obviously into the kitchen and hurried through to greet his guests wondering,—not suspecting in the least,—what good angel had been there to let them in.

Good fortune had favored Miranda. The neighbor had stayed longer than usual, perhaps in hopes of an invitation to stay to tea and share in the gingerbread she could smell being taken from the oven by Hannah, who occasionally varied her occupations by a turn at the culinary art. Hannah could make delicious gingerbread. Her grandmother had taught her when she was but a child.

Miranda stole into the kitchen when Hannah's back was turned and picked over her berries so fast that when Hannah came into the pantry to set her gingerbread to cool Miranda had nearly all her berries in the big yellow bowl ready to wash, and Hannah might conjecture if she pleased that Miranda had been some time picking them over. It is not stated just how thoroughly those berries were picked over. But Miranda cared little for that. Her mind was upon other things. The pantry window overlooked the hills and the woods. She could see if David and Marcia were coming back soon. She wanted to watch her play till the close, and had no fancy for having the curtain fall in the middle of the most exciting act, the rescue of the princess. But the talk in the sitting room went on and on. By and by Hannah Heath washed her hands, untied her apron, and taking her sunbonnet slipped over to Ann Bertram's for a pattern of her new sleeve. Miranda took the opportunity to be off again.

Swiftly down behind the currants she ran, and standing on the fence behind the corn she looked off across the wheat, but no sign of anybody yet coming out of the woods was granted her. She stood so a long time. It was growing dusk. She wondered if Harry Temple had shut the front door when he went out. But then David went in that way, and he would have closed it, of course. Still, he went away in a hurry, maybe it would be as well to go and look. She did not wish to be caught by her grandmother, so she stole along like a cat close to the dark berry bushes, and the gathering dusk hid her well. She thought she could see from the front of the fence whether the door looked as if it were closed. But there were people coming up the street. She would wait till they had passed before she looked over the fence.

They were two men coming, slowly, and in earnest conversation upon some deeply interesting theme. Each carried a heavy carpet-bag, and they walked wearily, as if their business were nearly over for the day and they were coming to a place of rest.

"This must be the house, I think," said one. "He said it was exactly opposite the Seceder church. That's the church, I believe. I was here once before."

"There doesn't seem to be a light in the house," said the other, looking up to the windows over the street. "Are you sure? Brother Spafford said he was coming directly home to let his wife know of our arrival."

"A little strange there's no light yet, for it is quite dark now, but I'm sure this must be the house. Maybe they are all in the kitchen and not expecting us quite so soon. Let's try anyhow," said the other, setting down his carpet-bag on the stoop and lifting the big brass knocker.

Miranda stood still debating but a moment. The situation was made plain to her in an instant. Not for nothing had she stood at Grandma Heath's elbow for years watching the movements of her neighbors and interpreting exactly what they meant. Miranda's wits were sharpened for situations of all kinds. Miranda was ready and loyal to those she adored. Without further ado she hastened to a sheltered spot she knew and climbed the picket fence which separated the Heath garden from the Spafford side yard. Before the brass knocker had sounded through the empty house the second time Miranda had crossed the side porch, thrown her sunbonnet upon a chair in the dark kitchen, and was hastening with noisy, encouraging steps to the front door.

She flung it wide open, saying in a breezy voice, "Just wait till I get a light, won't you, the wind blew the candle out."

There wasn't a particle of wind about that soft September night, but that made little difference to Miranda. She was part of a play and she was acting her best. If her impromptu part was a little irregular, it was at least well meant, boldly and bravely presented.

Miranda found a candle on the shelf and, stooping to the smouldering fire upon the hearth, blew and coaxed it into flame enough to light it.

"This is Mr. Spafford's home, is it not?" questioned the old gentleman whom Miranda had heard speak first on the sidewalk.

"Oh, yes, indeed," said the girl glibly. "Jest come in and set down. Here, let me take your hats. Jest put your bags right there on the floor."

"You are— Are you—Mrs. Spafford?" hesitated the courtly old gentleman.

"Oh, landy sakes, no, I ain't her," laughed Miranda well pleased. "Mis' Spafford had jest stepped out a bit when her husband come home, an' he's gone after her. You see she didn't expect her husband home till late to-night. But you set down. They'll be home real soon now. They'd oughter ben here before this. I 'spose she'd gone on further'n she thought she'd go when she stepped out."

"It's all right," said the other gentleman, "no harm done, I'm sure. I hope we shan't inconvenience Mrs. Spafford any coming so unexpectedly."

"No, indeedy!" said quick-witted Miranda. "You can't ketch Mis' Spafford unprepared if you come in the middle o' the night. She's allus ready fer comp'ny." Miranda's eyes shone. She felt she was getting on finely doing the honors.

"Well, that's very nice. I'm sure it makes one feel at home. I wonder now if she would mind if we were to go right up to our room and wash our hands. I feel so travel-stained. I'd like to be more presentable before we meet her," said the first gentleman, who looked very weary.

But Miranda was not dashed.

"Why, that's all right. 'Course you ken go right up. Jest you set in the keepin' room a minnit while I run up'n be sure the water pitcher's filled. I ain't quite sure 'bout it. I won't be long."

Miranda seated them in the parlor with great gusto and hastened up the back stairs to investigate. She was not at all sure which room would be called the guest room and whether the two strangers would have a room apiece or occupy the same together. At least it would be safe to show them one till the mistress of the house returned. She peeped into Marcia's room, and knew it instinctively before she caught sight of a cameo brooch on the pin cushion, and a rose colored ribbon neatly folded lying on the foot of the bed where it had been forgotten. That question settled, she thought any other room would do, and chose the large front room across the hall with its high four-poster and the little ball fringe on the valance and canopy. Having lighted the candle which stood in a tall glass candlestick on the high chest of drawers, she hurried down to bid her guests come up.

Then she hastened back into the kitchen and went to work with swift skilful fingers. Her breath came quickly and her cheeks grew red with the excitement of it all. It was like playing fairy. She would get supper for them and have everything all ready when the mistress came, so that there would be no bad breaks. She raked the fire and filled the tea kettle, swinging it from the crane. Then she searched where she thought such things should be and found a table cloth and set the table. Her hands trembled as she put out the sprigged china that was kept in the corner cupboard. Perhaps this was wrong, and she would be blamed for it, but at least it was what she would have done, she thought, if she were mistress of this house and had two nice gentlemen come to stay to tea. It was not often that Grandmother Heath allowed her to handle her sprigged china, to be sure, so Miranda felt the joy and daring of it all the more. Once a delicate cup slipped and rolled over on the table and almost reached the edge. A little more and it would have rolled off to the floor and been shivered into a dozen fragments, but Miranda spread her apron in front and caught it fairly as it started and then hugged it in fear and delight for a moment as she might have done a baby that had been in danger. It was a great pleasure to her to set that table. In the first place she was not doing it to order but because she wanted to please and surprise some one whom she adored, and in the second place it was an adventure. Miranda had longed for an adventure all her life and now she thought it had come to her.

When the table was set it looked very pretty. She slipped into the pantry and searched out the stores. It was not hard to find all that was needed; cold ham, cheese, pickles, seed cakes, gingerbread, fruit cake, preserves and jelly, bread and raised biscuit, then she went down cellar and found the milk and cream and butter. She had just finished the table and set out the tea pot and caddy of tea when she heard the two gentlemen coming down the stairs. They went into the parlor and sat down, remarking that their friend had a pleasant home, and then Miranda heard them plunge into a political discussion again and she felt that they were safe for a while. She stole out into the dewy dark to see if there were yet signs of the home-comers. A screech owl hooted across the night. She stood a while by the back fence looking out across the dark sea of whispering wheat. By and by she thought she heard subdued voices above the soft swish of the parting wheat, and by the light of the stars she saw them coming. Quick as a wink she slid over the fence into the Heath back-yard and crouched in her old place behind the currant bushes. So she saw them come up together, saw David help Marcia over the fence and watched them till they had passed up the walk to the light of the kitchen door. Then swiftly she turned and glided to her own home, well knowing the reckoning that would be in store for her for this daring bit of recreation. There was about her, however, an air of triumphant joy as she entered.

"Where have you ben to, Miranda Griscom, and what on airth you ben up to now?" was the greeting she received as she lifted the latch of the old green kitchen door of her grandmother's house.

Miranda knew that the worst was to come now, for her grandmother never mentioned the name of Griscom unless she meant business. It was a hated name to her because of the man who had broken the heart of her daughter. Grandma Heath always felt that Miranda was an out and out Griscom with not a streak of Heath about her. The Griscoms all had red hair. But Miranda lifted her chin high and felt like a princess in disguise.

"Ben huntin' hen's eggs down in the grass," she said, taking the first excuse that came into her head. "Is it time to get supper?"

"Hen's eggs! This time o' night an' dark as pitch. Miranda Griscom, you ken go up to your room an' not come down tell I call you!"

It was a dire punishment, or would have been if Miranda had not had her head full of other things, for the neighbor had been asked to tea and there would have been much to hear at the table. Besides, it was apparent that her disgrace was to be made public. However, Miranda did not care. She hastened to her little attic window, which looked down, as good fortune would have it, upon the dining-room windows of the Spafford house. With joy Miranda observed that no one had thought to draw down the shades and she might sit and watch the supper served over the way,—the supper she had prepared,—and might think how delectable the doughnuts were, and let her mouth water over the currant jelly and the quince preserves and pretend she was a guest, and forget the supper downstairs she was missing.

CHAPTER XVI

David made what apology he could for his absence on the arrival of his guests, and pondered in his heart who it could have been that they referred to as "the maid," until he suddenly remembered Miranda, and inwardly blessed her for her kindliness. It was more than he would have expected from any member of the Heath household. Miranda's honest face among the currant bushes when she had said, "You needn't be afraid of me, I'll keep still," came to mind. Miranda had evidently scented out the true state of the case and filled in the breach, taking care not to divulge a word. He blest her kindly heart and resolved to show his gratitude to her in some way. Could poor Miranda, sitting supperless in the dark, have but known his thought, her lonely heart would have fluttered happily. But she did not, and virtue had to bring its own reward in a sense of duty done. Then, too, there was a spice of adventure to Miranda's monotonous life in what she had done, and she was not altogether sad as she sat and let her imagination revel in what the Spaffords had said and thought, when they found the house lighted and supper ready. It was better than playing house down behind the barn when she was a little girl.

Marcia was the most astonished when she slipped down from her hurried toilet and found the table decked out in all the house afforded, fairly groaning under its weight of pickles, preserves, doughnuts, and pie. In fact, everything that Miranda had found she had put upon that table, and it is safe to say that the result was not quite as it would have been had the preparation of the supper been left to Marcia.

She stood before it and looked, and could not keep from laughing softly to herself at the array of little dishes of things. Marcia thought at first that one of the aunts must be here, in the parlor, probably entertaining the guests, and that the supper was a reproof to her for being away when she should have been at home attending to her duties, but still she was puzzled. It scarcely seemed like the aunts to set a table in such a peculiar manner. The best china was set out, it is true, but so many little bits of things were in separate dishes. There was half a mould of currant jelly in a large china plate, there was a fresh mould of quince jelly quivering on a common dish. All over the table in every available inch there was something. It would not do to call the guests out to a table like that. What would David say? And yet, if one of the aunts had set it and was going to stay to tea, would she be hurt? She tiptoed to the door and listened, but heard no sound save of men's voices. If an aunt had been here she was surely gone now and would be none the wiser if a few dishes were removed.

With swift fingers Marcia weeded out the things, and set straight those that were to remain, and then made the tea. She was so quick about it David had scarcely time to begin to worry because supper was not announced before she stood in the parlor door, shy and sweet, with a brilliant color in her cheeks. His little comrade, David felt her to be, and again it struck him that she was beautiful as he arose to introduce her to the guests. He saw their open admiration as they greeted her, and he found himself wondering what they would have thought of Kate, wild-rose Kate with her graceful witching ways. A tinge of sadness came into his face, but something suggested to him the thought that Marcia was even more beautiful than Kate, more like a half-blown bud of a thing. He wondered that he had never noticed before how her eyes shone. He gave her a pleasant smile as they passed into the hall, which set the color flaming in her cheeks again. David seemed different somehow, and that lonely, set-apart feeling that she had had ever since she came here to live was gone. David was there and he understood, at least a little bit, and they had something,—just something, even though it was but a few minutes in a lonely woods and some gentle words of his,—to call their very own together. At least that experience did not belong to Kate, never had been hers, and could not have been borrowed from her. Marcia sighed a happy sigh as she took her seat at the table.

The talk ran upon Andrew Jackson, and some utterances of his in his last message to Congress. The elder of the two gentlemen expressed grave fears that a mistake had been made in policy and that the country would suffer.

Governor Clinton was mentioned and his policy discussed. But all this talk was familiar to Marcia. Her father had been interested in public affairs always, and she had been brought up to listen to discussions deep and long, and to think about such things for herself. When she was quite a little girl her father had made her read the paper aloud to him, from one end to the other, as he lay back in his big chair with his eyes closed and his shaggy brows drawn thoughtfully into a frown. Sometimes as she read he would burst forth with a tirade against this or that man or set of men who were in opposition to his own pronounced views, and he would pour out a lengthy reply to little Marcia as she sat patient, waiting for a chance to go on with her reading. As she grew older she became proud of the distinction of being her father's *confidante* politically, and she was able to talk on such matters as intelligently and as well if not better than most of the men who came to the house. It was a position which no one disputed with her. Kate had been much too full of her own plans and Madam Schuyler too busy with household affairs to bother with politics and newspapers, so Marcia had always been the one called upon to read when her father's eyes were tired. As a consequence she was far beyond other girls of her age in knowledge on public affairs. Well she knew what Andrew Jackson thought about the tariff, and about the system of canals, and about improvements in general. She knew which men in Congress were opposed to and which in favor of certain bills. All through the struggle for improvements in New York state she had been an eager observer. The minutest detail of the Erie canal project had interested her, and she was never without her own little private opinion in the matter, which, however, seldom found voice except in her eager eyes, whose listening lights would have been an inspiration to the most eloquent speaker.

Therefore, Marcia as she sat behind her sprigged china teacups and demurely poured tea, was taking in all that had been said, and she drew her breath quickly in a way she had when she was deeply excited, as at last the conversation neared the one great subject of interest which to her seemed of most importance in the country at the present day, the project of a railroad run by steam.

Nothing was too great for Marcia to believe. Her father had been inclined to be conservative in great improvements. He had favored the Erie canal, though had feared it would be impossible to carry so great a project through, and Marcia in her girlish mind had rejoiced with a joy that to her was unspeakable when it had been completed and news had come that many packets were travelling day and night upon the wonderful new water way. There had been a kind of triumph in her heart to think that men who could study out these big schemes and plan it all, had been able against so great odds to carry out their project and prove to all unbelievers that it was not only possible but practicable.

Marcia's brain was throbbing with the desire for progress. If she were a man with money and influence she felt she would so much like to go out into the world and make stupid people do the things for the country that ought to be done. Progress had been the keynote of her upbringing, and she was teeming with energy which she had no hope could ever be used to help along that for which she felt her ambitions rising. She wanted to see the world alive, and busy, the great cities connected with one another. She longed to have free access to cities, to great libraries, to pictures, to wonderful music. She longed to meet great men and women, the men and women who were making the history of the world, writing, speaking, and doing things that were moulding public opinion. Reforms of all sorts were what helped along and made possible her desires. Why did not the people want a steam railroad? Why were they so ready to say it could never succeed, that it would be an impossibility; that the roads could not be made strong enough to bear so great weights and so constant wear and tear? Why did they interpose objections to every suggestion made by inventors and thinking men? Why did even her dear father who was so far in advance of his times in many ways, why did even he too shake his head and say that he feared it would never be in this country, at least not in his day, that it was impracticable?

The talk was very interesting to Marcia. She ate bits of her biscuit without knowing, and she left her tea untasted till it was cold. The younger of the two guests was talking. His name was Jervis. Marcia thought she had heard the name somewhere, but had not yet placed him in her mind:

"Yes," said he, with an eager look on his face, "it is coming, it is coming sooner than they think. Oliver Evans said, you know, that good roads were all we could expect one generation to do. The next must make canals, the next might build a railroad which should run by horse power, and perhaps the next would run a railroad by steam. But we shall not have to wait so long. We shall have steam moving railway carriages before another year."

"What!" said David, "you don't mean it! Have you really any foundation for such a statement?" He leaned forward, his eyes shining and his whole attitude one of deep interest. Marcia watched him, and a great pride began to glow within her that she belonged to him. She looked at the other men. Their eyes were fixed upon David with heightening pleasure and pride.

The older man watched the little tableau a moment and then he explained:

"The Mohawk and Hudson Company have just made an engagement with Mr. Jervis as chief engineer of their road. He expects to run that road by steam!"

He finished his fruit cake and preserves under the spell of astonishment he had cast upon his host and hostess.

David and Marcia turned simultaneously toward Mr. Jervis for a confirmation of this statement. Mr. Jervis smiled in affirmation.

"But will it not be like all the rest, no funds?" asked David a trifle sadly. "It may be years even yet before it is really started."

But Mr. Jervis' face was reassuring.

"The contract is let for the grading. In fact work has already begun. I expect to begin laying the track by next Spring, perhaps sooner. As soon as the track is laid we shall show them."

David's eyes shone and he reached out and grasped the hand of the man who had the will and apparently the means of accomplishing this great thing for the country.

"It will make a wonderful change in the whole land," said David musingly. He had forgotten to eat. His face was aglow and a side of his nature which Marcia did not know was uppermost. Marcia saw the man, the thinker, the writer, the former of public opinion, the idealist. Heretofore David had been to her in the light of her sister's lover, a young man of promise, but that was all. Now she saw something more earnest, and at once it was revealed to her what a man he was, a man like her father. David's eyes were suddenly drawn to meet hers. He looked on Marcia and seemed to be sharing his thought with her, and smiled a smile of comradeship. He felt all at once that she could and would understand his feelings about this great new enterprise, and would be glad too. It pleased him to feel this. It took a little of his loneliness away. Kate would never have been interested in these things. He had never expected such sympathy from her. She had been something beautiful and apart from his world, and as such he had adored her. But it was pleasant to have some one who could understand and feel as he did. Just then he was not thinking of his lost Kate. So he smiled and Marcia felt the glow of warmth from his look and returned it, and the two visitors knew that they were among friends who understood and sympathized.

"Yes, it will make a change," said the older man. "I hope I may live to see at least a part of it."

"If you succeed there will be many others to follow. The land will soon be a network of railroads," went on David, still musing.

"We shall succeed!" said Mr. Jervis, closing his lips firmly in a way that made one sure he knew whereof he spoke.

"And now tell me about it," said David, with his most engaging smile, as a child will ask to have a story. David could be most fascinating when he felt he was in a sympathetic company. At other times he was wont to be grave, almost to severity. But those who knew him best and had seen him thus melted into child-likeenthusiasm, felt his lovableness as the others never dreamed.

The table talk launched into a description of the proposed road, the road bed, the manner of laying the rails, their thickness and width, and the way of bolting them down to the heavy timbers that lay underneath. It was all intensely fascinating to Marcia. Mr. Jervis took knives and forks to illustrate and then showed by plates and spoons how they were fastened down.

David asked a question now and then, took out his note book and wrote down some things. The two guests were eager and plain in their answers. They wanted David to write it up. They wanted the information to be accurate and full.

"The other day I saw a question in a Baltimore paper, sent in by a subscriber, 'What is a railroad?'" said the old gentleman, "and the editor's reply was, 'Can any of our readers answer this question and tell us what is a railroad?'"

There was a hearty laugh over the unenlightened unbelievers who seemed to be only too willing to remain in ignorance of the march of improvement.

David finally laid down his note book, feeling that he had gained all the information he needed at present. "I have much faith in you and your skill, but I do not quite see how you are going to overcome all the obstacles. How, for instance, are you going to overcome the inequalities in the road? Our country is not a flat even one like those abroad where the railroad has been tried. There are sharp grades, and many curves will be necessary," said he.

Mr. Jervis had shoved his chair back from the table, but now he drew it up again sharply and began to move the dishes back from his place, a look of eagerness gleaming in his face.

Once again the dishes and cups were brought into requisition as the engineer showed a crude model, in china and cutlery, of an engine he proposed to have constructed, illustrating his own idea about a truck for the forward wheels which should move separately from the back wheels and enable the engine to conform to curves more readily.

Marcia sat with glowing cheeks watching the outline of history that was to be, not knowing that the little model before her, made from her own teacups and saucers, was to be the model for all the coming engines of the many railroads of the future.

Finally the chairs were pushed back, and yet the talk went on. Marcia slipped silently about conveying the dishes away. And still the guests sat talking. She could hear all they said even when she was in the kitchen washing the china, for she did it very softly and never a clink hid a word. They talked of Governor Clinton again and of his attitude toward the railroad. They spoke of Thurlow Weed and a number of others whose names were familiar to Marcia in the papers she had read to her father. They told how lately on the Baltimore and Ohio railroad Peter Cooper had experimented with a little locomotive, and had beaten a gray horse attached to another car.

Marcia smiled brightly as she listened, and laid the delicate china teapot down with care lest she should lose a word. But ever with her interest in the march of civilization, there were other thoughts mingling. Thoughts of David and of how he would be connected with it all. He would write it up and be identified with it. He was brave enough to face any new movement.

David's paper was a temperance paper. There were not many temperance papers in those days. David was brave. He had already faced a number of unpleasant circumstances in consequence. He was not afraid of sneers or sarcasms, nor of being called a fanatic. He had taken such a stand that even those who were opposed had to respect him. Marcia felt the joy of a great pride in David to-night.

She sang a happy little song at the bottom of her heart as she worked. The new railroad was an assured thing, and David was her comrade, that was the song, and the refrain was, "David, David, David!"

Later, after the guests had talked themselves out and taken their candles to their rooms, David with another comrade's smile, and a look in his eyes that saw visions of the country's future, and for this one night at least promised not to dream of the past, bade her good night.

She went up to her white chamber and lay down upon the pillow, whose case was fragrant of lavendar blossoms, dreaming with a smile of to-morrow. She thought she was riding in a strange new railroad train with David's arm about her and Harry Temple running along at his very best pace to try to catch them, but he could not.

Miranda, at her supperless window, watched the evening hours and thought many thoughts. She wondered why they stayed in the dining room so late, and why they did not go into the parlor and make Marcia play the"music box" as she called it; and why there was a light so long in that back chamber over the kitchen. Could it be they had put one of the guests there? Surely not. Perhaps that was David's study. Perhaps he was writing. Ah! She had guessed aright. David was sitting up to write while the inspiration was upon him.

But Miranda slept and ceased to wonder long before David's light was extinguished, and when he finally lay down it was with a body healthily weary, and a mind for the time free from any intruding thought of himself and his troubles.

He had written a most captivating article that would appear in his paper in a few days, and which must convince many doubters that a railroad was at last an established fact among them.

There were one or two points which he must ask the skilled engineer in the morning, but as he reviewed what he had written he felt a sense of deep satisfaction, and a true delight in his work. His soul thrilled with the power of his gift. He loved it, exulted in it. It was pleasant to feel that delight in his work once more. He had thought since his marriage that it was gone forever, but perhaps by and by it would return to console him, and he would be able to do greater things in the world because of his suffering.

Just as he dropped to sleep there came a thought of Marcia, pleasantly, as one remembers a flower. He felt that there was a comfort about Marcia, a something helpful in her smile. There was more to her than he had supposed. She was not merely a child. How her face had glowed as the men talked of the projected railroad, and almost she seemed to understand as they described the proposed engine with its movable trucks. She would be a companion who would be interested in his pursuits. He had hoped to teach Kate to understand his life work and perhaps help him some, but Kate was by nature a butterfly, a bird of gay colors, always on the wing. He would not have wanted her to be troubled with deep thoughts. Marcia seemed to enjoy such things. What if he should take pains to teach her, read with her, help cultivate her mind? It would at least be an occupation for leisure hours, something to interest him and keep away the awful pall of sadness.

How sweet she had looked as she lay asleep in the woods with the tears on her cheek like the dew-drops upon a rose petal! She was a dear little girl and he must take care of her and protect her. That scoundrel Temple! What were such men made for? He must settle him to-morrow.

And so he fell asleep.

CHAPTER XVII

Harry Temple sat in his office the next morning with his feet upon the table and his wooden armed chair tilted back against the wall.

He had letters to write, a number of them, that should go out with the afternoon coach, to reach the night packet. There were at least three men he ought to go and see at once if he would do the best for his employers, and the office he sat in was by no means in the best of order. But his feet were elevated comfortably on the table and he was deep in the pages of a story of the French Court, its loves and hates and intrigues.

It was therefore with annoyance that he looked up at the opening of the office door.

But the frown changed to apprehension, as he saw who was his visitor. He brought the chair legs suddenly to the floor and his own legs followed them swiftly. David Spafford was not a man before whom another would sit with his feet on a table, even to transact business.

There was a look of startled enquiry on Harry Temple's face. For an instant his self-complacency was shaken. He hesitated, wondering what tack to take. Perhaps after all his alarm was unnecessary. Marcia likely had been too frightened to tell of what had occurred. He noticed the broad shoulder, the lean, active body, the keen eye, and the grave poise of his visitor, and thought he would hardly care to fight a duel with that man. It was natural for him to think at once of a duel on account of the French court life from which his mind had just emerged. A flash of wonder passed through his mind whether it would be swords or pistols, and then he set himself to face the other man.

David Spafford stood for a full minute and looked into the face of the man he had come to shame. He looked at him with a calm eye and brow, but with a growing contempt that did not need words to express it. Harry Temple felt the color rise in his cheek, and his soul quaked for an instant. Then his habitual conceit arose and he tried to parry with his eye that keen piercing gaze of the other. It must have lasted a full minute, though it seemed to Mr. Temple it was five at the least. He made an attempt to offer his visitor a chair, but it was not noticed. David Spafford looked his man through and through, and knew him for exactly what he was. At last he spoke, quietly, in a tone that was too courteous to be contemptuous, but it humiliated the listener more even than contempt:

"It would be well for you to leave town at once."

That was all. The listener felt that it was a command. His wrath arose hotly, and beat itself against the calm exterior of his visitor's gaze in a look that was brazen enough to have faced a whole town of accusers. Harry Temple could look innocent and handsome when he chose.

"I do not understand you, sir!" he said. "That is a most extraordinary statement!"

"It would be well for you to leave town at once."

This time the command was imperative. Harry's eyes blazed.

"Why?" He asked it with that impertinent tilt to his chin which usually angered his opponent in any argument. Once he could break that steady, iron, self-control he felt he would have the best of things. He could easily persuade David Spafford that everything was all right if he could get him off his guard and make him angry. An angry man could do little but bluster.

"You understand very well," replied David, his voice still, steady and his gaze not swerving.

"Indeed! Well, this is most extraordinary," said Harry, losing control of himself again. "Of what do you accuse me, may I enquire?"

"Of nothing that your own heart does not accuse you," said David. And somehow there was more than human indignation in the gaze now: there was pity, a sense of shame for another soul who could lower himself to do unseemly things. Before that look the blood crept into Harry's cheek again. An uncomfortable sensation entirely new was stealing over him. A sense of sin—no, not that exactly,—a sense that he had made a mistake, perhaps. He never was very hard upon himself even when the evidence was clear against him. It angered him to feel humiliated. What a fuss to make about a little thing! What a tiresome old cad to care about a little flirtation with his wife! He wished he had let the pretty baby alone entirely. She was of no finer stuff than many another who had accepted his advances with pleasure. He stiffened his neck and replied with much haughtiness:

"My heart accuses me of nothing, sir. I assure you I consider your words an insult! I demand satisfaction for your insulting language, sir!" Harry Temple had never fought a duel, and had never been present when others fought, but that was the language in which a challenge was usually delivered in French novels.

"It is not a matter for discussion!" said David Spafford, utterly ignoring the other's blustering words. "I am fully informed as to all that occurred yesterday afternoon, and I tell you once more, it would be well for you to leave town at once. I have nothing further to say."

David turned and walked toward the door, and Harry stood, ignored, angry, crestfallen, and watched him until he reached the door.

"You would better ask your informant further of her part in the matter!" he hissed, suddenly, an open sneer in his voice and a covert implication of deep meaning.

David turned, his face flashing with righteous indignation. The man who was withered by the scorn of that glance wished heartily that he had not uttered the false sentence. He felt the smallness of his own soul, during the instant of silence in which his visitor stood looking at him.

Then David spoke deliberately:

"I knew you were a knave," said he, "but I did not suppose you were also a coward. A man who is not a coward will not try to put the blame upon a woman, especially upon an innocent one. You, sir, will leave town this evening. Any business further than you can settle between this and that I will see properly attended to. I warn you, sir, it will be unwise for you to remain longer than till the evening coach."

Perfectly courteous were David's tones, keen command was in his eye and determination in every line of his face. Harry could not recover himself to reply, could not master his frenzy of anger and humiliation to face the righteous look of his accuser. Before he realized it, David was gone.

He stood by the window and watched him go down the street with rapid, firm tread and upright bearing. Every line in that erect form spoke of determination. The conviction grew within him that the last words of his visitor were true, and that it would be wise for him to leave town. He rebelled at the idea. He did not wish to leave, for business matters were in such shape, or rather in such chaos, that it would be extremely awkward for him to meet his employers and explain his desertion at that time. Moreover there were several homes in the town open to him whenever he chose, where were many attractions. It was a lazy pleasant life he had been leading here, fully trusted, and wholly disloyal to the trust, troubled by no uneasy overseers, not even his own conscience, dined and smiled upon with lovely languishing eyes. He did not care to go, even though he had decried the town as dull and monotonous.

But, on the other hand, things had occurred—not the unfortunate little mistake of yesterday, of course, but others, more serious things—that he would hardly care to have brought to the light of day, especially through the keen sarcastic columns of David Spafford's paper. He had seen other sinners brought to a bloodless retribution in those columns by dauntless weapons of sarcasm and wit which in David Spafford's hands could be made to do valiant work. He did not care to be humiliated in that way. He could not brazen it out. He was convinced that the man meant what he said, and from what he knew of his influence he felt that he would leave no stone unturned till he had made the place too hot to hold him. Only Harry Temple himself knew how easy that would be to do, for no one else knew how many "mistakes" (?) Harry had made, and he, unfortunately for himself, did not know how many of them were not known, by any who could harm him.

He stood a long time clinking some sixpences and shillings together in his pocket, and scowling down the street after David had disappeared from sight.

"Blame that little pink-cheeked, baby-eyed fool!" he said at last, turning on his heel with a sigh. "I might have known she was too goody-goody. Such people ought to die young before they grow up to make fools of other people. Bah! Think of a wife like that with no spirit of her own. A baby! Merely a baby!"

Nevertheless, in his secret heart, he knew he honored Marcia and felt a true shame that she had looked into his tarnished soul.

Then he looked round about upon his papers that represented a whole week's hard work and maybe more before they were cleared away, and reflected how much easier after all it would be to get up a good excuse and go away, leaving all this to some poor drudge who should be sent here in his place. He looked around again and his eyes lighted upon his book. He remembered the exciting crisis in which he had left the heroine and down he sat to his story again. At least there was nothing demanding attention this moment. He need not decide what he would do. If he went there were few preparations to make. He would toss some things into his carpet-bag and pretend to have been summoned to see a sick and dying relative, a long-lost brother or something. It would be easy to invent one when the time came. Then he could leave directions for the rest of his things to be packed if he did not return, and get rid of the trouble of it all. As for the letters, if he was going what use to bother with them? Let them wait till his successor should come. It mattered little to him whether his employers suffered for his negligence or not so long as he finished his story. Besides, it would not do to let that cad think he had frightened him. He would pretend he was not going, at least during his hours of grace. So he picked up his book and went on reading.

At noon he sauntered back to his boarding house as usual for his dinner, having professed an unusually busy morning to those who came in to the office on business and made appointments with them for the next day. This had brought him much satisfaction as the morning wore away and he was left free to his book, and so before dinner he had come to within a very few pages of the end.

After a leisurely dinner he sauntered back to the office again, rejoicing in the fact that circumstances had so arranged themselves that he had passed David Spafford in front of the newspaper office and given him a most elaborate and friendly bow in the presence of four or five bystanders. David's look in return had meant volumes, and decided Harry Temple to do as he had been ordered, not, of course, because he had been ordered to do so, but because it would be an easier thing to do. In fact he made up his mind that he was weary of this part of the country. He went back to his book.

About the middle of the afternoon he finished the last pages. He rose up with alacrity then and began to think what he should do. He glanced around the room, sought out a few papers, took some daguerreotypes of girls from a drawer of his desk, gave a farewell glance around the dismal little room that had seen so much shirking for the past few months, and then went out and locked the door.

He paused at the corner. Which way should he go? He did not care to go back to the office, for his book was done, and he scarcely needed to go to his room at his boarding place yet either, for the afternoon was but half over and he wished his departure to appear to be entirely unpremeditated. A daring thought came into his head. He would walk past David Spafford's house. He would let Marcia see him if possible. He would show them that he was not afraid in the least. He even meditated going in and explaining to Marcia that she had made a great mistake, that he had been merely admiring her, and that there was no harm in anything he had said or done yesterday, that he was exceedingly grieved and mortified that she should have mistaken his meaning for an insult, and so on and so on. He knew well how to make such honeyed talk when he chose, but the audacity of the thing was a trifle too much for even his bold nature, so he satisfied himself by strolling in a leisurely manner by the house.

When he was directly opposite to it he raised his eyes casually and bowed and smiled with his most graceful air. True, he did not see any one, for Marcia had caught sight of him as she was coming out upon the stoop and had fled into her own room with the door buttoned, she was watching unseen from behind the folds of her curtain, but he made the bow as complete as though a whole family had been greeting him from the windows. Marcia, poor child, thought he must see her, and she felt frozen to the spot, and stared wildly through the little fold of her curtain with trembling hands and weak knees till he was passed. Well pleased at himself the young man walked on, knowing that at least three prominent citizens had seen him bow and smile, and that they would be witnesses, against anything David might say to the contrary, that he was on friendly terms with Mrs. Spafford.

Hannah Heath was sitting on the front stoop with her knitting. She often sat there dressed daintily of an afternoon. Her hands were white and looked well against the blue yarn she was knitting. Besides there was something domestic and sentimental in a stocking. It gave a cosy, homey, air to a woman, Hannah considered. So she sat and knitted and smiled at whomsoever passed by, luring many in to sit and talk with her, so that the stockings never grew rapidly, but always kept at about the same stage. If it had been Miranda, Grandmother Heath would have made some sharp remarks about the length of time it took to finish that blue stocking, but as it was Hannah it was all right.

Hannah sat upon the stoop and knitted as Harry Temple came by. Now, Hannah was not so great a favorite with Harry as Harry was with Hannah. She was of the kind who was conquered too easily, and he did not consider it worth his while to waste time upon her simperings usually. But this afternoon was different. He had nowhere to go for a little while, and Hannah's appearance on the stoop was opportune and gave him an idea. He would lounge there with her. Perchance fortune would favor him again and David Spafford would pass by and see him. There would be one more opportunity to stare insolently at him and defy him, before he bent his neck to obey. David had given him the day in which to do what he would, and he would make no move until the time was over and the coach he had named departed, but he knew that then he would bring down retribution. In just what form that retribution would come he was not quite certain, but he knew it would be severe.

So when Hannah smiled upon him, Harry Temple stepped daintily across the mud in the road, and came and sat down beside her. He toyed with her knitting, caught one of her plump white hands, the one on the side away from the street, and held it, while Hannah pretended not to notice, and drooped her long eyelashes in a telling way. Hannah knew how. She had been at it a good many years.

So he sat, toward five o'clock, when David came by, and bowed gravely to Hannah, but seemed not to see Harry. Harry let his eyes follow the tall figure in an insolent stare.

"What a dough-faced cad that man is!" he said lazily, "no wonder his little pink-cheeked wife seeks other society. Handsome baby, though, isn't she?"

Hannah pricked up her ears. Her loss of David was too recent not to cause her extreme jealousy of his pretty young wife. Already she fairly hated her. Her upbringing in the atmosphere of Grandmother Heath's sarcastic, ill-natured gossip had prepared her to be quick to see meaning in any insinuation.

She looked at him keenly, archly for a moment, then replied with drooping gaze and coquettish manner:

"You should not blame any one for enjoying your company."

Hannah stole sly glances to see how he took this, but Harry was an old hand and proof against such scrutiny. He only shrugged his shoulder carelessly, as though he dropped all blame like a garment that he had no need for.

"And what's the matter with David?" asked Hannah, watching David as he mounted his own steps, and thinking how often she had watched that tall form go down the street, and thought of him as destined to belong to her. The mortification that he had chosen some one else was not yet forgotten. It amounted almost to a desire for revenge.

Harry lingered longer than he intended. Hannah begged him to remain to supper, but he declined, and when she pressed him to do so he looked troubled and said he was expecting a letter and must hurry back to see if it came in the afternoon coach. He told her that a dear friend, a beloved cousin, was lying very ill, and he might be summoned at any moment to his bedside, and Hannah said some comforting little things in a caressing voice, and hoped he would find the letter saying the cousin was better. Then he hurried away.

It was easy at his boarding house to say he had been called away, and he rushed up to his room and threw some necessaries into his carpet-bag, scattering things around the room and helping out the impression that he was called away in a great hurry. When he was ready he looked at his watch. It was growing late. The evening coach left in half an hour. He knew its route well. It started at the village inn, and went down the old turnpike, stopping here and there to pick up passengers. There was always a convocation when it started. Perhaps David Spafford would be there and witness his obedience to the command given him. He set his lips and made up his mind to escape that at least. He would cheat his adversary of that satisfaction.

It would involve a sacrifice. He would have to go without his supper, and he could smell the frying bacon coming up the stairs. But it would help the illusion and he could perhaps get something on the way when the coach stopped to change horses.

He rushed downstairs and told his landlady that he must start at once, as he must see a man before the coach went, and she, poor lady, had no chance to suggest that he leave her a little deposit on the sum of his board which he already owed her. There was perhaps some method in his hurry for that reason also. It always bothered him to pay his bills, he had so many other ways of spending his money.

So he hurried away and caught a ride in a farm wagon going toward the Cross Roads. When it turned off he walked a little way until another wagon came along; finally crossed several fields at a breathless pace and caught the coach just as it was leaving the Cross Roads, which was the last stopping place anywhere near the village. He climbed up beside the driver, still in a breathless condition, and detailed to him how he had received word, just before the coach started, by a messenger who came across-country on horseback, that his cousin was dying.

After he had answered the driver's minutest questions, he sat back and reflected upon his course with satisfaction. He was off, and he had not been seen nor questioned by a single citizen, and by to-morrow night his story as he had told it to the driver would be fully known and circulated through the place he had just left. The stage driver was one of the best means of advertisement. It was well to give him full particulars.

The driver after he had satisfied his curiosity about the young man by his side, and his reasons for leaving town so hastily, began to wax eloquent upon the one theme which now occupied his spare moments and his fluent tongue, the subject of a projected railroad. Whether some of the sentiments he uttered were his own, or whether he had but borrowed from others, they were at least uttered with force and apparent conviction, and many a traveller sat and listened as they were retailed and viewed the subject from the standpoint of the loud-mouthed coachman.

514

A little later Tony Weller, called by some one "the best beloved of all coachmen," uttered much the same sentiments in the following words:

"I consider that the railroad is unconstitutional and an invader o' privileges. As to the comfort, as an old coachman I may say it,—vere's the comfort o' sittin' in a harm-chair a lookin' at brick walls, and heaps o' mud, never comin' to a public 'ouse, never seein' a glass o' ale, never goin' through a pike, never meetin' a change o' no kind (hosses or otherwise), but always comin' to a place, ven you comes to vun at all, the werry picter o' the last.

"As to the honor an' dignity o' travellin' vere can that be without a coachman, and vat's the rail, to sich coachmen as is sometimes forced to go by it, but an outrage and an hinsult? As to the ingen, a nasty, wheezin', gaspin', puffin', bustin' monster always out o' breath, with a shiny green and gold back like an onpleasant beetle; as to the ingen as is always a pourin' out red 'ot coals at night an' black smoke in the day, the sensiblest thing it does, in my opinion, is ven there's somethin' in the vay, it sets up that 'ere frightful scream vich seems to say, 'Now 'ere's two 'undred an' forty passengers in the werry greatest extremity o' danger, an' 'ere's their two 'undred an' forty screams in vun!'"

But such sentiments as these troubled Harry Temple not one whit. He cared not whether the present century had a railroad or whether it travelled by foot. He would not lift a white finger to help it along or hinder. As the talk went on he was considering how and where he might get his supper.

CHAPTER XVIII

The weather turned suddenly cold and raw that Fall, and almost in one day, the trees that had been green, or yellowing in the sunshine, put on their autumn garments of defeat, flaunted them for a brief hour, and dropped them early in despair. The pleasant woods, to which Marcia had fled in her dismay, became a mass of finely penciled branches against a wintry sky, save for the one group of tall pines that hung out heavy above the rest, and seemed to defy even snowy blasts.

Marcia could see those pines from her kitchen window, and sometimes as she worked, if her heart was heavy, she would look out and away to them, and think of the day she laid her head down beneath them to sob out her trouble, and awoke to find comfort. Somehow the memory of that little talk that she and David had then grew into vast proportions in her mind, and she loved to cherish it.

There had come letters from home. Her stepmother had written, a stiff, not unloving letter, full of injunctions to be sure to remember this, and not do that, and on no account to let any relative or neighbor persuade her out of the ways in which she had been brought up. She was attempting to do as many mothers do, when they see the faults in the child they have brought up, try to bring them up over again. At some of the sentences a wild homesickness took possession of her. Some little homely phrase about one of the servants, or the mention of a pet hen or cow, would bring the longing tears to her eyes, and she would feel that she must throw away this new life and run back to the old one.

School was begun at home. Mary Ann and Hanford would be taking the long walk back and forth together twice a day to the old school-house. She half envied them their happy, care-free life. She liked to think of the shy courting that she had often seen between scholars in the upper classes. Her imagination pleased itself sometimes when she was going to sleep, trying to picture out the school goings and home comings, and their sober talk. Not that she ever looked back to Hanford Weston with regret, not she. She knew always that he was not for her, and perhaps, even so early as that in her new life, if the choice had been given her whether she would go back to her girlhood again and be as she was before Kate had run away, or whether she would choose to stay here in the new life with David, it is likely she would have chosen to stay.

There were occasional letters from Squire Schuyler. He wrote of politics, and sent many messages to his son-in-law which Marcia handed over to David at the tea table to read, and which always seemed to soften David and bring a sweet sadness into his eyes. He loved and respected his father-in-law. It was as if he were bound to him by the love of some one who had died. Marcia thought of that every time she handed David a letter, and sat and watched him read it.

Sometimes little Harriet or the boys printed out a few words about the family cat, or the neighbors' children, and Marcia laughed and cried over the poor little attempts at letters and longed to have the eager childish faces of the writers to kiss.

But in all of them there was never a mention of the bright, beautiful, selfish girl around whom the old home life used to centre and who seemed now, judging from the home letters, to be worse than dead to them all. But since the afternoon upon the hill a new and pleasant intercourse had sprung up between David and Marcia. True it was confined mainly to discussions of the new railroad, the possibilities of its success, and the construction of engines, tracks, etc. David was constantly writing up the subject for his paper, and he fell into the habit of reading his articles aloud to Marcia when they were finished. She would listen with breathless admiration, sometimes combating a point ably, with the old vim she had used in her discussion over the newspaper with her father, but mainly agreeing with every word he wrote, and always eager to understand it down to the minutest detail.

He always seemed pleased at her praise, and wrote on while she put away the tea-things with a contented expression as though he had passed a high critic, and need not fear any other. Once he looked up with a quizzical expression and made a jocose remark about "our article," taking her into a sort of partnership with him in it, which set her heart to beating happily, until it seemed as if she were really in some part at least growing into his life.

But after all their companionship was a shy, distant one, more like that of a brother and sister who had been separated all their lives and were just beginning to get acquainted, and ever there was a settled sadness about the lines of David's mouth and eyes. They sat around one table now, the evenings when they were at home, for there were still occasional tea-drinkings at their friends' houses; and there was one night a week held religiously for a formal supper with the aunts, which David kindly acquiesced in—more for the sake of his Aunt Clarinda than the others,—whenever he was not detained by actual business. Then, too, there was the weekly prayer meeting held at "early candle light" in the dim old shadowed church. They always walked down the twilighted streets together, and it seemed to Marcia there was a sweet solemnity about that walk. They never said much to each other on the way. David seemed preoccupied with holy thoughts, and Marcia walked softly beside him as if he had been the minister, looking at him proudly and reverently now and then. David was often called upon to pray in meeting and Marcia loved to listen to his words. He seemed to be more intimate with God than the others, who were mostly old men and prayed with long, rolling, solemn sentences that put the whole community down into the dust and ashes before their Creator.

Marcia rather enjoyed the hour spent in the sombreness of the church, with the flickering candle light making grotesque forms of shadows on the wall and among the tall pews. The old minister reminded her of the one she had left at home, though he was more learned and scholarly, and when he had read the Scripture passages he would take his spectacles off and lay them across the great Bible where the candle light played at glances with the steel bows, and say: "Let us pray!" Then would come that soft stir and hush as the people took the attitude of prayer. Marcia sometimes joined in the prayer in her heart, uttering shy little petitions that were vague and indefinite, and had to do mostly with the days when she was troubled and homesick, and felt that David belonged wholly to Kate. Always her clear voice joined in the slow hymns that quavered out now and again, lined out to the worshippers.

Marcia and David went out from that meeting down the street to their home with the hush upon them that must have been upon the Israelites of old after they had been to the solemn congregation.

But once David had come in earlier than usual and had caught Marcia reading the Scottish Chiefs, and while she started guiltily to be found thus employed he smiled indulgently. After supper he said: "Get your book, child, and sit down. I have some writing to do, and after it is done I will read it to you." So after that, more and more often, it was a book that Marcia held in her hands in the long evenings when they sat together, instead of some useful employment, and so her education progressed. Thus she read Epictetus, Rasselas, The Deserted Village, The Vicar of Wakefield, Paradise Lost, the Mysteries of the Human Heart, Marshall's Life of Columbus, The Spy, The Pioneers, and The Last of the Mohicans.

She had been asked to sing in the village choir. David sang a sweet high tenor there, and Marcia's voice was clear and strong as a blackbird's, with the plaintive sweetness of the wood-robin's.

Hannah Heath was in the choir also, and jealously watched her every move, but of this Marcia was unaware until informed of it by Miranda. With her inherited sweetness of nature she scarcely credited it, until one Sunday, a few weeks after the departure of Harry Temple, Hannah leaned forward from her seat among the altos and whispered quite distinctly, so that those around could hear—it was just before the service—"I've just had a letter from your friend Mr. Temple. I thought you might like to know that his cousin got well and he has gone back to New York. He won't be returning here this year. On some accounts he thought it was better not."

It was all said pointedly, with double emphasis upon the "your friend," and "some accounts." Marcia felt her cheeks glow, much to her vexation, and tried to control her whisper to seem kindly as she answered indifferently enough.

"Oh, indeed! But you must have made a mistake. Mr. Temple is a very slight acquaintance of mine. I have met him only a few times, and I know nothing about his cousin. I was not aware even that he had gone away."

Hannah raised her speaking eyebrows and replied, quite loud now, for the choir leader had stood up already with his tuning-fork in hand, and one could hear it faintly twang:

"Indeed!"—using Marcia's own word—and quite coldly, "I should have thought differently from what Harry himself told me," and there was that in her tone which deepened the color in Marcia's cheeks and caused it to stay there during the entire morning service as she sat puzzling over what Hannah could have meant. It rankled in her mind during the whole day. She longed to ask David about it, but could not get up the courage.

She could not bear to revive the memory of what seemed to be her shame. It was at the minister's donation party that Hannah planted another thorn in her heart,—Hannah, in a green plaid silk with delicate undersleeves of lace, and a tiny black velvet jacket.

She selected a time when Lemuel was near, and when Aunt Amelia and Aunt Hortense, who believed that all the young men in town were hovering about David's wife, sat one on either side of Marcia, as if to guard her for their beloved nephew—who was discussing politics with Mr. Heath—and who never seemed to notice, so blind he was in his trust of her.

So Hannah paused and posed before the three ladies, and with Lemuel smiling just at her elbow, began in her affected way:

"I've had another letter from New York, from your friend Mr. Temple," she said it with the slightest possible glance over her shoulder to get the effect of her words upon the faithful Lemuel, "and he tells me he has met a sister of yours. By the way, she told him that David used to be very fond of her before she was married. I suppose she'll be coming to visit you now she's so near as New York."

Two pairs of suspicious steely eyes flew like stinging insects to gaze upon her, one on either side, and Marcia's heart stood still for just one instant, but she felt that here was her trying time, and if she would help David and do the work for which she had become his wife, she must protect him now from any suspicions or disagreeable tongues. By very force of will she controlled the trembling of her lips.

"My sister will not likely visit us this winter, I think," she replied as coolly as if she had had a letter to that effect that morning, and then she deliberately looked at Lemuel Skinner and asked if he had heard of the offer of prizes of four thousand dollars in cash that the Baltimore and Ohio railroad had just made for the most approved engine delivered for trial before June first, 1831, not to exceed three and a half tons in weight and capable of drawing, day by day, fifteen tons inclusive of weight of wagons, fifteen miles per hour. Lemuel looked at her blankly and said he had not heard of it. He was engaged in thinking over what Hannah had said about a letter from Harry Temple. He cared nothing about railroads.

"The second prize is thirty-five hundred dollars," stated Marcia eagerly, as though it were of the utmost importance to her.

"Are you thinking of trying for one of the prizes?" sneered Hannah, piercing her with her eyes, and now indeed the ready color flowed into Marcia's face. Her ruse had been detected.

"If I were a man and understood machinery I believe I would. What a grand thing it would be to be able to invent a thing like an engine that would be of so much use to the world," she answered bravely.

"They are most dangerous machines," said Aunt Amelia disapprovingly. "No right-minded Christian who wishes to live out the life his Creator has given him would ever ride behind one. I have heard that boilers always explode."

"They are most unnecessary!" said Aunt Hortense severely, as if that settled the question for all time and all railroad corporations.

But Marcia was glad for once of their disapproval and entered most heartily into a discussion of the pros and cons of engines and steam, quoting largely from David's last article for the paper on the subject, until Hannah and Lemuel moved slowly away. The discussion served to keep the aunts from inquiring further that evening about the sister in New York.

Marcia begged them to go with her into the kitchen and see the store of good things that had been brought to the minister's house by his loving parishioners. Bags of flour and meal, pumpkins, corn in the ear, eggs, and nice little pats of butter. A great wooden tub of doughnuts, baskets of apples and quinces, pounds of sugar and tea, barrels of potatoes, whole hams, a side of pork, a quarter of beef, hanks of yarn, and strings of onions. It was a goodly array. Marcia felt that the minister must be beloved by his people. She watched him and his wife as they greeted their people, and wished she knew them better, and might come and see them sometimes, and perhaps eventually feel as much at home with them as with her own dear minister.

She avoided Hannah during the remainder of the evening. When the evening was over and she went upstairs to get her wraps from the high four-poster bedstead, she had almost forgotten Hannah and her ill-natured, prying remarks. But Hannah had not forgotten her. She came forth from behind the bed curtains where she had been searching for a lost glove, and remarked that she should think Marcia would be lonely this first winter away from home and want her sister with her a while.

But the presence of Hannah always seemed a mental stimulus to the spirit of Marcia.

"Oh, I'm not in the least lonely," she laughed merrily. "I have a great many interesting things to do, and I love music and books."

"Oh, yes, I forgot you are very fond of music. Harry Temple told me about it," said Hannah. Again there was that disagreeable hint of something more behind her words, that aggravated Marcia almost beyond control. For an instant a cutting reply was upon her lips and her eyes flashed fire; then it came to her how futile it would be, and she caught the words in time and walked swiftly down the stairs. David watching her come down saw the admiring glances of all who stood in the hall below, and took her under his protection with a measure of pride in her youth and beauty that he did not himself at all realize. All the way home he talked with her about the new theory of railroad construction, quite contented in her companionship, while she, poor child, much perturbed in spirit, wondered how he would feel if he knew what Hannah had said.

David fell into a deep study with a book and his papers about him, after they had reached home. Marcia went up to her quiet, lonely chamber, put her face in the pillow and thought and wept and prayed. When at last she lay down to rest she did not know anything she could do but just to go on living day by day and helping David all she could. At most there was nothing to fear for herself, save a kind of shame that she had not been the first sister chosen, and she found to her surprise that that was growing to be deeper than she had supposed.

She wished as she fell asleep that her girl-dreams might have been left to develop and bloom like other girls', and that she might have had a real lover,—like David in every way, yet of course not David because he was Kate's. But a real lover who would meet her as David had done that night when he thought she was Kate, and speak to her tenderly.

One afternoon David, being wearied with an unusual round of taxing cares, came home to rest and study up some question in his library.

Finding the front door fastened, and remembering that he had left his key in his other pocket, he came around to the back door, and much preoccupied with thought went through the kitchen and nearly to the hall before the unusual sounds of melody penetrated to his ears. He stopped for an instant amazed, forgetting the piano, then comprehending he wondered who was playing. Perhaps some visitor was in the parlor. He would listen and find out. He was weary and dusty with the soil of the office upon his hands and clothes. He did not care to meet a visitor, so under cover of the music he slipped into the door of his library across the hall from the parlor and dropped into his great arm-chair.

Softly and tenderly stole the music through the open door, all about him, like the gentle dropping of some tender psalms or comforting chapter in the Bible to an aching heart. It touched his brow like a soft soothing hand, and seemed to know and recognize all the agonies his heart had been passing through, and all the weariness his body felt.

He put his head back and let it float over him and rest him. Tinkling brooks and gentle zephyrs, waving of forest trees, and twitterings of birds, calm lazy clouds floating by, a sweetness in the atmosphere, bells far away, lowing herds, music of the angels high in heaven, the soothing strain from each extracted and brought to heal his broken heart. It fell like dew upon his spirit. Then, like a fresh breeze with zest and life borne on, came a new strain, grand and fine and high, calling him to better things. He did not know it was a strain of Handel's music grown immortal, but his spirit recognized the higher call, commanding him to follow, and straightway he felt strengthened to go onward in the course he had been pursuing. Old troubles seemed to grow less, anguish fell away from him. He took new lease of life. Nothing seemed impossible.

Then she played by ear one or two of the old tunes they sang in church, touching the notes tenderly and almost making them speak the words. It seemed a benediction. Suddenly the playing ceased and Marcia remembered it was nearly supper time.

He met her in the doorway with a new look in his eyes, a look of high purpose and exultation. He smiled upon her and said: "That was good, child. I did not know you could do it. You must give it to us often." Marcia felt a glow of pleasure in his kindliness, albeit she felt that the look in his eyes set him apart and above her, and made her feel the child she was. She hurried out to get the supper between pleasure and a nameless unrest. She was glad of this much, but she wanted more, a something to meet her soul and satisfy.

CHAPTER XIX

The world had not gone well with Mistress Kate Leavenworth, and she was ill-pleased. She had not succeeded in turning her father's heart toward herself as she had confidently expected to do when she ran away with her sea captain. She had written a gay letter home, taking for granted, in a pretty way, the forgiveness she did not think it necessary to ask, but there had come in return a brief harsh statement from her father that she was no longer his daughter and must cease from further communication with the family in any way; that she should never enter his house again and not a penny of his money should ever pass to her. He also informed her plainly that the trousseau made for her had been given to her sister who was now the wife of the man she had not seen fit to marry.

Over this letter Mistress Kate at first stormed, then wept, and finally sat down to frame epistle after epistle in petulant, penitent language. These epistles following each other by daily mail coaches still brought nothing further from her irate parent, and my lady was at last forced to face the fact that she must bear the penalty of her own misdeeds; a lesson she should have learned much earlier in life.

The young captain, who had always made it appear that he had plenty of money, had spent his salary, and most of his mother's fortune, which had been left in his keeping as administrator of his father's estate; so he had really very little to offer the spoiled and petted beauty, who simply would not settle down to the inevitable and accept the fate she had brought upon herself and others. Day after day she fretted and blamed her husband until he heartily wished her back from whence he had taken her; wished her back with her straitlaced lover from whom he had stolen her; wished her anywhere save where she was. Her brightness and beauty seemed all gone: she was a sulky child insisting upon the moon or nothing. She waited to go to New York and be established in a fine house with plenty of servants and a carriage and horses, and the young captain had not the wherewithal to furnish these accessories to an elegant and luxurious life.

He had loved her so far as his shallow nature could love, and perhaps she had returned it in the beginning. He wanted to spend his furlough in quiet places where he might have a honeymoon of his ideal, bantering Kate's sparkling sentences, looking into her beautiful eyes, touching her rosy lips with his own as often as he chose. But Mistress Kate had lost her sparkle. She would not be kissed until she had gained her point, her lovely eyes were full of disfiguring tears and angry flashes, and her speech scintillated with cutting sarcasms, which were none the less hard to bear that they pressed home some disagreeable truths to the easy, careless spendthrift. The rose had lost its dew and was making its thorns felt.

And so they quarreled through their honeymoon, and Captain Leavenworth was not sorry when a hasty and unexpected end came to his furlough and he was ordered off with his ship for an indefinite length of time.

Even then Kate thought to get her will before he left, and held on her sullen ways and her angry, blameful talk until the last minute, so that he hurried away without even one good-bye kiss, and with her angry sentences sounding in his ears.

True, he repented somewhat on board the ship and sent her back more money than she could reasonably have expected under the circumstances, but he sent it without one word of gentleness, and Kate's heart was hard toward her husband.

Then with bitterness and anguish,—that was new and fairly astonishing that it had come to her who had always had her way,—she sat down to think of the man she had jilted. He would have been kind to her. He would have given her all she asked and more. He would even have moved his business to New York to please her, she felt sure. Why had she been so foolish! And then, like many another sinner who is made at last to see the error of his ways, she cast hard thoughts at a Fate which had allowed her to make so great a mistake, and pitied her poor little self out of all recognition of the character she had formed.

But she took her money and went to New York, for she felt that there only could she be at all happy, and have some little taste of the delights of true living.

She took up her abode with an ancient relative of her own mother's, who lived in a quiet respectable part of the city, and who was glad to piece out her small annuity with the modest sum that Kate agreed to pay for her board.

It was not long before Mistress Kate, with her beautiful face, and the pretty clothes which she took care to provide at once for herself, spending lavishly out of the diminishing sum her husband had sent her, and thinking not of the morrow, nor the day when the board bills would be due, became well known. The musty little parlor of the ancient relative was daily filled with visitors, and every evening Kate held court, with the old aunt nodding in her chair by the fireside.

Neither did the poor old lady have a very easy time of it, in spite of the promise of weekly pay. Kate laughed at the old furniture and the old ways. She demanded new things, and got them, too, until the old lady saw little hope of any help from the board money when Kate was constantly saying: "I saw this in a shop down town, auntie, and as I knew you needed it I just bought it. My board this week will just pay for it." As always, Kate ruled. The little parlor took on an air of brightness, and Kate became popular. A few women of fashion took her up, and Kate launched herself upon a gay life, her one object to have as good a time as possible, regardless of what her husband or any one else might think.

When Kate had been in New York about two months it happened one day that she went out to drive with one of her new acquaintances, a young married woman of about her own age, who had been given all in a worldly way that had been denied to Kate.

They made some calls in Brooklyn, and returned on the ferry-boat, carriage and all, just as the sun was setting.

The view was marvellous. The water a flood of pink and green and gold; the sails of the vessels along the shore lit up resplendently; the buildings of the city beyond sent back occasional flashes of reflected light from window glass or church spire. It was a picture worth looking upon, and Kate's companion was absorbed in it.

Not so Kate. She loved display above all things. She sat up statelily, aware that she looked well in her new frock with the fine lace collar she had extravagantly purchased the day before, and her leghorn bonnet with its real ostrich feather, which was becoming in the extreme. She enjoyed sitting back of the colored coachman, her elegant friend by her side, and being admired by the two ladies and the little girl who sat in the ladies' cabin and occasionally peeped curiously at her from the window. She drew herself up haughtily and let her soul "delight itself in fatness"—borrowed fatness, perhaps, but still, the long desired. She told herself she had a right to it, for was she not a Schuyler? That name was respected everywhere.

She bore a grudge at a man and woman who stood by the railing absorbed in watching the sunset haze that lay over the river showing the white sails in gleams like flashes of white birds here and there.

A young man well set up, and fashionably attired, sauntered up to the carriage. He spoke to Kate's friend, and was introduced. Kate felt in her heart it was because of her presence there he came. His bold black eyes told her as much and she was flattered.

They fell to talking.

"You say you spent the summer near Albany, Mr. Temple," said Kate presently, "I wonder if you happen to know any of my friends. Did you meet a Mr. Spafford? David Spafford?"

"Of course I did, knew him well," said the young man with guarded tone. But a quick flash of dislike, and perhaps fear had crossed his face at the name. Kate was keen. She analyzed that look. She parted her charming red lips and showed her sharp little teeth like the treacherous pearls in a white kitten's pink mouth.

"He was once a lover of mine," said Kate carelessly, wrinkling her piquant little nose as if the idea were comical, and laughing out a sweet ripple of mirth that would have cut David to the heart.

"Indeed!" said the ever ready Harry, "and I do not wonder. Is not every one that at once they see you, Madam Leavenworth? How kind of your husband to stay away at sea for so long a time and give us other poor fellows a chance to say pleasant things."

Then Kate pouted her pretty lips in a way she had and tapped the delighted Harry with her carriage parasol across the fingers of his hand that had taken familiar hold of the carriage beside her arm.

"Oh, you naughty man!" she exclaimed prettily. "How dare you! Yes, David Spafford and I were quite good friends. I almost gave in at one time and became Mrs. Spafford, but he was too good for me!"

She uttered this truth in a mocking tone, and Harry saw her lead and hastened to follow. Here was a possible chance for revenge. He was ready for any. He studied the lady before him keenly. Of what did that face remind him? Had he ever seen her before?

"I should judge him a little straitlaced for your merry ways," he responded gallantly, "but he's like all the rest, fickle, you know. He's married. Have you heard?"

Kate's face darkened with something hard and cruel, but her voice was soft as a cat's purr:

"Yes," she sighed, "I know. He married my sister. Poor child! I am sorry for her. I think he did it out of revenge, and she was too young to know her own mind. But they, poor things, will have to bear the consequences of what they have done. Isn't it a pity that that has to be, Mr. Temple? It is dreadful to have the innocent suffer. I have been greatly anxious about my sister." She lifted her large eyes swimming in tears, and he did not perceive the insincerity in her purring voice just then. He was thanking his lucky stars that he had been saved from any remarks about young Mrs. Spafford, whom her sister seemed to love so deeply. It had been on the tip of his tongue to suggest that she might be able to lead her husband a gay little dance if she chose. How lucky he had not spoken! He tried to say some pleasant comforting nothings, and found it delightful to see her face clear into smiles and her blue eyes look into his so confidingly. By the time the boat touched the New York side the two felt well acquainted, and Harry Temple had promised to call soon, which promise he lost no time in keeping.

Kate's heart had grown bitter against the young sister who had dared to take her place, and against the lover who had so easily solaced himself. She could not understand it.

She resolved to learn all that Mr. Temple knew about David, and to find out if possible whether he were happy. It was Kate's nature not to be able to give up anything even though she did not want it. She desired the life-long devotion of every man who came near her, and have it she would or punish him.

Harry Temple, meanwhile, was reflecting upon his chance meeting that afternoon and wondering if in some way he might not yet have revenge upon the man who had humbled him. Possibly this woman could help him.

After some thought he sat down and penned a letter to Hannah Heath, begemming it here and there with devoted sentences which caused that young woman's eyes to sparkle and a smile of anticipation to wreathe her lips. When she heard of the handsome sister in New York, and of her former relations with David Spafford, her eyes narrowed speculatively, and her fair brow drew into puzzled frowns. Harry Temple had drawn a word picture of Mrs. Leavenworth. Harry should have been a novelist. If he had not been too lazy he would have been a success. Gold hair! Ah! Hannah had heard of gold hair before, and in connection with David's promised wife. Here was a mystery and Hannah resolved to look into it. It would at least be interesting to note the effect of her knowledge upon the young bride next door. She would try it.

Meantime, the acquaintance of Harry Temple and Kate Leavenworth had progressed rapidly. The second sight of the lady proved more interesting than the first, for now her beautiful gold hair added to the charm of her handsome face. Harry ever delighted in beauty of whatever type, and a blonde was more fascinating to him than a brunette. Kate had dressed herself bewitchingly, and her manner was charming. She knew how to assume pretty child-like airs, but she was not afraid to look him boldly in the eyes, and the light in her own seemed to challenge him. Here was a delightful new study. A woman fresh from the country, having all the charm of innocence, almost as child-like as her sister, yet with none of her prudishness. Kate's eyes held latent wickedness in them, or he was much mistaken. She did not droop her lids and blush when he looked boldly and admiringly into her face, but stared him back, smilingly, merrily, daringly, as though she would go quite as far as he would. Moreover, with her he was sure he need feel none of the compunctions he might have felt with her younger sister who was so obviously innocent, for whether Kate's boldness was from lack of knowledge, or from lack of innocence, she was quite able to protect herself, that was plain.

So Harry settled into his chair with a smile of pleasant anticipation upon his face. He not only had the prospect before him of a possible ally in revenge against David Spafford, but he had the promise of a most unusually delightful flirtation with a woman who was worthy of his best efforts in that line.

Almost at once it began, with pleasant banter, adorned with personal compliments.

"Lovelier than I thought, my lady," said Harry, bowing low over the hand she gave him, in a courtly manner he had acquired, perhaps from the old-world novels he had read, and he brushed her pink finger tips with his lips in a way that signified he was her abject slave.

Kate blushed and smiled, greatly pleased, for though she had held her own little court in the village where she was brought up, and queened it over the young men who had flocked about her willingly, she had not been used to the fulsome flattery that breathed from Harry Temple in every word and glance.

He looked at her keenly as he stood back a moment, to see if she were in any wise offended with his salutation, and saw as he expected that she was pleased and flattered. Her cheeks had grown rosier, and her eyes sparkled with pleasure as she responded with a pretty, gracious speech.

Then they sat down and faced one another. A good woman would have called his look impudent—insulting. Kate returned it with a look that did not shrink, nor waver, but fearlessly, recklessly accepted the challenge. Playing with fire, were these two, and with no care for the fearful results which might follow. Both knew it was dangerous, and liked it the better for that. There was a long silence. The game was opening on a wider scale than either had ever played before.

"Do you believe in affinities?" asked the devil, through the man's voice.

The woman colored and showed she understood his deeper meaning. Her eyes drooped for just the shade of an instant, and then she looked up and faced him saucily, provokingly:

"Why?"

He admired her with his gaze, and waited, lazily watching the color play in her cheeks.

"Do you need to ask why?" he said at last, looking at her significantly. "I knew that you were my affinity the moment I laid my eyes upon you, and I hoped you felt the same. But perhaps I was mistaken." He searched her face.

She kept her eyes upon his, returning their full gaze, as if to hold it from going too deep into her soul.

"I did not say you were mistaken, did I?" said the rosy lips coquettishly, and Kate drooped her long lashes till they fell in becoming sweeps over her burning cheeks.

Something in the curve of cheek and chin, and sweep of dark lash over velvet skin, reminded him of her sister. It was so she had sat, though utterly unconscious, while he had been singing, when there had come over him that overwhelming desire to kiss her. If he should kiss this fair lady would she slap him in the face and run into the garden? He thought not. Still, she was brought up by the same father and mother in all likelihood, and it was well to go slow. He reached forward, drawing his chair a little nearer to her, and then boldly took one of her small unresisting hands, gently, that he might not frighten her, and smoothed it thoughtfully between his own. He held it in a close grasp and looked into her face again, she meanwhile watching her hand amusedly, as though it were something apart from herself, a sort of distant possession, for which she was in no wise responsible.

"I feel that you belong to me," he said boldly looking into her eyes with a languishing gaze. "I have known it from the first moment."

Kate let her hand lie in his as if she liked it, but she said:

"And what makes you think that, most audacious sir? Did you not know that I am married?" Then she swept her gaze up provokingly at him again and smiled, showing her dainty, treacherous, little teeth. She was so bewitchingly pretty and tempting then that he had a mind to kiss her on the spot, but a thought came to him that he would rather lead her further first. He was succeeding well. She had no mind to be afraid. She did her part admirably.

"That makes no difference," said he smiling. "That another man has secured you first, and has the right to provide for you, and be near you, is my misfortune of course, but it makes no difference, you are mine? By all the power of love you are mine. Can any other man keep my soul from yours, can he keep my eyes from looking into yours, or my thoughts from hovering over you, or—" he hesitated and looked at her keenly, while she furtively watched him, holding her breath and half inviting him—"or my lips from drinking life from yours?" He stooped quickly and pressed his lips upon hers.

Kate gave a quick little gasp like a sob and drew back. The aunt nodding over her Bible in the next room had not heard,—she was very deaf,—but for an instant the young woman felt that all the shades of her worthy patriarchal ancestors were hurrying around and away from her in horror. She had come of too good Puritan stock not to know that she was treading in the path of unrighteousness. Nevertheless it was a broad path, and easy. It tempted her. It was exciting. It lured her with promise of satisfying some of her untamed longings and impulses.

She did not look offended. She only drew back to get breath and consider. The wild beating of her heart, the tumult of her cheeks and eyes were all a part of a new emotion. Her vanity was excited, and she thrilled with a wild pleasure. As a duck will take to swimming so she took to the new game, with wonderful facility.

"But I didn't say you might," she cried with a bewildering smile.

"I beg your pardon, fair lady, may I have another?"

His bold, bad face was near her own, so that she did not see the evil triumph that lurked there. She had come to the turning of another way in her life, and just here she might have drawn back if she would. Half she knew this, yet she toyed with the opportunity, and it was gone. The new way seemed so alluring.

"You will first have to prove your right!" she said decidedly, with that pretty commanding air that had conquered so many times.

And in like manner on they went through the evening, frittering the time away at playing with edged tools.

A friendship so begun—if so unworthy an intimacy may be called by that sweet name—boded no good to either of the two, and that evening marked a decided turn for the worse in Kate Leavenworth's career.

CHAPTER XX

David had found it necessary to take a journey which might keep him away for several weeks.

He told Marcia in the evening when he came home from the office. He told her as he would have told his clerk. It meant nothing to him but an annoyance that he had to start out in the early winter, leave his business in other's hands for an indefinite period, and go among strangers. He did not see the whitening of Marcia's lips, nor the quick little movement of her hand to her heart. Even Marcia herself did not realize all that it meant to her. She felt as if a sudden shock had almost knocked her off her feet. This quiet life in the big house, with only David at intervals to watch and speak to occasionally, and no one to open her true heart to, had been lonely; and many a time when she was alone at night she had wept bitter tears upon her pillow,—why she did not quite know. But now when she knew that it was to cease, and David was going away from her for a long time, perhaps weeks, her heart suddenly tightened and she knew how sweet it had been growing. Almost the tears came to her eyes, but she made a quick errand to the hearth for the teapot, busying herself there till they were under control again. When she returned to her place at the table she was able to ask David some commonplace question about the journey which kept her true feeling quite hidden from him.

He was to start the next evening if possible. It appeared that there was something important about railroading coming up in Congress. It was necessary that he should be present to hear the debate, and also that he should see and interview influential men. It meant much to the success of the great new enterprises that were just in their infancy that he should go and find out all about them and write them up as only he whose heart was in it could do. He was pleased to have been selected for this; he was lifted for the time above himself and his life troubles, and given to feel that he had a work in the world that was worth while, a high calling, a chance to give a push to the unrolling of the secret possibilities of the universe and help them on their way.

Marcia understood it all, and was proud and glad for him, but her own heart which beat in such perfect sympathy with the work felt lonely and left out. If only she could have helped too!

There was no time for David to take Marcia to her home to stay during his absence. He spoke of it regretfully just as he was about to leave, and asked if she would like him to get some one to escort her by coach to her father's house until he could come for her; but she held back the tears by main force and shook her head. She had canvassed that question in the still hours of the night. She had met in imagination the home village with its kindly and unkindly curiosity, she had seen their hands lifted in suspicion; heard their covert whispers as to why her husband did not come with her; why he had left her so soon after the honeymoon; why—a hundred things. She had even thought of Aunt Polly and her acrid tongue and made up her mind that whatever happened she did not want to go home to stay.

The only other alternative was to go to the aunts. David expected it, and the aunts spoke of it as if nothing else were possible. Marcia would have preferred to remain alone in her own house, with her beloved piano, but David would not consent, and the aunts were scandalized at the suggestion. So to the aunts went Marcia, and they took her in with a hope in their hearts that she might get the same good from the visit that the sluggard in the Bible is bidden to find.

"We must do our duty by her for David's sake," said Aunt Hortense, with pursed lips and capable, folded hands that seemed fairly to ache to get at the work of reconstructing the new niece.

"Yes, it is our opportunity," said Aunt Amelia with a snap as though she thoroughly enjoyed the prospect. "Poor David!" and so they sat and laid out their plans for their sweet young victim, who all unknowingly was coming to one of those tests in her life whereby we are tried for greater things and made perfect in patience and sweetness.

It began with the first breakfast—the night before she had been company, at supper—but when the morning came they felt she must be counted one of the family. They examined her thoroughly on what she had been taught with regard to housekeeping. They made her tell her recipes for pickling and preserving. They put her through a catechism of culinary lore, and always after her most animated account of the careful way in which she had been trained in this or that housewifely art she looked up with wistful eyes that longed to please, only to be met by the hard set lips and steely glances of the two mentors who regretted that she should not have been taught their way which was so much better.

Aunt Hortense even went so far once as to suggest that Marcia write to her stepmother and tell her how much better it was to salt the water in which potatoes were to be boiled before putting them in, and was much offended by the clear girlish laugh that bubbled up involuntarily at the thought of teaching her stepmother anything about cooking.

"Excuse me," she said, instantly sobering as she saw the grim look of the aunt, and felt frightened at what she had done. "I did not mean to laugh, indeed I did not; but it seemed so funny to think of my telling mother how to do anything."

"People are never too old to learn," remarked Aunt Hortense with offended mien, "and one ought never to be too proud when there is a better way."

"But mother thinks there is no better way I am sure. She says that it makes potatoes soggy to boil them in salt. All that grows below the ground should be salted after it is cooked and all that grows above the ground should be cooked in salted water, is her rule."

"I am surprised that your stepmother should uphold any such superstitious ideas," said Aunt Amelia with a self-satisfied expression.

"One should never be too proud to learn something better," Aunt Hortense said grimly, and Marcia retreated in dire consternation at the thought of what might follow if these three notable housekeeping gentlewomen should come together. Somehow she felt a wicked little triumph in the thought that it would be hard to down her stepmother.

Marcia was given a few light duties ostensibly to "make her feel at home," but in reality, she knew, because the aunts felt she needed their instruction. She was asked if she would like to wash the china and glass; and regularly after each meal a small wooden tub and a mop were brought in with hot water and soap, and she was expected to handle the costly heirlooms under the careful scrutiny of their worshipping owners, who evidently watched each process with strained nerves lest any bit of treasured pottery should be cracked or broken. It was a trying ordeal.

The girl would have been no girl if she had not chafed under this treatment. To hold her temper steady and sweet under it was almost more than she could bear.

There were long afternoons when it was decreed that they should knit.

Marcia had been used to take long walks at home, over the smooth crust of the snow, going to her beloved woods, where she delighted to wander among the bare and creaking trees; fancying them whispering sadly to one another of the summer that was gone and the leaves they had borne now dead. But it would be a dreadful thing in the aunts' opinion for a woman, and especially a young one, to take a long walk in the woods alone, in winter too, and with no object whatever in view but a walk! What a waste of time!

There were two places of refuge for Marcia during the weeks that followed. There was home. How sweet that word sounded to her! How she longed to go back there, with David coming home to his quiet meals three times a day, and with her own time to herself to do as she pleased. With housewifely zeal that was commendable in the eyes of the aunts, Marcia insisted upon going down to her own house every morning to see that all was right, guiltily knowing that in her heart she meant to hurry to her beloved books and piano. To be sure it was cold and cheerless in the empty house. She dared not make up fires and leave them, and she dared not stay too long lest the aunts would feel hurt at her absence, but she longed with an inexpressible longing to be back there by herself, away from that terrible supervision and able to live her own glad little life and think her own thoughts untrammeled by primness.

Sometimes she would curl up in David's big arm-chair and have a good cry, after which she would take a book and read until the creeping chills down her spine warned her she must stop. Even then she would run up and down the hall or take a broom and sweep vigorously to warm herself and then go to the cold keys and play a sad little tune. All her tunes seemed sad like a wail while David was gone.

The other place of refuge was Aunt Clarinda's room. Thither she would betake herself after supper, to the delight of the old lady. Then the other two occupants of the house were left to themselves and might unbend from their rigid surveillance for a little while. Marcia often wondered if they ever did unbend.

There was a large padded rocking chair in Aunt Clarinda's room and Marcia would laughingly take the little old lady in her arms and place her comfortably in it, after a pleasant struggle on Miss Clarinda's part to put her guest into it. They had this same little play every evening, and it seemed to please the old lady mightily. Then when she was conquered she always sat meekly laughing, a fine pink color in her soft peachy cheek, the candle light from the high shelf making flickering sparkles in her old eyes that always seemed young; and she would say: "That's just as David used to do."

Then Marcia drew up the little mahogany stool covered with the worsted dog which Aunt Clarinda had worked when she was ten years old, and snuggling down at the old lady's feet exclaimed delightedly: "Tell me about it!" and they settled down to solid comfort.

There came a letter from David after he had been gone a little over a week. Marcia had not expected to hear from him. He had said nothing about writing, and their relations were scarcely such as to make it necessary. Letters were an expensive luxury in those days. But when the letter was handed to her, Marcia's heart went pounding against her breast, the color flew into her cheeks, and she sped away home on feet swift as the wings of a bird. The postmaster's daughter looked after her, and remarked to her father: "My, but don't she think a lot of him!"

Straight to the cold, lonely house she flew, and sitting down in his big chair read it.

It was a pleasant letter, beginning formally: "My dear Marcia," and asking after her health. It brought back a little of the unacquaintedness she had felt when he was at home, and which had been swept away in part by her knowledge of his childhood. But it went on quite happily telling all about his journey and describing minutely the places he had passed through and the people he had met on the way; detailing every little incident as only a born writer and observer could do, until she felt as if he were talking to her. He told her of the men whom he had met who were interested in the new project. He told of new plans and described minutely his visit to the foundry at West Point and the machinery he had seen. Marcia read it all breathlessly, in search of something, she knew not what, that was not there. When she had finished and found it not, there was a sense of aloofness, a sad little disappointment which welled up in her throat. She sat back to think about it. He was having a good time, and he was not lonely. He had no longing to be back in the house and everything running as before he had gone. He was out in the big glorious world having to do with progress, and coming in contact with men who were making history. Of course he did not dream how lonely she was here, and how she longed, if for nothing else, just to be back here alone and do as she pleased, and not to be watched over. If only she might steal Aunt Clarinda and bring her back to live here with her while David was away! But that was not to be thought of, of course. By and by she mustered courage to be glad of her letter, and to read it over once more.

That night she read the letter to Aunt Clarinda and together they discussed the great inventions, and the changes that were coming to pass in the land. Aunt Clarinda was just a little beyond her depth in such a conversation, but Marcia did most of the talking, and the dear old lady made an excellent listener, with a pat here, and a "Dearie me! Now you don't say so!" there, and a "Bless the boy! What great things he does expect. And I hope he won't be disappointed."

That letter lasted them for many a day until another came, this time from Washington, with many descriptions of public men and public doings, and a word picture of the place which made it appear much like any other place after all if it was the capitol of the country. And once there was a sentence which Marcia treasured. It was, "I wish you could be here and see everything. You would enjoy it I know."

There came another letter later beginning, "My dear little girl." There was nothing else in it to make Marcia's heart throb, it was all about his work, but Marcia carried it many days in her bosom. It gave her a thrill of delight to think of those words at the beginning. Of course it meant no more than that he thought of her as a girl, his little sister that was to have been, but there was a kind of ownership in the words that was sweet to Marcia's lonely heart. It had come to her that she was always looking for something that would make her feel that she belonged to David.

CHAPTER XXI

When David had been in New York about three weeks, he happened one day to pass the house where Kate Leavenworth was living.

Kate was standing listlessly by the window looking into the street. She was cross and felt a great depression settling over her. The flirtation with Harry Temple had begun to pall upon her. She wanted new worlds to conquer. She was restless and feverish. There was not excitement enough in the life she was living. She would like to meet more people, senators and statesmen—and to have plenty of money to dress as became her beauty, and be admired publicly. She half wished for the return of her husband, and meditated making up with him for the sake of going to Washington to have a good time in society there. What was the use of running away with a naval officer if one could not have the benefit of it? She had been a fool. Here she was almost to the last penny, and so many things she wanted. No word had come from her husband since he sent her the money at sailing. She felt a bitter resentment toward him for urging her to marry him. If she had only gone on and married David she would be living a life of ease now—plenty of money—nothing to do but what she pleased and no anxiety whatever, for David would have done just what she wanted.

Then suddenly she looked up and David passed before her!

He was walking with a tall splendid-looking man, with whom he was engaged in most earnest conversation, and his look was grave and deeply absorbed. He did not know of Kate's presence in New York, and passed the house in utter unconsciousness of the eyes watching him.

Kate's lips grew white, and her limbs seemed suddenly weak, but she strained her face against the window to watch the retreating figure of the man who had almost been her husband. How well she knew the familiar outline. How fine and handsome he appeared now! Why had she not thought so before? Were her eyes blind, or had she been under some strange enchantment? Why had she not known that her happiness lay in the way that had been marked out for her? Well, at least she knew it now.

She sat all day by that window and watched. She professed to have no appetite when pressed to come to the table, though she permitted herself to languidly consume the bountiful tray of good things that was brought her, but her eyes were on the street. She was watching to see if David would pass that way again. But though she watched until the sun went down and dusk sifted through the streets, she saw no sign nor heard the sound of his footsteps. Then she hastened up to her room, which faced upon the street also, and there, wrapped in blankets she sat in the cold frosty air, waiting and listening. And while she watched she was thinking bitter feverish thoughts. She heard Harry Temple knock and knew that he was told that she was not feeling well and had retired early. She watched him pause on the stoop thoughtfully as if considering what to do with the time thus unexpectedly thrown upon his hands, then saw him saunter up the street unconcernedly, and she wondered idly where he would go, and what he would do.

It grew late, even for New York. One by one the lights in the houses along the street went out, and all was quiet. She drew back from the window at last, weary with excitement and thinking, and lay down on the bed, but she could not sleep. The window was open and her ears were on the alert, and by and by there came the distant echo of feet ringing on the pavement. Some one was coming. She sprang up. She felt sure he was coming. Yes, there were two men. They were coming back together. She could hear their voices. She fancied she heard David's long before it was possible to distinguish any words. She leaned far out of her upper window till she could discern dim forms under the starlight, and then just as they were under the window she distinctly heard David say:

"There is no doubt but we shall win. The right is on our side, and it is the march of progress. Some of the best men in Congress are with us, and now that we are to have your influence I do not feel afraid of the issue."

They had passed by rapidly, like men who had been on a long day's jaunt of some kind and were hastening home to rest. There was little in the sentence that Kate could understand. She had no more idea whether the subject of their discourse was railroads or the last hay crop. The sentence meant to her but one thing. It showed that David companioned with the great men of the land, and his position would have given her a standing that would have been above the one she now occupied. Tears of defeat ran down her cheeks. She had made a bad mistake and she saw no way to rectify it. If her husband should die,—and it might be, for the sea was often treacherous—of course there were all sorts of possibilities,—but even then there was Marcia! She set her sharp little teeth into her red lips till the blood came. She could not get over her anger at Marcia. It would not have been so bad if David had remained her lone lorn lover, ready to fly to her if others failed. Her self-love was wounded sorely, and she, poor silly soul, mistook it for love of David. She began to fancy that after all she had loved him, and that Fate had somehow played her a mad trick and tied her to a husband she had not wanted.

Then out of the watchings of the day and the fancies of the night, there grew a thought—and the thought widened into a plan. She thought of her intimacy with Harry and her new found power. Might she perhaps exercise it over others as well as Harry Temple? Might she possibly lead back this man who had once been her lover, to bow at her feet again and worship her? If that might be she could bear all the rest. She began to long with intense craving to see David grovel at her feet, to hear him plead for a kiss from her, and tell her once more how beautiful she was, and how she fulfilled all his soul's ideals. She sat by the open window yet with the icy air of the night blowing upon her, but her cheeks burned red in the darkness, and her eyes glowed like coals of fire from the tawny framing of her fallen hair. The blankets slipped away from her throat and still she heeded not the cold, but sat with hot clenched hands planning with the devil's own strategy her shameless scheme.

By and by she lighted a candle and drew her writing materials toward her to write, but it was long she sat and thought before she finally wrote the hastily scrawled note, signed and sealed it, and blowing out her candle lay down to sleep.

The letter was addressed to David, and it ran thus:

"DEAR DAVID:"

"I have just heard that you are in New York. I am in great distress and do not know where to turn for help. For the sake of what we have been to each other in the past will you come to me?

"Hastily, your loving KATE."

She did not know where David was but she felt reasonably sure she could find out his address in the morning. There was a small boy living next door who was capable of ferreting out almost anything for money. Kate had employed him more than once as an amateur detective in cases of minor importance. So, with a bit of silver and her letter she made her way to his familiar haunts and explained most carefully that the letter was to be delivered to no one but the man to whom it was addressed, naming several stopping places where he might be likely to be found, and hinting that there was more silver to be forthcoming when he should bring her an answer to the note. With a minute description of David the keen-eyed urchin set out, while Kate betook herself to her room to dress for David's coming. She felt sure he would be found, and confident that he would come at once.

The icy wind of the night before blowing on her exposed throat and chest had given her a severe cold, but she paid no heed to that. Her eyes and cheeks were shining with fever. She knew she was entering upon a dangerous and unholy way. The excitement of it stimulated her. She felt she did not care for anything, right or wrong, sin or sorrow, only to win. She wanted to see David at her feet again. It was the only thing that would satisfy this insatiable longing in her, this wounded pride of self.

When she was dressed she stood before the mirror and surveyed herself. She knew she was beautiful, and she defied the glass to tell her anything else. She raised her chin in haughty challenge to the unseen David to resist her charms. She would bring him low before her. She would make him forget Marcia, and his home and his staid Puritan notions, and all else he held dear but herself. He should bend and kiss her hand as Harry had done, only more warmly, for instinctively she felt that his had been the purer life and therefore his surrender would mean more. He should do whatever she chose. And her eyes glowed with an unhallowed light.

She had chosen to array herself regally, in velvet, but in black, without a touch of color or of white. From her rich frock her slender throat rose daintily, like a stem upon which nodded the tempting flower of her face. No enameled complexion could have been more striking in its vivid reds and whites, and her mass of gold hair made her seem more lovely than she really was, for in her face was love of self, alluring, but heartless and cruel.

The boy found David, as Kate had thought he would, in one of the quieter hostelries where men of letters were wont to stop when in New York, and David read the letter and came at once. She had known that he would do that, too. His heart beat wildly, to the exclusion of all other thoughts save that she was in trouble, his love, his dear one. He forgot Marcia, and the young naval officer, and everything but her trouble, and before he had reached her house the sorrow had grown in his imagination into some great danger to protect her from which he was hastening.

She received him alone in the room where Harry Temple had first called, and a moment later Harry himself came to knock and enquire for the health of Mistress Leavenworth, and was told she was very much engaged at present with a gentleman and could not see any one, whereupon Harry scowled, and set himself at a suitable distance from the house to watch who should come out.

David's face was white as death as he entered, his eyes shining like dark jewels blazing at her as if he wouldabsorb the vision for the lonely future. She stood and posed,—not by any means the picture of broken sorrow he had expected to find from her note,—and let the sense of her beauty reach him. There she stood with the look on her face he had pictured to himself many a time when he had thought of her as his wife. It was a look of love unutterable, bewildering, alluring, compelling. It was so he had thought she would meet him when he came home to her from his daily business cares. And now she was there, looking that way, and he stood here, so near her, and yet a great gulf fixed! It was heaven and hell met together, and he had no power to change either.

He did not come over to her and bow low to kiss the white hand as Harry had done,—as she had thought she could compel him to do. He only stood and looked at her with the pain of an anguish beyond her comprehension, until the look would have burned through to her heart—if she had had a heart.

"You are in trouble," he spoke hoarsely, as if murmuring an excuse for having come.

She melted at once into the loveliest sorrow, her mobile features taking on a wan cast only enlivened by the glow of her cheeks.

"Sit down," she said, "you were so good to come to me, and so soon—" and her voice was like lily-bells in a quiet church-yard among the head-stones. She placed him a chair.

"Yes, I am in trouble. But that is a slight thing compared to my unhappiness. I think I am the most miserable creature that breathes upon this earth."

And with that she dropped into a low chair and hid her glowing face in a dainty, lace bordered kerchief that suppressed a well-timed sob.

Kate had wisely calculated how she could reach David's heart. If she had looked up then and seen his white, drawn look, and the tense grasp of his hands that only the greatest self-control kept quiet on his knee, perhaps even her mercilessness would have been softened. But she did not look, and she felt her part was well taken. She sobbed quietly, and waited, and his hoarse voice asked once more, as gently as a woman's through his pain:

"Will you tell me what it is and how I can help you?" He longed to take her in his arms like a little child and comfort her, but he might not. She was another's. And perhaps that other had been cruel to her! His clenched fists showed how terrible was the thought. But still the bowed figure in its piteous black sobbed and did not reply anything except, "Oh, I am so unhappy! I cannot bear it any longer."

"Is—your—your—husband unkind to you?" The words tore themselves from his tense lips as though they were beyond his control.

"Oh, no,—not exactly unkind—that is—he was not very nice before he went away," wailed out a sad voice from behind the linen cambric and lace, "and he went away without a kind word, and left me hardly any money— and he hasn't sent me any word since—and fa-father won't have anything to do with me any more—but—but— it's not that I mind, David. I don't think about those things at all. I'm so unhappy about you. I feel you do not forgive me, and I cannot stand it any longer. I have made a fearful mistake, and you are angry with me—I think about it at night"—the voice was growing lower now, and the sentences broken by sobs that told better than words what distress the sufferer would convey.

"I have been so wicked—and you were so good and kind—and now you will never forgive me—I think it will kill me to keep on thinking about it—" her voice trailed off in tears again.

David white with anguish sprang to his feet.

"Oh, Kate," he cried, "my darling! Don't talk that way. You know I forgive you. Look up and tell me you know I forgive you."

Almost she smiled her triumph beneath her sobs in the little lace border, but she looked up with real tears on her face. Even her tears obeyed her will. She was a good actress, also she knew her power over David.

"Oh, David," she cried, standing up and clasping her hands beseechingly, "can it be true? Do you really forgive me? Tell me again."

She came and stood temptingly near to the stern, suffering man wild with the tumult that raged within him. Her golden head was near his shoulder where it had rested more than once in time gone by. He looked down at her from his suffering height his arms folded tightly and said, as though taking oath before a court of justice:

"I do."

She looked up with her pleading blue eyes, like two jewels of light now, questioning whether she might yet go one step further. Her breath came quick and soft, he fancied it touched his cheek, though she was not tall enough for that. She lifted her tear-wet face like a flower after a storm, and pleaded with her eyes once more, saying in a whisper very soft and sweet:

"If you really forgive me, then kiss me, just once, so I may remember it always."

It was more than he could bear. He caught her to himself and pressed his lips upon hers in one frenzied kiss of torture. It was as if wrung from him against his will. Then suddenly it came upon him what he had done, as he held her in his arms, and he put her from him gently, as a mother might put away the precious child she was sacrificing tenderly, agonizingly, but finally. He put her from him thus and stood a moment looking at her, while she almost sparkled her pleasure at him through the tears. She felt that she had won.

But gradually the silence grew ominous. She perceived he was not smiling. His mien was like one who looks into an open grave, and gazes for the last time at all that remains of one who is dear. He did not seem like one who had yielded a moral point and was ready now to serve her as she would. She grew uneasy under his gaze. She moved forward and put out her hands inviting, yielding, as only such a woman could do, and the spell which bound him seemed to be broken. He fumbled for a moment in his waistcoat pocket and brought out a large roll of bills which he laid upon the table, and taking up his hat turned toward the door. A cold wave of weakness seemed to pass over her, stung here and there by mortal pride that was in fear of being wounded beyond recovery.

"Where are you going?" she asked weakly, and her voice sounded to her from miles away, and strange.

He turned and looked at her again and she knew the look meant farewell. He did not speak. Her whole being rose for one more mighty effort.

"You are not going to leave me—now?" There was angelic sweetness in the voice, pleading, reproachful, piteous.

"I must!" he said, and his voice sounded harsh. "I have just done that for which, were I your husband, I would feel like killing any other man. I must protect you against yourself,—against myself. You must be kept pure before God if it kills us both. I would gladly die if that could help you, but I am not even free to do that, for I belong to another."

Then he turned and was gone.

Kate's hands fell to her sides, and seemed stiff and lifeless. The bright color faded from her cheeks, and a cold frenzy of horror took possession of her. "Pure before God!" She shuddered at the name, and crimson shame rolled over forehead and cheek. She sank in a little heap on the floor with her face buried in the chair beside which she had been standing, and the waters of humiliation rolled wave on wave above her. She had failed, and for one brief moment she was seeing her own sinful heart as it was.

But the devil was there also. He whispered to her now the last sentence that David had spoken: "I belong to another!"

Up to that moment Marcia had been a very negative factor in the affair to Kate's mind. She had been annoyed and angry at her as one whose ignorance and impertinence had brought her into an affair where she did not belong, but now she suddenly faced the fact that Marcia must be reckoned with. Marcia the child, who had for years been her slave and done her bidding, had arisen in her way, and she hated her with a sudden vindictive hate that would have killed without flinching if the opportunity had presented at that moment. Kate had no idea how utterly uncontrolled was her whole nature. She was at the mercy of any passing passion. Hate and revenge took possession of her now. With flashing eyes she rose to her feet, brushing her tumbled hair back and wiping away angry tears. She was too much agitated to notice that some one had knocked at the front door and been admitted, and when Harry Temple walked into the room he found her standing so with hands clenched together, and tears flowing down her cheeks unchecked.

Now a woman in tears, when the tears were not caused by his own actions, was Harry's opportunity. He had ways of comforting which were as unscrupulous as they generally proved effective, and so with affectionate tenderness he took Kate's hand and held it impressively, calling her "dear." He spoke soothing words, smoothed her hair, and kissed her flushed cheeks and eyes. It was all very pleasant to Kate's hurt pride. She let Harry comfort her, and pet her a while, and at last he said:

"Now tell me all about it, dear. I saw Lord Spafford trail dejectedly away from here looking like death, and I come here and find my lady in a fine fury. What has happened? If I mistake not the insufferable cad has got badly hurt, but it seems to have ruffled the lady also."

This helped. It was something to feel that David was suffering. She wanted him to suffer. He had brought shame and humiliation upon her. She never realized that the thing that shamed her was that he thought her better than she was.

"He is offensively good. I *hate* him!" she remarked as a kitten might who had got hurt at playing with a mouse in a trap.

The man's face grew bland with satisfaction.

"Not so good, my lady, but that he has been making love to you, if I mistake not, and he with a wife at home." The words were said quietly, but there was more of a question in them than the tone conveyed. The man wished to have evidence against his enemy.

Kate colored uneasily and drooped her lashes.

Harry studied her face keenly, and then went on cautiously:

"If his wife were not your sister I should say that one might punish him well through her."

Kate cast him a hard, scrutinizing look.

"You have some score against him yourself," she said with conviction.

"Perhaps I have, my lady. Perhaps I too hate him. He is offensively good, you know."

There was silence in the room for a full minute while the devil worked in both hearts.

"What did you mean by saying one might punish him through his wife? He does not love his wife."

"Are you sure?"

"Quite sure."

"Perhaps he loves some one else, my lady."

"He does." She said it proudly.

"Perhaps he loves you, my lady." He said it softly like the suggestion from another world. The lady was silent, but he needed no other answer.

"Then indeed, the way would be even clearer,—were not his wife your sister."

Kate looked at him, a half knowledge of his meaning beginning to dawn in her eyes.

"How?" she asked laconically.

"In case his wife should leave him do you think my lord would hold his head so high?"

Kate still looked puzzled.

"If some one else should win her affection, and should persuade her to leave a husband who did not love her, and who was bestowing his heart"—he hesitated an instant and his eye traveled significantly to the roll of bills still lying where David had left them—"and his gifts," he hazarded, "upon another woman——"

Kate grasped the thought at once and an evil glint of eagerness showed in her eyes. She could see what an advantage it would be to herself to have Marcia removed from the situation. It would break one more cord of honor that bound David to a code which was hateful to her now, because its existence shamed her. Nevertheless, unscrupulous as she was she could not see how this was a possibility.

"But she is offensively good too," she said as if answering her own thoughts.

"All goodness has its weak spot," sneered the man. "If I mistake not you have found my lord's. It is possible I might find his wife's."

The two pairs of eyes met then, filled with evil light. It was as if for an instant they were permitted to look into the pit, and see the possibilities of wickedness, and exult in it. The lurid glare of their thoughts played in their faces. All the passion of hate and revenge rushed upon Kate in a frenzy. With all her heart she wished this might be. She looked her co-operation in the plan even before her hard voice answered:

"You need not stop because she is my sister."

He felt he had her permission, and he permitted himself a glance of admiration for the depths to which she could go without being daunted. Here was evil courage worthy of his teaching. She seemed to him beautiful enough and daring enough for Satan himself to admire.

"And may I have the pleasure of knowing that I would by so doing serve my lady in some wise?"

She drooped her shameless eyes and murmured guardedly, "Perhaps." Then she swept him a coquettish glance that meant they understood one another.

"Then I shall feel well rewarded," he said gallantly, and bowing with more than his ordinary flattery of look bade her good day and went out.

CHAPTER XXII

David stumbled blindly out the door and down the street. His one thought was to get to his room at the tavern and shut the door. He had an important appointment that morning, but it passed completely from his mind. He met one or two men whom he knew, but he did not see them, and passed them swiftly without a glance of recognition. They said one to another, "How absorbed he is in the great themes of the world!" but David passed on in his pain and misery and humiliation and never knew they were near him.

He went to the room that had been his since he had reached New York, and fastening the door against all intrusion fell upon his knees beside the bed, and let the flood-tide of his sorrow roll over him. Not even when Kate had played him false on his wedding morning had he felt the pain that now cut into his very soul. For now there was mingled with it the agony of consciousness of sin. He had sinned against heaven, against honor and love, and all that was pure and good. He was just like any bad man. He had yielded to sudden temptation and taken another man's wife in his arms and kissed her! That the woman had been his by first right, and that he loved her: that she had invited the kiss, indeed pleaded for it, his sensitive conscience told him in no wise lessened the offense. He had also caused her whom he loved to sin. He was a man and knew the world. He should have shielded her against herself. And yet as he went over and over the whole painful scene through which he had just passed his soul cried out in agony and he felt his weakness more and more. He had failed, failed most miserably. Acted like any coward!

The humiliation of it was unspeakable. Could any sorrow be like unto his? Like a knife flashing through the gloom of his own shame would come the echo of her words as she pleaded with him to kiss her. It was a kiss of forgiveness she had wanted, and she had put her heart into her eyes and begged as for her very life. How could he have refused? Then he would parley with himself for a long time trying to prove to himself that the kiss and the embrace were justified, that he had done no wrong in God's sight. And ever after this round of confused arguing he would end with the terrible conviction that he had sinned.

Sometimes Marcia's sweet face and troubled eyes would appear to him as he wrestled all alone, and seemed to be longing to help him, and again would come the piercing thought that he had harmed this gentle girl also. He had tangled her into his own spoiled web of life, and been disloyal to her. She was pure and true and good. She had given up every thing to help him and he had utterly forgotten her. He had promised to love, cherish, and protect her! That was another sin. He could not love and cherish her when his whole heart was another's. Then he thought of Kate's husband, that treacherous man who had stolen his bride and now gone away and left her sorrowing—left her without money, penniless in a strange city. Why had he not been more calm and questioned her before he came away. Perhaps she was in great need. It comforted him to think he had left her all the money he had with him. There was enough to keep her from want for a while. And yet, perhaps he had been wrong to give it to her. He had no right to give it!

He groaned aloud at the thought of his helplessness to help her helplessness. Was there not some way he could find out and help her without doing wrong?

Over and over he went through the whole dreadful day, until his brain was weary and his heart failed him. The heavens seemed brass and no answer came to his cry,—the appeal of a broken soul. It seemed that he could not get up from his knees, could not go out into the world again and face life. He had been tried and had failed, and yet though he knew his sin he felt an intolerable longing to commit it over again. He was frightened at his own weakness, and with renewed vigor he began to pray for help. It was like the prayer of Jacob of old, the crying out of a soul that would not be denied. All day long the struggle continued, and far into the night. At last a great peace began to settle upon David's soul. Things that had been confused by his passionate longings grew clear as day. Self dropped away, and sin, conquered, slunk out of sight. Right and Wrong were once more clearly defined in his mind. However wrong it might or might not be he was here in this situation. He had married Marcia and promised to be true to her. He was doubly cut off from Kate by her own act and by his. That was his punishment,—and hers. He must not seek to lessen it even for her, for it was God-sent. Henceforth his path and hers must be apart. If she were to be helped in any way from whatsoever trouble was hers, it was not permitted him to be the instrument. He had shown his unfitness for it in his interview that morning, even if in the eyes of the world it could have been at all. It was his duty to cut himself off from her forever. He must not even think of her any more. He must be as true and good to Marcia as was possible. He must do no more wrong. He must grow strong and suffer.

The peace that came with conviction brought sleep to his weary mind and body.

When he awoke it was almost noon. He remembered the missed appointment of the day before, and the journey to Washington which he had planned for that day. With a start of horror he looked at his watch and found he had but a few hours in which to try to make up for the remissness of yesterday before the evening coach left for Philadelphia. It was as if some guardian angel had met his first waking thoughts with business that could not be delayed and so kept him from going over the painful events of the day before. He arose and hastened out into the world once more.

Late in the afternoon he found the man he was to have met the day before, and succeeded in convincing him that he ought to help the new enterprise. He was standing on the corner saying the last few words as the two separated, when Kate drove by in a friend's carriage, surrounded by parcels. She had been on a shopping tour spending the money that David had given her, for silks and laces and jewelry, and now she was returning in high glee with her booty. The carriage passed quite near to David who stood with his back to the street, and she could see his animated face as he smiled at the other man, a fine looking man who looked as if he might be some one of note. The momentary glance did not show the haggard look of David's face nor the lines that his vigil of the night before had traced under his eyes, and Kate was angered to see him so unconcerned and forgetful of his pain of yesterday. Her face darkened with spite, and she resolved to make him suffer yet, and to the utmost, for the sin of forgetting her.

But David was in the way of duty, and he did not see her, for his guardian angel was hovering close at hand.

As the Fall wore on and the winter set in Harry's letters became less frequent and less intimate. Hannah was troubled, and after consultation with her grandmother, to which Miranda listened at the latch hole, duly reporting quotations to her adored Mrs. Spafford, Hannah decided upon an immediate trip to the metropolis.

"Hannah's gone to New York to find out what's become of that nimshi Harry Temple. She thought she had him fast, an' she's been holdin' him over poor Lemuel Skinner's head like thet there sword hangin' by a hair I heard the minister tell about last Sunday, till Lemuel, he don't know but every minute's gone'll be his last. You mark my words, she'll hev to take poor Lem after all, an' be glad she's got him, too,—and she's none too good for him neither. He's ben faithful to her ever since she wore pantalets, an' she's ben keepin' him off'n on an' hopin' an' tryin' fer somebody bigger. It would jes' serve her right ef she'd get that fool of a Harry Temple, but she won't. He's too sharp for that ef he *is* a fool. He don't want to tie himself up to no woman's aprun strings. He rather dandle about after 'em all an' say pretty things, an' keep his earnin's fer himself."

Hannah reached New York the week after David left for Washington. She wrote beforehand to Harry to let him know she was coming, and made plain that she expected his attentions exclusively while there, and he smiled blandly as he read the letter and read her intentions between the lines. He told Kate a good deal about her that evening when he went to call, told her how he had heard she was an old flame of David's, and Kate's jealousy was immediately aroused. She wished to meet Hannah Heath. There was a sort of triumph in the thought that she had scorned and flung aside the man whom this woman had "set her cap" for, even though another woman was now in the place that neither had. Hannah went to visit a cousin in New York who lived in a quiet part of the city and did not go out much, but for reasons best known to themselves, both Kate Leavenworth and Harry Temple elected to see a good deal of her while she was in the city. Harry was pleasant and attentive, but not more to one woman than to the other. Hannah, watching him jealously, decided that at least Kate was not her rival in his affections, and so Hannah and Kate became quite friendly. Kate had a way of making much of her women friends when she chose, and she happened to choose in this case, for it occurred to her it would be well to have a friend in the town where lived her sister and her former lover. There might be reasons why, sometime. She opened her heart of hearts to Hannah, and Hannah, quite discreetly, and without wasting much of her scanty store of love, entered, and the friendship was sealed. They had not known each other many days before Kate had confided to Hannah the story of her own marriage and her sister's, embellished of course as she chose. Hannah, astonished, puzzled, wondering, curious, at the tragedy that had been enacted at her very home door, became more friendly than ever and hated more cordially than ever the young and innocent wife who had stepped into the vacant place and so made her own hopes and ambitions impossible. She felt that she would like to put down the pert young thing for daring to be there, and to be pretty, and now she felt she had the secret which would help her to do so.

As the visit went on and it became apparent to Hannah Heath that she was not the one woman in all the world to Harry Temple, she hinted to Kate that it was likely she would be married soon. She even went so far as to say that she had come away from home to decide the matter, and that she had but to say the word and the ceremony would come off. Kate questioned eagerly, and seeing her opportunity asked if she might come to the wedding. Hannah, flattered, and seeing a grand opportunity for a wholesale triumph and revenge, assented with pleasure. Afterward as Hannah had hoped and intended, Kate carried the news of the impending decision and probable wedding to the ears of Harry Temple.

But Hannah's hint had no further effect upon the redoubtable Harry. Two days later he appeared, smiling, congratulatory, deploring the fact that she would be lost in a certain sense to his friendship, although he hoped always to be looked upon as a little more than a friend.

Hannah covered her mortification under a calm and condescending exterior. She blushed appropriately, said some sentimental things about hoping their friendship would not be affected by the change, told him how much she had enjoyed their correspondence, but gave him to understand that it had been mere friendship of course from her point of view, and Harry indulgently allowed her to think that he had hoped for more and was grieved but consolable over the outcome.

They waxed a trifle sentimental at the parting, but when Harry was gone, Hannah wrote a most touching letter to Lemuel Skinner which raised him to the seventh heaven of delight, causing him to feel that he was treading upon air as he walked the prosaic streets of his native town where he had been going about during Hannah's absence like a lost spirit without a guiding star.

"Dear Lemuel:" she wrote:—

"I am coming home. I wonder if you will be glad?

(Artful Hannah, as if she did not know!)

"It is very delightful in New York and I have been having a gay time since I came, and everybody has been most pleasant, but—

"'Mid pleasures and palaces though we may roam,

Still, be it ever so humble, there's no place like home.

A charm from the skies seems to hallow it there,

Which, go through the world, you'll not meet with elsewhere.

Home, home, sweet home!

There's no place like home.

"That is a new song, Lemuel, that everybody here is singing. It is written by a young American named John Howard Payne who is in London now acting in a great playhouse. Everybody is wild over this song. I'll sing it for you when I come home.

"I shall be at home in time for singing school next week, Lemuel. I wonder if you'll come to see me at once and welcome me. You cannot think how glad I shall be to get home again. It seems as though I had been gone a year at least. Hoping to see you soon, I remain

"Always your sincere friend,

"Hannah Heath."

And thus did Hannah make smooth her path before her, and very soon after inditing this epistle she bade good-bye to New York and took her way home resolved to waste no further time in chasing will-o-the-wisps.

When Lemuel received that letter he took a good look at himself in the glass. More than seven years had he served for Hannah, and little hope had he had of a final reward. He was older by ten years than she, and already his face began to show it. He examined himself critically, and was pleased to find with that light of hope in his eyes he was not so bad looking as he feared. He betook himself to the village tailor forthwith and ordered a new suit of clothes, though his Sunday best was by no means shiny yet. He realized that if he did not win now he never would, and he resolved to do his best.

On the way home, during all the joltings of the coach over rough roads Hannah Heath was planning two campaigns, one of love with Lemuel, and one of hate with Marcia Spafford. She was possessed of knowledge which she felt would help her in the latter, and often she smiled vindictively as she laid her neat plans for the destruction of the bride's complacency.

That night the fire in the Heath parlor burned high and glowed, and the candles in their silver holders flickered across fair Hannah's face as she dimpled and smiled and coquetted with poor Lemuel. But Lemuel needed no pity. He was not afraid of Hannah. Not for nothing had he served his seven years, and he understood every fancy and foible of her shallow nature. He knew his time had come at last, and he was getting what he had wanted long, for Lemuel had admired and loved Hannah in spite of the dance she had led him, and in spite of the other lovers she had allowed to come between them.

Hannah had not been at home many days before she called upon Marcia.

Marcia had just seated herself at the piano when Hannah appeared to her from the hall, coming in unannounced through the kitchen door according to old neighborly fashion.

Marcia was vexed. She arose from the instrument and led the way to the little morning room which was sunny and cosy, and bare of music or books. She did not like to visit with Hannah in the parlor. Somehow her presence reminded her of the evil face of Harry Temple as he had stooped to kiss her.

"You know how to play, too, don't you?" said Hannah as they sat down. "Your sister plays beautifully. Do you know the new song, 'Home, Sweet Home?' She plays it with so much feeling and sings it so that one would think her heart was breaking for her home. You must have been a united family." Hannah said it with sharp scrutiny in voice and eyes.

"Sit down, Miss Heath," said Marcia coolly, lowering the yellow shades that her visitor's eyes might not be troubled by a broad sunbeam. "Did you have a pleasant time in New York?"

Hannah could not be sure whether or not the question was an evasion. The utterly child-like manner of Marcia disarmed suspicion.

"Oh, delightful, of course. Could any one have anything else in New York?"

Hannah laughed disagreeably. She realized the limitations of life in a town.

"I suppose," said Marcia, her eyes shining with the thought, "that you saw all the wonderful things of the city. I should enjoy being in New York a little while. I have heard of so many new things. Were there any ships in the harbor? I have always wanted to go over a great ship. Did you have opportunity of seeing one?"

"Oh, dear me. No!" said Hannah. "I shouldn't have cared in the least for that. I'm sure I don't know whether there were any ships in or not. I suppose there were. I saw a lot of sails on the water, but I did not ask about them. I'm not interested in dirty boats. I liked visiting the shops best. Your sister took me about everywhere. She is a most charming creature. You must miss her greatly. You were a sly little thing to cut her out."

Marcia's face flamed crimson with anger and amazement. Hannah's dart had hit the mark, and she was watching keenly to see her victim quiver.

"I do not understand you," said Marcia with girlish dignity.

"Oh, now don't pretend to misunderstand. I've heard all about it from headquarters," she said it archly, laughing. "But then I don't blame you. David was worth it." Hannah ended with a sigh. If she had ever cared for any one besides herself that one was David Spafford.

"I do not understand you," said Marcia again, drawing herself up with all the Schuyler haughtiness she could master, till she quite resembled her father.

"Now, Mrs. Spafford," said the visitor, looking straight into her face and watching every expression as a cat would watch a mouse, "you don't mean to tell me your sister was not at one time very intimate with your husband."

"Mr. Spafford has been intimate in our family for a number of years," said Marcia proudly, her fighting fire up, "but as for my having 'cut my sister out' as you call it, you have certainly been misinformed. Excuse me, I think I will close the kitchen door. It seems to blow in here and make a draft."

Marcia left the room with her head up and her fine color well under control, and when she came back her head was still up and a distant expression was in her face. Somehow Hannah felt she had not gained much after all. But Marcia, after Hannah's departure, went up to her cold room and wept bitter tears on her pillow alone.

After that first visit Hannah never found the kitchen door unlocked when she came to make a morning call, but she improved every little opportunity to torment her gentle victim. She had had a letter from Kate and had Marcia heard? How often did Kate write her? Did Marcia know how fond Harry Temple was of Kate? And where was Kate's husband? Would he likely be ordered home soon? These little annoyances were almost unbearable sometimes and Marcia had much ado to keep her sweetness of outward demeanor.

People looked upon Lemuel with new respect. He had finally won where they had considered him a fool for years for hanging on. The added respect brought added self-respect. He took on new manliness. Grandmother Heath felt that he really was not so bad after all, and perhaps Hannah might as well have taken him at first. Altogether the Heath family were well pleased, and preparations began at once for a wedding in the near future.

And still David lingered, held here and there by a call from first one man and then another, and by important doings in Congress. He seemed to be rarely fitted for the work.

Once he was called back to New York for a day or two, and Harry Temple happened to see him as he arrived. That night he wrote to Hannah a friendly letter—Harry was by no means through with Hannah yet—and casually remarked that he saw David Spafford was in New York again. He supposed now that Mrs. Leavenworth's evenings would be fully occupied and society would see little of her while he remained.

The day after Hannah received that letter was Sunday.

The weeks had gone by rapidly since David left his home, and now the spring was coming on. The grass was already green as summer and the willow tree by the graveyard gate was tender and green like a spring-plume. All the foliage was out and fluttering its new leaves in the sunshine as Marcia passed from the old stone church with the two aunts and opened her little green sunshade. Her motion made David's last letter rustle in her bosom. It thrilled her with pleasure that not even the presence of Hannah Heath behind her could cloud.

However prim and fault-finding the two aunts might be in the seclusion of their own home, in public no two could have appeared more adoring than Amelia and Hortense Spafford. They hovered near Marcia and delighted to show how very close and intimate was the relationship between themselves and their new and beautiful niece, of whom in their secret hearts they were prouder than they would have cared to tell. In their best black silks and their fine lace shawls they walked beside her and talked almost eagerly, if those two stately beings could have anything to do with a quality so frivolous as eagerness. They wished it understood that David's wife was worthy of appreciation and they were more conscious than she of the many glances of admiration in her direction.

Hannah Heath encountered some of those admiring glances and saw jealously for whom they were meant. She hastened to lean forward and greet Marcia, her spiteful tongue all ready for a stab.

"Good morning, Mrs. Spafford. Is that husband of yours not home yet? Really! Why, he's quite deserted you. I call that hard for the first year, and your honeymoon scarcely over yet."

"He's been called back to New York again," said Marcia annoyed over the spiteful little sentences. "He says he may be at home soon, but he cannot be sure. His business is rather uncertain."

"New York!" said Hannah, and her voice was annoyingly loud. "What! Not again! There must be some great attraction there," and then with a meaning glance, "I suppose your sister is still there!"

Marcia felt her face crimsoning, and the tears starting from angry eyes. She felt a sudden impulse to slap Hannah. What if she should! What would the aunts say? The thought of the tumult she might make roused her sense of humor and a laugh bubbled up instead of the tears, and Hannah, watching, cat-like, could only see eyes dancing with fun though the cheeks were charmingly red. By Hannah's expression Marcia knew she was baffled, but Marcia could not get away from the disagreeable suggestion that had been made.

Yes, David was in New York, and Kate was there. Not for an instant did she doubt her husband's nobleness. She knew David would be good and true. She knew little of the world's wickedness, and never thought of any blame, as other women might, in such a suggestion. But a great jealousy sprang into being that she never dreamed existed. Kate was there, and he would perhaps see her, and all his old love and disappointment would be brought to mind again. Had she, Marcia, been hoping he would forget it? Had she been claiming something of him in her heart for herself? She could not tell. She did not know what all this tumult of feeling meant. She longed to get away and think it over, but the solemn Sunday must be observed. She must fold away her church things, put on another frock and come down to the oppressive Sunday dinner, hear Deacon Brown's rheumatism discussed, or listen to a long comparison of the morning's sermon with one preached twenty years ago by the minister, now long dead upon the same text. It was all very hard to keep her mind upon, with these other thoughts rushing pell-mell through her brain; and when Aunt Amelia asked her to pass the butter, she handed the sugar-bowl instead. Miss Amelia looked as shocked as if she had broken the great-grandmother's china teapot.

Aunt Clarinda claimed her after dinner and carried her off to her room to talk about David, so that Marcia had no chance to think even then. Miss Clarinda looked into the sweet shadowed eyes and wondered why the girl looked so sad. She thought it was because David stayed away so long, and so she kept her with her all the rest of the day.

When Marcia went to her room that night she threw herself on her knees beside the bed and tried to pray. She felt more lonely and heartsick than she ever felt before in her life. She did not know what the great hunger in her heart meant. It was terrible to think David had loved Kate. Kate never loved him in return in the right way. Marcia felt very sure of that. She wished she might have had the chance in Kate's place, and then all of a sudden the revelation came to her. She loved David herself with a great overwhelming love. Not just a love that could come and keep house for him and save him from the criticisms and comments of others; but with a love that demanded to be loved in return; a love that was mindful of every dear lineament of his countenance. The knowledge thrilled through her with a great sweetness. She did not seem to care for anything else just now, only to know that she loved David. David could never love her of course, not in that way, but she would love him. She would try to shut out the thought of Kate from him forever.

And so, dreaming, hovering on the edge of all that was bitter and all that was sweet, she fell asleep with David's letter clasped close over her heart.

CHAPTER XXIII

Marcia had gone down to her own house the next morning very early. She had hoped for a letter but none had come. Her soul was in torment between her attempt to keep out of her mind the hateful things Hannah Heath had said, and reproaching herself for what seemed to her her unseemly feeling toward David, who loved another and could never love her. It was not a part of her life-dream to love one who belonged to another. Yet her heart was his and she was beginning to know that everything belonging to him was dear to her. She went and sat in his place at the table, she touched with tenderness the books upon his desk that he had used before he went away, she went up to his room and laid her lips for one precious daring instant upon his pillow, and then drew back with wildly beating heart ashamed of her emotion. She knelt beside his bed and prayed: "Oh, God, I love him, I love him! I cannot help it!" as if she would apologize for herself, and then she hugged the thought of her love to herself, feeling its sweet pain drift through her like some delicious agony. Her love had come through sorrow to her, and was not as she would have had it could she have chosen. It brought no ray of happy hope for the future, save just the happiness of loving in secret, and of doing for the object loved, with no thought of a returned affection.

Then she went slowly down the stairs, trying to think how it would seem when David came back. He had been so long gone that it seemed as if perhaps he might never return. She felt that it had been no part of the spirit of her contract with David that she should render to him this wild sweet love that he had expected Kate to give. He had not wanted it. He had only wanted a wife in name.

Then the color would sweep over her face in a crimson drift and leave it painfully white, and she would glide to the piano like a ghost of her former self and play some sad sweet strain, and sometimes sing.

She had no heart for her dear old woods in these days. She had tried it one day in spring; slipped over the back fence and away through the ploughed field where the sea of silver oats had surged, and up to the hillside and the woods; but she was so reminded of David that it only brought heart aches and tears. She wondered if it was because she was getting old that the hillside did not seem so joyous now, and she did not care to look up into the sky just for the pure joy of sky and air and clouds, nor to listen to the branches whisper to the robins nesting. She stooped and picked a great handful of spring beauties, but they did not seem to give her pleasure, and by and by she dropped them from listless fingers and walked sedately down to the house once more.

On this morning she did not even care to play. She went into the parlor and touched a few notes, but her heart was heavy and sad. Life was growing too complex.

Last week there had come a letter from Harry Temple. It had startled her when it arrived. She feared it was some ill-news about David, coming as it did from New York and being written in a strange hand.

It had been a plea for forgiveness, representing that the writer had experienced nothing but deep repentance and sorrow since the time he had seen her last. He set forth his case in a masterly way, with little touching facts of his childhood, and lonely upbringing, with no mother to guide. He told her that her noble action toward him had but made him revere her the more, and that, in short, she had made a new creature of him by refusing to return his kiss that day, and leaving him alone with so severe a rebuke. He felt that if all women were so good and true men would be a different race, and now he looked up to her as one might look up to an angel, and he felt he could never be happy again on this earth until he had her written word of forgiveness. With that he felt he could live a new life, and she must rest assured that he would never offer other than reverence to any woman again. He further added that his action had not intended any insult to her, that he was merely expressing his natural admiration for a spirit so good and true, and that his soul was innocent of any intention of evil. With sophistry in the use of which he was an adept, he closed his epistle, fully clearing himself, and assuring her that he could have made her understand it that day if she had not left so suddenly, and he had not been almost immediately called away to the dying bed of his dear cousin. This contradictory letter had troubled Marcia greatly. She was keen enough to see that his logic was at fault, and that the two pages of his letter did not hang together, but one thing was plain, that he wished her forgiveness. The Bible said that one must forgive, and surely it was right to let him know that she did, though when she thought of the fright he had given her it was hard to do. Still, it was right, and if he was so unhappy, perhaps she had better let him know. She would rather have waited until David returned to consult him in the matter, but the letter seemed so insistent that she had finally written a stiff little note, in formal language, "Mrs. Spafford sends herewith her full and free forgiveness to Mr. Harry Temple, and promises to think no more of the matter."

She would have liked to consult some one. She almost thought of taking Aunt Clarinda into her confidence, but decided that she might not understand. So she finally sent off the brief missive, and let her troubled thoughts wander after it more than once.

She was standing by the window looking out into the yard perplexing herself over this again when there came a loud knocking at the front door. She started, half frightened, for the knock sounded through the empty house so insistently. It seemed like trouble coming. She felt nervous as she went down the hall.

It was only a little urchin, barefoot, and tow-headed. He had ridden an old mare to the door, and left her nosing at the dusty grass. He brought her a letter. Again her heart fluttered excitedly. Who could be writing to her? It was not David. Why did the handwriting look familiar? It could not be from any one at home. Father? Mother? No, it was no one she knew. She tore it open, and the boy jumped on his horse and was off down the street before she realized that he was gone.

"DEAR MADAM:" the letter read,

"I bring you news of your husband, and having met with an accident I am unable to come further. You will find me at the Green Tavern two miles out on the corduroy road. As the business is private, please come alone.

"A MESSENGER."

Marcia trembled so that she sat down on the stairs. A sudden weakness went over her like a wave, and the hall grew dark around her as though she were going to faint. But she did not. She was strong and well and had never fainted in her life. She rallied in a moment and tried to think. Something had happened to David. Something dreadful, perhaps, and she must go at once and find out. Still it must be something mysterious, for the man had said it was private. Of course that meant David would not want it known. David had intended that the man would come to her and tell her by herself. She must go. There was nothing else to be done. She must go at once and get rid of this awful suspense. It was a good day for the message to have come, for she had brought her lunch expecting to do some spring cleaning. David had been expected home soon, and she liked to make a bustle of preparation as if he might come in any day, for it kept up her good cheer.

Having resolved to go she got up at once, closed the doors and windows, put on her bonnet and went out down the street toward the old corduroy road. It frightened her to think what might be at the end of her journey. Possibly David himself, hurt or dying, and he had sent for her in this way that she might break the news gently to his aunts. As she walked along she conjured various forms of trouble that might have come to him. Now and then she would try to take a cheerful view, saying to herself that David might have needed more important papers, papers which he would not like everyone to know about, and had sent by special messenger to her to get them. Then her face would brighten and her step grow more brisk. But always would come the dull thud of possibility of something more serious. Her heart beat so fast sometimes that she was forced to lessen her speed to get her breath, for though she was going through town, and must necessarily walk somewhat soberly lest she call attention to herself, she found that her nerves and imagination were fairly running ahead, and waiting impatiently for her feet to catch up at every turning place.

At last she came to the corduroy road—a long stretch of winding way overlaid with logs which made an unpleasant path. Most of the way was swampy, and bordered in some places by thick, dark woods. Marcia sped on from log to log, with a nervous feeling that she must step on each one or her errand would not be successful. She was not afraid of the loneliness, only of what might be coming at the end of her journey.

But suddenly, in the densest part of the wood, she became conscious of footsteps echoing hers, and a chill laid hold upon her. She turned her head and there, wildly gesticulating and running after her, was Miranda!

Annoyed, and impatient to be on her way, and wondering what to do with Miranda, or what she could possibly want, Marcia stopped to wait for her.

"I thought—as you was goin' 'long my way"—puffed Miranda, "I'd jes' step along beside you. You don't mind, do you?"

Marcia looked troubled. If she should say she did then Miranda would think it queer and perhaps suspect something.

She tried to smile and ask how far Miranda was going.

"Oh, I'm goin' to hunt fer wild strawberries," said the girl nonchalantly clattering a big tin pail.

"Isn't it early yet for strawberries?" questioned Marcia.

"Well, mebbe, an' then ag'in mebbe 'tain't. I know a place I'm goin' to look anyway. Are you goin' 's fur 's the Green Tavern?"

Miranda's bright eyes looked her through and through, and Marcia's truthful ones could not evade. Suddenly as she looked into the girl's homely face, filled with a kind of blind adoration, her heart yearned for counsel in this trying situation. She was reminded of Miranda's helpfulness the time she ran away to the woods, and the care with which she had guarded the whole matter so that no one ever heard of it. An impulse came to her to confide in Miranda. She was a girl of sharp common sense, and would perhaps be able to help with her advice. At least she could get comfort from merely telling her trouble and anxiety.

"Miranda," she said, "can you keep a secret?"

The girl nodded.

"Well, I'm going to tell you something, just because I am so troubled and I feel as if it would do me good to tell it." She smiled and Miranda answered the smile with much satisfaction and no surprise. Miranda had come for this, though she did not expect her way to be so easy.

"I'll be mum as an oyster," said Miranda. "You jest tell me anything you please. You needn't be afraid Hannah Heath'll know a grain about it. She 'n' I are two people. I know when to shut up."

"Well, Miranda, I'm in great perplexity and anxiety. I've just had a note from a messenger my husband has sent asking me to come out to that Green Tavern you were talking about. He was sent to me with some message and has had an accident so he couldn't come. It kind of frightened me to think what might be the matter. I'm glad you are going this way because it keeps me from thinking about it. Are we nearly there? I never went out this road so far before."

"It ain't fur," said Miranda as if that were a minor matter. "I'll go right along in with you, then you needn't feel lonely. I guess likely it's business. Don't you worry." The tone was reassuring, but Marcia's face looked troubled.

"No, I guess that won't do, Miranda, for the note says it is a private matter and I must come alone. You know Mr. Spafford has matters to write about that are very important, railroads, and such things, and sometimes he doesn't care to have any one get hold of his ideas before they appear in the paper. His enemies might use them to stop the plans of the great improvements he is writing about."

"Let me see that note!" demanded Miranda. "Got it with you?" Marcia hesitated. Perhaps she ought not to show it, and yet there was nothing in the note but what she had already told the girl, and she felt sure she would not breathe a word to a living soul after her promise. She handed Miranda the letter, and they stopped a moment while she slowly spelled it out. Miranda was no scholar. Marcia watched her face eagerly, as if to gather a ray of hope from it, but she was puzzled by Miranda's look. A kind of satisfaction had overspread her homely countenance.

"Should you think from that that David was hurt—or ill—or—or—killed—or anything?" She asked the question as if Miranda were a wizard, and hung anxiously upon her answer.

"Naw, I don't reckon so!" said Miranda. "Don't you worry. David's all right somehow. I'll take care o' you. You go 'long up and see what's the business, an' I'll wait here out o' sight o' the tavern. Likely's not he might take a notion not to tell you ef he see me come along with you. You jest go ahead, and I'll be on hand when you get through. If you need me fer anything you jest holler out 'Randy!' good and loud an' I'll hear you. Guess I'll set on this log. The tavern's jest round that bend in the road. Naw, you needn't thank me. This is a real pretty mornin' to set an' rest. Good-bye."

Marcia hurried on, glancing back happily at her protector in a calico sunbonnet seated stolidly on a log with her tin pail beside her.

Poor stupid Miranda! Of course she could not understand what a comfort it was to have confided her trouble. Marcia went up to the tavern with almost a smile on her face, though her heart began to beat wildly as a slatternly girl led her into a big room at the right of the hall.

As Marcia disappeared behind the bend in the road, Miranda stealthily stole along the edge of the woods, till she stood hidden behind a clump of alders where she could peer out and watch Marcia until she reached the tavern and passed safely by the row of lounging, smoking men, and on into the doorway. Then Miranda waited just an instant to look in all directions, and sped across the road, mounting the fence and on through two meadows, and the barnyard to the kitchen door of the tavern.

"Mornin'! Mis' Green," she said to the slovenly looking woman who sat by the table peeling potatoes. "Mind givin' me a drink o' water? I'm terrible thirsty, and seemed like I couldn't find the spring. Didn't thare used to be a spring 'tween here'n town?"

"Goodness sakes! Randy! Where'd you come from? Water! Jes' help yourself. There's the bucket jes' from the spring five minutes since, an' there's the gourd hanging up on the wall. I can't get up, I'm that busy. Twelve to dinner to-day, an' only me to do the cookin'. 'Melia she's got to be upstairs helpin' at the bar."

"Who all you got here?" questioned Miranda as she took a draught from the old gourd.

"Well, got a gentleman from New York fur one. He's real pretty. Quite a beau. His clo'es are that nice you'd think he was goin' to court. He's that particular 'bout his eatin' I feel flustered. Nothin' would do but he hed to hev a downstairs room. He said he didn't like goin' upstairs. He don't look sickly, neither."

"Mebbe he's had a accident an' lamed himself," suggested Miranda cunningly. "Heard o' any accidents? How'd he come? Coach or horseback?"

"Coach," said Mrs. Green. "Why do you ask? Got any friends in New York?"

"Not many," responded Miranda importantly, "but my cousin Hannah Heath has. You know she's ben up there for a spell visitin' an' they say there was lots of gentlemen in love with her. There's one in particular used to come round a good deal. It might be him come round to see ef it's true Hannah's goin' to get married to Lem Skinner. Know what this fellow's name is?"

"You don't say! Well now it might be. No, I don't rightly remember his name. Seems though it was something like Church er Chapel. 'Melia could tell ye, but she's busy."

"Where's he at? Mebbe I could get a glimpse o' him. I'd jest like to know ef he was comin' to bother our Hannah."

"Well now. Mebbe you could get a sight o' him. There's a cupboard between his room an' the room back. It has a door both sides. Mebbe ef you was to slip in there you might see him through the latch hole. I ain't usin' that back room fer anythin' but a store-room this spring, so look out you don't stumble over nothin' when you go in fer it's dark as a pocket. You go right 'long in. I reckon you'll find the way. Yes, it's on the right hand side o' the hall. I've got to set here an' finish these potatoes er dinner'll be late. I'd like to know real well ef he's one o' Hannah Heath's beaux."

Miranda needed no second bidding. She slipped through the hall and store room, and in a moment stood before the door of the closet. Softly she opened it, and stepped in, lifting her feet cautiously, for the closet floor seemed full of old boots and shoes.

It was dark in there, very dark, and only one slat of light stabbed the blackness coming through the irregular shape of the latch hole. She could hear voices in low tones speaking on the other side of the door. Gradually her eyes grew accustomed to the light and one by one objects came out of the shadows and looked at her. A white pitcher with a broken nose, a row of bottles, a bunch of seed corn with the husks braided together and hung on a nail, an old coat on another nail.

Down on her knees beside the crack of light went Miranda. First her eye and then her ear were applied to the small aperture. She could see nothing but a table directly in front of the door about a foot away on which were quills, paper, and a large horn inkstand filled with ink. Some one evidently had been writing, for a page was half done, and the pen was laid down beside a word.

The limits of the latch hole made it impossible for Miranda to make out any more. She applied her ear and could hear a man's voice talking in low insinuating tones, but she could make little of what was said. It drove her fairly frantic to think that she was losing time. Miranda had no mind to be balked in her purpose. She meant to find out who was in that room and what was going on. She felt a righteous interest in it.

Her eyes could see quite plainly now in the dark closet. There was a big button on the door. She no sooner discovered it than she put up her hand and tried to turn it. It was tight and made a slight squeak in turning. She stopped but the noise seemed to have no effect upon the evenly modulated tones inside. Cautiously she moved the button again, holding the latch firmly in her other hand lest the door should suddenly fly open. It was an exciting moment when at last the button was turned entirely away from the door frame and the lifted latch swung free in Miranda's hand. The door opened outward. If it were allowed to go it would probably strike against the table. Miranda only allowed it to open a crack. She could hear words now, and the voice reminded her of something unpleasant. The least little bit more she dared open the door, and she could see, as she had expected, Marcia's bonnet and shoulder cape as she sat at the other side of the room. This then was the room of the messenger who had sent for Mrs. Spafford so peremptorily. The next thing was to discover the identity of the messenger. Miranda had suspicions.

The night before she had seen a man lurking near the Spafford house when she went out in the garden to feed the chickens. She had watched him from behind the lilac bush, and when he had finally gone away she had followed him some distance until he turned into the old corduroy road and was lost in the gathering dusk. The man she had seen before, and had reason to suspect. It was not for nothing that she had braved her grandmother and gone hunting wild strawberries out of season.

With the caution of a creature of the forest Miranda opened the door an inch further, and applied her eye to the latch hole again. The man's head was in full range of her eye then, and her suspicion proved true.

When Marcia entered the big room and the heavy oak door closed behind her her heart seemed almost choking her, but she tried with all her might to be calm. She was to know the worst now.

On the other side of the room in a large arm-chair, with his feet extended on another and covered by a travelling shawl, reclined a man. Marcia went toward him eagerly, and then stopped:

"Mr. Temple!" There was horror, fear, reproach in the way she spoke it.

"I know you are astonished, Mrs. Spafford, that the messenger should be one so unworthy, and let me say at the beginning that I am more thankful than I can express that your letter of forgiveness reached me before I was obliged to start on my sorrowful commission. I beg you will sit down and be as comfortable as you can while I explain further. Pardon my not rising. I have met with a bad sprain caused by falling from my horse on the way, and was barely able to reach this stopping place. My ankle is swollen so badly that I cannot step upon my foot."

Marcia, with white face, moved to the chair he indicated near him, and sat down. The one thought his speech had conveyed to her had come through those words "my sorrowful commission." She felt the need of sitting down, for her limbs would no longer bear her up, and she felt she must immediately know what was the matter.

"Mrs. Spafford, may I ask you once more to speak your forgiveness? Before I begin to tell you what I have come for, I long to hear you say the words 'I forgive you.' Will you give me your hand and say them?"

"Mr. Temple, I beg you will tell me what is the matter. Do not think any further about that other matter. I meant what I said in the note. Tell me quick! Is my husband—has anything happened to Mr. Spafford? Is he ill? Is he hurt?"

"My poor child! How can I bear to tell you? It seems terrible to put your love and trust upon another human being and then suddenly find—— But wait. Let me tell the story in my own way. No, your husband is not hurt, physically. Illness, and death even, are not the worst things that can happen to a mortal soul. It seems to me cruel, as I see you sit there so young and tender and beautiful, that I should have to hurt you by what I have to say. I come from the purest of motives to tell you a sad truth about one who should be nearest and dearest to you of all the earth. I beg you will look upon me kindly and believe that it hurts me to have to tell you these things. Before I begin I pray you will tell me that you forgive me for all I have to say. Put your hand in mine and say so."

Marcia had listened to this torrent of words unable to stop them, a choking sensation in her throat, fear gripping her heart. Some terrible thing had happened. Her senses refused to name the possibility. Would he never tell? What ailed the man that he wanted her hand in forgiveness? Of course she forgave him. She could not speak, and he kept urging.

"I cannot talk until I have your hand as a pledge that you will forgive me and think not unkindly of me for what I am about to tell you."

He must have seen how powerfully he wrought upon her, for he continued until wild with frantic fear she stumbled toward him and laid her hand in his. He grasped it and thanked her profusely. He looked at the little cold hand in his own, and his lying tongue went on:

"Mrs. Spafford, you are good and true. You have saved me from a life of uselessness, and your example and high noble character have given me new inspiration. It seems a poor gratitude that would turn and stab you to the heart. Ah! I cannot do it, and yet I must."

This was torture indeed! Marcia drew her hand sharply away and held it to her heart. She felt her brain reeling with the strain. Harry Temple saw he must go on at once or he would lose what he had gained. He had meant to keep that little hand and touch it gently with a comforting pressure as his story went on, but it would not do to frighten her or she might take sudden alarm.

"Sit down," he begged, reaching out and drawing a chair near to his own, but she stepped back and dropped into the one which she had first taken.

"You know your husband has been in New York?" he began. She nodded. She could not speak.

"Did you never suspect why he is there and why he stays so long?" A cold vise gripped Marcia's heart, but though she turned white she said nothing, only looked steadily into the false eyes that glowed and burned at her like two hateful coals of fire that would scorch her soul and David's to a horrid death.

"Poor child, you cannot answer. You have trusted perfectly. You thought he was there on business connected with his writing, but did it never occur to you what a very long time he has been away and that—that there might be some other reason also which he has not told? But you must know it now, my child. I am sorry to say it, but he has been keeping it from you, and those who love you think you ought to know. Let me explain. Very soon after he reached New York he met a lady whom he used to know and admire. She is a very beautiful woman, and though she is married is still much sought after. Your husband, like the rest of her admirers, soon lost his heart completely, and his head. Strange that he could so easily forget the pearl of women he had left behind! He went to see her. He showed his affection for her in every possible way. He gave her large sums of money. In fact, to make a long story short, he is lingering in New York just to be near her. I hesitate to speak the whole truth, but he has surely done that which you cannot forgive. You with your lofty ideas—Mrs. Spafford—he has cut himself off from any right to your respect or love.

"And now I am here to-day to offer to do all in my power to help you. From what I know of your husband's movements, he is likely to return to you soon. You cannot meet him knowing that the lips that will salute you have been pressed upon the lips of another woman, and that woman *your own sister*, dear Mrs. Spafford!

"Ah! Now you understand, poor child. Your lips quiver! You have reason to understand. I know, I know you cannot think what to do. Let me think for you." His eyes were glowing and his face animated. He was using all his persuasive power, and her gaze was fixed upon him as though he had mesmerized her. She could not resist the flood-tide of his eloquence. She could only look on and seem to be gradually turning to stone—frozen with horror.

He felt he had almost won, and with demoniacal skill he phrased his sentences.

"I am here for that purpose. I am here to help you and for no other reason. In the stable are horses harnessed and a comfortable carriage. My advice to you is to fly from here as fast as these fleet horses can carry you. Where you go is for you to say. I should advise going to your father's house. That I am sure is what will please him best. He is your natural refuge at such a time as this. If, however, you shrink from appearing before the eyes of the village gossips in your native town, I will take you to the home of a dear old friend of mine, hidden among the quiet hills, where you will be cared for most royally and tenderly for my sake, and where you can work out your life problem in the way that seems best to you. It is there that I am planning to take you to-night. We can easily reach there before evening if we start at once."

Marcia started to her feet in horror.

"What do you mean?" she stammered in a choking voice. "I could never go anywhere with you Mr. Temple. You are a bad man! You have been telling me lies! I do not believe one word of what you have said. My husband is noble and good. If he did any of those things you say he did he had a reason for it. I shall never distrust him."

Marcia's head was up grandly now and her voice had come back. She looked the man in the eye until he quailed, but still he sought to hold his power over her.

"You poor child!" and his voice was gentleness and forbearance itself. "I do not wonder in your first horror andsurprise that you feel as you do. I anticipated this. Sit down and calm yourself and let me tell you more about it. I can prove everything that I have said. I have letters here——" and he swept his hand toward a pile of letters lying on the table; Miranda in the closet marked well the position of those letters. "All that I have said is only too true, I am sorry to say, and you must listen to me——"

Marcia interrupted him, her eyes blazing, her face excited: "Mr. Temple, I shall not listen to another word you say. You are a wicked man and I was wrong to come here at all. You deceived me or I should not have come. I must go home at once." With that she started toward the door.

Harry Temple flung aside the shawl that covered his sometime sprained ankle and arose quickly, placing himself before her, forgetful of his invalid rôle:

"Not so fast, my pretty lady," he said, grasping her wrists fiercely in both his hands. "You need not think to escape so easily. You shall not leave this room except in my company. Do you not know that you are in my power? You have spent nearly an hour alone in my bedchamber, and what will your precious husband have to do with you after this is known?"

CHAPTER XXIV

Miranda's time had come. She had seen it coming and was prepared.

With a movement like a flash she pushed open the closet door, seized the pot of ink from the table, and before the two excited occupants of the room had time to even hear her or realize that she was near, she hurled the ink pot full into the insolent face of Harry Temple. The inkstand itself was a light affair of horn and inflicted only a slight wound, but the ink came into his eyes in a deluge blinding him completely, as Miranda had meant it should do. She had seen no other weapon of defense at hand.

Harry Temple dropped Marcia's wrists and groaned in pain, staggering back against the wall and sinking to the floor. But Miranda would not stay to see the effect of her punishment. She seized the frightened Marcia, dragged her toward the cupboard door, sweeping as she passed the pile of letters, finished and unfinished, into her apron, and closed the cupboard doors carefully behind her. Then she guided Marcia through the dark mazes of the store room to the hall, and pushing her toward the front door, whispered: "Go quick 'fore he gets his eyes open. I've got to go this way. Run down the road fast as you can an' I'll be at the meetin' place first. Hurry, quick!"

Marcia went with feet that shook so that every step seemed like to slip, but with beating heart she finally traversed the length of the piazza with a show of dignity, passed the loungers, and was out in the road. Then indeed she took courage and fairly flew.

Miranda, breathless, but triumphant, went back into the kitchen: "I guess 'tain't him after all," she said to the interested woman who was putting on the potatoes to boil. "He's real interesting to look at though. I'd like to stop and watch him longer but I must be goin'. I come out to hunt fer"—Miranda hesitated for a suitable object before this country-bred woman who well knew that strawberries were not ripe yet—"wintergreens fer Grandma," she added cheerfully, not quite sure whether they grew around these parts, "and I must be in a hurry. Good-bye! Thank you fer the drink."

Miranda whizzed out of the door breezily, calling a good morning to one of the hostlers as she passed the barnyard, and was off through the meadows and over the fence like a bird, the package of letters rustling loud in her bosom where she had tucked them before she entered the kitchen.

Neither of the two girls spoke for some minutes after they met, but continued their rapid gait, until the end of the corduroy road was in sight and they felt comparatively safe.

"Wal, that feller certainly ought to be strung up an' walluped, now, fer sure," remarked Miranda, "an I'd like to help at the wallupin'."

Marcia's overstrung nerves suddenly dissolved into hysterical laughter. The contrast from the tragic to the ridiculous was too much for her. She laughed until the tears rolled down her cheeks, and then she cried in earnest. Miranda stopped and put her arms about her as gently as a mother might have done, and smoothed her hair back from the hot cheek, speaking tenderly:

"There now, you poor pretty little flower. Jest you cry 's hard 's you want to. I know how good it makes you feel to cry. I've done it many a time up garret where nobody couldn't hear me. That old Satan, he won't trouble you fer a good long spell again. When he gets his evil eyes open, if he ever does, he'll be glad to get out o' these parts or I miss my guess. Now don't you worry no more. He can't hurt you one mite. An' don't you think a thing about what he said. He's a great big liar, that's what he is."

"Miranda, you saved me. Yes, you did. I never can thank you enough. If you hadn't come and helped me something awful might have happened!" Marcia shuddered and began to sob convulsively again.

"Nonsense!" said Miranda, pleased. "I didn't do a thing worth mentioning. Now you jest wipe your eyes and chirk up. We've got to go through town an' you don't want folks to wonder what's up."

Miranda led Marcia up to the spring whose location had been known to her all the time of course, and Marcia bathed her eyes and was soon looking more like herself, though there was a nervous tremor to her lips now and then. But her companion talked gaily, and tried to keep her mind from going over the events of the morning.

When they reached the village Miranda suggested they go home by the back street, slipping through a field of spring wheat and climbing the garden fence. She had a mind to keep out of her grandmother's sight for a while longer.

"I might's well be hung for a sheep's a lamb," she remarked, as she slid in at Marcia's kitchen door in the shadow of the morning-glory vines. "I'm goin' to stay here a spell an' get you some dinner while you go upstairs an' lie down. You don't need to go back to your aunt's till near night, an' you can wait till dusk an' I'll go with you. Then you needn't be out alone at all. I know how you feel, but I don't believe you need worry. He'll be done with you now forever, er I'll miss my guess. Now you go lie down till I make a cup o' tea."

Marcia was glad to be alone, and soon fell asleep, worn out with the excitement, her brain too weary to go over the awful occurrences of the morning. That would come later. Now her body demanded rest.

Miranda, coming upstairs with the tea, tiptoed in and looked at her,—one round arm thrown over her head, and her smooth peachy cheek resting against it. Miranda, homely, and with no hope of ever attaining any of the beautiful things of life, loved unselfishly this girl who had what she had not, and longed with all her heart to comfort and protect the sweet young thing who seemed so ill-prepared to protect herself. She stooped over the sleeper for one yearning moment, and touched her hair lightly with her lips. She felt a great desire to kiss the soft round cheek, but was afraid of wakening her. Then she took the cup of tea and tiptoed out again, her eyes shining with satisfaction. She had a self-imposed task before her, and was well pleased that Marcia slept, for it gave her plenty of opportunity to carry out her plans.

She went quickly to David's library, opened drawers and doors in the desk until she found writing materials, and sat down to work. She had a letter to write, and a letter, to Miranda, was the achievement of a lifetime. She did not much expect to ever have to write another. She plunged into her subject at once.

"DEAR MR. DAVID:" (she was afraid that sounded a little stiff, but she felt it was almost too familiar to say "David" as he was always called.)

"I ain't much on letters, but this one has got to be writ. Something happened and somebody's got to tell you about it. I'm most sure she wont, and nobody else knows cept me.

"Last night 'bout dark I went out to feed the chickens, an' I see that nimshi Harry Temple skulkin round your house. It was all dark there, an he walked in the side gate and tried to peek in the winders, only the shades was down an he couldn't see a thing. I thought he was up to some mischief so I followed him down the street a piece till he turned down the old corduroy road. It was dark by then an I come home, but I was on the watchout this morning, and after Mis' Spafford come down to the house I heard a horse gallopin by an I looked out an saw a boy get off an take a letter to the door an ride away, an pretty soon all in a hurry your wife come out tyin her bonnet and hurryin along lookin scared. I grabbed my sunbonnet an clipped after her, but she went so fast I didn't get up to her till she got on the old corduroy road. She was awful scared lookin an she didn't want me much I see, but pretty soon she up an told me she had a note sayin there was a messenger with news from you out to the old Green Tavern. He had a accident an couldn't come no further. He wanted her to come alone cause the business was private, so I stayed down by the turn of the road till she got in an then I went cross lots an round to the kitchen an called on Mis' Green a spell. She was tellin me about her boarders an I told her I thought mebbe one of em was a friend o' Hannah Heath's so she said I might peek through the key hole of the cubberd an see. She was busy so I went alone.

"Well sir, I jest wish you'd been there. That lying nimshi was jest goin on the sweetest, as respectful an nice a thankin your wife fer comin, an excusin himself fer sendin fer her, and sayin he couldn't bear to tell her what he'd come fer, an pretty soon when she was scared 's death he up an told her a awful fib bout you an a woman called Kate, whoever she is, an he jest poured the words out fast so she couldn't speak, an he said things about you he shouldn't uv, an you could see he was makin it up as he went along, an he said he had proof. So he pointed at a pile of letters on the table an I eyed em good through the hole in the door. Pretty soon he ups and perposes that he carry her off in a carriage he has all ready, and takes her to a friend of his, so she wont be here when you come home, cause you're so bad, and she gets up looking like she wanted to scream only she didn't dare, and she says he dont tell the truth, it wasn't so any of it, and if it was it was all right anyway, that you had some reason, an she wouldn't go a step with him anywhere. An then he forgets all about the lame ankle he had kept covered up on a chair pertendin it was hurt fallin off his horse when the coach brought him all the way fer I asked Mis' Green— and he ketches her by the wrists, and he says she can't go without him, and she needn't be in such a hurry fer you wouldn't have no more to do with her anyway after her being shut up there with him so long, an then she looked jest like she was going to faint, an I bust out through the door an ketched up the ink pot, it want heavy enough to kill him, an I slung it at him, an the ink went square in his eyes, an we slipped through the closet an got away quick fore anybody knew a thing.

"I brought all the letters along so here they be. I havn't read a one, cause I thought mebbe you'd ruther not. She aint seen em neither. She dont know I've got em. I hid em in my dress. She's all wore out with cryin and hurryin, and being scared, so she's upstairs now asleep, an she dont know I'm writing. I'm goin to send this off fore she knows, fer I think she wouldn't tell you fear of worryin you. I'll look after her es well's I can till you get back, but I think that feller ought to be strung up. But you'll know what to do, so no more at present from your obedient servent,

"MIRANDA GRISCOM."

Having at last succeeded in sealing her packet to her satisfaction and the diminishing of the stick of sealing wax she had found in the drawer, Miranda slid out the front door, and by a detour went to David Spafford's office.

"Good afternoon, Mr. Clark," she said to the clerk importantly. "Grandma sends her respecks and wants to know ef you'd be so kind as to back this letter fer her to Mr. David Spafford. She's writin' to him on business an' she don't rightly know his street an' number in New York."

Mr. Clark willingly wrote the address, and Miranda took it to the post office, and sped back to Marcia, happy in the accomplishment of her purpose.

In the same mail bag that brought Miranda's package came a letter from Aunt Clarinda. David's face lit up with a pleased smile. Her letters were so infrequent that they were a rare pleasure. He put aside the thick package written in his clerk's hand. It was doubtless some business papers and could wait.

Aunt Clarinda wrote in a fine old script that in spite of her eighty years was clear and legible. She told about the beauty of the weather, and how Amelia and Hortense were almost done with the house cleaning, and how Marcia had been going to their house every day putting it in order. Then she added a paragraph which David, knowing the old lady well, understood to be the *raison d'être* of the whole letter:

"I think your wife misses you very much, Davie, she looks sort of peeked and sad. It is hard on her being separated from you so long this first year. Men don't think of those things, but it is lonely for a young thing like her here with three old women, and you know Hortense and Amelia never try to make it lively for anybody. I have been watching her, and I think if I were you I would let the business finish itself up as soon as possible and hurry back to put a bit of cheer into that child. She's whiter than she ought to be."

David read it over three times in astonishment with growing, mingled feelings which he could not quite analyze.

Poor Aunt Clarinda! Of course she did not understand the situation, and equally of course she was mistaken. Marcia was not sighing for him, though it might be dull for her at the old house. He ought to have thought of that; and a great burden suddenly settled down upon him. He was not doing right by Marcia. It could not be himself of course that Marcia was missing, if indeed Aunt Clarinda was right and she was worried about anything. Perhaps something had occurred to trouble her. Could that snake of a Temple have turned up again? No, he felt reasonably sure he would have heard of that, besides he saw him not long ago on the street at a distance. Could it be some boy-lover at home whose memory came to trouble her? Or had she discovered what a sacrifice she had made of her young life? Whatever it was, it was careless and cruel in him to have left her alone with his aunts all this time. He was a selfish man, he told himself, to have accepted her quiet little sacrifice of all for him. He read the letter over again, and suddenly there came to him a wish that Marcia *was* missing him. It seemed a pleasant thought to have her care. He had been trying to train himself to the fact that no one would ever care for him again, but now it seemed dear and desirable that his sweet young companion should like to have him back. He had a vision of home as it had been, so pleasant and restful, always the food that he liked, always the thought for his wishes, and he felt condemned. He had not noticed or cared. Had she thought him ungrateful?

He read the letter over again, noting every mention of his wife in the account of the daily living at home. He was searching for some clue that would give him more information about her. And when he reached the last paragraph about missing him, a little tingle of pleasure shot through him at the thought. He did not understand it. After all she was his, and if it was possible he must help to make up to her for what she had lost in giving herself to him. If the thought of doing so brought a sense of satisfaction to him that was unexpected, he was not to blame in any wise.

Since his interview with Kate, and the terrible night of agony through which he had passed, David had plunged into his business with all his might. Whenever a thought of Kate came he banished it if possible, and if it would not go he got out his writing materials and went to work at an article, to absorb his mind. He had several times arisen in the night to write because he could not sleep, and must think.

When he was obliged to be in New York he had steadily kept away from the house where Kate lived, and never walked through the streets without occupying his mind as fully as possible so that he should not chance to see her. In this way his sorrow was growing old without having been worn out, and he was really regaining a large amount of his former happiness and interest in life. Not so often now did the vision of Kate come to trouble him. He thought she was still his one ideal of womanly beauty and grace and perfection of course, and always would be, but she was not for him to think upon any more. A strong true man he was growing, out of his sorrow. And now when the thought of Marcia came to him with a certain sweetness he could be glad that it was so, and not resent it. Of course no one could ever take the place of Kate, that was impossible.

So reflecting, with a pleasant smile upon his face, he opened Miranda's epistle.

Puzzled and surprised he began to read the strange chirography, and as he read his face darkened and he drew his brows in a heavy frown. "The scoundrel!" he muttered as he turned the sheet. Then as he went on his look grew anxious. He scanned the page quickly as if he would gather the meaning from the crooked ill-spelled words without taking them one by one. But he had to go slowly, for Miranda had not written with as much plainness as haste. He fairly held his breath when he thought of the gentle girl in the hands of the unscrupulous man of the world. A terrible fear gripped his heart, Marcia, little Marcia, so sweet and pure and good. A vision of her face as she lay asleep in the woods came between him and the paper. Why had he left her unprotected all these months?

Fool that he was! She was worth more than all the railroads put together. As if his own life was in the balance, he read on, growing sick with horror. Poor child! what had she thought? And how had his own sin and weakness been found out, or was it merely Harry Temple's wicked heart that had evolved these stories? The letter smote him with terrible accusation, and all at once it was fearful to him to think that Marcia had heard such things about him. When he came to her trust in him he groaned aloud and buried his face in the letter, and then raised it quickly to read to the end.

When he had finished he rose with sudden determination to pack his carpet-bag and go home at once. Marcia needed him, and he felt a strong desire to be near her, to see her and know she was safe. It was overwhelming. He had not known he could ever feel strongly again. He must confess his own weakness of course, and he would. She should know all and know that she might trust his after all.

But the motion of rising had sent the other papers to the floor, and in falling the bundle of letters that Miranda had enclosed, scattered about him. He stooped to pick them up and saw his own name written in Kate's handwriting. Old association held him, and wondering, fearful, not wholly glad to see it, he picked up the letter. It was an epistle of Kate's, written in intimate style to Harry Temple and speaking of himself in terms of the utmost contempt. She even stooped to detail to Harry an account of her own triumph on that miserable morning when he had taken her in his arms and kissed her. There were expressions in the letter that showed her own wicked heart, as nothing else could ever have done, to David. As he read, his soul growing sick within him,—read one letter after another, and saw how she had plotted with this bad man to wreck the life of her young sister for her own triumph and revenge,—the beautiful woman whom he had loved, and whom he had thought beautiful within as well as without, crumbled into dust before him. When he looked up at last with white face and firmly set lips, he found that his soul was free forever from the fetters that had bound him to her.

He went to the fireplace and laid the pile of letters among the embers, blowing them into a blaze, and watched them until they were eaten up by the fire and nothing remained but dead grey ashes. The thought came to him that that was like his old love. It was burnt out. There had not been the right kind of fuel to feed it. Kate was worthless, but his own self was alive, and please God he would yet see better days. He would go home at once to the child wife who needed him, and whom now he might love as she should be loved. The thought became wondrously sweet to him as he rapidly threw the things into his travelling bag and went about arrangements for his trip home. He determined that if he ever came to New York again Marcia should come with him.

CHAPTER XXV

Marcia hurried down to her own house early one morning. The phantoms of her experiences in the old Green Tavern were pursuing her.

Once there she could do nothing but go over and over the dreadful things that Harry Temple had said. In vain did she try to work. She went into the library and took up a book, but her mind would wander to David.

She sat down at the piano and played a few tender chords and sang an old Italian song which somebody had left at their house several years before:

"Dearest, believe,

When e'er we part:

Lonely I grieve,

In my sad heart:—"

With a sob her head dropped upon her hands in one sad little crash of wailing tones, while the sound died away in reverberation after reverberation of the strings till Marcia felt as if a sea of sound were about her in soft ebbing, flowing waves.

The sound covered the lifting of the side door latch and the quiet step of a foot. Marcia was absorbed in her own thoughts. Her smothered sobs were mingling with the dying sounds of the music, still audible to her fine ear.

David had come by instinct to his own home first. He felt that Marcia would be there, and now that he was come and the morning sun flooded everything and made home look so good he felt that he must find her first of all before his relationship with home had been re-established. He passed through kitchen, dining room and hall, and by the closed parlor door. He never thought of her being in there with the door closed. He glanced into the library and saw the book lying in his chair as she had left it, and it gave a touch of her presence which pleased him. He went softly toward the stairs thinking to find her. He had stopped at a shop the last thing and bought a beautiful creamy shawl of China crêpe heavily embroidered, and finished with long silken fringe. He had taken it from his carpet-bag and was carrying it in its rice paper wrappings lest it should be crushed. He was pleased as a child at the present he had brought her, and felt strangely shy about giving it to her.

Just then there came a sound from the parlor, sweet and tender and plaintive. Marcia had conquered her sobs and was singing again with her whole soul, singing as if she were singing to David. The words drew him strangely, wonderingly toward the parlor door, yet so softly that he heard every syllable.

"Dearest, believe,
When e'er we part:
Lonely I grieve,
In my sad heart:—
Thy faithful slave,
Languishing sighs,
Haste then and save—"

Here the words trailed away again into a half sob, and the melody continued in broken, halting chords that flickered out and faded into the shadows of the room.

David's heart was pierced with a belief that Aunt Clarinda was right and something was the matter with Marcia. A great trouble and tenderness, and almost jealousy, leaped up in his heart which were incomprehensible to him. Who was Marcia singing this song for? That it was a true cry from a lonely soul he could but believe. Was she feeling her prison-bars here in the lonely old house with only a forlorn man whose life and love had been thrown away upon another? Poor child! Poor child! If he might but save her from suffering, cover her with his own tenderness and make her content with that. Would it be possible if he devoted himself to it to make her forget the one for whom she was sighing; to bring peace and a certain sort of sweet forgetfulness and interest in other things into her life? He wanted to make a new life for her, his little girl whom he had so unthinkingly torn from the home nest and her future, and compelled to take up his barren way with him. He would make it up to her if such a thing were possible. Then he opened the door.

In the soft green light of the noonday coming through the shades Marcia's color did not show as it flew into her cheeks. Her hands grew weak and dropped upon the keys with a soft little tinkle of surprise and joy. She sprang up and came a step toward him, then clasped her hands against her breast and stopped shyly. David coming into the room, questioning, wondering, anxious, stopped midway too, and for an instant they looked upon one another. David saw a new look in the girl's face. She seemed older, much older than when he had left her. The sweet round cheeks were thinner, her mouth drooped sadly, pathetically. For an instant he longed to take her in his arms and kiss her. The longing startled him. So many months he had thought of only Kate in that way, and then had tried to teach himself never to think of Kate or any woman as one to be caressed by him, that it shocked him. He felt that he had been disloyal to himself, to honor,—to Kate—no—not to Kate, he had no call to be loyal to her. She had not been loyal to him ever. Perhaps rather he would have put it loyalty to Love for Love's sake, love that is worthy to be crowned by a woman's love.

With all these mingling feelings David was embarrassed. He came toward her slowly, trying to be natural, trying to get back his former way with her. He put out his hand stiffly to shake hands as he had done when he left, and timidly she put hers into it, yet as their fingers closed there leaped from one to the other a thrill of sweetness, that neither guessed the other knew and each put by in memory for closer inspection as to what it could mean. Their hands clung together longer than either had meant, and there was something pleasant to each in the fact that they were together again. David thought it was just because it was home, rest, and peace, and a relief from his anxiety about Marcia now that he saw she was all right. Marcia knew it was better to have David standing there with his strong fingers about her trembling ones, than to have anything else in the world. But she would not have told him so.

"That was a sweet song you were singing," said David. "I hope you were singing it for me, and that it was true! I am glad I am come home, and you must sing it again for me soon."

It was not in the least what he intended to say, and the words tumbled themselves out so tumultuously that he was almost ashamed and wondered if Marcia would think he had lost his mind in New York. Marcia, dear child, treasured them every word and hugged them to her heart, and carried them in her prayers.

They went out together and got dinner as if they had been two children, with a wild excited kind of glee; and they tried to get back their natural ways of doing and saying things, but they could not.

Instead they were forever blundering and halting in what they said; coming face to face and almost running over one another as they tried to help each other; laughing and blushing and blundering again.

When they each tried to reach for the tea kettle to fill the coffee pot and their fingers touched, each drew back and pretended not to notice, but yet had felt the contact sweet.

They were lingering over the dinner when Hannah Heath came to the door. David had been telling of some of his adventures in detail and was enjoying the play of expression on Marcia's face as she listened eagerly to every word. They had pushed their chairs back a little and were sitting there talking,—or rather David was talking, Marcia listening. Hannah stood for one jealous instant and saw it all. This was what she had dreamed for her own long years back, she and David. She had questioned much just what feeling there might be between him and Marcia, and now more than ever she desired to bring him face to face with Kate and read for herself what the truth had been. She hated Marcia for that look of intense delight and sympathy upon her face; hated her that she had the right to sit there and hear what David had to say—some stupid stuff about railroads. She did not see that she herself would have made an ill companion for a man like David.

As yet neither Marcia nor David had touched upon the subjects which had troubled them. They did not realize it, but they were so suddenly happy in each other's company they had forgotten for the moment. The pleasant converse was broken up at once. Marcia's face hardened into something like alarm as she saw who stood in the doorway.

"Why, David, have you got home at last?" said Hannah. "I did not know it." That was an untruth. She had watched him from behind Grandmother Heath's rose bush. "Where did you come from last? New York? Oh, then you saw Mrs. Leavenworth. How is she? I fell in love with her when I was there."

Now David had never fully taken in Kate's married name. He knew it of course, but in his present state of happiness at getting home, and his absorption in the work he had been doing, the name "Mrs. Leavenworth" conveyed nothing whatever to David's mind. He looked blankly at Hannah and replied indifferently enough with a cool air. "No, Miss Hannah, I had no time for social life. I was busy every minute I was away."

David never expected Hannah to say anything worth listening to, and he was so full of his subject that he had not noticed that she made no reply.

Hannah watched him curiously as he talked, his remarks after all were directed more to Marcia than to her, and when he paused she said with a contemptuous sneer in her voice, "I never could understand, David, how you who seem to have so much sense in other things will take up with such fanciful, impractical dreams as this railroad. Lemuel says it'll never run."

Hannah quoted her lover with a proud bridling of her head as if the matter were settled once and for all. It was the first time she had allowed the world to see that she acknowledged her relation to Lemuel. She was not averse to having David understand that she felt there were other men in the world besides himself. But David turned merry eyes on her.

"Lemuel says?" he repeated, and he made a sudden movement with his arm which sent a knife and spoon from the table in a clatter upon the floor.

"And how much does Lemuel know about the matter?"

"Lemuel has good practical common sense," said Hannah, vexed, "and he knows what is possible and what is not. He does not need to travel all over the country on a wild goose chase to learn that."

Now that she had accepted him Hannah did not intend to allow Lemuel to be discounted.

"He has not long to wait to be convinced," said David thoughtfully and unaware of her tart tone. "Before the year is out it will be a settled fact that every one can see."

"Well, it's beyond comprehension what you care, anyway," said Hannah contemptuously. "Did you really spend all your time in New York on such things? It seems incredible. There certainly must have been other attractions?"

There was insinuation in Hannah's voice though it was smooth as butter, but David had had long years of experience in hearing Hannah Heath's sharp tongue. He minded it no more than he would have minded the buzzing of a fly. Marcia's color rose, however. She made a hasty errand to the pantry to put away the bread, and her eyes flashed at Hannah through the close drawn pantry door. But Hannah did not give up so easily.

"It is strange you did not stay with Mrs. Leavenworth," she said. "She told me you were one of her dearest friends, and you used to be quite fond of one another."

Then it suddenly dawned upon David who Mrs. Leavenworth was, and a sternness overspread his face.

"Mrs. Leavenworth, did you say? Ah! I did not understand. I saw her but once and that for only a few minutes soon after I first arrived. I did not see her again." His voice was cool and steady. Marcia coming from the pantry with set face, ready for defence if there was any she could give, marvelled at his coolness. Her heart was gripped with fear, and yet leaping with joy at David's words. He had not seen Kate but once. He had known she was there and yet had kept away. Hannah's insinuations were false. Mr. Temple's words were untrue. She had known it all the time, yet what sorrow they had given her!

"By the way, Marcia," said David, turning toward her with a smile that seemed to erase the sternness in his voice but a moment before. "Did you not write me some news? Miss Hannah, you are to be congratulated I believe. Lemuel is a good man. I wish you much happiness."

And thus did David, with a pleasant speech, turn aside Hannah Heath's dart. Yet while she went from the house with a smile and a sound of pleasant wishes in her ears, she carried with her a bitter heart and a revengeful one.

David was suddenly brought face to face with the thing he had to tell Marcia. He sat watching her as she went back and forth from pantry to kitchen, and at last he came and stood beside her and took her hands in his looking down earnestly into her face. It seemed terrible to him to tell this thing to the innocent girl, now, just when he was growing anxious to win her confidence, but it must be told, and better now than later lest he might be tempted not to tell it at all.

"Marcia!" He said the name tenderly, with an inflection he had never used before. It was not lover-like, nor passionate, but it reached her heart and drew her eyes to his and the color to her cheeks. She thought how different his clasp was from Harry Temple's hateful touch. She looked up at him trustingly, and waited.

"You heard what I said to Hannah Heath just now, about—your——" He paused, dissatisfied—"about Mrs. Leavenworth"—it was as if he would set the subject of his words far from them. Marcia's heart beat wildly, remembering all that she had been told, yet she looked bravely, trustingly into his eyes.

"It was true what I told her. I met Mrs. Leavenworth but once while I was away. It was in her own home and she sent for me saying she was in trouble. She told me that she was in terrible anxiety lest I would not forgive her. She begged me to say that I forgave her, and when I told her I did she asked me to kiss her once to prove it. I was utterly overcome and did so, but the moment my lips touched hers I knew that I was doing wrong and I put her from me. She begged me to remain, and I now know that she was utterly false from the first. It was but a part she was playing when she touched my heart until I yielded and sinned. I have only learned that recently, within a few days, and from words written by her own hand to another. I will tell you about it all sometime. But I want to confess to you this wrong I have done, and to let you know that I went away from her that day and have never seen her since. She had said she was without money, and I left her all I had with me. I know now that that too was unwise,—perhaps wrong. I feel that all this was a sin against you. I would like you to forgive me if you can, and I want you to know that this other woman who was the cause of our coming together, and yet has separated us ever since we have been together, is no longer anything to me. Even if she and I were both free as we were when we first met, we could never be anything but strangers. Can you forgive me now, Marcia, and can you ever trust me after what I have told you?"

Marcia looked into his eyes, and loved him but the more for his confession. She felt she could forgive him anything, and her whole soul in her countenance answered with her voice, as she said: "I can." It made David think of their wedding day, and suddenly it came over him with a thrill that this sweet womanly woman belonged to him. He marvelled at her sweet forgiveness. The joy of it surprised him beyond measure.

"You have had some sad experiences yourself. Will you tell me now all about it?" He asked the question wistfully still holding her hands in a firm close grasp, and she let them lie nestling there feeling safe as birds in the nest.

"Why, how did you know?" questioned Marcia, her whole face flooded with rosy light for joy at his kind ways and relief that she did not have to open the story.

"Oh, a little bird, or a guardian angel whispered the tale," he said pleasantly. "Come into the room where we can be sure no Hannah Heaths will trouble us," and he drew her into the library and seated her beside him on the sofa.

"But, indeed, Marcia," and his face sobered, "it is no light matter to me, what has happened to you. I have been in an agony all the way home lest I might not find you safe and well after having escaped so terrible a danger."

He drew the whole story from her bit by bit, tenderly questioning her, his face blazing with righteous wrath, and darkening with his wider knowledge as she told on to the end, and showed him plainly the black heart of the villain who had dared so diabolical a conspiracy; and the inhumanity of the woman who had helped in the intrigue against her own sister,—nay even instigated it. His feelings were too deep for utterance. He was shaken to the depths. His new comprehension of Kate's character was confirmed at the worst. Marcia could only guess his deep feelings from his shaken countenance and the earnest way in which he folded his hands over hers and said in low tones filled with emotion: "We should be deeply thankful to God for saving you, and I must be very careful of you after this. That villain shall be searched out and punished if it takes a lifetime, and Miranda,—what shall we do for Miranda? Perhaps we can induce her grandmother to let us have her sometime to help take care of us. We seem to be unable to get on without her. We'll see what we can do sometime in return for the great service she has rendered."

But the old clock striking in the hall suddenly reminded David that he should go at once to the office, so he hurried away and Marcia set about her work with energy, a happy song of praise in her heart.

There was much to be done. David had said he would scarcely have time to go over to his aunts that night, so she had decided to invite them to tea. She would far rather have had David to herself this first evening, but it would please them to come, especially Aunt Clarinda. There was not much time to prepare supper to be sure, but she would stir up a gingerbread, make some puffy cream biscuits, and there was lovely white honey and fresh eggs and peach preserves.

So she ran to Deacon Appleby's to get some cream for her biscuits and to ask Tommy Appleby to harness David's horse and drive over for Aunt Clarinda. Then she hurried down to the aunts to give her invitation.

Aunt Clarinda sat down in her calico-covered rocking chair, wiped her dear old eyes and her glasses, and said, over and over again: "Dear child! Bless her! Bless her!"

It was a happy gathering that evening. David was as pleased as they could have desired, and looked about upon the group in the dining-room with genuine boyish pleasure. It did his heart good to see Aunt Clarinda there. It had never occurred to him before that she could come. He turned to Marcia with a light in his eyes that fully repaid her for the little trouble she had had in carrying out her plan. He began to feel that home meant something even though he had lost the home of his long dreams and ideals.

He talked a great deal about his trip, and in between the sentences, he caught himself watching Marcia, noting the curve of her round chin, the dimple in her left cheek when she smiled, the way her hair waved off from her forehead, the pink curves of her well-shaped ears. He found a distinct pleasure in noting these things and he wondered at himself. It was as if he had suddenly been placed before some great painting and become possessed of the knowledge wherewith to appreciate art to its fullest. It was as if he had heard a marvellous piece of music and had the eyes and ears of his understanding opened to take in the gracious melodies and majestic harmonies.

Aunt Clarinda watched his eyes, and Aunt Clarinda was satisfied. Aunt Hortense watched his eyes, jealously and sighed. Aunt Amelia watched his eyes and set her lips and feared to herself. "He will spoil her if he does like that. She will think she can walk right over him." But Aunt Clarinda knew better. She recognized the eternal right of love.

They took the three old ladies home in the rising of an early moon, Marcia walking demurely on the sidewalk with Aunt Amelia, while David drove the chaise with Aunt Clarinda and Aunt Hortense.

As he gently lifted Aunt Clarinda down and helped her to her room David felt her old hands tremble and press his arm, and when he had reached her door he stooped and kissed her.

"Davie," she said in the voice that used to comfort his little childish troubles, or tell him of some nice surprise she had for him, "Davie, she's a dear child! She's just as good as gold. She's the princess I used to put in all your fairy-tales. David, she's just the right one for you!" and David answered earnestly, solemnly, as if he were discovering a truth which surprised him but yet was not unwelcome. "I believe she is, Aunt Clarinda."

They drove to the barn and Marcia sat in the chaise in the sweet hay-scented darkness while David put up the horse by the cobwebby light of the lantern; then they walked quietly back to the house. David had drawn Marcia's hand through his arm and it rested softly on his coat sleeve. She was silently happy, she knew not why, afraid to think of it lest to-morrow would show her there was nothing out of the ordinary monotony to be happy about.

David was silent, wondering at himself. What was this that had come to him? A new pleasure in life. A little trembling rill of joy bubbling up in his heart; a rift in the dark clouds of fate; a show of sunshine where he had expected never to see the light again. Why was it so pleasant to have that little hand resting upon his arm? Was it really pleasant or was it only a part of the restfulness of getting home again away from strange faces and uncomfortable beds, and poor tables?

They let themselves into the house as if they were walking into a new world together and both were glad to be there again. When she got up to her room Marcia went and stood before the glass and looked at herself by the flickering flame of the candle. Her eyes were bright and her cheeks burned red in the centre like two soft deep roses. She felt she hardly knew herself. She tried to be critical. Was this person she was examining a pretty person? Would she be called so in comparison with Kate and Hannah Heath? Would a man,—would David,—if his heart were not filled,—think so? She decided not. She felt she was too immature. There was too much shyness in her glance, too much babyishness about her mouth. No, David could never have thought her beautiful, even if he had seen her before he knew Kate. But perhaps, if Kate had been married first and away and then he had come to their home, perhaps if he knew no one else well enough to love,—could he have cared for her?

Oh, it was a dreadful, beautiful thought. It thrilled through and through her till she hid her face from her own gaze. She suddenly kissed the hand that had rested on his sleeve, and then reproached herself for it. She loved him, but was it right to do so?

As for David, he was sitting on the side of his bed with his chin in his hands examining himself.

He had supposed that with the reading of those letters which had come to him but two short days before all possibility of love and happiness had died, but lo! he found himself thrilling with pleasure over the look in a girl's soft eyes, and the touch of her hand. And that girl was his wife. It was enough to keep him awake to try to understand himself.

CHAPTER XXVI

Hannah Heath's wedding day dawned bright enough for a less calculating bride.

David did not get home until half past three. He had been obliged to drive out to the starting place of the new railroad, near Albany, where it was important that he get a few points correctly. On the morrow was to be the initial trip, by the Mohawk and Hudson Railroad, of the first train drawn by a steam engine in the state of New York.

His article about it, bargained for by a New York paper, must be on its way by special post as soon after the starting of the train as possible. He must have all items accurate; technicalities of preparation; description of engine and coaches; details of arrangements, etc.; before he added the final paragraphs describing the actual start of the train. His article was practically done now, save for these few items. He had started early that morning on his long drive, and, being detained longer than he had expected, arrived at home with barely time to put himself into wedding garments, and hasten in at the last moment with Marcia who stood quietly waiting for him in the front hall. They were the last guests to arrive. It was time for the ceremony, but the bride, true to her nature to the last, still kept Lemuel waiting; and Lemuel, true to the end, stood smiling and patient awaiting her pleasure.

David and Marcia entered the wide parlor and shook hands here and there with those assembled, though for the most part a hushed air pervaded the room, as it always does when something is about to happen.

Soon after their arrival some one in purple silk came down the stairs and seated herself in a vacant chair close to where the bride was to stand. She had gold hair and eyes like forget-me-nots. She was directly opposite to David and Marcia. David was engrossed in a whispered conversation with Mr. Brentwood about the events of the morrow, and did not notice her entrance, though she paused in the doorway and searched him directly from amongst the company before she took her seat. Marcia, who was talking with Rose Brentwood, caught the vision of purple and gold and turned to face for one brief instant the scornful, half-merry glance of her sister. The blood in her face fled back to her heart and left it white.

Then Marcia summoned all her courage and braced herself to face what was to come. She forced herself to smile in answer to Rose Brentwood's question. But all the while she was trying to understand what it was in her sister's look that had hurt her so. It was not the anger,—for that she was prepared. It was not the scorn, for she had often faced that. Was it the almost merriment? Yes, there was the sting. She had felt it so keenly when as a little girl Kate had taken to making fun of some whim of hers. She could not see why Kate should find cause for fun just now. It was as if she by her look ignored Marcia's relation to David in scornful laugh and appropriated him herself. Marcia's inmost soul rebelled. The color came back as if by force of her will. She would show Kate,—or she would show David at least,—that she could bear all things for him. She would play well her part of wife this day. The happy two months that had passed since David came back from New York had made her almost feel as if she was really his and he hers. For this hour she would forget that it was otherwise. She would look at him and speak to him as if he had been her husband for years, as if there were the truest understanding between them,—as indeed, of a certain wistful, pleasant sort there was. She would not let the dreadful thought of Kate cloud her face for others to see. Bravely she faced the company, but her heart under Kate's blue frock sent up a swift and pleading prayer demanding of a higher Power something she knew she had not in herself, and must therefore find in Him who had created her. It was the most trustful, and needy prayer that Marcia ever uttered and yet there were no words, not even the closing of an eyelid. Only her heart took the attitude of prayer.

The door upstairs opened in a business-like way, and Hannah's composed voice was heard giving a direction. Hannah's silken tread began to be audible. Miranda told Marcia afterward that she kept her standing at the window for an hour beforehand to see when David arrived, and when they started over to the house. Hannah kept herself posted on what was going on in the room below as well as if she were down there. She knew where David and Marcia stood, and told Kate exactly where to go. It was like Hannah that in the moment of her sacrifice of the long cherished hopes of her life she should have planned a dramatic revenge to help carry her through.

The bride's rustle became at last so audible that even David and Mr. Brentwood heard and turned from their absorbing conversation to the business in hand.

Hannah was in the doorway when David looked up, very cold and beautiful in her bridal array despite the years she had waited, and almost at once David saw the vision in purple and gold like a saucy pansy, standing near her.

Kate's eyes were fixed upon him with their most bewitching, dancing smile of recognition, like a naughty little child who had been in hiding for a time and now peeps out laughing over the discomfiture of its elders. So Kate encountered the steadfast gaze of David's astonished eyes.

But there was no light of love in those eyes as she had expected to see. Instead there grew in his face such a blaze of righteous indignation as the lord of the wedding feast might have turned upon the person who came in without a wedding garment. In spite of herself Kate was disconcerted. She was astonished. She felt that David was challenging her presence there. It seemed to her he was looking through her, searching her, judging her, sentencing her, and casting her out, and presently his eyes wandered beyond her through the open hall door and out into God's green world; and when they came back and next rested upon her his look had frozen into the glance of a stranger.

Angry, ashamed, baffled, she bit her lips in vexation, but tried to keep the merry smile. In her heart she hated him, and vowed to make him bow before her smiles once more.

David did not see the bride at all to notice her, but the bride, unlike the one of the psalmist's vision whose eyes were upon "her dear bridegroom's face," was looking straight across the room with evident intent to observe David.

The ceremony proceeded, and Hannah went through her part correctly and calmly, aware that she was giving herself to Lemuel Skinner irrevocably, yet perfectly aware also of the discomfiture of the sweet-faced girl-wife who sat across the room bravely watching the ceremony with white cheeks and eyes that shone like righteous lights.

Marcia did not look at David. She was with him in heart, suffering with him, feeling for him, quivering in every nerve for what he might be enduring. She had no need to look. Her part was to ignore, and help to cover.

They went through it all well. Not once did Aunt Amelia or Aunt Hortense notice anything strange in the demeanor of their nephew or his wife. Aunt Clarinda was not there. She was not fond of Hannah.

As soon as the service was over and the relatives had broken the solemn hush by kissing the bride, David turned and spoke to Rose Brentwood, making some smiling remark about the occasion. Rose Brentwood was looking her very prettiest in a rose-sprigged delaine and her wavy dark hair in a beaded net tied round with a rose-colored lute-string ribbon.

Kate flushed angrily at this. If it had been Marcia to whom he had spoken she would have judged he did it out of pique, but a pretty stranger coming upon the scene at this critical moment was trying. And then, too, David's manner was so indifferent, so utterly natural. He did not seem in the least troubled by the sight of herself.

David and Marcia did not go up to speak to the bride at once. David stepped back into the deep window seat to talk with Mr. Brentwood, and seemed to be in no hurry to follow the procession who were filing past the calm bride to congratulate her. Marcia remained quietly talking to Rose Brentwood.

At last David turned toward his wife with a smile as though he had known she was there all the time, and had felt her sympathy. Her heart leaped up with new strength at that look, and her husband's firm touch as he drew her hand within his arm to lead her over to the bride gave her courage. She felt that she could face the battle, and with a bright smile that lit up her whole lovely face she marched bravely to the front to do or to die.

"I had about given up expecting any congratulations from you," said Hannah sharply as they came near. It was quite evident she had been watching for them.

"I wish you much joy, Mrs. Skinner," said David mechanically, scarcely feeling that she would have it for he knew her unhappy, dissatisfied nature.

"Yes," said Marcia, "I wish you may be happy,—as happy as I am!"

It was an impetuous, childish thing to say, and Marcia scarcely realized what words she meant to speak until they were out, and then she blushed rosy red. Was she happy? Why was she happy? Yes, even in the present trying circumstances she suddenly felt a great deep happiness bubbling up in her heart. Was it David's look and his strong arm under her hand?

Hannah darted a look at her. She was stung by the words. But did the girl-bride before her mean to flaunt her own triumphs in her face? Did she fully understand? Or was she trying to act a part and make them believe she was happy? Hannah was baffled once more as she had been before with Marcia.

Kate turned upon Marcia for one piercing instant again, that look of understanding, mocking merriment, which cut through the soul of her sister.

But did Marcia imagine it, or was it true that at her words to Hannah, David's arm had pressed hers closer as they stood there in the crowd? The thought thrilled through her and gave her greater strength.

Hannah turned toward Kate.

"David," she said, as she had always called him, and it is possible that she enjoyed the triumph of this touch of intimacy before her guest, "you knew my friend Mrs. Leavenworth!"

David bowed gravely, but did not attempt to put out his hand to take the one which Kate offered in greeting. Instead he laid it over Marcia's little trembling one on his arm as if to steady it.

"We have met before," said David briefly in an impenetrable tone, and turning passed out of the room to make way for the Brentwoods who were behind him.

Hannah scarcely treated the Brentwoods with decency, so vexed was she with the way things were turning out. To think that David should so completely baffle her. She turned an annoyed look at Kate, who flashed her blue eyes contemptuously as if to blame Hannah.

Soon the whole little gathering were in the dining-room and wide hall being served with Grandmother Heath's fried chicken and currant jelly, delicate soda biscuits, and fruit cake baked months before and left to ripen.

The ordeal through which they were passing made David and Marcia feel, as they sat down, that they would not be able to swallow a mouthful, but strangely enough they found themselves eating with relish, each to encourage the other perhaps, but almost enjoying it, and feeling that they had not yet met more than they would be able to withstand.

Kate was seated on the other side of the dining-room, by Hannah, and she watched the two incessantly with that half merry contemptuous look, toying with her own food, and apparently waiting for their acting to cease and David to put on his true character. She never doubted for an instant that they were acting.

The wedding supper was over at last. The guests crowded out to the front stoop to bid good-bye to the happy bridegroom and cross-looking bride, who seemed as if she left the gala scene reluctantly.

Marcia, for the instant, was separated from David, who stepped down upon the grass and stood to one side to let the bridal party pass. The minister was at the other side. Marcia had slipped into the shelter of Aunt Amelia's black silk presence and wished she might run out the back door and away home.

Suddenly a shimmer of gold with the sunlight through it caught her gaze, and a glimpse of sheeny purple. There, close behind David, standing upon the top step, quite unseen by him, stood her sister Kate.

Marcia's heart gave a quick thump and seemed to stop, then went painfully laboring on. She stood quite still watching for the moment to come when David would turn around and see Kate that she might look into his face and read there what was written.

Hannah had been put carefully into the carriage by the adoring Lemuel, with many a pat, and a shaking of cushions, and an adjustment of curtains to suit her whim. It pleased Hannah, now in her last lingering moment of freedom, to be exacting and show others what a slave her husband was.

They all stood for an instant looking after the carriage, but Marcia watched David. Then, just as the carriage wound around the curve in the road and was lost from view, she saw him turn, and at once knew she must not see his face as he looked at Kate. Closing her eyes like a flash she turned and fled upstairs to get her shawl and bonnet. There she took refuge behind the great white curtains, and hid her face for several minutes, praying wildly, she hardly knew what, thankful she had been kept from the sight which yet she had longed to behold.

As David turned to go up the steps and search for Marcia he was confronted by Kate's beautiful, smiling face, radiant as it used to be when it had first charmed him. He exulted, as he looked into it, that it did not any longer charm.

"David, you don't seem a bit glad to see me," blamed Kate sweetly in her pretty, childish tones, looking into his face with those blue eyes so like to liquid skies. Almost there was a hint of tears in them. He had been wont to kiss them when she looked like that. Now he felt only disgust as some of the flippant sentences in her letters to Harry Temple came to his mind.

His face was stern and unrecognizing.

"David, you are angry with me yet! You said you would forgive!" The gentle reproach minimized the crime, and enlarged the punishment. It was Kate's way. The pretty pout on the rosy lips was the same as it used to be when she chided him for some trifling forgetfulness of her wishes.

The other guests had all gone into the house now. David made no response, but, nothing daunted, Kate spoke again.

"I have something very important to consult you about. I came here on purpose. Can you give me some time to-morrow morning?"

She wrinkled her pretty face into a thousand dimples and looked her most bewitching like a naughty child who knew she was loved in spite of anything, and coquettishly putting her head on one side, added, in the tone she used of old to cajole him:

"You know you never could refuse me anything, David."

David did not smile. He did not answer the look. With a voice that recognized her only as a stranger he said gravely:

"I have an important engagement to-morrow morning."

"But you will put off the engagement." She said it confidently.

"It is impossible!" said David decidedly. "I am starting quite early to drive over to Albany. I am under obligation to be present at the starting of the new steam railroad."

"Oh, how nice!" said Kate, clapping her hands childishly, "I have wanted to be there, and now you will take me. Then I—we—can talk on the way. How like old times that will be!" She flashed him a smile of molten sunshine, alluring and transforming.

"That, too, is impossible, Mrs. Leavenworth. My wife accompanies me!" he answered her promptly and clearly and with a curt bow left her and went into the house.

Kate Leavenworth was angry, and for Kate to be angry, meant to visit it upon some one, the offender if possible, if not the nearest to the offender. She had failed utterly in her attempt to win back the friendship of her former lover. She had hoped to enjoy his attention to a certain extent and bathe her sad (?) heart in the wistful glances of the man she had jilted; and incidentally perhaps be invited to spend a little time in his house, by which she would contrive to have a good many of her own ways. A rich brother-in-law who adored one was not a bad thing to have, especially when his wife was one's own little sister whom one had always dominated. She was tired of New York and at this season of the year the country was much preferable. She could thus contrive to hoard her small income, and save for the next winter, as well as secure a possible entrance finally into her father's good graces again through the forgiveness of David and Marcia. But she had failed. Could it be that he cared for Marcia! That child! Scout the idea! She would discover at once.

Hurriedly she searched through the rooms downstairs and then went stealthily upstairs. Instinctively she went to the room where Marcia had hidden herself.

Marcia, with that strong upward breath of prayer had grown steady again. She was standing with her back to the door looking out of the window toward her own home when Kate entered the room. Without turning about she felt Kate's presence and knew that it was she. The moment had come. She turned around, her face calm and sweet, with two red spots upon her cheeks, and her bonnet,—Kate's bonnet and shawl, Kate's fine lace shawl sent from Paris—grasped in her hands.

They faced each other, the sisters, and much was understood between them in a flash without a word spoken. Marcia suddenly saw herself standing there in Kate's rightful place, Kate's things in her hands, Kate's garments upon her body, Kate's husband held by her. It was as if Kate charged her with all these things, as she looked her through and over, from her slipper tips to the ruffle around the neck. And oh, the scorn that flamed from Kate's eyes playing over her, and scorching her cheeks into crimson, and burning her lips dry and stiff! And yet when Kate's eyes reached her face and charged her with the supreme offense of taking David from her, Marcia's eyes looked bravely back, and were not burned by the fire, and she felt that her soul was not even scorched by it. Something about the thought of David like an angelic presence seemed to save her.

The silence between them was so intense that nothing else could be heard by the two. The voices below were drowned by it, the footstep on the stair was as if it were not.

At last Kate spoke, angered still more by her sister's soft eyes which gazed steadily back and did not droop before her own flashing onslaught. Her voice was cold and cruel. There was nothing sisterly in it, nothing to remind either that the other had ever been beloved.

"Fool!" hissed Kate. "Silly fool! Did you think you could steal a husband as you stole your clothes? Did you suppose marrying David would make him yours, as putting on my clothes seemed to make them yours? Well I can tell you he will never be a husband to you. He doesn't love you and he never can. He will always love me. He's as much mine as if I had married him, in spite of all your attempts to take him. Oh, you needn't put up your baby mouth and pucker it as if you were going to cry. Cry away. It won't do any good. You can't make a man yours, any more than you can make somebody's clothes yours. They don't fit you any more than he does. You look horrid in blue, and you know it, in spite of all your prinking around and pretending. I'd be ashamed to be tricked out that way and know that every dud I had was made for somebody else. As for going around and pretending you have a husband—it's a lie. You know he's nothing to you. You know he never told you he cared for you. I tell you he's mine, and he always will be."

"Kate, you're married!" cried Marcia in shocked tones. "How can you talk like that?"

"Married! Nonsense! What difference does that make? It's hearts that count, not marriages. Has your marriage made you a wife? Answer me that! Has it? Does David love you? Does he ever kiss you? Yet he came to see me in New York this winter, and took me in his arms and kissed me. He gave me money too. See this brooch?"—she exhibited a jeweled pin—"that was bought with his money. You see he loves me still. I could bring him to my feet with a word to-day. He would kiss me if I asked him. He is weak as water in my hands."

Marcia's cheeks burned with shame and anger. Almost she felt at the limit of her strength. For the first time in her life she felt like striking,—striking her own sister. Horrified over her feelings, and the rage which was tearing her soul, she looked up, and there stood David in the doorway, like some tall avenging angel!

Kate had her back that way and did not see at once, but Marcia's eyes rested on him hungrily, pleadingly, and his answered hers. From her sudden calmness Kate saw there was some one near, and turning, looked at David. But he did not glance her way. How much or how little he had heard of Kate's tirade, which in her passion had been keyed in a high voice, he never let them know and neither dared to ask him, lest perhaps he had not heard anything. There was a light of steel in his eyes toward everything but Marcia, and his tone had in it kindness and a recognition of mutual understanding as he said:

"If you are ready we had better go now, dear, had we not?"

Oh how gladly Marcia followed her husband down the stairs and out the door! She scarcely knew how she went through the formalities of getting away. It seemed as she looked back upon them that David had sheltered her from it all, and said everything needful for her, and all she had done was to smile an assent. He talked calmly to her all the way home; told her Mr. Brentwood's opinion about the change in the commerce of the country the new railroad was going to make; told her though he must have known she could not listen. Perhaps both were conscious of the bedroom window over the way and a pair of blue eyes that might be watching them as they passed into the house. David took hold of her arm and helped her up the steps of their own home as if she had been some great lady. Marcia wondered if Kate saw that. In her heart she blessed David for this outward sign of their relationship. It gave her shame a little cover at least. She glanced up toward the next house as she passed in and felt sure she saw a glimmer of purple move away from the window. Then David shut the door behind them and led her gently in.

CHAPTER XXVII

He made her go into the parlor and sit down and she was all unnerved by his gentle ways. The tears would come in spite of her. He took his own fine wedding handkerchief and wiped them softly off her hot cheeks. He untied the bonnet that was not hers, and flung it far into a corner in the room. Marcia thought he put force into the fling. Then he unfolded the shawl from her shoulders and threw that into another corner. Kate's beautiful thread lace shawl. Marcia felt a hysterical desire to laugh, but David's voice was steady and quiet when he spoke as one might speak to a little child in trouble.

"There now, dear," he said. He had never called her dear before. "There, that was an ordeal, and I'm glad, it's over. It will never trouble us that way again. Let us put it aside and never think about it any more. We have our own lives to live. I want you to go with me to-morrow morning to see the train start if you feel able. We must start early and you must take a good rest. Would you like to go?"

Marcia's face like a radiant rainbow answered for her as she smiled behind her tears, and all the while he talked David's hand, as tender as a woman's, was passing back and forth on Marcia's hot forehead and smoothing the hair. He talked on quietly to soothe her, and give her a chance to regain her composure, speaking of a few necessary arrangements for the morning's ride. Then he said, still in his quiet voice: "Now dear, I want you to go to bed, for we must start rather early, but first do you think you could sing me that little song you were singing the day I came home? Don't if you feel too tired, you know."

Then Marcia, an eager light in her eyes, sprang up and went to the piano, and began to play softly and sing the tender words she had sung once before when he was listening and she knew it not.

"Dearest, believe,
When e'er we part:
Lonely I grieve,
In my sad heart:—"

Kate, standing within the chintz curtains across the yard shedding angry tears upon her purple silk, heard presently the sweet tones of the piano, which might have been hers; heard her sister's voice singing, and began to understand that she must bear the punishment of her own rash deeds.

The room had grown from a purple dusk into quiet darkness while Marcia was singing, for the sun was almost down when they walked home. When the song was finished David stood half wistfully looking at Marcia for a moment. Her eyes shone to his through the dusk like two bright stars. He hesitated as though he wanted to say something more, and then thought better of it. At last he stooped and lifted her hand from the keys and led her toward the door.

"You must go to sleep at once," he said gently. "You'll need all the rest you can get." He lighted a candle for her and said good-night with his eyes as well as his lips. Marcia felt that she was moving up the stairs under a spell of some gentle loving power that surrounded her and would always guard her.

And it was about this time that Miranda, having been sent over to take a forgotten piece of bride's cake to Marcia, and having heard the piano, and stolen discreetly to the parlor window for a moment, returned and detailed for the delectation of that most unhappy guest Mrs. Leavenworth why she could not get in and would have to take it over in the morning:

"The window was open in the parlor and they were in there, them two, but they was so plum took up with their two selves, as they always are, that there wasn't no use knockin' fer they'd never hev heard."

Miranda enjoyed making those remarks to the guest. Some keen instinct always told her where best to strike her blows.

When Marcia had reached the top stair she looked down and there was David smiling up to her.

"Marcia," said he in a tone that seemed half ashamed and half amused, "have you, any—that is—things—that you had before—all your own I mean?" With quick intuition Marcia understood and her own sweet shame about her clothes that were not her own came back upon her with double force. She suddenly saw herself again standing before the censure of her sister. She wondered if David had heard. If not, how then did he know? Oh, the shame of it!

She sat down weakly upon the stair.

"Yes," said she, trying to think. "Some old things, and one frock."

"Wear it then to-morrow, dear," said David, in a compelling voice and with the sweet smile that took the hurt out of his most severe words.

Marcia smiled. "It is very plain," she said, "only chintz, pink and white. I made it myself."

"Charming!" said David. "Wear it, dear. Marcia, one thing more. Don't wear any more things that don't belong to you. Not a Dud. Promise me? Can you get along without it?"

"Why, I guess so," said Marcia laughing joyfully. "I'll try to manage. But I haven't any bonnet. Nothing but a pink sunbonnet."

"All right, wear that," said David.

"It will look a little queer, won't it?" said Marcia doubtfully, and yet as if the idea expressed a certain freedom which was grateful to her.

"Never mind," said David. "Wear it. Don't wear any more of those other things. Pack them all up and send them where they belong, just as quick as we get home."

There was something masterful and delightful in David's voice, and Marcia with a happy laugh took her candle and got up saying, with a ring of joy in her voice: "All right!" She went to her room with David's second good-night ringing in her ears and her heart so light she wanted to sing.

Not at once did Marcia go to her bed. She set her candle upon the bureau and began to search wildly in a little old hair-cloth trunk, her own special old trunk that had contained her treasures and which had been sent her after she left home. She had scarcely looked into it since she came to the new home. It seemed as if her girlhood were shut up in it. Now she pulled it out from the closet.

What a flood of memories rushed over her as she opened it! There were relics of her school days, and of her little childhood. But she had no time for them now. She was in search of something. She touched them tenderly, but laid them all out one after another upon the floor until down in the lower corner she found a roll of soft white cloth. It contained a number of white garments, half a dozen perhaps in all, finished, and several others cut out barely begun. They were her own work, every stitch, the first begun when she was quite a little girl, and her stepmother started to teach her to sew. What pride she had taken in them! How pleased she had been when allowed to put real tucks in some of them! She had thought as she sewed upon them at different times that they were to be a part of her own wedding trousseau. And then her wedding had come upon her unawares, with the trousseau ready-made, and everything belonged to some one else. She had folded her own poor little garments away and thought never to take them out again, for they seemed to belong to her dead self.

But now that dead self had suddenly come to life again. These hated things that she had worn for a year that were not hers were to be put away, and, pretty as they were, many of them, she regretted not a thread of them.

She laid the white garments out upon a chair and decided that she would put on what she needed of them on the morrow, even though they were rumpled with long lying away. She even searched out an old pair of her own stockings and laid them on a chair with the other things. They were neatly darned as all things had always been under her stepmother's supervision. Further search brought a pair of partly worn prunella slippers to light, with narrow ankle ribbons.

Then Marcia took down the pink sprigged chintz that she had made a year ago and laid it near the other things, with a bit of black velvet and the quaint old brooch. She felt a little dubious about appearing on such a great occasion, almost in Albany, in a chintz dress and with no wrap. Stay! There was the white crêpe shawl, all her own, that David had brought her. She had not felt like wearing it to Hannah Heath's wedding, it seemed too precious to take near an unloving person like Hannah. Before that she had never felt an occasion great enough. Now she drew it forth breathlessly. A white crêpe shawl and a pink calico sunbonnet! Marcia laughed softly. But then, what matter! David had said wear it.

All things were ready for the morrow now. There were even her white lace mitts that Aunt Polly in an unusual fit of benevolence had given her.

Then, as if to make the change complete, she searched out an old night robe, plain but smooth and clean and arrayed herself in it, and so, thankful, happy, she lay down as she had been bidden and fell asleep.

David in the room below pondered, strange to say, the subject of dress. There was some pride beneath it all, of course; there always is behind the great problem of dress. It was the rejected bonnet lying in the corner with its blue ribbons limp and its blue flowers crushed that made that subject paramount among so many others he might have chosen for his night's meditation.

He was going over to close the parlor window, when he saw the thing lying innocent and discarded in the corner. Though it bore an injured look, it yet held enough of its original aristocratic style to cause him to stop and think.

It was all well enough to suggest that Marcia wear a pink sunbonnet. It sounded deliciously picturesque. She looked lovely in pink and a sunbonnet was pretty and sensible on any one; but the morrow was a great day. David would be seen of many and his wife would come under strict scrutiny. Moreover it was possible that Kate might be upon the scene to jeer at her sister in a sunbonnet. In fact, when he considered it he would not like to take his wife to Albany in a sunbonnet. It behoved him to consider. The outrageous words which he had heard Mistress Leavenworth speak to his wife still burned in his brain like needles of torture: revelation of the true character of the woman he had once longed to call his own.

But that bonnet! He stood and examined it. What was a bonnet like? The proper kind of a bonnet for a woman in his wife's position to wear. He had never noticed a woman's bonnet before except as he had absent-mindedly observed them in front of him in meeting. Now he brought his mind to bear upon that bonnet. It seemed to be made up of three component parts—a foundation: a girdle apparently to bind together and tie on the head; and a decoration. Straw, silk and some kind of unreal flowers. Was that all? He stooped down and picked the thing up with the tips of his fingers, held it at arms length as though it were contaminating, and examined the inside. Ah! There was another element in its construction, a sort of frill of something thin,—hardly lace,—more like the foam of a cloud. He touched the tulle clumsily with his thumb and finger and then he dropped the bonnet back into the corner again. He thought he understood well enough to know one again. He stood pondering a moment, and looked at his watch.

Yes, it was still early enough to try at least, though of course the shop would be closed. But the village milliner lived behind her little store. It would be easy enough to rouse her, and he had known her all his life. He took his hat as eagerly as he had done when as a boy Aunt Clarinda had given him a penny to buy a top and permission to go to the corner and buy it before Aunt Amelia woke up from her nap. He went quietly out of the door, fastening it behind him and walked rapidly down the street.

Yes, the milliner's shop was closed, but a light in the side windows shining through the veiling hop-vines guided him, and he was presently tapping at Miss Mitchell's side door. She opened the door cautiously and peeped over her glasses at him, and then a bright smile overspread her face. Who in the whole village did not welcome David whenever he chanced to come? Miss Mitchell was resting from her labors and reading the village paper. She had finished the column of gossip and was quite ready for a visitor.

"Come right in, David," she said heartily, for she had known him all the years, "it does a body good to see you though your visits are as few and far between as angels' visits. I'm right glad to see you! Sit down." But David was too eager about his business.

"I haven't any time to sit down to-night, Miss Susan," he said eagerly, "I've come to buy a bonnet. Have you got one? I hope it isn't too late because I want it very early in the morning."

"A bonnet! Bless me! For yourself?" said Miss Mitchell from mere force of commercial habit. But neither of them saw the joke, so intent upon business were they. "For my wife, Miss Mitchell. You see she is going with me over to Albany to-morrow morning and we start quite early. We are going to see the new railroad train start, you know, and she seems to think she hasn't a bonnet that's suitable."

"Going to see a steam engine start, are you! Well, take care, David, you don't get too near. They do say they're terrible dangerous things, and fer my part I can't see what good they'll be, fer nobody'll ever be willin' to ride behind 'em, but I'd like to see it start well enough. And that sweet little wife of yours thinks she ain't got a good enough bonnet. Land sakes! What is the matter with her Dunstable straw, and what's become of that one trimmed with blue lutestrings, and where's the shirred silk one she wore last Sunday? They're every one fine bonnets and ought to last her a good many years yet if she cares fer 'em. The mice haven't got into the house and et them, hev they?"

"No, Miss Susan, those bonnets are all whole yet I believe, but they don't seem to be just the suitable thing. In fact, I don't think they're over-becoming to her, do you? You see they're mostly blue——"

"That's so!" said Miss Mitchell. "I think myself she'd look better in pink. How'd you like white? I've got a pretty thing that I made fer Hannah Heath an' when it was done Hannah thought it was too plain and wouldn't have it. I sent for the flowers to New York and they cost a high price. Wait! I will show it to you."

She took a candle and he followed her to the dark front room ghostly with bonnets in various stages of perfection.

It was a pretty thing. Its foundation was of fine Milan braid, creamy white and smooth and even. He knew at a glance it belonged to the higher order of things, and was superior to most of the bonnets produced in the village.

It was trimmed with plain white taffeta ribbon, soft and silky. That was all on the outside. Around the face was a soft ruching of tulle, and clambering among it a vine of delicate green leaves that looked as if they were just plucked from a wild rose bank. David was delighted. Somehow the bonnet looked like Marcia. He paid the price at once, declining to look at anything else. It was enough that he liked it and that Hannah Heath had not. He had never admired Hannah's taste. He carried it home in triumph, letting himself softly into the house, lighted three candles, took the bonnet out and hung it upon a chair. Then he walked around it surveying it critically, first from this side, then from that. It pleased him exceedingly. He half wished Marcia would hear him and come down. He wanted to see it on her, but concluded that he was growing boyish and had better get himself under control.

The bonnet approved, he walked back and forth through the kitchen and dining-room thinking. He compelled himself to go over the events of the afternoon and analyze most carefully his own innermost feelings. In fact, after doing that he began further back and tried to find out how he felt toward Marcia. What was this something that had been growing in him unaware through the months; that had made his homecoming so sweet, and had brightened every succeeding day; and had made this meeting with Kate a mere commonplace? What was this precious thing that nestled in his heart? Might he, had he a right to call it love? Surely! Now all at once his pulses thrilled with gladness. He loved her! It was good to love her! She was the most precious being on earth to him. What was Kate in comparison with her? Kate who had shown herself cold and cruel and unloving in every way?

His anger flamed anew as he thought of those cutting sentences he had overheard, taunting her own sister about the clothes she wore. Boasting that he still belonged to her! She, a married woman! A woman who had of her own free will left him at the last moment and gone away with another! His whole nature recoiled against her. She had sinned against her womanhood, and might no longer demand from man the homage that a true woman had a right to claim.

Poor little bruised flower! His heart went out to Marcia. He could not bear to think of her having to stand and listen to that heartless tirade. And he had been the cause of all this. He had allowed her to take a position which threw her open to Kate's vile taunts.

Up and down he paced till the torrent of his anger spent itself, and he was able to think more calmly. Then he went back in his thoughts to the time when he had first met Kate and she had bewitched him. He could see now the heartlessness of her. He had met her first at the house of a friend where he was visiting, partly on pleasure, partly on business. She had devoted herself to him during the time of her stay in a most charming way, though now he recalled that she had also been equally devoted to the son of the house whom he was visiting. When she went home she had asked him to come and call, for her home was but seven miles away. He had been so charmed with her that he had accepted the invitation, and, rashly he now saw, had engaged himself to her, after having known her in all face to face but a few days. To be sure he had known of her father for years, and he took a good deal for granted on account of her fine family. They had corresponded after their engagement which had lasted for nearly a year, and in that time David had seen her but twice, for a day or two at a time, and each time he had thought her grown more lovely. Her letters had been marvels of modesty, and shy admiration. It was easy for Kate to maintain her character upon paper, though she had had little trouble in making people love her under any circumstances. Now as he looked back he could recall many instances when she had shown a cruel, heartless nature.

Then, all at once, with a throb of joy, it came to him to be thankful to God for the experience through which he had passed. After all it had not been taken from him to love with a love enduring, for though Kate had been snatched from him just at the moment of his possession, Marcia had been given him. Fool that he was! He had been blind to his own salvation. Suppose he had been allowed to go on and marry Kate! Suppose he had had her character revealed to him suddenly as those letters of hers to Harry Temple had revealed it—as it surely would have been revealed in time, for such things cannot be hid,—and she had been his *wife!* He shuddered. How he would have loathed her! How he loathed her now!

Strangely enough the realization of that fact gave him joy. He sprang up and waved his hands about in silent delight. He felt as if he must shout for gladness. Then he gravely knelt beside his chair and uttered an audible thanksgiving for his escape and the joy he had been given. Nothing else seemed fitting expression of his feelings.

There was one other question to consider—Marcia's feelings. She had always been kind and gentle and loving to him, just as a sister might have been. She was exceedingly young yet. Did she know, could she understand what it meant to be loved the way he was sure he could love a woman? And would she ever be able to love him in that way? She was so silent and shy he hardly knew whether she cared for him or not. But there was one thought that gave him unbounded joy and that was that she was his wife. At least no one else could take her from him. He had felt condemned that he had married her when his heart was heavy lest she would lose the joy of life, but all that was changed now. Unless she loved some one else surely such love as his could compel hers and finally make her as happy as a woman could be made.

A twinge of misgiving crossed his mind as he admitted the possibility that Marcia might love some one else. True, he knew of no one, and she was so young it was scarcely likely she had left any one back in her girlhood to whom her heart had turned when she was out of his sight. Still there were instances of strong union of hearts of those who had loved from early childhood. It might be that Marcia's sometime-sadness was over a companion of her girlhood.

A great longing took possession of him to rush up and waken her and find out if she could ever care for him. He scarcely knew himself. This was not his dignified contained self that he had lived with for twenty-seven years.

It was very late before he finally went upstairs. He walked softly lest he disturb Marcia. He paused before her door listening to see if she was asleep, but there was only the sound of the katydids in the branches outside her window, and the distant tree-toads singing a fugue in an orchard not far away. He tiptoed to his room but he did not light his candle, therefore there was no light in the back room of the Spafford house that night for any watching eyes to ponder over. He threw himself upon the bed. He was weary in body yet his soul seemed buoyant as a bird in the morning air. The moon was casting long bars of silver across the rag carpet and white counterpane. It was almost full moon. Yes, to-morrow it would be entirely full. It was full moon the night he had met Marcia down by the gate, and kissed her. It was the first time he had thought of that kiss with anything but pain. It used to hurt him that he had made the mistake and taken her for Kate. It had seemed like an ill-omen of what was to come. But now, it thrilled him with a great new joy. After all he had given the kiss to the right one. It was Marcia to whom his soul bowed in the homage that a man may give to a woman. Did his good angel guide him to her that night? And how was it he had not seen the sweetness of Marcia sooner? How had he lived with her nearly a year, and watched her dainty ways, and loving ministry and not known that his heart was hers? How was it he had grieved so long over Kate, and now since he had seen her once more, not a regret was in his heart that she was not his; but a beautiful revelation of his own love to Marcia had been wrought in him? How came it?

And the importunate little songsters in the night answered him a thousand times: "Kate-did-it! Kate-she-did it! Yes she did! I say she did. Kate did it!"

Had angel voices reached him through his dreams, and suddenly given him the revelation which the little insects had voiced in their ridiculous colloquy? It was Kate herself who had shown him how he loved Marcia.

CHAPTER XXVIII

Slowly the moon rode over the house, and down toward its way in the West, and after its vanishing chariot the night stretched wistful arms. Softly the grey in the East tinged into violet and glowed into rose and gold. The birds woke up and told one another that the first of August was come and life was good.

The breath that came in the early dawn savored of new-mown hay, and the bird songs thrilled Marcia as if it were the day of her dreams.

She forgot all her troubles; forgot even her wayward sister next door; and rose with the song of the birds in her heart. This was to be a great day. No matter what happened she had now this day to date from. David had asked her to go somewhere just because he wanted her to. She knew it from the look in his eyes when he told her, and she knew it because he might have asked a dozen men to go with him. There was no reason why he need have taken her to-day, for it was distinctly an affair for men, this great wonder of machinery. It was a privilege for a woman to go. She felt it. She understood the honor.

With fingers trembling from joy she dressed. Not the sight of her pink calico sunbonnet lying on the chair, nor the thought of wearing it upon so grand an occasion, could spoil the pleasure of the day. Among so large a company her bonnet would hardly be noticed. If David was satisfied why what difference did it make? She was glad it would be early when they drove by the aunts, else they might be scandalized. But never mind! Trill! She hummed a merry little tune which melted into the melody of the song she had sung last night.

Then she smiled at herself in the glass. She was fastening the brooch in the bit of velvet round her neck, and she thought of the day a year ago when she had fastened that brooch. She had wondered then how she would feel if the next day was to be her own wedding day. Now as she smiled back at herself in the glass all at once she thought it seemed as if this was her wedding day. Somehow last night had seemed to realize her dreams. A wonderful joy had descended upon her heart. Maybe she was foolish, but was she not going to ride with David? She did not long for the green fields and a chance to run wild through the wood now. This was better than those childish pleasures. This was real happiness. And to think it should have come through David!

She hurried with the arrangement of her hair until her fingers trembled with excitement. She wanted to get downstairs and see if it were all really true or if she were dreaming it. Would David look at her as he had done last night? Would he speak that precious word "dear" to her again to-day? Would he take her by the hand and lead her sometimes, or was that a special gentleness because he knew she had suffered from her sister's words? She clasped her hands with a quick, convulsive gesture over her heart and looking back to the sweet face in the glass, said softly, "Oh, I love him, love him! And it cannot be wrong, for Kate is married."

But though she was up early David had been down before her. The fire was ready lighted and the kettle singing over it on the crane. He had even pulled out the table and put up the leaf, and made some attempt to put the dishes upon it for breakfast. He was sitting by the hearth impatient for her coming, with a bandbox by his side.

It was like another sunrise to watch their eyes light up as they saw one another. Their glances rushed together as though they had been a long time withholden from each other, and a rosy glow came over Marcia's face that made her long to hide it for a moment from view. Then she knew in her heart that her dream was not all a dream. David was the same. It had lasted, whatever this wonderful thing was that bound them together. She stood still in her happy bewilderment, looking at him, and he, enjoying the radiant morning vision of her, stood too.

David found that longing to take her in his arms overcoming him again. He had made strict account with himself and was resolved to be careful and not frighten her. He must be sure it would not be unpleasant to her before he let her know his great deep love. He must be careful. He must not take advantage of the fact that she was his and could not run away from him. If she dreaded his attentions, neither could she any more say no.

And so their two looks met, and longed to come closer, but were held back, and a lovely shyness crept over Marcia's sweet face. Then David bethought himself of his bandbox.

He took up the box and untied it with unaccustomed fingers, fumbling among the tissue paper for the handle end of the thing. Where did they take hold of bonnets anyway? He had no trouble with it the night before, but then he was not thinking about it. Now he was half afraid she might not like it. He remembered that Hannah Heath had pronounced against it. It suddenly seemed impossible that he should have bought a bonnet that a pretty woman had said was not right. There must be something wrong with it after all.

Marcia stood wondering.

"I thought maybe this would do instead of the sunbonnet," he said at last, getting out the bonnet by one string and holding it dangling before him.

Marcia caught it with deft careful hands and an exclamation of delight. He watched her anxiously. It had all the requisite number of materials,—one, two, three, four,—like the despised bonnet he threw on the floor—straw, silk, lace and flowers. Would she like it? Her face showed that she did. Her cheeks flushed with pleasure, and her eyes danced with joy. Marcia's face always showed it when she liked anything. There was nothing half-way about her.

"Oh, it is beautiful!" she said delightedly. "It is so sweet and white and cool with that green vine. Oh, I am glad, glad, glad! I shall never wear that old blue bonnet again." She went over to the glass and put it on. The soft ruching settled about her brown hair, and made a lovely setting for her face. The green vine twined and peeped in and out under the round brim and the ribbon sat in a prim bow beneath her pretty chin.

She gave one comprehensive glance at herself in the glass and then turned to David. In that glance was revealed to her just how much she had dreaded wearing her pink sunbonnet, and just how relieved she was to have a substitute.

Her look was shy and sweet as she said with eyes that dared and then drooped timidly:

"You—are—very—good to me!"

Almost he forgot his vow of carefulness at that, but remembered when he had got half across the room toward her, and answered earnestly:

"Dear, *you* have been very good to *me*."

Marcia's eyes suddenly sobered and half the glow faded from her face. Was it then only gratitude? She took off the bonnet and touched the bows with wistful tenderness as she laid it by till after breakfast. He watched her and misinterpreted the look. Was she then disappointed in the bonnet? Was it not right after all? Had Hannah known better than he? He hesitated and then asked her:

"Is there—— Is it—— That is—perhaps you would rather take it back and and choose another. You know how to choose one better than I. There were others I think. In fact, I forgot to look at any but this because I liked it, but I'm only a man——" he finished helplessly.

"No! No! No!" said Marcia, her eyes sparkling emphatically again. "There couldn't be a better one. This is just exactly what I like. I do not want anything else. And I—like it all the better because you selected it," she added daringly, suddenly lifting her face to his with a spice of her own childish freedom.

His eyes admired her.

"She told me Hannah Heath thought it too plain," he added honestly.

"Then I'm sure I like it all the better for that," said Marcia so emphatically that they both laughed.

It all at once became necessary to hurry, for the old clock in the hall clanged out the hour and David became aware that haste was imperative.

Early as Marcia had come down, David had been up long before her, his heart too light to sleep. In a dream, or perchance on the borders of the morning, an idea had come to him. He told Marcia that he must go out now to see about the horse, but he also made a hurried visit to the home of his office clerk and another to the aunts, and when he returned with the horse he had left things in such train that if he did not return that evening he would not be greatly missed. But he said nothing to Marcia about it. He laughed to himself as he thought of the sleepy look on his clerk's face, and the offended dignity expressed in the ruffle of Aunt Hortense's night cap all awry as she had peered over the balusters to receive his unprecedentedly early visit. The aunts were early risers. They prided themselves upon it. It hurt their dignity and their pride to have anything short of sudden serious illness, or death, or a fire cause others to arise before them. Therefore they did not receive the message that David was meditating another trip away from the village for a few days with good grace. Aunt Hortense asked Aunt Amelia if she had ever feared that Marcia would have a bad effect upon David by making him frivolous. Perhaps he would lose interest in his business with all his careering around the country. Aunt Amelia agreed that Marcia must be to blame in some way, and then discovering they had a whole hour before their usual rising time, the two good ladies settled themselves with indignant composure to their interrupted repose.

Breakfast was ready when David returned. Marcia supposed he had only been to harness the horse. She glanced out happily through the window to where the horse stood tied to the post in front of the house. She felt like waving her hand to him, and he turned and seemed to see her; rolling the whites of his eyes around, and tossing his head as if in greeting.

Marcia would scarcely have eaten anything in her excitement if David had not urged her to do so. She hurried with her clearing away, and then flew upstairs to arrange her bonnet before the glass and don the lovely folds of the creamy crêpe shawl, folding it demurely around her shoulders and knotting it in front. She put on her mitts, took her handkerchief folded primly, and came down ready.

But David no longer seemed in such haste. He made a great fuss fastening up everything. She wondered at his unusual care, for she thought everything quite safe for the day.

She raised one shade toward the Heath house. It was the first time she had permitted herself this morning to think of Kate. Was she there yet? Probably, for no coach had left since last night, and unless she had gone by private conveyance there would have been no way to go. She looked up to the front corner guest room where the windows were open and the white muslin curtains swayed in the morning breeze. No one seemed to be moving about in the room. Perhaps Kate was not awake. Just then she caught the flutter of a blue muslin down on the front stoop. Kate was up, early as it was, and was coming out. A sudden misgiving seized Marcia's heart, as when a little child, she had seen her sister coming to eat up the piece of cake or sweetmeat that had been given to her. Many a time had that happened. Now, she felt that in some mysterious way Kate would contrive to take from her her new-found joy.

She could not resist her,—David could not resist her,—no one could ever resist Kate. Her face turned white and her hand began to tremble so that she dropped the curtain she had been holding up.

Just then came David's clear voice, louder than would have been necessary, and pitched as if he were calling to some one upstairs, though he knew she was just inside the parlor where she had gone to make sure of the window fastening.

"Come, dear! Aren't you ready? It is more than time we started."

There was a glad ring in David's voice that somehow belied the somewhat exacting words he had spoken, and Marcia's heart leaped up to meet him.

"Yes, I'm all ready, dear!" she called back with a hysterical little laugh. Of course Kate could not hear so far, but it gave her satisfaction to say it. The final word was unpremeditated. It bubbled up out of the depths of her heart and made the red rush back into her cheeks when she realized what she had said. It was the first time she had ever used a term of endearment toward David. She wondered if he noticed it and if he would think her very— bold,—queer,—immodest, to use it. She looked shyly up at him, enquiring with her eyes, as she came out to him on the front stoop, and he looked down with such a smile she felt as if it were a caress. And yet neither was quite conscious of this little real by-play they were enacting for the benefit of the audience of one in blue muslin over the way. How much she heard, or how little they could not tell, but it gave satisfaction to go through with it inasmuch as it was real, and not acting at all.

David fastened the door and then helped Marcia into the carriage. They were both laughing happily like two children starting upon a picnic. Marcia was serenely conscious of her new bonnet, and it was pleasant to have David tuck the linen lap robe over her chintz frock so carefully. She was certain Kate could not identify it now at that distance, thanks to the lap robe and her crêpe shawl. At least Kate could not see any of her own trousseau on her sister now.

Kate was sitting on the little white seat in the shelter of the honeysuckle vine facing them on the stoop of the Heath house. It was impossible for them to know whether she was watching them or not. They did not look up to see. She was talking with Mr. Heath who, in his milking garb, was putting to rights some shrubs and plants near the walk that had been trampled upon during the wedding festivities. But Kate must have seen a good deal that went on.

David took up the reins, settled himself with a smile at Marcia, touched the horse with the tip of the whip, which caused him to spring forward in astonishment—that from David! No horse in town would have expected it of him. They had known him from babyhood, most of them, and he was gentleness itself. It must have been a mistake. But the impression lasted long enough to carry them a rod or two past the Heath house at a swift pace, with only time for a lifting of David's hat, prolonged politely,—which might or might not have included Kate, and they were out upon their way together.

Marcia could scarcely believe her senses that she was really here beside David, riding with him swiftly through the village and leaving Kate behind. She felt a passing pity for Kate. Then she looked shyly up at David. Would his gaiety pass when they were away, and would he grow grave and sad again so soon as he was out of Kate's sight? She had learned enough of David's principles to know that he would not think it right to let his thoughts stray to Kate now, but did his heart still turn that way in spite of him?

Through the town they sped, glad with every roll of the wheels that took them further away from Kate. Each was conscious, as they rolled along, of that day one year ago when they rode together thus, out through the fields into the country. It was a day much as that other one, just as bright, just as warm, yet oh, so much more radiant to both! Then they were sad and fearful of the future. All their life seemed in the past. Now the darkness had been led through, and they had reached the brightness again. In fact, all the future stretched out before them that fair morning and looked bright as the day.

They were conscious of the blueness of the sky, of the soft clouds that hovered in haziness on the rim of the horizon, as holding off far enough to spoil no moment of that perfect day. They were conscious of the waving grains and of the perfume of the buckwheat drifting like snow in the fields beyond the wheat; conscious of the meadow-lark and the wood-robin's note; of the whirr of a locust; and the thud of a frog in the cool green of a pool deep with brown shadows; conscious of the circling of mated butterflies in the simmering gold air; of the wild roses lifting fair pink petals from the brambly banks beside the road; conscious of the whispering pine needles in a wood they passed; the fluttering chatter of leaves and silver flash of the lining of poplar leaves, where tall trees stood like sentinels, apart and sad; conscious of a little brook that tinkled under a log bridge they crossed, then hurried on its way unmindful of their happy crossing; conscious of the dusty daisy beside the road, closing with a bumbling bee who wanted honey below the market price; conscious of all these things; but most conscious of each other, close, side by side.

It was all so dear, that ride, and over so soon. Marcia was just trying to get used to looking up into the dazzling light of David's eyes. She had to droop her own almost immediately for the truth she read in his was overpowering. Could it be? A fluttering thought came timidly to her heart and would not be denied.

"Can it be, can it be that he cares for me? He loves me. He loves me!" It sang its way in with thrill after thrill of joy and more and more David's eyes told the story which his lips dared not risk yet. But eyes and hearts are not held by the conventions that bind lips. They rushed into their inheritance of each other and had that day ahead, a day so rare and sweet that it would do to set among the jewels of fair days for all time and for any one.

All too soon they began to turn into roads where were other vehicles, many of them, and all going in the same direction. Men and women in gala day attire all laughing and talking expectantly and looking at one another as the carriages passed with a degree of familiar curiosity which betokens a common errand. Family coaches, farm wagons, with kitchen chairs for accommodation of the family; old one-horse chaises, carryalls, and even a stage coach or two wheeled into the old turnpike. David and Marcia settled into subdued quiet, their joy not expressing itself in the ripples of laughter that had rung out earlier in the morning when they were alone. They sought each other's eyes often and often, and in one of these excursions that David's eyes made to Marcia's face he noticed how extremely becoming the new bonnet was. After thinking it over he decided to risk letting her know. He was not shy about it now.

"Do you know, dear," he said,—there had been a good many "dear's" slipping back and forth all unannounced during that ride, and not openly acknowledged either. "Do you know how becoming your new bonnet is to you? You look prettier than I ever saw you look but once before." He kept his eyes upon her face and watched the sweet color steal up to her drooping eyelashes.

"When was that?" she asked coyly, to hide her embarrassment, and sweeping him one laughing glance.

"Why, that night, dear, at the gate, in the moonlight. Don't you remember?"

"Oh-h-h-h!" Marcia caught her breath and a thrill of joy passed through her that made her close her eyes lest the glad tears should come. Then the little bird in her heart set up the song in earnest to the tune of Wonder:"He loves me, He loves me, He loves me!"

He leaned a little closer to her.

"If there were not so many people looking I think I should have to kiss you now."

"Oh-h-h-h!" said Marcia drawing in her breath and looking around frightened on the number of people that were driving all about them, for they were come almost to the railroad now, and could see the black smoke of the engine a little beyond as it stood puffing and snorting upon its track like some sulky animal that had been caught and chained and harnessed and was longing to leap forward and upset its load.

But though Marcia looked about in her happy fright, and sat a trifle straighter in the chaise, she did not move her hand away that lay next David's, underneath the linen lap robe, and he put his own hand over it and covered it close in his firm hold. Marcia trembled and was so happy she was almost faint with joy. She wondered if she were very foolish indeed to feel so, and if all love had this terrible element of solemn joy in it that made it seem too great to be real.

They had to stop a number of times to speak to people. Everybody knew David, it appeared. This man and that had a word to speak with him, some bit of news that he must not omit to notice in his article, some new development about the attitude of a man of influence that was important; the change of two or three of those who were to go in the coaches on this trial trip.

To all of them David introduced his wife, with a ring of pride in his voice as he said the words "My wife," and all of them stopped whatever business they had in hand and stepped back to bow most deferentially to the beautiful woman who sat smiling by his side. They wondered why they had not heard of her before, and they looked curiously, enviously at David, and back in admiration at Marcia. It was quite a little court she held sitting there in the chaise by David's side.

Men who have since won a mention in the pages of history were there that day, and nearly all of them had a word for David Spafford and his lovely wife. Many of them stood for some time and talked with her. Mr. Thurlow Weed was the last one to leave them before the train was actually ready for starting, and he laid an urging hand upon David's arm as he went. "Then you think you cannot go with us? Better come. Mrs. Spafford will let you I am sure. You're not afraid are you, Mrs. Spafford? I am sure you are a brave woman. Better come, Spafford."

But David laughingly thanked him again as he had thanked others, and said that he would not be able to go, as he and his wife had other plans, and he must go on to Albany as soon as the train had started.

Marcia looked up at him half worshipfully as he said this, wondering what it was, instinctively knowing that it was for her sake he was giving up this honor which they all wished to put upon him. It would naturally have been an interesting thing to him to have taken this first ride behind the new engine "Dewitt Clinton."

Then, suddenly, like a chill wind from a thunder cloud that has stolen up unannounced and clutched the little wild flowers before they have time to bind up their windy locks and duck their heads under cover, there happened a thing that clutched Marcia's heart and froze all the joy in her veins.

CHAPTER XXIX

A coach was approaching filled with people, some of them Marcia knew; they were friends and neighbors from their own village, and behind it plodding along came a horse with a strangely familiar gait drawing four people. The driver was old Mr. Heath looking unbelievingly at the scene before him. He did not believe that an engine would be able to haul a train any appreciable distance whatever, and he believed that he had come out here to witness this entire company of fanatics circumvented by the ill-natured iron steed who stood on the track ahead surrounded by gaping boys and a flock of quacking ganders, living symbol of the people who had come to see the thing start; so thought Mr. Heath. He told himself he was as much of a goose as any of them to have let this chit of a woman fool him into coming off out here when he ought to have been in the hay field to-day.

By his side in all the glory of shimmering blue with a wide white lace bertha and a bonnet with a steeple crown wreathed about heavily with roses sat Kate, a blue silk parasol shading her eyes from the sun, those eyes that looked to conquer, and seemed to pierce beyond and through her sister and ignore her. Old Mrs. Heath and Miranda were along, but they did not count, except to themselves. Miranda was all eyes, under an ugly bonnet. She desired above all things to see that wonderful engine in which David was so interested.

Marcia shrunk and seemed to wither where she sat. All her bright bloom faded in an instant and a kind of frenzy seized her. She had a wild desire to get down out of the carriage and run with all her might away from this hateful scene. The sky seemed to have suddenly clouded over and the hum and buzz of voices about seemed a babel that would never cease.

David felt the arm beside his cringe, and shrink back, and looking down saw the look upon her sweet frightened face; following her glance his own face hardened into what might have been termed righteous wrath. But not a word did he say, and neither did he apparently notice the oncoming carriage. He busied himself at once talking with a man who happened to pass the carriage, and when Mr. Heath drove by to get a better view of the engine he was so absorbed in his conversation that he did not notice them, which seemed but natural.

But Kate was not to be thus easily foiled. She had much at stake and she must win if possible. She worked it about that Squire Heath should drive around to the end of the line of coaches, quite out of sight of the engine and where there was little chance of seeing the train and its passengers,—the only thing Squire Heath cared about. But there was an excellent view of David's carriage and Kate would be within hailing distance if it should transpire that she had no further opportunity of speaking with David. It seemed strange to Squire Heath, as he sat there behind the last coach patiently, that he had done what she asked. She did not look like a woman who was timid about horses, yet she had professed a terrible fear that the screech of the engine would frighten the staid old Heath horse. Miranda, at that, had insisted upon changing seats, thereby getting herself nearer the horse, and the scene of action. Miranda did not like to miss seeing the engine start.

At last word to start was given. A man ran along by the train and mounted into his high seat with his horn in his hand ready to blow. The fireman ceased his raking of the glowing fire and every traveller sprang into his seat and looked toward the crowd of spectators importantly. This was a great moment for all interested. The little ones whose fathers were in the train began to call good-bye and wave their hands, and one old lady whose only son was going as one of the train assistants began to sob aloud.

A horse in the crowd began to act badly. Every snort of the engine as the steam was let off made him start and rear. He was directly behind Marcia, and she turned her head and looked straight into his fiery frightened eyes, red with fear and frenzy, and felt his hot breath upon her cheek. A man was trying most ineffectually to hold him, but it seemed as if in another minute he would come plunging into the seat with them. Marcia uttered a frightened cry and clutched at David's arm. He turned, and seeing instantly what was the matter, placed his arm protectingly about her and at once guided his own horse out of the crowd, and around nearer to the engine. Somehow that protecting arm gave Marcia a steadiness once more and she was able to watch the wonderful wheels begin to turn and the whole train slowly move and start on its way. Her lips parted, her breath came quick, and for the instant she forgot her trouble. David's arm was still about her, and there was a reassuring pressure in it. He seemed to have forgotten that the crowd might see him—if the crowd had not been too busy watching something more wonderful. It is probable that only one person in that whole company saw David sitting with his arm about his wife—for he soon remembered and put it quietly on the back of the seat, where it would call no one's attention—and that person was Kate. She had not come to this hot dusty place to watch an engine creak along a track, she had come to watch David, and she was vexed and angry at what she saw. Here was Marcia flaunting her power over David directly in her face. Spiteful thing! She would pay her back yet and let her know that she could not touch the things that she, Kate, had put her own sign and seal upon. For this reason it was that at the last minute Kate allowed poor Squire Heath to drive around near the front of the train, saying that as David Spafford seemed to find it safe she supposed she ought not to hold them back for her fears. It needed but the word to send the vexed and curious Squire around through the crowd to a spot directly behind David's carriage, and there Miranda could see quite well, and Kate could sit and watch David and frame her plans for immediate action so soon as the curtain should fall upon this ridiculous engine play over which everybody was wild.

And so, amid shouts and cheers, and squawking of the geese that attempted to precede the engine like a white frightened body-guard down the track; amid the waving of handkerchiefs, the shouts of excited little boys, and the neighing of frightened horses, the first steam engine that ever drew a train in New York state started upon its initial trip.

Then there came a great hush upon the spectators assembled. The wheels were rolling, the carriages were moving, the train was actually going by them, and what had been so long talked about was an assured fact. They were seeing it with their own eyes, and might be witnesses of it to all their acquaintances. It was true. They dared not speak nor breathe lest something should happen and the great miracle should stop. They hushed simultaneously as though at the passing of some great soul. They watched in silence until the train went on between the meadows, grew smaller in the distance, slipped into the shadow of the wood, flashed out into the sunlight beyond again, and then was lost behind a hill. A low murmur growing rapidly into a shout of cheer arose as the crowd turned and faced one another and the fact of what they had seen.

"By gum! She kin do it!" ejaculated Squire Heath, who had watched the melting of his skeptical opinions in speechless amazement.

The words were the first intimation the Spaffords had of the proximity of Kate. They made David smile, but Marcia turned white with sudden fear again. Not for nothing had she lived with her sister so many years. She knew that cruel nature and dreaded it.

David looked at Marcia for sympathy in his smile at the old Squire, but when he saw her face he turned frowning toward those behind him.

Kate saw her opportunity. She leaned forward with honeyed smile, and wily as the serpent addressed her words to Marcia, loud and clear enough for all those about them to hear.

"Oh, Mrs. Spafford! I am going to ask a great favor of you. I am sure you will grant it when you know I have so little time. I am extremely anxious to get a word of advice from your husband upon business matters that are very pressing. Would you kindly change places with me during the ride home, and give me a chance to talk with him about it? I would not ask it but that I must leave for New York on the evening coach and shall have no other opportunity to see him."

Kate's smile was roses and cream touched with frosty sunshine, and to onlookers nothing could have been sweeter. But her eyes were coldly cruel as sharpened steel, and they said to her sister as plainly as words could have spoken: "Do you obey my wish, my lady, or I will freeze the heart out of you."

Marcia turned white and sick. She felt as if her lips had suddenly stiffened and refused to obey her when they ought to have smiled. What would all these people think of her, and how was she behaving? For David's sake she ought to do something, say something, look something, but what—what should she do?

While she was thinking this, with the freezing in her heart creeping up into her throat, the great tears beating at the portals of her eyes, and time standing suddenly still waiting for her leaden tongue to speak, David answered:

All gracefully 'twas done, with not so much as a second's hesitation,—though it had seemed so long to Marcia,—nor the shadow of a sign that he was angry:

"Mrs. Leavenworth," he said in his masterful voice, "I am sure my wife would not wish to seem ungracious, or unwilling to comply with your request, but as it happens it is impossible. We are not returning home for several days. My wife has some shopping to do in Albany, and in fact we are expecting to take a little trip. A sort of second honeymoon, you know,"—he added, smiling toward Mrs. Heath and Miranda; "it is the first time I have had leisure to plan for it since we were married. I am sorry I have to hurry away, but I am sure that my friend Squire Heath can give as much help in a business way as I could, and furthermore, Squire Schuyler is now in New York for a few days as I learned in a letter from him which arrived last evening. I am sure he can give you more and better advice than any I could give. I wish you good morning. Good morning, Mrs. Heath. Good morning, Miss Miranda!"

Lifting his hat David drove away from them and straight over to the little wayside hostelry where he was to finish his article to send by the messenger who was even then ready mounted for the purpose.

"My! Don't he think a lot of her though!" said Miranda, rolling the words as a sweet morsel under her tongue. "It must be nice to have a man so fond of you." This was one of the occasions when Miranda wished she had eyes in the back of her head. She was sharp and she had seen a thing or two, also she had heard scraps of her cousin Hannah's talk. But she sat demurely in the recesses of her deep, ugly bonnet and tried to imagine how the guest behind her looked.

All trembling sat Marcia in the rusty parlor of the little hostelry, while David at the table wrote with hurried hand, glancing up at her to smile now and then, and passing over the sheets as he finished them for her criticism. She thought she had seen the Heath wagon drive away in the home direction, but she was not sure. She half expected to see the door open and Kate walk in. Her heart was thumping so she could scarcely sit still and the brightness of the world outside seemed to make her dizzy. She was glad to have the sheets to look over, for it took her thoughts away from herself and her nameless fears. She was not quite sure what it was she feared, only that in some way Kate would have power over David to take him away from her. As he wrote she studied the dear lines of his face and knew, as well as human heart may ever know, how dear another soul had grown to hers.

David had not much to write and it was soon signed, approved, and sealed. He sent his messenger on the way and then coming back closed the door and went and stood before Marcia.

As though she felt some critical moment had come she arose, trembling, and looked into his eyes questioningly.

"Marcia," he said, and his tone was grave and earnest, putting her upon an equality with him, not as if she were a child any more. "Marcia, I have come to ask your forgiveness for the terrible thing I did to you in allowing you, who scarcely knew what you were doing then, to give your life away to a man who loved another woman."

Marcia's heart stood still with horror. It had come then, the dreadful thing she had feared. The blow was going to fall. He did not love her! What a fool she had been!

But the steady voice went on, though the blood in her neck and temples throbbed in such loud waves that she could scarcely hear the words to understand them.

"It was a crime, Marcia, and I have come to realize it more and more during all the days of this year that you have so uncomplainingly spent yourself for me. I know now, as I did not think then in my careless, selfish sorrow, that I was as cruel to you, with your sweet young life, as your sister was cruel to me. You might already have given your heart to some one else; I never stopped to inquire. You might have had plans and hopes for your own future; I never even thought of it. I was a brute. Can you forgive me? Sometimes the thought of the responsibility I took upon myself has been so terrible to me that I felt I could not stand it. You did not realize what it was then that you were giving, perhaps, but somehow I think you have begun to realize now. Will you forgive me?" He stopped and looked at her anxiously. She was drooped and white as if a blast had suddenly struck her and faded her sweet bloom. Her throat was hot and dry and she had to try three times before she could frame the words, "Yes, I forgive."

There was no hope, no joy in the words, and a sudden fear descended upon David's heart. Had he then done more damage than he knew? Was the child's heart broken by him, and did she just realize it? What could he do? Must he conceal his love from her? Perhaps this was no time to tell it. But he must. He could not bear the burden of having done her harm and not also tell her how he loved her. He would be very careful, very considerate, he would not press his love as a claim, but he must tell her.

"And Marcia, I must tell you the rest," he went on, his own words seeming to stay upon his lips, and then tumble over one another; "I have learned to love you as I never loved your sister. I love you more and better than I ever could have loved her. I can see how God has led me away from her and brought me to you. I can look back to that night when I came to her and found you there waiting for me, and kissed you,—darling. Do you remember?" He took her cold little trembling hands and held them firmly as he talked, his whole soul in his face, as if his life depended upon the next few moments. "I was troubled at the time, dear, for having kissed you, and given you the greeting that I thought belonged to her. I have rebuked myself for thinking since how lovely you looked as you stood there in the moonlight. But afterward I knew that it was you after all that my love belonged to, and to you rightfully the kiss should have gone. I am glad it was so, glad that God overruled my foolish choosing. Lately I have been looking back to that night I met you at the gate, and feeling jealous that that meeting was not all ours; that it should be shadowed for us by the heartlessness of another. It gives me much joy now to think how I took you in my arms and kissed you. I cannot bear to think it was a mistake. Yet glad as I am that God sent you down to that gate to meet me, and much as I love you, I would rather have died than feel that I have brought sorrow into your life, and bound you to one whom you cannot love. Marcia, tell me truly, never mind my feelings, tell me! Can you ever love me?"

Then did Marcia lift her flower-like face, all bright with tears of joy and a flood of rosy smiles, the light of seven stars in her eyes. But she could not speak, she could only look, and after a little whisper, "Oh, David, I think I have always loved you! I think I was waiting for you that night, though I did not know it. And look!"—with sudden thought——

She drew from the folds of her dress a little old-fashioned locket hung by a chain about her neck out of sight. She opened it and showed him a soft gold curl which she touched gently with her lips, as though it were something very sacred.

"What is it, darling?" asked David perplexed, half happy, half afraid as he took the locket and touched the curl more thrilled with the thought that she had carried it next her heart than with the sight of it.

"It is yours," she said, disappointed that he did not understand. "Aunt Clarinda gave it to me while you were away. I've worn it ever since. And she gave me other things, and told me all about you. I know it all, about the tops and marbles, and the spelling book, and I've cried with you over your punishments, and—I—love it all!"

He had fastened the door before he began to talk, but he caught her in his arms now, regardless of the fact that the shades were not drawn down, and that they swayed in the summer breeze.

"Oh, my darling! My wife!" he cried, and kissed her lips for the third time.

The world was changed then for those two. They belonged to each other they believed, as no two that ever walked through Eden had ever belonged. When they thought of the precious bond that bound them together their hearts throbbed with a happiness that well-nigh overwhelmed them.

A dinner of stewed chickens and little white soda biscuits was served them, fit for a wedding breakfast, for the barmaid whispered to the cook that she was sure there was a bride and groom in the parlor they looked so happy and seemed to forget anybody else was by. But it might have been ham and eggs for all they knew what it was they ate, these two who were so happy they could but look into each other's eyes.

When the dinner was over and they started on their way again, with Albany shimmering in the hot sun in the distance, and David's arm sliding from the top of the seat to circle Marcia's waist, David whispered:

"This is our real wedding journey, dearest, and this is our bridal day. We'll go to Albany and buy you a trousseau, and then we will go wherever you wish. I can stay a whole week if you wish. Would you like to go home for a visit?"

Marcia, with shining eyes and glowing cheeks, looked her love into his face and answered: "Yes, *now* I would like to go home,—just for a few days—and then back to our home."

And David looking into her eyes understood why she had not wanted to go before. She was taking her husband,*her* husband, not Kate's, with her now, and might be proud of his love. She could go among her old comrades and be happy, for he loved her. He looked a moment, comprehended, sympathized, and then pressing her hand close—for he might not kiss her, as there was a load of hay coming their way—he said: "Darling!" But their eyes said more.